Also by Mavis Gallant

The
COLLECTED
STORIES
of
Mavis Gallant

The

COLLECTED
STORIES

of

Mavis Gallant

RANDOM HOUSE   NEW YORK

All rights reserved under International and Pan-American Copyright Conventions. Published in the United States by Random House, Inc., New York.

Published in Canada by McClelland & Stewart, Inc., Toronto, as *The Selected Stories of Mavis Gallant*

All of the stories in this work were originally published in *The New Yorker*, except for "1933," which was originally published as "Declassé" in *Mademoiselle*.

Library of Congress Cataloging-in-Publication Data

Gallant, Mavis.
[Short stories]
The collected stories of Mavis Gallant / Mavis Gallant.
p.   cm.
ISBN 0-679-44886-1
I. Manners and customs—Fiction.   I. Title.
PR9199.3.G26A6   1996   96-6290
813'.54—dc20

Random House website address: http://www.randomhouse.com/

Printed in the United States of America on acid-free paper

2   4   6   8   9   7   5   3

First Edition

Book design by Lilly Langotsky

To

BILL MAXWELL

and to

DAN MENAKER

PREFACE

꙰

*S*amuel Beckett, answering a hopeless question from a Paris newspaper—
"Why do you write?"—said it was all he was good for: *"Bon qu'a ça."* Georges
Bernanos said that writing was like rowing a boat out to sea: The shoreline disappears, it is too late to turn back, and the rower becomes a galley slave. When Colette was seventy-five and crippled with arthritis she said that now, at last, she could
write anything she wanted without having to count on what it would bring in.
Marguerite Yourcenar said that if she had inherited the estate left by her mother
and then gambled away by her father, she might never have written another word.
Jean-Paul Sartre said that writing is an end in itself. (I was twenty-two and working on a newspaper in Montreal when I interviewed him. I had not asked him the
why of the matter but the *what*.) The Polish poet Aleksander Wat told me that it
was like the story of the camel and the Bedouin; in the end, the camel takes over.
So that was the writing life: an insistent camel.

I have been writing or just thinking about things to write since I was a child.
I invented rhymes and stories when I could not get to sleep and in the morning
when I was told it was too early to get up, and I uttered dialogue for a large
colony of paper dolls. Once, I was astonished to hear my mother say, "Oh, she
talks to herself all the time." I had not realized that that kind of speech could be
overheard, and, of course, I was not talking but supplying a voice. If I pin it down
as an adult calling, I have lived in writing, like a spoonful of water in a river, for
more than forty-five years. (If I add the six years I spent on a weekly newspaper—
The Standard, dead and buried now—it comes to more than fifty. At that time, at
home, I was steadily filling an old picnic hamper with notebooks and manuscripts. The distinction between journalism and fiction is the difference between
without and within. Journalism recounts as exactly and economically as possible
the weather in the street; fiction takes no notice of that particular weather but
brings to life a distillation of all weathers, a climate of the mind. Which is not

to say it need not be exact and economical: It is precision of a different order.)

I still do not know what impels anyone sound of mind to leave dry land and spend a lifetime describing people who do not exist. If it is child's play, an extension of make-believe—something one is frequently assured by persons who write about writing—how to account for the overriding wish to do that, just that, only that, and consider it as rational an occupation as riding a racing bike over the Alps? Perhaps the cultural attaché at a Canadian embassy who said to me "Yes, but what do you really do?" was expressing an adult opinion. Perhaps a writer is, in fact, a child in disguise, with a child's lucid view of grown-ups, accurate as to atmosphere, improvising when it tries to make sense of adult behavior. Peter Quennell, imagining Shakespeare, which means imagining the inexplicable, says that Shakespeare heard the secret summons and was sent along his proper path. The secret summons, the proper path, are what saints and geniuses hold in common. So do great writers, the semi-great, the good, the lesser, the dogged, the trudgers, and the merely anxious. All will discover that Paradise (everybody's future) is crisscrossed with hedges. Looking across a hedge to the green place where genius is consigned, we shall see them assembled, waiting to receive a collective reward if only they will agree on the source of the summons and the start of the proper path. The choir of voices floating back above the hedge probably will be singing, *"Bon qu'a ça,"* for want of knowing.

Janet Flanner, a great journalist of the age, the *New Yorker* correspondent in Paris for half a century, when on the brink of her eighties said she would rather have been a writer of fiction. The need to make a living, the common lot, had kept her from leaving something she did brilliantly and setting off for, perhaps, nowhere. She had published fiction, but not much and not satisfactorily. Now she believed her desire to write had been greater than her talent. Something was missing. My father, who was younger than Janet Flanner and who died in his early thirties, never thought of himself as anything but a painter. It may have been just as well—for him—that he did not go on to discover that he could never have been more than a dedicated amateur. He did not try and fail: In a sense, he never started out, except along the path of some firm ideal concerning life and art. The ideality required displacement; he went from England to Canada. His friends would recall him as levelheaded. No one ever heard him say that he had hoped for this or regretted that. His persona as an artist was so matter-of-fact, so taken for granted, so fully accepted by other people, that it was years until I understood what should have been obvious: He also had worked and gone to an office, before he became too ill to work at anything.

"What did you imagine you lived on?" said the family friend who had just let me know that my father was, after all, like most other people. He was with a firm that imported massive office furnishings of heavy wood and employed Englishmen. Not every business wanted Englishmen. They had a reputation for criticizing Canada and failing to pull their weight. Quite often they just filled posts where they could do no real harm or they held generic job titles. It created a small inflation of inspectors, controllers, estimators, managers, assistants, counselors, and vice-presidents. Some hung on to a military rank from the First World War and went about as captains and majors. This minor imperial sham survived into the 1930s, when the Depression caved in on jobs and pseudo-jobs alike.

At eighteen I went to look at the office building, which was a gray stone house on Beaver Hall Hill. I remembered having been taken there, wearing my convent school uniform of black serge with a clerical collar, and being introduced to a man with an English accent. My father was inclined to show me off, and I was used to it. What I had retained of the visit (or so it came back) was a glowing lampshade made of green glass and a polished desk of some dark wood and a shadowy room, a winter room. It was on Beaver Hall Hill, around the same time, that another stranger stopped me in the street because I looked so startlingly like my late father. The possibility of a grown daughter cannot have been uppermost: I had vanished from Montreal at ten and come back on my own. The legal age for making such decisions was twenty-one: I had made it at eighteen and hoped no one would notice. A few people in Montreal believed I had died. It was a rumor, a floating story with no setting or plot, and it had ceased to affect anyone, by now, except for a family of French Canadians who had been offering prayers every year on my birthday.

Years later, in a town called Châteauguay, I would hear a trailing echo of the report. We had spent summers there and, once, two whole winters. The paralyzing winter wind blowing from the Châteauguay River was supposed to be restorative for the frail. My mother, who never had a cold, breathed it in and said, sincerely, "Isn't it glorious!" I came back to Châteauguay fifty years after taking the Montreal train for the last time, across the bridge, over the river. I came with a television crew from Toronto. We were looking at places where I had been as a child. At one address in Montreal we had found a bank. My first school had become a vacant lot. The small building where I had rented my first independent apartment, installed my own furniture, filled shelves with books and political pamphlets (as many as possible of them banned in Quebec), hung pictures, bought inch by inch from Montreal painters, then a flourishing school, was now a students' residence, run-down, sagging, neglected. I would never have returned alone to Châteauguay. It was the last place where we had lived as a family. When my father died, I was told he had gone to England and would be back before long, and I had believed it. A television unit is composed of strangers, largely indifferent, intent on getting the assignment over and a flight home. Their indifference was what I needed: a thick glass wall against the effects of memory.

I drew a map of the place—town, river, bridge, railway station, Catholic church, Anglican church, Protestant school, houses along a road facing the river, even candy store—and gave it to the producer. Everything was exact, except perhaps the Protestant school, which we forgot to look for. I saw the remembered house, still standing, though greatly altered. The candy store had been turned into a ramshackle coffee shop with a couple of pool tables, the Duranseau farm replaced by a sign, RUE DURANSEAU, indicating not much of a street. I recognized Dundee Cottage, now called something else, and Villa Crépina, where the Crépin boys had lived. They threw stones at other people's dogs, especially English dogs. Their low evergreen hedge along the sidewalk still put out red berries. I had once been warned not to touch the leaves or berries, said to be poisonous. I ate only small quantities of leaves, and nothing happened. They tasted like strong tea, also forbidden, and desirable on that account. There was a fairy-tale look of danger about the berries. One could easily imagine long fairy-tale sleep.

At the café I spoke to some men sitting huddled at a counter. The place had gone silent when we came in speaking English. I asked if anyone had ever heard of families I remembered—the Duranseaus, whose children I had played with, or the tenants of Dundee Cottage, whose name suddenly returned and has again dissolved, or another elderly neighbor—elderly in recollection, perhaps not even forty—who complained to my mother when I said "bugger" and complained again when I addressed him, quite cheerfully, as "old cock." I had no idea what any of it meant. None of the men at the counter looked my way. Their hunched backs spoke the language of small-town distrust. Finally, a younger man said he was a relation of the Crépins. He must have been born a whole generation after the time when I picked a poisoned leaf whenever I went by his great-uncle's hedge. He knew about our house, so radically modified now, because of some child, a girl, who had lived there a long time before and been drowned in the river. He gave me his great-aunt's telephone number, saying she knew about every house and stone and tree and vanished person. I never called. There was nothing to ask. Another English Canadian family with just one child had lived on the same side of the river. They had a much larger house, with a stone wall around it, and the drowned child was a boy. The Protestant school was named after him.

The fear that I had inherited a flawed legacy, a vocation without the competence to sustain it, haunted me from early youth. It was the reason why I tore up more than I saved, why I was slow to show my work except to one or two friends—and then not often. When I was twenty-one, someone to whom I had given two stories, just to read, handed them to a local literary review, and I was able to see what a story looked like surrounded by poetry and other fiction. I sent another story to a radio station. They paid me something and read it over the air, and I discovered what my own work could sound like in a different voice. After that I went on writing, without attempting to have anything published or asking for an opinion, for another six years. By then I was twenty-seven and becoming exactly what I did not want to be: a journalist who wrote fiction along some margin of spare time. I thought the question of writing or stopping altogether had to be decided before thirty. The only solution seemed to be a clean break and a try: I would give it two years. What I was to live on during the two years does not seem to have troubled me. Looking back, I think my entire concentration was fixed on setting off. No city in the world drew me as strongly as Paris. (When I am asked why, I am unable to say.) It was a place where I had no friends, no connections, no possibility of finding employment should it be necessary—although, as I reasoned things, if I was to go there with a job and salary in mind, I might as well stay where I was—and where I might run out of money. That I might not survive at all, that I might have to be rescued from deep water and ignominiously shipped home, never entered my head. I believed that if I was to call myself a writer, I should live on writing. If I could not live on it, even simply, I should destroy every scrap, every trace, every notebook, and live some other way. Whatever happened, I would not enter my thirties as a journalist—or an anything else—with stories piling up in a picnic hamper. I decided to send three of my stories to *The New Yorker*, one after the other. One acceptance would be good enough. If all three were refused, I would take it as decisive. But then I did something that seems contradictory and odd: A few days before I put the first story in the mail (I was having all the trouble in the world measuring if it was all right or rubbish), I told the newspaper's managing editor I intended to quit. I think I was afraid of having a failure of nerve. Not long before, the newspaper had started a pension plan, and I had asked if I could keep out of it. I had worked in an office where I had watched people shuffle along to retirement time, and the sight had scared me. The managing editor thought I was dissatisfied about something. He sent me to someone else, who was supposed to find out what it was. In the second office, I was told I was out of my mind; it was no use training women, they always leave; one day I would come creeping back, begging for my old job; all reporters think they can write; I had the audacity to call myself a writer when I was like an architect who had never designed a house. I went back to my desk, typed a formal resignation, signed it, and turned it in.

The first story came back from *The New Yorker* with a friendly letter that said, "Do you have anything else you could show us?" The second story was taken. The third I didn't like anymore. I tore it up and sent the last of the three from Paris.

Newspaper work was my apprenticeship. I never saw it as a drag or a bind or a waste of time. I had no experience and would never have been taken on if there had been a man available. It was still very much a man's profession. I overheard an editor say, "If it hadn't been for the goddamned war, we wouldn't have hired even one of the goddamned women." The appalling labor laws of Quebec made it easy for newspapers to ban unions. I received half the salary paid to men and I had to hear, frequently and not only from men, that I had "a good job, for a girl." Apparently, by holding on to it I was standing in the way of any number of qualified men, each with a wife and three children to support. That was the accepted view of any young female journalist, unless she was writing about hemlines or three-fruit jam.

My method of getting something on paper was the same as for the fiction I wrote at home: I could not move on to the second sentence until the first sounded true. True to what? Some arrangement in my head, I suppose. I wrote by hand, in pencil, made multitudinous changes, erased, filled in, typed a clean page, corrected, typed. An advantage to early practice of journalism is said to be that it teaches one how to write fast. Whatever I acquired did not include a measure of speed. I was always on the edge of a deadline, and even on the wrong side. Thinking back on my outrageous slowness, I don't know why I wasn't fired a dozen times. Or, rather, perhaps I do: I could write intelligible English, I was cheaper by half than a man, and I seemed to have an unending supply of ideas for feature stories and interviews, or picture stories to work on with a photographer. It was the era of photo features. I liked inventing them. They were something like miniature scripts; I always saw the pictures as stills from a film. I knew Quebec to the core, and not just the English-speaking enclaves of Montreal. I could interview French Canadians without dragging them into English, a terrain of wariness and ill will. I suggested stories on subjects I wanted to know more about and places I wanted to see and people I was curious to meet. Only a few were turned down, usually because they scraped against political power or the sensibilities of advertisers. I wrote feature stories from the beginning; was an occasional critic, until I gave a film an impertinent review and a string of theatres canceled a number of ads; wrote a weekly column, until the head of an agency protested about a short item that poked fun at a radio commercial, at which point the column was dropped. All this is a minor part of the social history of an era, in a region of North America at a political standstill.

I managed to carve out an astonishing amount of autonomy, saved myself from writing on the sappy subjects usually reserved for women, and was not sacked— not even when someone wrote to protest about "that Marxist enfant terrible." (It was not a safe time or place for such accusations.) My salary was modest, but whole families were living on less. I had amassed an enormous mental catalog of places and people, information that still seeps into my stories. Journalism was a life I liked, but not the one I wanted. An American friend has told me that when we were fifteen I said I intended to write and live in Paris. I have no recollection of the conversation, but she is not one to invent anecdotes based on hindsight. It is about all I have in the way of a blueprint. The rest is memory and undisputed evidence.

The impulse to write and the stubbornness needed to keep going are supposed to come out of some drastic shaking up, early in life. There is even a term for it: the shock of change. Probably, it means a jolt that unbolts the door between perception and imagination and leaves it ajar for life, or that fuses memory and language and waking dreams. Some writers may just simply come into the world with overlapping vision of things seen and things as they might be seen. All have a gift for holding their breath while going on breathing: It is the basic requirement. If shock and change account for the rest of it, millions of men and women, hit hard and steadily, would do nothing but write; in fact, most of them don't. No childhood is immunized against disturbance. A tremor occurs underfoot when a trusted adult says one thing and means another. It brings on the universal and unanswerable wail "It's not fair!"—to which the shabby rejoinder that life isn't does nothing to restore order.

I took it for granted that life was tough for children and that adults had a good time. My parents enjoyed themselves, or seemed to. If I want to bring back a Saturday night in full summer, couples dancing on the front gallery (Quebec English for veranda), a wind-up gramophone and a stack of brittle records, all I need to hear is the beginning of "West End Blues." The dancers are down from Montreal or up from the States, where there is Prohibition. Prohibition would be out of the question in Quebec, although the rest of Canada enjoys being rather dry. I mention it just to say that there is no such thing as a Canadian childhood. One's beginnings are regional. Mine are wholly Quebec, English and Protestant, yes, but with a strong current of French and Catholic. My young parents sent me off on that current by placing me in a French convent school, for reasons never made plain. I remember my grandmother's saying, "Well, I give up." It was a singular thing to do and in those days unheard of. It left me with two systems of behavior, divided by syntax and tradition; two environments to consider, one becalmed in a long twilight of nineteenth-century religiosity; two codes of social behavior; much practical experience of the difference between a rule and a moral point.

Somewhere in this duality may be the exact point of the beginning of writing. All I am certain of is that the fragile root, the tentative yes or no, was made safe by reading. I cannot recall a time when I couldn't read; I do remember being read to and wanting to take the book and decipher it for myself. A friend of my parents recalled seeing my father trying to teach me the alphabet as I sat in a high chair. He held the book flat on a tray—any book, perhaps a novel, pulled off a shelf—and pointed out the capital letters. At a young age, apparently, I could translate at sight, English to French, reading aloud without stumbling. I was in no other way precocious: For years I would trail far behind other children in grasping simple sums or telling the time (I read the needles in reverse, five o'clock for seven) or separating left from right. I thought the eldest child in a family had been born last. At seven, I wondered why no one ever married some amiable dog. When my mother explained, I remained unenlightened. (The question possibly arose from my devoted reading of an English comic strip for children, *Pip and Squeak*, in which a dog and a penguin seem to be the parents of a rabbit named Wilfred.) I did not know there was a particular bodily difference between boys and girls until I was eight; I had thought it a matter of clothes, haircuts, and general temperament. At nine, I still looked for mermaids in the Châteauguay River. My father had painted for me a screen that showed mermaids, with long red hair, rising out of green waves. I had not yet seen an ocean, just lakes and rivers. The river across the road froze white in winter and thawed to a shade of clear golden brown. Apart from the error as to color, it seemed unlikely he would paint something untrue.

Four weeks after my fourth birthday, when I was enrolled as a boarder in my first school, run by a semi-cloistered order of teaching and missionary nuns, I brought, along with my new, strange, stiff, uncomfortable and un-English uniform and severely buttoned underclothes, some English storybooks from home. (I owned a few books in French, the gift of a doctor, a French Canadian specialist, who had attended me for a mastoid infection after scarlet fever and become a close friend of my parents. I was far too young to understand them. They were moral tales for older children, and even years later I would find them heavy going.) It was a good thing—to have books in English, that is—because I would hear and speak next to no English now, except in the summer holidays and at Christmas and Easter and on the odd weekend when I was fetched home. I always went back to school with new books, which had to be vetted; but no one knew any English and the nun who taught it could not speak it at all, and so the illustrations were scanned for decency and the books handed back, to be stored in the small night-table next to my bed.

I owe it to children's books—picture books, storybooks, then English and American classics—that I absorbed once and for all the rhythm of English prose, the order of words in an English sentence and how they are spelled. I was eight before I was taught to write and spell English in any formal way, and what I was taught I already knew. By then, English was irremovably entrenched as the language of imagination. Nothing supposed, daydreamed, created, or invented would enter my mind by way of French. In the paper-doll era, I made up a mishmash of English, French, and the mysterious Italian syllables in recordings of bel canto, which my mother liked and often played. I called this mixture "talking Marigold." Marigold faded soon, along with paper dolls. After that, for stories and storytelling there was only one sound.

The first flash of fiction arrives without words. It consists of a fixed image, like a slide or (closer still) a freeze frame, showing characters in a simple situation. For example, Barbara, Alec, and their three children, seen getting down from a train in the south of France, announced "The Remission." The scene does not appear in the story but remains like an old snapshot or a picture in a newspaper, with a caption giving all the names. The quick arrival and departure of the silent image can be likened to the first moments of a play, before anything is said. The difference is that the characters in the frame are not seen, but envisioned, and do not have to speak to be explained. Every character comes into being with a name (which I may change), an age, a nationality, a profession, a particular voice and accent, a family background, a personal history, a destination, qualities, secrets, an attitude toward love, ambition, money, religion, and a private center of gravity.

Over the next several days I take down long passages of dialogue. Whole scenes then follow, complete in themselves but like disconnected parts of a film. I do not deliberately invent any of this: It occurs. Some writers say they actually hear the words, but I think "hear" is meant to be in quotation marks. I do not hear anything: I know what is being said. Finally (I am describing a long and complex process as simply as I can), the story will seem to be entire, in the sense that nearly everything needed has been written. It is entire but unreadable. Nothing fits. A close analogy would be an unedited film. The first frame may have dissolved into sound and motion (Sylvie and her mother, walking arm in arm, in "Across the Bridge") or turn out to be the end (Jack and Netta in Place Masséna, in "The Moslem Wife") or something incidental, such as the young Angelo begging for coins from Walter, which barely figures in "An Unmarried Man's Summer."

Sometimes one sees immediately what needs to be done, which does not mean it can be done in a hurry: I have put aside elements of a story for months and even years. It is finished when it seems to tally with a plan I surely must have had in mind but cannot describe, or when I come to the conclusion that it cannot be written satisfactorily any other way; at least, not by me. A few times, the slow transformation from image to fiction has begun with something actually glimpsed: a young woman reading an airmail letter in the Paris Métro, early in the morning; a man in Berlin eating a plate of cold cuts, next to a lace curtain that filters gray afternoon light; an American mother, in Venice, struggling to show she is having a fine time, and her two tactful, attentive adolescent children. Sometimes, hardly ever, I have seen clearly that a character sent from nowhere is standing in for someone I once knew, disguised as thoroughly as a stranger in a dream. I have always let it stand. Everything I start glides into print, in time, and becomes like a house once lived in.

I was taught the alphabet three times. The first, the scene with the high chair, I remember nothing about. The second time, the letters were written in lacy capitals on a blackboard—pretty-looking, decorative; nuns' handwriting of the time. Rows of little girls in black, hands folded on a desk, feet together, sang the letters and then, in a rising scale, the five vowels. The third time was at the Protestant school, in Châteauguay. The schoolhouse had only two rooms, four grades to each. I was eight: It had been noticed that I was beginning to pronounce English proper nouns with French vowel sounds. (I do it to this day, thinking "Neek" for "Nike," "Ray-bok" for "Reebok." The first time I saw Ribena, a fruit drink, advertised in the London Underground, I said, "What is Reebayna?" It is the only trace of that lacy, pretty, sung alphabet.) At my new school it was taken for granted that French and Catholic teaching had left me enslaved to superstition and wholly ignorant. I was placed with the six-year-olds and told to recite the alphabet. I pronounced *G* with its French vowel sound, something like an English *J.* Our teacher pulled down over the blackboard a large, illustrated alphabet, like a wide window blind. I stood in front of the blind and was shown the letter *G.* Above it a large painted hand held a tipped water jug, to which clung, suspended, a single drop. The sound of *G* was the noise the drop would make in a water glass: it would say *gug.*

"The sound of *G* is *gug.* Say it after me. *Gug.*"

"*Gug.*"

"Everyone, now. *Gug, gug, gug.*"

"*Gug, gug, gug.*"

"What letter is it?"

"*G.*"

"What does it say?"

"*Gug.*"

"Don't forget it, now."

Whatever it was, it could never be sung.

The way the stories are arranged in this collection, as well as their selection, was left up to me. The original editor, Joe Fox, whose sad and sudden death some months ago has left him entirely alive in my mind, not yet a memory, had written, "Knowing you, I suspect that you're going to write back that *I* should decide. But . . . only *you* can decide, and only you can assemble your work in a way that pleases you." His book, or so I thought of it, was caught in midair by Kate Medina, and I thank her for her good catch and for her patience.

I keep the sketchiest sort of files, few letters and almost no records. As it turned out, I had published more stories than I had expected. This is a heavy volume, and if I had included everything, even nearly everything, it would have become one of those tomes that can't be read in comfort and that are no good for anything except as a weight on sliced cucumbers. I rejected straight humor and satire, which dates quickly, seven stories that were pieces of novels, stories that seemed to me not worth reprinting, stories I was tired of, and stories that bored me. I also removed more than a dozen stories that stood up to time but not to the practical requirement I've mentioned. Their inclusion would have made this collection as long as the *Concise Oxford* to "speedometer," or the whole of *The Oxford Book of American Verse* plus some of the *Oxford English,* as far as Sir Thomas Wyatt, or the King James Bible from Genesis to about the middle of Paul's first Epistle to the Romans.

With just a single exception all the stories were published in *The New Yorker.* Good and bad luck comes in waves. It was a wave of the best that brought me to William Maxwell, who read my first story and every other for the next twenty-five years. He has turned away the IOUs I have tried to hand him, which announce just simply that I owe him everything. And so I am writing another one here, with no possibility of any answer: I owe him everything. When we met for the first time, in the spring of 1950, I did not immediately connect him to the author of *The Folded Leaf*. He, of course, said nothing about himself at all. He asked just a few questions and let me think it was perfectly natural to throw up one's job and all one's friends and everything familiar and go thousands of miles away to write. He made it seem no more absurd or unusual than taking a bus to visit a museum. Everyone else I knew had quite the opposite to say; I felt suddenly like a stranded army with an unexpected ally. I was about to try something entirely normal and that (he made it sound obvious) I was unlikely to regret.

He seems to me the most American of writers and the most American of all the Americans I have known; but even as I say this, I know it almost makes no sense and that it is undefinable and that I am unable to explain what I mean. I can get myself out of it only by saying it is a compliment. When he retired, in the mid-seventies, I was inherited by a much younger editor, Daniel Menaker, whom he liked, trusted, and chose. Every writer/editor relationship is a kind of shotgun wedding; it works or it doesn't. There is no median way and no jogging along. Dan Menaker and I had the same dopey sense of humor. He would call across the Atlantic just to tell me a joke. It was because I knew I could make him laugh that I began to write straight satire, which gradually evolved into stories, such as the stories about Henri Grippes, the Montparnasse author and slum landlord. All the linked stories, silly or serious, at the end of this volume were written with Dan Menaker as first reader.

There is something I keep wanting to say about reading short stories. I am doing it now, because I may never have another occasion. Stories are not chapters of novels. They should not be read one after another, as if they were meant to follow along. Read one. Shut the book. Read something else. Come back later. Stories can wait.

CONTENTS

THE SEVENTIES

THE EIGHTIES AND NINETIES

LINNET MUIR

THE CARETTE SISTERS

ÉDOUARD, JULIETTE, LENA

HENRI GRIPPES

The

THIRTIES

and

FORTIES

THE MOSLEM WIFE

⁂

*I*n the south of France, in the business room of a hotel quite near to the house where Katherine Mansfield (whom no one in this hotel had ever heard of) was writing "The Daughters of the Late Colonel," Netta Asher's father announced that there would never be a man-made catastrophe in Europe again. The dead of that recent war, the doomed nonsense of the Russian Bolsheviks had finally knocked sense into European heads. What people wanted now was to get on with life. When he said "life," he meant its commercial business.

Who would have contradicted Mr. Asher? Certainly not Netta. She did not understand what he meant quite so well as his French solicitor seemed to, but she did listen with interest and respect, and then watched him signing papers that, she knew, concerned her for life. He was renewing the long lease her family held on the Hotel Prince Albert and Albion. Netta was then eleven. One hundred years should at least see her through the prime of life, said Mr. Asher, only half jokingly, for of course he thought his seed was immortal.

Netta supposed she might easily live to be more than a hundred—at any rate, for years and years. She knew that her father did not want her to marry until she was twenty-six and that she was then supposed to have a pair of children, the elder a boy. Netta and her father and the French lawyer shook hands on the lease, and she was given her first glass of champagne. The date on the bottle was 1909, for the year of her birth. Netta bravely pronounced the wine delicious, but her father said she would know much better vintages before she was through.

Netta remembered the handshake but perhaps not the terms. When the lease had eighty-eight years to run, she married her first cousin, Jack Ross, which was not at all what her father had had in mind. Nor would there be the useful pair of children—Jack couldn't abide them. Like Netta he came from a hotelkeeping family where the young were like blight. Netta had up to now never shown a scrap of maternal feeling over anything, but Mr. Asher thought Jack might have made an amiable parent—a kind one, at least. She consoled Mr. Asher on one count, by taking the hotel over in his lifetime. The hotel was, to Netta, a natural life; and so when Mr. Asher, dying, said, "She behaves as I wanted her to," he was right as far as the drift of Netta's behavior was concerned but wrong about its course.

The Ashers' hotel was not down on the seafront, though boats and sea could be had from the south-facing rooms.

Across a road nearly empty of traffic were handsome villas, and behind and to either side stood healthy olive trees and a large lemon grove. The hotel was painted a deep ocher with white trim. It had white awnings and green shutters and black iron balconies as lacquered and shiny as Chinese boxes. It possessed two tennis courts, a lily pond, a sheltered winter garden, a formal rose garden, and trees full of nightingales. In the summer dark, *belles-de-nuit* glowed pink, lemon, white, and after their evening watering they gave off a perfume that varied from plant to plant and seemed to match the petals' coloration. In May the nights were dense with stars and fireflies. From the rose garden one might have seen the twin pulse of cigarettes on a balcony, where Jack and Netta sat drinking a last brandy-and-soda before turning in. Most of the rooms were shuttered by then, for no traveler would have dreamed of being south except in winter. Jack and Netta and a few servants had the whole place to themselves. Netta would hire workmen and have the rooms that needed it repainted—the blue cardroom, and the red-walled bar, and the white dining room, where Victorian mirrors gave back glossy walls and blown curtains and nineteenth-century views of the Ligurian coast, the work of an Asher great-uncle. Everything upstairs and down was soaked and wiped and polished, and even the pictures were relentlessly washed with soft cloths and ordinary laundry soap. Netta also had the boiler overhauled and the linen mended and new monograms embroidered and the looking glasses resilvered and the shutters taken off their hinges and scraped and made spruce green again for next year's sun to fade, while Jack talked about decorators and expert gardeners and even wrote to some, and banged tennis balls against the large new garage. He also read books and translated poetry for its own sake and practiced playing the clarinet. He had studied music once, and still thought that an important life, a musical life, was there in the middle distance. One summer, just to see if he could, he translated pages of Saint-John Perse, which were as blank as the garage wall to Netta, in any tongue.

Netta adored every minute of her life, and she thought Jack had a good life too, with nearly half the year for the pleasures that suited him. As soon as the grounds and rooms and cellar and roof had been put to rights, she and Jack packed and went traveling somewhere. Jack made the plans. He was never so cheerful as when buying Baedekers and dragging out their stickered trunks. But Netta was nothing of a traveler. She would have been glad to see the same sun rising out of the same sea from the window every day until she died. She loved Jack, and what she liked best after him was the hotel. It was a place where, once, people had come to die of tuberculosis, yet it held no trace or feeling of danger. When Netta walked with her workmen through sheeted summer rooms, hearing the cicadas and hearing Jack start, stop, start some deeply alien music (alien even when her memory automatically gave her a composer's name), she was reminded that here the dead had never been allowed to corrupt the living; the dead had been dressed for an outing and removed as soon as their first muscular stiffness relaxed. Some were wheeled out in chairs, sitting, and some reclined on portable cots, as if merely resting.

That is why there is no bad atmosphere here, she would say to herself. Death has been swept away, discarded. When the shutters are closed on a room, it is for sleep or for love. Netta could think this easily because neither she nor Jack was ever sick. They knew nothing about insomnia, and they made love every day of their lives—they had married in order to be able to.

Spring had been the season for dying in the old days. Invalids who had struggled through the dark comfort of winter took fright as the night receded. They felt without protection. Netta knew about this, and about the difference between darkness and brightness, but neither affected her. She was not afraid of death or of the dead—they were nothing but cold, heavy furniture. She could have tied jaws shut and weighted eyelids with native instinctiveness, as other women were born knowing the temperature for an infant's milk.

"There are no ghosts," she could say, entering the room where her mother, then her father had died. "If there were, I would know."

Netta took it for granted, now she was married, that Jack felt as she did about light, dark, death, and love. They were as alike in some ways (none of them physical) as a couple of twins, spoke much the same language in the same accents, had the same jokes—mostly about other people—and had been together as much as their families would let them for most of their lives. Other men seemed dull to Netta—slower, perhaps, lacking the spoken shorthand she had with Jack. She never mentioned this. For one thing, both of them had the idea that, being English, one must not say too much. Born abroad, they worked hard at an Englishness that was innocently inaccurate, rooted mostly in attitudes. Their families had been innkeepers along this coast for a century, even before Dr. James Henry Bennet had discovered "the Genoese Rivieras." In one of his guides to the region, a "Mr. Ross" is mentioned as a hotel owner who will accept English bank checks, and there is a "Mr. Asher," reliable purveyor of English groceries. The most trustworthy shipping agents in 1860 are the Montale brothers, converts to the Anglican Church, possessors of a British *laissez-passer* to Malta and Egypt. These families, by now plaited like hair, were connections of Netta's and Jack's and still in business from beyond Marseilles to Genoa. No wonder that other men bored her, and that each thought the other both familiar and unique. But of course they were unalike too. When once someone asked them, "Are you related to Montale, the poet?" Netta answered, "What poet?" and Jack said, "I wish we were."

There were no poets in the family. Apart from the great-uncle who had painted landscapes, the only person to try anything peculiar had been Jack, with his music. He had been allowed to study, up to a point; his father had been no good with hotels—had been a failure, in fact, bailed out four times by his cousins, and it had been thought, for a time, that Jack Ross might be a dunderhead too. Music might do him; he might not be fit for anything else.

Information of this kind about the meaning of failure had been gleaned by Netta years before, when she first became aware of her little cousin. Jack's father and mother—the commercial blunderers—had come to the Prince Albert and Albion to ride out a crisis. They were somewhere between undischarged bankruptcy and annihilation, but one was polite: Netta curtsied to her aunt and uncle. Her eyes were on Jack. She could not read yet, though she could sift and classify attitudes. She drew near him, sucking her lower lip, her hands behind her back. For the first time she was conscious of the beauty of another child. He was younger than Netta, imprisoned in a portable-fence arrangement in which he moved tirelessly, crabwise, hanging on a barrier he could easily have climbed. He was as fair as his Irish mother and sunburned a deep brown. His blue gaze was not a baby's—it was too challenging. He was naked except for shorts that were large and seemed about to fall down. The sunburn, the undress were because his mother was reckless and rather odd. Netta—whose mother was perfect—wore boots, stockings, a longsleeved frock, and a white sun hat. She heard the adults laugh and say that Jack looked like a prizefighter. She walked around his prison, staring, and the blue-eyed fighter stared back.

The Rosses stayed for a long time, while the family sent telegrams and tried to raise money for them. No one looked after Jack much. He would lie on a marble step of the staircase watching the hotel guests going into the cardroom or the dining room. One night, for a reason that remorse was to wipe out in a minute, Netta gave him such a savage kick (though he was not really in her way) that one of his legs remained paralyzed for a long time.

"*Why* did you do it?" her father asked her—this in the room where she was shut up on bread and water. Netta didn't know. She loved Jack, but who would believe it now? Jack learned to walk, then to run, and in time to ski and play tennis; but her lifelong gift to him was a loss of balance, a sudden lopsided bend of a knee. Jack's parents had meantime been given a small hotel to run at Bandol. Mr. Asher, responsible for a bank loan, kept an eye on the place. He went often, in a hotel car with a chauffeur, Netta perched beside him. When, years later, the families found out that the devoted young cousins had become lovers, they separated them without saying much. Netta was too independent to be dealt with. Besides, her father did not want a rift; his wife had died, and he needed Netta. Jack, whose claim on music had been the subject of teasing until now, was suddenly sent to study in England. Netta saw that he was secretly dismayed. He wanted to be almost anything as long as it was impossible, and then only as an act of grace. Netta's father did think it was his duty to tell her that marriage was, at its best, a parched arrangement, intolerable without a flow of golden guineas and fresh blood. As cousins, Jack and Netta could not bring each other anything except stale money. Nothing stopped them: They were married four months after Jack became twenty-one. Netta heard someone remark at her wedding, "She doesn't need a husband," meaning perhaps the practical, matter-of-fact person she now seemed to be. She did have the dry, burned-out look of someone turned inward. Her dark eyes glowed out of a thin face. She had the shape of a girl of fourteen. Jack, who was large, and fair, and who might be stout at forty if he wasn't careful, looked exactly his age, and seemed quite ready to be married.

Netta could not understand why, loving Jack as she did, she did not look more like him. It had troubled her in the past when they did not think exactly the same thing at almost the same time. During the secret meetings of their long engagement she had noticed how even before a parting they were nearly apart—they had begun to "unmesh," as she called it. Drinking a last drink, usually in the buffet of a railway station, she would see that Jack was somewhere else, thinking about the next-best thing to Netta. The next-best thing might only be a book he wanted to finish reading, but it was enough to make her feel exiled. He often told Netta, "I'm not holding on to you. You're free," because he thought it needed saying, and of course he wanted freedom for himself. But to Netta "freedom" had a cold sound. Is that what I do want, she would wonder. Is that what I think he should offer? Their partings were often on the edge of parting forever, not just because Jack had said or done or thought the wrong thing but because between them they generated the high sexual tension that leads to quarrels. Barely ten minutes after agreeing that no one in the world could possibly know what they knew, one of them, either one, could curse the other out over something trivial. Yet they were, and remained, much in love, and when they were apart Netta sent him letters that were almost despairing with enchantment.

Jack answered, of course, but his letters were cautious. Her exploration of feeling was part of an unlimited capacity she seemed to have for passionate behavior, so at odds with her appearance, which had been dry and sardonic even in childhood. Save for an erotic sentence or two near the end (which Netta read first) Jack's messages might have been meant for any girl cousin he particularly liked. Love was memory, and he was no good at the memory game; he needed Netta there. The instant he saw her he knew all he had missed. But Netta, by then, felt forgotten, and she came to each new meeting aggressive and hurt, afflicted with the physical signs of her doubts and injuries—cold sores, rashes, erratic periods, mysterious temperatures. If she tried to discuss it he would say, "We aren't going over all that again, are we?" Where Netta was concerned he had settled for the established faith, but Netta, who had a wilder, more secret God, wanted a prayer a minute, not to speak of unending miracles and revelations.

When they finally married, both were relieved that the strain of partings and of tense disputes in railway stations would come to a stop. Each privately blamed the other for past violence, and both believed that once they could live openly, without interference, they would never have a disagreement again. Netta did not want Jack to regret the cold freedom he had vainly tried to offer her. He must have his liberty, and his music, and other people, and, oh, anything he wanted—whatever would stop him from saying he was ready to let her go free. The first thing Netta did was to make certain they had the best room in the hotel. She had never actually owned a room until now. The private apartments of her family had always been surrendered in a crisis: Everyone had packed up and moved as beds were required. She and Jack were hopelessly untidy, because both had spent their early years moving down hotel corridors, trailing belts and raincoats, with tennis shoes hanging from knotted strings over their shoulders, their arms around books and sweaters and gray flannel bundles. Both had done lessons in the corners of lounges, with cups and glasses rattling, and other children running, and English voices louder than anything. Jack, who had been vaguely educated, remembered his boarding schools as places where one had a permanent bed. Netta chose for her marriage a south-facing room with a large balcony and an awning of dazzling white. It was furnished with lemonwood that had been brought to the Riviera by Russians for their own villas long before. To the lemonwood Netta's mother had added English chintzes; the result, in Netta's eyes, was not bizarre but charming. The room was deeply mirrored; when the shutters were closed on hot afternoons a play of light became as green as a forest on the walls, and as blue as seawater in the glass. A quality of suspension, of disbelief in gravity, now belonged to Netta. She became tidy, silent, less introspective, as watchful and as reflective as her bedroom mirrors. Jack stayed as he was, luckily; any alteration would have worried her, just as a change in an often-read story will trouble a small child. She was intensely, almost unnaturally happy.

One day she overheard an English doctor, whose wife played bridge every afternoon at the hotel, refer to her, to Netta, as "the little Moslem wife." It was said affectionately, for the doctor liked her. She wondered if he had seen through walls and had watched her picking up the clothing and the wet towels Jack left strewn like clues to his presence. The phrase was collected and passed from mouth to mouth in the idle English colony. Netta, the last person in the world deliberately to eavesdrop (she lacked that sort of interest in other people), was sharp of hearing where her marriage was concerned. She had a special antenna for Jack, for his shades of meaning, secret intentions, for his innocent contradictions. Perhaps "Moslem wife" meant several things, and possibly it was plain to anyone with eyes that Jack, without meaning a bit of harm by it, had a way with women. Those he attracted were a puzzling lot, to Netta. She had already catalogued them—elegant elderly parties with tongues like carving knives; gentle, clever girls who flourished on the unattainable; untouchable-daughter types, canny about their virginity, wondering if Jack would be father enough to justify the sacrifice. There was still another kind—tough, sunburned, clad in dark colors—who made Netta think in the vocabulary of horoscopes: Her gem—diamonds. Her color—black. Her language—worse than Netta's. She noticed that even when Jack had no real use for a woman he never made it apparent; he adopted anyone who took a liking to him. He assumed—Netta thought— a tribal, paternal air that was curious in so young a man. The plot of attraction interested him, no matter how it turned out. He was like someone reading several novels at once, or like someone playing simultaneous chess.

Netta did not want her marriage to become a world of stone. She said nothing except, "Listen, Jack, I've been at this hotel business longer than you have. It's wiser not to be too pally with the guests." At Christmas the older women gave him boxes of expensive soap. "They must think someone around here wants a good wash," Netta remarked. Outside their fenced area of private jokes and private love was a landscape too open, too light-drenched, for serious talk. And then, when? Jack woke up quickly and early in the morning and smiled as naturally as children do. He knew where he was and the day of the week and the hour. The best moment of the day was the first cigarette. When something bloody happened, it was never before six in the evening. At night he had a dark look that went with a dark mood, sometimes. Netta would tell him that she could see a cruise ship floating on the black horizon like a piece of the Milky Way, and she would get that look for an answer. But it never lasted. His memory was too short to let him sulk, no matter what fragment of night had crossed his mind. She knew, having heard other couples all her life, that at least she and Jack never made the conjugal sounds that passed for conversation and that might as well have been bowwow and quack quack.

If, by chance, Jack found himself drawn to another woman, if the tide of attraction suddenly ran the other way, then he would discover in himself a great need to talk to his wife. They sat out on their balcony for much of one long night and he told her about his Irish mother. His mother's eccentricity—"Vera's dottiness," where the family was concerned—had kept Jack from taking anything seriously. He had been afraid of pulling her mad attention in his direction. Countless times she had faked tuberculosis and cancer and announced her own imminent death. A telephone call from a hospital had once declared her lost in a car crash. "It's a new life, a new life," her husband had babbled, coming away from the phone. Jack saw his father then as beautiful. Women are beautiful when they fall in love, said Jack; sometimes the glow will last a few hours, sometimes even a day or two.

"You know," said Jack, as if Netta knew, "the look of amazement on a girl's face . . ."

Well, that same incandescence had suffused Jack's father when he thought his wife had died, and it continued to shine until a taxi deposited dotty Vera with her cheerful announcement that she had certainly brought off a successful April Fool. After Jack's father died she became violent. "Getting away from her was a form of violence in me," Jack said. "But I did it." That was why he was secretive; that was why he was independent. He had never wanted any woman to get her hands on his life.

Netta heard this out calmly. Where his own feelings were concerned she thought he was making them up as he went along. The garden smelled coolly of jasmine and mimosa. She wondered who his new girl was, and if he was likely to blurt out a name. But all he had been working up to was that his mother—mad, spoiled, devilish, whatever she was—would need to live with Jack and Netta, unless Netta agreed to giving her an income. An income would let her remain where she was—at the moment, in a Rudolph Steiner community in Switzerland, devoted to medieval gardening and to getting the best out of Goethe. Netta's father's training prevented even the thought of spending the money in such a manner.

"You won't regret all you've told me, will you?" she asked. She saw that the new situation would be her burden, her chain, her mean little joke sometimes. Jack scarcely hesitated before saying that where Netta mattered he could never regret anything. But what really interested him now was his mother.

"Lifts give her claustrophobia," he said. "She mustn't be higher than the second floor." He sounded like a man bringing a legal concubine into his household, scrupulously anxious to give all his women equal rights. "And I hope she will make friends," he said. "It won't be easy, at her age. One can't live without them." He probably meant that he had none. Netta had been raised not to expect to have friends: You could not run a hotel and have scores of personal ties. She expected people to be polite and punctual and to mean what they said, and that was the end of it. Jack gave his friendship easily, but he expected considerable diversion in return.

Netta said dryly, "If she plays bridge, she can play with Mrs. Blackley." This was the wife of the doctor who had first said "Moslem wife." He had come down here to the Riviera for his wife's health; the two belonged to a subcolony of flat-dwelling expatriates. His medical practice was limited to hypochondriacs and rheumatic patients. He had time on his hands: Netta often saw him in the hotel reading room, standing, leafing—he took pleasure in handling books. Netta, no reader, did not like touching a book unless it was new. The doctor had a trick of speech Jack loved to imitate: He would break up his words with an extra syllable, some words only, and at that not every time. "It is all a matter of stu-hyle," he said, for "style," or, Jack's favorite, "Oh, well, in the end it all comes down to su-hex." "Uh-hebb and flo-ho of hormones" was the way he once described the behavior of saints—Netta had looked twice at him over that. He was a firm agnostic and the first person from whom Netta heard there existed a magical Dr. Freud. When Netta's father had died of pneumonia, the doctor's "I'm su-horry, Netta" had been so heartfelt she could not have wished it said another way.

His wife, Georgina, could lower her blood pressure or stop her heartbeat nearly at will. Netta sometimes wondered why Dr. Blackley had brought her to a soft climate rather than to the man at Vienna he so admired. Georgina was well enough to play fierce bridge, with Jack and anyone good enough. Her husband usually came to fetch her at the end of the afternoon when the players stopped for tea. Once, because he was obliged to return at once to a patient who needed him, she said, "Can't you be competent about anything?" Netta thought she understood, then, his resigned repetition of "It's all su-hex." "Oh, don't explain. You bore me," said his wife, turning her back.

Netta followed him out to his car. She wore an India shawl that had been her mother's. The wind blew her hair; she had to hold it back. She said, "Why don't you kill her?"

"I am not a desperate person," he said. He looked at Netta, she looking up at him because she had to look up to nearly everyone except children, and he said, "I've wondered why we haven't been to bed."

"Who?" said Netta. "You and your wife? Oh. You mean me." She was not offended; she just gave the shawl a brusque tug and said, "Not a hope. Never with a guest," though of course that was not the reason.

"You might have to, if the guest were a maharaja," he said, to make it all harmless. "I am told it is pu-hart of the courtesy they expect."

"We don't get their trade," said Netta. This had not stopped her liking the doctor. She pitied him, rather, because of his wife, and because he wasn't Jack and could not have Netta.

"I do love you," said the doctor, deciding finally to sit down in his car. "Ee-nee-ormously." She watched him drive away as if she loved him too, and might never see him again. It never crossed her mind to mention any of this conversation to Jack.

That very spring, perhaps because of the doctor's words, the hotel did get some maharaja trade—three little sisters with ebony curls, men's eyebrows, large heads, and delicate hands and feet. They had four rooms, one for their governess. A chauffeur on permanent call lodged elsewhere. The governess, who was Dutch, had a perfect triangle of a nose and said "whom" for "who," pronouncing it "whum." The girls were to learn French, tennis, and swimming. The chauffeur arrived with a hairdresser, who cut their long hair; it lay on the governess's carpet, enough to fill a large pillow. Their toe- and fingernails were filed to points and looked like a kitten's teeth. They came smiling down the marble staircase, carrying new tennis racquets, wearing blue linen skirts and navy blazers. Mrs. Blackley glanced up from the bridge game as they went by the cardroom. She had been one of those opposed to their having lessons at the English Lawn Tennis Club, for reasons that were, to her, perfectly evident.

She said, loudly, "They'll have to be in white."

"End whayt, pray?" cried the governess, pointing her triangle nose.

"They can't go on the courts except in white. It is a private club. Entirely white."

"Whum do they all think they are?" the governess asked, prepared to stalk on. But the girls, with their newly cropped heads, and their vulnerable necks showing, caught the drift and refused to go.

"Whom indeed," said Georgina Blackley, fiddling with her bridge hand and looking happy.

"My wife's seamstress could run up white frocks for them in a minute," said Jack. Perhaps he did not dislike children all that much.

"Whom could," muttered Georgina.

But it turned out that the governess was not allowed to choose their clothes, and so Jack gave the children lessons at the hotel. For six weeks they trotted around the courts looking angelic in blue, or hopelessly foreign, depending upon who saw them. Of course they fell in love with Jack, offering him a passionate loyalty they had nowhere else to place. Netta watched the transfer of this gentle, anxious gift. After they departed, Jack was bad-tempered for several evenings and then never spoke of them again; they, needless to say, had been dragged from him weeping.

When this happened the Rosses had been married nearly five years. Being childless but still very loving, they had trouble deciding which of the two would be the child. Netta overheard "He's a darling, but she's a sergeant major and no mistake. And so *mean.*" She also heard "He's a lazy bastard. He bullies her. She's a fool." She searched her heart again about children. Was it Jack or had it been Netta who had first said no? The only child she had ever admired was Jack, and not as a child but as a fighter, defying her. She and Jack were not the sort to have animal children, and Jack's dotty mother would probably soon be child enough for any couple to handle. Jack still seemed to adopt, in a tribal sense of his, half the women who fell in love with him. The only woman who resisted adoption was Netta—still burned-out, still ardent, in a manner of speaking still fourteen. His mother had turned up meanwhile, getting down from a train wearing a sly air of enjoy-ing her own jokes, just as she must have looked on the day of the April Fool. At first she was no great trouble, though she did complain about an ulcer-ated leg. After years of pretending, she at last had something real. Netta's policy of silence made Jack's mother confident. She began to make a mock-ery of his music: "All that money gone for nothing!" Or else, "The amount we wasted on schools! The hours he's thrown away with his nose in a book. All that reading—if at least it had got him somewhere." Netta noticed that he spent more time playing bridge and chatting to cronies in the bar now. She thought hard, and decided not to make it her business. His mother had once been pretty; perhaps he still saw her that way. She came of a ram-shackle family with a usable past; she spoke of the Ashers and the Rosses as if she had known them when they were tinkers. English residents who had a low but solid barrier with Jack and Netta were fences-down with his mad mother: They seemed to take her at her own word when it was about her-self. She began then to behave like a superior sort of guest, inviting large parties to her table for meals, ordering special wines and dishes at inconve-nient hours, standing endless rounds of drinks in the bar.

Netta told herself, Jack wants it this way. It is his home too. She began to live a life apart, leaving Jack to his mother. She sat wearing her own mother's shawl, hunched over a new, modern adding machine, punching out accounts. "Funny couple," she heard now. She frowned, smiling in her mind; none of these people knew what bound them, or how tied they were. She had the habit of dodging out of her mother-in-law's parties by saying, "I've got such an awful lot to do." It made them laugh, because they thought this was Netta's term for slave-driving the servants. They thought the staff did the work, and that Netta counted the profits and was too busy with bookkeeping to keep an eye on Jack—who now, at twenty-six, was as attractive as he ever would be.

A woman named Iris Cordier was one of Jack's mother's new friends. Tall, loud, in winter dully pale, she reminded Netta of a blond penguin. Her voice moved between a squeak and a moo, and was a mark of the distinguished literary family to which her father belonged. Her mother, a Frenchwoman, had been in and out of nursing homes for years. The Cordiers haunted the Riviera, with Iris looking after her parents and watching their diets. Now she lived in a flat somewhere in Roquebrune with the survivor of the pair—the mother, Netta believed. Iris paused and glanced in the business room where Mr. Asher had signed the hundred-year lease. She was on her way to lunch—Jack's mother's guest, of course.

"I say, aren't you Miss Asher?"

"I was." Iris, like Dr. Blackley, was probably younger than she looked. Out of her own childhood Netta recalled a desperate adolescent Iris with middle-aged parents clamped like handcuffs on her life. "How is your mother?" Netta had been about to say "How is Mrs. Cordier?" but it sounded servile.

"I didn't know you knew her."

"I remember her well. Your father too. He was a nice person."

"And still is," said Iris, sharply. "He lives with me, and he always will. French daughters don't abandon their parents." No one had ever sounded more English to Netta. "And your father and mother?"

"Both dead now. I'm married to Jack Ross."

"Nobody told me," said Iris, in a way that made Netta think, Good Lord, Iris too? Jack could not possibly seem like a patriarchal figure where she was concerned; perhaps this time the game was reversed and Iris played at being tribal and maternal. The idea of Jack, or of any man, flinging himself on that iron bosom made Netta smile. As if startled, Iris covered her mouth. She seemed to be frightened of smiling back.

Oh, well, and what of it, Iris too, said Netta to herself, suddenly turning back to her accounts. As it happened, Netta was mistaken (as she never would have been with a bill). That day Jack was meeting Iris for the first time.

The upshot of these errors and encounters was an invitation to Roque-brune to visit Iris's father. Jack's mother was ruthlessly excluded, even though Iris probably owed her a return engagement because of the lunch. Netta supposed that Iris had decided one had to get past Netta to reach Jack—an inexactness if ever there was one. Or perhaps it was Netta Iris wanted. In that case the error became a farce. Netta had almost no knowledge of private houses. She looked around at something that did not much interest her, for she hated to leave her own home, and saw Iris's father, apparently too old and shaky to get out of his armchair. He smiled and he nodded, meanwhile stroking an aged cat. He said to Netta, "You resemble your mother. A sweet woman. Obliging and quiet. I used to tell her that I longed to live in her hotel and be looked after."

Not by me, thought Netta.

Iris's amber bracelets rattled as she pushed and pulled everyone through introductions. Jack and Netta had been asked to meet a young American Netta had often seen in her own bar, and a couple named Sandy and Sandra Braunsweg, who turned out to be Anglo-Swiss and twins. Iris's long arms were around them as she cried to Netta, "Don't you know these babies?" They were, like the Rosses, somewhere in their twenties. Jack looked on, blue-eyed, interested, smiling at everything new. Netta supposed that she was now seeing some of the rather hard-up snobbish—snobbish what? "Intelligum-hen-sia," she imagined Dr. Blackley supplying. Having arrived at a word, Netta was ready to go home; but they had only just arrived. The American turned to Netta. He looked bored, and astonished by it. He needs the word for "bored," she decided. Then he can go home, too. The Riviera was no place for Americans. They could not sit all day waiting for mail and the daily papers and for the clock to show a respectable drinking time. They made the best of things when they were caught with a house they'd been rash enough to rent unseen. Netta often had them then *en pension* for meals: A hotel dining room was one way of meeting people. They paid a fee to use the tennis courts, and they liked the bar. Netta would notice then how Jack picked up any accent within hearing.

Jack was now being attentive to the old man, Iris's father. Though this was none of Mr. Cordier's business, Jack said, "My wife and I are first cousins, as well as second cousins twice over."

"You don't look it."

Everyone began to speak at once, and it was a minute or two before Netta heard Jack again. This time he said, "We are from a family of great . . ." It was lost. What now? Great innkeepers? Worriers? Skinflints? Whatever it was, old Mr. Cordier kept nodding to show he approved.

"We don't see nearly enough of young men like you," he said.

"True!" said Iris loudly. "We live in a dreary world of ill women down here." Netta thought this hard on the American, on Mr. Cordier, and on the male Braunsweg twin, but none of them looked offended. "I've got no time for women," said Iris. She slapped down a glass of whiskey so that it splashed, and rapped on a table with her knuckles. "Shall I tell you why? Because women don't tick over. They just simply don't tick over." No one disputed this. Iris went on: Women were underinformed. One could have virile conversations only with men. Women were attached to the past through fear, whereas men had a fearless sense of history. "Men tick," she said, glaring at Jack.

"I am not attached to a past," said Netta, slowly. "The past holds no attractions." She was not used to general conversation. She thought that every word called for consideration and for an answer. "Nothing could be worse than the way we children were dressed. And our mothers—the hard waves of their hair, the white lips. I think of those pale profiles and I wonder if those women were ever young."

Poor Netta, who saw herself as profoundly English, spread consternation by being suddenly foreign and gassy. She talked the English of expatriate children, as if reading aloud. The twins looked shocked. But she had appealed to the American. He sat beside her on a scuffed velvet sofa. He was so large that she slid an inch or so in his direction when he sat down. He was Sandra Braunsweg's special friend: They had been in London together. He was trying to write.

"What do you mean?" said Netta. "Write what?"

"Well—a novel, to start," he said. His father had staked him to one year, then another. He mentioned all that Sandra had borne with, how she had actually kicked and punched him to keep him from being too American. He had embarrassed her to death in London by asking a waitress, "Miss, where's the toilet?"

Netta said, "Didn't you mind being corrected?"

"Oh, no. It was just friendly."

Jack meanwhile was listening to Sandra telling about her English forebears and her English education. "I had many years of undeniably excellent schooling," she said. "Mitten Todd."

"What's that?" said Jack.

"It's near Bristol. I met excellent girls from Italy, Spain. I took *him* there to visit," she said, generously including the American. "I said, 'Get a yellow necktie.' He went straight out and bought one. I wore a little Schiaparelli. Bought in Geneva but still a real . . . A yellow jacket over a gray . . . Well, we arrived at my excellent old school, and even though the day was drizzly I said, 'Put the top of the car back.' He did so at once, and then he understood. The interior of the car harmonized perfectly with the yellow and gray." The twins were orphaned. Iris was like a mother.

"When Mummy died we didn't know where to put all the Chippendale," said Sandra. "Iris took a lot of it."

Netta thought, She is so silly. How can he respond? The girl's dimples and freckles and soft little hands were nothing Netta could have ever described: She had never in her life thought a word like "pretty." People were beautiful or they were not. Her happiness had always been great enough to allow for despair. She knew that some people thought Jack was happy and she was not.

"And what made you marry your young cousin?" the old man boomed at Netta. Perhaps his background allowed him to ask impertinent questions; he must have been doing so nearly forever. He stroked his cat; he was confident. He was spokesman for a roomful of wondering people.

"Jack was a moody child and I promised his mother I would look after him," said Netta. In her hopelessly un-English way she believed she had said something funny.

At eleven o'clock the hotel car expected to fetch the Rosses was nowhere. They trudged home by moonlight. For the last hour of the evening Jack had been skewered on virile conversations, first with Iris, then with Sandra, to whom Netta had already given "Chippendale" as a private name. It proved that Iris was right about concentrating on men and their ticking—Jack even thought Sandra rather pretty.

"Prettier than me?" said Netta, without the faintest idea what she meant, but aware she had said something stupid.

"Not so attractive," said Jack. His slight limp returned straight out of childhood. *She* had caused his accident.

"But she's not always clear," said Netta. "Mitten Todd, for example."

"Who're you talking about?"

"Who are *you*?"

"Iris, of course."

As if they had suddenly quarreled they fell silent. In silence they entered their room and prepared for bed. Jack poured a whiskey, walked on the clothes he had dropped, carried his drink to the bathroom. Through the half-shut door he called suddenly, "Why did you say that asinine thing about promising to look after me?"

"It seemed so unlikely, I thought they'd laugh." She had a glimpse of herself in the mirrors picking up his shed clothes.

He said, "Well, is it true?"

She was quiet for such a long time that he came to see if she was still in the room. She said, "No, your mother never said that or anything like it."

"We shouldn't have gone to Roquebrune," said Jack. "I think those bloody people are going to be a nuisance. Iris wants her father to stay here, with the cat, while she goes to England for a month. How do we get out of that?"

"By saying no."

"I'm rotten at no."

"I told you not to be too pally with women," she said, as a joke again, but jokes were her way of having floods of tears.

Before this had a chance to heal, Iris's father moved in, bringing his cat in a basket. He looked at his room and said, "Medium large." He looked at his bed and said, "Reasonably long." He was, in short, daft about measurements. When he took books out of the reading room, he was apt to return them with "This volume contains about 70,000 words" written inside the back cover.

Netta had not wanted Iris's father, but Jack had said yes to it. She had not wanted the sick cat, but Jack had said yes to that too. The old man, who was lost without Iris, lived for his meals. He would appear at the shut doors of the dining room an hour too early, waiting for the menu to be typed and posted. In a voice that matched Iris's for carrying power, he read aloud, alone: "Consommé. Good Lord, again? Is there a choice between the fish and the cutlet? I can't possibly eat all of that. A bit of salad and a boiled egg. That's all I could possibly want." That was rubbish, because Mr. Cordier ate the menu and more, and if there were two puddings, or a pudding and ice cream, he ate both and asked for pastry, fruit, and cheese to follow. One day, after Dr. Blackley had attended him for faintness, Netta passed a message on to Iris, who had been back from England for a fortnight now but seemed in no hurry to take her father away.

"Keith Blackley thinks your father should go on a diet."

"He can't," said Iris. "Our other doctor says dieting causes cancer."

"You can't have heard that properly," Netta said.

"It is like those silly people who smoke to keep their figures," said Iris. "Dieting."

"Blackley hasn't said he should smoke, just that he should eat less of everything."

"My father has never smoked in his life," Iris cried. "As for his diet, I weighed his food out for years. He's not here forever. I'll take him back as soon as he's had enough of hotels."

He stayed for a long time, and the cat did too, and a nuisance they both were to the servants. When the cat was too ailing to walk, the old man carried it to a path behind the tennis courts and put it down on the gravel to die. Netta came out with the old man's tea on a tray (not done for everyone, but having him out of the way was a relief) and she saw the cat lying on its side, eyes wide, as if profoundly thinking. She saw unlicked dirt on its coat and ants exploring its paws. The old man sat in a garden chair, wearing a panama hat, his hands clasped on a stick. He called, "Oh, Netta, take her away. I am too old to watch anything die. I know what she'll do," he said, indifferently, his voice falling as she came near. "Oh, I know that. Turn on her back and give a shriek. I've heard it often."

Netta disburdened her tray onto a garden table and pulled the tray cloth under the cat. She was angered at the haste and indecency of the ants. "It would be polite to leave her," she said. "She doesn't want to be watched."

"I always sit here," said the old man.

Jack, making for the courts with Chippendale, looked as if the sight of the two conversing amused him. Then he understood and scooped up the cat and tray cloth and went away with the cat over his shoulder. He laid it in the shade of a Judas tree, and within an hour it was dead. Iris's father said, "I've got no one to talk to here. That's my trouble. That shroud was too small for my poor Polly. Ask my daughter to fetch me."

Jack's mother said that night, "I'm sure you wish that I had a devoted daughter to take me away too." Because of the attention given the cat she seemed to feel she had not been nuisance enough. She had taken to saying, "My leg is dying before I am," and imploring Jack to preserve her leg,

should it be amputated, and make certain it was buried with her. She wanted
Jack to be close by at nearly any hour now, so that she could lean on him.
After sitting for hours at bridge she had trouble climbing two flights of
stairs; nothing would induce her to use the lift.

"Nothing ever came of your music," she would say, leaning on him. "Of
course, you have a wife to distract you now. I needed a daughter. Every
woman does." Netta managed to trap her alone, and forced her to sit while
she stood over her. Netta said, "Look, Aunt Vera, I forbid you, I absolutely
forbid you, do you hear, to make a nurse of Jack, and I shall strangle you
with my own hands if you go on saying nothing came of his music. You are
not to say it in my hearing or out of it. Is that plain?"

Jack's mother got up to her room without assistance. About an hour
later the gardener found her on a soft bed of wallflowers. "An inch to the
left and she'd have landed on a rake," he said to Netta. She was still alive
when Netta knelt down. In her fall she had crushed the plants, the yellow
minted *giroflées de Nice*. Netta thought that she was now, at last, for the first
time, inhaling one of the smells of death. Her aunt's arms and legs were
turned and twisted; her skirt was pulled so that her swollen leg showed. It
seemed that she had jumped carrying her walking stick—it lay across the
path. She often slept in an armchair, afternoons, with one eye slightly open.
She opened that eye now and, seeing she had Netta, said, "My son." Netta
was thinking, I have never known her. And if I knew her, then it was Jack
or myself I could not understand. Netta was afraid of giving orders, and of
telling people not to touch her aunt before Dr. Blackley could be summoned, because she knew that she had always been mistaken. Now Jack
was there, propping his mother up, brushing leaves and earth out of her
hair. Her head dropped on his shoulder. Netta thought from the sudden
heaviness that her aunt had died, but she sighed and opened that one eye
again, saying this time, "Doctor?" Netta left everyone doing the wrong
things to her dying—no, her murdered—aunt. She said quite calmly into
a telephone, "I am afraid that my aunt must have jumped or fallen from the
second floor."

Jack found a letter on his mother's night table that began, "Why blame
Netta? I forgive." At dawn he and Netta sat at a card table with yesterday's
cigarettes still not cleaned out of the ashtray, and he did not ask what Netta
had said or done that called for forgiveness. They kept pushing the letter
back and forth. He would read it and then Netta would. It seemed natural

for them to be silent. Jack had sat beside his mother for much of the night. Each of them then went to sleep for an hour, apart, in one of the empty rooms, just as they had done in the old days when their parents were juggling beds and guests and double and single quarters. By the time the doctor returned for his second visit Jack was neatly dressed and seemed wide awake. He sat in the bar drinking black coffee and reading a travel book of Evelyn Waugh's called *Labels*. Netta, who looked far more untidy and underslept, wondered if Jack wished he might leave now, and sail from Monte Carlo on the *Stella Polaris*.

Dr. Blackley said, "Well, you are a dim pair. She is not in pu-hain, you know." Netta supposed this was the roundabout way doctors have of announcing death, very like "Her sufferings have ended." But Jack, looking hard at the doctor, had heard another meaning. "Jumped or fell," said Dr. Blackley. "She neither fell nor jumped. She is up there enjoying a damned good thu-hing."

Netta went out and through the lounge and up the marble steps. She sat down in the shaded room on the chair where Jack had spent most of the night. Her aunt did not look like anyone Netta knew, not even like Jack. She stared at the alien face and said, "Aunt Vera, Keith Blackley says there is nothing really the matter. You must have made a mistake. Perhaps you fainted on the path, overcome by the scent of wallflowers. What would you like me to tell Jack?"

Jack's mother turned on her side and slowly, tenderly, raised herself on an elbow. "Well, Netta," she said, "I daresay the fool is right. But as I've been given quite a lot of sleeping stuff, I'd as soon stay here for now."

Netta said, "Are you hungry?"

"I should very much like a ham sandwich on English bread, and about that much gin with a lump of ice."

She began coming down for meals a few days later. They knew she had crept down the stairs and flung her walking stick over the path and let herself fall hard on a bed of wallflowers—had even plucked her skirt up for a bit of accuracy; but she was also someone returned from beyond the limits, from the other side of the wall. Once she said, "It was like diving and suddenly realizing there was no water in the sea." Again, "It is not true that your life rushes before your eyes. You can see the flowers floating up to you. Even a short fall takes a long time."

Everyone was deeply changed by this incident. The effect on the victim herself was that she got religion hard.

"We are all hopeless nonbelievers!" shouted Iris, drinking in the bar one afternoon. "At least, I hope we are. But when I see you, Vera, I feel there might be something in religion. You look positively temperate."

"I am allowed to love God, I hope," said Jack's mother.

Jack never saw or heard his mother anymore. He leaned against the bar, reading. It was his favorite place. Even on the sunniest of afternoons he read by the red-shaded light. Netta was present only because she had supplies to check. Knowing she ought to keep out of this, she still said, "Religion is more than love. It is supposed to tell you why you exist and what you are expected to do about it."

"You have no religious feelings at all?" This was the only serious and almost the only friendly question Iris was ever to ask Netta.

"None," said Netta. "I'm running a business."

"I love God as Jack used to love music," said his mother. "At least he said he did when we were paying for lessons."

"Adam and Eve had God," said Netta. "They had nobody *but* God. A fat lot of good that did them." This was as far as their dialectic went. Jack had not moved once except to turn pages. He read steadily but cautiously now, as if every author had a design on him. That was one effect of his mother's incident. The other was that he gave up bridge and went back to playing the clarinet. Iris hammered out an accompaniment on the upright piano in the old music room, mostly used for listening to radio broadcasts. She was the only person Netta had ever heard who could make Mozart sound like an Irish jig. Presently Iris began to say that it was time Jack gave a concert. Before this could turn into a crisis Iris changed her mind and said what he wanted was a holiday. Netta thought he needed something: He seemed to be exhausted by love, friendship, by being a husband, someone's son, by trying to make a world out of reading and sense out of life. A visit to England to meet some stimulating people, said Iris. To help Iris with her tiresome father during the journey. To visit art galleries and bookshops and go to concerts. To meet people. To talk.

This was a hot, troubled season, and many persons were planning journeys—not to meet other people but for fear of a war. The hotel had emptied out by the end of March. Netta, whose father had known there would never be another catastrophe, had her workmen come in, as usual. She could hear the radiators being drained and got ready for painting as she packed Jack's clothes. They had never been separated before. They kept telling each other that it was only for a short holiday—for three or four weeks. She was surprised at how neat marriage was, at how many years and feelings could be folded and put under a lid. Once, she went to the window so that he would not see her tears and think she was trying to blackmail him. Looking out, she noticed the American, Chippendale's lover, idly knocking a tennis ball against the garage, as Jack had done in the early summers of their life; he had come round to the hotel looking for a partner, but that season there were none. She suddenly knew to a certainty that if Jack were to die she would search the crowd of mourners for a man she could live with. She would not return from the funeral alone.

Grief and memory, yes, she said to herself, but what about three o'clock in the morning?

By June nearly everyone Netta knew had vanished, or, like the Blackleys, had started to pack. Netta had new tablecloths made, and ordered new white awnings, and two dozen rosebushes from the nursery at Cap Ferrat. The American came over every day and followed her from room to room, talking. He had nothing better to do. The Swiss twins were in England. His father, who had been backing his writing career until now, had suddenly changed his mind about it—now, when he needed money to get out of Europe. He had projects for living on his own, but they required a dose of funds. He wanted to open a restaurant on the Riviera where nothing but chicken pie would be served. Or else a vast and expensive café where people would pay to make their own sandwiches. He said that he was seeing the food of the future, but all that Netta could see was customers asking for their money back. He trapped her behind the bar and said he loved her; Netta made other women look like stuffed dolls. He could still remember the shock of meeting her, the attraction, the brilliant answer she had made to Iris about attachments to the past.

Netta let him rave until he asked for a loan. She laughed and wondered if it was for the chicken-pie restaurant. No—he wanted to get on a boat sailing from Cannes. She said, quite cheerfully, "I can't be Venus and Barclays Bank. You have to choose."

He said, "Can't Venus ever turn up with a letter of credit?"

She shook her head. "Not a hope."

But when it was July and Jack hadn't come back, he cornered her again.

Money wasn't in it now: His father had not only relented but had virtually ordered him home. He was about twenty-two, she guessed. He could still plead successfully for parental help and for indulgence from women. She said, no more than affectionately, "I'm going to show you a very pretty room."

A few days later Dr. Blackley came alone to say good-bye.

"Are you really staying?" he asked.

"I am responsible for the last eighty-one years of this lease," said Netta. "I'm going to be thirty. It's a long tenure. Besides, I've got Jack's mother and she won't leave. Jack has a chance now to visit America. It doesn't sound sensible to me, but she writes encouraging him. She imagines him suddenly very rich and sending for her. I've discovered the limit of what you can feel about people. I've discovered something else," she said abruptly. "It is that sex and love have nothing in common. Only a coincidence, sometimes. You think the coincidence will go on and so you get married. I suppose that is what men are born knowing and women learn by accident."

"I'm su-horry."

"For God's sake, don't be. It's a relief."

She had no feeling of guilt, only of amazement. Jack, as a memory, was in a restricted area—the tennis courts, the cardroom, the bar. She saw him at bridge with Mrs. Blackley and pouring drinks for temporary friends. He crossed the lounge jauntily with a cluster of little dark-haired girls wearing blue. In the mirrored bedroom there was only Netta. Her dreams were cleansed of him. The looking glasses still held their blue-and-silver-water shadows, but they lost the habit of giving back the moods and gestures of a Moslem wife.

About five years after this, Netta wrote to Jack. The war had caught him in America, during the voyage his mother had so wanted him to have. His limp had kept him out of the Army. As his mother (now dead) might have put it, all that reading had finally got him somewhere: He had spent the last years putting out a two-pager on aspects of European culture—part of a scrupulous effort Britain was making for the West. That was nearly all Netta knew. A Belgian Red Cross official had arrived, apparently in Jack's name, to see if she was still alive. She sat in her father's business room, wearing a coat and a shawl because there was no way of heating any part of the hotel now, and she tried to get on with the letter she had been writing in her head, on and off, for many years.

"In June, 1940, we were evacuated," she started, for the tenth or eleventh time. "I was back by October. Italians had taken over the hotel. They used the mirror behind the bar for target practice. Oddly enough it was not smashed. It is covered with spiderwebs, and the bullet hole is the spider. I had great trouble over Aunt Vera, who disappeared and was found finally in one of the attic rooms.

"The Italians made a pet of her. Took her picture. She enjoyed that. Everyone who became thin had a desire to be photographed, as if knowing they would use this intimidating evidence against those loved ones who had missed being starved. Guilt for life. After an initial period of hardship, during which she often had her picture taken at her request, the Italians brought food and looked after her, more than anyone. She was their mama. We were annexed territory and in time we had the same food as the Italians. The thin pictures of your mother are here on my desk.

"She buried her British passport and would never say where. Perhaps under the Judas tree with Mr. Cordier's cat, Polly. She remained just as mad and just as spoiled, and that became dangerous when life stopped being ordinary. She complained about me to the Italians. At that time a complaint was a matter of prison and of death if it was made to the wrong person. Luckily for me, there was also the right person to take the message.

"A couple of years after that, the Germans and certain French took over and the Italians were shut up in another hotel without food or water, and some people risked their well-being to take water to them (for not everyone preferred the new situation, you can believe me). When she was dying I asked her if she had a message for one Italian officer who had made such a pet of her and she said, 'No, why?' She died without a word for anybody. She was buried as 'Rossini,' because the Italians had changed people's names. She had said she was French, a Frenchwoman named Ross, and so some peculiar civil status was created for us—the two Mrs. Rossinis.

"The records were topsy-turvy; it would have meant going to the Germans and explaining my dead aunt was British, and of course I thought I would not. The death certificate and permission to bury are for a Vera Rossini. I have them here on my desk for you with her pictures.

"You are probably wondering where I have found all this writing paper. The Germans left it behind. When we were being shelled I took what few books were left in the reading room down to what used to be the wine cellar and read by candlelight. You are probably wondering where the candles came from. A long story. I even have paint for the radiators, large buckets that have never been opened.

"I live in one room, my mother's old sitting room. The business room can be used but the files have gone. When the Italians were here your mother was their mother, but I was not their Moslem wife, although I still had respect for men. One yelled '*Luce, luce,*' because your mother was showing a light. She said, 'Bugger you, you little toad.' He said, 'Granny, I said "*luce*," not "*Duce.*"'

"Not long ago we crept out of our shelled homes, looking like cave dwellers. When you see the hotel again, it will be functioning. I shall have painted the radiators. Long shoots of bramble come in through the card-room windows. There are drifts of leaves in the old music room and I saw scorpions and heard their rustling like the rustle of death. Everything that could have been looted has gone. Sheets, bedding, mattresses. The neighbors did quite a lot of that. At the risk of their lives. When the Italians were here we had rice and oil. Your mother, who was crazy, used to put out grains to feed the mice.

"When the Germans came we had to live under Vichy law, which meant each region lived on what it could produce. As ours produces nothing, we got quite thin again. Aunt Vera died plump. Do you know what it means when I say she used to complain about me?

"Send me some books. As long as they are in English. I am quite sick of the three other languages in which I've heard so many threats, such boasting, such a lot of lying.

"For a time I thought people would like to know how the Italians left and the Germans came in. It was like this: They came in with the first car moving slowly, flying the French flag. The highest-ranking French official in the region. Not a German. No, just a chap getting his job back. The Belgian Red Cross people were completely uninterested and warned me that no one would ever want to hear.

"I suppose that you already have the fiction of all this. The fiction must be different, oh very different, from Italians sobbing with homesickness in the night. The Germans were not real, they were specially got up for the events of the time. Sat in the white dining room, eating with whatever plates and spoons were not broken or looted, ate soups that were mostly water, were forbidden to complain. Only in retreat did they develop faces and I noticed then that some were terrified and many were old. A radio broadcast from some untouched area advised the local population not to attack them

as they retreated, it would make wild animals of them. But they were attacked by some young boys shooting out of a window and eight hostages
were taken, including the son of the man who cut the maharaja's daughters'
black hair, and they were shot and left along the wall of a café on the more
or less Italian side of the border. And the man who owned the café was
killed too, but later, by civilians—he had given names to the Gestapo once,
or perhaps it was something else. He got on the wrong side of the right side
at the wrong time, and he was thrown down the deep gorge between the two
frontiers.

"Up in one of the hill villages Germans stayed till no one was alive. I was
at that time in the former wine cellar, reading books by candlelight.

"The Belgian Red Cross team found the skeleton of a German deserter
in a cave and took back the helmet and skull to Knokke-le-Zoute as souvenirs.

"My war has ended. Our family held together almost from the
Napoleonic adventures. It is shattered now. Sentiment does not keep families whole—only mutual pride and mutual money."

This true story sounded so implausible that she decided never to send it. She
wrote a sensible letter asking for sugar and rice and for new books; nothing
must be older than 1940.

Jack answered at once: There were no new authors (he had been asking
people). Sugar was unobtainable, and there were queues for rice. Shoes had
been rationed. There were no women's stockings but lisle, and the famous
American legs looked terrible. You could not find butter or meat or tinned
pineapple. In restaurants, instead of butter you were given miniature golf
balls of cream cheese. He supposed that all this must sound like small beer
to Netta.

A notice arrived that a CARE package awaited her at the post office. It
meant that Jack had added his name and his money to a mailing list. She refused to sign for it; then she changed her mind and discovered it was not
from Jack but from the American she had once taken to such a pretty room.
Jack did send rice and sugar and delicious coffee but he forgot about books.
His letters followed; sometimes three arrived in a morning. She left them
sealed for days. When she sat down to answer, all she could remember were
implausible things.

Iris came back. She was the first. She had grown puffy in England—the
result of drinking whatever alcohol she could get her hands on and grimly

eating her sweets allowance: There would be that much less gin and chocolate for the Germans if ever they landed. She put her now wide bottom on
a comfortable armchair—one of the few chairs the first wave of Italians had
not burned with cigarettes or idly hacked at with daggers—and said Jack
had been living with a woman in America and to spare the gossip had let her
be known as his wife. Another Mrs. Ross? When Netta discovered it was
dimpled Chippendale, she laughed aloud.

"I've seen them," said Iris. "I mean I saw them together. King Charles and
a spaniel. Jack wiped his feet on her."

Netta's feelings were of lightness, relief. She would not have to tell Jack
about the partisans hanging by the neck in the arches of the Place Masséna
at Nice. When Iris had finished talking, Netta said, "What about his
music?"

"I don't know."

"How can you not know something so important?"

"Jack had a good chance at things, but he made a mess of everything,"
said Iris. "My father is still living. Life really is too incredible for some
of us."

A dark girl of about twenty turned up soon after. Her costume, a gray
dress buttoned to the neck, gave her the appearance of being in uniform. She
unzipped a military-looking bag and cried, in an unplaceable accent, "Hallo,
hallo, Mrs. Ross? A few small gifts for you," and unpacked a bottle of Haig,
four tins of corned beef, a jar of honey, and six pairs of American nylon
stockings, which Netta had never seen before, and were as good to have
under a mattress as gold. Netta looked up at the tall girl.

"Remember? I was the middle sister. With," she said gravely, "the typical middle-sister problems." She scarcely recalled Jack, her beloved. The
memory of Netta had grown up with her. "I remember you laughing," she
said, without loving that memory. She was a severe, tragic girl. "You were
the first adult I ever heard laughing. At night in bed I could hear it from
your balcony. You sat smoking with, I suppose, your handsome husband. I
used to laugh just to hear you."

She had married an Iranian journalist. He had discovered that political
prisoners in the United States were working under lamentable conditions in
tin mines. President Truman had sent them there. People from all over the
world planned to unite to get them out. The girl said she had been to Germany and to Austria, she had visited camps, they were all alike, and that was
already the past, and the future was the prisoners in the tin mines.

Netta said, "In what part of the country are these mines?"

The middle sister looked at her sadly and said, "Is there more than one part?"

For the first time in years, Netta could see Jack clearly. They were silently sharing a joke; he had caught it too. She and the girl lunched in a corner of the battered dining room. The tables were scarred with initials. There were no tablecloths. One of the great-uncle's paintings still hung on a wall. It showed the Quai Laurenti, a country road alongside the sea. Netta, who had no use for the past, was discovering a past she could regret. Out of a dark, gentle silence—silence imposed by the impossibility of telling anything real—she counted the cracks in the walls. When silence failed she heard power saws ripping into olive trees and a lemon grove. With a sense of deliverance she understood that soon there would be nothing left to spoil. Her great-uncle's picture, which ought to have changed out of sympathetic magic, remained faithful. She regretted everything now, even the three anxious little girls in blue linen. Every calamitous season between then and now seemed to descend directly from Georgina Blackley's having said "white" just to keep three children in their place. Clad in buttoned-up gray, the middle sister now picked at corned beef and said she had hated her father, her mother, her sisters, and most of all the Dutch governess.

"Where is she now?" said Netta.

"Dead, I hope." This was from someone who had visited camps. Netta sat listening, her cheek on her hand. Death made death casual: she had always known. Neither the vanquished in their flight nor the victors returning to pick over rubble seemed half so vindictive as a tragic girl who had disliked her governess.

Dr. Blackley came back looking positively cheerful. In those days men still liked soldiering. It made them feel young, if they needed to feel it, and it got them away from home. War made the break few men could make on their own. The doctor looked years younger, too, and very fit. His wife was not with him. She had survived everything, and the hardships she had undergone had completely restored her to health—which had made it easy for her husband to leave her. Actually, he had never gone back, except to wind up the matter.

"There are things about Georgina I respect and admire," he said, as husbands will say from a distance. His war had been in Malta. He had come here, as soon as he could, to the shelled, gnawed, tarnished coast (as if he had not seen enough at Malta) to ask Netta to divorce Jack and to marry him, or live with him—anything she wanted, on any terms.

But she wanted nothing—at least, not from him.

"Well, one can't defeat a memory," he said. "I always thought it was mostly su-hex between the two of you."

"So it was," said Netta. "So far as I remember."

"Everyone noticed. You would vanish at odd hours. Dis-huppear."

"Yes, we did."

"You can't live on memories," he objected. "Though I respect you for being faithful, of course."

"What you are talking about is something of which one has no specific memory," said Netta. "Only of seasons. Places. Rooms. It is as abstract to remember as to read about. That is why it is boring in talk except as a joke, and boring in books except for poetry."

"You never read poetry."

"I do now."

"I guessed that," he said.

"That lack of memory is why people are unfaithful, as it is so curiously called. When I see closed shutters I know there are lovers behind them. That is how the memory works. The rest is just convention and small talk."

"Why lovers? Why not someone sleeping off the wine he had for lunch?"

"No. Lovers."

"A middle-aged man cutting his toenails in the bathtub," he said with unexpected feeling. "Wearing bifocal lenses so that he can see his own feet."

"No, lovers. Always."

He said, "Have you missed him?"

"Missed who?"

"Who the bloody hell are we talking about?"

"The Italian commander billeted here. He was not a guest. He was here by force. I was not breaking a rule. Without him I'd have perished in every way. He may be home with his wife now. Or in that fortress near Turin where he sent other men. Or dead." She looked at the doctor and said, "Well, what would you like me to do? Sit here and cry?"

"I can't imagine you with a brute."

"I never said that."

"Do you miss him still?"

"The absence of Jack was like a cancer which I am sure has taken root, and of which I am bound to die," said Netta.

"You'll bu-hury us all," he said, as doctors tell the condemned.

"I haven't said I won't." She rose suddenly and straightened her skirt, as she used to do when hotel guests became pally. "Conversation over," it meant.

"Don't be too hard on Jack," he said.

"I am hard on myself," she replied.

After he had gone he sent her a parcel of books, printed on grayish paper, in warped wartime covers. All of the titles were, to Netta, unknown. There was *Fireman Flower* and *The Horse's Mouth* and *Four Quartets* and *The Stuff to Give the Troops* and *Better Than a Kick in the Pants* and *Put Out More Flags.* A note added that the next package would contain Henry Green and Dylan Thomas. She guessed he would not want to be thanked, but she did so anyway. At the end of her letter was "Please remember, if you mind too much, that I said no to you once before." Leaning on the bar, exactly as Jack used to, with a glass of the middle sister's drink at hand, she opened *Better Than a Kick in the Pants* and read, ". . . two Fascists came in, one of them tall and thin and tough looking; the other smaller, with only one arm and an empty sleeve pinned up to his shoulder. Both of them were quite young and wore black shirts."

Oh, thought Netta, I am the only one who knows all this. No one will ever realize how much I know of the truth, the truth, the truth, and she put her head on her hands, her elbows on the scarred bar, and let the first tears of her after-war run down her wrists.

The last to return was the one who should have been first. Jack wrote that he was coming down from the north as far as Nice by bus. It was a common way of traveling and much cheaper than by train. Netta guessed that he was mildly hard up and that he had saved nothing from his war job. The bus came in at six, at the foot of the Place Masséna. There was a deep blue late-afternoon sky and pale sunlight. She could hear birds from the public gardens nearby. The Place was as she had always seen it, like an elegant drawing room with a blue ceiling. It was nearly empty. Jack looked out on this sun-lighted, handsome space and said, "Well, I'll just leave my stuff at the bus office, for the moment"—perhaps noticing that Netta had not invited him anywhere. He placed his ticket on the counter, and she saw that he had not come from far away: he must have been moving south by stages. He carried an aura of London pub life; he had been in London for weeks.

A frowning man hurrying to wind things up so he could have his first drink of the evening said, "The office is closing and we don't keep baggage here."

"People used to be nice," Jack said.

"Bus people?"

"Just people."

She was hit by the sharp change in his accent. As for the way of speaking, which is something else again, he was like the heir to great estates back home after a Grand Tour. Perhaps the estates had run down in his absence. She slipped the frowning man a thousand francs, a new pastel-tinted bill, on which the face of a calm girl glowed like an opal. She said, "We shan't be long."

She set off over the Place, walking diagonally—Jack beside her, of course. He did not ask where they were headed, though he did make her smile by saying, "Did you bring a car?" expecting one of the hotel cars to be parked nearby, perhaps with a driver to open the door; perhaps with cold chicken and wine in a hamper, too. He said, "I'd forgotten about having to tip for every little thing." He did not question his destination, which was no farther than a café at the far end of the square. What she felt at that instant was intense revulsion. She thought, I don't want him, and pushed away some invisible flying thing—a bat or a blown paper. He looked at her with surprise. He must have been wondering if hardship had taught Netta to talk in her mind.

This is it, the freedom he was always offering me, she said to herself, smiling up at the beautiful sky.

They moved slowly along the nearly empty square, pausing only when some worn-out Peugeot or an old bicycle, finding no other target, made a swing in their direction. Safely on the pavement, they walked under the arches where partisans had been hanged. It seemed to Netta the bodies had been taken down only a day or so before. Jack, who knew about this way of dying from hearsay, chose a café table nearly under a poor lad's bound, dangling feet.

"I had a woman next to me on the bus who kept a hedgehog all winter in a basketful of shavings," he said. "He can drink milk out of a wineglass." He hesitated. "I'm sorry about the books you asked for. I was sick of books by then. I was sick of rhetoric and culture and patriotic crap."

"I suppose it is all very different over there," said Netta.

"God, yes."

He seemed to expect her to ask questions, so she said, "What kind of clothes do they wear?"

"They wear quite a lot of plaids and tartans. They eat at peculiar hours. You'll see them eating strawberries and cream just when you're thinking of having a drink."

She said, "Did you visit the tin mines, where Truman sends his political prisoners?"

"*Tin* mines?" said Jack. "No."

"Remember the three little girls from the maharaja trade?"

Neither could quite hear what the other had to say. They were partially deaf to each other.

Netta continued softly, "Now, as I understand it, she first brought an American to London, and then she took an Englishman to America."

He had too much the habit of women, he was playing too close a game, to waste points saying, "Who? What?"

"It was over as fast as it started," he said. "But then the war came and we were stuck. She became a friend," he said. "I'm quite fond of her"—which Netta translated as, "It is a subterranean river that may yet come to light." "You wouldn't know her," he said. "She's very different now. I talked so much about the south, down here, she finally found some land going dirt cheap at Bandol. The mayor arranged for her to have an orchard next to her property, so she won't have neighbors. It hardly cost her anything. He said to her, 'You're very pretty.' "

"No one ever had a bargain in property because of a pretty face," said Netta.

"Wasn't it lucky," said Jack. He could no longer hear himself, let alone Netta. "The war was unsettling, being in America. She minded not being active. Actually she was using the Swiss passport, which made it worse. Her brother was killed over Bremen. She needs security now. In a way it was sorcerer and apprentice between us, and she suddenly grew up. She'll be better off with a roof over her head. She writes a little now. Her poetry isn't bad," he said, as if Netta had challenged its quality.

"Is she at Bandol now, writing poetry?"

"Well, no." He laughed suddenly. "There isn't a roof yet. And, you know, people don't sit writing that way. They just think they're going to."

"Who has replaced you?" said Netta. "Another sorcerer?"

"Oh, *he* . . . he looks like George the Second in a strong light. Or like Queen Anne. Queen Anne and Lady Mary, somebody called them." Iris, that must have been. Queen Anne and Lady Mary wasn't bad—better than King Charles and his spaniel. She was beginning to enjoy his story. He saw it, and said lightly, "I was too preoccupied with you to manage another life. I couldn't see myself going on and on away from you. I didn't want to grow middle-aged at odds with myself."

But he had lost her; she was enjoying a reverie about Jack now, wearing one of those purple sunburns people acquire at golf. She saw him driving an open car, with large soft freckles on his purple skull. She saw his mistress's dog on the front seat and the dog's ears flying like pennants. The revulsion she felt did not lend distance but brought a dreamy reality closer still. He must be thirty-four now, she said to herself. A terrible age for a man who has never imagined thirty-four.

"Well, perhaps you have made a mess of it," she said, quoting Iris.

"What mess? I'm here. *He*—"

"Queen Anne?"

"Yes, well, actually Gerald is his name; he wears nothing but brown. Brown suit, brown tie, brown shoes. I said, '*He* can't go to Mitten Todd. He won't match.' "

"Harmonize," she said.

"That's it. Harmonize with the—"

"What about Gerald's wife? I'm sure he has one."

"Lucretia."

"No, really?"

"On my honor. When I last saw them they were all together, talking."

Netta was remembering what the middle sister had said about laughter on the balcony. She couldn't look at him. The merest crossing of glances made her start laughing rather wildly into her hands. The hysterical quality of her own laughter caught her in midair. What were they talking about? He hitched his chair nearer and dared to take her wrist.

"Tell me, now," he said, as if they were to be two old confidence men getting their stories straight. "What about you? Was there ever ..." The glaze of laughter had not left his face and voice. She saw that he would make her his business, if she let him. Pulling back, she felt another clasp, through a wall of fog. She groped for this other, invisible hand, but it dissolved. It was a lost, indifferent hand; it no longer recognized her warmth. She understood: He is dead ... Jack, closed to ghosts, deaf to their voices, was spared this. He would be spared everything, she saw. She envied him his imperviousness, his true unhysterical laughter.

Perhaps that's why I kicked him, she said. I was always jealous. Not of women. Of his short memory, his comfortable imagination. And I am going to be thirty-seven and I have a dark, an accurate, a deadly memory.

He still held her wrist and turned it another way, saying, "Look, there's paint on it."

"Oh, God, where is the waiter?" she cried, as if that were the one important thing. Jack looked his age, exactly. She looked like a burned-out child who had been told a ghost story. Desperately seeking the waiter, she turned to the café behind them and saw the last light of the long afternoon strike the mirror above the bar—a flash in a tunnel; hands juggling with fire. That unexpected play, at a remove, borne indoors, displayed to anyone who could stare without blinking, was a complete story. It was the brightness on the looking glass, the only part of a life, or a love, or a promise, that could never be concealed, changed, or corrupted.

Not a hope, she was trying to tell him. He could read her face now. She reminded herself, If I say it, I am free. I can finish painting the radiators in peace. I can read every book in the world. If I had relied on my memory for guidance, I would never have crept out of the wine cellar. Memory is what ought to prevent you from buying a dog after the first dog dies, but it never does. It should at least keep you from saying yes twice to the same person.

"I've always loved you," he chose to announce—it really was an announcement, in a new voice that stated nothing except facts.

The dark, the ghosts, the candlelight, her tears on the scarred bar—*they* were real. And still, whether she wanted to see it or not, the light of imagination danced all over the square. She did not dare to turn again to the mirror, lest she confuse the two and forget which light was real. A pure white awning on a cross street seemed to her to be of indestructible beauty. The window it sheltered was hollowed with sadness and shadow. She said with the same deep sadness, "I believe you." The wave of revulsion receded, sucked back under another wave—a powerful adolescent craving for something simple, such as true love.

Her face did not show this. It was set in adolescent stubbornness, and this was one of their old, secret meetings when, sullen and hurt, she had to be coaxed into life as Jack wanted it lived. It was the same voyage, at the same rate of speed. The Place seemed to her to be full of invisible traffic— first a whisper of tires, then a faint, high screeching, then a steady roar. If Jack heard anything, it could be only the blood in the veins and his loud, happy thought. To a practical romantic like Jack, dying to get Netta to bed right away, what she was hearing was only the uh-hebb and flo-ho of hormones, as Dr. Blackley said. She caught a look of amazement on his face: *Now* he knew what he had been deprived of. *Now* he remembered. It had been Netta, all along.

Their evening shadows accompanied them over the long square. "I still have a car," she remarked. "But no petrol. There's a train." She did keep on hearing a noise, as of heavy traffic rushing near and tearing away. Her own quiet voice carried across it, saying, "Not a hope." He must have heard that. Why, it was as loud as a shout. He held her arm lightly. He was as buoyant as morning. This *was* his morning—the first light on the mirror, the first cigarette. He pulled her into an archway where no one could see. What could I do, she asked her ghosts, but let my arm be held, my steps be guided?

Later, Jack said that the walk with Netta back across the Place Masséna was the happiest event of his life. Having no reliable counter-event to put in its place, she let the memory stand.

THE FOUR SEASONS

———

ᘓ❦ᘔ

I

*T*he school Carmela attended for much of six years was founded by
Dr. Barnes, a foreigner who had no better use for his money. It had two classrooms, with varnished desks nailed to the floor, and steel lockers imported
from England, and a playing field in which stray dogs collected. A sepia picture of the founder reading a book hung near a likeness of Mussolini. The two
frames were identical, which showed the importance of Dr. Barnes—at least
in Castel Vittorio. Over their heads the King rode horseback, wearing all his
medals. To one side, somewhat adrift on the same wall, was the Sacred Heart.
After Carmela was twelve and too old to bother with school anymore, she forgot all the history and geography she'd learned, but she remembered the men
in their brown frames, and Jesus with His heart on fire. She left home that
year, just after Easter, and came down to the Ligurian coast between Ven-
timiglia and Bordighera. She was to live with Mr. and Mrs. Unwin now, to
cook and clean and take care of their twin daughters. Tessa and Clare were the
children's names; Carmela pronounced them easily. The Unwins owned a
small printing press, and as there was a large Anglo-American colony in that
part of the world they never lacked for trade. They furnished letterhead stationery, circulars, and announcements for libraries, consulates, Anglican
churches, and the British Legion—some printed, some run off the mimeograph machine. Mr. Unwin was also a part-time real-estate agent. They lived
in a villa on top of a bald hill. Because of a chronic water shortage, nothing
would grow except cactus. An electric pump would have helped the matter,
but the Unwins were too poor to have one put in. Mrs. Unwin worked with

her husband in the printing office when she felt well enough. She was the victim of fierce headaches caused by pollen, sunshine, and strong perfumes. The Unwins had had a cook, a char, and a nanny for the children, but when Carmela joined the household they dismissed the last of the three; the first two had been gone for over a year now. From the kitchen one could look down a slope into a garden where flowering trees and shrubs sent gusts of scent across to torment Mrs. Unwin, and leaves and petals to litter her cactus bed. An American woman called "the Marchesa" lived there. Mrs. Unwin thought of her as an enemy—someone who deliberately grew flowers for the discomfort they created.

Carmela had never been anywhere except her own village and this house, but Mrs. Unwin had no way of knowing that. She pressed a cracked black change purse in Carmela's hand and sent her down the hill to the local market to fetch carrots and not over a pound of the cheapest stewing beef. Carmela saw walled villas, and a clinic with a windbreak of cypress trees and ocher walls and black licorice balconies. Near the shore, work had stopped on some new houses. One could look through them, where windows were still holes in the walls, and catch a glimpse of the sea. She heard someone comment in an Italian more precious than her own, "Hideous. I hope they fall down on top of the builder. Unwin put money in it, too, but he's bankrupt." The woman who made these remarks was sitting under the pale blue awning of a café so splendid that Carmela felt bound to look the other way. She caught, like her flash of the sea, small round tables and colored ices in silver dishes. All at once she recognized a chauffeur in uniform leaning with his back to a speckless motorcar. He was from Castel Vittorio. He gave no sign that he knew Carmela. Her real life was beginning now, and she never doubted its meaning. Among the powerful and the strange she would be mute and watchful. She would swim like a little fish, and learn to breathe underwater.

At the beginning, she did not always understand what was said, or what Mrs. Unwin expected. When Mrs. Unwin remarked, "The chestnut trees flower beautifully up where you come from, though, of course, the blossoms are death for *me*," Carmela stopped peeling vegetables for the English stew Mrs. Unwin was showing her how to make and waited for something more. "What have I said now to startle you?" said Mrs. Unwin. "You're like a little sparrow!" Carmela still waited, glancing sidelong, hair cut unevenly and pushed behind her ears. She wore a gray skirt, a cotton blouse, and sandals. A limp black cardigan hung on her shoulders. She did not own stockings, shoes, a change of underwear, a dressing gown, or a coat, but she had a medal on a chain, an inheritance from a Sicilian grandmother—the grandmother from whom she had her southern name. Mrs. Unwin had already examined Carmela's ears to see if the lobes were pierced. She couldn't stand that—the vanity of it, and the mutilation. Letting Carmela's ears go, she had said to her husband, "Good. Mussolini is getting rid of most of that. All but the medals."

"Have I pronounced 'chestnut' in some peculiar way? My Italian can't be that bad." She got a little green dictionary out of the pocket of her smock and ruffled its pages. She had to tilt her head and close an eye because of the cigarette she kept in her mouth. "I don't mean horse chestnuts," she said, the cigarette waving. "How very funny that is in Italian, by the way. I mean the Spanish chestnuts. They flower late in the season, I believe."

"Every flower has its season," said the child.

Carmela believed this conversation to have a malignant intent she could not yet perceive. The mixture of English and unstressed Italian was virtually impossible for her to follow. She had never seen a woman smoking until now.

"But your family *are* up the Nervia Valley?" Mrs. Unwin insisted. "Your father, your mother, your sisters and your cousins and your aunts?" She became jocular, therefore terrifying. "Maria, Liliana, Ignazio, Francamaria . . ." The names of remembered servants ran out.

"I think so," said Carmela.

Her mother had come down to Bordighera to work in the laundry room of a large hotel. Her little brother had been apprenticed to a stonemason. Her father was dead, perhaps. The black and the gray she wore were half-mourning.

"Mussolini is trying to get away from those oversized families," said Mrs. Unwin with confidence. She sat on a high stool, arranging flowers in a copper bowl. She squashed her cigarette suddenly and drank out of a teacup. She seemed to Carmela unnaturally tall. Her hands were stained, freckled, *old*, but she was the mother of Tessa and Clare, who were under three and still called "the babies." The white roses she was stabbing onto something cruel and spiked had been brought to the kitchen door by the chauffeur from Castel Vittorio. This time he had given Carmela a diffident nod.

"Do you know him?" said Mrs. Unwin instantly.

"I think I saw him in the town," said Carmela.

"Now, that is deceitful," said Mrs. Unwin, though without reproach. "He knows who *you* are, because he vouched for your whole family. 'Hardworking, sober, the pride of the Nervia Valley.' I hope there is to be none of that," she added, in another voice. "You know what I mean. Men, giggling, chatting men up in the doorway, long telephone calls."

The white roses were a peace offering: A dog belonging to the next-door neighbor had torn up something precious in the Unwins' garden. Mrs. Unwin suddenly said that *she* had no time to stroll out in pink chiffon, wearing a floppy hat and carrying a sprinkling can; no time to hire jazz bands for parties or send shuttlecocks flying over the hedge and then a servant to retrieve them; less time still to have a chauffeur as a lover. Carmela could not get the drift of this. She felt accused.

"I don't know, Signora," she said, as though some yes-or-no answer had been required point-blank.

Where the roses had come from everything was white, green, lavish, sweet-smelling. Plants Carmela could not have put a name to bent over with the weight of their blooms. She could faintly hear a radio. All of that belonged to the Marchesa. She was the one who had said, "Hideous."

Pollen carried on the wind from the Marchesa's garden felled Mrs. Unwin in May. She was also assaulted by a large treelike shrub on the Marchesa's side called a datura; some of its bell-like creamy flowers hung over the cactus patch. Their scent, stronger than jasmine, was poison to Mrs. Unwin's nervous system. From her darkened room she sent for Carmela. She opened a leather box with a little key and showed her a sapphire set in diamonds and a loose emerald. She told Carmela the names of the stones and said, "I do not believe in hiding. I am telling you where they are and that the key is in my handkerchief case." Again Carmela felt she had been accused.

The babies sat on their mother's bed meanwhile. They were placid, sleepy children with yellow hair Carmela enjoyed brushing; only one thing was tiring about them—they were too lazy to walk. One or the other had to be carried by Carmela, hooked like a little monkey above her left hip. She began to stand with her spine slightly bent to one side, as a habit. What she remembered of that spring was the weight of Clare or Tessa pulling her shoulder down, and that she was always hungry. Carmela had never known people to eat so little as the Unwins, not even among the poor. They shared a thin cutlet for lunch, or the vegetable remains of a stew, or had an egg apiece or a bit of cooked ham. The children's food and Carmela's was hardly more abundant. Mrs. Unwin did not mean to undernourish her own children; she sincerely believed that very little was enough. Also, meat was expensive. Fruit was expensive. So were cheese, butter, coffee, milk, and bread. The Unwins were pinched for money. They had a house, a printing establishment, furniture, a garden, a car, and they had Carmela, but they had nothing to spend. The drawing-room carpet was scuffed and torn, and the wine-red wallpaper displayed peony-shaped stains of paler dampmold. Mrs. Unwin counted out the coins she gave Carmela for shopping, and she counted the change.

On Fridays the Unwins would send Carmela across to France, where a few things, such as chocolate and bananas, were cheaper. That was not the only reason; it seemed that vegetables grown in Italy gave one typhoid fever. Carmela rode in a bus to within a few yards of the border, walked over (the customs men on both sides came to know her), and took a narrow road downhill to an avenue along the sea. She went as far as the marketplace, never beyond it. She always brought back a loaf of French bread, because it was one of the few things Mr. Unwin could eat with any pleasure. His chronically poor appetite was one of the reasons so little food came into the house. Carmela would break off one end of the loaf to eat on the spot. Then she would break off the other end, to make the loaf symmetrical, but she always kept that crust for later.

Carmela had two other reasons to be anxious that spring. One had to do with the room she slept in; the other was the sea. Although she had spent her life not many miles from the sea, it made her uneasy to be so close to it. At night she heard great waves knock against the foundations of the town. She dreamed of being engulfed, of seeking refuge on rooftops. Within the dream her death seemed inevitable. In the garden, coaxing the twins to walk, she said to the chauffeur from Castel Vittorio, "What happens when the sea comes out?"

In his shirtsleeves, walking the Marchesa's dogs on the road outside, he stopped and laughed at Carmela. "What do you mean, 'out'?"

"Out, up," said Carmela. "Up out of where it is now."

"It doesn't come up or out," he said. "It stays where it is."

"What is there where we can't see?"

"More water," he said. "Then Africa."

Carmela crossed herself—not out of a more ample fear but for the sake of her father, who had probably died there. He had been conscripted for a war and had never come back. There had been no word, no telegram, no congratulations from Mussolini, and of course no pension.

As for her room, it was off the pantry, almost higher than long, with a tiled floor and a good view, if one wanted that. Someone had died there—a relative of Mrs. Unwin's; he had come for a long visit and had been found on the tiles with an electric bell switch in his hand.

"A peaceful death," said Mrs. Unwin, utterly calmly, talking as if Carmela would need to know the history of the place. "Not even time to ring."

The old man's heart was delicate; he could not climb stairs. Who would have heard the bell? It rang somewhere in the passage. The servants they'd kept in those days slept out, and the Unwins took sleeping drafts, yellow and green, prepared in the kitchen and carried up to bed. Carmela felt the sad presence of the poor relation who had come ailing to a good climate and had been put in the meanest room; who had choked, panicked, grabbed for the bell, and fallen on it. The chauffeur from Castel Vittorio had still another version: This house had belonged to the old man. The Unwins had promised to look after him in his lifetime in exchange for the property. But so many debts had come with it that they could not raise any money on it. They were the next thing to paupers, and were known along the coast more or less as steady defaulters.

The chauffeur had often seen the uncle's ghost walking to and fro in the garden, and Carmela herself was often to hear the thud as his body fell between her bed and the door. Under the bed—as beneath any bed that she knew of—was a devil, or a demon, waiting to catch her. Not for a fortune would she have sat on the edge of the bed with her feet dangling. At night she burrowed beneath the bedclothes with a mole tunnel left for breathing. She made sure that every strand of hair was tucked out of sight.

Mornings were tender—first pink, then pearl, then blue. The house was quiet, the twins were awake and smiling. From their upstairs window the sea was a silken cushion. White sails floated—feathers. The breeze that came in was a friendly presence and the fragrance of the Marchesa's garden an extra gift. After a time Carmela's phantoms were stilled. The softness of that June lulled them. The uncle slept peacefully somewhere, and the devil under the bed became too drowsy to stretch out his hand.

II

Late in June, Carmela's little brother ran away from the stonemason and came to the kitchen door. His blond hair was dark with sweat and dirt and his face streaked with it. She gave him a piece of bread she had saved from a French loaf, and a cup of the children's milk out of the icebox. The larder was padlocked; Mrs. Unwin would be along to open it before teatime. Just as Carmela was rinsing the cup she heard, "Who is that, Carmela?" It was Mr., thank God, not Mrs.

"A beggar," said Carmela.

The babies' father was nearsighted. He wore thick glasses, never shouted, seldom smiled. He looked down at the boy in the doorway and said to him, "Why do you beg? Who sends you to do this?" The child's hand was clenched on something, perhaps a stolen something. Mr. Unwin was not unkind; he was firm. The small fist turned this and that way in his grasp, but he managed to straighten the fingers; all that he revealed was a squashed crust and a filthy palm. "Why do you beg?" he repeated. "No one needs to beg in modern Italy. Who sends you? Your father? Your mother? Do they sit idly at home and tell you to ask for money?" It was clear that he would never have put up with an injustice of that kind. The child remained silent, and soon Mr. Unwin found himself holding a hand he did not know what to do with. He read its lines, caked with dirt and marked clearly in an M-shape of blackness. "Where do you live?" he said, letting go. "You can't wander around up here. Someone will tell the police." He did not mean that he would.

"He is going back where he came from," said Carmela. The child looked at her with such adult sadness, and she turned away so gravely as she dried the cup and put it on a shelf, that Mr. Unwin would tell his wife later, in Carmela's hearing, "They were like lovers."

"Give him something," he said to Carmela, who replied that she would, without mentioning that the larder was padlocked; for surely he knew?

Carmela could understand English now, but nobody guessed that. When she heard the Unwins saying sometime after this that they wanted a stonemason because the zoning laws obliged them to grow a hedge or build a wall to replace the sagging wire that surrounded their garden, she kept still; and when they asked each other if it would be worthwhile speaking to Carmela, who might know of someone reliable and cheap, she wore the lightest, vaguest of looks on her face, which meant "No." It was the Marchesa who had lodged a complaint about the Unwins' wire. The unsightliness of it lowered the value of her own property. Mrs. Unwin promised her husband she would carry the bitterness of this to her grave.

The light that had sent the house ghosts to sleep brought Mrs. Unwin nothing but despair. She remained in her curtained bedroom and often forgot even to count the change Carmela returned in the black purse. Dr. Chaffee, of the clinic down the hill, called to see Mrs. Unwin. He wanted to look at the children, too; their father had told him how Tessa and Clare were too lazy to walk. Dr. Chaffee was not Italian and not English. The English physician who had been so good with children and so tactful with their parents had gone away. He was afraid of war. Mrs. Unwin thought this was poor of him. Mussolini did not want war. Neither did Hitler, surely? What did Dr. Chaffee think? He had lived in Berlin.

"I think that you must not feel anxious about a situation you can't change," he said. He still wore the strange dark clothes that must have been proper in another climate.

"I do not feel anxious," she said, her hands to her face.

Carmela parted the curtains a little so that the doctor could examine the twins by light of day. They were not lazy, he said. They had rickets. Carmela could have told him that. She also knew there was no cure for it.

Mrs. Unwin seemed offended. "Our English doctor called it softening of the bone."

"They must have milk," said Dr. Chaffee. "Not the skimmed stuff. Fresh fruit, cod-liver oil." He wrote on a pad as he spoke. "And in August you must get them away from the coast."

Mrs. Unwin's hands slid forward until they covered her face. "I was too old," she said. "I had no right to bring these maimed infants into the world."

Dr. Chaffee did not seem to be alarmed at this. He drew Carmela near, saying, "What about this child? How old is she?"

Carmela remembered she knew no English; she looked dumbly from one to the other. Dr. Chaffee repeated the question in Italian, straight to Carmela, and calling her "little girl."

"Nearly thirteen," said Carmela.

"Good God, she looks nine."

Mrs. Unwin's hands parted. She wore the grimace that was one of her ways of smiling. "I am remiss about everything, then? I didn't create her. Tell me how to make her look nearly thirteen."

"Partly heredity," he said.

They began to chat, and Mrs. Unwin to smile widely.

"I shall do whatever you say," said Mrs. Unwin.

After the doctor had departed—Carmela saw him in his dark suit pausing to look at the datura tree—Mrs. Unwin sent for her again. "The doctor says that part of your trouble must be spaghetti," she said seriously, as if she did not know to a crumb what Carmela was given at meals. "You are to eat meat, fresh vegetables. And take these. Now don't forget. Dr. Chaffee went to some trouble." She gave Carmela a small amber bottle of dark pills, which were said to be iron. Carmela never tasted any, of course. For one thing, she mistrusted medicines; but the bottle remained among her belongings for many years, and had the rank of a personal possession.

Another thing happened about that time: Mrs. Unwin paid Carmela the first installment of her wages.

Mrs. Unwin said that the doves in the Marchesa's garden made more noise than was required of birds. By seven in the morning, the sky was heavy and held the afternoon's thundershower. Carmela, rushing outside to bring in washing dried on the line, felt on her face a breeze that was like warm water. She moved through heat and housework that seemed like a long dream. Someone had placed an order with Mr. Unwin to have poems printed. Mrs. Unwin parted the curtains in her bedroom and in spite of her headaches, which nearly blinded her, stitched one hundred and fifty booklets by hand. One Friday, after shopping in the French market, Carmela went to see a marvel she had been told about—two rows of plane trees whose branches met to form a tunnel. The trunks of these trees turned out to be thick and awkward-looking; they blocked Carmela's view of shops from one sidewalk to the next. Like most trees, they simply stood in the way of anything interesting. She mentioned this to Mrs. Unwin, who walked to and fro in the kitchen, drinking out of a teacup, with a straw sun hat on her head.

"Where there are no trees there are no nightingales," said Mrs. Unwin. "When I am feeling well I like to hear them."

"What, those things that make a noise at night?"

"Not noise but song," said Mrs. Unwin, cradling her teacup.

"Every creature has its moment," said Carmela.

"What a prim creature *you* are," cried Mrs. Unwin, flinging her head back, showing her teeth. Carmela was glad she had made her laugh, but she resolved to be more careful than ever: This was as far as an exchange between them need ever go.

Because of what Dr. Chaffee had said, the Unwins rented an apartment in a village away from the coast for the month of August. They squeezed into the car with the twins and Carmela and much luggage, drove past the road leading to the Nervia Valley, and climbed back into hills Carmela had never seen.

"Weren't you born around here," said Mrs. Unwin, without desiring an answer.

Carmela, who thought she knew all Mrs. Unwin's voices now, did not reply, but Mr. Unwin said, "You know perfectly well it was that other road." It seemed to matter to him that his wife should have made a mistake.

The twins were shared by Mrs. Unwin and Carmela. Both of them wanted to sit on Carmela's lap. Mrs. Unwin was not at all jealous; some serious matters she found extremely comic. The girls slept, and when they woke and began to fret, Mr. Unwin stopped the car so they could both be moved to the back with Carmela. There was scarcely room even for her, small though Dr. Chaffee had said she was, for the back was piled with bedsheets and blankets and even saucepans. After four hours they came to a village that had grass everywhere, and wooden houses that were painted a soft brown. Their summer flat was half a house, with a long carved balcony, and mats instead of carpets, and red curtains on brass rings. It contained an exciting smell of varnish and fresh soap. The Unwins piled all the luggage in a heap on the floor and unpacked nothing to start with but a kettle and teapot and three pottery mugs. Carmela heard Mr. Unwin talking to the owner of this house in his strange nasal Italian and mentioning her, Carmela, as "the young lady who would be in charge." They drank tea meanwhile, Mrs. Unwin sitting on a bare mattress stuffed with horsehair, Carmela standing with her back to a wall. Mrs. Unwin talked to her as she had never done before and would never again. She still seemed to Carmela very large and ugly, but her face was smooth and she kept her voice low, and Carmela thought that perhaps she was not so old after all. She said, "If there is a war, we may not be able to get money out of England, such as there is. We shall never leave Italy. I have faith in the Movement. The Italians know they can trust us. The Germans are, well, as they have always been, and I'm afraid we British have made no effort to meet them halfway. Dr. Chaffee tells me you are as reliable as an adult, Carmela. I am going to believe him. I would like you to teach the twins the alphabet. Will you do that? Don't forget that the English alphabet has a W. Somewhere near the end. Teach them Italian poems and songs. Dr. Chaffee thinks I should have as few worries as possible just now. There will be a course of treatment at the clinic. Baths. Wet sheets. I suppose I must believe in magic." She went on like this, perched on the edge of the bare mattress, staring out over her tea mug, all knees and elbows, and Carmela did not move or answer or even sip her tea. She wanted to make the bed and put the twins in it, because they had missed their afternoon sleep—unless one counted the fitful dozing in the automobile. Mrs. Unwin said, "I had expected a better south than this one. First we went to Amalfi. I had left my son in England. A little boy. When I was allowed to visit him he said, 'How do you do?' No one would speak to me. We came back to Italy. The moonlight glittered on his eyes. Before the twins came. 'Do not think, but feel,' he said to me. Or the opposite. But it was only being tied again—this time with poverty, and the chatter of ill-bred people. No escape from it—marriage, childbirth, patriotism, the dark. The same circle—baptism, confirmation, prayers for the dead. Or else, silence."

From the doorway Mr. Unwin said, *"Ellen."* He came along with a walk Carmela had not seen before, slightly shambling. "What is in the cup?" he said.

She smiled at him and said, "Tea."

He took it, sniffed it. "So it is." He helped her up.

Unpacking, making beds, Carmela experienced a soft, exultant happiness. The Unwins were going back home early the next morning. Mr. Unwin gave Carmela a handful of money—pulled it out of his wallet without counting—and said, "That has got to last you, eh?" with an upward lift that denied this was an order. The money was more than she had ever been trusted with on the coast and actually more than she had seen at any one time. She put the twins to sleep with nightgowns round their pillows (she and Mrs. Unwin between them had forgotten to pack cases) and then shared the Unwins' picnic supper. New people in a new place, they told Carmela to go to bed without bothering about the dishes.

She was pulled out of a deep sleep by a thunderstorm. Her heart squeezed tight in uncontrollable terror. Through the beating of horses' hooves she heard Mr. Unwin speaking quietly. When the storm stopped, the house was perfectly still. She became prey to a hawkmoth and a mosquito. She pulled the sheet up over her head as she had against ghosts, and fell asleep and had the sea dream. She woke up still hearing a thin mosquito song nearby. Along the wall was a white ladder of slatted light that she took to be the light of morning. In her half-sleep she rose and unclasped the shutters and, looking out, saw a track of moon over the village as on the sea, and one pale street lamp, and a cat curled up on the road. The cat, wakened by being seen by Carmela, walked off lashing its tail. She had the true feeling that she was in a real place. She did not dream the sea dream again.

The next thing Carmela heard was the twins bouncing a ball and stumbling after it, still in their nightclothes. The Unwins, up even earlier, had made breakfast. They greeted Carmela as if she were one of their own. The storm had swept the sky clean. Oh, such happiness! Never before, never again. Soon after breakfast they went away, having plotted first with Carmela to distract the twins. In the late afternoon a mist came down so thick and low that Carmela, who had never seen anything like it before, thought it must be the smoke of trees on fire.

Without any warning, the Unwins drove up from the coast one Saturday with Mrs. Unwin's son, Douglas, who lived in England. He was taller even than the Unwins, and had a long face, dark straight hair, and horn-rimmed spectacles. With him was a girl he thought he might marry. "Don't be such a fool," Carmela heard Mrs. Unwin telling Douglas in the kitchen. No one suspected how much Carmela now understood. The girl had a reddish sunburn on her cheeks and nose. Her hair was cut rather like Carmela's, but held with metal grips. She unpacked a flimsy embroidery pattern and a large canvas and began stabbing at it with a flat needle. She was making a cushion. Carmela did not care for the colors, which were dark greens and browns. The girl shifted her gaze from the pattern to the canvas, back and forth. Her sunburn made her too cross to speak. Douglas told his mother she wasn't always quite so unfriendly. Carmela thought that to be as large and as ugly as these people was to be cursed.

They all crowded into the flat for one night. Mrs. Unwin went over Carmela's accounts, but did not ask how much money she had been given in the first place. The next day the parents departed, leaving Douglas and his irritable girl, whom Carmela had been told to call "Miss Hermione"— but of course she could not pronounce it. Miss Hermione took the Unwins' bedroom, Douglas was given Carmela's, and Carmela slept on a cot next to the twins. Every night, Miss Hermione said "No, I said *no*" to Douglas and slammed her door. Carmela supposed she sat behind the door embroidering. She also ate things she had brought in her suitcase. Carmela, who made Miss Hermione's bed every day, discovered chocolate crumbs. One night, when Miss Hermione had retired and was eating stale chocolate and embroidering a cushion, Douglas came into the kitchen where Carmela was washing up at the stone sink.

"Like some help?" he said. She knew no English, of course; did not even turn. He leaned against the drainboard, where she had to see him. He folded his arms and looked at Carmela. Then he began to whistle through his teeth as people do when they are bored, and then he must have reached up and tapped the lightbulb that hung on a cord. It was only the gesture of some-one bored again, but the rocking shadows and the tall ugly boy whistling were like Carmela's sea dream. She dropped her little string dishmop and ran out. She thought she heard herself screaming. "Oh, don't pretend!" he called after her, as mysterious as his mother had once seemed.

He *was* bored; he said so the next day. There was not a thing to do here except stare out at mountains. He went downstairs to where the owner of the house lived, and together they listened to bad news over the radio. He could not understand much of the Italian, but sometimes they caught the BBC broadcasts, and when Douglas did understand something it made the situation seem worse.

"Oh, let's leave, then, for God's sake," Miss Hermione said, folding her canvas neatly twice.

Douglas pressed his hands to his head, for all the world like his mother. He said, "I don't want to be caught up in it."

"Military life won't hurt you," Miss Hermione answered. Without em-broidery to keep her hands busy, she kept shifting and changing position; now she had her hands clasped round a knee, and she swung a long foot and played at pointing her toes.

The day they went off, there was a loud windstorm. They paid the land-lord to drive them as far as a bus station; Carmela never saw them again. Miss Hermione left a green hair ribbon behind. Carmela kept it for years.

As soon as these two had vanished, the wind dropped. Carmela and the twins climbed a little way out of the village and sat in deep grass. The sky held one small creamy cloud. At eye level were lacy grasses and, behind them, blue-black mountains. She tried to teach the twins the alphabet, but she was not certain where to put the W, and the girls were silly and would not listen; she did teach them songs.

III

In September she slipped back to a life she was sure of. She had taken its color. The sea was greener than anything except Mrs. Unwin's emerald, bluer than her sapphire, more transparent than blue, white, transparent glass. Wading with a twin at each hand, she saw their six feet underwater like sea creatures. The sun became as white as a stone; something stung in its heat, like fine, hard, invisible rain. War was somewhere, but not in Italy. Besides, something much more important than a war had taken place. It was this: A new English clergyman had arrived. Now that England was at war he did not know if he should stay. He told someone, who told the Unwins, that he would remain as long as he had a flock to protect. The Unwins, who were agnostics, wondered how to address him. His name was Dunn, but that was not the point. He was not the vicar, only a substitute. They had called his predecessor "Ted," straight out, but they did not propose to call Mr. Dunn "Horace." They decided to make it "Padre." "Padre" was not solemn, and marked an ironic distance they meant to keep with the Church; and it was not rude, either.

Carmela understood that the Unwins' relations with the rest of the foreign colony were endlessly complicated. There were two layers of English, like sea shelves. Near the bottom was a shelf of hotelkeepers, dentists, people who dealt in fruit and in wine—not for amusement but for a living. Nearer the light dwelt the American Marchesa, and people like Miss Barnes and her companion, Miss Lewis. These two lived in mean rooms almost in the attic of a hotel whose owner did not ask them to pay very much, because Miss Barnes was considered someone important—it was her father who had founded village schools and made a present of them to the Italian government. Between the two shelves the Unwins floated, bumping against the one or the other as social currents flung them upward or let them sink. Still lower than any of the English were Russians, Austrians, or Hungarians, rich and poor alike, whose preoccupation was said to be gaining British passports for their children. As passports could be had by marriage—or so the belief ran—the British colony kept a grip on its sons. Mrs. Unwin was heard by Carmela to remark that Hermione had this to be said for her—she was English to the core.

Mrs. Unwin still smiled sometimes, but not as she had in August. She showed a death grin now. When she was excited her skin became a mottled brick-and-white. Carmela had never seen Mrs. Unwin as smiling and as dappled as the afternoon Miss Barnes and Miss Lewis came to tea. Actually, Miss Barnes had called to see about having still more of her late father's poems printed.

"Carmela! Tea!" cried Mrs. Unwin.

Having been often told not to touch the good china, Carmela brought their tea in pottery mugs, already poured in the kitchen.

"Stupid!" said Mrs. Unwin.

"That is something of an insult," Miss Lewis remarked.

"Carmela knows I am more bark than bite," said Mrs. Unwin, with another of her smiles—a twitchy grimace.

But Miss Lewis went on, "You have been down here long enough to know the things one can and can't say to them."

Mrs. Unwin's face, no longer mottled, had gone the solid shade the English called Egyptian red. Carmela saw the room through Mrs. Unwin's eyes: It seemed to move and crawl, with its copper bowl, and novels from England, and faded cretonne-covered chairs, and stained wallpaper. All these dead things seemed to be on the move, because of the way Miss Lewis had spoken to Mrs. Unwin. Mrs. Unwin smiled unceasingly, with her upper lip drawn back.

Miss Barnes, in a wheelchair because she had sprained a knee, reached across and patted her companion's hand. "Charlotte is ever so bolshie," she remarked, taking on a voice and an accent that were obviously meant to make a joke of it. Her eyes went smoothly around the room, but all *she* chose to see or to speak of was the copper bowl, with dahlias in it this time.

"From the Marchesa. Such a pet. Always popping in with flowers!" Mrs. Unwin cried.

"Frances is a dear," said Miss Barnes.

"Ask Mr. Unwin to join us, Carmela," said Mrs. Unwin, trembling a little. After that she referred to the Marchesa as "Frances."

The pity was that this visit was spoiled by the arrival of the new clergyman. It was his first official parish call. He could not have been less welcome. He was a young man with a complexion as changeable as Mrs. Unwin's. He settled unshyly into one of the faded armchairs and said he had been busy clearing empty bottles out of the rectory. Not gin bottles, as they would have been in England, but green bottles with a sediment of red wine, like red dust. The whole place was a shambles, he added, though without complaining; no, it was as if this were a joke they were all young enough to share.

In the general shock Miss Barnes took over: Ted—Dr. Edward Stonehouse, rather—had been repatriated at the expense of his flock, with nothing left for doing up the rectory. He had already cost them a sum—the flock had twice sent him on a cure up to the mountains for his asthma. Everyone had loved Ted; no one was likely to care about the asthma or the anything else of those who came after. Miss Barnes made that plain.

"He left a fair library," said the young man, after a silence. "Though rather dirty."

"I should never have thought that of *Hymns Ancient and Modern*," said bolshie Miss Lewis.

"Dusty, I meant," said the clergyman vaguely. At a signal from Mrs. Unwin, Carmela, whose hands were steady, poured the clergyman's tea. "The changes I shall make won't cost any money," he said, pursuing some thought of his own. He came to and scanned their stunned faces. "Why, I was thinking of the notice outside, 'Evensong Every Day at Noon.' "

"Why change it?" said Miss Barnes in her wheelchair. "I admit it was an innovation of poor old Dr. Stonehouse's, but we are so used to it now."

"And *was* Evensong every day at noon?"

"No," said Miss Barnes, "because that is an hour when most people are beginning to think about lunch."

"More bread and butter, Carmela," said Mrs. Unwin.

Returning, Carmela walked into "The other thing I thought I might . . . do something about"—as if he were avoiding the word "change"—"is the church clock."

"The clock was a gift," said Miss Barnes, losing her firmness, looking to the others for support. "The money was collected. It was inaugurated by the Duke of Connaught."

"Surely not Connaught," murmured the clergyman, sounding to Carmela not quarrelsome but pleasantly determined. He might have been teasing them; or else he thought the entire conversation was a tease. Carmela peeped sideways at the strange man who did not realize how very serious they all were.

"My father was present," said Miss Barnes. "There is a plaque."

"Yes, I have seen it," he said. "No mention of Connaught. It may have been an oversight"—finally responding to the blinks and frowns of Miss Barnes's companion, Miss Lewis. "All I had hoped to alter was . . . I had thought I might have the time put right."

"What is wrong with the time?" said Mrs. Unwin, letting Miss Barnes have a rest.

"It is slow."

"It has always been slow," said Miss Barnes. "If you will look more carefully than you looked at the plaque, you will see a rectangle of cardboard upon which your predecessor printed in large capital letters the word 'slow'; he placed it beneath the clock. In this way the clock, which has historical associations for some of us—my father was at its inauguration—in this way the works of the clock need not be tampered with."

"Perhaps I might be permitted to alter the sign and add the word 'slow' in Italian." He *still* thought this was a game, Carmela could see. She stood nearby, keeping an eye on the plate of bread and butter and listening for the twins, who would be waking at any moment from their afternoon sleep.

"No Italian would be bothered looking at an English church clock," said Miss Barnes. "And none of us has ever missed a train. Mr. Dunn—let me give you some advice: Do not become involved with anything. We are a flock in need of a shepherd; nothing more."

"Right!" screamed Mrs. Unwin, white-and-brick-mottled again. "For God's sake, Padre . . . no involvement!"

The clergyman looked as though he had been blindfolded and turned about in a game and suddenly had the blindfold whipped off. Mr. Unwin had not spoken until now. He said deliberately, "I hope you are not a scholar, Padre. Your predecessor was, and his sermons were a great bore."

"Stonehouse a scholar?" said Mr. Dunn.

"Yes, I'm sorry to say. I might have brought my wife back to the fold, so to speak, but his sermons were tiresome—all about the Hebrews and the Greeks."

The clergyman caught Carmela staring at him, and noticed her. He smiled. The smile fixed his face in her memory for all time. It was not to her an attractive face—it was too fair-skinned for a man's; it had color that came and ebbed too easily. "Perhaps there won't be time for the Greeks and the Hebrews now," he said gently. "We *are* at war, aren't we?"

"We?" said Miss Barnes.

"Nonsense, Padre," said Mrs. Unwin briskly. "Read the newspapers."

"England," said the clergyman, and stopped.

Mr. Unwin was the calmest man in the world, but he could be as wild-looking as his wife sometimes. At the word "England" he got up out of his chair and went to fetch the Union Jack on a metal standard that stood out in the hall, leaning into a corner. The staff was too long to go through the door upright; Mr. Unwin advanced as if he were attacking someone with a long spear. "Well, Padre, what about this?" he said. The clergyman stared as if he had never seen any flag before, ever; as if it were a new kind of leaf, or pudding, or perhaps a skeleton. "Will the flag have to be dipped at the church door on Armistice Day?" said Mr. Unwin. "It can't be got through the door without being dipped. I have had the honor of carrying this flag for the British Legion at memorial services. But I shall no longer carry a flag that needs to be lowered now that England is at war. For I do agree with you, Padre, on that one matter. I agree that England *is* at war, rightly or wrongly. The lintel of the church door must be raised. You do see that? Your predecessor refused to have the door changed. I can't think why. It is worthless as architecture."

"You don't mean that," said Miss Barnes. "The door is as important to us as the time of Evensong."

"Then I shall say no more," said Mr. Unwin. He stood the flag in a corner and became his old self in a moment. He said to Carmela, "The Padre has had enough tea. Bring us some glasses, will you?" On which the three women chorused together, "Not for me!"

"Well, I expect you'll not forget your first visit," said Mr. Unwin.

"I am not likely to," said the young man.

By October the beach was windy and alien, with brown seaweed-laden waves breaking far inshore. A few stragglers sat out of reach of the icy spray. They were foreigners; most of the English visitors had vanished. Mrs. Unwin invented a rule that the little girls must bathe until October the fifteenth. Carmela felt pity for their blue, chattering lips; she wrapped towels around their bodies and held them in her arms. Then October the fifteenth came and the beach torment was over. She scarcely remembered that she had lived any life but this. She could now read in English and was adept at flickering her eyes over a letter left loose without picking it up. As for the Unwins, they were as used to Carmela as to the carpet, whose tears must have seemed part of the original pattern by now. In November Miss Barnes sent Mrs. Unwin into a paroxysm of red-and-white coloration by accepting an invitation to lunch. Carmela rehearsed serving and clearing for two days. The meal went off without any major upset, though Carmela did stand staring when Miss Barnes suddenly began to scream, "Chicken! Chicken! How wonderful! Chicken!" Miss Barnes did not seem to know why she was saying this; she finally became conscious that her hands were in the air and brought them down. After that, Carmela thought of her as "Miss Chicken." That day Carmela heard, from Miss Chicken, "Hitler will never make the Italians race-minded. They haven't it in them." Then, "Of course, Italian men are not to be taken seriously," from Miss Lewis, fanning herself absently with her little beaded handbag, and smiling at some past secret experience. Still later, Carmela heard Miss

Barnes saying firmly, "Charlotte is mistaken. Latins talk, but they would never hurt a fly."

Carmela also learned, that day, that the first sermon the new clergyman had preached was about chastity, the second on duty, the third on self-discipline. But the fourth sermon was on tolerance—"slippery ground," in Mrs. Unwin's opinion. And on the eleventh of November, at a special service sparsely attended, flag and all, by such members of the British Legion as had not fled, he had preached pacifism. Well—Italy was at peace, so it was all right. But there had been two policemen in mufti, posing as Anglican parishioners. Luckily they did not seem to understand any English.

"The Padre was trying to make a fool of me with that sermon," said Mrs. Unwin.

"Why you, Ellen?" said her husband.

"Because he knows my views," said Mrs. Unwin. "I've had courage enough to voice them."

Miss Lewis looked as if she had better say nothing; then she decided to remark, in a distant, squeaky voice, "I don't see why an agnostic ever goes to church at all."

"To see what he is up to," said Mrs. Unwin.

"Surely the police were there for that?"

Mr. Unwin said he had refused to attend the Armistice Day service; the matter of flag dipping had never been settled.

"I have written the Padre a letter," said Mrs. Unwin. "What do we care about the Greek this and the Hebrew that? We are all living on dwindled incomes and wondering how to survive. Mussolini has brought order and peace to this country, whether Mr. Dunn likes it or not."

"Hear, hear," said Miss Chicken. Mr. Unwin nodded in slow agreement. Miss Lewis looked into space and pursed her lips, like someone counting the chimes of a clock.

IV

In spite of the electricity rates, the kitchen light had to go on at four o'clock. Carmela, lifting her hand to the shelf of tea mugs, cast a shadow. At night she slept with her black cardigan round her legs. When she put a foot on the tiled floor she trembled with cold and with fear. She was afraid of the war and of the ghost of the uncle, which, encouraged by early darkness, could be seen in the garden again. Half the villas along the hill were shuttered. She looked at a faraway sea, lighted by a sun twice as far off as it had ever been before. The Marchesa was having a bomb shelter built in her garden. To make way for it, her rose garden had been torn out by the roots. So far only a muddy oblong shape, like the start of a large grave, could be seen from the Unwins' kitchen. Progress on it was by inches only; the men could not work in the rain, and this was a wet winter. Mrs. Unwin, who had now instigated a lawsuit over the datura tree, as the unique cause of her uneven health, stood on her terrace and shouted remarks—threats, perhaps—to the workmen on the far side of the Marchesa's hedge. She wore boots and a brown fur coat like a kimono. Among the men were Carmela's little brother and his employer. The employer, whose name was Lucio, walked slowly as far as the hedge.

"How would you like to do some really important work for us?" cried Mrs. Unwin.

Mr. Unwin would come out and look at his wife and go in the house again. He spoke gently to Carmela and the twins, but not often. There were now only two or three things he would eat—Carmela's vegetable soup, Carmela's rice and cheese, and French bread. Mrs. Unwin no longer spoke of the Marchesa as "Frances," and the chauffeur had given up coming round to the kitchen door. There was bad feeling over the lawsuit, which, as a civil case, could easily drag on for the next ten years. Then one day the digging ceased. The villa was boarded over. The Marchesa had taken her dogs to America, leaving everything, even the chauffeur, behind. Soon after Christmas, the garden began to bloom in waves of narcissi, anemones, irises, daffodils; then came the great white daisies and the mimosa; and then all the geraniums that had not been uprooted with the rosebushes flowered at once—white, salmon-pink, scarlet, peppermint-striped. The tide of color continued to run as long as the rains lasted. After that the flowers died off and the garden became a desert.

Mrs. Unwin said the Marchesa had bolted like a frightened hare. She, though untitled, though poor, would now show confidence in Mussolini and his wish for peace by having a stone wall built round her property. Lucio was employed. Mrs. Unwin called him "a dear old rogue." She was on tiptoe between headaches. The climate was right for her just now: no pollen. Darkness. Not too much sun. Long cold evenings. For a time she blossomed like the next-door garden, until she made a discovery that felled her again.

She and Mr. Unwin together summoned Carmela; together they pointed to a fair-haired boy carrying stones. Mr. Unwin said, "Who is he?"

"He is my brother," Carmela said.

"I have seen him before," said Mr. Unwin.

"He once visited me."

"But Carmela," said Mr. Unwin, as always softly. "You knew that we were looking about for a stonemason. Your own brother was apprenticed to Lucio. You never said a word. Why, Carmela? It is the same thing as lying."

Mrs. Unwin's voice had a different pitch: "You admit he is your brother?"

"Yes."

"You heard me saying I needed someone for the walls?"

"Yes."

"It means you don't trust me." All the joyous fever had left her. She was soon back in her brown kimono coat out on the terrace, ready to insult strangers again. There was only Lucio. No longer her "dear old rogue," he spat in her direction and shook his fist and called her a name for which Carmela did not have the English.

The Italians began to expel foreign-born Jews. The Unwins were astonished to learn who some of them were: They had realized about the Blums and the Wiesels, for that was evident, but it was a shock to have to see Mrs. Teodoris and the Delaroses in another light, or to think of dear Dr. Chaffee as someone in trouble. The Unwins were proud that this had not taken place in their country—at least not since the Middle Ages—but it might not be desirable if all these good people were to go to England now. Miss Barnes had also said she hoped some other solution could be found. They were all of them certainly scrambling after visas, but were not likely to obtain any by marriage; the English sons and daughters had left for home.

Carmela still went over to France every Friday. The frontier was open; there were buses and trains, though Dr. Chaffee and the others were prevented from using them. Sometimes little groups of foreign-born Jews were rounded up and sent across to France, where the French sent them back again, like the Marchesa's shuttlecocks. Jews waiting to be expelled from France to Italy were kept in the grounds of the technical school for boys; they sat there on their luggage, and people came to look at them through the fence. Carmela saw a straggling cluster of refugees—a new word—being marched at gunpoint up the winding street to the frontier on the French side. Among them, wearing his dark suit, was Dr. Chaffee. She remembered how she had not taken the pills he had given her—had not so much as unscrewed the metal cap of the bottle. Wondering if he knew, she looked at him with shame and apology before turning her head away. As though he had seen on her face an expression he wanted, he halted, smiled, shook his head. He was saying no to something. Terrified, she peeped again, and this time he lifted his hand, palm outward, in a curious greeting that was not a salute. He was pushed on. She never saw him again.

"What *is* all this talk?" said Mrs. Unwin. "Miss Lewis is full of it. Have you seen anything around the frontier, Carmela?"

"No, never," she said.

"I'm sure it is the Padre's doing," said Mrs. Unwin. "He preached about tolerance once too often. It worked the Italians up." She repeated to her husband Miss Barnes's opinion, which was that Mussolini did not know what was going on.

In March the wind blew as it had in the autumn. The east wind seemed to have a dark color to it. Twice on the same March night, Carmela was wakened by the beating of waves. At the market, people seemed to be picking their feet out of something gray and adhesive—their own shadows. The Italians began to change; even the clerks in the post office were cheeky with foreigners now. Mrs. Unwin believed the Padre was to blame. She went to listen to his Lenten sermons, and of course caught him out. He preached five Lenten messages, and with each the season advanced and the sea became light, then deep blue, and the Marchesa's garden brighter and sweeter-smelling. As he had in the autumn, the Padre started off carefully, choosing as his subjects patience, abstinence, and kindness. So far so good, said Mrs. Unwin. But the fourth sermon was on courage, the fifth on tyranny, on Palm Sunday he spoke about justice, and on Good Friday he took his text from Job: "Behold I cry out of wrong, but I am not heard: I cry aloud, but there is no judgment." On Easter Sunday he mentioned Hitler by name.

Mrs. Unwin looked up the Good Friday text and found at the top of the page "Job complaineth of his friends' cruelty." She read it out to her husband, adding, "That was meant for me."

"Why you?"

"Because I have hit, and where I hit I hit hard," she cried.

"What have you been up to?" His voice rose as much as ever it could or would. He noticed Carmela and fell silent.

Late in May, Mrs. Unwin won her case against the Marchesa. There was no precedent for the speed of the decision. Mr. Unwin thought the courts were bored with the case, but his wife took it to mean compensation for the Unwins' having not run away. All the datura branches overhanging the Unwins' garden were to be lopped off, and if Mrs. Unwin's headaches persisted the tree was to be cut down. The Unwins hired a man to do the pruning, but it was a small triumph, for the Marchesa was not there to watch.

The night before the man arrived to prune the tree, a warship sent playful searchlights over the hills and the town. The shore was lit as if with strings of yellow lanterns. The scent of the datura rose in the air like a bonfire. Mrs. Unwin suddenly said, "Oh, what does it matter now?" Perhaps it was not the datura that was responsible after all. But in the morning, when the man came with an axe and a saw, he would not be dismissed. He said, "You sent for me and I am here." Carmela had never seen him before. He told her she had no business to be working for foreigners and that soon there would be none left. He hacked a hole through the hedge and began to saw at the base of the datura.

"That's not our property!" Mrs. Unwin cried.

The man said, "You hired me and I am here," and kept on sawing.

On the road where the chauffeur had walked the Marchesa's dogs, a convoy of army lorries moved like crabs on the floor of the sea.

V

*T*he frontier was tightened on both sides for Jews—even those who were not refugees. Some of the refugees set off for Monaco by fishing boat; there was a rumor that from Monaco no one was turned back to Italy. They paid sums of money to local fishermen, who smuggled them along the coast by night and very often left them stranded on a French beach, and the game of battledore and shuttlecock began again. Carmela heard that one woman flung herself over the edge of the bridge into the gorge with the dried riverbed at the bottom that marked the line between Italy and France. Lucio gave up being a stonemason and bought a part interest in a fishing boat. He took Carmela's brother along.

Carmela's mother was given notice that the hotel where she worked was to close. She sent a message to Carmela telling her to stay where she was for as long as the Unwins could keep her, for at home they would be sorely in need of money now. Carmela's brother was perhaps earning something with the boat traffic of Jews, but how long could it last? And what was the little boy's share?

Carmela heard from someone in the local market that all foreigners were to be interned—even Miss Barnes. She gave a hint about it, because her own situation depended on the Unwins' now. Mrs. Unwin scolded Carmela for spreading rumors. That very day, the Unwins' mimeograph machine was seized and carried away, though whether for debts or politics Carmela could not be sure. Along with the machine the provincial police confiscated a pile of tracts that had been ordered by the British Legion and had to do with a garden party on the twenty-fourth of May, the birthday of Queen Victoria. The deepest official suspicion now surrounded this celebration, although in the past the Italian military commander of the region had always attended with his wife and daughters. Then the printing shop was suddenly pad-locked and sealed. Mr. Unwin was obliged to go to the police station and explain that he had paid his taxes and had not printed anything that was il-legal or opposed to Mussolini. While he was away, a carload of civil guards arrived and pounded on the door.

"They don't even speak good Italian," said Mrs. Unwin. "Here, Car-mela—find out what they want." But they were Calabrians and quite foreign to Carmela, in spite of her Sicilian grandmother. She told Mrs. Unwin she did not know what they were saying, either. At the same time, she decided to ask for her wages. She had not been paid after the first three months.

Mr. Unwin returned from the police station, but nothing was said in front of Carmela. The frontier was now closed to everyone. Carmela would never go shopping on the French side again. When she mentioned her wages Mrs. Unwin said, "But Carmela, you seemed so fond of the children!"

Early one afternoon, Mrs. Unwin burst into the kitchen. Her hair was wild, as if she had been pulling at it. She said, "It has happened, Carmela. Can you understand? Can you understand the horror of our situation? We can't get any money from England, and we can't draw anything out of the bank here. You must go home now, back to your family. We are leaving for England, on a coal boat. I am leaving with the children. Mr. Unwin will try to come later. You must go home now, today. Why are you crying?" she said, and now she really did tug her hair. "We'll pay you in full and with in-terest when it is all over."

Carmela had her head down on the kitchen table. Pains like wings pressed on her shoulders until her sobs tore them apart.

"Why are you crying?" said Mrs. Unwin again. "Nothing can happen to you. You'll be thankful to have the money after Mussolini has lost his war." She patted the child between her fragile shoulders. "And yet, how can he lose, eh? Even I don't see how. Perhaps we'll all laugh—oh, I don't know what I'm saying. Carmela, please. Don't alarm the children."

For the last time in her life, Carmela went into the room she had shared with a ghost and a demon. She knew that her mother would never believe her story and that she would beat her. "Good-bye, little girls," she said, though they were out of earshot. In this way she took leave without alarming them. She packed and went back to the kitchen, for want of knowing where to go. All this had happened while Carmela was clearing away after lunch. The larder was still unlocked. She took a loaf of bread and cut it in three pieces and hid the pieces in her case. Many years later, it came to her that in lieu of wages she should have taken a stone from the leather box. Only fear would have kept her from doing it, if she had thought of it. For the last time, she looked out over the Marchesa's shuttered villa. It had already been looted twice. Each time, the police had come and walked around and gone away again. The deep pit of the unfinished bomb shelter was used by all the neighborhood as a dump for unwanted litters of kittens. The chauffeur had prowled for a bit, himself something of a cat, and then he vanished, too.

When Mrs. Unwin searched Carmela's case—Carmela expected that; everyone did it with servants—she found the bread, looked at it without understanding, and closed the lid. Carmela waited to be told more. Mrs. Unwin kissed her forehead and said, "Best of luck. We are all going to need it. The children will miss you."

Now that the worst was over, Mr. Unwin appeared on the scene; he would drive Carmela as far as the Nervia Valley bus stop. He could not take her all the way home, because he had only so much petrol, and because of everything else he had to do before evening. This was without any doubt the worst day of the Unwins' lives.

"Is it wise of you to drive about so openly?" said his wife.

"You don't expect to hide and cringe? As long as I am free I shall use my freedom."

"So you said to me years ago," said his wife. This time Carmela did not consider the meaning of her smile. It had lost its importance.

Mr. Unwin carried Carmela's case to the car and stowed it in the luggage compartment. She sat up front in Mrs. Unwin's usual place. Mr. Unwin explained again that he would drive as far as the Nervia Valley road, where she could then continue by bus. He did not ask if there was any connection to Castel Vittorio or, should there be one, its frequency. They drove down the hill where Carmela had walked to the local market that first day. Most of the beautiful villas were abandoned now, which made them look incomplete. The Marchesa's word came back to her: "Hideous." They passed Dr. Chaffee's clinic and turned off on the sea road. Here was the stop where Carmela had waited for a bus to the frontier every Friday—every Friday of her life, it seemed. There was the café with the pale blue awning. Only one person, a man, sat underneath it today.

"*Hallo*," said Mr. Unwin. He braked suddenly and got out of the car. "Fond of ices, Padre?" he said.

"I've spent two nights talking to the police," said the clergyman. "I very much want to be seen."

"You too, eh?" Mr. Unwin said. He seemed to forget how much he still had to do before evening, and that he and the Padre had ever disagreed about tolerance or Hitler or dipping the flag. "Come along, Carmela," he called over his shoulder. "These young things are always hungry," he said lightly, as though Carmela had been eating him out of house and home.

"My party," said the Padre. Mr. Unwin did not contradict. There they were, police or not, war or not. It was one of the astonishing things that Carmela remembered later on. When an ice was brought and set before her she was afraid to eat it. First, it was too beautiful—pistachio, vanilla, tangerine, three colors in a long-stemmed silver dish that sat in turn upon a lace napkin and a glass plate. Carmela was further given cold water in a tall frosted glass, a long-handled delicate spoon with a flat bowl, and yet another plate containing three overlapping wafer biscuits. Her tears had weakened her; it was almost with sadness that she touched the spoon.

"I won't have it said that I ran away," said the clergyman. "One almost *would* like to run. I wasn't prepared for anonymous letters." The soft complexion that was like a girl's flushed. Carmela noticed that he had not shaved; she could not have imagined him bearded.

"Anonymous letters to the police?" said Mr. Unwin. "And in English?"

"First one. Then there were others."

"In *English?*"

"Oh, in English. They'd got the schoolmaster to translate them."

"Not even to my worst enemy—" Mr. Unwin began.

"No, I'm sure of that. But if I have inspired hatred, then I've failed. Some of the letters came to me. I never spoke of them. When there was no reaction then—I suppose it must have been interesting to try the police."

"Those you had—were they by hand?" said Mr. Unwin. "Let me see one. I shan't read it."

"I'm sorry, I've destroyed them."

Carmela looked across at the houses on which work had been suspended for more than a year—a monument to Mr. Unwin's qualifications as an investor of funds, she now understood; behind them was the sea that no longer could frighten her. She let a spoonful of pistachio melt in her mouth and swallowed regretfully.

"Of course you know the story," said Mr. Unwin. "You have heard the gossip."

"I don't listen to gossip," said the clergyman. They had no use for each other, and might never meet again. Carmela sensed that, if Mr. Unwin did not. "Nothing needs to be explained. What matters is, how we all come out of it. I've been told I may leave. My instructions *are* to leave. Hang them. They can intern me or do whatever they like. I won't have them believing that we can be bullied."

Mr. Unwin was speaking quietly; their words overlapped. He was going to explain, even if it was to no purpose now, whether the clergyman had any use for him or not. ". . . When we did finally marry we were so far apart that she hardly had a claim. I made her see a neurologist. He asked her if she was afraid of me." The lines of age around his eyes made him seem furtive. He had the look of someone impartial, but stubborn, too. "Having children was supposed to be good. To remove the guilt. To make her live in the present." They had come here, where there was a famous clinic and an excellent doctor—poor Dr. Chaffee. Gone now. Between her second breakdown and the birth of the twins, somewhere in that cleared-out period, they married. The Church of England did not always allow it. Old Ted Stonehouse had been lenient. For years they'd had nothing but holidays, a holiday life, always with the puritan belief that they would have to pay up. They had paid, he assured the younger man, for a look at their past—a wrecked past, a crippling accident. At times, he could see the debris along the road—a woman's shoe, a charred map. And they married, and had the twins, and the holiday came to an end. And she was beginning to be odd, cruel, drinking stuff out of teacups. She kept away from the babies. Was afraid of herself. Knew she was cruel. Cruel to her own great-uncle. Never once looked at his grave. Mr. Unwin had been to the grave not long ago, had stung his hands on nettles.

"Oh, I'd never weed a grave," said the clergyman. "I am like that, too."

"Well, Padre, we choose our lives," said Mr. Unwin. "I gave up believing in mine."

"Forget about believing in your life," said the younger man. "Think about the sacraments—whether you believe in them or not. You might arrive in a roundabout way. Do you see?"

"Arrive where?" said Mr. Unwin. "Arrive at what? I never get up in the morning without forcing myself to get out of bed, and without tears in my eyes. I have had to stop shaving sometimes because I could not see for tears. I've watched the sun rising through the tears of a child left in his first school. If ever I had taken a day in bed nothing would have made me get up again. Not my children, not my life, not my country. How I have envied Carmela, here—hearing her singing at her work."

"Well, and how about you, Carmela?" said the clergyman, quite glad to turn his attention to her, it seemed.

Carmela put her spoon down and said simply, "I have just eaten my way into Heaven."

"Then I haven't entirely failed," the clergyman said.

Mr. Unwin laughed, then blew his nose. "Let me give you a lift, Padre," he said. "Think twice about staying. If I were you I would get on that coal boat with the others."

They left Carmela at what they both seemed to think was a bus stop. Mr. Unwin set her case down and pressed money into her hand without counting it, as he had done last August.

"The children will miss you," he said, which must have been the Unwins' way of saying good-bye.

As soon as the car was out of sight she began to walk. There *was* a bus, but it was not here that it stopped for passengers. In any case it would not be along until late afternoon, and it did not go as far as Castel Vittorio. Within half an hour she was in a different landscape—isolated, lonely, and densely green. A farmer gave her a ride on a cart as far as Dolceacqua. She passed a stucco hotel where people sometimes came up from the coast in August to get away from the heat. It was boarded up like the villas she had left behind. After Dolceacqua she had to walk again. The villages along the valley were just as they'd been a year ago. She had forgotten about them. She did not want to lose the taste of the ices, but all she had kept was the look of them—the pink-orange, the pale green, the white with flecks of vanilla, like pepper. She shifted her cardboard suitcase with its rope strap from hand to hand. It was not heavy but cumbersome; certainly much lighter than one of the twins. Sometimes she stopped and crouched beside it in a position of repose she had also forgotten but now assumed naturally. This was a warm clear June day, with towering clouds that seemed like cream piled on a glass plate. She looked up through invisible glass to a fantastic tower of cream. The palms of the coast had given way to scrub and vineyards, then to oaks and beeches and Spanish chestnut trees in flower. She remembered the two men and their strange conversation; they were already the far past. A closer memory was the schoolhouse, and Dr. Barnes and Mussolini and the King in wooden frames. Mr. Unwin weeping at sunrise had never been vivid. He faded first. His tears died with him. The clergyman blushed like a girl and wished Mr. Unwin would stop talking. Both then were lost behind Dr. Chaffee in his dark suit stumbling up the hill. He lifted his hand. What she retained, for the present, was one smile, one gesture, one man's calm blessing.

THE FENTON CHILD

―――――

⚜

I

*I*n a long room filled with cots and undesired infants, Nora Abbott had her first sight of Neil, who belonged to Mr. and Mrs. Boyd Fenton. The child was three months old but weedy for his age, with the face of an old man who has lost touch with his surroundings. The coarse, worn, oversized gown and socks the nuns had got him up in looked none too fresh. Four large safety pins held in place a chafing and voluminous diaper. His bedding—the whole nursery, in fact—smelled of ammonia and carbolic soap and in some way of distress.

Nora was seventeen and still did not know whether she liked children or saw them as part of a Catholic woman's fate. If they had to come along, then let them be clear-eyed and talcum-scented, affectionate and quick to learn. The eyes of the Fenton baby were opaquely gray, so rigidly focused that she said to herself, He is blind. They never warned me. But as she bent close, wondering if his gaze might alter, the combs at her temples slipped loose and she saw him take notice of the waves of dark hair that fell and enclosed him. So, he perceived things. For the rest, he remained as before, as still as a doll, with both hands folded tight.

Like a doll, yes, but not an attractive one: No little girl would have been glad to find him under a Christmas tree. The thought of a rebuffed and neglected toy touched Nora deeply. She lifted him from his cot, expecting— though not precisely—the limpness of a plush or woolly animal: a lamb, say. But he was braced and resistant, a wooden soldier, every inch of him tense. She placed him against her shoulder, her cheek to his head, saying, "There you go. You're just grand. You're a grand little boy." Except for a fringe of down around his forehead, he was perfectly bald. He must have spent his entire life, all three months of it, flat on his back with his hair rubbing off on the pillow.

In a narrow aisle between rows of beds, Mr. Fenton and a French-Canadian doctor stood at ease. Actually, Dr. Alex Marchand was a pal from Mr. Fenton's Montreal regiment. What they had in common was the recent war and the Italian campaign. Mr. Fenton appeared satisfied with the state and condition of his son. (With her free hand Nora pulled back her hair so he could see the baby entirely.) The men seemed to take no notice of the rest of the room: the sixty-odd puny infants, the heavily pregnant girl of about fourteen, waxing the floor on her hands and knees, or the nun stand-ing by, watching hard to be sure they did not make off with the wrong child. The pregnant girl's hair had been cropped to the skull. She was dressed in a dun-colored uniform with long sleeves and prickly-looking black stock-ings. She never once looked up.

Although this was a hot and humid morning in late summer, real Mon-treal weather, the air a heavy vapor, the men wore three-piece dark suits, vest and all, and looked thoroughly formal and buttoned up. The doctor carried a panama hat. Mr. Fenton had stuck a carnation in his lapel, broken off from a bunch he had presented to the Mother Superior downstairs, a few minutes before. His slightly rash approach to new people seemed to appeal. Greeting him, the nuns had been all smiles, accepting without shadow his alien presence, his confident ignorance of French, his male sins lightly borne. The liquor on his breath was enough to knock the Mother Superior off her feet (he was steady on his) but she may have taken it to be part of the natural aura of men.

"Well, Nora!" said Mr. Fenton, a lot louder than he needed to be. "You've got your baby."

What did he mean? A trained nanny was supposed to be on her way over from England. Nora was filling in, as a favor; that was all. He behaved as if they had known each other for years, had even suggested she call him "Boyd." (She had pretended not to hear.) His buoyant nature seemed to re-quire a sort of fake complicity or comradeship from women, on short no-tice. It was his need, not Nora's, and in her mind she became all-denying. She was helping out because her father, who knew Mr. Fenton, had asked if she would, but nothing more. Mr. Fenton was in his late twenties, a married man, a father, some sort of Protestant—another race.

Luckily, neither the girl in uniform nor the attendant nun seemed to know English. They might otherwise have supposed Nora to be Neil's mother. She could not have been the mother of anyone. She had never let a man anywhere near. If ever she did, if ever she felt ready, he would be nothing like Mr. Fenton—typical Anglo-Montreal gladhander, the kind who said "Great to see you!" and a minute later forgot you were alive. She still had no image of an acceptable lover (which meant husband) but rather of the kind she meant to avoid. For the moment, it took in just about every type and class. What her mother called "having relations" was a source of dirty stories for men and disgrace for girls. It brought bad luck down even on married couples unless, like the Fentons, they happened to be well-off and knew how to avoid accidents and had no religious barrier that kept them from using their knowledge. When a mistake did occur—namely, Neil—they weren't strapped for cash or extra space. Yet they were helpless in some other way, could not tend to an infant without outside assistance, and for that reason had left Neil to founder among castaways for his first twelve weeks.

So Nora reasoned, gently stroking the baby's back. She wondered if he had managed to capture her thoughts. Apparently infants came into the world with a gift for mind reading, an instinct that faded once they began to grasp the meaning of words. She had been assured it was true by her late Aunt Rosalie, a mother of four. The time had come to take him out of this sour place, see him fed, washed, put into new clothes and a clean bed. But the two men seemed like guests at a disastrous party, unable to get away, rooted in place by a purely social wish to seem agreeable.

How sappy they both look, ran Nora's thoughts. As sappy as a couple of tenors. ("Sappy-looking as a tenor" was an expression of her father's.) I'll never get married. Who wants to look at some sappy face the whole day.

As though he had heard every silent word and wished to prove he could be lively and attentive, the doctor looked all around the room, for the first time, and remarked, "Some of these children, it would be better for everybody if they died at birth." His English was exact and almost without accent, but had the singsong cadence of French Montreal. It came out, "Most of these child*ren*, it would be bet*ter* for every*body* . . ." Nora held a low opinion of that particular lilt. She had been raised in two languages. To get Nora to answer in French, particularly after she had started attending an English high school, her mother would pretend not to understand English. I may not be one of your intellectuals, Nora decided (an assurance her father gave freely), but I sound English in English and French in French. She knew it was wrong of her to criticize an educated man such as Dr. Marchand, but he had said a terrible thing. It would have sounded bad spoken heedfully by the King himself. (The King, that August morning, was still George the Sixth.)

The stiff drinks Mr. Fenton had taken earlier in the day must have been wearing off. He seemed far away in his mind and somewhat put-upon. The doctor's remark brought him to. He said something about shoving off, turned easily to the nun, gave her a great smile. In answer, she placed a folded document in his hands, said a cool "Au revoir" to the doctor and did not look at Nora at all. In the hall outside Mr. Fenton stopped dead. He appealed to the doctor and Nora: "Look at this thing."

Nora shifted the baby to her right arm but otherwise kept her distance. "It's a certificate," she said.

"Baptismal," said the doctor. "He's been baptized."

"I can see that. Only, it's made out for 'Armand Albert Antoine.' She gave me the wrong thing. You'd better tell them," for of course he could not have made the complaint in French.

"Those are just foundling names," said the doctor. "They give two or three Christian names when there's no known family. I've seen even *four.* 'Albert' or 'Antoine' could be used as a surname. You see?"

"There damn well is a known family," said Mr. Fenton. "Mine. The name is Neil Boyd Fenton. When I make up my mind, it's made up for good. I never look back." But instead of returning the certificate he stuffed it, crumpled, into a pocket. "Nobody asked to have him christened here. I call that overstepping."

"They have to do it," said the doctor. "It is a rule." In the tone of someone trying to mend a quarrel, he went on, "Neil's a fine name." Nora knew for a fact he had suggested it. Mr. Fenton had never got round to finding a name, though he'd had three months to think it over. "There's another name I like. 'Earl.' Remember Earl Laine?"

"Yeah, I remember Earl." They started down a broad staircase, three in a row. Mr. Fenton was red in the face, either from his outburst or just the heat and weight of his dark clothes. Nora might have sympathized, but she had already decided not to do that: What can't be helped must be borne. Her mother had got her to wear a long-sleeved cotton jacket, over her white piqué dress, and a girdle and stockings, because of the nuns. The dress was short and allowed her knees to be seen. Nora had refused to let the hem down for just that one visit. Her small gold watch was a graduation present from her uncle and cousins. The blue bangle bracelets on her other wrist had belonged to her elder sister.

The mention of Earl Laine had started the men on a last-war story. She had already noticed their war stories made them laugh. They were not stories, properly speaking, but incidents they remembered by heart and told back and forth. Apparently, this Earl person had entered an Italian farmhouse ("shack" was the word Mr. Fenton actually used) and dragged a mattress off a bed. He wanted it for his tank, to make the tank more comfortable. A woman all in black had followed him out the door, clawing at the mattress, screaming something. When she saw there was no help for it, that Earl was bigger and stronger and laughing the whole time, she lay down in the road and thumped the ground with her fists.

"That Earl!" said the doctor, as one might speak of a bad but charming boy. "He'd do anything. Anything he felt like doing. Another time . . ."

"He was killed in '44," Mr. Fenton said. "Right? So how old would that make him now?"

It sounded very silly to Nora, like a conundrum in arithmetic, but the doctor replied, "He'd be around twenty-three." Dr. Marchand was older than Mr. Fenton but much younger than her father. He walked in a stately, deliberate way, like a mourner at a funeral. There was a wife-and-children air to him. Unlike Mr. Fenton he wore a wedding ring. Nora wondered if Mrs. Fenton and Mme. Marchand had ever met.

"Earl's people lived up in Montreal North," said Mr. Fenton. "I went to see them after I got back. They were Italians. Did you know that? He never said."

"I knew it the first time he opened his mouth," said the doctor. "His English wasn't right. It turned out his first language was some Sicilian dialect from Montreal North. Nobody in Italy could make it out, so he stayed with English. But it sounded funny."

"Not to me," said Mr. Fenton. "It was straight, plain Canadian."

The doctor had just been revealed as a man of deep learning. He understood different languages and dialects and knew every inch of Montreal far better than Nora or Mr. Fenton. He could construe a man's background from the sound of his words. No, no, he was not to be dismissed, whatever he had said or might still come out with. So Nora decided.

Downstairs, they followed a dark, waxed corridor to the front door, passing on the way a chapel recently vacated. The double doors, flung wide, revealed a sunstruck altar. Mr. Fenton's antipapal carnations (Nora gave them this attribute with no hard feelings) stood in a vase of cut glass, which shed rainbows. A strong scent of incense accompanied the visitors to the foyer, where it mingled with furniture polish.

"Is today something special?" said Mr. Fenton.

A blank occurred in the doctor's long list of reliable information. He stared at the wall, at a clock with Roman numerals. Only the hour mattered, he seemed to be telling himself. Nora happened to know that today, the twenty-third of August, was the feast of Saint Rosa de Lima, but she could not recall how Saint Rosa had lived or died. Nora's Aunt Rosalie, deceased, leaving behind three sons and a daughter and sad Uncle Victor, had in her lifetime taken over any saint on the calendar with a Rose to her name: not just Saint Rosalie, whose feast day on September fourth was hers by right, but Saint Rosaline (January) and Saint Rosine (March) and Rosa de Lima (today). It did not explain the special Mass this morning; in any case, Nora would have thought it wrong to supply an answer the doctor could not provide.

Although someone was on permanent duty at the door, making sure no stranger to the place wandered in, another and much older nun had been sent to see them off. She was standing directly under the clock, both hands resting on a cane, her back as straight as a yardstick. Her eyes retained some of the bluish-green light that often goes with red hair. The poor woman most likely had not much hair to speak of, and whatever strands remained were bound to be dull and gray. The hair of nuns died early, for want of light and air. Nora's sister, Geraldine, had the same blue-green eyes but not yet the white circle around the iris. She was in the process now of suppressing and concealing her hair, and there was no one to say it was a shame, that her hair was her most stunning feature. So it would continue, unless Gerry changed her mind and came home to stay and let Nora give her a shampoo with pure white almond-oil soap, followed by a vinegar rinse. She would need to sit at the kitchen window and let the morning sun brighten and strengthen her hair to the roots.

The old nun addressed Mr. Fenton: "Your beautiful flowers are gracing our little chapel." At least, that was how Dr. Marchand decided to translate her words. Nora would have made it, "Your flowers are in the chapel," but that might have sounded abrupt, and "gracing" was undoubtedly more pleasing to Mr. Fenton.

"That's good to hear," he said. A current of laughter set off by the story of Earl and the mattress still ran in his voice. Nora was afraid he might pat the nun on the cheek, or in some other way embarrass them horribly, but all he did was glance up at the clock, then at his watch, and make a stagy sort of bow—not mockingly, just trying to show he was not in his customary habitat and could get away with a gesture done for effect. The clock struck the half hour: twelve-thirty. They should have been sitting down to lunch at Mr. Fenton's house, along with his wife and Mrs. Clopstock, who was his wife's mother. Nora had never before been invited to a meal at a strange table. This overwhelming act of hospitality was her reason for wearing white earrings, white high-heeled shoes, and her sister's relinquished bracelets.

The hard midday light of the street stunned them quiet at first, then the baby set up a thin wail—his first message to Nora. I know, she told him. You're hungry, you're too hot. You need a good wash. You don't like being moved around. (For a second, she saw the hairline divide between being rescued and taken captive. The idea was too complex, it had no end or beginning, and she let it go.) You've dirtied yourself, too. In fact, you reek to high heaven. Never mind. We're going to put everything right. Trying to quiet him, she gave him one of her fingers to suck. Better to let him swallow a few germs and microbes than cry himself sick. Mr. Fenton had parked in shade, around the corner. It wasn't much of a walk.

"Nora can't remember the war," he said to the doctor, but really to her, trying the buddy business again. "She must have been in her cradle."

"I know it's over," she said, thinking to close the subject.

"Oh, it's that, all right." He sounded sorry, about as sorry as he could feel about anything.

The doctor had replaced his panama hat, after three times at achieving the angle he wanted. He made a reassuring sort of presence in the front seat—solid, reliable. Nothing would knock him over. Nora's father was thin and light as a blown leaf. The doctor said, "There's another name I like. 'Desmond.' "

"Des?" said Mr. Fenton. He struggled out of his jacket and vest and threw them on the backseat, next to Nora. His white carnation fell on the floor. The doctor remained fully dressed, every button fastened. "Des Butler?"

"He married an English girl," said the doctor. "Remember?"

"*Remember?* I was best man. She cried the whole time. She was called Beryl—no, Brenda."

"Well, she was in the family way," said the doctor.

"She hightailed it right back to England," said Mr. Fenton. "The Canadian taxpayers had to pay to bring her over. Nobody ever figured out where she got the money to go back. Even Des didn't know."

"Des never knew anything. He never knew what he should have known. All he noticed was she had gotten fat since the last time he saw her."

"She arrived with a bun in the oven," said Mr. Fenton. "Four, five months. Des had already been back in Canada for six. So . . ." He turned his attention to Nora. "Your dad get overseas, Nora?"

"He tried."

"And?"

"He was already thirty-nine and he had the two children. They told him he was more useful sticking to his job."

"We needed civilians, too," said Mr. Fenton, showing generosity. "Two, did you say? Ray's got two kids?"

"There's my sister, Gerry—Geraldine. She's a novice now, up in the Laurentians."

"Where?" He twisted the rearview mirror, so he could see her.

"Near St. Jerome. She's on the way to being a nun."

That shut him up, for the time being. The doctor reached up and turned the mirror the other way. While they were speaking, the baby had started to gush up some awful curdled stuff, which she had to wipe on the skirt of his gown. He had no luggage—not even a spare diaper. The men had rolled down the front windows, but the crossbreeze was sluggish and smelled of warm metal, and did nothing to lighten the presence of Neil.

"Want to open up back there?" said Mr. Fenton.

No, she did not. One of her boy cousins had come down with an infected ear, the result of building a model airplane while sitting in a draft.

"At that stage, they're only a digestive tube," said the doctor, fanning himself with his hat.

"How about the brain?" said Mr. Fenton. "When does the brain start to work?" He drove without haste, as he did everything else. His elbow rested easily in the window frame. Ashes from his cigarette drifted into Nora's domain.

"The brain is still primitive," the doctor said, sounding sure. "It is still in the darkness of early time." Nora wondered what "the darkness of time" was supposed to mean. Mr. Fenton must have been wondering too. He started to say something, but the doctor went on in his slow singsong way, "Only the soul is fully developed from birth. The brain . . ."

"Newborn, they've got these huge peckers," said Mr. Fenton. "I mean, really developed."

"The brain tries to catch up with the soul. For most people, it's a lifelong struggle."

"If you say so, Alex," Mr. Fenton said.

The baby wasn't primitive, surely. She examined his face. There wasn't a hair on him except the blond fluff around his forehead. Primitive man, shaggy all over, dragged his steps through the recollection of a movie she had seen. Speak for yourself, she wanted to tell the doctor. Neil is not *primitive.* He just wants to understand where he's going. Her duty was to hand over to its mother this bit of a child, an only son without a stitch to his name. Socks, gown, and diaper were fit to be burned, not worth a washtub of water. So her sister had gone through an open door and the door had swung to behind her. She had left to Nora everything she owned. So Marie Antoinette, younger than Nora, had been stripped to the skin when she reached the border of France, on the way to marry a future king. Total strangers had been granted the right to see her nude. The clothes she had been wearing were left on the ground and she was arrayed in garments so heavy with silver and embroidery she could hardly walk. Her own ladies-in-waiting, who spoke her native language, were turned back. (Nora could not remember where Marie Antoinette had started out.) "For we brought nothing . . . ," Nora's Methodist Abbott grandmother liked to point out, convinced that Catholics never cracked a Bible and had to be kept informed. "Naked we came . . ." was along the same line. Nora knew how to dress and undress under a bathrobe, quick as a mouse. No earthquake, no burglar, no stranger suddenly pushing a door open would find Nora without at least one thing on, even if it was only a bra.

". . . from Mac McIvor," the doctor was telling Mr. Fenton. "He's out in Vancouver now. It's a big change from Montreal."

"He'll crawl back here one day, probably sooner than he thinks," said Mr. Fenton. Something had made him cranky, perhaps the talk about souls. "I consider it a privilege to live in Montreal. I was born on Crescent and that's where I intend to die. Unless there's another war. Then it's a toss-up."

"Crescent's a fine street," said the doctor. "Nice houses, nice stores." He paused and let the compliment sink in, a way of making peace. "He's buying a place. Property's cheap out there."

"It's a long way off," said Mr. Fenton. "They can't get people to go and live there. That's why everything's so cheap."

"Not being married, he doesn't need a lot of room," the doctor said. "It's just a bungalow, two rooms and a kitchen. He can eat in the kitchen. It's a nice area. A lot of gardens."

"Sure, there are stores on Crescent now, but they're high-quality," said Mr. Fenton. "I could sell the house for a hell of a lot more than my father ever paid. Louise wants me to. She can't get used to having a dress shop next door. She wants a lawn and a yard and a lot of space between the houses."

"Mac's got a fair-size garden. That won't break his neck. Out there, there's no winter. You stick something in the ground, it grows."

"My father hung on to the house all through the Depression," said Mr. Fenton. "It'll take a lot more than a couple of store windows to chase me away." So saying, he made a sudden rough swerve into his street, having almost missed the corner.

It jolted the baby, who had just fallen asleep. Before he could start to cry or do anything else that could make him unpopular, she lifted him to the window. "See the houses?" she said. "One of them's yours." A few had fancy dress shops on the first floor. Others were turned into offices, with uncurtained front windows and neon lights, blazing away in broad daylight. The double row of houses ran straight down to St. Catherine Street without a break, except for some ashy lanes. Short of one of these, Mr. Fenton pulled up. He retrieved his vest and jacket, got out, and slammed the door. It was the doctor who turned back to help Nora struggle out of the car, held her arm firmly, even adjusted the strap of her white shoulder bag. He wasn't trying anything, so she let him. Anyone could tell he was a family man.

Neil seemed more awkward to hold than before, perhaps because she was tired. Shielding his eyes from sunlight, she turned his face to a narrow house of pale gray stone. On her street, it would indicate three two-bedroom flats, not counting the area. She was about to ask, "Is the whole thing yours?" but it might make her sound as if she had never been anywhere, and the last thing she wanted was Mr. Fenton's entire attention. In the shadow of steps leading up to the front door, at a window in the area, a hand lifted a net curtain and let it fall. So, someone knew that Neil was here. For his sake, she took precedence and climbed straight to the door. The men barely noticed. Mr. Fenton, in shirtsleeves, vest and jacket slung over a shoulder, spoke of heat and thirst. Halfway up, the doctor paused and said, "Boyd, isn't that the alley where the girl was supposed to have been raped?"

"They never caught him," said Mr. Fenton at once. "It was dark. She didn't see his face. Some kids had shot out the alley light with an air gun.

Her father tried to sue the city, because of the light. It didn't get him anywhere. Ray Abbott knows the story. Light or no light, it wasn't a city case."

"What was she doing by herself in a dark lane?" said the doctor. "Did she work around here?"

"She lived over on Bishop," said Mr. Fenton. "She was visiting some friend and took a shortcut home. Her father was a principal." He named the school. Nora had never heard of it.

"English," said Dr. Marchand, placing the story in context.

"They moved away. Some crazy stories went around, that she knew the guy, they had a date."

"I knew a case," said the doctor. "An old maid. She set the police on a married man. He never did anything worse than say hello."

"It was hard on Louise, something like that going on just outside. Nobody heard a thing until she ran down to the area and started banging on the door and screaming."

"Louise did that?"

"This girl. Missy let her in and gave her a big shot of brandy. Missy's a good head. She said, 'If you don't quit yelling I'll call the police.' "

"Her English must be pretty good now," said the doctor.

"Missy's smart. When my mother-in-law hired her, all she could say was, 'I cook, I clean.' Now she could argue a case in court. She told Louise, 'Some guy grabs *me* in a lane, I twist him like a wet mop.' Louise couldn't get over it." He became lighthearted suddenly, which suited him better. "We shouldn't be scaring Nora with all this." Nora found that rich, considering the things that had been said in the car. She was at the door, waiting. He had to look up.

He took the last steps slowly. Of course, he was closer to thirty than twenty and not in great shape. All that booze and his lazy way of moving were bound to tell. On the landing he had to catch his breath. He said, "Don't worry, Nora. This end of Crescent is still good. It isn't as residential as when I was a kid but it's safe. Anyway, it's safe for girls who don't do dumb things."

"I'm not one for worrying," she said. "I don't wander around on my own after dark and I don't answer strangers. Anyways, I won't ever be spending the night here. My father doesn't like me to sleep away."

A word she knew but had never thought of using—"morose"—came to mind at the slow change in his face. Sulky or deeply pensive (it was hard to tell), he began searching the pockets of his vest and jacket, probably looking for his latchkey. The doctor reached across and pressed the doorbell. They heard it jangle inside the house. Without Dr. Marchand they might have remained stranded, waiting for the earth to turn and the slant of the sun to alter and allow them shade. Just as she was thinking this, wondering how Mr. Fenton managed to get through his day-by-day life without having the doctor there every minute, Dr. Marchand addressed her directly: "*On ne dit pas* 'anyways.' *C'est commun. Il faut toujours dire* 'anyway.' "

The heat of the day and the strain of events had pushed him off his rocker. There was no other explanation. Or maybe he believed he was some kind of bilingual marvel, a real work of art, standing there in his undertaker suit, wearing that dopey hat. Nora's father knew more about anything than he did, any day. He had information about local politics and the private dealings of men who were honored and admired, had their pictures in the *Gazette* and the *Star*. He could shake hands with anybody you cared to mention; could tell, just by looking at another man, what that man was worth. When he went to Blue Bonnets, the racetrack, a fantastic private intuition told him where to put his money. He often came home singing, his hat on the back of his head. He had an office to himself at City Hall, no duties anybody could figure, but unlimited use of a phone. He never picked a quarrel and never took offense. "Never let anyone get under your skin," he had told Gerry and Nora. "Consider the source."

She considered the source: Dr. Marchand had spent a horrible morning, probably, trying to sidestep Mr. Fenton's temporary moods and opinions. Still, the two of them were friends, like pals in a movie about the Great War, where actors pledged true loyalty in a trench before going over the top. Wars ran together, like the history of English kings, kept alive in tedious stories repeated by men. As a boring person he was easy to forgive. As a man he had a cold streak. His reproof stung. He had made her seem ignorant. Mr. Fenton didn't know a word of French, but he must have caught the drift.

Just as Nora's mother could predict a change in the weather from certain pains in her wrists, so the baby sensed a change in Nora. His face puckered. He let out some more of that clotted slobber, followed by a weak cough and a piercing, choking complaint. "Oh, stop," she said, hearing a rush of footsteps. She gave him a gentle shake. "Where's my little man? Where's my soldier?" Her piqué dress, which had been fresh as an ironed handkerchief just a few hours before, was stained, soiled, crumpled, wetted, damaged by Neil. She kissed his head. All she could find to say, in a hurry, was "Be good." The door swung open. Without being bidden Nora entered the house. The doctor removed his hat, this time with a bit of a flourish. Mr. Fenton, she noticed, was still looking for a key.

In rooms glimpsed from the entrance hall the shades were drawn against the burning street. A darker and clammier heat, like the air of an August night, condensed on her cheeks and forehead. She smiled at two women, dimly perceived. The younger had the figure of a stout child, wore her hair cut straight across her eyebrows, and had on what Nora took to be a white skirt. In the seconds it took for her pupils to widen, her eyes to focus anew, she saw that the white skirt was a white apron. In the meantime, she had approached the young woman, said, "Here's your sweet baby, Mrs. Fenton," and given him up.

"Well, Missy, you heard what Nora said," said Mr. Fenton. He could enjoy that kind of joke, laugh noisily at a mistake, but Missy looked as if a tide had receded, leaving her stranded and unable to recognize anything along the shore. All she could say was "There's a bottle ready," in a heavy accent.

"Give it to him right away," said the older woman, who could not be anyone but Mrs. Clopstock, the mother-in-law from Toronto. "That sounds to me like a hunger cry." Having made the observation, she took no further notice of Neil, but spoke to the two men: "Louise is really knocked out by the heat. She doesn't want any lunch. She said to say hello to you, Alex."

The doctor said, "Once she sees him, she'll take an interest. I had another case, just like that. I can tell you all about it."

"Yes, tell us, Alex," said Mrs. Clopstock. "Do tell us. You can tell us about it at lunch. We have to talk about something."

It pleased Nora that Dr. Marchand, for the first time, had made a "th" mistake in English, saying "dat" for "that." He wasn't so smart, after all. Just the same, she had spoiled Neil's entrance into his new life; as if she had crossed the wrong line. The two errors could not be matched. The doctor could always start over and get it right. For Nora and Neil, it had been once and for all.

II

Nora's uncle, Victor Cochefert, was the only member of her family, on either side, with much of consequence to leave in a will. He had the place he lived in—four bedrooms and double garage and a weeping willow on the lawn—and some flats he rented to the poor and improvident, in the east end of the city. He was forever having tenants evicted, and had had beer bottles thrown at his car. The flats had come to him through his marriage to Rosalie, daughter of a notary. Her father had drawn up a tight, grim marriage contract, putting Rosalie in charge of her assets, but she had suffered an early stroke, dragged one foot, and left everything up to Victor. The other relatives were lifelong renters, like most of Montreal. None were in want but only Victor and Rosalie had been to Florida.

Her own father's financial arrangements were seen by the Cocheferts as eccentric and somewhat obscure. He never opened his mouth about money but was suspected of being better off than he cared to let on; yet the Abbotts continued to live in a third-floor walk-up flat, with an outside staircase and linoleum-covered floors on which scatter rugs slipped and slid underfoot. His wife's relations admired him for qualities they knew to exist behind his great wall of good humor; they had watched him saunter from the dark bureau where he had stood on the far side of a counter, wearing an eyeshade (against what light?), registering births and delivering certificates, to a private office in City Hall. He had moved along nonchalantly, whistling, hands in his pockets—sometimes in other people's, Victor had hinted. At the same time, he held Ray in high regard, knowing that if you showed confidence, made him an accomplice, he could be trusted. He had even confided to Ray a copy of his will.

Victor's will was locked up in a safe in Ray's small office, where nothing was written on the door. "Nothing in the safe except my lunch," Ray often remarked, but Nora once had seen it wide open and had been impressed by the great number of files and dossiers inside. When she asked what these were, her father had laughed and said, "Multiple-risk insurance policies," and called her pie-face and sniffy-nose. She thought he must be proud to act as custodian to any part of Victor's private affairs. Victor was associate in a firm of engineers, established since 1900 on St. James Street West. The name of the company was Macfarlane, Macfarlane & Macklehurst. It was understood that when Macfarlane Senior died or retired, "Cochefert" would figure on the letterhead—a bit lower and to the right, in smaller print. Three other people with French surnames were on staff: a switchboard operator, a file clerk, and a bilingual typist. During working hours they were expected to speak English, even to one another. The elder Macfarlane harbored the fear that anything said in an unknown language could be about him.

Nora's father knew the exact reason why Uncle Victor had been hired: It had to do with Quebec provincial government contracts. Politicians liked to deal in French and in a manner they found pertinent and to the point. Victor used English when he had to, no more and no less, as he waited. He was waiting to see his name figure on the firm's stationery, and he pondered the retreat and obscuration of the English. "The English" had names such as O'Keefe, Murphy, Llewellyn, Morgan-Jones, Ferguson, MacNab, Hoefer, Oberkirch, Aarmgaard, Van Roos, or Stavinsky. Language was the clue to native origin. He placed the Oberkirches and MacNabs by speech and according to the street where they chose to live. Nora's father had escaped his close judgment, was the English exception, even though no one knew what Ray thought or felt about anything. The well-known Anglo reluctance to show deep emotion might be a shield for something or for nothing. Victor had told his wife this, and she had repeated it to Nora's mother.

He had taken the last war to be an English contrivance and had said he would shoot his three sons rather than see them in uniform. The threat had caused Aunt Rosalie to burst into sobs, followed by the three sons, in turn, as though they were performing a round of weeping. The incident took place at a dinner given to celebrate the Cochefert grandparents' golden wedding anniversary—close relatives only, twenty-six place settings, small children perched on cushions or volumes of the Littré dictionary. The time was six days after the German invasion of Poland and three after Ray had tried to enlist. Victor was in such a state of pacifist conviction that he trembled all over. His horn-rimmed glasses fell in his plate. He said to Nora's father, "I don't mean this for you."

Ray said, "Well, in my family, if Canada goes to war, we go too," and left it at that. He spoke a sort of French he had picked up casually, which not everyone understood. Across the table he winked at Nora and Geraldine, as if to say, "It's all a lot of hot air." His favorite tune was "Don't Let It Bother You." He could whistle it even if he lost money at Blue Bonnets.

Just before Victor's terrible outburst, the whole table had applauded the arrival of the superb five-tier, pink-and-white anniversary cake, trimmed with little gold bells. Now, it sat at the center of the table and no one had the heart to cut it. The chance that one's children could be shot seemed not contrary to reason but prophetic. It was an unlucky age. The only one of Victor's progeny old enough to get into uniform and be gunned down by her father was his daughter, Ninon—Aunt Rosalie's Ninette. For years Victor and Rosalie had been alone with Ninette; then they had started having the boys. She was eighteen that September, just out of her convent school, could read and speak English, understand every word of Latin in the Mass, play anything you felt like hearing on the piano; in short, was ready to become a superior kind of wife. Her historical essay, "Marie-Antoinette, Christian Queen and Royal Martyr," had won a graduation medal. Aunt Rosalie had brought the medal to the dinner, where it was passed around and examined on both sides. As for "Marie-Antoinette," Victor had had it printed on cream-colored paper and bound in royal blue, with three white fleurs-de-lys embossed on the cover, and had presented a copy to every person he was related to or wished to honor.

Nora was nine and had no idea what or where Poland might be. The shooting of her cousins by Uncle Victor lingered as a possibility but the wailing children were starting to seem a bit of a nuisance. Ninette stood up—not really a commanding presence, for she was small and slight—and said something about joining the armed forces and tramping around in boots. Since none of them could imagine a woman in uniform, it made them all more worried than ever; then they saw she had meant them to smile. Having restored the party to good humor, more or less, she moved around the table and made her little brothers stop making that noise, and cleaned their weepy, snotty faces. The three-year-old had crawled under the table, but Ninette pulled him out and sat him hard on his chair and tied his napkin around his neck, good and tight. She liked the boys to eat like grown-ups and remember every instructive thing she said: The Reverend Mother had told Victor she was a born teacher. If he would not allow her to take further training (he would not) he ought to let Ninette give private lessons, in French or music. Nothing was more conducive to moral disaster than a good female mind left to fester and rot. Keeping busy with lessons would prevent Ninette from dwelling on imponderables, such as where one's duty to parents ends and what was liable to happen on her wedding night. The Reverend Mother did not care how she talked to men. She was more circumspect with women, having high regard for only a few. Uncle Victor thought that was the best stand for the director of an exceptional convent school.

Having thoroughly daunted her little brothers, Ninette gave each of her troubled parents a kiss. She picked up a big silver cake knife—an 1889 wedding present, like the dictionary—and sliced the whole five-tier edifice from top to bottom. She must have been taught how to do it as part of her studies, for the cake did not fall apart or collapse. "There!" she said, as if life held nothing more to be settled. Before she began to serve the guests, in order, by age, she undid the black velvet ribbon holding her hair at the nape of her neck and gave it to Geraldine. Nora watched Ninette closely during the cake operation. Her face in profile was self-contained, like a cat's. Ray had remarked once that all the Cochefert women, his own wife being the single exception, grew a mustache by the age of eighteen. Ninette showed no trace of any, but Nora did perceive she had on mascara. Uncle Victor seemed not to have noticed. He wiped his glasses on his napkin and looked around humbly, as though all these people were too good for him, the way he always emerged from tantrums and tempers. He said nothing else about the war or the English, but as soon as he started to feel more like himself, remarked that it was no use educating women: It confused their outlook. He hoped Ray had no foolish and extravagant plans for Nora and Geraldine. Ray went on eating quietly and steadily, and was first to finish his cake.

Nora's father was a convert, but he fitted in. He had found the change no more difficult than digging up irises to put in tulips. If something annoying occurred—say, some new saint he thought shouldn't even have been in the running—he would say, "I didn't sign on for that." Nora's mother had had a hard time with him over Assumption. He came from Prince Edward Island. Nora and Geraldine had been taken down there, just once, so Ray's mother could see her grandchildren. All her friends and neighbors seemed to be called Peters or White. Nora was glad to be an Abbott, because there weren't so many. They traveled by train, sitting up all night in their clothes, and were down to their last hard-boiled egg at the end of the journey. Their Abbott grandmother said, "Three days of sandwiches." Of course it had not been anything like three days, but Nora and Gerry were trained not to contradict. (Their mother had made up her mind not to understand a word of English.)

Grandmother Abbott had curly hair, a striking shade of white, and a pink face. She wore quite nice shoes but had been forced to cut slits in them to accommodate her sore toes. Her apron strings could barely be tied, her waist was that thick around. She said to Gerry, "You take after your grandpa's side," because of the red-gold hair. The girls did not yet read English, and so she deduced they could not read at all. She told them how John Wesley and his brothers and sisters had each learned the alphabet on the day they turned five. It was achieved by dint of being shut up in a room with Mrs. Wesley, and receiving nothing to eat or drink until the recitation ran smoothly from A to Z.

"That's a Methodist birthday for you," said Ray. It may have stirred up memories, for he became snappy and critical, as he never was at home. He stood up for Quebec, saying there was a lot of good in a place where a man could have a beer whenever he felt like it, and no questions asked. In Quebec, you could buy beer in grocery stores. The rest of Canada was pretty dry, yet in those parched cities, on a Saturday night, even the telephone poles were reeling-drunk. Nora was proud of him for having all that to say. On their last evening a few things went wrong, and Ray said, "Tough corn and sour apple pie. That's no meal for a man." He was right. Her mother would never have served it. No wonder he had stayed in Montreal.

On a warm spring afternoon the war came to an end. Nora was fifteen and going to an English high school. She knew who George Washington was and the names of the Stuart kings but not much about Canada. A bunch of fatheads—Ray's assessment—swarmed downtown and broke some store windows and overturned a streetcar, to show how glad they felt about peace. No one knew what to expect or what was supposed to happen without a war. Even Ray wasn't sure if his place on the city payroll was safe, with all the younger men coming back and shoving for priority. Uncle Victor decided to evict all his tenants, give the flats a coat of paint, and rent them to veterans at a higher price. Ninette and Aunt Rosalie went to Eaton's and stood in one of the first lines for nylon stockings. Nora's mother welcomed the end of rationing on principle, although no one had gone without. Geraldine had been moping for years: She had yearned to be the youngest novice in universal history and now it was too late. Ray had kept saying, "Nothing doing. There's a war on." He wanted the family to stick together in case Canada was invaded, forgetting how eager he had been to leave at the very beginning, though it was true that in 1939 the entire war was expected to last about six months.

Now Gerry sat around weeping because she could leave home. When Ray said she had to wait another year, she suddenly stopped crying and began to sort the clothes and possessions she was giving up. The first thing she turned over to Nora was the black velvet ribbon Ninette had unfastened all those years ago. It was as good as new; Gerry never wore anything out. To Nora it seemed the relic of a distant age. The fashion now was curved combs and barrettes and hair clips studded with colored stones. Gerry went on separating her clothes into piles until the last minute and went away dry-eyed, leaving an empty bed in the room she had shared with Nora all Nora's life.

The next person to leave was Ninette. She came down with tuberculosis and had to be sent to a place in the Laurentians—not far from Gerry's convent. She never wrote, for fear of passing germs along by mail. If Nora wanted to send a letter, she had to give it, unsealed, to Aunt Rosalie. The excuse was that Ninette had to be shielded from bad news. Nora had no idea what the bad news might be. Ninette had never married. Her education had gone to waste, Nora often heard. She had inherited her father's habit of waiting, and now life had played her a mean trick. She had slapped her little brothers around for their own good and given private French lessons. Her favorite book was still her own "Marie-Antoinette." Perhaps she secretly had hoped to be martyred and admired. Ray had thought so: "The trouble with Ninette was all that goddamn queen stuff."

"Was," he had said. She had fallen into their past. After a short time Nora began to forget about her cousin. It was impossible to go on writing to someone who never replied. The family seemed to see less of Aunt Rosalie and Uncle Victor. Tuberculosis was a disgraceful disease, a curse of the poor, said to run through generations. Some distant, driven ancestor, a victim of winter and long stretches of émigré hunger, had bequeathed the germ, across three centuries, perhaps. The least rumor concerning Ninette could blight the life of brothers and cousins. The summer after she vanished, Aunt Rosalie had a second stroke and two weeks later died.

One person who came well out of the war was Ray. He was in the same office, an adornment to the same payroll, and still had friends all over. He had devised a means of easing the sorrow of childless couples by bringing them together with newborn babies no one wanted to bring up. He had the satisfaction of performing a kindness, a Christian act, and the pleasure of experiencing favors returned. "Ray doesn't quite stand there with his hand out," Uncle Victor had been heard to say. "But a lot of the time he finds something in it." Ray had his own letter paper now, with "Cadaster/*Cadastre*" printed across the top. "Cadaster" had no connection to his job, as far as anyone could tell. He had found sheaves of the paper in a cardboard box, about to be carted away. The paper was yellowed and brittle around the edges. He enjoyed typing letters and signing his name in a long scrawl. He had once said he wanted his children to have names he could pronounce, and to be able to speak English at his own table if he felt like it. Both wishes had been granted. He was more cheerful than any man Nora had ever heard of and much happier than poor Uncle Victor.

Nora had to herself the room she had shared with her sister. She placed Gerry's framed high school graduation portrait on the dresser and kissed the glass, and spread her belongings in all the dresser drawers. Before long, her mother moved in and took over the empty bed. She was having her change of life and had to get up in the night to put on a fresh nightgown and replace the pillowcases soaked with sweat. After about a week of it, Ray came to the door and turned on the overhead light. He said, "How long is it going on for?"

"I don't know. Go back to bed. You need your sleep."

He walked away, leaving the light on. Nora went barefoot to switch it off. She said, "What does it feel like, exactly?"

Her mother's voice in the dark sounded girlish, like Gerry's. "As if somebody dipped a towel in boiling-hot water and threw it over your head."

"I'm never getting married," Nora said.

"Being married has nothing to do with it."

"Will it happen to Gerry?"

"Nuns get all the women's things," said her mother.

The August heat wave and her mother's restlessness kept Nora awake. She thought about the secretarial school where she was to begin a new, great phase of her life on the Tuesday after Labor Day—twelve days from tomorrow. Her imagination traveled along unknown corridors and into classrooms where there were rows of typewriters, just delivered from the factory; the pencils, the erasers, the spiral notebooks had never been touched. All the girls were attractive-looking and serious-minded. At a front-row desk (should they be seated in alphabetical order) was Miss Nora Abbott, with her natural bilingual skills and extensive wardrobe—half of it Gerry's.

As children, she and Gerry had taken parental magic on trust, had believed their mother heard their unspoken thoughts and listened from a distance to their most secret conversations. Now her mother said, "Can't you get to sleep, Nora? You're all impressed about taking that course. Are you wanting to leave home with your first paycheck? Papa wouldn't want that."

"Gerry was eighteen when she went away."

"We knew where she was going."

"I'll be over nineteen by the time I start to work."

"And starting off at fifteen dollars a week, if you're lucky."

Nora said, "I've been wondering how Dad's going to manage to pay for the course. It's two hundred dollars, not counting the shorthand book."

"It's not for you to worry about," said her mother. "He's paid the hundred deposit. The rest isn't due until December."

"Uncle Victor had to chip in."

"Uncle Victor didn't *have* to do anything. When he helps out, it's because he wants to. Your father doesn't beg."

"Why couldn't he pay the whole hundred dollars on his own? Did he lose some of it at Blue Bonnets?"

Her mother sat up all of a sudden and became a looming presence in the dark. "Did you ever have to go to bed on an empty stomach?" she said. "You and Gerry always had a new coat every winter."

"Gerry did. I got the hand-me-down. Grandma Abbott sent Gerry presents because she had red hair."

"Gerry's old coats looked as if they came straight from the store. She never got a spot or a stain on any of her clothes. Grandmother Abbott sent her a chocolate Easter egg once. It broke up in the mail and your father told her not to bother with any more parcels."

"Why would Uncle Victor have to lend Dad fifty dollars? What does he do with his money?"

"Did you ever have to go without shoes?" said her mother. "Did you ever miss a hot meal? Who gave you the gold chain and the twenty-four-karat crucifix for your First Communion?"

"Uncle Victor."

"Well, and who was he trying to be nice to? Your father. He's been the best father in the world and the best husband. If I go before he does, I want you to look after him."

I'll be married by then, Nora thought. "It's girls that look after their old dads," Ray had said when Victor had once commiserated with him for not having a son. Ninette was now back from the place in the Laurentians— cured, it was said—and had taken Aunt Rosalie's place, seeing to it that the boys did their homework and Uncle Victor got his meals on time. She wore her hair short (apparently the long hair had been taking all the strength) and had put on weight. Her manner had changed more than her appearance. She was twenty-six, unlikely to find a husband. A nagging, joyless religiosity had come over her. Nora had seen her only once since her return: Ninette had instructed Nora to pray for her, as though she were gradually growing used to giving spiritual orders. Nora had said to herself, She's like a sergeant-major. The whole family had been praying for Ninette for well over a year, without being pushed. Perhaps she had chosen this new, bossy way of behaving over another possibility, which was to sit with her head in her hands, thinking, Unfair! Either way, she was not good company.

Nora said to her mother, "You mean you want me to look after Dad the way Ninette takes care of Uncle Victor?"

"Poor Ninette," her mother said at once. "What else can she do now." Who would marry Ninette, she was trying to say. Ninette kept herself to herself; it may have been that one kept away from her—not unkindly, not dismissing the devaluation of her life, but for fear of ill luck and its terrible way of spreading by contact.

In the next room, Ray thumped on the wall and said, "Either we all get up and waltz or we pipe down and get some sleep."

Her last waking thoughts were about Gerry. When the time came to take over Ray's old age—for she had assumed her mother's wild requirement to be a prophecy—Gerry might decide to leave her convent and keep house for him. She could easily by then have had enough: Ray believed her vocation to be seriously undermined by a craving for peanut clusters and homemade fudge. In a letter she had run on about her mother's celebrated Queen of Sheba chocolate cake, artfully hollowed and filled with chocolate mousse and whipped cream. Nora tried to see Gerry and Ray old and middle-aged, with Gerry trying to get him to drink some hot soup; her imagination went slack. Old persons were said to be demanding and difficult, but Gerry would show endless patience. Would she? Was she, any more than most people, enduring and calm? Nora could not remember. Only a year or so had gone by, but the span of separation had turned out to be longer and more effacing than ordinary time.

The next morning, and in spite of the heat, Ray requested pancakes and sausages for breakfast. No two of the Abbotts ever ate the same thing; Nora's mother stood on her feet until the family was satisfied. Then she cleared away plates, bowls, and coffee cups and made herself a pot of strong tea. Ray picked his teeth, and suddenly asked Nora if she wanted to do a favor for a couple he knew: It involved fetching this couple's baby and keeping an eye on it just a few hours a day, until the end of the week. The infant's mother had suffered a nervous breakdown at his birth, and the child had been placed in a home and cared for by nuns.

"Why can't they hire a nurse?" Nora said.

"She's on her way over from England. They're just asking you to be around till she comes. It's more than just a good turn," her father said. "It's a Christian act."

"A Christian act is one where you don't get paid," Nora said.

"Well, you've got nothing better to do for the moment," he said. "You wouldn't want to take money for this. If you take the money, you're a nursemaid and have to eat in the kitchen."

"I eat in the kitchen at home." She could not shake off the picture of Ray as old and being waited on by Gerry. "Do you know them?" she said to her mother, who was still standing, eating toast.

"Your mother doesn't know them," said Ray.

"I just saw the husband once," said his wife. "It was around the time when Ninette had to stop giving lessons. Mrs. Fenton used to come once a week. She must have started being depressed before the baby came along, because she couldn't concentrate or remember anything. Taking lessons was supposed to pull her mind together. He brought a book belonging to Ninette and I think he paid for some lessons his wife still owed. Ninette wasn't around. Aunt Rosalie introduced us. That was all."

"You never told me about that," said Ray.

"What was he like?" said Nora.

Her mother answered, in English, "Like an English."

Nora and her father took the streetcar down to the stone building where Ray had worked before moving into his office at City Hall. He put on his old green eyeshade and got behind an oak counter. He was having a good time, playing the role of a much younger Ray Abbott, knowing all the while he had the office and the safe and connections worth a gold mine. Mr. Fenton and his doctor friend were already waiting, smoking under a dilapidated NO SMOKING sign. Nora felt not so much shy as careful. She took in their light hot-weather clothes—the doctor's pale beige jacket, with wide lapels, and Mr. Fenton's American-looking seersucker. The huge room was dark and smelled of old books and papers. It was not the smell of dirt, though the place could have done with a good cleanout.

Nora and the men stood side by side, across from her father. Another person, whom she took to be a regular employee, was sitting at a desk, reading the *Gazette* and eating a Danish. Her father had in front of him a ledger of printed forms. He filled in the blank spaces by hand, using a pen, which he dipped with care in black ink. Mr. Fenton dictated the facts. Before giving the child's name or its date of birth, he identified his wife and, of course, himself: They were Louise Marjorie Clopstock and Boyd Markham Forrest Fenton. He was one of those Anglos with no Christian name, just a string of surnames. Ray lifted the pen over the most important entry. He peered up, merry-looking as a squirrel. It was clear that Mr. Fenton either could not remember or make up his mind. "Scott?" he said, as if Ray ought to know.

The doctor said, "Neil Boyd Fenton," pausing heavily between syllables. "Not Neil Scott?"

"You said you wanted 'Neil Boyd.' "

Nora thought, You'd think Dr. Marchand was the mother. Ray wrote the name carefully and slowly, and the date of birth. Reading upside down, she saw that the Fenton child was three months old, which surely was past the legal limit of registration. Her father turned the ledger around so Mr. Fenton could sign, and said "Hey, Vince" to the man eating Danish. He came over and signed too, and then it was the doctor's turn.

Mr. Fenton said, "Shouldn't Nora be a witness?" and her father said, "I think we could use an endorsement from the little lady," as if he had never seen her before. To the best of Nora's knowledge, all the information recorded was true, and so she signed her name to it, along with the rest.

Her father sat down where Vince had been, brushed away some crumbs, and ran a cream-colored document into a big clackety typewriter, older than Nora, most likely. When he had finished repeating the names and dates in the ledger, he fastened a red seal to the certificate and brought it back to the counter to be signed. The same witnesses wrote their names, but only Nora, it seemed, saw her father's mistakes: He had typed "Nell" for "Neil" and "Frenton" for "Fenton" and had got the date of birth wrong by a year, giving "Nell Frenton" the age of fifteen months. The men signed the certificate without reading it. If she and her father had been alone, she could have pointed out the mistakes, but of course she could not show him up in front of strangers.

The doctor put his fountain pen away and remarked, "I like Neil for a name." He spoke to Mr. Fenton in English and to Ray and Nora not at all. At the same time he and Nora's father seemed to know each other. There was an easiness of acquaintance between them; a bit cagey perhaps. Mr. Fenton seemed more like the sort of man her father might go with to the races. She could imagine them easily going on about bets and horses. Most of the babies Ray was kind enough to find for unhappy couples were made known by doctors. Perhaps he was one of them.

It was decided between Ray and Mr. Fenton that Nora would be called for, the next morning, by Mr. Fenton and the doctor. They would all three collect the child and take him home. Nora was invited to lunch. Saying good-bye, Mr. Fenton touched her bare arm, perhaps by accident, and asked her to call him "Boyd." Nothing in her manner or expression showed she had heard.

That evening, Ray and his wife played cards in the kitchen. Nora was ironing the starched piqué dress she would wear the next day. She said, "They gave up their own baby for adoption, or what?"

"Maybe they weren't expecting a child. It was too much for them," her mother said.

"Give us a break," said Ray. "Mrs. Fenton wasn't in any shape to look after him. She had *her* mother down from Toronto because she couldn't even run the house. They've got this D.P. maid always threatening to quit."

"Does he mind having his mother-in-law around the whole time?" said Nora.

"He sure doesn't." Nora thought he would add some utterly English thing like "She's got the money," but Ray went on, "She's on his side. She wants them together. The baby's the best thing that could happen."

"Maybe there was a mistake at the hospital," said Nora's mother, trying again. "The Fentons got some orphan by mistake and their own baby went to the home."

"And then the truth came out," said Nora. It made sense.

"Now when you're over there, don't you hang out with that maid," Ray said. "She can't even speak English. If somebody says to you to eat in the kitchen, I want you to come straight home."

"I'm not leaving home," said Nora. "I'm not sure if I want to go back to their place after tomorrow."

"Come on," said Ray. "I promised."

"You promised. I didn't."

"Leave your dress on the ironing board," said her mother. "I'll do the pleats."

Nora switched off the iron and went to stand behind her father. She put her hands on his shoulders. "Don't worry," she said. "I'm not going to let you down. You might as well throw your hand in. I saw Maman's."

III

*O*bliged to take the baby from Nora, Missy now held him at arm's length, upright between her hands, so that no part of him could touch her white apron. Nora thought, He'll die from his own screaming. Missy's face said she was not enjoying the joke. Perhaps she thought Mr. Fenton had put Nora up to it. His laughter had said something different: Whatever blunders he might have committed until now, choosing Missy to be the mother of a Fenton was not among them.

"You'd better clean him up right away," said Mrs. Clopstock.

Missy, whose silences were astonishingly powerful, managed to suggest that cleaning Neil up was not in her working agreement. She did repeat that a bottle was ready for some reason, staring hard at the doctor.

"The child is badly dehydrated," he said, as if replying to Missy. "He should be given liquid right away. He is undernourished and seriously below his normal weight. As you can tell, he has a bad case of diarrhea. I'll take his temperature after lunch."

"Is he really sick?" said Nora.

"He may have to be hospitalized for a few days." He was increasingly solemn and slower than ever.

"Hospitalized?" said Mr. Fenton. "We've only just got him here."

"The first thing is to get him washed and changed," said Mrs. Clopstock.

"I'll do it," said Nora. "He knows me."

"Missy won't mind."

Sensing a private exchange between Mrs. Clopstock and Missy, Nora held still. She felt a child's powerful desire to go home, away from these strangers. Mrs. Clopstock said, "Let us all please go and sit down. We're standing here as if we were in a hotel lobby."

"I can do it," Nora said. She said again, "He knows me."

"Missy knows where everything is," said Mrs. Clopstock. "Come along, Alex, Boyd. Nora, don't you want to wash your hands?"

"I'm feeling dehydrated too," said Mr. Fenton. "I hope Missy put something on ice."

Nora watched Missy turn and climb the stairs and disappear around the bend in the staircase. There'll be a holy row about this, she thought. I'll be gone.

"It was very nice meeting you," she said. "I have to leave now."

"Come on, Nora," said Mr. Fenton. "Anybody could have made the same mistake. You came in out of bright sunlight. The hall was dark."

"Could we please, please go and sit down?" said his mother-in-law.

"All right," he said, still to Nora. "It's O.K. You've had enough. Let's have a bite to eat and I'll drive you home."

"You may have to take Neil to the hospital."

Mrs. Clopstock took the doctor's arm. She was a little woman in green linen, wearing pearls and pearl earrings. Aunt Rosalie would have seen right away if they were real. The two moved from the shaded hall to a shaded room.

Mr. Fenton watched them go. "Nora," he said, "just let me have a drink and I'll drive you home."

"I don't need to be driven home. I can take the Sherbrooke bus and walk the rest of the way."

"Can you tell me what's wrong? It can't be my mother-in-law. She's a nice woman. Missy's a little rough, but she's nice too."

"Where's Mrs. Fenton?" said Nora. "Why didn't she at least come to the door? It's her child."

"You're not dumb," he said. "You're not Ray's girl for nothing. It's hers and it isn't."

"We all signed," Nora said. "I didn't sign to cover up some story. I came here to do a Christian act. I wasn't paid anything."

"What do you mean by 'anything'? You mean not enough?"

"Who's Neil?" she said. "I mean, who *is* he?"

"He's a Fenton. You saw the register."

"I mean, *who* is he?"

"He's my son. You signed the register. You should know."

"I believe you," she said. "He has English eyes." Her voice dropped. He had to ask her to repeat something. "I said, was it Ninette?"

It took him a second or so to see what she was after. He gave the same kind of noisy laugh as when she had tried to place the child in Missy's arms. "Little Miss Cochefert? Until this minute I thought you were the only sane person in Montreal."

"It fits," said Nora. "I'm sorry."

"Well, I'll tell you," he said. "I don't know. There are two people that know. Your father, Ray Abbott, and Alex Marchand."

"Did you pay my dad?"

"*Pay* him? I paid him for *you*. We wouldn't have asked anyone to look after Neil for nothing."

"About Ninette," she said. "I just meant that it fits."

"A hundred women in Montreal would fit, when it comes to that. The truth is, we don't know, except that she was in good health."

"Who was the girl in the lane? The one you were talking about."

"Just a girl in the wrong place. Her father was a school principal."

"You said that. Did you know her?"

"I never saw her. Missy and Louise did. Louise is my wife."

"I know. How much did you give my dad? Not for Neil. For me."

"Thirty bucks. Some men don't make that in a week. If you have to ask, it means you never got it."

"I've never had thirty dollars in one piece in my life," she said. "In my family we don't fight over money. What my dad says, goes. I've never had to go without. Gerry and I had new coats every winter."

"Is that the end of the interrogatory? You'd have made a great cop. I agree, you can't stay. But would you just do one last Christian act? Wash your hands and comb your hair and sit down and have lunch. After that, I'll put you in a taxi and pay the driver. If you don't want me to, my mother-in-law will."

"I could help you take him to the hospital."

"Forget the Fenton family," he said. "Lunch is the cutoff."

Late in the afternoon Ray came home and they had tea and sandwiches at the kitchen table. Nora was wearing Gerry's old white terry-cloth robe. Her washed hair was in rollers.

"There was nothing to it, no problem," she said again. "He needed a hospital checkup. He was run-down. I don't know which hospital."

"I could find out," said Ray.

"I think they don't want anybody around."

"What did you eat for lunch?" said her mother.

"Some kind of cold soup. Some kind of cold meat. A fruit salad. Iced tea. The men drank beer. There was no bread on the table."

"Pass Nora the peanut butter," said Ray.

"Did you meet Mr. Fenton because of Ninette," said Nora, "or did you know him first? Did you know Dr. Marchand first, or Mr. Fenton?"

"It's a small world," said her father. "Anyways, I've got some money for you."

"How much?" said Nora. "No, never mind. I'll ask if I ever need it."

"You'll never need anything," he said. "Not as long as your old dad's around."

"You know that Mrs. Clopstock?" said Nora. "She's the first person I've ever met from Toronto. I didn't stare at her, but I took a good look. Maman, how can you tell real pearls?"

"They wouldn't be real," said Ray. "The real ones would be on deposit. Rosalie had a string of pearls."

"They had to sell them on account of Ninette," said her mother.

"Maybe you could find out the name of the hospital," Nora said. "He might like to see me. He knows me."

"He's already forgotten you," her mother said.

"I wouldn't swear to that," said Ray. "I can remember somebody bending over my baby buggy. I don't know who it was, though."

He will remember that I picked him up, Nora decided. He will remember the smell of the incense. He will remember the front door and moving into the dark hall. I'll try to remember him. It's the best I can do.

She said to Ray, "What's the exact truth? Just what's on paper?"

"Nora," said her mother. "Look at me. Look me right in the face. Forget that child. He isn't yours. If you want children, get married. All right?"

"All right," her father answered for her. "Why don't you put on some clothes and I'll take you both to a movie." He began to whistle, not "Don't Let It Bother You," but some other thing just as easy.

The

FIFTIES

———
⚜

THE OTHER PARIS

———

❧

$\mathcal{B}$y the time they decided what Carol would wear for her wedding (white with white flowers), it was the end of the afternoon. Madame Germaine removed the sketchbooks, the scraps of net and satin, the stacks of *Vogue;* she had, already, a professional look of anxiety, as if it could not possibly come out well. One foresaw seams ripped open, extra fittings, even Carol's tears.

Odile, Carol's friend, seemed disappointed. "White isn't *original,*" she said. "If it were me, I would certainly not be married in all that rubbish of lace, like a First Communion." She picked threads from her skirt fastidiously, as if to remove herself completely from Carol and her unoriginal plans.

I wonder if anyone has ever asked Odile to marry him, Carol thought, placidly looking out the window. As her wedding approached, she had more and more the engaged girl's air of dissociation: Nothing mattered until the wedding, and she could not see clearly beyond it. She was sorry for all the single girls of the world, particularly those who were, like Odile, past thirty. Odile looked sallow and pathetic, huddled into a sweater and coat, turning over samples of lace with a disapproving air. She seemed all of a piece with the day's weather and the chilly air of the dressmaker's flat. Outside, the street was still damp from a rain earlier in the day. There were no trees in sight, no flowers, no comforting glimpse of park. No one in this part of Paris would have known it was spring.

"Even *blue,*" said Odile. But there was evidently no conversation to be had with Carol, who had begun to hum, so she said to the dressmaker, "Just imagine! Miss Frazier came to Paris to work last autumn, and fell in love with the head of her department."

"Non!" Madame Germaine recoiled, as if no other client had ever brought off such an extraordinary thing.

"Fell in love with Mr. Mitchell," said Odile, nodding. "At first sight, *le coup de foudre.*"

"At first sight?" said the dressmaker. She looked fondly at Carol.

"Something no one would have expected," said Odile. "Although Mr. Mitchell is charming. *Charming.*"

"I think we ought to go," said Carol.

Odile looked regretfully, as if she had more to say. Carol made an appointment for the following day, and the two left the flat together, Odile's sturdy heels making a clatter as they went down the staircase.

"Why were you so funny just then?" Odile said. "I didn't say anything that wasn't true, and you know how women like that love to hear about weddings and love and everything. And it's such a wonderful story about you and Mr. Mitchell. I tell it to everyone."

This, Carol thought, could not be true, for Odile was rarely interested in anyone but herself, and had never shown the least curiosity about Carol's plans, other than offering to find a dressmaker.

"It was terribly romantic," Odile said, "whether you admit it or not. You and Mr. Mitchell. Our Mr. Mitchell."

It penetrated at last that Odile was making fun of her.

People had assured Carol so often that her engagement was romantic, and she had become so accustomed to the word, that Odile's slight irony was perplexing. If anyone had asked Carol at what precise moment she fell in love, or where Howard Mitchell proposed to her, she would have imagined, quite sincerely, a scene that involved all at once the Seine, moonlight, barrows of violets, acacias in flower, and a confused, misty background of the Eiffel Tower and little crooked streets. This was what everyone expected, and she had nearly come to believe it herself.

Actually, he had proposed at lunch, over a tuna-fish salad. He and Carol had known each other less than three weeks, and their conversation until then had been limited to their office—an American government agency—and the people in it. Carol was twenty-two; no one had proposed to her before, except an unsuitable medical student with no money and eight years' training still to go. She was under the illusion that in a short time she would be so old no one would ask her again. She accepted at once, and Howard celebrated by ordering an extra bottle of wine. Both would have liked champagne, as a more emphatic symbol of the unusual, but each was too diffident to suggest it.

The fact that Carol was not in love with Howard Mitchell did not dismay her in the least. From a series of helpful college lectures on marriage she had learned that a common interest, such as a liking for Irish setters, was the true basis for happiness, and that the illusion of love was a blight imposed by the film industry, and almost entirely responsible for the high rate of divorce. Similar economic backgrounds, financial security, belonging to the same church—these were the pillars of the married union. By an astonishing coincidence, the fathers of Carol and Howard were both attorneys and both had been defeated in their one attempt to get elected a judge. Carol and Howard were both vaguely Protestant, although a serious discussion of religious beliefs would have gravely embarrassed them. And Howard, best of all, was sober, old enough to know his own mind, and absolutely reliable. He was an economist who had had sense enough to attach himself to a corporation that continued to pay his salary during his loan to the government. There was no reason for the engagement or the marriage to fail.

Carol, with great efficiency, nearly at once set about the business of falling in love. Love required only the right conditions, like a geranium. It would wither exposed to bad weather or in dismal surroundings; indeed, Carol rated the chances of love in a cottage or a furnished room at zero. Given a good climate, enough money, and a pair of good-natured, *intelligent* (her college lectures had stressed this) people, one had only to sit back and watch it grow. All winter, then, she looked for these right conditions in Paris. When, at first, nothing happened, she blamed it on the weather. She was often convinced she would fall deeply in love with Howard if only it would stop raining. Undaunted, she waited for better times.

Howard had no notion of any of this. His sudden proposal to Carol had been quite out of character—he was uncommonly cautious—and he alternated between a state of numbness and a state of self-congratulation. Before his engagement he had sometimes been lonely, a malaise he put down to overwork, and he was discontented with his bachelor households, for he did not enjoy collecting old pottery or making little casserole dishes. Unless he stumbled on a competent housemaid, nothing ever got done. This in itself would not have spurred him into marriage had he not been seriously unsettled by the visit of one of his sisters, who advised him to marry some nice girl before it was too late. "Soon," she told him, "you'll just be a person who fills in at dinner."

Howard saw the picture at once, and was deeply moved by it. Retreating by inches, he said he knew of no one who would do.

Nonense, his sister said. There were plenty of nice girls everywhere. She then warned him not to marry a French girl, who might cause trouble once he got her home to Chicago, or a Catholic, because of the children, and to avoid anyone fast, nervous, divorced, or over twenty-four. Howard knew a number of girls in Paris, most of whom worked in his office or similar agencies. They struck him as cheerful and eager, but aggressive—not at all what he fancied around the house. Just as he was becoming seriously baffled by this gap in his life, Carol Frazier arrived.

He was touched by her shy good manners, her earnest college French. His friends liked her, and, more important, so did the wives of his friends. He had been seriously in love on earlier occasions, and did not consider it a reliable emotion. He and Carol got on well, which seemed to him a satisfactory beginning. His friends, however, told him that she was obviously in love with him and that it was pretty to see. This he expected, not because he was vain but because one took it for granted that love, like a harmless familiar, always attended young women in friendships of this nature. Certainly he was fond of Carol and concerned for her comfort. Had she complained of a toothache, he would have seen to it that she got to a dentist. Carol was moved to another department, but they met every day for lunch and dinner, and talked without discord of any kind. They talked about the job Howard was returning to in Chicago; about their wedding, which was to take place in the spring; and about the movies they saw together. They often went to parties, and then they talked about everyone who had been there, even though they would see most of them next day, at work.

It was a busy life, yet Carol could not help feeling that something had been missed. The weather continued unimproved. She shared an apartment in Passy with two American girls, a temporary ménage that might have existed anywhere. When she rode the Métro, people pushed and were just as rude as in New York. Restaurant food was dull, and the cafés were full of Coca-Cola signs. No wonder she was not in love, she would think. Where was the Paris she had read about? Where were the elegant and expensive-looking women? Where, above all, were the men, those men with their gay good looks and snatches of merry song, the delight of English lady novelists? Traveling through Paris to and from work, she saw only shabby girls bundled into raincoats, hurrying along in the rain, or men who needed a haircut. In the famous parks, under the drizzly trees, children whined peevishly and were slapped. She sometimes thought that perhaps if she and Howard had French friends . . . She suggested it to him.

"You have a French friend," said Howard. "How about Odile?"

But that was not what Carol meant. Odile Pontmoret was Howard's secretary, a thin, dark woman who was (people said) the niece of a count who had gone broke. She seldom smiled and, because her English was at once precise and inaccurate, often sounded sarcastic. All winter she wore the same dark skirt and purple pullover to work. It never occurred to anyone to include her in parties made up of office people, and it was not certain that she would have come anyway. Odile and Carol were friendly in an impersonal way. Sometimes, if Howard was busy, they lunched together. Carol was always careful not to complain about Paris, having been warned that the foreign policy of her country hinged on chance remarks. But her restraint met with no answering delicacy in Odile, whose chief memory of her single trip to New York, before the war, was that her father had been charged twenty-four dollars for a taxi fare that, they later reasoned, must have been two dollars and forty cents. Repeating this, Odile would look indignantly at Carol, as if Carol had been driving the taxi. "And there was no service in the hotel, no service at all," Odile would say. "You could drop your nightgown on the floor and they would sweep around it. And still expect a tip."

These, her sole observations of America, she repeated until Carol's good nature was strained to the limit. Odile never spoke of her life outside the office, which Carol longed to hear about, and she touched on the present only to complain in terms of the past. "Before the war, we traveled, we went everywhere," she would say. "Now, with our poor little franc, everything is finished. I work to help my family. My brother publicizes wines—*Spanish* wines. We work and work so that our parents won't feel the change and so that Martine, our sister, can study music."

Saying this, she would look bewildered and angry, and Carol would have the feeling that Odile was somehow blaming her. They usually ate in a restaurant of Odile's choice—Carol was tactful about this, for Odile earned less than she did—where the food was lumpy and inadequate and the fluorescent lighting made everyone look ill. Carol would glance around at the neighboring tables, at which sat glum and noisy Parisian office workers and shop clerks, and observe that everyone's coat was too long or too short, that the furs were tacky.

There must be more to it than this, she would think. Was it possible that these badly groomed girls liked living in Paris? Surely the sentimental songs about the city had no meaning for them. Were many of them in love, or— still less likely—could any man be in love with any of them?

Every evening, leaving the building in which she and Howard worked, she would pause on the stair landing between the first and second floors to look through the window at the dark winter twilight, thinking that an evening, a special kind of evening, was forming all over the city, and that she had no part in it. At the same hour, people streamed out of an old house across the street that was now a museum, and Carol would watch them hurrying off under their umbrellas. She wondered where they were going and where they lived and what they were having for dinner. Her interest in them was not specific; she had no urge to run into the street and introduce herself. It was simply that she believed they knew a secret, and if she spoke to the right person, or opened the right door, or turned down an unexpected street, the city would reveal itself and she would fall in love. After this pause at the landing, she would forget all her disappointments (the Parma violets she had bought that were fraudulently cut and bound, so that they died in a minute) and run the rest of the way down the stairs, meaning to tell Howard and see if he shared her brief optimism.

On one of these evenings, soon after the start of the cold weather, she noticed a young man sitting on one of the chairs put out in an inhospitable row in the lobby of the building for job seekers. He looked pale and ill, and the sleeves of his coat were short, as if he were still growing. He stared at her with the expression of a clever child, at once bold and withdrawn. She had the impression that he had seen her stop at the window on the landing and that he was, for some reason, amused. He did not look at all as if he belonged there. She mentioned him to Howard.

"That must have been Felix," Howard said. "Odile's friend." He put so much weight on the word "friend" that Carol felt there was more, a great deal more, and that, although he liked gossip as well as anyone else, he did not find Odile's affairs interesting enough to discuss. "He used to wait for her outside every night. Now I guess he comes in out of the rain."

"But she's never mentioned him," Carol protested. "And he must be younger than she is, and so pale and funny-looking! Where does he come from?"

Howard didn't know. Felix was Austrian, he thought, or Czech. There was something odd about him, for although he obviously hadn't enough to eat, he always had plenty of American cigarettes. That was a bad sign. "Why are you so interested?" he said. But Carol was not interested at all.

After that, Carol saw Felix every evening. He was always polite and sometimes murmured a perfunctory greeting as she passed his chair. He continued to look tired and ill, and Carol wondered if it was true that he hadn't enough to eat. She mentioned him to Odile, who was surprisingly willing to discuss her friend. He was twenty-one, she said, and without relatives. They had all been killed at the end of the war, in the final bombings. He was in Paris illegally, without a proper passport or working papers. The police were taking a long time to straighten it out, and meanwhile, not permitted to work, Felix "did other things." Odile did not say what the other things were, and Carol was rather shocked.

That night, before going to sleep, she thought about Felix, and about how he was only twenty-one. She and Felix, then, were closer in age than he was to Odile or she herself was to Howard. When I was in school, he was in school, she thought. When the war stopped, we were fourteen and fifteen. ... But here she lost track, for where Carol had had a holiday, Felix's parents had been killed. Their closeness in age gave her unexpected comfort, as if someone in this disappointing city had some tie with her. In the morning she was ashamed of her disloyal thoughts—her closest tie in Paris was, after all, with Howard—and decided to ignore Felix when she saw him again. That night, when she passed his chair, he said "Good evening," and she was suddenly acutely conscious of every bit of her clothing: the press of the belt at her waist, the pinch of her earrings, the weight of her dress, even her gloves, which felt as scratchy as sacking. It was a disturbing feeling; she was not sure that she liked it.

"I don't see why Felix should just sit in that hall all the time," she complained to Howard. "Can't he wait for Odile somewhere else?"

Howard was too busy to worry about Felix. It occurred to him that Carol was being tiresome, and that this whining over who sat in the hall was only one instance of her new manner. She had taken to complaining about their friends, and saying she wanted to meet new people and see more of Paris. Sometimes she looked at him helplessly and eagerly, as if there were something he ought to be saying or doing. He was genuinely perplexed; it seemed to him they got along well and were reasonably happy together. But Carol was changing. She hunted up odd, cheap restaurants. She made him walk in the rain. She said that they ought to see the sun come up from the steps of the Sacré-Coeur, and actually succeeded in dragging him there, nearly dead of cold. And, as he might have foreseen, the expedition came to nothing, for it was a rainy dawn and a suspicious gendarme sent them both home.

At Christmas, Carol begged him to take her to the carol singing in the Place Vendôme. Here, she imagined, with the gentle fall of snow and the small, rosy choirboys singing between lighted Christmas trees, she would find something—a warm memory that would, later, bring her closer to Howard, a glimpse of the Paris other people liked. But, of course, there was no snow. Howard and Carol stood under her umbrella as a fine, misty rain fell on the choristers, who sang over and over the opening bars of *"Il est né, le Divin Enfant,"* testing voice levels for a broadcast. Newspaper photographers drifted on the rim of the crowd, and the flares that lit the scene for a newsreel camera blew acrid smoke in their faces. Howard began to cough. Around the square, the tenants of the Place emerged on their small balconies. Some of them had champagne glasses in their hands, as if they had interrupted an agreeable party to step outside for a moment. Carol looked up at the lighted open doorways, through which she could see a painted ceiling, a lighted chandelier. But nothing happened. None of the people seemed beautiful or extraordinary. No one said, "Who *is* that charming girl down there? Let's ask her up!"

Howard blew his nose and said that his feet were cold; they drifted over the square to a couturier's window, where the Infant Jesus wore a rhinestone pin and a worshiping plaster angel extended a famous brand of perfume. "It just looks like New York or something," Carol said, plaintive with disappointment. As she stopped to close her umbrella, the wind carried to her feet a piece of mistletoe and, glancing up, she saw that cheap tinsel icicles and bunches of mistletoe had been tied on the street lamps of the square. It looked pretty, and rather poor, and she thought of the giant tree in Rockefeller Center. She suddenly felt sorry for Paris, just as she had felt sorry for Felix because he looked hungry and was only twenty-one. Her throat went warm, like the prelude to a rush of tears. Stooping, she picked up the sprig of mistletoe and put it in her pocket.

"Is this all?" Howard said. "Was this what you wanted to see?" He was cold and uncomfortable, but because it was Christmas, he said nothing impatient, and tried to remember, instead, that she was only twenty-two.

"I suppose so."

They found a taxi and went on to finish the evening with some friends from their office. Howard made an amusing story of their adventure in the Place Vendôme. She realized for the first time that something could be perfectly accurate but untruthful—they had not found any part of that evening funny—and that this might cover more areas of experience than the occasional amusing story. She looked at Howard thoughtfully, as if she had learned something of value.

The day after Christmas, Howard came down with a bad cold, the result of standing in the rain. He did not shake it off for the rest of the winter, and Carol, feeling guiltily that it was her fault, suggested no more excursions. Temporarily, she put the question of falling in love to one side. Paris was not the place, she thought; perhaps it had been, fifty years ago, or whenever it was that people wrote all the songs. It did not occur to her to break her engagement.

She wore out the winter working, nursing Howard's cold, toying with office gossip, and, now and again, lunching with Odile, who was just as unsatisfactory as ever. It was nearly spring when Odile, stopping by Carol's desk, said that Martine was making a concert debut the following Sunday. It was a private gathering, a subscription concert. Odile sounded vague. She dropped two tickets on Carol's desk and said, walking away, "If you want to come."

"If I *want* to!"

Carol flew away to tell Howard at once. "It's a sort of private musical thing," she said. "There should be important musicians there, since it's a debut, and all Odile's family. The old count—everyone." She half expected Odile's impoverished uncle to turn up in eighteenth-century costume, his hands clasped on the head of a cane.

Howard said it was all right with him, provided they needn't stand out in the rain.

"Of course not! It's a *concert*." She looked at the tickets; they were handwritten slips bearing mimeographed numbers. "It's probably in someone's house," she said. "In one of those lovely old drawing rooms. Or in a little painted theater. There are supposed to be little theaters all over Paris that belong to families and that foreigners never see."

She was beside herself with excitement. What if Paris had taken all winter to come to life? Some foreigners lived there forever and never broke in at all. She spent nearly all of one week's salary on a white feather hat, and practiced a few graceful phrases in French. *"Oui, elle est charmante,"* she said to her mirror. *"La petite Martine est tout à fait ravissante. Je connais très bien Odile. Une coupe de champagne? Mais oui, merci bien. Ah, voici mon fiancé! Monsieur Mitchell, le Baron de ..."* and so forth.

She felt close to Odile, as if they had been great friends for a long time. When, two days before the concert, Odile remarked, yawning, that Martine was crying night and day because she hadn't a suitable dress, Carol said, "Would you let me lend her a dress?"

Odile suddenly stopped yawning and turned back the cuffs of her pullover as if it were a task that required all her attention. "That would be very kind of you," she said, at last.

"I mean," said Carol, feeling gauche, "would it be all right? I have a lovely pale green tulle that I brought from New York. I've only worn it twice."

"It sounds very nice," said Odile.

Carol shook the dress out of its tissue paper and brought it to work the next day. Odile thanked her without fervor, but Carol knew by now that that was simply her manner.

"We're going to a private musical debut," she wrote to her mother and father. "The youngest niece of the Count de Quelquechose . . . I've lent her my green tulle." She said no more than that, so that it would sound properly casual. So far, her letters had not contained much of interest.

The address Odile had given Carol turned out to be an ordinary, shabby theater in the Second Arrondissement. It was on an obscure street, and the taxi driver had to stop and consult his street guide so often that they were half an hour late. Music came out to meet them in the empty lobby, where a poster said only J. S. BACH. An usher tiptoed them into place with ill grace and asked Carol please to have some thought for the people behind her and remove her hat. Carol did so while Howard groped for change for the usher's tip. She peered around: The theater was less than half filled, and the music coming from the small orchestra on the stage had a thin, echoing quality, as if it were traveling around an empty vault. Odile was nowhere in sight. After a moment, Carol saw Felix sitting alone a few rows away. He smiled—much too familiarly, Carol thought. He looked paler than usual, and almost deliberately untidy. He might at least have taken pains for the concert. She felt a spasm of annoyance, and at the same time her heart began to beat so quickly that she felt its movement must surely be visible.

Whatever is the matter with me, she thought. If one could believe all the arch stories on the subject, this was traditional for brides-to-be. Perhaps, at this unpromising moment, she had begun to fall in love. She turned in her seat and stared at Howard; he looked much as always. She settled back and began furnishing in her mind the apartment they would have in Chicago. Sometimes the theater lights went on, startling her out of some problem involving draperies and venetian blinds; once Howard went out to smoke. Carol had just finished papering a bedroom green and white when Martine walked onstage, with her violin. At the same moment, a piece of plaster bearing the painted plump foot of a nymph detached itself from the ceiling and crashed into the aisle, just missing Howard's head. Everyone stood up to look, and Martine and the conductor stared at Howard and Carol furiously, as if it were their fault. The commotion was horrifying. Carol slid down in her seat, her hands over her eyes. She retained, in all her distress, an impression of Martine, who wore an ill-fitting blue dress with a little jacket. She had not worn Carol's pretty tulle; probably she had never intended to.

Carol wondered, miserably, why they had come. For the first time, she noticed that all the people around them were odd and shabby. The smell of stale winter coats filled the unaired theater; her head began to ache, and Martine's violin shrilled on her ear like a pennywhistle. At last the music stopped and the lights went on. The concert was over. There was some applause, but people were busy pulling on coats and screaming at one another from aisle to aisle. Martine shook hands with the conductor and, after looking vaguely around the hall, wandered away.

"Is this all?" said Howard. He stood up and stretched. Carol did not reply. She had just seen Felix and Odile together. Odile was speaking rapidly and looked unhappy. She wore the same skirt and pullover Carol had seen all winter, and she was carrying her coat.

"Odile!" Carol called. But Odile waved and threaded her way through the row of seats to the other side of the theater, where she joined some elderly people and a young man. They went off together backstage.

Her family, Carol thought, sickening under the snub. And she didn't introduce me, or even come over and speak. She was positive now that Odile had invited her only to help fill the hall, or because she had a pair of tickets she didn't know what to do with.

"Let's go," Howard said. Their seats were near the front. By the time they reached the lobby, it was nearly empty. Under the indifferent eyes of the usher, Howard guided Carol into her coat. "They sure didn't put on much of a show for Martine," he said.

"No, they didn't."

"No flowers," he said. "It didn't even have her name on the program. No one would have known."

It had grown dark, and rain poured from the edge of the roof in an unbroken sheet. "You stay here," said Howard. "I'll get a taxi."

"No," said Carol. "Stay with me. This won't last." She could not bring herself to tell him how hurt and humiliated she was, what a ruin the afternoon had been. Howard led her behind the shelter of a billboard.

"That dress," he went on. "I thought you'd lent her something."

"I had. She didn't wear it. I don't know why."

"Ask Odile."

"I don't care. I'd rather let it drop."

He agreed. He felt that Carol had almost knowingly exposed herself to an indignity over the dress, and pride of that nature he understood. To distract her, he spoke of the job waiting for him in Chicago, of his friends, of his brother's sailboat.

Against a background of rain and Carol's disappointment, he sounded, without meaning to, faintly homesick. Carol picked up his mood. She looked at the white feather hat the usher had made her remove and said suddenly, "I wish I were home. I wish I were in my own country, with my own friends."

"You will be," he said, "in a couple of months." He hoped she would not begin to cry.

"I'm tired of the way everything is here—old and rotten and falling down."

"You mean that chunk of ceiling?"

She turned from him, exasperated at his persistently missing the point, and saw Felix not far away. He was leaning against the ticket booth, looking resignedly at the rain. When he noticed Carol looking at him, he said, ignoring Howard, "Odile's backstage with her family." He made a face and went on, "No admission for us foreigners."

Odile's family did not accept Felix; Carol had barely absorbed this thought, which gave her an unexpected and indignant shock, when she realized what he had meant by "us foreigners." It was rude of Odile to let her family hurt her friend; at the same time, it was even less kind of them to include Carol in a single category of foreigners. Surely Odile could see the difference between Carol and this pale young man who "did other things." She felt that she and Felix had been linked together in a disagreeable way, and that she was floating away from everything familiar and safe. Without replying, she bent her head and turned away, politely but unmistakably.

"Funny kid," Howard remarked as Felix walked slowly out into the rain, his hands in his pockets.

"He's horrible," said Carol, so violently that he stared at her. "He's not funny. He's a parasite. He lives on Odile. He doesn't work or anything, he just hangs around and stares at people. Odile says he has no passport. Well, why doesn't he *get* one? Any man can work if he wants to. Why are there people like that? All the boys I ever knew at home were well brought up and manly. I never knew anyone like Felix."

She stopped, breathless, and Howard said, "Well, let Odile worry."

"Odile!" Carol cried. "Odile must be crazy. What is she thinking of? Her family ought to put a stop to it. The whole thing is terrible. It's bad for the office. It ought to be stopped. Why, he'll never marry her! Why should he? He's only a boy, an orphan. He needs friends, and connections, and somebody his own age. Why should he marry Odile? What does he want with an old maid from an old, broken-down family? He needs a good meal, and—and help." She stopped, bewildered. She had been about to say "and love."

Howard, now beyond surprise, felt only a growing wave of annoyance. He did not like hysterical women. His sisters never behaved like that.

"I want to go *home*," said Carol, nearly wailing.

He ran off to find a taxi, glad to get away. By "home" he thought she meant the apartment she shared with the two American girls in Passy.

For Carol, the concert was the end, the final *clou*. She stopped caring about Paris, or Odile, or her feelings for Howard. When Odile returned her green dress, nicely pressed and folded in a cardboard box, she said only, "Just leave it on my desk." Everyone seemed to think it normal that now her only preoccupation should be the cut of her wedding dress. People began giving parties for her. The wash of attention soothed her fears. She was good-tempered, and did not ask Howard to take her to tiresome places. Once again he felt he had made the right decision, and put her temporary waywardness down to nerves. After a while, Carol began lunching with Odile again, but she did not mention the concert.

As for Felix, Carol now avoided him entirely. Sometimes she waited until Odile had left the office before leaving herself. Again, she braced herself and walked briskly past him, ignoring his "Good evening." She no longer stopped on the staircase to watch the twilight; her mood was different. She believed that something fortunate had happened to her spirit, and that she had become invulnerable. Soon she was able to walk by Felix without a tremor, and after a while she stopped noticing him at all.

"Have you noticed winter is over?" Odile said. She and Carol had left the dressmaker's street and turned off on a broad, oblique avenue. "It hasn't rained for hours. This was the longest winter I remember, although I think one says this every year."

"It was long for me, too," Carol said. It was true that it was over. The spindly trees of the avenue were covered with green, like a wrapping of tissue. A few people sat out in front of shops, sunning themselves. It was, suddenly, like coming out of a tunnel.

Odile turned to Carol and smiled, a rare expression for her. "I'm sorry I was rude at Madame Germaine's just now," she said. "I don't know what the matter is nowadays—I am dreadful to everyone. But I shouldn't have been to you."

"Never mind," said Carol. She flushed a little, for Howard had taught her to be embarrassed over anything as direct as an apology. "I'd forgotten it. In fact, I didn't even notice."

"Now you are being nice," said Odile unhappily. "Really, there is something wrong with me. I worry all the time, over money, over Martine, over Felix. I think it isn't healthy." Carol murmured something comforting but indistinct. Glancing at her, Odile said, "Where are you off to now?"

"Nowhere. Home, I suppose. There's always something to do these days."

"Why don't you come along with me?" Odile stopped on the street and took her arm. "I'm going to see Felix. He lives near here. Oh, he would be so surprised!"

"Felix?" Automatically Carol glanced at her watch. Surely she had something to do, some appointment? But Odile was hurrying her along. Carol thought, Now, this is all wrong. But they had reached the Boulevard de Grenelle, where the Métro ran overhead, encased in a tube of red brick. Light fell in patterns underneath; the boulevard was lined with ugly shops and dark, buff-painted cafés. It was a far cry from the prim street a block or so away where the dressmaker's flat was. "Is it far?" said Carol nervously. She did not like the look of the neighborhood. Odile shook her head. They crossed the boulevard and a few crooked, narrow streets filled with curbside barrows and marketing crowds. It was a section of Paris Carol had not seen; although it was on the Left Bank, it was not pretty, not picturesque. There were no little restaurants, no students' hotels. It was simply down-and-out and dirty, and everyone looked ill-tempered. Arabs lounging in doorways looked at the two girls and called out, laughing.

"Look straight ahead," said Odile. "If you look at them, they come up and take your arm. It's worse when I come alone."

How dreadful of Felix to let Odile walk alone through streets like this, Carol thought.

"Here," said Odile. She stopped in front of a building on which the painted word "Hôtel" was almost effaced. They climbed a musty-smelling staircase, Carol taking care not to let her skirt brush the walls. She wondered nervously what Howard would say when he heard she had visited Felix in his hotel room. On a stair landing, Odile knocked at one of the doors. Felix let them in. It took a few moments, for he had been asleep. He did not look at all surprised but with a slight bow invited them in, as if he frequently entertained in his room.

The room was so cluttered, the bed so untidy, that Carol stood bewildered, wondering where one could sit. Odile at once flung herself down on the bed, dropping her handbag on the floor, which was cement and gritty with dirt.

"I'm tired," she said. "We've been choosing Carol's wedding dress. White, and *very* pretty."

Felix's shirt was unbuttoned, his face without any color. He glanced sidelong at Carol, smiling. On a table stood an alcohol stove, some gaudy plastic bowls, and a paper container of sugar. In the tiny washbasin, over which hung a cold-water faucet, were a plate and a spoon, and, here and there on the perimeter, Felix's shaving things and a battered toothbrush.

"Do sit on that chair," he said to Carol, but he made no move to take away the shirt and sweater and raincoat that were bundled on it. Everything else he owned appeared to be on the floor. The room faced a court and was quite dark. "I'll heat up this coffee," Felix said, as if casting about for something to do as a host. "Miss Frazier, sit down." He put a match to the stove and a blue flame leaped along the wall. He stared into a saucepan of coffee, sniffed it, and added a quantity of cold water. "A new PX has just been opened," he said to Odile. He put the saucepan over the flame, apparently satisfied. "I went around to see what was up," he said. "Nothing much. It is really sad. Everything is organized on such a big scale now that there is no room for little people like me. I waited outside and finally picked up some cigarettes—only two cartons—from a soldier."

He talked on, and Carol, who was not accustomed to his conversation, could not tell if he was joking or serious. She had finally decided to sit down on top of the raincoat. She frowned at her hands, wondering why Odile didn't teach him to make coffee properly and why he talked like a criminal. For Carol, the idea that one might not be permitted to work was preposterous. She harbored a rigid belief that anyone could work who sincerely wanted to. Picking apples, she thought vaguely, or down in a mine, where people were always needed.

Odile looked at Carol, as if she knew what she was thinking. "Poor Felix doesn't belong in this world," she said. "He should have been killed at the end of the war. Instead of that, every year he gets older. In a month, he will be twenty-two."

But Odile was over thirty. Carol found the gap between their ages distasteful, and thought it indelicate of Odile to stress it. Felix, who had been ineffectively rinsing the plastic bowls in cold water, now poured the coffee out. He pushed one of the bowls toward Odile; then he suddenly took her hand and, turning it over, kissed the palm. "*Why* should I have been killed?" he said.

Carol, breathless with embarrassment, looked at the brick wall of the court. She twisted her fingers together until they hurt. How can they act like this in front of me, she thought, and in such a dirty room? The thought that they might be in love entered her head for the first time, and it made her ill. Felix, smiling, gave her a bowl of coffee, and she took it without meeting his eyes. He sat down on the bed beside Odile and said happily, "I'm glad you came. You both look beautiful."

Carol glanced at Odile, thinking, Not beautiful, not by any stretch of good manners. "French girls are all attractive," she said politely.

"Most of them are frights," said Felix. No one disputed it, and no one but Carol appeared distressed by the abrupt termination of the conversation. She cast about for something to say, but Odile put her bowl on the floor, said again that she was tired, lay back, and seemed all at once to fall asleep.

Felix looked at her. "She really can shut out the world whenever she wants to," he said, suggesting to Carol's startled ears that he was quite accustomed to seeing her fall asleep. Of course, she might have guessed, but why should Felix make it so obvious? She felt ashamed of the way she had worried about Felix, and the way she had run after Odile, wanting to know her family. This was all it had come to, this dirty room. Howard was right, she thought. It doesn't pay.

At the same time, she was perplexed at the intimacy in which she and Felix now found themselves. She would have been more at ease alone in a room with him than with Odile beside him asleep on his bed.

"I must go," she said nervously.

"Oh, yes," said Felix, not stopping her.

"But I can't find my way back alone." She felt as if she might cry.

"There are taxis," he said vaguely. "But I can take you to the Métro, if you like." He buttoned his shirt and looked around for a jacket, making no move to waken Odile.

"Should we leave her here?" said Carol. "Shouldn't I say good-bye?"

He looked surprised. "I wouldn't think of disturbing her," he said. "If she's asleep, then she must be tired." And to this Carol could think of nothing to say.

He followed her down the staircase and into the street, dark now, with stripes of neon to mark the cafés. They said little, and because she was afraid of the dark and the Arabs, Carol walked close beside him. On the Boulevard de Grenelle, Felix stopped at the entrance to the Métro.

"Here," he said. "Up those steps. It takes you right over to Passy."

She looked at him, feeling this parting was not enough. She had criticized him to Howard and taught herself to ignore him, but here, in a neighborhood where she could not so much as find her way, she felt more than ever imprisoned in the walls of her shyness, unable to say, "Thank you," or "Thanks for the coffee," or anything perfunctory and reasonable. She had an inexplicable and uneasy feeling that something had ended for her, and that she would never see Felix, or even Odile, again.

Felix caught her look, or seemed to. He looked around, distressed, at the Bar des Sportifs, and the *sportifs* inside it, and said, "If you would lend me a little money, I could buy you a drink before you go."

His unabashed cadging restored her at once. "I haven't time for a drink," she said, all briskness now, as if he had with a little click dropped into the right slot. "But if you'll promise to take Odile to dinner, I'll lend you two thousand francs."

"Fine," said Felix. He watched her take the money from her purse, accepted it without embarrassment, and put it in the pocket of his jacket.

"Take her for a nice dinner somewhere," Carol repeated.

"Of course."

"Oh!" He exasperated her. "Why don't you act like other people?" she cried. "You can't live like this all the time. You could go to America. Mr. Mitchell would help you. I know he would. He'd vouch for you, for a visa, if I asked him to."

"And Odile? Would Mr. Mitchell vouch for Odile too?"

She glanced at him, startled. When Felix was twenty-five, Odile would be nearly forty. Surely he had thought of this? "She could go, too," she said, and added, "I suppose."

"And what would we do in America?" He rocked back and forth on his heels, smiling.

"You could work," she said sharply. She could not help adding, like a scold, "For once in your life."

"As cook and butler," said Felix thoughtfully, and began to laugh. "No, don't be angry," he said, putting out his hand. "One has to wait so long for American papers. I know, I used to do it. To sit there all day and wait, or stand in the queue—how could Odile do it? She has her job to attend to. She has to help her family."

"In America," said Carol, "she would make more money, she could help them even more." But she could not see clearly the picture of Felix and Odile combining their salaries in a neat little apartment and faithfully remitting a portion to France. She could not imagine what on earth Felix would do for a living. Perhaps he and Odile would get married; something told her they would not. "I'm sorry," she said. "It's really your own business. I shouldn't have said anything at all." She moved away, but Felix took her hand and held it.

"You mean so well," he said. "Odile is right, you know. I ought to have been killed, or at least disappeared. No one knows what to do with me or where I fit. As for Odile, her whole family is overdue. But we're not—how does it go in American papers, under the photographs?—'Happy Europeans find new life away from old cares.' We're not that, either."

"I suppose not. I don't know." She realized all at once how absurd they must look, standing under the Métro tracks, holding hands. Passersby looked at them, sympathetic.

"You shouldn't go this way, looking so hurt and serious," he said. "You're so nice. You mean so well. Will you go to prom with me?"*

Her heart leaped as if he, Felix, had said he loved her. But no, she corrected herself. Not Felix but some other man, some wonderful person who did not exist.

Odile loved her. Her hand in his, she remembered how he had kissed Odile's palm, and she felt on her own palm the pressure of a kiss; but not from Felix. Perhaps, she thought, what she felt was the weight of his love for Odile, from which she was excluded, and to which Felix now politely and kindly wished to draw her, as if his and Odile's ability to love was their only hospitality, their only way of paying debts. For a moment, standing under the noisy trains on the dark, dusty boulevard, she felt that she had at last opened the right door, turned down the right street, glimpsed the vision

*Odile loves you."

toward which she had struggled on winter evenings when, standing on the staircase, she had wanted to be enchanted with Paris and to be in love with Howard.

But that such a vision could come from Felix and Odile was impossible. For a moment she had been close to tears, like the Christmas evening when she found the mistletoe. But she remembered in time what Felix was—a hopeless parasite. And Odile was silly and immoral and old enough to know better. And they were not married and never would be, and they spent heaven only knew how many hours in that terrible room in a slummy quarter of Paris.

No, she thought. What she and Howard had was better. No one could point to them, or criticize them, or humiliate them by offering to help.

She withdrew her hand and said with cold shyness, "Thank you for the coffee, Felix."

"Oh, that." He watched her go up the steps to the Métro, and then he walked away.

Upstairs, she passed a flower seller and stopped to buy a bunch of violets, even though they would be dead before she reached home. She wanted something pretty in her hand to take away the memory of the room and the Arabs and the dreary cafés and the messy affairs of Felix and Odile. She paid for the violets and noticed as she did so that the little scene—accepting the flowers, paying for them—had the gentle, nostalgic air of something past. Soon, she sensed, the comforting vision of Paris as she had once imagined it would overlap the reality. To have met and married Howard there would sound romantic and interesting, more and more so as time passed. She would forget the rain and her unshared confusion and loneliness, and remember instead the Paris of films, the street lamps with their tinsel icicles, the funny concert hall where the ceiling collapsed, and there would be, at last, a coherent picture, accurate but untrue. The memory of Felix and Odile and all their distasteful strangeness would slip away; for "love" she would think, once more, "Paris," and, after a while, happily married, mercifully removed in time, she would remember it and describe it and finally believe it as it had never been at all.

ACROSS THE BRIDGE

———

✤

*W*e were walking over the bridge from the Place de la Concorde, my mother and I—arm in arm, like two sisters who never quarrel. She had the invitations to my wedding in a leather shopping bag: I was supposed to be getting married to Arnaud Pons. My father's first cousin, Gaston Castelli, deputy for a district in the south, had agreed to frank the envelopes. He was expecting us at the Palais Bourbon, at the other end of the bridge. His small office looked out on nothing of interest—just a wall and some windows. A typist who did not seem to work for anyone in particular sat outside his door. He believed she was there to spy on him, and for that reason had told my mother to keep the invitations out of sight.

I had been taken to see him there once or twice. On the wall were two photographs of Vincent Auriol, president of the Republic, one of them signed, and a picture of the restaurant where Jean Jaurès was shot to death; it showed the façade and the waiters standing in the street in their long white aprons. For furniture he had a Louis Philippe armchair, with sticking plaster around all four legs, a lumpy couch covered with a blanket, and, for visitors, a pair of shaky varnished chairs filched from another room. When the Assembly was in session he slept on the couch. (Deputies were not supposed actually to live on the premises, but some of those from out of town liked to save on hotel bills.) His son Julien was fighting in Indochina. My mother had already cautioned me to ask how Julien was getting along and when he thought the war would be over. Only a few months earlier she might have hinted about a wedding when Julien came back, pretending to make a joke of it, but it was too late now for insinuations: I was nearly at the altar with someone else. My marrying Julien was a thought my parents and Cousin Gaston had enjoyed. In some way, we would have remained their children forever.

When Cousin Gaston came to dinner he and Papa discussed their relations in Nice and the decadent state of France. Women were not expected to join in: Maman always found a reason to go off to the kitchen and talk things over with Claudine, a farm girl from Normandy she had trained to cook and wait. Claudine was about my age, but Maman seemed much freer with her than with me; she took it for granted that Claudine was informed about all the roads and corners of life. Having no excuse to leave, I would examine the silver, the pattern on my dinner plate, my own hands. The men, meanwhile, went on about the lowering of morality and the lack of guts of the middle class. They split over what was to be done: Our cousin was a Socialist, though not a fierce one. He saw hope in the new postwar managerial generation, who read Marx without becoming dogmatic Marxists, while my father thought the smart postwar men would be swept downhill along with the rest of us.

Once, Cousin Gaston mentioned why his office was so seedily fitted out. It seemed that the government had to spend great sums on rebuilding roads; they had gone to pieces during the war and, of course, were worse today. Squads of German prisoners of war sent to put them right had stuffed the roadbeds with leaves and dead branches. As the underlay began to rot, the surfaces had collapsed. Now repairs were made by French workers— unionized, Communist-led, always on the verge of a national strike. There was no money left over.

"There never has been any money left over," Papa said. "When there is, they keep it quiet."

He felt uneasy about the franking business. The typist in the hall might find out and tell a reporter on one of the opposition weeklies. The reporter would then write a blistering piece on nepotism and the misuse of public funds, naming names. (My mother never worried. She took small favors to be part of the grace of life.)

It was hot on the bridge, July in April. We still wore our heavy coats. Too much good weather was not to be trusted. There were no clouds over the river, but just the kind of firm blue sky I found easy to paint. Halfway across, we stopped to look at a boat with strings of flags, and tourists sitting along the bank. Some of the men had their shirts off. I stared at the water and saw how far below it was and how cold it looked, and I said, "If I weren't a Catholic, I'd throw myself in."

"Sylvie!"—as if she had lost me in a crowd.

"We're going to so much trouble," I said. "Just so I can marry a man I don't love."

"How do you know you don't love him?"

"I'd know if I did."

"You haven't tried," she said. "It takes patience, like practicing scales. Don't you want a husband?"

"Not Arnaud."

"What's wrong with Arnaud?"

"I don't know."

"Well," after a pause, "what *do* you know?"

"I want to marry Bernard Brunelle. He lives in Lille. His father owns a big textile business—the factories, everything. We've been writing. He doesn't know I'm engaged."

"Brunelle? Brunelle? Textiles? From Lille? It sounds like a mistake. In Lille they just marry each other, and textiles marry textiles."

"I've got one thing right," I said. "I want to marry Bernard."

My mother was a born coaxer and wheedler; avoided confrontation, preferring to move to a different terrain and beckon, smiling. One promised nearly anything just to keep the smile on her face. She was slim and quick, like a girl of fourteen. My father liked her in flowered hats, so she still wore the floral bandeaux with their wisps of veil that had been fashionable ten years before. Papa used to tell about a funeral service where Maman had removed her hat so as to drape a mantilla over her hair. An usher, noticing the hat beside her on the pew, had placed it with the other flowers around the coffin. When I repeated the story to Arnaud he said the floral-hat anecdote was one of the world's oldest. He had heard it a dozen times, always about a different funeral. I could not see why Papa would go on telling it if it were not true, or why Maman would let him. Perhaps she was the first woman it had ever happened to.

"You say that Bernard has written to you," she said, in her lightest, prettiest, most teasing manner. "But where did he send the letters? Not to the house. I'd have noticed."

No conspirator gives up a network that easily. Mine consisted of Chantal Nauzan, my trusted friend, the daughter of a general my father greatly admired. Recently Papa had begun saying that if I had been a boy he might have wanted a career in the Army for me. As I was a girl, he did not want me to do anything too particular or specific. He did not want to have to say,

"My daughter is . . ." or "Sylvie does . . ." because it might make me sound needy or plain.

"Dear Sylvie," my mother went on. "Look at me. Let me see your eyes. Has he written 'marriage' in a letter signed with his name?" I looked away. What a question! "Would you show me the letter—the important one? I promise not to read the whole thing." I shook my head no. I was not sharing Bernard. She moved to new ground, so fast I could barely keep up. "And you would throw yourself off a bridge for him?"

"Just in my thoughts," I said. "I think about it when Arnaud makes me listen to records—all those stories about women dying, Brünnhilde and Mimi and Butterfly. I think that for the rest of my life I'll be listening to records and remembering Bernard. It's all I have to look forward to, because it is what you and Papa want."

"No," she said. "It is not at all what we want." She placed the leather bag on the parapet and turned it upside down over the river, using both hands. I watched the envelopes fall in a slow shower and land on the dark water and float apart. Strangers leaned on the parapet and stared, too, but nobody spoke.

"Papa will know what to do next," she said, altogether calmly, giving the bag a final shake. "For the time being, don't write any more letters and don't mention Bernard. Not to anyone."

I could not have defined her tone or expression. She behaved as if we had put something over on life, or on men; but that may be what I have read into it since. I looked for a clue, wondering how she wanted me to react, but she had started to walk on, making up the story we would tell our cousin, still waiting in his office to do us a good turn. (In the end, she said the wedding had to be postponed owing to a death in Arnaud's family.)

"Papa won't be able to have Monsieur Pons as a friend now," she remarked. "He's going to miss him. I hope your Monsieur Brunelle in Lille can make up the loss."

"I have never met him," I said.

I could see white patches just under the surface of the river, quite far along. They could have been candy papers or scraps of rubbish from a barge. Maman seemed to be studying the current, too. She said, "I'm not asking you to tell me how you met him."

"In the Luxembourg Gardens. I was sketching the beehives."

"You made a nice watercolor from that sketch. I'll have it framed. You can hang it in your bedroom."

Did she mean now or after I was married? I was taller than she was: When I turned my head, trying to read her face, my eyes were level with her smooth forehead and the bandeau of daisies she was wearing that day. She said, "My girl," and took my hand—not possessively but as a sort of welcome. I was her kind, she seemed to be telling me, though she had never broken an engagement that I knew. Another of my father's stories was how she had proposed to him, had chased and cornered him and made the incredible offer. He was a young doctor then, new to Paris. Now he was an ear specialist with a large practice. His office and secretary and waiting room were in a separate wing of the apartment. When the windows were open, in warm weather, we could hear him laughing and joking with Melle Coutard, the secretary. She had been with him for years and kept his accounts; he used to say she knew all his bad secrets. My mother's people thought he was too southern, too easily amused, too loud in his laughter. My Castelli great-grandparents had started a wholesale fruit business, across from the old bus terminal at Nice. The whole block was empty now and waiting to be torn down, so that tall buildings could replace the ocher warehouses and stores with their dark red roofs. CASTELLI was still painted over a doorway, in faded blue. My father had worked hard to lose his local accent, which sounded comical in Paris and prevented patients from taking him seriously, but it always returned when he was with Cousin Gaston. Cousin Gaston cherished his own accent, polished and refined it: His voters mistrusted any voice that sounded north of Marseilles.

I cannot say what was taking place in the world that spring; my father did not like to see young women reading newspapers. Echoes from Indochina came to me, and news of our cousin Julien drifted around the family, but the war itself was like the murmur of a radio in a distant room. I know that it was the year of *Imperial Violets,* with Luis Mariano singing the lead. At intermission he came out to the theater lobby, where his records were on sale, and autographed programs and record sleeves. I bought "Love Is a Bouquet of Violets," and my mother and I got in line, but when my turn came I said my name so softly that she had to repeat it for me. After the performance he took six calls and stood for a long time throwing kisses.

My mother said, "Don't start to dream about Mariano, Sylvie. He's an actor. He may not mean a word he says about love."

I was not likely to. He was too old for me, and I supposed that actors were nice to everybody in the same way. I wanted plenty of children and a

husband who would always be there, not traveling and rehearsing. I wanted
him to like me more than other people. I dreamed about Bernard Brunelle.
I was engaged to Arnaud Pons.

Arnaud was the son of another man my father admired, I think more
than anyone else. They had got to know each other through one of my father's patients, a M. Tarre. My father had treated him for a chronically
abscessed ear—eight appointments—and, at the end, when M. Tarre
asked if he wanted a check at once or preferred to send a bill, my father
answered that he took cash, and on the nail. M. Tarre inquired if that was
his usual custom. My father said it was the custom of every specialist he
had ever heard of, on which M. Tarre threatened to drag him before an
ethics committee. "And your secretary, too!" he shouted. We could hear
him in the other wing. "Your accomplice in felony!" My mother pulled
me away from the window and said I was to go on being nice to Melle
Coutard.

It turned out that M. Tarre was retired from the Ministry of Health and
knew all the rules. Papa calmed him down by agreeing to meet a lawyer M.
Tarre knew, called Alexandre Pons. He liked the sound of the name, which
had a ring of the south. Even when it turned out that those particular Ponses
had been in Paris for generations, my father did not withdraw his goodwill.

M. Pons arrived a few days later, along with M. Tarre, who seemed to
have all the time in the world. He told my father that a reprimand from an
ethics committee was nothing compared with a charge of tax fraud. Imagine, M. Pons said, a team of men in English-style suits pawing over your accounts. He turned to his friend Tarre and continued, "Over yours, too.
Once they get started."

M. Tarre said that his life was a house of glass, anyone was welcome to
look inside, but after more remarks from M. Pons, and a couple of generous suggestions from my father, he agreed to let the thing drop.

As a way of thanking M. Pons, as well as getting to know him better,
Papa asked my mother to invite him to dinner. For some reason, M. Pons
waited several days before calling to say he had a wife. She turned out to be
difficult, I remember, telling how she had fainted six times in eighteen
months, and announcing, just as the roast lamb was served, that the smell of
meat made her feel sick. However, when my mother discovered there was
also a Pons son, aged twenty-six, unmarried, living at home, and working in
the legal department of a large maritime-insurance firm, she asked them
again, this time with Arnaud.

During the second dinner Maman said, "Sylvie is something of an artist. Everything on the dining-room walls is Sylvie's work."

Arnaud looked around, briefly. He was silent, though not shy, with a thin face and brown hair. His mind was somewhere else, perhaps in livelier company. He ate everything on his plate, sometimes frowning; when it was something he seemed to like, his expression cleared. He glanced at me, then back at my depictions of the Roman countryside and the harbor at Naples in 1850. I was sure he could see they were replicas and that he knew the originals, and perhaps despised me.

"They are only copies," I managed to say.

"But full of feeling," said Maman.

He nodded, as if acknowledging a distant and somewhat forward acquaintance—a look neither cold nor quite welcoming. I wondered what his friends were like and if they had to pass a special test before he would consent to conversation.

After dinner, in the parlor, there was the usual difficulty over coffee. Claudine was slow to serve, and particularly slow to collect the empty cups. A chinoiserie table stood just under the chandelier, but Maman made sure nothing ever was placed on it. She found an excuse to call attention to the marble floor, because she took pleasure in the icy look of it, but no one picked up the remark. Mme. Pons was first to sit down. She put her cup on the floor, crossed her legs, and tapped her foot to some tune playing in her head. Perhaps she was recalling an evening before her marriage when she had danced wearing a pleated skirt and ropes of beads: I had seen pictures of my mother dressed that way.

I had settled my own cup predicament by refusing coffee. Now I took a chair at some distance from Mme. Pons: I guessed she would soon snap out of her dream and start to ask personal questions. I looked at my hands and saw they were stained with paint. I sat on them: Nobody paid attention.

My mother was showing Arnaud loose sketches and unframed watercolors of mine that she kept in a folder—more views of Italy, copies, and scenes in Paris parks drawn from life.

"Take one! Take one!" she cried.

My father went over to see what kind of taste Arnaud had. He had picked the thing nearest him, a crayon drawing of Vesuvius—not my best work. My father laughed, and said my idea of a volcano in eruption was like a haystack on fire.

✳   ✳   ✳

Bernard's father did not respond to my father's first approach—a letter that began: "I understand that our two children, Bernard and Sylvie, are anxious to unite their destinies." Probably he was too busy finding out if we were solvent, Papa said.

My mother canceled the wedding dates, civil and church. There were just a few presents that had to be returned to close relatives. The names of the other guests had dissolved in the Seine. "It should be done quickly," she had told my father, once the sudden change had been explained half a dozen times and he was nearly over the shock. He wondered if haste had anything to do with disgrace, though he could hardly believe it of me. No, no, nothing like that, she said. She wanted to see me safe and settled and in good hands. Well, of course, he wanted something like that, too.

As for me, I was sure I had been put on earth to marry Bernard Brunelle and move to Lille and live in a large stone house. ("Brick," my friend Chantal corrected, when I told her. "It's all brick up in Lille.") A whole floor would be given over to my children's nurseries and bedrooms and classrooms. They would learn English, Russian, German, and Italian. There would be tutors and governesses, holidays by the sea, ponies to ride, birthday parties with huge pink cakes, servants wearing white gloves. I had never known anyone who lived exactly that way, but my vision was so precise and highly colored that it had to be prompted from Heaven. I saw the curtains in the children's rooms, and their smooth hair and clear eyes, and their neat schoolbooks. I knew it might rain in Lille, day after day: I would never complain. The weather would be part of my enchanted life.

By this time, of course, Arnaud had been invited by my father to have an important talk. But then my father balked, saying he would undertake nothing unless my mother was there. After all, I had two parents. He thought of inviting Arnaud to lunch in a restaurant—Lipp, say, so noisy and crowded that any shock Arnaud showed would not be noticed. Maman pointed out that one always ended up trying to shout over the noise, so there was a danger of being overheard. In the end, Papa asked him to come round to the apartment, at about five o'clock. He arrived with daffodils for my mother and a smaller bunch for me. He believed Papa was planning a change in the marriage contract: He would buy an apartment for us outright instead of granting a twenty-year loan, adjustable to devaluation or inflation, interest-free.

They received him in the parlor, standing, and Maman handed him the sealed rejection she had helped me compose. If I had written the narrowest kind of exact analysis it would have been: "I have tried to love you, and can't. My feelings toward you are cordial and full of respect. If you don't want me to hate the sight of you, please go away." I think that is the truth about any such failure, but nobody says it. In any case, Maman would not have permitted such a thing. She had dictated roundabout excuses, ending with a wish for his future happiness. What did we mean by happiness for Arnaud? I suppose, peace of mind.

Papa walked over to the window and stood drumming on the pane. He made some unthinking remark—that he could see part of the Church of Saint-Augustin, the air was so clear. In fact, thick, gray, lashing rain obscured everything except the nearest rank of trees.

Arnaud looked up from the letter and said, "I must be dreaming." His clever, melancholy face was the color of the rain. My mother was afraid he would faint, as Mme. Pons so liked doing, and hurt his head on the marble floor. The chill of the marble had worked through everyone's shoes. She tried to edge the men over to a carpet, but Arnaud seemed paralyzed. Filling in silence, she went on about the floor: The marble came from Italy; people had warned her against it; it was hard to keep clean and it held the cold.

Arnaud stared at his own feet, then hers. Finally, he asked where I was.

"Sylvie has withdrawn from worldly life," my mother said. I had mentioned nothing in my letter about marrying another man, so he asked a second, logical question: Was I thinking of becoming a nun?

The rain, dismantling chestnut blossoms outside, sounded like gravel thrown against the windows. I know, because I was in my bedroom, just along the passage. I could not see him then as someone frozen and stunned. He was an obstacle on a railway line. My tender and competent mother had agreed to push him off the track.

That evening I said, "What if his parents turn up here and try to make a fuss?"

"They wouldn't dare," she said. "You were more than they had ever dreamed of."

It was an odd, new way of considering the Ponses. Until then, their education and background and attention to things of the past had made up for an embarrassing lack of foresight: They had never acquired property for their only son to inherit. They lived in the same dim apartment, in a lamentable quarter, which they had first rented in 1926, the year of their marriage. It was on a street filled with uninviting stores and insurance offices, east of the Saint-Lazare station, near the old German church. (Arnaud had taken me to the church for a concert of recorded music. I had never been inside a Protestant church before. It was spare and bare and somehow useful-looking, like a large broom closet. I wondered where they hatched the Protestant plots Cousin Gaston often mentioned, such as the crushing of Mediterranean culture by peaceful means. I remember that I felt lonely and out of place, and took Arnaud's hand. He was wearing his distant, listening-to-music expression, and seemed not to notice. At any rate, he didn't mind.)

Families such as the Ponses had left the area long before, but Arnaud's father said his belongings were too ancient and precious to be bumped down a winding staircase and heaved aboard a van. Papa thought he just wanted to hang on to his renewable lease, which happened to fall under the grace of a haphazard rent-control law: He still paid just about the same rent he had been paying before the war. Whatever he saved had never been squandered on paint or new curtains. His eleven rooms shared the same degree of decay and looked alike: You never knew if you were in a dining room or somebody's bedroom. There were antique tables and bedsteads everywhere. All the mirrors were stained with those dark blotches that resemble maps. Papa often wondered if the Ponses knew what they really looked like, if they actually saw themselves as silvery white, with parts of their faces spotted or missing.

One of the first things Mme. Pons had ever shown me was a mute harpsichord, which she wanted to pass on to Arnaud and me. To get it to look right—never mind the sound—would have required months of expert mending, more than Arnaud could afford. Looking around for something else to talk about, I saw in a far, dim corner a bathtub and washstand, valuable relics, in their way, streaked and stained with age. Someone had used them recently: The towels on a rack nearby looked damp. I had good reason for thinking the family all used the same towels.

What went wrong for M. Pons, the winter of my engagement? Even Papa never managed to find out. He supposed M. Pons had been giving too much taxation advice, on too grand a scale. He took down from his front door the brass plate mentioning office hours and went to work in a firm that did not carry his name. His wife had an uncommon past, at once aristocratic and vaguely bohemian. My parents wondered what it could mean. My children would inherit a quarter share of blue blood, true, but they might also come by a tendency to dance naked in Montmartre. Her father had been killed in the First World War, leaving furniture, a name, and a long tradition of perishing in battle. She was the first woman in her circle ever to work. Her mother used to cry every morning as she watched her pinning her hat on and counting her lunch money. Her name was Marie-Eugénie-Paule-Diane. Her husband called her Nenanne—I never knew why.

Arnaud had studied law, for the sake of family tradition, but his true calling was to write opinions about music. He wished he had been a music critic on a daily newspaper, incorruptible and feared. He wanted to expose the sham and vulgarity of Paris taste; so he said. Conductors and sopranos would feel the extra edge of anxiety that makes for a good performance, knowing the incorruptible Arnaud Pons was in the house. (Arnaud had no way of judging whether he was incorruptible, my father said. He had never tried earning a living by writing criticism in Paris.)

We spent most of our time together listening to records, while Arnaud told me what was wrong with Toscanini or Bruno Walter. He would stop the record and play the same part again, pointing out the mistakes. The music seemed as worn and shabby as the room. I imagined the musicians in those great orchestras of the past to be covered with dust, playing on instruments cracked, split, daubed with fingerprints, held together with glue and string. My children in Lille had spotless instruments, perfectly tuned. Their music floated into a dark garden drenched with silent rain. But then my thoughts would be overtaken by the yells and screams of one of Arnaud's doomed sopranos—a Tosca, a Mimi—and I would shut my eyes and let myself fall. A still surface of water rose to meet me. I was not dying but letting go.

Bernard's father answered Papa's second approach, which had been much like the first. He said that his son was a student, with no roof or income of his own. It would be a long time before he could join his destiny to anyone's, and it would not be to mine. Bernard had no inclination for me; none whatever. He had taken me to be an attractive and artistic girl, anxious to please, perhaps a bit lonely. As an ardent writer of letters, with pen friends as far away as Belgium, Bernard had offered the hand of epistolary comradeship. I had grabbed the hand and called it a commitment. Bernard was ready to swear in court (should a lawsuit be among my father's insane intentions) that he had taken no risks and never dropped his guard with an unclaimed young person, encountered in a public park. (My parents were puzzled by "unclaimed." I had to explain that I used to take off my engagement ring and carry it loose in a pocket. They asked why. I could not remember.)

M. Brunelle, the answer went on, hoped M. Castelli would put a stop to my fervent outpourings in the form of letters. Their agitated content and their frequency—as many as three a day—interfered with Bernard's studies and, indeed, kept him from sleeping. Surely my father did not want to see me waste the passion of a young heart on a delusion that led nowhere ("on a chimera that can only run dry in the Sahara of disappointment" was what M. Brunelle actually wrote). He begged my father to accept the word of a gentleman that my effusions had been destroyed. "Gentleman" was in English and underlined.

My parents shut themselves up in their bedroom. From my own room, where I sat at the window, holding Bernard's messages, I could hear my father's shouts. He was blaming Maman. Eventually she came in, and I stood up and handed her the whole packet: three letters and a postcard.

"Just the important one," she said. "The one I should have made you show me last April. I want the letter that mentions marriage."

"It was between the lines," I said, watching her face as she read.

"It was nowhere." She seemed sorry for me, all at once. "Oh, Sylvie, Sylvie. My poor Sylvie. Tear it up. Tear every one of them up. All this because you would not try to love Arnaud."

"I thought he loved me," I said. "Bernard, I mean. He never said he didn't."

The heaven-sent vision of my future life had already faded; the voices of my angelic children became indistinct. I might, now, have been turning the pages of an old storybook with black-and-white engravings.

I said, "I'll apologize to Papa and ask him to forgive me. I can't explain what happened. I thought he wanted what I wanted. He never said that he didn't. I promise never to paint pictures again."

I had not intended the remark about painting pictures. It said itself. Before I could take it back, Maman said, "Forgive you? You're like a little child. Does forgiveness include sending our most humble excuses to the Brunelle family and our having to explain that our only daughter is a fool? Does it account for behavior no sane person can understand? Parents knew what they were doing when they kept their daughters on a short lead. My mother read every letter I wrote until I was married. We were too loving, too lenient."

Her face looked pinched and shrunken. Her love, her loyalties, whatever was left of her youth and charm pulled away from me to be mustered in favor of Papa. She stood perfectly still, almost at attention. I think we both felt at a loss. I thought she was waiting for a signal so she could leave the room. Finally, my father called her. I heard her mutter, "Please get out of my way," though I was nowhere near the door.

My friend Chantal—my postal station, my go-between—came over as soon as she heard the news. It had been whispered by my mother to Chantal's mother, over the telephone, in a version of events that absolved me entirely and turned the Brunelles into fortune-hunting, come-lately provincial merchants and rogues. Chantal knew better, though she still believed the Brunelles had misrepresented their case and came in for censure. She had brought chocolates to cheer me up; we ate most of a box, sitting in a corner of the salon like two travelers in a hotel lobby. She wore her hair in the newest style, cut short and curled thickly on her forehead. I have forgotten the name of the actress who started the fashion: Chantal told me, but I could not take it in.

Chantal was a good friend, perhaps because she had never taken me seriously as a rival; and perhaps in saying this I misjudge her. At any rate, she lost no time in giving me brisk advice. I ought to cut my hair, change my appearance. It was the first step on the way to a new life. She knew I loved children and might never have any of my own: I had no idea how to go about meeting a man or how to hang on to one if he drifted my way. As the next-best thing, I should enter a training college and learn to teach nursery classes. There wasn't much to it, she said. You encouraged them to draw with crayons and sing and run in circles. You put them on pots after lunch and spread blankets on the floor for their afternoon nap. She knew plenty of girls who had done this after their engagements, for some reason, collapsed.

She had recently got to know a naval lieutenant while on a family holiday in the Alps, and now they were planning a Christmas wedding. Perhaps I could persuade my family to try the same thing; but finding a fiancé in the mountains was a new idea—to my mother chancy and doubtful, while my father imagined swindlers and foreigners trampling snow in pursuit of other men's daughters.

Since the fiasco, as he called it, Papa would not look at me. When he had anything to say he shouted it to Maman. They did not take their annual holiday that year but remained in the shuttered apartment, doing penance for my sins. The whole world was away, except us. From Normandy, Claudine sent my mother a postcard of the basilica at Lisieux and the message "My maman, being a mother, respectfully shares your grief"—as if I had died.

At dinner one night—curtains drawn, no one saying much—Papa suddenly held up his hands, palms out. "How many hands do you count?" he said, straight to me.

"Two?" I made it a question in case it was a trick.

"Right. Two hands. All I needed to pull me to the top of my profession. I gave my wife the life she wanted, and I gave my daughter a royal upbringing."

I could sense my mother's close attention, her wanting me to say whatever Papa expected. He had drunk most of a bottle of Brouilly by himself and seemed bound for headlong action. In the end, his message was a simple one: He had forgiven me. My life was a shambles and our family's reputation gravely injured, but I was not wholly to blame. Look at the young men I'd had to deal with: neutered puppies. No wonder there were so many old maids now. I had missed out on the only virile generation of the twentieth century, the age group that took in M. Pons, Cousin Gaston, and, of course, Papa himself.

"We were a strong rung on the ladder of progress," he said. "After us, the whole ladder broke down." The name of Pons, seldom mentioned, seemed to evoke some faraway catastrophe, recalled by a constant few. He bent his head and I thought, Surely he isn't going to cry. I recalled how my mother had said, "We were too loving." I saw the storehouse in Nice and our name in faded blue. There were no more Castellis, except Julien in Indochina. I put my napkin over my face and began to bawl.

Papa cheered up. "Two hands," he said, this time to Maman. "And no help from any quarter. Isn't that true?"

"Everybody admired you," she said. She was clearing plates, fetching dessert. I was too overcome to help; besides, she didn't want me. She missed Claudine. My mother sat down again and looked at Papa, leaving me out. I was a dreary guest, like Mme. Pons getting ready to show hysteria at the sight of a veal chop. They might have preferred her company to mine, given the choice. She had done them no harm and gave them reasons to laugh. I refused dessert, though no one cared. They continued to eat their fresh figs poached in honey, with double cream: too sugary for Maman, really, but a great favorite of Papa's. "The sweeter the food, the better the temper" was a general truth she applied to married life.

*　*　*

My mother dreamed she saw a young woman pushed off the top of a tall building. The woman plunged headfirst, with her wedding veil streaming. The veil materialized the next day, as details of the dream returned. At first Maman described the victim as a man, but the veil confirmed her mistake. She mentioned her shock and horror at my remark on the bridge. The dream surely had been sent as a reminder: I was not to be crossed or harshly contradicted or thrust in the wrong direction. Chantal's plans for my future had struck her as worse than foolery: They seemed downright dangerous. I knew nothing about little children. I would let them swallow coins and crayon stubs, leave a child or two behind on our excursions to parks and squares, lose their rain boots and sweaters. Nursery schools were places for nuns and devoted celibates. More to the point, there were no men to be found on the premises, save the occasional inspector, already married, and underpaid. Men earning pittance salaries always married young. It was not an opinion, my mother said. It was a statistic.

Because of the dream she began to show her feelings through hints and silences or by telling anecdotes concerning wretched and despairing spinster teachers she had known. I had never heard their names before and wondered when she had come across all those Martines and Georgettes. My father, closed to dreams, in particular the threatening kind, wanted to know why I felt such an urge to wipe the noses and bottoms of children who were no relation of mine. Dealing with one's own offspring was thankless enough. He spoke of the violent selfishness of the young, their mindless questions, their love of dirt. Nothing was more deadening to an adult intellect than a child's cycle of self-centered days and long, shapeless summers.

I began to sleep late. Nothing dragged me awake, not even the sound of Papa calling my mother from room to room. At noon I trailed unwashed to the kitchen and heated leftover coffee. Claudine, having returned to claim all my mother's attention, rinsed lettuce and breaded cutlets for lunch, and walked around me as though I were furniture. One morning Maman brought my breakfast on a tray, sat down on the edge of the bed, and said Julien had been reported missing. He could be a prisoner or he might be dead. Waiting for news, I was to lead a quiet life and to pray. She was dressed to go out, I remember, wearing clothes for the wrong season—all in pale blue, with a bandeau of forget-me-nots and her turquoise earrings and a number of little chains. Her new watch, Papa's latest present, was the size of a coin. She had to bring it up to her eyes.

"It isn't too late, you know," she said. I stared at her. "Too late for Arnaud."

I supposed she meant he could still be killed in Indochina, if he wanted that. To hear Cousin Gaston and Papa, one could imagine it was all any younger man craved. I started to say that Arnaud was twenty-seven now and might be too old for wars, but Maman broke in: Arnaud had left Paris and gone to live in Rennes. Last April, after the meeting in the parlor, he had asked his maritime-insurance firm to move him to a branch office. It had taken months to find him the right place; being Arnaud, he wanted not only a transfer but a promotion. Until just five days ago he had never been on his own. There had always been a woman to take care of him; namely, Mme. Pons. Mme. Pons was sure he had already started looking around in Rennes for someone to marry. He would begin with the girls in his new office, probably, and widen the circle to church and concerts.

"It isn't too late," said Maman.

"Arnaud hates me now," I said. "Besides, I can work. I can take a course in something. Mme. Pons worked."

"We don't know what Mme. Pons did."

"I could mind children, take them for walks in the afternoon."

My double file of charges, hand in hand, stopped at the curb. A policeman held up traffic. We crossed and entered the court of an ancient abbey, now a museum. The children clambered over fragments of statues and broken columns. I showed them medieval angels.

Mme. Pons did not want a strange daughter-in-law from a provincial city, my mother said. She wanted me, as before.

For the first time I understood about the compact of mothers and the conspiracy that never ends. They stand together like trees, shadowing and protecting, shutting out the view if it happens to suit them, letting in just so much light. She started to remove the tray, though I hadn't touched a thing.

"Get up, Sylvie," she said. It would have seemed like an order except for the tone. Her coaxing, teasing manner had come back. I was still wondering about the pale blue dress: Was she pretending it was spring, trying to pick up whatever had been dropped in April? "It's time you had your hair cut. Sometimes you look eighteen. It may be part of your trouble. We can lunch at the Trois Quartiers and buy you some clothes. We're lucky to have Papa. He never grumbles about spending."

My mother had never had her own bank account or signed a check. As a married woman she would have needed Papa's consent, and he preferred to hand over wads of cash, on demand. Melle Coutard got the envelopes ready and jotted the amounts in a ledger. Owing to a system invented by M. Pons, the money was deducted from Papa's income tax.

"And then," said Maman, "you can go to the mountains for two weeks." It was no surprise: Chantal and her lieutenant wanted to return to Chamonix on a lovers' pilgrimage, but General Nauzan, Chantal's father, would not hear of it unless I went, too. It was part of my mission to sleep in her room: The Nauzans would not have to rush the wedding or have a large and healthy baby appear seven months after the ceremony, to be passed off as premature. So I would not feel like an odd number—in the daytime, that is—the lieutenant would bring along his brother, a junior tennis champion, aged fifteen.

(We were well into our first week at Chamonix before Chantal began to disappear in the afternoon, leaving me to take a tennis lesson from the champion. I think I have a recollection of her telling me, late at night, in the darkness of our shared room, "To tell you the truth, I could do without all that side of it. Do you want to go with him tomorrow, instead of me? He thinks you're very nice." But that kind of remembering is like trying to read a book with some of the pages torn out. Things are said at intervals and nothing connects.)

I got up and dressed, as my mother wanted, and we took the bus to her hairdresser's. She called herself Ingrid. Pasted to the big wall mirror were about a dozen photographs cut from *Paris Match* of Ingrid Bergman and her little boy. I put on a pink smock that covered my clothes and Ingrid cut my long hair. My mother saved a few locks, one for Papa, the others in case I ever wanted to see what I had once been like, later on. The two women decided I would look silly with curls on my forehead, so Ingrid combed the new style sleek.

What Chantal had said was true: I looked entirely different. I seemed poised, sharp, rather daunting. Ingrid held a looking glass up so I could see the back of my head and my profile. I turned my head slowly. I had a slim neck and perfect ears and my mother's forehead. For a second a thought flared, and then it died: With her blue frock and blue floral hat and numerous trinkets Maman was like a little girl dressed up. I stared and stared, and the women smiled at each other. I saw their eyes meet in the mirror. They thought they were watching emerging pride, the kind that could make me strong. Even vanity would have pleased them; any awakening would do.

I felt nothing but the desire for a life to match my changed appearance.

It was a longing more passionate and mysterious than any sort of love. My role could not be played by another person. All I had to do now was wait for my true life to reveal itself and the other players to let me in.

My father took the news from Indochina to be part of a family curse. He had hoped I would marry Julien. He would have had Castelli grandchildren. But Julien and I were too close in age and forever squabbling. He was more like a brother. "Lover" still held a small quantity of false knowledge. Perhaps I had always wanted a stranger. Papa said the best were being taken, as in all wars. He was sorry he had not been gunned down in the last one. He was forty-nine and had survived to see his only daughter washed up, a decent family nearly extinct, the whole nation idle and soft.

He repeated all these things, and more, as he drove me to the railway station where I was to meet Chantal, the lieutenant, and the junior champion. His parting words reproached me for indifference to Julien's fate, and I got on the train in tears.

My mother was home, at the neat little desk where she plotted so many grave events. For the first time in her life, she delivered an invitation to dinner by telephone. I still have the letter she sent me in Chamonix, describing what they had had to eat and what Mme. Pons had worn: salmon pink, sleeveless, with spike heels and fake pearls. She had also worn my rejected engagement ring. Mme. Pons could get away with lack of judgment and taste, now. We were the suppliants.

My father had been warned it would be fish, because of Mme. Pons, but he forgot and said quite loudly, "Are you trying to tell me there's nothing after the turbot? Are the butchers on strike? Is it Good Friday? Has the whole world gone crazy? Poor France!" he said, turning to M. Pons. "I mean it. These changes in manners and customs are part of the decline."

The two guests pretended not to hear. They gazed at my painting of the harbor at Naples—afraid, Papa said later, we might try to give it to them.

When Papa asked if I'd enjoyed myself in the Alps I said, "There was a lot of tennis." It had the dampening effect I had hoped for, and he began to talk about a man who had just deserted from the Army because he was a pacifist, and who ought to be shot. Maman took me aside as soon as she could and told me her news: Arnaud was still undecided. His continued license to choose was like a spell of restless weather. The two mothers studied the sky. How long could it last? He never mentioned me, but Mme. Pons was sure he was waiting for a move.

"What move?" I said. "A letter from Papa?"

"You can't expect Papa to write any more letters," she said. "It has to come from you."

Once again, I let my mother dictate a letter for Arnaud. I had no idea what to say; or, rather, of the correct way of saying anything. It was a formal request for an appointment, at Arnaud's convenience, at the venue of his choice. That was all. I signed my full name: Sylvie Mireille Castelli. I had never written to anyone in Rennes before. I could not imagine his street. I wondered if he lived in someone else's house or had found his own apartment. I wondered who made his breakfast and hung up his clothes and changed the towels in the bathroom. I wondered how he would feel when he saw my handwriting; if he would burn the letter, unread.

He waited ten days before saying he did not mind seeing me, and suggested having lunch in a restaurant. He could come to Paris on a Sunday, returning to Rennes the same day. It seemed to me an enormous feat of endurance. The fastest train, in those days, took more than three hours. He said he would let me know more on the matter very soon. The move to Rennes had worn him down and he needed a holiday. He signed "A. Pons." ("That's new," my father said, about the invitation to lunch. He considered Arnaud's approach to money to be conservative, not to say nervous.)

He arrived in Paris on the third Sunday in October, finally, almost a year to the day from our first meeting. I puzzled over the timetable, wondering why he had chosen to get up at dawn to catch a train that stopped everywhere when there was a direct train two hours later. Papa pointed out the extra-fare sign for the express. "And Arnaud . . . ," he said, but left it at that.

Papa and I drove to the old Montparnasse station, where the trains came in from the west of France. Hardly anyone remembers it now: a low gray building with a wooden floor. I have a black-and-white postcard that shows the curb where my father parked his Citroën and the station clock we watched and the door I went through to meet Arnaud face-to-face. We got there early and sat in the car, holding hands sometimes, listening to a Sunday-morning program of political satire—songs and poems and imitations of men in power—but Papa soon grew tired of laughing alone and switched it off. He smoked four Gitanes from a pack Uncle Gaston had left behind. When his lighter balked he pretended to throw it away, trying to make me smile. I could see nothing funny about the loss of a beautiful silver lighter, the gift of a patient. It seemed wasteful, not amusing. I ate some expensive chocolates I found in the glove compartment: Melle Coutard's, I think.

He kept leaning forward to read the station clock, in case his watch and my watch and the dashboard clock were slow. When it was time, he kissed me and made me promise to call the minute I knew the time of Arnaud's return train, so he could come and fetch me. He gave me the names of two or three restaurants he liked, pointing in the direction of the Boulevard Raspail—places he had taken me that smelled of cigars and red Burgundy. They looked a bit like station buffets, but were more comfortable and far more expensive. I imagined that Arnaud and I would be walking along the boulevard in the opposite direction, where there were plenty of smaller, cheaper places. Papa and Cousin Gaston smoked Gitanes in memory of their student days. They did, sometimes, visit the restaurants of their youth, where the smells were of boiled beef and fried potatoes and dark tobacco, but they knew the difference between a sentimental excursion and a good meal.

As I turned away, my heart pounding enough to shake me, I heard him say, "Remember, whatever happens, you will always have a home," which was true but also a manner of speaking.

The first passenger off the train was a girl with plastic roses pinned to her curly hair. She ran into the arms of two other girls. They looked alike, in the same long coats with ornamental buttons, the same frothy hair and plastic hair slides. One of the Parisians took the passenger's cardboard suitcase and they went off, still embracing and chattering. Chantal had warned me not to speak to any man in the station, even if he seemed respectable. She had described the sad girls who came from the west, a deeply depressed area, to find work as maids and waitresses, and the gangsters who hung around the train gates. They would pick the girls up and after a short time put them on the street. If a girl got tired of the life and tried to run away, they had her murdered and her body thrown in the Seine. The crimes were never solved; nobody cared.

Actually, most of the men I saw looked like citified Breton farmers. I had a problem that seemed, at the moment, far more acute than the possibility of being led astray and forced into prostitution. I had no idea what to say to Arnaud, how to break the ice. My mother had advised me to talk about Rennes if conversation ran thin. I could mention the great fire of 1720 and the fine houses it had destroyed.

Arnaud walked straight past me and suddenly turned back. On his arm he carried a new raincoat with a plaid lining. He was wearing gloves; he took one off to shake hands.

I said, "I've had my hair cut."

"So I see."

That put a stop to 1720, or anything else, for the moment. We crossed the Boulevard du Montparnasse without touching or speaking. He turned, as I had expected, in the direction of the cheaper restaurants. We read and discussed the menus posted outside. He settled on Rougeot. Not only did Rougeot have a long artistic and social history, Arnaud said, but it offered a fixed-price meal with a variety of choice. Erik Satie had eaten here. No one guessed how poor Satie had been until after his death, when Cocteau and others had visited his wretched suburban home and learned the truth. Rilke had eaten here, too. It was around the time when he was discovering Cézanne and writing those letters. I recognized Arnaud's way of mentioning famous people, pausing before the name and dropping his voice.

The window tables were already taken. Arnaud made less fuss than I expected. Actually, I had never been alone at a restaurant with Arnaud; it was my father I was thinking of, and how violently he wanted whatever he wanted. Arnaud would not hang up his coat. He had bought it just the day before and did not want a lot of dirty garments full of fleas in close touch. He folded it on a chair, lining out. It fell on the floor every time a waiter went by.

I memorized the menu so I could describe it to Maman. Our first course was hard-boiled eggs with mayonnaise, then we chose the liver. Liver was something his mother would not have in the house, said Arnaud. As a result, he and his father were chronically lacking in iron. I wanted to ask where he ate his meals now, if he had an obliging landlady who cooked or if he had the daily expense of a restaurant; but it seemed too much like prying.

The red wine, included in the menu, arrived in a thick, stained decanter. Arnaud asked to be shown the original label. The waiter said the label had been thrown away, along with the bottle. There was something of a sneer in his voice, as if we were foreigners, and Arnaud turned away coldly. The potatoes served with the liver had been boiled early and heated up: We both noticed. Arnaud said it did not matter; because of the wine incident, we were never coming back. "We" suggested a common future, but it may have been a slip of the tongue; I pretended I hadn't heard. For dessert I picked custard flan and Arnaud had prunes in wine. Neither of us was hungry by then, but dessert was included, and it would have been a waste of money to skip a course. Arnaud made some reference to this.

I want to say that I never found him mean. He had not come to Paris to charm or impress me; he was here to test his own feelings at the sight of me and to find out if I understood what getting married meant—in particular, to him. His conversation was calm and instructive. He told me about "situations," meaning the entanglements people got into when they were characters in novels and plays. He compared the theater of Henry de Montherlant with Jean Anouilh's: how they considered the part played by innocent girls in the lives of more worldly men. To Anouilh a girl was a dove, Arnaud said, an innocent dressed in white, ultimately and almost accidentally destroyed. Montherlant saw them as ignorant rather than innocent—more knowing than any man suspected, unlearned and crass.

All at once he said a personal thing: "You aren't eating your dessert."

"There's something strange on it," I said. "Green flakes."

He pulled my plate over and scraped the top of the flan with my spoon. (I had taken one bite and put the spoon down.) "Parsley," he said. "There was a mistake made in the kitchen. They took the flan for a slice of quiche."

"I know it is paid for," I said. "But I can't."

I was close to tears. It occurred to me that I sounded like Mme. Pons. He began to eat the flan, slowly, using my spoon. Each time he put the spoon in his mouth I said to myself, He must love me. Otherwise it would be disgusting. When he had finished, he folded his napkin in the exact way that always annoyed my mother and said he loved me. Oh, not as before, but enough to let him believe he could live with me. I was not to apologize for last spring or to ask for forgiveness. As Cosima had said to Hans von Bülow, after giving birth to Wagner's child, forgiveness was not called for—just understanding. (I knew who Wagner was, but the rest bewildered me utterly.) I had blurted out something innocent, impulsive, Arnaud continued, and my mother—herself a child—had acted as though it were a mature decision. My mother had told his mother about the bridge and the turning point; he understood that, too. He knew all about infatuation. At one time he had actually believed my drawing of Vesuvius could bring him luck, and had carried it around with the legal papers in his briefcase. That was how eaten up by love he had been, at twenty-six. Well, that kind of storm and passion of the soul was behind him. He was twenty-seven, and through with extremes. He blamed my mother, but one had to take into account her infantile nature. He was inclined to be harder on Bernard—speaking the name easily, as if "Bernard Brunelle" were a character in one of the plays he had just mentioned. Brunelle was a vulgar libertine, toying with the feelings of an untried and trustful girl and discarding her when the novelty wore off. He, Arnaud, was prepared to put the clock back to where it had stood exactly a second before my mother wrenched the wedding invitations out of my hands and hurled them into the Seine.

Seated beside a large window that overlooked the terrace and boulevard were the three curly-haired girls I had noticed at the station. They poured wine for each other and leaned into the table, so that their heads almost touched. Above them floated a flat layer of thin blue smoke. Once I was married, I thought, I would smoke. It would give me something to do with my hands when other people talked, and would make me look as if I were enjoying myself. One of the girls caught me looking, and smiled. It was a smile of recognition, but hesitant, too, as if she wondered if I would want to acknowledge her. She turned back, a little disappointed. When I looked again, I had a glimpse of her in profile, and saw why she had seemed familiar and yet diffident: She was the typist who sat outside Cousin Gaston's office, who had caused Gaston and Papa so much anxiety and apprehension. She was just eighteen—nineteen at most. How could they have taken her for a spy? She was one of three kittenish friends, perhaps sisters, from the poorest part of France.

Look at it this way, Arnaud was saying. We had gone through tests and trials, like Tamino and Pamina, and had emerged tempered and strong. I must have looked blank, for he said, a little sharply, "In *The Magic Flute.* We spent a whole Sunday on it. I translated every word for you—six records, twelve sides."

I said, "Does she die?"

"No," said Arnaud. "If she had to die we would not be sitting here." Now, he said, lowering his voice, there was one more thing he needed to know. This was not low curiosity on his part, but a desire to have the whole truth spread out—"like a sheet spread on green grass, drying in sunshine" was the way he put it. My answer would make no difference; his decisions concerning me and our future were final. The question was, Had Bernard Brunelle *succeeded* and, if so, to what extent? Was I entirely, or partly, or not at all the same as before? Again, he said the stranger's name as if it were an invention, a name assigned to an imaginary life.

It took a few moments for me to understand what Arnaud was talking about. Then I said, "Bernard Brunelle? Why, I've never even kissed him. I saw him only that once. He lives in Lille."

✻   ✻   ✻

His return train did not leave for another hour. I asked if he would like to walk around Montparnasse and look at the famous cafés my father liked, but the sidewalk was spotted with rain, and I think he did not want to get his coat wet. As we crossed the boulevard again, he took my arm and remarked that he did not care for Bretons and their way of thinking. He would not spend his life in Rennes. Unfortunately, he had asked for the transfer and the firm had actually created a post for him. It would be some time before he could say he had changed his mind. In the meantime, he would come to Paris every other weekend. Perhaps I could come to Rennes, too, with or without a friend. We had reached the age of common sense and could be trusted. Some of the beaches in Brittany were all right, he said, but you never could be sure of the weather. He preferred the Basque coast, where his mother used to take him when he was a child. He had just spent four weeks there, in fact.

I did not dare ask if he had been alone; in any case, he was here, with me. We sat down on a bench in the station. I could think of nothing more to say. The great fire of 1720 seemed inappropriate as a topic for someone who had just declared an aversion to Bretons and their history. I had a headache, and was just as glad to be quiet. I wondered how long it would take to wean him away from the Pons family habit of drinking low-cost wine. He picked up a newspaper someone had left behind and began to read yesterday's news. There was more about the pacifist deserter; traitors (I supposed they must be that) were forming a defense committee. I thought about Basque beaches, wondering if they were sand or shale, and if my children would be able to build sand castles.

Presently Arnaud folded the paper, in the same careful way he always folded a table napkin, and said I ought to follow Chantal's suggestion and get a job teaching in a nursery school. (So Maman had mentioned that to Mme. Pons, too.) I should teach until I had enough working time behind me to claim a pension. It would be good for me in my old age to have an income of my own. Anything could happen. He could be killed in a train crash or called up for a war. My father could easily be ruined in a lawsuit and die covered with debts. There were advantages to teaching, such as long holidays and reduced train fares.

"How long would it take?" I said. "Before I could stop teaching and get my pension."

"Thirty-five years," said Arnaud. "I'll ask my mother. She had no training, either, but she taught private classes. All you need is a decent background and some recommendations."

Wait till Papa hears this, I thought. He had imagined everything possible, even that she had been the paid mistress of a Romanian royal.

Arnaud said a strange thing then: "You would have all summer long for your art. I would never stand in your way. In fact, I would do everything to help. I would mind the children, take them off your hands."

In those days men did not mind children. I had never in my life seen a married man carrying a child except to board a train or at a parade. I was glad my father hadn't heard. I think I was shocked: I believe that, in my mind, Arnaud climbed down a notch. More to the point, I had not touched a brush or drawing pencil since the day my mother had read the letter from Bernard—the important one. Perhaps if I did not paint and draw and get stains on my hands and clothes Arnaud would be disappointed. Perhaps, like Maman, he wanted to be able to say that everything hanging on the walls was mine. What he had said about not standing in my way was unusual, certainly; but it was kind, too.

We stood up and he shook and then folded his coat, holding the newspaper under his arm. He pulled his gloves out of his coat pocket, came to a silent decision, and put them back. He handed me the newspaper, but changed his mind: He would work the crossword puzzle on the way back to Rennes. By the end of the day, I thought, he would have traveled some eight hours and have missed a Sunday-afternoon concert, because of me. He started to say good-bye at the gate, but I wanted to see him board the train. A special platform ticket was required: He hesitated until I said I would buy it myself, and then he bought it for me.

From the step of the train he leaned down to kiss my cheek.

I said, "Shall I let it grow back?"

"What?"

"My hair. Do you like it short or long?"

He was unable to answer, and seemed to find the question astonishing. I walked along the platform and saw him enter his compartment. There was a discussion with a lady about the window seat. He would never grab or want anything he had no claim on, but he would always establish his rights, where they existed. He sat down in the place he had a right to, having shown his seat reservation, and opened the paper to the puzzle. I waited until the train pulled away. He did not look out. In his mind I was on my way home.

I was not quite sure what to do next, but I was certain of one thing: I would not call Papa. Arnaud had not called his family, either. We had behaved like a real couple, in a strange city, where we knew no one but each other. From the moment of his arrival until now we had not been separated, not once. I decided I would walk home. It was a long way, much of it up-hill once I crossed the river, but I would be moving along, as Arnaud was moving with the train. I would be accompanying him during at least part of his journey.

I began to walk, under a slight, not a soaking, drizzle, along the boule-vard, alongside the autumn trees. The gray clouds looked sculptured, the traffic lights unnaturally bright. I was sitting on a sandy beach somewhere along the Basque coast. A red ribbon held my long hair, kept it from blow-ing across my face. I sat in the shade of a white parasol, under a striped towel. My knees were drawn up to support my sketch pad. I bent my head and drew my children as they dug holes in the sand. They wore white sun hats. Their arms and legs were brown.

By the time I reached the Invalides the rain had stopped. Instead of tak-ing the shortest route home, I had made a wide detour west. The lights gleamed brighter than ever as night came down. There were yellow streaks low in the sky. I skirted the little park and saw old soldiers, survivors of wars lovingly recalled by Cousin Gaston and Papa, sitting on damp benches. They lived in the veterans' hospital nearby and had nothing else to do. I turned the corner and started down toward the Seine, walking slowly. I still had a considerable distance to cover, but it seemed unfair to arrive home be-fore Arnaud; that was why I had gone so far out of my way. My parents could think whatever they liked: that he had taken a later train, that I had got wet finding a taxi. I would never tell anyone how I had traveled with Ar-naud, not even Arnaud. It was a small secret, insignificant, but it belonged to the true life that was almost ready to let me in. And so it did; and, yes, it made me happy.

THE LATEHOMECOMER

―――――

When I came back to Berlin out of captivity in the spring of 1950, I discovered I had a stepfather. My mother had never mentioned him. I had been writing from Brittany to "Grete Bestermann," but the "Toeppler" engraved on a brass plate next to the bellpull at her new address turned out to be her name, too. As she slipped the key in the lock, she said quietly, "Listen, Thomas. I'm Frau Toeppler now. I married a kind man with a pension. This is his key, his name, and his apartment. He wants to make you welcome." From the moment she met me at the railway station that day, she must have been wondering how to break it.

I put my hand over the name, leaving a perfect palm print. I said, "I suppose there are no razor blades and no civilian shirts in Berlin. But some ass is already engraving nameplates."

Martin Toeppler was an old man who had been a tram conductor. He was lame in one arm as the result of a working accident and carried that shoulder higher than the other. His eyes had the milky look of the elderly, lighter round the rim than at the center of the iris, and he had an old woman's habit of sighing, "Ah, yes, yes." The sigh seemed to be his way of pleading, "It can't be helped." He must have been forty-nine, at the most, but aged was what he seemed to me, and more than aged—useless, lost. His mouth hung open much of the time, as though he had trouble breathing through his nose, but it was only because he was a chronic talker, always ready to bite down on a word. He came from Franconia, near the Czech border, close to where my grandparents had once lived.

"Grete and I can understand each other's dialects," he said—but we were not a dialect-speaking family. My brother and I had been made to say "bread" and "friend" and "tree" correctly. I turned my eyes to my mother, but she looked away.

Martin's one dream was to return to Franconia; it was almost the first thing he said to me. He had inherited two furnished apartments in a town close to an American military base. One of the two had been empty for years. The occupants had moved away, no one knew where—perhaps to Sweden. After their departure, which had taken place at five o'clock on a winter morning in 1943, the front door had been sealed with a government stamp depicting a swastika and an eagle. The vanished tenants must have died, perhaps in Sweden, and now no local person would live in the place, because a whole family of ghosts rattled about, opening and shutting drawers, banging on pipes, moving chairs and ladders. The ghosts were looking for a hoard of gold that had been left behind, Martin thought. The second apartment had been rented to a family who had disappeared during the confused migrations of the end of the war and were probably dead, too; at least they were dead officially, which was all that mattered. Martin intended to modernize the two flats, raise them up to American standards—he meant by this putting venetian blinds at the windows and gas-heated water tanks in the bathrooms—and let them to a good class of American officer, too foreign to care about a small-town story, too educated to be afraid of ghosts. But he would have to move quickly; otherwise his inheritance, his sole postwar capital, his only means of getting started again, might be snatched away from him for the sake of shiftless and illiterate refugees from the Soviet zone, or bombed-out families still huddled in barracks, or for latehomecomers. This last was a new category of persons, all one word. It was out of his mouth before he remembered that I was one, too. He stopped talking, and then he sighed and said, "Ah, yes, yes."

He could not keep still for long: He drew out his wallet and showed me a picture of himself on horseback. He may have wanted to substitute this country image for any idea I had of him on the deck of a tram. He held the snapshot at arm's length and squinted at it. "That was Martin Toeppler once," he said. "It will be Martin Toeppler again." His youth, and a new right shoulder and arm, and the hot, leafy summers everyone his age said had existed before the war were waiting for him in Franconia. He sounded like a born winner instead of a physically broken tram conductor on the losing side. He put the picture away in a cracked celluloid case, pocketed his wallet, and called to my mother, "The boy will want a bath."

My mother, who had been preparing a bath for minutes now, had been receiving orders all her life. As a girl she had worked like a slave in her mother's village guesthouse, and after my father died she became a servant again, this time in Berlin, to my powerful Uncle Gerhard and his fat wife. My brother and I spent our winters with her, all three sleeping in one bed sometimes, in a cold attic room, sharing bread and apples smuggled from Uncle Gerhard's larder. In the summer we were sent to help our grand-mother. We washed the chairs and tables, cleaned the toilets of vomit, and carried glasses stinking with beer back to the kitchen. We were still so small we had to stand on stools to reach the taps.

"It was lucky you had two sons," Uncle Gerhard said to my mother once. "There will never be a shortage of strong backs in the family."

"No one will exploit my children," she is supposed to have replied, though how she expected to prevent it only God knows, for we had no roof of our own and no money and we ate such food as we were given. Our uni-forms saved us. Once we had joined the Hitler Jugend, even Uncle Gerhard never dared ask, "Where are you going?" or "Where have you been?" My brother was quicker than I. By the time he was twelve he knew he had been trapped; I was sixteen and a prisoner before I understood. But from our mother's point of view we were free, delivered; we would not repeat her life. That was all she wanted.

In captivity I had longed for her and for the lost paradise of our poverty, where she had belonged entirely to my brother and to me and we had slept with her, one on each side. I had written letters to her full of remorse for past neglect and containing promises of future goodness: I would work hard and look after her forever. These letters, sent to blond, young, soft-voiced Grete Bestermann, had been read by Grete Toeppler, whose graying hair was pinned up in a sort of oval balloon, and who was anxious and thin, as afraid of things to come as she was of the past. I had not recognized her at the sta-tion, and when she said timidly, "Excuse me? Thomas?" I thought she was her own mother. I did not know then, or for another few minutes, that my grandmother had died or that my rich Uncle Gerhard, now officially de-Nazified by a court of law, was camped in two rooms carved out of a ruin, raising rabbits for a living and hoping that no one would notice him. She had last seen me when I was fifteen. We had been moving toward each other since early this morning, but I was exhausted and taciturn, and we were both shy, and we had not rushed into each other's arms, because we had each been afraid of embracing a stranger. I had one horrible memory of her, but it may have been only a dream. I was small, but I could speak and walk. I came into a room where she was nursing a baby. Two other women were with her. When they saw me they started to laugh, and one said to her, "Give some to Thomas." My mother leaned over and put her breast in my mouth. The taste was disgustingly sweet, and because of the two women I felt humiliated: I spat and backed off and began to cry. She said something to the women and they laughed harder than ever. It must have been a dream, for who could the baby have been? My brother was eleven months older than I.

She was cautious as an animal with me now, partly because of my reaction to the nameplate. She must have feared there was more to come. She had been raised to respect men, never to interrupt their conversation, to see that their plates were filled before hers—even, as a girl, to stand when they were sitting down. I was twenty-one, I had been twenty-one for three days, I had crossed over to the camp of the bullies and strangers. All the while Martin was talking and boasting and showing me himself on horseback, she crept in and out of the parlor, fetching wood and the briquettes they kept by the tile stove, carrying them down the passage to build a fire for me in the bathroom. She looked at me sidelong sometimes and smiled with her hand before her mouth—a new habit of hers—but she kept silent until it was time to say that the bath was ready.

My mother spread a towel for me to stand on and showed me a chair where, she said, Martin always sat to dry his feet. There was a shelf with a mirror and comb but no washbasin. I supposed that he shaved and they cleaned their teeth in the kitchen. My mother said the soap was of poor quality and would not lather, but she asked me, again from behind the screen of her hand, not to leave it underwater where it might melt and be wasted. A stone underwater might have melted as easily. "There is a hook for your clothes," she said, though of course I had seen it. She hesitated still, but when I began to unbutton my shirt she slipped out.

The bath, into which a family could have fitted, was as rough as lava rock. The water was boiling hot. I sat with my knees drawn up as if I were in the tin tub I had been lent sometimes in France. The starfish scar of a grenade wound was livid on one knee, and that leg was misshapen, as though it had been pressed the wrong way while the bones were soft. Long underwear I took to be my stepfather's hung over a line. I sat looking at it, and at a stiff thin towel hanging next to it, and at the water condensing on the cement walls, until the skin of my hands and feet became as ridged and soft as corduroy.

There is a term for people caught on a street crossing after the light has changed: "pedestrian-traffic residue." I had been in a prisoner-of-war camp at Rennes when an order arrived to repatriate everyone who was under eighteen. For some reason, my name was never called. Five years after that, when I was in Saint-Malo, where I had been assigned to a druggist and his wife as a "free worker"—which did not mean free but simply not in a camp—the police sent for me and asked what I was doing in France with a large "PG," for *"prisonnier de guerre,"* on my back. Was I a deserter from the Foreign Legion? A spy? Nearly every other prisoner in France had been released at least ten months before, but the file concerning me had been lost or mislaid in Rennes, and I could not leave until it was found—I had no existence. By that time the French were sick of me, because they were sick of the war and its reminders, and the scheme of using the prisoners the Americans had taken to rebuild the roads and bridges of France had not worked out. The idea had never been followed by a plan, and so some of the prisoners became farm help, some became domestic servants, some went into the Foreign Legion because the food was better, some sat and did nothing for three or four years, because no one could discover anything for them to do. The police hinted to me that if I were to run away no one would mind. It would have cleared up the matter of the missing file. But I was afraid of putting myself in the wrong, in which case they might have an excuse to keep me forever. Besides, how far could I have run with a large "PG" painted on my jacket and trousers? Here, where it would not be necessary to wear a label, because "latehomecomer" was written all over me, I sensed that I was an embarrassment, too; my appearance, my survival, my bleeding gums and loose teeth, my chronic dysentery and anemia, my craving for sweets, my reticence with strangers, the cast-off rags I had worn on arrival, all said "war" when everyone wanted peace, "captivity" when the word was "freedom," and "dry bread" when everyone was thinking "jam and butter." I guessed that now, after five years of peace, most of the population must have elbowed onto the right step of the right staircase and that there was not much room left for pedestrian-traffic residue.

My mother came in to clean the tub after I was partly dressed. She used fine ash from the stove and a cloth so full of holes it had to be rolled into a ball. She said, "I called out to you but you didn't hear. I thought you had fallen asleep and drowned."

I was hard of hearing because of the anti-aircraft duty to which I'd been posted in Berlin while I was still in high school. After the boys were sent to the front, girls took our places. It was those girls, still in their adolescence, who defended the grown men in uniform down in the bunkers. I wondered if they had been deafened, too, and if we were a generation who would never hear anything under a shout. My mother knelt by the tub, and I sat on Martin's chair, like Martin, pulling on clean socks she had brought me. In a low voice, which I heard perfectly, she said that I had known Martin in my childhood. I said I had not. She said then that my father had known him. I stood up and waited until she rose from her knees, and I looked down at her face. I was afraid of touching her, in case we should both cry. She muttered that her family must surely have known him, for the Toepplers had a burial plot not far from the graveyard where my grandmother lay buried, and some thirty miles from where my father's father had a bakery once. She was looking for any kind of a link.

"I wanted you and Chris to have a place to stay when you came back," she said, but I believed she had not expected to see either of us again and that she had been afraid of being homeless and alone. My brother had vanished in Czechoslovakia with the Schörner army. All of that army had been given up for dead. My Uncle Gerhard, her only close relative, could not have helped her even if it had occurred to him; it had taken him four years to become officially and legally de-Nazified, and now, "as white as a white lilac," according to my mother, he had no opinions about anything and lived only for his rabbits.

"It is nice to have a companion at my age," my mother said. "Someone to talk to." Did the old need more than conversation? My mother must have been about forty-two then. I had heard the old men in prison camp comparing their wives and saying that no hen was ever too tough for boiling.

"Did you marry him before or after he had this apartment?"

"After." But she had hesitated, as if wondering what I wanted to hear.

The apartment was on the second floor of a large dark block—all that was left of a workers' housing project of the 1920s. Martin had once lived somewhere between the bathroom window and the street. Looking out, I could easily replace the back walls of the vanished houses, and the small balconies festooned with brooms and mops, and the moist oily courtyard. Winter twilight must have been the prevailing climate here until an air raid let the seasons in. Cinders and gravel had been raked evenly over the crushed masonry now; the broad concourse between the surviving house—ours—and the road beyond it that was edged with ruins looked solid and flat.

But no, it was all shaky and loose, my mother said. Someone ought to cause a cement walk to be laid down; the women were always twisting their ankles, and when it rained you walked in black mud, and there was a smell of burning. She had not lost her belief in an invisible but well-intentioned "someone." She then said, in a hushed and whispery voice, that Martin's first wife, Elke, was down there under the rubble and cinders. It had been impossible to get all the bodies out, and one day a bulldozer covered them over for all time. Martin had inherited those two apartments in a town in Franconia from Elke. The Toepplers were probably just as poor as the Bestermanns, but Martin had made a good marriage.

"She had a dog, too," said my mother. "When Martin married her she had a white spitz. She gave it a bath in the bathtub every Sunday." I thought of Martin Toeppler crossing this new wide treacherous front court and saying, "Elke's grave. Ah, yes, yes." I said it, and my mother suddenly laughed loudly and dropped her hand, and I saw that some of her front teeth were missing.

"The house looks like an old tooth when you see it from the street," she said, as though deliberately calling attention to the very misfortune she wanted to hide. She knew nothing about the people who had lived in this apartment, except that they had left in a hurry, forgetting to pack a large store of black-market food, some pretty ornaments in a china cabinet, and five bottles of wine. "They left without paying the rent," she said, which didn't sound like her.

It turned out to be a joke of Martin Toeppler's. He repeated it when I came back to the parlor wearing a shirt that I supposed must be his, and with my hair dark and wet and combed flat. He pointed to a bright rectangle on the brown wallpaper. "That is where they took Adolf's picture down," he said. "When they left in a hurry without paying the rent."

My father had been stabbed to death one night when he was caught tearing an election poster off the schoolhouse wall. He left my mother with no money, two children under the age of five, and a political reputation. After that she swam with the current. I had worn a uniform of one kind or another most of my life until now. I remembered wearing civilian clothes once, when I was fourteen, for my confirmation. I had felt disguised, and wondered what to do with my hands; from the age of seven I had stuck my thumbs in a leather belt. I had impressions, not memories, of my father. Pictures were frozen things; they told me nothing. But I knew that when my hair was wet I looked something like him. A quick flash would come back out of a mirror, like a secret message, and I would think, There, that is how he was. I sat with Martin at the table, where my mother had spread a lace cloth (the vanished tenants') and over which the April sun through lace curtains laid still another design. I placed my hands flat under lace shadows and wondered if they were like my father's, too.

She had put out everything she could find to eat and drink—a few sweet biscuits, cheese cut almost as thin as paper, dark bread, small whole tomatoes, radishes, slices of salami arranged in a floral design on a dish to make them seem more. We had a bottle of fizzy wine that Martin called champagne. It had a brown tint, like watered iodine, and a taste of molasses. Through this murk bubbles climbed. We raised our glasses without saying what we drank to, other than my return. Perhaps Martin drank to his destiny in Franconia with the two apartments. I had a plan, but it was my own secret. By a common accord, there was no mutual past. Then my mother spoke from behind the cupped hand and said she would like us to drink to her missing elder son. She looked at Martin as she said this, in case the survival of Chris might be a burden, too.

Toward the end of that afternoon, a neighbor came in with a bottle of brandy—a stout man with three locks of slick gray hair across his skull. All the fat men of comic stories and of literature were to be Willy Wehler to me, in the future. But he could not have been all that plump in Berlin in 1950; his chin probably showed the beginnings of softness, and his hair must have been dark still, and there must have been plenty of it. I can see the start of his baldness, the two deep peninsulas of polished skin running from the corners of his forehead to just above his ears. Willy Wehler was another Franconian. He and Martin began speaking in dialect almost at once. Willy was at a remove, however—he mispronounced words as though to be funny, and he would grin and look at me. This was to say that he knew better, and he knew that I knew. Martin and Willy hated Berlin. They sounded as if they had been dragged to Berlin against their will, like displaced persons. In their eyes the deepest failure of a certain political authority was that it had enticed peace-loving persons with false promises of work, homes, pensions, lives afloat like little boats at anchor; now these innocent provincials saw they had been tricked, and they were going back where they had started from. It was as simple to them as that—the equivalent of an insurance company's no longer meeting its obligations. Willy even described the life he would lead now in a quiet town, where, in sight of a cobbled square with a fountain and an equestrian statue, he planned to open a perfume-and-cosmetics shop; people wanted beauty now. He would live above the shop—he was not too proud for that—and every morning he would look down on his blue store awnings, over window boxes stuffed with frilled petunias. My stepfather heard this with tears in his eyes, but perhaps he was thinking of his two apartments and of Elke and the spitz. Willy's future seemed so real, so close at hand, that it was almost as though he had dropped in to say good-bye. He sat with his daughter on his knees, a baby not yet three. This little girl, whose name was Gisela, became a part of my life from that afternoon, and so did fat Willy, though none of us knew it then. The secret to which I had drunk my silent toast was a girl in France, who would be a middle-aged woman, beyond my imagining now, if she had lived. She died by jumping or accidentally falling out of a fifth-floor window in Paris. Her parents had locked her in a room when they found out she was corresponding with me.

This was still an afternoon in April in Berlin, the first of my freedom. It was one day after old Adolf's birthday, but that was not mentioned, not even in dialect or in the form of a Berlin joke. I don't think they were avoiding it; they had simply forgotten. They would always be astonished when other people turned out to have more specific memories of time and events.

This was the afternoon about which I would always say to myself, "I should have known," and even "I knew"—knew that I would marry the baby whose movements were already so willful and quick that her father complained, "We can't take her anywhere," and sat holding both her small hands in his; otherwise she would have clutched at every glass within reach. Her winged brows reminded me of the girl I wanted to see again. Gisela's eyes were amber in color, and luminous, with the whites so pure they seemed blue. The girl in France had eyes that resembled dark petals, opaque and velvety, and slightly tilted. She had black hair from a Corsican grandmother, and long fine lashes. Gisela's lashes were stubby and thick. I found that I was staring at the child's small ears and her small perfect teeth, thinking all the while of the other girl, whose smile had been spoiled by the malnutrition and the poor dentistry of the Occupation. I should have realized then, as I looked at Willy and his daughter, that some people never go without milk and eggs and apples, whatever the landscape, and that the sparse feast on our table had more to do with my mother's long habit of poverty—a kind of fatalistic incompetence that came from never having had enough money—than with a real shortage of food. Willy had on a white nylon shirt, which was a luxury then. Later, Martin would say to me, "That Willy! Out of a black uniform and into the black market before you could say 'democracy,' " but I never knew whether it was a common Berlin joke or something Martin had made up or the truth about Willy.

Gisela, who was either slow to speak for her age or only lazy, looked at me and said, "Man"—all she had to declare. Her hair was so silky and fine that it reflected the day as a curve of mauve light. She was all light and sheen, and she was the first person—I can even say the first *thing*—I had ever seen that was unflawed, without shadow. She was as whole and as innocent as a drop of water, and she was without guilt.

Her hands, released when her father drank from his wineglass, patted the tablecloth, seized a radish, tried to stuff it in his mouth.

My mother sat with her chair pushed back a few respectful inches. "Do you like children, Thomas?" she said. She knew nothing about me now except that I was not a child.

The French girl was sixteen when she came to Brittany on a holiday with her father and mother. The next winter she sent me books so that I would not drop too far behind in my schooling, and the second summer she came to my room. The door to the room was in a bend of the staircase, halfway between the pharmacy on the ground floor and the flat where my employers lived. They were supposed to keep me locked in this room when I wasn't working, but the second summer they forgot or could not be bothered, and in any case I had made a key with a piece of wire by then. It was the first room I'd had to myself. I whitewashed the walls and boxed in the store of potatoes they kept on the floor in a corner. Bunches of wild plants and herbs the druggist used in prescriptions hung from hooks in the ceiling. One whole wall was taken up with shelves of drying leaves and roots—walnut leaves for treating anemia, chamomile for fainting spells, thyme and rosemary for muscular cramps, and nettles and mint, sage and dandelions. The fragrance in the room and the view of the port from the window could have given me almost enough happiness for a lifetime, except that I was too young to find any happiness in that.

How she escaped from her parents the first afternoon I never knew, but she was a brave, careless girl and had already escaped from them often. They must have known what could happen when they locked that wild spirit into a place where the only way out was a window. Perhaps they were trying to see how far they could go with a margin of safety. She left a message for them: "To teach you a lesson." She must have thought she would be there and not there, lost to them and yet able to see the result. There was no message for me, except that it is a terrible thing to be alone; but I had already learned it. She must have knelt on the windowsill. The autumn rain must have caught her lashes and hair. She was already alien on the windowsill, beyond recognition.

I had made my room as neat for her as though I were expecting a military inspection. I wondered if she knew how serious it would be for both of us if we were caught. She glanced at the view, but only to see if anyone could look in on us, and she laughed, starting to take off her pullover, arms crossed; then stopped and said, "What is it—are you made of ice?" How could she know that I was retarded? I had known nothing except imagination and solitude, and the preying of old soldiers; and I was too old for one and repelled by the other. I thought she was about to commit the sacrifice of her person—her physical self and her immortal soul. I had heard the old men talking about women as if women were dirt, but needed for "that." One man said he would cut off an ear for "that." Another said he would swim the Atlantic. I thought she would lie in some way convenient to me and that she would feel nothing but a kind of sorrow, which would have made it a pure gift. But there was nothing to ask; it was not a gift. It was her decision and not a gift but an adventure. She hadn't come here to look at the harbor, she told me, when I hesitated. I may even have said no, and it might have been then that she smiled at me over crossed arms, pulling off her sweater, and said, "Are you made of ice?" For all her jauntiness, she thought she was deciding her life, though she continued to use the word "adventure." I think it was the only other word she knew for "love." But all we were settling was her death, and my life was decided in Berlin when Willy Wehler came in with a bottle of brandy and Gisela, who refused to say more than "Man." I can still see the lace curtains, the mark on the wallpaper, the china ornaments left by the people who had gone in such a hurry—the chimney sweep with his matchstick broom, the girl with bobbed orange hair sitting on a crescent moon, the dog with the ruff around his neck—and when I remember this I say to myself, "I must have known."

We finished two bottles of Martin's champagne, and then my mother jumped to her feet to remove the glasses and bring others so that we could taste Willy Wehler's brandy.

"The dirty Belgian is still hanging around," he said to Martin, gently rocking the child, who now had her thumb in her mouth.

"What does he want?" said my stepfather. He repeated the question; he was slow and he thought that other people, unless they reacted at once and with a show of feeling, could not hear him.

"He was in the Waffen-S.S.—he says. He complains that the girls here won't go out with him, though only five or six years ago they were like flies."

"They are afraid of him," came my mother's timid voice. "He stands in the court and stares. . . ."

"I don't like men who look at pure young girls," said Willy Wehler. "He said to me, 'Help me; you owe me help.' He says he fought for us and nobody thanked him."

"He did? No wonder we lost," said Martin. I had already seen that the survivors of the war were divided into those who said they had always known how it would all turn out and those who said they had been indifferent. There are also those who like wars and those who do not. Martin had never been committed to winning or to losing or to anything—that explained his jokes. He had gained two apartments and one requisitioned flat in Berlin. He had lost a wife, but he often said to me later that people were better off out of this world.

"In Belgium he was in jail," said Willy. "He says he fought for us and then he was in jail and now we won't help him and the girls won't speak to him."

"Why is he here?" my stepfather suddenly shouted. "Who let him in? All this is his own affair, not ours." He rocked in his chair in a peculiar way, perhaps only imitating the gentle motion Willy made to keep Gisela asleep and quiet. "Nobody owes him anything," cried my stepfather, striking the table so that the little girl started and shuddered. My mother touched his arm and made a sort of humming sound, with her lips pressed together, that I took to be a signal between them, for he at once switched to another topic. It was a theme of conversation I was to hear about for many years after that afternoon. It was what the old men had to say when they were not boasting about women or their own past, and it was this: What should the Schörner army have done in Czechoslovakia to avoid capture by the Russians, and why did General Eisenhower (the villain of the story) refuse to help?

Eisenhower was my stepfather's left hand, General Schörner was his right, and the Russians were a plate of radishes. I turned very slightly to look at my mother. She had that sad cast of feature women have when their eyes are fixed nowhere. Her hand still lay lightly on Martin Toeppler's sleeve. I supposed then that he really was her husband and that they slept in the same bed. I had seen one or two closed doors in the passage on my way to the bath. Of my first prison camp, where everyone had been under eighteen or over forty, I remembered the smell of the old men—how they stopped being clean when there were no women to make them wash—and I remembered their long boasting. And yet, that April afternoon, as the sunlight of my first hours of freedom moved over the table and up along the brown wall, I did my boasting, too. I told about a prisoner I had captured. It seemed to be the thing I had to say to two men I had never seen before.

"He landed in a field just outside my grandmother's village," I told them. "I was fourteen. Three of us saw him—three boys. We had French rifles captured in the 1870 war. He'd had time to fold his parachute and he was sitting on it. I knew only one thing in English; it was 'Hands up.'"

My stepfather's mouth was open, as it had been when I first walked into the flat that day. My mother stood just out of sight.

"We advanced, pointing our 1870 rifles," I went on, droning, just like the old prisoners of war. "We all now said, 'Hands up.' The prisoner just—" I made the gesture the American had made, of chasing a fly away, and I realized I was drunk. "He didn't stand up. He had put everything he had on the ground—a revolver, a wad of German money, a handkerchief with a map of Germany, and some smaller things we couldn't identify at once. He had on civilian shoes with thick soles. He very slowly undid his watch and handed it over, but we had no ruling about that, so we said no. He put the watch on the ground next to the revolver and the map. Then he slowly got up and strolled into the village, with his hands in his pockets. He was chewing gum. I saw he had kept his cigarettes, but I didn't know the rule about that, either. We kept our guns trained on him. The schoolmaster ran out of my grandmother's guesthouse—everyone ran to stare. He was excited and kept saying in English, 'How do you do? How do you do?' but then an officer came running, too, and he was screaming, 'Why are you interfering? You may ask only one thing: Is he English or American.' The teacher was glad to show off his English, and he asked, 'Are you English or American?' and the American seemed to move his tongue all round his mouth before he answered. He was the first foreigner any of us had ever seen, and they took him away from us. We never saw him again."

That seemed all there was to it, but Martin's mouth was still open. I tried to remember more. "There was hell because we had left the gun and the other things on the ground. By the time they got out to the field, someone had stolen the parachute—probably for the cloth. We were in trouble over that, and we never got credit for having taken a prisoner. I went back to the field alone later on. I wanted to cry, for some reason—because it was over. He was from an adventure story to me. The whole war was a Karl May adventure, when I was fourteen and running around in school holidays with a gun. I found some small things in the field that had been overlooked—pills for keeping awake, pills in transparent envelopes. I had never seen that before. One envelope was called 'motion sickness.' It was a crime to keep anything, but I kept it anyway. I still had it when the Americans captured me, and they took it away. I had kept it because it was from another world. I would look at it and wonder. I kept it because of *The Last of the Mohicans,* because, because."

This was the longest story I had ever told in my life. I added, "My grandmother is dead now." My stepfather had finally shut his mouth. He looked at my mother as if to say that she had brought him a rival in the only domain that mattered—the right to talk everyone's ear off. My mother edged close to Willy Wehler and urged him to eat bread and cheese. She was still in the habit of wondering what the other person thought and how important he might be and how safe it was to speak. But Willy had not heard more than a sentence or two. That was plain from the way the expression on his face came slowly awake. He opened his eyes wide, as if to get sleep out of them, and—evidently imagining I had been talking about my life in France—said, "What were you paid as a prisoner?"

I had often wondered what the first question would be once I was home. Now I had it.

"Ha!" said my stepfather, giving the impression that he expected me to be caught out in a monstrous lie.

"One franc forty centimes a month for working here and there on a farm," I said. "But when I became a free worker with a druggist the official pay was three thousand francs a month, and that was what he gave me." I paused. "And of course I was fed and housed and had no laundry bills."

"Did you have bedsheets?" said my mother.

"With the druggist's family, always. I had one sheet folded in half. It was just right for a small cot."

"Was it the same sheet as the kind the family had?" she said, in the hesitant way that was part of her person now.

"They didn't buy sheets especially for me," I said. "I was treated fairly by the druggist, but not by the administration."

"Aha," said the two older men, almost together.

"The administration refused to pay my fare home," I said, looking down into my glass the way I had seen the men in prison camp stare at a fixed point when they were recounting a grievance.

"A prisoner of war has the right to be repatriated at administration expense. The administration would not pay my fare because I had stayed too
long in France—but that was their mistake. I bought a ticket as far as Paris
on the pay I had saved. The druggist sold me some old shoes and trousers
and a jacket of his. My own things were in rags. In Paris I went to the
YMCA. The YMCA was supposed to be in charge of prisoners' rights. The
man wouldn't listen to me. If I had been left behind, then I was not a prisoner, he said; I was a tourist. It was his duty to help me. Instead of that, he
informed the police." For the first time my voice took on the coloration of
resentment. I knew that this complaint about a niggling matter of train fare
made my whole adventure seem small, but I had become an old soldier. I remembered the police commissioner, with his thin lips and dirty nails, who
said, "You should have been repatriated years ago, when you were sixteen."

"It was a mistake," I told him.

"Your papers are full of strange mistakes," he said, bending over them.
"There, one capital error. An omission, a grave omission. What is your
mother's maiden name?"

"Wickler," I said.

I watched him writing "W-i-e-c-k-l-a-i-r," slowly, with the tip of his
tongue sticking out of the corner of his mouth as he wrote. "You have been
here for something like five years with an incomplete dossier. And what
about this? Who crossed it out?"

"I did. My father was not a pastry cook."

"You could be fined or even jailed for this," he said.

"My father was not a pastry cook," I said. "He had tuberculosis. He was
not allowed to handle food."

Willy Wehler did not say what he thought of my story. Perhaps not having any opinion about injustice, even the least important, had become a
habit of his, like my mother's of speaking through her fingers. He was on
the right step of that staircase I've spoken of. Even the name he had given
his daughter was a sign of his sensitivity to the times. Nobody wanted to
hear the pagan, Old Germanic names anymore—Sigrun and Brunhilde and
Sieglinde. Willy had felt the change. He would have called any daughter
something neutral and pretty—Gisela, Marianne, Elisabeth—anytime after
the battle of Stalingrad. All Willy ever had to do was sniff the air.

He pushed back his chair (in later years he would be able to push a table
away with his stomach) and got to his feet. He had to tip his head to look
up into my eyes. He said he wanted to give me advice that would be useful

to me as a latehomecomer. His advice was to forget. "Forget everything," he said. "Forget, forget. That was what I said to my good neighbor Herr Silber when I bought his wife's topaz brooch and earrings before he emigrated to Palestine. I said, 'Dear Herr Silber, look forward, never back, and forget, forget, forget.' "

The child in Willy's arms was in the deepest of sleeps. Martin Toeppler followed his friend to the door, they whispered together; then the door closed behind both men.

"They have gone to have a glass of something at Herr Wehler's," said my mother. I saw now that she was crying quietly. She dried her eyes on her apron and began clearing the table of the homecoming feast. "Willy Wehler has been kind to us," she said. "Don't repeat that thing."

"About forgetting?"

"No, about the topaz brooch. It was a crime to buy anything from Jews."

"It doesn't matter now."

She lowered the tray she held and looked pensively out at the wrecked houses across the street. "If only people knew beforehand what was allowed," she said.

"My father is probably a hero now," I said.

"Oh, Thomas, don't travel too fast. We haven't seen the last of the changes. Yes, a hero. But too late for me. I've suffered too much."

"What does Martin think that he died of?"

"A working accident. He can understand that."

"You could have said consumption. He did have it." She shook her head. Probably she had not wanted Martin to imagine he could ever be saddled with two sickly stepsons. "Where do you and Martin sleep?"

"In the room next to the bathroom. Didn't you see it? You'll be comfortable here in the parlor. The couch pulls out. You can stay as long as you like. This is your home. A home for you and Chris." She said this so stubbornly that I knew some argument must have taken place between her and Martin.

I intended this room to be my home. There was no question about it in my mind. I had not yet finished high school; I had been taken out for antiaircraft duty, then sent to the front. The role of adolescents in uniform had been to try to prevent the civilian population from surrendering. We were expected to die in the ruins together. When the women ran pillowcases up flagpoles, we shinnied up to drag them down. We were prepared to hold the line with our 1870 rifles until we saw the American tanks. There had not been tanks in our Karl May adventure stories, and the Americans, finally, were not out of *The Last of the Mohicans*. I told my mother that I had to go back to high school and then I would apply for a scholarship and take a degree in French. I would become a schoolmaster. French was all I had from my captivity; I might as well use it. I would earn money doing translations.

That cheered her up. She would not have to ask the ex–tram conductor too many favors. "Translations" and "scholarship" were an exalted form of language, to her. As a schoolmaster, I would have the most respectable job in the family, now that Uncle Gerhard was raising rabbits. "As long as it doesn't cost *him* too much," she said, as if she had to say it and yet was hoping I wouldn't hear.

It was not strictly true that all I had got out of my captivity was the ability to speak French. I had also learned to cook, iron, make beds, wait on table, wash floors, polish furniture, plant a vegetable garden, paint shutters. I wanted to help my mother in the kitchen now, but that shocked her. "Rest," she said, but I did not know what "rest" meant. "I've never seen a man drying a glass," she said, in apology. I wanted to tell her that while the roads and bridges of France were still waiting for someone to rebuild them I had been taught how to make a tomato salad by the druggist's wife; but I could not guess what the word "France" conveyed to her imagination. I began walking about the apartment. I looked in on a store cupboard, a water closet smelling of carbolic, the bathroom again, then a room containing a high bed, a brown wardrobe, and a table covered with newspapers bearing half a dozen of the flowerless spiky dull green plants my mother had always tended with so much devotion. I shut the door as if on a dark past, and I said to myself, I am free. This is the beginning of life. It is also the start of the good half of a rotten century. Everything ugly and corrupt and vicious is behind us. My thoughts were not exactly in those words, but something like them. I said to myself, This apartment has a musty smell, an old and dirty smell that sinks into clothes. After a time I shall probably smell like the dark parlor. The smell must be in the cushions, in the bed that pulls out, in the lace curtains. It is a smell that creeps into nightclothes. The blankets will be permeated. I thought, I shall get used to the smell, and the smell of burning in the stone outside. The view of ruins will be my view. Every day on my way home from school I shall walk over Elke. I shall get used to the wood staircase, the bellpull, the polished nameplate, the white enamel fuses in the hall—my mother had said, "When you want light in the parlor you give the center fuse in the lower row a half turn." I looked at a framed draw-

ing of cartoon people with puffy hair. A strong wind had blown their umbrella inside out. They would be part of my view, like the ruins. I took in
the ancient gas bracket in the kitchen and the stone sink. My mother, washing glasses without soap, smiled at me, forgetting to hide her teeth. I reex-
amined the tiled stove in the parlor, the wood and the black briquettes that
would be next to my head at night, and the glass-fronted cabinet full of the
china ornaments God had selected to survive the Berlin air raids. These
would be removed to make way for my books. For Martin Toeppler need
not imagine he could count on my pride, or that I would prefer to starve
rather than take his charity, or that I was too arrogant to sleep on his dusty
sofa. I would wear out his soap, borrow his shirts, spread his butter on my
bread. I would hang on Martin like an octopus. He had a dependent now—
a ravenous, egocentric, latehomecoming high school adolescent of twenty-
one. The old men owed this much to me—the old men in my prison camp
who would have sold mother and father for an extra ounce of soup, who had
already sold their children for it; the old men who had fouled my idea of
women; the old men in the bunkers who had let the girls defend them in
Berlin; the old men who had dared to survive.

    The bed that pulled out was sure to be all lumps. I had slept on worse.
Would it be wide enough for Chris, too?

    People in the habit of asking themselves silent useless questions look for
answers in mirrors. My hair was blond again now that it had dried. I looked
less like my idea of my father. I tried to see the reflection of the man who
had gone out in the middle of the night and who never came back. You
don't go out alone to tear down election posters in a village where nobody
thinks as you do—not unless you *want* to be stabbed in the back. So the
family had said.

    "You were well out of it," I said to the shadow that floated on the glass
panel of the china cabinet, though it would not be my father's again unless
I could catch it unaware.

    I said to myself, It is quieter than France. They keep their radios low.

    In captivity I had never suffered a pain except for the cramps of hunger
the first years, which had been replaced by a scratching, morbid anxiety, and
the pain of homesickness, which takes you in the stomach and the throat.
Now I felt the first of the real pains that were to follow me like little dogs
for the rest of my life, perhaps: The first compressed my knee, the second
tangled the nerves at the back of my neck. I discovered that my eyes were
sensitive and that it hurt to blink.

This was the hour when, in Brittany, I would begin peeling the potatoes for dinner. I had seen food my mother had never heard of—oysters, and artichokes. My mother had never seen a harbor or a sea.

My American prisoner had left his immediate life spread on an alien meadow—his parachute, his revolver, his German money. He had strolled into captivity with his hands in his pockets.

"I know what you are thinking," said my mother, who was standing behind me. "I know that you are judging me. If you could guess what my life has been—the whole story, not only the last few years—you wouldn't be hard on me."

I turned too slowly to meet her eyes. It was not what I had been thinking. I had forgotten about her, in that sense.

"No, no, nothing like that," I said. I still did not touch her. What I had been moving along to in my mind was: Why am I in this place? Who sent me here? Is it a form of justice or injustice? How long does it last?

"Now we can wait together for Chris," she said. She seemed young and happy all at once. "Look, Thomas. A new moon. Bow to it three times. Wait—you must have something silver in your hand." I saw that she was hurrying to finish with this piece of nonsense before Martin came back. She rummaged in the china cabinet and brought out a silver napkin ring—left behind by the vanished tenants, probably. The name on it was "Meta"—no one we knew. "Bow to the moon and hold it and make your wish," she said. "Quickly."

"You first."

She wished, I am sure, for my brother. As for me, I wished that I was a few hours younger, in the corridor of a packed train, clutching the top of the open window, my heart hammering as I strained to find the one beloved face.

SEÑOR PINEDO

───────

❧

*B*ecause there was nothing to separate our rooms but the thinnest of plaster partitions, it sometimes seemed as if the Pinedos—Señor, Señora, and baby José María—and I were really living together. Every morning, we four were roused by the same alarm clock. At night, we all went to bed to the sound of Señora Pinedo's prayers. She prayed in a bored, sleepy voice, invoking a great many saints of the Spanish calendar, while her husband, a fussy Madrid civil servant, followed along with the responses.

"San Juan de la Cruz . . . ," Señora Pinedo would say, between yawns. "San Agustín de Cantórbery . . . Santa Anatolia . . ."

"Pray for us!" her husband would command after every name.

After the prayers, I would hear them winding the clock and muffling door and window against harmful, wayward drafts of the night air. Then, long after all the lights in the *pension* we lived in had been put out, and against a background of the restless, endless racket of the Madrid night, their voices would sound almost against my ear as they talked about money.

"I have only one dress for the summer, and it's too tight," the Señora would say, into the dark. "José María's doctor came right to the house today. I pretended I was out. 'I know she never goes out,' he said. By Monday, we have to pay the interest on the silver crucifix at the Monte de Piedad, or we lose it." The Monte de Piedad was the municipal pawnshop, a brisk, banklike place into which occasionally vanished not only the crucifix but also José María's silver christening cup and Señora Pinedo's small radio.

"I know," Señor Pinedo would reply, with somewhat less authority than he used in his prayers. Or, "It can't be helped."

Sometimes the baby cried, interrupting the sad little catalogue of complaints. He would cry again in the morning, jolted by the alarm, and I would hear Señor Pinedo swearing to himself as he stumbled about the room getting dressed and preparing José María's early-morning *biberón* of dark wheat flour and milk. Señora Pinedo never rose until much later; it was understood that, having given birth to José María a few months before, she had done nearly as much as could be expected of her. Hours after her husband had gone off to his ministry desk and his filing trays, she would inch her way out of bed, groaning a little, and, after examining her face for signs of age (she was twenty-three), complete her toilette by drawing on a flowered cotton wrapper that at night hung on a gilded wall candle bracket, long fallen away from its original use.

"Is it a nice day?" she would call, knocking on the wall. Our windows faced the same direction, but she liked to be reassured. "Shall I go out? What would you do in my place?" It took several minutes of talking back and forth before the problem could be settled. If the day seemed to lack promise, she turned on the radio and went back to bed. Otherwise, she dragged a chair out to the courtyard balcony that belonged to both our rooms and sat in the sun, plucking her eyebrows and screaming companionably at the neighbors. Since it was well known that crying developed the lungs, José María was usually left indoors, where he howled and whimpered in a crib trimmed with shabby ribbons. His cries, the sound of the radio, and Señor Pinedo's remarks all came through the wall as if it had been a sieve.

The Pinedos and I did, in a sense, share a room, for the partition divided what had once been the drawing room of a stately third-floor flat. The wall was designed with scrupulous fairness; I had more space and an extra window, while the Pinedos had the pink marble fireplace, the candle brackets, and some odd lengths of green velvet drapery gone limp with age. Each side had a door leading out to the balcony, and one semicircle of plaster roses on the ceiling, marking the place where a chandelier had hung.

Like many *pensions* in Madrid, the flat had once housed a rich middle-class family. The remnants of the family, Señorita Elvira Gómez and her brother, lived in two cramped rooms off the entrance hall. The rest of the house was stuffed with their possessions—cases of tropical birds, fat brocaded footstools, wardrobes with jutting, treacherous feet. Draperies and muslin blinds maintained the regulation *pension* twilight. In the Pinedos' room, the atmosphere was particularly dense, for to the mountain of furnishings provided for their comfort they had added all the odds and ends of a larger household. Chairs, tables, and chimneypiece were piled with plates and glasses that were never used, with trinkets and paperweights shaped like charging bulls or Walt Disney gnomes. In one corner stood a rusty camping stove, a relic of Señora Pinedo's hearty, marching youth. The stove was now used for heating José María's bottles.

Added to this visual confusion was the noise. The baby wept tirelessly, but most of the heavy sounds came from the radio, which emitted an unbroken stream of jazz, flamenco, roaring *fútbol* games, the national anthem, Spanish operetta with odd, muddled overtones of Viennese, and, repeatedly, a singing commercial for headache tablets. The commercial was a particular favorite with Señora Pinedo. *"Okal!"* she would sing whenever it came on the air. *"Okal! Okal es un producto superior!"* There were three verses and three choruses, and she sang them all the way through. Sometimes it was too much for Señor Pinedo, and I would hear him pitting his voice against the uproar of his room in a despairing quaver of *"Silencio!"* He was a thin, worried-looking man, who bore an almost comic resemblance to Salvador Dalí. Nevertheless, he was a Spanish husband and father, and his word, by tradition, was law. *"Silencio!"* he commanded.

"Viva a tableta Okal!" sang his wife.

I had arrived at the *pension* on a spring morning, for a few weeks' stay. Señorita Elvira warned me about the noise next door, without for a moment proposing that anything might be done about it. Like so many of the people I was to encounter in Madrid, she lived with, and cherished, a galaxy of problems that seemed to trail about her person. The Pinedo radio was one. Another stemmed from the fact that she didn't report her lodgers to the police and pay the tax required for running a *pension.* No government inspector ever visited the house, nor, I discovered from the porter downstairs, had anyone so much as asked why so many people came and went from our floor. Still Señorita Elvira lived in a frenzy of nervous apprehension, shared, out of sympathy, by her tenants.

On my first day, she ushered me in with a rapid succession of warnings, as dolorous and pessimistic as the little booklets of possible mishaps that accompany the sale of English cars. First, if a government inspector asked me questions, I was to say nothing, nothing at all. Then (frantically adjusting her helmet of tortoiseshell hairpins), I was not to use the electric fan in the room, because of the shaky nature of the fuses; I was to sign a little book whenever I made a telephone call; I was not to hang clothes on the balcony railing, because of some incoherent reason that had to do with the neighbors; and, finally, I was not to overtip the maid, who, although she earned the sturdy sum of two hundred pesetas—or five dollars—a month, became so giddy at the sight of money there was no keeping her in the kitchen. All her tenants were distinguished, Señorita Elvira said—*muy, muy* distinguished—and the most distinguished of all was my neighbor, Señor Pinedo. No matter how noisy I might find my accommodations, I was to remember how distinguished he was, and be consoled.

Later in the morning, I met my distinguished neighbor's wife. She was sunning herself on the balcony in nightgown and wrapper, her bare feet propped flat against the warm railing. Her hair was tied back with a grubby ribbon, and on the upper and lower lids of her eyes, which were lovely, she had carefully applied makeup, in the Arab manner.

"I heard the old one," she said, evidently meaning Señorita Elvira. "Do you like music? Then you won't mind the radio. Will you be here long? Did you bring many bags? Do you like children? Do children where you come from cry at night?"

"I don't think so," I said. "Not after a certain age." It seemed to me a strange sort of introductory conversation. The courtyard, formed by adjoining apartment blocks, was so narrow that women on balconies across the way could hear, and were listening with interest.

"Some babies are forced not to cry," said Señora Pinedo. "Many are drugged, to make them sleep. *Qué horror!*"

An assenting murmur went around the court. Suddenly maternal, Señora Pinedo went indoors and fetched José María. For the next few minutes— until it bored her—she entertained him by shaking a ring of bells in his face, so that he shrieked with annoyance.

The courtyard, crisscrossed with lines of washing that dripped onto the cobbles below, seemed to be where the most active life of the apartment houses took place. Children played under the constant rain from the laundry, and the balconies were crowded with women sewing, preparing vegetables, and even cooking on portable charcoal stoves. The air was cloudy with frying olive oil. In spite of the sun, everyone, and particularly the children, seemed to me inordinately pale—perhaps because they had not yet shaken off the effects of the tiring Castilian winter. Against a wall that made a right angle with ours hung a huge iron block attached to a cable. At irregular intervals it rose and descended, narrowly scraping between the balconies. I asked Señora Pinedo about it finally, and she explained that it was the weight that counterbalanced the elevator in the building around the corner.

Sometimes the little boys playing in the courtyard would sit on the block, holding on to the cable from which it was suspended, and ride up as far as the second-floor balconies, where they would scramble off; frequently the elevator would stall before they had traveled any distance. From our third-floor balcony, the children below looked frail and small. I asked Señora Pinedo if the block wasn't dangerous.

"It is, without doubt," she said, but with a great dark-rimmed glance of astonishment; it was clear that this thought had never before entered her head. "But then," she added, as if primly repeating a lesson, "in Spain we do things our own way."

Only after meeting Señor Pinedo could I imagine where she had picked up this petulant and, in that context, meaningless phrase. He arrived at two o'clock for his long lunch-and-siesta break. Señora Pinedo and I were still on the balcony, and José María had, miraculously, fallen asleep on his mother's lap. Señor Pinedo carried out one of Señorita Elvira's billowing chairs and sat down, looking stiff and formal. He wore a sober, badly cut suit and a large, cheap signet ring, on which was emblazoned the crossed arrows of the Falange. He told me, as if it were important this be made very clear, that he and his wife were living in such crowded quarters only temporarily. They were used to much finer things. I had the impression that they were between apartments.

"Yes, we've been here four and a half years," said Señora Pinedo, cheerfully destroying the impression. "We were married and came right here. My trousseau linen is in a big box under the bed."

"But you are not to suppose from this that there is a housing problem in Spain," said Señor Pinedo. "On the contrary, our urban building program is one of the most advanced in Europe. We are ahead of England. We are ahead of France."

"Then why don't we have a nice little house?" his wife interrupted dreamily. "Or an apartment? I would like a salon, a dining room, three bedrooms, a balcony for flowers, and a terrace for the laundry. In my uncle's house, in San Sebastián, the maids have their own bathroom."

"If you are interested," said Señor Pinedo to me, "I could bring you some interesting figures from the Ministry of Housing."

"The maids have their own bathtub," said Señora Pinedo, bouncing José María. "How many people in Madrid can say the same? Twice every month, they have their own hot water."

"I will bring you the housing figures this evening," Señor Pinedo promised. He rose, hurried his wife indoors before she could tell me anything more about the maids in San Sebastián, and bowed in the most ceremonious manner, as if we would not be meeting a few moments later in the dining room.

That evening, he did indeed bring home from his office a thick booklet that bore the imprint of the Ministry of Housing. It contained pictures of a workers' housing project in Seville, and showed smiling factory hands moving into their new quarters. The next day, there was something else—a chart illustrating the drop in infant mortality. And after that came a steady flow of pamphlets and graphs, covering milk production, the exporting of olive oil, the number of miles of railroad track constructed per year, the improved lot of agricultural workers. With a triumphant smile, as if to say, "Aha! *Here's* something you didn't know!" Señor Pinedo would present me with some new document, open it, and show me photographs of a soup kitchen for nursing mothers or of tubercular children at a summer camp.

The Pinedos and I were not, of course, the only tenants of Señorita Elvira's flat. Apart from the tourists, the honeymooning couples from the province, and the commercial travelers, there was a permanent core of lodgers, some of whom, although young, appeared to have lived there for years. These included a bank clerk, a student from Zaragoza, a civil engineer, a bullfighters' impresario, and a former university instructor of Spanish literature, who, having taken quite the wrong stand during the Civil War—he had been neutral—now dispensed hand lotion and aspirin in a drugstore on the Calle del Carmen. There was also the inevitable Englishwoman, one of the queer Mad Megs who seem to have been born and bred for *pension* life. This one, on hearing me speak English in the dining room, looked at me with undisguised loathing, picked up knife, fork, plate, and wineglass, and removed herself to the far corner of the room; the maid followed with the Englishwoman's own private assortment of mineral water, digestive pills, Keen's mustard, and English chop sauce.

All these people, with the exception of the Englishwoman, seemed to need as much instruction as I did in the good works performed by the state. Every new bulletin published by the Ministry of Propaganda was fetched home by Señor Pinedo and circulated through the dining room, passing from hand to hand. All conversation would stop, and Señor Pinedo would eagerly search the readers' faces, waiting for someone to exclaim over, say, the splendid tidings that a new luxury train had been put into operation between Madrid and the south. Usually, however, the only remark would come from the impresario, a fat, noisy man who smoked cigars and wandered about the halls in his underwear. Sometimes he entertained one of his simpleminded clients in our dining room; on these occasions, Señorita Elvira, clinging gamely to her boast that everyone was *muy, muy* distinguished, kept the conversation at her table at a rattling pitch in order to drown out the noise matador and impresario managed to make with their food and wine.

"How much did this thing cost?" the impresario would ask rudely, holding Señor Pinedo's pamphlet at arm's length and squinting at it. "Who made the money on it? What's it good for?"

"Money?" Señor Pinedo would cry, seriously upset. "Good for?" Often, after such an exchange, he was unable to get on with his meal, and sat hurt and perplexed, staring at his plate in a rising clatter of dishes and talk.

Sometimes his arguments took on a curious note of pleading, as if he believed that these people, with their genteel pretensions, their gritty urban poverty that showed itself in their clothes, their bad-tasting cigarettes, their obvious avoidance of such luxuries as baths and haircuts, should understand him best. "Am I rich?" he would ask. "Did I make black-market money? Do I have a big house, or an American car? I don't love myself, I love Spain. I've sacrificed everything for Spain. I was wounded at seventeen. Seventeen! And I was a volunteer. No one recruited me."

Hearing this declaration for the twentieth time, the tenants in the dining hall would stare, polite. It was all undoubtedly interesting, their faces suggested; it was even important, perhaps, that Señor Pinedo, who had not made a dishonest céntimo, sat among them. In another year, at another period of life, they might have been willing to reply; however, at the moment, although their opinions were not dead, they had faded, like the sepia etching of the Chief of State that had hung in the entrance hall for more than thirteen years and now blended quietly with the wallpaper.

In Señor Pinedo's room, between the portraits of film stars tacked up by his wife, hung another likeness, this one of José Antonio Primo de Rivera, the founder of the Falange, who was shot by the Republicans during the Civil War.

"He was murdered," Señor Pinedo said to me one day when I was visiting the Pinedos in their room. "Murdered by the Reds." He looked at the dead leader's face, at the pose, with its defiant swagger, the arms folded over the famous blue shirt. "Was there ever a man like that in your country?" Under the picture, on a shelf, he kept an old, poorly printed edition of José

Antonio's speeches and a framed copy of the Call to Arms, issued on the greatest day of Señor Pinedo's life. Both these precious things he gave me to read, handling the book with care and reverence. "Everything is here," he assured me. "When you have read these, you will understand the true meaning of the movement, not just foreign lies and propaganda."

Everything was there, and I read the brave phrases of revolution that had appealed to Señor Pinedo at seventeen. I read of a New Spain, mighty, Spartan, and feared abroad. I read of the need for austerity and sacrifice. I read the promise of land reform, the denunciation of capitalism, and, finally, the Call to Arms. It promised "one great nation for all, and not for a group of privileged."

I returned the book and the framed declaration to Señor Pinedo, who said mysteriously, "Now you know," as if we shared a great secret.

That spring, there was an unseasonable heat wave in Madrid; by the time Easter approached, it was as warm as a northern June. The week before Palm Sunday, the plane trees along the Calle de Alcalá were in delicate leaf, and on the watered lawns of the Ministry of War roses drooped on thin tall stalks, like the flowers in Persian art. Outside the ministry gates, sentries paced and wheeled, sweating heroically in their winter greatcoats.

The table in the entrance hall of the *pension* was heaped with palms, some of them as tall as little trees. Señorita Elvira planned to have the entire lot blessed and then affixed to the balconies on both sides of the house; she believed them effective against a number of dangers, including lightning. The Chief of State, dusted and refreshed after a spring-cleaning, hung over the palms, gazing directly at a plaster Santa Rita, who was making a parochial visit. She stood in a small house that looked like a sentry box, to which was tacked a note explaining that her visit brought good fortune to all and that a minimum fee of two pesetas was required in exchange. It seemed little enough in return for good fortune, but Señor Pinedo, who sometimes affected a kind of petulant anticlericalism, would have no part of the pink-faced little doll, and said that he was not planning to go to church on Palm Sunday—an announcement that appeared to shock no one at all.

On Saturday night, four of us accidentally came home at the same time and were let into the building and then into the *pension* by the night porter. Señor Pinedo had been to the cinema. The stills outside the theater had promised a rich glimpse of American living, but in line with some imbecility of plot (the hero was unable to love a girl with money) all the characters had to pretend to be poor until the last reel. They wore shabby clothes, and walked instead of riding in cars. Describing the movie, Señor Pinedo sounded angry and depressed. He smelled faintly of the disinfectant with which Madrid cinemas are sprayed.

"If I belonged to the Office of Censorship," he said, "I would have had the film banned." Catching sight of Santa Rita, he added, "And no one can make me go to church."

Later, from my side of the partition, I heard him describing the film, scene by scene, to his wife, who said, *"Sí, claro"* sleepily, but with interest, from time to time. Then they said their prayers. The last voice in the room that night came from the radio. *"Viva Franco!"* it said, signing off. *"Arriba España!"*

It seemed to me not long afterward that I heard the baby crying. It was an unusual cry—he sounded frightened—and, dragged abruptly awake, I sat up and saw that it was daylight. If it was José María, he was outside. That was where the cry had come from. Señor Pinedo was out of bed. I heard him mutter angrily as he scraped a chair aside and went out to the balcony. It wasn't the baby, after all, for Señora Pinedo was talking to him indoors, saying, "It's nothing, only noise." There was a rush of voices from the courtyard and, in our own flat, the sound of people running in the corridor and calling excitedly. I pulled on a dressing gown and went outside.

Señor Pinedo, wearing a raincoat, was leaning over the edge of the balcony. In the well of the court, a little boy lay on his back, surrounded by so many people that one could not see the cobblestones. The spectators seemed to have arrived, as they do at Madrid street accidents, from nowhere, panting from running, pale with the fear that something had been missed. On the wall at right angles to ours there was a mark that, for a moment, I thought was paint. Then I realized that it must be blood.

"It was the elevator," Señor Pinedo said to me, waving his hand toward the big iron block that now hung, motionless, just below the level of the second-floor balconies. "I knew someone would be hurt," he said with a kind of gloomy triumph. "The boys never left it alone."

The little boy, whose name was Jaime Gámez, and who lived in the apartment directly across from our windows, had been sitting astride the block, grasping the cable, and when the elevator moved, he had been caught between the block and the wall.

"One arm and one leg absolutely crushed," someone announced from the courtyard, calling the message around importantly. The boy's father arrived. He had to fight through the crowd in the court. Taking off his coat, he wrapped Jaime in it, lifted him up, and carried him away. Jaime's face looked white and frightened. Apparently he had not yet begun to experience the pain of his injuries, and was simply stunned and shocked.

By now, heads had appeared at the windows on all sides of the court, and the balconies were filled with people dressed for church or still in dressing gowns. The courtyard suddenly resembled the arena of a bullring. There was the same harsh division of light and shadow, as if a line had been drawn, high on the opposite wall. The faces within the area of sun were white and expressionless, with that curious Oriental blankness that sometimes envelops the whole arena during moments of greatest emotion.

Some of the crowd of strangers down below sauntered away. The elevator began to function again, and the huge weight creaked slowly up the side of the house. Across the court, Jaime's family could be heard crying and calling inside their flat. After a few moments, the boy's mother, as if she were too distracted to stay indoors, or as if she had to divert her attention to inconsequential things, rushed out on her balcony and called to someone in the apartment above ours. On a chair in the sun was Jaime's white sailor suit, which he was to have worn to church. It had long trousers and a navy-blue collar. It had been washed and ironed, and left to dry out thoroughly in the sun. On a stool beside it was his hat, a round sailor hat with *"España"* in letters of gold on the blue band.

"Look at his suit, all ready!" cried Jaime's mother, as if one tragedy were not enough. "And his palms!" She disappeared into the dark apartment, and ran out again to the hard light of the morning carrying the palms Jaime was to have taken to church for the blessing. They were wonderfully twisted and braided into a rococo shape, and dangling and shining all over them were gilt and silver baubles that glinted in the sun.

"Terribly bad luck," said Señor Pinedo. I stared at him, surprised at this most Anglo-Saxon understatement. "If the palms had been blessed earlier," he went on, "this might not have happened, but, of course, they couldn't have known. Not that I have beliefs like an old woman." He gazed at the palms in an earnest way, looking like Salvador Dalí. "Doña Elvira believes they keep off lightning. I wouldn't go so far. But I still think . . ." His voice dropped, as if he were not certain, or not deeply interested in, what he did think.

Someone called the mother. She went inside, crying, carrying the palms and the sailor suit. A few of the people around the courtyard had drifted indoors, but most of them seemed reluctant to leave the arena, where—one never knew—something else of interest might take place. They looked down through the tangle of clotheslines to the damp stones of the court, talking in loud, matter-of-fact voices about the accident. They spoke of hospitalization, of amputation—for the rumor that Jaime's hand was to be amputated had started even before I came out—and of limping and crutches and pain and expense.

"The poor parents," someone said. A one-armed child would be a terrible burden, and useless. Everyone agreed, just as, on my first day, they had all agreed with Señora Pinedo that it was bad to drug one's children.

Señor Pinedo, beside me, drew in his breath. "Useless?" he said loudly. "A useless child? Why, the father can claim compensation for him—a lifetime pension."

"From the angels?" someone shouted up.

"From the building owners, first," Señor Pinedo said, trying to see who had spoken. "But also from our government. Haven't any of you thought of that?"

"No," said several voices together, and everyone laughed.

"Of course he'll have a pension!" Señor Pinedo shouted. He looked around at them all and said, "Wasn't it promised? Weren't such things promised?" People hung out of windows on the upper floors, trying to see him under the overhang of the balcony. "I guarantee it!" Señor Pinedo said. He leaned over the railing and closed his fist like an orator, a leader. The railing shook.

"Be careful," I said, unheard.

He brought his fist down on the railing, which must have hurt. "I guarantee it," he said. "I work in the office of pensions."

"Ah!" That made sense. Influence was something they all understood. "He must be related to little Jaime," I heard someone say, sounding disappointed. "Still, that's not a bad thing, a pension for life." They discussed it energetically, citing cases of deserving victims who had never received a single céntimo. Señor Pinedo looked around at them all. For the first time since I had known him, he was smiling happily. Finally, when it seemed quite clear that nothing more was to happen, the chatter died down, and even the most persistent observers, with a last look at the blood, the cobbles, and the shuttered windows of Jaime's flat, went indoors.

Señor Pinedo and I were the last to leave the court. We parted, and through the partition I heard him telling his wife that he had much to do that week, a social project connected with the hurt child. In his happiness, he sounded almost childlike himself, convinced, as he must convince others, of the truth and good faith of the movement to which he had devoted his life and in which he must continue to believe.

Later, I heard him repeating the same thing to the *pension* tenants as they passed his door on the way to church. There was no reply. It was the silence of the dining room when the bulletins were being read, and as I could not see his listeners' faces, I could not have said whether the silence was owing to respect, delight, apathy, or a sudden fury of some other emotion so great that only silence could contain it.

BY THE SEA

At the beginning of the afternoon, just before the luncheon gongs were due to be sounded at the *pensions* and villas along the cliff, a lull would descend on the beach. It was July; the beach was a baking stretch of shore on the south coast of Spain. At this hour, the sun shone straight overhead. To the west, Gibraltar wavered in heat. The cliffs behind the beach held the warmth of the day and threw it back to the sand. Only the children, protected with sun oil and porous straw hats, seemed not to mind; they paddled in the scummy surf, dug the blistering sands, and communicated in a private language. Heat fell on the bamboo roof of the pavilion and bar. The bar and the tables and the sticky, salty, half-naked tourists were covered alike with zebra stripes of light and shade. Nowhere was cool enough or dark enough. The glasses on the tables were filled to the brim with ice. No one said much.

In the neutral area of tables between the English tourists and the French sat the Tuttlingens, from Stuttgart, and Mrs. Owens, who was American. They lived in the same *pension*, Villa Margate (whose owner, like many of the permanent residents of this corner of Spain, was English), and, being neither English nor French, had drifted together. Mrs. Owens watched the beach, where her son, aged five, was busy with bucket and spade. She and the Tuttlingens, bored with one another, wished the luncheon gong would be struck at the Margate, so that they would have an excuse to separate.

"She is an extraordinary woman," Dr. Tuttlingen suddenly remarked. "Heat does not bother her. Nothing does."

The others stared, and nodded, agreeing. Mrs. Parsters, a white towel draped on her neck like a boa, was coming toward them. She wore her morning costume—a chaste swimming suit made of cretonne, and flopping carpet slippers. Leaving the slippers above the waterline, Mrs. Parsters had put one bare foot into the surf. The bathing, she said, was impossible. "It's not that it's warm, and it's not that it's cold. It's all the damned insects and jellyfish, not to mention the orange peelings from the cruise ship that went by this morning."

As far as anyone sitting in the pavilion could tell, Mrs. Parsters was speaking only to Bobby, her dog, part of whose ancestry was revealed in a noble spitz tail he wore furled on his back like a Prince of Wales plume. A few of the languid tourists looked over, but it was clear, even to innocent newcomers, unfamiliar with beach protocol, that Mrs. Parsters had nothing to say to any of them. She stopped at the pavilion steps and surveyed the scattered children, all of them busy, each child singing or muttering softly to himself.

"You are building neatly," she said to Mrs. Owens's little boy. She said it with such positive approval that he stopped and stared at what he was doing, perplexed. "Where is your father?" she asked. She had been wondering this ever since Mrs. Owens's arrival.

"Home," said the child, with unnecessary pathos.

"And is he coming here?"

"No." Dismissing her, he began piling sand. "Not ever."

"How easily Americans divorce!" said Mrs. Parsters, walking on.

Mrs. Owens, who had heard all this, wondered if it was worth the bother of explaining that she was happily married. But she was a little overwhelmed by Mrs. Parsters. "It's so hot" was all that she finally said as Mrs. Parsters approached.

Acknowledging this but refusing to be defeated by it, Mrs. Parsters looked up and down the pavilion. None of her own friends were about; she would have to settle for the Tuttlingens and Mrs. Owens. Mrs. Owens was young, anxious, and fluffy-haired. She lacked entirely the air of competence Mrs. Parsters expected—even demanded—of Americans. She looked, Mrs. Parsters thought, as if her husband had been in the habit of leaving her around in strange places. At some point, undoubtedly, he had forgotten to pick her up. Tuttlingen, running to fat at the waist, and with small red veins high on the cheekbones, was a doctor, a profession that had Mrs. Parsters's complete approval. As for Frau Tuttlingen, the less said the better. A tart, thought Mrs. Parsters, without malice. There was no moral judgment involved; a fact was a fact.

Mrs. Owens and Frau Tuttlingen looked up as if her appearance were a heaven-sent diversion. Their conversation—what existed of it—had become hopelessly single-tracked. Dr. Tuttlingen was emigrating to the United States in the autumn, and wanted as much information as Mrs. Owens could provide. At the beginning, she had been pleased, racking her memory for production and population figures, eager to describe her country, its civil and social institutions. But that was not the kind of information Dr. Tuttlingen was after.

"How much do you get for a gram of gold in America?" he said, interrupting her.

"Goodness, I don't know," Mrs. Owens said, flustered.

"You mean you don't know what you would get for, say, a plain unworked link bracelet of twenty-two-karat gold, weighing, in all, fifty grams?" It was incredible that she, a citizen, should not know such things.

During these interrogations, Frau Tuttlingen, whose first name was Heidemarie, combed her long straw-colored hair and gazed, bored, out to sea. She was much younger than Dr. Tuttlingen. "America," she sometimes remarked sadly, as if the name held for her a meaning unconnected with plain link bracelets and grams of gold. She would turn and look at Dr. Tuttlingen. It was a long look, full of reproach.

"As far as I am concerned, the Tuttlingens hold no mystery," Mrs. Parsters had told Mrs. Owens one morning shortly after Mrs. Owens's arrival. "Do you know why she gives him those long melting looks? It's because they aren't married, that's why." Mrs. Parsters, who had never bestowed on anyone, including the late Mr. Parsters, a look that could even remotely be called melting, had sniffed with scorn. "Look at that," she had said, gesturing toward the sea. "Is that the behavior of a married couple?" It was morning; the water had not yet acquired its midday consistency of soup. Dr. Tuttlingen and Heidemarie stood ankle-deep. He held her by the waist and seemed to be saying, "Come, you see, it's not dangerous at all!" When Dr. Tuttlingen was not about, Heidemarie managed to swim adequately by herself, even venturing out quite far. On that occasion, however, she squealed and flung her arms around his neck as a warm, salty ripple broke against them on its way to shore. Dr. Tuttlingen led her tenderly back to the beach. "Of course they're not married," said Mrs. Parsters. "It fairly *shouts!* Damned old goat! But age has nothing to do with it."

Their suspect condition did not, it appeared, render them socially impossible. Mrs. Parsters had lived in this tiny English pocket of Spain much too long to be taken aback; over the years, any number of people had turned up in all manner of situations. Often she sat with the Tuttlingens, asking clever leading questions, trying to force them into an equivocal statement, while Mrs. Owens, who considered immorality sacred, blushed.

Mrs. Parsters now drew up a wicker chair and sat down facing Heidemarie. She inspected, as if from a height, the left side of the pavilion, where it was customary for the French tourists to gather. Usually, they chattered like agitated seagulls. They sat close to the railings, the better to harass their young, drank Spanish wine (shuddering and making faces and all but spitting it out), and spent an animated but refreshing holiday reading the Paris papers and comparing their weekly *pension* bills. But this afternoon the heat had felled them. Mrs. Parsters sniffed and said faintly, "Bus conductors." She held the belief that everyone in France, male or female, earned a living driving some kind of vehicle. She had lived in Spain for twenty years, and during the Civil War had refused to be interned, evacuated, or deported, but after everything was over, she had made a brief foray over the Pyrenees, in search of tea and other comforts. Traffic in Spain was nearly at a halt, and she had returned with the impression that everything in France was racing about on wheels. Now, dismissing the French, who could only be put down to one of God's most baffling whims, she turned her gaze to the right, where the English sat, working crossword puzzles. They were a come-lately lot, she thought, a frightening symptom of what her country had become while her back was turned.

"You might just order me a bottle of mineral water," she said to Dr. Tuttlingen, and he did so at once.

It was unusual for Mrs. Parsters to favor them with a visit at this hour. Usually she spent the hour or so before lunch in a special corner of the pavilion, playing fierce bridge with a group of cronies, all of whom looked oddly alike. Their beach hats sat level with their eyebrows, and the smoke of their black-market cigarettes from Gibraltar made them squint as they contemplated their hands. Although they spoke of married sons and of nephews involved in distinguished London careers, their immediate affections were expended on yappy little beasts like Mrs. Parsters's Bobby who prowled around the bridge table begging for the sugar lodged at the bottom of the gin-and-lime glasses. It was because of the dogs, newcomers were told, that these ladies lived in Spain. They had left England years before because of the climate, had prolonged their absence because of the war, of

Labour, of the income tax; now, released from at least two of these excuses, they remembered their dogs and vowed never to return to the British Isles until the brutal six-month quarantine law was altered or removed. The ladies were not about this afternoon; they were organizing a bazaar—a periodic vestigial activity that served no purpose other than the perpetuation of a remembered rite and that bore no relation whatsoever to their life in Spain. Flowers would be donated, knitted mufflers offered and, astoundingly, sold.

Mrs. Parsters sipped her mineral water and sighed; this life, with its routine and quiet pleasures, would soon be behind her. She was attached to this English beachhead; here she had survived a husband, two dogs, and a war. But, as she said, she had been away too long. "It's either go back now or never," she had told Mrs. Owens. "If I wait until I'm really old, I shall be like those wretched Anglo-Indians who end their days poking miserably about some muddy country garden, complaining and catching bronchitis. Besides, I've seen too much here. I've seen too many friends come and go." She did not mention the fact that her decision had been greatly facilitated by the death of a cousin who had left her a house and a small but useful income. Her chief problem in England, she had been told, would be finding a housemaid. Mrs. Parsters, anticipating this, had persuaded Carmen, her adolescent Spanish cook, to undertake the journey with her. Not only had Mrs. Parsters persuaded Carmen's parents to let her go but she had wangled for her charge a passport and exit visa, had paid the necessary deposit to the Spanish government, and had guaranteed Carmen's support to the satisfaction of Her Majesty's immigration officials. That done, prepared to relax, Mrs. Parsters discovered that Carmen was wavering. Sometimes Carmen felt unable to part with her mother; again it was her fiancé. This morning, she had wept in the kitchen and said she could not leave Spain without three large pots of begonias she had raised from cuttings. Mrs. Parsters began to suspect that her spadework had been for nothing.

"Life is one sacrifice after another," she said now, imagining that Carmen, and not Heidemarie, sat before her.

"That is true," said Heidemarie. She looked sadly at Dr. Tuttlingen and said, as she so often did, "America."

He's not taking you, Mrs. Parsters thought, watching Heidemarie. The words flashed into her head, just like that. Past events had proved her intuitions almost infallible. You're not married, and he's not taking you to America. Mrs. Parsters began to drum on the table, thinking.

Beside her, Dr. Tuttlingen was pursuing his investigation of the American way of life. "What is the cost in America of a pure-white diamond weighing four hundred milligrams?" He looked straight into Mrs. Owens's eyes and brought out each word with pedantic care.

"Well, really, that's something I just don't know," Mrs. Owens said, gazing helplessly around.

"I have a nephew in South Africa," said Mrs. Parsters. "He would know."

Dr. Tuttlingen was not at all interested in South Africa. Annoyed at being interrupted, he said, with heavy, sarcastic interest, "Cigarettes are cheap in South Africa, yes?"—a remark intended to put Mrs. Parsters in her place.

"*Very* expensive," said Mrs. Parsters, drinking mineral water as if the last word on emigration had now been uttered.

Dr. Tuttlingen turned back to his cicerone, relentless. "What is the cost in America of one hundred pounds of roasted coffee beans?"

In her distraction, Mrs. Owens forgot how to multiply by one hundred. "Oh dear," she said. "Just let me think."

"I know a place where one can have tea for five pesetas," said Mrs. Parsters.

"Goodness! Where?" cried Mrs. Owens, grateful for the change of subject.

"Unavailable today, I'm afraid. It's being done up for the bazaar. It is run by a girl from Glasgow, for holders of British passports only." She added, graciously, "I believe that she will accept Americans."

"What do you get with this tea?" said Dr. Tuttlingen, suspicious but not noticeably offended.

"Tea," said Mrs. Parsters, "with a choice of toast or biscuits."

Dr. Tuttlingen looked as if he would not have taken the tea, or the talisman passport, as a gift. "I am going to swim now," he announced, rising and patting his stomach. "Hot or cold, rain or shine, exercise before a meal is good for the health." He trotted down to the sea, elbows tucked in.

The three women watched him go. Mrs. Owens relaxed. Heidemarie began to comb her hair. She opened a large beach bag of cracked patent leather and drew from it a lipstick and glass. With delicate attention, she gave herself a lilac mouth. She bit the edge of a long red nail and looked at it, mournfully.

"What a pretty shade," Mrs. Parsters said.

"He doesn't want to take me to America," said Heidemarie. "He said it on the eleventh of July, on the thirteenth of July, and again this morning."

"He doesn't, eh?" Mrs. Parsters sounded neither triumphant nor surprised. "You haven't managed it very cleverly, have you?"

"No," admitted Heidemarie. She reached down and picked up Bobby and held him on her lap. Her round pink face struggled, as if in the grip of an intolerable emotion. The others waited. At last it came. "I like dogs so much," she said.

"*Do* you?" said Mrs. Parsters. "Bobby, of course, is particularly likable. There are a great many dogs in England."

"I like dogs," said Heidemarie again, hugging Bobby. "And all the animals. I like horses. A horse is intelligent. A horse has some heart. I mean a horse will try to understand."

"In terms of character, no man is the slightest match for a horse," Mrs. Parsters agreed.

Mrs. Owens, trying hard to follow the strange rabbit paths of this dialogue, turned almost involuntarily at the mention of horses and stared at the bar. Sometimes a half door behind the bar would swing open, revealing an old, whiskery horse belonging to one of the waiters. The horse would gaze at them all, bemused and kindly, greeted from the French side of the pavilion with enthusiastic seagull cries of *"Tiens! Tiens! Bonjour, mon coco!"*

Heidemarie released Bobby. She looked as if she might cry.

"Now, then," said Mrs. Parsters, drawing toward herself Dr. Tuttlingen's empty chair. "You won't help yourself by weeping and mewing. Come and sit here." Obediently, Heidemarie moved over. "You must not take these things so seriously," Mrs. Parsters went on. "Time heals everything. Look at Mrs. Owens."

Mrs. Owens took a deep breath, deciding the time had come to explain, once and for all, that she was not divorced. But, as so frequently happened, by the time she had formulated the sentence, the conversation had moved along.

"I wanted to see New York," said Heidemarie, drooping.

"Perfectly commendable," said Mrs. Parsters.

"*He* says I'm better off in Stuttgart."

"Oh, he does, does he?" Mrs. Parsters turned to look at the sea, where Dr. Tuttlingen, flat on his back, was thrashing briskly away from shore. "The impudence! I'd like to hear him say that to *me*. You want to give that man a surprise. Make a plan of your own. Show him how independent you are."

"Yes," said Heidemarie, biting the lilac tip of the straw in her glass. After a moment, she added, "But I am not."

"Nonsense," said Mrs. Parsters. "Don't let me hear such words. Was it for this that foolish women chained themselves to lampposts? Snap your fingers in his face. Tell him you can take care of yourself. Tell him you can work."

Heidemarie repeated "work" with such melancholy that Mrs. Owens was touched. She tried to recall what accomplishments one could expect from a young, unmarried person of Heidemarie's disposition, summoning and dismissing images of her as an airline hostess, a kindergarten teacher, and a smiling receptionist. "Can you type?" she asked, wishing to be helpful.

"No, Heidemarie doesn't type," said Mrs. Parsters, answering for her. "But I'm certain she can do other things. I'm positive that Heidemarie can cook, and keep house, and market far more economically than my ungrateful Carmen!" Heidemarie nodded, gloomy, at this iteming of her gifts. "My ungrateful Carmen," said Mrs. Parsters, pursuing her own indomitable line of thought. "I said to her this morning, 'It isn't so much a cook I require as an intelligent assistant, with just enough maturity to make her reliable.' A few light duties," Mrs. Parsters said, looking dreamily out to sea. Suddenly, she seemed to remember they had been discussing Heidemarie. "I have only one piece of advice for you, my dear, and that is leave him before he leaves you. Show him you have a plan of your own."

"I haven't," said Heidemarie.

"I might just think of something," said Mrs. Parsters, with a smile.

"We all might," said Mrs. Owens kindly. "I might think of something, too." She wondered why this innocent offer should cause Mrs. Parsters to look so exasperated.

Farther along the beach, Dr. Tuttlingen was pursuing his daily course of exercise, trotting up and down the sands under the blazing sun. He looked determined and inestimably pleased with himself. He trotted over to the pavilion, climbed the steps, and drew up to them, panting. "I forgot to ask you," he said to Mrs. Owens, who at once looked apprehensive. "What is the average income tax paid by a doctor in a medium-sized city in America?"

"I don't know," said Mrs. Owens. "I mean it's not the sort of thing you ask—"

"I expect it's a great deal," said Mrs. Parsters.

Dr. Tuttlingen began to hop, first on one foot, then on the other. "Water in the ears," he explained. He seemed happy. He sat down and pinched Heidemarie above the elbow. "As long as we don't have to pay too much, eh?" he said.

"I don't understand the 'we,' " said Heidemarie, morose. "On July the eleventh, and again on July the thirteenth, and again this morning—"

"Ah," said the Doctor, obviously enjoying this. "That was a joke. Do you think I would leave you all alone in Stuttgart, with all the Americans?"

From the top of the cliff came the quavering note of the luncheon gong at Villa Margate, followed by the clapper bell of the *pension* next door. On both sides of the pavilion there was a stir, like the wind.

"Oh, well," said Mrs. Parsters, watching the beach colony leave like a file of ants. She looked moody. Mrs. Owens wondered why.

"Good-bye, everyone," said Heidemarie. Her whole demeanor had changed; she looked at Mrs. Owens and Mrs. Parsters as if she felt sorry for them.

"Life—" began Mrs. Parsters. "Oh, the hell with it." She said to Mrs. Owens, "And I expect that you, too, have some concrete plan?"

"Oh, dear, no," said Mrs. Owens, distracted, beckoning to her child. "I'm just waiting here for my husband. He's in Gibraltar on business. The fact is, you know, I'm not really divorced, or anything like that. I'm just waiting here. He's going to pick me up."

"I rather expected that," said Mrs. Parsters, cheering up. One of her guesses, at least, had been nearly right. "Just so long as he doesn't forget you, my dear."

Waiters walked about, listless, collecting glasses, pocketing tips. Nothing moved between the pavilion and the sea. Mrs. Parsters, Bobby, Mrs. Owens, and her child plowed through sand on their way to the steps that led up from the beach.

WHEN WE
WERE NEARLY YOUNG

❧

*I*n Madrid, nine years ago, we lived on the thought of money. Our friendships were nourished with talk of money we expected to have, and what we intended to do when it came. There were four of us—two men and two girls. The men, Pablo and Carlos, were cousins. Pilar was a relation of theirs. I was not Spanish and not a relation, and a friend almost by mistake. The thing we had in common was that we were all waiting for money.

Every day I went to the Central Post Office, and I made the rounds of the banks and the travel agencies, where letters and money could come. I was not certain how much it might be, or where it was going to arrive, but I saw it riding down a long arc like a rainbow. In those days I was always looking for signs. I saw signs in cigarette smoke, in the way ash fell, and in the cards. I laid the cards out three times a week, on Monday, Wednesday, and Friday. Tuesday, Thursday, and Saturday were no good, because the cards were mute or evasive; and on Sundays they lied. I thought these signs—the ash, the smoke, and so on—would tell me what direction my life was going to take and what might happen from now on. I had unbounded belief in free will, which most of the people I knew despised, but I was superstitious, too. I saw inside my eyelids at night the nine of clubs, which is an excellent card, and the ten of hearts, which is better, morally speaking, since it implies gain through effort. I saw the aces of clubs and diamonds, and the jack of diamonds, who is the postman. Although Pablo and Pilar and Carlos were not waiting for anything in particular—indeed, had nothing to wait for, except a fortune—they were anxious about the postman, and relieved when he turned up. They never supposed that the postman would not arrive, or that his coming might have no significance.

Carlos and Pablo came from a town outside Madrid. They had no near relatives in the city, and they shared a room in a flat on Calle Hortaleza. I lived in a room along the hall; that was how we came to know one another. Pilar, who was twenty-two, the youngest of the four of us, lived in a small flat on her own. She had been married to Carlos's stepbrother at seventeen, and had been a widow three years. She was eager to marry again, but feared she was already too old. Carlos was twenty-nine, the oldest. Pablo and I came in between.

Carlos worked in a bank. His salary was so small that he could barely subsist on it, and he was everywhere in debt. Pablo studied law at the University of Madrid. When he had nothing to do, he went with me on my rounds. These rounds took up most of the day, and had become important, for, after a time, the fact of waiting became more valid than the thing I was waiting for. I knew that I would feel let down when the waiting was over. I went to the post office, to three or four banks, to Cook's, and American Express. At each place, I stood and waited in a queue. I have never seen so many queues, or so many patient people. I also gave time and thought to selling my clothes. I sold them to the gypsies in the flea market. Once I got a dollar-fifty for a coat and a skirt, but it was stolen from my pocket when I stopped to buy a newspaper. I thought I had jostled the thief, and when I said "Sorry" he nodded his head and walked quickly away. He was a man of about thirty. I can still see his turned-up collar and the back of his head. When I put my hand in my pocket to pay for the paper, the money was gone. When I was not standing in queues or getting rid of clothes, I went to see Pilar. We sat out on her balcony when it was fine, and next to her kitchen stove when it was cold. We were not ashamed to go to the confectioner's across the street and bargain in fractions of pennies for fifty grams of chocolate, which we scrupulously shared. Pilar was idle, but restful. Pablo was idle, but heavy about it. He was the most heavily idle person I have ever known. He was also the only one of us who had any money. His father sent him money for his room and his meals, and he had an extra allowance from his godfather, who owned a hotel on one of the coasts. Pablo was dark, curly-haired, and stocky, with the large head and opaque eyes you saw on the streets of Madrid. He was one of the New Spaniards—part of the first generation grown to maturity under Franco. He was the generation they were so proud of in the newspapers. But he must be—he *is*—well over thirty now, and no longer New. He had already calculated, with paper and pencil, what the future held, and decided it was worth only half a try.

We stood in endless queues together in banks, avoiding the bank where Carlos worked, because we were afraid of giggling and embarrassing him. We shelled peanuts and gossiped and held hands in the blank, amiable waiting state that had become the essence of life. When we had heard the ritual "No" everywhere, we went home.

Home was a dark, long flat filled with the sound of clocks and dripping faucets. It was a *pension*, of a sort, but secret. In order to escape paying taxes, the owners had never declared it to the police, and lived in perpetual dread. A girl had given me the address on a train, warning me to say nothing about it to anyone. There was one other foreign person—a crazy old Englishwoman. She never spoke a word to me and, I think, hated me on sight. But she did not like Spaniards any better; one could hear her saying so when she talked to herself. At first we were given meals, but after a time, because the proprietors were afraid about the licensing and the police, that stopped, and so we bought food and took it to Pilar's, or cooked in my room on an alcohol stove. We ate rationed bread with lumps of flour under the crust, and horrible ersatz jam. We were always vaguely hungry. Our craving for sweet things was limitless; we bought cardboard pastries that seemed exquisite because of the lingering sugary taste they left in the mouth. Sometimes we went to a restaurant we called "the ten-peseta place" because you could get a three-course meal with wine and bread for ten pesetas—about twenty-three cents then. There was also the twelve-peseta place, where the smell was less nauseating, although the food was nearly as rank. The décor in both restaurants was distinctly un-European. The cheaper the restaurant, the more cheaply Oriental it became. I remember being served calves' brains in an open skull.

One of the customers in the ten-peseta restaurant was a true madman, with claw hands, sparse hair, and dying skin. He looked like a monkey, and behaved like one I had known, who would accept grapes and bananas with pleasure, and then, shrieking with hate at some shadowy insult, would dance and gibber and try to bite. This man would not eat from his plate. He was beyond even saying the plate was poisoned; that had been settled long ago. He shoveled his food onto the table, or onto pieces of bread, and scratched his head with his fork, turning and muttering with smiles and scowls. Everyone sat still when he had his seizures—not in horror, even less with compassion, but still, suspended. I remember a coarse-faced sergeant slowly lowering his knife and fork and parting his heavy lips as he stared; and I remember the blankness in the room—the waiting. What will happen next?

What does it mean? The atmosphere was full of cold, secret marveling. But nobody moved or spoke.

We often came away depressed, saying that it was cheaper and pleasanter to eat at home; but the stove was slow, and we were often too hungry to linger, watching water come to the boil. But food was cheap enough; once, by returning three empty Valdepeñas wine bottles, I bought enough food for three. We ate a lot of onions and potatoes—things like that. Pilar lived on sweet things. I have seen her cook macaroni and sprinkle sugar on it and eat it up. She was a pretty girl, with a pointed face and blue-black hair. But she was an untidy, a dusty sort of girl, and you felt that in a few years something might go wrong; she might get swollen ankles or grow a mustache.

Her flat had two rooms, one of which was rented to a young couple. The other room she divided with a curtain. Behind the curtain was the bed she had brought as part of her dowry for the marriage with Carlos's stepbrother. There was a picture of María Felix, the Mexican actress, on the wall. I would like to tell a story about Pilar, but nobody will believe it. It is how she thought, or pretended to think, that the Museo Romantico was her home. This was an extraordinary museum—a set of rooms furnished with all the trappings of the romantic period. Someone had planned it with love and care, but hardly any visitors came. If any did wander in when we were around, we stared them out. The cousins played the game with Pilar because they had no money and nothing better to do. I see Pilar sitting in an armchair, being elegant, and the boys standing or lounging against a mantelpiece; I say "boys" because I never thought of them as men. I am by the window, with my back turned. I disapprove, and it shows. I feel like a prig. I tip the painted blind, just to see the street and be reassured by a tram going by. It *is* the twentieth century. And Pilar cries, in unaffected anguish, "Oh, make her stop. She is spoiling everything."

I can hear myself saying grandly, "I don't want your silly fairy tales. I'm trying to get rid of my own."

Carlos says, "I've known people like you before. You think you can get rid of all the baggage—religion, politics, ideas, everything. Well, you won't."

The other two yawn, quite rightly. Carlos and I are bores.

Of them all, I understood Carlos best, but we quarreled about anything. We could have quarreled about a piece of string. He was pessimistic, and I detested this temperament; worse, I detested his face. He resembled a certain kind of Swiss or South African or New Zealander. He was suspicious and faintly Anglo-Saxon-looking. It was not the English bun-face, or the Swiss canary, or the lizard, or the hawk; it was the unfinished, the undecided face that accompanies the rotary sprinkler, the wet martini, pussyfooting in love and friendship, expense-account foolery, the fear of the open heart. He made me think of a lawyer who had once told me, in all sincerity, "Bad things don't happen to nice people." It was certainly not Carlos's fault; I might have helped my prejudices, which I had dragged to Spain with my passport, but he could not help the way he looked. Pablo was stupid, but cheerful. Pilar was demented, but sweet. What was needed—we agreed to this many times—was a person who was a composite of all our best qualities, which we were not too modest to name. Home from the Romantic Museum, they made me turn out the cards. I did the Petit Jeu, the Square, the Fan, and the Thirteen, and the Fifteen. There was happy news for everyone except Carlos, but, as it was Sunday, none of it counted.

Were they typical Spaniards? I don't know what a typical Spaniard is. They didn't dance or play the guitar. Truth and death and pyromania did not lurk in their dark eyes; at least I never saw it. They were grindingly hard up. The difference between them and any three broke people anywhere else was in a certain passiveness, as though everything had been dealt in advance. Barring catastrophe, death, and revolution, nothing could happen anymore. When we walked together, their steps slowed in rhythm, as if they had all three been struck with the same reluctance to go on. But they did go on, laughing and chattering and saying what they would do when the money came.

We began keeping diaries at about the same time. I don't remember who started it. Carlos's was secret. Pilar asked how to spell words. Pablo told everything before he wrote it down. It was a strange occupation, considering the ages we were, but we hadn't enough to think about. Poverty is not a goad but a paralysis. I have never been back to Madrid. My memories are of squares and monuments, of things that are free or cheap. I see us huddled in coats, gloved and scarfed, fighting the icy wind, pushing along to the ten-peseta place. In another memory it is so hot that we can scarcely force ourselves to the park, where we will sit under elm trees and look at newspapers. Newspapers are the solace of the worried; one absorbs them without having to read. I sometimes went to the libraries—the British Institute, and the American one—but I could not for the life of me have put my nose in a book. The very sight of poetry made me sick, and I could not make sense of a novel, or even remember the characters' names.

Oddly enough, we were not afraid. What was the worst that could happen? No one seemed to know. The only fear I remember was an anxiety we had caught from Carlos. He had rounded twenty-nine and saw down a corridor we had not yet reached. He made us so afraid of being thirty that even poor Pilar was alarmed, although she had eight years of grace. I was frightened of it, too. I was not by any means in first youth, and I could not say that the shape of my life was a mystery. But I felt I had done all I could with free will, and that circumstances, the imponderables, should now take a hand. I was giving them every opportunity. I was in a city where I knew not a soul, save the few I had come to know by chance. It was a city where the mentality, the sound of the language, the hopes and possibilities, even the appearance of the people in the streets, were as strange as anything I might have invented. My choice in coming here had been deliberate: I had a plan. My own character seemed to me ill-defined; I believed that this was unfortunate and unique. I thought that if I set myself against a background into which I could not possibly merge, some outline would present itself. But it hadn't succeeded, because I adapted too quickly. In no time at all, I had the speech and the movements and the very expression on my face of seedy Madrid.

I was with Pablo more than anyone, but I remember Carlos best. I regret now how much we quarreled. I think of the timorous, the symbolic, stalemate of our chess games. I was not clever enough to beat him, but he was not brave enough to win. The slowing down of our respective positions on the board led to immobility of thought. I sat nervously smoking, and Carlos sat with his head in his hands. Thought suspended, fear emerged. Carlos's terror that he would soon be thirty and that the effective part of his life had ended with so little to show haunted him and stunned his mind. He would never be anything but the person he was now. I remember the dim light, the racket in the street, the silence inside the flat, the ticking of the Roman-numbered clock in the hall. Time was like water dropping— Madrid time. And I would catch his fear, and I was afraid of the movement of time, at once too quick and too slow. After that came a revolt and impatience. In his company I felt something I had never felt before—actively northern. Seeing him passive, head on hands, I wanted to urge and exhort and beg him to do something: act, talk, sing, dance, finish the game of chess—anything at all. At no period was I as conscious of the movement and meaning of time; and I had chosen the very city where time dropped, a drop from the roof of a cave, one drop at a time.

We came to a financial crisis at about the same moment. Pablo's godfather stopped sending money to him—that was a blow. Pilar's lodgers left. I had nothing more to sell. There was Carlos's little salary, but there were also his debts, and he could not be expected to help his friends. He looked more vaguely Anglo-Saxon, more unfinished and decent than ever. I wished there was something to kick over, something to fight. There was the Spanish situation, of course, and I had certainly given a lot of thought to it before coming to Spain, but now that I was here and down-and-out I scarcely noticed it. I would think, "*I* am free," but what of it? I was also hungry. I dreamed of food. Pilar dreamed of things chasing her, and Pablo dreamed of me, and Carlos dreamed he was on top of a mountain preaching to multitudes, but I dreamed of baked ham and Madeira sauce. I suspected that my being here and in this situation was all folly, and that I had been trying to improve myself—my moral condition, that is. My financial condition spoke for itself. It was like Orwell, in Paris, reveling in his bedbugs. If that was so, then it was all very plain, and very Protestant, but I could not say more for it than that.

One day I laid out forty-eight cards—the Grand Jeu. The cards predicted treachery, ruin, illness, accidents, letters bringing bad news, disaster, and pain.

I made my rounds. In one of the places, the money had come, and I was saved. I went out to the university, where the fighting had been, eleven or twelve years before. It looked like a raw suburban housing development, with its mud, its white buildings and puny trees. I waited in the café where Pablo took his bitter coffee, and when he came in I told him the news. We rode into the heart of Madrid on a swaying tram. Pablo was silent—I thought because he was delighted and overwhelmed; actually, he must have been digesting the astonishing fact that I had been expecting something and that my hanging around in banks was not a harmless mania, like Pilar in the Romantic Museum.

My conception of life (free will plus imponderables) seemed justified again. The imponderables were in my pocket, and free will began to roll. I decided, during the tram ride, to go to Mallorca, hire a villa, invite the three for a long holiday, and buy a dog I had seen. We got down from the tram and bought white, tender, delicious, unrationed bread, weighed out by the pound; and three roasted chickens, plus a pound of sweet butter and two three-liter bottles of white Valdepeñas. We bought some nougat and chestnut paste. I forget the rest.

Toward the end of our dinner, and before the end of the wine, Carlos made one bitter remark: "The difference between you and us is that in the end something will always come for you. Nothing will ever come from anywhere for any of us. You must have known it all along."

No one likes to be accused of posturing. I was as irritated as I could be, and quickly turned the remark to his discredit. He was displaying self-pity. Self-pity was the core of his character. It was in the cards; all I could ever turn out for him were plaintive combinations of twos and threes—an abject fear of anonymous threats, and worry that his friends would betray him. This attack silenced him, but it showed that my character was in no way improved by my misfortunes. I defended myself against the charge of pretending. My existence had been poised on waiting, and I had always said I was waiting for something tangible. But they had thought I was waiting in their sense of the word—waiting for summer and then for winter, for Monday and then for Tuesday, waiting, waiting for time to drop into the pool.

We did not talk about what we could do with money now. I was thinking about Mallorca. I knew that if I invited them they would never come. They were polite. They understood that my new fortune cast me out. There was no evasion, but they were nice about it. They had no plans, and simply closed their ranks. We talked of a longer future, remembering Carlos and his fear. We talked of our thirties as if we were sliding toward an icy subterranean water; as if we were to be submerged and frozen just as we were: first Carlos, then Pablo and me, finally little Pilar. She had eight years to wait, but eight would be seven, and seven six, and she knew it.

I don't know what became of them, or what they were like when their thirtieth year came. I left Madrid. I wrote, for a time, but they never answered. Eventually they were caught, for me, not by time but by the freezing of memory. And when I looked in the diary I had kept during that period, all I could find was descriptions of the weather.

THE ICE WAGON GOING
DOWN THE STREET

―――――

❧

*N*ow that they are out of world affairs and back where they started, Peter Frazier's wife says, "Everybody else did well in the international thing except us."

"You have to be crooked," he tells her.

"Or smart. Pity we weren't."

It is Sunday morning. They sit in the kitchen, drinking their coffee, slowly, remembering the past. They say the names of people as if they were magic. Peter thinks, Agnes Brusen, but there are hundreds of other names. As a private married joke, Peter and Sheilah wear the silk dressing gowns they bought in Hong Kong. Each thinks the other a peacock, rather splendid, but they pretend the dressing gowns are silly and worn in fun.

Peter and Sheilah and their two daughters, Sandra and Jennifer, are visiting Peter's unmarried sister, Lucille. They have been Lucille's guests seventeen weeks, ever since they returned to Toronto from the Far East. Their big old steamer trunk blocks a corner of the kitchen, making a problem of the refrigerator door; but even Lucille says the trunk may as well stay where it is, for the present. The Fraziers' future is so unsettled; everything is still in the air.

Lucille has given her bedroom to her two nieces, and sleeps on a camp cot in the hall. The parents have the living-room divan. They have no privileges here; they sleep after Lucille has seen the last television show that interests her. In the hall closet their clothes are crushed by winter overcoats. They know they are being judged for the first time. Sandra and Jennifer are waiting for Sheilah and Peter to decide. They are waiting to learn where these exotic parents will fly to next. What sort of climate will Sheilah consider? What job will Peter consent to accept? When the parents are ready, the children will make a decision of their own. It is just possible that Sandra and Jennifer will choose to stay with their aunt.

The peacock parents are watched by wrens. Lucille and her nieces are much the same—sandy-colored, proudly plain. Neither of the girls has the father's insouciance or the mother's appearance—her height, her carriage, her thick hair and sky-blue eyes. The children are more cautious than their parents; more Canadian. When they saw their aunt's apartment they had been away from Canada nine years, ever since they were two and four; and Jennifer, the elder, said, "Well, now we're home." Her voice is nasal and flat. Where did she learn that voice? And why should this be home? Peter's answer to anything about his mystifying children is, "It must be in the blood."

On Sunday morning Lucille takes her nieces to church. It seems to be the only condition she imposes on her relations: The children must be decent. The girls go willingly, with their new hats and purses and gloves and coral bracelets and strings of pearls. The parents, ramshackle, sleepy, dim in the brain because it is Sunday, sit down to their coffee and privacy and talk of the past.

"We weren't crooked," says Peter. "We weren't even smart."

Sheilah's head bobs up; she is no drowner. It is wrong to say they have nothing to show for time. Sheilah has the Balenciaga. It is a black afternoon dress, stiff and boned at the waist, long for the fashions of now, but neither Sheilah nor Peter would change a thread. The Balenciaga is their talisman, their treasure; and after they remember it they touch hands and think that the years are not behind them but hazy and marvelous and still to be lived.

The first place they went to was Paris. In the early fifties the pick of the international jobs was there. Peter had inherited the last scrap of money he knew he was ever likely to see, and it was enough to get them over: Sheilah and Peter and the babies and the steamer trunk. To their joy and astonishment they had money in the bank. They said to each other, "It should last a year." Peter was fastidious about the new job; he hadn't come all this distance to accept just anything. In Paris he met Hugh Taylor, who was earning enough smuggling gasoline to keep his wife in Paris and a girl in Rome. That impressed Peter, because he remembered Taylor as a sour scholarship student without the slightest talent for life. Taylor had a job, of course. He hadn't said to himself, I'll go over to Europe and smuggle gasoline. It gave Peter an idea; he saw the shape of things. First you catch your fish. Later, at an international party, he met Johnny Hertzberg, who told him Germany was the place. Hertzberg said that anyone who came out of Germany broke now was too stupid to be here, and deserved to be back home at a desk. Peter nodded, as if he had already thought of that. He began to think about Germany. Paris was fine for a holiday, but it had been picked clean. Yes, Germany. His money was running low. He thought about Germany quite a lot.

That winter was moist and delicate; so fragile that they daren't speak of it now. There seemed to be plenty of everything and plenty of time. They were living the dream of a marriage, the fabric uncut, nothing slashed or spoiled. All winter they spent their money, and went to parties, and talked about Peter's future job. It lasted four months. They spent their money, lived in the future, and were never as happy again.

After four months they were suddenly moved away from Paris, but not to Germany—to Geneva. Peter thinks it was because of the incident at the Trudeau wedding at the Ritz. Paul Trudeau was a French-Canadian Peter had known at school and in the Navy. Trudeau had turned into a snob, proud of his career and his Paris connections. He tried to make the difference felt, but Peter thought the difference was only for strangers. At the wedding reception Peter lay down on the floor and said he was dead. He held a white azalea in a brass pot on his chest, and sang, "Oh, hear us when we cry to Thee for those in peril on the sea." Sheilah bent over him and said, "Peter, darling, get up. Pete, listen, every single person who can do something for you is in this room. If you love me, you'll get up."

"I do love you," he said, ready to engage in a serious conversation. "She's so beautiful," he told a second face. "She's nearly as tall as I am. She was a model in London. I met her over in London in the war. I met her there in the war." He lay on his back with the azalea on his chest, explaining their history. A waiter took the brass pot away, and after Peter had been hauled to his feet he knocked the waiter down. Trudeau's bride, who was freshly out of an Ursuline convent, became hysterical; and even though Paul Trudeau and Peter were old acquaintances, Trudeau never spoke to him again. Peter says now that French-Canadians always have that bit of spite. He says Trudeau asked the embassy to interfere. Luckily, back home there were still a few people to whom the name "Frazier" meant something, and it was to these people that Peter appealed. He wrote letters saying that a French-Canadian combine was preventing his getting a decent job, and could anything be done? No one answered directly, but it was clear that

what they settled for was exile to Geneva: a season of meditation and remorse, as he explained to Sheilah, and it was managed tactfully, through Lucille. Lucille wrote that a friend of hers, May Fergus, now a secretary in
Geneva, had heard about a job. The job was filing pictures in the information service of an international agency in the Palais des Nations. The pay
was so-so, but Lucille thought Peter must be getting fed up doing nothing.

Peter often asks his sister now who put her up to it—what important
person told her to write that letter suggesting Peter go to Geneva?

"Nobody," says Lucille. "I mean, nobody in the way *you* mean. I really
did have this girl friend working there, and I knew you must be running
through your money pretty fast in Paris."

"It must have been somebody pretty high up," Peter says. He looks at his
sister admiringly, as he has often looked at his wife.

Peter's wife had loved him in Paris. Whatever she wanted in marriage she
found that winter, there. In Geneva, where Peter was a file clerk and they
lived in a furnished flat, she pretended they were in Paris and life was still
the same. Often, when the children were at supper, she changed as though
she and Peter were dining out. She wore the Balenciaga, and put candles on
the card table where she and Peter ate their meal. The neckline of the dress
was soiled with makeup. Peter remembers her dabbing on the makeup with
a wet sponge. He remembers her in the kitchen, in the soiled Balenciaga,
patting on the makeup with a filthy sponge. Behind her, at the kitchen table,
Sandra and Jennifer, in buttonless pajamas and bunny slippers, ate their supper of marmalade sandwiches and milk. When the children were asleep, the
parents dined solemnly, ritually, Sheilah sitting straight as a queen.

It was a mysterious period of exile, and he had to wait for signs, or signals, to know when he was free to leave. He never saw the job any other way.
He forgot he had applied for it. He thought he had been sent to Geneva because of a misdemeanor and had to wait to be released. Nobody pressed him
at work. His immediate boss had resigned, and he was alone for months in
a room with two desks. He read the *Herald Tribune,* and tried to discover how
things were here—how the others ran their lives on the pay they were officially getting. But it was a closed conspiracy. He was not dealing with adventurers now but civil servants waiting for pension day. No one ever
answered his questions. They pretended to think his questions were a form
of wit. His only solace in exile was the few happy weekends he had in the

late spring and early summer. He had met another old acquaintance, Mike Burleigh. Mike was a serious liberal who had married a serious heiress. The Burleighs had two guest lists. The first was composed of stuffy people they felt obliged to entertain, while the second was made up of their real friends, the friends they wanted. The real friends strove hard to become stuffy and dull and thus achieve the first guest list, but few succeeded. Peter went on the first list straightaway. Possibly Mike didn't understand, at the beginning, why Peter was pretending to be a file clerk. Peter had such an air—he might have been sent by a universal inspector to see how things in Geneva were being run.

Every Friday in May and June and part of July, the Fraziers rented a sky-blue Fiat and drove forty miles east of Geneva to the Burleighs' summer house. They brought the children, a suitcase, the children's tattered picture books, and a token bottle of gin. This, in memory, is a period of water and water birds; swans, roses, and singing birds. The children were small and still belonged to them. If they remember too much, their mouths water, their stomachs hurt. Peter says, "It was fine while it lasted." Enough. While it lasted Sheilah and Madge Burleigh were close. They abandoned their husbands and spent long summer afternoons comparing their mothers and praising each other's skin and hair. To Madge, and not to Peter, Sheilah opened her Liverpool childhood with the words "rat poor." Peter heard about it later, from Mike. The women's friendship seemed to Peter a bad beginning. He trusted women but not with each other. It lasted ten weeks. One Sunday, Madge said she needed the two bedrooms the Fraziers usually occupied for a party of sociologists from Pakistan, and that was the end. In November, the Fraziers heard that the summer house had been closed, and that the Burleighs were in Geneva, in their winter flat; they gave no sign. There was no help for it, and no appeal.

Now Peter began firing letters to anyone who had ever known his late father. He was living in a mild yellow autumn. Why does he remember the streets of the city dark, and the windows everywhere black with rain? He remembers being with Sheilah and the children as if they clung together while just outside their small shelter it rained and rained. The children slept in the bedroom of the flat because the window gave on the street and they could breathe air. Peter and Sheilah had the living-room couch. Their window was not a real window but a square on a well of cement. The flat seemed damp as a cave. Peter remembers steam in the kitchen, pools under the sink, sweat on the pipes. Water streamed on him from the children's clothes, washed and dripping overhead. The trunk, upended in the children's room, was not quite unpacked. Sheilah had not signed her name to this life; she had not given in. Once Peter heard her drop her aitches. "You kids are lucky," she said to the girls. "I never 'ad so much as a sit-down meal. I ate chips out of a paper or I 'ad a butty out on the stairs." He never asked her what a butty was. He thinks it means bread and cheese.

The day he heard "You kids are lucky" he understood they were becoming in fact something they had only *appeared* to be until now—the shabby civil servant and his brood. If he had been European he would have ridden to work on a bicycle, in the uniform of his class and condition. He would have worn a tight coat, a turned collar, and a dirty tie. He wondered then if coming here had been a mistake, and if he should not, after all, still be in a place where his name meant something. Surely Peter Frazier should live where "Frazier" counts? In Ontario even now when he says "Frazier" an absent look comes over his hearer's face, as if its owner were consulting an interior guide. What is Frazier? What does it mean? Oil? Power? Politics? Wheat? Real estate? The creditors had the house sealed when Peter's father died. His aunt collapsed with a heart attack in somebody's bachelor apartment, leaving three sons and a widower to surmise they had never known her. Her will was a disappointment. None of that generation left enough. One made it: the granite Presbyterian immigrants from Scotland. Their children, a generation of daunted women and maiden men, held still. Peter's father's crowd spent: They were not afraid of their fathers, and their grandfathers were old. Peter and his sister and his cousins lived on the remains. They were left the rinds of income, of notions, and the memories of ideas rather than ideas intact. If Peter can choose his reincarnation, let him be the oppressed son of a Scottish parson. Let Peter grow up on cuffs and iron principles. Let him make the fortune! Let him flee the manse! When he was small his patrimony was squandered under his nose. He remembers people dancing in his father's house. He remembers seeing and nearly understanding adultery in a guest room, among a pile of wraps. He thought he had seen a murder; he never told. He remembers licking glasses wherever he found them—on windowsills, on stairs, in the pantry. In his room he listened while Lucille read Beatrix Potter. The bad rabbit stole the carrot from the good rabbit without saying please, and downstairs was the noise of the party—the roar of the crouched lion. When his father died he saw the chairs upside down and the bailiff's chalk marks. Then the doors were sealed.

He has often tried to tell Sheilah why he cannot be defeated. He remembers his father saying, "Nothing can touch us," and Peter believed it and still does. It has prevented his taking his troubles too seriously. Nothing can be as bad as this, he will tell himself. It is happening to me. Even in Geneva, where his status was file clerk, where he sank and stopped on the level of the men who never emigrated, the men on the bicycles—even there he had a manner of strolling to work as if his office were a pastime, and his real life a secret so splendid he could share it with no one except himself.

In Geneva Peter worked for a woman—a girl. She was a Norwegian from a small town in Saskatchewan. He supposed they had been put together because they were Canadians; but they were as strange to each other as if "Canadian" meant any number of things, or had no real meaning. Soon after Agnes Brusen came to the office she hung her framed university degree on the wall. It was one of the gritty, prideful gestures that stand for push, toil, and family sacrifice. He thought, then, that she must be one of a family of immigrants for whom education is everything. Hugh Taylor had told him that in some families the older children never marry until the youngest have finished school. Sometimes every second child is sacrificed and made to work for the education of the next-born. Those who finish college spend years paying back. They are white-hot Protestants, and they live with a load of work and debt and obligation. Peter placed his new colleague on scraps of information. He had never been in the West.

She came to the office on a Monday morning in October. The office was overheated and painted cream. It contained two desks, the filing cabinets, a map of the world as it had been in 1945, and the Charter of the United Nations left behind by Agnes Brusen's predecessor. (She took down the Charter without asking Peter if he minded, with the impudence of gesture you find in women who wouldn't say boo to a goose; and then she hung her college degree on the nail where the Charter had been.) Three people brought her in—a whole committee. One of them said, "Agnes, this is Pete Frazier. Pete, Agnes Brusen. Pete's Canadian, too, Agnes. He knows all about the office, so ask him anything."

Of course he knew all about the office: He knew the exact spot where the cord of the venetian blind was frayed, obliging one to give an extra tug to the right.

The girl might have been twenty-three: no more. She wore a brown tweed suit with bone buttons, and a new silk scarf and new shoes. She clutched an unscratched brown purse. She seemed dressed in going-away presents. She said, "Oh, I never smoke," with a convulsive movement of her hand, when Peter offered his case. He was courteous, hiding his disappointment. The people he worked with had told him a Scandinavian girl was arriving, and he had expected a stunner. Agnes was a mole: She was small and brown, and round-shouldered as if she had always carried parcels or younger children in her arms. A mole's profile was turned when she said good-bye to her committee. If she had been foreign, ill-favored though she was, he might have flirted a little, just to show that he was friendly; but their being Canadian, and suddenly left together, was a sexual damper. He sat down and lit his own cigarette. She smiled at him, questionably, he thought, and sat as if she had never seen a chair before. He wondered if his smoking was annoying her. He wondered if she was fidgety about drafts, or allergic to anything, and whether she would want the blind up or down. His social compass was out of order because the others couldn't tell Peter and Agnes apart. There was a world of difference between them, yet it was she who had been brought in to sit at the larger of the two desks.

While he was thinking this she got up and walked around the office, almost on tiptoe, opening the doors of closets and pulling out the filing trays. She looked inside everything except the drawers of Peter's desk. (In any case, Peter's desk was locked. His desk is locked wherever he works. In Geneva he went into Personnel one morning, early, and pinched his application form. He had stated on the form that he had seven years' experience in public relations and could speak French, German, Spanish, and Italian. He has always collected anything important about himself—anything useful. But he can never get on with the final act, which is getting rid of the information. He has kept papers about for years, a constant source of worry.)

"I know this looks funny, Mr. Ferris," said the girl. "I'm not really snooping or anything. I just can't feel easy in a new place unless I know where everything is. In a new place everything seems so hidden."

If she had called him "Ferris" and pretended not to know he was Frazier, it could only be because they had sent her here to spy on him and see if he had repented and was fit for a better place in life. "You'll be all right here," he said. "Nothing's hidden. Most of us haven't got brains enough to have secrets. This is Rainbow Valley." Depressed by the thought that they were having him watched now, he passed his hand over his hair and looked outside to the lawn and the parking lot and the peacocks someone gave the Palais des Nations years ago. The peacocks love no one. They wander about the parked cars looking elderly, bad-tempered, mournful, and lost.

Agnes had settled down again. She folded her silk scarf and placed it just so, with her gloves beside it. She opened her new purse and took out a notebook and a shiny gold pencil. She may have written

> Duster for desk
> Kleenex
> Glass jar for flowers
> Air-Wick because he smokes
> Paper for lining drawers

because the next day she brought each of these articles to work. She also brought a large black Bible, which she unwrapped lovingly and placed on the left-hand corner of her desk. The flower vase—empty—stood in the middle, and the Kleenex made a counterpoise for the Bible on the right.

When he saw the Bible he knew she had not been sent to spy on his work. The conspiracy was deeper. She might have been dispatched by ghosts. He knew everything about her, all in a moment: He saw the ambition, the terror, the dry pride. She was the true heir of the men from Scotland; she was at the start. She had been sent to tell him, "You can begin, but not begin again." She never opened the Bible, but she dusted it as she dusted her desk, her chair, and any surface the cleaning staff had overlooked. And Peter, the first days, watching her timid movements, her insignificant little face, felt, as you feel the approach of a storm, the charge of moral certainty round her, the belief in work, the faith in undertakings, the bread of the Black Sunday. He recognized and tasted all of it: ashes in the mouth.

After five days their working relations were settled. Of course, there was the Bible and all that went with it, but his tongue had never held the taste of ashes long. She was an inferior girl of poor quality. She had nothing in her favor except the degree on the wall. In the real world, he would not have invited her to his house except to mind the children. That was what he said to Sheilah. He said that Agnes was a mole, and a virgin, and that her tics and mannerisms were sending him round the bend. She had an infuriating habit of covering her mouth when she talked. Even at the telephone she put up her hand as if afraid of losing anything, even a word. Her voice was nasal and flat. She had two working costumes, both dull as the wall. One was the brown suit, the other a navy-blue dress with changeable collars. She dressed for no one; she dressed for her desk, her jar of flowers, her Bible, and her box of Kleenex. One day she crossed the space between the two desks and stood over Peter, who was reading a newspaper. She could have spoken to him from her desk, but she may have felt that being on her feet gave her authority. She had plenty of courage, but authority was something else.

"I thought—I mean, they told me you were the person . . ." She got on with it bravely: "If you don't want to do the filing or any work, all right, Mr. Frazier. I'm not saying anything about that. You might have poor health or your personal reasons. But it's got to be done, so if you'll kindly show me about the filing I'll do it. I've worked in Information before, but it was a different office, and every office is different."

"My dear girl," said Peter. He pushed back his chair and looked at her, astonished. "You've been sitting there fretting, worrying. How insensitive of me. How trying for you. Usually I file on the last Wednesday of the month, so you see, you just haven't been around long enough to see a last Wednesday. Not another word, please. And let us not waste another minute." He emptied the heaped baskets of photographs so swiftly, pushing "Iran—Smallpox Control" into "Irish Red Cross" (close enough), that the girl looked frightened, as if she had raised a whirlwind. She said slowly, "If you'll only show me, Mr. Frazier, instead of doing it so fast, I'll gladly look after it, because you might want to be doing other things, and I feel the filing should be done every day." But Peter was too busy to answer, and so she sat down, holding the edge of her desk.

"There," he said, beaming. "All done." His smile, his sunburst, was wasted, for the girl was staring round the room as if she feared she had not inspected everything the first day after all; some drawer, some cupboard, hid a monster. That evening Peter unlocked one of the drawers of his desk and took away the application form he had stolen from Personnel. The girl had not finished her search.

"How could you *not* know?" wailed Sheilah. "You sit looking at her every day. You must talk about *something*. She must have told you."

"She did tell me," said Peter, "and I've just told you."

It was this: Agnes Brusen was on the Burleighs' guest list. How had the Burleighs met her? What did they see in her? Peter could not reply. He knew that Agnes lived in a bed-sitting room with a Swiss family and had her meals with them. She had been in Geneva three months, but no one had ever seen her outside the office. "You *should* know," said Sheilah. "She must have something, more than you can see. Is she pretty? Is she brilliant? What is it?"

"We don't really talk," Peter said. They talked in a way: Peter teased her and she took no notice. Agnes was not a sulker. She had taken her defeat like a sport. She did her work and a good deal of his. She sat behind her Bible, her flowers, and her Kleenex, and answered when Peter spoke. That was how he learned about the Burleighs—just by teasing and being bored. It was a January afternoon. He said, "*Miss* Brusen. Talk to me. Tell me everything. Pretend we have perfect rapport. Do you like Geneva?"

"It's a nice clean town," she said. He can see to this day the red and blue anemones in the glass jar, and her bent head, and her small untended hands.

"Are you learning beautiful French with your Swiss family?"

"They speak English."

"Why don't you take an apartment of your own?" he said. Peter was not usually impertinent. He was bored. "You'd be independent then."

"I am independent," she said. "I earn my living. I don't think it proves anything if you live by yourself. Mrs. Burleigh wants me to live alone, too. She's looking for something for me. It mustn't be dear. I send money home."

Here was the extraordinary thing about Agnes Brusen: She refused the use of Christian names and never spoke to Peter unless he spoke first, but she would tell anything, as if to say, "Don't waste time fishing. Here it is."

He learned all in one minute that she sent her salary home, and that she was a friend of the Burleighs. The first he had expected; the second knocked him flat.

"She's got to come to dinner," Sheilah said. "We should have had her right from the beginning. If only I'd known! But *you* were the one. You said she looked like—oh, I don't even remember. A Norwegian mole."

She came to dinner one Saturday night in January, in her navy-blue dress, to which she had pinned an organdy gardenia. She sat upright on the edge of the sofa. Sheilah had ordered the meal from a restaurant. There was lobster, good wine, and a *pièce-montée* full of kirsch and cream. Agnes refused the lobster; she had never eaten anything from the sea unless it had been sterilized and tinned, and said so. She was afraid of skin poisoning. Someone in her family had skin poisoning after having eaten oysters. She touched her cheeks and neck to show where the poisoning had erupted. She sniffed her wine and put the glass down without tasting it. She could not eat the cake because of the alcohol it contained. She ate an egg, bread and butter, a sliced tomato, and drank a glass of ginger ale. She seemed unaware she was creating disaster and pain. She did not help clear away the dinner plates. She sat, adequately nourished, decently dressed, and waited to learn why she had been invited here—that was the feeling Peter had. He folded the card table on which they had dined, and opened the window to air the room.

"It's not the same cold as Canada, but you feel it more," he said, for something to say.

"Your blood has gotten thin," said Agnes.

Sheilah returned from the kitchen and let herself fall into an armchair. With her eyes closed she held out her hand for a cigarette. She was performing the haughty-lady act that was a family joke. She flung her head back and looked at Agnes through half-closed lids; then she suddenly brought her head forward, widening her eyes.

"Are you skiing madly?" she said.

"Well, in the first place there hasn't been any snow," said Agnes. "So nobody's doing any skiing so far as I know. All I hear is people complaining because there's no snow. Personally, I don't ski. There isn't much skiing in the part of Canada I come from. Besides, my family never had that kind of leisure."

"Heavens," said Sheilah, as if her family had every kind.

I'll bet they had, thought Peter. On the dole.

Sheilah was wasting her act. He had a suspicion that Agnes knew it was an act but did not know it was also a joke. If so, it made Sheilah seem a fool, and he loved Sheilah too much to enjoy it.

"The Burleighs have been wonderful to me," said Agnes. She seemed to have divined why she was here, and decided to give them all the information they wanted, so that she could put on her coat and go home to bed. "They had me out to their place on the lake every weekend until the weather got cold and they moved back to town. They've rented a chalet for the winter, and they want me to come there, too. But I don't know if I will or not. I don't ski, and, oh, I don't know—I don't drink, either, and I don't always see the point. Their friends are too rich and I'm too Canadian."

She had delivered everything Sheilah wanted and more: Agnes was on the first guest list and didn't care. No, Peter corrected: doesn't know. Doesn't care and doesn't know.

"I thought with you Norwegians it was in the blood, skiing. And drinking," Sheilah murmured.

"Drinking, maybe," said Agnes. She covered her mouth and said behind her spread fingers, "In our family we were religious. We didn't drink or smoke. My brother was in Norway in the war. He saw some cousins. Oh," she said, unexpectedly loud, "Harry said it was just terrible. They were so poor. They had flies in their kitchen. They gave him something to eat a fly had been on. They didn't have a real toilet, and they'd been in the same house about two hundred years. We've only recently built our own home, and we have a bathroom and two toilets. I'm from Saskatchewan," she said. "I'm not from any other place."

Surely one winter here had been punishment enough? In the spring they would remember him and free him. He wrote Lucille, who said he was lucky to have a job at all. The Burleighs had sent the Fraziers a second-guest-list Christmas card. It showed a Moslem refugee child weeping outside a tent. They treasured the card and left it standing long after the others had been given the children to cut up. Peter had discovered by now what had gone wrong in the friendship—Sheilah had charged a skirt at a dressmaker to Madge's account. Madge had told her she might, and then changed her mind. Poor Sheilah! She was new to this part of it—to the changing humors of independent friends. Paris was already a year in the past. At Mardi Gras, the Burleighs gave their annual party. They invited everyone, the damned and the dropped, with the prodigality of a child at prayers. The invitation said "in costume," but the Fraziers were too happy to wear a disguise. They might not be recognized. Like many of the guests they expected to meet at the party, they had been disgraced, forgotten, and rehabilitated. They would be anxious to see one another as they were.

On the night of the party, the Fraziers rented a car they had never seen before and drove through the first snowstorm of the year. Peter had not driven since last summer's blissful trips in the Fiat. He could not find the switch for the windshield wiper in this car. He leaned over the wheel. "Can you see on your side?" he asked. "Can I make a left turn here? Does it look like a one-way?"

"I can't imagine why you took a car with a right-hand drive," said Sheilah.

He had trouble finding a place to park; they crawled up and down unknown streets whose curbs were packed with snow-covered cars. When they stood at last on the pavement, safe and sound, Peter said, "This is the first snow."

"I can see that," said Sheilah. "Hurry, darling. My hair."

"It's the first snow."

"You're repeating yourself," she said. "Please hurry, darling. Think of my poor shoes. My *hair*."

She was born in an ugly city, and so was Peter, but they have this difference: She does not know the importance of the first snow—the first clean thing in a dirty year. He would have told her then that this storm, which was wetting her feet and destroying her hair, was like the first day of the English spring, but she made a frightened gesture, trying to shield her head. The gesture told him he did not understand her beauty.

"Let me," she said. He was fumbling with the key, trying to lock the car. She took the key without impatience and locked the door on the driver's side; and then, to show Peter she treasured him and was not afraid of wasting her life or her beauty, she took his arm and they walked in the snow down a street and around a corner to the apartment house where the Burleighs lived. They were, and are, a united couple. They were afraid of the party, and each of them knew it. When they walk together, holding arms, they give each other whatever each can spare.

Only six people had arrived in costume. Madge Burleigh was disguised as Manet's "Lola de Valence," which everyone mistook for Carmen. Mike was an Impressionist painter, with a straw hat and a glued-on beard. "I am all of them," he said. He would rather have dressed as a dentist, he said, welcoming the Fraziers as if he had parted from them the day before, but Madge wanted him to look as if he had created her. "You know?" he said.

"Perfectly," said Sheilah. Her shoes were stained and the snow had softened her lacquered hair. She was not wasted: She was the most beautiful woman there.

About an hour after their arrival, Peter found himself with no one to talk to. He had told about the Trudeau wedding in Paris and the pot of azaleas, and after he mislaid his audience he began to look round for Sheilah. She was on a window seat, partly concealed by a green velvet curtain. Facing her, so that their profiles were neat and perfect against the night, was a man. Their conversation was private and enclosed, as if they had in minutes covered leagues of time and arrived at the place where everything was implied, understood. Peter began working his way across the room, toward his wife, when he saw Agnes. He was granted the sight of her drowning face. She had dressed with comic intention, obviously with care, and now she was a ragged hobo, half tramp, half clown. Her hair was tucked up under a bowler hat. The six costumed guests who had made the same mistake—the ghost, the gypsy, the Athenian maiden, the geisha, the Martian, and the apache—were delighted to find a seventh; but Agnes was not amused; she was gasping for life. When a waiter passed with a crowded tray, she took a glass without seeing it; then a wave of the party took her away.

Sheilah's new friend was named Simpson. After Simpson said he thought perhaps he'd better circulate, Peter sat down where he had been. "Now look, Sheilah," he began. Their most intimate conversations have taken place at parties. Once at a party she told him she was leaving him; she didn't, of course. Smiling, blue-eyed, she gazed lovingly at Peter and said rapidly, "Pete, shut up and listen. That man. The man you scared away. He's a big wheel in a company out in India or someplace like that. It's gorgeous out there. Pete, the *servants*. And it's warm. It never never snows. He says there's heaps of jobs. You pick them off the trees like . . . orchids. He says it's even easier now than when we owned all those places, because now the poor pets can't run anything and they'll pay *fortunes*. Pete, he says it's warm, it's heaven, and Pete, they pay."

A few minutes later, Peter was alone again and Sheilah part of a closed, laughing group. Holding her elbow was the man from the place where jobs grew like orchids. Peter edged into the group and laughed at a story he hadn't heard. He heard only the last line, which was "Here comes another tunnel." Looking out from the tight laughing ring, he saw Agnes again, and he thought, I'd be like Agnes if I didn't have Sheilah. Agnes put her glass down on a table and lurched toward the doorway, head forward. Madge Burleigh, who never stopped moving around the room and smiling, was still smiling when she paused and said in Peter's ear, "Go with Agnes, Pete. See that she gets home. People will notice if Mike leaves."

"She probably just wants to walk around the block," said Peter. "She'll be back."

"Oh, stop thinking about yourself, for once, and see that that poor girl gets home," said Madge. "You've still got your Fiat, haven't you?"

He turned away as if he had been pushed. Any command is a release, in a way. He may not want to go in that particular direction, but at least he is going somewhere. And now Sheilah, who had moved inches nearer to hear what Madge and Peter were murmuring, said, "Yes, go, darling," as if he were leaving the gates of Troy.

Peter was to find Agnes and see that she reached home: This he repeated to himself as he stood on the landing, outside the Burleighs' flat, ringing for the elevator. Bored with waiting for it, he ran down the stairs, four flights, and saw that Agnes had stalled the lift by leaving the door open. She was crouched on the floor, propped on her fingertips. Her eyes were closed.

"Agnes," said Peter. "*Miss* Brusen, I mean. That's no way to leave a party. Don't you know you're supposed to curtsy and say thanks? My God, Agnes, anybody going by here just now might have seen you! Come on, be a good girl. Time to go home."

She got up without his help and, moving between invisible crevasses, shut the elevator door. Then she left the building and Peter followed, remembering he was to see that she got home. They walked along the snowy pavement, Peter a few steps behind her. When she turned right for no reason, he turned, too. He had no clear idea where they were going. Perhaps she lived close by. He had forgotten where the hired car was parked, or what it looked like; he could not remember its make or its color. In any case, Sheilah had the key. Agnes walked on steadily, as if she knew their destination, and he thought, Agnes Brusen is drunk in the street in Geneva and dressed like a tramp. He wanted to say, "This is the best thing that ever happened to you, Agnes; it will help you understand how things are for some of the rest of us." But she stopped and turned and, leaning over a low hedge, retched on a frozen lawn. He held her clammy forehead and rested his hand on her arched back, on muscles as tight as a fist. She straightened up and drew a breath but the cold air made her cough. "Don't breathe too deeply," he said. "It's the worst thing you can do. Have you got a handkerchief?" He passed his own handkerchief over her wet weeping face, upturned like the face of one of his little girls. "I'm out without a coat," he said, noticing it. "We're a pair."

"I never drink," said Agnes. "I'm just not used to it." Her voice was sweet and quiet. He had never seen her so peaceful, so composed. He thought she must surely be all right, now, and perhaps he might leave her here. The trust in her tilted face had perplexed him. He wanted to get back to Sheilah and have her explain something. He had forgotten what it was, but Sheilah would know. "Do you live around here?" he said. As he spoke, she let herself fall. He had wiped her face and now she trusted him to pick her up, set her on her feet, take her wherever she ought to be. He pulled her up and she stood, wordless, humble, as he brushed the snow from her tramp's clothes. Snow horizontally crossed the lamplight. The street was silent. Agnes had lost her hat. Snow, which he tasted, melted on her hands. His gesture of licking snow from her hands was formal as a handshake. He tasted snow on her hands and then they walked on.

"I never drink," she said. They stood on the edge of a broad avenue. The wrong turning now could lead them anywhere; it was the changeable avenue at the edge of towns that loses its houses and becomes a highway. She held his arm and spoke in a gentle voice. She said, "In our house we didn't smoke or drink. My mother was ambitious for me, more than for Harry and the others." She said, "I've never been alone before. When I was a kid I would get up in the summer before the others, and I'd see the ice wagon going down the street. I'm alone now. Mrs. Burleigh's found me an apartment. It's only one room. She likes it because it's in the old part of town. I don't like old houses. Old houses are dirty. You don't know who was there before."

"I should have a car somewhere," Peter said. "I'm not sure where we are."

He remembers that on this avenue they climbed into a taxi, but nothing about the drive. Perhaps he fell asleep. He does remember that when he paid the driver Agnes clutched his arm, trying to stop him. She pressed extra coins into the driver's palm. The driver was paid twice.

"I'll tell you one thing about us," said Peter. "We pay everything twice." This was part of a much longer theory concerning North American behavior, and it was not Peter's own. Mike Burleigh had held forth about it on summer afternoons.

Agnes pushed open a door between a stationer's shop and a grocery, and led the way up a narrow inside stair. They climbed one flight, frightening beetles. She had to search every pocket for the latchkey. She was shaking with cold. Her apartment seemed little warmer than the street. Without speaking to Peter she turned on all the lights. She looked inside the kitchen and the bathroom and then got down on her hands and knees and looked under the sofa. The room was neat and belonged to no one. She left him standing in this unclaimed room—she had forgotten him— and closed a door behind her. He looked for something to do—some useful action he could repeat to Madge. He turned on the electric radiator in the fireplace. Perhaps Agnes wouldn't thank him for it; perhaps she would rather undress in the cold. "I'll be on my way," he called to the bathroom door.

She had taken off the tramp's clothes and put on a dressing gown of orphanage wool. She came out of the bathroom and straight toward him. She pressed her face and rubbed her cheek on his shoulder as if hoping the contact would leave a scar. He saw her back and her profile and his own face in the mirror over the fireplace. He thought, This is how disasters happen. He saw floods of seawater moving with perfect punitive justice over reclaimed land; he saw lava covering vineyards and overtaking dogs and stragglers. A bridge over an abyss snapped in two and the long express train, suddenly V-shaped, floated like snow. He thought amiably of every kind of disaster and thought, This is how they occur.

Her eyes were closed. She said, "I shouldn't be over here. In my family we didn't drink or smoke. My mother wanted a lot from me, more than from Harry and the others." But he knew all that; he had known from the day of the Bible, and because once, at the beginning, she had made him afraid. He was not afraid of her now.

She said, "It's no use staying here, is it?"

"If you mean what I think, no."

"It wouldn't be better anywhere."

She let him see full on her blotched face. He was not expected to do anything. He was not required to pick her up when she fell or wipe her tears. She was poor quality, really—he remembered having thought that once. She left him and went quietly into the bathroom and locked the door. He heard taps running and supposed it was a hot bath. He was pretty certain there would be no more tears. He looked at his watch: Sheilah must be home, now, wondering what had become of him. He descended the beetles' staircase and for forty minutes crossed the city under a windless fall of snow.

The neighbor's child who had stayed with Peter's children was asleep on the living-room sofa. Peter woke her and sent her, sleepwalking, to her own door. He sat down, wet to the bone, thinking, I'll call the Burleighs. In half an hour I'll call the police. He heard a car stop and the engine running and a confusion of two voices laughing and calling good night. Presently Sheilah let herself in, rosy-faced, smiling. She carried his trench coat over her arm. She said, "How's Agnes?"

"Where were you?" he said. "Whose car was that?"

Sheilah had gone into the children's room. He heard her shutting their window. She returned, undoing her dress, and said, "Was Agnes all right?"

"Agnes is all right. Sheilah, this is about the worst . . ."

She stepped out of the Balenciaga and threw it over a chair. She stopped and looked at him and said, "Poor old Pete, are you in love with Agnes?" And then, as if the answer were of so little importance she hadn't time for it, she locked her arms around him and said, "My love, we're going to Ceylon."

Two days later, when Peter strolled into his office, Agnes was at her desk. She wore the blue dress, with a spotless collar. White and yellow freesias were symmetrically arranged in the glass jar. The room was hot, and the spring snow, glued for a second when it touched the window, blurred the view of parked cars.

"Quite a party," Peter said.

She did not look up. He sighed, sat down, and thought if the snow held he would be skiing at the Burleighs' very soon. Impressed by his kindness to Agnes, Madge had invited the family for the first possible weekend.

Presently Agnes said, "I'll never drink again or go to a house where people are drinking. And I'll never bother anyone the way I bothered you."

"You didn't bother me," he said. "I took you home. You were alone and it was late. It's normal."

"Normal for you, maybe, but I'm used to getting home by myself. Please never tell what happened."

He stared at her. He can still remember the freesias and the Bible and the heat in the room. She looked as if the elements had no power. She felt neither heat nor cold. "Nothing happened," he said.

"I behaved in a silly way. I had no right to. I led you to think I might do something wrong."

"*I* might have tried something," he said gallantly. "But that would be my fault and not yours."

She put her knuckle to her mouth and he could scarcely hear. "It was because of you. I was afraid you might be blamed, or else you'd blame yourself."

"There's no question of any blame," he said. "Nothing happened. We'd both had a lot to drink. Forget about it. Nothing *happened.* You'd remember if it had."

She put down her hand. There was an expression on her face. Now she sees me, he thought. She had never looked at him after the first day. (He has since tried to put a name to the look on her face; but how can he, now, after so many voyages, after Ceylon, and Hong Kong, and Sheilah's nearly leaving him, and all their difficulties—the money owed, the rows with hotel managers, the lost and found steamer trunk, the children throwing up the foreign food?) She sees me now, he thought. What does she see?

She said, "I'm from a big family. I'm not used to being alone. I'm not a suicidal person, but I could have done something after that party, just not to see anymore, or think or listen or expect anything. What can I think when I see these people? All my life I heard, Educated people don't do this, educated people don't do that. And now I'm here, and you're all educated people, and you're nothing but pigs. You're educated and you drink and do everything wrong and you know what you're doing, and that makes you worse than pigs. My family worked to make me an educated person, but they didn't know you. But what if I didn't see and hear and expect anything anymore? It wouldn't change anything. You'd all be still the same. Only *you* might have thought it was your fault. You might have thought you were to blame. It could worry you all your life. It would have been wrong for me to worry you."

He remembered that the rented car was still along a snowy curb somewhere in Geneva. He wondered if Sheilah had the key in her purse and if she remembered where they'd parked.

"I told you about the ice wagon," Agnes said. "I don't remember everything, so you're wrong about remembering. But I remember telling you that. That was the best. It's the best you can hope to have. In a big family, if you want to be alone, you have to get up before the rest of them. You get up early in the morning in the summer and it's you, you, once in your life alone in the universe. You think you know everything that can happen. . . . Nothing is ever like that again."

He looked at the smeared window and wondered if this day could end without disaster. In his mind he saw her falling in the snow wearing a tramp's costume, and he saw her coming to him in the orphanage dressing gown. He saw her drowning face at the party. He was afraid for himself. The story was still unfinished. It had to come to a climax, something threatening to him. But there was no climax. They talked that day, and afterward nothing else was said. They went on in the same office for a short time, until Peter left for Ceylon; until somebody read the right letter, passed it on for the right initials, and the Fraziers began the Oriental tour that should have made their fortune. Agnes and Peter were too tired to speak after that morning. They were like a married couple in danger, taking care.

But what were they talking about that day, so quietly, such old friends? They talked about dying, about being ambitious, about being religious, about different kinds of love. What did she see when she looked at him— taking her knuckle slowly away from her mouth, bringing her hand down to the desk, letting it rest there? They were both Canadians, so they had this much together—the knowledge of the little you dare admit. Death, near death, the best thing, the wrong thing—God knows what they were telling each other. Anyway, nothing happened.

*　　*　　*

When, on Sunday mornings, Sheilah and Peter talk about those times, they take on the glamour of something still to come. It is then he remembers Agnes Brusen. He never says her name. Sheilah wouldn't remember Agnes. Agnes is the only secret Peter has from his wife, the only puzzle he pieces together without her help. He thinks about families in the West as they were fifteen, twenty years ago—the iron-cold ambition, and every member pushing the next one on. He thinks of his father's parties. When he thinks of his father he imagines him with Sheilah, in a crowd. Actually, Sheilah and Peter's father never met, but they might have liked each other. His father admired good-looking women. Peter wonders what they were doing over there in Geneva—not Sheilah and Peter, *Agnes* and Peter. It is almost as if they had once run away together, silly as children, irresponsible as lovers. Peter and Sheilah are back where they started. While they were out in world affairs picking up microbes and debts, always on the fringe of disaster, the fringe of a fortune, Agnes went on and did—what? They lost each other. He thinks of the ice wagon going down the street. He sees something he has never seen in his life—a Western town that belongs to Agnes. Here is Agnes—small, mole-faced, round-shouldered because she has always carried a younger child. She watches the ice wagon and the trail of ice water in a morning invented for her: hers. He sees the weak prairie trees and the shadows on the sidewalk. Nothing moves except the shadows and the ice wagon and the changing amber of the child's eyes. The child is Peter. He has seen the grain of the cement sidewalk and the grass in the cracks, and the dust, and the dandelions at the edge of the road. He is there. He has taken the morning that belongs to Agnes, he is up before the others, and he knows everything. There is nothing he doesn't know. He could keep the morning, if he wanted to, but what can Peter do with the start of a summer day? Sheilah is here, it is a true Sunday morning, with its dimness and headache and remorse and regrets, and this is life. He says, "We have the Balenciaga." He touches Sheilah's hand. The children have their aunt now, and he and Sheilah have each other. Everything works out, somehow or other. Let Agnes have the start of the day. Let Agnes think it was invented for her. Who wants to be alone in the universe? No, begin at the beginning: Peter lost Agnes. Agnes says to herself somewhere, Peter is lost.

THE REMISSION

*W*hen it became clear that Alec Webb was far more ill than anyone had cared to tell him, he tore up his English life and came down to die on the Riviera. The time was early in the reign of the new Elizabeth, and people were still doing this—migrating with no other purpose than the hope of a merciful sky. The alternative (Alec said to his only sister) meant queueing for death on the National Health Service, lying on a regulation mattress and rubber sheet, hearing the breath of other men dying.

Alec—as obituaries would have it later—was husband to Barbara, father to Will, Molly, and James. It did not occur to him or to anyone else that the removal from England was an act of unusual force that could rend and lacerate his children's lives as well as his own. The difference was that their lives were barely above ground and not yet in flower.

The five Webbs arrived at a property called Lou Mas in the course of a particularly hot September. Mysterious Lou Mas, until now a name on a deed of sale, materialized as a pink house wedged in the side of a hill between a motor road and the sea. Alec identified its style as Edwardian-Riviera. Barbara supposed he must mean the profusion of balconies and parapets, and the slender pillars in the garden holding up nothing. In the new southern light everything looked to her brilliant and moist, like color straight from a paintbox. One of Alec's first gestures was to raise his arm and shield his eyes against this brightness. The journey had exhausted him, she thought. She had received notice in dreams that their change of climates was irreversible; not just Alec but none of them could go back. She did not tell him so, though in better times it might have interested that part of his mind he kept fallow: Being entirely rational, he had a prudent respect for second sight.

The children had never been in a house this size. They chased each other and slid along the floors until Alec asked, politely, if they wouldn't mind playing outside, though one of the reasons he had wanted to come here was to be with them for the time remaining. Dispatched to a flagged patio in front of the house, the children looked down on terraces bearing olive trees, then a railway line, then the sea. Among the trees was a cottage standing empty which Barbara had forbidden them to explore. The children were ten, eleven, and twelve, with the girl in the middle. Since they had no school to attend, and did not know any of the people living around them, and as their mother was too busy to invent something interesting for them to do, they hung over a stone balustrade waving and calling to trains, hoping to see an answering wave and perhaps a decapitation. They had often been warned about foolish passengers and the worst that could happen. Their mother came out and put her arms around Will, the eldest. She kissed the top of his head. "Do look at that sea," she said. "Aren't we lucky?" They looked, but the vast, flat sea was a line any of them could have drawn on a sheet of paper. It was there, but no more than there; trains were better—so was the ruined cottage. Within a week James had cut his hand on glass breaking into it, but by then Barbara had forgotten her injunction.

The sun Alec had wanted turned out to be without compassion, and he spent most of the day indoors, moving from room to room, searching for some gray, dim English cave in which to take cover. Often he sat without reading, doing nothing, in a room whose one window, none too clean, looked straight into the blank hill behind the house. Seepage and a residue of winter rainstorms had traced calm yellowed patterns on its walls. He guessed it had once been assigned to someone's hapless, helpless paid companion, who would have marveled at the thought of its lending shelter to a dying man. In the late afternoon he would return to his bedroom, where, out on the balcony, an angular roof shadow slowly replaced the sun. Barbara unfolded his deck chair on the still burning tiles. He stretched out, opened a book, found the page he wanted, at once closed his eyes. Barbara knelt in a corner, in a triangle of light. She had taken her clothes off, all but a sun hat; bougainvillea grew so thick no one could see. She said, "Would you like me to read to you?" No; he did everything alone, or nearly. He was—always—bathed, shaved, combed, and dressed. His children would not remember him unkempt or disheveled, though it might not have mattered to them. He did not smell of sweat or sickness or medicine or fear.

When it began to rain, later in the autumn, the children played indoors. Barbara tried to keep them quiet. There was a French school up in the town, but neither Alec nor Barbara knew much about it; and, besides, there was no use settling them in. He heard the children asking for bicycles so they could ride along the motor road, and he heard Barbara saying no, the road was dangerous. She must have changed her mind, for he next heard them discussing the drawbacks and advantages of French bikes. One of the children—James, it was—asked some question about the cost.

"You're not to mention things like that," said Barbara. "You're not to speak of money."

Alec was leaving no money and three children—four, if you counted his wife. Barbara often said she had no use for money, no head for it. "Thank God I'm Irish," she said. "I haven't got rates of interest on the brain." She read Irishness into her nature as an explanation for it, the way some people attributed their gifts and failings to a sign of the zodiac. Anything natively Irish had dissolved long before, leaving only a family custom of Catholicism and another habit, fervent in Barbara's case, of anticlerical passion. Alec supposed she was getting her own back, for a mysterious reason, on ancestors she would not have recognized in Heaven. Her family, the Laceys, had been in Wales for generations. Her brothers considered themselves Welsh.

It was Barbara's three Welsh brothers who had put up the funds for Lou Mas. Houses like this were to be had nearly for the asking, then. They stood moldering at the unfashionable end of the coast, damaged sometimes by casual shellfire, difficult to heat, costly to renovate. What the brothers had seen as valuable in Lou Mas was not the villa, which they had no use for, but the undeveloped seafront around it, for which each of them had a different plan. The eldest brother was a partner in a firm of civil engineers; another managed a resort hotel and had vague thoughts about building one of his own. The youngest, Mike, who was Barbara's favorite, had converted from the RAF to commercial flying. Like Alec, he had been a prisoner of war. The two men had that, but nothing else, in common. Mike was the best traveled of the three. He could see, in place of the pink house with its thick walls and high ceilings, one of the frail, domino-shaped blocks that were starting to rise around the Mediterranean basin, creating a vise of white plaster at the rim of the sea.

Because of United Kingdom income-tax laws, which made it awkward for the Laceys to have holdings abroad, Alec and Barbara had been registered as owners of Lou Mas, with Desmond, the engineer, given power of attorney. This was a manageable operation because Alec was entirely honorable, while Barbara did not know a legal document from the ace of diamonds. So that when the first scouts came round from the local British colony to find out what the Webbs were like and Barbara told them Lou Mas belonged to her family she was speaking the truth. Her visitors murmured that they had been very fond of the Vaughan-Thorpes and had been sorry to see them go—a reference to the previous owners, whose grandparents had built Lou Mas. Barbara did not suppose this to be a snub: She simply wondered why it was that a war out of which her brothers had emerged so splendidly should have left Alec, his sister, and the unknown Vaughan-Thorpes worse off than before.

The scouts reported that Mr. Webb was an invalid, that the children were not going to school, that Mrs. Webb must at one time have been pretty, and that she seemed to be spending a good deal of money, either her husband's or her own. When no improvements were seen in the house, the grounds, or the cottage, it began to be taken for granted that she had been squandering, on trifles, rather more than she had.

Her visitors were mistaken: Barbara never spent more than she had, but only the total of all she could see. What she saw now was a lump of money like a great block of marble, from which she could chip as much as she liked. It had come by way of Alec's sister. Alec's obstinate refusal to die on National Health had meant that his death had somehow to be paid for. Principle was a fine thing, one of Barbara's brothers remarked, but it came high. Alec's earning days were done for. He had come from a long line of medium-rank civil servants who had never owned anything except the cottages to which they had eventually retired, and which their heirs inevitably sold. Money earned, such as there was, disappeared in the sands of their male progeny's education. Girls were expected to get married. Alec's sister, now forty-four, had not done so, though she was no poorer or plainer than most. "I am better off like this," she had told Alec, perhaps once too often. She was untrained, unready, unfitted for any life save that of a woman civilian's in wartime; peace had no use for her, just as the postwar seemed too fast, too hard, and too crowded to allow for Alec. Her only asset was material: a modest, cautiously invested sum of money settled on her by a godparent, the income from which she tried to add to by sewing. Christening robes had been her special joy, but fewer babies were being baptized with pomp, while nylon was gradually replacing the silks and lawns she worked with such care. Nobody wanted the bother of ironing flounces and tucks in a world without servants.

Barbara called her sister-in-law "the mouse." She had small brown eyes; was vegetarian; prayed every night of her life for Alec and for the parents who had not much loved her. "If they would just listen to me," she was in the habit of saying—about Alec and Barbara, for instance. She never complained about her compressed existence, which seemed to her the only competent one at times; at least it was quiet. When Alec told her that he was about to die, and wanted to emigrate, and had been provided with a house but with nothing to run it on, she immediately offered him half her capital. He accepted in the same flat way he had talked about death—out of his driving need, she supposed, or because he still held the old belief that women never need much. She knew she had made an impulsive gesture, perhaps a disastrous one, but she loved Alec and did not want to add to her own grief. She was assured that anything left at the end would be returned enriched and amplified by some sort of nimble investment, but as Alec and his family intended to live on the capital she did not see how this could be done.

Alec knew that his sister had been sacrificed. It was merely another of the lights going out. Detachment had overtaken him even before the journey south. Mind and body floated on any current that chose to bear them.

For the first time in her life Barbara had enough money, and no one to plague her with useless instructions. While Alec slept, or seemed to, she knelt in the last triangle of sun on the balcony reading the spread-out pages of the *Continental Daily Mail*. It had been one thing to have no head for money when there was none to speak of; the present situation called for percipience and wit. Her reading informed her that dollars were still stronger than pounds. (Pounds were the decaying cottage, dollars the Edwardian house.) Alec's background and training made him find the word "dollars" not overnice, perhaps alarming, but Barbara had no class prejudice to hinder her. She had already bought dollars for pounds, at a giddy loss, feeling each time she had put it over on banks and nations, on snobs, on the financial correspondent of the *Mail*, on her own clever brothers. (One of the Webbs' neighbors, a retired Army officer, had confided to Alec that he was expecting the Russians to land in the bay below their villas at any time. He intended to die fighting on his doorstep; however, should anything happen to prevent his doing so, he had kept a clutch of dollars tucked in the pocket of an old dressing gown so that he and his mother could buy their way out.)

In Alec's darkened bedroom she combed her hair with his comb. Even if he survived he would have no foothold on the 1950s. She, Barbara, had been made for her time. This did not mean she wanted to live without him. Writing to one of her brothers, she advised him to open a hotel down here. Servants were cheap—twenty or thirty cents an hour, depending on whether you worked the official or the free-market rate. In this letter her brother heard Barbara's voice, which had stayed high and breathless though she must have been thirty-four. He wondered if this was the sort of prattle poor dying old Alec had to listen to there in the south.

"South" was to Alec a place of the mind. He had not deserted England, as his sad sister thought, but moved into one of its oldest literary legends, the Mediterranean. His part of this legend was called Rivabella. Actually, "Rivebelle" was written on maps and road signs, for the area belonged to France—at least, for the present. It had been tugged between France and Italy so often that it now had a diverse, undefinable character and seemed to be remote from any central authority unless there were elections or wars. At its heart was a town sprawled on the hill behind Lou Mas and above the motor road. Its inhabitants said "Rivabella"; they spoke, among themselves, a Ligurian dialect with some Spanish and Arabic expressions mixed in, though their children went to school and learned French and that they descended from a race with blue eyes. What had remained constant to Rivabella was its poverty, and the groves of ancient olive trees that only the strictest of laws kept the natives from cutting down, and the look and character of the people. Confined by his illness, Alec would never meet more of these than about a dozen; they bore out the expectation set alight by his reading, seeming to him classless and pagan, poetic and wise, imbued with an instinctive understanding of light, darkness, and immortality. Barbara expected them to be cunning and droll, which they were, and to steal from her, which they did, and to love her, which they seemed to. Only the children were made uneasy by these strange new adults, so squat and ill-favored, so quarrelsome and sly, so destructive of nature and pointlessly cruel to animals. But, then, the children had not read much, were unfamiliar with films, and had no legends to guide them.

Barbara climbed up to the town quite often during the first weeks, looking for a doctor for Alec, for a cook and maid, for someone to give lessons to the children. There was nothing much to see except a Baroque church from which everything removable had long been sold to antiquarians, and a crumbling palace along the very dull main street. In one of the palace rooms she was given leave to examine some patches of peach-colored smudge she was told were early Renaissance frescoes. Some guidebooks referred to these, with the result that a number of the new, hardworking breed of postwar traveler panted up a steep road not open to motor traffic only to find that the palace belonged to a cranky French countess who lived alone with her niece and would not let anyone in. (Barbara, interviewing the niece for the post of governess, had been admitted but was kept standing until the countess left the room.) Behind the palace she discovered a town hall with a post office and a school attached, a charming small hospital—where a doctor was obtained for Alec—and a walled graveyard. Only the graveyard was worth exploring; it contained Victorian English poets who had probably died of tuberculosis in the days when an enervating climate was thought to be good for phthisis, and Russian aristocrats who had owned some of the English houses, and Garibaldian adventurers who, like Alec, had never owned a thing. Most of these graves were overgrown and neglected, with the headstones all to one side, and wild grasses grown taller than roses. The more recent dead seemed to be commemorated by marble plaques on a high concrete wall; these she did not examine. What struck her about this place was its splendid view: She could see Lou Mas, and quite far into Italy, and of course over a vast stretch of the sea. How silly of all those rich foreigners to crowd down by the shore, with the crashing noise of the railway. I would have built up here in a minute, she thought.

Alec's new doctor was young and ugly and bit his nails. He spoke good English, and knew most of the British colony, to whose colds, allergies, and perpetually upset stomachs he ministered. British ailments were nursery ailments; what his patients really wanted was to be tucked up next to a nursery fire and fed warm bread-and-milk. He had taken her to be something like himself—an accomplice. "My husband is anything but childish," she said gently. She hesitated before trotting out her usual Irish claim, for she was not quite certain what he meant.

"Rivabella has only two points of cultural interest," he said. "One is the market on the church square. The other is the patron saint, St. Damian. He appears on the church roof, dressed in armor, holding a flaming sword in the air. He does this when someone in Rivabella seems to be in danger." She saw, in the way he looked at her, that she had begun her journey south a wife and mother whose looks were fading, and arrived at a place where her face seemed exotic. Until now she had thought only that a normal English family had taken the train, and the caricature of one had descended. It amounted to the same thing—the eye of the beholder.

From his balcony Alec saw the hill as a rough triangle, with a few straggling farms beneath the gray-and-umber town (all he could discern was its color) and the apex of graveyard. This, in its chalky whiteness, looked like an Andalusian or a North African village washed up on the wrong part of the coast. It was alien to the lush English gardens and the foreign villas, which tended to pinks, and beiges, and to a deep shade known as Egyptian red. Within those houses was a way of being he sensed and understood, for it was a smaller, paler version of colonial life, with chattering foreign servants who might have been budgerigars, and hot puddings consumed under brilliant sunlight. Rules of speech and regulations for conduct were probably observed, as in the last days of the dissolving Empire. Barbara had told him of one: it was bad form to say "Rivebelle" for "Rivabella," for it showed one hadn't known about the place in its rich old days, or even that Queen Victoria had mentioned *"pretty* little Rivabella" to the Crown Princess of Prussia in one of her affectionate letters.

"All snobs," said Barbara. "Thank God I'm Irish," though there was something she did in a way mind: Saying "Rivebelle" had been one of her first mistakes. Another had been hiring a staff without taking advice. She was also suspected of paying twice the going rate, which was not so much an economic blunder as a social affront. "All snobs" was not much in the way of ammunition, but then, none of the other villas could claim a cook, a maid, a laundress, a gardener, and a governess marching down from Rivabella, all of them loyal, devoted, cheerful, hardworking, and kind.

She wrote to her pilot brother, the one she loved, telling him how self-reliant people seemed to be here, what pride they took in their jobs, how their philosophy was completely alien to the modern British idea of strife and grab. "I would love it if you would come and stay for a while. We have more rooms than we know what to do with. You and I could talk." But no one came. None of them wanted to have to watch poor old Alec dying.

The children would recall later on that their cook had worn a straw hat in the kitchen, so that steam condensing on the ceiling would not drop on her head, and that she wore the same hat to their father's funeral. Barbara would remind them about the food. She had been barely twenty at the beginning of the war, and there were meals for which she had never stopped feeling hungry. Three times a day, now, she sat down to cream and butter and fresh bread, new-laid eggs, jam you could stand a spoon in: breakfasts out of a storybook from before the war. As she preferred looking at food to eating it, it must have been the *idea* of her table spread that restored richness to her skin, luster to her hair. She had been all cream and gold, once, but war and marriage and Alec's illness and being hard up and some other indefinable disappointment had skimmed and darkened her. And yet she felt shot through with happiness sometimes, or at least by a piercing clue as to what bliss might be. This sensation, which she might have controlled more easily in another climate, became so natural, so insistent, that she feared sometimes that its source might be religious and that she would need to reject—out of principle—the felicity it promised. But no; she was, luckily, too earthbound for such nonsense. She could experience sudden felicity merely seeing her cook arrive with laden baskets, or the gardener crossing the terrace with a crate of flowering plants. (He would bed these out under the olive trees, where they perished rapidly.) Lou Mas at such times seemed to shrink to a toy house she might lift and carry; she would remember what it had been like when the children were babies still, and hers alone.

Carrying Alec's breakfast tray, she came in wearing the white dressing gown that had been his sister's parting gift to her. Her hair, which she now kept thick and loose, was shades lighter than it had been in England. He seemed barely to see her. But, then, everything dazzled him now. She buttered toast for him, and spread it with jam, saying, "Do try it, darling. You will never taste jam like this again." Of course, it thundered with prophecy. Her vision blurred—not because of tears, for she did not cry easily. It was as if a sheet of pure water had come down with an enormous crashing sound, cutting her off from Alec.

Now that winter was here, he moved with the sun instead of away from it. Shuffling to the balcony, he leaned on her shoulder. She covered him with blankets, gave him a book to read, combed his hair. He had all but stopped speaking, though he made an effort for strangers. She thought, What would it be like to be shot dead? Only the lingering question contained in a nightmare could account for this, but her visionary dreams had left her, probably because Alec's fate, and so to some measure her own, had been decided once and for all. Between house and sea the gardener crouched with a trowel in his hand. His work consisted of bedding-out, and his imagination stopped at salvia: The ground beneath the olive trees was dark red with them. She leaned against the warm parapet and thought of what he might see should he look up—herself, in white, with her hair blazing in the sun. But when he lifted his face it was only to wipe sweat from it with the shirt he had taken off. A dream of loss came back: She had been ordered to find new names for refugee children whose names had been forgotten. In real life, she had wanted her children to be called Giles, Nigel, and Samantha, but Alec had interfered. All three had been conceived on his wartime leaves, before he was taken prisoner. The children had her gray eyes, her skin that freckled, her small bones and delicate features (though Molly showed signs of belonging to a darker, sturdier race), but none of them had her richness, her shine. They seemed to her and perhaps to each other thin and dry, like Alec.

Everything Mademoiselle said was useless or repetitive. She explained, " 'Lou Mas' means 'the farm,' " which the children knew. When they looked out the dining-room window she remarked, "You can see Italy." She came early in order to share their breakfast; the aunt she lived with, the aunt with the frescoes, kept all the food in their palace locked up. "What do you take me for?" she sometimes asked them, tragically, of some small thing, such as their not paying intense attention. She was not teaching them much, only some French, and they were picking this up faster now than she could instruct. Her great-grandfather had been a French volunteer against Garibaldi (an Italian bandit, she explained); her grandfather was founder of a nationalist movement; her father had been murdered on the steps of his house at the end of the war. She was afraid of Freemasons, Socialists, Protestants, and Jews, but not of drowning or falling from a height or being attacked by a mad dog. When she discovered that the children had been christened (Alec having considered baptism a rational start to agnostic life), she undertook their religious education, which was not at all what Barbara was paying for.

After lunch, they went upstairs to visit Alec. He lay on his deck chair, tucked into blankets, as pale as clouds. James suddenly wailed out, believing he was singing, "We'll ring all the bells and kill all the Protestants." Silence, then James said, "Are there any left? Any Protestants?"

"I am left, for one," said his father.

"It's a good thing we came down here, then," said the child calmly. "They couldn't get at you."

Mademoiselle said, looking terrified, "It refers to old events in France."

"It wouldn't have mattered." His belief had gone to earth as soon as he had realized that the men he admired were in doubt. His conversation, like his reading, was increasingly simple. He was reading a book about gardening. He held it close to his face. Daylight tired him; it was like an intruder between memory and the eye. He read, "Nerine. Guernsey Lily. Ord. Amaryllidaceae. First introduced, 1680." Introduced into England, that meant. "Oleander, 1596. East Indian Rose Bay, 1770. Tamarind Tree, 1633. Chrysanthemum, 1764." So England had flowered, become bedecked, been bedded-out.

The book had been given him by a neighbor. The Webbs not only had people working for them, and delicious nursery food to eat, and a garden running down to the sea, but distinguished people living on either side— Mr. Edmund Cranefield of Villa Osiris to the right, and Mrs. Massie at Casa Scotia on the left. To reach their houses you had to climb thirty steps to the road, then descend more stairs on their land. Mr. Cranefield had a lift, which looked like a large crate stood on its side. Within it was a kitchen chair. He sat on the chair and was borne up to the road on an electric rail. No one had ever seen him doing this. When he went to Morocco during the worst of the winter, he had the lift disconnected and covered with rugs, the pond drained and the fish put in tanks, and his two peacocks, who screamed every dawn as if a fox were at them, boarded for a high fee with a private zoo. Casa Scotia belonged to Mrs. Massie, who was lame, wore a tweed cape, never went out without a hat, walked with a stick, and took a good twenty minutes to climb her steps.

Mr. Cranefield was a novelist, Mrs. Massie the author of a whole shelf of gardening books. Mr. Cranefield never spoke of his novels or offered to lend them; he did not even say what their titles were. "You must tell me every one!" Barbara cried, as if she were about to rush out and return with a wheelbarrow full of books by Mr. Cranefield.

He sat upstairs with Alec, and they talked about different things, quite often about the war. Just as Barbara was beginning to imagine Mr. Cranefield did not like her, he invited her to tea. She brought Molly along for protection, but soon saw he was not drawn to women—at least, not in the way she supposed men to be. She wondered then if she should keep Will and James away from him. He showed Barbara and Molly the loggia where he worked on windless mornings; a strong mistral had once blown one hundred and forty pages across three gardens—some were even found in a hedge at Casa Scotia. On a table were oval picture frames holding the likeness of a fair girl and a fair young man. Looking more closely, Barbara saw they were illustrations cut out of magazines. Mr. Cranefield said, "They are the pair I write about. I keep them there so that I never make a mistake."

"Don't they bore you?" said Barbara.

"Look at all they have given me." But the most dispossessed peasant, the filthiest housemaid, the seediest nail-biting doctor in Rivabella had what he was pointing out—the view, the sea. Of course, a wave of the hand cannot take in everything; he probably had more than this in reserve. He turned to Molly and said kindly, "When you are a little older you can do some typing for me," because it was his experience that girls liked doing that— typing for Mr. Cranefield while waiting for someone to marry. Girls were fond of him: He gave sound advice about love affairs, could read the future in handwriting. Molly knew nothing about him, then, but she would recall later on how Mr. Cranefield, who had invented women deep-sea divers, women test pilots, could not imagine—in his innocence, in his manhood— anything more thrilling to offer a girl when he met one than "You can type."

Barbara broke in, laughing: "She is only eleven."

This was true, but it seemed to Molly a terrible thing to say.

Mrs. Massie was not shy about bringing *her* books around. She gave several to Alec, among them *Flora's Gardening Encyclopaedia*, seventeenth edition, considered her masterpiece. All her books were signed "Flora," though it was not her name. She said about Mr. Cranefield, "Edmund is a great, pampered child. Spoiled by adoring women all his life. Not by me." She sat straight on the straightest chair, her hands clasped on her stick. "I do my own typing. My own gardening, too," though she did say to James and Will, "You can help in the garden for pocket money, if you like."

In the spring, the second Elizabeth was crowned. Barbara ordered a television set from a shop in Nice. It was the first the children had seen. Two men carried it with difficulty down the steps from the road, and soon became tired of lifting it from room to room while Barbara decided where she wanted it. She finally chose a room they kept shut usually; it had a raised platform at one end and until the war had been the site of amateur theatricals. The men set the box down on the stage and began fiddling with antennae and power points, while the children ran about arranging rows of chairs. One of the men said they might not have a perfect view of the Queen the next day, the day of the Coronation, because of Alps standing in the way. The children sat down and stared at the screen. Horizontal lightning streaked across its face. The men described implosion, which had killed any number of persons all over the world. They said that should the socket and plug begin to smoke, Barbara was to make a dash for the meter box and pull out the appropriate fuse.

"The appropriate fuse?" said Barbara. The children minded sometimes about the way she laughed at everything.

When the men had gone, they trooped upstairs to tell Alec about the Alps and implosion. He was resting in preparation for tomorrow's ceremony, which he would attend. It was clear to Molly that her father would not be able to get up and run if there was an accident. Kneeling on the warm tiles (this was in June) she pressed her face to his hand. Presently he slipped the hand away to turn a page. He was reading more of the book Mrs. Massie had pounded out on her 1929 Underwood—four carbons, single-spaced, no corrections, every page typed clean: "Brussels Sprouts—see Brassica." Brassica must be English, Alec thought. That was why he withdrew his hand—to see about Brassica. What use was his hand to Molly or her anxiety to him now? Why hold her? Why draw her into his pale world? She was a difficult, dull, clumsy child, something of a moper when her brothers teased her but sulky and tough when it came to Barbara. He had watched Barbara, goaded by Molly, lose control of herself and slap the girl's face, and he had heard Molly's pitiful credo: "You can't hurt me. My vaccination hurt worse than that." "Hurt more," Alec in silence had amended. "Hurt me *more* than that."

He found Brassica. It was Borecole, Broccoli, Cabbage, Cauliflower. His eyes slid over the rest of what it was until, "Native to Europe—BRITAIN," which Mrs. Massie had typed in capital letters during the war, with a rug around her legs in unheated Casa Scotia, waiting for the Italians or the Germans or the French to take her away to internment in a lorry. He was closer in temper to Mrs. Massie than to anyone else except his sister, though he had given up priorities. His blood was white (that was how he saw it), and his lungs and heart were bleached, too, and starting to disintegrate like snowflakes. He was a pale giant, a drained Gulliver, cast up on the beach, open territory for invaders. (Barbara and Will were sharing a paperback about flying saucers, whose occupants had built Stonehenge.) Alec's intrepid immigrants, his microscopic colonial settlers had taken over. He had been easy to subdue, being courteous by nature, diffident by choice. He had been a civil servant, then a soldier; had expected the best, relied on good behavior; had taken to prison camp thin books about Calabria and Greece; had been evasive, secretive, brave, unscrupulous only sometimes—had been English and middle class, in short.

That night Alec had what the doctor called "a crisis" and Alec termed "a bad patch." There was no question of his coming down for Coronation the next day. The children thought of taking the television set up to him, but it was too heavy, and Molly burst into tears thinking of implosion and accidents and Alec trapped. In the end the Queen was crowned in the little the-ater, as Barbara had planned, in the presence of Barbara and the children, Mr. Cranefield and Mrs. Massie, the doctor from Rivabella, a neighbor called Major Lamprey and his old mother, Mrs. Massie's housekeeper, Bar-bara's cook and two of her grandchildren, and Mademoiselle. One after the other these people turned their heads to look at Alec, gasping in the door-way, holding on to the frame. His hair was carefully combed and parted low on one side, like Mr. Cranefield's, and he had dressed completely, though he had a scarf around his neck instead of a tie. He was the last, the very last, of a kind. Not British but English. Not Christian so much as Anglican. Not Anglican but giving the benefit of the doubt. His children would never feel what he had felt, suffer what he had suffered, relinquish what he had done without so that this sacrament could take place. The new Queen's voice flowed easily over the Alps—thin, bored, ironed flat by the weight of what she had to remember—and came as far as Alec, to whom she owed her crown. He did not think that, precisely, but what had pulled him to his feet, made him stand panting for life in the doorway, would not occur to James or Will or Molly—not then, or ever.

He watched the rest of it from a chair. His breathing bothered the oth-ers: It made their own seem too quiet. He ought to have died that night. It would have made a reasonable ending. This was not a question of getting rid of Alec (no one wanted that) but of being able to say later, "He got up and dressed to see the Coronation." However, he went on living.

A nurse came every day, the doctor almost as often. He talked quietly to Barbara in the garden. A remission as long as this was unknown to him; it smacked of miracles. When Barbara would not hear of that, he said that Alec was holding on through willpower. But Alec was not holding on. His invaders had pushed him off the beach and into a boat. The stream was white and the shoreline, too. Everything was white, and he moved peace-fully. He had glimpses of his destination—a room where the hems of thin curtains swept back and forth on a bare floor. His vision gave him green bronze doors sometimes; he supposed they were part of the same room.

He could see his children, but only barely. He had guessed what the boys might become—one a rebel, one turned inward. The girl was a question mark. She was stoic and sentimental, indifferent sometimes to pleasure and pain. Whatever she was or could be or might be, he had left her behind. The boys placed a row of bricks down the middle of the room they shared. In the large house they fought for space. They were restless and noisy, untutored and bored. "I'll always have a packet of love from my children," Barbara had said to a man once (not Alec).

At the start of their second winter one of the Laceys came down to investigate. This was Ron, the hotelkeeper. He had dark hair and was thin and pale and walked softly. When he understood that what Barbara had written about servants and dollars was true, he asked to see the accounts. There were none. He talked to Barbara without raising his voice; that day she let everyone working for her go with the exception of the cook, whom Ron had said she was to keep because of Alec. He seemed to feel he was in a position of trust, for he ordered her—there was no other word for it—to place the children at once in the Rivabella town school: Lou Mas was costing the Lacey brothers enough in local taxes—they might as well feel they were getting something back. He called his sister "Bab" and Alec "Al." The children's parents suddenly seemed to them strangers.

When Ron left, Barbara marched the children up to Rivabella and made them look at the church. They had seen it, but she made them look again. She held the mistaken belief that religion was taught in French state schools, and she wanted to arm them. The children knew by now that what their mother called "France" was not really France down here but a set of rules, a code for doing things, such as how to recite the multiplication table or label a wine. Instead of the northern saints she remembered, with their sorrowful preaching, there was a southern St. Damian holding up a blazing sword. Any number of persons had seen him; Mademoiselle had, more than once.

"I want you to understand what superstition is," said Barbara, in clear, carrying English. "Superstition is what is wrong with Uncle Ron. He believes what he can't see, and what he sees he can't believe in. Now, imagine intelligent people saying they've seen this—this apparition. This St. George, or whatever." The church had two pink towers, one bearing a cross and the other a weather vane. St. Damian usually hovered between them. "In armor," said Barbara.

To all three children occurred, "Why not?" Protect me, prayed the girl. Vanquish, said Will. Lead, ordered the youngest, seeing only himself in command. He looked around the square and said to his mother, "Could we go, soon, please? Because people are looking."

That winter Molly grew breasts; she thought them enormous, though each could have been contained easily in a small teacup. Her brothers teased her. She went about with her arms crossed. She was tall for her age, and up in the town there was always some man staring. Elderly neighbors pressed her close. Major Lamprey, calling on Alec, kissed her on the mouth. He smelled of gin and pipe smoke. She scrubbed her teeth for minutes afterward. When she began to menstruate, Barbara said, "Now, Molly, you are to keep away from men," as if she weren't trying to.

The boys took their bicycles and went anywhere they wanted. In the evening they wheeled round and round the church square. Above them were swallows, on the edge of the square men and boys. Both were starting to speak better French than English, and James spoke dialect better than French. Molly disliked going up to Rivabella, unless she had to. She helped Barbara make the beds and wash the dishes and she did her homework and then very often went over to talk to Mr. Cranefield. She discovered, by chance, that he had another name—E. C. Arden. As E. C. Arden he was the author of a series of thumbed, comfortable novels (it was Mrs. Massie who lent Molly these), one of which, called *Belinda at Sea*, was Molly's favorite book of any kind. It was about a girl who joined the crew of a submarine, disguised as a naval rating, and kept her identity a secret all the way to Hong Kong. In the end, she married the submarine commander, who apparently had loved her all along. Molly read *Belinda at Sea* three or four times without ever mentioning to Mr. Cranefield she knew he was E. C. Arden. She thought it was a matter of deep privacy and that it was up to him to speak of it first. She did, however, ask what he thought of the saint on the church roof, using the name Barbara had, which was St. George.

"What," said Mr. Cranefield. "That Ethiopian?"

The girl looked frightened—not of Ethiopians, certainly, but of confusion as to person, the adult world of muddle. Even Mr. Cranefield was *also* E. C. Arden, creator of Belinda.

Mr. Cranefield explained, kindly, that up at Rivabella they had made a patron saint out of a mixture of St. Damian, who was an intellectual, and St. Michael, who was not, and probably a local pagan deity as well. St. Michael accounted for the sword, the pagan for the fire. Reliable witnesses had seen the result, though none of these witnesses were British. "We aren't awfully good at seeing saints," he said. "Though we do have an eye for ghosts."

Another thing still troubled Molly, but it was not a matter she could mention: She did not know what to do about her bosom—whether to try to hold it up in some way or, on the contrary, bind it flat. She had been granted, by the mistake of a door's swinging wide, an upsetting glimpse of Mrs. Massie changing out of a bathing suit, and she had been worried about the future shape of her own body ever since. She pored over reproductions of statues and paintings in books belonging to Mr. Cranefield. The Eves and Venuses represented were not reassuring—they often seemed to be made of India rubber. There was no one she could ask. Barbara was too dangerous; the mention of a subject such as this always made her go too far and say things Molly found unpleasant.

She did remark to both Mrs. Massie and Mr. Cranefield that she hated the Rivabella school. She said, "I would give anything to be sent home to England, but I can't leave my father."

After a long conversation with Mrs. Massie, Mr. Cranefield agreed to speak to Alec. Interfering with other people was not his way, but Molly struck him as being pathetic. Something told him that Molly was not useful leverage with either parent and so he mentioned Will first: Will would soon be fourteen, too old for the school at Rivabella. Unless the Webb children were enrolled, and quickly, in good French establishments—say, in lycées at Nice—they would become unfit for anything save menial work in a foreign language they could not speak in an educated way. Of course, the ideal solution would be England, if Alec felt he could manage that.

Alec listened, sitting not quite straight in his chair, wearing a dressing gown, his back to a window. He found all light intolerable now. Several times he lifted his hand as if he were trying to see through it. No one knew why Alec made these odd gestures; some people thought he had gone slightly mad because death was too long in coming. He parted his lips and whispered, "French school . . . If you would look after it," and then, "I would be grateful."

Mr. Cranefield dropped his voice too, as if the gray of the room called for hush. He asked if Alec had thought of appointing a guardian for them. The hand Alec seemed to want transparent waved back and forth, stiffly, like a shut ivory fan.

All that Barbara said to Mr. Cranefield was "Good idea," once he had assured her French high schools were not priest-ridden.

"It might have occurred to *her* to have done something about it," said Mrs. Massie, when this was repeated.

"Things do occur to Barbara," said Mr. Cranefield. "But she doesn't herself get the drift of them."

The only disturbing part of the new arrangement was that the children had been assigned to separate establishments, whose schedules did not co-incide; this meant they would not necessarily travel in the same bus. Molly had shot up as tall as Will now. Her hair was dark and curled all over her head. Her bones and her hands and feet were going to be larger, stronger, than her mother's and brothers'. She looked, already, considerably older than her age. She was obstinately innocent, turning her face away when Barbara, for her own good, tried to tell her something about men.

Barbara imagined her willful, ignorant daughter being enticed, trapped, molested, impregnated, and disgraced. *And* ending up wondering how it happened, Barbara thought. She saw Molly's seducer, brutish and dull. I'd get him by the throat, she said to herself. She imagined the man's strong neck and her own small hands, her brittle bird-bones. She said, "You are never, ever to speak to a stranger on the bus. You're not to get in a car with a man—not even if you know him."

"I don't know any man with a car."

"You could be waiting for a bus on a dark afternoon," said Barbara. "A car might pull up. Would you like a lift? No, you must answer. No and no and no. It is different for the boys. There are the two of them. They could put up a fight."

"Nobody bothers boys," said Molly.

Barbara drew breath but for once in her life said nothing.

Alec's remission was no longer just miraculous—it had become unreasonable. Barbara's oldest brother hinted that Alec might be better off in England, cared for on National Health: They were paying unholy taxes for just such a privilege. Barbara replied that Alec had no use for England, where the Labour government had sapped everyone's self-reliance. He believed in having exactly the amount of suffering you could pay for, no less and no more. She knew this theory did not hold water, because the Laceys and Alec's own sister had done the paying. It was too late now; they should have thought a bit sooner; and Alec was too ravaged to make a new move.

The car that, inevitably, pulled up to a bus stop in Nice was driven by a Mr. Wilkinson. He had just taken Major Lamprey and the Major's old mother to the airport. He rolled his window down and called to Molly, through pouring rain, "I say, aren't you from Lou Mas?"

If he sounded like a foreigner's Englishman, like a man in a British joke, it was probably because he had said so many British-sounding lines in films set on the Riviera. Eric Wilkinson was the chap with the strong blue eyes and ginger mustache, never younger than thirty-four, never as much as forty, who flashed on for a second, just long enough to show there was an Englishman in the room. He could handle a uniform, a dinner jacket, tails, a monocle, a cigarette holder, a swagger stick, a polo mallet, could open a cigarette case without looking like a gigolo, could say without being an ass about it, "Bless my soul, wasn't that the little Maharani?" or even, "Come along, old boy—fair play with Monica, now!" Foreigners meeting him often said, "That is what the British used to be like, when they were still all right, when the Riviera was still fit to live in." But the British who knew him were apt to glaze over: "You mean Wilkinson?" Mrs. Massie and Mr. Cranefield said, "Well, Wilkinson, what are you up to now?" There was no harm to him: His one-line roles did not support him, but he could do anything, even cook. He used his car as a private taxi, driving people to airports, meeting them when they came off cruise ships. He was not a chauffeur, never said "sir," and at the same time kept a certain distance, was not shy about money changing hands—no fake pride, no petit bourgeois demand for a slipped envelope. Good-natured. Navy blazer. Summer whites in August. Wore a tie that carried a message. What did it stand for? A third-rate school? A disgraced, disbanded regiment? A club raided by the police? No one knew. Perhaps it was the symbol of something new altogether. "Still playing in those films of yours, Wilkinson?" He would flash on and off— British gent at roulette, British Army officer, British diplomat, British political agent, British anything. Spoke his line, fitted his monocle, pressed the catch on his cigarette case. His ease with other people was genuine, his financial predicament unfeigned. He had never been married, and had no children that he knew of.

"By Jove, it's nippy," said Wilkinson, when Molly had settled beside him, her books on her lap.

What made her do this—accept a lift from a murderer of schoolgirls? First, she had seen him somewhere safe once—at Mr. Cranefield's. Also, she was wet through, and chilled to the heart. Barbara kept refusing or neglecting or forgetting to buy her the things she needed: a lined raincoat, a jersey the right size. (The boys were wearing hand-me-down clothes from England now, but no one Barbara knew of seemed to have a daughter.) The sleeves of her old jacket were so short that she put her hands in her pockets, so that Mr. Wilkinson would not despise her. He talked to Molly as he did to everyone, as if they were of an age, informing her that Major Lamprey and his mother were flying to Malta to look at a house. A number of people were getting ready to leave the south of France now; it had become so seedy and expensive, and all the wrong people were starting to move in.

"What kind of wrong people?" She sat tense beside him until he said, "Why, like Eric Wilkinson, I should think," and she laughed when his own laugh said she was meant to. He was nice to her; even later, when she thought she had reason to hate him, she would remember that Wilkinson had been nice. He drove beyond his destination—a block of flats that he waved at in passing and that Molly in a confused way supposed he owned. They stopped in the road behind Lou Mas; she thanked him fervently, and then, struck with something, sat staring at him: "Mr. Wilkinson," she said. "Please—I am not allowed to be in cars with men alone. In case someone happened to see us, would you mind just coming and meeting my mother? Just so she can see who you are?"

"God bless my soul," said Wilkinson, sincerely.

Once, Alec had believed that Barbara was not frightened by anything, and that this absence of fear was her principal weakness. It was true that she had begun drifting out of her old life now, as calmly as Alec drifted away from life altogether. Her mock phrase for each additional Lou Mas catastrophe had become "the usual daily developments." The usual developments over seven rainy days had been the departure of the cook, who took with her all she could lay her hands on, and a French social-security fine that had come down hard on the remains of her marble block of money, reducing it to pebbles and dust. She had never filled out employer's forms for the people she had hired, because she had not known she was supposed to and none of them had suggested it; for a number of reasons having to do with government offices and tax files, none of them had wanted even this modest income to be registered anywhere. As it turned out, the gardener had also been receiving unemployment benefits, which, unfairly, had increased the amount of the fine Barbara had to pay. Rivabella turned out to be just as grim and bossy as England—worse, even, for it kept up a camouflage of wine and sunshine and olive trees and of amiable southern idiots who, if sacked, thought nothing of informing on one.

She sat at the dining-room table, wearing around her shoulders a red cardigan Molly had outgrown. On the table were the Sunday papers Alec's sister continued to send faithfully from England, and Alec's lunch tray, exactly as she had taken it up to him except that everything on it was now cold. She glanced up and saw the two of them enter—one stricken and guilty-looking, the other male, confident, smiling. The recognition that leaped between Barbara and Wilkinson was the last thing that Wilkinson in his right mind should have wanted, and absolutely everything Barbara now desired and craved. Neither of them heard Molly saying, "Mummy, this is Mr. Wilkinson. Mr. Wilkinson wants to tell you how he came to drive me home."

It happened at last that Alec had to be taken to the Rivabella hospital, where the local poor went when it was not feasible to let them die at home. Eric Wilkinson, new family friend, drove his car as far as it could go along a winding track, after which they placed Alec on a stretcher; and Wilkinson, Mr. Cranefield, Will, and the doctor carried him the rest of the way. A soft April rain was falling, from which they protected Alec as they could. In the rain the doctor wept unnoticed. The others were silent and absorbed. The hospital stood near the graveyard—shamefully near, Wilkinson finally remarked, to Mr. Cranefield. Will could see the cemetery from his father's new window, though to do so he had to lean out, as he'd imagined passengers doing and having their heads cut off in the train game long ago. A concession was made to Alec's status as owner of a large villa, and he was given a private room. It was not a real sickroom but the place where the staff went to eat and drink when they took time off. They cleared away the plates and empty wine bottles and swept up most of the crumbs and wheeled a bed in.

The building was small for a hospital, large for a house. It had been the winter home of a Moscow family, none of whom had come back after 1917. Alec lay flat and still. Under a drift of soot on the ceiling he could make out a wreath of nasturtiums and a bluebird with a ribbon in its beak.

At the window, Will said to Mr. Cranefield, "We can see Lou Mas from here, and even your peacocks."

Mr. Cranefield fretted, "They shouldn't be in the rain."

Alec's neighbors came to visit. Mrs. Massie, not caring who heard her (one of the children did), said to someone she met on the hospital staircase, "Alec is a gentleman and always will be, but Barbara . . . Barbara." She took a rise of the curved marble stairs at a time. "If the boys were girls they'd be sluts. As it is, they are ruffians. Their old cook saw one of them stoning a cat to death. And now there is Wilkinson. Wilkinson." She moved on alone, repeating his name.

Everyone was saying "Wilkinson" now. Along with "Wilkinson" they said "Barbara." You would think that having been married to one man who was leaving her with nothing, leaving her dependent on family charity, she would have looked around, been more careful, picked a reliable kind of person. "A foreigner, say," said Major Lamprey's mother, who had not cared for Malta. Italians love children, even other people's. She might have chosen—you know—one of the cheerful sort, with a clean shirt and a clean white handkerchief, proprietor of a linen shop. The shop would have kept Barbara out of mischief.

No one could blame Wilkinson, who had his reasons. Also, he had said all those British-sounding lines in films, which in a way made him all right. Barbara had probably said she was Irish once too often. "What can you expect?" said Mrs. Massie. "Think how they were in the war. They keep order when there is someone to bully them. Otherwise ..." The worst she had to say about Wilkinson was that he was preparing to flash on as the colonel of a regiment in a film about desert warfare; it had been made in the hilly country up behind Monte Carlo.

"Not a grain of sand up there," said Major Lamprey. He said he wondered what foreigners thought they meant by "desert."

"A colonel!" said Mrs. Massie.

"Why not?" said Mr. Cranefield.

"They must think he looks it," said Major Lamprey. "Gets a fiver a day, I'm told, and an extra fiver when he speaks his line. He says, 'Don't underestimate Rommel.' For a fiver I'd say it," though he would rather have died.

The conversation veered to Wilkinson's favor. Wilkinson was merry; told irresistible stories about directors, unmalicious ones about film stars; repeated comic anecdotes concerning underlings who addressed him as "Guv." "I wonder who they can be?" said Mrs. Massie. "It takes a Wilkinson to find them." Mr. Cranefield was more indulgent; he had to be. A sardonic turn of mind would have been resented by E. C. Arden's readers. The blond-headed pair on his desk stood for a world of triumphant love, with which his readers felt easy kinship. The fair couple, though competent in any domain, whether restoring a toppling kingdom or taming a tiger, lived on the same plane as all human creatures except England's enemies. They raised the level of existence—raised it, and flattened it.

Mr. Cranefield—as is often and incorrectly said of children—lived in a world of his own, too, in which he kept everyone's identity clear. He did not confuse St. Damian with an Ethiopian, or Wilkinson with Raffles, or Barbara with a slut. This was partly out of the habit of neatness and partly because he could not make up his mind to live openly in the world he wanted, which was a homosexual one. He said about Wilkinson and Barbara and the blazing scandal at Lou Mas, "I am sure there is no harm in it. Barbara has too much to manage alone, and it is probably better for the children to have a man about the place."

When Wilkinson was not traveling, he stayed at Lou Mas. Until now his base had been a flat he'd shared with a friend who was a lawyer and who was also frequently away. Wilkinson left most of his luggage behind; there was barely enough of his presence to fill a room. For a reason no one understood Barbara had changed everyone's room around: She and Molly slept where Alec had been, the boys moved to Barbara's room, and Wilkinson was given Molly's bed. It seemed a small bed for so tall a man.

Molly had always slept alone, until now. Some nights, when Wilkinson was sleeping in her old room, she would waken just before dawn and find that her mother had disappeared. Her feeling at the sight of the empty bed was one of panic. She would get up, too, and go in to Will and shake him, saying, "She's disappeared."

"No, she hasn't. She's with Wilkinson." Nevertheless, he would rise and stumble, still nearly sleeping, down the passage—Alec's son, descendant of civil servants, off on a mission.

Barbara slept with her back against Wilkinson's chest. Outside, Mr. Cranefield's peacocks greeted first light by screaming murder. Years from now, Will would hear the first stirrings of dawn and dream of assassinations. Wilkinson never moved. Had he shown he was awake, he might have felt obliged to say a suitable one-liner—something like "I say, old chap, you are a bit of a trial, you know."

Will's mother picked up the nightgown and robe that lay white on the floor, pulled them on, flung her warm hair back, tied her sash—all without haste. In the passage, the door shut on the quiet Wilkinson, she said tenderly, "Were you worried?"

"Molly was."

Casual with her sons, she was modest before her daughter. Changing to a clean nightdress, she said, "Turn the other way." Turning, Molly saw her mother, white and gold, in the depths of Alec's mirror. Barbara had her arms raised, revealing the profile of a breast with at its tip the palest wash of rose, paler than the palest pink flower. (Like a Fragonard, Barbara had been told, like a Boucher—not by Alec.) What Molly felt now was immense relief. It was not the fate of every girl to turn into India rubber. But in no other way did she wish to resemble her mother.

Like the residue left by winter rains, awareness of Barbara and Wilkinson seeped through the house. There was a damp chill about it that crept to the bone. One of the children, Will, perceived it as torment. Because of the mother defiled, the source of all such knowledge became polluted, probably forever. The boys withdrew from Barbara, who had let the weather in. James imagined ways of killing Wilkinson, though he drew the line at killing Barbara. He did not want her dead, but different. The mother he wanted did not stand in public squares pointing crazily up to invisible saints, or begin sleeping in one bed and end up in another.

Barbara felt that they were leaving her; she put the blame on Molly, who had the makings of a prude, and who, at worst, might turn out to be something like Alec's sister. Barbara said to Molly, "I had three children before I was twenty-three, and I was alone, and there were all the air raids. The life I've tried to give you and the boys has been so different, so happy, so free." Molly folded her arms, looked down at her shoes. Her height, her grave expression, her new figure gave her a bogus air of maturity: She was only thirteen, and she felt like a pony flicked by a crop. Barbara tried to draw near: "My closest friend is my own daughter," she wanted to be able to say. "I never do a thing without talking it over with Molly." So she would have said, laughing, her bright head against Molly's darker hair, if only Molly had given half an inch.

"What a cold creature you are," Barbara said, sadly. "You live in an ice palace. There is so little happiness in life unless you let it come near. I always at least had an *idea* about being happy." The girl's face stayed shut and locked. All that could cross it now was disappointment.

One night when Molly woke Will, he said, "I don't care where she is." Molly went back to bed. Fetching Barbara had become a habit. She was better off in her room alone.

When they stopped coming to claim her, Barbara perceived it as mortification. She gave up on Molly, for the moment, and turned to the boys, sat curled on the foot of their bed, sipping wine, telling stories, offering to share her cigarette, though James was still twelve. James said, "He told us it was dangerous to smoke in bed. People have died that way." "He" meant Alec. Was this all James would remember? That he had warned about smoking in bed?

James, who was embarrassed by this attempt of hers at making them equals, thought she had an odd smell, like a cat. To Will, at another kind of remove, she stank of folly. They stared at her, as if measuring everything she still had to mean in their lives. This expression she read as she could. Love for Wilkinson had blotted out the last of her dreams and erased her gift of second sight. She said unhappily to Wilkinson, "My children are prigs. But, then, they are only half mine."

Mademoiselle, whom the children now called by her name—Geneviève—still came to Lou Mas. Nobody paid her, but she corrected the children's French, which no longer needed correcting, and tried to help with their homework, which amounted to interference. They had always in some way spared her; only James, her favorite, sometimes said, "No, I'd rather work alone." She knew now that the Webbs were poor, which increased her affection: Their descent to low water equaled her own. Sometimes she brought a packet of biscuits for their tea, which was a dull affair now the cook had gone. They ate the biscuits straight from the paper wrapping: Nobody wanted to wash an extra plate. Wilkinson, playing at British something, asked about her aunt. He said "Madame la Comtesse." When he had gone, she cautioned the children not to say that but simply "your aunt." But as Geneviève's aunt did not receive foreigners, save for a few such as Mrs. Massie, they had no reason to ask how she was. When Geneviève realized from something said that Wilkinson more or less lived at Lou Mas, she stopped coming to see them. The Webbs had no further connection with Rivabella then except for their link with the hospital, where Alec still lay quietly, still alive.

Barbara went up every day. She asked the doctor, "Shouldn't he be having blood transfusions—something of that kind?" She had never been in a hospital except to be born and to have her children. She was remembering films she had seen: bottles dripping liquids, needles taped to the crook of an arm, nursing sisters wheeling oxygen tanks down white halls.

The doctor reminded her that this was Rivabella—a small town where half the population lived without employment. He had been so sympathetic at first, so slow to present a bill. She could not understand what had changed him; but she was hopeless at reading faces now. She could scarcely read her children's.

She bent down to Alec, so near that her eyes would have seemed enormous had he been paying attention. She told him the name of the scent she was wearing; it reminded her and perhaps Alec, too, of jasmine. Eric had brought it back from a dinner at Monte Carlo, given to promote this very perfume. He was often invited to these things, where he represented the best sort of Britishness. "Eric is being the greatest help," she said to Alec, who might have been listening. She added, for it had to be said sometime, "Eric has very kindly offered to stay at Lou Mas."

Mr. Cranefield and Mrs. Massie continued to plod up the hill, she with increasing difficulty. They brought Alec what they thought he needed. But he had no addictions, no cravings, no use for anything now but his destination. The children were sent up evenings. They never knew what to say or what he could hear. They talked as if they were still eleven or twelve, when Alec had stopped seeing them grow.

To Mr. Cranefield they looked like imitations of English children— loud, humorless, dutiful, clear. "James couldn't come with us tonight," said Molly. "He was quite ill, for some reason. He brought his dinner up." All three spoke the high, thin English of expatriate children who, unknowingly, mimic their mothers. The lightbulb hanging crooked left Alec's face in shadow. When the children had kissed Alec and departed, Mr. Cranefield could hear them taking the hospital stairs headlong, at a gallop. The children were young and alive, and Alec was forty-something and nearly always sleeping. Unequal chances, Mr. Cranefield thought. They can't really beat their breasts about it. When Mrs. Massie was present, she never failed to say, "Your father is tired," though nobody knew if Alec was tired or not.

The neighbors pitied the children. Meaning only kindness, Mr. Cranefield reminded Molly that one day she would type, Mrs. Massie said something more about helping in the garden. That was how everyone saw them now— grubbing, digging, lending a hand. They had become Wilkinson's second-hand kin but without his panache, his ease in adversity. They were Alec's offspring: stiff. Humiliated, they overheard and garnered for memory: "We've asked Wilkinson to come over and cook up a curry. He's hours in the kitchen, but I must say it's worth every penny." "We might get Wilkinson to drive us to Rome. He doesn't charge all that much, and he's such good company." Always Wilkinson, never Eric, though that was what Barbara had called him from their first meeting. To the children he was, and remained, "Mr. Wilkinson," friend of both parents, occasional guest in the house.

The rains of their third southern spring were still driving hard against the villa when Barbara's engineer brother wrote to say they were letting Lou Mas. Everything dripped wet as she stood near a window, with bougainvillea soaked and wild-looking on one side of the pane and steam forming on the other, to read this letter. The new tenants were a family of planters who had been forced to leave Malaya; it had a connection with political events, but Barbara's life was so full now that she never looked at the papers. They would be coming there in June, which gave Barbara plenty of time to find another home. He—her brother—had thought of giving her the Lou Mas cottage, but he wondered if it would suit her, inasmuch as it lacked electric light, running water, an indoor lavatory, most of its windows, and part of its roof. This was not to say it could not be fixed up for the Webbs in the future, when Lou Mas had started paying for itself. Half the rent obtained would be turned over to Barbara. She would have to look hard, he said, before finding brothers who were so considerate of a married sister. She and the children were not likely to suffer from the change, which might even turn out to their moral advantage. Barbara supposed this meant that Desmond—the richest, the best-educated, the most easily flabbergasted of her brothers—was still mulling over the description of Lou Mas Ron must have taken back.

With Wilkinson helping, the Webbs moved to the far side of the hospital, on a north-facing slope, away from the sea. Here the houses were tall and thin with narrow windows, set in gardens of raked gravel. Their neighbors included the mayor, the more prosperous shopkeepers, and the coach of the local football team. Barbara was enchanted to find industrial activity she had not suspected—a thriving ceramics factory that produced figurines of monks whose heads were mustard pots, dogs holding thermometers in their paws, and the patron saint of Rivabella wearing armor of pink, orange, mauve, or white. These were purchased by tourists who had trudged up to the town in the hope of seeing early Renaissance frescoes.

Barbara had never missed a day with Alec, not even the day of the move. She held his limp hand and told him stories. When he was not stunned by drugs, or too far lost in his past, he seemed to be listening. Sometimes he pressed her fingers. He seldom spoke more than a word at a time. Barbara described to him the pleasures of moving, and how pretty the houses were on the north side, with their gardens growing gnomes and shells and tinted bottles. Why make fun of such people, she asked his still face. They probably knew, by instinct, how to get the best out of life. She meant every word, for she was profoundly in love and knew that Wilkinson would never leave her except for a greater claim. She combed Alec's hair and bathed him; Wilkinson came whenever he could to shave Alec and cut his nails and help Barbara change the bedsheets; for it was not the custom of the hospital staff to do any of this.

Sometimes Alec whispered, "Diana," who might have been either his sister or Mrs. Massie. Barbara tried to remember her old prophetic dreams, from that time when, as compensation for absence of passion, she had been granted second sight. In none had she ever seen herself bending over a dying man, listening to him call her by another woman's name.

They lived, now, in four dark rooms stuffed with furniture, some of it useful. Upstairs resided the widow of the founder of the ceramics factory. She had been bought out at a loss at the end of the war, and disapproved of the new line of production, especially the monks. She never interfered, never asked questions—simply came down once a month to collect her rent, which was required in cash. She did tell the children that she had never seen the inside of an English villa, but did not seem to think her exclusion was a slight; she took her bearings from a very small span of the French middle-class compass.

Barbara and Wilkinson made jokes about the French widow-lady, but the children did not. To replace their lopped English roots they had grown the sensitive antennae essential to wanderers. They could have drawn the social staircase of Rivabella on a blackboard, and knew how low a step, now, had been assigned to them. Barbara would not have cared. Wherever she stood now seemed to suit her. On her way home from the hospital she saw two men, foreigners, stop and stare and exchange remarks about her. She could not understand the language they spoke, but she saw they had been struck by her beauty. One of them seemed to be asking the other, "Who can she be?" In their new home she took the only bedroom—an imposing matrimonial chamber. When Wilkinson was in residence he shared it as a matter of course. The boys slept on a pullout sofa in the dining room, and Molly had a couch in a glassed-in verandah. The verandah contained their landlady's rubber plants, which Molly scrupulously tended. The boys had stopped quarreling. They would never argue or ever say much to each other again. Alec's children seemed to have been collected under one roof by chance, like strays, or refugees. Their narrow faces, their gray eyes, their thinness and dryness, were similar, but not alike; a stranger would not necessarily have known they were of the same father and mother. The boys still wore secondhand clothes sent from England; this was their only connection with English life.

On market days Molly often saw their old housemaid or the laundress. They asked for news of Alec, which made Molly feel cold and shy. She was dressed very like them now, in a cotton frock and rope-soled shoes from a market stall. "Style is all you need to bring it off," Barbara had assured her, but she had none, at least not that kind. It was Molly who chose what the family would eat, who looked at prices and kept accounts and counted her change. Barbara was entirely busy with Alec at the hospital, and with Wilkinson at home. With love, she had lost her craving for nursery breakfasts. She sat at table smoking, watching Wilkinson telling stories. When Wilkinson was there, he did much of the cooking. Molly was grateful for that.

The new people at Lou Mas had everyone's favor. If there had been times when the neighbors had wondered how Barbara and Alec could possibly have met, the Malayan planter and his jolly wife were an old novel known by heart. They told about jungle terrorists, and what the British ought to be doing, and they described the owner of Lou Mas—a Welshman who was planning to go into politics. Knowing Barbara to be Irish, no one could place the Welshman. The story started up that Barbara's family were bankrupt and had sold Lou Mas to a Welsh war profiteer.

Mrs. Massie presented the new people with *Flora's Gardening Encyclopaedia*. "It is by way of being a classic," she said. "Seventeen editions. I do all my typing myself."

"Ah, well, poor Barbara," everyone said now. What could you expect? Luckily for her, she had Wilkinson. Wilkinson's star was rising. "Don't underestimate Rommel" had been said to some effect—there was a mention in the *Sunday Telegraph*. "Wilkinson goes everywhere. He's invited to everything at Monte Carlo. He must positively live on lobster salad." "Good for old Wilkinson. Why shouldn't he?" Wilkinson had had a bad war, had been a prisoner somewhere.

Who imagined that story, Mr. Cranefield wondered. Some were mixing up Wilkinson with the dying Alec, others seemed to think Alec was already dead. By August it had become established that Wilkinson had been tortured by the Japanese and had spent the years since trying to leave the memory behind. He never mentioned what he'd been through, which was to his credit. Barbara and three kids must have been the last thing he wanted, but that was how it was with Wilkinson—too kind for his own good, all too ready to lend a hand, to solve a problem. Perhaps, rising, he would pull the Webbs with him. Have you seen that girl hanging about in the market? You can't tell her from the butcher's child.

From Alec's bedside Barbara wrote a long letter to her favorite brother, the pilot, Mike. She told about Alec, "sleeping so peacefully as I write," and described the bunch of daisies Molly had put in a jug on the windowsill, and how well Will had done in his finals ("He will be the family intellectual, a second Alec"), and finally she came round to the matter of Wilkinson: "You probably saw the rave notice in the *Telegraph*, but you had no way of knowing of course it was someone I knew. Well, here is the whole story. Please, Mike, do keep it to yourself for the moment, you know how Ron takes things sometimes." Meeting Eric had confirmed her belief there was something in the universe more reasonable than God—at any rate more logical. Eric had taken a good look at the Lou Mas cottage and thought something might be done with it after all. "You will adore Eric," she promised. "He is marvelous with the children and so kind to Alec," which was true.

"Are you awake, love?" She moistened a piece of cotton with mineral water from a bottle that stood on the floor (Alec had no table) and wet his lips with it, then took his hand, so light it seemed hollow, and held it in her own, telling him quietly about the Lou Mas cottage, where he would occupy a pleasant room overlooking the sea. He flexed his fingers; she bent close: "Yes, dear; what is it, dear?" For the first time since she'd known him he said, "Mother." She waited; but no, that was all. She saw herself on his balcony at Lou Mas in her white dressing gown, her hair in the sun, saw what the gardener would have been struck by if only he had looked up. She said to herself, I gave Alec three beautiful children. That is what he is thanking me for now.

Her favorite brother had been away from England when her letter came, so that it was late in September when he answered to call her a bitch, a trollop, a crook, and a fool. He was taking up the question of her gigolo boyfriend with the others. They had been supporting Alec's family for three years. If she thought they intended to take on her lover (this written above a word scratched out); and here the letter ended. She went white, as her children did, easily. She said to Wilkinson, "Come and talk in the car, where we can be quiet," for they were seldom alone.

She let him finish reading, then said, in a voice that he had never heard before but that did not seem to surprise him—"I grew up blacking my brothers' boots. Alec was the first man who ever held a door open for me."

He said, "Your brothers all did well," without irony, meaning there was that much to admire.

"Oh," she said, "if you are comparing their chances with Alec's, if that's what you mean—the start Alec had. Well, poor Alec. Yes, a better start. I often thought, Well, there it is with him, that's the very trouble—a start too good."

This exchange, this double row of cards faceup, seemed all they intended to reveal. They instantly sat differently, she straighter, he more relaxed.

Wilkinson said, "Which one of them actually owns Lou Mas?"

"Equal shares, I think. Though Desmond has power of attorney and makes all the decisions. Alec and I *own* Lou Mas, but only legally. They put it in our name because we were emigrating. It made it easier for them, with all the taxes. We had three years, and not a penny in rent."

Wilkinson said, in a kind of anguish, "Oh, God bless my soul."

It was Wilkinson's English lawyer friend in Monte Carlo who drew up the papers with which Alec signed his share of Lou Mas over to Barbara and Alec and Barbara revoked her brother's power of attorney. Alec, his obedient hand around a pen and the hand firmly held in Barbara's, may have known what he was doing but not why. The documents were then put in the lawyer's safe to await Alec's death, which occurred not long after.

The doctor, who had sat all night at the bedside, turning Alec's head so that he would not strangle vomiting (for that was not the way he wished him to die), heard him breathing deeply and ever more deeply and then no longer. Alec's eyes were closed, but the doctor pressed the lids with his fingers. Believing in his own and perhaps Alec's damnation, he stood for a long time at the window while the roof and towers of the church became clear and flushed with rose; then the red rim of the sun emerged, and turned yellow, and it was as good as day.

There was only one nurse in the hospital, and a midwife on another floor. Summoning both, he told them to spread a rubber sheet under Alec, and wash him, and put clean linen on the bed.

At that time, in that part of France, scarcely anyone had a telephone. The doctor walked down the slope on the far side of Rivabella and presented himself unshaven to Barbara in her nightdress to say that Alec was dead. She dressed and came at once; there was no one yet in the streets to see her and to ask who she was. Eric followed, bringing the clothes in which Alec would be buried. All he could recall of his prayers, though he would not have said them around Barbara, were the first words of the Collect: "Almighty God, unto whom all hearts be open, all desires known, and from whom no secrets are hid."

Barbara had a new friend—her French widowed landlady. It was she who arranged to have part of Barbara's wardrobe dyed black within twenty-four hours, who lent her a black hat and gloves and a long crêpe veil. Barbara let the veil down over her face. Her friend, whose veil was tied around her hat and floated behind her, took Barbara by the arm, and they walked to the cemetery and stood side by side. The Webbs' former servants were there, and the doctor, and the local British colony. Some of the British thought the other woman in black must be Barbara's Irish mother:

Only the Irish poor or the Royal Family ever wore mourning of that kind.

The graveyard was so cramped and small, so crowded with dead from the time of Garibaldi and before, that no one else could be buried. The coffins of the recent dead were stored in cells in a thick concrete wall. The cells were then sealed, and a marble plaque affixed in lieu of a tombstone. Alec had to be lifted to shoulder level, which took the strength of several persons—the doctor, Mr. Cranefield, Barbara's brothers, and Alec's young sons. (Wilkinson would have helped, but he had already wrenched his shoulder quite badly carrying the coffin down the hospital steps.) Molly thrust her way into this crowd of male mourners. She said to her mother, "Not you—you never loved him."

God knows who might have heard that, Barbara thought.

Actually, no one had, except for Mrs. Massie. Believing it to be true, she dismissed it from memory. She was composing her own obituary: "Two generations of gardeners owed their . . ." "Two generations of readers owed their gardens . . ."

"Our Father," Alec's sister said, hoping no one would notice and mistake her for a fraud. Nor did she wish to have a scrap of consideration removed from Barbara, whose hour this was. Her own loss was beyond remedy, and so not worth a mention. There was no service—nothing but whispering and silence. To his sister, it was as if Alec had been left, stranded and alone, in a train stalled between stations. She had not seen him since the day he left England, and had refused to look at him dead. Barbara was aware of Diana, the mouse, praying like a sewing machine somewhere behind her. She clutched the arm of the older widow and thought, I know, I know, but she can get a job, can't she? I was working when I met Alec, wasn't I? But what Diana Webb meant by "work" was the fine stitching her own mother had done to fill time, not for a living. In Diana's hotel room was a box containing the most exquisite and impractical child's bonnet and coat made from some of the white silk Alec had sent her from India, before the war. Perhaps a luxury shop in Monte Carlo or one of Barbara's wealthy neighbors would be interested. Perhaps there was an Anglican clergyman with a prosperous parish. She opened her eyes and saw that absolutely no one in the cemetery looked like Alec—not even his sons.

The two boys seemed strange, even to each other, in their dark, new suits. The word "father" had slipped out of their grasp just now. A marble plaque on which their father's name was misspelled stood propped against the wall. The boys looked at it helplessly.

Is that all, people began wondering. What happens now?

Barbara turned away from the wall and, still holding the arm of her friend, led the mourners out past the gates.

It was I who knew what he wanted, the doctor believed. He had told me long before. Asked me to promise, though I refused. I heard his last words. The doctor kept telling himself this. I heard his last words—though Alec had not said anything, had merely breathed, then stopped.

"Her father was a late Victorian poet of some distinction," Mrs. Massie's obituary went on.

Will, who was fifteen, was no longer a child, did not look like Alec, spoke up in that high-pitched English of his: "Death is empty without God." Now where did that come from? Had he heard it? Read it? Was he performing? No one knew. Later, he would swear that at that moment a vocation had come to light, though it must have been born with him—bud within the bud, mind within the mind. I will buy back your death, he would become convinced he had said to Alec. Shall enrich it; shall refuse the southern glare, the southern void. I shall pay for your solitude, your humiliation. Shall demand for myself a stronger life, a firmer death. He thought, later, that he had said all this, but he had said and thought only five words.

As they shuffled out, all made very uncomfortable by Will, Mrs. Massie leaned half on her stick and half on James, observing, "You were such a little boy when I saw you for the first time at Lou Mas." Because his response was silence, she supposed he was waiting to hear more. "You three must stick together now. The Three Musketeers." But they were already apart.

Major Lamprey found himself walking beside the youngest of the Laceys. He told Mike what he told everyone now—why he had not moved to Malta. It was because he did not trust the Maltese. "Not that one can trust anyone here," he said. "Even the mayor belongs to an anarchist movement, I've been told. Whatever happens, I intend to die fighting on my own doorstep."

The party was filing down a steep incline. "You will want to be with your family," Mrs. Massie said, releasing James and leaning half her weight on Mr. Cranefield instead. They picked up with no trouble a conversation dropped the day before. It was about how Mr. Cranefield—rather, his other self, E. C. Arden—was likely to fare in the second half of the 1950s: "It is a question of your not being too modern and yet not slipping back," Mrs. Massie said. "I never have to worry. Gardens don't change."

"I am not worried about new ideas," he said. "Because there are none. But words, now. 'Permissive.' "

"What's that?"

"It was in the *Observer* last Sunday. I suppose it means something. Still. One mustn't. One can't. There are limits."

Barbara met the mayor coming the other way, too late, carrying a wreath with a purple ribbon on which was written, in gold, "From the Municipality—Sincere Respects." Waiting for delivery of the wreath had made him tardy. "For a man who never went out, Alec made quite an impression," Mrs. Massie remarked.

"His funeral was an attraction," said Mr. Cranefield.

"Can one call that a funeral?" She was still thinking about her own.

Mike Lacey caught up to his sister. They had once been very close. As soon as she saw him she stood motionless, bringing the line behind her to a halt. He said he knew this was not the time or place, but he had to let her know she was not to worry. She would always have a roof over her head. They felt responsible for Alec's children. There were vague plans for fixing up the cottage. They would talk about it later on.

"Ah, Mike," she said. "That is so kind of you." Using both hands she lifted the veil so that he could see her clear gray eyes.

The procession wound past the hospital and came to the church square. Mr. Cranefield had arranged a small after-funeral party, as a favor to Barbara, who had no real home. Some were coming and some were not; the latter now began to say good-bye. Geneviève, whose face was like a pink sponge because she had been crying so hard, flung herself at James, who let her embrace him. Over his governess's dark shoulder he saw the faces of people who had given him secondhand clothes, thus (he believed) laying waste to his life. He smashed their faces to particles, left the particles dancing in the air like midges until they dissolved without a sound. Wait, he was thinking. Wait, wait.

Mr. Cranefield wondered if Molly was going to become her mother's hostage, her moral bail—if Barbara would hang on to her to show that Alec's progeny approved of her. He remembered Molly's small, anxious face, and how worried she had been about St. George. "You will grow up, you know," he said, which was an odd thing to say, since she was quite tall. They walked down the path Wilkinson had not been able to climb in his car. She stared at him. "I mean, when you grow up you will be free." She shook her head. She knew better than that now, at fourteen: There was no freedom except to cease to love. She would love her brothers when they had stopped thinking much about her: women's fidelity. This would not keep her from fighting them, inch by inch, over money, property, remnants of the past: women's insecurity. She would hound them and pester them about

Alec's grave, and Barbara's old age, and where they were all to be buried: women's sense of order. They would by then be another James, an alien Will, a different Molly.

Mr. Cranefield's attention slipped from Molly to Alec to the funeral, to the extinction of one sort of Englishman and the emergence of another. Most people looked on Wilkinson as a prewar survival, what with his "I say's" and "By Jove's," but he was really an English mutation, a new man, wearing the old protective coloring. Alec would have understood his language, probably, but not the person behind it. A landscape containing two male figures came into high relief in Mr. Cranefield's private image of the world, as if he had been lent trick spectacles. He allowed the vision to fade. Better to stick to the blond pair on his desk; so far they had never let him down. I am not impulsive, or arrogant, he explained to himself. No one would believe the truth about Wilkinson even if he were to describe it. I shall not insist, he decided, or try to have the last word. I am not that kind of fool. He breathed slowly, as one does when mortal danger has been averted.

The mourners attending Mr. Cranefield's party reached the motor road and began to straggle across: It was a point of honor for members of the British colony to pay absolutely no attention to cars. The two widows had fallen back, either so that Barbara could make an entrance, or because the older woman believed it would not be dignified for her to exhibit haste. A strong west wind flattened the black dresses against their breasts and lifted their thick veils.

How will he hear me, Molly wondered. You could speak to someone in a normal grave, for earth is porous and seems to be life, of a kind. But how to speak across marble? Even if she were to place her hands flat on the marble slab, it would not absorb a fraction of human warmth. She had to tell him what she had done—how it was she, Molly, who had led the intruder home, let him in, causing Alec, always courteous, to remove himself first to the hospital, then farther on. Disaster, the usual daily development, had to have a beginning. She would go back to the cemetery, alone, and say it, whether or not he could hear. The disaster began with two sentences: "Mummy, this is Mr. Wilkinson. Mr. Wilkinson wants to tell you how he came to drive me home."

Barbara descended the steps to Mr. Cranefield's arm in arm with her new friend, who was for the first time about to see the inside of an English house. "Look at that," said the older widow. One of the peacocks had taken shelter from the wind in Mr. Cranefield's electric lift. A minute earlier Alec's sister had noticed, too, and had thought something that seemed irrefutable: No power on earth would ever induce her to eat a peacock.

Who is to say I never loved Alec, said Barbara, who loved Wilkinson. He was high-handed, yes, laying down the law as long as he was able, but he was always polite. Of course I loved him. I still do. He will have to be buried properly, where we can plant something—white roses. The mayor told me that every once in a while they turn one of the Russians out, to make room. There must be a waiting list. We could put Alec's name on it. Alec gave me three children. Eric gave me Lou Mas.

Entering Mr. Cranefield's, she removed her dark veil and hat and revealed her lovely head, like the sun rising. Because the wind had started blowing leaves and sand, Mr. Cranefield's party had to be moved indoors from the loggia. This change occasioned some confusion, in which Barbara did not take part; neither did Wilkinson, whose wrenched shoulder was making him feel ill. She noticed her children helping, carrying plates of small sandwiches and silver buckets of ice. She approved of this; they were obviously well brought up. The funeral had left Mr. Cranefield's guests feeling hungry and thirsty and rather lonely, anxious to hold on to a glass and to talk to someone. Presently their voices rose, overlapped, and created something like a thick woven fabric of blurred design, which Alec's sister (who was not used to large social gatherings) likened to a flying carpet. It was now, with Molly covertly watching her, that Barbara began in the most natural way in the world to live happily ever after. There was nothing willful about this: She was simply borne in a single direction, though she did keep seeing for a time her black glove on her widowed friend's black sleeve.

Escorting lame Mrs. Massie to a sofa, Mr. Cranefield said they might as well look on the bright side. (He was still speaking about the second half of the 1950s.) Wilkinson, sitting down because he felt sick, and thinking the remark was intended for him, assured Mr. Cranefield, truthfully, that he had never looked anywhere else. It then happened that every person in the room, at the same moment, spoke and thought of something other than Alec. This lapse, this inattention, lasting no longer than was needed to say "No, thank you" or "Oh, really?" or "Yes, I see," was enough to create the dark gap marking the end of Alec's span. He ceased to be, and it made absolutely no difference after that whether or not he was forgotten.

The

SIXTIES

THE CAPTIVE NIECE

—————

❧

*W*ithout the slightest regard for her feelings or the importance of this day, he had said, "Bring back a sandwich or some bread and pâté, will you, anything you see—oh, and the English papers." He spoke as if she were going out on a common errand or an ordinary walk—to look at the Eiffel Tower, for instance. A telephone dangled on the wall just above his head; all he had to do was reach. It was true that her hotel gave no meals except breakfast, but he might have made a show of trying. He lay on the bed and watched her preparing for the interview. Her face in the bathroom mirror seemed frightened and small. She gave herself eyes and a mouth, and with them an air of decision. Knowing he was looking on made her jumpy; she kicked the bathroom door shut, but then, as though fearing a reprimand, opened it gently.

He took no notice, no more than her aunt had ever taken of her tantrums, and when she came, repentant, tearful almost, to kiss him good-bye, he simply held out the three postcards he had been writing—identical views of the Seine for his children in England. How could he? There was only one reason—he was evil and jealous and trying to call thunderbolts down on her head. An old notion of economy prevented her from throwing the cards out the window—they were stamped, and stamps seemed for some reason more precious than coins. "I don't *want* them," she said. Her hand struck nervously on the bottle of wine beside the bed.

"No, that's dangerous," he said quickly, thinking he saw what she was up to. She was something of a thrower, not at him, but away from him, and always with the same intention—to make him see he had, in some way, slighted her. As he might have done with a frantic puppy, he diverted her with a pack of cigarettes and the corkscrew.

"I don't want them, leave me alone!" she cried, and flung them out the open window into the court. "This is your fault," she said, "and now you've got nothing to smoke." But he had a whole carton of cigarettes, bought on the plane, the day before.

He had to console her. "I know," he said, "I know. But do bring another corkscrew, will you? I really can't use my teeth."

Oh, she would pay him out! For this, and for the past, and for failing to see her as she was.

Hours later he was exactly as she had left him—reading, under a torn red lampshade, on the ashy bed. The room smelled of smoke and hot iron radiators. You would not have known that a woman had ever lived in it. The first thing she did was open the window, but the air was cold and the rain too noisy, and she had to close it again. He did not say, "Oh, it's you," or "There you are," or anything that might infuriate her and set her off again. He said, as if he remembered what her day had been about, "How did it go?"

She had no desire except to win his praise. "Leget wants me," she said. "I don't mean for this film, but another next summer. He's getting me a teacher for French and a teacher only for French diction. What do you think of *that?* He said it was a pity I had spoken English all my life, because it's so bad for the teeth. Funny that Aunt Freda never thought of it—she was so careful about most things."

"You could hardly have expected her to bring you up in a foreign language," he said. "She was English. Millions of people speak English."

"Yes, and look at them!" She had never heard about the effects of English until today, but it was as if she had known it forever. She could see millions and millions of English-speaking people—black, Asian, and white—each with a misshapen upper jaw. Like her Aunt Freda, he had never been concerned. She gave him a look of slight pity. "Well, it's happened," she went on. "I shall be working in Paris, really working, and with *him.*" She untied her damp head scarf and unbuttoned her coat. "When I am R and F that coat will be lined with mink," she said. "Coat sixteen guineas, lining six thousand." R and F meant "rich and famous." His response was usually "When I am old and ill and poor ..." She remembered that he was ill, and she had not brought him his sandwich. She dropped on her knees beside the bed. "Are you all right? Feeling better?" The poor man lay there with an attack of lumbago—at least she supposed that was what it was. He had never been unwell before, not for a second. Perhaps he had put something out of joint carrying his things at the airport, but that seemed unlikely. He had come with just one small case and a typewriter, as if he were meeting her for the weekend instead of for life.

"I'm all right," he said. "Tell me about Leget."

She stammered, "He thinks I've got . . . something. A presence. He said that the minute he saw me, when I walked in. . . . He said he had been hoping to talk to me, alone—to talk about me."

"Clever man," he said. "I don't blame him. I know what he means—I saw it when you were seventeen. It's more than a face, more than drive. I thought then that I'd never been close to it before."

The child in her, told it was singular, felt a rush of love. She said with new urgency, "Are you better? Oh, I forgot to say . . . he asked who had brought me up. I told him I had no parents. He asked who was, well, *responsible* for me."

"Did you tell him?"

"Of course. I said, my aunt."

"Your aunt! Did you happen to mention she was dead?"

"I told him she'd died reaching for a drink, and how she was born pickled, and how her mind had never been original or sharp, but I loved her and owed her so much. She taught me how to sit and walk and move. Leget said, 'Yes, but your general culture'—don't make a face, darling, it's not the same in French. I told him it was just old detective stories and that the time before I was born seemed a lovely summer day full of detectives rushing to save pretty girls. I never thought about love. I used to just think, When I meet the nice detective . . ."

He had heard this many times. "Let me know when you do meet him," he said.

"Perhaps you won't like me when I'm R and F," she said. "So it won't matter what I tell you. Perhaps you'd rather I just stayed what you called me once, Aunt Freda's captive niece. You're sick of hearing about her. You're already sick of Leget, and I'm absolutely certain you're sick of me."

He got up by rolling on his side and gripping the edge of the mattress. He was dressed except for his trousers, and in the abjection of pain did not mind looking foolish. He took his jacket off and as he did so heard the lining tear. He stood looking at the bookshelf nailed beside the bed, giving his attention to the tattered Penguins, and *Sélections du Reader's Digest*, out of which Gitta proposed to improve her French. He looked at the Beaujolais he could not open, and the empty bottle of Haig. He said, and meant it now, "I am old and ill and poor." He was thirty-nine. What seems to the traveler ten or twenty years, he remembered, may in real time be ten thousand. In the nineteen years Gitta will have to travel before she overtakes me—but she never will, not unless the lumbago turns out to be fatal. He was old and ill, and he would be poor because he would give everything from now on to his wife and children. He would never buy drink again except in duty-free airport shops. "I'll have to do a hell of a lot of traveling," he remarked.

"What? Oh, you're being silly. Please sit down. Or lie down. Or take something."

"It's the same if I stand." He began to explain that the aspirin he had swallowed earlier would not dissolve because he had nothing to wash it down with; and that pain was lodged like fishhooks beneath the skin. "But I'll take one more aspirin," he said, to appease Gitta rather than the pain.

She was barely listening, looking intently now at the dark rain, or at her face on the window. She must have been recalling her triumph—her conquest. Turning to him slowly she said, "Why do you have your shirt tucked in that way? It looks funny." She added, "I've never seen anyone else do that."

"You've been knocking around with a lot of damn foreigners in Paris," he said. "Don't even know how to keep their clothes on."

She came to him, awkwardly for a girl who had been taught how to move, and touched his head for fever. "It's nothing. You aren't sick at all." Pain stuck to fragrance like glue; the scent of her hand became a source of uneasiness. Had he really expected to keep her to himself? He knew of one anguish, and that was the separation from his children; but Gitta had been a child, and more—they had been lovers since she was seventeen. He found the aspirin in an open suitcase and hobbled to the bathroom. Clutching the basin, he stood on one foot and flexed his knee.

"Is it that bad?" she said, without sympathy because his forehead was cool. "You're making a horrible face." He looked, as if he had only one minute left, at the walls, which seemed newly papered, and the white ceiling.

"I'm trying out the nerve," he said, as though that meant anything. He reached up to the light over the mirror and he thought the nerve had frayed and split. He imagined a ragged sort of string tied round his spine. "It's more like needles and pins now," he presently said.

"I thought men never had pains," she said. "Only neurotic women." He could not guess the direction of her thoughts, for their knowledge of each other was intimate, not general. "Who gave you the electric toothbrush?" she asked.

"No one. I bought it."

"What did you want a thing like that for?" He realized that she thought she had caught him out and that his wife had given it to him—probably for Father's Day, with a ribbon around it. She was still thin-skinned about his family, even now, after he had proved there was nothing but her. His children were altogether taboo; their very names carried misfortune. Giving her the cards to post—his attempt to bring about a casual order—must have seemed such a violation of safety that she was probably amazed at finding them both here, intact.

He started to answer but the habit of clandestine holidays cut him short, for they heard a high-pitched exchange in English outside the door: ". . . sent in an unsealed envelope to save sixpence." "I should have torn it up." "So I did."

She smiled at him. The day was still safe; the complicity between them had from the beginning been as important as love.

Of course she needed him, she said to herself. Without him, she would never have known about love, only about gratitude, affection, claustrophobia. She sat on the bed and spread the torn coat on her knee. The lining was rent under the arm; with difficulty she joined the ragged seams. The material seemed stiff and old, and it was unpleasant to handle. Intellectual sweat, she said deep within her mind.

"The first time you saw me with Aunt Freda you said, 'She is using you as a *femme de charme*,' remember? But she had been kind, as always, and she'd bought me a sumptuous velvet skirt and a leather jacket, and I didn't see why I couldn't wear them together. I must have been a sight. I thought all *you* could see were my bitten nails."

"You and your aunt were too tied up," he said. "Too dependent on each other." He sounded as if the aunt were to blame for a flaw in Gitta; at least that was the meaning she selected. She could have straightened out the right and wrong of it, but what would their lives become, with so many explanations? She imagined them, a worn-out old couple in a traveler's climate, not speaking much—explanations having devoured conversation long ago—pretending to be all right when anyone looked at them. "Women are bad for each other," he said. She thought he was describing her life without him, but perhaps it was another woman's—he'd had nothing but daughters. She felt, obscurely, that a searing discussion had taken place.

Settling into an armchair he groaned sincerely. He said, "Well, you liked old Leget. That's a good thing."

She looked up and said simply, "I told you. I worship him. I would do anything he asked."

"Don't ever tell him that."

"I mean it. I worshiped his films before I ever knew you knew him. It's talent I love. I'd do anything."

"So you said. What *has* he asked you to do?"

"It's just one scene, to tell you the truth. I . . . I sort of sleepwalk through American Express. Don't laugh. *Stop* it! I don't mean walking in my sleep. You know how sometimes you feel no one can see you, because you are so intent—looking for a friend, let's say—and suddenly you wake up and notice everybody staring? I can't explain it the way he does. Actually, I don't need to say anything. I just am. I exist. I'm me, Gitta."

"You aren't you if you don't open your mouth. Also, if you don't talk, it means he pays you a good deal less."

"Don't be so small. You know very well I am paid and how much. It doesn't come out of his pocket. I'm not some little tart he picked up in the Café Select."

"I'm going to be sorry I introduced you to Leget," he said. "You're doting."

"He doesn't care for women," she said primly, and, as if one statement completed the other, "He has his wife."

She wondered if he was trying to tell her she owed him the interview. But she remembered all that she owed him, particularly now, when he had given up everything for her—his children, and the room he was used to working in, and his wife answering the telephone (she could imagine no other use for her), and perhaps his job. He might go into a news agency here, but it was a comedown. That might be the greatest loss of all; it was the only one he mentioned. But she was astute enough at times to guess he might not speak of what bothered him most. How could she match his sacrifice? She had rid herself of everything that might divert a scrap of her love; she had thrown away a small rabbit with nylon fur, a bracelet made of painted wooden links, both highly charged with the powers of fortune. It was not enough; she was frightened without her talismans, and they were still not on an equal footing. She often said to him now, "Never leave me."

She cut off the thread and went on, "Leget is young to be married. I mean, so definitely married."

"There's no age limit." He was not yet divorced. He had jumped without a net—at his time of life! When he had talked gently to her in the old days, at the beginning, it had been about herself. Now, as he composed a new message in which he figured, she heard the word "compulsive," or perhaps it was "impulsive"—she could not take it in. She felt utterly an impostor, sewing for a grown person who ought to look after his own clothes, as if sewing were a translation of devotion. He was unwell, of course, and out of his element. Inactive, he seemed to disappear. We are all selfish, she decided. She had been devoted to her aunt, but selfishness was a green fly, unobserved, the color of the leaf. She murmured, as she had many times in the past two days, "Don't leave me," but it was only a new exorcism. She had shed her talismans—oh, mistake! If he made love to her, that might be a way out of their predicament; it seemed, in fact, the only way. But when he crept onto the bed, behind her back, it was only because he'd had enough of sitting in the chair.

"I'm not going out," she said suddenly. "Ring downstairs and see if they can send someone out to the café for you."

She turned and saw that he was watching her closely. Just as his hand went to the telephone she said, "Darling, a hideous thing happened today. I didn't tell you. When I was coming home after seeing Leget, the rain started pelting, so I stopped in a doorway, and some man, a sort of workingman, was there, in the dark. I had the feeling if I said '*Partez!*' he would go, and I was ashamed to think it—to think he was inferior, I mean. All at once he moved between me and the street, and when I looked back I saw the building was empty—it was being torn down from the inside. The outside walls were all that was left. I got my back against the wall, and as he walked toward me I pushed him away with both hands, with all my might. He opened his mouth—it was full of blood. He sort of fell against me; some of it got on my coat. He staggered back and fell in a heap, and I left him. I walked away very slowly to show I wasn't frightened, but I was so upset that I went in a café and had a drink and watched their television for about an hour. I was afraid if I came straight back to you I might be hysterical and it might bother you."

"You probably aren't hungry then, are you?" he said.

"Of course I'm hungry. I'm as hungry as you are. You know perfectly well I haven't eaten the whole day."

He seemed to take it for granted she was making this up—she could tell. He had known her to do it before, when she was anxious to change the meaning of a situation, but in those days she had been living with her aunt, and trying to make her life seem vivid and interesting to him.

"Why didn't you shout, or call someone?"

"Because I wanted to show him I wasn't afraid of him."

"Weren't you?"

"I wanted to kill him. I was murderous."

"That's understandable," he said. "You'll realize tomorrow, or when you wake up in the night, that you were frightened. What shall I ask them to fetch you from the café? A ham sandwich? Two sandwiches?"

"I don't care." She was bitterly offended, alone, astray, for he was making little of the danger she had been in. All he seemed to have on his mind was food. He spoke into the telephone, explained that he was very ill. Sandwiches, he said, and he knew the French for "corkscrew."

She said, "What if it isn't real? What if I made it up?"

"Even if you have, it's frightened you. You've frightened yourself."

"Aren't you?"

"I wasn't in on it."

"Aren't you frightened that I wanted to kill someone?"

"I haven't got round to that," he said. "If you invented it *only* to frighten me, I'll try to respond."

"All right. I made it up to worry you, let's say. But there's blood on the sleeve of my coat. As for you, you only got this lumbago because you don't want us to be happy. Now that your wife knows, you don't enjoy making love to me."

"Be an angel," he said. "Don't say too much more now."

"As long as Aunt Freda had me," she said, "you had me and all the rest. She kept me for you. And she didn't mind your being married, because it meant I'd never leave her. There, that's what I think. Do you want to go back? Aunt Freda said men never leave home unless their wives are hell."

"My wife wasn't hell."

"Then there's no explanation, is there?"

"There bloody well is, and you know what it is."

"We're like children, aren't we?" she said. "In a way?"

Knowing more than she did about children, he said, sadly, "No, not at all."

She started to answer, "If anything goes wrong now, I suppose I have no one to blame but myself," which came out, without her meaning it that way, "no one to love but myself."

She was frightened, as he had predicted, in the night. She supposed that the man who had come out of the shadows of the courtyard and was now blocking her way to the street intended to kill her. "I don't need to die," she said, meaning that she did not want to be transformed; that life was manageable. He stood with his arms spread, hands dangling, as though imitating a clumsy bird. "Oh, look," she cried. "It isn't fair!" for the bus she wanted slipped away from the curb. No one could see her in here, and there was nothing left of the queue she had abandoned so as to shelter from the rain. "I'm late as it is," she said. It seemed her only grievance.

She supposed he knew no English. "If only I'd said 'Get out' the instant I saw you," she raged at him. "You'd have gone. You'd have respected the tone. All you deserve from me is commands. 'Get out,' I ought to have said. 'Get out!'"

The steps of his curious bird dance brought him near. He stretched his mouth so that she saw the bloody gums. He had been in a fight. She smelled the breath of someone frightened; she saw his eyes. She understood that he had no plans for her: He was drunk and vacant, like her aunt. She remembered the subdual of drinks, the easy victories. "I'm going out that door," she said. Her triumphs over her aunt had been of this order. Feelings about other people she had never specifically understood sent her toward him—into his arms, he might have thought. He was afflicted with the worst of curses—obscurity, a life without meaning—while she would never be forgotten, unless she let some fool destroy her. When they were almost as close as lovers she pushed him away, one hand on the other and both on his throat. He should have fallen back and cracked his head and made an end to it, but instead he knelt, sagged; his face, in passing, knocked against the sleeve of her coat. "Oh, you'll be all right," she said. She spoke in the *jeune Anglaise* voice she had only that day been advised to lose.

"*Partez,*" she said softly in the dark, and again, a little louder, "*Partez!*" and then, as he began to come awake, "Would you be very unhappy? Would you miss me? Is it true you don't believe a word I say?"

QUESTIONS AND ANSWERS

———

⁘

*R*omanians notoriously are marked by delusions of eminence and persecution, and Madame Gisèle does not encourage them among her clientele. She never can tell when they are trying to acquire information, or present some grievance that were better taken to a doctor or the police. Like all expatriates in Paris, they are concerned with the reactions of total strangers. She is expected to find in the cards the functionary who sneered, the flunky who behaved like a jailer, the man who, for no reason, stared too long at the plates of the car. Madame Gisèle prefers her settled clients—the married women who sit down to say, "When is my husband going to die?" and "What about the man who smiles at me every morning on the bus?" She can find him easily: There he is—the jack of hearts. One of the queens is not far away, along with the seven of diamonds turned upside down. Forget about him. He is supporting his mother and has already deserted a wife.

Amalia Moraru has been visiting Madame Gisèle for two years now. She has been so often, and her curiosity is so flickering and imprecise, that Madame Gisèle charges her for time, like a garage. Amalia asks questions about her friend Marie.

"Marie used to be so pretty," Amalia begins, taking no notice of Madame Gisèle's greeting, which is "You again!" "Thirty years ago we used to say she looked French. That was a compliment in Bucharest. You know, we are a Latin race in that part of the country. . . ."

Madame Gisèle, who is also Romanian but from one of the peripheral provinces, replies, "Who cares?" She and Amalia both speak their language badly. Amalia was educated in French, which was the fashion for Bucharest girls of her background thirty years ago, while the fortune-teller is at home in a Slavic-sounding dialect.

"Marie must be very ill now," Amalia says cautiously, "to have stopped looking so French. Last night in the Place du Marché St.-Honoré, people were staring at her. She smiles at anyone. My husband thinks she has lost her mind. Her legs are swollen. What do you see? Heart trouble? Circulation?"

"Overwork. What makes you think *you* look French?"

A long glance in the magic hand mirror, lying face upward on the table, assures Amalia that if she does not seem French it is entirely to her credit. Her collar is pressed, her hair is coiled and railed in by pins. She tries something else: "I have Marie's new X rays—the ones she's had taken for the Americans."

"I've already told you, I am not a doctor."

"You could look at them. You can tell so much from just a snapshot sometimes."

"I can in a normal consultation. You brought me a picture once. You said, 'This is my old friend in Bucharest. Do you see a journey for her?' 'Everyone travels,' I told you. But I did look, and I did see a journey. . . ."

"You even saw the broken lightbulbs in the train, and the unswept floors," says Amalia, encouraging her.

"I know what Romanian trains have been like since the war. Your friend came to Paris. What more did you want?"

"Why hasn't she said anything about the money certain people owe her? What does Marie think about certain people when she is alone?"

Madame Gisèle will not look in the hand mirror, or the ball, she will not burn candles to collect the wax, because Amalia pays a low rate for her time. She does keep one hand on the cards, in case a question should be asked she feels she can answer. The seven of hearts would indicate the trend of Marie's most secret thoughts, but Madame Gisèle cannot find it. When she does, nothing around it makes sense.

"*Succès légers en amour,*" announces Madame Gisèle, who is accustomed to making such statements in French.

"Jesus Maria. We are talking about an old woman. Try again."

"*Cadeau agréable.*"

"She buys presents, but I've already told you that. What is she thinking *this minute?*"

"Cut the cards yourself. Left hand . . . *Naissance,*" says Madame Gisèle, examining the result. "Monday is a bad day. Go home and come back on a Friday."

Amalia supposes that on this April day Marie is collecting more information about herself for the Americans. Marie hopes to emigrate before long. From time to time she receives a letter requesting a new piece of evidence for her file. She is enjoying April, or pretends to. She waddles to the flower market when she can, and has already brought Amalia the first yellow daffodils of the year. "Make a wish," says Marie. Her teeth are like leaves in winter now. Does she really think the Americans will let her into the country with that ruined smile? "The first daffodils—wish on them, Amalia. Wish for something." Marie is always wishing. Amalia could understand it in a young person, but at Marie's age what is it all about?

This is not a pleasant April. Some mornings the air is so white and still you might expect a fall of snow, and at night the sky expands, as it does in December.

"Marie is lucky," Amalia remarks to Madame Gisèle. "She came here when there was plenty of work, and nobody thinks of saying 'refugee' anymore. She has her own passport. Dino and I have never had one. She doesn't know how things were for us fifteen, sixteen years ago. We gave a pearl ring for one CARE parcel, but it had been sold three times and there was nothing in it except rancid butter and oatmeal."

Madame Gisèle is trying again for the seven of hearts. Amalia feels a draft and tugs the collar of her coat around her neck. All over Paris the heating has been turned off too soon. Marie must suffer with the cold. She is a *corsetière*, and kneels to fat women all day. Her legs, her knees, her wrists, her fingers are bloated—she looks like a carving in stone.

"*Rendez-vous la nuit*," says Madame Gisèle. "Look, I am sick of your friend Marie. Either she knows and is laughing at us or it is you bringing low-class spirits in the room."

"Not laughing—wishing."

On an April evening Marie, in slow march time, approaches her house and sixth-floor room in the Place du Marché St.-Honoré. Her legs are thick as boots. Crossing the street she suddenly stands still and begins to watch the sky. You would think her mind was drifting if you could see her, choosing to block traffic at the worst moment of the day, staring at the new moon and the planet Venus. She is making a wish. Amalia, who lives on the same square, has seen her doing it. Marie stares as if the sky were a reflecting sheet; perhaps what Marie sees against blue Venus is the streaky movement of cars behind her, and the shadow of her own head.

Peering into Madame Gisèle's magic hand mirror again to see what *she* can see, Amalia does not recognize her own face. Two years ago, when she knew that Marie would be coming to Paris, Amalia dyed her graying hair. Later, she saw her reflection in the glass covering an old photograph of Marie (the photograph taken to Madame Gisèle for mystical guesswork) and she saw two faces and believed them to be both her own. What am I now, she wondered. I am the one I left and the other one I became. Marie is still herself. . . . Now Amalia knows she was mistaken; Marie is also two. When Marie did arrive in Paris, when she got down from the train that terrifying morning and lumbered toward them, out of the past, holding out her arms, Dino and Amalia would never have known her if Marie had not cried out their names. They had been waiting all night for the past, and they were embraced by a ridiculous stranger who had no one to love but them. Dino pushed out his lips in the Eastern grimace of triumph and contempt, but close to his frightened heart, with his work permit and residence permit and proof of existence and assurance of identity and evidence of domicile, he carried—still carries—a folded piece of paper covered with figures in red ink. It is a statement of account for Marie, if ever she should ask for it. It will show how little Dino received for the rings and gold pieces she gave Amalia when Dino and Amalia left Bucharest sixteen years ago. "Send for me later," Marie had said, and they kissed on the promise. Dino has a round face, blond hair, small uptilted blue eyes, and a nose like a cork on a bottle, but of course he is pure Romanian—a Latin, that is. There is not a drop of foreign blood in any of them: no Greek, no Turkish, no Magyar, no Slav, no Teuton, no Serb. He is represented in the cards by the king of clubs, a dark card, but Amalia prefers it to diamonds. Diamonds mean "stranger."

Madame Gisèle turns the hand mirror facedown, because when Amalia looks in it she is getting more than her money's worth.

"Oh, why did Marie ever come here?" Amalia says. In Bucharest they would have given her a pension, in time. They might have sent her to a rest home on the Black Sea. Who will look after her during the long, last illness every émigré dreads? Amalia wonders, What if Marie is insane?

With the word "insane" she is trying to describe Marie's wishing, her belief that the planets can hear. Amalia is an old expatriate; she knows how to breathe underwater. Marie is too old to learn. She belongs to ir-recoverable time—that has been the trouble from the beginning. She came to Paris nearly two years ago, and has been wishing for something ever since.

This is a common story. Madame Gisèle's clients are forever worried about lunacy in friends and loved ones. With her left hand she cuts the deck and peers at the queen of diamonds—the stranger, the mortal enemy, the gossip and poisoner of the mind. Surely not Marie?

"Your friend is not insane," says Madame Gisèle abruptly. "She found work without your help. She has found a room to live in."

"Yes, by talking to a Romanian on the street! What Romanian? What do we know about him? She talks to anybody. Why did she leave certain people who made a home for her even when they had no room, and even bought her a bed? She found work, yes, but she spends like a fool. Why does she bring certain people the first strawberries of the season? They haven't asked for anything. They can live on soup and apples. Marie is old and sick and silly. She says, 'Look, Amalia, look at the new moon.' What do you know about Marie? You don't know anything."

"Why do you come, if you don't want to hear what I say?" shouts Madame Gisèle, in her village dialect. "Your brain is mildewed, your husband murdered his mother, your friend is a whore!"

These are standard insults and no more offensive than a sneeze. *"Parlons français,"* says Amalia, folding her hands on Marie's X rays. She will furnish proof of Marie's dementia, if she can—it seems an obligation suddenly.

"I am the last to deny that Marie was a whore," she begins. "She was kept by a married man. When Dino and I were engaged and I brought him to her flat for the first time, she answered the door dressed in her underwear. But remember that in Bucharest we are a Latin race, and in the old days it was not uncommon for a respectable man to choose an apartment, select the furniture, and put a woman in it. After this man's wife died, he would have married Marie, but it was too late. He was too ill. Marie nursed this man when he was dying. She could have left with Dino and me but she stayed."

"It was easier for two to come out then than three," says Madame Gisèle, to whom this is not a complete story. "Certain people may have encouraged her to stay behind."

"If everyone left, what would become of the country?" says Amalia, which is what every old émigré has to say about new arrivals. "Listen to me. I think Marie is insane."

✤   ✤   ✤

One day, soon after Marie had come to Paris, before she had found work in a shop by talking to a Romanian on the street, Amalia walked with her in the gardens of the Champs-Élysées. It was by no means a promenade; Amalia was on one of the worried errands that make up her day—this time, going to the snack bar where the cook, who is from Bucharest, saves stale bread for people who no longer need it. Once you have needed this bread, you cannot think of its going to anyone else. Marie walked too slowly—her legs hurt her, and she was admiring the avenue. Amalia left her under a chestnut tree. If the tree had opened and encased Marie, Amalia would have thought, God is just, for Marie was a danger, and her presence might pull Amalia and Dino back and down to trouble with the police, which is to say the floor of the sea.

"Listen, Marie," began Amalia to herself, having disposed of Marie on a bench. "We never sent for you because we never were ready. You've seen the hole we live in? We bought it with your rings. We sleep in a cupboard—it has no windows. That piece of cotton hanging is a door. We call this a dining room because it has a table and three chairs—we bought the third chair when we knew you were coming. There is your new bed, between the chair and the curtain. Dino will curse you every time he stumbles against it. The trees of Paris? The flower stalls? We have the biggest garage of Paris in the middle of our square. The square should be called Place du Garage St.-Honoré now. I want to tell you also that most of the things you gave me were worth nothing. Only diamonds matter, and the best were stolen when we were coming through Bulgaria and Greece. When we first came to live here, where the garage stands now there were baskets of fruit and flowers."

Returning with her newspaper parcel of stale bread, Amalia looks for Marie. Marie has vanished. Amalia understands that some confused wishing of her own, some abracadabra pronounced without knowing its powers, has caused her old friend to disintegrate. She, Amalia, will be questioned about it.

Marie is not far away. She has left the bench and is sitting on the ground. Pigeons cluster around her—they go to anyone. Her eyes are globed with tears. The tears are suspended, waiting, and every line of her body seems hurt and waiting for greater pain. Whatever has hurt her is nothing to what is to come. Amalia rushes forward, calling. Marie is not crying at all. She holds out a chestnut. "Look," she says.

"Where did it come from?" cries Amalia wildly, as if she has forgotten where she is.

Marie gets to her feet like a great cow. "It was still in its case; it must be left over from last year."

"They turn dark and ugly in a minute," says Amalia, and she throws it away.

As proof of madness this is fairly thin, except for the part about sitting on the ground. Amalia, remembering that she is paying for time, now takes the tack that Madame Gisèle is concealing what she knows. "It is up to you to convince me," she says. *"Will Marie go to America?"*

"Everyone travels," says Madame Gisèle.

Well, that is true. The American consulate is full of ordinary tourists who can pay their passage and will see, they hope, Indian ceremonial dances. Amalia is told that scholars are admitted to the great universities for a year, two years, with nothing required, not even a knowledge of English. Who will want Marie, who actually does speak a little English but has nonsensical legs, no relations, and thinks she can sell corsets in a store? Marie filled out the forms they gave her months ago, and received a letter saying, "You are not legible."

"How funny," said the girl in the consulate when Marie and Amalia returned with the letter. "They mean eligible."

"What does it mean?" said Marie.

"It is a mistake, but it means you can't go to the United States. Not as your situation is now."

"If it is a mistake—"

"One word is a mistake."

"Then the whole letter might be wrong."

To Amalia, standing beside her, Marie seems unable to support something just then—perhaps the weight of her own clothes. Amalia reviews her friend's errors—her broken English, her plucked eyebrows, her flat feet in glossy shoes, the fact that she stayed in Romania when it was time to leave and left when it was better to stay. "Will my clothes be all right for there?" says Marie, because Amalia is staring.

"You may not be going. Didn't you hear the young lady?"

"This isn't the last word, or the last letter. You will see." Marie is confident—she shows her broken teeth.

Madame Gisèle is interested, though she has heard this before. She cuts the deck and says, "Here it is—*réception d'une missive peu compréhensible.*"

"Pff—fourteen months ago that was," says Amalia. "Then they wrote and asked for centimeter-by-centimeter enlargements of the pictures of her lungs. You haven't told me why Marie left the friends who had bought her a bed."

"Because she found a room by talking to another Romanian on the street."

"That is true. But she had the room for days, weeks even, before she decided to leave."

"Something must have made her decide," says Madame Gisèle. "No one can say I am not trying, but your questions are not clear. I am expecting another client, and I have to take the dog out."

"There must be another reason. Look again."

Every evening when she came home from work, Marie helped Amalia chop the vegetables for the evening soup. They sat face-to-face across a thick board on which were the washed leeks, the potatoes, the onions, and the parsley. Amalia wondered if she and Marie looked the same, with their hands misshapen and twisted and the false meekness of their bent heads. Living had bent them, Amalia would begin to say, and emigration, and being women, and oh, she supposed, the war. "At least you didn't marry a peasant," Amalia said once. "At least I know what class I am from. My ancestors could read and write from the time of Julius Caesar, and my grandfather owned his own house." Marie said nothing. "If only we had been men," said Amalia, "or had any amount of money, or lived on a different continent . . ." She looked up, dreaming, the knife in abeyance.

Sometimes Amalia spoke of Dino. Sometimes she giggled as if she and Marie were still Bucharest girls, convent-trained, French-prattling, with sleek Turkish hair, Greek noses, long amber eyes, and not a drop of foreign blood. "Your apartment, Marie?" It was white and gold, Amalia remembered, and there was a row of books that turned out to be not Balzac at all but a concealed bar. There was an original pastel drawing of a naked girl on a diving board, and a musical powder box that played "Valentine." "After I married Dino, we came back sometimes and sat on the white chairs and watched your friends dancing—do you remember, Marie?—and we waited until they had gone, and you would lend us a little money—we always paid it back—and you gave me a fox scarf, and a pin that showed a sleeping fawn, and a hat made of sequins, and perfume from France—Shalimar. I kept the empty bottle. Your life was French. . . ." It has always seemed that the old flat furnished by Marie's dead friend is the real Paris, and the row of Balzac that turns into a bar is the truth about France. "Dino was apprenticed to a glovemaker at the beginning," Amalia said, "and his hands had a queer smell, something to do with the leather, and he never dared ask the girls to dance." Marie went on chopping leeks, holding the knife by the handle and blade in both swollen hands. Amalia said, "He's afraid of you, Marie, because you remember all that. He was always mean and stingy, and he hasn't changed. Remember the first present he ever gave me?"

"A gold locket," said Marie gently.

"Gold? Don't make me laugh. I put it around my neck and said, 'I'll never take it off,' and he said, 'You had better sometimes because the yellow will wear off.' "

She laughed, laughing into the past as if she were no longer afraid of it. "He hasn't changed. I thought of leaving him. Yes, I was going to write to you and say, 'I am leaving him now.' But by then we had so many years of worry behind us, and everywhere I looked that worry was like a big stone in the road."

Marie nodded, as if she knew. She never said much, never confided. Amalia snatched away the last of the vegetables and said, "Let me finish. You are so slow," and then Dino came in and slapped the table with the flat of his hand, so as to send the women flying apart, one to put the soup on the stove and the other to go out and buy the evening paper, which he had forgotten. It happens every night for a year, it can happen all your life, Amalia was thinking, and suddenly you have all those years like a stone. But Marie once sat quietly and said, "Listen, Dino," so carefully that he did seem to hear. "I am not your slave. Perhaps I will be a slave one day, but I don't want to learn the habit of slavery. I am well and strong, and my whole life is before me, and I am working, and I have a room. Yes, I am going to live alone now. Oh, not far away, but somewhere else."

"Who wants you?" Dino shouted, but he was in a cold sweat because of all Marie knew, and because she had never asked about the rings she gave them. Amalia was thinking, She is too ill to live alone. What if she dies? And the rings—she has said nothing about the rings. Why is she leaving me?

She looked around to see what they had done to Marie, but there was no hint of cruelty or want of gratitude in the room. Marie would never guess that Amalia had been to Madame Gisèle, saying, "How do you kill it—the buoyancy, the credulity, the blindness to everything harsh?"

"Marie," Amalia would like to say, "will you admit that working and getting older and dying matter, and can't be countered by the first hyacinth of the year?" But Marie went on packing. Amalia consoled herself: Marie's mind had slipped. She was mad.

Marie straightened up from her packing and smiled. "Three people can't live together. You and Dino will be better alone."

"No, don't leave us alone together," Amalia cried. There must have been some confusion in the room at that moment, because nobody heard.

Last autumn one serious thing happened to Marie—she was in trouble with the police. She says that at the Préfecture—the place every émigré is afraid of—they shut her in a room one whole day. Had she been working without a permit? Did she change her address without reporting it? Could her passport be a forgery? Marie only says, "A policeman was rude to me, and I told him never to do it again." Released in the evening, having been jeered at, sequestered, certainly insulted, she crossed the street and began to admire the flower market. She bought a bunch of ragged pink asters and spent the last money she had in her pocket (it seems that at the Préfecture she was made to pay a large fine) on coffee and cakes. She can describe every minute of her adventures after she left the Préfecture: how she bought the asters, with Amalia in mind, how she sat down at a white marble table in a tearoom, and the smoking coffee she admired in the white china cup, and the color the coffee was when the milk was poured in, and how good it was, how hot. She shares, in the telling, a *baba au rhum.* You can see the fork pressing on the very last crumb, and the paper-lace *napperon* on the plate. Now she chooses to walk along the Seine, between the ugly evening traffic and the stone parapet above the quay. She is walking miles the wrong way. She crosses a bridge she likes the look of, then another, and sees a clock. It is half past six. From the left of the wooden footbridge that joins Île Saint-Louis and the Île de la Cité, she looks back and falls in love with the sight of Notre Dame; the scanty autumn foliage beneath it is bright gold. Everything is gold but the sky, which is mauve, and contains a new moon. She has spent all her money, and cannot wish on the new moon without a coin in her hand. She stops a passerby by touching him on the arm. Stiff with outrage, he refuses to let her hold even a one-centime piece so that she can wish. She has to wish on the moon without a coin, holding a second-class Métro ticket instead—all that her pocket now contains. She turns the ticket over as if it were silver, and wishes for something with all her heart.

Marie tells Dino and Amalia about it. It can only irritate them, but she hasn't sense enough to keep it to herself. They are concerned about the police: "What happened? What did they say?"

"Nothing," says Marie. "They gave me a card. I can stay in France another year."

"Not a year; three months," says Dino angrily. "It is three months and three months and three months . . ." She shows the card to him. It is the red card—she may stay a year. That is the beginning. Probably she can stay forever.

"They have made a mistake," says Dino.

The police never make a mistake. She is an elderly refugee with a chronic illness and no money, and she has broken some rule and even lectured a policeman, they have shut her up a whole day, and yet they have given her this. Dino returns the card—he holds it as if it were crystal.

"If I were afraid of policemen," says Marie, casually putting the object in her purse, "I wouldn't have left Romania with a passport, and I wouldn't be here with you now."

They are gagged with shame at what they suspect about each other's thoughts. Before she came, each of them hoped she would be arrested at some frontier and taken off the train. They never wanted her.

Amalia, from this moment, considers Marie a witch. What does she say to herself when she turns a Métro ticket over, staring at the new moon? Wishes have no power to correct the past—even credulous Marie must know it. Madame Gisèle says most women ask about their husbands, or other men. When Amalia goes to Madame Gisèle, it is to ask about Marie.

"I think I know your secret," Madame Gisèle said once.

Amalia's heart stopped. Which secret, which one?

"I don't think you are telling me about a real person. Why do I never turn up the right cards or find out what she is thinking? For all I know, she is just someone you've invented, or it's another way of talking about yourself. That has happened to me before."

Amalia laughed, in her April coat with the neat collar. "Is that what you think? Marie is my old friend. You have seen her picture. I have centimeter-by-centimeter enlargements of her lungs."

"If she had committed suicide and you were wondering why—I've had cases of that."

"She never will. Marie will go on and on."

"There is your answer—Marie will go on and on. I don't know what you want from me. I can't give you any answers. Go home, Amalia. Never come back here. Go away."

Marie kill herself? You would have to smother Marie; put the whole map of Paris over her face and hold it tight.

Amalia rehearses for her next session with Madame Gisèle: "I want to show her the slums sometimes, show her my hands, my hair when it isn't dyed, show her what my life has been. It becomes a hysterical film speeded up. . . . You should see her going to work every morning. She can hardly put one crippled foot down after the other. She goes by two kiosks on her way to the Métro station and stops and reads the newspapers. She comes to dinner every Sunday, bringing a bottle of champagne and a box of pastry—her crooked finger under the pink bowknot on the box. She brings the first strawberries, the first melon in summer, the first lilacs; she smiles and tells about her work, her letters from the Americans; she says she went to the Opéra-Comique—she is fond of *Louise*—and she smiles and we see her teeth. She brings cigarettes for Dino. She has never asked for an account. Dino has it ready, but she has never asked. You would think something had been settled for Marie, sorted out a long time ago."

Amalia thinks they might forgive Marie if she insulted them—if she stamped her foot, called them liars and cheats. She could have their respect that way. Failing respect, she might still have their pity. "Weep," they would tell her. "Admit you are no luckier than we are, that every move was a mistake, that you are one of the dead. Be one of us, and be loved." Once Marie said, "You should have had children, Amalia. Émigrés need them; otherwise they die of suffocation." She thinks they need a repository for their hopes and dreams. What about her own? "Make a wish," Marie will say, as if there was still something to wish for. They ought to do it: put their faces so close they cannot see each other's eyes and say, "We wish—we wish—but first we must know what Marie has wished for us."

ERNST IN CIVILIAN CLOTHES

———————

❧

Opening a window in Willi's room to clear the room of cigarette smoke, Ernst observes that the afternoon sky has not changed since he last glanced at it a day or two ago. It is a thick winter blanket, white and gray. Nothing moves. The black cobbles down in the courtyard give up a design of wet light. More light behind the windows now, and the curtains become glassy and clear. The life behind them is implicit in its privacy. Forms are poised at stove and table, before mirrors, insolently unconcerned with Ernst. His neighbors on this court in the Rue de Lille in Paris do not care if he peers at them, and he, in turn, may never be openly watched. Nevertheless, he never switches on the table lamp, dim though it is, without fastening Willi's cretonne curtains together with a safety pin. He feels so conspicuous in his new civilian clothes, idling the whole day, that it would not astonish him if some civic-minded and diligent informer had already been in touch with the police.

On a January afternoon, Ernst the civilian wears a nylon shirt, a suede tie, a blazer with plastic buttons, and cuffless trousers so tapered and short that when he sits down they slide to his calf. His brown military boots—unsuccessfully camouflaged for civilian life with black Kiwi—make him seem anchored. These are French clothes, and, all but the boots, look as if they had been run up quickly and economically by a little girl. Willi, who borrowed the clothes for Ernst, was unable to find shoes his size, but is pleased, on the whole, with the results of his scrounging. It is understood (by Willi) that when Ernst is back in Germany and earning money, he will either pay for the shirt, tie, blazer, and trousers or else return them by parcel post. Ernst will do neither. He has already forgotten the clothes were borrowed in

Willi's name. He will forget he lived in Willi's room. If he does remember, if a climate one day brings back a January in Paris, he will simply weep. His debts and obligations dissolve in his tears. Ernst's warm tears, his good health, and his poor memory are what keep him afloat.

In an inside pocket of the borrowed jacket are the papers that show he is not a deserter. His separation from the Foreign Legion is legal. For reasons not plain this afternoon, his life is an endless leave without the hope and the dread of return to the barracks. He is now like any man who has begged for a divorce and was shocked when it was granted. The document has it that he is Ernst Zimmermann, born in 1927, in Mainz. If he were to lose that paper, he would not expect any normal policeman to accept his word of honor. He is not likely to forget his own name, but he could, if cornered, forget the connection between an uncertified name and himself. Fortunately, his identification is given substance by a round purple stamp on which one can read *"Préfecture de Police."* Clipped to the certificate is a second-class railway ticket to Stuttgart, where useful Willi has a brother-in-law in the building trade. Willi has written that Ernst is out of the Legion, and needs a job, and is not a deserter. The brother-in-law is rich enough to be jovial; he answers that even if Ernst is a deserter he will take him on. This letter perplexes Ernst. What use are papers if the first person you deal with as a civilian does not ask to see even copies of them? What is Ernst, if his papers mean nothing? He knows his name and his category (ex-Legionnaire) but not much more. He does not know if he is German or Austrian. His mother was Austrian and his stepfather was German. He was born before Austria became Germany, but when he was taken prisoner by the Americans in April 1945, Austria and Germany were one. Austrians are not allowed to join the Foreign Legion. If he were Austrian now and tried to live in Austria, he might be in serious trouble. Was he German or Austrian in September 1945, when he became a Legionnaire because the food was better on their side of the prison camp? His mother *is* Austrian, but he has chosen the stepfather; he is German. He looks at the railway posters with which Willi has decorated the room, and in a resolution that must bear a date (January 28, 1963) he decides, My Country. A new patriotism, drained from the Legion, flows over a field of daffodils, the casino at Baden-Baden, a gingerbread house, part of the harbor at Hamburg, and a couple of seagulls.

Actually, there may be misstatements in his papers. Only his mother, if she is still living, and still cares, could make the essential corrections. He was really born in the Voralberg in 1929. When he joined the Legion, he said he was eighteen, for there were advantages in both error and accuracy then; prisoners under eighteen received double food rations, but prisoners who joined the Foreign Legion thought it was the fastest way home. Ernst is either thirty-four or thirty-six. He pledged his loyalty to official papers years ago—to officers, to the Legion, to stamped and formally attested facts. It is an attested fact that he was born in Mainz. Mainz is a place he passed through once, in a locked freight car, when he was being transported to France with a convoy of prisoners. He does not know why the Americans who took him prisoner in Germany sent him to France. Willi says to this day that the Americans sold their prisoners at one thousand five hundred francs a head, but Ernst finds such suppositions taxing. During one of the long, inexplicable halts on the mysterious voyage, where arrival and traveling were equally dreaded, another lad in man's uniform, standing crushed against Ernst, said, "We're in Mainz." "Well?" "Mainz is finished. There's nothing left." "How do you know? We can't see out," said Ernst. "There is nothing left anywhere for us," said the boy. "My father says this is the Apocalypse." What an idiot, Ernst felt; but later on, when he was asked where he came from, he said, without hesitating, and without remembering why, "Mainz."

Ernst is leaving Paris tomorrow morning. He will take the Métro to the Gare de l'Est at an hour when the café windows are fogged with the steam of rinsed floors. The Métro quais will smell of disinfectant and cigarette butts. Willi will probably carry his duffel bag and provide him with bread and chocolate to eat on the train. He is leaving before he is deported. He has no domicile and no profession; he is a vagabond without a home (his home was the Legion) and without a trade (his trade was the Legion, too). Some ex-Legionnaires have come out of it well. András is a masseur, Thomas a car washer, Carlo lives with a prostitute, Dietrich is a night watchman, Vieko has a scholarship and is attending courses in French civilization, Piotr is seen with a smart interior decorator, Lothar is engaged to marry a serious French girl. Ernst has nothing, not even his pension. He waited for the pension, but now he has given up. He is not bitter but feels ill-used. Also, he thinks he looks peculiar. He has not been to Germany since he was carried through Mainz eighteen years ago, and he is wearing civilian clothes as normal dress for the first time since he was seven years old.

His Austrian mother was desperately poor even after she married his stepfather, and when Ernst put on his Hitler Youth uniform at seven, it meant, mostly, a great saving in clothes. He has been in uniform ever since. His uniforms have not been lucky. He has always been part of a defeated army. He has fought for Germany and for France and, according to what he has been told each time, for civilization.

He wore civilian clothes for one day, years ago, when he was confirmed, and then again when he was sixteen and a Werewolf, but those were not normal occasions. When he was confirmed a Christian, and created a Werewolf, he felt disguised and curiously concealed. He is disguised and foreign to himself today, looking out of Willi's window at the sky and the cobbles and the neighbors in the court. He looks shabby and unemployed, like the pictures of men in German street crowds before the Hitler time.

It is quite dark when the little boy, holding his mother's hand with one hand and a cone with roasted chestnuts in the other, enters the court. The mother pushes the heavy doors that hide the court from the street, and the pair enter slowly, as if they had tramped a long way in heavy snow. They have returned safely, once again, from their afternoon stroll in the Jardin des Tuileries. The chestnuts were bought from the old Algerian beside the pond near the Place de la Concorde. The smoke of the blue charcoal fire was darker than the sky, and the smell of chestnuts burning is more pungent than their taste. In a cone of newspaper (a quarter page of *France-Soir*) they warm the heart and hand.

Four days ago Ernst followed these two. They live up above Willi's room. He was curious to know where they were going. The walk came to nothing. When the boy and his mother reached the object of their outing— the old man, the chestnuts, the frozen pond—they turned around and came away, between the black, stripped trees and the cold statues Ernst thinks of as trees. Mercury is a tree; the Rape of Deidamia is another tree. They skirted a sea of feeding pigeons, out of which rose a brave old maniac of a woman with a cotton scarf on her head. It is an illegal act to scatter crumbs for the birds of Paris, but on this Siberian day the guardians of the peace are too frozen to act. The mother, the child, and Ernst behind them, plod on snow like sifted sugar, past the Roman emperors, past the straw-covered beds of earth. In great peril they cross the Quai des Tuileries. The traffic light changes from green to red without warning when they are half over, and they stand still, creating a whirlpool. Along the Pont Royal the wind strikes like an enemy, from every direction at once. After a sunless day there is a pale orange cloud on the Gare d'Orsay. The spires of Notre Dame and the stalled buses in the traffic block on the Pont du Carousel appear nacreous and white, as if in moonlight. The mother and child are engulfed and nearly trampled suddenly by released civil servants running away from their offices behind the Gare d'Orsay. They run as if there were lions behind them. It has never been as cold as this in Paris. Breath is visible; Ernst's emerges from marble lungs. The mother and child face the last hazard of the journey—the Quai Anatole France. Even when they have the green light in their favor, they are caught by cars turning right off the Pont Royal. There are two policemen here to protect them, and there are traffic lights to be obeyed, but every person and every thing is submerged by the dark and the cold and the torrent of motorcars and a fear like a fear of lions.

Tiring of this, Ernst threads his way across, against the light, leaving the child and the woman trembling on the curb. He had wondered about them, and wondered where they went every day, and now he knows. That was four days ago. He has seldom been out of Willi's room since.

"Hurry," says the mother when she and the child reach the middle of the court. She takes the chestnuts and the boy's gloves, and the child vanishes behind the rotting wooden door of the courtyard lavatory. The mother, waiting, looks up at a window for a friend. She has a crony—a hag Ernst sees in the store where he and she, without speaking, buy the same ink-thick, unlabeled red wine. She buys one liter at a time, Ernst several. Her window is just below his, to the left.

The mother might be twenty-six. She stands in cold light from an open window. Her upturned face is broad and white, the angora beret on her head is white moss. She has wrapped a tatty fur around her neck, like an old Russian countess. Her handbag seems the old displaced-person sort, too—big, and bulging with canceled passports. She speaks in the thin voice of this city, the high plucked wire of a voice that belittles the universe.

"I've had enough, and I've told him so," she says, without caring who might hear. It sounds at least the start of a tragedy, but then she invites the hag, who, with a tablecloth around her head, is hanging out the window, to stop by and share the television later on. At half past seven there will be a program called *L'Homme du XXe Siècle.*

Ernst followed this woman because she was fit for his attention. He would have sought a meeting somewhere, but the weather was against it. He could not have brought her to Willi's room, because Willi has scruples about gossip and neighbors. Ernst could have gone upstairs (he does not doubt his success for a moment), but the walls are cardboard and he would have drawn notice to his marked civilian self.

*   *   *

Early in the morning, the mother's voice is fresh and quick. The father leaves for work at six o'clock. She takes the child to school at a quarter to eight. The child calls her often: "*Maman*, come here." "*Maman*, look." She rushes about, clattering with brooms. At nine she goes to market, and she returns at ten, calling up to her crony that she has found nothing, nothing fit to eat, but the basket is full of something; she is bent sideways with the weight of it. By noon, after she has gone out once more to fetch the child for lunch, her voice begins to rise. Either the boy refuses what she has cooked for him or does not eat quickly enough, but his meal is dogged with the repeated question "Are you going to obey?" He is dragged back to school weeping. Both are worn out with this, and their late-afternoon walk is exhausted and calm. In the evening the voice climbs still higher. "You will see, when your father comes home!" It is a bird shrieking. Whatever the child has done or said is so monstrously disobedient that she cannot wait for the father to arrive. She has to chase the child and catch him before she can beat him. There is the noise of running, a chair knocked down, something like marbles, perhaps the chestnuts, rolling on the floor. "You *will* obey me!" It is a promise of the future now. The caught child screams. If the house were burning, if there were lions on the stairs, he could not scream more. All round the court the neighbors stay well away from their windows. It is no one's concern. When his mother beats him, the child calls for help, and calls, "*Maman.*" His true mother will surely arrive and take him away from his mother transformed. Who else can he appeal to? It makes sense. Ernst has heard grown men call for their mothers. He knows about submission and punishment and justice and power. He knows what the child does not know—that the screaming will stop, that everything ends. He did not learn a trade in the Foreign Legion, but he did learn to obey.

Good-natured Willi danced a java this morning, with an imaginary girl in his arms. Fortunately, he had no partner, for she would have been kicked to bits. His thick hands described circles to the music from the radio, and his thick legs kicked sideways and forward. Ernst saw the soles of Willi's shoes and his flying unmilitary hair, and his round face red with laughter. When the music stopped, he stopped, and after he had regained his breath, used it to repeat that he would come home early to cook the stew for their last supper. Willi then went off to work. Today he is guide and interpreter for seventeen men from a German firm that makes bath salts. He will show them the Emperor's tomb and the Eiffel Tower and leave them to their fate up in Pigalle. As Willi neither smokes nor drinks, and is not even objectively interested in pictures of naked dancers, he can see no advantage in spending an evening there. He weighs the free banquet against the waste of time and chooses time. He will tell them what the limit price is for a bottle of champagne and abandon them, seventeen of them, in hats, scarves, overcoats, and well-soled shoes, safe in an establishment where *Man spricht Deutsch.* Then he will hurry home to cut up the leeks and carrots for Ernst's last stew. Willi has a sense of responsibility, and finds most people noisier and sillier than they were ten years ago. He does not know that ten years have gone by. His face does not reflect the change of time, rate, and distance. He is small in stature, as if he had not begun his adolescent growth. He looks and speaks about as he did when he and Ernst were prisoners in the west of France eighteen years ago.

This morning, before attending to his seventeen men from the bath-salts factory, Willi went to the market and came back with a newspaper some-one had dropped in a bus shelter. What a find! Twenty-five centimes of fresh news! He also had a piece of stewing beef and a marrow bone, and he unfolded an old journal to reveal four carrots and two leeks. The grocer weighed the vegetables and the journal together, so that Willi was cheated, but he was grateful to be allowed to purchase any vegetables at all. The only vegetables on public sale that morning were frozen Brussels sprouts.

"It is like wartime," says Willi, not displeased that it is like wartime. He might enjoy the privations of another war, without the killing. He thinks privation is good for people. If you give Willi a piece of chocolate, he gives half of it away to someone else and puts the rest aside until it has turned stale and white. Then he eats it, slowly and thankfully, and says it is delicious. Lying on the floor, Ernst has watched Willi working—typing translations at four francs a page. His blunt fingers work rapidly. His eyes never look up from the paper beside the machine. He has taught himself to translate on sight, even subjects about which he cares nothing, such as neon tubes and historical principles. They have come only a short distance from their camp in 1945, where someone said to Ernst, "You have lost the war. You are not ordinary prisoners. You may never go home again." At the other end of the camp, on the far side of a fence, the Foreign Legion recruits played soccer and threw leftover food into garbage cans; and so Ernst left Willi with his bugs, his potato peelings, his diseased feet, his shorn head, and joined the Legion. Willi thought he would get home faster by staying where he was. They were both bad guessers. Willi is still in Paris, typing translations, guiding visiting businessmen, playing S.S. officers in films about the last war. It is a way of living, not quite a life. Ernst teases Willi because he works hard for little money, and because he worries about things of no consequence—why children are spoiled, why girls lose their virtue, why wars are lost, won, or started. He tells Willi, "Do you want to go to your grave with nothing but this behind you?" If Ernst really believes what he says, how can one explain the expression he takes on then, when he suddenly rolls over on the floor and says, "Girls are nothing, Willi. You haven't missed much. You're better off the way you are."

This is a long day without daylight. Ernst's duffel bag is packed. He has nothing to do. He has forgotten that Willi asked him to put the marrow bone and stewing beef in a pan of water on the electric plate no later than four o'clock. In the paper found at the bus shelter Ernst discovers that because of the hard winter—the coldest since 1880—the poor are to be given fifty kilos of free coal. Or else it is one hundred and fifty or one hundred kilos; he cannot understand the news item, which gives all three figures. Gas is to be free for the poor (if consumed moderately) until March 31. Willi's gas heater flames the whole day, because Ernst, as a civilian, is sensitive to weather. Ernst will let Willi pay the bill, and, with some iridescent memory of something once read, he will believe that Willi had free gas—and, who knows, perhaps free rent and light!—all winter long. When Ernst believes an idea suitable for the moment, it becomes true. He has many troubles, and if you believe one-tenth of anything he tells you, he will say you are decent.

Once, Ernst was a Werewolf concealed in civilian clothes. His uniform was gone, and his arms and identity papers buried in the mud outside a village whose name he cannot remember. It begins with L. He lay on the ground vomiting grass, bark, and other foods he had eaten. He had been told to get rid of the papers but not the arms. He disobeyed. He walked all one night to the town where his mother and stepfather were. The door was locked, because the forced-labor camps were open now and ghosts in rags were abroad and people were frightened of them. His mother opened the door a crack when she recognized the Werewolf's voice (but not his face or his disguise) and she said, "You can't stay here." There was a smell of burning. They were burning his stepfather's S.S. uniform in the cellar. Ernst's mother kissed him, but he had already turned away. The missed embrace was a salute to the frightening night, and she shut the door on her son and went back to her husband. Even if she had offered him food, he could not have swallowed. His throat closed on his breath. He could not swallow his own spit. He cannot now remember his own age or what she was like. He is either thirty-four or thirty-six, and born in Mainz.

Willi is always reading about the last war. He cuts up newspapers and pastes clippings in scrapbooks. All this is evidence. Willi is waiting for the lucid, the wide-awake, and above all the rational person who will come out of the past and say with authority, "This was true," and "This was not." The photographs, the films, the documents, the witnesses, and the survivors could have been invented or dreamed. Willi searches the plain blue sky of his childhood and looks for a stain of the evil he has been told was there. He cannot see it. The sky is without spot.

"What was wrong with the Hitler Youth?" says Willi. What was wrong with being told about Goethe Rilke Wagner Schiller Beethoven?

Ernst, when he listens to Willi, seems old and sly. He looks like a corrupted old woman. Many of the expressions of his face are womanish. He is like the old woman who says to the young girl, "Have nothing to do with anyone. Stay as you are." He knows more than Willi because he has been a soldier all his life. He knows that there are no limits to folly and pain except fatigue and the failing of imagination. He has always known more than Willi, but he can be of no help to him, because of his own lifesaving powers of forgetfulness.

It is the twentieth anniversary of Stalingrad, and the paper found at the bus stop is full of it. Stalingrad—now renamed—is so treated that it seems a defeat all around, and a man with a dull memory, like Ernst, can easily think that France and Germany fought on the same side twenty years ago. Or else there were two separate wars, one real and one remembered. It must have been a winter as cold as this, a winter gray on white and full of defeat. Ernst turns on the radio and, finding nothing but solemn music, turns it off. From the court he hears a romantic tune sung by Charles Aznavour and is moved by it. On an uncrowded screen a line of ghosts shuffles in snow, limps through the triumphant city, and a water cart cleans the pavement their feet have touched. Ernst, the eternally defeated, could know the difference between victory and failure, if he would apply his mind to it; but he has met young girls in Paris who think Dien Bien Phu was a French victory, and he has let them go on thinking it, because it is of no importance. Ernst was in Indochina and knows it was a defeat. There is no fear in the memory. Sometimes another, younger Ernst is in a place where he must save someone who calls, *"Mutti!"* He advances; he wades in a flooded cellar. There is more fear in dreams than in life. What about the dream where someone known—sometimes a man, sometimes a woman—wears a mask and wig? The horror of the wig! He wakes dry-throated. Willi has always been ready to die. If the judge he is waiting for says, "This is true, and you were not innocent," he says he will be ready to die. He could die tomorrow. But Ernst, who has been in uniform since he was seven, and defeated in every war, has never been prepared.

In the court it snowed and rained and the rain froze on the windows. By three o'clock he could not see without a light. He pinned the curtains together, switched on the table lamp, and lay down on the floor. In the paper he read the following:

> *A l'occasion d'un premier colloque*
> *européen*
> LE "DOPING" HUMAIN
> *a été défini et condamné*

It must mean something. Would Willi cut this out and paste it in a scrapbook? Willi, who will be home in two or three hours, is made sick by the smell of cigarette smoke, and so Ernst gets up, undoes the curtains, and airs the room. He must have fallen asleep over the paper, for it is quite dark, and the child and his mother have returned from their walk. The room is cold and smells of the courtyard instead of cigarettes. He shuts the window and curtains and looks for something to read. Willi has saved a magazine article by an eminent author in which it is claimed that young Werewolves were animals. Their training had lowered the barrier between wolves and men. Witnesses heard them howling in the night. When the judge arrives, Willi will say to him, "What about this?" Ernst begins the article but finds it long-winded. He grins, suddenly, reading, without knowing he has shown his teeth. If he were seen at this moment, an element of folklore would begin to seep through Europe, where history becomes folklore in a generation: "On the Rue de Lille, a man of either thirty-six or thirty-four, masquerading in civilian clothes, became a wolf." He reads: "Witnesses saw them eating babies and tearing live chickens apart." He buried his arms and his identity in the mud outside a village whose name he cannot remember. He vomited bark and grass and the yellow froth of fear. He was in a peasant's jacket stiff with grease and sweat. Ernst is rusting and decomposing in the soft earth near a village. Under leaves, snow, dandelions, twigs, his shame molders. Without papers he was no one; without arms he was nothing. Without papers and without arms he walked as if in a fever, asking himself constantly what he had forgotten. In the village whose name began with L, he saw an American. He sat throwing a knife at a mark on a wall. He would get up slowly, go over to the wall, pull out the knife, walk slowly back, sit down, balance the knife, and aim at the mark, holding the knife by the blade.

Ernst is going home, but not to that village. He could never find it again. He does not know what he will find. Willi, who goes home every year at Christmas, returns disgusted. He hates the old men who sit and tell stories. "Old men in their forties," says Willi, who does not know he will soon be old. The old men rub their sleeves through beer rings and say that if the Americans had done this, if von Paulus had done that, if Hitler had died a year sooner . . . finger through the beer rings, drawing a line, and an arrow, and a spear.

Having aired the room, and frozen it, Ernst lights another cigarette. He is going home. In Willi's scrapbook he turns over unpasted clippings about the terrorist trials in Paris in 1962. Two ex-Legionnaires, deserters, were tried—he will read to the end, if he can keep awake. Two ex-Legionnaires were shot by a firing squad because they had shot someone else. It is a confusing story, because some of the clippings say "bandits" and some say "patriots." He does not quite understand what went on, and the two terrorists could not have understood much, either, because when the death sentence was spoken they took off their French decorations and flung them into the courtroom and cried, "Long Live France!" and "Long Live French Algeria!" They were not French, but they had been in the Legion, and probably did not know there were other things to say. That was 1962—light-years ago in political time.

Ernst is going home. He has decided, about a field of daffodils, My Country. He will not be shot with "Long Live" anything on his lips. No. He will not put on a new uniform, or continue to claim his pension, or live with a prostitute, or become a night watchman in Paris. What will he do?

When Ernst does not know what to do, he goes to sleep. He sits on the floor near the gas heater with his knees drawn up and his head on his arms. He can sleep in any position, and he goes deeply asleep within seconds. The room is as sealed as a box and his duffel bag an invisible threat in a corner. He wades in the water of a flooded cellar. His pocket light is soaked; the damp batteries fail. There is another victim in the cellar, calling *"Mutti,"* and it is his duty to find him and rescue him and drag him up to the light of day. He wades forward in the dark, and knows, in sleep, where it is no help to him, that the voice is his own.

Ernst, on his feet, stiff with the cold of a forgotten dream, makes a new decision. Everyone is lying; he will invent his own truth. Is it important if one-tenth of a lie is true? Is there a horror in a memory if it was only a dream? In Willi's shaving mirror now he wears the face that no superior officer, no prisoner, and no infatuated girl has ever seen. He will believe only what *he* knows. It is a great decision in an important day. Life begins with facts: He is Ernst Zimmermann, ex-Legionnaire. He has a ticket to Stuttgart. On the twenty-eighth of January, in the coldest winter since 1880, on the Rue de Lille, in Paris, the child beaten by his mother cries for help and calls, *"Maman, Maman."*

AN UNMARRIED MAN'S
SUMMER

❧

*T*he great age of the winter society Walter Henderson frequents on the French Riviera makes him seem young to himself and a stripling to his friends. In a world of elderly widows his relative youth appears a virtue, his existence as a bachelor a precious state. All winter long he drives his sporty little Singer over empty roads, on his way to parties at Beaulieu, or Roquebrune, or Cap Ferrat. From the sea he and his car must look like a drawing of insects: a firefly and a flea. He drives gaily, as if it were summer. He is often late. He has a disarming gesture of smoothing his hair as he makes his apologies. Sometimes his excuse has to do with Angelo, his hilarious and unpredictable manservant. Or else it is Mme. Rossi, the *femme de ménage*, who has been having a moody day. William of Orange, Walter's big old ginger tomcat, comes into the account. As Walter describes his household, he is the victim of servants and pet animals, he is chief player in an endless imbroglio of intrigue, swindle, cuckoldry—all of it funny, of course; haven't we laughed at Molière?

"*Darling* Walter," his great friend Mrs. Wiggott has often said to him. "This could only happen to *you*."

He tells his stories in peaceful dining rooms, to a circle of loving, attentive faces. He is surrounded by the faces of women. Their eyes are fixed on his dotingly, but in homage to another man: a young lover killed in the 1914 war; an adored but faithless son. "Naughty Walter," murmurs Mrs. Wiggott. "*Wicked* boy." Walter must be wicked, for part of the memory of every vanished husband or lover or son is the print of his cruelty. Walter's old friends are nursing bruised hearts. Mrs. Wiggott's injuries span four husbands, counted on four arthritic fingers—the gambler, the dipsomaniac, the dago, and poor Wiggott, who ate a good breakfast one morning and walked straight in front of a train. "None of my husbands was from my own walk of life," Mrs. Wiggott has said to Walter. "I made such mistakes with men, trying to bring them up to my level. I've often thought, Walter, if only I had met *you* forty years ago!"

"Yes, indeed," says Walter heartily, smoothing his hair.

They have lost their time sense in this easy climate; when Mrs. Wiggott was on the lookout for a second husband forty years ago, Walter was five.

"If your life isn't exactly the way you want it to be by the time you are forty-five," said Walter's father, whom he admired, "not much point in continuing. You might as well hang yourself." He also said, "Parenthood is sacred. Don't go about creating children right and left"; this when Walter was twelve. Walter's Irish grandmother said, "Don't touch the maids," which at least was practical. "I stick to the women who respect and admire me," declared his godfather. He was a bachelor, a great diner-out. "What good is beauty to a boy?" Walter's mother lamented. "I have such a plain little girl, poor little Eve. Couldn't it have been shared?" "Nothing fades faster than the beauty of a boy." Walter has read that, but cannot remember where.

A mosaic picture of Walter's life early in the summer of his forty-fifth year would have shown him dead center, where nothing can seem more upsetting than a punctured tire or more thrilling than a sunny day. On his right is Angelo, the comic valet. Years ago, Angelo followed Walter through the streets of a shadeless, hideous town. He was begging for coins; that was their introduction. Now he is seventeen, and quick as a knife. In the mosaic image, Walter's creation, he is indolent, capricious, more trouble than he is worth. Mme. Rossi, the *femme de ménage,* is made to smile. She is slovenly but good-tempered, she sings, her feet are at ease in decaying shoes. Walter puts it about that she is in love with a driver on the Monte Carlo bus. That is the role he has given her in his dinner-party stories. He has to say something about her to bring her to life. The cat, William of Orange, is in Angelo's arms. As a cat, he is film star, prizefighter, and stubbornness itself; as a personality, he lives in a cloud of black thoughts. The figures make a balanced and nearly perfect design, supported by a frieze of pallida iris in mauve, purple, and white.

The house in the background, the stucco façade with yellow shutters, three brick steps, and Venetian door, is called Les Anémones. It belongs to two spinsters, Miss Cooper and Miss Le Chaine. They let Walter live here, rent-free, with the understanding that he pay the property taxes, which are small, and keep the garden alive and the roof in repair. Miss Cooper is headmistress of a school in England; Miss Le Chaine is her oldest friend. When Miss Cooper retires from her post fifteen years from now, she and Miss Le Chaine plan to come down to the Riviera and live in Les Anémones forever. Walter will then be sixty years of age and homeless. He supposes he ought to be doing something about it; he ought to start looking around for another place. He sees himself, aged sixty, Mrs. Wiggott's permanent guest, pushing her in a Bath chair along the Promenade des Anglais at Nice. It is such a disgusting prospect that he hates Mrs. Wiggott because of the imaginary chair.

Walter knows that pushing a Bath chair would be small return for everything Mrs. Wiggott has done for him: It was Mrs. Wiggott who persuaded Miss Cooper and Miss Le Chaine there might be a revolution here—nothing to do with politics, just a wild upheaval of some kind. (Among Walter's hostesses, chaos is expected from week to week, and in some seasons almost hourly.) With revolution a certain future, is it not wise to have someone like Walter in charge of one's house? Someone who will die on the brick doorstep, if need be, in the interests of Miss Cooper and Miss Le Chaine? Having had a free house for many years, and desiring the arrangement to continue, Walter will feel he has something to defend. So runs Mrs. Wiggott's reasoning, and it does sound sane. It sounded sane to the two ladies in England, luckily for him. He does not expect a revolution, because he does not expect anything; he would probably defend Les Anémones because he couldn't imagine where else he might go. This house is a godsend, because Walter is hard up. In spite of the total appearance of the mosaic, he has to live very carefully indeed, never wanting anything beyond the moment. He has a pension from the last war, and he shares the income of a small trust fund with his sister, Eve, married and farming in South Africa. When anyone asks Walter why he has never married, he smiles and says he cannot support a wife. No argument there.

This picture belongs to the winter months. Summer is something else. In all seasons the sea is blocked from his view by a large hotel. From May to October, this hotel is festooned with drying bathing suits. Its kitchen sends the steam of tons of boiled potatoes over Walter's hedge. His hostesses have fled the heat; his telephone is still. He lolls on a garden chair, rereading his boyhood books—the Kipling, the bound albums of *Chums*. He tries to give Angelo lessons in English literature, using his old schoolbooks, but Angelo is silly, laughs; and if Walter persists in trying to teach him anything, he says he feels sick. Mme. Rossi carries ice up from the shop in a string bag. It is half melted when she arrives, and it leaves its trail along the path and over the terrace and through the house to the kitchen. In August, even she goes to the mountains, leaving Walter, Angelo, and the cat to get on as best they can. Walter wraps a sliver of ice in a handkerchief and presses the handkerchief to his wrists. He is deafened by cicadas and nauseated by the smell of jasmine. His skin does not sweat; most of his body is covered with puckered scars. Twenty years ago, he was badly burned. He reads, but does not quite know what he is reading. Fortunately, his old books were committed to memory years before.

At last the good weather fades, the crowds go away. The hotel closes its shutters. His hostesses return. They have survived the season in Scotland and Switzerland—somewhere rainy and cold. They are back now, in time for the winter rain. All at once Walter's garden seems handsome, with the great fig tree over the terrace, and the Judas tree waiting for its late-winter flowering. After Christmas the iris will bloom, and Walter will show his tottering visitors around. "I put in the iris," he explains, "but, of course, Miss Cooper shall have them when I go." This sounds as though he means to die on the stroke of sixty, leaving the iris as a mauve-and-white memorial along the path. "Naughty Walter," Mrs. Wiggott chides him. "Morbid boy." Yet the only morbid remark he has ever made in her presence went unheard, or at least unanswered: "I wish it had been finished off for me in the last war." That last war, recalled by fragments of shell dug up in Riviera gardens, was for many of his present friends the last commerce with life, if life means discomfort, bad news. They still see, without reading them, the slogans praising Mussolini, relics of the Italian occupation of the coast. Walter has a faded old *Viva* on the door to his garage. He thought he might paint over it one day, but Mrs. Wiggott asked him not to. Her third husband was a high-up Fascist, close to Mussolini. Twenty years ago, she wore a smart black uniform, tailored for her in Paris, and she had a jaunty tasseled hat. She was the first foreign woman to give her wedding ring to the great Italian gold collection; at least she says she was. But Walter has met two other women, one Belgian and one American, who claim the same thing.

He lay in a garden chair that summer—the summer he had not hanged himself, having arranged life exactly as he wanted it—unshaven, surviving, when a letter arrived that contained disagreeable news. His sister and brother-in-law had sold their African farm, were flying to England, and intended to stop off and have a short holiday with him on the way. His eyes were blood-shot. He did not read the letter more than twice. He had loved his sister, but she had married a farmer, a Punch squire, blunt, ignorant, Anglo-Irish. Walter, who had the same mixture in his blood, liked to think that Frank Osborn had "the worst of both." Frank was a countryman. He despised city life, yet the country got the better of him every time. In twelve years in Africa, he and Eve had started over twice. He attracted bad luck. Once, Eve wrote Walter asking if he would let some of the capital out of the trust whose income they shared. She and Frank wanted to buy new equipment, expand. They had two children now, a girl and a boy. She hinted that halv-ing the income was no longer quite fair. Walter answered the letter with-out making any mention of her request, and was thankful to hear no more about it.

Now, dead center of summer, she was making a new claim: She was de-manding a holiday. Walter saw pretty clearly what had happened. Although Frank and Eve had not yet been dispossessed in South Africa, they were leaving while the going was good. Eve wrote that no decent person could stand the situation down there, and Walter thought that might well be the truth, but only part of it; the rest of the truth was they had failed. They kept trying, which was possibly to their credit; but they had failed. Five days after the arrival of this letter came a second letter, giving the date of their ar-rival—August fifteenth.

On the fifteenth of August, Walter stood upon his terrace in an attitude of welcome. A little behind him was Angelo, excited as only an Italian can be by the idea of "family." William of Orange sat on the doorstep, between two tubs, each holding an orange tree. Walter had not met the family at the airport, because there was not room for them all in the Singer, and because Eve had written a third letter, telling him not to meet them. The Osborns were to be looked after by a man from Cook's, who was bringing to the air-port a Citroën Frank had hired. In the Citroën they proposed to get from the airport to Walter, a distance of only thirty-odd miles, but through sum-mer traffic and over unfamiliar roads. Walter thought of them hanging out the car windows, shouting questions. He knew there were two children, but pictured six. He thought of them lost, and the six children in tears.

Toward the end of the afternoon, when Walter had been pacing the ter-race, or nervously listening, for the better part of the day, Angelo shouted that he heard children's voices on the other side of the hedge. Walter instantly took up a new position. He seemed to be protecting the house against the expected revolution. Then—there was no mistaking it—he heard car doors slammed, and the whole family calling out. He stared down the path to the gate, between the clumps of iris Angelo had cut back after the last flowering. The soil was dry and hard and clay. He was still thinking of that, of the terrible soil he had to contend with here, when Eve rushed at him. She was a giantess, around his neck almost before he saw her face. He had her damp cheek, her unsophisticated talcum smell. She was crying, but that was probably due to fatigue. She drew back and said to him, "You're not a minute older, darling, except where you've gone gray." What remarkable eyes she must have, Walter thought, and what gifts of second sight; for his hair was *slightly* gray, but only at the back. Eve was jolly and loud. It had been said in their childhood that she should have been a boy. Frank came along with a suitcase in each hand. He put the cases down. "Well, old Frank," said Walter. Frank replied with astonishment, "Why, it's Walter!"

The two children stared at their uncle and then at Angelo. They were not timid, but seemed to Walter without manners or charm. Eve had written that Mary, the elder, was the image of Walter in appearance and in character. He saw a girl of about eleven with lank yellow hair, and long feet in heavy sandals. Her face was brown, her lashes rabbit-white. The boy was half his sister's size, and entirely Osborn; that is, he had his father's round red face. He showed Walter a box he was holding. "There's a hamster in it," he said, and explained in a piping voice that he had bought it from a boy at the airport.

"They don't waste any time when it comes to complicating life," said Frank proudly.

Angelo stood by, smiling, waiting to be presented. Keeping Angelo as a friend and yet not a social friend was a great problem for Walter. Angelo lacked the sophistication required to make the change easily. Walter decided he would not introduce him, but the little Osborn boy suddenly turned to the valet and smiled. The two, Johnny and Angelo, seemed to be struck shy. Until then, Walter had always considered Angelo someone partly unreal, part of his personal mosaic. Once, Angelo had been a figure on the wall of a baroque church; from the wall he came toward Walter, with his hand out, cupped for coins. The church had been intended from its beginnings to blister and crack, to set off black hair, appraising black eyes. The four elements of Angelo's childhood were southern baroque, malaria, idleness, and hunger. They were what he would go back to if Walter were to tire of him, or if he should decide to leave. Now the wall of the church disappeared, and so did a pretty, wheedling boy. Angelo was seventeen, dumpy, nearly coarse. "Nothing fades faster than the beauty of a boy." Angelo looked shrewd; he looked as if he might have a certain amount of common sense—that most defeating of qualities, that destroyer.

The family settled on the terrace, in the wicker chairs that belonged with the house, around the chipped garden table that was a loan from Mrs. Wiggott. They were sprawling, much at ease, like an old-fashioned *Chums* picture of colonials. They praised Angelo, who carried in the luggage and then gave them tea, and the children smiled at him, shyly still.

"They've fallen for him," Eve said.

"What?" It seemed to Walter such an extraordinary way to talk. The children slid down from their chairs (without permission, the bachelor uncle observed) and followed Angelo around the side of the house.

"They don't love *us* much at the moment," Eve said. "We've taken them away from their home. They don't think anything of the idea. They'll get over it. But it's natural for them to turn to someone else, don't you think? Tell Angelo to watch himself with Mary. She's a seething mass of feminine wiles. She's always after something."

"She doesn't get anything out of *me*," said Mary's father.

"You don't even notice when she does, that's how clever she is," said Eve.

"I told her I'd buy her something at the airport, because Johnny had the hamster," said Frank. "She said she didn't want anything."

"She doesn't want just anything you offer," said Eve. "That's where she's wily. She thinks about what she wants and then she goes after it without saying anything. It's a game. I tell you, she's feminine. More power to her. I'm glad."

"Angelo hasn't much to worry about," said Walter. "I don't think she could get much out of him, because he hasn't got anything. Although I do pay him; I'm a stickler about that. He has his food and lodging and clothes, and although many people would think that enough, I give him pocket money as well." This had an effect he had not expected. His sister and brother-in-law stared as if he had said something puzzling and incomplete. Walter felt socially obliged to go on speaking. In the dry afternoon he inspected their tired faces. They had come thousands of miles by plane, and then driven here in an unknown car. They were still polite enough to listen and to talk. He remembered one of his most amusing stories, which Mrs. Wiggott frequently asked him to repeat. It was about how he had sent Angelo and William of Orange to Calabria one summer so that Angelo could visit his people and William of Orange have a change of air. Halfway through the journey, Angelo had to give it up and come back to Les Anémones. William of Orange hadn't stopped howling from the time the train started to move. "You understand," said Walter, "he couldn't leave William of Orange shut up in his basket. It seemed too cruel. William of Orange *wouldn't* keep still, Angelo daren't let him *out*, because he was in such a fury he would have attacked the other passengers. Also, William of Orange was being desperately sick. It was an Italian train, third class. You can imagine the counsel, the good advice! Angelo tried leaving the basket partly open, so that William of Orange could see what was going on but not jump out, but he only screamed all the more. Finally Angelo bundled up all his things, the presents he'd been taking his family and William of Orange in his basket, and he got down at some stop and simply took the next train going the other direction. I shall never forget how they arrived early in the morning, having traveled the whole night and walked from the . . ."

"This is a dreadful story," said Eve, slowly turning her head. "It's sad."

Frank said nothing, but seemed to agree with his wife. Walter supposed they thought the cat and the valet should not have been traveling at all; they had come up from South Africa, where they had spent twelve years bullying blacks. He said, "They were traveling third class."

Mary, his niece, sauntered back to the table, as if she had just learned a new way of walking. She flung herself in a chair and picked up her father's cigarettes. She began playing with them, waiting to be told not to. Neither parent said a word.

"And how was your journey?" said Walter gravely.

The girl looked away from the cigarettes and said, "In a way, I've forgotten it."

"No showing off, please," said Eve.

"There's a kind of holiday tonight," said the girl. "There'll be fireworks, all that. Angelo says we can see them from here. He's making Johnny sleep now, on two chairs in the kitchen. He wanted me to sleep, too, but I wouldn't, of course. He's fixing a basket for the hamster up where the cat can't get it. We're going to have the fireworks at dinner, and then he'll take us down to the harbor, he says, to see the people throwing confetti and all that."

"The fireworks won't be seen from our dining room, I fear," said Walter.

"We're having our dinner out here, on the terrace," said the girl. "He says the mosquitoes are awful and you people will have to smoke."

"Do the children always dine with you?" said Walter.

There was no answer, because William of Orange came by, taking their attention. Mary put out her hand, but the cat avoided it. Walter looked at the determined child who was said to resemble him. She bent toward the cat, idly calling. Her hair divided, revealing a delicate ear. The angle of her head lent her expression something thoughtful and sad; it was almost an exaggerated posture of wistfulness. Her arms and hands were thin, but with no suggestion of fragility. She smiled at the cat and said, "*He* doesn't care. He doesn't care what we say." Her bones were made of something tough and precious. She was not pretty, no, but quite lovely, in spite of the straight yellow hair, the plain way she was dressed. Walter knew instantly what he would have given her to wear. He thought, Ballet lessons ... beautiful French, and saw himself the father of a daughter. The mosaic expanded; there was room for another figure, surely? Yes—but to have a daughter one needed a wife. That brought everything down to normal size again. He smiled to himself, thinking how grateful he was that clods like Frank Osborn could cause enchanting girls to appear, all for the enjoyment of vicarious fathers. It was a new idea, one he would discuss next winter with Mrs. Wiggott. He could develop it into a story. It would keep the old dears laughing for weeks.

Angelo strung paper lanterns on wires between branches of the fig tree. The children were fogged with sleep, but bravely kept their heads up, waiting for the fireworks he had said would be set off over the sea. Neither of them remarked that the sea was hidden by the hotel; they trusted Angelo to produce the sea as he produced their dinner. Walter's nephew slept with his eyes wide. Angelo's lanterns were reflected in his eyes—pinpoints of cobalt blue.

From the table they heard the crowd at the harbor, cheering every burst. Colored smoke floated across the dark sky. The smell of jasmine, which ordinarily made Walter sick, was part of the children's night.

"Do you know my name?" said the little boy, as Angelo moved around the table collecting plates. "It's Johnny." He sighed, and put his head down where the plate had been. Presently Angelo came out of the house wearing a clean white pullover and with his hair well oiled. Johnny woke up as if he had heard a bell. "Are you taking us to the harbor?" he said. "Now?"

Mary, Johnny, and Angelo looked at Eve. It was plain to Walter that these children should not be anywhere except in bed. He was furious with Angelo.

"Is there polio or anything here?" said Eve lazily. Now it was Walter's turn. The children—all three—looked at him with something like terror. He was about to deny them the only pleasure they had ever been allowed; that was what their looks said. Without waiting for his answer about polio, Eve said the children could go.

The candles inside the paper lanterns guttered and had to be blown out. The Osborns smoked conscientiously to keep mosquitoes away. In the light of a struck match, Walter saw his sister's face, her short graying hair. "That's a nice lad," she said.

"The kids are mad about him," said Frank.

"They are besotted," said Eve. "I'm glad. You couldn't have planned a better welcome, Walter dear," and in the dark she briefly covered his hand with hers.

The family lived in Miss Cooper's house as if it were a normal place to be. They were more at home than Walter had ever been. Mornings, he heard them chattering on the terrace or laughing in the kitchen with Angelo. Eve and Angelo planned the meals, and sometimes they went to the market together. The Osborns took over the household food expenses, and Walter, tactfully, made no mention of it. Sometimes the children had their meals in the kitchen with Angelo and the hamster and the cat. But there was no order, no system, to their upbringing. They often dined with the adults. The parents rose late, but not so late as Walter. They seemed to feel it would be impolite to go off to the beach or the market until Walter's breakfast was over. He was not accustomed to eating breakfast, particularly during the hot weather, but he managed to eat an egg and some cold toast, only because they appeared to expect it.

"Change has got to come in South Africa," said Eve one morning as Walter sat down to a boiled egg. The family had eaten. The table was covered with ashes, eggshells, and crumbs.

"Why at our expense?" said Frank.

"Frank is an anarchist, although you wouldn't think it at times," said Eve, with pride.

Married twelve years and still talking, Walter thought. Frank and Eve were in accord on one thing—that there was bad faith on all sides in South Africa. They interrupted each other, explaining apartheid to Walter, who did not want to hear anything about it. Frank repeated that no decent person could stand by and accept the situation, and Eve agreed; but she made no bones about the real reason for their having left. They had failed, failed. The word rolled around the table like a wooden ball.

So Frank was an anarchist, was he, Walter thought, snipping at his egg. Well, he could afford to be an anarchist, living down there, paying next to no income tax. He said, "You will find things different in England."

"An English farm, aha," said Frank, and looked at Eve.

"Just so long as it isn't a poultry farm," said Walter, getting on with his revolting breakfast. The egg had given him something to say. "I have seen people try that."

"As a matter of fact, it *is* a poultry farm," said Eve. Frank's face was earnest and red; this farm had a history of arguments about it. Eve went on, "You see, we try one thing after the other. We're obliged to try things, aren't we? We have two children to educate."

"I wouldn't want to live without doing something," said Frank. "Even if I could afford to. I mean to say that I'm not brainy and it's better for me if I have something to do."

"Walter used to think it better," said Eve. She went on, very lightly, "I did envy Walter once. Walter, think of the money that was spent educating you. They wouldn't do it for a girl. Ah, how I used to wish we could have exchanged, then." Having said this, she rounded on her husband, as if it were Frank who had failed to give Walter credit, had underestimated him, dragging schoolroom jealousy across the lovely day. Frank must be told: Walter in Hong Kong in a bank. Walter in amateur theatricals, the image of Douglas Fairbanks. He was marvelous in the war; he was burned from head to foot. He was hours swimming in flames in the North Sea. He should have had the Victoria Cross. Everyone said so.

The two children, sitting nearby sorting colored pebbles they had brought up from the beach, scarcely glanced at their courageous uncle. The impossibility of his ever having done anything splendid was as clear to them as it was to Walter. He agreed with the children—for it had all of it gone, and he wanted nothing but the oasis of peace, the admiration of undemanding old women, the winter months. If he was irritated, it was only by his sister's puritanical insistence on working. Would the world have been a happier place if Walter had remained in Hong Kong in a bank? Luckily, there was William of Orange to talk about. There was William of Orange now, stalking an invisible victim along the terrace wall. Up in the fig tree he went, with his killer's face, his marigold eyes. "Oh, the poor birds!" Eve cried. "He's after birds!" She saw him stretch out his paw, spread like a hand, and then she saw him detach ripe figs and let them fall on the paved terrace. She had never seen a cat do that before. She said that William of Orange was perfectly sweet.

"He doesn't care what you think about him," said Mary, looking up from her heap of stones.

"You know, darling," said Eve, laughing at Walter, "if you aren't careful, you'll become an old spinster with a pussycat."

Frank sat on the terrace wall wearing a cotton shirt and oversize Army shorts. He was burned reddish brown. His arms and legs were covered with a coating of thick fair hair. "What is the appeal about cats?" he said kindly. "I've always wanted to know. I can understand having them on a farm, if they're good mousers." He wore a look of great sincerity most of the time, as if he wanted to say, "Please tell me what you are thinking. I so much want to know."

"I like them because they are independent," said Walter. "They don't care what you think, just as Mary says. They don't care if you like them. They haven't the slightest notion of gratitude, and they never pretend. They take what you have to offer, and away they go."

"That's what all cat fanciers say," said Frank. "But it's hard for someone like me to understand. That isn't the way you feel about people, is it? Do you like people who just take what you can give them and go off?"

Angelo came out of the house with a shopping basket over one arm and a straw sun hat on his head. He took all his orders from Eve now. There had never been a discussion about it; she was the woman of the house, the mother.

"It would be interesting to see what role the cat fancier *is* trying on," said Walter, looking at Angelo. "He says he likes cats because they don't like anyone. I suppose he is proving he is so tough he can exist without affection."

"I couldn't," said Frank, "and I wouldn't want to try. Without Eve and the children and . . ."

The children jumped to their feet and begged to go to market with Angelo. They snatched at his basket, arguing whose turn it was to carry it. How Angelo strutted; how he grew tall! All this affection, this admiration, Walter thought—it was as bad as overtipping.

✻   ✻   ✻

The family stayed two weeks, and then a fortnight more. They were brown, drowsy, and seemed reluctant to face England and the poultry farm. They were enjoying their holiday, no doubt about that. On the beach they met a professor of history who spoke a little English, and a retired consul who asked them to tea. They saw, without knowing what to make of it, a monument to Queen Victoria. They heard people being comic and noisy, they bought rice-and-spinach pies to eat on the beach, and ice cream that melted down to powder and water. They ate melons and peaches nearly as good as the fruit back in Africa, and they buried the peach stones and the melon skins and the ice-cream sticks and the greasy piecrusts in the sand. They drove along the coast as far as Cannes, in the Parma-violet Citroën Frank had hired, sight unseen, from South Africa. He had bought his new farm in the same way. Walter was glad his friends were away, for he was ashamed to be seen in the Citroën. It was a vulgar automobile. He told Frank that the DS was considered exclusively the property of concierges' sons and successful grocers.

"I'm not even that," said Frank.

The seats were covered with plastic leopard skin. At every stop, the car gave a great sigh and sank down like a tired dog. The children loved this. They sat behind, with Eve between them, telling riddles, singing songs. They quarreled across their mother as if she were a hedge. "Silly old sow," Walter heard his nephew saying. He realized the boy was saying it to Eve. His back stiffened. Eve saw.

"Why shouldn't he say it, if he wants to?" she said. "He doesn't know what it means. Do you want me to treat them the way we were treated? Would you like to see some of that?"

"No," said Walter, after a moment.

"Well, then. I'm trying another way."

Walter said, "I don't believe one person should call another a silly old sow." He spoke without turning his head. The children were still as mice; then the little boy began to cry.

They drove home in the dark. The children slept, and the three adults looked at neon lights and floodlit palm trees without saying much. Suddenly Eve said, "Oh, I like *that*." Walter looked at a casino; at the sea; at the Anglican church, which was thirty years old, Riviera Gothic. "That church," she said. "It's like home."

"Alas," said Walter.

"Terrible, is it?" said his brother-in-law, who had not bothered to look.

"I think I'll make up my own mind," said Eve. So she had sat, with her face set, when Walter tried to introduce her to some of his friends and his ideas, fifteen years before. She had never wanted to be anything except a mother, and she would protect anyone who wanted protection—Walter as well. But nothing would persuade her that a church was ugly if it was familiar and reminded her of home.

Walter did not desire Eve's protection. He did not think he could use anything Eve had to give. Sometimes she persuaded him to come to the beach with the family, and then she fussed over him, seeing that the parasol was fixed so that he had full shade. She knew he did not expose his arms and legs to the sun, because of his scars. She made him sit on an arrangement of damp, sandy towels and said, "There. Isn't that nice?" In an odd way, she still admired him; he saw it, and was pleased. He answered her remarks (about Riviera people, French politics, the Mediterranean climate, and the cost of things) with his habitual social fluency, but it was the children who took his attention. He marveled at their singleness of purpose, the energy they could release just in tearing off their clothes. They flung into the water and had to be bullied out. Mauve-lipped, chattering, they said, "What's there to do *now?*"

"Have you ever wanted to be a ballet dancer?" Walter asked his niece.

"No," she said, with scorn.

One day Angelo spent the morning with them. Frank had taken the car to the Citroën garage and looked forward to half a day with the mechanics there. In a curious way Angelo seemed to replace the children's father. He organized a series of canals and waterways and kept the children digging for more than an hour. Walter noticed that Angelo was doing none of the work himself. He stood over them with his hand on one hip—peacock lad, cock of the walk. When an Italian marries, you see this change, Walter thought. He treats his servants that way, and then his wife. He said, "Angelo, put your clothes on and run up to the bar and bring us all some cold drinks."

"Oh, Uncle Walter," his niece complained.

"I'll go, Uncle Walter," said the little boy.

"Angelo will go," Walter said. "It's his job."

Angelo pulled his shorts over his bathing suit and stood, waiting for Walter to drop money in his hand.

"Don't walk about naked," Walter said. "Put on your shirt."

Eve was knitting furiously. She sat with her cotton skirt hitched up above her knees and a cotton bolero thrown over her head to keep off the sun.

From this shelter her sunglasses gleamed at him, and she said in her plain, loud voice, "I don't like this, Walter, and I haven't been liking it for some time. It's not the kind of world I want my children to see."

"I'm not responsible for the Riviera," said Walter.

"I mean that I don't like your bullying Angelo in front of them. They admire him so. I don't like any of it. I mean to say, the master-servant idea. I think it's bad taste, if you want my opinion."

"Are you trying to tell me you didn't have a servant in South Africa?"

"You know perfectly well what I mean. Walter, what *are* you up to? That sad, crumbling house. Nothing has been changed or painted or made pretty in it for years. You don't seem to have any friends here. Your telephone never rings. It hasn't rung once since I've been here. And that poor boy."

"Poor?" said Walter. "Is that what he's been telling you? You should have seen the house I rescued him from. You should just see what he's left behind him. Twelve starving sisters and brothers, an old harridan of a mother—and a grandmother. He's so frightened of her even at this distance that he sends her every penny I give him. Twelve sisters and brothers . . ."

"He must miss them," said Eve.

"I've sent him home," Walter said. "I sent him for a visit with a first-class ticket. He sold the first-class ticket and traveled third. If I hadn't been certain he wanted to give the difference to his people, I should never have had him back. I hate deceit. If he didn't get home that time it was because the cat was worrying him. I've told you the story. You said it was sad. But it was his idea, taking the cat."

"He eyes the girls in the market," said Eve. "But he never speaks."

"Let him," said Walter. "He is free to do as he likes."

"Perhaps he doesn't think he is."

"I can assure you he is, and knows it. If he is devoted to me because I've been kind to him, it's his own affair."

"It's probably too subtle for me," she said. She pulled her skirts a little higher and stroked her veined, stretched legs. She was beyond vanity. "But I still think it's all wrong. He's sweet with the children, but he's a little afraid of me."

"Perhaps you think he should be familiar with women and call them silly old sows."

"No, not at his age," she said mildly. "Johnny is still a baby, you know. I don't expect much from him." She was veering away from a row.

"My telephone never rings because my friends are away for the summer," he said. "This summer crowd has nothing to do with my normal life." He had to go on with that; her remark about the telephone had annoyed him more than anything else.

Yet he wanted her to approve of him; he wanted even Frank to approve of him. He was pushed into seeing himself through their eyes. He preferred his own images, his own creations. Once, he had loved a woman much older than himself. He saw her, by chance, after many years, when she was sixty. "What will happen when I am sixty?" he wanted to say. He wondered if Eve, with her boundless concern for other people, had any answer to that. What will happen fifteen years from now, when Miss Cooper claims the house?

That night, William of Orange, who lost no love on anyone, pulled himself onto the terrace table, having first attained a chair, and allowed Walter to scratch his throat. When he had had enough, he slipped away and dropped off the table and prowled along the wall. Eve was upstairs, putting the children to bed. It was a task she usually left to Angelo. Walter understood he and Frank had been deliberately left together alone. He knew he was about to be asked a favor. Frank leaned over the table. His stupid, friendly face wore its habitual expression of deep attention: *I am so interested in you. I am trying to get the point of everything you say.* He was easy enough; he never suggested Walter should be married, or working at something. He began to say that he missed South Africa. They had sold their property at a loss. He said he was starting over again for the last time, or so he hoped. He was thirty-seven. He had two children to educate. His face was red as a balloon. Walter let him talk, thinking it was good for him.

"We can always use another person on a farm—another man, that is," said Frank.

"I wouldn't be much use to you, I'm afraid," said Walter.

"No. Well, I meant to say . . . We shall have to pack up soon. I think next week."

"We shall miss you," said Walter. "Angelo will be shattered."

"We're going to drive the Citroën up to Paris," said Frank, suddenly lively, "and turn it in to Cook's there. We may never have a chance to do that trip again. Wonderful for the kids." He went off on one of his favorite topics—motors and mileage—and was diverted from whatever request he had been prodded by Eve to make. Walter was thankful it had been so easy.

Unloved, neglected, the hamster chewed newspaper in its cage. The cage hung from the kitchen ceiling, and rocked with every draft. Angelo remembered to feed the hamster, but as far as the children were concerned it might have been dead. William of Orange claimed them now; he threw up hair balls and string, and behaved as if he were poisoned. Angelo covered his coat with olive oil and pushed mashed garlic down his throat. He grew worse; Angelo found him on the steps one morning, dying, unable to move his legs. He sat with the cat on his knees and roared, as William of Orange had howled on the train in his basket. The cat was dying of old age. Walter assured everyone it was nothing more serious than that. "He came with the house," he repeated again and again. "He must be the equivalent of a hundred and two."

Angelo's grief terrified the children. Walter was frightened as well, but only because too much was taking place. The charming boy against the baroque wall had become this uncontrolled, bellowing adolescent. The sight of his niece's delicate ear, the lamps reflected in his nephew's eyes, his sister's disapproval of him on the beach, his brother-in-law's soulless exposition of his personal disaster—each was an event. Any would have been a stone to mark the season. Any would have been enough. He wanted nothing more distressing than a spoiled dinner, nothing more lively than a drive along the shore. He thought, In three days, four at the most, they will disappear. William of Orange is old and dying, but everything else will be as before. Angelo will be amusing and young. Mrs. Wiggott will invite me to dine. The telephone will ring.

The children recovered quickly, for they saw that William of Orange was wretched but not quite dead. They were prepared to leave him and go to the beach as usual, but Angelo said he would stay with the cat. The children were sorry for Angelo now. Johnny sat next to Angelo on the step, frowning in a grown-up way, rubbing his brown knees. "Tell me one thing," he said to Angelo from under his sun hat. "Is William of Orange your father or something like that?" That night the little boy wet his bed, and Walter had a new horror. It was the sight of a bedsheet with a great stain flapping on the line.

Fortunately for Walter, the family could no longer put off going away. "There is so much to do," said Eve. "We got the Citroën delivered, but we didn't do a thing about the children's schools. I wonder if the trunks have got to London? I expect there hasn't been time. I hope they get there before the cold weather. All the children's clothes are in them."

"You are preposterous parents," Walter said. "I suppose you know that."

"We are, aren't we?" said Eve cheerfully. "You don't understand how much one has to *do*. If only we could leave the children somewhere, even for a week, while we look at schools and everything."

"You had your children because you wanted them," said Walter. "I suppose."

"Yes, we did," said Frank. It was the only time Walter ever saw his easy manner outdistanced. "We wanted them. So let's hear no more about leaving them. Even for a week."

Only one rainy day marred the holiday, and as it was the last day, it scarcely counted. It was over—the breather between South Africa and England, between home for the children and a new home for Eve. They crowded into the sitting room, waiting for lunch. They had delayed leaving since early that morning, expecting, in their scatterbrained way, that the sky would clear. The room smelled of musty paper and of mice. Walter suddenly remembered what it was like in winter here, and how Angelo was often bored. His undisciplined relations began pulling books off the shelves and leaving them anywhere.

"Are all these yours?" Mary asked him. "Are they old?"

"These shelves hold every book I have ever bought or had given me since I was born," said Walter. And the children looked again at the dark green and dark wine covers.

"I know *Kim*," said Mary, and she opened it and began to read in a monotonous voice, " 'He sat, in defiance of municipal orders, astride the gun Zam-Zammeh on her brick platform opposite the old Ajaibgher.' "

"I can still see him," said Eve. "I can see Kim."

"I can't see him as I saw him," said Walter.

"Never could bear Kipling, personally," Frank said. "He's at the bottom of all the trouble we're having now. You only have to read something like 'Wee Willie Winkie' to understand that."

"Why is the gun 'her'?" Mary asked.

"Because in an English education it's the only thing allowed to be female," said Frank. "That and boats." He hadn't wanted the change; that was plain. For Eve's sake, Walter hoped it was a change for the good.

"This book is all scribbled in," Mary complained. She began to turn at random, reading the neat hand that had been Walter's at twelve: " 'Shows foresight,' " she read. " 'Local color. More color. Building up the color. Does not wish to let women interfere with his career.' That's underlined, Uncle Walter," she said, breaking off. " 'A deceiver. Kim's strong will—or white blood? Generous renunciation. Sympathetic. Shows off. Sly. Easily imposed on. Devout. Persistent. Enterprising.' "

"That will do," said Frank. " 'Shows off' is the chief expression where you're concerned."

"Those notes were how Kipling was introduced to me, and I used them when I was teaching Angelo," said Walter. "Angelo doesn't like Kipling, either. You can keep the book, if you want it."

"Thank you very much," said Mary automatically. She placed the book more or less where it had been, as if she recognized that this was a bogus gesture.

"Thank you, darling Walter," said Eve, and she picked up the book and stroked the cover, dirtying her hand. "Johnny will love it, later on."

Walter's first dinner invitation of the autumn season arrived by post eight days after the Osborns had gone. In the same mail were three letters, each addressed by his sister. Eve thanked him for his great kindness; he would never know what it had meant, the holiday it had been. They were in a hotel, and it was a great change from the south. In a P.S. she said they were moving to the new farm soon. The children were their great worry. She went on about schools. The postscript was longer than the body of the letter.

The other two envelopes, although addressed by Eve, contained letters from Mary and Johnny. The boy spelled difficult words correctly, simple words hopelessly, and got his own name wrong.

"Dear Uncle Walter," he wrote. "Thank you for letting us stay at your house." A row of dots led out to the margin, where he had added, "and for Kim." The text of the letter went on, "It was the most exciting, and enjoyable time I have ever had. Please tell Angelo on the way back we were fined for overtaking in a village, but we got safley out of France. I hope the hamster is well and happy. Tell Angelo there are two very small kittens down in the kitchin of the hotel where we now rent two rooms. They are sweat, white, snowballs, also there is a huge golden labridore, he is very stuppid. Love from Johny."

The girl's letter had been written on a line guide. Her hand was firm. "Dear Uncle Walter," she said. "Thank you for letting us sleep in your house and for everything too. We had a lovely time. Will you please tell Angelo that on the way to Paris Daddy was fined 900 francs for overtaking in a village. He was livid. On Monday I had two teeth out, one on each side. I hope the hamster is healthy. Will you please tell Angelo that our trunks have arrived with my books and he can have one as a present from me, if he will tell me which one he likes best.

Successful Show Jumping
Bridle Wise
Pink and Scarlet
The Young Rider

"These are my favorites and so I would like him to have one. Also, here is a poem I have copied out for him from a book.

FROM THE DREAM OF AN OLD MELTONIAN
by W. Bromley Davenport
Though a rough-riding world may bespatter your breeches
Though sorrow may cross you, or slander revile,
Though you plunge overhead in misfortune's blind ditches,
Shun the gap of deception—the hand gate of guile.

"Tell Angelo we miss him, and William of Orange, and the hamster too. Thank you again for everything. Your affectionate niece, Mary."

Walking to the kitchen with the letters in his hand, he tried to see the passionate child—dancer, he had thought—on the summer beach. But although eight days had passed, no more, he had forgotten what she was like. He tried to think of England then. Someone had told him the elms were going, because of an American disease. He knew that all this thinking and drifting was covering one displeasure, one blister on his pride: It was Mary's letter he had been waiting for.

"These letters are intended for you," he said, and put them in Angelo's hands. "They were addressed to me by mistake. Or perhaps the family didn't know your full name. I didn't know you were interested in horses, by the way."

Angelo sat at the kitchen table, cleaning the hamster's cage. Mme. Rossi sat facing him. Neither of them rose. "Master-servant," Eve had said. She ought to have seen Angelo's casual manner now, the way he accepted his morning's post—as though Walter were the servant. The boy's secretive face bent over the letters. Already Angelo's tears were falling. Walter watched, exasperated, as the ink dissolved.

"You can't keep on crying every time I mention the children," he said. "Look at the letters now. You won't be able to read them."

"He is missing the family," Mme. Rossi said. "Even though they made more work for him. He cries the whole day."

Of course he was missing the family. He was missing the family, the children were missing him. Walter looked at the boy's face, which seemed as closed and vain as a cat's. "They meant more work for you," he said. "Did you hear that?"

"We could have kept the children," Angelo mumbled. His lips hung open. His face was Negroid, plump. One day he would certainly be fat.

"What, brought them up?"

"Only for one week," said Angelo, wiping his eyes.

"It seems to me you overheard rather a good deal." Another thought came to him: It would have been a great responsibility. He felt aggrieved that Angelo did not take into consideration the responsibilities Walter already had—for instance, he was responsible for Angelo's being in France. If Angelo were to steal a car and smash it, Walter would have to make good the loss. He was responsible for the house, which was not his, and for William of Orange, who was no better and no worse, but lay nearly paralyzed in a cardboard box, demanding much of Angelo's attention. Now he was responsible for a hamster in a cage.

"They would have taken me on the farm," Angelo said.

"Nonsense." Walter remembered how Eve avoided a brawl, and he imitated her deliberately mild manner. He understood now that they had been plotting behind his back. He had raised Angelo in cotton wool, taught him Kipling and gardening and how to wash the car, fed him the best food . . . "My brother-in-law is Irish," he said. "You mustn't think his promises are real."

The boy sat without moving, expressionless, sly. He was waiting for Walter to leave the room so that he could have the letters to himself.

"Would you like to go home, Angelo?" Walter said. "Would you like to go back and live in Italy, back with your family?" Angelo shook his head. Of course he would say no to that; for one thing, they relied on his pocket money—on the postal orders he sent them. An idea came to Walter. "We shall send for your mother," he said. The idea was radiant now. "We shall bring your old mother here for a visit. Why not? That's what we shall do. Bring your mother here. She can talk to you. I'm sure that is all you need."

"Can you imagine that lazy boy on an English farm?" said Walter to Mrs. Wiggott. "That is what I said to him: 'Have you ever worked as a farmer?

Do you know what it means?' " He blotted imaginary tears with his sleeve to show how Angelo had listened. His face was swollen, limp.

"Stop it, Walter," said Mrs. Wiggott. "I shall *perish.*"

"And so now the mother is coming," said Walter. "That is where the situation has got to. They will all sit in the kitchen eating my food, gossiping in Calabrian. I say 'all' because of course she is bound to come with a *covey* of cousins. But I am hoping that when I have explained the situation to the old woman she can reason with Angelo and make him see the light."

"Darling Walter," said Mrs. Wiggott. "This could only happen to you."

"If only I could explain things to Angelo in *our* terms," said Walter. "How to be a good friend, a decent host, all the rest. Not to expect too much. How to make the best of life, as we do."

"As we do," said Mrs. Wiggott, solemn now.

"Live for the minute, I would like to tell him. Look at the things I put up with, without complaint. The summer I've had! Children everywhere. Eggs and bacon in the *hottest* weather. High tea—my brother-in-law's influence, of course. Look at the house I live in. Ugly box, really. I never complain."

"That is true," said his old friend.

"No heat in winter. Not an anemone in the garden. Les Anémones, they called it, and not an anemone on the place. Nothing but a lot of irises, and I put those in myself."

APRIL FISH

❧

*B*ecause I was born on the first day of April, I was given April as a
Christian name. Here in Switzerland they make Avril of it, which sounds
more like a sort of medicine than a month of spring. "Take a good dose of
Avril," I can imagine Dr. Ehrmann saying, to each of the children. Today
was the start of the fifty-first April. I woke up early and sipped my tea, careful not to disturb the dogs sleeping on the foot of the bed on their own Red
Cross blanket. I still have nightmares, but the kind of terror has changed. In
the hanging dream I am no longer the victim. Someone else is hanged. Last
night, in one harrowing dream, one of my own adopted children drowned,
there, outside the window, in the Lake of Geneva. I rushed about on the
grass, among the swans. I felt dew on my bare feet; the hem of my velvet
dressing gown was dark with it. I saw very plainly the children's toys: the
miniature tank Igor has always wanted, and something red—a bucket and
spade, perhaps. My hair came loose and tumbled down my back. I can still
feel the warmth and the comfort of it. It was auburn, leaf-colored, as it used
to be. I think I saved Igor; the memory is hazy. I seemed very competent and
sure of my success. As I sat in bed, summing up my progress in life as measured by dreams, trying not to be affected by the sight of the rain streaming
in rivulets from the roof (I was not depressed by the rain, but by the thought
that I could rely on no one, *no one,* to get up on the roof and clear out the
weeds and grass that have taken root and are choking the gutter), the children trooped in. They are home for Easter, all three—Igor, with his small
thief's eyes, and Robert, the mulatto, who will not say *"Maman"* in public
because it makes him shy, and Ulrich, whose father was a famous jurist and
his mother a brilliant, beautiful girl but who will never be anything but dull

and Swiss. There they were, at the foot of the bed, all left behind by careless parents, dropped like loose buttons and picked up by a woman they call *Maman.*

"*Bon anniversaire,*" said Igor, looking already like any postal clerk in Moscow, and the two others muttered it in a ragged way, like a response in church. They had brought me a present, an April fish, but not made of chocolate. It was the glass fish from Venice everyone buys, about twenty inches long, transparent and green—the green of geranium leaves, with chalky white stripes running from head to tail. These children have lived in my house since infancy, but their taste is part of their skin and hearts and fingernails. The nightmare I ought to be having is a projection into the future, a vision of the girls they will marry and the houses they will have—the glass coffee tables and the Venetian-glass fish on top of the television, unless that space has already been taken up with a lump of polished olive root.

Igor advanced and put the fish down very carefully on the table beside me, and, as he could think of nothing else, began again, "*Bon anniversaire, Maman.*" They had nothing to tell me. Their feet scuffled and scratched on the floor—the rug, soiled by the dogs, was away being cleaned.

"What are you going to do today?" I said.

"Play," said Robert, after a silence.

A morning concert struck up on the radio next to me, and I looked for something—an appreciation, a reaction to the music—in their eyes, but they had already begun pushing each other and laughing, and I knew that the music would soon be overlaid by a second chorus, from me, "Don't touch. Don't tease the dogs," all of it negative and as bad for them as for me. I turned down the music and said, "Come and see the birthday present that came in the mail this morning. It is a present from my brother, who is your uncle." I slipped on my reading glasses and spread the precious letter on the counterpane. "It is an original letter written by Dr. Sigmund Freud. He was a famous doctor, and that is his handwriting. Now I shall teach you how to judge from the evidence of letters. The writing paper is ugly and cheap—you all see that, do you?—which means that he was a miser, or poor, or lacked aesthetic feeling, or did not lend importance to worldly matters. The long pointed loops mean a strong sense of spiritual values, and the slope of the lines means a pessimistic nature. The margin widens at the bottom of the page, like the manuscript of Keats's 'Ode to a Nightingale.' You remember that I showed you a photograph of it? Who remembers? Ulrich? Good for Ulrich. It means that Dr. Freud was the same kind of person as

Keats. Keats was a poet, but he died. Dr. Freud is also dead. I am sorry to say that the signature denotes conceit. But he was a great man, quite right to be sure of himself."

"What does the letter say?" said Igor, finally.

"It is not a letter written to me. It is an old letter—see the date? It was sent about thirty years before any of you were born. It was written probably to a colleague—look, I am pointing. To another doctor. Perhaps it is an opinion about a patient."

"Can't you read what it says?" said Igor.

I tried to think of a constructive answer, for "I can't read German" was too vague. "Someday you, and Robert, and even Ulrich will read German, and then you will read the letter, and we shall all know what Dr. Freud said to his colleague. I would learn German," I went on, "if I had more time."

As proof of how little time I have, three things took place all at once: My solicitor, who only rings up with bad news, called from Lausanne, Maria-Gabriella came in to remove the breakfast tray, and the dogs woke up and began to bark. Excessive noise seems to affect my vision: I saw the room as blurry and one-dimensional. I waved to Maria-Gabriella—discreetly, for I should never want the children to feel *de trop* or rejected—and she immediately understood and led them away from me. The dogs stopped barking, all but poor blind old Sarah, who went on calling dismally into a dark private room in which she hears a burglar. Meanwhile, Maître Gossart was telling me, from Lausanne, that I was not to have one of the Vietnam children. None of them could be adopted; when their burns have healed, they are all to be returned to Vietnam. That was the condition of their coming. He went on telling it in such a roundabout way that I cut him off with "Then I am not to have one of the burned children?" and as he still rambled I said, "But I want a little girl!" I said, "Look here. I want one of the Vietnam babies, and I want a girl." The rain was coming down harder than ever. I said, "Maître, this is a filthy, rotten, bloody country, and if it weren't for the income tax I'd pack up and leave. Because of the income tax I am not free. I am compelled to live in Switzerland."

Maria-Gabriella found me lying on the pillows with my eyes full of tears. As she reached for the tray, I wanted to say, "Knock that fish off the table before you go, will you?" but it would have shocked her, and puzzled the boys had they come to learn of it. Maria-Gabriella paused, in fact, to admire the fish, and said, "They must have saved their pocket money for weeks." It occurred to me then that *poisson d'avril* means a joke, it means playing an

April-fool joke on someone. No, the fish is not a joke. First of all, none of them has that much imagination, the fish was too expensive, and, finally, they wouldn't dare. To tell the truth, I don't really want them. I don't even want the Freud letter. I wanted the little Vietnam girl. Yes, what I really want is a girl with beautiful manners, I have wanted her all my life, but no one will ever give me one.

IN TRANSIT

❧

*A*fter the Cook's party of twenty-five Japanese tourists had departed for Oslo, only four people were left in the waiting room of the Helsinki airport—a young French couple named Perrigny, who had not been married long, and an elderly pair who were identifiably American. When they were sure that the young people two benches forward could not understand them, the old people went on with a permanent, flowing quarrel. The man had the habit of reading signs out loud, though perhaps he did it only to madden his wife. He read the signs over the three doors leading out to the field: " 'Oslo.' 'Amsterdam.' 'Copenhagen.' . . . I don't see 'Stockholm.' "

She replied, "What I wonder is what I have been to you all these years."

Philippe Perrigny, who understood English, turned around, pretending he was looking at Finnish pottery in the showcases on their right. He saw that the man was examining timetables and tickets, all the while muttering "Stockholm, Stockholm," while the woman looked away. She had removed her glasses and was wiping her eyes. How did she arrive at that question here, in the Helsinki airport, and how can he answer? It has to be answered in a word: everything/nothing. It was like being in a country church and suddenly hearing the peasant priest put a question no one cares to consider, about guilt or duty or the presence of God, and breathing with relief when he has got past that and on to the prayers.

"In the next world we will choose differently," the man said. "At least I know you will."

The wild thoughts of the younger man were: They are chained for the rest of this life. Too old to change? Only a brute would leave her now? They are walking toward the door marked AMSTERDAM, and she limps. That is why they cannot separate. She is an invalid. He has been looking after her for years. They are going through the Amsterdam door, whatever their tickets said. Whichever door they take, they will see the circular lanes of suburbs, and the family cars outside each house, and in the backyard a blue pool. All across northern Europe streets are named after acacia trees, but they may not know that.

Perrigny was on his wedding trip, but also on assignment for his Paris paper, and he assembled the series on Scandinavia in his mind. He had been repeating for four years now an article called "The Silent Cry," and neither his paper nor he himself had become aware that it was repetitious. He began to invent again, in the style of the Paris weeklies: "It was a silent anguished cry torn from the hearts and throats ..." No. "It was a silent song, strangled ..." "It was a silent passionate hymn to ..." This time the beginning would be joined to the blue-eyed puritanical north; it had applied to Breton farmers unable to get a good price for their artichokes, to the Christmas crowd at the Berlin Wall, to Greece violated by tourists, to Negro musicians performing at the Olympia music hall, to miserable Portuguese fishermen smuggled into France and dumped on the labor market, to poets writing under the influence of drugs.

The old man took his wife's hand. She was still turned away, but dry-eyed now, and protected by glasses. To distract her while their tickets were inspected he said rapidly, "Look at the nice restaurant, the attractive restaurant. It is part outside and part inside, see? It is inside *and* outside."

Perrigny's new wife gently withdrew her hand from his and said, "Why did you leave her?"

He had been expecting this, and said, "Because she couldn't concentrate on one person. She was nice to everybody, but she couldn't concentrate enough for a marriage."

"She was unfaithful."

"That too. It came from the same lack of concentration. She had been married before."

"Oh? She was old?"

"She's twenty-seven now. She was afraid of being twenty-seven. She used to quote something from Jane Austen—an English writer," he said as Claire frowned. "Something about a woman that age never being able to hope for anything again. I wonder what she did hope for."

"The first husband left her, too?"

"No, he died. They hadn't been married very long."

"You *did* leave her?" said the girl, for fear of a possible humiliation—for fear of having married a man some other woman had thrown away.

"I certainly did. Without explanations. One Sunday morning I got up and dressed and went away. I came back when she wasn't there and took my things away—my tape recorder, my records. I came back twice for my books. I never saw her again except to talk about the divorce."

"Weren't you unhappy, just walking out that way? You make it sound so easy."

"I don't admire suffering," he said, and realized he was echoing his first wife. Suffering was disgusting to her; the emblem of dirt was someone like Kafka alone in a room distilling blows and horror.

"Nobody admires suffering," said the girl, thinking of aches and cramps. "She had a funny name."

"Yes, terrible. Shirley. She always had to spell it over the phone. Suzanne Henri Irma Robert Louis Émile Yvonne. It is not pronounced as it is spelled."

"Were you really in love with her?"

"I was the first time I saw her. The mistake was that I married her. The mystery was why I ever married her."

"Was she pretty?"

"She had lovely hair, like all the American girls, but she was always cutting it and making it ugly. She had good legs, but she wore flat shoes. Like all the Americans, she wore her clothes just slightly too long, and with the flat shoes . . . she never looked dressed. She was blind as a mole and wore dark glasses because she had lost the other ones. When she took her glasses off, sometimes she looked ruthless. But she was worried and impulsive, and thought men had always exploited her."

Claire said, "How do I know you won't leave me?" but he could tell from her tone she did not expect an answer to that.

Their flight was called. They moved out under COPENHAGEN, carrying their cameras and raincoats. He was glad this first part of the journey was over. He and Claire were together the whole twenty-four hours. She was good if he said he was working, but puzzled and offended if he read. Attending to her, he made mistakes. In Helsinki he had gone with her to buy clothes. Under racks of dresses he saw her legs and bare feet. She came out, smiling, holding in front of herself a bright dress covered with suns. "You can't wear it in Paris," he said, and he saw her face change, as if he had dark-

ened some idea she'd had of what she might be. In a park, yesterday, beside
a tall spray of water, he found himself staring at another girl, who sat feeding squirrels. He admired the back of her neck, the soft parting of her hair,
her brown shoulder and arm. Idleness of this kind never happened in what
he chose to think of as real life—as if love and travel were opposed to living, were a dream. He drew closer to his new wife, this blond summer child,
thinking of the winter honeymoon with his first wife. He had read her hand
to distract her from the cold and rain, holding the leaf-palm, tracing the extremely shallow head line (no judgment, he informed her) and the choppy
life—an American life, he had said, folding the leaf. He paid attention to
Claire, because he had admired another girl and had remembered something
happy with his first wife, all in a minute. How would Claire like to help him
work, he said. Together they saw how much things cost in shopwindows,
and she wrote down for him how much they paid for a meal of fried fish
and temperance beer. Every day had to be filled as never at home. A gap of
two hours in a strange town, in transit, was like being shut up in a stalled
lift with nothing to read.

Claire would have given anything to be the girl in the park, to have that
neck and that hair *and* stand off and see it, all at once. She saw the homage
he paid the small ears, the lobes pasted. She had her revenge in the harbor,
later, when a large group of tourists mistook her for someone famous—for
an actress, she supposed. She had been told she looked like Catherine
Deneuve. They held out cards and papers and she signed her new name,
"Claire Perrigny," "Claire Perrigny," over and over, looking back at him
with happy, triumphant eyes. Everything flew and shrieked around them—
the seagulls, the wind, the strangers calling in an unknown language something she took to mean "Your name, your name!"

"They think I am famous!" she called, through her thick flying hair. She
smiled and grinned, in conspiracy, because she was not famous at all, only a
pretty girl who had been married eight days. Her tongue was dark with the
blueberries she had eaten in the market—until Philippe had told her, she
hadn't known what blueberries were. She smiled her stained smile, and tried
to catch her soaring skirt between her knees. Compassion, pride, tenderness,
jealousy, and acute sick misery were what he felt in turn. He saw how his
first wife had looked before he had ever known her, when she was young and
in love.

O LASTING PEACE

❧

*T*hough my Aunt Charlotte, my sad mother, my Uncle Theo, and I all live together, and can see each other as often as we need to, when Uncle Theo has something urgent to tell me he comes here, to the Civic Tourist and Travel Bureau. He gets in line, as if he were waiting to ask about the Bavarian Lakes and Mountains Program or the Ludwig the Second Bus Circuit. He slides close to the counter. I glance over, and suddenly have to look down; Uncle Theo is so small he is always a surprise. He grins, scared to death of me. He is totally bald now, not a hair to stretch sideways. He looks like a child's drawing of two eyes and a smile. After a furtive trip to Berlin last summer he edged along the queue to say he had called on my father, who is his brother and Aunt Charlotte's brother, too.

"Hilde, everything has gone wrong for him," said Uncle Theo, gripping the counter as if that might keep me from sending him away. "Do you remember how he couldn't stand cigarette smoke? How none of you could smoke when he was around?" Do I remember? It was one of the reasons my younger brother cleared out, leaving me to support half the household. "Well, *she* smokes all the time," said Uncle Theo. "She blows smoke in his face and so do her friends. She even eggs them on."

"Her friends," I repeated, writing it down. My expression was open but reserved. To anyone watching, Uncle Theo is supposed to be a client like any other.

"Low friends," said Uncle Theo. "Low Berliners in shady Berlin rackets. The kind of people who live in abandoned stores. No curtains, just whitewashed windows." At the word "shady" I did look as if I had seen my uncle somewhere before, but he is one more respectable survivor now, a hero of yesterday. "Ah, your poor father's kitchen," he went on lamenting. "Grease on the ceiling that deep," showing thumb and finger. "They're so down they've had to rent the parlor and the bedroom. They sleep on a mattress behind the front door."

"He's got what he wanted."

"Well, it had been going on between them for a long time, eh?" Embarrassment made him rise on his toes; it was almost a dance step. "After fifteen years she and your mother joined up and told him to choose. Your mother didn't understand what she was doing. She thought it was like some story on television."

My father left us five winters ago, at the age of sixty-three. I still have in mind the sight of my mother in a faint on the sofa and my Aunt Charlotte with an apron over her face, rocking and crying. I remember my Uncle Theo whispering into the telephone and my Aunt Charlotte taking the damp corner of her apron to wipe the leaves of the rubber plant. I came home from work on a dark evening to find this going on. I thought my Uncle Theo had been up to something. I went straight to my mother and gave her a shake. I was not frightened—she faints at will. I said, "Now you see what Uncle Theo is really like." She opened her eyes, sniffling. Her nylon chignon, which looks like a pound of butter sometimes, was askew on the pillow. She answered, "Be nice to poor Theo, he never had a wife to look after him." "Whose fault is that?" I said. I did not know yet that my father had gone, or even that such a thing might ever happen. Now it seems that my mother had been expecting it for fifteen years. A lifetime won't be enough to come to the end of their lies and their mysteries. I am the inspector, the governess, the one they tell stories to. And yet they depend on me! Without me they would be beggars, outcasts! Aunt Charlotte and my mother would wash windows in schoolhouses; they would haul buckets of dirty water up the stairs of office buildings; they would stand on vacant lots selling plastic combs and miniature Christmas trees!

My Uncle Theo began describing her—that other one. His face was as bright as if he were reciting a list of virtues: "I never did understand my brother. She has no taste, no charm, no looks, no culture, no education. She has a birthmark here," touching the side of his nose.

"I'm busy, Uncle Theo."

"We must send him money," he said, getting round to it.

"Well?" I said to the person next in line, over Uncle Theo's head.

"Hilde, we must send the poor old man money," he said, hanging on the counter. "A little every month, just the two of us." Uncle Theo thinks everyone else is old and poor. "Hilde—he's a night porter in a hospital. He doesn't like anything about the job. He can't eat the food."

Sometimes Uncle Theo will come here to intercede for our neighbors, having heard I have started legal action again. We have East German refugees in the next apartment—loud, boorish Saxons, six to a room. They send everything through the wall, from their coarse songs to their bedbugs. Long ago they were given a temporary housing priority, and then the city forgot them. The truth is these people live on priorities. They have wormed their way into everything. Ask anyone who it is that owns the laundries, the best farmlands, the electronics industry; you will always get the same answer: "East German refugees." At one time a popular riddle based on this subject went the rounds. Question: "Who were the three greatest magicians of all time?" Answer: "Jesus, because he turned water into wine. Hitler, because he turned Jews into soap. Adenauer, because he turned East German refugees into millionaires." Very few people can still repeat this without a mistake. Only 2 percent of the readers of our morning paper still consider Hitler "a great figure." My own sister-in-law cannot say who Adenauer was, or what made him famous. As for Jesus, even I have forgotten what that particular miracle was about. A story that once made people laugh now brings nothing but "Who?" or "What?" or even *"Be careful."* It is probably best not to try to remember.

At a quarter to two this Christmas Eve, my Uncle Theo turned up here again. The watchman was already dressed in his overcoat, standing by the glass doors with a bunch of keys in his hand. The banks, the grocers, the bookshops, the hairdressers were shut tight. The street outside looked dead, for those who weren't down with Asian flu were just getting over it. Uncle Theo slipped in past the porter. He wore his best winter pelisse with the seal collar and his seal hat. He looked smaller than ever, because of the greatcoat and because of a huge brown paper parcel he was carrying. He made as if to come straight over, but I frowned and looked down. The cashier was on sick leave, too, and I was doing double duty. I knew the parcel was our Christmas goose. Uncle Theo buys one every year. Now, that he chooses well; it is not an imported Polish bird but a local goose, a fine one. I stood there counting money, twenty-five, thirty, fifty, and I heard Uncle Theo saying, "She is my niece." In my position I cannot murmur, "Oh, shut up," but I imagined him bound and trussed, like the goose, and with adhesive tape across his mouth. He was speaking to a man standing before him in the queue, a tall fellow wearing one of those square fur caps with earflaps. The cap had certainly come from Russia. I guessed at once that the man was a show-off. Uncle Theo was telling him his history, of course, and probably mine as well—that I spoke four, or even seven, languages and that the tourist office could not manage without me. What a waste of time, and how foolish of Uncle Theo! Even from behind the counter I could see the show-off's wedding ring. None of the staff was happy. We were almost the only people still working in the whole city. It was one of the days when you can smell the central heating, like an aluminum saucepan burning. I looked sharply at Hausen, my assistant. He has devised a way of reading a newspaper in a desk drawer, folded in quarters. He can even turn the pages, with movements so economical only I can see them. You would never guess that he was reading—he seems to be looking for pencils. "Take some of these people over, will you?" I called out. Hausen didn't respond, and the line didn't move. Uncle Theo's voice was now clear: "I also happened to be in Calcutta when the end of the world was expected. That was February fifth, 1962. The Calcutta stock exchange closed down. People left their homes and slept in tents. Imagine—the stock exchange affected. Everyone waiting. Eminent persons, learned professors." Uncle Theo shook his head.

"You were there on business, I suppose," said the man in the square cap. He had to stand in profile so they could go on talking. It made an untidy sort of queue. Uncle Theo looked ridiculous. The pelisse swamps him.

"No, no. I was retired long ago," he said. "Forcibly retired. My factories were bombed. I made a little porcelain—pretty stuff. But my vocation was elsewhere." Having let that sink in, he put on his quotations voice and said, " 'And now, like many another wreck, I am throwing myself into the arms of literature.' I found much to inspire me in India. The holy men. The end of the world on February fifth, 1962. The moon. The moon in India has no phases. It is full all the year round."

In a job like mine it would be best not to have relatives at all. Nothing of Uncle Theo's is quite the truth or entirely a lie. The remark about the moon was a mistake, caused by his lack of schooling. For "factories" he meant "one workroom," and for "porcelain" he meant "hand-painted ashtrays." It is true about the literature, though. Two of his poems have been set to music and sung by our choral society. "In Autumn, in Summer, in Autumn, in Summer," with the voices fading on the last word, is not without effect. The other, which begins, "O peace, O peace, O lasting peace, we all demand a lasting peace," is less successful. It sounds preachy, even when sung in a lively way.

"Will someone please take over these people," I said, this time loud enough so that Hausen couldn't pretend not to hear. The whole queue shuffled obediently to the left—all but the last two. These were Uncle Theo and his new friend, of course. The friend made for me and put a traveler's check down on the counter. I looked at it. It had been signed "F. T. Gellner" and countersigned "F. Thomas Gellner." Haste, carelessness, perhaps. But the T on the top line was a printer's capital, while the second was written in script. I pushed the check back with one finger: "Sorry, it's not the same signature."

He pretended not to see what I meant, then said, "Oh, that. I can cross out the 'Thomas' and put the initial on, can't I?"

"Not on a traveler's. Next person, please," I said, even though the next was Uncle Theo, who had no business here.

"I'll write a personal check," said the man, getting a pen out first.

"This is not a bank," I said. "We cash traveler's checks as a favor to clients."

"But the banks are closed."

"Yes," I said. "It is Christmas Eve. It isn't only the 'Thomas,' but also your capitals. The two signatures are absolutely not the same."

"Is that all?" he cried out, so happily (thinking it was settled) that even deaf Hausen looked over. "I write one way sometimes, then another. Let me show you—my driver's license, my passport ..." He started tumbling papers out of an inside pocket. "I should be more careful," he said to me, trying to play at being friends.

"It is not my business to examine your driver's license," I said. "The two signatures are not the same."

He looked round the office and said, "Isn't there anyone else I can see?"

"It is Christmas Eve," I said, "and I am in charge. The manager is at home with Asian flu. Would you like his number?"

Uncle Theo stuck his head out sideways, like a little boiled egg with a hat on it, and said, "I can vouch for the gentleman." He must have forgotten who and where he was. "I can sign anything you like," he said. "My name is important locally."

"There is nothing to sign and I do not need your name." Important lo-

cally? Where is his name? On the war memorial? Have they called a street
after him? His name is not even on a civil registry—he never married, even
though there has been a shortage of husbands since Bismarck.

The man took no more notice of Uncle Theo; he had finally understood
that the honorary assistant head of the choral society was of no use to anyone. To be rid of the incident, I said, "Sign another traveler's in my presence."

"That was my last one."

Uncle Theo repeated, "I can vouch for the gentleman. I have seen the
gentleman buying in shops—spending," said my uncle, making a circle of
his thumb and forefinger for emphasis under the brown paper parcel, as if
we were poor villagers for whom the very sight of money was a promise of
honor.

"Ask your hotel to cash a check," I said. "I'm sorry but I cannot deal with
you any longer. It is Christmas Eve."

"I'm not in a hotel. I mean that I am staying here with friends." Of
course, I had seen the "friends." She was waiting outside, trying to seem casual, wearing one of those reddish fur coats. Snow fell on her hair.

"Ask your friends to lend you something."

"You could save me that embarrassment," he said, trying for friendliness
again.

"It is not my business to save you embarrassment," I said, glancing at his
wedding ring.

Even when he had got as far as the door, and the watchman was preparing to lock it behind him, he kept looking back at me. I made a point of
being taken up by Uncle Theo, who now stood woebegone and scuffling his
feet, shifting his burden from arm to arm.

"That wasn't kind, Hilde," he began. "The poor man—he'll have a sad
Christmas."

"Be quick, Uncle Theo. What do you want?"

"Tonight," he said, "when we are eating our dinner, and the candles are
lighted on the Christmas tree . . ."

"Yes?"

"Try not to cry. Let the girls enjoy themselves. Don't think of sad
things." The girls are my mother and Aunt Charlotte.

"What else is there?" I said. I could have piled all our sad Christmases on
the counter between us—the Christmas when I was thirteen and we were

firebombed, and saved nothing except a knife and fork my mother had owned when she was little. She still uses them; "Traudi" is engraved on the handle of each. It worries my mother to find anything else next to her plate. It makes her feel as if no one considered her—as if she were devalued in her own home. I remember another Christmas and my father drinking wine with Uncle Theo; wine slowed him down, we had to finish his sentences for him. They say that when he left us he put an apple in his pocket. My Aunt Charlotte packed some of his things afterward and deposited them with a waiter he knew. The next Christmas, my Uncle Theo, the only man of the house now, drank by himself and began to caper like a little goat, round and round the tree. I looked at the table, beautifully spread with a starched cloth, and I saw four large knives and forks, as for four enormous persons. Aunt Charlotte had forgotten about my mother.

"Oh, my own little knife and fork, I can't see them!" cried my mother, coming in at that moment, in blue lace down to her ankles.

"Oh, my own little arse," said Uncle Theo, in my mother's voice, still dancing.

He was just as surprised as we were. He stared all round to see who could have said such a thing. My mother locked herself in her room. My Aunt Charlotte tapped on the door and said, "We only want you to eat a little compote, dear Traudi."

"Then you will have to bring it here," said my mother. But after saying that, she would not open the door. We knew she would come out in time to watch *The Nutcracker,* and so we left the house, pretending we were about to pay our Christmas visits a day early. We sat in the railway station for a long time, as if we were waiting for someone. When we came back, we found she had put the short chain lock on the front door of the apartment, so that all the keys in the world wouldn't let you in. Here we were, all three wearing hats, and hoping our neighbors would not peep out to see who was doing all the ringing. Finally someone did emerge—a grubby little boy. Behind him we could see a large party round a table, looking out and laughing at us, with their uneducated mouths wide open. We said courteously that our relative must have fallen asleep and, being slightly deaf, could not hear the doorbell.

"We knew there must be a deaf person in that apartment," said someone at the table.

"There is no Christmas in India," said Uncle Theo, becoming one of their party. "It has no meaning there." I was glad to see that my aunt and I looked decent. "My sister-in-law once had a great emotional shock," said Uncle Theo, accepting a glass. "Christmas is so sad."

A gust of feeling blew round the table. Yes, Christmas is sad. Everyone has a reason for jumping out the window at Christmas and in the spring. Meanwhile I was calling our number, and I could hear our telephone ringing on the other side of the wall. The neighbors' wallpaper is covered with finger marks, like my sister-in-law's. "Why not send for the police?" someone said. My aunt looked as if she wanted to throw an apron over her face and cry, which was all she did when her own brother left. "Well, Uncle?" I said. Everyone looked at the man who had been to India. Before he could decide, the little boy who had opened the door said, "I can get round by the balconies." Do you see how easy it is for these people to spy on us? They must have done it hundreds of times. All he had to do was straddle the partition between the two balconies, which he did, knocking down the flowerpots covered with squares of plastic for the winter. My aunt frowned at me, as if to say it didn't matter. He cupped his hands round his eyes, peering through the panes of the double glass doors. Then he pounded with both fists, breathing hard, his cheeks as red as if they had been slapped. "The lady is just sitting on the floor watching television," he said finally.

"Stone-deaf," said Uncle Theo, keeping up the story.

"She is dead," wailed my aunt. "My sister-in-law has had a stroke."

"Break the panes," I cried to the child. "Use a flowerpot. Be careful not to cut yourself." I was thinking of blood on the parquet floor.

She was not dead, of course, but only sulking and waiting for *The Nutcracker.* She said she had fainted. We helped her to an armchair. It was difficult after that to turn the neighbors out, and even harder to return to our original status; they would stop us on the stairs and ask for news of "the poor sick lady." A year was needed to retreat to "Good morning," and back again to nothing but an inclination of the head. For although we put lighted candles in the windows on Christmas Eve as a reminder of German separation, it seems very different when masses of refugees move in next door, six to a room, and entirely without culture. It would be good to have everyone under one flag again, but the Saxons in Saxony, et cetera, please.

With all this behind me, the Christmas memories of my life, what could I say except, "What else is there?"

"Try not to think at all," said Uncle Theo, grinning with nervousness and his anxious little bandit's eyes darting everywhere. "Bandit" is perhaps too much; he never had a gram of civic feeling, let us say. "I have tickets to *The Gypsy Baron*," he said. So that was what he had come to tell me!

"What do you mean, Uncle Theo?"

"For the four of us, the day after Christmas."

"Out of the question," I said.

"Now, why, Hilde? The girls like music."

"Use your head, Uncle Theo. I can't talk now."

What did he mean, *why?* It was out of the question, that was all. First, the flu epidemic. People were coughing and sneezing without covering their faces.

"I wanted you to have two days to think it over," said Uncle Theo. He gave me the impression that he was sliding, crawling. I don't know why he is so afraid of me.

It seemed so evident: It is wrong to take them out to the theater, or anywhere in the cold. It disturbs their habits. They are perfectly happy with their television. They have their own warm little theater in our parlor. My mother is always allowed to choose the program, as you may imagine. She settles in with a bowl of walnuts on her lap. My aunt never sees the beginning of anything, because she walks round examining her plants. She sits down finally, and the others tell her the plot, when there is one. Uncle Theo drinks white wine and laughs at everything. One by one they fall asleep in their chairs. I wake them up and send them off to bed while the late news predicts the next day's weather. Why drive them out in the cold to see an operetta? And then, how are we supposed to get there? The car has been put away for the winter, with the insurance suspended and the battery disconnected. Say that we get it out and in running order—where does Uncle Theo expect me to park? I suppose I might go earlier in the day, on foot, and pick out the streets near the theater where parking might be allowed. Or we could *all* go very early and sit in the car until the theater opens. But we would have to keep the engine running and the heater on, and we would be certain to have blinding headaches within the hour. We might walk, but these old persons get terribly warm in their overcoats, and then they perspire and catch chills and fever. I am surprised that the city is letting the play be produced at this time.

All this I explained to Uncle Theo in the calmest voice imaginable.

He said, "I had better turn the tickets in."

"Why?" I said. "Why do that? As you say, the girls like music. Why deprive them of an outing? I only want you to realize, for once, the possible results of your actions."

Why is it that everyone is depressed by hearing the truth? I tell the office manager about Hausen reading newspapers in a desk drawer. His face puckers. He wishes I had never brought it up. He looks out the window; he has decided to forget it. He will forget it. I have never said a thing; he is not obliged to speak to Hausen, let alone sack him. When my brother married a girl with a chin like a Turkish slipper, I warned him what his children would be like—that he would be ashamed to have them photographed because of their ugly faces.

I say to my mother, "How can you giggle over nothing? One son was killed, the other one never comes to see you, and your husband left you for another woman at the age of sixty-three." Half an hour later, unless someone has hurt her feelings, or changed the television program without asking, she has forgotten her own life's story. The family say Uncle Theo is a political hero, but isn't he just a man who avoided going to war? He was called up for military service after Stalingrad. At the medical examination he pointed out his age, his varicose veins, his blood pressure, but none of that helped. He was fit for service—for the next wholesale offering, in Uncle Theo's view. He put on his clothes, still arguing, and was told to take a file with his name on it to a room upstairs. It was on his way up that he had his revelation. Everything concerning his person was in that file. If the file disappeared, then Uncle Theo did, too. He turned and walked straight out the front door. He did not destroy the file, in case they should come round asking; he intended to say he had not understood the instructions. No one came, and soon after this his workroom was bombed and the file became ashes. When Uncle Theo was arrested it was for quite another reason, having to do with black-market connections. He went first to prison, then, when the jail was bombed, to a camp. Here he wore on his striped jacket the black sleeve patch that meant "antisocial." It is generally thought that he wore the red patch, meaning "political." As things are now, it gives him status. But it was not so at the time, and he himself has told me that the camp was run by that antisocial element. It was they who had full control of the internal order, the margarine racket, the extra-soup racket, the cigarette traffic. Uncle Theo was there less than a month, all told, but it changed his outlook for life.

Now consider my situation: eighteen years with the Civic Tourist and Travel Bureau, passed over for promotion because I am female, surrounded at home by aged children who can't keep their own histories straight. They have no money, no property, no future, no recorded past, nothing but secrets. My parents never explained themselves. For a long time I thought they kept apple juice in our cellar locker. After my father left us I went down and counted eighteen bottles of white wine. Where did it come from? "Tell me the truth," I have begged them. "Tell me everything you remember." They sit smiling and sipping wine out of postwar glasses. My mother cracks walnuts and passes the bowl around. That is all I have for an answer.

Sometimes on my way home I take the shortcut through the cemetery. The long bare snowy space is where Russian prisoners used to be buried. When the bodies were repatriated, even the gravestones were taken—all but two. Perhaps the families forgot to claim the bodies; or perhaps they were not really prisoners but impostors of some kind. Whatever the reason, two fairly clean stones stand alone out of the snow, with nothing around them. Nearby are the graves of Russian prisoners from the 1914 war. The stones are old and dark and tipped every way. The more I think of it the more I am certain those two could not have been Russians.

Yesterday in the cemetery, at six o'clock, there were lovers standing motionless, like a tree. I had to step off the path; snow came over the tops of my boots. I saw candles burning in little hollows on some of the graves, and Christmas trees on the graves of children. What shall I do when I have to bury the family? Uncle Theo speaks of buying a plot, but in the plot he has in mind there is no room for me and he knows it. I should have married, and when I died I'd be buried with my in-laws—that is what Uncle Theo says to himself. When you speak about dying he looks confused. His face loses its boiled-egg symmetry. Then he says, "Cheer up, Hilde, it can't be so bad or they would have found a way to stop it by now."

He was a guard in the prisoner-of-war camp. I forgot to mention that. In fact that was how he got out of his own camp; they were so desperate that they asked for volunteers from among the antisocial element—the thieves, the pimps, the black marketeers. Most of them went to the Eastern front and died there. Uncle Theo, undersized and elderly, became a guard not too far from home. Even there he got on well, and when the Russian prisoners broke out at the end, they did not hang him or beat him to death but simply tied him to a tree. They told him a phrase he was to repeat phonetically if Russian troops got there before the others. Luckily for him the Americans turned up first; all he has ever been able to say in a foreign language is *"Pro domo sua,"* and he must have learned that phonetically, too. He hardly went to school. Uncle Theo was able to prove he had once been arrested, and that turned out to be in his favor. Now he has a pension, and is considered a hero, which is annoying. He was never a member of any party. He does not go to church. *"Pro domo sua,"* he says, closing an eye.

Uncle Theo applied for war reparations in 1955. He offered his record—destruction of porcelain factory, unjust imprisonment, pacifist convictions, humane and beloved guard in prisoner-of-war camp—and in 1960 he received a lump sum and a notice of a pension to follow. He immediately left for India, with a touring group composed mostly of little widows. But he decided not to marry any of them. He brought us a scarf apiece and a set of brass bowls. It was after his return that he wrote "O Lasting Peace."

One last thing: Without my consent, without even asking me, Uncle Theo advertised for a husband for me. This was years ago, before he had his pension. He gave my age as "youthful," my face and figure as "gracious," my world outlook as "modern," and my upbringing as "delicate." There was too much unemployment at the time, and so no one answered. Eleven years later he ran the same notice, without changing a word. The one person who answered was invited—by Uncle Theo—to call and see if he wanted me. I saw the candidate through a fog of shame. I remember his hair, which sprang from his forehead in a peculiar way, like black grass, and that he sat with his feet turned in and the toe of one shoe over the other. He was not really a fool, but only strange, like all persons who do not really intend to go through with the wedding. My aunt, my mother, and my uncle stated my qualities for me and urged him to eat fruitcake. My mother had to say, "Hilde has been so many years with the tourist office that we can't even count them," which knocked out the "youthful" bit, even if he had been taken in by it. It was a few days after a Christmas; fresh candles were lighted on the tree. The candidate turned his head, swallowing. Everyone wanted him to say something. "Won't the curtains catch fire?" he asked. I'm sure Uncle Theo would have picked up the tree and moved it if he had been able, he was that excited by his guest. Then the man finished eating his cake and went away, and I knew we would not hear about him again; and that was a good riddance.

"You are so anxious to have this apartment to yourselves," I said to my family. "You have made yourselves cheap over a peasant who sits with one foot on the other. How would you pay the rent here without me? Don't you understand that I can't leave you?" At the same time, I wanted to run out on the balcony screaming, "Come back!" but I was afraid of knocking the flowerpots over. I've forgotten why I wanted to mention this.

AN ALIEN FLOWER

*M*y daughter wept when the news reached us here in Cologne that Bibi had died. It was the first loss by death she had ever experienced, except for that of our old brown poodle, and it affected her to the point of fantasy. She accused me of having murdered Bibi; of having treated her like a servant; of having been jealous of her brains and her beauty (her beauty?); and, finally, of having driven her out of our house with my capricious demands, my moods, and my coldness.

Everyone knows what it is like now to be judged by spoiled, ignorant children. Of course we never considered Bibi a servant! That is a pure invention. From the very beginning—when we were, in fact, her employers—she ate at our table and called us Julius and Helga. There were hundreds of thousands of girls like Bibi in those days, just as poor and alone. No person was ever considered to blame for his own poverty or solitude. You would never have dreamed of hinting it could be his own fault. You never knew what that person's past might be, or what unspoken grudge he might be hiding. There was also a joint past that lay all around us in heaps of charred stone. The streets still smelled of terror and ashes, particularly after rain. Every stone held down a ghost, or a frozen life, or a dreadful secret. No one was inferior, because everyone was. A social amnesty had been declared.

Bibi must have been in her early twenties then. She was a refugee, from Silesia. In the town she named as her birthplace everyone had died or run away. She had no friends, no family, and no money, but she must have been given some sort of education at one time, because she had been accepted in high school here, in the terminal class. How she got in is a mystery. There was no room for anyone, and students were selected like grains of sand. People of all ages were trying to go to school—middle-aged men, prisoners of war coming back and claiming an education. In those days, so many papers and documents had been burned that people like Bibi could say anything they liked about themselves. Still, she had passed some sort of entrance examination—she must have. She had also found a place to live, and she supported herself doing sewing and ironing and minding babies—whatever she could find. We had her Tuesday, Thursday, and Saturday, for housework; three evenings a week. Her dinner was part of her wages, but as the evening meal was nothing but soup she did not have to give up her ration tickets. After she had been with us for a while, one of her teachers told Julius that Bibi was brilliant. Yes, brilliant. Without any real culture, without . . . but brilliant all the same. As soon as Julius was certain it was true, he found a part-time job for Bibi in the first re-search laboratory they were establishing then at Possner. Possner was looking for bright young people with a promising future and no past. It was an incredible stroke of fortune for someone in Bibi's situation. She stayed at Possner on that part-time basis until she published her thesis in 1955. (Possner sent her to the university.) After that she went on to a much, much better job. From the time she met Julius, Bibi had nothing but luck.

Her thesis was called "The Occurrence of Alkaloids in the"—in the something. In a word beginning with A. I could look it up—there must be twelve copies or even more down in the wine cellar. "The Occurrence" was nearly a book—eighty-two pages long, not counting the pages of thanks and the dedications. Julius has a whole page to himself: "To Doctor Engi-neer Julius Lauer, of the firm of Possner (Cologne), my Heartfelt Grati-tude." The copies are well bound in that brown paper that imitates bark. Possner must have paid.

Bibi was something of a friend, finally. My daughter called her Aunt and was taught to respect her. She even lived with us for a time—for ten years in our old house, and for several months in the house we have now. She em-igrated to an American branch of Possner and she died over there.

I don't think she ever wanted to marry. She never mentioned it. She had peculiar opinions and was no good at hiding what she thought. After the age of thirty she became insistent. She would insist on the same thing over and over—usually something to do with the harsh side of life. She felt shy about some ugly scars she had on her legs, and wore thick stockings even in summer, and would never go on a beach.

Even if I had ever considered Bibi less than myself, how could I have shown it? By having her eat in the kitchen alone? In the days when we met Bibi the kitchen was a privileged place, the only warm room anyone had. Julius worked nearly every evening then and I was glad to have Bibi's company. As she sewed and ironed I sat nearby, reading, sometimes talking to her, wishing she would stop whistling and singing but not liking to say so. She had several odious habits. For instance, she owned only one pair of stockings and was afraid of wearing them out. As soon as she arrived she would take them off and drape them over the back of a chair. Once, Heidi, the old brown poodle we had, licked Bibi's bare legs under the table.

"Heidi, you swine!" Bibi wailed. I have forgotten to say how funny she looked and sounded when she was young. She had short blond hair that stuck out like stiff flower petals, and she spoke with a coarse, droll, regional accent that turned her simplest remarks into comedy. "Heidi, you swine" became a joke between Julius and me until the day he was informed she was brilliant. After that, I lost my bearings where Bibi was concerned, for now she was part of Possner, and Possner was also Julius, and neither Julius nor Possner were to be laughed at. Possner was a small industrial complex then—nothing compared with a great house such as Bayer; but to Julius it was a new force in the nation, an elite army for which he enlisted the best of recruits. Julius was, I suppose, a lieutenant in the industry-army. He knew he would go up and up as this new army grew. I knew it too, and that was why I had asked for help—why I had Bibi. I was afraid that if I became a housewife Julius would find me dull and would leave me behind. Every morning, instead of scrubbing and dusting, I read a newspaper. The papers were thin; the news was boring and censored, or, rather, "approved." I would begin at the back, with the deaths and the cinema advertisements, and work forward to the political news. In the afternoon I walked Heidi and tried to read books belonging to Julius. Of that period of my "education" I remember long, sleepy winter afternoons, and I see myself trying to keep awake. I also spent hours in queues, because meat, clothing, and even matches were hard to find.

Like Bibi, I had no friends; I had no family, except Julius. I was not from Cologne but from Dortmund. Anyone who had ever known me or loved me had been killed in one period of seven weeks. I was a year or two older than Bibi—about twenty-four. I was not as pretty as my daughter is now, though my wedding picture shows me with soft chestnut hair. In the picture I look as though someone had just scolded me. I was nervous in those days and easily startled. I worried about gas escaping, burglars at the windows, and bicycles ridden by drunken criminals; I was also afraid of being thought too stupid for Julius and unworthy of being his wife.

I can still see us in our kitchen, under the faintest of lightbulbs, with three plates of soup on the table and a plate for Heidi, the poodle, on the floor. Heidi had belonged to Julius's parents. "Four old survivors," said Julius, though Heidi was old and we three were young.

Julius was made a captain and we took our first holiday. We went to Rome. I remember a long train journey during which we ate hard-boiled-egg sandwiches and slept in our clothes. The shops dazzled me; I wanted to buy presents for dozens of people, but I had only Bibi. I chose a marble darning egg and a pair of sandals that were the wrong size. I had thought of her feet as enormous, but to my surprise they were narrow and fine. She could not take two steps in the new sandals without sliding. She kept the shoes as a souvenir. Julius found them in her trunk, wrapped in white tissue paper, after she died.

A change in Bibi's status came at about that time. Julius had wangled an excellent scholarship for her. With that, and the money she earned at Possner, Bibi could afford an apartment. She said she was happy as she was, but Julius wanted Possner employees to live decently. Also, she roomed with a family of refugees, and Julius did not want her to waste her mental energies talking about the tides of history. I can truthfully say that Julius has never discussed historical change. Do leaves speak? Are mountains asked to have an opinion? Bibi still resisted, saying there was no such thing as a flat in Cologne; but Julius found one. He personally moved her to her new quarters—one room, gas ring, and sink. Just about what she was leaving, except that now she lived alone. I don't know how the room was furnished—Bibi never invited me to see it. She still came to us for three weekly evenings of housework, still ate her bread and soup and put the money we paid her aside. We were astonished at the size of her savings account when we saw her bankbook years later.

Julius was not so much concerned with Bibi as with Possner. When he helped other people it was because he was helping the firm. His life was his work; his faith was in Possner's future. I believed in Julius. In one of the books belonging to him—the books that gave me so much trouble on winter afternoons—I read that belief, like love, could not be taken by storm. I knew that Julius lied sometimes, but so do all divinities. Divinities invented convenient fables and they appeared in strange disguises, but they were never mistaken. I believed, because he said it, that we would not live among ashes forever, and that he would give me a new, beautiful house. Because he vouched for Bibi's genius I had to believe in it too. It was my duty to imagine Bibi ten years from now with a Nobel Prize for chemistry. This was another Bibi, tall and gracious and speaking pure German. She had stopped singing tunes from *The Merry Wives of Windsor* in such an annoying way, she no longer sat like an elephant or laughed with her mouth wide open or held bread on the palm of her hand to spread it with margarine.

If, in this refined and comfortable future, I corrected Bibi's manners it was a sign that the postwar social amnesty could not go on. In fact, the rules of difference were restored long before the symphony orchestras were full strength, the prisoners were home, the schools were rebuilt. Seeing where Bibi was going, I began wondering where she had started out. Her name, Beate Brüning, was honest and plain. She hinted that once she had not lived like other people and had missed some of her schooling on that account. Why? Had she been ill, or delinquent? Was she, as well as Silesian, slightly foreign? Sometimes male ancestors had been careless about the women they married. Perhaps Bibi had been unable to give a good account of herself. My textbook of elementary biology in high school explained about the pure and the impure, beginning with plant life. Here was the picture of an upright, splendid, native plant, and next to it the photograph of a spindly thing that never bloomed and that was in some way an alien flower. Bibi's round face, her calm eyes, her expression of sweetness and anxiety to please spoke of nothing but peasant sanity; still, she was different; she was "other." She never mentioned her family or said how they had died. I could only guess that they must have vanished in the normal way of a recent period—killed at the front, or lost without trace in the east, or burned alive in air raids. Who were the Brünings? Was she ashamed of them? Were they Socialists, radicals, troublemakers, black marketeers, prostitutes, wife-beaters, informers, Witnesses of Jehovah?

After she died no one came forward to claim her bank account, though Julius was scrupulous about advertising. Whoever the Brünings were, Bibi was their survivor, and she was as pure as the rest of us in the sense that she was alone, swept clean of friends and childhood myths and of childhood itself. But someone, at some time, must have existed and must have called her Bibi. A diminutive is not a thing you invent for yourself.

Of course, my life was not composed of these long speculations, but of subthemes, common questions and answers. One day new information about Julius came into my hands. As I stood on a chair to fetch a pair of bedsheets down from the high shelf of a cupboard, a folded blanket and an old jacket belonging to him came slipping down on top of me. I clutched at the edge of the shelf to steady myself and had under my fingers someone's diary. Still standing on the chair, I let the diary fall open. I read how Julius and an unknown girl—the writer of the diary—had pushed the girl's bed close to a window one sunny winter afternoon. "No one could see us," the girl felt obliged to note, as if she were writing for some other person. A bombed wall outlined in snow was their only neighbor. The sky was winter blue.

Now I am free was my first thought, but what did I mean? I wanted to live with Julius, not without him. I did not know what I meant.

I remembered the new, beautiful house he had promised, with the clock from Holland, the wallpaper from France, the swimming-pool tiles from Italy. I sat down and read the diary through.

On the girl's birthday Julius took her to a restaurant, but friends "connected with him professionally" came in. After twisting and turning and trying to hide his face, Julius sent her to the ladies' room with instructions to wait there for five minutes and then go home without stopping to speak to him. "What a bad ending for an evening that began with such promise," the diarist remarked. Did she live in Cologne? "Two nights," she recorded, or "one afternoon," or "one and one-half hours," followed by "did everything," then "everything," then finally just the initial of the word, as if she herself were no longer surprised or enchanted. One dull lonely weekend when she had not seen Julius for days, she wrote, "The sun is shining on all the rooftops and filling every heart with gladness while I   Over the rooftops the sun shines but I   My heart is sad though the sun is filling every heart . . ."

"Helga, are you all right?"

Here was Bibi breaking in—anxious, good, and extremely comic. Her accent would have made even tragedy seem hilarious, I thought then. I began to laugh, and blurted out, "Julius has always had other women, but now he leaves their belongings where I can find them." Bibi's look of shock was on my behalf. ". . . always had women," I repeated. "I said I didn't mind." The truth was that each time had nearly killed me. Also, the girls were poor things, sometimes barely literate. Looking down at the diary on my lap I thought, Well, at least this one can spell, and I am his wife, and he treats me with consideration, and he has promised me a house.

"Oh, Helga," Bibi cried, kneeling and clutching my hands, "you have always been kind to me." She muttered something else. I made her repeat it. "I don't understand; I don't keep that sort of a diary" was what Bibi had said.

So in the same hour I found out about Bibi and Julius too. Here was my situation: I was pregnant, and I should not have been standing on a chair to begin with. I was ill. I had such violent spasms sometimes that Julius would ask if I was trying to vomit the baby. I had absolutely no one but Julius, and nowhere to go. Moreover, as I have said, I did not *want* to live without him. As for Bibi, when I was feeling at my most wretched she was the only person the smell of whose skin and hair did not turn my stomach. I could not stand the scent of soap, or cologne, or food cooking, or milk, or smoke, or other people. Bibi looked after me. Once she said shyly, "I know, I know that mixture of hunger and nausea, when all you long for is good white bread." I remember sweating and trembling and thinking that it was she, it was Bibi, who was the good white bread. I never hated Bibi. I may have pitied her. I knew a little about Julius and I had a fear of explosions. I could have said to Julius, "I know about Bibi and you." What next? Bibi then departs and Julius and I are alone. He knows I know, which means we live in ruins and ashes forever. All I could feel was Bibi's utter misery; I saw her stricken face, her rough hands, and then I began to cry too, and we two— we two grown-up war orphans—dried each other's tears. I am quite certain Bibi never knew I had understood.

It was Bibi who saw me into the clinic where Roma was born. Julius was in Belgium. I asked Bibi to send him a telegram concerning the baby's name. "I want Roma because that was where she was conceived," I told her. "Don't put 'conceived' in the telegram. Julius will understand."

She nodded and said something in her ridiculous accent and went out the door. In a sense I never saw her again; I mean that this was the last I saw of a certain young, good-hearted Bibi. Julius came back before receiving the telegram; perhaps she hadn't sent it. It was two days before I remembered to ask about Bibi, and another before she was found. She had taken gardénal. She was alive, but she had been in a long, untended coma. The flesh on her legs had begun to alter, and she had to stay for a long time in the hospital—the hospital where Roma was born—after her skin-graft operations. That was why she wore thick stockings forever after, even in summer.

No one told me, at first. Julius made up a story. He said Bibi had met a young engineer and had run away with him. It sounded unlike her, but it was also unlike him to be so inventive, so I thought it must be true. I sat up against a starched pillowcase Bibi had brought me from home, and I invited Julius to admire Roma's hands and feet. He said that Bibi's lover was named Wolfgang, and we laughed and thought of Bibi on her wedding night saying, "Wolfgang, you swine!"

All Bibi was ever able to explain to me later was that somewhere between my room and the front door of the hospital she had asked God to strike her with lightning. She stood still and counted up to ten; ten seconds was the limit she gave Him to prove He could hear. Nothing happened. She saw a rubbery begonia on a windowsill; an aide pushing along a trolley of tea mugs; a father and two children waiting on a bench with the patience of the ignorant. She could not recall whether or not she had ever sent the telegram. She next remembered being at home, in the room Julius had insisted would be in keeping with her new position, and that there she had taken gardénal. The gardénal was in the form of large flat tablets, like salt pills. She said she had "always" had them, even in her refugee camp. For someone who had access to every sort of modern poison at Possner, she had chosen an old-fashioned, feminine way of death. She broke up the tablets patiently, one after the other, sitting on the edge of her bed. She was obliged to swallow so much water that she began to be sick on it, and finally she heated a little milk on the gas ring. The milk probably saved her.

She had imagined dying would be like a slow anesthetic; she thought death could be inhaled, like fresh air. But it was a black cloak being blown down on one, she told me—like a cape slipping off a hook and falling in soft folds over your hands and face.

* * *

By the time Bibi was well enough to tell me these things, Julius had forgotten her, and had all but forgotten me. He was in love with no one but Roma, a baby ten days old, named for a holiday. This was a quiet love affair that gave us all a period of relative peace. I don't believe he visited Bibi once, though he paid for her private room, the skin-graft operations, and her long convalescence. Bibi begged to be put in a ward, for being alone made her feel miserable, but Julius refused. She finally came home to us, because I needed someone; my health had broken down. I had fits of crying so prolonged that my eyelids became allergic to daylight and I had to spend hours lying down in the dark. Bibi worked part-time at Possner, looked after Roma, ran the house, and saw that I was allowed to recover very, very slowly.

Julius was now a major, and we moved into the first of our new, beautiful homes. We had a room for Bibi, next to Roma's. She kept that room for ten years and never once made a change in it. She would not admit any furniture except a bed, a wardrobe, a small bookcase that served as her night table, and a lamp. She did not correspond with anyone. Her books, concerned with one subject, were called *Tetrahedron Letters, The Chemistry of Steroids, Steroid Reactions*, and so on. I tried to read her thesis but I could not take in "... washed repeatedly in a solution of bicarbonate of soda, then in distilled water, and dried on sulphate of sodium. After evaporation, a residue of 8.78 ..." I discovered that she kept a journal, but it told me nothing. "Monday—Conversation with Arab student in canteen. Interesting." "Tuesday—*Funtumia latifolia* is a tree in Western Africa. Flowers white. Wood white. Used for matches, fruit crates." "Wednesday—Heidi dead." "Thursday—Roma draws Papa, Mama, Aunt Bibi, self, a tombstone for Heidi. Accept drawing as gift." "Friday—Menses." "Saturday—Allied powers forbid demonstration against rearmament." "Sunday—Visit kennel. New puppy for Roma. Roma undecided." This was Bibi's journal in a typical week.

Bibi had no sense of beauty. It was impossible to make her room attractive or interesting, and I avoided showing it to strangers. She never left a towel or a toothbrush in the bathroom she and Roma shared. I sometimes wondered if she had been raised in an orphanage, where every other bed held a potential thief. All her life she used only the smallest amount of water. At first, when she washed dishes I could never persuade her to rinse them. Water was something to be rationed, but I never learned why. She could keep a cake of soap or a tube of toothpaste for months. She wanted to live owning nothing, using nothing. On the other hand, once an object had come into her hands, and if she did not give it away immediately, to be parted from it later on was anguish. Sometimes I took her handbag and dumped it upside down. I would get rid of the broken comb, the thumbed mirror, the pencil stubs, and replace all this rubbish with something clean and new. But she was miserable until everything became old, cracked, and "hers" again. Most refugees talked too much. Bibi said too little, and that in disturbing fragments. Drink went straight to her head. At our parties I looked out for her, and when I saw the bad signs—her eyes pressed to slits, her head thrown back, a trusting smile—I would take her glass away. Once, during a dinner party, her voice floated over the rest of the talk: "Some adolescents, under difficult circumstances, were instructed in algebra and physics by distinguished professors. A gypsy girl named Angela, who had been in a concentration camp, was taught to read and write by a woman doctor of philosophy whose husband had been shot in the cellar of a prison in Moscow in 1941."

After that, I came to a quiet agreement with Julius that Bibi be given nothing to drink except when we were alone. I could not expect Julius's guests to abandon their own homes and their own television to hear nothing but disjointed anecdotes. This was the year when every television network celebrated the anniversary of the liberation of the concentration camps. Roma sat on a low stool with her elbows on her knees and saw everything. We now had a fifth person in the family, a young man from Possner named Michael. Julius had brought him in. Michael must already have decided to marry Julius's daughter if only he could remain important to Julius while Roma was growing up. I noticed that he thought Aunt Bibi was also someone who had to be pleased. In a way, Michael was a new kind of Bibi. The firm intended to send him to an advanced course in business management, just as Bibi had been sent to the university.

Michael was trying to take the political temper of the house. He would stand up and sit down and seem alternately interested in Roma's television program and wretchedly uneasy. He wondered if he would bother the three older people by too much attention to the screen, or lose Roma forever by not showing enough interest. Roma was so young then that Michael, at twenty-two, must have seemed like a parent. Bibi sat reading a speech Julius was to make at a congress where English would be the working language. From time to time she glanced at the screen, then went on making corrections with a green pencil. Her English was better than Julius's, but he said it was too perfect. Afterward he would alter half the changes she had made, saying, "It may be good English, but nobody talks that way." The look on Bibi's face as she glanced at the screen seemed to me overly patient, as though "the children," as she called Roma and Michael, were in above their heads. What does it matter now, she seemed to be telling herself. As for me, I went about my business. I never interfered with Roma, and certainly never with Julius in the room. As I watched the program, my allegiances shifted back and forth. Sometimes I hated the men and women who had done something in my name, and sometimes I hated the victims—yes, passionately. It is not normal conversation to talk about old deaths. No matter what was shown on television, no matter what we had to reconsider or see in a new light, my house was large and I had no servant except for an Italian half the day. Even with Bibi helping after work in the evenings, the house was too much for me. I saw that Roma's myths might include misery and sadness, but my myths were bombed, vanished, and whatever remained had to be cleaned and polished and kept bright. At times like these, Bibi seemed to know more than I did. She seemed so lofty, so superior, with her knowledge of hardship, that I wanted to scream at her, "Damn you, Bibi, I saw my mother running, running out of a burning house with her hair on fire. Her hands and face were like black paper when she died." Then the program came to an end and Julius stood before the screen lecturing Michael. He said, "A mission in life—a goal. Without an ideal, life is nothing." He stood with his hands behind his back. He has never smoked, not even when cigarettes were hard to get and everyone craved them. He is frugal, neat; every other day he eats nothing for dinner but yogurt. He said, "These unfortunate people you have just seen had a mission." Michael, the future executive, sat worshiping every word that fell from Julius. "Oh, a highly spiritual mission," said Julius easily. "A goal of a highly—spiritual—nature. That is why they are remembered." Bibi said (had she been drinking too much?), "Encouraging people to buy synthetic products they don't really need will be Michael's mission. Do you think it compares?"

The roof did not cave in. Julius merely laughed. How soft, how easy Julius had become!

"Papa is so short that when he sits down he looks like a little dog begging for sugar," said his beloved Roma, somewhere about that period. Roma had just tasted her first champagne. Julius smiled and touched her bright hair. It was shameful, but once Roma had made that remark about the little dog Julius began appearing in my dreams in that form. He was a terrier who simply would not stop barking. Roma was growing up, but he did not seem jealous. He had, in fact, selected the husband he wanted for her. He chose Michael when Roma was only fourteen or so, and began to train him, and then he went back to having other women again.

The girl and the diary had long been forgotten. Some new person called Julius on the telephone day after day. He trailed the long wire of the bedroom phone to his bathroom. Even Roma would never have dared to listen to an extension; he could smile if Roma was impertinent and pretty and had just drunk a glass of wine, but he could also be frightening. I have never seen anyone outstare him. He would take the phone to the bathroom and talk for a long time. The ringing stopped. In the weeks of lull that followed I dreamed of gunfire, of someone who claimed to be my mother, and of dogs. Julius suddenly ordered me to go with him on a long business journey to Hong Kong, Japan, California, and Vancouver. He said he was sick of traveling alone. I understood that he wanted protection from a woman who had become tiresome—someone who was either over there and waiting, or planning to follow. I remembered the telephone and the peculiar long ring of long-distance calls, the ring that continued after you lifted the receiver. Sometimes I thought I would take Roma and vanish, but the thought never lasted. I did not want to live outside my own house.

"If it is only for the sake of company, then take Bibi," I said. "Roma is at a delicate age. I can't leave her. Bibi has never been anywhere. You said you wanted her to study at one of the Anglo-Saxon universities." He had said that once, but fifteen years ago. However, because the idea had once been his, he now decided it would do Bibi, and thus Possner, some good. There was something else—being honorably rid of her. It was obvious that the idea of traveling with Bibi for company bored him. She was an old friend of the family now, plain and pedantic. He was a busy man with not much time for conversation. He had personal and professional acquaintances in South Africa, Argentina, Sweden, Milan, and many other places I had never seen. He was still very kind to young people if they were worth his while and knew how to make good use of an education. In what manner was he ever less than fair to Bibi? What would Bibi have done without Julius? How many refugees would have given years of their lives to have been in Bibi's place? Julius was very fit. He did yoga exercises every Sunday. I had given in to twin beds, but I refused the idea of separate rooms.

Bibi accepted the interesting journey and the chance to study at an Anglo-Saxon university without thanks and without joy. It meant an interruption of work that interested her, and she was frightened of planes. "It will be like a fairy tale," she said sadly. She must have been remembering stories where little children are abandoned in deep woods by parents who no longer can feed them. She was thinking of dark branches, night, crows spreading their wings, inch-high demons squealing a hideous language.

"Well, of course you are thinking of fairy tales," I said. "But do remember you are a grown woman." I looked at her pale cheeks and tried to see another Bibi, with spokes of sunflower hair. She had nothing in common with Julius now except an adoration for Roma. I had showed her that other girl's diary and she had been shocked. "An *ignorant* person," she said, and I saw how little she knew about him. If Bibi herself had not at one time had the *appearance* of an inferior, if she had not said "Heidi, you swine!" in a farm girl's accent, then Julius would never have looked at her twice.

Julius, who was good at arrangements, abandoned Bibi at a university in the west of Canada and came home alone. Her wounded, homesick letters followed, one a day. She told about a sign reading GAS AT CITY PRICES, which she never understood and which became the symbol of everything she never would grasp over there. She went to an Italian grocery and stood weeping because it was Europe. She had knifelike memories of towns and streets. Every girl reminded her of Roma. She wrote that she had suddenly learned she was old and plain. Her gestures were awkward; her hair was changing color with age. She entered a bookstore and found a shelf of German poetry. She congratulated the owner, who said, "Oh, we try" so sarcastically that she knew her accent and her appearance were offensive. She wanted to answer, but the English Julius had considered "too perfect" turned out to be full of holes. She became frightened of shops and when she went into one she would stand near the door, not daring to say what she wanted, letting other customers push in front of her. She stopped a stranger in the street to ask a direction. "Go to hell," he said. She counted the weeks, days, and minutes until she could be with us again. The first person she embraced at the airport was Roma.

Roma whispered, "Michael thinks he has me, but wait and see. Papa said he could live with us, but I would never let anyone take Aunt Bibi's room."

I heard, and thought, Now I shall have Bibi for the rest of my life.

Was that such a bad prospect? While Bibi had been gaining experience and writing those despairing letters, I had fallen ill. One day Julius asked me to unpack a suitcase for him and I found myself unable to move or speak. This passed, but the attack returned each time Julius gave me an order. The neurologist he sent me to said that my paralytic seizures were caused by nothing more serious than a calcium deficiency. I was instructed to eat sixty grams of cheese four times a day. With Bibi there, I had no more calcium problems. She took over her old duties of ironing and washing the supper dishes—anything the Italian had forgotten or had left undone—and I began reading again. I read fewer books and more magazines. Possner now owned several. It was at Julius's suggestion that a sign was put up in the editorial offices of each, saying YOUR READERS NEVER WENT TO HIGH SCHOOL.

Julius was now a colonel, and we moved here, to the newest and best of our homes. It was our house, and Julius put it in my name, as he had promised me long ago. Every windowpane belongs to me.

I knew quite a great deal about Julius; not everything. One summer evening we sat on our terrace, all five of us, with a portable television between us, and the remains of a sunset. Julius went indoors to fetch a bottle of white wine. With two wives and a daughter to serve him he need not have lifted a finger, but he was particular about wine (his cellar is shock-proof and soundproof) and he thought no one else knew how to take the cork out of a bottle. Presently I followed to see if he had everything he needed. He was in the kitchen with a glass of wine in his hand, and he stood sipping it in front of a mirror, deep in silent conversation. "What a good time you and I are having," he might have been saying. He smiled, and his face went wry. "Oh, you know how it is sometimes," he might have said now. He was seducing someone in the mirror—only it was himself. Julius was watching Julius seducing Julius. I remembered how confident he was when he was in love. I went back to the terrace and sat down.

I said, "Julius is a brilliant, clever man." No one answered. That opinion was the rule of the house.

The sunset died; Michael switched on lights hidden in trees and at the bottom of the pool. Waiting for the evening news, we watched, with some disgust, a beer-drinking contest.

"Why show this to us?" said Julius. He had a bouquet of long-stemmed glasses between his fingers. He set the glasses down carefully. "No one here is Bavarian."

"Right," cried Michael. "We are not Bavarian! Roma is not, and her mother is from Dortmund, and Aunt Bibi is from . . . and . . . and *you* are from . . ." He should have known where Julius was born. He must surely have read the vital facts about Julius in Possner house publications often enough. ". . . here, in Cologne," Michael gasped, correctly.

On the screen a slight girl downed a stein of beer in six seconds. Her throat worked in anguish and tension. She turned out to be a Berliner, not a Bavarian, either. She said she had noticed her gift of rapid drinking when still very young. It worked with milk or beer, but not so well with water.

As soon as the news came on, Julius showed signs of annoyance. The conversational aspect of world affairs has always been an irritant to him. What good is talk? In the middle of a remark about the Common Market he turned it off. He said that everyone was incompetent.

Michael the sycophant said, "Why don't you send very efficient well-trained men from Possner into politics? You could take someone promising and give him a sound education and launch him in a good party—in fact, you could launch several in all parties. Then no matter who was elected you would be certain everything would run efficiently. . . ." He always let his sentences run down. Even when a sentence normally might have come to a stop, it sounded as if the end were nowhere. Sometimes my future son-in-law looked like a terrier too, peering from one large human to the other, wondering who would slip him a morsel of something good.

"Wouldn't that strike you as immoral, Michael?" Here was Bibi sitting in the shadows—lumpy, wearing heavy stockings, saying prickly, difficult things. Bibi is raving, I thought. It seemed to me that the girl's voice had grown rasping. A "girl," I called her, but the person determined to spoil our enjoyment of the summer weather was nearly forty, had popping blue eyes, and had failed as an emigrant.

As if Bibi's remark weren't enough, now impertinent Roma spoke up:

"You aren't much of a generation to talk about morality." This was annoying, for it meant she was mixing up the generations and making us older than we really were.

Bibi laughed and said, "Little girl, what do you know about some of us?"

"Enough of that," said Julius, who did not need to shout to be frightening. "Enough from Bibi. Bibi, don't you dare touch my daughter's innocence."

My heart was pounding. For the first time I felt that Julius and I were thinking as one. Our marriage was our house. I said to myself, Here we are together in the fortress. The bodies pile up outside. Don't look at them. I forgave him for Bibi, the girl of the diary, the twin beds, the long-distance calls, for being a peacock who preened before mirrors. I put a hundred injuries and injustices behind me.

Bibi had pushed her chair back and risen and, after hesitating, looking over our heads and all round the garden, she walked away, down the sloping lawn. The pool, the trees, the imported white camellias in pots were beautifully lighted. We—particularly Roma—had looked charming, I thought, and now here was one person walking out of the picture. Michael suddenly said, "The neighbors!" and pressed a switch—a foolish gesture that left us sitting in semidarkness. Later he said he thought Bibi was about to drown herself in the pool and that our neighbors, excited by the sound of a quarrel (What sound? We were speaking quietly), might peer at us through field glasses.

"Turn the lights on immediately," said Julius, without moving.

We saw Roma clinging to Bibi and we heard her sobbing, "I didn't mean you, I meant everybody else."

"Now they have made my daughter cry on a lovely summer evening," said Julius, but quite casually, as if it were only one complaint on a long list of misdemeanors. But we were able to laugh, finally, because Michael, in his anxiety, had pressed all the buttons he could find, causing the gate in the driveway to slide back and forth, the garage doors to open and shut, and the pool in the garden to blink like a star. The lilies on the surface of the pool flashed negative-positive-negative. (It was thanks to an idea of Bibi's that Julius had been able to grow the lilies; their roots feed on a chemical mixture encased in a sphere. Even with flowers the pool looks sterile. I always found the water lilies unpleasant; they attract dragonflies.) I had a vision that cramped my stomach, of Bibi facedown among the negative-positive lilies, with dragonflies darting at her wet hair.

Bibi now let Roma lead her back to us. Julius poured wine as if nothing had happened, and he answered Michael's question. He said, "An idea similar to yours was discussed, but we have decided against it." We all let Julius have the last word.

Bibi finally died in America, by gas. She had gone out to an American branch of Possner at her own request. She left her passport and bankbook and some loose money on her kitchen table. The money was weighed down with the marble darning egg I had brought her from Italy years before. She named Julius as her closest living relative and Roma as her direct heir. There was also a sealed letter for Julius, which the police had opened before he arrived. Julius flew over, of course, though he was not a relative. After twenty years of Bibi we still did not know if she had any real family. In the letter she said she willed her body to a medical school, but since she also said she hoped there was enough money on the table to pay for a modest funeral, no one could tell exactly what she had wanted. Because of the circumstances there was a police autopsy. Julius brought back a photocopy of her letter— the police kept the original. Instead of telling why she had wanted to kill herself Bibi explained that she had chosen early morning so that she would be discovered at some time during the day and not after dark. She knew of accidents that had been caused by someone's turning on a light in a room filled with gas. I said to Julius that all she needed to have done was turn off the electricity; there must have been a switch somewhere in the apartment. But no, said Julius, Bibi had probably thought of that too. What if she remained alone and undiscovered for days, as she had after that first failed mess of a try with gardénal? Some stranger might have broken down the door, tried a light, and, failing to find one, might have absentmindedly struck a match. This sounded involved, not very sensible. Actually, she was found in broad daylight and no one was hurt.

Later, much later, on an evening when Julius was in a pleasant mood, I asked him about that girl's diary—if he knew how it had come to be on the shelf of a linen cupboard. It took him minutes to understand what I was talking about, and then he said the diary belonged to a silly uneducated person. He could not recall anything about a shelf. He was certain, in fact, that he had thrown the diary, unread, in a wastebasket.

"What did she mean by 'everything'?" I said.

He did not remember.

"You can see how unimportant she was," Julius said. "I wanted to have nothing to do with her, and so she sent me the diary so I could read about her soul. We are discussing an imaginary situation. There was no evidence that I was involved. My name was not mentioned anywhere," Julius concluded.

We were sitting on the terrace during this conversation. Julius, not yet fifty, had been made a general, and we drank to his triumph and his life. I had the nausea and dizziness of the repeated moment, as though we had sat in exactly the same position once before and I had heard Julius explain the same portion of his past. I saw the water lilies.

"I have dreams about Bibi," I said.

"She had an incurable illness," he replied.

This had never been mentioned. The water lilies seemed enormous. "Was it in the autopsy report?"

"Naturally."

Divinities invent convenient fables, but they are never mistaken. It must have been true; Bibi had an incurable illness and died to spare herself useless pain. Our conversation could have ended there, since we had no further use for it. Unfortunately I had still another question.

"That first time," I said. "The first time you traveled over there with Bibi for company and left her and came back alone. You remember? The day you were to leave, something happened. I was in the living room with Roma when we heard shrieks of hysterical laughter from the hall. Roma ran out ahead of me and began to scream in the same strident way. Bibi was in front of the looking glass trying on a hat. It was a hat specially bought for the journey. An ignoble hat. A disgusting and hideous hat of cheap turquoise jersey. She had no taste—any salesgirl could fob off anything. The salesgirl had told her she had a bad hairline, and this criminal hat covered her head from the eyebrows to the nape of her neck. Michael the subaltern, having already seen that you were laughing, was doubled up, yelling, outdoing himself in laughter. You said to Roma, 'I shall take you to a corner of the airport where the wind can blow it away.' Roma—she was fifteen or sixteen—said, 'Aunt Bibi looks like a little piglet dressed up as an actress.' At that, Bibi, who had been laughing too, moved away from the mirror and said, 'That was unkind.' All at once you saw I was not laughing at all. You turned and knelt down to buckle a suitcase as if the scene did not concern you anymore. Bibi was finished then. Michael had felt the shift of power too. *I* mattered."

All this had been meant to lead up to a question, but I had lost it. Anyway, Julius had stopped listening almost from the beginning. He sipped his wine and looked attentive, but his thoughts were floating. In the same voice, as if continuing my boring anecdote, I said, "... and tigers and zebras and ants and bees ..."

"Yes, yes," said Julius, pretending to hear.

"Oh, Julius, Julius," I said in the same voice. "Now a general, tomorrow a field marshal. Last night in a dream I had you were nothing but a little dog who kept on barking, and Bibi had to thrash you to make you stop."

THE END OF THE WORLD

────────

❧

I never like to leave Canada, because I'm disappointed every time. I've felt disappointed about places I haven't even seen. My wife went to Florida with her mother once. When they arrived there, they met some neighbors from home who told them about a sign saying NO CANADIANS. They never saw this sign anywhere, but they kept hearing about others who did, or whose friends had seen it, always in different places, and it spoiled their trip for them. Many people, like them, have never come across it but have heard about it, so it must be there somewhere. Another time I had to go and look after my brother Kenny in Buffalo. He had stolen a credit card and was being deported on that account. I went down to vouch for him and pay up for him and bring him home. Neither of us cared for Buffalo.

"What have they got here that's so marvelous?" I said.

"Proust," said Kenny.

"What?"

"Memorabilia," he said. He was reading it off a piece of paper.

"Why does a guy with your education do a dumb thing like swiping a credit card?" I said.

"Does Mother know?" said Kenny.

"Mum knows, and Lou knows, and I know, and Beryl knows. It was in the papers. 'Kenneth Apostolesco, of this city . . .' "

"I'd better stay away," my brother said.

"No, you'd better not, for Mum's sake. We've only got one mother."

"Thank God," he said. "Only one of each. One mother and one father. If I had more than one of each, I think I'd still be running."

It was our father who ran, actually. He deserted us during the last war.

He joined the Queen's Own Rifles, which wasn't a Montreal regiment—he couldn't do anything like other people, couldn't even join up like anyone else—and after the war he just chose to go his own way. I saw him downtown in Montreal one time after the war. I was around twelve, delivering prescriptions for a drugstore. I knew him before he knew me. He looked the way he had always managed to look, as if he had all the time in the world. His mouth was drawn in, like an old woman's, but he still had his coal-black hair. I wish we had his looks. I leaned my bike with one foot on the curb and he came down and stood by me, rocking on his feet, like a dancer, and looking off over my head. He said he was night watchman at a bank and that he was waiting for the Army to fix him up with some teeth. He'd had all his teeth out, though there wasn't anything wrong with them. He was eligible for new ones provided he put in a claim that year, so he thought he might as well. He was a bartender by profession, but he wasn't applying for anything till he'd got his new teeth. "I've told them to hurry it up," he said. "I can't go round to good places all gummy." He didn't ask how anyone was at home.

I had to leave Canada to be with my father when he died. I was the person they sent for, though I was the youngest. My name was on the back page of his passport: "In case of accident or death notify WILLIAM APOSTOLESCO. Relationship: Son." I was the one he picked. He'd been barman on a ship for years by then, earning good money, but he had nothing put by. I guess he never expected his life would be finished. He collapsed with a lung hemorrhage, as far as I could make out, and they put him off at a port in France. I went there. That was where I saw him. This town had been shelled twenty years ago and a lot of it looked bare and new. I wouldn't say I hated it exactly, but I would never have come here of my own accord. It was worse than Buffalo in some ways. I didn't like the food or the coffee, and they never gave you anything you needed in the hotels—I had to go out and buy some decent towels. It didn't matter, because I had to buy everything for my father anyway—soap and towels and Kleenex. The hospital didn't provide a thing except the bedsheets, and when a pair of those was put on the bed it seemed to be put there once and for all. I was there twenty-three days and I think I saw the sheets changed once. Our grandfathers had been glad to get out of Europe. It took my father to go back. The hospital he was in was an old convent or monastery. The beds were so close together you could hardly get a chair between them. Women patients were always wandering around the men's wards, and although I wouldn't swear to it, I think some of them had their beds there, at the far end. The patients were given crocks of tepid water to wash in, not by their beds but on a long table in the middle of the ward. Anyone too sick to get up was just out of luck unless, like my father, he had someone to look after him. I saw beetles and cockroaches, and I said to myself, This is what a person gets for leaving home.

My father accepted my presence as if it were his right—as if he hadn't lost his claim to any consideration years ago. So as not to scare him, I pretended my wife's father had sent me here on business, but he hardly listened, so I didn't insist.

"Didn't you drive a cab one time or other?" he said. "What else have you done?"

I wanted to answer, "You know what I've been doing? I've been supporting your wife and educating your other children, practically single-handed, since I was twelve."

I had expected to get here in time for his last words, which ought to have been "I'm sorry." I thought he would tell me where he wanted to be buried, how much money he owed, how many bastards he was leaving behind, and who was looking out for them. I imagined them in ports like this, with no-good mothers. *Somebody* should have been told—telling me didn't mean telling the whole world. One of the advantages of having an Old Country in the family is you can always say the relations that give you trouble have gone there. You just say, "He went back to the Old Country," and nobody asks any questions. So he could have told me the truth, and I'd have known and still not let the family down. But my father never confided anything. The trouble was he didn't know he was dying—he'd been told, in fact, he was getting better—so he didn't act like a dying man. He used what breath he had to say things like "I always liked old Lou," and you would have thought she was someone else's daughter, a girl he had hardly known. Another time he said, "Did Kenny do well for himself? I heard he went to college."

"Don't talk," I said.

"No, I mean it. I'd like to know how Kenny made out."

He couldn't speak above a whisper some days, and he was careful how he pronounced words. It wasn't a snobbish or an English accent—nothing that would make you grit your teeth. He just sounded like a stranger. When I was sent for, my mother said, "He's dying a pauper, after all his ideas. I hope he's satisfied." I didn't answer, but I said to myself, This isn't a question of satisfaction. I wanted to ask her, "Since you didn't get along with him and

he didn't get along with you, what did you go and have three children for?"
But those are the questions you keep to yourself.

"What's your wife like?" my father croaked. His eyes were interested. I
hadn't been prepared for this, for how long the mind stayed alive and how
frivolous it went on being. I thought he should be more serious. *"Wife,"* my
father insisted. "What about her?"

"Obedient" came into my head, I don't know why; it isn't important.
"Older than me," I said, quite easily, at last. "Better educated. She was a
kindergarten teacher. She knows a lot about art." Now, why that, of all the
side issues? She doesn't like a bare wall, that's all. "She prefers the Old Masters," I said. I was thinking about the Scotch landscape we've got over the
mantelpiece.

"Good, good. Name?"

"You know—*Beryl.* We sent you an announcement, to that place in Mexico where you were then."

"That's right, Beryl." "Burrull" was what he actually said.

I felt reassured, because my father until now had sounded like a strange
person. To have "Beryl" pronounced as I was used to hearing it made up for
being alone here and the smell of the ward and the coffee made of iodine. I
remembered what the Old Master had cost—one hundred and eighty dollars in 1962. It must be worth more now. Beryl said it would be an investment. Her family paid for half. She said once, about my father, "One day
he'll be sick; we'll have to look after him." "We can sell the painting," I said.
"I guess I can take care of my own father."

It happened—I was here, taking care of him; but he spoiled it now by
saying, "You look like you've done pretty well. That's not a bad suit you've
got on."

"Actually," I said, "I had to borrow from Beryl's father so as to get here."

I thought he would say, "Oh, I'm sorry," and I had my next answer ready,
about not begrudging a cent of it. But my father closed his eyes, smiling, saving up more breath to talk about nothing.

"I liked old Lou," he said distinctly. I was afraid he would ask, "Why
doesn't she write to me?" and I would have to say, "Because she never forgave you," and he was perfectly capable of saying then, "Never forgave me
for what?" But instead of that he laughed, which was the worst of the choking and wheezing noises he made now, and when he had recovered he said,
"Took her to Eaton's to choose a toy village. Had this shipment in, last one

in before the war. Summer '39. The old man saw the ad, wanted to get one for the kid. Old man came—each of us had her by the hand. Lou looked round, but every village had something the matter, as far as Her Royal Highness was concerned. The old man said, 'Come on, Princess, hurry it up,' but no, she'd of seen a scratch, or a bad paint job, or a chimney too big for a cottage. The old man said, 'Can't this kid make up her mind about anything? She's going to do a lot more crying than laughing,' he said, 'and that goes for you, too.' He was wrong about me. Don't know about Lou. But she was smart that time—not to want something that wasn't perfect."

He shut his eyes again and breathed desperately through his mouth. The old man in the story was his father, my grandfather.

"Nothing is perfect," I said. I felt like standing up so everyone could hear. It wasn't sourness but just the way I felt like reacting to my father's optimism.

Some days he seemed to be getting better. After two weeks I was starting to wonder if they hadn't brought me all this way for nothing. I couldn't go home and come back later, it had to be now; but I couldn't stay on and on. I had already moved to a cheaper hotel room. I dreamed I asked him, "How much longer?" but luckily the dream was in a foreign language—so foreign I don't think it was French, even. It was a language no one on earth had ever heard of. I wouldn't have wanted him to understand it, even in a dream. The nurses couldn't say anything. Sometimes I wondered if they knew who he was—if they could tell one patient from another. It was a big place, and poor. These nurses didn't seem to have much equipment. When they needed sterile water for anything, they had to boil it in an old saucepan. I got to the doctor one day, but he didn't like it. He had told my father he was fine, and that I could go back to Canada anytime—the old boy must have been starting to wonder why I was staying so long. The doctor just said to me, "Family business is of no interest to me. You look after your duty and I'll look after mine." I was afraid that my dream showed on my face and that was what made them all so indifferent. I didn't know how much time there was. I wanted to ask my father why he thought everything had to be perfect, and if he still stood by it as a way of living. Whenever he was reproached about something—by my mother, for instance—he just said, "Don't make my life dark for me." What could you do? He certainly made her life dark for her. One year when we had a summer cottage, he took a girl from the village, the village tramp, out to an island in the middle of the lake. They got caught in a storm coming back, and around fifty people stood on shore waiting to see the canoe capsize and the sinners drown. My mother had told us to stay in the house, but when Kenny said, to scare me, "I guess the way things are, Mum's gone down there to drown herself," I ran after her. She didn't say anything to me, but took her raincoat off and draped it over my head. It would have been fine if my father had died then—if lightning had struck him, or the canoe gone down like a stone. But no, he waded ashore—the slut, too, and someone even gave her a blanket. It was my mother that was blamed, in a funny way. "Can't you keep your husband home?" this girl's father said. I remember that same summer some other woman saying to her, "You'd better keep your husband away from my daughter. I'm telling you for your own good, because my husband's got a gun in the house." Someone did say, "Oh, poor Mrs. Apostolesco!" but my mother only answered, "If you think that, then I'm poor for life." That was only one of the things he did to her. I'm not sure if it was even the worst.

It was hard to say how long he had been looking at me. His lips were trying to form a word. I bent close and heard, "Sponge."

"Did you say 'sponge'? Is 'sponge' what you said?"

"Sponge," he agreed. He made an effort: "Bad night last night. Awful. Wiped everything with my sponge—blood, spit. Need new sponge."

There wasn't a bed table, just a plastic bag that hung on the bedrail with his personal things in it. I got out the sponge. It needed to be thrown away, all right. I said, "What color?"

"Eh?"

"This," I said, and held it up in front of him. "The new one. Any special color?"

"Blue." His voice broke out of a whisper all at once. His eyes were mocking me, like a kid seeing how far he can go. I thought he would thank me now, but then I said to myself, You can't expect anything; he's a sick man, and he was always like this.

"Most people think it was pretty good of me to have come here," I wanted to explain—not to boast or anything, but just for the sake of conversation. I was lonely there, and I had so much trouble understanding what anybody was saying.

"Bad night," my father whispered. "Need sedation."

"I know. I tried to tell the doctor. I guess he doesn't understand my French."

He moved his head. "Tip the nurses."

"You don't mean it!"

"Don't make me talk." He seemed to be using a reserve of breath. "At least twenty dollars. The ward girls less."

I said, "Jesus God!" because this was new to me and I felt out of my depth. "They don't bother much with you," I said, talking myself into doing it. "Maybe you're right. If I gave them a present, they'd look after you more. Wash you. Maybe they'd put a screen around you—you'd be more private then."

"No, thanks," my father said. "No screen. Thanks all the same."

We had one more conversation after that. I've already said there were always women slopping around in the ward, in felt slippers, and bathrobes stained with medicine and tea. I came in and found one—quite young, this one was—combing my father's hair. He could hardly lift his head from the pillow, and still she thought he was interesting. I thought, Kenny should see this.

"She's been telling me," my father gasped when the woman had left. "About herself. Three children by different men. Met a North African. He adopts the children, all three. Gives them his name. She has two more by him, boys. But he won't put up with a sick woman. One day he just doesn't come. She's been a month in another place; now they've brought her here. Man's gone. Left the children. They've been put in all different homes, she doesn't know where. Five kids. Imagine."

I thought, You left *us*. He had forgotten; he had just simply forgotten that he'd left his own.

"Well, we can't do anything about her, can we?" I said. "She'll collect them when she gets out of here."

"If she gets out."

"That's no way to talk," I said. "Look at the way she was talking and walking around ..." I could not bring myself to say "and combing your hair." "Look at how *you* are," I said. "You've just told me this long story."

"She'll seem better, but she'll get worse," my father said. "She's like me, getting worse. Do you think I don't know what kind of ward I'm in? Every time they put the screen around a patient, it's because he's dying. If I had TB, like they tried to make me believe, I'd be in a TB hospital."

"That just isn't true," I said.

"Can you swear I've got TB? You can't."

I said without hesitating, "You've got a violent kind of TB. They had no place else to put you except here. The ward might be crummy, but the med-icine . . . the medical care . . ." He closed his eyes. "I'm looking you straight in the face," I said, "and I swear you have this unusual kind of TB, and you're almost cured." I watched, without minding it now, a new kind of bug crawling along the base of the wall.

"Thanks, Billy," said my father.

I really was scared. I had been waiting for something without knowing what it would mean. I can tell you how it was: It was like the end of the world.

"I didn't realize you were worried," I said. "You should of asked me right away."

"I knew you wouldn't lie to me," my father said. "That's why I wanted you, not the others."

That was all. Not long after that, he couldn't talk. He had deserted his whole family once, but I was the one he abandoned twice. When he died, a nurse said to me, "I am sorry." It had no meaning, from her, yet only a few days before, it was all I thought I wanted to hear.

NEW YEAR'S EVE

On New Year's Eve the Plummers took Amabel to the opera.

"Whatever happens tonight happens every day for a year," said Amabel, feeling secure because she had a Plummer on either side.

Colonel Plummer's car had broken down that afternoon; he had got his wife and their guest punctually to the Bolshoi Theater, through a storm, in a bootleg taxi. Now he discovered from his program that the opera announced was neither of those they had been promised.

His wife leaned across Amabel and said, "Well, which is it?" She could not read any Russian and would not try.

She must have known it would take him minutes to answer, for she sat back, settled a width of gauzy old shawl on her neck, and began telling Amabel the relative sizes of the Bolshoi and some concert hall in Vancouver the girl had never heard of. Then, because it was the Colonel's turn to speak, she shut her eyes and waited for the overture.

The Colonel was gazing at the program and putting off the moment when he would have to say that it was *Ivan Susanin,* a third choice no one had so much as hinted at. He wanted to convey that he was sorry and that the change was not his fault. He took bearings: He was surrounded by women. To his left sat the guest, who mewed like a kitten, who had been a friend of his daughter's, and whose name he could not remember. On the right, near the aisle, two quiet unknown girls were eating fruit and chocolates. These two smelled of oranges; of clothes worn a long time in winter; of light recent sweat; of women's hair. Their arms were large and bare. When the girl closest to him moved slightly, he saw a man's foreign wristwatch. He wondered who she was, and how the watch had come to her, but he had been here two years now—long enough to know he would never be answered. He also wondered if the girls were as shabby as his guest found everyone in Moscow. His way of seeing women was not concerned with that sort of evidence: Shoes were shoes, a frock was a frock.

The girls took no notice of the Colonel. He was invisible to them, wiped out of being by a curtain pulled over the inner eye.

He felt his guest's silence, then his wife's. The visitor's profile was a kitten's, to match her voice. She was twenty-two, which his Catherine would never be. Her gold dress, packed for improbable gala evenings, seemed the size of a bathing suit. She was divorcing someone, or someone in Canada had left her—he remembered that, but not her name.

He moved an inch or two to the left and muttered, "It's *Ivan.*"

"What?" cried his wife. "What did you say?"

In the old days, before their Catherine had died, when the Colonel's wife was still talking to him, he had tried to hush her in public places sometimes, and so the habit of loudness had taken hold.

"It isn't *Boris.* It isn't *Igor.* It's *Ivan.* They must both have had sore throats."

"Oh, well, bugger it," said his wife.

Amabel supposed that the Colonel's wife had grown peculiar through having lived so many years in foreign parts. Having no one to speak to, she conversed alone. Half of Mrs. Plummer's character was quite coarse, though a finer Mrs. Plummer somehow kept order. Low-minded Mrs. Plummer chatted amiably and aloud with her high-minded twin—far more pleasantly than the whole of Mrs. Plummer ever talked to anybody.

"Serves you right," she said.

Amabel gave a little jump. She wondered if Mrs. Plummer's remark had anything to do with the opera. She turned her head cautiously. Mrs. Plummer had again closed her eyes.

The persistence of memory determines what each day of the year will be like, the Colonel's wife decided. Not what happens on New Year's Eve. This morning I was in Moscow; between the curtains snow was falling. The day had no color. It might have been late afternoon. Then the smell of toast came into my room and I was back in my mother's dining room in Victoria, with the gros-point chairs and the framed embroidered grace on the wall. A little girl I had been ordered to play with kicked the baseboard, waiting for us to finish our breakfast. A devilish little boy, Hume something, was on my mind. I was already attracted to devils; I believed in their powers. My

mother's incompetence about choosing friends for me shaped my life, because that child, who kicked the baseboard and left marks on the paint ...

When she and her husband had still been speaking, this was how Frances
Plummer had talked. She had offered him hours of reminiscence, and the
long personal thoughts that lead to quarrels. In those days red wine had
made her aggressive, whiskey made him vague.

Not only vague, she corrected; stubborn too. *Speak?* said one half of Mrs.
Plummer to the other. Did we speak? We yelled!

The quiet twin demanded a fairer portrait of the past, for she had no
memory.

Oh, he was a shuffler, back and forth between wife and mistress, said the
virago, who had forgotten nothing. He'd desert one and then leave the
other—flag to flag, false convert, double agent, reason why a number of
women had long, hilly conversations, like the view from a train—monotonous, finally. That was the view a minute ago, you'd say. Yes, but look now.

The virago declared him incompetent; said he had shuffled from embassy
to embassy as well, pushed along by a staunch ability to retain languages, an
untiring recollection of military history and wars nobody cared about.
What did he take with him? His wife, for one thing. At least she was here,
tonight, at the opera. Each time they changed countries he supervised the
packing of a portrait of his mother, wearing white, painted when she was
seventeen. He had nothing of Catherine's: When Catherine died, Mrs.
Plummer gave away her clothes and her books, and had her little dog put to
sleep.

How did it happen? In what order? said calm Mrs. Plummer. Try and
think it in order. He shuffled away one Easter; came shuffling back; and
Catherine died. It is useless to say "Serves you right," for whatever served
him served you.

The overture told Amabel nothing, and by the end of the first act she still
did not know the name of the opera or understand what it was about. Earlier in the day the Colonel had said, "There is some uncertainty—sore
throats here and there. The car, now—you can see what has happened. It
doesn't start. If our taxi should fail us, and isn't really a taxi, we might arrive at the Bolshoi too late for me to do anything much in the way of explaining. But you can easily figure it out for yourself." His mind cleared; his
face lightened. "If you happen to see Tartar dances, then you will know it
is *Igor.* Otherwise it is *Boris.*"

The instant the lights rose, Amabel thrust her program at him and said, "What does that mean?"

"Why, *Ivan.* It's *Ivan.*"

"There are two words, aren't there?"

"Yes. What's-His-Name had a sore throat, d'you see? We knew it might all be changed at any moment. It was clever of them to get these printed in time."

Mrs. Plummer, who looked like the Red Queen sometimes, said, "A life for the tsar," meanwhile staring straight ahead of her.

"Used to be, used to be," said the Colonel, and he smiled at Amabel, as if to say to her, "Now you know."

The Plummers did not go out between acts. They never smoked, were seldom thirsty or hungry, and they hated crowds. Amabel stood and stretched so that the Russians could appreciate her hair, her waist, her thin arms, and, for those lucky enough to glimpse them, her thighs. After a moment or two Mrs. Plummer thought the Russians had appreciated Amabel enough, and she said very loudly, "You might be more comfortable sitting down."

"*Lakmé* is coming," said the Colonel, for it was his turn to speak. "It's far and away my favorite opera. It makes an awful fool of the officer caste." This was said with ambiguous satisfaction. He was not really disowning himself.

"How does it do that?" said Amabel, who was not more comfortable sitting down.

"Why, an officer runs off with the daughter of a temple priest. No one would ever have got away with that. Though the military are awful fools most of the time."

"You're that class—caste, I mean—aren't you?"

The Colonel supposed that like most people he belonged to the same caste as his father and mother. His father had worn a wig and been photographed wearing it just before he died. His mother, still living, rising eighty, was given to choked melancholy laughter over nothing, a habit carried over from a girlhood of Anglican giggling. It was his mother the Colonel had wanted in Moscow this Christmas—not Amabel. He had wanted to bring her even if it killed her; even if she choked to death on her own laughter as she shook tea out of a cup because her hand trembled, or if she laughed and said, "My dear boy, nobody forced you to marry Frances."

The Colonel saw himself serene, immune to reminders; observed a new Colonel Plummer crowned with a wig, staring out of a photograph, in the uniform his father had worn at Vimy Ridge; sure of himself and still, faded to a plain soft neutral color; unhearing, at peace—dead, in short. He had dreamed of sending the plane ticket, of meeting his mother at the airport with a fur coat over his arm in case she had come dressed for the wrong winter; had imagined giving her tea and watching her drink it out of a glass set in a metal base decorated all over with Soviet cosmonauts; had sat beside her here, at the Bolshoi, at a performance of *Eugene Onegin*, which she once had loved. It seemed fitting that he now do some tactful, unneeded, appreciated thing for her, at last—she who had never done anything for him.

One evening his wife had looked up from the paperback spy novel she was reading at dinner and—having waited for him to notice she was neither eating nor turning pages—remarked that Amabel Bacon, who had been Amabel Fisher, that pretty child Catherine roomed with in school, had asked if she might come to them for ten days at Christmas.

"Nothing for children here," he said. "And not much space."

"She must be twenty-two," said his wife, "and can stay in a hotel."

They stared at each other, as if they were strangers in a crush somewhere and her earring had caught on his coat. Their looks disentangled. That night Mrs. Plummer wrote to Amabel saying that they did not know any young people; that Mrs. Plummer played bridge from three to six every afternoon; that the Colonel was busy at the embassy; that it was difficult to find seats at the ballet; that it was too cold for sight-seeing; Lenin's tomb was temporarily closed; there was nothing in the way of shopping; the Plummers, not being great mixers, avoided parties; they planned to spend a quiet Christmas and New Year's; and Amabel was welcome.

Amabel seemed to have forgotten her question about the officer caste. "... hissing and whispering behind us the whole time" was what she was saying now. "I could hardly hear the music." She had a smile ready, so that if the Colonel did look at her he would realize she was pleased to be at the Bolshoi and not really complaining. "I suppose you know every note by heart, so you aren't bothered by extra noise." She paused, wondering if the Colonel was hard of hearing. "I hate whispering. It's more bothersome than something loud. It's like that hissing you get on stereo sometimes, like water running."

"Water running?" said the Colonel, not deafly but patiently.

"I mean the people behind us."

"A mother explaining to a child," he said, without looking.

Amabel turned, pretending she was only lifting her long, soft hair away from her neck. She saw a little girl, wearing a white hair ribbon the size of a melon, leaning against, and somehow folded into, a seal-shaped mother. The two shared a pear, bite for bite. Everyone around them was feeding, in fact. It's a zoo, Amabel thought. On the far side of the Colonel, two girls munched on chocolates. They unwrapped each slowly, and dropped the paper back in the box. Amabel sighed and said, "Are they happy? Cheap entertainment isn't everything. Once you've seen *Swan Lake* a hundred times, what is there to do here?"

Mrs. Plummer slapped at her bangles and said, "We were told when we were in Morocco that children with filthy eye diseases and begging their food were perfectly happy."

"Well, at least they have the sun in those places," said Amabel. She had asked the unanswerable only because she herself was so unhappy. It was true that she had left her husband—it was not the other way around—but he had done nothing to keep her. She had imagined pouring all this out to dead Catherine's mother, who had always been so kind on school holidays because Amabel's parents were divorced; who had invited her to Italy once, and another time to Morocco. Why else had Amabel come all this way at Christmastime, if not to be adopted? She had fancied herself curled at the foot of Mrs. Plummer's bed, Mrs. Plummer with a gray braid down on one shoulder, her reading spectacles held between finger and thumb, her book— one of the thick accounts of somebody's life at Cambridge, the reading of the elderly—slipping off the counterpane as she became more and more engrossed in Amabel's story. She had seen Mrs. Plummer handing her a deep blue leather case stamped with dead Catherine's initials. The lid, held back by Mrs. Plummer, was lined with sky-blue moire; the case contained Catherine's first coral bracelet, her gold sleeper rings, her first locket, her chains and charm bracelets, a string of pearls, her childless godmother's engagement ring. . . . "I have no one to leave these to, and Catherine was so fond of you," said a fantastic Mrs. Plummer.

None of it could happen, of course: From a chance phrase Amabel learned that the Plummers had given everything belonging to Catherine to the gardener's children of that house in Italy where Catherine caught spinal meningitis and died. Moreover, Amabel never saw so much as the wallpaper of Mrs. Plummer's bedroom. When she hinted at her troubles, said something about a wasted life, Mrs. Plummer cut her off with, "Most lives are wasted. All are shortchanged. A few are tragic."

The Plummers lived in a dark, drab, high-ceilinged flat. They had somehow escaped the foreigners' compound, but their isolation was deeper, as though they were embedded in a large block of ice. Amabel had been put in a new hotel, to which the Colonel conducted her each night astonishingly early. They ate their dinner at a nursery hour, and as soon as Amabel had drunk the last of the decaffeinated coffee the Plummers served, the Colonel guided her over the pavement to where his Rover was waiting and freezing, then drove her along streets nearly empty of traffic, but where lights signaled and were obeyed, so that it was like driving in a dream. The sidewalks were dark with crowds. She wiped the mist away from the window with her glove, and saw people dragging Christmas trees along—not for Christmas, for the New Year, Colonel Plummer told her. When he left her in the hotel lobby it was barely half past eight. She felt as if her visit were a film seen in fragments, with someone's head moving back and forth in front of her face; or as if someone had been describing a story while a blind flapped and a window banged. In the end she would recall nothing except shabby strangers dragging fir trees through the dark.

"Are you enjoying it?" said Mrs. Plummer, snatching away from the Colonel a last-ditch possibility. He had certainly intended to ask this question next time his turn came round.

"Yes, though I'd appreciate it more if I understood," said Amabel. "Probably."

"Don't you care for music?"

"I love music. Understood Russian, I meant."

Mrs. Plummer did not understand Russian, did not need it, and did not miss it. She had not heard a thing said to her in French, or in Spanish, let alone any of the Hamitic tongues, when she and the Colonel were in Morocco; and she had not cared to learn any Italian in Italy. She went to bed early every night and read detective novels. She was in bed before nine unless an official reason kept her from going. She would not buy new clothes now; would not trouble about her hair, except for cutting it. She played bridge every afternoon for money. When she had enough, she intended to leave him. Dollars, pounds, francs, crowns, lire, deutsche marks, and guldens were rolled up in nylon stockings and held fast with elastic bands.

But of course she would never be able to leave him: She would never have enough money, though she had been saving, and rehearsing her farewell, for years. She had memorized every word and seen each stroke of punctuation, so that when the moment arrived she would not be at a loss. The parting speech would spring from her like a separate Frances. Sentences streamed across a swept sky. They were pure, white, unblemished by love or compassion. She felt a complicity with her victim. She leaned past their guest and spoke to him and drew his attention to something by touching his hand. He immediately placed his right hand, the hand holding the program, over hers, so that the clasp, the loving conspiracy, was kept hidden.

So it appeared to Amabel—a loving conspiracy. She was embarrassed, because they were too old for this; then she was envious, then jealous. She hated them for flaunting their long understanding, making her seem discarded, left out of a universal game. No one would love her the way the Colonel loved his wife. Mrs. Plummer finished whatever trivial remark she had considered urgent and sat back, very straight, and shook down her Moroccan bangles, and touched each of her long earrings to see if it was still in place—as if the exchange of words with the Colonel had in fact been a passionate embrace.

Amabel pretended to read the program, but it was all in Russian; there wasn't a word of translation. She wished she had never come.

The kinder half of Mrs. Plummer said aloud to her darker twin, "Oh, well, she is less trouble than that damned military-cultural mission last summer."

Tears stood in Amabel's eyes and she had to hold her head as stiffly as Mrs. Plummer did; otherwise the tears might have spilled on her program and thousands of people would have heard them fall. Later, the Plummers would drop her at her hotel, which could have been in Toronto, in Caracas, or in Amsterdam; where there was no one to talk to, and where she was not loved. In her room was a tapped cream-colored telephone with framed instructions in a secret alphabet, and an oil painting of peonies concealing a microphone to which a Russian had his ear glued around the clock. There were three thousand rooms in the hotel, which meant three thousand microphones and an army of three thousand listeners. Amabel kept her coat, snow boots, and traveler's checks on a chair drawn up to the bedside, and she slept in her bra and panties in case they came to arrest her during the night.

"My bath runs sand," she said. Mrs. Plummer merely looked with one eye, like a canary.

"In my hotel," said Amabel. "Sand comes out of the tap. It's in the bathwater."

"Speak to the manager," said Mrs. Plummer, who would not put up with complaints from newcomers. She paused, conceding that what she had just advised was surrealistic. "I've found the local water clean. I drink quarts of it."

"But to bathe in . . . and when I wash my stockings . . ."

"One thing you will never hear of is typhoid here," said the Colonel, kindly, to prevent his wife from saying, "Don't wash your damned stockings." He took the girl's program and looked at it, as if it were in some way unlike his own. He turned to the season's events on the back page and said, "Oh, it isn't *Lakmé* after all," meanwhile wondering if that was what had upset her.

Amabel saw that she would never attract a man again; she would never be loved, for she had not held even the Colonel's attention. First he sat humming the music they had just heard, then he was hypnotized by the program, then he looked straight up at the ceiling and brought his gaze down to the girls sitting next to the aisle. What was so special about them? Amabel leaned forward, as if looking for a dropped glove. She saw two heads, bare round arms, a pink slip strap dropped on the curve of a shoulder. One of the girls divided an orange, holding it out so the juice would not drip on her knees.

They all look like servants, thought the unhappy guest. I can't help it. That's what they look like. They dress like maids. I'm having a rotten time. She glanced at the Colonel and thought, They're his type. But he must have been good-looking once.

The Colonel was able to learn the structure of any language, given a few pages of colloquial prose and a dictionary. His wife was deaf to strangers, and she barely noticed the people she could not understand. As a result, the Colonel had grown accustomed to being alone among hordes of ghosts. With Amabel still mewing beside him, he heard in the ghost language only he could capture, "Yes, but are you happy?"

His look went across the ceiling and came down to the girls. The one who had whispered the question was rapt; she held a section of orange suspended a few inches from her lips as she waited. But the lights dimmed. "Cht," her friend cautioned. She gathered up the peelings on her lap in a paper bag.

Mrs. Plummer suddenly said clearly to herself or to Amabel, "My mother used to make her children sing. If you sing, you must be happy. That was another idea of happiness."

Amabel thought, Every day of the year will be like tonight.

He doesn't look at women now, said Mrs. Plummer silently. Doesn't dare. Every girl is a wife screaming for justice and revenge; a mistress deserted, her life shrunk down to a postage stamp; a daughter dead.

He walked away in Italy, after a violent drinking quarrel, with Catherine there in the house. Instead of calling after him, Mrs. Plummer sat still for an hour, then remembered she had forgotten to leave some money for the postman for Easter. It was early morning; she was dressed; neither of them had been to bed. She found an envelope, the kind she used for messages to servants and the local tradesmen, and crammed a thousand-lire note inside. She was sober and cursing. She scribbled the postman's name. Catherine, in the garden, on her knees, tore out the pansy plants she had put in the little crevices between paving stones the day before. She looked up at her mother.

"Have you had your breakfast?" her mother said.

"It's no use chasing *them*," Catherine answered. "They've gone."

That was how he had done it—the old shuffler: chosen the Easter holiday, when his daughter was home from school, down in Italy, to creep away. And Catherine understood, for she said "them," though she had never known that the other person existed. Well, of course he came shuffling back, because of Catherine. All was safe: Wife was there, home safe, daughter safe, books in place, wine cellar intact, career unchipped. He came out of it scot-free, except that Catherine died. Was it accurate to say, "Serves you right"? Was it fair?

Yes! Yes! "Serves you right!"

Amabel heard, and supposed it could only have to do with the plot of the opera. She said to herself, It will soon be over.

The thing he was most afraid of now was losing his memory. Sometimes he came to breakfast wearing two kinds of shoes. He could go five times to a window to see if snow was falling and forget each time why he was standing there. He had thrown three hundred dollars in a wastepaper basket and carefully kept an elastic band. It was of extreme importance that he remember his guest's name. The name was royal, or imperial, he seemed to recall. Straight down an imperial tree he climbed, counting off leaves: Julia, Octavia, Livia, Cleopatra—not likely—Messalina, Claudia, Domitia. Antonia? It was a name with two *a*'s but with an *m* and not an *n*.

"Marcia," he said in the dark, half turning to her.

"It's Amabel, actually," she said. "I don't even know a Marcia." Like a child picking up a piece of glass and innocently throwing it, she said, "I don't think Catherine knew any Marcias either."

The woman behind them hissed for silence. Amabel swung round, abruptly this time, and saw that the little girl had fallen asleep. Her ribbon was askew, like a frayed birthday wrapping.

The Colonel slept for a minute and dreamed that his mother was a reed, or a flower. "If only you had always been like that!" he cried, in the dream.

Amabel thought that the scene of the jewel case still might take place: A tap at the hotel-room door tomorrow morning, and there would be Mrs. Plummer, tall and stormy, in her rusty-orange ancient mink, with her square fur bonnet, first visitor of the year, starting the new cycle with a noble gesture. She undid a hastily wrapped parcel, saying, "Nothing really valuable—Catherine was too young." But no, for everything of Catherine's belonged to the gardener's children in Italy now. Amabel rearranged tomorrow morning: Mrs. Plummer brought *her own case* and said, "I have no one to leave anything to except a dog hospital," and there was Amabel, sitting up in bed, hugging her knees, loved at last, looking at emeralds.

Without speaking, Colonel Plummer and his wife each understood what the other had thought of the opera, the staging, and the musical quality of the evening; they also knew where Mrs. Plummer would wait with Amabel while he struggled to the cloakroom to fetch their wraps.

He had taken great care to stay close behind the two girls. For one thing, he had not yet had the answer to "Are you happy?" He heard now, "I am twenty-one years old and I have not succeeded ..." and then he was wrenched out of the queue. Pushing back, pretending to be armored against unknown forces, like his wife, he heard someone insult him and smiled uncomprehendingly. No one knew how much he understood—except for his wife. It was as though he listened to stones, or snow, or trees speaking. "... even though we went to a restaurant and I paid for his dinner," said the same girl, who had not even looked round, and for whom the Colonel had no existence. "The next night he came to the door very late. My parents were in bed. He had come from some stuffy place—his coat stank. But he looked clean and important. He always does. We went into the kitchen. He said he had come up because he cared and could not spend an evening without seeing me, and then he said he had no money, or had lost his money somewhere. I did not want my mother to hear. I said, 'Now I know why you came to see me.' I gave him money—how could I refuse? He knows we keep it in the same drawer as the knives and forks. He could have helped himself, but instead he was careful not to look at the drawer at all. When he wants to show tenderness, he presses his face to my cheek, his lips as quiet as his forehead—it is like being embraced by a dead animal. I was ashamed to think he knew I would always be there waiting. He thinks he can come in whenever he sees a light from the street. I have no advantage from my loyalty, only disadvantages."

Her friend seemed to be meditating deeply. "If you are not happy, it might be your fault," she said.

The cloakroom attendant flung first the girls' coats and woollen caps on the counter, and then their boots, which had been stored in numbered cubbyholes underneath, and it was the Colonel's turn to give up plastic tokens in exchange for his wife's old fur-lined cloak, Amabel's inadequate jacket, his own overcoat—but of course the girls were lost, and he would never see them again. What nagged at him was that disgraceful man. Oh, he could imagine him well enough: an elegant black marketeer, speaking five languages, wearing a sable hat, following tourists in the snow, offering icons in exchange for hard currency. It would explain the watch and perhaps even the chocolates and oranges. "His coat stank" and "he looked clean and important" were typically feminine contradictions, of unequal value. He thought he saw the girls a moment later, but they may have been two like them, leaning on a wall, holding each other's coats as they tugged their boots on; then he saw them laughing, collapsed in each other's arms. This is unusual, he told himself, for when do people laugh in public anywhere in the north—not only in this sullen city? He thought, as though suddenly superior to the person he had been only a minute ago, what an iron thing it would be never to regret one's losses.

His wife and Amabel looked too alert, as if they had been discussing him and would now pretend to talk about something else.

"That didn't take long," remarked Mrs. Plummer, meaning to say that it had. With overwhelming directness she said, "The year still has an hour to run, so Amabel tells me, and so we had better take her home with us for a drink."

"Only an hour left to change the year ahead," said Amabel without tact.

The Colonel knew that the city was swept by a Siberian blizzard and that their taxi would be nowhere in sight. But outside he saw only the dust of snow sifting past streetlights. The wind had fallen; and their driver was waiting exactly where he had promised. Colonel Plummer helped Amabel down the icy steps of the opera house, then went back for his wife. Cutting off a possible question, she said, "I can make a bed for her somewhere."

Wait, he said silently, looking at all the strangers disappearing in the last hour of the year. Come back, he said to the girls. Who are you? Who was the man?

Amabel's little nose was white with cold. Though this was not her turn to speak, Mrs. Plummer glanced down at her guest, who could not yet hear, saying, " 'He is not glad that he is going home, nor sorry that he has not had time to see the city. . . .' "

"It's 'the *sights* of the city,' I think," said the Colonel. "I'll look it up." He realized he was not losing his memory after all. His breath came and went as if he were still very young. He took Amabel's arm and felt her shiver, though she did not complain about the weather and had her usual hopeful smile ready in case he chose to look. Hilarity is happiness, he thought, sadly, remembering those two others. Is it?

Mrs. Plummer took her turn by remarking, "Used to read the same books," to no one in particular.

Without another word, the Plummers climbed into the taxi and drove with Amabel back to the heart of their isolation, where there was no room for a third person; but the third person knew nothing about this, and so for Amabel the year was saved.

The

SEVENTIES

IN THE TUNNEL

⚜

$\mathcal{S}$arah's father was a born widower. As she had no memory of a mother, it was as though Mr. Holmes had none of a wife and had been created perpetually bereaved and knowing best. His conviction that he must act for two gave him a jocular heaviness that made the girl react for a dozen, but his jokes rode a limitless tide of concern. He thought Sarah was subjective and passionate, as small children are. She knew she was detached and could prove it. A certain kind of conversation between them was bound to run down, wind up, run down again: You are, I'm not, yes, no, you should, I won't, you'll be sorry. Between eighteen and twenty, Sarah kept meaning to become a psychosociologist. Life would then be a tribal village through which she would stalk soft-footed and disguised: That would show him who was subjective. But she was also a natural *amoureuse,* as some girls were natural actresses, and she soon discovered that love refused all forms of fancy dress. In love she had to show her own face, and speak in a true voice, and she was visible from all directions.

One summer, after a particularly stormy spring, her father sent her to Grenoble to learn about French civilization—actually, to get her away from a man he always pretended to think was called Professor Downcast. Sarah raged mostly over the harm her father had brought to Professor Downcast's career, for she had been helping with his "Urban and Regional Studies of the Less Privileged in British Columbia," and she knew he could not manage without her. She did not stay long in Grenoble; she had never intended to. She had decided beforehand that the Alps were shabby, the cultural atmosphere in France was morbid and stifling, and that every girl she met would be taking the civilization course for the wrong reason. She packed and caught a bus down the Napoleon Route to the Mediterranean.

Professor Downcast had been forced to promise he would not write, and so, of course, Sarah would not write her father. She wanted to have new friends and a life that was none of his business. The word "Riviera" had predicted yellow mornings and snowy boats, and crowds filling the streets in the way dancers fill a stage. Her mind's eye had kept them at a distance so that they shimmered and might have been plumed, like peacocks. Up close, her moralist's eye selected whatever was bound to disappoint: a stone beach skirted with sewage, a promenade that was really a through speedway, an eerie bar. For the first time she recognized prostitutes; they clustered outside her hotel, gossiping, with faces like dead letters. For friends she had a pair of middle-aged tourists who took her sight-seeing and warned her not to go out at night by herself. Grenoble had been better after all. Who was to blame? She sent her father a letter of reproach, of abuse, of cold reason, and also of apology—the postmark was bound to be a shock. She then began waiting round American Express for an answer. She was hoping it would be a cable saying "Come on home."

His feelings, when he got round to describing them, filled no more than one flimsy typewritten page. She thought she was worth more than that. What now? She walked out of American Express, still reading her letter. A shadow fell over the page. At the same time a man's soft voice said, "Don't be frightened."

She looked up, not frightened—appraising. The man was about twice her age, and not very tall. He was dressed in clean, not too new summer whites, perhaps the remains of a naval officer's uniform. His accent was English. His eyes were light brown. Once he had Sarah's attention, and had given her time to decide what her attention would be, he said his name was Roy Cooper and asked if she wouldn't like to have lunch with him somewhere along the port.

Of course, she answered: It was broad daylight and there were policemen everywhere—polite, old-fashioned, and wearing white, just like Roy Cooper. She was always hungry, and out of laziness had been living on pizzas and ice cream. Her father had never told her to keep experience at bay. For mystery and horror he had tried to substitute common sense, which may have been why Sarah did not always understand him. She and Roy Cooper crossed the promenade together. He held her arm to guide her through traffic, but let go the minute they reached the curb. "I've been trying to talk to you for days now," he said. "I was hoping you might know someone I knew, who could introduce us."

"Oh, I don't know anyone *here*," said Sarah. "I met a couple of Americans in my hotel. We went to see this sort of abandoned chapel. It has frescoes of Jesus and Judas and . . ." He was silent. "Their name was Hayes?"

He answered that his car was parked over near the port in the shade. It was faster to walk than drive, down here. He was staying outside Nice; otherwise he wouldn't bother driving at all.

They moved slowly along to the port, dragging this shapeless conversation between them, and Sarah was just beginning to wonder if he wasn't a friend of her father's, and if this might be one of her father's large concrete jokes, when he took her bare arm in a way no family friend would have dared and said look here, what about this restaurant? Again he quickly dropped her arm before she could tug away. They sat down under an awning with a blue tablecloth between them. Sarah frowned, lowered her eyes, and muttered something. It might have been a grace before eating had she not seemed so determined; but her words were completely muffled by the traffic grinding by. She leaned forward and repeated, "I'd like to know what your motives are, exactly." She did not mean anything like "What do you want?" but "What is it? Why Roy Cooper? Why me?" At the back of her mind was the idea that he deserved a lesson: She would eat her lunch, get up, coolly stroll away.

His answer, again miles away from Sarah's question, was that he knew where Sarah was staying and had twice followed her to the door of the hotel. He hadn't dared to speak up.

"Well, it's a good thing you finally did," she said. "I was only waiting for a letter, and now I'm going back to Grenoble. I don't like it here."

"Don't do that, don't leave." He had a quiet voice for a man, and he knew how to slide it under another level of sound and make himself plain. He broke off to order their meal. He seemed so at ease, so certain of other people and their reactions—at any moment he would say he was the ambassador of a place where nothing mattered but charm and freedom. Sarah was not used to cold wine at noon. She touched the misty decanter with her fingertips and wet her forehead with the drops. She wanted to ask his motives again but found he was questioning hers—laughing at Sarah, in fact. Who was she to frown and cross-examine, she who wandered around eating pizzas alone? She told him about Professor Downcast and her father—she had to, to explain what she was doing here—and even let him look at her father's letter. Part of it said, "My poor Sarah, no one ever seems to interest you unless he is

    no good at his job

    small in stature; I wonder why?

    'Marxist-Leninist' (since you sneer at 'Communist' and will not allow its use around the house)

    married or just about to be

    in debt to God and humanity.

I am not saying you should look for the opposite in every case, only for some person who doesn't combine all these qualities at one time."

"I'm your father's man," said Roy Cooper, and he might well have been, except for the problem of height. He was a bachelor, and certainly the opposite of a Marxist-Leninist: He was a former prison inspector whose career had been spent in an Asian colony. He had been retired early when the Empire faded out and the New Democracy that followed no longer required inspection. As for "debt to God and humanity," he said he had his own religion, which made Sarah stare sharply at him, wondering if his idea of being funny was the same as her father's. Their conversation suddenly became locked; an effort would be needed to pull it in two, almost a tug-of-war. I could stay a couple of days or so, she said to herself. She saw the south that day as she would see it finally, as if she had picked up an old dress and first wondered, then knew, how it could be changed to suit her.

They spent that night talking on a stony beach. Sarah half lay, propped on an elbow. He sat with his arms around his knees. Behind him, a party of boys had made a bonfire. By its light Sarah told him all her life, every season of it, and he listened with the silent attention that honored her newness. She had scarcely reached the end when a fresh day opened, streaky and white. She could see him clearly: Even unshaven and dying for sleep he was the ambassador from that easy place. She tossed a stone, a puppy asking for a game. He smiled, but still kept space between them, about the distance of the blue tablecloth.

They began meeting every day. They seemed to Sarah to be moving toward each other without ever quite touching; then she thought they were traveling in the same direction, but still apart. They could not turn back, for there was nothing to go back to. She felt a pause, a hesitation. The conversation began to unlock; once Sarah had told all her life she could not think of anything to say. One afternoon he came to the beach nearly two hours late. She sensed he had something to tell her, and waited to hear that he had a wife, or was engaged, or on drugs, or had no money. In the most casual voice imaginable he asked Sarah if she would spend the rest of her holiday with him. He had rented a place up behind Nice. She would know all his friends, quite openly; he did not want to let her in for anything squalid or mean. She could come for a weekend. If she hated it, no hard feelings. It was up to her.

This was new, for of course she had never *lived* with anyone. Well, why not? In her mind she told her father, After all, it was a bachelor you wanted for me. She abandoned her textbooks and packed instead four wooden bowls she had bought for her father's sister and an out-of-print Matisse poster intended for Professor Downcast. Now it would be Roy's. He came to fetch her that day in the car that was always parked somewhere in shade—it was a small open thing, a bachelor's car. They rolled out of Nice with an escort of trucks and buses. She thought there should have been carnival floats spilling yellow roses. Until now, this was her most important decision, for it supposed a way of living, a style. She reflected on how no girl she knew had ever done quite this, and on what her father would say. He might not hear of it; at least not right away. Meanwhile, they made a triumphant passage through blank white suburbs. Their witnesses were souvenir shops, a village or two, a bright solitary supermarket, the walls and hedges of villas. Along one of these flowering barriers they came to a stop and got out of the car. The fence wire looked tense and new; the plumbago it supported leaned every way, as if its life had been spared but only barely. It was late evening. She heard the squeaky barking of small dogs, and glimpsed, through an iron gate, one of those stucco bungalows that seem to beget their own palm trees. They went straight past it, down four shallow garden steps, and came upon a low building that Sarah thought looked like an Indian lodge. It was half under a plane tree. Perhaps it was the tree, whose leaves were like plates, that made the house and its terrace seem microscopic. One table and four thin chairs was all the terrace would hold. A lavender hedge surrounded it.

"They call this place The Tunnel," Roy said. She wondered if he was already regretting their adventure; if so, all he had to do was drive her back at once, or even let her down at a bus stop. But then he lit a candle on the table, which at once made everything dark, and she could see he was smiling as if in wonder at himself. The Tunnel was a long windowless room with an arched whitewashed ceiling. In daytime the light must have come in from the door, which was protected by a soft white curtain of mosquito netting. He groped for a switch on the wall, and she saw there was next to no furniture. "It used to be a storage place for wine and olives," he said. "The Reeves fixed it up. They let it to friends."

"What are Reeves?"

"People—nice people. They live in the bungalow."

She was now in this man's house. She wondered about procedure: whether to unpack or wait until she was asked, and whether she had any domestic duties and was expected to cook. Concealed by a screen was a shower bath; the stove was in a cupboard. The lavatory, he told her, was behind the house in a garden shed. She would find it full of pictures of Labour leaders. The only Socialist the Reeves could bear was Hugh Dalton (Sarah had never heard of him, or most of the others, either), because Dalton had paid for the Queen's wedding out of his own pocket when she was a slip of a girl without a bean of her own. Sarah said, "What did he want to do that for?" She saw, too late, that he meant to be funny.

He sat down on the bed and looked at her. "The Reeves versus Labour," he said. "Why should you care? You weren't even born." She was used to hearing that every interesting thing had taken place before her birth. She had a deadly serious question waiting: "What shall I do if you feel remorseful?"

"If I am," he said, "you'll never know. That's a promise."

It was not remorse that overcame him but respectability: First thing next day, Sarah was taken to meet his friends, landlords, and neighbors, Tim and Meg Reeve. "I want them to like you," he said. Wishing to be liked by total strangers was outside anything that mattered to Sarah; all the same, quickened by the new situation and its demands, she dressed and brushed her hair and took the path between the two cottages. The garden seemed a dry, cracked sort of place. The remains of daffodils lay in brown ribbons on the soil. She looked all round her, at an olive tree, and yesterday's iron gate, and at the sky, which was fiercely azure. She was not as innocent as her father still hoped she might turn out to be, but not as experienced as Roy thought, either. There was a world of knowledge between last night and what had gone before. She wondered, already, if violent feelings were going to define the rest of her life, or simply limit it. Roy gathered her long hair in his hand

and turned her head around. They'd had other nights, or attempts at nights, but this was their first morning. Whatever he read on her face made him say, "You know, it won't always be as lovely as this." She nodded. Professor Downcast had a wife and children, and she was used to fair warnings. Roy could not guess how sturdy her emotions were. Her only antagonist had been her father, who had not touched her self-confidence. She accepted Roy's caution as a tribute: *He*, at least, could see that Sarah was objective.

Roy rang the doorbell, which set off a gunburst of barking. The Reeves' hall smelled of toast, carpets, and insect spray. She wanted southern houses to smell of jasmine. "Here, Roy," someone called, and Roy led her by the hand into a small sitting room where two people, an old man and an old woman, sat in armchairs eating breakfast. The man removed a tray from his knees and stood up. He was gaunt and tall, and looked oddly starched, like a nurse coming on duty. "Jack Sprat could eat no fat" came to Sarah's mind. Mrs. Reeve was—she supposed—obese. Sarah stared at her; she did not know how to be furtive. Was the poor woman ill? No, answered the judge who was part of Sarah too. Mrs. Reeve is just greedy. Look at the jam she's shoveled on her plate.

"Well, this is Sarah Holmes," said Roy, stroking her hair, as if he was proving at the outset there was to be no hypocrisy. "We'd adore coffee."

"You'd better do something about it, then," said the fat woman. "We've got tea here. You know where the kitchen is, Roy." She had a deep voice, like a moo. "You, Sarah Holmes, sit down. Find a pew with no dog hair, if you can. Of course, if you're going to be fussy, you won't last long around *here*— eh, boys? You can make toast if you like. No, never mind. I'll make it for you."

It seemed to Sarah a pretty casual way for people their age to behave. Roy was older by a long start, but the Reeves were *old*. They seemed to find it natural to have Roy and Sarah drift over for breakfast after a night in the guesthouse. Mr. Reeve even asked quite kindly, "Did you sleep well? The plane tree draws mosquitoes, I'm afraid."

"I'll have that tree down yet," said Mrs. Reeve. "Oh, I'll have it down one of these days. I can promise you that." She was dressed in a bathrobe that looked like a dark parachute. "We decided not to have eggs," she said, as though Sarah had asked. "Have 'em later. You and Roy must come back for lunch. We'll have a good old fry-up." Here she attended to toast, which meant shaking and tapping an antique wire toaster set on the table before her. "When Tim's gone—bless him—I shall never cook a meal again," she said. "Just bits and pieces on a tray for the boys and me." The boys were dogs, Sarah guessed—two little yappers up on the sofa, the color of teddy-bear stuffing.

"I make a lot of work for Meg," Mr. Reeve said to Sarah. "The break-fasts—breakfast every day, you know—and she is the one who looks after the Christmas cards. Marriage has been a bind for her. She did a marvelous job with evacuees in the war. And poor old Meg loathed kids, still does. You'll never hear her say so. I've never known Meg to complain."

Mrs. Reeve had not waited for her husband to die before starting her widow's diet of tea and toast and jam and gin (the bottle was there, by the toaster, along with a can of orange juice). Sarah knew about this, for not only was her father a widower but they had often spent summers with a widowed aunt. The Reeves seemed like her father and her aunt grown elderly and dis-torted. Mrs. Reeve now unwrapped a chocolate bar, which caused a fit of snorting and jostling on the sofa. "No chockie bits for boys with bad man-ners," she said, feeding them just the same. Yes, there she sat, a widow with two dogs for company. Mr. Reeve, delicately buttering and eating the toast meant for Sarah, murmured that when he *did* go he did not want poor Meg to have any fuss. He seemed to be planning his own modest gravestone; in a heightened moment of telepathy Sarah was sure she could see it too. To Sarah, the tall old man had already ceased to be. He was not Mr. Reeve, Roy's friend and landlord, but an ectoplasmic impression of somebody like him, leaning forward, lips slightly parted, lifting a piece of toast that was cav-ing in like a hammock with a weight of strawberry jam. Panic was in the room, but only Sarah felt it. She had been better off, safer, perhaps happier even, up in Grenoble, trying not to yawn over *"Tout m'afflige, et me nuit, et con-spire à me nuire."* What was she doing here, indoors, on this glowing day, with these two snivelly dogs and these gluttonous old persons? She turned swiftly, hearing Roy, and in her heart she said, in a quavering spoiled child's voice, I want to go home. (How many outings had she ruined for her father. How many picnics, circuses, puppet shows, boat rides. From how many attempted holidays had he been fetched back with a telegram from whichever relation had been trying to hold Sarah down for a week. The strong brass chords of "I want my own life" had always been followed by this dismal piping.)

Roy poured their coffee into pottery mugs and his eyes met Sarah's. His said, Yes, these are the Reeves. They don't matter. I only want one thing, and that's to get back to where we were a few hours ago.

So they were to be conspirators: She liked that.

The Reeves had now done with chewing, feeding, swallowing, and brushing crumbs, and began placing Sarah. Who was she? Sarah Holmes, a little transatlantic pickup, a student slumming round for a summer? What had she studied? Sociology, psychology, and some economics, she told them.

"Sounds Labour" was Mr. Reeve's comment.

She simplified her story and mentioned the thesis. "Urban and Regional Studies of the Less Privileged in British Columbia," as far as Mr. Reeve was concerned, contained only one reassuring word, and that was "British." Being the youngest in the room, Sarah felt like the daughter of the house. She piled cups and plates on one of the trays and took them out to the kitchen. The Reeves were not the sort of people who would ever bother to whisper: She heard that she was "a little on the tall side" and that her proportions made Roy seem slight and small, "like a bloody dago." Her hair was too long; the fringe on her forehead looked sparse and pasted down with soap. She also heard that she had a cast in one eye, which she did not believe.

"One can't accuse her of oversmartness," said Mrs. Reeve.

Roy, whose low voice had carrying qualities, said, "No, Meg. Sarah's jeans are as faded, as baggy, as those brown corduroys of yours. However, owing to Sarah's splendid and enviable shape, hers are not nearly so large across the beam end." This provoked two laughs—a cackle from Jack Sprat and a long three-note moo from his wife.

"Well, Roy," said Tim Reeve, "all I can say is, you amaze me. How do you bring it off?"

What about me? said Sarah to herself. How do *I* bring it off?

"At least she's had sense enough not to come tramping around in high-heeled shoes, like some of our visitors," said Mrs. Reeve—her last word for the moment.

Roy warned Sarah what lunch—the good old fry-up—would be. A large black pan the Reeves had brought to France from England when they emigrated because of taxes and Labour would be dragged out of the oven; its partner, a jam jar of bacon fat, stratified in a wide extent of suety whites, had its permanent place on top of the stove. The lowest, or Ur, line of fat marked the very first fry-up in France. A few spoonfuls of this grease, releasing blue smoke, received tomatoes, more bacon, eggs, sausages, cold boiled potatoes. To get the proper sausages they had to go to a shop that imported them, in Monte Carlo. This was no distance, but the Reeves' car had been paid for by Tim, and he was mean about it. He belonged to a generation that had been in awe of batteries: Each time the ignition was turned on, he thought the car's lifeblood was seeping away. When he became too stingy with the car, then Meg would not let him look at television: The set was hers. She would push it on its wheeled table over bumpy rugs into their bedroom and put a chair against the door.

Roy was a sharp mimic and he took a slightly feminine pleasure in mocking his closest friends. Sarah lay on her elbow on the bed as she had lain on the beach and thought that if he was disloyal to the Reeves then he was all the more loyal to her. They had been told to come back for lunch around three; this long day was in itself like a whole summer. She said, "It sounds like a movie. Are they happy?"

"Oh, blissful," he answered, surprised, and perhaps with a trace of reproval. It was as if he were very young and she had asked an intimate question about his father and mother.

The lunch Roy had described was exactly the meal they were given. She watched him stolidly eating eggs fried to a kind of plastic lace, and covering everything with mustard to damp out the taste of grease. When Meg opened the door to the kitchen she was followed by a blue haze. Tim noticed Sarah's look—she had wondered if something was burning—and said, "Next time you're here that's where we'll eat. It's what we like. We like our kitchen."

"Today we are honoring Sarah," said Meg Reeve, as though baiting Roy.

"So you should," he said. It was the only attempt at sparring; they were all much too fed and comfortable. Tim, who had been to Monte Carlo, had brought back another symbol of their roots, the Hovis loaf. They talked about his shopping, and the things they liked doing—gambling a little, smuggling from Italy for sport. One thing they never did was look at the Mediterranean. It was not an interesting sea. It had no tides. "I do hope you aren't going to bother with it," said Tim to Sarah. It seemed to be their private measure for a guest—that and coming round in the wrong clothes.

The temperature in full sun outside the sitting-room window was thirty-three degrees centigrade. "What does it mean?" said Sarah. Nobody knew. Tim said that 16°C. was the same thing as 61°F. but that nothing else corresponded. For instance, 33°C. could not possibly be 33°F. No, it felt like a lot more.

After the trial weekend Sarah wrote to her father, "I am in this interesting old one-room guesthouse that belongs to an elderly couple here. It is in their garden. They only let reliable people stay in it." She added, "Don't worry, I'm working." If she concealed information she did not exactly lie: She thought she *was* working. Instead of French civilization taught in airless classrooms she would study expatriates at first hand. She decided to record the trivia first—how visitors of any sort were a catastrophe, how a message from old friends staying at Nice brought Tim back from the telephone wearing the look of someone whose deepest feelings have been raked over.

"Come on, Tim, what was it?" his wife would call. "The who? What did they want? An invitation to their hotel? Damned cheek. More likely a lot of free drinks here, that's what they want." They lived next to gas fires with all the windows shut, yelling from room to room. Their kitchen was comfortable providing one imagined it was the depth of January in England and that sleet was battering at the garden. She wanted to record that Mr. Reeve said "heith" and "strenth" and that they used a baby language with each other—walkies, tummy, spend-a-penny. When Sarah said "cookie" it made them laugh; a minute later, feeding the dogs a chocolate cookie, Meg said, "Here, have a chockie bicky." If Tim tried to explain anything, his wife interrupted with "Come on, get to Friday." Nobody could remember the origin of the phrase; it served merely to rattle him.

Sarah meant to record this, but Professor Downcast's useful language had left her. The only words in her head were so homespun and plain she was ashamed to set them down. The heat must have flattened her brain, she thought. The Reeves, who never lowered their voices for anyone, bawled one night that "old Roy was doting and indulgent" and "the wretched girl is in love." That was the answer. She had already discovered that she could live twenty-four hours on end just with the idea that she was in love; she also knew that a man could think about love for a while but then he would start to think about something else. What if Roy never did? Sarah Cooper didn't sound bad; Mrs. R. Cooper was better. But Sarah was not that foolish. She was looking ahead only because she and Roy had no past. She did say to him, "What do you do when you aren't having a vacation?"

"You mean in winter? I go to Marbella. Sometimes Kenya. Where my friends are."

"Don't you work?"

"I did work. They retired me."

"You're too young to be retired. My father isn't even retired. You should write your memoirs—all that colonial stuff."

He laughed at her. She was never more endearing to him than when she was most serious; that was not her fault. She abandoned the future and re-arranged their short history to suit herself. Every word was recollected later in primrose light. Did it rain every Sunday? Was there an invasion of red ants? She refused the memory. The Reeves' garden incinerator, which was never cleaned out, set oily smoke to sit at their table like a third person. She drank her coffee unaware of this guest, seeing nothing but butterflies danc-ing over the lavender hedge. Sarah, who would not make her own bed at home, insisted now on washing everything by hand, though there was a laundry in the village. Love compelled her to buy enough food for a family of seven. The refrigerator was a wheezy old thing, and sometimes Roy got up and turned it off in the night because he could not sleep for its sighing. In the morning Sarah piled the incinerator with spoiled meat, cheese, and peaches, and went out at six o'clock to buy more and more. She was never so bathed in love as when she stood among a little crowd of villagers at a bus stop—the point of creation, it seemed—with her empty baskets; she desperately hoped to be taken for what the Reeves called "part of the local populace." The market she liked was two villages over; the buses were tum-brels. She could easily have driven Roy's car or had everything sent from shops, but she was inventing fidelities. Once, she saw Meg Reeve, wearing a floral cotton that compressed her figure and gave her a stylized dolphin shape, like an ornament on a fountain. On her head was a straw hat with a polka-dot ribbon. She found a place one down and across the aisle from Sarah, who shrank from her notice for fear of that deep voice letting the world know Sarah was not a peasant. Meg unfolded a paper that looked like a prescription; slid her glasses along her nose; held them with one finger. She always sat with her knees spread largely. In order not to have Meg's thigh crushing his, her neighbor, a priest in a dirty cassock, had to squeeze against the window.

She doesn't care, Sarah said to herself. She hasn't even looked to see who is there. When she got down at the next village Meg was still rereading the scrap of paper, and the bus rattled on to Nice.

Sarah never mentioned having seen her; Meg was such a cranky, unpre-dictable old lady. One night she remarked, "Sarah's going to have trouble landing Roy," there, in front of him, on his own terrace. "He'll never marry." Roy was a bachelor owing to the fact he had too many rich friends, and because men were selfish. . . . Here Meg paused, conceding that this might sound wrong. No, it sounded right; Roy was a bachelor because of the selfishness of men, and the looseness and availability of young women.

"True enough, they'll do it for a ham sandwich," said Tim, as if a supply of sandwiches had given him the pick of a beach any day.

His wife stared at him but changed her mind. She plucked at her fork and said, "When Tim's gone—bless him—I shall have all my meals out. Why bother cooking?" She then looked at her plate as if she had seen a mouse on it.

"It's all right, Meg," said Roy. "Sarah favors the cooking of the under-developed countries. All our meals are raw and drowned in yogurt." He said it so kindly Sarah had to laugh. For a time she had tried to make them all eat out of her aunt's bowls, but the untreated wood became stained and Roy found it disgusting. The sight of Sarah scouring them out with ashes did not make him less squeamish. He was, in fact, surprisingly finicky for some-one who had spent a lifetime around colonial prisons. A dead mosquito made him sick—even the mention of one.

"It is true that Roy has never lacked for pretty girls," said Tim. "We should know, eh, Roy?" Roy and the Reeves talked quite a lot about his personal affairs, as if a barrier of discretion had long ago been breached. They were uncomfortable stories, a little harsh sometimes for Sarah's taste. Roy now suddenly chose to tell about how he had met his future brother-in-law in a brothel in Hong Kong—by accident, of course. They became the best of friends and remained so, even after Roy's engagement was broken off.

"Why'd she dump you?" Sarah said. "She found out?"

Her way of asking plain questions froze the others. They looked as if winter had swept over the little terrace and caught them. Then Roy took Sarah's hand and said, "I'm ashamed to say I wasn't gallant—I dumped the lady."

"Old Roy probably thought, um, matrimony," said Tim. "Eh, Meg?" This was because marriage was supposed to be splendid for Tim but some-how confining for his wife.

"She said I was venomous," said Roy, looking at Sarah, who knew he was not.

"She surely didn't mean venomous," said Tim. "She meant something more like, moody." Here he lapsed into a mood of his own, staring at the candles on the table, and Sarah remembered her shared vision of his unas-suming gravestone; she said to Roy in an undertone, "Is anything wrong with him?"

"Wrong with him? Wrong with old Tim? Tim!" Roy called, as if he were out of sight instead of across the table. "When was the last time you ever had a day's illness?"

"I was sick on a Channel crossing—I might have been ten," said Tim.

"Nothing's the matter with Tim, I can promise you that," said his wife. "Never a headache, never a cold, no flu, no rheumatism, no gout, nothing."

"Doesn't feel the amount he drinks," said Roy.

"Are you ever sick, Mrs. Reeve?" Sarah asked.

"Oh, poor Meg," said Tim immediately. "You won't get a word out of her. Never speaks of herself."

"The ailments of old parties can't possibly interest Sarah," said Meg. "Here, Roy, give Sarah something to drink," meaning that her own glass was empty. "My niece Lisbet will be here for a weekend. Now, *that's* an interesting girl. She interviews people for jobs. She can see straight through them, mentally speaking. She had stiff training—had to see a trick cyclist for a year."

"I abhor that subject," said Roy. "No sensible prison governor ever allowed a trick cyclist anywhere near. The good were good and the bad were bad and everyone knew it."

"Psycho-whatnot does not harm if the person is sound," said Meg. "Lisbet just went week after week and had a jolly old giggle with the chap. The firm was paying."

"A didactic analysis is a waste of time," said Sarah, chilling them all once more.

"I didn't say that or anything like it," said Meg. "I said the firm was paying. But you're a bit out of it, Roy," turning to him and heaving her vast garments so Sarah was cut out. "Lisbet said it did help her. You wouldn't believe the number of people she turns away, whatever their education. She can tell if they are likely to have asthma. She saves the firm thousands of pounds every year."

"Lisbet can see when they're queer," said Tim.

"What the hell do you mean?" said Roy.

"What did she tell you?" said Meg, now extremely annoyed. "Come on, Tim, get to Friday."

But Tim had gone back to contemplating his life on the Other Side, and they could obtain nothing further.

Sarah forgot all about Mrs. Reeve's niece until Lisbet turned up, wearing a poncho, black pants, and bracelets. She was about Roy's age. All over her head was a froth of kinky yellow hair—a sort of Little Orphan Annie wig. She stared with small blue eyes and gave Sarah a boy's handshake. She said, "So you're the famous one!"

Sarah had come back from the market to find them all drinking beer in The Tunnel. Her shirt stuck to her back. She pulled it away and said, "Famous one what?" From the way Lisbet laughed she guessed she had been described as a famous comic turn. Roy handed Sarah a glass without looking at her. Roy and Tim were talking about how to keep Lisbet amused for the weekend. Everything was displayed—the night racing at Cagnes, the gambling, the smuggling from Italy, which bored Sarah but which even Roy did for amusement. "A picnic," Sarah said, getting in something she liked. Also, it sounded cool. The Hayeses, those anxious tourists at her hotel in Nice, suddenly rose up in her mind offering advice. "There's this chapel," she said, feeling a spiky nostalgia, as if she were describing something from home. "Remember, Roy, I mentioned it? Nobody goes there. . . . You have to get the keys from a café in the village. You can picnic in the churchyard; it has a gate and a wall. There's a river where we washed our hands. The book said it used to be a pagan place. It has these paintings now, of the Last Judgment, and Jesus, naturally, and one of Judas after he hung himself."

"Hanged," said Roy and Lisbet together.

"Hanged. Well, somebody had really seen a hanging—the one who painted it, I mean."

"Have you?" said Roy, smiling.

"No, but I can imagine."

"No," he said, still smiling. "You can't. All right, I'm for the picnic. Sunday, then. We'll do Italy tomorrow."

His guests got up to leave. Tim suddenly said, for no reason Sarah could see, "I'm glad I'm not young."

As soon as the others were out of earshot Roy said, "God, what a cow! Planeloads of Lisbets used to come out to Asia looking for civil-service husbands. Now they fly to Majorca and sleep with the waiters."

"Why do we have to be nice to her, if you feel like that?" said Sarah.

"Why don't you know about these things without asking?" said Roy.

My father didn't bring me up well, Sarah thought, and resolved to write and tell him so. Mr. Holmes would not have been nice to Lisbet and then called her a cow. He might have done one or the other, or neither. His dilemma as a widower was insoluble; he could never be too nice for fear of someone's taking it into her head that Sarah wanted a mother. Also, he was not violent about people, even those he had to eliminate. That was why he gave them comic names. "Perhaps you are right," she said to Roy, without being any more specific. He cared for praise, however ambiguous; and so they had a perfect day, and a perfect night, but those were the last: In the morning, as Sarah stood on the table to tie one end of a clothesline to the plane tree, she slipped, had to jump, landed badly, and sprained her ankle. By noon the skin was purple and she had to cut off her canvas shoe. The foot needed to be bandaged, but not by Roy: The very sight of it made him sick. He could not bear a speck of dust anywhere, or a chipped cup. She remembered the wooden bowls, and how he'd had to leave the table once because they looked a little doubtful, not too clean. Lisbet was summoned. Kneeling, she wrapped Sarah's foot and ankle in strips of a torn towel and fixed the strips with safety pins.

"It'll do till I see a doctor," Sarah said.

Lisbet looked up. How small her eyes were! "You don't want a doctor for that, surely?"

"Yes, I do. I think it should be X-rayed," Sarah said. "It hurts like anything."

"Of course she doesn't," said Roy.

Getting well with the greatest possible amount of suffering, and with your bones left crooked, was part of their code. It seemed to Sarah an unreasonable code, but she did not want to seem like someone making a fuss. All the same, she said, "I feel sick."

"Drink some brandy," said Lisbet.

"Lie down," said Roy. "We shan't be long." It would have been rude not to have taken Lisbet on the smuggling expedition just because Sarah couldn't go.

In the late afternoon Meg Reeve strolled down to see how Sarah was managing. She found her standing on one foot hanging washing on a line. The sight of Sarah's plaid slacks, bought on sale at Nice, caused Meg to remark, "My dear, are you a Scot? I've often wondered, seeing you wearing those." Sarah let a beach towel of Roy's fall to the ground.

"Damn, it'll have to be washed again," she said.

Meg had brought Roy's mail. She put the letters on the table, facedown, as if Sarah were likely to go over the postmarks with a magnifying glass. The dogs snuffled and snapped at the ghosts of animal-haters. "What clan?" said Meg.

"Clan? Oh, you're still talking about my slacks. Clan *salade niçoise*, I guess."

"Well, you must not wear tartan," said Meg. "It is an insult to the family, d'you see? I'm surprised Roy hasn't . . . Ticky! Blue! Naughty boys!"

"Oh, the dogs come down here and pee all over the terrace every day," said Sarah.

"Roy used to give them chockie bits. They miss being spoiled. But now he hasn't time for them, has he?"

"I don't know. I can't answer for him. He has time for what interests him."

"Why do you hang your washing where you can see it?" said Meg. "Are you Italian?" Sarah made new plans; next time the Reeves were invited she would boil Ticky and Blue with a little sugar and suet and serve them up as pudding. I must look angelic at this moment, she thought.

She said, "No, I'm not Italian. I don't think so."

"There are things I could never bring myself to do," said Meg. "Not in my walk of life."

The sociologist snapped to attention. Easing her sore ankle, Sarah said, "Please, what is your walk of life, exactly?"

It was so dazzling, so magical, that Meg could not name it, but merely mouthed a word or two that Sarah was unable to lip-read. A gust of incinerator smoke stole between them and made them choke. "As for Tim," said Meg, getting her breath again, "you, with all your transatlantic money, couldn't buy what Tim has in his veins."

Sarah limped indoors and somehow found the forgotten language. "Necessity for imparting status information," she recorded, and added "erroneous" between "imparting" and "status." She was still, in a way, half in love with Professor Downcast.

She discovered this was a conversation neither Roy nor Lisbet could credit. They unpacked their loot from Italy on the wobbly terrace table— plastic table mats, plastic roses, a mermaid paperweight, a bottle of apéritif that smelled like medicine, a Florentine stamp box . . . "Rubbish, garbage," Sarah said in her mind. "But Roy is happy." Also, he was drunk. So was Lisbet.

"Meg could not have said those things," said Roy, large-eyed.

"Meg doesn't always understand Sarah," said Lisbet. "The accent."

"Mrs. Reeve was doing the talking," said Sarah.

"She wouldn't have talked that way to an Englishwoman," said Roy, swinging round to Sarah's side.

"Wouldn't have dared," said Lisbet. She shouted, "Wouldn't have dared to me!"

"As for Tim, well, Tim really is the real thing," said Roy. "I mean to say that Tim really *is*."

"So is my aunt," said Lisbet, but Roy had disappeared behind the white net curtain, and they heard him fall on the bed. "He's had rather a lot," said Lisbet. Sarah felt anxiety for Roy, who had obviously had a lot of every-thing—perhaps of Lisbet too. And there was still the picnic next day, and no one had bought any food for it. Lisbet looked glowing and superb, as if she had been tramping in a clean wind instead of sitting crouched in a twilit bar somewhere on the Italian side. She should have been haggard and gray.

"Who was driving?" Sarah asked her.

"Took turns."

"What did you talk about?" She was remembering his "God, what a cow!"

"Capital punishment, apartheid, miscegenation, and my personal prob-lems with men. That I seem cold, but I'm not really."

"Boys, boys, boys!" That was Meg Reeve calling her dogs. They rolled out of the lavender hedge like a pair of chewed tennis balls. They might well have been eavesdropping. Sarah gave a shiver, and Lisbet laughed and said, "Someone's walking on your grave."

The sunlight on the terrace next morning hurt Roy's eyes; he made little flapping gestures, meaning Sarah was not to speak. "What were you drink-ing in Italy?" she said. He shook his head. Mutely, he took the dried laun-dry down and folded it. Probably, like Meg, he did not much care for the look of it. "I've made the picnic," Sarah next offered. "No reason why I can't come—we won't be doing much walking." She stood on one leg, like a stork. The picnic consisted of anything Sarah happened to find in the re-frigerator. She included plums in brandy because she noticed a jar of them, and iced white wine in a thermos. At the last minute she packed olives, salted peanuts, and several pots of yogurt.

"Put those back," said Roy.

"Why? Do you think they'll melt?"

"Just do as I say, for once. Put them back."

"Do you know what I think?" said Sarah after a moment. "I think we're starting out on something my father would call The Ill-Fated Excursion."

For the first time ever, she saw Roy looking angry. The vitality of the look made him younger, but not in a nice way. He became a young man, an ugly one. "Liz will have to drive," he said. "I've got a blinding headache, and you can't, not with *that*." He could not bring himself to name her affliction. "How do you know about this place?" he said. "Who took you there?"

"I told you. Some Americans in my hotel. Haynes—no, Hayes."

"Yes, I can imagine." He looked at her sidelong and said, "Just who were you sleeping with when I collected you?"

She felt what it was like to blush—like a rash of needles and pins. He knew every second of her life, because she had told it to him that night on the beach. What made her blush was that she sensed he was only pretending to be jealous. It offended her. She said, "Let's call the picnic off."

"I don't want to."

She was not used to quarrels, only to tidal waves. She did not understand that they were quarreling now. She wondered again what he had been drinking over in Italy. Her ankle felt in a vise, but that was the least of it. They set off, all three together, and Lisbet drove straight up into the hills as if pursuing escaped prisoners. They shot past towns Sarah had visited with the Americans, who had been conscientious about churches; she saw, open-and-shut, views they had stopped to photograph. When she said, "Look," nobody heard. She sat crumpled in the narrow backseat, with the picnic sliding all over as they rounded the mountain curves, quite often on the wrong side.

"That was the café, back there, where you get the key," Sarah had to say twice—once very loudly. Lisbet braked so they were thrown forward and then reversed like a bullet ricocheting. "Sarah knows about this," said Roy, as if it were a good thing to know about. That was encouraging. She gripped her ankle between her hands and set her foot down. She tested her weight and managed to walk and hop to the cool café, past the beaded curtain. She leaned on the marble counter; she had lost something. Was it her confidence? She wanted someone to come and take her home, but was too old to want that; she knew too many things. She said to the man standing behind the counter, "*J'ai mal*," to explain why she did not take the keys from him and at once go out. His reaction was to a confession of sorrow and grief; he poured out something to drink. It was clear as water, terribly strong, and smelled of warm fruit. When she gestured to show him she had no money, he said, "*Ça va.*" He was kind; the Hayeses, such an inadequate substitute for peacocks, had been kind too. She said to herself, "How awful if I should cry."

The slight inclination of Roy's head when she handed the keys to him meant he might be interested. She felt emboldened: "One's for the chapel, the other's the gate. There isn't a watchman or anything. It's too bad, because people write on the walls."

"Which way?" Lisbet interrupted. She chased her prisoners another mile or so.

Sarah had told them no one ever came here, but they were forced to park behind a car with Swiss license plates. Next to the gate sat a large party of picnickers squeezed round a card table. There was only one man among them, and Sarah thought it must be a harem and the man had been allowed several wives for having been reasonable and Swiss until he was fifty. She started to tell this to Roy, but he had gone blank as a monument; she felt overtaken by her father's humor, not her own. Roy gave the harem an empty look that reminded her of the prostitutes down in Nice, and now she knew what their faces had been saying. It was "I despise you." The chapel was an icebox; and she saw Roy and Lisbet glance with some consternation at the life of Jesus spread around for anyone to see. They would certainly have described themselves as Christians, but they were embarrassed by Christ. They went straight to Judas, who was more reassuring. Hanged, disemboweled, his stomach and liver exposed to ravens, Judas gave up his soul. His soul was a small naked creature. Perceiving Satan, the creature held out its arms.

"Now, *that* man must have eaten Sarah's cooking," said Roy, and such were their difficulties that she was grateful to hear him say anything. But he added, "A risk many have taken, I imagine." This was to Lisbet. Only Sarah knew what he meant. She fell back and pretended to be interested in a rack of postcards. The same person who trusted visitors not to write their names on paintings had left a coin box. Sarah had no money and did not want to ask Roy for any. She stole a reproduction of the Judas fresco and put it inside her shirt.

Roy and Lisbet ate some of the picnic. They sat where Sarah had sat with the Americans, but it was in no way the same. Of course, the season was later, the river lower, the grass drooping and dry. The shadows of clouds made them stare and comment, as if looking for something to say. Sarah was relieved when the two decided to climb up in the maquis, leaving her "to rest a bit"—this was Lisbet. "Watch out for snakes," Sarah said, and got from Roy one blurred, anxious, puzzled look, the last straight look he ever gave her. She sat down and drank all the brandy out of the jar of plums. Roy had an attitude about people she had never heard of: Nothing must ever go wrong. An accident is degrading for the victim. She undid the toweling strips and looked at her bloated ankle and foot. Of course, it was ugly; but it was part of a living body, not a corpse, and it hurt Sarah, not Roy. She tipped out the plums so the ants could have a party, drank some of the white wine, and, falling asleep, thought she was engaged in an endless and heated discussion with some person who was in the wrong.

She woke up cramped and thirsty on the backseat of the car. They were stopped in front of the café and must have been parked for some time, for they were in an oblique shadow of late afternoon. Roy was telling Lisbet a lie: He said he had been a magistrate and was writing his memoirs. Next he told her of hangings he'd seen. He said in his soft voice, "Don't you think some people are better out of the way?" Sarah knew by heart the amber eyes and the pupils so small they seemed a mistake sometimes. She was not Sarah now but a prisoner impaled on a foreign language, seeing bright, light, foreign eyes offering something nobody wanted—death. "Flawed people, born rotten," Roy went on.

"Oh, everyone thinks that now," said Lisbet.

They were alike, with fortunes established in piracy. He liked executions; she broke people before they had a chance to break themselves. Lisbet stroked the back of her own neck. Sarah had noticed before that when Lisbet was feeling sure of herself she made certain her neck was in place. Neurotic habit, Sarah's memory asked her to believe; but no, it was only the gesture of someone at ease in a situation she recognized. Tranquil as to her neck, Lisbet now made sure of her hair. She patted the bright steel wool that must have been a comfort to her mother some thirty-five—no, forty—years before.

I am jealous, Sarah said to herself. How unwelcome. Jealousy is only . . . the jealous person is the one keeping something back and so . . .

"Oh, keys, always keys," said Roy, shaking them. He slammed out in a way that was surely rude to Lisbet. She rested her arm over the back of the seat and looked at Sarah. "You drank enough to stun a rhinoceros, little girl," she said. "We had to take you out behind the chapel and make you be sick before we could let you in the car." Sarah began to remember. She saw Roy's face, a gray flash in a cracked old film about a catastrophe. Lisbet said, "Look, Sarah, how old are you? Aren't you a bit out of your depth with Roy?" She might have said more, but a native spitefulness, or a native prudence, prevented her. She flew to Majorca the next day, as Roy had predicted, leaving everyone out of step.

Now Roy began hating; he hated the sea, the Reeves, the dogs, the blue of plumbago, the mention of Lisbet, and most of all he hated Sarah. The Reeves laughed and called it "old Roy being bloody-minded again," but

Sarah was frightened. She had never known anyone who would simply refuse to speak, who would take no notice of a question. Meg said to her, "He misses that job of his. It came to nothing. He tried to give a lot of natives a sense of right and wrong, and then some Socialist let them vote."

"Yes, he liked that job," Sarah said slowly. "One day he'd watch a hanging, and the next he'd measure the exercise yard to see if it was up to standard." She said suddenly and for no reason she knew, "I've disappointed him."

Their meals were so silent that they could hear the swelling love songs from the Reeves' television, and the Reeves' voices bawling away at each other. Sarah's throat would go tight. In daytime the terrace was like an oven now, and her ankle kept her from sleeping at night. Then Roy gave up eating and lay on the bed looking up at the ceiling. She still went on shopping, but now it took hours. Mornings, before leaving, she would place a bowl of coffee for him, like an offering; it was still there, at the bedside, cold and oily-looking now, when she came back. She covered a tray with leaves from the plane tree—enormous powdery leaves, the size of her two hands—and she put cheese on the leaves, and white cheese covered with pepper, a Camembert, a salty goat cheese he had liked. He did not touch any. Out of a sort of desperate sentiment, she kept the tray for days, picking chalky pieces off as the goat cheese grew harder and harder and became a fossil. He must have eaten sometimes; she thought of him gobbling scraps straight from the refrigerator when her back was turned. She wrote a letter to her father that of course she did not send. It said, "I've been having headaches lately. I wind a thread around a finger until the blood can't get past and that starts a new pain. The headache is all down the back of my neck. I'm not sure what to do next. It will be terrible for you if I turn out to have a brain tumor. It will cost you a lot of money and you may lose your only child."

One dawn she knew by Roy's breathing that he was awake. Every muscle was taut as he pulled away, as if to touch her was defilement. No use saying what they had been like not long before, because he could not remember. She was a disgusting object because of a cracked ankle, because she had drunk too much and been sick behind a chapel, and because she had led an expedition to look at Jesus. She lay thinking it over until the dawn birds stopped and then she sat up on the edge of the bed, feeling absolutely out of place because she was undressed. She pulled clothes on as fast as she could and packed whatever seemed important. After she had pushed her suitcase out the door, she remembered the wooden bowls and the poster. These she took along the path and threw in the Reeves' foul incinerator, as if to get rid of all traces of witchery, goodness, and love. She realized she was leaving, a decision as final and as stunning as her having crossed the promenade in Nice with Roy's hand on her arm.

She said through the white netting over the door, "I'm sorry, Roy." It was not enough; she added, "I'm sorry I don't understand you more." The stillness worried her. She limped near and bent over him. He was holding his breath, like a child in temper. She said softly, "I could stay a bit longer." No answer. She said, "Of course, my foot will get better, but then you might find something else the matter with me." Still no answer, except that he began breathing. Nothing was wrong except that he was cruel, lunatic, Fascist—No, not even that. Nothing was wrong except that he did not love her. That was all.

She lugged her suitcase as far as the road and sat down beside it. Overnight a pocket of liquid the size of a lemon had formed near the anklebone. Her father would say it was all her own fault again. Why? Was it Sarah's fault that she had all this loving capital to invest? What was she supposed to do with it? Even if she always ended up sitting outside a gate somewhere, was she any the worse for it? The only thing wrong now was the pain she felt, not of her ankle but in her stomach. Her stomach felt as if it was filled up with old oyster shells. Yes, a load of old, ugly, used-up shells was what she had for stuffing. She had to take care not to breathe too deeply, because the shells scratched. In her research for Professor Downcast she had learned that one could be alcoholic, crippled, afraid of dying and of being poor, and she knew these things waited for everyone, even Sarah; but nothing had warned her that one day she would not be loved. That was the meaning of "less privileged." There was no other.

Now that she had vanished, Roy would probably get up, and shave, and stroll across to the Reeves, and share a good old fry-up. Then, his assurance regained, he would start prowling the bars and beaches, wearing worn immaculate whites, looking for a new, unblemished story. He would repeat the first soft words, "Don't be frightened," the charm, the gestures, the rituals, and the warning "It won't always be lovely." She saw him out in the open, in her remembered primrose light, before he was trapped in the tunnel again and had to play at death. "Roy's new pickup," the Reeves would bawl at each other. "I said, Roy's new one . . . he hardly knows how to get rid of her."

At that, Sarah opened her mouth and gave a great sobbing cry; only one, but it must have carried, for next thing she heard was the Reeves' door, and, turning, she saw Tim in a dressing gown, followed by Meg in her parachute of a robe. Sarah stood up to face them. The sun was on her back. She clutched the iron bars of the gate because she had to stand like a stork again. From their side of it, Tim looked down at her suitcase. He said, "Do you want—are you waiting to be driven somewhere?"

"To the airport, if you feel like taking me. Otherwise I'll hitch."

"Oh, please don't do that!" He seemed afraid of another outburst from her—something low-pitched and insulting this time.

"Come in this minute," said Meg. "I don't know what you are up to, but we do have neighbors, you know."

"Why should I care?" said Sarah. "They aren't my neighbors."

"You *are* a little coward," said Meg. "Running away only because ..." There were so many reasons that of course she hesitated.

Without unkind intention Sarah said the worst thing: "It's just that I'm too young for all of you."

Meg's hand crept between the bars and around her wrist. "Somebody had to be born before you, Sarah," she said, and unlocked her hand and turned back to the house. "Yes, boys, dear boys, here I am," she called.

Tim said, "Would you like—let me see—would you like something to eat or drink?" It seemed natural for him to talk through bars.

"I can't stay in the same bed with someone who doesn't care," said Sarah, beginning to cry. "It isn't right."

"It is what most people do," said Tim. "Meg has the dogs, and her television. She has everything. We haven't often lived together. We gradually stopped. When did we last live together? When we went home once for the motor show." She finally grasped what he meant by "live together." Tim said kindly, "Look, I don't mean to pry, but you didn't take old Roy too much to heart, did you? He wasn't what you might call the love of your life?"

"I don't know yet."

"Dear, dear," said Tim, as if someone had been spreading bad news. He seemed so much more feminine than his wife; his hands were powdery—they seemed dipped in talcum. His eyes were embedded in a little volcano of wrinkles that gave him in full sunlight the look of a lizard. A white lizard, Sarah decided. "This has affected Meg," he said. "The violence of it. We shall talk it over for a long time. Well. You have so much more time. You will bury all of us." His last words were loud and sudden, almost a squawk, because Meg, light of tread and silent on her feet, had come up behind him. She wore her straw hat and carried her morning glass of gin and orange juice.

"Sarah? She'll bury you," said Meg. "Fetch the car, Tim, and take Sarah somewhere. Come along. Get to Friday. Tim." He turned. "Dress first," she said.

The sun which had turned Tim into a white lizard now revealed a glassy stain on Meg's cheek, half under her hair. Sarah's attention jumped like a child's. She said, "Something's bitten you. Look. Something poisonous."

Meg moved her head and the poisoned bite vanished under the shade of her hat. "Observant. Tim has never noticed. Neither has Roy. It is only a small malignant thing," she said indifferently. "I've been going to the hospital in Nice twice a week for treatment. They burned it—that's the reason for the scar."

"Oh, Meg," said Sarah, drawn round the gate. "Nobody knew. That was why you went to Nice. I saw you on the bus."

"I saw you," said Meg, "but why talk when you needn't? I get plenty of talk at home. May I ask where you are going?"

"I'm going to the airport, and I'll sit there till they get me on a plane."

"Well, Sarah, you may be sitting for some time, but I know you know what you are doing," said Meg. "I am minding the summer heat this year. I feel that soon I won't be able to stand it anymore. When Tim's gone I won't ever marry again. I'll look for some woman to share expenses. If you ever want to come back for a holiday, Sarah, you have only to let me know."

And so Tim, the battery of his car leaking its lifeblood all over French roads, drove Sarah down to Nice and along to the airport. Loyal to the Reeve standards, he did not once glance at the sea. As for Sarah, she sat beside him crying quietly, first over Meg, then over herself, because she thought she had spent all her capital on Roy and would never love anyone again. She looked for the restaurant with the blue tablecloths, and for the beach where they had sat talking for a night, but she could not find them; there were dozens of tables and awnings and beaches, all more or less alike.

"You'll be all right?" said Tim. He wanted her to say yes, of course.

She said, "Tim, Roy needs help."

He did not know her euphemisms any more than she understood his. He said, "Help to do what?"

"Roy is unhappy and he doesn't know what he wants. If you're over forty and you don't know what you want, well, I guess someone should tell you."

"My dear Sarah," said the old man, "that is an unkind thing to say about a friend we have confidence in."

She said quickly, "Don't you see, before he had a life that suited him, inspecting people in jails. They didn't seem like people *or* jails. It kept him happy, it balanced ..." Suddenly she gave a great shiver in the heat of the morning and heard Lisbet laugh and say, "Someone's walking on your grave." She went on, "For example, he won't eat."

"Don't you worry about that," cried Tim, understanding something at last. "Meg will see that he eats." Right to the end, everyone was at crosspurposes. "Think of it this way," said Tim. "You had to go home sometime."

"Not till September."

"Well, look on the happy side. Old Roy ... matrimony. You might not enjoy it, you know, unless you met someone like Meg." He obviously had no idea what he was saying anymore, and so she gave up talking until he set her down at the departures gate. Then he said, "Good luck to you, child," and drove away looking indescribably happy.

Sarah kept for a long time the picture of Judas with his guts spilling and with his soul (a shrimp of a man, a lesser Judas) reaching out for the Devil. It should have signified Roy, or even Lisbet, but oddly enough it was she, the victim, who felt guilty and maimed. Still, she was out of the tunnel. Unlike Judas she was alive, and that was something. She was so much younger than all those other people: As Tim had said, she would bury them all. She tacked the Judas card over a map of the world on a wall of her room. Plucked from its origins it began to flower from Sarah's; here was an image that might have followed her from the nursery. It was someone's photo, a family likeness, that could bear no taint of pain or disaster. One day she took the card down, turned it over, and addressed it to a man she was after. He was too poor to invite her anywhere and seemed too shy to make a move. He was also in terrible trouble—back taxes, ex-wife seizing his salary. He had been hounded from California to Canada for his political beliefs. She was in love with his mystery, his hardships, and the death of Trotsky. She wrote, "This person must have eaten my cooking. Others have risked it so please come to dinner on Friday, Sarah." She looked at the words for seconds before hearing another voice. Then she remembered where the card was from, and she understood what the entire message was about. She could have changed it, but it was too late to change anything much. She was more of an *amoureuse* than a psycho-anything, she would never use up her capital, and some summer or other would always be walking on her grave.

IRINA

~❧~

One of Irina's grandsons, nicknamed Riri, was sent to her at Christmas. His mother was going into hospital, but nobody told him that. The real cause of his visit was that since Irina had become a widow her children worried about her being alone. The children, as Irina would call them forever, were married and in their thirties and forties. They did not think they were like other people, because their father had been a powerful old man. He was a Swiss writer, Richard Notte. They carried his reputation and the memory of his puritan equity like an immense jar filled with water of which they had been told not to spill a drop. They loved their mother, but they had never needed to think about her until now. They had never fretted about which way her shadow might fall, and whether to stay in the shade or get out by being eccentric and bold. There were two sons and three daughters, with fourteen children among them. Only Riri was an only child. The girls had married an industrial designer, a Lutheran minister (perhaps an insolent move, after all, for the daughter of a militant atheist), and an art historian in Paris. One boy had become a banker and the other a lecturer on Germanic musical tradition. These were the crushed sons and loyal daughters to whom Irina had been faithful, whose pictures had traveled with her and lived beside her bed.

Few of Notte's obituaries had even mentioned a family. Some of his literary acquaintances were surprised to learn there had been any children at all, though everyone paid homage to the soft, quiet wife to whom he had dedicated his books, the subject of his first rapturous poems. These poems, conventional verse for the most part, seldom translated out of German except by unpoetical research scholars, were thought to be the work of his youth. Actually, Notte was forty when he finally married, and Irina barely nineteen. The obituaries called Notte the last of a breed, the end of a Tolstoyan line of moral lightning rods—an extinction which was probably hard on those writers who came after him, and still harder on his children. However, even to his family the old man had appeared to be the very archetype of a respected European novelist—prophet, dissuader, despairingly opposed to evil, crack-voiced after having made so many pronouncements. Otherwise, he was not all that typical as a Swiss or as a Western, liberal, Protestant European, for he neither saved, nor invested, nor hid, nor disguised his material returns.

"What good is money, except to give away?" he often said. He had a wife, five children, and an old secretary who had turned into a dependent. It was true that he claimed next to nothing for himself. He rented shabby, ramshackle houses impossible to heat or even to clean. Owning was against his convictions, and he did not want to be tied to a gate called home. His room was furnished with a cot, a lamp, a desk, two chairs, a map of the world, a small bookshelf—no more, not even carpets or curtains. Like his family, he wore thick sweaters indoors as out, and crouched over inadequate electric fires. He seldom ate meat—though he did not deprive his children—and drank water with his meals. He had married once—once and for all. He could on occasion enjoy wine and praise and restaurants and good-looking women, but these festive outbreaks were on the rim of his real life, as remote from his children—as strange and as distorted to them—as some other country's colonial wars. He grew old early, as if he expected old age to suit him. By sixty, his eyes were sunk in pockets of lizard skin. His hair became bleached and lustrous, like the scrap of wedding dress Irina kept in a jeweler's box. He was photographed wearing a dark suit and a woman's plaid shawl—he was always cold by then, even in summer—and with a rakish felt hat shading half his face. His wife still let a few photographers in, at the end—but not many. Her murmured "He is working" had for decades been a double lock. He was as strong as Rasputin, his enemies said; he went on writing and talking and traveling until he positively could not focus his eyes or be helped aboard a train. Nearly to the last, he and Irina swung off on their seasonal cycle of journeys to Venice, to Rome, to cities where their married children lived, to Liège and Oxford for awards and honors. His place in a hotel dining room was recognizable from the door because of the pills, drops, and powders lined up to the width of a dinner plate. Notte's hypochondria had been known and gently caricatured for years. His sons, between them, had now bought up most of the original drawings: Notte, in infant's clothing, downing his medicine like a man (he had missed the Nobel); Notte quarreling with Aragon and throwing up Surrealism; a grim female figure called "Existentialism" taking his pulse; Notte catching Asian flu on a cultural trip to Peking. During the final months of his life his children noticed that their mother had begun acquiring medicines of her own, as if hoping by means of mirror-magic to draw his ailments into herself.

If illness became him, it was only because he was fond of ritual, the children thought—even the hideous ceremonial of pain. But Irina had not been intended for sickness and suffering; she was meant to be burned dry and consumed by the ritual of him. The children believed that the end of his life would surely be the death of their mother. They did not really expect Irina to turn her face to the wall and die, but an exclusive, even a selfish, alliance with Notte had seemed her reason for being. As their father grew old, then truly old, then old in mind, and querulous, and unjust, they observed the patient tenderness with which she heeded his sulks and caprices, his almost insane commands. They supposed this ardent submission of hers had to do with love, but it was not a sort of love they had ever experienced or tried to provoke. One of his sons saw Notte crying because Irina had buttered toast for him when he wanted it dry. She stroked the old man's silky hair, smiling. The son hated this. Irina was diminishing a strong, proud man, making a senile child of him, just as Notte was enslaving and debasing her. At the same time the son felt a secret between the two, a mystery. He wondered then, but at no other time, if the secret might not be Irina's invention and property.

Notte left a careful will for such an unworldly person. His wife was to be secure in her lifetime. Upon her death the residue of income from his work would be shared among the sons and daughters. There were no gifts or bequests. The will was accompanied by a testament which the children had photocopied for the beauty of the handwriting and the charm of the text. Irina, it began, belonged to a generation of women shielded from decisions, allowed to grow in the sun and shade of male protection. This flower, his flower, he wrote, was to be cherished now as if she were her children's child.

"In plain words," said Irina, at the first reading, in a Zurich lawyer's office, "I am the heir." She was wearing dark glasses because her eyes were tired, and a tight hat. She looked tense and foreign.

Well, yes, that was it, although Notte had put it more gracefully. His fa-

vorite daughter was his literary executor, entrusted with the unfinished manuscripts and the journals he had kept for sixty-five years. But it soon became
evident that Irina had no intention of giving these up. The children adored
their mother, but even without love as a factor would not have made a case
of it; Notte's lawyer had already told them about disputes ending in maze-
like litigation, families sundered, contents of a desk sequestered, diaries rotting in bank vaults while the inheritors thrashed it out. Besides, editing
Notte's papers would keep Irina busy and an occupation was essential now.
In loving and unloving families alike, the same problem arises after a death:
What to do about the widow?

Irina settled some of it by purchasing an apartment in a small Alpine
town. She chose a tall, glassy, urban-looking building of the kind that made
conservationist groups send round-robin letters, accompanied by incrimi-
nating photographs, to newspapers in Lausanne. The apartment had a hall,
an up-to-date kitchen, a bedroom for Irina, a spare room with a narrow bed
in it, one bathroom, and a living room containing a couch. There was a
glassed-in cube of a balcony where in a pinch an extra cot might have fitted,
but Irina used the space for a table and chairs. She ordered red lampshades
and thick curtains and the pale furniture that is usually sold to young couples. She seemed to come into her own in that tight, neutral flat, the children thought. They read some of the interviews she gave, and approved: She
said, in English and Italian, in German and French, that she would not be a
literary widow, detested by critics, resented by Notte's readers. Her firm dif-
fidence made the children smile, and they were proud to read about her dignified beauty. But as for her intelligence—well, they supposed that the
interviewers had confused fluency with wit. Irina's views and her way of expressing them were all camouflage, simply part of a ladylike undereducation,
long on languages and bearing, short on history and arithmetic. Her origins
were Russian and Swiss and probably pious; the children had not been
drawn to that side of the family. Their father's legendary peasant childhood,
his isolated valley-village had filled their imaginations and their collective
past. There was a sudden April lightness in her letters now that relieved and
yet troubled them. They knew it was a sham happiness. Nature's way of
protecting the survivor from immediate grief. The crisis would come later,
when her most secret instincts had built a seawall. They took turns invad-
ing her at Easter and in the summer, one couple at a time, bringing a child
apiece—there was no room for more. Winter was a problem, however, for
the skiing was not good just there, and none of them liked to break up their

families at Christmastime. Not only was Irina's apartment lacking in beds but there was absolutely no space for a tree. Finally, she offered to visit them, in regular order. That was how they settled it. She went to Bern, to Munich, to Zurich, and then came the inevitable Christmas when it was not that no one wanted her but just that they were all doing different things.

She had written in November of that year that a friend, whom she described, with some quaintness, as "a person," had come for a long stay. They liked that. A visit meant winter company, lamps on at four, China tea, conversation, the peppery smell of carnations (her favorite flower) in a warm room. For a week or two of the visit her letters were blithe, but presently they noticed that "the person" seemed to be having a depressing effect on their mother. She wrote that she had been working on Notte's journals for three years now. Who would want to read them except old men and women? His moral and political patterns were fossils of liberalism. He had seen the cracks in the Weimar Republic. He had understood from the beginning what Hitler meant. If at first he had been wrong about Mussolini, he had changed his mind even before Croce changed his, and had been safely back on the side of democracy in time to denounce Pirandello. He had given all he could, short of his life, to the Spanish Republicans. His measure of Stalin had been so wise and unshakably just that he had never been put on the Communist index—something rare for a Western Socialist. No one could say, ever, that Notte had hedged or retreated or kept silent when a voice was needed. Well, said Irina, what of it? He had written, pledged, warned, signed, declared. And what had he changed, diverted, or stopped? She suddenly sent the same letter to all five children: "This Christmas I don't want to go anywhere. I intend to stay here, in my own home."

They knew this was the crisis and that they must not leave her to face it alone, but that was the very winter when all their plans ran down, when one daughter was going into hospital, another moving to a different city, the third probably divorcing. The elder son was committed to a Christmas with his wife's parents, the younger lecturing in South Africa—a country where Irina, as Notte's constant reflection, would certainly not wish to set foot. They wrote and called and cabled one another: What shall we do? Can you? Will you? I can't.

Irina had no favorites among her children, except possibly one son who had been ill with rheumatic fever as a child and required long nursing. To him she now confided that she longed for her own childhood sometimes, in order to avoid having to judge herself. She was homesick for a time when nothing had crystallized and mistakes were allowed. Now, in old age, she had no excuse for errors. Every thought had a long meaning; every motive had angles and corners, and could be measured. And yet whatever she saw and thought and attempted was still fluid and vague. The shape of a table against afternoon light still held a mystery, awaited a final explanation. You looked for clarity, she wrote, and the answer you had was paleness, the flat white cast that a snowy sky throws across a room.

Part of this son knew about death and dying, but the rest of him was a banker and thoroughly active. He believed that, given an ideal situation, one should be able to walk through a table, which would save time and round-about decisions. However, like all of Notte's children he had been raised with every awareness of solid matter too. His mother's youthful, yearning, and probably religious letter made him feel bland and old. He told his wife what he thought it contained, and she told a sister-in-law what she thought he had said. Irina was tired. Her eyesight was poor, perhaps as a result of prolonged work on those diaries. Irina did not need adult company, which might lead to morbid conversation; what she craved now was a symbol of innocent, continuing life. An animal might do it. Better still, a child.

Riri did not know that his mother would be in hospital the minute his back was turned. Balanced against a tame Christmas with a grandmother was a midterm holiday, later, of high-altitude skiing with his father. There was also some further blackmail involving his holiday homework, and then the vague state of behavior called "being reasonable"—that was all anyone asked. They celebrated a token Christmas on the twenty-third, and the next day he packed his presents (a watch and a tape recorder) and was put on a plane at Orly West. He flew from Paris to Geneva, where he spent the real Christmas Eve in a strange, bare apartment into which an aunt and a large family of cousins had just moved. In the morning he was wakened when it was dark and taken to a six o'clock train. He said good-bye to his aunt at the station, and added, "If you ask the conductor or anyone to look after me, I'll—" Whatever threat was in his mind he seemed ready to carry out. He wore an RAF badge on his jacket and carried a Waffen-S.S. emblem in his pocket. He knew better than to keep it in sight. At home they had al-ready taken one away but he had acquired another at school. He had Astérix comic books for reading, chocolate-covered hazelnuts for support, and his personal belongings in a fairly large knapsack. He made a second train on his own and got down at the right station.

He had been told that he knew this place, but his memory, if it was a memory, had to do with fields and a picnic. No one met him. He shared a taxi through soft snow with two women, and paid his share—actually more than his share, which annoyed the women; they could not give less than a child in the way of a tip. The taxi let him off at a dark, shiny tower on stilts with granite steps. In the lobby a marble panel, looking like the list of names of war dead in his school, gave him his grandmother on the eighth floor. The lift, like the façade of the building, was made of dark mirrors into which he gazed seriously. A dense, thoughtful person looked back. He took off his glasses and the blurred face became even more remarkable. His grandmother had both a bell and a knocker at her door. He tried both. For quite a long time nothing happened. He knocked and rang again. It was not nervousness that he felt but a new sensation that had to do with a shut, foreign door.

His grandmother opened the door a crack. She had short white hair and a pale face and blue eyes. She held a dressing gown gripped at the collar. She flung the door back and cried, "Darling Richard, I thought you were arriving much later. Oh," she said, "I must look dreadful to you. Imagine finding me like this, in my dressing gown!" She tipped her head away and talked between her fingers, as he had been told never to do, because only liars cover their mouths. He saw a dark hall and a bright kitchen that was in some disorder, and a large, dark, curtained room opposite the kitchen. This room smelled stuffy, of old cigarettes and of adults. But then his grandmother pushed the draperies apart and wound up the slatted shutters, and what had been dark, moundlike objects turned into a couch and a bamboo screen and a round table and a number of chairs. On a bookshelf stood a painting of three tulips that must have fallen out of their vase. Behind them was a sky that was all black except for a rainbow. He unpacked a portion of the things in his knapsack—wrapped presents for his grandmother, his new tape recorder, two school textbooks, a notebook, a Bic pen. The start of this Christmas lay hours behind him and his breakfast had died long ago.

"Are you hungry?" said his grandmother. He heard a telephone ringing as she brought him a cup of hot milk with a little coffee in it and two fresh croissants on a plate. She was obviously someone who never rushed to answer any bell. "My friend, who is an early riser, even on Christmas Day, went out and got these croissants. Very bravely, I thought." He ate his new breakfast, dipping the croissants in the milk, and heard his grandmother saying, "Well, I must have misunderstood. But he managed. . . . He didn't bring his skis. Why not? . . . I see." By the time she came back he had a book open. She watched him for a second and said, "Do you read at meals at home?"

"Sometimes."

"That's not the way I brought up your mother."

He put his nose nearer the page without replying. He read aloud from the page in a soft schoolroom plainchant: " 'Go, went, gone. Stand, stood, stood. Take, took, taken.' "

"Richard," said his grandmother. When he did not look up at once, she said, "I know what they call you at home, but what are you called in school?"

"Riri."

"I have three Richard grandsons," she said, "and not one is called Richard exactly."

"I have an Uncle Richard," he said.

"Yes, well, he happens to be a son of mine. I never allowed nicknames. Have you finished your breakfast?"

"Yes."

"Yes who? Yes what? What is your best language, by the way?"

"I am French," he said, with a sharp, sudden, hard hostility, the first tense bud of it, that made her murmur, "So soon?" She was about to tell him that he was not French—at least, not really—when an old man came into the room. He was thin and walked with a cane.

"Alec, this is my grandson," she said. "Riri, say how do you do to Mr. Aiken, who was kind enough to go out in this morning's snow to buy croissants for us all."

"I knew he would be here early," said the old man, in a stiff French that sounded extremely comical to the boy. "Irina has an odd ear for times and trains." He sat down next to Riri and clasped his hands on his cane; his hands at once began to tremble violently. "What does that interesting-looking book tell you?" he asked.

" 'The swallow flew away,' " answered Irina, reading over the child's head. " 'The swallow flew away with my hopes.' "

"Good God, let me look at that!" said the old man in his funny French. Sure enough, those were the words, and there was a swallow of a very strange blue, or at least a sapphire-and-turquoise creature with a swallow's tail. Riri's grandmother took her spectacles out of her dressing-gown pocket and brought the book up close and said in a loud, solemn way, " 'The swallows will have flown away.' " Then she picked up the tape recorder, which was the size of a glasses case, and after snapping the wrong button on and off, causing agonizing confusion and wastage, she said with her mouth against it, " 'When shall the swallows have flown away?' "

"No," said Riri, reaching, snatching almost. As if she had always given in to men, even to male children, she put the book down and the recorder too, saying, "Mr. Aiken can help with your English. He has the best possible accent. When he says 'the girl' you will think he is saying 'de Gaulle.' "

"Irina has an odd ear for English," said the old man calmly. He got up slowly and went to the kitchen, and she did too, and Riri could hear them whispering and laughing at something. Mr. Aiken came back alone carrying a small glass of clear liquid. "The morning heart-starter," he said. "Try it." Riri took a sip. It lay in his stomach like a warm stone. "No more effect on you than a gulp of milk," said the old man, marveling, sitting down close to Riri again. "You could probably do with pints of this stuff. I can tell by looking at you you'll be a drinking man." His hands on the walking stick began to tremble anew. "I'm not the man I was," he said. "Not by any means." Because he did not speak English with a French or any foreign accent, Riri could not really understand him. He went on, "Fell down the staircase at the Trouville casino. Trouville, or that other place. Shock gave me amnesia. Hole in the stair carpet—must have been. I went there for years," he said. "Never saw a damned hole in anything. Now my hands shake."

"When you lift your glass to drink they don't shake," called Riri's grandmother from the kitchen. She repeated this in French, for good measure.

"She's got an ear like a radar unit," said Mr. Aiken.

Riri took up his tape recorder. In a measured chant, as if demonstrating to his grandmother how these things should be done, he said, " 'The swallows would not fly away if the season is fine.' "

"Do you know what any of it means?" said Mr. Aiken.

"He doesn't need to know what it means," Riri's grandmother answered for him. "He just needs to know it by heart."

They were glassed in on the balcony. The only sound they could hear was of their own voices. The sun on them was so hot that Riri wanted to take off his sweater. Looking down, he saw a chalet crushed in the shadows of two white blocks, not so tall as their own. A large, spared spruce tree suddenly seemed to retract its branches and allow a great weight of snow to slip off. Cars went by, dogs barked, children called—all in total silence. His grandmother talked English to the old man. Riri, when he was not actually eating, read *Astérix in Brittany* without attracting her disapproval.

"If people can be given numbers, like marks in school," she said, "then children are zero." She was enveloped in a fur cloak, out of which her hands and arms emerged as if the fur had dissolved in certain places. She was pink with wine and sun. The old man's blue eyes were paler than hers. "Zero." She held up thumb and forefinger in an O. "I was there with my five darling zeros while he ... You are probably wondering if I was *ever* happy. At the beginning, in the first days, when I thought he would give me interesting books to read, books that would change all my life. Riri," she said, shading her eyes, "the cake and the ice cream were, I am afraid, the end of things for the moment. Could I ask you to clear the table for me?"

"I don't at home." Nevertheless he made a wobbly pile of dishes and took them away and did not come back. They heard him, indoors, starting all over: " 'Go, went, gone.' "

"I have only half a memory for dates," she said. "I forget my children's birthdays until the last minute and have to send them telegrams. But I know *that* day. . . ."

"The twenty-sixth of May," he said. "What I forget is the year."

"I know that I felt young."

"You were. You *are* young," he said.

"Except that I was forty if a day." She glanced at the hands and wrists emerging from her cloak as if pleased at their whiteness. "The river was so sluggish, I remember. And the willows trailed in the river."

"Actually, there was a swift current after the spring rains."

"But no wind. The clouds were heavy."

"It was late in the afternoon," he said. "We sat on the grass."

"On a raincoat. You had thought in the morning those clouds meant rain."

"A young man drowned," he said. "Fell out of a boat. Funny, he didn't try to swim. So people kept saying."

"We saw three firemen in gleaming metal helmets. They fished for him so languidly—the whole day was like that. They had a grappling hook. None of them knew what to do with it. They kept pulling it up and taking the rope from each other."

"They might have been after water lilies, from the look of them."

"One of them bailed out the boat with a blue saucepan. I remember that. They'd got that saucepan from the restaurant."

"Where we had lunch," he said. "Trout, and a coffee cream pudding. You left yours."

"It was soggy cake. But the trout was perfection. So was the wine. The bridge over the river filled up slowly with holiday people. The three firemen rowed to shore."

"Yes, and one of them went off on a shaky bicycle and came back with a coil of frayed rope on his shoulders."

"The railway station was just behind us. All those people on the bridge were waiting for a train. When the firemen's boat slipped off down the river, they moved without speaking from one side of the bridge to the other, just to watch the boat. The silence of it."

"Like the silence here."

"This is planned silence," she said.

Riri played back his own voice. A tinny, squeaky Riri said, " 'Go, went, gone. Eat, ate, eaten. See, saw, sen.' "

" 'Seen'!" called his grandmother from the balcony. " 'Seen,' not 'sen.' His mother made exactly that mistake," she said to the old man. "Oh, stop that," she said. He was crying. "Please, please stop that. How could I have left five children?"

"Three were grown," he gasped, wiping his eyes.

"But they didn't know it. They didn't know they were grown. They still don't know it. And it made six children, counting him."

"The secretary mothered him," he said. "All he needed."

"I know, but you see she wasn't his wife, and he liked saying to strangers 'my wife,' 'my wife this,' 'my wife that.' What is it, Riri? Have you come to finish doing the thing I asked?"

He moved close to the table. His round glasses made him look desperate and stern. He said, "Which room is mine!" Darkness had gathered round him in spite of the sparkling sky and a row of icicles gleaming and melting in the most dazzling possible light. Outrage, a feeling that consideration had been wanting—that was how homesickness had overtaken him. She held his hand (he did not resist—another sign of his misery) and together they explored the apartment. He saw it all—every picture and cupboard and doorway—and in the end it was he who decided that Mr. Aiken must keep the spare room and he, Riri, would be happy on the living-room couch.

The old man passed them in the hall; he was obviously about to rest on the very bed he had just been within an inch of losing. He carried a plastic bottle of Evian. "Do you like the bland taste of water?" he said.

Riri looked boldly at his grandmother and said, "Yes," bursting into un-explained and endless-seeming laughter. He seemed to feel a relief at this substitute for impertinence. The old man laughed too, but broke off, coughing.

At half past four, when the windows were as black as the sky in the paint-ing of tulips and began to reflect the lamps in a disturbing sort of way, they drew the curtains and had tea around the table. They pushed Riri's books and belongings to one side and spread a cross-stitched tablecloth. Riri had hot chocolate, a croissant left from breakfast and warmed in the oven, which made it deliciously greasy and soft, a slice of lemon sponge cake, and a ba-nana. This time he helped clear away and even remained in the kitchen, talk-ing, while his grandmother rinsed the cups and plates and stacked them in the machine.

The old man sat on a chair in the hall struggling with snow boots. He was going out alone in the dark to post some letters and to buy a newspa-per and to bring back whatever provisions he thought were required for the evening meal.

"Riri, do you want to go with Mr. Aiken? Perhaps you should have a walk."

"At home I don't have to."

His grandmother looked cross; no, she looked worried. She was biting something back. The old man had finished the contention with his boots and now he put on a scarf, a fur-lined coat, a fur hat with earflaps, woolen gloves, and he took a list and a shopping bag and a different walking stick, which looked something like a ski pole. His grandmother stood still, as if dreaming, and then (addressing Riri) decided to wash all her amber neck-laces. She fetched a wicker basket from her bedroom. It was lined with or-ange silk and filled with strings of beads. Riri followed her to the bathroom and sat on the end of the tub. She rolled up her soft sleeves and scrubbed the amber with laundry soap and a stiff brush. She scrubbed and rinsed and then began all over again.

"I am good at things like this," she said. "Now, unless you hate to dis-cuss it, tell me something about your school."

At first he had nothing to say, but then he told her how stupid the younger boys were and what they were allowed to get away with.

"The younger boys would be seven, eight?" Yes, about that. "A hopeless generation?"

He wasn't sure; he knew that his class had been better.

She reached down and fetched a bottle of something from behind the bathtub and they went back to the sitting room together. They put a lamp between them, and Irina began to polish the amber with cotton soaked in turpentine. After a time the amber began to shine. The smell made him homesick, but not unpleasantly. He carefully selected a necklace when she told him he might take one for his mother, and he rubbed it with a soft cloth. She showed him how to make the beads magnetic by rolling them in his palms.

"You can do that even with plastic," he said.

"Can you? How very sad. It is dead matter."

"Amber is too," he said politely.

"What do you want to be later on? A scientist?"

"A ski instructor." He looked all round the room, at the shelves and curtains and at the bamboo folding screen, and said, "If you didn't live here, who would?"

She replied, "If you see anything that pleases you, you may keep it. I want you to choose your own present. If you don't see anything, we'll go out tomorrow and look in the shops. Does that suit you?" He did not reply. She held the necklace he had picked and said, "Your mother will remember seeing this as I bent down to kiss her good night. Do you like old coins? One of my sons was a collector." In the wicker basket was a lacquered box that contained his uncle's coin collection. He took a coin but it meant nothing to him; he let it fall. It clinked, and he said, "We have a dog now." The dog wore a metal tag that rang when the dog drank out of a china bowl. Through a sudden rainy blur of new homesickness he saw that she had something else, another lacquered box, full of old canceled stamps. She showed him a stamp with Hitler and one with an Italian king. "I've kept funny things," she said. "Like this beautiful Russian box. It belonged to my grandmother, but after I have died I expect it will be thrown out. I gave whatever jewelry I had left to my daughters. We never had furniture, so I became attached to strange little baskets and boxes of useless things. My poor daughters—I had precious little to give. But they won't be able to wear rings any more than I could. We all come into our inherited arthritis, these knotted-up hands. Our true heritage. When I was your age, about, my mother was dying of . . . I wasn't told. She took a ring from under her pillow and folded my hand on it. She said that I could always sell it if I had to, and no one need know. You see, in those days women had nothing of their own. They were like brown paper parcels tied with string. They were handed like parcels from their fathers to their husbands. To make the parcel look attractive it was decked with curls and piano lessons, and rings and gold coins and banknotes and shares. After appraising all the decoration, the new owner would undo the knots."

"Where is that ring?" he said. The blur of tears was forgotten.

"I tried to sell it when I needed money. The decoration on the brown paper parcel was disposed of by then. Everything thrown, given away. Not by me. My pearl necklace was sold for Spanish refugees. Victims, flotsam, the injured, the weak—they were important. I wasn't. The children weren't. I had my ring. I took it to a municipal pawnshop. It is a place where you take things and they give you money. I wore dark glasses and turned up my coat collar, like a spy." He looked as though he understood that. "The man behind the counter said that I was a married woman and I needed my husband's written consent. I said the ring was mine. He said nothing could be mine, or something to that effect. Then he said he might have given me something for the gold in the band of the ring but the stones were worthless. He said this happened in the finest of families. Someone had pried the real stones out of their setting."

"Who did that?"

"A husband. Who else would? Someone's husband—mine, or my mother's or my mother's mother's, when it comes to that."

"With a knife?" said Riri. He said, "The man might have been pretending. Maybe he took out the stones and put in glass."

"There wasn't time. And they were perfect imitations—the right shapes and sizes."

"He might have had glass stones all different sizes."

"The women in the family never wondered if men were lying," she said. "They never questioned being dispossessed. They were taught to think that lies were a joke on the liar. That was why they lost out. He gave me the price of the gold in the band, as a favor, and I left the ring there. I never went back."

He put the lid on the box of stamps, and it fitted; he removed it, put it back, and said, "What time do you turn on your TV?"

"Sometimes never. Why?"

"At home I have it from six o'clock."

The old man came in with a pink-and-white face, bearing about him a smell of cold and of snow. He put down his shopping bag and took things out—

chocolate and bottles and newspapers. He said, "I had to go all the way to the station for the papers. There is only one shop open, and even then I had to go round to the back door."

"I warned you that today was Christmas," Irina said.

Mr. Aiken said to Riri, "When I was still a drinking man this was the best hour of the day. If I had a glass now, I could put ice in it. Then I might add water. Then if I had water I could add whiskey. I know it is all the wrong way around, but at least I've started with a glass."

"You had wine with your lunch and gin instead of tea and I believe you had straight gin before lunch," she said, gathering up the beads and coins and the turpentine and making the table Riri's domain again.

"Riri drank that," he said. It was so obviously a joke that she turned her head and put the basket down and covered her laugh with her fingers, as she had when she'd opened the door to him—oh, a long time ago now.

"I haven't a drop of anything left in the house," she said. That didn't matter, the old man said, for he had found what he needed. Riri watched and saw that when he lifted his glass his hand did not tremble at all. What his grandmother had said about that was true.

They had early supper and then Riri, after a courageous try at keeping awake, gave up even on television and let her make his bed of scented sheets, deep pillows, a feather quilt. The two others sat for a long time at the table, with just one lamp, talking in low voices. She had a pile of notebooks from which she read aloud and sometimes she showed Mr. Aiken things. He could see them through the chinks in the bamboo screen. He watched the lamp shadows for a while and then it was as if the lamp had gone out and he slept deeply.

The room was full of mound shapes, as it had been that morning when he arrived. He had not heard them leave the room. His Christmas watch had hands that glowed in the dark. He put on his glasses. It was half past ten. His grandmother was being just a bit loud at the telephone; that was what had woken him up. He rose, put on his slippers, and stumbled out to the bathroom.

"Just answer yes or no," she was saying. "No, he can't. He has been asleep for an hour, two hours, at least. . . . Don't lie to me—I am bound to find the truth out. Was it a tumor? An extrauterine pregnancy? . . . Well, look. . . . Was she or was she not pregnant? What can you mean by 'not exactly'? If you don't know, who will?" She happened to turn her head, and saw him and said without a change of tone, "Your son is here, in his pajamas; he wants to say good night to you."

She gave up the telephone and immediately went away so that the child could talk privately. She heard him say, "I drank some kind of alcohol."

So that was the important part of the day: not the journey, not the necklace, not even the strange old guest with the comic accent. She could tell from the sound of the child's voice that he was smiling. She picked up his bathrobe, went back to the hall, and put it over his shoulders. He scarcely saw her: He was concentrated on the distant voice. He said, in a matter-of-fact way, "All right, good-bye," and hung up.

"What a lot of things you have pulled out of that knapsack," she said.

"It's a large one. My father had it for military service."

Now, why should that make him suddenly homesick when his father's voice had not? "You are good at looking after yourself," she said. "Independent. No one has to tell you what to do. Of course, your mother had sound training. Once when I was looking for a nurse for your mother and her sisters, a great peasant woman came to see me, wearing a black apron and black buttoned boots. I said, 'What can you teach children?' And she said, 'To be clean and polite.' Your grandfather said, 'Hire her,' and stamped out of the room."

His mother interested, his grandfather bored him. He had the Christian name of a dead old man.

"You will sleep well," his grandmother promised, pulling the feather quilt over him. "You will dream short dreams at first, and by morning they will be longer and longer. The last one of all just before you wake up will be like a film. You will wake up wondering where you are, and then you will hear Mr. Aiken. First he will go round shutting all the windows, then you will hear his bath. He will start the coffee in an electric machine that makes a noise like a door rattling. He will pull on his snow boots with a lot of cursing and swearing and go out to fetch our croissants and the morning papers. Do you know what day it will be? The day after Christmas." He was almost asleep. Next to his watch and his glasses on a table close to the couch was an Astérix book and Irina's Russian box with old stamps in it. "Have you decided you want the stamps?"

"The box. Not the stamps."

He had taken, by instinct, the only object she wanted to keep. "For a special reason?" she said. "Of course, the box is yours. I am only wondering."

"The cover fits," he said.

She knew that the next morning he would have been here forever and that at parting time, four days later, she would have to remind him that leaving was the other half of arriving. She smiled, knowing how sorry he would be to go and how soon he would leave her behind. "This time yesterday . . . ," he might say, but no more than once. He was asleep. His mouth opened slightly and the hair on his forehead became dark and damp. A doubled-up arm looked uncomfortable but Irina did not interfere; his sunken mind, his unconscious movements, had to be independent, of her or anyone, particularly of her. She did not love him more or less than any of her grandchildren. You see, it all worked out, she was telling him. You, and your mother, and the children being so worried, and my old friend. Anything can be settled for a few days at a time, though not for longer. She put out the light, for which his body was grateful. His mind, at that moment, in a sunny icicle brightness, was not only skiing but flying.

POTTER

---

*P*iotr was almost forty-one when he fell in love with Laurie Bennett. She lived in Paris, for no particular reason he knew; that is, she had not been drawn by work or by any one person. She seemed young to him, about half his age. Her idea of history began with the Vietnam War; Genesis was her own Canadian childhood. She was spending a legacy of careless freedom with an abandon Piotr found thrilling to watch, for he had long considered himself to be bankrupt—of belief, of love, of license to choose. Here in Paris he was shackled, held, tied to a visa, then to the system of mysterious favors on which his Polish passport depended. His hands were attached with a slack rope and a slipknot. If he moved abruptly, the knot tightened. He had a narrow span of gestures, a prudent range. His new world of love seemed too wide for comfort sometimes, though Laurie occupied it easily.

He called his beloved "Lah-ow-rie," which made her laugh. She could not pronounce "Piotr" and never tried; she said Peter, Prater, Potter, and Otter, and he answered to all. Why not? He loved her. If she took some forms of injustice for granted, it was because she did not know they were unjust. Piotr was supposed to know *by instinct* every shade of difference between Victoria, British Columbia, and Charlottetown, Prince Edward Island, whereas he, poor Potter, came out of a cloudy Eastern plain bereft of roads, schools, buses, elevators, perhaps even frontiers—this because she could not have found Warsaw on a map. She knew he was a poet and a teacher, but must have considered him a radical exception. She had been touchingly pleased when he showed her poems of his in an American university quarterly. Three pages of English were all he had needed to get past her cultural customs barrier. She kept a copy of the review in a plastic bag, and so far as he knew had never read more than his name on the cover. None of this disturbed him. It was not as a poet that Laurie had wanted Piotr but as a lover—thank God. The surprise to him after their first conversations was that there were any roads, schools, etc., in Canada, though she talked often of an Anglican boarding school where she had been "left" and "abandoned" and which she likened to a concentration camp. "You've really never heard of it, Potter?" It seemed incredible that a man of his education knew nothing about Bishop Purse School or its famous headmistress, Miss Ellen Jones. Bishop Purse, whatever its advantages, had not darkened Laurie's sunny intelligence with anything like geography, history, or simple arithmetic. She had the handwriting of a small boy and could not spell even in her own language. For a long time Piotr treasured a letter in which he was described as "a really sensative person," and Laurie herself as "mixed-up in some ways but on the whole pretty chearfull."

Her good nature made her entirely exotic. Piotr was accustomed to people who could not look at a letter without saying eagerly, "Bad news?" He had known women who set aside a little bit of each day for spells of soft, muted weeping. The problem with Polish women, as Piotr saw it, was that they had always just been or were just about to be deserted by their men. At the first rumor of rejection (a fragment of gossip overheard, some offhand evidence of a lover's neglect) they gave way at once, stopped combing their hair, stopped making their beds. They lay like starfish, smoking in the strewn, scattered way of the downhearted. He saw them, collectively, wet-cheeked and feverish, heard a chorus of broken voices gasping out the dreadful story of male treachery. Out of the fear of losing the man at hand would grow a moist determination to find another to take his place. Piotr was separated from his wife, he was irresolute, and he never had quite what he wanted. What he did not want was a feather bed of sadness. He knew that unhappiness is catching and wondered if happiness might not be infectious, too. All that he needed was to love a happy person and get her to love him.

"Am I too cheerful?" Laurie asked. "They say I am sometimes. I've been told. It puts people off. You know, like 'It's nothing to laugh about.' " *I've been told.* There, at the beginning, she had given him the raw material of future anguish, if only he had been alert. But it had come linked with another statement, which was that if Potter was not exactly her first lover he was certainly among the first, and the first ever to please her—a preposterous declaration he accepted on the spot.

Piotr met Laurie through a cousin he had in Paris, an émigré bachelor who worked at a travel agency. Piotr had never seen Marek's office. Meeting Piotr for lunch in one of the smoky café-bars around the Place de l'Opéra, Marek would look at his watch and whisper, "I have to meet someone very high up in Swiss television," or "the editor of the most important newspaper, the most politically powerful man south of the Loire," or "a countess who controls absolutely everything at the Quai d'Orsay." Although he did not say so, it sounded to Piotr very much like social survival in Warsaw. By means of his affability, his ease with languages, and a certain amount of cultural soft-soaping, Marek had acquired a French circle of acquaintance, of which he was extremely proud. But it was a fragile affair, like a child with a constant chest cold. He lavished great amounts of time, care, and worry on keeping it alive, which did not prevent him from knowing every name, event, scandal, and political maneuver in the local Polish colony. He knew so much, in fact, that he was widely believed to be working for the French police. Like most informers—should that have been his story—he was often hard up and often had unexpected money to spend. He lived in the run-down area east of the Hôtel de Ville. The street seemed drab and gritty to Piotr, but his cousin assured him that it was thought fashionable in the highest reaches of bohemia. His rooms were next door to a synagogue and one flight up from an undertaker's. When, as it sometimes happened, nighttime outbursts of anti-Semitism caused swastikas to be chalked on the synagogue, a few usually spilled along to the undertaker's somber window and over the door and staircase leading to Marek's. The swastikas gave rise to another legend: Marek had been a double agent in the French Resistance. Actually, he had been nowhere near France, and had been barely thirteen by the end of the war. Rumor also had him working for Israel (possibly because of the proximity of the synagogue) and for the CIA. His quarters contained large soft lumps of furniture, gray in color, considered "modern," and "American," which had undoubtedly been shipped by airfreight from Washington in exchange for information about Mr. X, who had bought a controlling interest in a toy shop, or little Miss Y, who had triumphantly terminated another school year. The chairs and sofas had in fact been the gift of a Swiss decorator from Bern, who owed Marek money or favors or help of some kind—the explanation always faded out. Although he was far more interested in men than in girls, there were usually more girls than men at his parties. The most beautiful young women Piotr had ever seen climbed the unlighted staircase, undaunted by the matter-of-fact trappings of death on the ground floor or the occasional swastika. Piotr marveled at his cousin's ease with women, at the casual embracing and hand-holding. It was as though the girls, having nothing to fear, or much to hope for, enjoyed trying out the lesser ornaments of seduction. The girls were Danish, German, French, and American. They were students, models, host-esses at trade fairs, hesitant fiancées, restless daughters. Their uniform the year Piotr met Laurie was blue jeans and velvet blazers. They were nothing like the scuffed, frayed girls he saw in the Latin Quarter, so downcast of face, so dejected of hair and hem that he had to be convinced by Marek they were well-fed children of the middle classes and not the rejects of a failing economy. Marek's girls kept their hair long and glossy, their figures trim. They discussed their thoughts, but not their feelings, with a solemn hauteur Piotr found endlessly touching. But he did not find them lighthearted. They were simply less natively given to despair than Polish women. He was look-ing for someone, though no one could have told. Perhaps his cousin knew. Why else did he keep on inviting Piotr with all those pretty women? One scowling French girl almost won Piotr when he noticed that the freckles across her nose were spots of russet paint. She was severe, and held her cig-arette like a ruler, but she must have been very humble alone with her mir-ror. "Help me," she must have implored the glass. "Help me to be suitable, wanted." She remarked to Piotr, "How can anyone write poetry today? Per-sonally, I reject the absolute." Piotr had no idea what she meant. He had never asked her, or any woman, to accept the absolute. He had been toying with the hope that she might accept him. Before he could even conceive of an answer, Laurie Bennett intervened. She simply came up to Piotr and told him her name. She had blue eyes, fair hair down to her shoulders, and a gap between her upper front teeth.

"I've never wanted to have it fixed," she told Piotr. "It's supposed to be lucky."

"Are you lucky?" said Piotr.

"Naturally. Who isn't? Aren't you?"

They sat down, Piotr in a Swiss armchair, the girl on the floor. Remarks in a foreign language often left him facing an imaginary brick wall. Lucky? Before he could answer she said, "You're the famous cousin? From there?"—with a wave that indicated a world of bad train connections and terrible food. "Do you know Solzhenitsyn? If Solzhenitsyn were to walk in here, I'd get right down on my knees and thank him."

"What for?" said Piotr.

"*I* don't know. I thought you might."

"He isn't likely to come in," said Piotr. "So you won't have to make a fool of yourself."

She was already kneeling, as it happened, sitting on her heels at Piotr's feet. She slid nearer, placed her glass of rosy wine on the arm of his chair, her elbow on his knee: "I was just trying to show you I sympathized." He wanted to touch her hair but clasped his hands instead. His cousin had told him he looked like a failed priest sometimes. He did, in fact, inspire confessions rather than passion from women.

In his later memories he thought it must have been then that Laurie began to tell about her neglected childhood and her school. She did not sound in the least mournful, though the story was as dismaying as the smiling girl could make it. After Bishop Purse, what she had hated most was someone called "my brother Ken." "My brother Ken" was so neurotically snobbish that he'd had a breakdown trying to decide between a golden and a Labrador. His wife, whose name sounded like "Bobber Ann," took the case to a psychotherapist, who advised buying one of each. Piotr did not know Laurie was talking about dogs, and after she explained he found the incident even more mystifying. What he loved at once was her built-up excitement. She was ignited by her own stories and at the end could scarcely finish for laughing. Yes, her brother's wife was Bobber Ann. Barbara, that is—she had been imitating Bobber Ann's Toronto accent. "Actually, my brother Ken's a mean sort of bugger," said Laurie, happily. "And she, Bobber Ann, she wears white gloves all the time, cleans 'em with bread crumbs—it's true. How long are you in Paris for, Otter, Potter, I can't pronounce it. Would you come to a party, if I gave one?"

She was living then in a borrowed apartment on Avenue Mozart. The name of this street remained incantatory to Piotr long after he knew he would never see Laurie again. He remembered of the strange rooms their stern blue walls, a plant that looked like a heap of lettuce leaves, which Laurie kept forgetting to water, and rows and rows of grim sepia views of bridges and rivers.

"My friends are well printed, eh?" said Laurie. Her friends worked at UNESCO "or some kind of culture racket like it." As the last English-speaking stragglers left her party, having finished off the last of the absent hosts' duty-free gin, Laurie said, with no particular emphasis, "No, you, Potter, you stay."

✳   ✳   ✳

The place on Avenue Mozart was one of so many that in time Piotr stopped counting. Her home was never her own but rooms she camped in while the owners were away. Sometimes she had a dog to walk or a budgerigar to feed, but mostly just the run of the house. She told Piotr she moved on because she wanted peace and could never find it. He supposed, not unkindly, that she had heard some such statement at one of Marek's parties. A year after Avenue Mozart, the B page of his address book was such a hedgehog of scratched-out directions that he bought a book for Laurie alone. He recorded in it the enchanting names of her Paris streets, and mysterious Poste Restante or American Express directions for Cannes, Crans-sur-Sierre, Munich, Portugal, Normandy, Gstaad, Madrid. She sent him bright scraps of news about eccentric living quarters, funny little jobs that never lasted for long, and she sent Piotr all, yes, all of her love. Word came from sunny beaches that Laurie was eating too much, she was lazy and brown and drinking delicious wine. Often she sounded alone. If she wrote "we," there seemed to be three of them; she traveled with couples, never the same pair twice. "You and I will come here together," she would promise, of places he would never see in his lifetime. He had told her about the passport and how having it for even three weeks was an erratic favor, because once, twenty years ago now, he had been arrested for political lèse-majesté. He explained, but she kept forgetting. She had no memory, except of her school days; she was like a blackboard wiped clean every week or so. Laurie could not recall restaurants where their most important conversations had taken place. Her life seemed to him fragile and silvery, like a Christmas bauble. When he and Laurie were apart, which was to say nearly always, her life reflected a female, Western mystery: It reflected hotel rooms and crouched skiers and glasses of wine and distorted faces. He could hear her voice and remembered her light hair. He was exiled from Laurie—never Laurie from Piotr. She simply picked up her world and took it with her. He resented his exile. He wanted to take her world, compress it, make sparkling dust of it. He could almost have made himself hate her, because of her unthinking, pointless freedom, her casual way with frontiers. She went from place to place without noticing where she was—he could tell that. What was she doing? Eating, drinking, loving probably, being silly. But even her silliness was a tie, a conspiracy. It had drawn him, made him share private jokes that stayed alive, compelled him to send drawings, pictures, reminders, whatever would strengthen the bond. But by the time these arrived Laurie had usually forgotten the joke and was on to another.

She was not always silly. He saw a face of true unhappiness sometimes, and always because of him—because she loved him and there was half a continent between them; because he had children; because the wife he no longer lived with, had admired but never loved, was like a book he could neither read nor shut. It seemed to him then that he bore a disease that might infect the confident girl and cripple her. He saw the self-doubt on her face, and the puzzled wretchedness. When she said, "There must be something wrong with me," he heard his wife, too.

They parted twice; they had to. Piotr had to go back. Laurie picked up her life and never wondered about his; at least, she never asked. In Warsaw he woke up each morning with the same question: Is there a letter? Her letters were funny, friendly, loving, misspelled. They were not a substitute for Laurie; they were like medicine that can quiet a symptom but not the root of the malady. She phoned sometimes but he preferred the voice in his mind, and the calls left him empty.

The second time he came to Paris, it was at the end of a hot summer. He found her over an art gallery on Boulevard Malesherbes. She told him that Proust had lived somewhere near, perhaps in the next house. She was unsure who Proust was. Like the Solzhenitsyn remark, it was made to please; it was Laurie's way of paying a compliment to someone she considered clever.

They lived behind closed shutters because of the heat, and came out to the still steaming streets after dark. He noticed that she was wearing a new watch with a white strap. The watch was transparent, with a multitude of stars spinning inside.

"I've always had it," she said when he asked where such a marvel was to be found. She wore it for sleep and in love—that was how he happened to see it. He observed Laurie (she did not see him looking) removing the watch and kissing it before taking a bath. A little later she said, "I picked it up in Zurich once," and then, such was her capacity for forgetting, "It was a birthday present." When the time came to accompany Piotr to the airport she suddenly produced a car. To Piotr, who did not know one automobile from another, it was merely cream-colored and small. "It belongs to the girl who owns the apartment," she said, though until now she had spoken of the owners as "they." At the airport, at the last minute, she said she and Piotr had better forget each other. These separations were killing her inch by inch. She could not look at him, did not want him to touch her. It was a shifting, evasive misery, like a dying animal's. She said, "I'm taking the car and driving somewhere. I don't know where. I don't even know where I'll be sleeping tonight. I can't go back and sleep alone in that apartment."

"Will you write?" said Piotr.

She turned, weeping, and ran.

For weeks he was stunned by her absence, her silence, her grief, his own guilt. Out of need, out of vanity, he had tampered with a young life. He had not expected this gift of deep sentiment. Perhaps he did not know what to do with it. He knew nothing about women; he had been in jail at the age when he should have been learning. Perhaps Laurie, so lighthearted and careless, had a capacity for passion that overshot Piotr. He had learned in prison that fasting, like any deprivation, made fullness impossible. He had been sick after eating an apple; it was like eating a wet stone. The solitude of prison made anyone else's presence exhausting, and the absence of love in his life now made love the transformed apple—the wet stone he could not taste or digest.

Three days after returning to Warsaw he broke an ankle—just like that, stupidly, stepping off a curb. He wrote into the silence of Paris that he was handicapped, in pain, but the pain was nothing to his longing for Laurie. Weeks later, she answered that she still loved him and no one else. She seemed upset about the ankle; in some way she blamed herself. They were now as they had been, in love, miles apart, with no hope of meeting. He was flattered that she recalled enough of him to say she still loved him—she who had no memory.

Piotr became forty-three. After delayed, drawn-out, finger-crossed, and breath-holding negotiations he obtained a new passport and a three-month visa for France, where he had been invited to give a series of lectures. A young woman was coming to Warsaw, in exchange, to instruct Polish students on tendencies in French poetry since 1950. Piotr silently wished her luck. His departure date had been twice postponed, so he was in a state of tension, dizziness, and unbearable control when he boarded the Air France plane on a cold day of autumn. Until the plane lifted he expected to be recalled because they had all changed their minds. The steward's unintelligible welcome over the intercom seemed for a sickening moment to be meant for him—the plane was going to land so that Professor S—— could be removed. Among a dozen gifts for his love in Piotr's luggage were two she had asked for: Polish birth-control pills, superior to any on the Western market (they prevented conception and also made you lose weight), and a soporific potion that was excitingly habit-forming and provided its addicts with the vivid, colorful dreams of opium sleep. In this way, wrote Laurie, sleep was less boring.

Marek met him in Paris, and wept as they embraced. He had taken a hotel room without a bath for his cousin in order to spare his limited funds. He gave Piotr confusing instructions about a locked bathroom down the hall, advice about the French franc exchange (Piotr had in his possession the allowed one hundred dollars and nothing more), and all the local Polish gossip. Piotr, who had never lied to Marek except over Laurie, invented a university dinner. Fifteen minutes after Marek departed, Piotr, carrying the smaller of his two suitcases, took a taxi to Laurie's new address. The names of her streets were to haunt him all his life: Avenue Mozart, Boulevard Malesherbes, Impasse Adrienne, Place Louis-Marin, Rue de l'Yvette, Rue Sisley, Rue du Regard. This year she occupied a studio-and-bath on the top floor of a new house in Rue Guynemer.

"It's my own, Potter. It isn't borrowed" was the first thing she said to him. "It costs the earth." Then, incoherently, "I'm not always here. Sometimes I go away."

The studio was bright, as neat and almost as bare as a cell, and smelled of fresh paint. So that was what Laurie was like, too. He found her face a shade thinner, her figure a trace fuller; but the hair, the eyes, the voice—no change. Now he recalled her perfume, and the smell beneath the fragrance. She laughed at his suitcase, because, suddenly embarrassed, he tried to conceal it behind the door; laughed at a beret he wore; laughed because she loved him but still she would not make love: "I can't, not yet, not just like that." Their evening fitted his memory of older evenings—Laurie greedy with a menu, telling Piotr in a suddenly prim voice all about wines. She was certainly repeating a lesson, but Piotr felt immeasurably secure, and tolerant of the men she might be quoting. Laurie said, "Isn't this marvelous?"— taking his happiness for granted simply because she was so entirely alive. He remembered how, once out, she hated to go home. "But it's a children's hour," she protested when he said at midnight that he was tired. Four hours later, as they sat in a harsh café, she said, "Potter, I'm so glad I was born," lifting her straight soft hair away from her neck in a ritual gesture of gladness. He took this to be a tribute to his presence. Piotr did not love being alive, but he absolutely did not want to die, which was another thing. At their table a drunk slept deeply with his head on his arms. The day behind

Piotr lay in shreds, like the old Métro tickets and strips of smudged paper on the café floor. Laurie said that the papers were receipts—the café was an offtrack betting shop. Like the old story about the golden and the Labrador, this information contained an insoluble mystery. All he knew was that in a hell of urban rubbish Laurie was glad she'd been born. Exhaustion gave Piotr hallucinations; he saw doors yawning in blank walls, dark flights of steps, nuns hovering, but still he did not lose track of the night. The night had to end, and even Laurie would be bound to admit that it was time to go home.

They had the next day, a night, a day of sun and long walks, and a night again. From Laurie's window he looked across to the Luxembourg Gardens, which were golden, rust brown, and the darkest green, like a profound shade of night. Each morning he walked to his hotel, unmade his bed, and asked for mail and messages. On the third morning the porter handed Piotr an envelope from his cousin containing a loan in French money, an advance on his university fees. He counted out fifteen hundred francs. The last barrier between Piotr and peace of mind dissolved.

On his way back to Laurie he bought croissants, a morning paper, and cigarettes. He knew that he would never be as happy again. He found Laurie dressed in jeans and a Russian tunic, packing a suitcase. The bed was made, the sheets they had slept in were folded on a chair; through the doorway he could see their damp towels hanging side by side on the shower rail. She looked up, smiled, and said she was going to Venice.

"When?"

"Today. In a couple of hours. I'm meeting this friend of mine." He suddenly imagined the girl with the painted freckles. "You'll be busy for the next few days anyway," she went on. "You put off coming to Paris twice, remember. I couldn't put off my friend anymore. I didn't tell you before, because I didn't want to spoil things when you arrived."

He carried her suitcase to the Gare Saint-Lazare. At the station she put coins in a machine that distributed second-class tickets. He looked around and said, "Do you go to Venice from here?"

"No, they're local trains. We're meeting at a station out of town. It saves driving through Paris, with the traffic and all."

An enormous hope was contained in "we're meeting." He understood, at last, that Laurie was going to Venice with a man. Laurie seemed unaware that he had not taken it in until now, or unaware that it mattered. She was hungry; she had missed her breakfast. CAFÉ DE LA PASSERELLE gleamed in green neon at the end of a dark buffet. Laurie chose from among twenty empty tables as if her choice could make any difference. Piotr, sleepwalking now, ordered and ate apricot pie. The café was shaped like a corridor, with dusty windows on either wall. He and Laurie had exchanged climates, seasons, places—for the windows looked out on slanting rain and deserted streets. Laurie slid back her cuff so that she could keep an eye on her watch. Piotr was silent. She said—sulking, almost—Now, why? What harm was there in her taking a few days off with an old friend while he had so many other things to do?

"It's an old story, you know," she said. "Hardly worth the trouble of breaking off. He always takes me somewhere for my birthday." She stopped, as if wondering how to explain what the old friendship was based on. She said, simply, "You know how it is. He got me young."

"Do you love him?"

"No, nothing like that. I love you. But we planned this trip ages ago. I couldn't be sure you would ever get to Paris. I don't want to hurt his feelings. You'd like him, Potter. Honestly you would. He speaks three different languages. He's independent—enjoys running his own business. I don't even make a dent in his life."

"Does he love you?"

"I keep telling you, it isn't like that. We aren't really lovers. I mean, not as you and I are. We sleep together—well, if we find ourselves in the same bed."

"Try not to find yourself," said Piotr.

"What?" She seemed as candid, as confident, as tender as always. Her eyes were as clear as a child's. Her hand shook suddenly. What was coming now? The unloved childhood? The day her mother left her at Bishop Purse School? The school must have provided clean sheets and warm rooms and regular meals, but she was of a world that took these remarkable gifts for granted. His wife, younger then than Laurie was now, had stolen food for Piotr when he lay in a prison infirmary absolutely certain he was about to die. She had been a prisoner, too, dispatched as medical aide and cleaner. She stopped at the foot of his cot. When she started talking she couldn't stop. He saw that her amber eyes focused nowhere—her "in-looking eyes," he was to call them. Because of the eyes and the mad rush of words and the danger she was calling down on them he had thought, The girl is insane. Then sanely, quietly, she said, "I have some bread for you." You could not compare Laurie Bennett with a person of that quality. All the same, Piotr had guessed: His wife was insane, but only with him. Danger had reached him after he seemed well out of it, only to be caught on the danger a couple create for each other.

"Look, Potter," said Laurie. "If you mind all that much, I won't go. I'll talk to him."

"When?"

"Now; soon. But I'd be sad. He's a good friend. Why would he want to take me to Venice, except out of friendship? He doesn't need *me*. He knows all kinds of interesting people. I'd be poorer without him—really alone." She was already making women's gestures of leaving, straightening the spoon in its saucer, gathering in whatever belonged to her, bringing her affairs close—protecting herself. "Don't come to the train," she said. "Drink your coffee, read the paper. Look, I've even brought it along. Keep the key to my room. You'll stay there, won't you? As we arranged? If you mind about the concierge seeing you—not that she cares—just use the garage instead of the front door. That's how the married ladies in the building meet their lovers. I'll write," she said. "I'll write to your hotel."

He pushed his chair back. As he got to his feet his ankle gave way. "Oh, Potter, your poor ankle!" Laurie said. "I was on a sailing holiday when you broke it. I was at Lake Constance and I wasn't getting my mail. I wasn't seeing newspapers or anything, and when I finally got back to Paris someone told me there'd been this war on in the Middle East. All those dead and it was already over and I hadn't known a thing—not about your ankle, not anything." She smiled, kissed him, picked up her suitcase, and walked away. Without knowing why, he touched his forehead. He was wearing his beret, which Marek had implored him not to do in Paris; the beret made Piotr look like an out-of-town intellectual, like a teacher from the provinces, like a priest from a working-class parish. What did it matter? Any disguise would do to hide the shame of being Piotr.

Only a few men now were left in the café—Algerians reading want ads, middle-aged stragglers clearly hating Piotr because he was alone and demented, like half the universe. Later, he had no memory of having taken the Métro, only that when he came back up to daylight the rain had stopped. He walked on wet leaves. Like the married women's lovers he entered Laurie's building by way of the garage, slipping and sliding because the slope was abrupt and the soles of his shoes had grown damp. Her room was airless now, with sun newly ablaze on the shut window. He was starting a new day, the third day since this morning. His croissants were still on the table. He picked them up, thinking that it was better to leave nothing. Then he saw there was nothing much he could leave, because Laurie had packed his things. Piotr's suitcase stood locked, buckled, next to the chair on which were folded the sheets they had slept in. Her neatness erased him. The extra towel on the shower rail might have been anyone's. He was wiped out by her clothes' hanging just so, by her sweaters and shirts in plastic boxes, by the prim order of the bouillon cubes and Nescafé and yellow bowls on a shelf, by the books—presents, probably—lined up by size beneath the window. He saw the review containing his poems, still honored by its dustproof bag. What he had never noticed before was that the bag also held a thin yellow book of verse, the Insel-Bücherei edition of Christian Morgenstern's *Palmström* poems. Piotr had once translated some of these, entirely for pleasure. When he was arrested he had had scraps of paper in his pocket covered with choppy phrases in Polish and German that became entirely sinister when read by the police. "Well, you see," said a blond, solemn Piotr of twenty years ago, "Morgenstern was not much understood and finally he was mad, but the poems in their way are funny."

"Why a German?" The sarcasm of the illiterate. "Aren't there enough mad Poles?"

"There soon will be," said Piotr, to his own detriment.

Now, in Laurie's room, even the yellow binding seemed to speak to him. Where had it come from? Someone, another doting Potter, had offered it to her, thinking, Love something I love and you are sure to love me. Who? The flyleaf said nothing. He turned the pages slowly and, on the same page as a poem called "The Dreamer," came upon a color snapshot of two people in an unknown room. Piotr recognized Laurie but not the man. The man was fair, like Piotr, but somewhat younger. His hair was brushed. He wore a respectable suit and a dark red tie. What Piotr saw at once about his face was that it was genuinely cheerful. Here, at last, caught by chance, was the *bon naturel* Piotr had hopelessly been seeking from woman to woman. Laurie, naked except for her wristwatch, sat on the arm of his chair, with her legs curled like the tail of a mermaid. One hand was slipped behind the man's neck. She held a white shower cap, probably the very cap now hanging on a tap in the next room.

A casual happiness suffused this picture. Piotr was looking at people who did not know or really understand how lucky they were. A sun risen for the lovers alone shone in at the window behind them and made Laurie's hair

white and sparkling, like light seen through an icicle. Those were Piotr's immediate, orderly thoughts. He sensed the particular eroticism of the clothed
man and the naked girl and only then felt the shock, like a door battered in.
The door collapsed, and Piotr saw whatever he had been dreading since he
had dared to fall in love—solitude, cruelty, the loneliness of dying: All
of that.

Laurie had deliberately left the picture for him to find. She had gone to
a foreign bookshop, perhaps the place in the Rue du Dragon that she had
pointed out to him, saying she once worked there for a week before they realized she spoke nothing but English, and chose the very book that was
bound to catch his eye. She had then staged the picture. Piotr's wife, in *her*
calculated dementia, had recorded her own lovemaking with another man
on a tape on which Piotr had been assembling the elements of a course in
Russian poetry. Recalling this, he remembered that where his wife had been
frantic Laurie was only heedless. The book and the picture were part of the
blithe indifference of the two lovers, no more.

He was suddenly overcome with a need to shut his eyes, to be blessed by
darkness. He lay flat on the bed and said to himself. What can I give her? I
am never here. When he rose and looked at the picture again, it seemed to
him it was not where he had left it. Also, in the neat row of clothing he saw
a hanger askew. Where there had been only Piotr's croissants on the table
there was now, as well, an enamel four-leaf-clover pin, open, as if it had
parted from its wearer unnoticed. The door had to be locked from within;
he tested the handle and saw he had forgotten to turn the key. Anyone
might have entered while Piotr had his eyes shut and examined the snapshot
and put it in the wrong place. Laurie, he now saw, had a coarse face, small,
calculating blue eyes, and a greedy, vacuous expression. What he had mistaken for gaiety had been nothing but guile. The man seemed more sympathetic somehow. For one thing, he was decently dressed. He looked sane.
There was nothing *wrong* with that man, really, except for the peculiar business of having set up a camera in the first place. He was a Western European by dress, haircut, expression. He was not a Latin. Nor was this an
English face. Piotr sensed a blunt sureness about him. He would be sure before, during, and after any encounter. He would not feel any of Piotr's anx-
iousness over pleasing Laurie and pleasing himself. He might have been a
young officer of solid yeoman origins, risen from the ranks, in the old Imperial Army—a character in a pre-1914 Viennese novel, say. He became
then, and for all time, "the Austrian" in Piotr's mind.

Piotr replaced the picture where he now thought it must have been, next to a poem called "Korf in Berlin." No one had entered the room—he knew that. The clover pin had fallen from Laurie's tunic. It was normal for a hanger to be askew when someone even as neat as Laurie had packed in a hurry.

He went out the front door this time, brave enough to confront the concierge and give up Laurie's key.

"Bennett," he said, and on receiving no answer said it again.

"I heard you." She seemed blurred and hostile. He had to narrow his eyes to keep her in focus. The trees in the Luxembourg Gardens were indistinct, as if seen through tears. He found himself caught in a crocodile of schoolboys. A harridan in a polo coat screamed at them, at Piotr, too, "Watch your step, keep together!" Piotr began to search for something that could protect him—trees in a magic ring around a monument might be suitable. As soon as he had selected a metal chair not too close to anyone the sun vanished. A north wind came at him. Leaves rolled over and over along the damp path. He sat on the edge of a forbidden grass plot, staring at a bust he at first took to be Lenin's. He still wore his reading glasses—the reason the concierge had seemed undefined. The bust was in fact a monument to Paul Verlaine.

The grass had kept its midsummer green; when the sun came out briefly the tree shadows were still summer's shadows. But the season was autumn, and he saw a gleaming chestnut lying among the split casings. He would have picked it up, but someone might have seen.

Laurie had escaped from her locked room. It was not her face, not her hair, but her voice and her voice in her letters that pursued Piotr. *He. We. I.* "*He* always takes me somewhere for my birthday." "*We* took the *tellypherique* and walked down from the reservoir." "*I* was on a sailing holiday at Lake Constance." It had been *we* in the Italian Tyrol—"We take lovely picnics up behind the hotel, you can hear bells from the other valley." *We* turned up again in Rome, at Crans-sur-Sierre, at a hotel in Normandy. *We* were old friends—James and Nancy, Mike and Sylvia, Hans and Heidi. *We* existed in a few letters, long enough to spin out a holiday, then fell over Laurie's horizon. Piotr's only balm was that *he* was wiped out. There was a big X over his ugly face. Laurie, or *I,* had been alone for at least the time it took to remember Piotr and write him an eager, loving letter full of spelling mistakes. Piotr had been with her in Portugal, in Switzerland; she had generously included him by making herself, for a few minutes, alone and available. Perhaps Laurie had been alone in her mind, truly loyal to Piotr—*he* meanwhile in the bar of the hotel? In the shower? Off on some disloyal pretext of his own so that he could slip an *I* message to his wife?

She was a good girl, all the same, for she had always taken care to give Piotr a story so plausible he could believe it without despising himself. Now that she had told him the truth, he was as bitter as if she had deceived him. Why shouldn't Laurie be taken for holidays? Did he want her alone, crabbed, disheveled, soured? The only shadow over her life that Piotr knew of had been Piotr himself. Her voice resumed: "I am taking the car and driving . . ." Whose car, by the way? Piotr moved his feet and struck his suitcase. His ankle made a snapping sound. There was no pain, but the noise was disconcerting, as if the bones were speaking to him. She had left him at the airport; she had not known where she would be sleeping that night. "That time you broke your ankle . . . I was on a sailing holiday at Lake Constance." Yes, and something else, about a war in the Middle East. The fragments were like smooth-grained panels of wood. The panels slid together, touched, fitted. Her wild journey to forget Piotr had only one direction: to Lake Constance, where someone was waiting.

There were aspects of Laurie's behavior that, for the sake of his sanity, Piotr had refused to consider. Now, sitting on a cold metal chair, eyes fixed on a chestnut he was too self-conscious to pick up, he could not keep free of his knowledge; it was like the dark wind that struck through the circle of trees. She had used him, made an audience of him, played on his feelings, and she was at this moment driving to Venice with—the element of farce in every iniquity—Piotr's Polish birth-control pills. Moreover, she had entirely forgotten Piotr. His grief was so beyond jealousy that he seemed truly beside himself; there was a Piotr in a public park, trying hard to look like other people, and a Piotr divorced from that person. His work, his childhood, his imprisonment, his marriage, his still mysterious death were rolled in a compact ball, spinning along the grass, away from whatever was left of him. Then, just as it seemed about to disappear, the two Piotrs came together again. The shock of the joining put him to sleep. His head fell forward; he pulled it up with a start. He may have slept for a second, no more. No one had noticed—he looked for that. The brief death had cleansed him. His only thought now was that his memory was better than hers and so he knew what they were losing. As for Laurie's abuse of him, it was simply that she did not know the meaning of words, their precision, their power—why, she could not even spell them. She did not realize when she was lying, because she did not know what words were about. This new, gentle tolerance made Piotr wonder: What if his feeling for Laurie was no more than tenderness, and what if Piotr was incapable of love other than the kind he could give his children? His wife had said this—had screamed it. She did not want his friendship, his loyalty, his affection, his devotion, his companionship. She wanted what he had finally bestowed on Laurie; at least, he thought he had.

He gave his first lecture and poetry reading in an amphitheater that was usually used by an institute of Polish civilization for showing films and for talks by visiting art historians. Most of the audience was made up of the Polish colony. A few had come to hear him read, but most of them were there to see what he looked like. The colony was divided that night not into its usual social or political splinters but over the issue of how Piotr was supposed to have treated his wife. All were agreed on the first paragraphs of Piotr's story: There were clues and traces in his early poems concerning the girl who saved his life. He and the girl had married, had lived for years on his earnings as an anonymous translator. Here came the first split in public opinion, for some said that it was really his wife who had done all the work, while Piotr, idle, served a joyous apprenticeship for his later career of pursuing girl students. Others maintained that his wife was ignorant of foreign languages; also, only Piotr could have made something readable out of the translated works.

Next came the matter of his wife's lovers: No one denied them, but what about Piotr's affairs? Also, what about his impotence? For he was held to be satyr and eunuch and in some ineffable way to be both at once. Perhaps he was merely impotent. Who, then, had fathered his wife's two—or four, or six—children? Names were offered, of men powerful in political and cultural circles.

Piotr had tried to kill his wife—some said by flinging her down a flight of stone steps, others said by defenestration. He had rushed at her with a knife, and to save herself she had jumped through a window, landing easily, but scarring her face on the broken panes. A pro-Piotr faction had the wife a heavy drinker who had stumbled while carrying a bottle and glass. The symmetry of the rumors had all factions agreed on the beginning (the couple meeting in prison) and on the end—Piotr collecting his wife's clothes in a bundle and leaving them on the doorstep of her latest lover.

Before starting his lecture Piotr looked at the expectant faces and wondered which story was current now. After the lecture, strangers crowded up to congratulate him. He was pleased to see one of them, an old sculptress his parents had known before the war. When she smiled her face became as flat and Oriental and as wrinkled as tissue paper. Maria, as virginal as her name, had once been a militant; quite often such women automatically became civil servants, referred to by a younger generation as "the aunts of the Revolution." Her reward had been of a different order: Summoned to Moscow by someone she trusted, arrested casually, released at random, she had lived in Paris for years. She never mentioned her past, and yet she was in it still, for her knowledge of Paris was only knowledge about bus stops. Her mind, ardent and young, moved in the direction of dazzling changes, but these were old changes now—from 1934 to 1935, say. Piotr recalled her spinster's flat, with the shaky, useless tables, the dull, green, beloved plants, the books in faded jackets, the lumpy chairs, the divans covered in odd lengths of homespun materials in orchard colors—greengage, grape, plum. Her references had been strict, dialectical, until they became soft and forgiving, with examples drawn from novels got by heart. He did not know of any experience of passion, other than politics, in Maria's life. Her work as a sculptress had been faithful and scrupulous and sentimental; seeing it, years before, one should have been able to tell her future. She had never asked him questions. Few women had mattered; she was one: a discreet, mistaken old woman he had seen twice since his childhood, with whom he talked of nothing but politics and art. These were subjects so important to him that their conversations seemed deeply personal. Maria did not praise Piotr's lecture but said only, "I heard every word," meaning, "I was listening." There were too many people; they could not speak. They agreed to meet, and just at that moment another woman, with dry red hair and a wide, nervous grin, pushed her way past Maria and said to Piotr, "My husband and I would think it an honor if you came to stay with us. We have a large flat, we are both out all day, and you would be private. We admire your work." She had something Piotr considered a handicap in a woman, which was that she showed her gums. "You are probably in a hotel," she said, "but just come to us when your money runs out."

Piotr kept the card she gave him, and later Marek examined it and said, "I know who they are. She is a doctor. No, no, they are not political, nothing like that. You would be all right there."

Was it because of the lecture? Because of seeing Maria? Because he had been invited by the doctor? Piotr now considered Laurie's absence with a sense of deliverance, as if a foreign object had been removed from his life. She had always lied. He recalled how she could tremble at will—how she had once spilled a cup of coffee, explaining later that she was attracted to him at that moment but felt too diffident to say so. She had let him think she was inexperienced in order to torture him, had kept him in her bed for hours of hesitation and monologue, insisting that she was afraid of a relationship that might be too binding, that she was afraid of falling in love with him—this after the party where she had said, "You, Potter, you stay." Afterward she told Piotr that she'd had her first lover at fifteen. Old family friend, she said, with children about her age. He used to take her home for holidays from Bishop Purse. She was his substitute for a forbidden daughter, said Laurie, calmly, drinking coffee without spilling it this time. Piotr should have smacked her, kicked her, cut up her clothes with scissors and hung the rags all over the lamps and furniture. He should have followed her around Paris, calling insults, making a fool of her in restaurants. As he was incapable of doing anything even remotely violent, it was just as well she had gone. Relief made him generous: He reminded himself that she had added to his life. She had given Piotr whatever love was left over from her love for herself. You could cut across any number of lies and reach the person you wanted, he decided, but no one could get past narcissism. It was like the crust of the earth.

He slept soundly that night and part of the next afternoon. Marek had left books at his hotel, the new novels of the autumn season. Nothing in them gave Piotr a clue to the people he saw in the streets, but the fresh appearance of the volumes, their clean covers, the smooth paper and fanciful titles put still more distance between himself and his foolish love affair. After dark his cousin arrived to take him to a French dinner party. Piotr had been accepted by a celebrated, beautiful hostess named Eliane, renowned for her wit, her lovers, and her dislike of foreigners. She had been to Piotr's lecture. At the dinner party she planned to place Piotr on her right. Marek was afraid that Piotr did not take in what this signified in terms of glory. Any of the people at that lecture would have given an arm and a leg if the sacrifice had meant getting past Eliane's front door.

Piotr asked, "What does she do?"

They traveled across Paris by taxi. Marek continued his long instructions, telling Piotr what Eliane was likely to talk about and what she thought about poetry and Poland. Piotr was not to contradict anything, even if he knew it to be inaccurate; above all, he was not to imagine that anything said to him was ever meant to be funny. Marek and Piotr would be the only foreign guests. He begged Piotr not to address any remark to him in Polish in anyone's hearing. Answering Piotr's question finally, he said that Eliane did not "do" anything. "You must get over the habit of defining women in terms of employment," he concluded.

During the preliminary drink—a thimble of sweet port—Marek did not leave his cousin's side. The hostess was the smallest woman Piotr had ever seen, just over dwarf size. She wore a long pink dress and had rings on every finger. To Piotr's right, at table, sat a pregnant girl with soft dark hair and a meek profile. He smiled at her. She stared at a point between his eyes. His smile had been like a sentence uttered too soon. Marek's expression signaled that Piotr was to turn and look at his hostess. Eliane said to him gravely, "Have you ever eaten salmon before?" She next said, "I heard your lecture." Piotr, still bemused by the salmon question, made no reply. She continued, "The poetry you recited was not in French, and I could not understand it." She waited; he waited, too. "Were you *greatly* influenced by Paul Valéry?" Piotr considered this. His hostess turned smoothly to the man on her left, who wore a red ribbon and a rosette on his lapel.

"Cézanne was a Freemason," Piotr heard him saying. "So was Braque. So was Juan Gris. So was Soutine. No one who was not a Freemason has ever had his work shown in a national museum."

The pregnant girl's social clockwork gave her Piotr along with the next course. "Is this your first visit to Paris?" she said. Her eyes danced, rolled almost. She tossed her head, as a nervous pony might. Where the rest of the table was concerned, she and Piotr were telling each other something deliciously amusing and private.

"It is my third trip as an adult. I came once with my parents when I was a child." He wondered if his discovery of chestnut meringues at Rumpelmayer's tearoom in 1938 was of the slightest interest.

"The rest of the time you were always in your pretty Poland?" The laugh that accompanied this was bewildering to him. "What could have been keeping you there all this time?" In another context, in a world more familiar, the look on the girl's face would have been an invitation. But what Piotr could see, and the others could not, was that she was not really looking at him at all.

"Well, at one time I was in prison," he said, "and sometimes translating books, and sometimes teaching at a university. Sometimes the progression goes in reverse, and your poet begins at the university and ends in jail."

"Have you ever had veal cooked this way before?" she said, after a quick glance to see if their hostess was ready to take on Piotr again. "It is typically French. But not typically Parisian. No, it is typically provincial. Eliane likes doing these funny provincial things." She paused again. Piotr was still hers. "And where did you learn your good French and your charming manners?" she said. "In Poland?"

"The hardest thing to learn was not to spit on the table," said Piotr.

After that both women left him in peace. But of course he was not in peace, for Marek was watching. He did not reproach Piotr, but Piotr knew he would not be invited to a French evening again.

Perhaps because he had slept too much in the afternoon, he found that night long and full of dark misery. He awoke at the worst possible hour, at four, when it was too late to read—his eyes watered and would not focus—and too early to get up. He heard the chimes of the hotel clock downstairs striking five, then six. He slept lightly and woke on the stroke of seven. His body had taken over and was trying to show him that the nonchalance about Laurie had been a false truce. Feeling dull and sick, he shaved at the basin in his room, and asked the maid to unlock the door down the hall so that he could have a bath. He entered the steamy room, with its cold walls and opaque windows, reminding himself that Laurie was a foreign object, that he had a life of his own, that he had a center of gravity. His body reacted to this show of independence with stomach cramps and violent nausea. His mouth went dry when he returned to his room to find a breakfast tray waiting. The skin around his mouth felt attacked by small stinging insects. A headache along his hairline prevented him from unfolding the morning paper or reading a letter from home. The day was sunny, and he saw now that the commonplace sayings about crossed love were all true: The weather mocked him; he craved darkness and rain. His unhappiness was a disease. Strangers would see signs of it, and would despise him.

He loved her. For more than two years now his waking thought had been, Is there a letter? He wanted to reach across to her, straight to Venice, but she had to want him—otherwise he was a demand, a claim, a dead weight on her life; he was like the soft, curled-up, dejected women who seemed to make an equal mess of love and cigarette ash. Laurie was in Venice, on a snowy beach. (The Venice of his imagining was all blue and white.) She lay immodestly close to a cloudy man. Piotr could not really see him. Perhaps he was placid, like the Austrian, or thin and worried, like Piotr. Perhaps he was a disgusting boulevardier with cheeks like boiled shrimp. "He speaks three languages ... enjoys running his own business." Oh, inferior, callous, stupid!

Piotr told his diminished self, My poems are translated into ... I have corresponded with ... been invited by ... I can lecture in Polish, Russian, Lithuanian, German, English, French, and I can also ...

Laurie had assured Piotr that no one, ever, had been like him. She had said, "To think that until now I thought I was just one more frigid North American!" Piotr had believed. He wanted to compose a scream of a letter: Where are you? Why don't you send me a telegram, give me a sign? I haunt the hotel office where mail is kept. I mistake the hotel bill for a message saying you have come back. They say that mail from Italy is slow, but I see other people receiving letters with Italian stamps. I wake at dawn wondering if today will be the day of the letter.

His torment was intensified by the number of mail deliveries; there were three a day, with a fourth for parcels (should she show she remembered him by sending a book). The porter, sorting letters, would see Piotr hovering and call, "Nothing!" and Piotr would scurry away as if he had been caught in some shameful voyeur posture. He now heard and saw "Venice" everywhere: When he bought fruit he found it stamped on an orange. He even said, "God," though until now he had thought there was no God to hear him.

Piotr had still not received any money from the university. He was used to administrative languor, but the francs his cousin had advanced him were melting fast and Piotr did not want to ask Marek for more. The day came when he decided to leave his hotel and move in with the doctor and her husband. Marek approved of the address, which was close to the École Militaire; he had unearthed what he thought of as useful information: The doctor and her husband had emigrated to France, separately, before the war. They had met in a Polish Resistance network operating out of Grenoble. The marriage was not a happy one. The husband had a mistress and an illegitimate daughter, with whom he spent every Sunday. The doctor was certain to fall in love with Piotr, Marek said.

Piotr did not care for the street, which seemed to him frozen and hostile. There was a desperate, respectable shabbiness about the house. Laurie would never have lived there. In the icy stairwell an elevator creaked on swaying cables. The halls were dim. Tenants rode in the lift and crossed in passageways without speaking, staring flatly. He imagined each high-ceilinged apartment occupied by one person, living alone, working in a ministry, eating ready-made food on the edge of a table at night. His hostess welcomed him as an old acquaintance and made up his bed in the room she had once used for private consultations. Vestiges of the old regime remained—the powerful lights overhead, the washbasin in a corner, a leather folding screen. Under his bed he discovered a case of books. None were newer than the early 1950s; probably it was then that the couple's marriage had broken down. The French bindings had gone from white to yellow. There were a number of volumes about the war. Piotr, a decade or so younger than the heroic generation, had always been faintly irritated by them.

The doctor was on the staff of a clinic in the Thirteenth Arrondissement, where she now had an office and received her private patients. She gave Piotr a ring of house keys and the key to a letter box downstairs in the court. This led Piotr to new hauntings. He could not bring himself to cross the courtyard without peering through the slot of the box, even if he had looked only half an hour before. He expected word from Laurie at any time: His old hotel might easily receive a special-delivery letter and send it around by messenger. Sometimes a gleam of light on the metal lining of the box could have been a letter, and the hope he felt almost made up for the disappointment. He also had a new worry: A lump, like a large black stone, filled his chest. He felt it when he woke up in the morning. The first thing he heard was an alarm clock in the doctor's bedroom shortly before six, and then he would become aware of the stone. He would hear the doctor's husband getting up and listening to the six o'clock news in the bathroom. He was small and bald and polite to Piotr. He did not really have to get up before six. He simply did not want to be alone with his wife more than he had to. The doctor actually said so to Piotr, staring at him craftily and boldly, obviously hoping for some oblique, similar confidence about his wife. Piotr noticed that when the pair were alone they argued in French. It was their language for reproach and for justification. He would remember how he had parted from his wife and given up his children so that the children would not have to hear adult violence from their dark bedroom. Often in the night Piotr heard the doctor's singsong complaint, which had an almost poetical rhythm to it. She said that her husband was a miser who did not love her. He deprived her of money; he deprived her of warmth. If the husband replied—a low grumble of words in which Piotr caught "never" and "idea"—her voice became discordant, choppy, like a child banging crazily on piano keys. He heard,

"Some men are cruel, but at least they are intelligent. How you must be gloating. You think *you* have come out of this safely. Well, you may not have a chance to gloat for long."

Sometimes the doctor had breakfast with Piotr. She told him how she had studied medicine in France, and about the war and the Resistance, adding, inevitably, "You are too young to remember." She said, "My husband was brave in that war. But he does not understand an educated woman and should never have married one." What she really wanted to talk about was Piotr and his wife. She looked, she stared, she hoped, she waited. Piotr was used to that.

He gave his second lecture, in French, in a basement classroom. This time he had a row of well-dressed, perfumed Frenchwomen—the inevitable *femmes du monde* attracted by the foreign poet—including, to his surprise, the pregnant girl from the fatal dinner party. A number of students, lowering as though Piotr intended in some way to mislead them, slumped at the back of the room. After the lecture a young man wearing a military-service haircut got up to ask if Piotr considered himself right-wing. Piotr said no.

"I heard they only let Fascists out."

"I have not been let out like a dog," said Piotr amiably. "I am here like any ordinary lecturer."

A girl applauded. One of the well-dressed women called him *"Maître."* Piotr pulled his beret down to his ears and scuttled out to the street. The students had been suspicious, the women distant and puzzled. What did they expect? He remembered Laurie's smile, her light voice, how suddenly her expression could alter as one quick wave of feeling followed another. He remembered that she had loved him and tried to make him happy, and that he was on his way to the doctor's silent flat. The stone in his chest expanded and pressed on his lungs. All that prevented him from weeping in the street was the thought that he had never seen a man doing that. In his room, he was overtaken. He was surprised at how warm tears were—surely warmer than blood. He said to himself, Well, at least I am crying over something real, and that was odd, for he believed that he lived in reality, that he had to. The stone dissolved, and he understood now about crying. But the feverish convalescence that followed the tears was unpleasant, and after a few hours the stone came back.

And so continued the most glorious autumn anyone in Paris could remember. The rainy morning of Laurie's departure had given way to blue and gold. And yet when Piotr, a haunter of anonymous parks now, sat with his back in shade, he felt a chill, as if the earth were tipping him into the dark. Marek, forgiving him for his French dinner fiasco, invited him to a new restaurant in the Latin Quarter. Piotr had the habit of eating anything put before him without tasting or noticing much. He could hear Laurie's voice mockingly describing their meal: "Mushrooms in diesel oil, steak broiled over moldy straw, Beaujolais like last year's vinegar." The other diners were plain-looking couples in their thirties and forties with *Le Monde* or *Le Nouvel Observateur* folded next to their plates. He noticed all this as if he were saving up facts to tell Laurie. The cousins' conversation was quiet gossip about Poles. They recalled a writer who had once been such a power in Warsaw that his objection to a student newspaper had sent Piotr to jail and Marek into exile. Now this man was teaching in America, where he was profoundly respected as someone who had been under the whip and survived to tell. He still had his sparse black teeth, said Marek, whose knowledge of such details was endless, and the university at which he taught had offered to have them replaced by something white and splendid. But the fact was that the writer who had broken other men's lives in the 1950s was afraid of the dentist.

Marek ordered a second bottle of wine and said, "Every day I wonder what I am doing in Paris. I have no real friends. I have enemies who chalk swastikas on my staircase. I speak seven languages. My maternal grandmother was the daughter of a princess. Who cares about that here? Perhaps I should go back to Poland." This was a normal émigré monologue; Piotr did not attempt to reply. They walked in the mild night, along bright streets, threading their way past beggars and guitar players, stopping to look at North African pastry shops. Piotr was troubled by the beggars—the bedraggled whining mothers with drugged, dozing babies, the maimed men exhibiting their blindness and the stumps of arms and legs for cash. "Yugoslav gangs," said Marek, shrugging. He reminded Piotr that begging was part of freedom. Men and women, here, were at liberty to beg their rent, their drink, their children's food. Piotr looked at him but could see no clue, no double meaning. Marek had settled for something, once and for all, just as Piotr had done in an entirely other existence. As they neared the Seine he had a childlike Christmas feeling of expectancy, knowing that the lighted flank of Notre Dame church would be reflected, trembling, on the dark water. He was forgetting Laurie—oh, surely he was! He decided that he would write about their story, fact on fact. Writing would remove the last trace of Laurie from his mind and heart. He was not a writer of prose and only an intermittent keeper of diaries, but he began then and there taking the cool historical measure of Laurie and love. He felt bold enough to say something about Laurie Bennett, and something else about Venice.

"Oh, Laurie—Laurie is in Florence," said Marek. "I had a card." Between Piotr's ribs the stone grew twice its size. "She travels," Marek went on. "An older man gives her money." He dropped the only important subject in the world to go on talking about himself.

"The older man," said Piotr. "Is he her lover?"

"She has never produced him," said Marek. "You always see Laurie alone. I have known her for years. You can never look at Laurie and look at another man and say 'sleeping with.' But this man—she was so innocent when she first came to Paris that she tried to declare him to the police as her source of income and nearly got herself kicked out of the country. That was years ago now."

Years ago? Piotr had never questioned her real age. Laurie looked young, and she talked about her school days as if they were just behind her. Perhaps she was someone who refused to have anything to do with time. In that case her youthfulness implied a lack of understanding: Just as she spelled words wrong because she did not know what words meant, she could not be changed by time because she did not know what change was about.

Piotr awoke the next morning with a flaming throat and a pain in his left shoulder. He could scarcely get his clothes on or swallow or speak. His hostess sat wearing a wrapper, hunched over a pot of strong tea. Today was Sunday.

"Mass in the morning, horse races in the afternoon," she said, referring to her husband, who had vanished. Piotr remembered what Marek had said about the illegitimate child. The doctor gave Piotr dark bread, cream cheese, and plum jam, and waited to hear—about his wife, of course. She never stopped waiting. From the kitchen he could see the room he had just left. He thought of his bed and wished he were in it, but then he would be her prisoner and she might talk to him all morning long.

Outside, above the courtyard, thin autumn clouds slid over the sun. He could hear the cold sound of water slopped on the cobblestones and traffic like a dimmed helicopter. His life seemed to have solidified overnight. Its substance was translucid, like jasper. He was contained in everything he had ever said and done. As for his pain, it was an anxious mystery. My shoulder, my throat, my ribs: Is it a fatal angina? Cancer of the trachea? Of the lungs? The left side of his body was rotting with illness within the jasper shell of his life.

He said to the doctor, "I may have caught a chill." He heard himself describing every one of his symptoms, as if each were a special grievance.

The doctor heard him out. "I think it is just something I call bachelor's ailment," she said. "You ought to have a mistress, if only to give you something real to worry about." Perhaps she meant this kindly, but even a doctor can have curious motives, especially one who shows her gums when she laughs, and whose husband gets up early to avoid being alone with her. "Do you want to see someone at my clinic?"

"No. It will go away."

"Suit yourself."

He delivered his third lecture through a tight, cindery throat. The room was filled with students this time, smoking, fidgeting, reading, whispering. He wondered what they were doing indoors on a glowing day. They showed little interest and asked only a few of their puzzling questions. After the lecture a plump man who introduced himself as a journalist invited Piotr to the terrace of the Brasserie Balzar. He wore a nylon turtleneck pullover and blazer and a large chrome-plated watch. Piotr supposed that he must have been sent by Marek—one of his cousin's significant connections. The reporter drank beer. Piotr, whose vitals rejected even its smell now, had weak tea, and even his tea seemed aggressive.

The reporter had a long gulp of his beer and said, "Are you one of those rebel poets?"

"Not for a second," said Piotr fervently.

"What about the letter you sent to *Pravda* and that *Pravda* refused to print?"

"I have never written to *Pravda*," said Piotr.

The reporter scribbled away, using many more words than Piotr had. Piotr remarked, "I am not a Soviet poet. I am a Polish lecturer, officially invited by a French university."

At this the reporter wrote harder than ever, and then asked Piotr about the Warsaw Legia—which Piotr, after a moment of brick wall, was able to recognize as the name of a football team—and about its great star, Robert Gadocha, whom Piotr had never heard of at all. The reporter shook Piotr's hand and departed. Piotr meant to make a note of the strange meeting and to ask Marek about the man, but as he opened his pocket diary he saw something of far greater importance—today was the sixteenth of October, the feast day of St. Jadwiga. His hostess, whose name this was, had particularly wanted him to be there for dinner. He went to a Swiss film about a girl in love with a married dentist, slept comfortably until the renunciation scene, and remembered when he came out that he would have to bring his hostess a present. Buying flowers, he glanced across the shop and saw the Austrian. He was with an old woman—his mother, perhaps. She moved back and forth, pointing and laughing in a way Piotr took to be senile. As she bent her topknot over calla lilies Piotr saw the Austrian clearly. Oh, it was the same man, with the wide forehead and slight smile. He gave the babbling old woman all his attention and charm. But when he and Piotr stood side by side, each of them paying—one for lilies, one for roses—Piotr saw that he was older than the Austrian in the picture, and that his arms and shoulders were stiff, slightly paralyzed. The senile old mother was efficient and brisk; it was she who carried the flowers. The Austrian was back in Venice, where he belonged. Is that where I want him, Piotr wondered.

The entire apartment, even Piotr's part of it, smelled of food cooking. The doctor had waved and tinted her hair and darkened her lashes. Her husband was dressed in a dark suit and somber tie. His gift to his wife, a pair of coral earrings, reposed on a velvet cushion on the dining-room table. The guests, remnants of the couple's old, happy days in the Resistance, sat stiffly, drinking French apéritifs. They were "little" Poles; Marek would not have known their names, or wished to. Their wives were French, so that the conversation was in French and merely polite. No one came in unexpectedly, as friends usually did for a name day. St. Jadwiga, incarnated in Paris, seemed to Piotr prim and middle-class. From Heaven his mind moved naturally to Venice, where he saw a white table and white chairs on the edge of a blue square. But perhaps Venice was quite other—perhaps it was all dark stone.

He had trouble swallowing his drink. A demon holding a pitchfork sat in his throat. Sometimes the pitchfork grazed his ear. The three men and Jadwiga soon slipped into Polish and reminiscences of the war. The French wives chatted to each other, and then the doctor drew their chairs close to the television set. She had been one of a delegation of doctors who that day had called on the minister of health; if they looked hard they might see a glimpse of her. All seven stared silently at the clockface now occupying the screen. The seconds ticked over. As soon as the news began, the doctor's husband began closing the shutters and drawing the curtains. It was a noisy performance, and Piotr saw that the doctor had tears in her eyes. Piotr thought of how this sniping went on night after night, with guests or without. He stared at lights reflected on the glassy screen, like fragments of a planet. A clock on the marble mantel had hands that never moved. The mirror behind the clock was tipped at an angle, so that Piotr could see himself. His hostess, following her most important guest's gaze, cried that the clock worked perfectly; her husband kept forgetting to wind it! At this everyone smiled at Piotr, as if to say, "So that is what poets wonder about!"

Dinner was further delayed because of a television feuilleton everyone in the room except Piotr had been following for seventeen weeks. A girl named Vanessa had been accused of euthanasia on the person of her aunt, named Ingrid, who had left Vanessa a large fortune. Anthony, a police detective from the Sûreté whose role it was to bully Vanessa into a hysterical confession, was suspected by all in the room (save Piotr). Anthony was a widower. His young daughter, Samantha, had left home because she wanted to be a championship swimmer. Anthony was afraid Samantha would die of heart failure as her mother, Pamela, had. Samantha did not know that at the time of her mother's death there had been whispers about euthanasia. The detective's concern for Samantha's inherited weakness was proof to everyone (except Piotr) that he had been innocent of Pamela's death. The dead aunt's adopted son, Flavien, who had been contesting the will, and who had been the cause of poor Vanessa's incarceration in the Santé prison, now said he would not testify against her after all. Piotr's France, almost entirely out of literature, had given him people sensibly called Albertine, Berthe, Marcel, and Colette. This flowering of exotic names bewildered him, but he did not think it worth mentioning. He had a more precise thought, which was that if his throat infection turned out to be cancer it would remove the need for wondering about anything. He invented advice he would leave his children: "Never try to make an unhappy person happy. It is a waste of life, and you will defeat your own natural goodness." In the looking glass behind the stopped clock Piotr was ugly and old.

Before going to sleep that night he read the account he had written of his love for Laurie. It had turned into a long wail, something for the ear, a babbling complaint. Describing Laurie, he had inevitably made two persons of her. Behind one girl—unbreakably jaunty, lacking only in imagination—came a smaller young woman who was fragile and untruthful and who loved out of fear. He had never sensed any fear in Laurie. He decided he would never write in that way about his life again.

He was pulled out of a long dream about airports by his own choked coughing. His left lung was on fire and a new pain, like an electric wire, ran along his arm to the tip of his little finger. He tried to suppress the coughing because another burst would kill him, and as he held his breath he felt a chain being forged, link by link, around his chest. The last two links met; the chain began to tighten. Before he could suffocate, a cough broke from him and severed the chain. He was shaking, covered in icy sweat. Panting, unable to raise himself on an elbow because of the pain, he gasped, "Help me." He may have fainted. The room was bright; the doctor bent over him. She swabbed his arm—he felt the cold liquid but not the injection. He wanted to stay alive. That overrode everything.

Piotr awoke fresh and rested, as though nothing had happened in the night. Nevertheless he let his hostess make an appointment at her clinic. "I still think it is bachelor's ailment," she grumbled, but she spoke with a false gruffness that meant she might be unsure.

"It is a chill in the throat," he said. Oh, to be told there were only six weeks to live! To settle scores; leave nothing straggling; to go quietly. Everything had failed him: his work (because it inevitably fell short of his vision), his marriage, politics, and now, because of Laurie, he had learned something final about love. He had been to jail for nothing, a poet for nothing, in love for nothing. And yet, in the night, how desperately he had craved his life—his own life, not another's. Also, how shamefully frightened he had felt. Laurie had told him once that he was a coward.

"All married men of your kind are scared," she had said, calmly. This took place at the small table of one of the drugstores she favored. Piotr said he was not married, not really. "I'll tell you if you're married *and* scared," she said. She looked at him over a steaming coffee cup. "Supposing I bought a Matisse and gave it to you."

"How could you?"

"We're imagining. Say I went without a winter coat to buy you a Matisse."

"A Matisse what?"

"Anything. Signed."

"For a winter coat?"

"Can't you imagine anything, Potter? Your lovely Matisse arrives in Warsaw. You unwrap it. It is a present from me. You know that it comes with my love. It's the sign of love and of going without." The trouble was that he *could* see it. He could see himself unrolling the picture. It was the head of a woman. "Would you hang it up on the wall?"

"Of course."

"And tell people where it came from?"

"What people?"

"If your wife came to see you, what would you say?"

"That it came from Paris."

"From someone who loved you?"

"It isn't her business," said Piotr.

"You see?" said Laurie. "You'd never dare. You're just a married man, and a frightened one. As frightened as any. You're even scared of an *ex*-wife. The day you can tell her where your Matisse came from, the day you say, 'I'm proud that any girl ever could have loved me that much,' then you'll know you've stopped being a scared little guy."

The Matisse was as real to him now as the car in which she had rushed away from the airport. Laurie could never in a lifetime have bought a Matisse. "Matisse" was only a name, the symbol of something famous and costly. She could accuse Piotr of fear because she was not certain what fear was; at least, she had never been frightened. Piotr thought this over coolly. Her voice, which had sung in his mind since her departure, suddenly left him. It had died on the last words, "scared little guy."

How silent my life will be now, Piotr said to himself. Yet it seemed to him that his anguish was diminishing, leaving behind it only the faint, daily anxiety any man can endure. A few days later he actually felt slow happiness, like water rising, like a tide edging in. He sat drinking black tea with Maria in her cramped little flat full of bric-a-brac and sagging divans. He saw sun on a window box and felt the slow tide. Maria was talking about men and women. She used books for her examples and the names of characters in novels as if they were friends: "Anna lived on such a level of idiocy, really." "If Natasha had not had all those children . . ." "Lavretsky was too resigned." Piotr decided this might be the soundest way of getting at the truth. Experience had never brought him near to the truth about anything. If he had fled Warsaw, forsaken his children, tried to live with Laurie, been abandoned by her, he would have been washed up in rooms like Maria's. He would have remembered to put clean sheets on the bed when he had a new girl in the offing, given tea to visitors from the home country, quoted from authors, spoken comic-sounding French and increasingly old-fashioned Polish until everyone but a handful of other émigrés had left him behind.

At ten in the morning, by appointment, Piotr arrived at the clinic where his hostess had her office. She had drawn a map and had repeated her instructions in every form except Braille. The clinic was a nineteenth-century brick house, miles from a Métro stop and unknown to buses. He approached it through streets of condemned houses with empty windows. A nurse directed him out to a mossy yard that smelled of mushrooms, and across to a low, shabby building, where the dim light, the atmosphere of dread and of waiting, the smell of ether and of carbolic were like any prison infirmary on inspection day. He joined a dozen women and one other man sitting around the four sides of a room. A kitchen table, dead center, held last winter's magazines. No one looked at these except Piotr, who tiptoed to the table and back. The room was so silent that he could hear one of the women swallowing saliva. Then from next door came the sound of thuds and iron locks. His prison memories, reviving easily, said, Someone is dying. They have gone out, all of them, and left a prisoner to die alone.

"My throat," he rehearsed. "I have no fever, no other symptoms, nothing seriously the matter, nothing but an incurable cancer of the throat."

A few mornings later his hostess knocked at the bedroom door and came in without waiting. His pajama jacket was undone. He groped for his glasses and put them on, as if they dressed him. The doctor placed a small glass tube filled with pink tablets on the night table.

"I still think it is bachelor's ailment," she said. "But if the pain should leave your throat, where you seem to want it to be, and you feel something here," placing an impudent hand on his chest, "take two of these half an hour apart. As soon as you get back to Warsaw, go into hospital for serious tests. I'll give you your dossier before you leave, with a letter for your doctor."

"What is it?"

"Just do as I tell you. It isn't serious."

"I'll imagine the worst," said Piotr.

"Imagining the worst protects you from it."

The worst was not a final illness; it was still a Venice built of white stone, with white bridges and statues. On a snowy street Laurie studied the menu outside a restaurant. Hand in hand with the Austrian, she said, "I'd rather go home and make love." Piotr's hand closed around the vial of pills. He guessed that the medicine was a placebo, but it could be a remedy for the worst. A placebo might accidentally attack the secret enemy that, unknown to the most alert and intelligent doctors in Paris, was slowly killing Piotr.

The worst, as always, turned out to be something simple. The French teacher sent to Poland in exchange for Piotr had wandered from her subject. Finding her students materialistic and coarsely bourgeois, she had tried to fire them with revolutionary ideals and had been expelled from the country. In retaliation, Piotr was banished from France. Marek accompanied his cousin to police headquarters. He seemed as helpless as Piotr and for once had no solutions. Piotr received a five-day reprieve to wind up his affairs. He would not give another lecture, and unless Laurie came back he would never see her again. Marek questioned him—grilled him, in fact: Who was the reporter he had talked to at the Balzar? Could Piotr describe him? Was he a Pole, an American? What about the pregnant girl—had Piotr offended her, had he made foolish and untranslatable jokes during that day's lecture? Piotr answered patiently, but Marek was not satisfied. There must have been Someone, he said, meaning the shadowy Someone who dogged their lives, who fed émigré fears and fantasies. In Marek's experience Someone always turned out to have a name, to be traceable. When, barely two days later, Someone informed Piotr that he had violated his agreement (that is, he was leaving) and therefore would not receive any money, he gazed at the unreadable signature and knew for certain that no human brain could be behind this; it was entirely the work of some bureaucratic machine performing on its own. Marek continued to grumble and to speculate about Someone, while Piotr settled for the machine. It was a restful solution and one he had learned to live with.

Except for his debt to Marek, which he now had no means of repaying, Piotr had no regrets about leaving. He seemed to have been sleeping in the doctor's old office forever, hearing her wounded voice in the night, assaulted by the strident news broadcast at six, measuring the size of today's stone in his chest, opening the shutters to a merciless sky, thinking of the mailbox and the key and the message from Laurie. Piotr suddenly realized that he had gone in and out of the house twice that day without looking for a letter. That was freedom! It was like the return to life after a long illness, like his wife feeding him smuggled soup out of a jar and saying, "You *will* get better." When he called Maria to say good-bye, she took the news of his leaving calmly. Piotr was only another novel. She turned the pages slowly. Sometimes in novels there is bound to be a shock. She invited him to tea, as though he had just arrived and their best conversations were yet to come. On his way to this last visit Piotr forced himself to look in the letter box, out of distant sympathy for the victim he had once been. Inside, propped at an angle, was a view of San Pietro in Venice and a message in Laurie's childish hand, with the inevitable spelling mistake:

It is over.

My friend and I seperating forever.

It is you I love.

Back Monday 8 P.M. Please meet chez moi.

"Love" was underlined three times.

Piotr had been condemned to death by hanging but now the blindfold was removed. He descended the gallows steps to perfect safety. The hangman untied his hands, lit his cigarette. He was given a passport good for all countries and for eternity. His first poems had just been published. He had fallen in love and she loved him, she was "really chearfull," and love, love, love was underlined three times. Today was Monday; there were still four hours to wait. The courtyard and the dull street beyond it became as white as Piotr's imagined Venice. He stood in the transformed street and said to himself that he was forty-three and that at last, for the first time, a woman had given something up for him. Laurie had turned from the person who provided travel, friendship, warmth, material help (somebody was certainly paying for the seventh-floor studio) for the sake of Piotr. She had done it without asking him to underwrite her risk, without a guarantee. Now he understood the fable about the Matisse, about loving and doing without.

He began to walk slowly toward a bus stop. Now, think about this, he told himself. She is alone except for that one brother who never writes. She has no training, no real education to speak of, and no money, and money is oxygen here in the West. Well, she has me, he thought. She has only me, and she could have anyone. The feeling that her silvery world depended on him now made it all the more mysterious and desirable. Now, be practical, he said. Now, be practical. . . . But he did not know what to be practical about; it was part of his new, thrilling role as Laurie's protector. What next? Piotr was separated, not divorced. He would return to Warsaw, divorce his wife, come back to France, and marry Laurie. He wondered how he had been so obtuse until now, why he had not thought of this sooner. Laurie had never mentioned any such arrangement—another proof of her generosity. He would apply for a post in France, perhaps at a provincial university. He would read poetry aloud to the wives of doctors and notaries and they would imagine he had escaped from Siberia and it was Russian they were hearing.

Piotr had forgotten that he was expelled, might never be allowed out of Poland or back into France in his lifetime, that he owed money to Marek, that he was entangled, hobbled, bound. His children became remote and silent, as if they had never existed outside their father's imagination.

Piotr, who never discussed his private affairs, told Maria about Laurie. His account of the long journey leading up to the arrival of the postcard, and Maria's reaction to it, created a third person in the room. She was a quiet, noble girl who without a trace of moral blackmail had traded safety for love. "She is the wonderful woman you deserve," said Maria, listening intently. Before bliss submerged him completely Piotr was able to see Maria and himself as two figures bobbing in the wake of a wreck. Their hopefulness about love had survived prisons. And yet every word he was saying seemed to him like part of a long truth. His new Laurie resembled the imaginary Matisse she had sent to Warsaw, which he had unrolled with wonder and admiration: She was motionless, mute, she was black-on-white, and she never looked at him.

"Promise me one thing," said Maria. "That you will not ask her any questions. Promise." He promised. Leaning forward, she took Piotr's face in her hands and kissed him. "I wish you so much happiness," she said.

His unpacked suitcase at his feet, Piotr sat on the edge of the bed. Laurie lay on her side, her head on her arm. The ashtray between them did not prevent her from sprinkling the white coverlet with ash. She had been under the shower when he arrived and she still wore a toweling bathrobe. Her hair, damp and darkened, lay flat on her neck and cheek and gave her a tight, sleek, unknown quality.

"Oh, it was all right when we were tramping around looking at those damned churches," she said. "But right from the beginning I knew it was going wrong. I felt something in him—a sort of disapproval of me. Everything he'd liked until now he started to criticize. Those Catholics—they always go back to what they were. Sex was wrong, living was wrong. Only God was O.K. He said why didn't I work, why didn't I start training to be a nurse. He said there was a world shortage of nurses. 'You could be having a useful life,' he said. It was horrible, Potter. I just don't know what went wrong. I thought maybe he'd met a girl he liked better than me. I kept fishing, but he wouldn't say. He was comparing—I could tell that. He said, 'All *you* ever think about is your lunch and your breakfast'—something like that."

Piotr said, "What is the business he so enjoys running?"

"Watch straps."

"Watch straps?"

"That's what he was doing in Italy. Buying them. We were in Florence, Milan. Venice was the holiday part. You should have seen the currency he smuggled in—Swiss, American. The stuff was falling out of his pockets like oak leaves. His mind was somewhere else the whole time. We weren't really together. We were just two travelers who happened to be sharing a room."

"You didn't happen to find yourself in the same bed?" said Piotr. He moved the ashtray out of the way and edged a box of paper handkerchiefs into its place. Although her face did not crumple or her voice change, tears were forming and spilling along her cheek and nose.

"Oh, sometimes, after a good dinner. He said a horrible thing. He said, 'Sometimes I can't bear to touch you.' No, no, we were just two travelers," she said, blowing her nose. "We each had our own toothpaste, he had his cake of soap. I didn't bring any soap and when we were moving around, changing hotels, he'd pack his before I'd even had my bath. I'd be there in the bathtub and he'd already packed his soap. He'd always been nice before. I just don't know. I'll never understand it. Potter, I can't face going out. I haven't eaten all day, but I still can't face it. Could you just heat some water and pour it over a soup cube for me?"

"Watch straps," said Piotr in a language she could not understand. He turned on the little electric plate. "Watch straps."

"He pretended he was doing it for me," said Laurie, lying flat on her back now. "Letting me go so I could create my own life. Those Catholics. He just wanted to be free for some other reason. To create his, I suppose."

"Is he still young enough for that?" said Piotr. "To create a whole life?"

"He's younger than you are, if that's young."

"I thought it might have been a much older person," said Piotr. "Your first friend of all. He took you home for holidays, out of Bishop Purse."

"*That* one. No-o-o. What finally happened with *him* was, his wife got sick. She got this awful facial neuralgia. It made a saint out of him. Believe me, Potter, when you get mixed up with a married man you're mixed up with his wife, too. They work as a team. Even when she doesn't know, she knows. It's an inside job. They went all over the place seeing new doctors. She used to scream with pain in hotel rooms. It's the sickness of unhappy wives—did you know?"

"I know about the ailment of bachelors. I thought you said it was the Venice person"—he was about to say "the Austrian"—"who knew you when you were young."

"Everybody got me young, when it comes to that. Oh," she said, suddenly alert, sitting up, dry-eyed, "don't sit there looking superior."

"I am standing," said Piotr. "I am here like a dog on its hind legs with a bowl of soup."

She took the bowl, with a scowl that would have meant ingratitude had its source been anything but mortification. "Well," she said abruptly, "I couldn't count on you, could I? You come and go and you've got those children. Who do they live with?"

"Their mother."

A tremor, like a chill, ran over her, and he recalled how she had trembled and spilled her coffee long ago. "How old are they?"

"Twelve and six."

"Why did you have the second one?" (Her first sensible observation.) "Girls?"

"Two boys."

"I hope they die."

"I don't," said Piotr.

"Do they love you?"

He hesitated; where love was concerned he had lost his bearings. He said, "They seem to eat up love and wait for more."

"Is there always more?"

"So far."

"They're like me, then," said Laurie.

"No, for children it is real food. It adds to their bones."

"Then it's not like me. I soak it up and it disappears and I feel undernourished. Do they like you?"

"They are excited and happy when they see me but hardly notice when I go."

"That's because you bring them presents." She began to cry, hard this time. "They won't need you much longer. They've got their mother. I really need you. I need you more than they do. I need any man more than his children do."

Piotr found sheets in the wardrobe and made the bed; he found pajamas in one of her plastic boxes, and the Polish sleeping potion in the bathroom. He counted out the magic drops. "Now sleep," he said. Something was missing: "Where is your white watch?"

"I don't know. I must have lost it. I lost it ages ago," she said, and turned on her side.

Piotr hung up Laurie's bathrobe and emptied the ashtray. He rinsed the yellow bowl and put it back on the shelf. He still had to break the news of his going; he did not feel banished but rather as if it were he who had decided to leave, who had established his own fate. Who gave you the *Palmström* poems, said Piotr silently. Another Potter? The man who had you at fifteen and then shipped you to Europe when you started getting in his way? Was it the Austrian? The man in Venice who suddenly feels he is sinning and can't bear to touch you? At the back of his mind was a small, anxious, jealous Piotr, for whom he felt little sympathy.

Laurie, though fresh from a shower, had about her a slightly sour smell, the scent that shock and terror produce on the skin. She was young, so that it was no worse than fresh yeast, or the odor of bread rising—the aura of the living, not yet of the dead. He remembered his wife and how her skin, then her voice, then her mind had become acid. "Am I plain?" she had said. "Am I diseased? Don't you consider me a normal woman?" You are good, you are brave, you are an impeccable mother to your children, but I don't want you, at least not the way you want me to, had been his answer. And so she became ugly, ill, haunted—all that he dreaded in women. It seemed to him that he saw the first trace of this change in the sleeping Laurie. She had lost her credentials, her seal of aristocracy. She had dropped to a lower division inhabited by Piotr's wife and Piotr himself; they were inferiors, unable to command loyalty or fidelity or even consideration in exchange for passion. Her silvery world, which had reflected nothing but Piotr's desperate inventions, floated and sank in Venice. This is what people like Maria and me are up against, he thought—our inventions. We belong either in books or in prison, out of the way. Romantic people are a threat to civilization. That man in Venice who wanted to make a nurse of poor Laurie was a romantic, too, a dangerous lunatic.

Laurie lay breathing deeply and slowly, in a sleep full of colored dreams—dreams of an imaginary Matisse, a real Lake Constance, a real Venice, dark and sad. "On a sailing holiday at Lake Constance . . ." Even now, when it no longer mattered, the truth of this particular dream clamped on Piotr's chest like the ghost of an old pain. Quietly, in order not to disturb her, he took one of his pink placebos. He thought of how frightened she would be if she woke to find him in the grip of an attack—she would be frightened of nearly everything now. He could still see the car hurtling all over the map as Laurie tried to run away from him and what she called "the situation." He could see it even though the journey had been only in her imagination, then in his. She had flown to Zurich, probably, and been met by, certainly, the man whose business was watch straps, or even ... It doesn't matter now, he said. She had been telling the truth, because her mind had been in flight.

He lay down beside her and, reaching out, switched off the light. The pattern of reflected streetlights that sprang to life on the ceiling had, for three nights long ago, been like the vault of Heaven. After tonight Laurie would watch it alone—at any rate, without Piotr. Poor Laurie, he thought. Poor, poor Laurie. He felt affection, kindness—less than he could feel for his children, less than the obligation he still owed his wife. Out of compassion he stroked her darkened hair. No one but Piotr himself could have taken the measure of his disappointment as he said, So there really was nothing in it, was there? So this was all it ever was—only tenderness. An immense weight of blame crushed him, flattened him, and by so doing cleansed and absolved him. I was incapable of any more feeling than this. I never felt more than kindness. There was nothing in it from the beginning. It was only tenderness, after all.

BAUM, GABRIEL,
1 9 3 5 – (   )

———

Uncle August

At the start of the 1960s Gabriel Baum's only surviving relative, his Uncle August, turned up in Paris. There was nothing accidental about this; the International Red Cross, responding to an appeal for search made on Gabriel's behalf many years before, had finally found Gabriel in Montparnasse and his uncle in the Argentine. Gabriel thought of his uncle as "the other Baum," because there were just the two of them. Unlike Gabriel's father and mother, Uncle August had got out of Europe in plenty of time. He owned garages in Rosario and Santa Fe and commercial real estate in Buenos Aires. He was as different from Gabriel as a tree is from the drawing of one; nevertheless Gabriel saw in him something of the old bachelor he too might become.

Gabriel was now twenty-five; he had recently been discharged from the French Army after twenty months in Algeria. Notice of his uncle's arrival reached him at a theater seating two hundred persons where he had a part in a play about J. K. Huysmans. The play explained Huysmans's progress from sullen naturalism to mystical Christianity. Gabriel had to say, "But Joris Karl has written words of penetrating psychology," and four or five other things.

The two Baums dined at the Bristol, where Gabriel's uncle was staying. His uncle ordered for both, because Gabriel was taking too long to decide. Uncle August spoke German and Spanish and the pale scrupulous French and English that used to be heard at spas and in the public rooms of large, airy hotels. His clothes were old-fashioned British; watch and luggage were

Swiss. His manners were German, prewar—pre-1914, that is. To Gabriel, his uncle seemed to conceal an obsolete social mystery; but a few Central Europeans, still living, would have placed him easily as a tight, unyielding remainder of the European shipwreck.

The old man observed Gabriel closely, watching to see how his orphaned nephew had been brought up, whether he broke his bread or cut it, with what degree of confidence he approached his asparagus. He was certainly pleased to have discovered a younger Baum and may even have seen Gabriel as part of God's subtle design, bringing a surrogate son to lighten his old age, one to whom he could leave Baum garages; on the other hand it was clear that he did not want just any Baum calling him "Uncle."

"I have a name," he said to Gabriel. "I have a respected name to protect. I owe it to my late father." He meant his own name: August Ernest Baum, b. Potsdam 1899–( ).

After dinner they sat for a long time drinking brandy in the hushed dining room. His uncle was paying for everything.

He said, "But were your parents ever married, finally? Because we were never told he had actually *married* her."

Gabriel at that time seemed to himself enduringly healthy and calm. His hair, which was dark and abundant, fell in locks on a surprisingly serene forehead. He suffered from only two complaints, which he had never mentioned. The first had to do with his breathing, which did not proceed automatically, like other people's. Sometimes, feeling strange and ill, he would realize that heart and lungs were suspended on a stopped, held breath. Nothing disastrous had come of this. His second complaint was that he seemed to be haunted, or inhabited, by a child—a small, invisible version of himself, a Gabriel whose mauled pride he was called on to salve, whose claims against life he was forced to meet with whatever thin means time provided, whose scores he had rashly promised to settle before realizing that debt and payment never interlock. His uncle's amazing question and the remark that followed it awoke the wild child, who began to hammer on Gabriel's heart.

He fixed his attention on a bottle—one of the dark bottles whose labels bear facsimiles of gold medals earned at exhibitions no one has ever heard of, in cities whose names have been swept off the map: Breslau 1884, Dantzig 1897, St. Petersburg 1901.

"The only time I ever saw her, they certainly were not married," his uncle resumed. "It was during the very hot autumn of 1930. He had left the university announcing that he would earn his living writing satirical poetry. My father sent me to Berlin to see what was going on. *She* was going on. Her dress had short sleeves. She wore no stockings. She had a clockwork bear she kept winding up and sending round the table. She was hopelessly young. 'Have you thought about the consequences?' I asked him. 'No degree. Low-grade employment all your life. Your father's door forever closed to you. And what about *her*? Is she an heiress? Will her father adopt you?' She was said to be taking singing lessons," he added, as if there were something wrong with that.

"Shut him up," ordered the younger Gabriel, but Gabriel was struggling for breath.

"I have lost everything and everyone but I still have a name," said his uncle. "I have a name to protect and defend. There is always the trace of a marriage certificate somewhere. Even when the registry office was bombed. Even when the papers had to be left behind. How old were you the last time you saw them?"

"Eight," said Gabriel, now in control.

"Were they together?"

"Oh, yes."

"Did they have time to say good-bye?"

"They left me with a neighbor. The neighbor said they'd be back."

"Where was this?"

"Marseilles. We were supposed to be from Alsace, but their French sounded wrong. People noticed I wasn't going to school. Someone reported them."

"Sounded wrong!" said his uncle. "Everything must have sounded wrong from the minute he left the university. It is a terrible story," he said, after a moment. "No worse than most, but terrible all the same. Why, why did he wait until the last minute? And once he had got to Marseilles what prevented him from getting on a boat?"

"He was a man of action," said Gabriel.

If his uncle wanted another Baum, he did not want a frivolous one. He said, "He was much younger than I was. I never saw him after 1930. He went his own way. After the war I had the family traced. Everybody was dead—camps, suicide, old age. In his case, no one knew what had happened. He disappeared. Of course, it took place in a foreign country. Only the Germans kept accurate records. I wish you knew something about the marriage. I know that my late father would not have wanted a bastard in the family."

Uncle August visited Nice, Lugano, and Venice, which he found greatly changed, then he returned to South America. He sent long letters to Gabriel several times a year, undeterred by the fact that he seldom received an answer. He urged his nephew to take a strong, positive line with his life and above all to get out of Paris, which had never amounted to more than an émigré way station. Its moral climate invited apathy and rot.

Gabriel read his uncle's letters in La Méduse, a *bar-tabac* close to the old Montparnasse railway station. Actors and extras for television were often recruited there; no one remembered how or why this arrangement had come about. Gabriel usually sat with his back to the window, at a table to the right of the door facing the bar. He drank draft beer or coffee and looked at magazines other customers had left behind. Glancing up from one of his uncle's letters, he saw the misted window in the mirror behind the bar. In a polluted winter fog neon glowed warmly—the lights of home.

His uncle wrote that he had liquidated his holdings at a loss and was thinking of settling in South Africa. He must have changed his mind, for a subsequent letter described him retired and living near a golf course, looked after by the housekeeper he had often told Gabriel about—his first mention of any such person. A heart attack made it tiring for him to write. The housekeeper sent news. Gabriel, who did not know Spanish, tried to get the drift. She signed "Anna Meléndes," then "Anna Baum."

Gabriel was playing a Brecht season in a suburban cultural center when word came that his uncle had died. *The Caucasian Chalk Circle* and *Mother Courage* alternated for an audience of schoolchildren and factory workers brought in by the busload, apparently against their will. Gabriel thought of Uncle August, his obstinacy and his pride, and truly mourned him. His uncle had left him an envelope he did not bother to open, being fairly certain it did not contain a check.

No Baum memorial existed, and so he invented one. Upon its marble surface he inscribed:

Various Baums:	Gone
Father:	1909–1943 (probably)
Mother:	1912–1943 (probably)
Uncle:	1899–1977
Gabriel B.:	1935–( )

Beneath the last name he drew a line, meaning to say this was the end. He saw, however, that the line, far from ending the Baum question, created a new difficulty: It left the onlooker feeling that these dates and names were factors awaiting a solution. He needed to add the dead to the living, or subtract the living from the dead—to come to some conclusion.

He thought of writing a zero, but the various Baums plus four others did not add up to nothing. His uncle by dying had not diminished the total number of Baums but had somehow increased it. Gabriel, with his feet on the finish line and with uncounted Baums behind him, was a variable quantity: For some years he had been the last of the Baums, then there had been two of them. Now he was unique again.

Someone else would have to work it out, he decided—someone unknown to him, perhaps unborn. In the meantime he had the memorial in his head, where it could not be lost or stolen.

Gabriel's Liselotte

Soon after Gabriel's uncle's visit, a generation of extremely pretty German girls suddenly blossomed in Paris. There would be just that one flowering— that one bright growth. They came because their fathers were dead or exiled under unremarkable names. Some of them were attracted to Gabriel— Gabriel as he was, with the dark locks, the serene brow—and he was drawn in turn, as to a blurred reflection, a face half recalled.

Gabriel at that time still imagined that everyone's life must be about the same, something like a half-worked crossword puzzle. He was always on the lookout for definitions and new solutions. When he moved close to other people, however, he saw that their lives were not puzzles but problems set in code, no two of which ever matched.

The pretty girls went home, finally, whistled back by solemn young men with solemn jobs. They had two children apiece, were probably rinsing the gray out of their hair now. (Gabriel cut his own as short as possible as it grew scarce.) He remembered Freya, who had thrown herself in the Seine over a married man, but who could swim, and Barbara, whose abortion two or three of them had felt bound to pay for, and Marie, who had gone to Alsace and had nearly been crowned Miss Upper Rhine before they found out she was a foreigner. Gabriel's memory dodging behind one name after the other brought him face-to-face with his Liselotte. Daughter of a dead man and a whore of a mother (which seemed to be a standard biography then), embarked on the au-pair adventure, pursuing spiritual cleanness through culture, she could be seen afternoons in Parc Monceau reading books of verse whose close print and shoddy bindings seemed to assure a cultural warranty. There was something meek about the curve of her neck. She had heard once that if one were arrested and held without trial it was an aid to sanity to have an anthology of poems in one's head. Poor Liselotte, whose aid to sanity never got beyond *"Le ciel est, par-dessus le toit, Si bleu, si calme!"* held the book flat on her knees, following the words with her finger.

"Who would want to arrest you?" Gabriel asked.

"You never know."

Well, that was true. Thinking there might be a better career for her he gave her lines to try. She practiced, "Is it tonight that you *die?*" "Is it *tonight* that *you* die?" Gabriel counted six, seven, eight shades of green around the place in Parc Monceau, where she sat asking this. He used to take the No. 84 bus to see her—he who never went out of Montparnasse unless he had to, who had never bothered to learn about bus routes or the names of streets. For the sake of Liselotte he crossed the Seine with prim, gloved women, with old men wearing slivers of ribbon to mark this or that war. Liselotte, now seeking improvement by way of love, made him speak French to her. She heard, memorized, and recited back to him without flaw his life's story. He had promised the child-Gabriel he would never marry a German, but it was not that simple; in an odd way she did not seem German *enough.*

She had learned her lines for nothing. The director he introduced her to also thought she did not look German. She was one of the brown-eyed Catholic girls from around Speyer. She prayed for Gabriel, but his life after the prayers was the same as before. She had a catch in her voice, almost a stammer; she tried to ask Gabriel if he wanted to marry her, but the word caught. He said to himself that she might not enjoy being Liselotte Baum after having been Liselotte Pfligge. Her stepfather, Wilhelm Pfligge—of Swiss origin, she said—had tried to rape her; still, she had his name. Gabriel thought that if the custom of name-changing had been reversed and he had been required, through marriage, to become Gabriel Pfligge, he might have done so without cringing, or at least with tact. Perhaps he would have been expected to call Wilhelm Pfligge "Papa." He saw Papa Pfligge with a mustache, strangely mottled ears, sporty shoes, a springy walk, speaking with his lips to Gabriel's ear: "We both love Liselotte so much, eh?"

While Gabriel continued to develop this, giving Papa Pfligge increasingly preposterous things to say, Liselotte gave up on love and culture and the au-pair adventure and went home. He accompanied her to the Gare de l'Est and

lifted her two cases to the overhead rack. Then he got down and stood on
the gray platform and watched her being borne away. The train was blurred,
as if he were looking at it through Liselotte's tears.

For a time her letters were like the trail of a child going ever deeper into
the woods. He could not decide whether or not to follow; while he was still
deciding, and not deciding, the trail stopped and the path became overgrown behind her.

The Interview

Until he could no longer write letters, Gabriel's uncle nagged him with useless advice. Most of it was about money. Owing to Gabriel's inability to
produce his father's marriage certificate (in fact, he never tried), his uncle
could not in all conscience leave him Baum possessions. It was up to
Gabriel, therefore, to look after his own future. He begged Gabriel to find
a job with some large, benevolent international firm. It would give him the
assurance of money coming in, would encourage French social-security bu-
reaucrats to take an interest in him, and would put him in the way of receiving an annuity at the age of sixty-five.

"Sixty-five is your next step," his uncle warned, for Gabriel's thirtieth
birthday.

He counseled Gabriel to lay claim to those revenues known as "German
money," but Gabriel's parents had vanished without trace; there was no way
of proving they had not taken ship for Tahiti. And it would not have been
in Gabriel's power to equate banknotes to a child's despair. His uncle fell
back on the Algerian War. Surely Gabriel was entitled to a pension? No, he
was not. War had never been declared. What Gabriel had engaged in was a
long tactical exercise for which there was no compensation except experience.

The Algerian-pension affair rankled with Gabriel. He had to fill out employment forms that demanded assurance that he had "fulfilled his military
obligations." Sometimes it was taken for granted he had been rejected out
of hand. There was no rational basis for this; he supposed it must be because of "Profession: Actor." After his return he continued to take an interest in the war. He was like someone who has played twenty minutes of a
match and has to know the outcome. As far as he could make out, it had
ended in a draw. The excitement died down, and then no one knew what to

put in the magazines and political weeklies anymore. Some journalists tried to interest Gabriel in Brittany, where there was an artichoke glut; others hinted that the new ecumenicity beginning to seep out of Rome was really an attack on French institutions. Gabriel doubted this. Looking for news about his pension, he learned about the Western European consumer society and the moral wounds that were being inflicted on France through full employment. Between jobs, he read articles about people who said they had been made unhappy by paper napkins and washing machines.

Most of the customers in La Méduse were waiting for a television call. The rest were refugees, poets' widows, and foreign students looking for work to supplement their scholarships. Up at the bar, where drinks were cheaper, were clustered the second-generation émigré actors Gabriel thought of as bachelor orphans. Unlike Gabriel, they had been everywhere—to Brazil, where they could not understand the language, and to New York, where they complained about the climate, and to Israel, where they were disappointed with the food. Now they were in Paris, where they disliked the police.

Sometimes Dieter Pohl shared Gabriel's table. He was a Bavarian Gabriel's age—thirty—who played in films about the Occupation. Dieter had begun as a private, had been promoted to lieutenant, and expected to become a captain soon. He had two good facial expressions, one for victory and one for defeat. Advancing, he gazed keenly upward, as if following a hawk to the vanishing point. Sometimes he pressed binoculars to his eyes. Defeat found him staring at his boots. He could also be glimpsed marching off into captivity with a bandage around his head. The captivity scene took place in the last episode. Gabriel, enrolled as a victim, had generally been disposed of in the first. His rapid disappearance was supposed to establish the tone of the period for audiences too young to recall it.

It was around this time, when French editorial alarm about the morally destructive aspect of Western prosperity was at its most feverish, that a man calling himself Briseglace wandered into the bar and began asking all the aliens and strangers there if they were glad to be poor. He said that he was a journalist, that his wife had left him for a psychiatrist, and that his girlfriend took tickets in a cinema farther along the street. He said that the Montparnasse railway station was to be torn down and a dark tower built in its place; no one believed him. He wore a tie made of some yellow Oriental stuff. His clothes looked as if they had been stitched by nuns on a convent sewing machine. Gabriel and his generation had gone into black—

black pullovers, black leather jackets, soft black boots. Their haircuts still spoke of military service and colonial wars. Briseglace's straggling, grayish locks, his shapeless and shabby and oddly feminine-looking overcoat, his stained fingers and cheap cigarettes, his pessimism and his boldness and his belief in the moral advantages of penury all came straight from the Latin Quarter of the 1940s. He was the Occupation; he was the Liberation, too. The films that Dieter and Gabriel played in grew like common weeds from the heart of whatever young man he once had been. Gabriel's only feeling, seeing him, was disgust at what it meant to grow old.

The dark garments worn in La Méduse gave the place the appearance of a camp full of armed militia into which Briseglace, outdated civilian, had stumbled without cause. Actually, the leather jackets covered only perpetual worry. Some people thought Briseglace was with the CIA, others saw a KGB agent with terrifying credentials. The orphans were certain he was an in-spector sent to see if their residence permits were forgeries. But his questions led only to one tame conclusion, which he begged them to ratify: It was that being poor they were free, and being free they were happy.

Released from immediate danger, a few of the aliens sat and stood straighter, looked nonchalant or offended, depending on how profound their first terrors had been. Dieter declared himself happy in a profession that had brought him moral satisfaction and material comfort, and that provided the general public with notions of history. Some of those at the bar identified themselves as tourists, briefly in Paris, staying at comfortable hotels. Some-one mentioned the high prices that had to be paid for soccer stars. Another recalled that on the subject of personal riches Christ had been ambiguous yet reassuring. Briseglace wrote everything down. When he paid for his coffee he asked for the check, which he had to turn in for expenses. Gabriel, who had decided to have nothing to do with him, turned the pages of *Paris-Match.*

Six weeks later Gabriel emerged in the pages of a left-wing weekly as "Gabriel B., spokesman for the flotsam of Western Europe."

"His first language was German," Gabriel read. "Lacking the rudder of political motivation, his aimless wanderings have cast him up in Montpar-nasse, in the sad fragrance of coffee machines. Do you think he eats in the Jewish quarter, at Jo Goldenberg's, at La Rose d'Or? Never. You will find Gabriel B. gnawing veal cutlets at the Wienerwald, devouring potato dumplings at the Tannhaüser. For Gabriel B. this bizarre nourishment con-stitutes a primal memory, from infancy to age twelve." "Seven," Gabriel scrupulously corrected, but it was too late, the thing was in print. "This handsome Prince of Bohemia has reached the fatal age of thirty. What can he do? Where can he go? Conscience-money from the wealthy German republic keeps him in cigarettes. A holdover from bad times, he slips through the good times without seeing them. The Western European consumer society is not so much an economic condition as a state of mind."

Gabriel read the part about the Prince of Bohemia two or three times. He wondered where the Wienerwald was. In the picture accompanying the article was Dieter Pohl, with his eyes inked over so that he could not be identified and use the identification as an excuse for suing the magazine.

There was no explaining it; Dieter was sure he had not sat for a portrait; Gabriel was positive he had not opened his mouth. He thought of posting the article to Uncle August, but his uncle would take it to be a piece of downright nonsense, like the clockwork bear. Dieter bought half a dozen copies of the magazine for his relatives in Bavaria; it was the first time that a picture of him had ever been published anywhere.

Gabriel's escape from annihilation in two real wars (even though one had been called something else) had left him with reverence for unknown forces. Perhaps Briseglace had been sent to nudge him in some new direction. Perhaps the man would turn up again, confessing he had never been a journalist and had been feigning not in order to harm Gabriel but to ensure his ultimate safety.

Nothing of the kind ever happened, of course. Briseglace was never seen again in La Méduse. The only reaction to the interview came from a cousin of Dieter's called Helga. She did not read French easily and had understood some of it to mean that Dieter was not eating enough. She sent him a quantity of very good gingerbread in a tin box and begged him, not for the first time, to pack his things and come home and let a woman look after his life.

Unsettling Rumors

As he grew older and balder, stouter, and more reflective, Gabriel found himself at odds with the few bachelors he still saw in Montparnasse. They tended to cast back to the 1960s as the springtime of life, though none of them had been all that young. Probably because they had outlived their parents and were without children, they had no way of measuring time. To Gabriel the decade now seemed to have been like a south wind making everyone fretful and jumpy. The colder their prospects, the steadier his friends had become. They slept well, cashed their unemployment checks without grumbling, strolled along the boulevards through a surf of fallen leaves, and discarded calls to revolution, stood in peaceful queues in front of those cinemas that still charged no more than eleven francs. Inside, the seats and carpets were moldering slowly. Half the line shuffling up to the ticket office was probably out of work. His friends preferred films in which women presented no obstacles and created no problems and were shown either naked or in evening dress.

Much of Gabriel's waking time was now spent like this, too—not idly, but immersed in the present moment.

Soon after the Yom Kippur War, a notice had been posted in La Méduse: OWING TO THE ECONOMIC SITUATION NO ONE MAY SIT FOR MORE THAN THIRTY MINUTES OVER A SINGLE ORDER. The management had no legal means of enforcing this; still the notice hung there, a symptom of a new harshness, the sourness engendered by the decline.

"That sign was the end of life as we knew it in the sixties," said Dieter Pohl. He was a colonel now, and as fussy as a monarch at a review about a badge misplaced or a button undone. Gabriel had no equivalent staircase to climb; who ever has heard of a victim's being promoted? Still, he had acquired a variety of victim experiences. Gabriel had been shot, stoned, drowned, suffocated, and marked off for hanging; had been insulted and betrayed; had been shoved aboard trains and dragged out of them; had been flung from the back of a truck with such accidental violence that he had broken his collarbone. His demise, seen by millions of people, some eating their dinner, was still needed in order to give a push to the old dishonorable plot—told ever more simply now, like a fable—while Dieter's fate was still part of its moral.

On this repeated game of death and consequences Dieter's seniority depended. He told Gabriel that the French would be bored with entertainment based on the Occupation by about 1982; by that time he would have been made a general at least once, and would have saved up enough money to buy a business of some kind in his native town.

He often spoke as if the parting were imminent, though he was still only a colonel: "Our biographies are not the same, and you are a real actor, who took lessons, and a real soldier, who fought in a real war. But look at the result—we ended up in the same place, doing the same work, sitting at the same table. Years and years without a disagreement. It is a male situation. Women would never be capable of such a thing."

Gabriel supposed Dieter to mean that women, inclined by nature to quick offense and unending grudges, were not gifted for loyal friendship. Perhaps it was true, but it seemed incomplete. Even the most solitary of the women he could observe—the poets' widows, for instance, with their crocheted berets, their mysterious shopping bags, their fat, waddling dogs—did not cluster together like anxious pigeons on the pretext of friendship. Each one came in alone and sat by herself, reading whatever fascinating stuff she could root out of the shopping bag, staring at strangers with ever-fresh interest, sometimes making comments about them aloud.

A woman can always get some practical use from a torn-up life, Gabriel decided. She likes mending and patching it, making sure the edges are straight. She spreads the last shred out and takes its measure: "What can I do with this remnant? How long does it need to last?" A man puts on his life ready-made. If it doesn't fit, he will try to exchange it for another. Only a fool of a man will try to adjust the sleeves or move the buttons; he doesn't know how.

Some of the older customers were now prey to unsettling rumors. La Méduse was said to have been sold by its owner, a dour Breton with very small eyes. It would soon be converted to a dry cleaner's establishment, as part of the smartening-up of Montparnasse. The chairs, the glasses, the thick, grayish cups and saucers, the zinc-covered bar, the neon tubes on the ceiling—sociological artifacts—had been purchased at roaring prices for a museum in Stockholm. It seemed far-fetched to Gabriel but not impossible; the Montparnasse station had been torn down, and a dark ugly tower had been put in its place. He remembered how Briseglace had predicted this.

Gabriel had noticed lately that he was not seeing Paris as it was but the way it had stayed in his mind; he still saw butchers and grocers and pastry shops, when in reality they had become garages and banks. There was a new smell in the air now, metallic and hot. He was changing too. Hunger was drawn to his attention by a feeling of sadness and loss. He breathed without effort. The child-Gabriel had grown still. Occupation films had fallen off a little, but Gabriel had more resources than Dieter. He wore a checked cap and sang the "Internationale"; he was one of a committee bringing bad news to Seneca. He had a summer season playing Flavius in *Julius Caesar*, and another playing Aston in *The Caretaker* and the zoo director in *The Bedbug*. These festivals were staged in working-class suburbs the inhabitants of which had left for the Côte d'Azur. During one of those summers La Méduse changed hands, shut for three months, and opened with rows of booths, automobile seats made of imitation leather, orange glass lamp-shades, and British First World War recruiting posters plastered on the walls. The notice about not sitting for more than thirty minutes had vanished, replaced by an announcement that ice cream and hamburgers could be obtained. Washrooms and telephones were one flight up instead of in the basement; there was someone on hand to receive tips and take messages. At each table was a bill of fare four pages long and a postcard advertising the café, which customers could send to their friends if they wanted to. The card showed a Medusa jellyfish with long eyelashes and a ribbon on its head, smiling out of a tiny screen. Beneath this one could read:

PUB LA MÉDUSE
THE OLDEST AND MOST CELEBRATED
MEETING-PLACE FOR TELEVISION
STARS IN PARIS

Gabriel tried a number of booths before finding one that suited him. Between the automobile seat and a radiator was a space where he could keep magazines. The draft beer was of somewhat lower quality than before. The main difference between the old place and the new one was its smell. For a time he could not identify it. It turned out to be the reek of a chicory drink, the color of boot polish, invented to fight inflation. The addition of sugar made it nauseating, and it was twice as expensive as coffee had ever been.

The Surrender

Dieter heard that a thirteen-hour television project about the Occupation was to be launched in the spring; he had seen the outline.

He said, "For the moment they just need a few people to be deported and to jump off the train."

Some old-timers heard Dieter say, "They want to deport the Poles," and some heard, "They are rounding up the foreign-born Socialists," and others swore he had asked for twelve Jews to be run over by a locomotive.

Dieter wore a new civilian winter costume, a light brown fur-lined winter coat and a Russian cap. He ate roasted chestnuts, which he peeled with his fingernails. They were in a cornucopia made of half a page of Le Quotidien de Paris. In the old Méduse eating out of newspaper would have meant instant expulsion. Dieter spread the paper on Gabriel's table, sat down, and told him about the film. It would begin with a group of Resistance fighters who were being deported jumping out of a train. Their group would include a coal miner, an anti-Semitic aristocrat, a Communist militant, a peasant with a droll Provençal accent, a long-faced Protestant intellectual, and a priest in doubt about his vocation. Three Jews will be discovered to have jumped or fallen with them: one aged rabbi, one black-market operator, and one anything.

The one anything will be me, Gabriel decided, helping himself to chestnuts. He saw, without Dieter's needing to describe them, the glaring lights, the dogs straining at their leads, the guards running and blowing whistles, the stalled train, a rainstorm, perhaps.

The aristo will be against taking the extra three men along, Dieter said, but the priest will intercede for them. The miner, or perhaps the black-market man, will stay behind to act as decoy for the dogs while the others all get in a rowboat and make for the maquis. The peasant will turn out to be a British intelligence agent named Scott. The Protestant will fall out of the rowboat; the priest will drown trying to save him; the Communist—

"We know all that," Gabriel interrupted. "Who's there at the end?"

The aristo, said Dieter. The aristo and the aged rabbi will survive twelve episodes and make their way together back to Paris for the Liberation. There they will discover Dieter and his men holed up in the Palais du Luxembourg, standing fast against the local Resistance and a few policemen. The rabbi will die next to the Medici fountain, in the arms of the aristo.

Gabriel thought this did not bode well for the future, but Dieter reassured him: The aristo will now be a changed man. He will storm the Palais and be seen at the end writing MY FRIENDS REMEMBERED on the wall while Dieter and the others file by with their hands up.

"What about the one anything?" said Gabriel. "How long does he last?"

"Dear friend and old comrade," said Dieter, "don't take offense at this. Ten years ago you would have been the first man chosen. But now you are at the wrong age. Who cares what happens to a man of forty-three? You aren't old enough or young enough to make anyone cry. The fact is— forgive me for saying so—but you are the wrong age to play a Jew. A uniform has no age," he added, because he was also forty-three. "And no one is expected to cry at the end, but just to be thoughtful and satisfied."

While Gabriel sat mulling this over, Dieter told him about the helmets the Germans were going to wear. Some were heavy metal, museum pieces;

they gave their wearers headaches and left red marks on the brow. A certain number of light plastic helmets would be distributed, but only to officers. The higher one's rank, the lighter the helmet. What Dieter was getting around to was this: He wondered if Gabriel might not care to bridge this stage of his Occupation career by becoming a surrendering officer, seen in the last episode instead of vanishing after the first. He would be a colonel in the Wehrmacht (humane, idealistic, opposed to extreme measures) while Dieter would have to be the S.S. one (not so good). He and Dieter would both have weightless helmets and comfortable, well-cut uniforms.

Gabriel supposed that Dieter was right, in a way. Certainly, he was at a bad age for dangerous antics. It was time for younger men to take their turn at jumping off moving vehicles, diving into ice-cold streams, and dodging blank shot; nor had he reached that time of life when he could die blessing and inspiring those the script had chosen to survive him. As an officer, doomed to defeat, he would at least be sure of his rank and his role and of being in one piece at the end.

Two weeks later Dieter announced to the old-timers that the whole first scene had been changed; there would now be a mass escape from a convoy of lorries, with dozens of men gunned down on the spot. The original cast was reduced, with the Protestant, the Communist, and the miner eliminated completely. This new position caused some argument and recrimination, in which Gabriel did not take part. All he had to wait for now was the right helmet and good weather.

The usual working delays occurred, so that it was not until May that the last of the Baums tried on his new uniform. Dieter adjusted the shoulders of the tunic and set the plastic helmet at a jaunty angle. Gabriel looked at himself. He removed the helmet and put it back on straight. Dieter spoke encouragingly; he seemed to think that Gabriel was troubled about seeming too stout, too bald, too old for his rank.

"There is nothing like a uniform for revealing a man's real age to him," said Dieter. "But from a distance everyone in uniform looks the same."

Gabriel in his new uniform seemed not just to be looking at himself in a glass but actually to be walking through it. He moved through a liquid mirror, back and forth. With each crossing his breath came a little shorter.

Dieter said generously, "A lot of soldiers went bald prematurely because the helmets rubbed their hair."

The surrender was again delayed, this time on account of bad weather. One sodden afternoon, after hanging about in the Luxembourg Gardens for hours, Dieter and Gabriel borrowed capes from a couple of actors who were playing policemen and, their uniforms concealed, went to a post office so that Dieter could make a phone call. His cousin, Helga, destined by both their families to be his bride, had waited a long time; just when it was beginning to look as if she had waited too long for anything, a widower proposed. She was being married the next day. Dieter had to call and explain why he could not be at the wedding; he was held up waiting for the surrender.

Helga talked to Dieter without drawing breath. He listened for a while, then handed the receiver to Gabriel. Helga continued telling Dieter, or Gabriel, that her husband-to-be had a grandchild who could play the accordion. The child was to perform at the wedding party. The accordion was almost as large as the little girl, and twice as heavy.

"You ought to see her fingers on the keyboard," Helga yelled. "They fly—fast, fast."

Gabriel gave the telephone to Dieter, who assumed a look of blank concentration. When he had heard enough he beckoned to Gabriel. Gabriel pressed the receiver to his ear and learned that Helga was worried. She had dreamed that she was married and that her husband would not make room for her in his apartment. When she wanted to try the washing machine, he was already washing his own clothes. "What do you think of the dream?" she said to Gabriel. "Can you hear me? I still love you." Gabriel placed the receiver softly on a shelf under the telephone and waved Dieter in so that he could say good-bye.

They came out of the post office to a drenching rain. Dieter wondered what shape their uniforms would be in by the time they surrendered. Gabriel argued that after the siege of the Palais du Luxembourg the original uniforms must have shown wear. Dieter answered that it was not up to him or Gabriel to decide such things.

Rain fell for another fortnight, but, at last, on a cool shining June day, they were able to surrender. During one of the long periods of inextricable confusion, Dieter and Gabriel walked as far as the Delacroix monument and sat on its rim. Dieter was disappointed in his men. There were no real Germans among them, but Yugoslavs, Turks, North Africans, Portuguese, and some unemployed French. The Resistance forces were not much better, he said. There had been complaints. Gabriel had to agree that they were a bedraggled-looking lot. Dieter recalled how in the sixties there used to be real Frenchmen, real Germans, authentic Jews. The Jews had played deportation the way they had seen it in films, and the Germans had surrendered according to film tradition, too, but there had been this difference: They had at least been doing something their parents had done before them. They had not only the folklore of movies to guide them but—in many cases—firsthand accounts. Now, even if one could assemble a true cast of players, they would be trying to imitate their grandfathers. They were at one remove too many. There was no assurance that a real German, a real Frenchman would be any more plausible now than a Turk.

Dieter sighed, and glanced up at the houses on the other side of the street edging the park. "It wouldn't be bad to live up there," he said. "At the top, with one of those long terraces. They grow real trees on them—poplars, birches."

"What would it cost?"

"Around a hundred and fifty million francs," said Dieter. "Without the furniture."

"Anyone can have a place like that with money," said Gabriel. "The interesting thing would be to live up there without it."

"How?"

Gabriel took off his helmet and looked deeply inside it. He said, "I don't know."

Dieter showed him the snapshots of his cousin's wedding. Helga and the groom wore rimless spectacles. In one picture they cut a cake together; in another they tried to drink out of the same champagne glass. Eyeglasses very like theirs, reduced in size, were worn by a plain little girl. On her head was a wreath of daisies. She was dressed in a long, stiff yellow gown. Gabriel could see just the hem of the dress and the small shoes, and her bashful anxious face and slightly crossed eyes. Her wrists were encircled by daisies, too. Most of her person was behind an accordion. The accordion seemed to be falling apart; she had all she could do to keep it together.

"My cousin's husband's granddaughter," said Dieter. He read Helga's letter: " 'She can play anything—fast, fast. Her fingers simply fly over the keyboard.' "

Gabriel examined every detail of the picture. The child was dazzled and alarmed, and the accordion was far too heavy. "What is her name?" he said.

Dieter read more of the letter and said, "Erna."

"Erna," Colonel Baum repeated. He looked again at the button of a face, the flower bracelets, the feet with the heels together—they must have told her to stand that way. He gave the snapshot back without saying anything.

A crowd had collected in the meantime, drawn by the lights and the equipment and the sight of the soldiers in German uniform. Some asked if they might be photographed with them; this often happened when a film of that kind was made in the streets.

An elderly couple edged up to the two officers. The woman said, in German, in a low voice, "What are you doing here?"

"Waiting to surrender," said Dieter.

"I can see that, but what are you *doing*?"

"I don't know," said Dieter. "I've been sitting on the edge of this monument for thirty-five years. I'm still waiting for orders."

The man tried to give them cigarettes, but neither colonel smoked. The couple took pictures of each other standing between Dieter and Gabriel, and went away.

Why is it, said Gabriel to himself, that when I was playing a wretched, desperate victim no one ever asked to have his picture taken with me? The question troubled him, seeming to proceed from the younger Gabriel, who had been absent for some time now. He hoped his unruly tenant was not on his way back, screaming for a child's version of justice, for an impossible world.

Some of the men put their helmets upside down on the ground and tried to make the visitors pay for taking their pictures. Dieter was disturbed by this. "Of course, you were a real soldier," he said to Gabriel unhappily. "All this must seem inferior." They sat without saying anything for a time and then Dieter began to talk about ecology. Because of ecology, there was a demand in Bavaria for fresh bread made of authentic flour, salt, water, and yeast. Because of unemployment, there were people willing to return to the old, forgotten trades, at which one earned practically nothing and had to work all night. The fact was that he had finally saved up enough money and had bought a bakery in his native town. He was through with the war, the Occupation, the Liberation, and captivity. He was going home.

This caused the most extraordinary change in Gabriel's view of the park. All the greens in it became one dull color, as if thunderous clouds had gathered low in the sky.

"You will always be welcome," said Dieter. "Your room will be ready, a bed made up, flowers in a vase. I intend to marry someone in the village—someone young."

Gabriel said, "If you have four or five children, how can you keep a spare room?"

Still, it was an attractive thought. The greens emerged again, fresh and bright. He saw the room that could be his. Imagine being wakened in a clean room by birds singing and the smell of freshly baked bread. Flowers in a vase—Gabriel hardly knew one from the other, only the caged flowers of parks. He saw, in a linen press, sheets strewn with lavender. His clothes hung up or folded. His breakfast on a white tablecloth, under a lime tree. A basket of warm bread, another of boiled eggs. Dieter's wife putting her hand on the white coffeepot to see if it was still hot enough for Gabriel. A jug of milk, another of cream. Dieter's obedient children drinking from mugs, their chins on the rim of the table. Yes, and the younger Gabriel, revived and outraged and jealous, thrashing around in his heart, saying, Think about empty rooms, letters left behind, cold railway stations washed down with disinfectant, dark glaciers of time. And, then, Gabriel knew nothing about the country. He could not see himself actually *in* it. He had never been to the country except to jump out of trains. It was only in films that he had seen mist lifting or paths lost in ferns.

They surrendered all the rest of the afternoon. The aristo wrote "MY FRIENDS REMEMBERED" on the wall while Dieter and Gabriel led some Turks and Yugoslavs and some unemployed Frenchmen into captivity. The aristo did not even bother to turn around and look. Gabriel was breathing at a good rhythm—not too shallow, not too fast. An infinity of surrenders had preceded this one, in color and in black-and-white, with music and without. A long trail of application forms and employment questionnaires had led Gabriel here: "Baum, Gabriel, b. 1935, Germany, nat. French, mil. serv. obl. fulf." (Actually, for some years now his date of birth had rendered the assurance about military service unnecessary.) Country words ran meanwhile in Gabriel's head. He thought, Dense thickets, lizards and snakes, a thrush's egg, a bee, lichen, wild berries, dark thorny leaves, pale mushrooms. Each word carried its own fragrance.

At the end of the day Dieter's face was white and tired and perfectly blank. He might have been listening to Helga. The aristo came over, smoking a cigarette. About twenty-three years before this, he and Gabriel had performed before a jury in a one-act play of Jules Renard's. The aristo had received an honorable mention, Gabriel a first. The aristo hadn't recognized Gabriel until now because of the uniform. He said, "What's the matter with him?"

Dieter sat slumped in an iron chair belonging to the park administration, staring at his boots. He jerked his head up and looked around, crying, "Why? Where?" and something else Gabriel didn't catch.

Gabriel hoped Dieter was not going to snap now, with the bakery and the flowers and the children in sight. "Well, well, old friend!" said Dieter, clutching Gabriel and trying to get to his feet. "Save your strength! Don't take things to heart! You'll dance at my wedding!"

"Exhaustion," said the aristo.

Gabriel and Dieter slowly made their way to the street, where Volkswagen buses full of actors were waiting. The actors made signs meaning to tell them to hurry up; they were all tired and impatient and anxious to change into their own clothes and get home. Dieter leaned on his old friend. Every few steps he stopped to talk excitedly, as people put to a great strain will do, all in a rush, like the long babbling of dreams.

"You'll have to walk faster," said Gabriel, beginning to feel irritated. "The buses won't wait forever, and we can be arrested for wearing these uniforms without a reason."

"There's a very good reason," said Dieter, but he seemed all at once to recover.

That night at La Méduse Dieter drew the plan of the bakery and the large apartment above it, with an X marking Gabriel's room. He said that Gabriel would spend his summers and holidays there, and would teach Dieter's children to pronounce French correctly. The light shining out of the orange glass lampshade made the drawing seem attractive and warm. It turned out that Dieter hadn't actually bought the bakery but had made a down payment and was negotiating for a bank loan.

The proprietor of La Méduse now came over to their table, accompanied by a young couple—younger than Dieter and Gabriel, that is—to whom he had just sold the place. He introduced them, saying, "My oldest customers. You know their faces, of course. Television."

The new owners shook hands with Gabriel and Dieter, assuring them that they did not intend to tamper with the atmosphere of the old place; not for anything in the world would they touch the recruiting posters or the automobile seats.

After they had gone Dieter seemed to lose interest in his drawing; he folded it in half, then in half again, and finally put his glass down on it. "They are a pair of crooks, you know," he said. "They had to get out of Bastia because they had swindled so many people they were afraid of being murdered. Apparently they're going to turn La Méduse into a front for the Corsican Mafia." Having said this, Dieter gave a great sigh and fell silent. Seeing that he had given up talking about the bakery and Gabriel's room,

Gabriel drew a magazine out from behind the radiator and began to read. Dieter let him go on reading for quite a while before he sighed again. Gabriel did not look up. Dieter unfolded the drawing and smoothed it flat. He examined it, made a change or two with a pencil, and said something indistinct.

Gabriel said, "What?" without raising his head. Dieter answered, "My father lived to be ninety."

SPECK'S IDEA

―――――

࿇

$\mathcal{S}$andor Speck's first art gallery in Paris was on the Right Bank, near the Church of St. Elisabeth, on a street too narrow for cars. When his block was wiped off the map to make way for a five-story garage, Speck crossed the Seine to the shadow of Saint-Julien-le-Pauvre, where he set up shop in a picturesque slum protected by law from demolition. When this gallery was blown up by Basque separatists, who had mistaken it for a travel agency exploiting the beauty of their coast, he collected his insurance money and moved to the Faubourg Saint-Germain.

Here, at terrifying cost, he rented four excellent rooms—two on the loggia level, and a clean dry basement for framing and storage. The entrance, particularly handsome, was on the street side of an eighteenth-century *hôtel particulier* built around an elegant court now let out as a parking concession. The building had long before been cut up into dirty, decaying apartments, whose spiteful, quarrelsome, and avaricious tenants were forgiven every failing by Speck for the sake of being the Count of this and the Prince of that. Like the flaking shutters, the rotting windowsills, the slops and oil stains in the ruined court, they bore a Proustian seal of distinction, like a warranty, making up for his insanely expensive lease. Though he appreciated style, he craved stability even more. In the Faubourg, he seemed at last likely to find it: Not a stone could be removed without the approval of the toughest cultural authorities of the nation. Three Marxist embassies installed in former ducal mansions along the street required the presence of armed policemen the clock around. The only commercial establishments anywhere near Speck's—a restaurant and a bookstore—seemed unlikely targets for firebombs: The first catered to lower-echelon civil servants, the second was painted royal blue, a conservative color he found reassuring. The book-store's name, Amandine, suggested shelves of calm regional novels and ac-counts of travel to Imperial Russia signed "A Diplomat." Pasted inside the window, flat on the pane, was an engraving that depicted an old man, bearded and mitered, tearing a small demon limb from limb. The old man looked self-conscious, the imp resigned. He supposed that this image con-cealed a deep religious meaning, which he did not intend to plumb. If it was holy, it was respectable; as the owner of the gallery across the street, he needed to know nothing more.

Speck was now in the parish of St. Clotilde, near enough to the church for its bells to give him migraine headaches. Leaves from the church square blew as far as his door—melancholy reminders of autumn, a season bad for art. (Winter was bad, too, while the first chestnut leaves unfolding heralded the worst season of all. In summer the gallery closed.) In spite of his con-stant proximity to churches he had remained rational. Generations of highly intellectual Central European agnostics and freethinkers had left in his bones a mistrust of the bogs and quicksands that lie beyond reality per-ceived. Neither loss nor grief nor guilt nor fear had ever moved him to ap-peal to the unknown—any unknown, for there were several. Nevertheless, after signing his third lease in seven years, he decided to send Walter, his Swiss assistant, a lapsed Calvinist inching toward Rome, to light a candle at St. Clotilde's. Walter paid for a five-franc taper and set it before St. Joseph, the most reliable intermediary he could find: A wave of postconciliar puri-tanism seemed to have broken at St. Clotilde's, sweeping away most of the mute and obliging figures to whom desires and gratitude could be expressed. Walter was willing to start again in some livelier church—Notre Dame de Paris, for instance—but Speck thought enough was enough.

On a damp October evening about a year after this, there could be seen in Speck's window a drawing of a woman drying her feet (Speck permanent collection); a poster announcing the current exhibition, "Paris and Its In-fluence on the Tirana School, 1931–2"; five catalogues displayed attrac-tively; and the original of the picture on the poster—a shameless copy of Foujita's *Mon Intérieur* reentitled *Balkan Alarm Clock*. In defiance of a govern-ment circular reminding Paris galleries about the energy crisis Speck had left the lights on. This was partly to give the lie to competitors who might be putting it about that he was having money troubles. He had set the burglar alarm, bolted the security door, and was now cranking down an openwork iron screen whose Art Nouveau loops and fronds allowed the works inside to be seen but nothing larger than a mouse to get in. The faint, floating sadness he always felt while locking up had to do with the time. In his experience, love affairs and marriages perished between seven and eight o'clock, the hour of rain and no taxis. All over Paris couples must be parting forever, leaving like debris along the curbs the shreds of canceled restaurant dates, useless ballet tickets, hopeless explanations, and scraps of pride; and toward each of these disasters a taxi was pulling in, the only taxi for miles, the light on its roof already dimmed in anticipation to the twin dots that in Paris mean "occupied." But occupied by whom?

"You take it."

"No, you. You're the one in a hurry."

The lover abandoned under a dripping plane tree would feel a damp victory of a kind, awarding himself a first-class trophy for selfless behavior. It would sustain him ten seconds, until the departing one rolled down the taxi window to hurl her last flint: "You Fascist!" Why was this always the final shot, the coup de grâce delivered by women? Speck's wife, Henriette, book critic on an uncompromising political weekly, had said it three times last spring—here, in the street, where Speck stood locking the iron screen into place. He had been uneasily conscious of his wellborn neighbors, hanging out their windows, not missing a thing. Henriette had then gone away in a cab to join her lover, leaving Speck, the gallery, her job—everything that mattered.

He mourned Henriette; he missed her steadying influence. Her mind was like a one-way thoroughfare, narrow and flat, maintained in repair. As he approached the age of forty he felt that his own intellect needed not just a direction but retaining walls. Unless his thoughts were nailed down by gallery business they tended to glide away to the swamps of imagination, behind which stretched the steamier marshland of metaphysics. Confessing this to Henriette was unlikely to bring her back. There had been something brisk and joyous about her going—her hailing of a taxi as though of a friend, her surprised smile as the third "Fascist!" dissolved in the April night like a double stroke from the belfry of St. Clotilde's. He supposed he would never see her again now, except by accident. Perhaps, long after he had forgotten Henriette, he would overhear someone saying in a restaurant, "Do you see that poor mad intellectual talking to herself in the corner? That is Henriette, Sandor Speck's second wife. Of course, she was very different then; Speck kept her in shape."

While awaiting this sop, which he could hardly call consolation, he had Walter and the gallery. Walter had been with him five years—longer than either of his marriages. They had been years of spiritual second-thinking for Walter and of strain and worry for Speck. Walter in search of the Eternal was like one of those solitary skippers who set out to cross an ocean only to capsize when barely out of port. Speck had been obliged to pluck his assistant out of Unitarian waters and set him on the firm shore of the Trinity. He had towed him to Transubstantiation and back; had charted the shoals and perils of careless prayer. His own aversion to superstitious belief made Speck particularly scrupulous; he would not commit himself on Free Will, for instance, uncertain if it was supposed to be an uphill trudge wearing tight boots or a downhill slide sitting on a tea tray. He would lie awake at night planning Walter's dismissal, only to develop a traumatic chest cold if his assistant seemed restless.

"What will the gallery do without you?" he would ask on the very morning he had been meaning to say, "Walter, sit down, please. I've got something to tell you." Walter would remind him about saints and holy men who had done without everything, while Speck would envision the pure hell of having to train someone new.

On a rainy night such as this, the street resembled a set in a French film designed for export, what with the policemen's white rain capes aesthetically gleaming and the lights of the bookstore, the restaurant, and the gallery reflected, quivering, in European-looking puddles. In reality, Speck thought, there was not even hope for a subplot. Henriette had gone forever. Walter's mission could not be photographed. The owner of the restaurant was in his eighties; the waiters were poised on the brink of retirement. As for the bookseller, M. Alfred Chassepoule, he seemed to spend most of his time wiping blood off the collected speeches of Mussolini, bandaging customers, and sweeping up glass. The fact was that Amandine's had turned out to have a fixed right-wing viewpoint, which made it subject to attack by commandos wielding iron bars. Speck, who had chosen the street for its upper-class hush, had grown used to the hoarse imprecation of the left and shriller keening of the right; he could tell the sob of an ambulance from the wail of a police van. The commerce of art is without bias: When insurance inspectors came round to ask what Speck might have seen, he invariably replied, "Seen where?" to which Walter, unsolicited, would add, "And I am Swiss."

Since Henriette's departure, Speck often ate his meals in the local restaurant, which catered to his frugal tastes, his vegetarian principles, and his desire to be left in peace. On the way, he would pause outside Amandine's, just enough to mark the halt as a comforting bachelor habit. He would glance over the secondhand books, the yellowing pamphlets, and the overpriced cartoons. The tone of the window display seemed old-fashioned rather than dangerous, though he knew that the slogan crowning the arrangement, "Europe for Europeans," echoed from a dark political valley. But even that valley had been full of strife and dissension and muddle, for hadn't the Ur-Fascists, the Italian ones, been in some way against an all-Europe? At least, some of their poets were. But who could take any of that seriously now? Nothing political had ever struck Speck as being above the level of a low-grade comic strip. On the cover of one volume, Uncle Sam shook hands with the Russian Bear over prostrate Europe, depicted as a maiden in a dead faint. A drawing of a spider on a field of banknotes (twelve hundred francs with frame, nine hundred without) jostled the image of a crablike hand clawing away at the map of France. Pasted against the pane, survivor of uncounted assaults, the old man continued to dismember his captive imp. Walter had told Speck he believed the old man to be St. Amand, Apostle of Flanders, Bishop in 430. "Or perhaps," said Walter, after thinking it over, "435." The imp probably stood for Flemish paganism, which the Apostle had been hard put to it to overcome.

From the rainy street Speck could see four or five of Amandine's customers—all men; he had never noticed a woman in the place—standing, reading, books held close to their noses. They had the weak eyes, long chins, and sparse, sparrow-colored hair he associated with low governmental salaries. He imagined them living with grim widowed mothers whose company they avoided after work. He had seen them, or young men like them, staggering out of the store, cut by flying glass, kicked and beaten as they lay stunned on the pavement; his anxious imagination had set them on their feet, booted and belted, the right signal given at last, swarming across to the gallery, determined to make Speck pay for injuries inflicted on them by total strangers. He saw his only early Chagall (quite likely authentic) ripped from its frame; Walter, his poor little spectacles smeared with blood, lambasted with the complete Charles Maurras, fourteen volumes, full morocco; Speck himself, his ears offended by acute right-wing cries of "Down with foreign art!" attempting a quick counterstroke with *Significant Minor French Realists, Twentieth Century*, which was thick enough to stun an ox. Stepping back from the window, Speck saw his own smile reflected. It was pinched and tight, and he looked a good twenty years older than thirty-nine.

* * *

His restaurant, crammed with civil servants at noon, was now nearly empty. A smell of lunchtime pot roast hung in the air. He made for his own table, from which he could see the comforting lights of the gallery. The waiter, who had finally stopped asking how Henriette was liking Africa, brought his dinner at once, setting out like little votive offerings the raw-carrot salad, the pot-roast vegetables without the meat, the quarter ounce of low-fat cheese, and a small pear. It had long been established that Speck did not wish to be disturbed by the changing of plates. He extracted a yellow pad and three pencils from his briefcase and placed them within the half circle of dishes. Speck was preparing his May-June show.

The right show at the right time: It was trickier than getting married to the right person at any time. For about a year now, Paris critics had been hinting at something missing from the world of art. These hints, poignant and patriotic on the right, neo-nationalist and pugnacious on the left, wistful but insistent dead center, were all in essence saying the same thing: "The time has come." The time had come; the hour had struck; the moment was ripe for a revival of reason, sanity, and taste. Surely there was more to art than this sickness, this transatlantic blight? Fresh winds were needed to sweep the museums and galleries. Two days ago there had been a disturbing article in *Le Monde* (front page, lower middle, turn to page 26) by a man who never took up his pen unless civilization was in danger. Its title—"Redemption Through Art—Last Hope for the West?"—had been followed by other disturbing questions: When would the merchants and dealers, compared rather unfairly to the money changers driven from the temple, face up to their share of responsibility as the tattered century declined? Must the flowering gardens of Western European culture wilt and die along with the decadent political systems, the exhausted parliaments, the shambling elections, the tired liberal impulses? What of the man in the street, too modest and confused to mention his cravings? Was he not gasping for one remedy and one only—artistic renovation? And where was this to come from? "In the words of Shakespr," the article concluded, supposedly in English, "That is the qustn."

As it happened, Speck had the answer: Say, a French painter, circa 1864–1949, forgotten now except by a handful of devoted connoisseurs. Populist yet refined, local but universal, he would send rays, beacons, into the thickening night of the West, just as Speck's gallery shone bravely into the dark street. Speck picked up a pencil and jotted rapidly: "Born in France, worked in Paris, went his own way, unmindful of fashion, knowing his hour would strike, his vision be vindicated. Catholical, as this retrospective so eloquently . . ." Just how does "catholical" come in, Speck wondered, forking up raw carrots. Because of ubiquity, the ubiquity of genius? No; not genius—leave that for the critics. His sense of harmony, then—his discretion.

Easy, Speck told himself. Easy on the discretion. This isn't interior decoration.

He could see the notices, knew which of the critics would write "At last," and "It has taken Sandor Speck to remind us." Left, right, and center would unite on a single theme: how the taste of two full generations had been corrupted by foreign speculation, cosmopolitan decadence, and the cultural imperialism of the Anglo-Saxon hegemony.

"The calm agnostic face," Speck wrote happily, "the quiet Cartesian voice are replaced by the snarl of a nation betrayed (1914), as startling for the viewer as a child's glimpse of a beloved adult in a temper tantrum. The snarl, the grimace vanish (1919) as the serene observer of Universal Will (1929) and of Man's responsibility to himself return. But we are left shaken. We have stopped trusting our feelings. We have been shown not only the smile but the teeth."

Here Speck drew a wavy line and turned to the biography, which was giving him trouble. On a fresh yellow page he tried again:

1938—Travels to Nice. Sees Mediterranean.
1939—Abandons pacifist principle. Lies about age. Is mobilized.
1940—Demobilized.
1941—

It was here that Speck bogged down. Should he say, "Joins Resistance"? "Resistance" today meant either a heroic moment sadly undervalued by the young or a minor movement greatly inflated in order to absolve French guilt. Whatever it is, thought Speck, it is not chic. The youngest survivor must be something like seventy-three. They know nothing about art, and never subscribe to anything except monuments. Some people read "Resistance" in a chronology and feel quite frankly exasperated. On the other hand, what about museums, state-subsidized, Resistance-minded on that account? He chewed a boiled leek and suddenly wrote, "1941—Conversations with Albert Camus." I wonder where all this comes from, Speck said to himself. Inspiration was what he meant.

These notes, typed by Walter, would be turned over to the fashionable historian, the alarming critic, the sound political figure unlikely to be thrown out of office between now and spring, whom Speck would invite to write the catalogue introduction. "Just a few notes," Speck would say tactfully. "Knowing how busy you are." Nothing was as inspiriting to him as the thought of his own words in print on a creamy catalogue page, even over someone else's name.

Speck took out of his briefcase the Directoire snuffbox Henriette had given him about a fortnight before suddenly calling him "Fascist." (Unexpected feminine generosity—first firm sign of adulterous love affair.) It contained three after-dinner tablets—one to keep him alert until bedtime, another to counter the stimulating effect of the first, and a third to neutralize the germ known as Warsaw flu now ravaging Paris, emptying schools and factories and creating delays in the postal service. He sat quietly, digesting, giving the pills a chance to work.

He could see the structure of the show, the sketchbooks and letters in glass cases. It might be worthwhile lacquering the walls black, concentrating strong spots on the correspondence, which straddled half a century, from Degas to Cocteau. The scrawl posted by Drieu la Rochelle just before his suicide would be particularly effective on black. Céline was good; all that crowd was back in vogue now. He might use the early photo of Céline in regimental dress uniform with a splendid helmet. Of course, there would be word from the left, too, with postcards from Jean Jaurès, Léon Blum, and Paul Éluard, and a jaunty get-well message from Louis Aragon and Elsa. In the first room Speck would hang the stiff, youthful landscapes and the portraits of the family, the artist's first models—his brother wearing a sailor suit, the awkward but touching likeness of his sister (*Germaine-Isabelle at the Window*).

"Yes, yes," Speck would hear in the buzz of voices at the opening. "Even from the beginning you can tell there was *something.*" The "something" became bolder, firmer in the second room. See his cities; watch how the streets turn into mazes, nets, prison corridors. Dark palette. Opaqueness, the whole canvas covered, immensities of indigo and black. "Look, 1929; he was doing it before What's-His-Name." Upstairs, form breaking out of shadow: bread, cheese, wine, wheat, ripe apples, grapes.

Hold it, Speck told himself. Hold the ripeness. This isn't social realism.

He gathered up the pencils, the snuffbox, and the pad, and put them back in the briefcase. He placed seventy francs, tip included, in a saucer. Still he sat, his mind moving along to the second loggia room, the end room, the important one. Here on the neutral walls would be the final assurance, the serenity, the satire, the power, and the vision for which, at last, the time had come. For that was the one thing Speck was sure of: The bell had rung, the hour had struck, the moment was at hand.

Whose time? Which hour? Yes—whose, which, what? That was where he was stuck.

The street was now empty except for the policemen in their streaming capes. The bookstore had put up its shutter. Speck observed the walls of the three Marxist embassies. Shutters and curtains that once had shielded the particular privacy of the aristocracy—privacy open to servants but not to the street—now concealed the receptions and merry dinner parties of people's democracies. Sometimes at this hour gleaming motorcars rolled past the mysterious gates, delivering passengers Speck's fancy continued to see as the Duchesse de Guermantes and anyone she did not happen to despise. He knew that the chauffeurs were armed and that half the guests were spies; still, there was nothing to stop a foreign agent from having patrician tastes, or from admiring Speck's window as he drove by.

"This gallery will be an oasis of peace and culture," Walter had predicted as they were hanging the first show, "Little-Known Aspects of Post-Decorator Style." "An oasis of peace and culture in the international desert."

Speck breathed germ-laden night air. Boulevard theaters and music halls were deserted, their managers at home writing letters to the mayor of Paris deploring the decline of popular entertainment and suggesting remedies in the form of large cash subsidies. The sluggish river of autumn life congealed and stagnated around millions of television sets as Parisians swallowed aspirin and drank the boiling-hot Scotch believed to be a sovereign defense against Warsaw flu.

A few determined intellectuals slunk, wet, into the Métro on their way to cultural centers where, in vivid translations from the German, actors would address the occasional surly remark to the audience—that loyal, anxious, humorless audience in its costly fake working-class clothes. Another contingent, dressed in Burberry trench coats, had already fought its way into the Geographical Institute, where a lecture with colored slides, "Ramblings in Secret Greenland," would begin, after a delay owing to trouble with the projection machine, at about nine-twenty. The advantage of slides over films was that they were not forever jumping about and confusing one, and the voice describing them belonged to a real speaker. When the lights went up, one could see him, talk to him, challenge him over the thing he had said about shamanism on Disko Island. What had drawn the crowd was not Greenland but the word "secret." In no other capital city does the population wait more trustfully for the mystery to be solved, the conspiracy laid bare, the explanation of every sort of vexation to be supplied: why money slumps, why prices climb, why it rains in August, why children are ungrateful. The answers might easily come from a man with a box of slides.

In each of the city's twenty administrative districts, Communists, distinguished by the cleanliness of their no-iron shirts, the sobriety of their washable neckties, and the modesty of their bearing, moved serenely toward their local cell meetings. I must persuade Walter to take out membership sometime, Speck thought. It might be useful and interesting for the gallery and it would take his mind off salvation.

Walter was at this moment in the Church of St. Gervais, across the Seine, where an ecumenical gathering of prayer, music, and debate on Unity of Faith had been marred the week before by ugly scuffling between middle-aged latecomers and young persons in the lotus position, taking up too much room. Walter had turned to his neighbor, a stranger to him, and asked courteously, "Is it a string ensemble tonight, or just the organ?" Mistaken for a traditionalist demanding the Latin Mass, he had been punched in the face and had to be led to a side chapel to mop up his nosebleed. God knows what they might do to him tonight, Speck thought.

As for Speck himself, nine-thirty found him in good company, briskly tying the strings of his Masonic apron. No commitment stronger than prudence kept him from being at St. Gervais, listening for a voice in the night of the soul, or at a Communist Party cell meeting, hoping to acquire a more wholesome slant on art in a doomed society, but he had already decided that only the Infinite could be everywhere at once. The Masonic Grand Architect of the Universe laid down no rules, appointed no prophets, required neither victims nor devotion, and seemed content to exist as a mere possibility. At the lodge Speck rubbed shoulders with men others had to be content to glimpse on television. He stood now no more than three feet away from Kléber Schaumberger, of the Alsatian Protestant banking Schaumbergers; had been greeted by Olivier Ombrine, who designed all the Arabian princesses' wedding gowns; could see, without craning, the plume of white hair belonging to François-Xavier Blum-Bloch-Weiler—former ambassador, historian, member of the French Academy, author of a perennially best-selling book about Vietnam called *When France Was at the Helm*. Speck kept the ambassador's family tree filed in his head. The Blum-Bloch-Weilers, heavy art collectors, produced statesmen, magistrates, anthropologists, and generals, and were on no account to be confused with the Blum-Weiler-Blochs, their penniless and mystical cousins, who produced poets, librarians, and Benedictine monks.

Tonight Speck followed the proceedings mechanically; his mind was set on the yellow pad in his briefcase, now lying on the backseat of his car. Direct address and supplication to the unknown were frowned on here. Order reigned in a complex universe where the Grand Architect, insofar as he existed, was supposed to know what he was doing. However, having nowhere to turn, Speck decided for the first time in his life to brave whatever cosmic derangement might ensue and to unburden himself.

Whoever and whatever you are, said Speck silently, as many had said before him, remember in my favor that I have never bothered you. I never called your attention to the fake Laurencin, the stolen Magritte, the Bonnard the other gallery was supposed to have insured, the Maurice Denis notebook that slipped through my fingers, the Vallotton woodcut that got lost between Paris and Lausanne. All I want . . . But there was no point in his insisting. The Grand Architect, if he was any sort of omnipresence worth considering, knew exactly what Speck needed now: He needed the tiny, enduring wheel set deep in the clanking, churning machinery of the art trade—the artist himself.

Speck came out to the street refreshed and soothed, feeling that he had shed some of his troubles. The rain had stopped. A bright moon hung low. He heard someone saying, ". . . hats." On the glistening pavement a group of men stood listening while Senator Antoine Bellefeuille told a funny story. Facts from the Bellefeuille biography tumbled through Speck's mind: twenty years a deputy from a rich farming district, twice a cabinet minister, now senator; had married a sugar-beet fortune, which he inherited when his wife died; no children; his mother had left him majority shares in milk chocolate, which he had sold to invest in the first postwar plastics; owned a racing stable in Normandy, a château in Provence, one of the last fine houses of Paris; had taken first-class degrees in law and philosophy; had gone into politics almost as an afterthought.

What had kept the old man from becoming Prime Minister, even President of the Republic? He had the bearing, the brains, the fortune, and the connections. Too contented, Speck decided, observing his lodge brother by moonlight. But clever, too; he was supposed to have kept copies of files from the time he had been at Justice. He splashed around in the arts, knew the third-generation dealers, the elegant bachelor curators. He went to openings, was not afraid of new movements, but he never bought anything. Speck tried to remember why the wealthy Senator who liked art never bought pictures.

"She was stunning," the Senator said. "Any man of my generation will tell you that. She came down Boulevard Saint-Michel on her husband's arm. He barely reached her shoulder. She had a smile like a fox's. Straight little animal teeth. Thick red-gold hair. A black hat tilted over one eye. And what a throat. And what hands and arms. A waist no larger than this," said the Senator, making a circle with his hands. "As I said, in those days men wore hats. You tipped a bowler by the brim, the other sort you picked up by the crown. I was so dazzled by being near her, by having the famous Lydia Cruche smile at me, I forgot I was wearing a bowler and tried to pick it up by the crown. You can imagine what a fool I looked, and how she laughed."

And of course they laughed, and Speck laughed, too.

"Her husband," said the Senator. "Hubert Cruche. A face like a gargoyle. Premature senile dementia. He'd been kicked by Venus at some time or other"—the euphemism for syphilis. "In those days the cure was based on mercury—worse than the disease. He seemed to know me. There was light in his eyes. Oh, not the light of intelligence. It was too late for that, and he'd not had much to begin with. He recognized me for a simple reason. I had already begun to assemble my Cruche collection. I bought everything Hubert Cruche produced for sixteen years—the oils, the gouaches, the pastels, the watercolors, the etchings, the drawings, the woodcuts, the posters, the cartoons, the book illustrations. Everything."

That was it, Speck remembered. That was why the Senator who liked art never bought so much as a wash drawing. The house was full of Cruches; there wasn't an inch to spare on the walls.

With a monarch's gesture, the Senator dismissed his audience and stepped firmly toward the chauffeur, who stood holding the door of his Citroën. He said, perhaps to himself, perhaps to Speck, thin and attentive in the moonlight, "I suppose I ought to get rid of my Cruches. Who ever thinks about Cruche now?"

"No," said Speck, whom the Grand Architect of the Universe had just rapped over the head. The Senator paused—benevolent, stout. "Don't get rid of the Cruches," said Speck. He felt as if he were on a distant shore, calling across deep cultural waters. "Don't sell! Hang on! Cruche is coming back!"

Cruche, Cruche, Hubert Cruche, sang Speck's heart as he drove homeward. Cruche's hour had just struck, along with Sandor Speck's. At the core of the May-June retrospective would be his lodge brother's key collection: "Our thanks, in particular ... who not only has loaned his unique and invaluable ... but who also ... and who ..." Recalling the little he knew of Cruche's obscure career, Speck made a few changes in the imaginary catalogue, substituting with some disappointment *The Power Station at Gagny-sur-Orme* for *Misia Sert on Her Houseboat*, and *Peasant Woman Sorting Turnips* for *Serge Lifar as Petrouchka*. He wondered if he could call Cruche heaven-sent. No; he would not put a foot beyond coincidence, just as he had not let Walter dash from saint to saint once he had settled for St. Joseph. And yet a small flickering marsh light danced upon the low-lying metaphysical ground he had done so much to avoid. Not only did Cruche overlap to an astonishing degree the painter in the yellow notebook but he was exactly the sort of painter that made the Speck gallery chug along. If Speck's personal collection consisted of minor works by celebrated artists, he considered them his collateral for a rainy, bank-loan day. Too canny to try to compete with international heavyweights, unwilling to burden himself with insurance, he had developed as his specialty the flattest, palest, farthest ripples of the late-middle-traditional Paris school. This sensible decision had earned him the admiration given the devoted miniaturist who is no threat to anyone. "Go and see Sandor Speck," the great lions and tigers of the trade would tell clients they had no use for. "Speck's the expert."

Speck was expert on barges, bridges, cafés at twilight, nudes on striped counterpanes, the artist's mantelpiece with mirror, the artist's street, his staircase, his bed made and rumpled, his still life with half-peeled apple, his summer in Mexico, his wife reading a book, his girlfriend naked and dejected on a kitchen chair. He knew that the attraction of customer to picture was always accidental, like love; it was his business to make it overwhelming. Visitors came to the gallery looking for decoration and investment, left it believing Speck had put them on the road to a supreme event. But there was even more to Speck than this, and if he was respected for anything in the trade it was for his knack with artists' widows. Most dealers hated them. They were considered vain, greedy, unrealistic, and tougher than bulldogs. The worst were those whose husbands had somehow managed the rough crossing to recognition only to become washed up at the wrong end of the beach. There the widow waited, guarding the wreckage. Speck's skill in dealing with them came out of a certain sympathy. An artist's widow was bound to be suspicious and adamant. She had survived the discomfort and confusion of her marriage; had lived through the artist's drinking, his avarice, his affairs, his obsession with constipation, his feuds and quarrels, his cowardice with dealers, his hypocrisy with critics, his depressions (which always fell at the most joyous seasons, blighting Christmas and spring); and then—oh, justice!—she had outlasted him.

Transfiguration arrived rapidly. Resurrected for Speck's approval was an ardent lover, a devoted husband who could not work unless his wife was around, preferably in the same room. If she had doubts about a painting, he at once scraped it down. Hers was the only opinion he had ever trusted. His last coherent words before dying had been of praise for his wife's autumnal beauty.

Like a swan in muddy waters, Speck's ancient Bentley cruised the suburbs where his painters had lived their last resentful seasons. He knew by heart the damp villa, the gravel path, the dangling bellpull, the shrubbery containing dead cats and plastic bottles. Indoors the widow sat, her walls plastered with portraits of herself when young. Here she continued the struggle begun in the Master's lifetime—the evicting of the upstairs tenant—her day made lively by the arrival of mail (dusty beige of anonymous threats, grim blue of legal documents), the coming and going of process servers, the outings to lawyers. Into this spongy territory Speck advanced, bringing his tactful presence, his subtle approximation of courtship, his gift for listening. Thin by choice, pale by nature, he suggested maternal need. Socks and cuff links suggested breeding. The drift of his talk suggested prosperity. He sent his widows flowers, wooed them with food. Although their taste in checks and banknotes ran to the dry and crisp, when it came to eating they craved the sweet, the sticky, the moist. From the finest pastry shops in Paris Speck brought soft macaroons, savarins soaked in rum, brioches stuffed with almond cream, mocha cake so tender it had to be eaten with a spoon. Sugar was poison to Speck. Henriette had once reviewed a book that described how refined sugar taken into one's system turned into a fog of hideous green. Her brief, cool warning, "A Marxist Considers Sweets," unreeled in Speck's mind if he was confronted with a cookie. He usually pretended to eat, reducing a mille-feuille to paste, concealing the wreck of an éclair under napkin and fork. He never lost track of his purpose—the prying of paintings out of a dusty studio on terms anesthetizing to the artist's widow and satisfactory to himself.

The Senator had mentioned a wife; where there had been wife there was relict. Speck obtained her telephone number by calling a rival gallery and pretending to be looking for someone else. "Cruche's widow can probably tell you," he finally heard. She lived in one of the gritty suburbs east of Paris, on the far side of the Bois de Vincennes—in Speck's view, the wrong direction. The pattern of his life seemed to come unfolded as he dialed. He saw himself stalled in industrial traffic, inhaling pollution, his Bentley pointed toward the seediest mark on the urban compass, with a vanilla cream cake melting beside him on the front seat.

She answered his first ring; his widows never strayed far from the telephone. He introduced himself. Silence. He gave the name of the gallery, mentioned his street, recited the names of painters he showed.

Presently he heard "D'you know any English?"

"Some," said Speck, who was fluent.

"Well, what do you want?"

"First of all," he said, "to meet you."

"What for?"

He cupped his hand round the telephone, as if spies from the embassies down the street were trying to overhear. "I am planning a major Cruche show. A retrospective. That's what I want to talk to you about."

"Not unless I know what you want."

It seemed to Speck that he had already told her. Her voice was languid and nasal and perfectly flat. An index to English dialects surfaced in his mind, yielding nothing useful.

"It will be a strong show," he went on. "The first big Cruche since the 1930s, I believe."

"What's that got to do with me?"

He wondered if the Senator had forgotten something essential—that Lydia Cruche had poisoned her husband, for instance. He said, "You probably own quite a lot of his work."

"None of it's for sale."

This, at last, was familiar; widows' negotiations always began with "No." "Actually, I am not proposing to buy anything," he said, wanting this to be clear at the start. "I am offering the hospitality of my gallery. It's a gamble I am willing to take because of my firm belief that the time—"

"What's the point of this show?"

"The point?" said Speck, his voice tightening as it did when Walter was being obtuse. "The point is getting Cruche back on the market. The time has come—the time to . . . to attack. To attack the museums with Hubert Cruche."

As he said this, Speck saw the great armor-plated walls of the Pompidou Art Center and the chink in the armor through which an 80 × 95 Cruche 1919 abstract might slip. He saw the provincial museums, cheeseparing, saving on lightbulbs, but, like the French bourgeoisie they stood for, so much richer than they seemed. At the name "Cruche" their curators would wake up from neurotic dreams of forced auction sales, remembering they had millions to get rid of before the end of the fiscal year. And France was the least of it; London, Zurich, Stockholm, and Amsterdam materialized as frescoes representing the neoclassical façades of four handsome banks. Overhead, on a Baroque ceiling, nymphs pointed their rosy feet to gods whose chariots were called "Tokyo" and "New York." Speck lowered his voice as if he had portentous news. Museums all over the world, although they did not yet know this, were starving for Cruche. In the pause that followed he seemed to feel Henriette's hand on his shoulder, warning him to brake before enthusiasm took him over the cliff.

"Although for the moment Cruche is just an idea of mine," he said, stopping cold at the edge. "Just an idea. We can develop the idea when we meet."

A week later, Speck parked his car between a ramshackle shopping center— survivor of the building boom of the sixties—and a municipal low-cost housing project that resembled a jail. In the space bounded by these structures crouched the late artist's villa, abiding proof in stucco that the taste of earlier generations had been as disastrous as today's. He recognized the shards of legal battle: Center and block had left the drawing board of some state-employed hack as a unit, only to be wedged apart by a widow's refusal to sell. Speck wondered how she had escaped expropriation. Either she knows someone powerful, he thought, or she can make such a pest of herself that they were thankful to give up.

A minute after having pushed the gate and tugged the rusted wire bellpull, he found himself alone in a bleak sitting room, from which his hostess had been called by a whistling kettle. He sat down on a faded sofa. The furniture was of popular local design, garnished with marble and ormolu. A television set encrusted with gilt acanthus leaves sat on a sideboard, like an objet d'art. A few rectangular shadings on the wallpaper showed where pictures had hung.

The melancholy tinged with foreboding Speck felt between seven and eight overtook him at this much earlier hour. The room was no more hideous than others he had visited in his professional quest for a bargain, but this time it seemed to daunt him, recalling sieges and pseudo courtships and expenditures of time, charm, and money that had come to nothing. He got up and examined a glass-fronted bookcase with nothing inside. His features, afloat on a dusty pane, were not quite as pinched as they had been the other night, but the image was still below par for a man considered handsome. The approach of a squeaking tea cart sent him scurrying back to the sofa, like a docile child invited somewhere for the first time.

"I was just admiring——" he began.

"I've run out of milk," she said. "I'm sure you won't mind your tea plain." With this governessy statement she handed him a cup of black Ceylon, a large slice of poisonous raisin cake, and a Mickey Mouse paper napkin.

Nothing about Cruche's widow tallied with the Senator's description. She was short and quite round, and reminded Speck of the fat little dogs one saw being reluctantly exercised in Paris streets. The abundant red-gold hair of the Senator's memory, or imagination, had gone ash-gray and was, in any case, pinned up. The striking fact of her person was simply the utter blankness of her expression. Usually widows' faces spoke to him. They said, "I am lonely," or "Can I trust you?" Lydia Cruche's did not suggest that she had so much as taken Speck in. She chose a chair at some distance from Speck, and proceeded to eat her cake without speaking. He thought of things to say, but none of them seemed appealing.

At last, she said, "Did you notice the supermarket next door?"

"I saw a shopping center."

"The market is part of it. You can get anything there now—bran, frozen pizzas, maple syrup. That's where I got the cake mix. I haven't been to Paris for three years."

Speck had been born in France. French education had left him the certainty that he was a logical, fair-minded person imbued with a culture from which every other Western nation was obliged to take its bearings. French was his first language; he did not really approve of any other. He said, rather coldly, "Have you been in this country long?"

"Around fifty years."

"Then you should know some French."

"I don't speak it if I don't have to. I never liked it."

He put down his cup, engulfed by a wave of second-generation distress. She was his first foreign widow. Most painters, whatever their origins, had sense enough to marry Frenchwomen—unrivaled with creditors, thrifty hoarders of bits of real estate, endowed with relations in country places where one could decamp in times of need and war.

"Perhaps, where you come from—" he began.

"Saskatchewan."

His tea had gone cold. Tannic scum had collected on its surface. She said, "This idea of yours, this show—what was it you called it? The hospitality of your gallery? I just want to say don't count on me. Don't count on me for anything. I don't mind showing you what I've got. But not today. The studio hasn't been dusted or heated for years, and even the light isn't working."

In Speck's experience, this was about average for a first attempt. Before making for civilization he stopped at a florist's in the shopping center and ordered two dozen roses to be delivered to Mme. Cruche. While these were lifted, dripping, from a plastic pail, he jotted down a warm message on his card, crossing out the engraved "Dr. Sandor Speck." His title, earned by a thesis on French neo-humanism and its ups and downs, created some confusion in Paris, where it was taken to mean that Speck could cure slipped disks and gastric ulcers. Still, he felt that it gave a grip to his name, and it was his only link with all the freethinking, agnostic Specks, who, though they had not been able to claim affinity by right of birth with Voltaire and Descartes, had probably been wise and intelligent and quite often known as "Dr."

As soon as he got back to the gallery, he had Walter look up Saskatchewan in an atlas. Its austere oblong shape turned his heart to ice. Walter said that it was one of the right-angled territories that so frequently contain oil. Oil seemed to Speck to improve the oblong. He saw a Chirico chessboard sliding off toward a horizon where the lights of derricks twinkled and blinked.

He let a week go by before calling Lydia Cruche.

"I won't be able to show you those roses of yours," she said. "They died right off."

He took the hint and arrived with a spray of pale green orchids imported from Brazil. Settled upon the faded sofa, which was apparently destined to be his place, he congratulated his hostess on the discovery of oil in her native plain.

"I haven't seen or heard of the place since Trotsky left the Soviet Union," she said. "If there is oil, I'd sooner not know about it. Oil is God's curse." The iron silence that followed this seemed to press on Speck's lungs. "That's a bad cough you've got there, Doctor," she said. "Men never look after those things. Who looks after you?"

"I look after myself," said Speck.

"Where's your wife? Where'd she run off to?"

Not even "Are you married?" He saw his hostess as a tough little pagan figure, with a goddess's gift for reading men's lives. He had a quick vision of himself clasping her knees and sobbing out the betrayal of his marriage, though he continued to sit upright, crumbling walnut cake so that he would not have to eat it.

"My wife," he said, "insofar as I can still be said to have one, has gone to live in a warm climate."

"She run off alone? Women don't often do that. They haven't got that kind of nerve."

Stepping carefully, for he did not wish to sound like a stage cuckold or a male fool, Speck described in the lightest possible manner how Henriette had followed her lover, a teacher of literature, to a depressed part of French-speaking Africa where the inhabitants were suffering from a shortage of Racine. Unable to halt once he had started, he tore on toward the edge: Henriette was a hopeless nymphomaniac (she had fallen in love) who lacked any sense of values (the man was broke); she was at the same time a grasping neurotic (having sunk her savings in the gallery, she wanted a return with 14 percent interest).

"You must be thankful you finally got rid of her," said Lydia Cruche. "You must be wondering why you married her in the first place."

"I felt sorry for Henriette," he said, momentarily forgetting any other reason. "She seemed so helpless." He told about Henriette living in her sixth-floor walk-up, working as slave labor on a shoddy magazine. A peasant from Alsace, she had never eaten anything but pickled cabbage until Speck drove his Bentley into her life. Under his tactful guidance she had tasted her first fresh truffle salad at Le Récamier; had worn her first mink-lined Dior raincoat; had published her first book-length critical essay, "A Woman Looks at Edgar Allan Poe." And then she had left him—just like that.

"You trained her," said Lydia Cruche. "Brought her up to your level. And now she's considered good enough to marry a teacher. You should feel proud. You shouldn't mind what happened. You should feel satisfied."

"I'm not satisfied," said Speck. "I do mind." He realized that something had been left out of his account. "I loved her." Lydia Cruche looked straight at him, for once, as though puzzled. "As you loved Hubert Cruche," he said.

There was no response except for the removal of crumbs from her lap. The goddess, displeased by his mortal impertinence, symbolically knocked his head off her knee.

"Hube liked my company," she finally said. "That's true enough. After he died I saw him sitting next to the television, by the radiator, where his mother usually crouched all winter looking like a sheep with an earache. I was just resting here, thinking of nothing in particular, when I looked up and noticed him. He said, 'You carry the seed of your death.' I said, 'If that's the case, I might as well put my head in the oven and be done with it.' 'Non,' he said, 'ce n'est pas la peine.' Now, his mother was up in her room, making lists of all the things she had to feel sorry about. I went up and said, 'Madame,' because you can bet your boots she never got a 'Maman' out of me, 'Hube was in the parlor just now.' She answered, 'It was his mother he wanted. Any message was for me.' I said that if that was so, then all he needed to do was to materialize upstairs and save me the bother of climbing. She gave me some half-baked reason why he preferred not to, and then she *did* die. Aged a hundred and three. It was in *France-Soir*."

The French she had spoken rang to Speck like silver bells. Everything about her had changed—voice, posture, expression. If he still could not see the Lydia Cruche of the Senator's vision, at least he could believe in her.

"Do you talk to your husband often?" he said, trying to make it sound like a usual experience.

"How could I talk to Hube? He's dead and buried. I hope you don't go in for ghosts, Dr. Speck. I would find that very silly. That was just some kind of accident—a visitation. I never saw him again or ever expect to. As for his mother, there wasn't a peep out of her after she died. And here I am, alone in the Cruche house." It was hard to say if she sounded glad or sorry. "I gather you're on your own, too. God never meant men and women to live by themselves, convenient though it may seem to some of us. That's why he throws men and women together. Coincidence is God's plan."

So soon, thought Speck. It was only their second meeting. It seemed discourteous to draw attention to the full generation that lay between them; experience had taught him that acknowledging any fragment of this dangerous subject did more harm than good. When widows showed their cards, he tried to look like a man with no time for games. He thought of the young André Malraux, dark and tormented, the windblown lock on the worried brow, the stub of a Gauloise sending up a vagabond spiral of smoke. Unfortunately, Speck had been born forty years too late for the model; he belonged to a much reedier generation of European manhood. He thought of the Pope. White-clad, serene, he gazed out on St. Peter's Square, over the subdued heads of one hundred thousand artists' widows, not one of whom would dare.

"So this was the Cruche family home," he said, striking out, he hoped, in a safe direction.

"The furniture was his mother's," said Lydia Cruche. "I got rid of most of it, but there was stuff you couldn't pay them to cart away. *Sa petite Maman adorable*," she said softly. Again Speck heard the string of silver bells. "I thought she was going to hang around forever. They were a tough family—peasants from the west of France. She took good care of him. Cooked him sheep's heart, tripe and onions, big beefsteaks they used to eat half raw. He was good-looking, a big fellow, big for a Frenchman. At seventy you'd have taken him for forty. Never had a cold. Never had a headache. Never said he was tired. Drank a liter of Calvados every other day. One morning he just keeled over, and that was that. I'll show you a picture of him sometime."

"I'd also like to see *his* pictures," said Speck, thankful for the chance. "The pictures you said you had upstairs."

"You know how I met Hube? People often ask me that. I'm surprised you haven't. I came to him for lessons."

"I didn't know he taught," said Speck. His most reliable professional trait was his patience.

"He didn't. I admired him so much that I thought I'd try anyway. I was eighteen. I rang the bell. His mother let me in. I never left—he wouldn't let me go. His mother often said if she'd known the future she'd never have answered the door. I must have walked about four miles from a tram stop, carrying a big portfolio of my work to show him. There wasn't even a paved street then—just a patch of nettles out front and some vacant lots."

Her work. He knew he had to get it over with: "Would you like to show me some of your things, too?"

"I burned it all a long time ago."

Speck's heart lurched. "But not his work?"

"It wasn't mine to burn. I'm not a criminal." Mutely, he looked at the bare walls. "None of Hube's stuff ever hung in here," she said. "His mother couldn't stand it. We had everything *she* liked—Napoleon at Waterloo, lighthouses, coronations. I couldn't touch it when she was alive, but once she'd gone I didn't wait two minutes."

Speck's eighteenth-century premises were centrally heated. The system, which dated from the early 1960s, had been put in by Americans who had once owned most of the second floor. With the first dollar slide of the Nixon era they had wisely sold their holdings and gone home, without waiting for the calamity still to come. Their memorial was an expensive, casual gift nobody knew what to do with; it had raised everyone's property taxes, and it cost a fortune to run. Tenants, such as Speck, who paid a fat share of the operation, had no say as to when heat was turned on, or to what degree of temperature. Only owners and landlords had a vote. They voted overwhelmingly for the lowest possible fuel bills. By November there was scarcely a trace of warmth in Speck's elegant gallery, his cold was entrenched for the winter, and Walter was threatening to quit. Speck was showing a painter from Bruges, sponsored by a Belgian cultural-affairs committee. Cost-sharing was not a habit of his—it lowered the prestige of the gallery—but in a tight financial season he sometimes allowed himself a breather. The painter, who clearly expected Speck to put him under contract, talked of moving to Paris.

"You'd hate it here," said Speck.

Belgian television filmed the opening. The Belgian Royal Family, bidden by Walter, on his own initiative, sent regrets signed by aides-de-camp on paper so thick it would scarcely fold. These were pinned to the wall, and drew more attention than the show itself. Only one serious critic turned up. The rooms were so cold that guests could not write their names in the visitors' book—their hands were too numb. Walter, perhaps by mistake, had invited Blum-Weiler-Blochs instead of Blum-Bloch-Weilers. They came in a horde, leading an Afghan hound they tried to raffle off for charity.

The painter now sat in the gallery, day after day, smoking black cigarettes that smelled of mutton stew. He gave off a deep professional gloom, which affected Walter. Walter began to speak of the futility of genius—a sure sign of melancholia. Speck gave the painter money so that he could smoke in cafés. The bells of St. Clotilde's clanged and echoed, saying to Speck's memory, "Fascist, Fascist, Fascist." Walter reminded Speck that November was bad for art. The painter returned from a café looking cheerful. Speck wondered if he was enjoying Paris and if he would decide to stay; he stopped giving him money and the gallery became once more infested with mutton stew and despair. Speck began a letter to Henriette imploring her to come back. Walter interrupted it with the remark that Rembrandt, Mozart, and Dante had lived in vain. Speck tore the letter up and started another one saying that a Guillaumin pastel was missing and suggesting that Henriette had taken it to Africa. Just as he was tearing this up, too, the telephone rang.

"I finally got Hube's stuff all straightened out," said Lydia Cruche. "You might as well come round and look at it this afternoon. By the way, you may call me Lydia, if you want to."

"Thank you," said Speck. "And you, of course, must call me—"

"I wouldn't dream of it. Once a doctor always a doctor. Come early. The light goes at four."

Speck took a pill to quiet the pounding of his heart.

In her summing-up of his moral nature, a compendium that had preceded her ringing "Fascist"'s, Henriette had declared that Speck appraising an artist's work made her think of a real-estate loan officer examining Chartres Cathedral for leaks. It was true that his feeling for art stopped short of love; it had to. The great cocottes of history had shown similar prudence. Madame de Pompadour had eaten vanilla, believed to arouse the senses, but such recklessness was rare. Cool but efficient—that was the professional ticket. No vanilla for Speck; he knew better. For what if he were to allow passion for painting to set alight his common sense? How would he be able to live then, knowing that the ultimate fate of art was to die of anemia in safe-deposit vaults? Ablaze with love, he might try to organize raids and rescue parties, dragging pictures out of the dark, leaving sacks of onions instead. He might drop the art trade altogether, as Walter kept intending to do, and turn his talents to cornering the onion market. The same customers would ring at election time, saying, "Dr. Speck, what happens to my onion collection if the left gets in? Shouldn't we try to unload part of it in New York now, just to be on the safe side?" And Speck, unloading onions of his own in Tokyo, would answer, "Don't worry. They can't possibly nationalize all the onions. Besides, they aren't going to win."

Lydia seemed uninterested in Speck's reaction to Cruche. He had expected her to hang about, watching his face, measuring his interest, the better to nail her prices; but she simply showed him a large, dim, dusty, north-facing room in which canvases were thickly stacked against the walls and said, "I wasn't able to get the light fixed. I've left a lamp. Don't knock it over. Tea will be ready when you are." Presently he heard American country music rising from the kitchen (Lydia must have been tuned to the BBC) and he smelled a baking cake. Then, immersed in his ice-cold Cruche encounter, he noticed nothing more.

About three hours later he came downstairs, slowly, wiping dust from his hands with a handkerchief. His conception of the show had been slightly altered, and for the better, by the total Cruche. He began to rewrite the catalogue notes: "The time has come for birth ..." No—"for rebirth. In a world sated by overstatement the moment is ripe for a calm ..." How to avoid "statement" and still say "statement"? The Grand Architect was keeping Speck in mind. "For avouchment," said Speck, alone on the stairs. It was for avouchment that the time had come. It was also here for hard business. His face became set and distant, as if a large desk were about to be shoved between Lydia Cruche and himself.

He sat down and said, "This is going to be a strong show, a powerful show, even stronger than I'd hoped. Does everything I've looked at upstairs belong to you outright? Is there anything which for any reason you are not allowed to lend, show, or sell?"

"Neither a borrower nor a lender be," said Lydia, cutting caramel cake.

"No. Well, I am talking about the show, of course."

"No show," she said. "I already told you that."

"What do you mean, no show?" said Speck.

"What I told you at the beginning. I told you not to count on me. Don't drop boiled frosting on your trousers. I couldn't get it to set."

"But you changed your mind," said Speck. "After saying 'Don't count on me,' you changed your mind."

"Not for a second."

"Why?" said Speck, as he had said to the departing Henriette. "Why?"

"God doesn't want it."

He waited for more. She folded her arms and stared at the blank television set. "How do you know that God doesn't want Hubert Cruche to have a retrospective?"

"Because He said so."

His first thought was that the Grand Architect had granted Lydia Cruche something so far withheld from Sandor Speck: a plain statement of intention. "Don't you know your Commandments?" she asked. "You've never heard of the graven image?"

He searched her face for the fun, the teasing, even the malice that might give shape to this conversation, allow him to take hold of it. He said, "I can't believe you mean this."

"You don't have to. I'm sure you have your own spiritual pathway. Whatever it is, I respect it. God reveals himself according to each person's mental capacity."

One of Speck's widows could prove she descended from Joan of Arc. Another had spent a summer measuring the walls of Toledo in support of a theory that Jericho had been in Spain. It was Speck's policy never to fight the current of eccentricity but to float with it. He said cautiously, "We are all held in a mysterious hand." Generations of Speck freethinkers howled from their graves; he affected not to hear them.

"I am a Japhethite, Dr. Speck. You remember who Noah was? And his sons, Ham, Shem, and Japheth? What does that mean to you?" Speck looked as if he possessed Old Testament lore too fragile to stand exposure. "Three," said Lydia. "The sacred number. The first, the true, the only source of Israel. That crowd Moses led into the desert were just Egyptian malcontents. The true Israelites were scattered all over the earth by then. The Bible hints at this for its whole length. Japheth's people settled in Scotland. Present-day Jews are impostors."

"Are you connected to this Japheth?"

"I do not make that claim. My Scottish ancestors came from the border country. The Japhethites had been driven north long before by the Roman invasion. The British Israelite movement, which preceded ours, proved that the name 'Hebrides' was primitive Gaelic for 'Hebrew.' The British Israelites were distinguished pathfinders. It was good of you to have come all the way out here, Dr. Speck. I imagine you'll want to be getting back."

After backing twice into Lydia's fence, Speck drove straight to Galignani's bookshop, on Rue de Rivoli, where he purchased an English Bible. He intended to have Walter ransack it for contra-Japhethite pronouncements. The orange dust jacket surprised him; it seemed to Speck that Bibles were usually black. On the back flap the churches and organizations that had sponsored this English translation were listed, among them the National Bible Society of Scotland. He wondered if this had anything to do with Japheth.

As far as Speck could gather from passages Walter marked during the next few days, art had never really flourished, even before Moses decided to put a stop to it. Apart from a bronze snake cast at God's suggestion (Speck underscored this for Lydia in red), there was nothing specifically cultural, though Ezekiel's visions had a certain surrealistic splendor. As Speck read the words "the terrible crystal," its light flooded his mind, illuminating a simple question: Why not forget Hubert Cruche and find an easier solution for the cultural penury of the West? The crystal dimmed. Speck's impulsive words that October night, "Cruche is coming back," could not be reeled in. Senator Bellefeuille was entangled in a promise that had Speck at one end and Lydia at the other. Speck had asked if he might examine his lodge brother's collection and had been invited to lunch. Cruche *had* to come back.

Believing Speck's deliverance at hand, Walter assailed him with texts and encouragement. He left biblical messages on Speck's desk so that he had to see them first thing after lunch. Apparently the British Israelite movement had truly existed, enjoying a large and respectable following. Its premise that it was the British who were really God's elect had never been challenged, though membership had dwindled at mid-century; Walter could find no trace of Lydia's group, however. He urged Speck to drive to the north of Scotland, but Speck had already decided to abandon the religious approach to Cruche.

"No modern translation conveys the word of Japheth or of God," Lydia had said when Speck showed her Walter's finds. There had been something unusual about the orange dust jacket, after all. He did not consider this a defeat. Bible reading had raised his spirits. He understood now why Walter found it consoling, for much in it consisted of the assurance of downing one's enemies, dashing them against stones, seeing their children reduced to beggary and their wives to despair. Still, he was not drawn to deep belief: He remained rational, skeptical, anxious, and subject to colds, and he had not succeeded in moving Lydia Cruche an inch.

Lunch at Senator Bellefeuille's was balm. Nothing was served that Speck could not swallow. From the dining room he looked across at the dark November trees of the Bois de Boulogne. The Senator lived on the west side of Paris—the clients' side. A social allegory in the shape of a city separated Speck from Lydia Cruche. The Senator's collection was fully insured, free from dust, attractively framed or stored in racks built to order.

Speck began a new catalogue introduction as he ate lunch. "The Bellefeuille Cruches represent a unique aspect of Cruche's vision," he composed, heartily enjoying fresh crab soufflé. "Not nearly enough has been said about Cruche and the nude."

The Senator broke in, asking how much Cruche was likely to fetch after the retrospective. Speck gave figures to which his choice of socks and cuff links lent authority.

"Cruche-and-the-nude implies a definition of Woman," Speck continued, silently, sipping coffee from a gold-rimmed cup. "Lilith, Eve, temptress, saint, child, mother, nurse—Cruche delineated the feminine factor once and for all."

The Senator saw his guest to the door, took his briefcase from the hands of a manservant, and bestowed it on Speck like a diploma. He told Speck he would send him a personal invitation list for the Cruche opening next May. The list would include the estranged wife of a respected royal pretender, the publisher of an influential morning paper, the president of a nationalized bank, and the highest-ranking administrative official of a thickly populated area. Before driving away, Speck took a deep breath of west-end air. It was cool and dry, like Speck's new expression.

That evening, around closing time, he called Lydia Cruche.

He had to let her know that the show could go on without her. "I shall be showing the Bellefeuille Cruches," he said.

"The *what?*"

Speck changed the subject. "There is enormous American interest," he said, meaning that he had written half a dozen letters and received prudent answers or none at all. He was accustomed to the tense excitement "American interest" could arouse. He had known artists to enroll in crash courses at Berlitz, the better to understand prices quoted in English.

Lydia was silent; then she said, slowly, "Don't ever mention such a thing again. Hube was anti-American—especially during the war." As for Lydia, she had set foot in the United States once, when a marshmallow roast had taken her a few yards inside North Dakota, some sixty years before.

The time was between half past seven and eight. Walter had gone to early dinner and a lecture on lost Atlantis. The Belgian painter was back in Bruges, unsold and unsung. The cultural-affairs committee had turned Speck's bill for expenses over to a law firm in Brussels. Two Paris galleries had folded in the past month and a third was packing up for America, where Speck gave it less than a year. Painters set adrift by these frightening changes drifted to other galleries, shipwrecked victims trying to crawl on board waterlogged rafts. On all sides Speck heard that the economic decline was irreversible. He knew one thing—art had sunk low on the scale of consumer necessities. To mop up a few back bills, he was showing part of his own collection—his last-ditch old-age-security reserve. He clasped his hands behind his neck, staring at a Vlaminck India ink on his desk. It had been certified genuine by an expert now serving a jail sentence in Zurich. Speck was planning to flog it to one of the ambassadors down the street.

He got up and began turning out lights, leaving just a spot in the window. To have been anti-American during the Second World War in France had a strict political meaning. Any hope of letters from Louis Aragon and Elsa withered and died: Hubert Cruche had been far right. Of course, there was right and right, thought Speck as he triple-locked the front door. Nowadays the Paris intelligentsia drew new lines across the past, separating coarse collaborators from fine-drawn intellectual Fascists. One could no longer lump together young hotheads whose passionate belief in Europe had led them straight to the Charlemagne Division of the Waffen-S.S. and the soft middle class that had stayed behind to make money on the black market. Speck could not quite remember why *pure* Fascism had been better for civilization than the other kind, but somewhere on the safe side of the barrier there was bound to be a slot for Cruche. From the street, he considered a page of Charles Despiau sketches—a woman's hand, her breast, her thigh. He thought of the Senator's description of that other, early Lydia and of the fragments of perfection Speck could now believe in, for he had seen the Bellefeuille nudes. The familiar evening sadness caught up with him and lodged in his heart. Posterity forgives, he repeated, turning away, crossing the road on his way to his dinner.

Speck's ritual pause brought him up to St. Amand and his demon just as M. Chassepoule leaned into his window to replace a two-volume work he had probably taken out to show a customer. The bookseller drew himself straight, stared confidently into the night, and caught sight of Speck. The two greeted each other through glass. M. Chassepoule seemed safe, at ease, tucked away in a warm setting of lights and friends and royal blue, and yet he made an odd little gesture of helplessness, as if to tell Speck, "Here I am, like you, overtaxed, hounded, running an honest business against dreadful odds." Speck made a wry face of sympathy, as if to answer that he knew, he knew. His neighbor seemed to belong to an old and desperate breed, its back to the wall, its birthright gnawed away by foreigners, by the heathen, by the blithe continuity of art, by Speck himself. He dropped his gaze, genuinely troubled, examining the wares M. Chassepoule had collected, dusted, sorted, and priced for a new and ardent generation. The work he had just put back in the window was *La France Juive*, by Édouard Drumont. A handwritten notice described it as a classic study, out of print, hard to find, and in good condition.

Speck thought, A few years ago, no one would have dared put it on display. It has been considered rubbish for fifty years. Édouard Drumont died poor, alone, cast off even by his old friends, completely discredited. Perhaps his work was always being sold, quietly, somewhere, and I didn't know. Had he been Walter and superstitious, he might have crossed his fingers; being Speck and rational, he merely shuddered.

Walter had a friend—Félicité Blum-Weiler-Bloch, the owner of the Afghan hound. When Walter complained to her about the temperature of the gallery, she gave him a scarf, a sweater, an old flannel bedsheet, and a Turkey carpet. Walter decided to make a present of the carpet to Speck.

"Get that thing out of my gallery," said Speck.

"It's really from Félicité."

"I don't want her here, either," said Speck. "Or the dog."

Walter proposed spreading the carpet on the floor in the basement. "I spend a lot of time there," he said. "My feet get cold."

"I want it out," said Speck.

Later that day Speck discovered Walter down in the framing room, holding a vacuum cleaner. The Turkey carpet was spread on the floor. A stripe of neutral color ran through the pattern of mottled reds and blues. Looking closer, Speck saw it was warp and weft. "Watch," said Walter. He switched on the vacuum; another strip of color vanished. "The wool lifts right out," said Walter.

"I told you to get rid of it," said Speck, trembling.

"Why? I can still use it."

"I won't have my gallery stuffed with filth."

"You'll never have to see it. You hardly ever come down here." He ran the vacuum, drowning Speck's reply. Over the noise Walter yelled, "It will look better when it's all one color."

Speck raised his voice to the right-wing pitch heard during street fights: "Get it out! Get it out of my gallery!"

Like a telephone breaking into a nightmare, delivering the sleeper, someone was calling, "Dr. Speck." There on the stairs stood Lydia Cruche, wearing an ankle-length fur coat and a brown velvet turban. "I thought I'd better have a look at the place," she said. "Just to see how much space you have, how much of Cruche you can hold."

Still trembling, Speck took her hand, which smelled as if she had been peeling oranges, and pressed it to his lips.

That evening, Speck called the Senator: Would he be interested in writing the catalogue introduction? No one was better fitted, said Speck, over senatorial modesty. The Senator had kept faith with Cruche. During his years of disappointment and eclipse Cruche had been heartened, knowing that guests at the Senator's table could lift their eyes from quail in aspic to feast on *Nude in the Afternoon.*

Perhaps his lodge brother exaggerated just a trifle, the Senator replied, though it was true that he had hung on to his Cruches even when their value had been wiped out of the market. The only trouble was that his recent prose had been about the capital-gains-tax project, the Common Market sugar-beet subsidy, and the uninformed ecological campaign against plastic containers. He wondered if he could write with the same persuasiveness about art.

"I have taken the liberty of drawing up an outline," said Speck. "Just a few notes. Knowing how busy you are."

Hanging up, he glanced at his desk calendar. Less than six weeks had gone by since the night when, by moonlight, Speck had heard the Senator saying "... hats."

A few days before Christmas Speck drove out to Lydia's with a briefcase filled with documents that were, at last, working papers: the list of exhibits from the Bellefeuille collection, the introduction, and the chronology in which there were gaps for Lydia to fill. He still had to draw up a financial arrangement. So far, she had said nothing about it, and it was not a matter Speck cared to rush.

He found another guest in the house—a man somewhat younger than he, slightly bald and as neat as a mouse.

"Here's the doctor I was telling you about," said Lydia, introducing Speck.

Signor Vigorelli of Milan was a fellow-Japhethite—so Speck gathered from their conversation, which took up, in English, as though he had never come in. Lydia poured Speck's tea in an offhand manner he found wounding. He felt he was being treated like the hanger-on in a Russian play. He smashed his lemon cupcake, scattering crumbs. The visitor's plate looked cleaner than his. After a minute of this, Speck took the catalogue material out of his briefcase and started to read. Nobody asked what he was reading. The Italian finally looked at his watch (expensive, of a make Speck recognized) and got to his feet, picking up car keys that had been lying next to his plate.

"That little man had an Alfa Romeo tag," said Speck when Lydia returned after seeing him out.

"I don't know why you people drive here when there is perfectly good bus service," she said.

"What does he do?"

"He is a devout, religious man."

For the first time, she sat down on the sofa, close to Speck. He showed her the introduction and the chronology. She made a number of sharp and useful suggestions. Then they went upstairs and looked at the pictures. The studio had been cleaned, the light repaired. Speck suddenly thought, I've done it—I've brought it off.

"We must discuss terms," he said.

"When you're ready," she replied. "Your cold seems a lot better."

Inching along in stagnant traffic, Speck tried one after the other the FM state-controlled stations on his car radio. He obtained a lecture about the cultural oppression of Cajuns in Louisiana, a warning that the road he was now driving on was saturated, and the disheartening squeaks and wails of a circumcision ceremony in Ethiopia. On the station called France-Culture someone said, "Henri Cruche."

"Not Henri, excuse me," said a polite foreigner. "His name was Hubert. Hubert Cruche."

"Strange that it should be an Italian to discover an artist so essentially French," said the interviewer.

Signor Vigorelli explained that his admiration for France was second only to his intense feelings about Europe. His career had been consecrated to enhancing Italian elegance with French refinement and then scattering the result abroad. He believed that the unjustly neglected Cruche would be a revelation and might even bring the whole of Western art to its senses.

Speck nodded, agreeing. The interview came to an end. Wild jungle drums broke forth, heralding the announcement that there was to be a reading of medieval Bulgarian poetry in an abandoned factory at Nanterre. It was then and then only that Speck took in the sense of what he had heard. He swung the car in a wild U-turn and, without killing himself or anyone else, ran into a tree. He sat quietly, for about a minute, until his breathing became steady again, then unlocked his safety belt and got out. For a long time he stood by the side of the road, holding his briefcase, feeling neither shock nor pain. Other drivers, noticing a man alone with a wrecked car, picked up speed. He began to walk in Lydia's direction. A cruising prostitute, on her way home to cook her husband's dinner, finally agreed to drop him off at a taxi stand. Speck gave her two hundred francs.

Lydia did not seem at all surprised to see him. "I'd invite you to supper," she said. "But all I've got is a tiny pizza and some of the leftover cake."

"The Italian," said Speck.

"Yes?"

"I've heard him. On the radio. He says he's got Cruche. That he discovered him. My car is piled up in the Bois. I tried to turn around and come back here. I've been walking for hours."

"Sit down," said Lydia. "There, on the sofa. Signor Vigorelli is having a big Cruche show in Milan next March."

"He can't," said Speck.

"Why can't he?"

"Because Cruche is mine. He was my idea. No one can have my idea. Not until after June."

"Then it goes to Trieste in April," said Lydia. "You could still have it by about the tenth of May. If you still want it."

If I want it, said Speck to himself. If I want it. With the best work sold and the insurance rates tripled and the commissions shared out like candy. And with everyone saying Speck jumped on the bandwagon, Speck made the last train.

"Lydia, listen to me," he said. "I invented Hubert Cruche. There would be no Hubert Cruche without Sandor Speck. This is an unspeakable betrayal. It is dishonorable. It is wrong." She listened, nodding her head. "What happens to me now?" he said. "Have you thought about that?" He knew better than to ask, "Why didn't you tell me about him?" Like all dissembling women, she would simply answer, "Tell you what?"

"It might be all the better," she said. "There'll be that much more interest in Hube."

"Interest?" said Speck. "The worst kind of interest. Third-rate, tawdry interest. Do you suppose I can get the Pompidou Center to look at a painter who has been trailing around in Trieste? It had to be a new idea. It had to be strong."

"You'll save on the catalogue," she said. "He will probably want to share."

"It's my catalogue," said Speck. "I'm not sharing. Senator Bellefeuille . . . my biography . . . never. The catalogue is mine. Besides, it would look as if he'd had the idea."

"He did."

"But after me," said Speck, falling back on the most useless of all lover's arguments. "*After* me. I was there first."

"So you were," she said tenderly, like any woman on her way out.

Speck said, "I thought you were happy with our arrangement."

"I was. But I hadn't met him yet. You see, he was so interested in the Japhethite movement. One day he opened the Bible and put his finger on something that seemed to make it all right about the graven image. In Ecclesiastes, I think."

Speck gave up. "I suppose it would be no use calling for a taxi?"

"Not around here, I'm afraid, though you might pick one up at the shopping center. Shouldn't you report the accident?"

"Which accident?"

"To the police," she said. "Get it on record fast. Make it a case. That squeezes the insurance people. The phone's in the hall."

"I don't care about the insurance," said Speck.

"You will care, once you're over the shock. Tell me exactly where it happened. Can you remember? Have you got your license? Registration? Insurance?"

Speck sank back and closed his eyes. He could hear Lydia dialing; then she began to speak. He listened, exactly as Cruche must have listened, while Lydia, her voice full of silver bells, dealt with creditors and dealers and Cruche's cast-off girlfriends and a Senator Bellefeuille more than forty years younger.

"I wish to report an accident," Lydia sang. "The victim is Dr. S. Speck. He is still alive—luckily. He was forced off the road in the Bois de Vincennes by a tank truck carrying high-octane fuel. It had an Italian plate. Dr. Speck was too shaken to get the number. Yes, I saw the accident, but I couldn't see the number. There was a van in the way. All I noticed was 'MI.' That must stand for Milan. I recognized the victim. Dr. Speck is well known in some circles . . . an intimate friend of Senator Antoine Bellefeuille, the former minister of . . . that's right." She talked a few minutes longer, then came back to Speck. "Get in touch with the insurance people first thing tomorrow," she said, flat Lydia again. "Get a medical certificate—you've had a serious emotional trauma. It can lead to jaundice. Tell your doctor to write that down. If he doesn't want to, I'll give you the name of a doctor who will. You're on the edge of nervous depression. By the way, the police will be towing your car to a garage. They know they've been very remiss, letting a foreign vehicle with a dangerous cargo race through the Bois. It might have hit a bus full of children. They must be looking for that tanker all over Paris. I've made a list of the numbers you're to call."

Speck produced his last card: "Senator Bellefeuille will never allow his Cruches to go to Milan. He'll never let them out of the country."

"Who—Antoine?" said Lydia. "Of course he will."

She cut a cupcake in half and gave him a piece. Broken, Speck crammed the whole thing in his mouth. She stood over him, humming. "Do you know that old hymn, Dr. Speck—'The day Thou gavest, Lord, is ended'?"

He searched her face, as he had often, looking for irony, or playfulness— a gleam of light. There floated between them the cold oblong on the map and the Chirico chessboard moving along to its Arctic destination. Trees dwindled to shrubs and shrubs to moss and moss to nothing. Speck had been defeated by a landscape.

Although Speck by no means considered himself a natural victim of hard luck, he had known disappointment. Shows had fallen flat. Galleries had been blown up and torn down. Artists he had nursed along had been lured away by siren dealers. Women had wandered off, bequeathing to Speck the warp and weft of a clear situation, so much less interesting than the ambiguous patterns of love. Disappointment had taught him rules: The first was that it takes next to no time to get used to bad news. Rain began to fall as he walked to the taxi stand. In his mind, Cruche was already being shown in Milan and he was making the best of it.

He gazed up and down the bleak road; of course there were no taxis. Inside a bus shelter huddled a few commuters. The thrust of their lives, their genetic destiny obliged them to wait for public transport—unlike Speck, thrown among them by random adventures. A plastic-covered timetable announced a bus to Paris every twenty-three minutes until five, every sixteen minutes from four to eight, and every thirty-one minutes thereafter. His watch had stopped late in the afternoon, probably at the time of the accident. He left the shelter and stood out in the wet, looking at windows of shops, one of which might contain a clock. He stood for a minute or two

staring at a china tea set flanked by two notices, HAND PAINTED and CHRIST-
MAS IS COMING, both of which he found deeply sad. The tea set had been
decorated with reproductions of the Pompidou Art Center, which was gradually replacing the Eiffel Tower as a constituent feature of French design.
The day's shocks caught up with him: He stared at the milk jug, feeling surprise because it did not tell him the time. The arrival of a bus replaced this
perplexity with one more pressing. He did not know what was needed on
suburban buses—tickets or tokens or a monthly pass. He wondered whether
the drivers accepted banknotes, and gave change, with civility.

"Dr. Speck, Dr. Speck!" Lydia Cruche, her raincoat open and flying, waving a battered black umbrella, bore down on him out of the dark. "You were
right," she said, gasping. "You were there first." Speck took his place at the
end of the bus queue. "I mean it," she said, clutching his arm. "He can wait."

Speck's second rule of disappointment came into play: The deceitful one
will always come back to you ten seconds too late. "What does it mean?"
he said, wiping rain from the end of his nose. "Having it before him means
what? Paying for the primary expenses and the catalogue and sweetening the
Paris critics and letting him rake in the chips?"

"Wasn't that what you wanted?"

"Your chap from Milan thought he was first," said Speck. "He may not
want to step aside for me—a humble Parisian expert on the entire Cruche
context and period. You wouldn't want Cruche to miss a chance at Milan,
either."

"Milan is ten times better for money than Paris," she said. "If that's what
we're talking about. But of course we aren't."

Speck looked down at her from the step of the bus. "Very well," he said.
"As we were."

"I'll come to the gallery," she called. "I'll be there tomorrow. We can
work out new terms."

Speck paid his fare without trouble and moved to the far end of the bus.
The dark shopping center with its windows shining for no one was a
Magritte vision of fear. Lydia had already forgotten him. Having tampered
with his pride, made a professional ass of him, gone off with his idea and
returned it dented and chipped, she now stood gazing at the Pompidou
Center tea set, perhaps wondering if the ban on graven images could possibly extend to this. Speck had often meant to ask her about the Mickey
Mouse napkins. He thought of the hoops she had put him through—God,
and politics, and finally the most dangerous one, which was jealousy. There

seemed to be no way of rolling down the window, but a sliding panel at the top admitted half his face. Rising from his seat, he drew in a gulp of wet suburban air and threw it out as a shout: "Fascist! Fascist! Fascist!"

Not a soul in the bus turned to see. From the look of them, they had spent the best Sundays of their lives shuffling in demonstrations from Place de la République to Place de la Nation, tossing "Fascist"s around like confetti. Lydia turned slowly and looked at Speck. She raised her umbrella at arm's length, like a trophy. For the first time, Speck saw her smile. What was it the Senator had said? "She had a smile like a fox's." He could see, gleaming white, her straight little animal teeth.

The bus lurched away from the curb and lumbered toward Paris. Speck leaned back and shut his eyes. Now he understood about that parting shot. It was amazing how it cleared the mind, tearing out weeds and tree stumps, flattening the live stuff along with the dead. "Fascist" advanced like a regiment of tanks. Only the future remained—clean, raked, ready for new growth. New growth of what? Of Cruche, of course—Cruche, whose hour was at hand, whose time was here. Speck began to explore his altered prospects. "New terms," she had said. So far, there had been none at all. The sorcerer from Milan must have promised something dazzling, swinging it before her eyes as he had swung his Alfa Romeo key. It would be foolish to match the offer. By the time they had all done with bungling, there might not be enough left over to buy a new Turkey carpet for Walter.

I was no match for her, he thought. No match at all. But then, look at the help she had—that visitation from Cruche. "Only once," she said, but women always said that: "He asked if he could see me just once more. I couldn't very well refuse." Dead or alive, when it came to confusion and double-dealing, there was no such thing as "only once." And there had been not only the departed Cruche but the very living Senator Bellefeuille— "Antoine"; who had bought every picture of Lydia for sixteen years, the span of her early beauty. Nothing would ever be the same again between Speck and Lydia, of course. No man could give the same trust and confidence the second time around. All that remained to them was the patch of landscape they held in common—a domain reserved for the winning, collecting, and sharing out of profits, a territory where believer and skeptic, dupe and embezzler, the loving and the faithless could walk hand in hand. Lydia had a talent for money. He could sense it. She had never been given much chance to use it, and she had waited so much longer than Speck.

He opened his eyes and saw rain clouds over Paris glowing with light—

the urban aurora. It seemed to Speck that he was entering a better weather zone, leaving behind the gray, indefinite mist in which the souls of discarded lovers are said to wander. He welcomed this new and brassy radiation. He saw himself at the center of a shadeless drawing, hero of a sort of cartoon strip, subduing Lydia, taming Henriette. Fortunately, he was above petty grudges. Lydia and Henriette had been designed by a bachelor God who had let the creation get out of hand. In the cleared land of Speck's future, a yellow notebook fluttered and lay open at a new page. The show would be likely to go to Milan in the autumn now; it might be a good idea to slip a note between the Senator's piece and the biographical chronology. If Cruche had to travel, then let it be with Speck's authority as his passport.

The bus had reached its terminus, the city limit. Speck waited as the rest of the passengers crept inch by inch to the doors. He saw, with immense relief, a rank of taxis half a block long. He alighted and strode toward them, suddenly buoyant. He seemed to have passed a mysterious series of tests, and to have been admitted to some new society, the purpose of which he did not yet understand. He was a saner, stronger, wiser person than the Sandor Speck who had seen his own tight smile on M. Chassepoule's window only two months before. As he started to get into a taxi, a young man darted toward him and thrust a leaflet into his hand. Speck shut the door, gave his address, and glanced at the flier he was still holding. Crudely printed on cheap pink paper was this:

FRENCHMEN!
FOR THE SAKE OF EUROPE, FIGHT
THE GERMANO-AMERICANO-ISRAELO
HEGEMONY!
Germans in Germany!
Americans in America!
Jews in Israel!
For a True Europe, For One Europe,
Death to the Anti-European Hegemony!

Speck stared at this without comprehending it. Was it a Chassepoule statement or an anti-Chassepoule plea? There was no way of knowing. He turned it over, looking for the name of an association, and immediately forgot what he was seeking. Holding the sheet of paper flat on his briefcase, he began to write, as well as the unsteady swaying of the cab would let him.

"It was with instinctive prescience that Hubert Cruche saw the need for a Europe united from the Atlantic to the . . . That Cruche skirted the murky zone of partisan politics is a tribute to his . . . even though his innocent zeal may have led him to the brink . . . early meeting with the young idealist and future statesman A. Bellefeuille, whose penetrating essay . . . close collaboration with the artist's wife and most trusted critic . . . and now, posthumously . . . from Paris, where the retrospective was planned and brought to fruition by the undersigned . . . and on to Italy, to the very borders of . . ."

Because this one I am keeping, Speck decided; this one will be signed: "By Sandor Speck." He smiled at the bright, wet streets of Paris as he and Cruche, together, triumphantly crossed the Alps.

FROM THE FIFTEENTH
DISTRICT

Although an epidemic of haunting, widely reported, spread through the Fifteenth District of our city last summer, only three acceptable complaints were lodged with the police.

Major Emery Travella, 31st Infantry, 1914–18, Order of the Leopard, Military Beech Leaf, Cross of St. Lambert First Class, killed while defusing a bomb in a civilian area 9 June, 1941, Medal of Danzig (posthumous), claims he is haunted by the entire congregation of St. Michael and All Angels on Bartholomew Street. Every year on the Sunday falling nearest the anniversary of his death, Major Travella attends Holy Communion service at St. Michael's, the church from which he was buried. He stands at the back, close to the doors, waiting until all the communicants have returned to their places, before he approaches the altar rail. His intention is to avoid a mixed queue of dead and living, the thought of which is disgusting to him. The congregation sits, hushed and expectant, straining to hear the Major's footsteps (he drags one foot a little). After receiving the Host, the Major leaves at once, without waiting for the Blessing. For the past several years, the Major has noticed that the congregation doubles in size as 9 June approaches. Some of these strangers bring cameras and tape recorders with them; others burn incense under the pews and wave amulets and trinkets in what they imagine to be his direction, muttering pagan gibberish all the while. References he is sure must be meant for him are worked into the sermons: "And he that was dead sat up, and began to speak" (Luke 7:15), or "So Job died, being old and full of days" (Job 42:17). The Major points out that he never speaks and never opens his mouth except to receive Holy Communion. He lived about sixteen thousand and sixty days, many of which he does not remember. On 23 September, 1914, as a young private, he was crucified to a cart wheel for five hours for having failed to salute an equally young lieutenant. One ankle was left permanently impaired.

The Major wishes the congregation to leave him in peace. The opacity of the living, their heaviness and dullness, the moisture of their skin, and the dustiness of their hair are repellent to a man of feeling. It was always his habit to avoid civilian crowds. He lived for six years on the fourth floor in Block E, Stoneflower Gardens, without saying a word to his neighbors or even attempting to learn their names. An affidavit can easily be obtained from the former porter at the Gardens, now residing at the Institute for Victims of Senile Trauma, Fifteenth District.

Mrs. Ibrahim, aged thirty-seven, mother of twelve children, complains about being haunted by Dr. L. Chalmeton of Regius Hospital, Seventh District, and by Miss Alicia Fohrenbach, social investigator from the Welfare Bureau, Fifteenth District. These two haunt Mrs. Ibrahim without respite, presenting for her ratification and approval conflicting and unpleasant versions of her own death.

According to Dr. Chalmeton's account, soon after Mrs. Ibrahim was discharged as incurable from Regius Hospital he paid his patient a professional call. He arrived at a quarter past four on the first Tuesday of April, expecting to find the social investigator, with whom he had a firm appointment. Mrs. Ibrahim was discovered alone, in a windowless room, the walls of which were coated with whitish fungus a quarter of an inch thick, which rose to a height of about forty inches from the floor. Dr. Chalmeton inquired, "Where is the social investigator?" Mrs. Ibrahim pointed to her throat, reminding him that she could not reply. Several dark-eyed children peeped into the room and ran away. "How many are yours?" the Doctor asked. Mrs. Ibrahim indicated six twice with her fingers. "Where do they sleep?" said the Doctor. Mrs. Ibrahim indicated the floor. Dr. Chalmeton said, "What does your husband do for a living?" Mrs. Ibrahim pointed to a workbench on which the Doctor saw several pieces of finely wrought jewelry; he thought it a waste that skilled work had been lavished on what seemed to be plastics and base metals. Dr. Chalmeton made the patient as comfortable as he could, explaining that he could not administer drugs for the relief of pain until the social investigator had signed a receipt for them. Miss Fohrenbach arrived at five o'clock. It had taken her forty minutes to find a suitable parking space: The street appeared to be poor, but everyone living on it owned one or two cars. Dr. Chalmeton, who was angry at having been kept waiting, declared he would not be responsible for the safety of his patient in a room filled with mold. Miss Fohrenbach retorted that the District could not resettle a family of fourteen persons who were foreign-born when there was a long list of native citizens waiting for accommodation. Mrs. Ibrahim had in any case relinquished her right to a domicile in the Fifteenth District the day she lost consciousness in the road and allowed an ambulance to transport her to a hospital in the Seventh. It was up to the hospital to look after her now. Dr. Chalmeton pointed out that housing of patients is not the business of hospitals. It was well known that the foreign poor preferred to crowd together in the Fifteenth, where they could sing and dance in the streets and attend one another's weddings. Miss Fohrenbach declared that Mrs. Ibrahim could easily have moved her bed into the kitchen, which was somewhat warmer and which boasted a window. When Mrs. Ibrahim died, the children would be placed in foster homes, eliminating the need for a larger apartment. Dr. Chalmeton remembers Miss Fohrenbach's then crying, "Oh, why do all these people come here, where nobody wants them?" While he was trying to think of an answer, Mrs. Ibrahim died.

In her testimony, Miss Fohrenbach recalls that she had to beg and plead with Dr. Chalmeton to visit Mrs. Ibrahim, who had been discharged from Regius Hospital without medicines or prescriptions or advice or instructions. Miss Fohrenbach had returned several times that April day to see if the Doctor had arrived. The first thing Dr. Chalmeton said on entering the room was "There is no way of helping these people. Even the simplest rules of hygiene are too complicated for them to follow. Wherever they settle, they spread disease and vermin. They have been responsible for outbreaks of aphthous stomatitis, hereditary hypoxia, coccidioidomycosis, gonorrheal arthritis, and scleroderma. Their eating habits are filthy. They never wash their hands. The virus that attacks them breeds in dirt. We took in the patient against all rules, after the ambulance drivers left her lying in the courtyard and drove off without asking for a receipt. Regius Hospital was built and endowed for ailing Greek scholars. Now it is crammed with unteachable persons who cannot read or write." His cheeks and forehead were flushed, his speech incoherent and blurred. According to the social investigator, he was the epitome of the broken-down, irresponsible old rascals the

Seventh District employs in its public services. Wondering at the effect this ranting of his might have on the patient, Miss Fohrenbach glanced at Mrs. Ibrahim and noticed she had died.

Mrs. Ibrahim's version of her death has the social investigator arriving first, bringing Mrs. Ibrahim a present of a wine-colored dressing gown made of soft, quilted silk. Miss Fohrenbach explained that the gown was part of a donation of garments to the needy. Large plastic bags, decorated with a moss rose, the emblem of the Fifteenth District, and bearing the words "Clean Clothes for the Foreign-Born," had been distributed by volunteer workers in the more prosperous streets of the District. A few citizens kept the bags as souvenirs, but most had turned them in to the Welfare Bureau filled with attractive clothing, washed, ironed, and mended, and with missing buttons replaced. Mrs. Ibrahim sat up and put on the dressing gown, and the social investigator helped her button it. Then Miss Fohrenbach changed the bed linen and pulled the bed away from the wall. She sat down and took Mrs. Ibrahim's hand in hers and spoke about a new, sunny flat containing five warm rooms which would soon be available. Miss Fohrenbach said that arrangements had been made to send the twelve Ibrahim children to the mountains for special winter classes. They would be taught history and languages and would learn to ski.

The Doctor arrived soon after. He stopped and spoke to Mr. Ibrahim, who was sitting at his workbench making an emerald patch box. The Doctor said to him, "If you give me your social-security papers, I can attend to the medical insurance. It will save you a great deal of trouble." Mr. Ibrahim answered, "What is social security?" The Doctor examined the patch box and asked Mr. Ibrahim what he earned. Mr. Ibrahim told him, and the Doctor said, "But that is less than the minimum wage." Mr. Ibrahim said, "What is a minimum wage?" The Doctor turned to Miss Fohrenbach, saying, "We really must try and help them." Mrs. Ibrahim died. Mr. Ibrahim, when he understood that nothing could be done, lay facedown on the floor, weeping loudly. Then he remembered the rules of hospitality and got up and gave each of the guests a present—for Miss Fohrenbach a belt made of Syriac coins, a copy of which is in the Cairo Museum, and for the Doctor a bracelet of precious metal engraved with pomegranates, about sixteen pomegranates in all, that has lifesaving properties.

Mrs. Ibrahim asks that her account of the afternoon be registered with the police as the true version and that copies be sent to the Doctor and the social investigator, with a courteous request for peace and silence.

* * *

Mrs. Carlotte Essling, née Holmquist, complains of being haunted by her husband, Professor Augustus Essling, the philosopher and historian. When they were married, the former Miss Holmquist was seventeen. Professor Essling, a widower, had four small children. He explained to Miss Holmquist why he wanted to marry again. He said, "I must have one person, preferably female, on whom I can depend absolutely, who will never betray me even in her thoughts. A disloyal thought revealed, a betrayal even in fantasy, would be enough to destroy me. Knowing that I may rely upon some one person will leave me free to continue my work without anxiety or distraction." The work was the Professor's lifelong examination of the philosopher Nicholas de Malebranche, for whom he had named his eldest child. "If I cannot have the unfailing loyalty I have described, I would as soon not marry at all," the Professor added. He had just begun work on *Malebranche and Materialism.*

Mrs. Essling recalls that at seventeen this seemed entirely within her possibilities, and she replied something like "Yes, I see," or "I quite understand," or "You needn't mention it again."

Mrs. Essling brought up her husband's four children and had two more of her own, and died after thirty-six years of marriage at the age of fifty-three. Her husband haunts her with proof of her goodness. He tells people that Mrs. Essling was born an angel, lived like an angel, and is an angel in eternity. Mrs. Essling would like relief from this charge. "Angel" is a loose way of speaking. She is astonished that the Professor cannot be more precise. Angels are created, not born. Nowhere in any written testimony will you find a scrap of proof that angels are "good." Some are merely messengers; others have a paramilitary function. All are stupid.

After her death, Mrs. Essling remained in the Fifteenth District. She says she can go nowhere without being accosted by the Professor, who, having completed the last phase of his work *Malebranche and Mysticism,* roams the streets, looking in shopwindows, eating lunch twice, in two different restaurants, telling his life story to waiters and bus drivers. When he sees Mrs. Essling, he calls out, "There you are!" and "What have you been sent to tell me?" and "Is there a message?" In July, catching sight of her at the open-air fruit market on Dulac Street, the Professor jumped off a bus, upsetting barrows of plums and apricots, waving an umbrella as he ran. Mrs. Essling had to take refuge in the cold-storage room of the central market, where, years ago, after she had ordered twenty pounds of raspberries and currants for making jelly, she was invited by the wholesale fruit dealer, Mr. Lobrano, aged twenty-nine, to spend a holiday with him in a charming southern city whose Mediterranean Baroque churches he described with much delicacy of feeling. Mrs. Essling was too startled to reply. Mistaking her silence, Mr. Lobrano then mentioned a northern city containing a Gothic cathedral. Mrs. Essling said that such a holiday was impossible. Mr. Lobrano asked for one good reason. Mrs. Essling was at that moment four months pregnant with her second child. Three stepchildren waited for her out in the street. A fourth stepchild was at home looking after the baby. Professor Essling, working on his *Malebranche and Money*, was at home, too, expecting his lunch. Mrs. Essling realized she could not give Mr. Lobrano one good reason. She left the cold-storage room without another word and did not return to it in her lifetime.

Mrs. Essling would like to be relieved of the Professor's gratitude. Having lived an exemplary life is one thing; to have it thrown up at one is another. She would like the police to send for Professor Essling and tell him so. She suggests that the police find some method of keeping him off the streets. The police ought to threaten him; frighten him; put the fear of the Devil into him. Philosophy has made him afraid of dying. Remind him about how he avoided writing his *Malebranche and Mortality*. He is an old man. It should be easy.

THE PEGNITZ JUNCTION

She was a bony slow-moving girl from a small bombed Baroque German city, where all that was worthwhile keeping had been rebuilt and which now looked as pink and golden as a pretty child and as new as morning. By the standards of a few years ago she would have been thought plain; she was so tall that she bumped her head getting in and out of airplanes, and in her childhood she had often been told that her feet were like canal boats. Her light hair would have been brown, about the color of brown sugar, if she had not rinsed it in chamomile and whenever possible dried it in sunlight; she could not use a commercial bleach because of some vague promise she had given her late grandmother when she was fourteen.

She had a striking density of expression in photographs, though she seemed unchanging and passive in life, and had caught sight of her own face looking totally empty-minded when, in fact, her thoughts and feelings were pushing her in some wild direction. She had heard a man say of her that you could leave her in a café for two hours and come back to find she was still smoking the same cigarette. She had done some modeling, not well paid, in middling ready-to-wear centers such as Berlin and Zurich, but now she was trying to be less conscious of her body. She was at one of those turnings in a young life where no one can lead, no one can help, but where someone for the sake of love might follow.

She lived with her family and was engaged to marry a student of theology, but the person closest to her was Herbert, who was thirty-one, divorced, and who with the help of a housekeeper was bringing up his only child. Unlike the student of theology, he had not put up barriers such as too much talk, self-analysis, or second thoughts. In fact, he tended to limit the number of subjects he would discuss. He had no hold on her mind, and no interest in gaining one. The mind that he constantly took stock of was his child's; apparently he could not be captivated in the same way by two people at once. He often said he thought he could not live without her, but a few minutes after making such a declaration he seemed unable to remember what he had just said, or to imagine how his voice must have sounded to her.

After they had known each other about seven months, they came to Paris for a holiday, all three of them—she, Herbert, and the child, who was called little Bert. Christine had just turned twenty-one and considered this voyage a major part of her emancipation. It was during the peak of a heat wave—the warmest July on record since 1873. They remained for a week, in an old hotel that had not been repainted for years because it was marked for demolition. They had two dusty, velvety rooms with a bathroom between. The bathroom was as large as the bedrooms together and had three doors, one of which gave on the passage. Leaving the passage door unlocked soon turned out to be a trick of little Bert's—an innocent trick; the locks were unlike those he was used to at home and he could not stop fiddling with them. The view from every window was of a church covered with scaffolding from top to bottom, the statue of a cardinal lying on its side, and a chestnut tree sawed in pieces. During the week of their stay nothing moved or was changed until a sign went up saying that a new car park was to be built under the church and that after its completion the chestnut tree would be replaced by something more suited to the gassy air of cities. The heat at night made sheets, blankets, curtains, blinds, or nightclothes unthinkable: She would lie awake for a long time, with a lock of her hair across her eyes to screen out the glare of a street lamp. Sometimes she woke up to find herself being inspected from head to foot by little Bert, who had crept to their room in search of his father. It was his habit to waken at two, and on finding the bed next to his empty, to come padding along in bare feet by way of the bathroom. Through her hair she would watch him taking a long look at her before he moved round the bed and began whimpering to Herbert that he was all alone and afraid of the dark.

Herbert would turn at once to little Bert. His deepest feelings were linked to the child. He sometimes could reveal anguish, of which only the child was the source. His first move was always to draw the sheet over Christine, to protect little Bert from the shock of female nakedness. Without a breath of reproach he would collect his dressing gown, glasses, watch, cigarettes, and lighter and take little Bert by the hand.

"I'm sorry," quavered the child.

"It's all right."

Then she would hear the two of them in the bathroom, where little Bert made the longest possible incident out of drinking a glass of water. The next day Herbert could not always recall how he had got from one bed to the other, and once, during the water-drinking rite, he had sleepily stuck a toothbrush in his mouth and tried to light it.

On their last night in Paris (which little Bert was to interrupt, as he had all the others) Herbert said he would never forget the view from the window or the shabby splendor of the room. "Both rooms," he corrected; he would not leave out little Bert. That day the Paris airports had gone on strike, which meant they had to leave by train quite early in the morning. Christine woke up alone at five. The others were awake too—she could hear little Bert's high-pitched chattering—but the bathroom was still empty. She waited a polite minute or so and then began to run her bath. Presently, above the sound of rushing water, she became aware that someone was pounding on the passage door and shouting. She called out, "What?" but before she could make a move, or even think of one, the night porter of the hotel had burst in. He was an old man without a tooth in his head, habitually dressed in trousers too large for him and a pajama top. He opened his mouth and screamed, "Stop the noise! Take all your belongings out of here! I am locking the bathroom—every door!"

At first, of course, she thought that the man was drunk; then the knowledge came to her—she did not know how, but never questioned it either— that he suffered from a form of epilepsy.

"It is too late," he kept repeating. "Too late for noise. Take everything that belongs to you and clear out."

He meant too *early*—Herbert, drawn by the banging and shouting, kept telling him so. Five o'clock was too *early* to be drawing a bath. The hotel was old and creaky anyway, and when you turned the taps it sounded as though fifty plumbers were pounding on the pipes. That was all Herbert had to say. He really seemed extraordinarily calm, picking up toothbrushes and jars and tubes without standing his ground for a second. It was as if he were under arrest, or as though the porter's old pajama top masked his badge of office, his secret credentials. The look on Herbert's face was abstract and soft, as if he had already lived this, or always had thought that he might.

The scented tub no one would ever use steamed gently; the porter pulled the stopper, finally, to make sure. She said, "You are going to be in trouble over this."

"Never mind," said Herbert. He did not want any unpleasantness in France.

She held her white toweling robe closed at the throat and with the other hand swept back her long hair. Without asking her opinion, Herbert put everything back in her dressing case and snapped it shut. She said to the porter in a low voice, "You filthy little swine of a dog of a bully."

Herbert's child looked up at their dazed, wild faces. It was happening in French; he would never know what had been said that morning. He hugged a large bath sponge to his chest.

"The sponge isn't ours," said Herbert, as though it mattered.

"Yes. It's mine."

"I've never seen it before."

"Its name is Bruno," said little Bert.

Unshaven, wearing a rather short dressing gown and glasses that sat crookedly, Herbert seemed unprepared to deal with sponges. He had let all three of them be pushed along to Christine's room and suffered the door to be padlocked behind him. "We shall never come to this hotel again," he remarked. Was that all? No, more: "And I intend to write to the Guide Michelin and the Tourist Office."

But the porter had left them. His answer came back from the passage: "Dirty Boches, you spoiled my holiday in Bulgaria. Everywhere I looked I saw Germans. The year before in Majorca. The same thing. Germans, Germans."

Through tears she did not wish the child to observe, Christine stared at larches pressing against the frame of the window. They had the look they often have, of seeming to be wringing wet. She noticed every detail of their bedraggled branches and red cones. The sky behind them was too bright for comfort. She took a step nearer and the larches were not there. They belonged to her school days and to mountain holidays with a score of little girls—a long time ago now.

Herbert did not enlarge on the incident, perhaps for the sake of little Bert. He said only that the porter had behaved strangely and that he really would write to the Guide Michelin. Sometimes Herbert meant more than he said; if so, the porter might have something to fear. She began to pack, rolling her things up with none of the meticulous folding and pleating of a week ago, when she had been preparing to come here with her lover. She buckled the lightest of sandals on her feet and tied her hair low on her neck, using a scarf for a ribbon. She had already shed her robe and pulled on a sleeveless dress. Herbert kept little Bert's head turned the other way, though the child had certainly seen all he wanted to night after night.

Little Bert would have breakfast on the French train, said Herbert, to distract him. He had never done *that* before.

"I have never been on a train" was the reply.

"It will be an exciting experience," said Herbert; like most parents, he was firm about pleasure. He promised to show little Bert a two-star restaurant at the Gare de l'Est. That would be fun. The entire journey, counting a stopover in Strasbourg and a change of trains, would take no more than twelve hours or so; this was fast, as trains go, but it might seem like a long day to a child. He was counting on little Bert's cooperation, Herbert concluded somberly.

After a pause, during which little Bert began to fidget and talk to his bath sponge, Herbert came back to the subject of food. At Strasbourg they would have time for a quick lunch, and little Bert had better eat his . . .

"Plum tart," said little Bert. He was a child who had to be coaxed to eat at every meal, yet who always managed to smell of food, most often of bread and butter.

. . . because the German train would not have a restaurant car, Herbert went on calmly. His actual words were, "Because there will be no facilities for eating on the second transport."

Christine thought that Herbert's information left out a great deal. Little Bert did not know what a two-star restaurant was, and would certainly have refused every dish set before him had he been taken to one. Also, the appalling schedule Herbert had just described meant that the boy would have nothing to eat or drink from about eleven in the morning until past his bedtime. She suggested they buy a picnic lunch and a bottle of mineral water before leaving. Her impression of the week just past was that little Bert had to be fed water all day and part of the night. But Herbert said no, that the smell of food on trains made him—Herbert—feel sick. It was the thing he hated most in the world, next to singing. The train would be staffed with vendors of sandwiches and milk and whatever little Bert wanted. Herbert did not foresee any food or drink problem across the Rhine.

Well, that was settled, though leaving early had destroyed Herbert's plans for exposing the Louvre to little Bert and finding out what he had to say about the Postal Museum. "Too bad," said Herbert.

"Yes, too bad." She knew now that there had been only one purpose to this holiday: to see how she got along with little Bert.

Herbert let the child carry the sponge to the station, hoping he would forget it on the way. But he continued to address it as "Bruno" and held it up to their taxi window to see Paris going by.

"The porter seemed drugged," said Herbert. "There was something hysterical, irrational. What did he mean by 'too late'? He meant 'too early'!"

"He was playing," said little Bert, who had the high, impudent voice of the spoiled favorite. "He wanted you to play too."

Herbert smiled. "Grown people don't play that way," he said. "They mean what they say." His scruples made him add, "Sometimes." Then, so that little Bert would not be confused, he said, "*I* mean what I say." To prove it he began looking for the two-star restaurant as soon as they had reached the station. He looked right and left and up at a bronze plaque on the wall. The plaque commemorated a time of ancient misery, so ancient that two of the three travelers had not been born then, and Herbert, the eldest, had been about the age of little Bert. An instinct made him turn little Bert's head the other way, though the child could barely read in German, let alone French.

"I can't protect him forever," he said to Christine. "Think of what the porter said."

It was a sad, gnawing moment, but once they were aboard the express to Strasbourg they forgot about it. They had a first-class compartment to themselves. Herbert opened one smooth morning paper after the other. He offered them to Christine but she shook her head. She carried a paperback volume of Dietrich Bonhoeffer's essays tucked in behind her handbag. For some reason she thought that Herbert might tease her. They moved on to breakfast in the dining car, where Herbert insisted on speaking French. Little Bert was truly cooperative this time and did not interrupt or keep whimpering, "What are you saying?" He propped the object Herbert had begun to refer to as "that damned sponge" behind the menu card, asked for a drop of coffee to color his milk, and ate toasted brioche without being coaxed. When the conductor came by to check their tickets little Bert suddenly repeated a French phrase of Herbert's, which was, *"Oh, en quel honneur?"* Everyone who heard it smiled, except Christine; she knew he had not meant to be funny, though Herbert believed the child had a precocious sense of humor. He did not go so far as to write down little Bert's remarks, but made a point of remembering them, though they were nothing but accidents.

The early start and the trouble at the hotel must have made Herbert jumpy. He kept lighting one cigarette after another so carelessly that sometimes he had two going at once. He looked at Christine and told her in French that she was overdressed. She smiled without replying; it was the end of the holiday, too late for anything except remarks. She glanced out at men fishing in ditches, at poplar shadows stretched from fence to fence, and finally—Herbert could tease her or not—she opened her book.

Little Bert was beside her in a second. He stood leaning, breathing unpleasantly on her bare arm. He laid a jammy hand over the page and said, "What are you doing?"

"Standing on my head."

"Don't," said Herbert. "Children can't understand sarcasm. Christine is reading, little Bert."

"But he can *see* that I'm reading, can't he?"

"What are you reading?" said the child.

"A book for an examination."

"When is it?" he said, as if knowing they had been expecting another "what?"

"In two days' time at eight in the morning."

Still he did not remove his paw from the page. "Can you read to me?" he said. "Read a story about Bruno."

"Herbert," she said suddenly, in her slow voice. "Do you ever think that nothing passes unobserved? That someone might be recording all your private expressions? The faces you think no one sees? And that this might be on film, stored away with tons and tons of other microfilm? For instance, your reaction to the porter—it wasn't a reaction at all. You were sleep-walking."

"Who would want a record of that?" said Herbert. *"En quel honneur."*

"Read a story where Bruno has sisters and brothers," said little Bert.

"I'll read after Strasbourg," said Christine. She was too inexperienced to know this was a pledge, though Herbert's manner told her so at once.

"If Christine wants to study I'll read," he said.

Oh, he was so foolish with the child! Like a servant, like a humble tutor with a crown prince. She would never marry Herbert—never. Not unless he placed the child in the strictest of boarding schools, for little Bert's own sake. Was it fair to the child, was it honest, to bring him up without discipline, without religion, without respect, belief, or faith? Wasn't it simply Herbert's own self-indulgence, something connected with his past? It happened that little Bert's mother had run away. Not only did Herbert-the-amiable forgive his wife, but he sent her money whenever she needed it. In a sense he was paying her to stay away from little Bert. He'd had bad luck with his women. His own mother had been arrested and put in a camp when he was three. She had been more pious than political, one of a flock milling around a stubborn pastor. After she came home she would sit on a chair for hours, all day sometimes, munching scraps of sweet food. She grew enormous—Herbert recalled having to help her with her shoes. She died early and stayed in his mind as a bloated sick woman eating sugar and telling bitter stories—how the Slav prisoners were selfish, the Dutch greedy, the French self-seeking and dirty, spreaders of lice and fleas. She had gone into captivity believing in virtue and learned she could steal. Went in loving the poor, came out afraid of them; went in for the hounded, came out a racist; went in generous, came out grudging; went in with God, came out alone. And left Herbert twice, once under arrest, and once to die. Herbert did not believe for a second that the Dutch were this or the French were that; he went to France often, said that French was the sole language of culture, there was no poetry in English, something else was wrong with Russian and Italian. At the same time he thought nothing of repeating his mother's remarks.

Christine came up out of her thoughts, which were quite far from their last exchange. She said, "Everyone thinks other people are dirty and that they won't cooperate. We think it about the Slavs, the Slavs think it about the Jews, the Jews think it about the Arabs ..."

Herbert said, "Oh, a Christian sermon? *En quel honneur?*" and stared hard at the two cigarettes lit by mistake and crowding the little ashtray. His mother's life had never been recorded, and even if it had been he would not have moved an inch to see the film. Her life and her death gave him such mixed feelings, made him so sad and uncomfortable, that he would say nothing except "Oh, a Christian sermon?" when something reminded him of it.

"Now, little Bert," said his father at eleven o'clock. "We are almost at Strasbourg. I know you are not used to eating your lunch quite so early, but we are victims of the airport strikes and I am counting on you to understand that." He drew the child close to him. "If there are shower-baths in the station ..."

"We'll eat our plum tart," said little Bert.

"We'll have to be quick and alert from the time we arrive," said Herbert.

He had more than that to say, but little Bert had put Bruno between his face and his father's and Herbert had no wish to address himself to a bath sponge. He began stuffing toothbrushes and everything they would need for their showers into his briefcase, not at all out of sorts.

Christine jumped down and made a dash in the right direction as soon as the train stopped. But the great haste recommended by Herbert had been for nothing: There were no showers. Nevertheless she paid her fee of one franc fifty centimes, which allowed her a threadbare dark blue square of toweling, a sliver of wrapped soap, four sheets of glassy paper, and a receipt for the money. She showed the receipt to an attendant carrying a mop and a bucket and wearing rubber waders, who looked at it hard and waited for a tip before unlocking a tiled cubicle containing a washbasin. The tiles rose very high and the ceiling was lost in twilight. The place was not really dirty, but coarse and institutional. She took off her dress and sandals and stood on the square of towel. Noise from the platform seemed to seep between the cracked tiling and to swirl and echo along the ceiling. Even the trains sounded sad, as though they were used to ferry poor and weary passengers—refugees perhaps. The cubicle was as cold as a cellar; no sun, no natural light had ever touched the high walls. She stepped from the towel to her sandals—she did not dare set a foot on the cement floor, which looked damp and gritty. In these surroundings her small dressing case with its modest collection of lotions and soap seemed a wasteful luxury. She said to herself, If this is something you pay for, what are their jails like?

Outside she discovered a new little Bert, subdued and teary.

"He wanted his lunch first," said Herbert. "So we changed our plan. But he ate too fast and threw up on the buffet floor. Nothing has worked as we intended, but perhaps there will be some unexpected facility on the German train."

Little Bert held on to his sponge and hiccuped softly. His face was streaked and none too clean. He looked like a runaway child who had been found in a coalbin and who was now being taken home against his will.

The German train crossed the Rhine at a snail's pace and then refused to move another foot. Until it moved, the toilets and washrooms would be locked. They sat for a long time, discontented but not complaining, gazing out at freight sheds, and finally were joined by a man as tall as Herbert, wearing a blond beard. He had a thick nose, eyes as blue as a doll's, and a bald spot like a tonsure. He dropped his luggage and at once went back to the corridor, where he pulled down the top half of the window, folded his arms on it, and stared hard as if he had something to look at. But there was nothing on his side except more freight sheds and shell-pocked gray hangars. The feeling aboard this train was of glossed-over poverty. Even the plump customs man shuffling through seemed poor, though his regulation short-sleeved shirt was clean, and his cap, the green of frozen peas, rode at a proper angle. Something of a lout, he leaned out the window of their compartment and bawled in dialect to someone dressed as he was. Herbert sat up straight and squashed his cigarette. He was a pacifist and antistate, but he expected a great deal in the way of behavior from civil servants, particularly those wearing a uniform.

Little Bert had been settled in one of the corner seats; the other was reserved for someone who had not yet appeared. Christine and Herbert sat facing each other. They were both so tall that for the rest of the afternoon someone or other would be tripping over their legs and feet. At last the freight sheds began to glide past the windows.

Christine said, "I don't feel as if I were going home." He did not consider this anything like the start of a conversation. She said, "The heat is unbelievable. My dress is soaked through. Herbert, I believe this train has a steam engine. How can they, when we have first-class tickets?" That at least made him smile; she had been outraged by the undemocratic Paris Métro with its first- and second-class cars. Foul smoke streamed past the window at which the bearded man still stood. The prickly velvet stuff their seats were covered in scratched her legs and arms. The cloth was hideous in color, and stamped with a pointless design. The most one could say was that it would do for first class.

"All we need here are lace curtains," Herbert remarked.

"Yes, and a fringed lampshade. My grandmother's parlor looked like this."

Little Bert, who seemed about to say what *he* thought of the furnishings, shut his mouth again; the owner of the window seat had arrived. This was an old woman carrying bags and parcels and a heavy-looking case that she lifted like a feather to the rack before Herbert could help. She examined her ticket to see if it matched the number at the window seat, sat down, pulled out the drop-leaf shelf under the sill, and placed upon it some food, a box of paper handkerchiefs, a bundle of postcards, and a bottle of eau de cologne, all drawn from a large carryall on which was printed WINES OF GERMANY. She sprinkled eau de cologne on a handkerchief and rubbed it into her face. She had sparse orange-blond hair done up in a matted beehive, a long nose, small gray eyes, and wore a printed dress and thick black shoes. As soon as she had rubbed her face thoroughly she opened a plastic bag of caramels. She did not wait to finish eating one caramel before unwrapping the next, and before long she had her mouth full.

Christine said to Herbert in French, "The German train may have unexpected facilities." The air coming in at the window was hot and dry. The houses they passed looked deserted. "What would you call the color of these seats?" she asked him.

"We've said it: middle-class."

"That's an impression, not a color. Would you say mustard?"

"Dried orange peel."

"Faded bloodstains."

"Melted raspberry sherbet."

"Persimmons? No, they're pretty."

"I have never eaten one," said Herbert. He was not at all interested.

Little Bert spoke up and said, "Vomited plum tart," quite seriously, which made the woman in the corner say "Hee hee" in a squeaky tone of voice. "Read to me," said little Bert quickly, taking this to be universal attention.

"It isn't a book for children," Christine said. But then she saw that the woman in the corner was beginning to stare at them curiously, and so she pretended to read: " 'It was the fourteenth of July in Paris. Bruno put on his blue-and-gold uniform with the tassels and buttons shining . . .' "

"No, no," said Herbert. "Nothing military."

"Well, you read then." She handed the book across. Herbert glanced at the title, then at the flyleaf to see if it was Christine's. He pretended to read: " 'Bruno had a camera. He wore it on a strap around his neck. He had already dropped one in the lake so this one was not quite so expensive. He took pictures of Marianne, the housekeeper . . .' "

" 'Who was really a beautiful princess instead of an ugly old gossip,' " said Christine.

"Don't," said Herbert. "She loves him." He went on: " 'He took pictures of a little boy his own age . . .' "

"Is Bruno a bear or a boy?" said Christine.

"A male cub, I imagine," said Herbert.

"It's a sponge," said the offended child. He threw it down and went out to where the bearded man was still gazing at the dull landscape. All this was only half a gesture, for he did not know what to do next.

"That's sulking," said Christine. "Don't let him, Herbert. For his own sake make him behave." The woman in the corner looked again, trying to make sense of this odd party. Christine supposed that it was up to her to be-have like a mother. Perhaps she ought to pick up the sponge, go out to lit-tle Bert, stoop down until their faces were nearly level, and say something like, "You mustn't be touchy. I'm not used to touchy people. I don't know how to be with them." Or, more effectively, "Your father wants you to come back at once." She realized how she might blackmail little Bert if ever she married Herbert, and was ashamed. It was an inherited method, straight from her late grandmother's velvet parlor. But by now Herbert was trying to show little Bert something interesting out the window, and little Bert was crying hard. She heard the bearded man telling Herbert that he was a Nor-wegian, a bass baritone, and that he had been asked to teach a summer course in Germany. His teaching method was inspired by yoga. He seemed to expect something from Herbert, but Herbert merely mouthed "Ah," and left it at that. He was trying to get little Bert to blow his nose. Then, after an exchange she was unable to hear, all three disappeared down the corri-dor, perhaps looking for a conductor. The toilets and washrooms were still locked.

A few minutes after this, at a place called Bietigheim, their carriage was overrun by a horde of fierce little girls who had been lined up in squads on a station platform for some time, heels together and eyes front. Now there was no holding them. "Girls, girls!" their camp monitor screamed, running alongside the train. "Move along! Move along to second class!" They took not the slightest notice; she was still calling and blowing a whistle as the train pulled away.

Christine and the old woman sat helplessly watching while their com-partment was taken over by a commando, led by a bossy little blonde of about eleven. Six children pushed into the four empty seats, pulling up the armrests and making themselves at home. "These places are taken," said Christine. The commando pretended not to hear. All six wore knee-length white lace socks and homemade cotton frocks in harsh colors. For all their city toughness, they seemed like country children. Their hair, loose and un-braided, was clasped here and there with plastic barrettes. The child sitting in Herbert's place had large red hands and the haunted face of a widow. An-other was plump and large, with clotted veins on her cheeks, as if she were already thirty-five and had been eating puddings and drinking beer since her wedding day. When she got up suddenly the others giggled; the pattern of the first-class velvet was imprinted on her fat thighs. As for the bossy one, the little gangster, showy as a poppy in red and green, she could not leave the others alone, but seem compelled to keep kicking and teasing them.

"No standing in first class!" This voice, growing louder and nearer, was so comically Bavarian that even the two adults had to laugh, though more discreetly than the children, who were simply doubled over. The voice was very like Herbert's, imitating a celebrated Bavarian politician addressing a congress of peasants. But Herbert was not unexpectedly being funny out there in the corridor, and the voice belonged to the conductor, now seen for the first time. He stumbled along saying "*No* standing," quite hopelessly, not really expecting anyone to obey, for who could possibly be afraid of such a jolly little person? He was only repeating something out of a tiresome rules book, and the children knew it. They leaned out the windows (also forbidden) trailing souvenir streamers of purple crepe paper, past miles of larches with bedraggled branches, past a landscape baked and blind. The bossy blonde peeped out to the corridor and giggled and covered her mouth. She had small green eyes and resembled a thief. Yes, Christine could easily see her snatching something and concealing it—a ring left on a washstand, say. She took her hand away to offer a gap-toothed smile to Herbert, struggling along past girls and crepe paper and long tangled hair and piles of luggage as if wading in seaweed. Instead of evicting the children at once he said a few comic words, which convulsed them anew, and asked for his briefcase. They would have murdered one another for the sake of being the favorite. The bossy blonde won, of course. She smiled adoringly. He appraised her as though she were twenty. All this took less than a minute. They were approaching Stuttgart.

The little girls filed off the train, leaving a curiously adult smell of sweat behind, followed by Herbert, the Norwegian, and little Bert. These three were still in pursuit of food and running water. She saw Herbert look at his watch. He had his briefcase in one hand and held on to little Bert with the other. The girls buzzed and swarmed. They seemed quite ordinary now; they were only children home from camp, waiting to be picked up by parents. The little gangster was overtaken by a mad mother pushing a pram and a grandmother who was the mother grown mean and fearful, plaintive and soft. The mother opened her thin mouth and cried to the little blonde, who was shaking hands all round with the friends she had so lately been abusing, "While you take hours to say good-bye to everyone, your poor grandmother is standing waiting . . ."

Waiting for what? said Christine to herself.

The grandmother put on the look of someone whose patience will never be rewarded enough. Her face said, "No one need think *I* ask for favors." A lie, Christine decided. She asked for nothing but favors.

The once bossy, once confident little girl who had led the commando raid was all seriousness now, all worry, looking older than her grandmother ever would. She tried to say that she was sorry, but according to family timing it was too late. For a second longer Christine saw her small, upturned, elderly face.

"That was my grandmother," said Christine. "Such a blackmailer. So humble." She wondered if she had said this aloud, but the woman in the corner was busy with a chocolate bar and to all appearances had heard nothing except whatever went on in her own head.

Herbert and little Bert had not found everything they wanted at Stuttgart, but at least there had been time to brush their teeth. The Norwegian had become quite a friend of Herbert's now; at least, he seemed to imagine he had. He asked easily, casually, what Herbert's profession might be. Trying not to smoke, Herbert folded his hands and said he was an engineer. He described a method of clearing waste from rivers which consisted of causing an infinite number of tiny bubbles to rise from the bottom of the waters, each little bubble gathering and bearing upward a particle of poisonous trash, which could then be raked off at the top. Herbert's information stopped there. If he had created an image of hand rakes, garden rakes, twig brooms; of women in bare feet and men in clogs raking away at the surface of ponds and inlets, he said nothing to change it. He was scrupulous about providing correct information but did not feel obliged to answer for pictures raised in the imagination. Christine thought that she knew what "information" truly was, and had known for some time. She could see it plainly, in fact; it consisted of fine silver crystals forming a pattern, dancing, separating, dissolving in a glittering trail along the window. The crystals flowed swiftly, faster than smoke, more beautiful and less durable than snowflakes. The woman in the corner said "Chck chck," admiring Herbert's method, and unfolded a new shopping bag labeled YOUR BEAUTICIAN HAS THE ANSWERS.

It was from the woman that the silvery crystals took their substance; she was the source. *It started this way*, Christine understood. She looked carefully at the woman who was creating information, all the while peeling paper stuck to a cream bun. She licked her fingers before taking the first bite. *This was the beginning. Two first cousins from Muggendorf married two first cousins from Doos. Emigrated to the U.S.A., all four together. Two cousins, boy and girl, married to two cousins, girl and boy. The men got work right away in Flushing. Flushing was full of mosquitoes but these were got rid of in time for the World's Fair. First factory ever to make good-class kitchen units for the unpretentious home. Disguised stove, vanishing sink, disappearing refrigerator, all that. First indoor barbecue, first electric spit for use in the smaller American residential facility. During the conflict the factory converted to making submarine galley units, after the war reconverted to kitchen conveniences, all the wiser for the experience.*

The woman had finished her bun. She wet a handkerchief with eau de cologne, washed her hands and passed the handkerchief around the back of her neck. The trees rushing by were reflected in her eyes. *We never lived in Flushing because of the mosquitoes. Settled at once in Elmhurst and remained without a break for forty-seven years. Lived in a duplex residence. First rented then bought the upper, were later in a position to purchase the lower. Rented the downstairs place to white Lutherans of which there was no shortage. Never owned a car—never needed one. Never went anywhere. Other couple had bungalow with heated garage, car, large yard and barbecue. Never used the barbecue—she couldn't cook. Arrangement was that they would come to us for their evening meal. Had every evening meal together for forty-seven years. She didn't shop, couldn't market, never learned any English. I cooked around seventeen thousand suppers, all told. Never a disagreement. Never an angry word. Nothing but good food and family loyalty. I cooked fresh chicken soup, pea soup with bacon, my own goulash soup, hot beer soup, soup with dumplings, soup with rice, soup with noodles, prepared my own cabbage in brine, made fresh celery salad, potato salad our way, potato dumplings, duck with red cabbage, cod with onions, plum dumplings, horseradish salad, sweet and sour pork our way, goose giblets with turnips. Man in Brownsville made real bratwurst, used to go over on Saturday to get it fresh. I made apple cake, apple tart, apple dumplings, roast knuckle of pork, kidneys in vinegar sauce, cherry compote our way, cheese noodles, onion tart, trotters five different ways, cinnamon cookies, no brook trout—never saw any real brook trout.*

"Do you want to read to me?" said little Bert, seeing that Christine was not doing anything in particular.

She opened the book with her customary slowness, which seemed to irritate the child and drive him to refuse the very thing he wanted. She said, "Bruno drives a racing car?"

"No."

"Bruno and the cowboys?"

"No."

"Bruno and the wicked stepmother?" This time Herbert said "No" just as little Bert seemed about to say "Yes."

They came for dinner every night, at first on foot, then when they got the car they would drive the three blocks.

She was saved from inventing more about Bruno by the passage of one of the vendors Herbert had promised. Though his trolley was marked COCA-COLA, he had only a tepid local drink to sell. He had no ice, no cups, and so few straws that he was reluctant to give any away. Christine took a can of whatever it was, and the one straw he grudgingly allowed her. She saw she had made a mistake: Herbert would not let little Bert have soft drinks, even in an emergency, because they were bad for the teeth, and of course he would not drink in front of the thirsty child. When she realized this she put the can down on the floor.

"Read!" said little Bert.

The woman in the corner, who had also bought a can of whatever it was, drank slowly, making a noise with her straw. *Nobody was ever as close as we were, two cousins married to two cousins. Never a cross answer, always found plenty of pleasant things to say.*

"I'm sorry about the drink, little Bert," said his father. "But you see, there are days when everything goes wrong from early morning, and even the weather is against you. That is what life is like. Of course it isn't like that *all* the time; otherwise people would get discouraged."

"Read out of your book," the child said, leaning on Christine. "Read how Bruno bit the other children."

"On the contrary, it says on this page that Bruno was an obedient sponge," said Christine. Raising her head, she looked at Herbert: "But sometimes on those days one feels more. More than just one's irritation, I mean. Everything opens, like a pomegranate. More things have gone wrong than one imagined. You begin to see that too."

"Little Bert has never seen a pomegranate," said Herbert. There were forms of conversation he simply refused to accept.

The woman in the corner had sucked up the last drops from the bottom of the can, and now began eating again. *Not only did I cook thousands of suppers, but they went on diets. Bananas and skimmed milk. The men lasted one day, she lasted two.*

"The Coca-Cola man," said little Bert—but no, this time the vendor had powdered coffee and a jug of hot water, which he was selling only to passengers who happened to have cups in their luggage; he had run out of plastic mugs. The woman pulled a pottery stein out of her WINES OF GERMANY bag and bought about an inch of coffee. Drinking it, she fanned herself with her chiffon scarf, complaining, "Too hot, too hot."

Half the time they all ate something different—this one rice, that one potatoes, the other one cornflakes and brown sugar. I was the one that stood there dishing it all up. Always on my feet. After she had finished the coffee she ate grapes, an apple, mint sweets, and raisin cookies. *I never got used to the electric stove. But I had to have it electric. It came from the factory.*

A smell of rot began to fill the compartment. The grape seeds and stems, the apple core, and the papers the sweets had been in had immediately become garbage. The Norwegian was clearly disturbed—nauseated, in fact. He kept moving in and out to the passage, trying to catch the slightest breath of fresh air. Each time he came back he stared at Christine.

Christine was conscious of her bare brown arms because she could see the Norwegian eyeing them. She raised them, nervously toying with her scarf. Herbert sat as calm as an incarnation of Buddha, even when their direction changed and the sun fell directly on him; even when the woman beside him shut the window because the hot breeze touched her beehive of hair. He must have been as hot and uncomfortable as the rest of them, but nothing would ever make him say so.

To escape the Norwegian's staring, Christine went out to the corridor and stood with her arms resting on the lowered window. She could see a road, a low wall, and a private park filled with shade trees sloping up to a small mock-Gothic castle built of reddish stone. Two cream-colored cars were drawn up before the gates—the Mercedes belonging to Uncle Ludwig and a Volvo driven by the horrible Jürgen, who was Uncle Ludwig's contact man. Jürgen was large and strong, weighed more than two hundred pounds, and had a beaked nose and eyes so sunken he looked blind.

It was like Uncle Ludwig to make everyone get out at the gates instead of driving straight in. He still dressed as he had when he was poor; he had on the trousers of one suit and the jacket of another, a narrow tie bought years ago out of a barrow, and metal-tipped boots. His clothes tended to be loose-fitting because he carried wads of money all over his person, paid everything in cash, kept his records in his head. Uncle Ludwig never carried a gun; Jürgen did. Along with these two, the party included Uncle Bebo, Aunt Barbara, Aunt Eva, Uncle Max, and Uncle Georg with Aunt Milena. These two were father and mother to a little boy who got out last of all and gave his hand to a grandmother. Grandmother was dressed in a long skirt and a blouse of dark blue embroidered with daisies of a lighter blue, so small they looked like dots. Upon the skirt was an apron of yet another blue, with a hem of starched glossy pleats. She was in shades of blue from her chin to her wrists and right down to the tops of her shoes, which were black and polished, without buckles or any nonsense. Grandmother had a wide mouth, eyes like currants, high cheekbones, and a little blunt nose. She was not much taller than her grandson.

The whole party shook itself out. The women straightened their skirts and blew what they hoped would be cooler air on each other's necks; the men wiped their wet foreheads with folded handkerchiefs and replaced their hats. They turned at the same time and smiled their respects to the estate steward, who had a broken neck and wore a cast like a white chimney. Close behind him came a thin man in country tweeds; he looked to them more English than German, because of all the aristocratic British scoundrels they had seen in films. He strolled down to them with his feet hidden in a low cloud of house dogs, who did not let up barking. He was not English, of course, but as removed from them as any foreigner might have been. He spoke with such a correct and beautiful accent that Grandmother could make out only a word or two. She looked away, blushed, and performed a deep curtsy.

Jürgen muttered, "The family came for the drive," to which the steward said affably that they could visit, with a great wave that seemed to waft them up the green hill and indoors.

"The castle is a museum," said Uncle Bebo. He was the only one in the family who had traveled much in peacetime.

Uncle Ludwig, who always sounded like a piece of metal machinery, said, "Yes—visit!" which was something of an order. He and his man Jürgen had come here to see about buying thousands of Christmas trees for the market next December. The steward, part of whose job it was to talk about money, removed himself to an alley of lime trees with the horrible Jürgen, while Uncle Ludwig and the thin man sat down on a stone bench carved with pineapples and began a discussion about the cathedral at Freiburg. Uncle Ludwig did not know if he had ever seen the cathedral or only pictures of it, and did not care whether he had or had not. Now that he was rich he was not thought ignorant anymore, but simply eccentric. He sat patiently, letting Jürgen get on with it.

The rest of the party marched on to the castle, led by Uncle Bebo. Knowing about museums, Uncle Bebo had some loose change ready, five marks in all, with which to tip the guide. It was a long walk, all uphill. The hot weather, plus Uncle Bebo's jokes, made them feel silly and drunk. Giggling and hitting each other, they trooped in and up a great flight of stairs— Uncle Bebo said that in castle-museums the ticket office was one floor up. They opened doors on museum rooms furnished to look as if someone lived in them. Uncle Bebo fingered the draperies and even tried the beds, while Aunt Barbara, who had one problem on outings, and one only, began to look for a sign saying LADIES.

"That will be downstairs," much-traveled Uncle Bebo said. He led the descent, opened another great door, and saw what he took to be the staff of the museum eating lunch. He swung his arm back, the confident gesture of a know-it-all, and the others followed him into a large dining room where some ten or twelve persons of all ages stared back at them without speaking.

"Good appetite!" the visitors cried. They urged the staff to take no notice, please—to eat up their veal and dumplings while the dish was still hot. Uncle Bebo tried to see if the guide to be tipped was here, but none of the stunned faces showed the required signs of leadership. The men at lunch wore country jackets with bone buttons. The women seemed so dowdy that nobody remembered later what they were wearing. The visitors were in their Sunday urban best—meaning, for the aunts, pinkish nylon stockings, flowered drip-dry frocks, white no-iron cardigans, Aunt Barbara in a no-iron skirt from Italy and shoes with needle heels and her hair rolled up in blond thimbles. The men wore high collars and stiff shiny ties, had hair newly trimmed so that a crescent of skin left each ear looking stranded. The men smelled of aftershave lotion—lilac and carnation—that they'd been given last Christmas by the family women.

The visitors followed Uncle Bebo once around the table. They paused when he did, to squint at an oval portrait, nodded when he said, "Baroque!" and cried out with wonder at the sweet bell-tone when he snapped his fingernails on a crystal punch bowl—all the while renewing their smiles and encouraging remarks to the staff. Finally all headed toward another door at the end of the room. This one had a pointed lintel beneath which Uncle Bebo paused for the last time. He raised his fist (still clenched around the five marks), looked up at the lintel, back at the frozen people of all ages clutching their knives and forks, did not cry, "Death to upper-class swine!"

as they might have feared in their collective bad dream, but only, "This door is Gothic! No mistake!" and led the visitors on, the marks in his knuckles going *cling-cling-cling*. Granny turned back, smiled, curtsied deeply, and gave them a blessing.

Now they began to look for THIS WAY OUT, for there had not been all that much to see in the museum. Aunt Barbara was still watching for the door she wanted. Uncle Bebo clamped his teeth together and made a hissing sound to torment Aunt Barbara, so that she couldn't stop laughing, which was no help either. All at once they were outside again in the handsome park, with Aunt Barbara searching hard for a row of shrubs or a tree large enough to conceal her. As soon as she saw what she needed she cried to her mother-in-law, "Oh, Granny, a lovely tree, a thick fat beautiful tree," and galloped off, hiking up her Italian pleated skirt. The grandmother was slower, bothered by her long petticoats—two of them navy blue, two of white linen-and-cotton, one of lawn—and mysterious bloomers that were long in the leg and had never been seen by her own daughters: They were washed apart, hung to dry between pillowcases, and ironed by Granny in the dead of night.

Granny grasped the edge of the innermost petticoat. The trick was to bundle all the other skirts within it and hang on to the hem with her teeth. Just as she had a good hold on the hem she happened to see two boys of sixteen or so running with large black dogs on leads in and out of shade down the sloping lawn. The dogs were barking and the boys were calling to the women, "Stop! Stop!"

But then from far away, from within the alley of lime trees, another cry sounded, and, running too, breaking free of the trees, came the steward, the horrible Jürgen, then sly-eyed Uncle Ludwig, and the owner of the trees with his little cloud of house dogs. Before these two parties could meet and lambaste each other with sticks and fists it was established that the ugliest of the intruders—Uncle Ludwig—was that godsent figure who might purchase thousands of Christmas trees. The boys backed off, pulled their dogs in short, and said, "We didn't know."

Aunt Barbara seemed thoroughly pleased to see everyone; she always liked a crowd. But she was bothered because her skirt was not hanging as she wanted it to, her undergarments having become tangled and twisted. She had to unzip the placket of her skirt, so that it looked as if she meant to take it off; but all she did was give a good wiggle and shake, and when everything had settled she zipped it up again and cried, "Oh, the dear sweet beautiful dogs!" So everything ended well, and as the two boys led Granny back up to the little castle, through the still sunny day filled with such exquisite green lights and shadows, she could be heard saying that she had known all along it could not have been a museum; the beds looked too soft.

Now all this family of visitors save one, the child, were struck dead before long. Five of them carried the germ of the cancer that would destroy them, and one died of a stroke. The little boy was allowed to grow up, but his parents were killed when a military helicopter exploded over a crowded highway on a Saturday afternoon. As for the horrible Jürgen, he was found murdered in a parking lot. A man who signed an IOU for five hundred marks in Jürgen's favor disappeared one day. The man's wife said he was dead, but Jürgen had yet to see an account of the funeral. He grew tired of waiting and went to call on the widow. She was obstinate, said she knew nothing about a debt, that her husband was buried. The death certificate had been lost. There was no stone on the grave because she had no money to pay for one. When she began to contradict herself, turned vague and weepy, Jürgen gave up talking and looked to see what he could take instead of the money. He lifted a coffee table out of the way and began rolling up a small rug. All the while he was doing this the widow howled that it was her best carpet, the only thing she owned worth selling. True—everything else was trash, probably bought secondhand to begin with.

Instead of crossing the road to the parking lot Jürgen strode down to the corner and the traffic lights (he was law-abiding) and around the corner; made a detour to compare his new rug with some in a store window; turned up a side street and back to the parking lot across from the widow's place. There he saw one of her sons, aged about thirteen. "What now?" Jürgen sang out. He held the rug overhead, thinking the kid would grab for it. He was good-tempered, laughing. He had an advantage; not only was he powerful and large, but he was not afraid of harming anyone.

The kid broke into a run, with a hand behind his back.

"You don't want to do that," said Jürgen. He was ready to cripple the kid with a knee and step on his right hand, but only if he had to. He must have seemed like a great statue to the boy, standing with both arms straight up supporting the carpet. Jürgen brought his knee up too high and too soon; he was used to fighting with men. The kid bent gracefully over the knee and pushed the length of the blade of a kitchen knife above the buckle of Jürgen's belt.

* * *

The train trembled and slid round a curve, out of sight of the dappled lawn and the people climbing slowly up to the castle, on their last excursion together. Christine moved back to the compartment to make way for a vendor in a white coat pulling an empty trolley.

"We have had drinks without ice," said Herbert. "Coffee without cups. Now nothing at all."

The woman in the corner fanned herself briskly with a fan improvised out of postcards. *They came over every night and for lunch on Sundays. When the other couple had God's own darling, our precious Carol Ann, they would bring her in a basket lined with dotted Swiss. I remember Carol Ann's first veal cutlet. I had a wooden hammer—no American butcher knew how to slice veal thin enough. Later they went on their diets, wanted broiled steaks, string beans, Boston lettuce, fat-free yogurts. Carol Ann the little cow came home from summer camp with a taste for cold meat loaf made from stray cats and chili sauce. The little bitch grew older, demanded baker's cakes, baker's pies, cupcakes in cellophane, ready-mix peach ice cream, frozen lasagna, pineapple chunks, canned chop suey, canned spaghetti, while the big cow, the little cow's mother, got a craving for canned fudge sauce their way, poured it over everything, poured it over my fresh spice cake. I stopped making spice cake.*

"We could move, you know," said Christine to Herbert. "I've noticed one or two empty compartments."

"I have seen them too," said Herbert, "but the seats in those compartments have been reserved and we would eventually have to come back here."

"It's just that I don't feel well," she said.

"Heat and hunger and thirst," said Herbert. He shrugged, though not through indifference; he meant that he was powerless to help.

They wanted Aunt Jemima pancakes, corn syrup, maple syrup, hot onion rolls, thousand-island dressing, butter that would give you jaundice just to look at, carrots grated in lemon Jell-O, and as for the piglet Carol Ann, one whole winter she would not eat anything but bottled sandwich spread on ready-sliced bread, said only Jews and krauts and squareheads ate the dark. Had been told this by her best friend at that time, Rose of Sharon Jasakowicz.

"There's too much interference!" said Christine, though little Bert was not being a bother at all, was nowhere near her. She sprang up and went back to the corridor, untied her scarf and let the wind lift her hair. The Norwegian stood close beside her and showed her his yoga method of breathing, pinching his nostrils and puffing like a bullfrog. The train stopped more and more erratically, sometimes every eight or nine minutes. Presently she noticed they were standing in a station yard that seemed so hopeless, so unlikely to offer even the most primitive sort of buffet, that none of them made a move to go out. The yard buildings were saturated with heat, gray with drought, and the shrubs and trees beyond the station contained not a drop of moisture in their trunks and stems. A loudspeaker carried a man's voice along the empty platform: "All the windows on the train are to be shut until further orders."

"They can't mean this train," said the Norwegian.

Herbert, evidently annoyed by such a senseless direction, immediately went off to find the conductor. The woman in the corner began peeling an orange with her teeth. "I have diabetes, I am always hungry," she said suddenly, apparently to little Bert.

Herbert soon came back with an answer: There had been grass and brush fires along the tracks. "They may even have been set deliberately," he said. She could hear him explaining calmly to little Bert about the fires, so the child would not be alarmed.

"We can't shut all the windows in this heat," said Christine. "Certainly not for long." No one answered her.

After the train had quit the gray station yard she continued to stand at the open window, her hair flying like the little girls' purple crepe-paper streamers. Each time the train approached a curve she imagined the holocaust they might become. She thought of the ties consumed, flakes of fire on the compartment ceilings, sparks burned black on the first-class velvet. All the same, she kept hold of the two window handles, ready to slide the pane up at the first hint of danger. No one challenged her except for the bun-faced conductor, who asked if she had heard the order.

"Yes, but there aren't any fires," she said. "We need air." It was true that there were no signs of trouble except for burned-out patches of grass. Not even a trace of ash remained on the sky, not even a cinder. The conductor continued to look at her in his jolly way, head to one side, a smile painted on his face, looking as round and as stuffed as a little clown. "All right," she said. "I shall close the window, at least until Backnang. Then you can say that we all obeyed you."

"The train has been rerouted because of the danger," he said. "No Backnang."

"That seems fairly high-handed of you," she began, but of course she was wasting her breath. He was only a subaltern; he had no real power.

With its shut window, the compartment was unbearable now. Even little Bert was looking green.

"I was going to tell you about the change," said Herbert. "But you were having a yoga lesson and I didn't want to interrupt. We go through Coburg now. We shall be a couple of hours late, I imagine. I believe we change trains. Coburg is a pretty place," he added, to console her.

"Will it be explained at the station at home?" she said. "Someone is supposed to be meeting me."

"Meeting *us*," Herbert corrected, because in the eyes of these strangers he and Christine were married. The truth was that they would separate at their home station as if they were strangers.

The woman in the corner emptied one of her plastic bags of all the food it contained and filled it with the rubbish. *Sundays I had them for the two meals. They wanted just soup for supper, with cold ham and iceberg lettuce, dressing their way. The men ate Harvard beets in the factory canteen; they started wanting them. They wanted two or three different kinds of pizzas, mushroom ketchup, mustard pickles.*

Little Bert kept an eye on Christine. "You never finished reading," he said.

"I can't remember what I was reading about," she said.

"What is the book called?" he said.

"*All About Bruno*," said Christine. "What else could it be?"

"No, that might confuse him," said Herbert. "He knows Bruno is his own invention. The book is supposed to tell Christine how to think, little Bert. The Bruno story might be there. I don't say it is."

"Now who is confusing?" said Christine.

"But *is* the Bruno story inside?" said little Bert. "Look again," he urged Christine.

She looked, or pretended to. "Bruno goes to the moon?"

"No, I know about the moon."

"Bruno goes to an antiauthoritarian kindergarten?"

"Don't tease him," said Herbert.

"The kindergarten," said little Bert. He leaned against her, out of fatigue, apparently. She might have felt pity for the fragile neck and the tired shadows around his eyes, but there were also the dirty knuckles, the bread-and-butter breath, the high insistent voice.

During the Depression the factory laid off, nobody was buying the kitchen units. I went to collect the relief, he was too ashamed. They didn't send you checks in those days, you had to go round and see them. The other couple still came for dinner. We ate beans, sardines, peanut butter, macaroni. You could get lambs' kidneys for twenty cents, nobody in the USA ate them. Also heart, tongue. He was laid off from February 16, 1931, to September 23, 1932. Went back part-time. I did part-time work cooking in Carol Ann's school. She called me

"Mrs.," *would never say I was a relative. My cousin-in-law never worked, always had headaches, had to lie down a lot, never learned English. Then the factory picked up full speed, getting ready for the conflict. I fed them all through the war, stood at the electric stove, making oxtail soup on the one hand, baked squash on the other, bread and milk when my cousin had his ulcer.*

"I have something he might like to look at," the woman in the corner said. She offered little Bert part of her collection of postcards, but he put both hands behind his back and pressed even closer to Christine. Taking no notice of him, the woman began handing the cards around clockwise, starting with Herbert. "My friends on their summer holidays," she said. Herbert passed on the dog-eared coffee-stained views of Dubrovnik, Edinburgh, Abidjan, Pisa, Madrid, Sofia, Nice. "Very nice," she said, encouraging Herbert. "Very nice people."

The Norwegian looked at each card seriously, turned it over, examined the stamp, read the woman's name and address, and tilted the card at an angle to read the message. The messages were aslant, consisted of a few words only, and ended in exclamation marks. He read aloud, " 'Very nice friendly people here!' "

The woman was smiling, handing the cards around, but her mind was elsewhere. *We never took the citizenship so we never voted. Were never interested in voting. During more than forty years we would only have voted four times anyway. Would have voted:*

In 1932—for repeal.

In 1936—against government interference and wild spending. Against a second term.

In 1940—against wild utterances and attempts to drag the USA into the conflict on the wrong side. The President of the USA at that time was a Dutch Jew, his father a diamond cutter from Rotterdam, stole the Russian Imperial jewels after the Bolshevik revolution, had to emigrate to avoid capture and prison sentence. Within ten years they were running the whole country. Had every important public figure tied up—Walter Winchell, everybody. Their real name was Roszenfeldt.

In 1944—against a Fourth Term. My cousin had a picture, it looked like a postcard, that showed the President behind bars. Caption said, "Fourth Term Hell!!!!!! I'm in for Life!!!!!"

Apart from those four times we would never have voted.

"We are on an electric line again," Herbert told little Bert, who could not have had the faintest idea what this meant. The child looked wilted with heat. Their conductor had opened all the windows—there seemed to be no further news about fires—but nothing could move the leaden air.

"I want it all in order," Herbert said to Christine. "I really do intend to write a letter. Most of the toilets are still locked—true? There isn't a drop of drinking water. The first vendor had no ice and no paper cups. The second had nothing but powdered coffee. The third had nothing at all. All three were indifferent."

"True," said the woman, answering in place of Christine. She took off her black shoes and put her feet on top of them as if they were pillows.

The conductor returned to check their seat reservations for the third or fourth time. "This is only a flag stop," he said, as their train slowed. To make it easier for him, those who were in the wrong places—Christine, the Norwegian, and little Bert—moved to where they were supposed to be. The train was now inching along past a level crossing, then gave a great groan and stopped, blocking the crossroad. The barriers must have been down for some time because a long line of traffic had formed, and some of the drivers, perspiring and scarlet, had got out to yell protests and shake their fists. The sight of grown people making fools of themselves was new to little Bert, or perhaps the comic side of it struck him for the first time; he laughed until he was breathless and had to be thumped on the back. The woman in the corner kept an apple between her teeth while she looked in her purse for the ticket. Her eyes were stretched, her mouth strained, but there was no room on the table now, not even for an apple. As for the three men— Herbert, the conductor, and the Norwegian—something about the scene on the road had set them off dreaming; the look on their faces was identical. Christine could not quite put a name to it.

The woman found her ticket and got rid of the apple.

My husband said that if the President got in for a fourth term he would jump in deep water. That was an expression they used for suicide where he came from, because they had a world-famous trout stream. Not deep, though. Where he came from everybody was too poor to buy rope, so they said the thing about jumping. That was all the saying amounted to.

To be truthful, said Christine to herself, all three of them seem to be thinking of rape. She wondered if the victim could be the pregnant young woman—a girl really, not as old as Christine—who was running along beside the tracks, making straight for the first-class carriage. Probably not; she was unmistakably an American Army wife, and you could have counted on one hand the American wives raped by German men. There existed, in fact, a mutual antipathy, which was not the case when the sexes were reversed. *But*—here Christine imitated Herbert explaining something—we are not going to explore the attraction between German girls, famous for their docility, and American men, perhaps unjustly celebrated for theirs. We are going to learn something more about Herbert.

Christine suddenly wondered if her lips had moved—if it was plain to anyone that her mind was speaking. At that second she noticed a fair, rosy, curly, simpering, stupid-looking child, whose bald and puffy papa kept punching the crossing barrier. Julchen Knopp was her name. Her skirt, as short as a tutu, revealed rows of ruffled lace running across her fat bottom.

They brought up the heiress Carol Ann American style—the parents were chauffeur and maid. The mother couldn't be chauffeur because she never learned to drive. My husband was crazy about Carol Ann. He called her Shirley Temple. I called her Shirley Bimbo, but not to her face.

At some distance from the smirking Julchen, agape with admiration but not daring to speak, stood four future conscripts of the new antiauthoritarian army: They were Dietchen Klingebiel, who later became a failed priest; Ferdinandchen Mickefett, who was to open the first chic drugstore at Wuppertal; Peter Sutitt, arrested for doping racehorses in Ireland; and Fritz Förster, who was sent to Africa to count giraffes for the United Nations and became a mercenary.

What she had just seen now was the decline of the next generation. What could prevent it? A new broom? A strong hand? The example of China? There was no limit to mediocrity, even today: The conductor had lied too easily; this was nothing like a flag stop. They had been standing still for at least seven minutes. Punctilious Herbert was far too besotted with Julchen Knopp to notice or protest. She felt an urgent need to make him pay for this, and tried to recall what it was he had said he hated most, along with the smell of food in railway compartments. As soon as they were moving again and the conductor had left off staring and gone away, she turned to the Norwegian and said, "Do please show us your yoga breathing method, and do let us hear you sing."

"Some people imagine that yoga is a joke," said the Norwegian. "Some others don't care about singing." Nevertheless he seemed willing to perform for Herbert and little Bert and the insatiable passenger in the corner. He shut the door, which instantly made the compartment a furnace, sat down where little Bert should have been, pinched his nostrils between thumb and forefinger, and produced the puffing bullfrog sounds Christine had already heard. He let his nose go and said in a normal voice, "I sing in five languages. First, a Finnish folk song, the title of which means 'Do Not Leave,' or 'Stay,' or 'Do Not Depart.' " He looked at Herbert. Perhaps he knew that Herbert had been teasing Christine, calling the Norwegian "your bearded cavalier."

The Norwegian pulled out the drop leaf at his end of the window and beat a rhythm upon it. His eyes all but vanished as he sang. His mouth was like a fish. As for Herbert, he suddenly resembled little Bert—eyes circled and tired, skin over the temples like tissue paper. She thought that he must be exhausted by the heat and by his worry over the child, and she remembered that although he hated the smell of food he had not said a word about it. The singing was tiring, finally; it filled the compartment and seemed to leave everyone short of breath. She got up and crossed to Herbert's side, and he, with the Norwegian's eyes fixed upon him, began stroking her arm with his fingertips, kissing her ear—things he never did in public and certainly not in front of little Bert. She sat quite still until the voice fell silent.

The woman in the corner and little Bert applauded for a long time. Herbert said, "Well. Thank you very much. That was generous of you. Yes, I think that was generous. . . ."

Having said what he thought, Herbert got up and left abruptly, but nobody minded. All of them, except for the woman, departed regularly in search of a drink, a conductor, or an unlocked washroom. Little Bert curled up with his face to the wall and began to breathe slowly and deeply. The Norwegian, still in little Bert's seat, tucked his head in the corner. His hands relaxed; his mouth came open. His breathing was louder and slower than the child's. From the corner facing his came *First the block around us got Catholic then it got black. That's the way it usually goes. I can tell you when it got Catholic—around the time of Lend-Lease. We remained in the neighborhood because there was a Lutheran school for the child. Good school. Some Germans, some Swiss, Swedes, Norwegians, Alsatians, the odd Protestant Pole from Silesia—Rose of Sharon was one. Seven other girls were called Carol Ann—most popular name. Later Carol Ann threw the school up to us, said it was ghetto, said she had to go to speech classes at the age of twenty to learn to pronounce "th." Much good did "th" do our little society queen—first husband a bigamist, second a rent collector. Th. Th. Th.*

This was followed by a dead silence. Herbert beckoned Christine from the corridor. She thought he wanted to stand at the window and talk and smoke, but he smiled and edged her along to one of the empty compartments at the end of their carriage. They sat down close together out of the sun and in a pleasant draft, for there was no one here who could ask them to shut the window. But then Herbert slid the door to, and undid the plushy useless curtains held back by broad ties. The curtains were too narrow to meet and would serve only to attract attention to the compartment.

"Someone might look in," Christine said.

"Who might?"

"Anybody going by."

"The whole train is asleep."

"Or if we stop at a station . . ."

"No scheduled stops. You know we've been rerouted."

It reminded her of the joke about Lenin saying, "Stop worrying, the train's sealed!" She wondered if this was a good time to tell it.

Herbert said, "Now that we're alone, tell me something."

"What?"

"Isn't it a bit of a pose, your reading? Why did you say you were reading for an exam?"

"I didn't say it was my exam," she said.

"You said that it was in two days' time."

"Yes. Well, I imagine that will be for students of theology who have failed their year."

"Of course," said Herbert. "That accounts for the Bonhoeffer. Well. Our Little Christian. What good does it do him if *you* read?"

"It may do me good, and what is good for me is good for both of you. Isn't that so?" For the second time that day her vision was shaken by tears.

"Chris."

"I do love you," she said. "But there has been too much interference."

"What, poor little Bert?" No, she had not meant interference of that kind. "You mean from *him*, then?" Sometimes Herbert tried to find out how much she lied to her official fiancé and whether she felt the least guilt. "What did you tell him about Paris?" he said.

"Nothing. It's got nothing to do with him."

"Does he think you love him?" said Herbert, blotting up her tears as though she were little Bert.

"I think that I could live with him," said Christine. "Perhaps there is more to living than what I have with you." She was annoyed because he was doing exactly what her fiancé always did—veering off into talk and analysis.

"It is easy to love two people at once," said Herbert, more sure of her than ever now. "But it can be a habit, a pattern of living; before it becomes too much a habit you ought to choose." He had seen the theology student

and did not take him seriously as a rival. She glanced out to the empty corridor. "Don't look there," said Herbert.

"What if we are arrested?"

Perhaps he would not mind. Perhaps he saw himself the subject of a sen-
sational case, baying out in a police court the social criticism he saved up to
send to newspapers. She remembered the elaborate lies and stories she had
needed for the week in Paris and wondered if they were part of the pattern
he had mentioned. Suddenly Herbert begged her to marry him—tomorrow,
today. He would put little Bert in boarding school; he could not live without her; there would never again be interference. Herbert did not hear what
he was saying and his words did not come back to him, not even as an echo.
He did not forget the promise; he had not heard it. Seconds later it was as
if nothing had been said. The corridor was empty, and outside were the
same plain of dried grass and the blind, hot, gray stucco box-houses they
had been seeing all afternoon. She felt angry with Herbert, hateful even, because he had an unfailing hold on her and used it.

She said, "Herbert, that Norwegian is not interested in me; he is interested in you. And you know it."

Herbert accepted the accusation as though he were used to every kind of
homage. He was tall, intelligent, brave, and good-looking. He was generous
and truthful. A good parent, a loyal friend. Never bore grudges. His family
was worthy of him, on both sides. His distinguished officer father had performed his duty, nothing worse; his mother had defended her faith to the
extreme limit. He was thirty-one and had made only one error in a lifetime:
He had married a girl who ran away. He sat still and did not protest use-
lessly or say, "Unhealthy imagination. Projecting your own morbid desires.
Insane jealousy," though he may have been thinking it. He accepted the
Norwegian as a compliment.

She plunged on recklessly, just as she had kept the window open when
there could have been fires, and said, "If it's men you want, you needn't
think I am going to be a screen for you." He turned slightly and said, "Only
one thing matters now—this train, which is running all over the map."

She did not wish to lose him. She *was* afraid of choosing—that was
true—and she was not certain about little Bert. When he kept his head
turned the other way, she quickly told the story about Lenin. He smiled, no
more. There was a way out of their last exchange, but where? She had tried
telling her joke with a Russian accent, but of course it didn't come off. She
knew nothing about him. One thing she had noticed: When he had to speak

on the telephone sometimes he would say "Berlin speaking," like a television announcer, or imitate some political figure, or talk broad Bavarian, which he did well, but it took seconds to get the real conversation moving, which was strange for a man as busy and practical as Herbert. She looked round for a change of subject—the landscape was hopeless—and said, "These seats aren't reserved. Why not move our things here?"

"No point, we've nearly arrived," said Herbert, and he opened the door and walked out, as if there were no reason for their being alone now. He strode along the rattling corridor with Christine behind him.

Interference came out to meet her halfway:

During the conflict we were enemy aliens. Went to be registered in a post office with spit all over the floor. From there to the police. Just as dirty. The jails must be really something once you're in them. Police had orders, had to tell us we couldn't go to the beaches anymore. Big joke on them—we never went anyway, didn't even own bathing suits! Were given our territorial limits: could go into Jackson Heights as far as the corner of Northern and 81st. Never went, never wanted to. We could take the train from Woodside to Corona, or from Woodside to Rego Park, we had the choice, and ride back and forth as much as we liked. Never did, never cared to. We could walk as far as Mount Zion Cemetery but never did—didn't know anyone in it. Could ride the subway from Woodside to Junction Boulevard and back as much as we wanted, or Rego Park to 65th and back. Never did it once that I remember. The men could take the train to Flushing, they still worked at the same place, closely watched to see they didn't sabotage the submarine galley units. They had three stations from home to work, were warned not to get off at the wrong one. They never did. The thing was we never wanted to go anywhere except the three blocks between our two homes. The only thing we missed was the fresh bratwurst. We never went anywhere because we never wanted to! The joke was on the whole USA!

They were a happy party in the compartment now. Herbert seemed to feel he had put something over on the universe, and Christine felt she had an edge on both the Norwegian and little Bert. The other three were feeling splendid because they had slept. All were filled with optimism and energy, as if it were early morning. The Norwegian in particular was lively and refreshed and extremely talkative. Inevitably, being a foreigner, he began to do what Herbert called "opening up the dossier."

"On the subject of German reparations I remain open-minded," the Norwegian said amiably. "Some accepted the money and invested it, some refused even to apply. I knew of a lawyer whose entire career consisted of handling reparations cases, from the time he left law school until he retired after a heart attack."

"I am open-minded too," said Herbert, every bit as amiable as the Norwegian.

The woman in the corner spoke up: "What I keep asking myself is where does the money come from?" She looked at Herbert, as if he should know. "And these payments go on! And on! Where does it all come from?"

"Don't worry," said Herbert. "The beneficiaries die younger than most other people. They die early for their age groups. Actuarial studies are reassuring on that point."

It was impossible for the two strangers to tell if Herbert was glad or sorry.

"It is only right that you pay," said the Norwegian, though not aggressively.

"Of course it is right," said Herbert, smiling. "However, I object to your use of 'you.' "

At this the conversation ran out. Christine removed herself from what might have been her share of feeling by opening her book. Instantly little Bert was beside her. "Read," he said.

She read, " 'Bruno lived in a house of his own. He had a bedroom, a living room, a dining room ...' "

"And a playroom."

"All right. 'The living room had red curtains, the bedroom had blue curtains ...' "

"No," said little Bert. "Red in the playroom."

Herbert looked at them both; across his face was written, "It's working. They're friends." The woman in the corner had closed her eyes after the abrupt ending of the last conversation, but her mind was awake. *The other couple bought a car when the neighborhood went. The three blocks weren't safe, they thought. Sometimes they were late for dinner because someone had parked in front of their garage. Otherwise they were always on time. At first they came just for lunch on Sundays, then got in the habit of staying for supper because Jack Benny came on at seven. The only words my sister-in-law ever learned in English were "Jello again." Once learned, never forgotten. Before the blacks came we had the Catholics. That was the way it went. Once I was waiting with my sister-in-law to cross the street in front of the house when a lot of little girls in First Communion dresses crossed without waiting for the light. So near you could touch them. I said to her, "You've got to admit they look nice in the white, like little snow fairies." One of those little girls turned right around and said in German, "We're not snow fairies, you old sow, we're angels—ANGELS!"*

Their train slowed at an unknown station, then changed its mind and picked up speed, but not before they'd been given a chance to see a detachment of conscripts of the Army of the Federal Republic in their crumpled uniforms and dusty boots and with their long hair hanging in strings. She saw them as she imagined Herbert must be seeing them: small, round-shouldered, rather dark. Blond, blue-eyed genes were on the wane in Europe.

Herbert's expression gradually changed to one of brooding. He seemed to be dwelling on a deep inner hurt. His eyes narrowed, as if he had been cornered by beams of electric light. Christine knew that he felt intense disgust for men-at-arms in general, but for untidy soldiers in particular. His pacifism was certainly real—little Bert was not allowed to have any military toys. His look may have meant that even to a pacifist soldiers are supposed to seem like soldiers; they should salute smartly, stare you frankly in the face, keep their shoes shined and their hair trimmed. The Norwegian turned his mouth down, as though soldiering were very different where he came from. He exchanged a glance with Herbert—it was the first that Herbert returned. The woman in the corner opened her little eyes, shook her head, and said "Chck chck," marveling that such spectacles were allowed.

The principal of Carol Ann's school had good ideas for raising money. One was the sale of crosses for one ninety-eight. Black crosses with the words HE DIED FOR YOU *in white. Meant to be hung on a bedroom wall, the first thing a child would see in the morning. Character building. First of all my cousin did not want any cross in the house. Then he said he wouldn't mind having just the one so long as nobody said "crucifix." He couldn't stand that word—too Catholic. Then his wife said she didn't want a black cross because the black didn't match anything in the room. Everything in Carol Ann's bedroom was powder blue and white. My cousin then said he did not want to see a cross with any person on it. Once you accept a cross with a person on it, they're in, he said, meaning the Catholics. My cousin was stricter than your average Lutheran. His wife said what about a white cross with powder-blue lettering? My cousin was really worked up; he said, "Over my dead body will a black cross called a crucifix and with any person on it enter my home." Finally Carol Ann got a white cross with no person on it and no words to read. It cost a little more, two forty-nine, on account of the white paint. The principal of that school had good ideas but went too far sometimes, though his aim was just to make people better Christians. The school earned quite a lot on the sale of the crosses, which went toward buying a dishwasher cut-rate from the Flushing factory. All the children were good Christians and the principal strove to make some better.*

They were all tired now and beginning to look despondent. Luckily the next station stop was a pretty one, with gingerbread buildings and baskets of petunias hanging everywhere. The woman stirred and smiled to herself, as if reminded of all the charming places she had ever lived in during the past. The Norwegian leaped to his feet. "Good luck," said Herbert. He had given up trying to find water, toilets, food.

My cousin-in-law never understood the television. She'd say, "Are they the good ones or the bad ones?" We'd say this one's bad, that one's good. She would say, "Then why are they dressed the same way?" If the bad and the good had the same kind of suits on she couldn't follow.

"Read something about Bruno," said little Bert. "Read about Bruno not doing as he's told."

" 'The fact was that Bruno could not always tell right from wrong,' " read Christine severely. " 'When he was in Paris he whistled and called to other people's dogs. He did not know that it is not polite to call other people's dogs, even in a friendly way. He ate everything with his fingers. He put his fingers in the pickle jar.' "

"Careful. Our housekeeper does that," said Herbert.

"Read about Bruno's sisters and brothers," said little Bert. "What did *they* do?"

" 'Bruno had five brothers. All five were named Georg. But Georg was pronounced five different ways in the family, so there was no mistake. They were called the Yursh, the Shorsh, the Goysh . . .' "

"Christine, *please*," said Herbert. "It's silly. The child is not an idiot."

"But, Herbert, it happens to be true! All five brothers had five different godfathers named George, so they were each called Georg. Is there a law against it?"

He searched and said, "No."

"Well then. 'The Goysh, the Jairsh . . .' "

"Don't confuse him," said Herbert.

"Oh, God, Herbert, you are the one confused. My father knew them. They existed. Only one survived the war, the Yursh. He was already old when I met him. He might be dead now."

"Well, all that is confusing for children," said Herbert.

"You're not reading," little Bert complained, but just then the Norwegian came back carrying an ice-cream cone. Little Bert took it without saying thank you and at once began eating in the most disgusting manner, licking up the melting edges, pushing the ice down inside the cone, and biting off the end.

"Herbert," said Christine. "Please make him stop. Make him eat properly."

"Eat properly," said Herbert, smiling.

Conscious of so many adult eyes on him, little Bert began to lark about with the ice cream and make a fool of himself, at which everyone except Herbert looked the other way.

There was a plan to save some German cities, those with interesting old monuments. The plan was to put Jews in the attics of all the houses. The Allies would never have dropped a bomb. What a difference it might have made. Later we learned this plan had been sabotaged by the President of the USA. Too bad. It could have saved many famous old statues and quite a few lives.

"Now, little Bert," said Herbert, trying to clean the child's sticky face with a handkerchief, "we shall be leaving this train about two minutes from now. Another nice train will then take us to a place called Pegnitz. Pegnitz is a railway junction. This means that from Pegnitz there are any number of trains to take us home."

Little Bert could not have been listening carefully, for he said, "Are we home now?"

"No, but it is almost like being home, because we know where we're going."

"That's not the same as being home," said little Bert. He turned swiftly from Herbert and his eyes grew wide and amazed as the pregnant Army wife, holding a wall for support, moved past their door. He looked at Christine and opened his mouth, but before he could ask anything loud and embarrassing, their conductor came in with new information: They must not wander too far away from the station during the stopover. They would soon see that they were just a few feet from a barbed-wire frontier, where someone had been shot to death only a week ago. They must pay close attention to signs and warnings concerning hostile police guards, guns, soldiers, dogs, land mines. Although this was good mushroom country, it was not really safe. Someone had been blown up not long ago while reaching for *Cantharellus cibarius*. The train to Pegnitz would be an unscheduled emergency transport for stranded passengers (theirs was not the only train to have been diverted), and this new transport might turn up at any moment. They were not to worry about their luggage: The conductor would look after everything. The train might arrive at any time, either five minutes or half an hour from now. All danger from the fires was over, the jolly conductor added. His hair was as shiny as leather and he bounded from one foot to the other as he gave the good news.

Herbert took down the woman's suitcase. She stuffed all her plastic bags and leftover food into the WINES OF GERMANY carryall. *I came back to Germany to bury my poor husband and look after his grave. Very rare for me to miss a day at the grave. I had to go and see about some investments. Otherwise I'm at the grave every morning with a watering can.*

As they shuffled along the corridor Herbert told Christine that he had folded and sealed his imaginary letter of protest about the train and was mailing it in his head to papers in Frankfurt, Hamburg, West Berlin, Munich, and Bonn; to three picture magazines, a trade journal, an engineering review, a powerful newsweekly, and a famous TV commentator—but not to any part of the opposition press. He wanted to throw rocks at official bungling, but the same rocks must not strike the elected government. His letter mentioned high-handedness, lives disrupted without thought or care, blind obedience to obsolete orders, pigheaded officials, buck-passing, locked toilets, shortage of drinking water, absence of someone responsible, danger to health, indifference to others. Among the victims he mentioned a small child, an old woman, a visiting foreigner who would be left with a poor impression, a pregnant American, and a tall girl who wore nothing but size-eleven sandals and a short linen frock, who was traveling almost naked, in fact.

Hand in hand, perhaps wanting to avoid further instructions, Christine and little Bert made for the barbed wire they had been told to avoid. They walked along a sandy road that was strewn with candy wrappers, cigarette butts, bottle caps, and bent straws, like any sightseers' road anywhere. Little Bert's hand felt as soft as the sand underfoot and as grubby as the rubbish on it. His natural surroundings were rust, wires, rain-washed warnings, sweet melting foods.

"Your father is getting you something to drink," she said, though he had not complained of thirst or of anything, and seemed content with promises. She showed him frontier posts looped with rusted wire like birthday ribbons. "You can die of tetanus if you catch your hand on it," she said. They stood on a height of land from which she could see two little villages flanking a smoking factory and a few scattered farmhouses with their windows boarded up on one side. No one in those houses could lean on the sill and observe little Bert, or Christine, or the barefooted old woman cutting grass for rabbits right to the first strands of rust, or a couple moving along at a crouch because they were hunting for mushrooms. Stern cautions against doing this had been nailed here and there, but people were used to these by now.

Little Bert began to play at hopping off the path. "You may step off one side, but not the other," she warned him. He no more questioned this than he had the meaning of tetanus. He appeared to have an inborn knowledge of what the frontier was about.

He was bored, however. "What are you looking at?" he said, with a return of his Paris whine. Being small he could not see farther than the first barrier. She counted off for him a fence, a tract of low scrub, fence again, scrub, more fence, deep-ditch trap, fence, trap again probably, fences clean and bright in the sun as they moved farther east. Shading her eyes, she found herself looking at a man in uniform who was looking at her through field glasses. He looked at her and at little Bert, who was tugging her hand and wailing, "Let's walk."

The child's bratty voice made another man turn; he was a civilian with a scarred hairline, strolling along the sandy road too with his hands behind his back. He seemed to measure everything he gazed on—seemed to estimate, memorize, and add to a sum of previous knowledge. He knew about the smoking factory on the other side and about its parasite villages; he remembered when there had been the rumor, years ago, that the factory, with its technicians and engineers, was to be dismantled and moved. No one had told him so: He was too little then to be trusted. He knew something had frightened the adults; he could read their mute predictions. All bicycles had been confiscated, even the children's. He had walked up the main street to the top of his village, which was shabby and countrylike. You could still find milk and an egg sometimes if you were not an informer. There he saw Marie sitting on a wheelbarrow, with her hair cut like a boy's (lice were rampant), blond and ragged; she was eating bread—or rather, sucking on a wide crust spread with boiled rhubarb. Bare dirty feet, eyes in the distance, dreamy: He thought later that he had seen clouds on her eyes, like clouds on a clean sky. But perhaps all that her eyes had reflected was stupidity. She swung her feet, which did not reach the ground because of the tilt of the barrow. The geese Marie was there to watch watched Sigi approaching with pure blue eyes outlined in orange that could have been drawn with a wax crayon, so thick was the tracing and the color so true. The geese looked at him with one eye at a time, the way the Ancient Egyptians looked at people. His mother caught up with him before he could say anything final to Marie, either "I love you" or "Good-bye." He had been told not to play with Marie and to keep away from that part of the village—he had been told again only this morning. His mother was looking for milk. She hid the canister in a basket, under a napkin camouflaged with the wild sorrel and plantain they ate as vegetables now.

Sigi left Marie still pensive, still occupied with her bread crust. He walked with his hand in his mother's. His mother said, "Did the Marie ask you any questions?" But Marie hardly ever spoke. His mother said that minding geese was too big a job for a little child; a long prison sentence was the punishment now for misappropriation of domestic fowl.

He was prepared for the end, perhaps the end of everything living, and he knew that endings were in blood. He decided to take to his execution *Peoples of the World*, a school prize of his father's, which was in perfect condition; his father never smudged or creased anything he owned and washed his hands before taking down a book. In this book were the Ancient Egyptians looking with one eye at a time precisely like Marie's geese. He closed his eyes so that his last memory would be of Marie.

"Why are you walking with your eyes shut?" asked his mother.

"I'm pretending to be blind."

"God will strike you blind if you play such wicked games." Normally she would have gone on to say exactly why God would want to do a thing like that. Her abrupt silence was part of the end of everything.

When she woke him up that night and dressed him (he could dress himself) she was still tongue-tied, and when *he* asked something she put her hand on his mouth.

"Tape it?" said his father, of Sigi's mouth. She shook her head. "God help us if you don't keep it shut, Sigi," said his father, bringing Him into it again. After he was dressed they gave him a glass of milk and told him to drink all of it. But they could not wait for him to finish drinking and when he was only halfway through his father removed the glass. His parents wore heavy coats and carried knapsacks. Sigi took *Peoples of the World* from under his pillow.

"No, you will need both hands," his father said. He pinched Sigi's arm, like the witch testing Hansel, and asked, "Will he be warm enough?"

The signs of the end of the world were being dressed in the night, the milky glass left on the table, and his mother's silence. She did not even ask why he had taken *Peoples of the World* to bed. Much later he fell asleep again. His father was carrying him, and woke him suddenly by setting him on his feet in a plowed field. Unable to move, paralyzed, he heard a strange man cursing him, and suddenly his mother cried from another corner of darkness, "Run!" So he plunged at a crouch between ropes of barbed wire as if he had been trained for this all his life. The man cursing him for his slowness grabbed Sigi and dragged him facedown. He looked up to see who it was and left a piece of his scalp on a wire. No matter how he combed his hair ever after the scar reappeared.

They went to live in Essen. He hated the food, school, traffic, accents, streets. No grass, no air to breathe. He would say to himself, "When I turn *this* corner, Marie will be here." Years later somebody sent a long letter with news of the village. Part of it was, "As for the Marie, she is so fat and stupid she falls off her bicycle."

"Some of them have bicycles" was all Sigi's father gleaned from this important letter.

His mother had kept a newspaper account of their adventure. He *knew* there had been just the three of them besides the unseen man who had cursed him, but the paper said they had been thirty-seven, the technical staff of the small lens factory and their wives and children.

He walked just in front of Christine and little Bert, holding a hand to his head because of the scar—a bad habit. He suddenly turned and came back so that they seemed to be walking toward a meeting point. She saw that he knew she knew everything; the expression on his face was one of infinite sorrow.

What are you doing here? she tried to ask as they nearly met. Why spend a vacation in a dead landscape? Why aren't you with all those others in Majorca and Bulgaria? Why bother to look? The houses are shuttered on one side. No one sees you except a policeman with field glasses. Marie wouldn't look even if she remembered you. Wouldn't, couldn't—she has forgotten how. Her face turns the other way now. Decide what the rest of your life is to be. Whatever you are now you might be forever, give or take a few conversions and lapses from faith. Besides, she said, as they silently passed each other, you know this was not the place. It must have been to the north.

Herbert had never seen such a hideous station or such a squalid town—so he said now, catching up to them. Prussian taste, he said, and all Napoleon's fault. By what right did Napoleon turn us over to the Prussians, he wanted to know. *En quel honneur?* He sounded as though he might write a letter to the newspapers complaining about Napoleon. He had discovered something curious, he went on: a coffeehouse on stilts. Part of its attraction, other than a trio of musicians (fiddle, accordion, xylophone), was the view it afforded of the ditches and mantraps over there. From the coffeehouse verandah you could even see a man in uniform looking through field glasses. "You don't see that often," said Herbert, but he meant the orchestra. He continued in French, for he did not want little Bert to hear: The verandah on stilts was full of guest workers talking Turkish, Croatian, and North African dialects. Though needed for the economy, the guest workers had brought with them new strains of tuberculosis, syphilis, and amoebic complaints that resisted antibiotics. Everyone knew this, but the government was hushing it up. Herbert had proof, in fact, but he would not make it public, for he did not wish to favor the opposition. But here was what he was getting at— Herbert did not want little Bert, young and vulnerable, to drink out of the same glasses as foreign disease-bearers. On the other hand, he must not breathe the slightest whiff of racial animosity. Therefore would Christine please engage the child's attention until they had passed the coffeehouse?

They were moving back slowly, she holding little Bert's hand, and he not fretting to be nearer his father, quite happy with her. Presently they found they were four abreast with the scarred stranger, all walking at the same pace. It would have seemed awkward to have drawn back or hurried ahead. Just as, shyly silent, they came level with the coffeehouse, the stranger spoke up: "That place is always packed with foreigners."

"What place?" said little Bert at once.

"Do you object to them?" said Herbert, in his most pleasant tone of voice.

"I don't know much about them. I never travel. My father was in Montenegro. The partisans gave him a bad time. I think I wasn't born yet. I'm not sure of the year. Forty-three?"

"I hope they gave him a bad time," said Herbert, who always said such things with a smile. People who did not know him had to think again, wondering what they had heard. No one knew how to deal with Herbert's ambiguities. "I hope they gave him a *very* bad time."

Could I have heard this? the scarred man seemed to appeal to Christine.

Suit yourself, she seemed to answer. I wasn't born either.

"Now the children of the partisans come here as guest workers," said Herbert, still smiling. "And we all drink coffee together. What could be better?"

The stranger edged away, went over to an old man standing by himself on the station platform, and began to speak urgently in a low voice. The old man came up to his shoulder. He had not a tooth in his mouth, not a hair on his head, and was about the age and the size of the night porter in their Paris hotel. He was dressed in clean tennis shoes without laces, old Army trousers, and a worn regional jacket over an open shirt. He rocked heel to toe as he listened, then said loudly to whatever it was the scarred man had asked, "I wouldn't know. I don't know any names around here. I'm a refugee too."

"His feelings are hurt," said Christine, as the stranger drifted away. "Look at the way he hangs his head. I'm sure he was asking a direction. Now, why did you answer that way?" she asked the old man. "I'm sure you are not a refugee at all. What didn't you like about the poor creature?"

"He's not from around here," said the old man. "He's from somewhere else, and that's enough for me."

"And you," she said to Herbert. "What didn't you like about him? Such a harmless lonely person."

He tightened his hold on her arm. "I saw the way he was watching you. Don't you know a policeman when you see one?"

She looked again, but the man had crossed the tracks and vanished. Anything he might have wanted to let her know was damped out by a stronger current; their companion with the WINES OF GERMANY shopping bag could not be far away. *On a hot day like today every plant on a grave can wither. Family spies on his side of the family inspect the grave, waiting for a leaf to fall or a flower to droop. But usually I'm right there with the watering can. He was fussy about the grave, often spoke of how he wanted it.*

"There isn't a restaurant," said Herbert, again in French. "It's hard on little Bert. Only a newsstand. I think on a day like today one might allow a comic book. Do you agree?"

But she was not the child's mother: She would not be drawn.

Herbert's answer to her silence was to march into the waiting room and across to a newsstand. She knew that by making an issue over something unimportant she had simply proved once again that willful obstinacy was part and parcel of a slow-moving nature. She suffered from its effects as much as Herbert did. Holding little Bert, she trailed along behind him, thinking that she would show her affection for Herbert now by being particularly nice to little Bert.

Herbert waited for the curator of the local museum to be served before choosing the mildest of the comic books on display. The curator walked off, reading the local paper as he walked. A ferocious war of opinion took up three of its pages. Was it about the barbed wire? About the careless rerouting of trains that had stranded dozens of passengers in this lamentable, godforsaken, Prussian-looking town? No, it was about an exhibition of photographs Dr. Ischias had commissioned and sponsored for his new museum—an edifice so bold in conception and structure that it was known throughout the region as "the teacup with mumps." Dr. Ischias was used to Philistine aggression; indeed, he secretly felt that his job depended to some extent upon the frequency and stridency of the attacks. But it seemed to him now that some of the letters in today's paper might have been written a good fifty years in the past. This time he was accused not just of taking the public for dimwits, but also of sapping morals and contributing to the artistic decline of a race.

"Once again" (he now read, walking out of the waiting room, holding the paper to his nose) "art has not known how to toe the mark or draw the line. Can filth be art? If so, let us do without it. Let us do without the photographer in question and his archangel, the curator with the funny name."

Well ... that was unpleasant. Perhaps the show had been a mistake. It happened that the photographer in question had reproduced every inch of a model he said was his wife; in fact, the exhibition was entitled "Marriage." These pictures had been blown up and cropped so peculiarly that only an abstract, grainy surface remained. As the newspaper had to admit, most adults honestly did not know what the pictures were about. However, most children, with their instinctive innocence, never failed to recognize that this or that form was really part of something else, which they named quite eagerly. And the local paper did not tiptoe round the matter, but asked, in a four-column double head on page two:

ARE GERMAN WOMEN BABOONS
AND MUST THEY ALWAYS EXHIBIT THEIR BACKSIDES?

This was followed up by a cartoon drawing of a creature, a gorilla probably, with his head under the dark hood of an old-fashioned camera on a tripod, about to take the picture of three Graces, or three Rhine maidens, or three stout local matrons who had somehow lost their clothes.

Now all this was libel—every word, and the drawing too. The curator folded his copy of the paper and began to walk up and down the platform, composing an answer.

Christine knew that Herbert could have helped him, because he was good at that kind of letter, taking a droll, dry tone, ending with, "Of course I am prepared to withdraw my allegations at any time," mockingly humble. His letters always drew a deluge of new correspondence, praising and honoring Doctor Engineer Herbert B. But the curator did not know that Doctor Engineer Herbert B. was just behind him; in any case he was not doing badly with his own reply: "A ray of light has just as much chance of penetrating into the thick swamp of the German middle-class mind as . . ." He clasped and unclasped his hands, the newspaper tucked high under one arm. "The myth of German womanhood, a myth belied every day . . ." Walking up and down the platform near the sandy road, seen by the man in uniform looking through field glasses. "As for the photographer in question, his international status places him above . . ." "Only the small-minded could possibly . . ." "People who never set foot in museums until drawn by the promise of pornography can hardly judge . . ." "Only children should be allowed into art galleries . . ." Excellent. That had never been said.

Meanwhile the photographer had descended from a local train and started to tell a story about grass fires. He was wearing his tartan waistcoat with George the Fourth buttons, his cream corduroy jacket from Rome, his cream silk turtleneck sweater, an American peace emblem on a chain, dark green shorts, Japanese sandals, and, because the sandals pinched, a pair of brown socks. His legs were tanned and covered with blond fur. Although slim and fit, he seemed older than usual. This was on account of his teeth. He had recently acquired two new bridges, upper and lower, which took years off his face but were a torture, so today he had changed back to the earlier set. The dentist had told the photographer's wife, "His jaw is underdeveloped, like a child's, difficult to fit."

And she answered, "Yes, I see. Classic, aesthetic—no?"

"Well, jaws are always classical," said the dentist.

The photographer wanted to look a bit younger for the sake of his wife. Every season the difference in time between them seemed to increase. Most young wives of middle-aged men bridged the gap by looking older, but his wife grew more and more childlike. On their honeymoon in Florence he had shown her the marble likeness of a total stranger, saying, "There, the ideal—classic, aesthetic," and so forth; and she told her mother later and they had a good laugh. When the dentist made the remark about his jaws she saved it up for her mother too. Now the dentist had said he could make a third lot of teeth that would make the photographer appear to be twenty-eight and would not hurt as much as the last set, but the work would cost six hundred marks more.

As soon as he saw the photographer the curator began to shout everything he had just been thinking about the newspaper. The very sight of the photographer with his collapsed face and brown socks made the curator feel tense. He had to defend art as far as the first row of barbed wire, but he would have preferred doing this without ever meeting an artist, for they took up time. The curator's angry voice carried along the platform to the waiting room, where a cultural traveling group, tossed up between trains like Christine and the others, sat hungry and miserable with their cultural group leader. These people distinctly heard the curator say that he was opposed to womanhood. They put their heads together and began to whisper.

The group were on their way to the opera and had dressed for a cultural evening in July—that is, the men in white dinner jackets and the women with long skirts, and fur stoles they hugged around themselves in spite of the heat. They knew pretty well what the curator was yelling about because the most revolting of the photographs had been shown on television and in the picture magazines, and had been discussed in a syndicated editorial of the opposition press. The result was that this little frontier town, with its teacup-with-mumps museum, its reputation for pornography, and its forward-looking curator, was quite famous now. Most members of the group had actually heard the curator mouthing cultural insults in their own living rooms, with the color TV lending a strange mauve tinge to his ears and chin. The photographer had scarcely been interviewed at all. He had nothing in the way of a social theory; he could only bleat that he loved his wife and thought marriage was noble and fulfilling. For some reason this irritated the public. He said nothing but simple and gentle things, yet everyone hated him and people had written letters to the government saying he ought to be lynched.

Now he walked along the platform with the curator in the boiling heat and said he had been wondering if the caricature of himself as a gorilla might not be just a little libelous. And the curator, sweating and cross, sick to death of art and artists, looked down at his legs and socks and snapped, "Oh, it's probably not libelous at all."

Little Bert stayed close to Christine and curled his hand tightly around her fingers. She remembered how he had wakened night after night in a strange room and found himself alone in the dark. At first he had not even known how the foreign light switch worked. She and Herbert had spoken French much of the time; no wonder the child had finally preferred to have conversation with a sponge.

"You'll soon be home," she said. "Are you hungry?"

The station buffet had run out of food and the newsstand sold nothing to eat except cough drops and chewing gum. Little Bert did not seem to notice; at least he did not say he was hungry. He was only slightly interested in the comic book. He was taking in the opera party, all in their sixties or so, looking rather alike. They sat facing one another on two long rows of benches, the women holding their fat knees together under their long gowns. Perhaps these people did not know each other well, except for their cultural meetings. There was too much shy laughter, and too many Oh, do you think so's after every remark. What they had in common at this moment was their need of comfort; here they were, forced to change trains, the new train late, and the women in particular having a bad time of it, their makeup melting in the heat and having to hear their sex and station in life criticized by the trumpet-voiced curator. Luckily to console them they had their own cultural group leader, a match for the curator any day.

The group leader, whose long chin all but hid his collar, and whose eyes seemed startled and wise because his glasses magnified them, sat with one hand on each knee, legs wide apart, shoulders forward. It was not quite the position of a cultured person, more the way a train conductor might perch between rounds, but this might have been only because the bench was so narrow. He spoke to them softly, looking from face to face, and leaning left and right for those sharing his bench.

Within a few minutes he had wiped out of their memories every vexation and discomfort they had been feeling. He mentioned

Bach
Brahms
Mozart
Mahler
Wagner
Schubert
Goethe
Schiller
Luther and Luther's Bible
Kant
Hegel
the Mann brothers, Thomas and Heinrich;
    true connoisseurs prefer the latter
Brecht—yes, Brecht
several Strausses
Schopenhauer
Gropius

and went on until he had mentioned perhaps one hundred familiar names. Just as everyone was beginning to feel pleasantly lulled, and even to feel oddly well fed, though a moment ago they had all been saying that they could eat the wooden benches, their leader suddenly said, "The Adolf-time . . ."

In the silence that followed he looked into every face, one after the other, sadly and accusingly, like a dog about to be left behind; the reproachful silence and sliding dog's glance went on for so long that one could have heard a thought. Christine did hear some, in fact: They were creaking thoughts, as old chairs creak. The whole cultural group held its breath and the thoughts creaked, "Oh, God, where is this kind of talk taking us?" Finally the cultural leader had to end his sentence because they could not go on holding their breath that way, especially those who were stout and easily winded. He concluded, ". . . was a sad time for art in this country."

Who could disagree? Certainly no cultivated person on his way to the opera. Yes, a sad time for art, though no one could remember much preoccupation with art at the time, rather more with coal and margarine. There had been no public exhibitions of women showing their private parts like baboons, if *that* was art. There had been none of that, said some of the creaking thoughts. Yet others creaked, "But stop! What does he mean when he says 'art'? For isn't music art too?" There had been concerts, hadn't there? And the Ring Cycle, never before so rich and full of meaning, and *The Magic Flute*, with its mysterious trials, the Mass in B Minor, the various Passions, and the Ninth Symphony almost whenever you wanted it? There must have been architecture, sculpture, historical memoirs, bookbinding, splendid color films. Plays, ballet—all that went on. Cranach, Dürer, the museums. Surely the cultural leader must have meant that it was a sad time *in general*, especially toward the end.

He was still speaking: "As I stood before the new opera house, the same house you are about to see—if our train ever does arrive—" (smiles and anxiety) "a distinguished foreigner said to me, 'If only you Germans had thought more about *that* . . .'" pointing as the distinguished foreigner had pointed, but really indicating a gap between two women sitting with their knees clenched. He continued, "'. . . instead of material things, it would have been better for you and for everybody . . .'"

Following this closely, little Bert turned to where the man had pointed and saw nothing but the newsstand, which was not any kind of a house. Christine saw little Bert looking at a row of pornographic magazines, the sort that were sold everywhere now, and wanted to cover his eyes, but as Herbert had said, one could not protect him forever.

The cultural group exhaled, then breathed in deeply and gently. The women did something melancholy with the corners of their mouths. "As for the orchestras in those days," said the leader cheerfully, "they played like cows and they knew it. I remember how one execrable fiddle said to another, equally vile, 'Are you a Party member too?' "

This was a comic story—it must be. Their sad faces began to clear. All the same, no one was doing much more than breathing carefully in and out. Their creaking thoughts were scattered and lost as two new people, the Norwegian and the American Army wife, appeared. The Norwegian greeted Herbert rather formally; the girl marched up to the newsstand, and after giving the rack of pornography a short, cool glance, indicated, somewhere beyond it, *Time, Life,* and *Newsweek.*

"They take their culture with them," said the Norwegian. "And what a culture it has become. Drugs, madness, sadism, poverty, lice, syphilis, and several other diseases believed to have died out in the Middle Ages."

"The girl is German," said Herbert, smiling.

"Oh, Herbert, no," said Christine. "Everything about her ... the hat ... the shell necklace ... everything ... the hair. She could not be anything but what she is."

"I agree," said Herbert. "German. Now, little Bert," he went on, "do you see the train which is just arriving? It will take us to Pegnitz. Once there we are almost home. Pegnitz is a junction. Trains go through every few minutes, in all directions. In *most* directions," he corrected.

Now that their transport was here a number of those who had been grumbling at the delay suddenly decided that they did not want this train after all; they would wait for the regular service, or hire taxis, or send telegrams asking their relatives to come and pick them up in cars. Finally, after a certain amount of elbowing and jostling, only the hungry woman, the cultural group going to the opera, the Norwegian, some German soldiers with hair like pirate wigs, the pregnant American girl, and little Bert's party climbed aboard. This train was neat, swept, cool; the first-class carriage was not crowded and had plastic-leather seats. The opera party immediately spread out and filled three compartments. The hungry woman, caught up in the platoon of soldiers, disappeared, swept on to second class. But she could not have been far away: *The arrangement was we each got 50 percent of the estate under a separate property agreement. He never thought I would survive him. All his plans were for how he would dispose of my 50 percent once I had passed on. His 50 percent was to be for himself, and half of mine for him, and half for the little movie star Shirley Bimbo. He never never thought I'd be there after him. I had this diabetes, pneumonia three times, around the change of life I got nervous and lost all my hair, had to do the cooking wearing a turban. Later I got a women's complaint, had the works out, better to get it over with. No wonder he never thought I could survive him. He left his 50 percent to the little lamb of God, Carol Ann. What the dumb bastard didn't know was that I would get my half plus 67 percent of his half because we were married in Muggendorf under a completely different set of laws and we never took the citizenship. So think that over in your grave, Josef Schneider! He turned out to have more than anyone knew. There were the savings, the property, some home appliances, the TV and that—but what he had salted away besides was nobody's business. It's invested over here now. Safer.*

This time they shared their compartment with the American girl, who buried her pretty nose in her magazines. There was nothing else for her to do; she could not understand what they were saying. The missing traveler drew nearer. *He asked to be cremated and the ashes brought to Muggendorf and buried. He left eight hundred dollars just for somebody to tend the plot. I signed a promise to look after the grave; the money's being held. If I keep the grave looking good for five years running I get the eight hundred dollars. Only one year to go. Always had said he wanted his ashes scattered on the trout stream at Muggendorf. Must have changed his mind. Just as well. Might be a fine for doing it. Pollution.* She saw them, perhaps had been looking for them, and came in and sat down. As Herbert had said, it was as good as being home.

A woman we knew had this happen—her husband said he wanted his ashes flung to the winds from a dune by the North Sea. No planes in those days, had to take the ashes over by boat. Went up to Holstein, would climb on a dune, change her mind. Hated to part with poor Jobst. Noticed more and more barbed wire along the dunes, didn't know why. Never read the papers, had got out of the habit in the USA. Dreamed that Jobst appeared and said the world would experience a terrible catastrophe if she didn't scatter his ashes. Went back to the beach as near as she could to the sea, flung one handful east, one south, one west, was about to turn north when somebody grabbed her arm, two men with revolvers, the conflict had begun, they thought she was making signs to submarines.

They arrived at Pegnitz at dusk. Everyone began to shuffle along the corridor, peering out at the station they had been told was a junction. The train seemed becalmed in an infinity of tracks meeting, merging, and sliding away. Little Bert said to his sponge, "There are cows, one black, one brown, one dappled." But of course no cows were to be seen in the yard, only lights flashing and signal stations like sentry boxes. The woman sorted out the food she had left—biscuits, chocolates, grapes, oranges, macaroons, portions of cheese in thin silver paper—and placed everything in one clean plastic bag which she unfolded out of her purse, and on which was printed

CANARY BED

WARM, HYGIENIC, AGREEABLE

Above these words was the drawing of a canary tucked up in sheets and blankets for the night. *Shirley Bimbo, Shirley Bimbo,* she was telling herself.

All of them got to their feet too soon, as people do when they are tired of traveling. The train seemed to coast slowly and endlessly along a long platform. Christine stood between the Norwegian and little Bert, who put his nose on the window, making it white and button-shaped. When he glanced up at her he had two round patches of dirt, one on his forehead.

"Again," exclaimed the Norwegian.

"What?"

He did not mean little Bert. He was glaring at a detachment of conscripts lounging and sitting slumped on their luggage, yelling at one another and laughing foolishly. Christine said, "They are only farmers' sons who have been drafted, you know. Poor lads who have never studied anything. Boys like that must exist everywhere, even where you come from." But then she remembered how kind he had been to little Bert, and how generous about singing. She tried to agree with him: "I must say, they aren't *attractive.* They do seem to be little and ugly." She paused. "It's not their fault."

"They always looked that way," said the Norwegian. "They were always very little and very ugly, but they frightened us."

Christine had none of Herbert's amiable ambiguities. She said sadly, "We don't even know each other's names."

He pinched his nostrils and did a few seconds' puffing without making a reply. The important part of the journey had ended, as far as he was concerned, because he had finally said what he thought.

Yet it isn't over, she said to herself. She saw threads, crystals, flying horizontally like driven snow, and she caught as clear as the summer night a new tone on a different channel: *Dear Ken   sorry I haven't written sooner but you know how it is Dear Ken   sorry I haven't written sooner but you know how it is*

"Now, be ready," called Herbert over his shoulder. He had seen their new train standing empty on the far side of the tracks. "Christine? Little Bert?" Little Bert clasped his sponge and was ready. Herbert opened a door on which was written DO NOT OPEN and helped the other two down. But after making a run for it they found the carriages were dark and the doors locked, and that a sign hanging upside down said COBURG-PEGNITZ, which was more or less where they had come from. "You must never do this, little Bert," said Herbert.

"Never do what?"

"Open the wrong door and cross the tracks. You could be killed or arrested."

They made their way to the platform by lawful means, through an underpass. The station was crammed with passengers who had been turned out of a number of rerouted trains, shouting, arguing, complaining, and asking questions. The American girl stood gazing up at PEGNITZ as if she could not believe what she saw. She seemed fragile and lonely.

"Help her," said Christine. "She doesn't understand. Herbert, you can speak English."

"*En quel honneur?*" said Herbert. "Her German is probably better than little Bert's."

Perhaps it was true, or else when she was among Germans she did not want to hear what they said. She had just returned from the square behind the station where the bus to Pottenstein was usually parked. But everything had been changed around; there wasn't even a schedule in sight, and everyone on the platform was trying to find out when some train would come by to take them away from Pegnitz. She was seven and a half months pregnant, she had been traveling for hours now, and her back ached. All at once she turned and looked at Herbert. He looked back—respectfully, she believed. She pushed her way over to him through the crowd on the platform and said in her haughtiest English, "Sir! Vare iss ze boss to Buttonshtah?" which was enough to tell any careful census taker (Herbert, for one) her nationality, schooling, region, village—what part of village, even, if one was particular over details.

The fact of the matter was that she was on her way home to Pottenstein and that her shape was bound to be something of a shock to her parents. However, once they had recovered consciousness they would certainly try to help. For instance, they had a friend, a garage mechanic who had worked for two years in America and knew the customs. He had returned to Pottenstein for two reasons: One, when Americans invited him to their houses they would offer him something to drink and never a bite to eat, which showed that they were not refined; and two, he had been offended by the anti-German tone of the television commercials for a certain brand of coffee. This man would be called in to look at the letter she had intercepted, stolen, read in secret, and reread until she could see every word with her eyes tight shut. He would tell her how to use the letter in order to further her case—providing she had a case at all.

Just as Christine understood all this from the beginning, just as information arrived in the form of an unwieldy package the color of bricks, Herbert, with sober face, began to speak with the accent of their train conductor. He said she was not far from Buttonshtah, only a few miles. He believed there existed a bus service.

"I know, but vare iss ze boss?" she complained, before she remembered that she was not supposed to know any German, let alone German spoken with that accent. She had been deceived by the look of Herbert; he was nothing more than a local product like herself. "Country pipples," she said, and showed them what it was to walk off with your nose in the air. Christine caught again, faintly, *Dear Ken   sorry I haven't written sooner but you know how it is*

Herbert did not want to rub it in but he did say, "You know, an American could live fifty years in Pottenstein without knowing it was Buttonshtah."

The Norwegian still thought the girl might be an American. He said that perhaps she had mistaken the P of "Pegnitz" for the first letter of "Pottenstein," and been too disturbed to read the rest. But Herbert laughed and said no American would do that either.

By now Christine knew all this. Herbert, who knew nothing, had fixed upon the essence of it: The girl was ashamed of being thought German by other Germans.

Little Bert tugged at Christine, trying to tell her something. "Is there time?" she asked Herbert.

She saw him nod before a new wave of soldiers pushed him back. He'll write a letter about *that*, she thought. Little Bert was very good about standing in the queue outside the door marked LADIES and neither giggled nor stared once inside. She found it curious that he had asked her and not his father; it was certainly the first time. When they came out Herbert was nowhere in sight; there were twice as many people as before milling about and protesting, and they saw the cultural group, quite red in the face now, the women clutching their furs as if the inhabitants of Pegnitz were bandits.

Their leader had lost his spectacles and was barely recognizable without them. His eyes were small and blue, and he looked insane.

"A short wait. In there," said the stationmaster, running past Christine with a long list of passengers' names in his hand.

"We can sit down for a few minutes," said Christine. "In any case, we could never find your father in this confusion." She saw a place on a bench and squeezed little Bert in beside her. Nearly every inch of bench was occupied by women carrying luggage tied with string. A window on the side opposite the platform gave onto the freight yards.

"Read to me," said little Bert.

She noticed that some of the women glanced at them with consternation, even disapproval. It was true that little Bert seemed spoiled and that his voice was often annoying to adults.

"I suppose we seem like a funny-looking pair," she said to him. "Both of us filthy, and you with your bath sponge."

"The ladies are funny too," he said.

The women sat grouped by nationality—Polish, French, Greek, Russian, Dutch. Her eyes caught on the Frenchwomen, who were thin and restless, with cheeks flushed either by rouge or tuberculosis, and hair swept up and forward and frizzed with tongs. They were almost uniformly dressed in navy-blue suits and white blouses, and their shoes had thick wooden soles. Their glance was hostile, bright, and missed nothing.

But they are not dirty, she said to herself. No more than we are at this moment. I shall tell the truth about it, if I'm asked. Herbert hasn't washed or shaved since yesterday. He brushed his teeth at Stuttgart, nothing more. As for little Bert . . .

"Whatever happens," she said to little Bert swiftly, "we must not become separated. We must never leave each other. You must stop calling me 'the lady' when you speak to your father. Try to learn to say 'Christine.' "

The child sighed, as he did sometimes when Herbert took too long to explain. "Read," he said sleepily.

"I can't remember a thing about Bruno."

"Look in your book."

"My mind is a blank." Nevertheless she opened it near the beginning and read the first thing she came to: " 'Shame and remorse are generally mistaken for one another.' It's no good reading that." She leaned against the child and felt his comforting breath on her arm.

"What happens then?" said little Bert after a pause. "That's not what you were reading before."

Their familiar bun-faced conductor now made an appearance. "Oh, thank God," said Christine. "He'll know about the train." He had stopped just inside the door. He scowled at the waiting women and, being something of a comedian, did an excellent impersonation of someone throwing a silent tantrum. First he turned red and his eyes started, then all the color left his face and he could not part his lips, could only gesticulate. It was extremely clever and funny. Little Bert applauded and laughed, which drew the conductor's attention. He walked over to them slowly with his thumbs in his belt and stopped a few inches away, rocking on his heels. Suddenly he prodded the bath sponge.

"What have you got there?" he asked. "Who said you could have it?"

"Don't use that tone with the child," said Christine. "Children don't always understand games."

"Yes, I do," protested little Bert.

She was surprised to feel the panic—stronger than mere disapproval—that the other women were signaling now. She wondered if they weren't simply *pretending* to take fright. It was so evident that he had no power! Why, even the little girls from the summer camp had not been taken in.

He retreated a step—to lend the distance authority required, perhaps—and cried, "Who told you to come here?"

"Please lower your voice," she said. "We aren't playing. We have every right to sit where we choose, and the child has a right to his toy."

"Sponge," said little Bert. "Not toy."

The conductor leaned over them, his face so near that she could see specks of gold in his brown eyes. He said, "You won't say bad things about me, will you?"

"To the stationmaster? I'm not sure."

"No, to anyone. If anyone asks."

"You were rude a moment ago," she reminded him.

"But I was kind on the train. I let you keep the window open when we went through the fire zone." True enough, but had he really been *kind*? "You'll testify for me, then?" he said. "If you are asked?"

"What about these passengers?" she said, meaning the other women. "You were making faces—scaring them. They're still frightened." Indeed, some of them looked positively ill with terror. However, now that Christine had shown him up he was unlikely to begin playing again; the game would have no point. "Perhaps you would like to find out about our train?" she said. "The child is quite tired."

He waddled away, either because he was anxious to show he was still the harmless creature he had been on the train, or because she had alarmed him and he wanted to escape.

"Read, now," said little Bert. "What happens?"

"I don't know any more."

"It's in your book," he said.

Dear Ken   sorry I haven't written sooner but you know how it is The girl was still searching for the bus to Pottenstein. Or perhaps she had given it up, couldn't face the family, knew the letter was hopeless as evidence. It was faint and faded now—committed to a dull mind, to no real purpose. A mush like a mixture of snow and ashes surrounded the information. *I suppose several people figure I squared up on you   I don't think you thought that   I came to within a hair of getting busted and for all practical purposes I did get busted when I got to the airport I was still trippppping*

I went to the rest room to change   I didn't have a poplin shirt or a tie   it took me a long time to get myself together

I looked like something from woodstock with a uniform on   do you remember the guy in munich who tried to get us to go to his car   well, I met him in the rest room   he had gotten scared about bringing it into the states so he was trying to get rid of it   he was in bad shape too   I processed out with him   as I was

"Why aren't you reading?" said little Bert. Only stubbornness still kept him awake.

"There's too much interference," she said. "I'm waiting for it to stop."

going through the customs line there were three guys ahead of me   they searched the first guy as if they thought he had a ton of smack   they asked him to empty his pockets well, when I saw this the first thing I did was turn white, the second thing I did was fall out of line and look for a place to get rid of what I had on me   the room was full of people

I sat down on the convair belt that brought our bags into the room   there I took it out of my pockets and put it under the belt, never to see it again   I ran back and got in line

I was next by then   the guy took one look at me and knew I was scared to death he went over me with a fine-tooth comb and I was never so glad not to have it on me in my life   we left there and went to ft dix   it was about 9:00 pm   they took our records and sent us to bed   next morning we got up cleaned the barracks and went on police call   after that we turned in to supply one set of greens, one poplin shirt, one over-

coat, one field jacket   I didn't have any of this and it didn't matter   that's all you have to have and they don't care if you have it or not   after that you get a lot of crap about being a veteran, some of which is good to know   then you go and get paid and that's the last thing

after I was paid I took a cab to the airport. there I went to the rest room removed my uniform threw it in the trash can, dressed went back up and got a ticket to toledo where my mother lives   I stayed with her for two weeks trying to decide what I was going to do next first I thought of sending you the 170 I owe you getting a job, but things were so screwed up there I had to leave or go crazy   you will see what I mean when you get out   you won't believe it   it's like being in a crazy house here and you are the only one sane so I left and came here the trip cost me about 150   I've spent some money since I've been out here and I have about 42 now   I've been looking for a job every day I've been offered a lot of jobs most of them are 80 or 90 a week clear   the reason I haven't taken any of them is they don't pay enough   you draw 65 clear a week drawing unemployment so working forty hours you only draw 15 more a week   no one is giving the good jobs right now because the economy is slow   the only thing I have to pay besides you is 12 a week to my sister for staying here so I'll be sending you money every week until I get you paid off   it really sucks living here with my sister and her husband   he's a nice guy but he and my sister are really concerned over me and they think I'm a great guy and when I'm here with them they never leave me alone   they're great, it's just that they get on my nerves   you'll understand this better once you get out   when you come over we could take a place together   write and tell me if the junk you had was good or not and how you all came out on it   don't bring any back with you—mail it   it's like gold here   my other advice is get out of the army first and forget about her. Once you're out she can't touch you   tell her you want to find a job first   you're crazy if you do it any other way   tell her you can't support a family till you're twenty-one (joke) I hope we can get together after you get out   answer this letter right away   tomorrow I'm going to get some grass I'll send you some good luck Ken   love PS it's 80° and I'm going to the beach

"Is it finished?" said little Bert.

"I suppose so. Though nothing is ever finished," said Christine. She had been disappointed by both the substance and quality of this information.

"You never finished a story," Little Bert said.

"I realize that. I'm sorry." He did not reply; living with adults had accustomed him as much to apologies as to promises.

She was always running, Herbert complained suddenly. *She streaked off like a hare. I went after. She doubled back. I tripped and fell. There we were, together. She seemed confident and competent, and I thought she did not need to be looked after. I must have dozed off. She woke me quite roughly saying, "You are supposed to be awake and making decisions. You are the man. That's how I've always heard it was played." The day she left she cut a lock of the child's hair. It was flaxen then. She took it close to the roots along the hairline. Destructive. Careless. When she needed money she sent the lock back to me. I understood immediately, sent money to a post-office address which was all she gave me, and returned the lock as well. After long-distance dialing was installed in the remotest villages she took to calling me late at night, never from the same place twice. So she said. Other people paid, without knowing it. You could tell she had her hand around the mouthpiece. She would say a few words and laugh. I never knew what she wanted. One night I heard, "Do you still love me?" I thought for a long time, wanting to give her a complete answer. After a while I said, "Are you still there?" She called again late in the winter. I said, "The answer to your last question is yes." She hung up quietly. Then silence. She was twenty-six, would now be twenty-eight.*

This fell like dirty cinders. As information, it offered nothing except the fact that Herbert was not far from the waiting room. Perhaps it had no connection with him; in this particular game no one was allowed an unfair advantage. It was old and tarnished stuff which had come to her by error. Complete information concerning Herbert had certainly been caught by someone who had no use for it. It was like the Pottenstein letter—each person involved with it was now in a different place, moving steadily in a new direction. A day of indecision could make all the difference between silvery flakes and mud.

Little Bert yawned and pressed the sponge against his mouth. His muffled voice said, "Read!"

The trouble about the grave is that he's got family living around Muggendorf. My cousin-in-law tipped them off. They're watching the grave closely. At the first sign of drought, weeds, plant lice, cyclamen mites, leafhoppers, thrips, borers, whiteflies, beetles feeding, they'll take color photographs of the disaster and use them as evidence. Which would mean the end of the eight hundred dollars.

"What are we waiting for now?" said little Bert.

"For the conductor to tell us about our train. It is much cooler in here." She had been going to add, "and there is less interference," but that wasn't true. At least the other women were silent; ever since Christine had put the conductor in his place they seemed afraid of her too.

"Read," said little Bert. "You never finished anything."

"What do you want as a beginning this time?"

"Whatever it says."

"I did read you a bit of that," she said. "You didn't like it."

Last Sunday they happened to find one bare spot and they planted an ageratum. A re-

proach. What nobody understands is that it isn't usual to buy a plot for just a can of ashes. I would have kept them at home, but his will had one whole page of special instructions. What can you put on a plot that size? Not much bigger than a cat's grave and the stone takes up room. The begonias are choking the roses and vice versa.

Little Bert yawned again, even wider. "You'll soon be home," she said.

"What do we do when we get home?" He had been away for a whole week, plus this long day.

And yet they managed to find room for one ageratum. Only one year to go. Hang on, I keep telling myself. Hang on for the eight hundred dollars. Worth hanging on for. After that I'll be ready to go. Plot purchased and paid up. Nowhere near him.

"You're not reading," said little Bert.

She waited a few seconds longer, until the air was clear. Perhaps the silent women were attracting everything to themselves without being conscious of it. Then she distinctly heard Herbert saying, *"En quel honneur?"* It was loud, for him, and rather frantic. She guessed it must have been his response to a piece of irritating news—that there would be a long delay, for instance. She wondered if she and little Bert should go out to him; but the child was tired and once they had left the waiting room they would have to stand, perhaps for a long time. While she was wondering and weighing, as reluctant as ever to make up her mind, a great stir started up in the gray and wintry-looking freight yards they could see from the window. Lights blazed, voices bawled in dialect, a dog barked. As if they knew what this animation meant and had been waiting for it, the women picked up their parcels and filed out without haste and without looking back.

"No, you stay here," said Christine, holding little Bert, who had made a blind move forward. He looked at her, puzzled perhaps, but not really frightened. When the door had closed softly behind the last of them she felt a relief, as at the cessation of pain. She relaxed her grip on the child, as if he were someone she loved but was not afraid of losing.

"Read," said little Bert. "Look in the book."

"I'll read for a minute," she said. "Then we will have to do something else."

"What?"

"I don't know," she said. "Go out, or wait here. I'm sorry to be so uncertain." He sat as near to her as when the room had been full. She opened her book and saw, " 'The knowledge of good and evil is therefore separation from God. Only against God can man know good and evil.' Well," she said, "no use going on with that. Don't be frightened, by the way," she told little Bert, who was not frightened of anything, though in Paris he had pretended to be afraid of the dark.

That was the end of it. He's in Muggendorf and I'm hanging on. When Carol Ann learned to pronounce "th" did that make her a better Christian? Perhaps it did. Perhaps it took just that one thing to make her a better Christian.

She had been hoping all day to have the last word, without interference. She held little Bert and said aloud, "Bruno had five brothers, all named Georg. But Georg was pronounced five different ways in the family, so there was no confusion. They were called the Goysh, the Yursh, the Shorsh . . ."

The

EIGHTIES

and

NINETIES

LUC AND HIS FATHER

❧

*T*o the astonishment of no one except his father and mother, Luc Clairevoie failed the examination that should have propelled him straight into one of the finest schools of engineering in Paris; failed it so disastrously, in fact, that an examiner, who knew someone in the same ministry as Luc's father, confided it was the sort of labor in vain that should be written up. Luc's was a prime case of universal education gone crazy. He was a victim of the current belief that any student, by dint of application, could answer what he was asked.

Luc's father blamed the late President de Gaulle. If de Gaulle had not opened the schools and universities to hordes of qualified but otherwise uninteresting young people, teachers would have had more time to spare for Luc. De Gaulle had been dead for years, but Roger Clairevoie still suspected him of cosmic mischief and double-dealing. (Like his wife, Roger had never got over the loss of Algeria. When the price of fresh fruit went high, as it did every winter, the Clairevoies told each other it was because of the loss of all those Algerian orchards.)

Where Luc was concerned, they took a practical course, lowered their sights to a lesser but still elegant engineering school, and sent Luc to a crammer for a year to get ready for a new trial. His mother took Luc to the dentist, had his glasses changed, and bought him a Honda 125 to make up for his recent loss of self-esteem. Roger's contribution took the form of long talks. Cornering Luc in the kitchen after breakfast, or in his own study, now used as a family television room, Roger told Luc how he had been graduated with honors from the noblest engineering institute in France; how he could address other alumni using the second person singular, even by Christian name, regardless of whether they spoke across a ministerial desk or a lunch table. Many of Roger's fellow-graduates had chosen civil-service careers. They bumped into one another in marble halls, under oil portraits of public servants who wore the steadfast look of advisers to gods; and these distinguished graduates, Roger among them, had a charming, particular way of seeming like brothers—or so it appeared to those who could only envy them, who had to keep to "Have I the honor of" and "If Mr. Assistant Under-Secretary would be good enough to" and "Should it suit the convenience." To this fraternity Luc could no longer aspire, but there was still some hope for future rank and dignity: He could become an engineer in the building trades. Luc did not reply; he did not even ask, "Do you mean houses, or garages, or what?" Roger supposed he was turning things over in his mind.

The crammer he went to was a brisk, costly examination factory in Rennes, run by Jesuits, with the reputation for being able to jostle any student, even the dreamiest, into a respectable institute for higher learning. The last six words were from the school's brochure. They ran through Roger Clairevoie's head like an election promise.

Starting in September, Luc spent Monday to Friday in Rennes. Weekends, he came home by train, laden with books, and shut himself up to study. Sometimes Roger would hear him trying chords on his guitar: pale sound without rhythm or sequence. When Luc had studied enough, he buckled on his white helmet and roared around Paris on the Honda. (The promise of a BMW R/80 was in the air, as reward or consolation, depending on next year's results.) On the helmet Luc had lettered IN CASE OF ACCIDENT DO NOT REMOVE. "You see, he does think of things," his mother said. "Luc thinks of good, useful things."

Like many Parisian students, Luc was without close friends, and in Rennes he knew nobody. His parents were somewhat relieved when, in the autumn, he became caught like a strand of seaweed on the edge of a political discussion group. The group met every Sunday afternoon in some member's house. Once, the group assembled at the Clairevoies'; Simone Clairevoie, pleased to see that Luc was showing interest in adult problems, served fruit juice, pâté sandwiches, and two kinds of ice cream. Luc's friends did not paint slogans on the sidewalk, or throw petrol bombs at police stations, or carry weapons (at least, Roger hoped not), or wear ragtag uniforms bought at the flea market. A few old men talked, and the younger men, those Luc's age, sat on a windowsill or on the floor, and seemed to listen. Among the speakers the day they came to the Clairevoies' was a retired journalist, once thought ironic and alarming, and the former secretary of a minor visionary, now in decrepit exile in Spain. Extremist movements were banned, but, as Roger pointed out to his wife, one could not really call this a movement. There was no law against meeting on a winter afternoon to consider the false starts of history. Luc never said much, but his parents supposed he must be taking to heart the message of the failed old men; and it was curious to see how Luc could grasp a slippery, allusive message so easily when he could not keep in mind his own private destiny as an engineer. Luc could vote, get married without permission, have his own bank account, run up bills. He could leave home, though a course so eccentric had probably not yet occurred to him. He was of age; adult; a grown man.

The Clairevoies had spent their married life in an apartment on the second floor of a house of venturesome design, built just after the First World War, in a quiet street near the Bois de Boulogne. The designer of the house, whose name they could never recall, had been German or Austrian. Roger, when questioned by colleagues surprised to find him in surroundings so bizarre, would say, "The architect was Swiss," which made him sound safer. Students of architecture rang the bell to ask if they might visit the rooms and take photographs. Often they seemed taken aback by the sight of the furniture, a wedding gift from Roger's side of the family, decorated with swans and sphinxes; the armchairs were as hard and uncompromising as the Judgment Seat. To Roger, the furniture served as counterpoise to the house, which belonged to the alien Paris of the 1920s, described by Roger's father as full of artists and immigrants of a shiftless kind—the flotsam of Europe.

The apartment, a wedding present from Simone's parents, was her personal choice. Roger's people, needing the choice explained away, went on saying for years that Simone had up-to-date ideas; but Roger was not sure this was true. After all, the house was some forty years old by the time the Clairevoies moved in. The street, at least, barely changed from year to year, unless one counted the increasing number of prostitutes that drifted in from the Bois. Directly across from the house, a café, the only place of business in sight, served as headquarters for the prostitutes' rest periods, conversations, and quarrels. Sometimes Roger went there when he ran out of cigarettes. He knew some of the older women by sight, and he addressed them courteously; and they, of course, were polite to him. Once, pausing under the awning to light a cigarette, he glanced up and saw Luc standing at a window, the curtain held aside with an elbow. He seemed to be staring at nothing in particular, merely waiting for something that might fix his attention. Roger had a middle-aged, paternal reflex: Is that what he calls studying? If Luc noticed his father, he gave no sign.

Simone Clairevoie called it the year of shocks. There had been Luc's failure, then Roger had suffered a second heart attack, infinitely more frightening than the first. He was home all day on convalescent leave from his ministry, restless and bored, smoking on the sly, grudgingly walking the family dog by way of moderate exercise. Finally, even though all three Clairevoies had voted against it, a Socialist government came to power. Simone foresaw nothing but further decline. If Luc failed again, it would mean a humble career, preceded by a tour of Army duty—plain military service, backpack and drill, with the sons of peasants and Algerian delinquents. Roger would never be able to get him out of it: He knew absolutely no one in the new system of favors. Those friends whose careers had not been lopped sat hard on their jobs, almost afraid to pick up the telephone. Every call was bad news. The worst news would be the voice of an old acquaintance, harking back to a foundered regime and expecting a good turn. Although the Clairevoies seldom went to church now—the new Mass was the enemy—Simone prayed hard on Christmas Eve, singling out in particular St. Odile, who had been useful in the past, around a time when Roger had seemed to regret his engagement to Simone and may have wanted to break it off.

Soon after the New Year, however, there came a message from the guidance counselor of the Jesuit school, summoning the Clairevoies for "a frank and open discussion."

"About being immortal?" said Roger to Simone, recalling an alarming talk with another Jesuit teacher long ago.

"About your son," she replied.

A card on his door identified the counselor as "F.-X. Rousseau, Orientation." Orientation wore a track suit and did not look to Roger like a Jesuit, or even much like a priest. Leaning forward (the Clairevoies instinctively drew back), he offered American cigarettes before lighting his own. It was not Luc's chances of passing that seemed to worry him but Luc's fragmented image of women. On the Rorschach test, for instance, he had seen a ballet skirt and a pair of legs, and a female head in a fishing net.

"You brought me here to tell me what?" said Roger. "My son has poor eyesight?"

Simone placed her hand on Father Rousseau's desk as she might have touched his sleeve. She was saying, Be careful. My husband is irritable, old-fashioned, ill. "I think that Father Rousseau is trying to tell us that Luc has no complete view of women because Luc has no complete view of himself as a man. Is that it?"

Father Rousseau added, "And he cannot see his future because he can't see himself."

It was Roger's turn to remonstrate with Luc. Simone suggested masculine, virile surroundings for their talk, and so he took Luc to the café across the street. There, over beer for Luc and mineral water for Roger, he told Luc about satisfaction. It was the duty of children to satisfy their parents. Roger, by doing extremely well at his studies, had given Luc's grandparents this mysterious pleasure. They had been able to tell their friends, "Roger has given us great satisfaction." He took Luc on a fresh tour of things to come, showing him the slow-grinding machinery of state competitive examinations against which fathers measured their sons. He said, Your future. If you fail. A poor degree is worse than none. Thousands of embittered young men, all voting Socialist. If you fail, you will sink into the swamp from which there is no rising. Do you want to sell brooms? Sweep the streets? Sell tickets in the Métro? Do you want to spend your life in a bank?

"Not that there is anything wrong with working in a bank," he corrected. Encrusted in his wife's family was a small rural bank with a staff of seventeen. Simone did not often see her provincial cousins, but the bank was always mentioned with respect. To say "a small bank" was no worse than saying "a small crown jewel." Simone, in a sense, personified a reliable and almost magical trade; she had brought to Roger the goods and the dream. What had Roger brought? Hideous Empire furniture and a dubious nineteenth-century title Simone scarcely dared use because of the Communists.

Only the word "Socialist" seemed to stir Luc. "We need a good little civil war," he declared, as someone who has never been near the ocean might announce, "We need a good little tidal wave"—so Roger thought.

He said, "There are no good little civil wars." But he knew what was said of him: that his heart attacks had altered his personality, made him afraid. On a November day, Roger and his father had followed the coffin of Charles Maurras, the nationalist leader, jailed after the war for collaboration. "My son," said Roger's father, introducing Roger to thin-faced men, some wearing the Action Française emblem. Roger's father had stood for office on a Royalist platform, and had come out of the election the last of five candidates, one an impertinent youngster with an alien name, full of z's and k's. He was not bitter; he was scornful and dry, and he wanted Roger to be dry and proud. Roger had only lately started to think, My father always said, and, My father believed. As he spoke, now, to Luc about satisfaction and failure, he remembered how he had shuffled behind the hearse of a dead old man, perhaps mistaken, certainly dispossessed. They got up to leave, and Roger bowed to an elderly woman he recognized. His son had already turned away.

In order to give Luc a fully virile image, Simone redecorated his room. The desk lamp was a galleon in full sail with a bright red shade—the color of decision and activity. She took down the photograph of Roger's graduating class and hung a framed poster of Che Guevara. Stepping back to see the effect, she realized Guevara would never do. The face was feminine, soft. She wondered if the whole legend was not a hoax and if Guevara had been a woman in disguise. Guevara had no political significance, of course; he had become manly, decorative kitsch. (The salesman had assured her of this; otherwise, she would never have run the risk of offending Roger.) As she removed the poster she noticed for the first time a hole drilled in the wall. She put her eye to it and had a partial view of the maid's bathroom, used in the past by a succession of au-pair visitors, in Paris to improve their French and to keep an eye on a younger Luc.

She called Roger and made him look: "Who says Luc has no view of women?"

Roger glanced round at the new curtains and bedspread, with their pattern of Formula I racing cars. Near the bed someone—Luc, probably—had tacked a photo of Hitler. Roger, without saying anything, took it down. He did not want Luc quite that manly.

"You can't actually see the shower," said Simone, trying the perspective again. "But I suppose that when she stands drying on the mat . . . We'd better tell him."

"Tell Luc?"

"Rousseau. Orientation."

Not "Father Rousseau," he noticed. It was not true that women were devoted guardians of tradition. They rode every new wave like so much plankton. My father was right, he decided. He always said it was a mistake to give them the vote. He said they had no ideas—just notions. My father was proud to stand up for the past. He was proud to be called a Maurrassien, even when Charles Maurras was in defeat, in disgrace. But who has ever heard of a Maurrassienne? The very idea made Roger smile. Simone, catch-ing the smile, took it to mean a sudden feeling of tolerance, and so she chose the moment to remind him they would have an au-pair guest at Easter—oh, not to keep an eye on Luc; Luc was too old. (She sounded sorry.) But Luc had been three times to England, to a family named Brunt, and now, in all fairness, it was the Clairevoies' obligation to have Cassandra.

"Another learner?" Roger was remembering the tall, glum girls from northern capitals and their strides in colloquial French: That is my friend. He did not sleep in my bed—he spent the night on the doormat. I am homesick. I am ill. A bee has stung me. I am allergic and may die.

"You won't have to worry about Cassandra," Simone said. "She is a ma-ture young woman of fifteen, a whole head taller than Luc."

Simone clipped a leash to the dog's collar and grasped Roger firmly by the arm. She was taking two of her charges for a walk, along streets she used to follow when Luc was still in his pram. On Boulevard Lannes a taxi stopped and two men wearing white furs, high-heeled white boots, and Marilyn Monroe wigs got out and made for the Bois. Roger knew that transvestites worked the fringe of the Bois now, congregating mostly toward the Porte Maillot, where there were hotels. He had heard the women in the café across the street complaining that the police were not vigilant enough, much the way an established artisan might grumble about black-market labor. Roger had imagined them vaguely as night creatures, glittering and sequined, caught like dragonflies in the headlights of roving automobiles. This pair was altogether real, and the man who had just paid the taxi driver shut his gold-mesh handbag with the firm snap of a housewife settling the butcher's bill. The dog at once began to strain and bark.

"Brazilians," said Simone, who watched educational television in the af-ternoon. "They send all their money home."

"But in broad daylight," said Roger.

"They don't earn as much as you think."

"There could be little children playing in the Bois."

"We can't help our children by living in the past," said Simone. Roger wondered if she was having secret talks with Father Rousseau. "Stop that," she told the barking dog.

"He's not deliberately trying to hurt their feelings," Roger said. Because he disliked animals—in particular, dogs—he tended to make excuses for the one they owned. Actually, the dog was an accident in their lives, pur-chased only after the staff psychologist in Luc's old school had said the boy's grades were poor because he had no siblings to love and hate, no rivals for his parents' attention, no responsibility to any living creature.

"A dog will teach my son to add and subtract?" said Roger. Simone had wondered if a dog would make Luc affectionate and polite, more grateful for his parents' devotion, aware of the many sacrifices they had made on his behalf.

Yes, yes, they had been assured. A dog could do all that.

Luc was twelve years old, the puppy ten weeks. Encouraged to find a name for him, Luc came up with "Mongrel." Simone chose "Sylvestre." Sylvestre spent his first night in Luc's room—part of the night, that is. When he began to whine, Luc put him out. After that, Sylvestre was fed, trained, and walked by Luc's parents, while Luc continued to find school a mystery and to show indifference and ingratitude. Want of thanks is a parent's lot, but blindness to simple arithmetic was like an early warning of catastrophe. Luc's parents had already told him he was to train as an engineer.

"Do you know how stiff the competition is?" his mother asked.

"Yes."

"Do you want to be turned down by the best schools?"

"I don't know."

"Do you want to be sent to a third-rate school, miles from home? Have you thought about that?"

Roger leaned on Simone, though he did not need to, and became querulous: "Sylvestre and I are two old men."

This was not what Simone liked to talk about. She said, "Your family never took you into consideration. You slept in your father's study. You took second best."

"It didn't feel that way."

"Look at our miserable country house. Look at your cousin Henri's estate."

"His godmother gave it to him," said Roger, as though she needed reminding.

"He should have given you compensation."

"People don't do that," said Roger. "All I needed was a richer godmother."

"The apartment is mine," said Simone, as they walked arm in arm. "The furniture is yours. The house in the country is yours, but most of the furniture belongs to me. You paid for the pool and the tennis court." It was not unpleasant conversation.

Roger stopped in front of a pastry shop and showed Simone a chocolate cake. "Why can't we have that?"

"Because it would kill you. The specialist said so."

"We could have oysters," Roger said. "I'm allowed oysters."

"Luc will be home," said Simone. "He doesn't like them."

Father Rousseau sent for the Clairevoies again. This time he wore a tweed jacket over a white sweater, with a small crucifix on one lapel and a Solidarność badge on the other. After lighting his cigarette he sat drumming his fingers, as if wondering how to put his grim news into focus. At last he said, "No one can concentrate on an exam and on a woman. Not at the same time."

"Women?" cried Simone. "What women?"

"Woman," Roger corrected, unheard.

There was a woman in Luc's life. It seemed unbelievable, but it was so.

"French?" said Roger instantly.

Father Rousseau was unable to swear to it. Her name was Katia, her surname Martin, but if Martin was the most common family name in France it might be because so many foreigners adopted it.

"I can find out," Simone interrupted. "What's her age?"

Katia was eighteen. Her parents were divorced.

"That's bad," said Simone. "Who's her father?"

She lived in Biarritz with her mother, but came often to Paris to stay with her father and brother. Her brother belonged to a political debating society.

"I've seen him," said Simone. "I know the one. She's a terrorist. Am I right?"

Father Rousseau doubted it. "She is a spoiled, rich, undereducated young woman, used to having her own way. She is also very much in love."

"With Luc?" said Roger.

"Luc is a Capricorn," said Simone. "The most levelheaded of all the signs."

So was Katia, Father Rousseau said. She and Luc wrote "Capricorn loves Capricorn" in the dust on parked cars.

"Does Luc want to marry her?" said Simone, getting over the worst.

"He wants something." But Father Rousseau hoped it would not be Katia. She seemed to have left school early, after a number of misadventures. She was hardly the person to inspire Luc, who needed a model he could copy. When Katia was around, Luc did not even pretend to study. When she was in Biarritz, he waited for letters. The two collected lump sugar from cafés but seemed to have no other cultural interest.

"She's from a rich family?" Simone said. "And she has just the one brother?"

"Luc has got to pass his entrance examination," said Roger. "After he gets his degree he can marry anyone he likes."

" 'Rich' is a relative term," said Simone, implying that Father Rousseau was too unworldly to define such a thing.

Roger said, "How do you know about the sugar and 'Capricorn loves Capricorn' and how Luc and Katia got to know each other?"

"Why, from Katia's letters, of course," said Father Rousseau, sounding surprised.

"Did you keep copies?" said Simone.

"Do you know that Luc is of age, and that he could take you to court for reading his mail?" said Roger.

Father Rousseau turned to Simone, the rational parent. "Not a word of reproach," he warned her. "Just keep an eye on the situation. We feel that Luc should spend the next few weeks at home, close to his parents." He would come back to Rennes just before the examination, for last-minute heavy cramming. Roger understood this to be a smooth Jesuitical manner of getting rid of Luc.

Luc came home, and no one reproached him. He promised to work hard and proposed going alone to the country house, which was near Auxerre. Simone objected that the place had been unheated all winter. Luc replied that he would live in one room and take his meals in the village. Roger guessed that Luc intended to spend a good amount of time with Cousin Henri, who lived nearby, and whom Luc—no one knew why—professed to admire. Cousin Henri and Roger enjoyed property litigation of long standing, but as there was a dim, far chance of Henri's leaving something to Luc, Roger said nothing. And as Simone pointed out, meaning by this nothing unkind or offensive, any male model for Luc was better than none.

In the meantime, letters from Katia, forwarded from Rennes, arrived at the Paris apartment. Roger watched in pure amazement the way Simone managed to open them, rolling a kitchen match under the flap. Having read the letter, she resealed it without trace. The better the quality of the paper, the easier the match trick, she explained. She held a page up to the light, approving the watermark.

"We'll need a huge apartment, because we will have so many children," Katia wrote. "And we'll need space for the sugar collection."

The only huge apartment Simone could think of was her own. "They wish we were dead," she told Roger. "My son wishes I were out of the way." She read aloud, " 'What would you be without me? One more little French-man, eternally studying for exams.' "

"What does she mean by 'little Frenchman'?" said Roger. He decided that Katia must be foreign—a descendant of White Russians, perhaps. There had been a colony in Biarritz in his father's day, the men gambling away their wives' tiaras before settling down as headwaiters and croupiers. Luc was entangled in a foreign love affair; he was already alien, estranged. Roger had seen him standing at the window, like an idle landowner in a Russian novel. What did Roger know about Russians? There were the modern ones, dressed in gray, with bulldog faces; there were the slothful, mournful people in books, the impulsive and slender women, the indecisive men. But it had been years since Roger had opened a novel; what he saw were overlapping images, like stills from old films.

" 'Where are you, where are you?' " read Simone. " 'There is a light in your parents' room, but your windows are dark. I'm standing under the awning across the street. My shoes are soaked. I am too miserable to care.'

"She can't be moping in the rain and writing all at the same time," said Simone. "And the postmark is Biarritz. She comes to Paris to stir up trou-ble. How does she know which room is ours? Luc is probably sick of her. He must have been at a meeting."

Yes, he had probably been at a meeting, sitting on the floor of a pale room, with a soft-voiced old man telling him about an older, truer Europe. Luc was learning a Europe caught in amber, unchanging, with trees for gods. There was no law against paganism and politics, or soft-voiced old men.

At least there are no guns, Roger told himself. And where had Simone learned the way to open other people's letters? He marveled at Katia's doing for his son what no woman had ever done for him; she had stood in the rain, crying probably, watching for a light.

Ten days before Easter, Cassandra Brunt arrived. Her father was a civil ser-vant, like Roger. He was also an author: Two books had been published, one about Napoleon's retreat from Moscow, the other about the failure of the Maginot Line and the disgraceful conduct of the French officer class. Both had been sent to the Clairevoies, with courteous inscriptions. When

Simone had gone over to England alone, to see if the Brunts would do for Luc, Mrs. Brunt confided that her husband was more interested in the philosophy of combat than in success and defeat. He was a dreamer, and that was why he had never got ahead. Simone replied that Roger, too, had been hampered by guiding principles. As a youth, he had read for his own pleasure. His life was a dream. Mrs. Brunt suggested a major difference: Mr. Brunt was no full-time dreamer. He had written five books, two of which had been printed, one in 1952 and one in 1966. The two women had then considered each other's child, decided it was sexless and safe and that Luc and Cassandra could spend time under the same roof. After that, Luc crossed the Channel for three visits, while Simone managed not to have Cassandra even once. Her excuse was the extreme youth of Cassandra and the dangers of Paris. Now that Cassandra was fifteen Mrs. Brunt, suddenly exercising her sense of things owed, had written to say that Cassandra was ready for perils and the French.

Roger and Simone met Cassandra at the Gare du Nord. The moment he saw her, Roger understood she had been forced by her parents to make the trip, and that they were ruining her Easter holiday. He marveled that a fifteen-year-old of her size and apparent strength could be bullied into anything.

"I'll be seeing Luc, what fun," said Cassandra, jackknifed into the car, her knees all but touching her chin. "It will be nice to see Luc," she said sadly. Her fair hair almost covered her face.

"Luc is at our country residence, studying with all the strength of his soul," said Simone. "He is in the Yonne," she added. Cassandra looked puzzled. Roger supposed that to a foreigner it must sound as though Luc had fallen into a river.

There had been no coaxing Luc, no pleading; no threat was strong enough to frighten him. They could keep the BMW; they could stop his allowance; they could put him in jail. He would not come to Paris to welcome Cassandra. He was through with England, through with the Brunts— through, for that matter, with his mother and father. Katia had taken their place.

"We'll have her in Paris for a week, alone," Simone had wailed. Luc's argument was unassailable; alone, he could study. Once they were all there, he would have to be kind to Cassandra, making conversation and showing her the village church. Simone put the blame on Mrs. Brunt, who had insisted in a wholly obtuse way on having her rights.

"How are your delicious parents?" she asked, turning as well as the seat belt allowed, seeming to let the car drive itself in Paris traffic.

"Daddy's at home now. He's retired from the minstrel."

"The ministry," said Simone deeply. Cassandra's was the only English she had ever completely understood. "My husband has also retired from public service. It was too much for his heart. He is much younger than Mr. Brunt, I believe."

"Daddy was a late starter," said Cassandra. "But he'll last a long time. At least, I hope so."

Like the dog bought to improve Luc's arithmetic; like the tropical fish Simone had tended for Luc, and eventually mourned; like the tennis court in which Luc had at once lost interest and on which Roger had had his first heart attack, so Cassandra fell to Luc's parents. With Simone, she watched television; with Roger, she walked uphill and down, to parks and museums.

"What was your minstrel?" she asked Roger, as they marched toward the Bois.

"Years ago, when there was a grave shortage of telephones, thanks to President de Gaulle—" Roger began. "Do you recall that unhappy time?"

"I'm afraid I'm dreffly ignorant."

"I was good at getting friends off the waiting list. That was what I did best."

He clutched her arm, dragging her out of the way of buses and taxis that rushed from the left while Cassandra looked hopelessly right.

"You like the nature?" he said, letting Sylvestre run free in the Bois. "The trees?"

"My mother does. Though this is hardly nature, is it?"

Sylvestre loped, snuffling, into a club of dusty shrubbery. He gave a yelp and came waddling out. All Roger saw of the person who had kicked him was a flash of white boot.

"You have them in England?" said Roger.

"Have what?"

"That. Male, female. Prostitutes."

"Yes, of course. But they aren't vile to animals."

"You like the modern art?" Roger asked, breathless, as they plodded up the stalled escalators of the Beaubourg museum.

"I'm horribly old-fashioned, I'm afraid."

Halfway, he paused to let his heart rest. His heart was an old pump, clogged and filthy. Cassandra's heart was of bright new metal; it beat more quietly and regularly than any clock.

Above the city stretched a haze of pollution, unstirring, all of an even color. The sun suffused the haze with amber dye, which by some grim alchemy was turned into dun. Roger saw through the haze to a forgotten city, unchanging, and it was enough to wrench the heart. A hand, reaching inside the rib cage, seemed to grasp the glutted machine. He knew that some part of the machine was intact, faithful to him; when his heart disowned him entirely he might as well die.

Cassandra, murmuring that looking down made her feel giddy, turned her back. Roger watched a couple, below, walking hand in hand. He was too far away to see their faces. They were eating out of a shared paper bag. The young man looked around, perhaps for a bin. Finding none, he handed the bag to the girl, who flung it down. The two were dressed nearly alike, in blue jackets and jeans. Simone had assured Roger that Katia was French, but he still saw her Russian. He saw Katia in winter furs, with a fur hat, and long fair hair over a snowy collar. She removed a glove and gave the hand, warm, to Luc to hold.

"I'm afraid I must be getting lazy," Cassandra remarked. "I found that quite a climb."

The couple in blue had turned a corner. Of Luc and Katia there remained footsteps on lightly fallen snow.

"This place reminds me of a giant food processor," said Cassandra. "What does it make you think of?"

"Young lovers," Roger said.

Cassandra had a good point in Simone's eyes: She kept a diary, which Simone used to improve her English.

"The Baron has sex on the brain," Simone read. "Even a museum reminds him of sex. In the Bois de Boulogne he tried to twist the conversation around to sex and bestiality. You have to be careful every minute. Each time we have to cross the road he tries to squeeze my arm."

When Cassandra had been shown enough of Paris, Simone packed the car with food that Luc liked to eat and drove south and east with the dog, Roger, and Cassandra. They stopped often during the journey so that Cassandra, who sat in the back of the car, could get out and be sick. They found Luc living like an elderly squatter in a ground-floor room full of toast crusts. It was three in the afternoon, and he was still wearing pajamas. Inevitably, Cassandra asked if he was ill.

"Katia's been here," said Simone, going round the house and opening shutters. "I can tell. It's in the air."

Luc was occupying the room meant for Cassandra. He showed no willingness to give it up. He took slight notice of his parents, and none whatever of their guest. It seemed to Roger that he had grown taller, but this was surely an illusion, a psychological image in Roger's mind. His affair, if Roger could call it that, had certainly made him bolder. He mentioned Katia by name, saying that one advantage of living alone was that he could read his mail before anyone else got to it. Roger foresaw a holiday of bursting quarrels. He supposed Cassandra would go home and tell her father, the historian, that the French were always like that.

On the day they arrived, Simone intercepted and read a letter. Katia, apparently in answer to some questioning from Luc, explained that she had almost, but not entirely, submitted to the advances of a cousin. (Luc, to forestall his mother, met the postman at the gate. Simone, to short-circuit Luc, had already picked up the letters that interested her at the village post office.) Katia's near seduction had taken place in a field of barley, while her cousin was on leave from military service. A lyrical account of clouds, birds, and crickets took up most of a page.

Roger would not touch the letter, but he listened as Simone read aloud. It seemed to him that some coarse appreciation of the cousin was concealed behind all those crickets and birds. Katia's blithe candor was insolent, a slur on his son. At the same time, he took heart: If a cousin was liable for Army duty, some part of the family must be French. On the other hand, who would rape his cousin in a barley field, if not a Russian?

"You swore Katia was French," he said, greatly troubled.

He knew nothing of Katia, but he did know something about fields. Roger decided he did not believe a word of the story. Katia was trying to turn Luc into a harmless and impotent bachelor friend. The two belonged in a novel of the early 1950s. (Simone, as Roger said this, began to frown.) "Luc is the good, kind man she can tell stories to," he said. "Her stories will be more and more about other men." As Simone drew breath, he said quickly, "Not that I see Luc in a novel."

"No, but I can see you in the diary of a hysterical English girl," said Simone, and she told him about Cassandra.

Roger, scarcely listening, went on, "In a novel, Katia's visit would be a real-estate tour. She would drive up from Biarritz with her mother and take pictures from the road. Katia's mother would find the house squat and suburban, and so Luc would show them Cousin Henri's. They would take pictures of that, too. Luc would now be going round with chalk and a tape measure, marking the furniture he wants to sell once we're buried, planning the rooms he will build for Katia when the place is his."

All at once he felt the thrust of the next generation, and for the first time he shared some of Simone's fear of the unknown girl.

"The house is yours," said Simone, mistaking his meaning. "The furniture is mine. They can't change that by going round with a piece of chalk. There's always the bank. She can't find *that* suburban." The bank had recently acquired a new and unexpected advantage: It was too small to be nationalized. "Your son is a dreamer," said Simone. "He dreams he is studying, and he fails his exams. He dreams about sex and revolutions, and he waits around for letters and listens to old men telling silly tales."

Roger remembered the hole drilled in the wall. An au-pair girl in the shower was Luc's symbol of sexual mystery. From the great courtesans of his grandfather's time to the prettiest children of the poor in bordellos to a girl glimpsed as she stood drying herself—what a decline! Here was the true comedown, the real debasement of the middle class. Perhaps he would write a book about it; it would at least rival Mr. Brunt's opus about the decline of French officers.

"She can't spell," said Simone, examining the letter again. "If Luc marries her, he will have to write all her invitations and her postcards." What else did women write? She paused, wondering.

"Her journal?" Roger said.

In Cassandra's journal Simone read, "They expect such a lot from that poor clod of a Luc." That night at dinner Simone remarked, "My father once said he could die happy. He had never entertained a foreigner or shaken hands with an Englishman."

Cassandra stared at Roger as if to say, "Is she joking?" Roger, married twenty-three years, thought she was not. Cassandra's pale hair swung down as she drooped over her plate. She began to pick at something that, according to her diary, made her sick: underdone lamb, cooked the French way, stinking of garlic and spilling blood.

At dawn there was a spring thunderstorm, like the start of civil war. The gunfire died, and a hard, steady rain soaked the tennis court and lawn. Roger got up, first in the household, and let the dog out of the garage, where it slept among piles of paperbacks and rusting cans of weed killer. Roger was forty-eight that day; he hoped no one would notice. He thought he saw yellow roses running along the hedge, but it was a shaft of sunlight. In the kitchen, he found a pot with the remains of last night's coffee and heated some in a saucepan. While he drank, standing, looking out the window, the sky cleared entirely and became soft and blue.

"Happy birthday."

He turned his head, and there was Cassandra in the doorway, wearing a long gypsy skirt and an embroidered nightshirt, with toy rings on every finger. "I thought I'd dress because of Sunday," she explained. "I thought we might be going to church."

"I could offer you better coffee in the village," said Roger. "If you do not mind the walk." He imagined her diary entry: "The Baron tried to get me alone on a country road, miles from any sign of habitation."

"The dog will come, too," he assured her.

They walked on the rim of wet fields, in which the freed dog leaped. The hem of Cassandra's skirt showed dark where it brushed against drenched grasses. Roger told her that the fields and woods, almost all they could see, had belonged to his grandparents. Cousin Henri owned the land now.

Cassandra knew; when Simone was not talking about Luc and Katia and the government, she talked about Cousin Henri.

"My father wants to write another book, about Torquemada and Stalin and, I think, Cromwell," Cassandra said. "The theme would be single-mindedness. But he can't get down to it. My mother doesn't see why he can't write for an hour, then talk to her for an hour. She asks him to help look for things she's lost, like the keys to the car. Before he retired, she was never bored. Now that he's home all day, she wants company and she loses everything."

"How did he write his other books?" said Roger.

"In the minstrel he had a private office and secretary. Two, in fact. He expected to write even more, once he was free, but he obviously won't. If he were alone, I could look after him." That was unexpected. Perhaps Luc knew just how unexpected Cassandra could be, and that was why he stayed away from her. "I don't mean I imagine my mother not there," she said. "I only meant that I could look after him, if I had to."

Half a mile before the village stood Cousin Henri's house. Roger told Cassandra why he and Henri were not speaking, except through lawyers. Henri had been grossly favored by their mutual grandparents, thanks to the trickery of an aunt by marriage, who was Henri's godmother. The aunt, who was very rich as well as mad and childless, had acquired the grandparents' domain, in their lifetime, by offering more money than it was worth. She had done this wicked thing in order to hand it over, intact, unshared, undivided, to Henri, whom she worshiped. The transaction had been brought off on the wrong side of the law, thanks to a clan of Protestants and Freemasons.

Cassandra looked puzzled and pained. "You see, the government of that time . . . ," said Roger, but he fell silent, seeing that Cassandra had stopped understanding. When he was overwrought he sounded like his wife. It was hardly surprising: He was simply repeating, word for word, everything Simone had been saying since they were married. In his own voice, which was ironic and diffident, he told Cassandra why Cousin Henri had never married. At the age of twenty Henri had been made trustee of a family secret. Henri's mother was illegitimate—at any rate, hatched from a cuckoo's egg. Henri's father was not his mother's husband but a country neighbor. Henri had been warned never to marry any of the such-and-such girls, because he might be marrying his own half sister. Henri might not have wanted to: The such-and-suches were ugly and poor. He had used the secret as good reason not to marry anyone, had settled down in the handsomest house in the Yonne (half of which should have been Roger's), and had peopled the neighborhood with his random children.

They slowed walking, and Cassandra looked at a brick-and-stucco box, and some dirty-faced children playing on the steps.

"There, behind the farmhouse," said Roger, showing a dark, severe manor house at the top of a straight drive.

"It looks more like a monastery, don't you think?" said Cassandra. Although Roger seemed to be waiting, she could think of nothing more to say. They walked on, toward Cassandra's breakfast.

On the road back, Roger neither looked at Cousin Henri's house nor mentioned it. They were still at some distance from home when they began to hear Simone: "Marry her! Marry Katia! Live with Katia! I don't care what you do. Anything, anything, so long as you pass your exam." Roger pushed open the gate and there was Simone, still in her dressing gown, standing on a lawn strewn with Luc's clothes, and Luc at the window, still in pajamas. Luc heaved a chair over the sill, then a couple of pillows and a whole armful of books. Having yelled something vile about the family (they were in disagreement later about what it was), he jumped out, too, and landed easily in a flower bed. He paused to pick up shoes he had flung out earlier, ran awkwardly across the lawn, pushed through a gap in the hedge, and vanished.

"He'll be back," said Simone, gathering books. "He'll want his breakfast. He really is a remarkable athlete. With proper guidance, Luc could have done anything. But Roger never took much interest."

"What was that last thing he said?" said Cassandra.

"Fools," said Simone. "But a common word for it. Never repeat that word, if you want people to think well of you."

"Spies," Roger had heard. In Luc's room he found a pair of sunglasses on the floor. He had noticed Luc limping as he made for the hedge; perhaps he had sprained an ankle. He remembered how Luc had been too tired to walk a dog, too worn out to feed a goldfish. Roger imagined him, now, wandering in muddy farmyards, in shoes and pajamas, children giggling at him—the Clairevoies' mooncalf son. Perhaps he had gone to tell his troubles to that other eccentric, Cousin Henri.

Tears came easily since Roger's last attack. He had been told they were caused by the depressant effect of the pills he had to take. He leaned on the window frame, in the hope of seeing Luc, and wept quietly in the shelter of Luc's glasses.

"It's awfully curious of me," said Cassandra, helping Simone, "but what's got into Luc? When he stayed with us, in England, he was angelic. Your husband seems upset, too."

"The *Baron*," said Simone, letting it be known she had read the diary and was ready for combat, "the *Baron* is too sensible. Today is his birthday. He is forty-eight—nearly fifty."

Roger supposed she meant "sensitive." To correct Simone might create a diversion, but he could not be sure of what kind. To let it stand might bewilder the English girl; but, then, Cassandra was born bewildered.

Luc came home in time for dinner, dressed in a shirt and corduroys belonging to Cousin Henri. His silence, Roger thought, challenged them for questions; none came. He accepted a portion of Roger's birthday cake, which, of course, Roger could not touch, and left half on his plate. "Even as a small child, Luc never cared for chocolate," Simone explained to Cassandra.

The next day, only food favored by Luc was served. Simone turned over a letter from Katia. It was brief and cool in tone: Katia had been exercising horses in a riding school, helping a friend.

The Clairevoies, preceded by Luc on the Honda, packed up and drove back to Paris. This time Cassandra was allowed to sit in front, next to Simone. Roger and the dog shared the backseat with Luc's books and a number of parcels.

They saw Cassandra off at the Gare du Nord. Roger was careful not to take her arm, brush against her, or otherwise inspire a mention in her diary. She wore a T-shirt decorated with a grinning mouth. "It's been really lovely," she said. Roger bowed.

Her letter of thanks arrived promptly. She was planning to help her father with his book on Stalin, Cromwell, and Torquemada. He wanted to include a woman on the list, to bring the work in line with trends of the day. Cassandra had suggested Boadicea, Queen of the Iceni. Boadicea stood for feminine rectitude, firmness, and true love of one's native culture. So Cassandra felt.

"Cassandra has written a most learned and affectionate letter," said Simone, who would never have to see Cassandra again. "I only hope Luc was as polite to the Brunts." Her voice held a new tone of maternal grievance and maternal threat.

Luc, who no longer found threats alarming, packed his books and took the train for Rennes. Katia's letters seemed to have stopped. Searching Luc's room, Simone found nothing to read except a paperback on private ownership. "I believe he is taking an interest in things," she told Roger.

It was late in May when the Clairevoies made their final trip to Rennes. Suspecting what awaited them, Simone wore mourning—a dark linen suit, black sandals, sunglasses. Father Rousseau had on a dark suit and black tie. After some hesitation he said what Roger was waiting to hear: It was useless to make Luc sit for an examination he had not even a remote chance of passing. Luc was unprepared, now and forever. He had, in fact, disappeared, though he had promised to come back once the talk with his parents was over. Luc had confided that he would be content to live like Cousin Henri, without a degree to his name, and with a reliable tenant farmer to keep things running.

My son is a fool, said Roger to himself. Katia, who was certainly beautiful, perhaps even clever, loved him. She stood crying in the street, trying to see a light in his room.

"Luc's cousin is rich," said Simone. "Luc is too pure to understand the difference. He will have to learn something. What about computer training?"

"Luc has a mind too fluid to be restrained," said Father Rousseau.

"Literature?" said Simone, bringing up the last resort.

Roger came to life. "Sorting letters in the post office?"

"Machines do that," said Father Rousseau. "Luc would have to pass a test to show he understands the machine. I have been wondering if there might be in Luc's close environment a family affair." The Clairevoies fell silent. "A family business," Father Rousseau repeated. "Families are open, airy structures. They take in the dreamy as well as the alert. There is always an extra corner somewhere."

Like most of her women friends, Simone had given up wearing jewelry: The streets were full of anarchists and muggers. One of her friends knew of someone who had had a string of pearls ripped off her neck by a bearded intellectual of the Mediterranean type—that is, quite dark. Simone still kept, for luck, a pair of gold earrings, so large and heavy they looked fake. She touched her talisman earrings and said, "We have in our family a bank too small to be nationalized."

"Congratulations," said Father Rousseau, sincerely. When he got up to see them to the door, Roger saw he wore running shoes.

It fell to Roger to tell Luc what was to become of him. After military service of the most humdrum and unprotected kind, he would move to a provincial town and learn about banks. The conversation took place late one night in Luc's room. Simone had persuaded Roger that Luc needed to be among his own things—the galleon lamp, the Foreign Legion recruiting poster that had replaced Che Guevara, the photograph of Simone that replaced Roger's graduating class. Roger said, somewhat shyly, "You will be that much closer to Biarritz."

"Katia is getting married," said Luc. "His father has a riding school." He said this looking away, rolling a pencil between thumb and finger, something like the way his mother had rolled a kitchen match. Reflected in the dark window, Luc's cheeks were hollowed, his eyes blazing and black. He looked almost a hero and, like most heroes, lonely.

"What happened to your friends?" said Roger. "The friends you used to see every Sunday."

"Oh, that . . . that fell apart. All the people they ever talked about were already dead. And some of the parents were worried. You were the only parents who never interfered."

"We wanted you to live your own life," said Roger. "It must have been that. Could you get her back?"

"You can do anything with a woman if you give her enough money."

"Who told you a thing like that?" In the window Roger examined the reflected lamp, the very sight of which was supposed to have made a man of Luc.

"Everyone. Cousin Henri. I told her we owned a bank, because Cousin Henri said it would be a good thing to tell her. She asked me how to go about getting a bank loan. That was all."

Does he really believe he owns a bank, Roger wondered. "About money," he said. "Nothing of Cousin Henri's is likely to be ours. Illegitimate children are allowed to inherit now, and my cousin," said Roger with some wonder, "has acknowledged everyone. I pity the schoolteacher. All she ever sees is the same face." This was not what Luc was waiting to hear. "You will inherit everything your mother owns. I have to share with my cousin, because that is how our grandparents arranged it." He did not go on about the Freemasons and Protestants, because Luc already knew.

"It isn't fair," said Luc.

"Then you and your mother share my share."

"How much of yours is mine?" said Luc politely.

"Oh, something at least the size of the tennis court," said Roger.

On Luc's desk stood, silver-framed, another picture of Simone, a charming one taken at the time of her engagement. She wore, already, the gold earrings. Her hair was in the upswept balloon style of the time. Her expression was smiling, confident but untried. Both Luc and Roger suddenly looked at it in silence.

It was Simone's belief that, after Katia, Luc had started sleeping with one of her own friends. She thought she knew the one: the Hungarian wife of an architect, fond of saying she wished she had a daughter the right age for Luc. This was a direct sexual compliment, based on experience, Simone thought. Roger thought it meant nothing at all. It was the kind of empty declaration mothers mistook for appreciation. Simone had asked Roger to find out what he could, for this was the last chance either of them would ever have to talk to Luc. From now on, he would undoubtedly get along better with his parents, but where there had been a fence there would be a wall. Luc was on his own.

Roger said, "It was often thought, in my day, mainly by foreigners who had never been to France, that young men began their lives with their mother's best friend. Absurd, when you consider it. Why pick an old woman when you can have a young one?" "*Buy* a young one," he had been about to say, by mistake. "Your mother's friends often seem young to me. I suppose it has to do with their clothes—so loose, unbuttoned. The disorder is already there. My mother's best friends wore armor. It was called the New Look, invented by Christian Dior, a great defender of matronly virtue." A direct glance from Luc—the first. "There really was a Mr. Dior, just as I suppose there was a Mr. Mercedes and a Mr. Benz. My mother and her friends were put into boned corsets, stiff petticoats, wide-brimmed, murderous hats. Their nails were pointed, and as red as your lampshade. They carried furled parasols with silver handles and metal-edged handbags. Even the heels of their shoes were contrived for braining people. No young man would have gone anywhere near." Luc's eyes met Roger's in the window. "I have often wondered," said Roger, "though I'm not trying to make it my business, what you and Katia could have done. Where could you have taken her? Well, unless she had some private place of her own. There's more and more of that. Daughters of nice couples, people we know. Their own apartment, car, money. Holidays no one knows where. Credit cards, bank accounts, abortions. In my day, we had a miserable amount of spending money, but we had the girls in the Rue Spontini. Long after the bordellos were closed, there was the Rue Spontini. Do you know who first took me there? Cousin Henri. Not surprising, considering the life he has led since. Henri called it 'the annex,' because he ran into so many friends from his school. On Thursday afternoons, that was." A slight question in Luc's eyes. "Thursday was our weekly holiday, like Wednesdays for you. I don't suppose every Wednesday—no, I'm sure you don't. Besides, even the last of those places vanished years ago. There were Belgian girls, Spanish girls from Algeria. Some were so young—oh, very young. One told me I was like a brother. I asked Cousin Henri what she meant. He said he didn't know."

Luc said, "Katia could cry whenever she wanted to." Her face never altered, but two great tears would suddenly brim over and course along her cheeks.

The curtains and shutters were open. Anyone could look in. There was no one in the street—not even a ghost. How real Katia and Luc had seemed; how they had touched what was left of Roger's heart; how he had loved them. Giving them up forever, he said, "I always admired that picture of your mother."

Simone and Roger had become engaged while Roger was still a lieutenant in Algeria. On the night before their wedding, which was to take place at ten o'clock in the morning in the church of Saint-Pierre de Chaillot, Roger paid a wholly unwelcome call. Simone received him alone, in her dressing gown, wearing a fine net over her carefully ballooned hair. Her parents, listening at the door, took it for granted Roger had caught a venereal disease in a North African brothel and wanted the wedding postponed; Simone supposed he had met a richer and prettier girl. All Roger had to say was that he had seen an Algerian prisoner being tortured to death. Simone had often asked Roger, since then, why he had tried to frighten her with something that had so little bearing on their future. Roger could not re-member what his reason had been.

He tried, now, to think of something important to say to Luc, as if the essence of his own life could be bottled in words and handed over. Sylvestre, wakened by a familiar voice, came snuffling at the door, expecting at this un-suitable hour to be taken out. Roger remarked, "Whatever happens, don't get your life all mixed up with a dog's."

OVERHEAD IN A BALLOON

───────

❦

*A*ymeric had a family name that Walter at first didn't catch. He had come into the art gallery as "A. Régis," which was how he signed his work. He must have been close to sixty, but only his self-confidence had kept pace with time. His eyes shone, young and expectant, in an unlined and rosy face. In spite of the face, almost downy, he was powerful-looking, with a wrestler's thrust of neck and hunched shoulders. Walter, assistant manager of the gallery, was immediately attracted to Aymeric, as to a new religion— this time, one that might work.

Painting portraits on commission had seen Aymeric through the sunnier decades, but there were fewer clients now, at least in Europe. After a brief late flowering of Moroccan princes and Pakistani generals, he had given up. Now he painted country houses. Usually he showed the front with the white shutters and all the ivy, and a stretch of lawn with white chairs and a teapot and cups, and some scattered pages of *Le Figaro*—the only newspaper, often the only anything, his patrons read. He had a hairline touch and could reproduce *Le Figaro*'s social calendar, in which he cleverly embedded his client's name and his own. Some patrons kept a large magnifying glass on a table under the picture, so that guests, peering respectfully, could appreciate their host's permanent place in art.

Unfortunately, such commissions never amounted to much. These were not the great homes of France (they had all been done long ago, and in times of uncertainty and anxious thrift the heirs and owners were not of a mind to start over) but weekend places. Aymeric was called in to immortalize a done-up village bakery, a barn refurbished and brightened with the yellow awnings *Dallas* had lately made so popular. They were not houses meant to be handed on but slabs of Paris-area real estate, to be sold and sold again, each time with a thicker garnish of improvements. Aymeric had by now worked his territory to the farthest limit of the farthest flagged terrace within a two-hour drive from Paris in any direction; it had occurred to him that a show, a sort of retrospective of lawns and *Figaros*, would bring fresh patronage, perhaps even from abroad. (As Walter was to discover, Aymeric was blankly unprofessional, with that ignorance of the trade peculiar to its fringe.) It happened that one of the Paris Sunday supplements had published a picture story on Walter's gallery, with captions that laid stress on the establishment's boldness, vitality, visibility, international connections, and financial vigor. The supplement project had cost Walter's employer a packet, and Walter was not surprised that one of the photographs showed him close to collapse, leaning for support against the wall safe in his private office. The accompanying article described mobbed openings, private viewings to which the police were summoned to keep order, and potential buyers lined up outside in below-freezing weather, bursting in the minute the doors were opened to grab everything off the walls. The name of the painter hardly mattered; the gallery's reputation was enough.

Who believes this, Walter had wondered, turning the slippery, rainbow pages. Then Aymeric had lumbered in, pink and hopeful, believing.

He had dealt with, and been dealt with by, Walter's employer, known privately to Walter as "Trout Face." Aymeric showed courteous amazement when he heard just how much a show of that kind would cost. The uncultured talk about money was the gallery's way of refusing him, though a clause in the rejection seemed to say that something might still be feasible, in some distant off-season, provided that Aymeric was willing to buy all his own work. He declined, politely. For that matter, Trout Face was civil, too.

Walter, from behind his employer's back, had been letting Aymeric know by means of winks and signs that he might be able to help. (In the end, he was no help.) He managed to make an appointment to meet Aymeric in a café not far away, on Boulevard Saint-Germain. There, a few hours later, they sat on the glass-walled sidewalk terrace—it was March, and still cold—with Walter suddenly feeling Swiss and insufficient as Aymeric delicately unfolded a long banner of a name. Walter had already introduced himself, much more briefly: "Obermauer." He pointed, because the conversation could not get going again, and said, "That's my Métro station, over there. Solférino."

They had been through some of Aymeric's troubles and were sliding,

Walter hoped, along to his own. These were, in order, that for nine years his employer had been exploiting him; that he had a foot caught in the steel teeth of his native Calvinism and was hoping to ease it free without resorting to a knife; that the awfully nice Dominican who had been lending books to him had brusquely advised him to try psychoanalysis. Finally, the apartment building he lived in had just been sold to a chain of health clubs, and everybody had to get out. It seemed a great deal to set loose on a new friend, so Walter mentioned only that he had a long underground ride to work every day, with two changes.

Aymeric replied that from the Notre-Dame-des-Champs station there was no change. That was how he had come, lugging his portfolio to show Walter's employer. "I was too soft with him, probably," Aymeric resumed. His relatives had already turned out to be his favorite topic. "The men in my family are too tolerant. Our wives leave us for brutes."

Leaning forward the better to hear Aymeric, who had dropped to a mutter, Walter noticed that his hair was dyed, pale locks on a ruddy forehead. His voice ran like clockwork, drawling to a stop and then, wound up tight, picking up again, like a refreshed countertenor. His voice was like the signature that required a magnifying glass; what he had to say was clear, but a kind of secret.

Walter said he was astonished at the number of men willing to admit, with no false pride, that their wives had left them.

"Oh, well, they do that nowadays," said Aymeric. "They wait for the children to." To? He must have meant "to grow up, to leave home."

"Are there children?" He imagined Aymeric lingering outside the fence of a schoolyard, trying to catch a glimpse of his estranged children, ducking behind a parked car when a teacher looked his way.

"Grandchildren."

Walter continued to feel sympathy. His employer, back in the days when he had been training Walter to be a gallery instrument as silent and reliable as the lock on the office safe, had repeatedly warned him that wives were death to the art trade. Degas had remained a bachelor. Did Walter know why? Because Degas did not want to have a wife looking at his work at the end of the day and remarking, "That's pretty."

They had finally got the conversation rolling evenly. Aymeric, wound up and in good breath, revealed that he and his cousin Robert and Robert's aged mother occupied a house his family had lived in forever. Actually, it was on one floor of an apartment building, but nearly the whole story—

three sides of the court. For a long time, it had been a place the women of the family could come back to when their husbands died or began showing the indifference that amounts to desertion. Now that Paris had changed so much, it was often the men who returned. (Walter noticed that Aymeric said "Paris" instead of "life," or "manners," or "people.") Probably laziness of habit had made him say they had lived forever between the Luxembourg Gardens and the Boulevard Raspail. Raspail was less than a century old, and could scarcely count as a timeless landmark. Still, when Aymeric looked down at the damp cobblestones in the court, out of his kitchen window, he could not help feeling behind him the line of ancestors who had looked out, too, wondering, like Aymeric, if it really would be a mortal sin to jump.

Robert, his cousin, owned much of the space. It was space one carved up, doled out anew, remodeled; it was space on which one was taxed. Sixty square meters had just been sold to keep the city of Paris from grabbing twice that amount for back taxes. Another piece had gone to pay their share in mending the roof. Over the years, as so many single, forsaken adults had tried to construct something nestlike, cushioning, clusters of small living quarters had evolved, almost naturally, like clusters of coral. All the apartments connected; one could walk from end to end of the floor without having to step out to a landing. They never locked their doors. Members of the same family do not steal from one another, and they have nothing to hide. Aymeric said this almost sternly. Robert's wife had died, he added, just as Walter opened his mouth to ask. Death was the same thing as desertion.

Walter did not know what to answer to all this, especially to the part about locks. A good, stout bolt seemed to him a sensible and not an unfriendly precaution. "And lead us not into temptation," he was minded to quote, but it was too soon to begin that ambiguous sort of exchange.

At that moment Walter's employer appeared across the boulevard, at the curb, trying to flag a taxi by waving his briefcase. None stopped, and he moved away, perhaps to a bus stop. Walter wondered where he was going, then remembered that he didn't care.

"I hate him," he told Aymeric. "I *hate* him. I dream he is in danger. A patrol car drives up and the execution squad takes him away. I dream he is drinking coffee after dinner and far off in the night you can hear the patrol car, coming to get him."

Aymeric wondered what bound Walter to that particular dealer. There were other employers in Paris, just as dedicated to art.

"I hate art, too," said Walter. "Oh, I don't mean that I hate what you do.

That, at least, has some meaning—it lets people see how they imagine they live."

Aymeric's tongue rested on his lower lip as he considered this. Walter explained that he had to spend another eleven years working for Trout Face if he was to get the full benefit of a twenty-year pension fund. In eleven years, he would be forty-six. He hoped there was still enjoyment to be had at that age.

"When you are drawing retirement pay, I'll be working for a living," Aymeric said. He let his strong, elderly hands rest on the table—evidence, of a kind.

"At first, when I thought I could pull my funds out at any time, I used to give notice," Walter went on. "When I stopped giving notice, he turned mean. I dreamed last night that there was a bomb under the floor of the gallery. He nearly blew himself up digging it out. He was saved. He is always saved. He escapes, or the thing doesn't explode, or the chief of the execution squad changes his mind."

"Robert has a book about dreams," said Aymeric. "He can look it up. I want him to meet you."

About four weeks after this, Walter moved into two rooms, kitchen, and bathroom standing empty between Robert's quarters and his mother's. It was Robert who looked after the practical side of the household and to whom Walter paid a surprisingly hefty rent; but he was on a direct Métro line, and within reach of friendship, and, for the first time since he had left Bern to work in Paris, he felt close to France.

That spring Robert's mother had grown old. She could not always remember where she was, or the age of her two children. At night she roamed about, turning on lights, opening bedroom doors. (Walter, who felt no responsibility toward her, kept his locked.) She picked up curios and trinkets and left them anywhere. Once a month Robert and Aymeric traded back paperweights and snuffboxes.

One night she entered her son's bedroom at two in the morning, pulled open a drawer, and began throwing his shirts on the floor. She was packing to send him on a summer holiday. Halfway through (her son pretended to be asleep), she turned her mind to Aymeric. Aymeric woke up a few minutes later to find his aunt in bed beside him, with her finger in her mouth. He got up and spent the rest of the night in an armchair.

"Why don't you knock her out with pills?" Walter asked him.

"We can't do that. It might kill her."

What's the difference, said Walter's face. "Then shut her up in her own bedroom."

"She might not like that. By the way, here's your phone bill."

Walter was surprised at the abruptness of the deadlock. Aymeric did not so much change the subject as tear it up. Walter could not understand many things—the amount of his telephone bill, for instance. He did most of his calling from the gallery, dialing his parents in Bern with the warm feeling that he was putting one over on Trout Face. He had been astonished to learn that he was supposed to pay a monthly fee for using the elevator. Apparently, it was the custom of the house. Aymeric was turning out to be less of a new religion than Walter had expected. For one thing, he was seldom there. His old life moved on, in an unseen direction, and he did not offer to bring Walter along. He seemed idle yet at the same time busy. He hardly ever sat down without giving the impression that he was trying to get to his feet; barely entered a room without starting to edge his way out of it. Running his fingers through his pale, abundant hair, he said, "I've got an awful lot to do."

Reading in bed one night, Walter glanced up and had the eerie sight of a doorknob silently turning. "Let me in," Robert's mother called. Her voice was sweet and pitched to childhood. "The latch is caught, and I can't use both hands." Walter tied the sash of the Old England dressing gown his employer had given him one Christmas, when they were still getting along.

She had put on lipstick and eye shadow. "I'm taking my children to Mass," she said, "and I thought I'd just leave this with you." She opened her fist, clenched like a baby's, and offered Walter a round gold snuffbox with a cameo portrait on its lid. He set the box down on a marble-topped table and led her through a labyrinth of low-ceilinged rooms to Robert's bedroom door, where he left her. She went straight in, turning on an overhead light.

By morning, the box had drawn in the cold of the marble, but it became warm in Walter's hand. He and his employer were barely speaking; they often used sign language to show that something had to be moved or hung up or taken down. Walter seemed to be trying to play a guessing game until he opened his hand, as Robert's mother had done.

"Just something I picked up," he said, as if he had been combing secondhand junk stores and was no fool.

"Picked up where?" said his employer, appreciating the weight and feel of the gold. He changed his spectacles for a stronger pair, ran his thumb lightly and affectionately over the cameo. "Messalina," he said. "Look at those curls." He held the box at eye level, tipping it slightly, and said, "Glued on. An amateur job. Where did you say you got it?"

"I happened to pick it up."

"Well, you'd better put it back." A bright spot moved on his bald head as he leaned into the light. "Or, wait; leave it. I'll look at it again." He wrapped the box in a paper handkerchief and locked it up in his safe.

"I brought it just to show you," said Walter.

His employer motioned as if he were pushing a curtain aside with the back of his right hand. It meant, "Go away."

Robert was in charge of a small laboratory on the Rue de Vaugirard. He sat counting blood cells in a basement room. Walter imagined Robert pushing cells along the wire of an abacus, counting them off by ten. (He was gently discouraged from paying a visit. Robert explained there was no extra chair.) In the laboratory they drew and analyzed blood samples. Patients came in with their doctor's instructions, social-security number, often a thick file of medical history they tried to get Robert to read, and blood was taken from a vein in the crook of the arm. The specimen had to be drawn before breakfast; even a cup of coffee could spoil the result. Sometimes patients fainted and were late for appointments. Robert revived them with red wine.

Each morning, Robert put on a track suit and ran in the Luxembourg Gardens, adroitly slipping past runners whose training program had them going the other way. Many of the neighborhood shopkeepers ran. The greengrocer and the Spaniard from the hardware store signaled greetings with their eyes. It was not etiquette to stop and talk, and they had to save breath.

Walter admired Robert's thinness, his clean running shoes, his close-cropped gray hair. When he was not running, he seemed becalmed. He could sit listening to Walter as if he were drifting and there was nothing but Walter in sight. Walter told him about his employer, and the nice Dominican, and how both, in their different spheres, had proved disappointing. He refrained from mentioning Aymeric, whose friendship had so quickly fallen short of Walter's. He did not need to be psychoanalyzed, he said. No analysis could resolve his wish to attain the Church of Rome, or remove the Protestant martyrs who stood barring the way.

Sometimes Robert made a controlled and quiet movement while Walter was speaking, such as moving a clean silver ashtray an inch. No one was allowed to smoke in his rooms, but they were furnished with whatever one might require. Walter confessed that he admired everything French, even the ashtrays, and Robert nodded his head, as if to say that for an outsider it was bound to be so.

Robert got up at five and cleaned his rooms. (Aymeric had someone who came in twice a week.) He ran, then came back to change and eat a light breakfast before going to work. The first thing he did at five was to put on a record of Mozart's Concerto in C Major for Flute and Harp. He opened his windows; everyone except Walter-the-Swiss slept with them tight shut. The allegro moved in a spiral around the courtyard, climbed above the mended roof, and became thin and celestial.

Walter usually woke up in the middle of the andantino. It was much too early to get up. He turned on his side, away from the day. The mysterious sadness he felt on waking he had until now blamed on remoteness from God. Now he was beginning to suppose that people really must be made in His image, for their true face was just as concealed and their true where-abouts as obscure. A long, dangerous trapeze swoop of friendship had borne him from Aymeric's to Robert's side of the void, but all Robert had done was make room for Walter on the platform. He was accommodating, noth-ing more. Walter knew that he was too old at thirty-five for those giddy, hopeful swings. One of these days he was going to lose momentum and be left dangling, without a safety net.

He could hear music, a vacuum cleaner, and sparrows. The nice Do-minican had assured him that God would still be there when his analysis had run its course. From his employer he had learned that sadness was supposed to be borne with every outward sign of elegance. Walter had no idea what that was supposed to mean. It meant nothing.

By the rondo allegro, Robert's mother would begin shaking Aymeric awake. Aymeric guided her back to her own apartment and began to boil water and grind coffee for her breakfast. She always asked him what he was doing in her private quarters, and where he had put his wife. She owned a scratched record of "Luna Rossa" sung by Tino Rossi, to which she could listen twelve times running without losing interest. It was a record of the old, breakable kind, and Walter wondered why someone didn't crack it on the edge of a sink. He thought of Farinelli, the castrato who every evening for ten years had to sing the same four tunes to the King of Spain. Nothing had been written about the King's attendants—whether at the end of ten years there were any of them sane.

In his own kitchen, Aymeric brewed lime-flower tea. Later, an egg timer would let him know he was ready for coffee. If he drank coffee too soon, his digestive system became flooded with acid, which made him feel ill. Whenever Robert talked about redistributing the space, Aymeric would remark that he would be dead before long and they could do as they liked with his rooms. His roseate complexion concealed an ashen inner reality, he believed. Any qualified doctor looking at him saw at once that he was meant to be pale. He followed the tea with a bowl of bran (bought in a health-food store) soaked in warm water. After that, he was prepared for breakfast.

When Aymeric was paying a weekend visit to a new patron, in some remodeled village abattoir, he ate whatever they gave him. Artist-in-residence, he had no complaints. On the first evening, sipping a therapeutic Scotch (it lowered blood pressure and made arterial walls elastic), he would tactfully, gradually, drop his chain-link name: he was not only "A. Régis" but "Aymeric Something Something de Something de Saint-Régis." Like Picasso, he said, he had added his mother's maiden name. His hostess, rapidly changing her mind about dinner, would open a tin of foie gras and some bottled fruit from Fauchon's. On Monday, he would be driven home, brick-colored, his psychic image more ashen than ever. Rich food made him dream. He dreamed that someone had snubbed him. Sometimes it was the Archbishop of Paris, more often the Pope.

In a thick, thumbed volume he kept at his bedside, Robert looked up all their dreams. Employer, execution squad, patrol car, arrest combined to mean bright days ahead for someone especially dear to the dreamer. Animals denoted treachery. Walter, when not granted a vision of his employer's downfall, dreamed about dormice and moles. Treachery, Robert repeated, closing the book. The harmless creatures were messengers of betrayal.

Coming up from underground at the Chambre des Députés station (his personal stop at Solférino was closed for repair) one day, Walter looked around. On a soft May morning, this most peaceful stretch of Boulevard Saint-Germain might be the place where betrayal would strike. He crossed the road so that he would not have to walk in front of the Ministry of Defense, where men in uniform might make him say that his dreams about patrol cars were seditious. After a block or so he crossed back and made his way, with no further threats or dangers, to his place of work.

Immersion in art had kept him from spiritual knowledge. What he had mistaken for God's beckoning had been a dabbling in colors, sentiment cut loose and set afloat by the sight of a stained-glass window. Years before, when he was still training Walter, his employer had sent him to museums, with a list of things to examine and ponder. God is in art, Walter had decided; then, God *is* art. Today, he understood: Art is God's enemy. God hates art, the trifling rival creation.

Aymeric, when Walter announced his revelation, closed his eyes. Closing his eyes, he seemed to go deaf. It was odd, because last March, in the café, he had surely been listening. Robert listened. His blue gaze never wavered from a point just above Walter's head. When Walter had finished, Robert said that as a native Catholic he did not have to worry about God and art, or God and anything. All the worrying had already been done for him. Walter replied that no one had ever finished with worrying, and he offered to lend Robert books.

Robert returned Walter's books unread. He was showing the native Catholic resistance to religious history and theology. He did not want to learn more about St. Augustine and St. Thomas Aquinas than he had been told years before, in his private school. Having had the great good luck to be born into the only true faith, he saw no reason to rake the subject over. He did not go in for pounding his head on an open door. (Those were Robert's actual words.)

Robert's favorite topic was not God but the administration of the city of Paris, to which he felt bound by the ownership of so many square meters of urban space. He would look withdrawn and Gothic when anyone said, "The city does such a lot for the elderly now." The latest folderol was having old people taken up for helicopter rides, at taxpayers' expense. Robert's mother heard about the free rides while toying with a radio. Robert borrowed his sister's car and drove his mother to the helicopter field near the Porte de Versailles, where they found a group of pensioners waiting their turn. He was told he could not accompany his mother aloft: He was only forty-nine.

"I don't need anyone," his mother said. She unpinned her hat of beige straw and handed it to him. He watched strangers help her aboard, along with three other old women and a man with a limp. Robert raised his hands to his ears, hat and all, against the noise. His mother ascended rapidly. In less than twenty minutes she was back, making sure, before she would tell him about the trip, that he had not damaged her hat. The old gentleman had an arthritic leg, which he had stuck out at an awkward angle, inconveniencing one of the ladies. The pilot had spoken once, to say, "You can see Orléans." When the helicopter dipped, all the old hens screamed, she said. In her own mind, except now and then, she was about twenty-eight. She made Robert promise he would write a letter to the authorities, telling them there should be a cassette on board with a spoken travelogue and light music. She pulled on her hat, and in its lacy shadow resembled her old black-and-white snapshots, from the time before Robert.

One evening, Walter asked Aymeric if Monique de Montrepos, Robert's sister, had ever done anything, any sort of work. He met a drowsy, distant stare. Walter had blundered into a private terrain, but the fault was Aymeric's—never posted his limits. Aymeric told scandalous and demeaning stories about his relatives; Walter thought that half of them were invented, just for the purpose of teasing Walter and leading his speculations about the family astray. And yet Aymeric backed off a simple question, something like, "Does Robert's sister work?"

Finally Aymeric yielded and said Monique could infer character from handwriting. Walter's picture of a gypsy in a trailer remained imprinted even after Aymeric assured him that she worked with a team of psychotherapists, in the clean, glassy rooms of a modern office building in Montparnasse. Instead of dropping the matter, Walter wanted to know if she had undergone the proper kind of training; without that, he said, it was the same thing as analyzing handwriting by mail order.

Aymeric thought it over and said that her daughters were well educated and that one of them had traveled to Peru and got on quite well in Peruvian. This time, Walter had sense enough to keep quiet.

By June, Robert's mother had become too difficult for him to manage alone, and so his sister, Monique, who did not live with her husband, turned her apartment over to one of her daughters and moved in to help. Her name was added to the list of tenants hanging from the concierge's doorknob. Walter asked Aymeric if "Montrepos" was a Spanish name. Walter was thinking of the Empress Eugénie, born Montijo, he said.

One would need to consult her husband, Aymeric replied. Aymeric thought that Gaston de Montrepos had been born Dupuy or Dupont or Durand or Dumas. His childhood was spent in one of the weedier Paris suburbs, in a bungalow called Mon Repos. The name was painted, pale green on a rose background, on an enamel plaque just over the doorbell. Most family names had a simple, sentimental origin, if one cared to look them up. (Walter doubted that this applied to Obermauer.) Monique was a perfect specimen of the paratroop aristocracy, Aymeric went on. He was referring not to a regiment of grandees about to jump in formation but to a recognizable upper-class physical type, stumping along on unbreakable legs. Aymeric represented a more perishable race; the mother with the spun-out surname had left him bones that crumbled, teeth that dissolved in the gum, fine, unbiddable hair. (There was no doubt that Aymeric was haunted by the subject of hair. He combed his own with his fingers all the while he was speaking. The pale tint Walter had observed last March had since been deepened to the yellow of high summer.) Monique's husband had also carried a look of impermanence, in spite of his unassuming background. Monique's father had at first minded about the name. Some simple names he would not have objected to—Rothschild, for instance. He would have let his only daughter be buried as "Monique de Rothschild" any day. Even though. Yes, even though. Gaston had some sort of patronage appointment in the Senate, checking stationery supplies. He had spent most of his working life reading in the Luxembourg when it was fine, and eating coffee éclairs in Pons on rainy afternoons.

After Gaston Dumas or Dupuy had asked for Monique's hand and been turned down, and after Monique had tried to kill herself by taking port wine and four aspirin tablets, Gaston had come back with the news that he was called Montrepos. He showed them something scribbled in his own hand on a leaf torn off a Senate memo pad.

Well, said her father, if Monique wanted that.

Walter soon saw that it was not true about Monique's stumpy legs. For the rest, she was something like Aymeric—blooming, sound. Unlike him, she made free with friendly slaps and punches. Her pat on the back was enough to send one across the room; a knuckle ground into one's arm was a sign of great good spirits. She kissed easily—noisy peasant smacks on both cheeks. She kissed the concierge for bringing good tidings with the morning mail (a check from Gaston, now retired and living in Antibes); kissed Aymeric's cleaning woman for unpaid favors, such as washing her underclothes. The concierge and the cleaning woman were no more familiar with Monique than with Robert or Aymeric. If anything, they showed a faint, cautious reserve. Women who joke and embrace too easily are often quick to mount a high horse. Of Walter they took the barest notice, in spite of the size of his tips.

Monique soon overflowed two rooms and a third belonging to Robert. She shared her mother's bathroom and Robert's kitchen, striding through

Walter's apartment without asking if her perpetual trespassing suited him. In Robert's kitchen she left supper dishes to soak until morning. Robert could not stand that, and he washed and dried them before going to bed. Soon after he had fallen asleep, his mother would come in and ask him what time it was.

"He was her favorite," Monique told Walter. "Poor Robert. He's paying for it now. It's a bad idea to be a mother's favorite. It costs too much later on."

Entering without knocking, Monique let herself fall into one of Walter's cretonne-covered armchairs. She crossed her legs and asked if anyone ever bought the stuff one saw in windows of art galleries. Walter hardly knew how to begin his reply. It would have encouraged him if Monique had worn clothes that rustled. Rustle in women's dress, the settling of a skirt as a woman sat down, smoothing it with both hands, suggested feminine expectancy. Do explain, the taffeta hiss said. Tell about spies, interest rates, the Americans, Elizabeth Taylor. Is Hitler somewhere, still alive? But all that was the far past—his boyhood. He had grown adult in a world where clothes told one nothing. As soon as he thought of an answer, Monique shouted at him, "What? What did you say?" When she made a move, it was to knock something over. In Walter's sitting room she upset a cut-glass decanter, breaking the stopper; another time it was a mahogany plant stand and a Chinese pot holding a rare kind of fern. He offered sponge cakes and watched in distress as she swept the crumbs onto the floor.

"You've got the best space in the house," she said, looking around.

Soon after that remark, after giving himself time to think about it, Walter started locking all his doors.

Monique and Robert began by discussing Walter's apartment, and moved along to the edge of a quarrel.

"In any case," said Robert, "you should be under your husband's roof. That is the law. You should never have left him."

"Nobody left. It's been like this for years." Monique did not mention that she had come here to help; he knew that. He did not say that he was grateful.

"The law is the law," Robert said.

"Not anymore."

"It was a law when you got married," he said. "The husband is head of the family, he chooses the domicile, the wife is obliged to live under his roof, and he is obliged to receive her there. Under his roof."

"That's finished. If you still bothered to go to weddings, you'd know."

"It was still binding when you married him. He should be offering you a roof."

"He can't," said Monique, flinging out her arm and hitting Robert's record player, which resisted the shock. "It's about to cave in from the weight of the mortgage."

"Well," said Robert, forgetting Gaston for a moment, "he has a lease and he pays his rent regularly. And I am still paying for mending *my* roof." After a pause he said, "Aymeric says Gaston has a rich woman in Antibes."

"I was said to have been a rich young one."

"There is space for you here, always," said Robert instantly. There would be even more, later on. When the time came, they would knock all the flats into one and divide up the new space obtained.

"Look up 'harp' in your dream book," she said. "I dreamed I was giving a concert."

Robert usually got the dream book out on Sundays. The others saved up their weeknight dreams. Aymeric continued to dream he had been slighted. It was a dream of contradiction, and meant that in real life he was deeply appreciated. Robert's mother dreamed she was polishing furniture, which prophesied good luck with the opposite sex. Monique played tennis in a downpour: Her affections would be returned. Robert went to answer the doorbell—the sign of a happy surprise. They began each new week reassured and smiling—all but Walter. He had been dreaming about moles and dormice again.

As the summer weather settled in, and with Monique there to care for their mother, Robert began spending weekends out of town. He took the Dijon train at the Gare de Lyon and got off at Tonnerre. Monique found canceled railway tickets in wastepaper baskets. Walter had a sudden illumination: Robert must be attending weekend retreats in a monastery. That thin, quiet face belonged to a world of silence. Then, one day, Robert mentioned that there was a ballooning club in Tonnerre. Balloons were quieter than helicopters. Swaying in silence, between the clouds and the Burgundy Canal, he had been able to reach a decision. He did not say what about.

He accepted books from Walter to read in the train. They piled up at his bedside as he kept forgetting to give them back. Some he owned up to having lost. Walter could see them overhead, St. Augustine and St. Thomas Aquinas, drifting and swaying. He had no wish to ascend in a balloon. He had seen enough balloons in engravings. Virtually anything portrayed as art turned his stomach. There was hardly anything he could look at without feeling sick. In any case, Robert did not invite him.

Sometimes they watched television together. Aymeric had an old black-and-white set with only two channels. Monique had a Japanese portable, but the screen was too small for her mother to enjoy. They all liked Walter's set, which had a large screen and more buttons than there would ever be channels in France. One Saturday when Robert was not ballooning, he suddenly said he was getting married. It was just in the middle of *Dallas*. They were about a year behind Switzerland, and Monique had been asking Walter, whose occasional trips to Bern kept him up to date, to tell them how it would all turn out. Aymeric switched off the sound, upon which Robert's mother went straight to sleep.

Robert said only that his first marriage had been so happy that he could hardly wait to start over. The others sat staring at him. Walter had a crazy idea, which he kept to himself: Would Robert get married overhead in a balloon? "I am happy," Robert said, once or twice. Walter fixed his eyes on the bright, silent screen.

Monique prepared their mother's meals and carried them from Robert's kitchen on a tray. She had to make a wide detour around Walter's locked apartment. Everything was stone cold by the time the old lady had been coaxed to sit down. Their mother had her own kitchen, but she filled the oven with whatever came to hand when she was tidying—towels, a shoebox full of old Bic pens. Once, Monique found a bolster folded in two, looking like a bloated loaf. She disconnected the stove, so that her mother could not turn on the gas and start a fire.

Robert showed them a picture of his bride-to-be. She and Robert stood smiling, with arms linked, both wearing track suits. "Does she run as well as float?" said Aymeric. He turned the snapshot over and read a date and the initial B.

"Brigitte," said Robert.

"Brigitte what?"

"I don't want anyone driving to Tonnerre for long talks," said Robert. He did say that she taught French grammar to semi-delinquents in a technical high school. She was trying to obtain a transfer to a Paris suburb.

There could be no question of the capital itself: One had to know someone, and there was a waiting list ten years long.

Monique's arrival was followed closely by a new shock from the administrative authorities of Paris: a telephone number old people could call in the summertime, free of charge, in case their families were away and they felt lonely. Robert's mother dialed the number on Aymeric's phone. The woman at the other end—young, from the sound of her—seemed surprised to hear that Robert's mother lived with a son, a daughter, and a nephew, all attentive; had the use of a large television set with plenty of buttons and dials; and still suffered from feelings of neglect and despair. She was afraid of dying alone in the dark. All night long, she tried to stay on her feet.

The young voice reminded her about old people who had absolutely no one, who lived at the top of six steep flights of stairs, who did not dare go down to buy a packet of macaroni for fear of the long climb back. Robert's mother replied that the lives of such people were at the next-to-final stage of hopelessness and terror. Her own meals were brought to her on a tray. She was not claiming more for her sentiments than blind panic.

Aymeric took the telephone out of her hand, said a few words into it, and hung up. His aunt gave him her sweet, steady smile before remarking, "Your poor mother, Aymeric, was nothing much to look at."

Walter, trying to find a place to go for his summer holiday where there would be no reminders of art, fell back on Switzerland and his mother and father. He scrubbed and vacuumed his rooms and put plastic dust sheets over the furniture. Just before calling for a taxi to take him to the airport, he asked Robert if he could have a word with him. He was more than usually nervous, and kept flexing his hands. Terrible things had been said at the gallery that day; Walter had threatened his employer with the police. Robert could not understand the story—something incoherent to do with the office safe. He removed a bundle of clothes fresh from the launderette (he did his own ironing) and invited Walter to sit down. Walter wanted to know if the imminent change in Robert's life and Monique's constant hints about the best space in the house meant that Walter's apartment was coveted. "Coveted" was a heavy word, but Robert finally answered, "You've got your lease."

"According to the law," said Walter, more and more fussed, "you can throw me out if you can prove you need the space." Robert sat quietly, and seemed to be waiting for something else. "I've got to be sure I have a home

to come back to—a home I can keep for a long time. This time I really intend to give notice. I don't care about the pension. He's making me an accomplice in crime. I'll stay just until he can train a replacement for me. If he
sees I am worried about something else as well, it will give him the upper
hand. And then, I'm like you and Aymeric. I feel as if my own family had
been living here forever." Robert at this looked at him with a terrible po-
liteness. Walter rushed on, mentioning a matter that other tenants, he
thought, would have brought up first. Since moving in, he had painted the
kitchen, paved the bathroom with imported tiles, and hung custom-made
curtains on rods designed to fit the windows. All this, he said, constituted
an embellishment of space.

"Your vacation will do you good," said Robert.

Walter gave Robert his house keys and said he hoped Monique would
feel free to use his apartment as a passageway while he was gone. Handing
them over, he was reminded of another gesture—his hand, outstretched,
opening to reveal the snuffbox.

Their mother had begun polishing furniture, as in some of her dreams. A
table in Walter's sitting room was like a pond. Everything else was dusty.
The plastic sheets lay like crumpled parachutes in a corner. On Aymeric's
birthday, late in August, he and Robert and Monique sat at the polished
table eating pastries out of a box. Robert picked out a few of the kind his
mother liked and put them aside for her on a plate. They could hear her, in
Walter's bedroom, telling City Hall that they had disconnected her stove.

Perhaps because there was an empty chair, Robert suddenly said that
Brigitte was immensely sociable and liked to entertain. She played first-class
bridge. She had somehow managed to obtain a transfer to Paris after all.
They would be getting married in October.

"How did she do it?" Aymeric asked.

"She knows someone."

They fell silent, admiring the empty chair.

"Who wants the last strawberry tart?" said Monique. When no one answered, she cut it in three.

"We will have to rearrange the space," said Robert. He traced lines with
his finger on the polished table and, with the palm of his hand, wiped something out.

Aymeric said, "Try to find out what she did with that snuffbox. I wanted
to give it to you as a wedding present."

"I'll look again in the oven," Monique said.

"Ask her carefully," said Aymeric. "Don't frighten her. Sometimes she remembers."

Robert went on tracing invisible lines.

Walter came back in September to find his kitchen under occupation, full of rusted sieves and food mills and old graters. On the stove was a saucepan of strained soup for the old woman's supper; a bowl of pureed apricots stood uncovered in the sink. He removed everything to the old woman's kitchen.

I was brought up so soundly, he said to himself. He had respected his parents; now he admired them. At home, nothing had made him feel worried or tense, and he hadn't minded his father's habit of reading the newspaper aloud while Walter tried to watch television. When his father answered the telephone, his mother called, "What do they want?" from the kitchen. His father always repeated everything the caller said, so that his mother would not miss a word of the conversation. There were no secrets, no mysteries. What Walter saw of his parents was probably all there was.

After cleaning his rooms and unpacking his suitcase, Walter called on Robert. He had meant to ask how they had spent their holidays, if in spite of the old lady they had managed to get away, but instead he found himself telling about a remarkable dream he'd had in Switzerland: A large badger had burst into the gallery and taken Walter's employer hostage. Trout Face had said, "You're not getting away with this. I'm not having anybody running around here with automatic weapons." It was not a nightmare, said Walter. He had seen himself, aloof and nonchalant, enjoying the incident.

Robert said he would look it up. That night he made a neat stack of the books Walter had lent him—all that he could still find—and left it outside his locked front door. He wrote on the back of a page torn off a calendar, "Dream of badger taking man hostage means a change of residence, for which the dreamer should be prepared. R." He rewrote this several times, changing a word here and there. In the morning, after starting the record and opening all the windows, he sat down and read his message again. He kept running his finger over the note, as he had traced new boundaries on Walter's table, and seemed to be wondering if there was any point in trying to say the same thing some other way.

KINGDOM COME

After having spent twenty-four years in the Republic of Saltnatek, where he established the first modern university, recorded the vocabulary and structure of the Saltnatek tongue, and discovered in a remote village an allophylian language unknown except to its speakers, Dr. Domini Missierna returned to Europe to find that nobody cared. Saltnatek was neither lush nor rich nor seductive, nor poor enough to arouse international pity. The university survived on grants left over from the defense budget, and even Missierna had to admit he had not attracted teachers of the first order. He had wasted his vitality chasing money for salaries and equipment, up to the day when an ungrateful administration dismissed him and the latest revolutionary council, thanking him for nothing, put him on a plane.

He was still in mourning for his Saltnatek years. It grieved him to hear, at a linguistic congress in Helsinki, younger colleagues in the most offhand way confusing Saltnatek with Malta and Madagascar. Saltnatek consisted of an archipelago of naked islands, one of which had been a port of call for cruise ships early in the century. Most tourists had not even bothered to go ashore: There was nothing to admire except straight rows of undecorated houses, and nothing to buy except shells of giant sea snails, on which the nation's artists had carved in a spiral pattern WHEN THIS YOU SEE, REMEMBER ME. The motto was thought to have been copied from the lid of a snuffbox found in the pocket of a drowned naval officer during the Napoleonic Wars. (Missierna supposed the box was probably a lucky piece, even though it had not turned out to be providential. He kept this to himself; he was not in the business of offering speculations.) Even that trifling commerce had come to a stop when, just after the First World War, a society for the protection of sea snails urged a boycott of mutilated shells—a prohibition that caused Saltnatek great bewilderment and economic distress.

In Helsinki, his heart galloping, his voice trembling sometimes, Missierna disclosed the existence of a complex and living language, spoken by an inbred population that produced children of much thievishness, cunning, and blank beauty. He stood on a stage too large for him, fuzzily lighted, in an auditorium the size of a concert hall. Nine men and three women sat, singly, in the first fifteen rows. They were still and unresponsive, and as soon as he had finished reading they got up in the same quiet way and filed out. There were no questions: He had brought back to Europe one more system, and no one knew how to make the old ones work.

If he was disappointed, it was in part because he was no longer young, and it was almost too late for his competence, perhaps his genius, to receive the rewards it deserved. Although he was far less vain than any of the substandard teachers he had interviewed and hired for Saltnatek, he still hoped that at least one conclusion might be named for him, so that his grandchildren, coming across his name in a textbook, could say, "So this is what he was like—modest, creative." But all that anyone said at the Helsinki congress was "You have demonstrated nothing that cannot be shown through Hungarian."

During the years when he was so obsessively occupied, Europe had grown small, become depleted, as bald in spirit as Saltnatek's sandy and stony islands. The doubting voices were thin and metallic. No one was listening. His colleagues said, "One step after the other," and "One at a time." They trod upon discarded rules of address, raked the ground to find shreds of sense and reason. Salvation was in the dust or it was nowhere. Even if he were to reveal twenty new and orderly and poetic methods of creating order by means of words, he would be told, "We had better deal with matters underfoot, closer to home."

He was a divorced parent, which meant he had children and grandchildren but no place in particular to go. Saltnatek had been like a child, and he had stayed with it longer than with any other, had seen it into maturity, and it had used and rejected him, as children do, as it is their right. It was not in his nature to put out emotional ultimatums. In the past, it could have been his business—he should have made it his business—to observe the patterns of exchange among his real children, even if the information, tabulated, had left him depressed and frightened. He could have taken them as an independent republic and applied for entry. Even now, he considered inviting himself for next Christmas. He would surely obtain the limited visa no one dares refuse a homeless old man, a distinguished relative, not poor, needing only consideration—notice taken of his deafness, his stiff shoulder, his need to get up and eat breakfast at five o'clock, his allergies to butter and white wine.

What to take on the Christmas exploration? The first rule of excursions into uncankered societies is: Don't bring presents. Not unless one wants to face charges of corruption. But then, like any scholar fending off a critic, he could justify the gifts, telling himself that another visitor might taint the society in a manner deadlier still, whereas he, Missierna, sat lightly. He had been a featherweight on his children; he had scarcely gone near them. A present from parent to child surely reinforces a natural tie. When they were young, he used to bring home one wristwatch and make them draw lots. For professional trips he had packed radio batteries; his travels had taught him that new republics run out of them soon. He had taken ski boots wherever there were snowy mountains, except in places where snow was sacred. He had always shown a sense of patience, a good-tempered approach to time, as he cut through the thorn patch of transit visas, six-month-residence permits, five-year research grants. To enter one's own family, he supposed, one needed to fill out forms. All he would have to understand was the slant of the questions.

From his hotel room in Helsinki, Missierna saw the Baltic and gulls skimming over the whitecaps. At night ghosts floated along the horizon. He took it for granted they were ghosts—having lived among people who saw a great many—and not simply the white shadows of summer.

An insurance actuarial study gave him six more years to live if he went on as he was, eight if he gave up smoking, nine and a half if he adopted an optimistic outlook. What about white magic? What about trying to add a few more summer nights by means of poems and incantations? Why not appeal to a saint—a saint so obscure that the direct line from Missierna's mind to the saint's memory of a mind would be clean, without the clutter of other, alien voices? He could begin by repeating his own name, before deciding what conjury should come next.

His grandchildren surely lived on magic. There was fresh daylight every morning. Clothes dropped on the floor were found clean and folded. A gray-haired man at the congress, who said he had once been Missierna's student, had told him that very soon, by law, children were going to be asked to acknowledge their parents, instead of the other way. There would be some cold refusals, Missierna supposed, and some selfish ones, and some inspired by embarrassment. There might be cases of simple antipathy, too. Most children would probably accept their parents, out of pity, or to keep a strong thread of filiation, or to claim an inheritance, or to conform to an astral pattern. Some, to avoid the sight of adult tears. A few might show the blind trust that parents pray for. The new insecurity, the terror of being cast off, was already causing adults to adopt the extreme conservatism that is usually characteristic of the very young. A mistrust of novelty and change surely accounted for Missierna's sparse audience, the silence in the auditorium, the unwillingness to know something more.

In Saltnatek, toward the end, he had heard some of the cool remarks that said, plainly, he was not a father; heard them from students he had taught, reared, nurtured, and who now were ready to send him packing: "You can't say we didn't warn you." "I tried to tell you that someday you'd be sorry." "I'm sorry if you're sorry. But that's all I have to be sorry about." From his own children there had been monitory signals, too, which he had mistaken for pertness: "Can't you ask a waitress for a cup of coffee without telling your life story?" "Other parents don't take the wrong bus." "Please don't get up and dance. It makes you look so silly." Their eyes were clean, pure, but bedeviled by unease and mortification. The eyes of children are the eyes of petit bourgeois, he decided. They can't help it; they are born wondering if their parents are worth what the bus driver thinks.

For twenty-four years the eyes of Saltnatek had appraised him, and had then turned away. He had become to himself large and awkward—a parent without authority, dispossessed, left to stumble around in an airport, as if he were sick or drunk.

He could still recite by rote the first test sentences he had used for his research:

"Now that you mention it, I see what you mean."

"There is no law against it, is there?"

"I am not comfortable, but I hope to be comfortable soon."

"Anyone may write to him. He answers all letters."

"Look it up. You will see that I was right all along."

At the outset, in Saltnatek, he had asked for a governmental ruling to put a clamp on the language: The vocabulary must not grow during the period of his field work. Expansion would confuse the word count. They had not been sure what to call him. Some had said "Father," which was close in sound to his name, as they pronounced it. His own children had for a while avoided saying even "you," dropping from their greetings such sentences as "What did you bring us?" and "Are you staying long?" They were like long-term patients in a hospital, or rebels interned. Their expression, at once careful and distant, seemed to be telling him, "If you intend to keep coming and going, then at least bring us something we need."

His children were not proud of him. It was his own fault; he had not told them enough. Perhaps he seemed old, but he appeared young to himself. In the shaving mirror he saw the young man he had been at university. In his dreams, even his bad dreams, he was never more than twenty-one.

Saltnatek was his last adventure. He would turn to his true children, whether they welcomed the old explorer or not. Or he could find something else to do—something tranquil; he could watch Europe as it declined and sank, with its pettiness and faded cruelty, its crabbed richness and sentimentality. Something might be discovered out of shabbiness—some measure taken of the past and the present, now that they were ground and trampled to the same shape and size. But what if he had lost his mixture of duty and curiosity, his professional humility, his ruthlessness? In that case, he could start but he would never finish.

At Helsinki he heard young colleagues describing republics they had barely seen. They seemed to have been drawn here and there for casual, private reasons. He did not like the reasons, and he regretted having mentioned, in his lecture, sibling incest in that village in Saltnatek. He had been careful to admit he had relied on folklore and legends, and would never know what went on when the children tore all their clothes off. Repeated actions are religious, but with children one can never decide if they are heathen, atheistic, agnostic, pantheistic, animist; if there remains a vestige of a ritual, a rattled-off prayer.

Say that he used his grandchildren as a little-known country: He would need to scour their language for information. What did they say when they thought "infinity"? In Saltnatek, in the village, they had offered him simple images—a light flickering, a fire that could not be doused, a sun that rose and set in long cycles, a bright night. Everything and nothing.

Perhaps they were right, and only the present moment exists, he thought. How they view endlessness is their own business. But if I start minding my own business, he said to himself, I have no more reason to be.

Was there any cause to feel uneasy about the present moment in Europe? What was wrong with it? There was no quarrel between Wales and Turkey.

Italy and Schleswig-Holstein were not at war. It was years since some part of the population, running away, had dug up and carried off its dead. It seemed to him now that his life's labor—the digging out, the coaxing and bribing to arrive at secret meanings—amounted to exhumation and flight.

The village children had wanted white crash helmets and motorcycles. He had given them helmets but said he could not bring in the bikes, which were dangerous, which would make the ancient windows rattle and the babies cry. Besides, there were no roads. Some of the village women turned the helmets into flowerpots, but the helmets were airtight, there was no drainage, the plants died. The helmets would never rot. Only the maimed giant snails, thrown back into the ocean, could decay. Missierna, the day he resolved that helmets do not die, and so have no hope of resurrection, wondered whether the time had come to stop thinking.

He should not have mentioned in his lecture that the village children were of blank but unusual beauty, that they wanted steep new roads and motorcycles. It might induce plodding, leaden, salacious scholars to travel there and seduce them, and to start one more dull and clumsy race.

All this he thought late at night in his hotel room and in the daytime as he walked the streets of Helsinki. He visited the Saltnatek consulate, because he was curiously forlorn, like a parent prevented by court order from having any more say in his children's fate and education. He entered a bookstore said to be the largest in Europe, and a department store that seemed to be its most expensive. On a street corner he bought chocolate ice cream in a plastic cone. He did not return the cone, as he was supposed to. He believed he had paid for it. He crossed a busy road, saying to himself, The cone is mine. I'm not giving it up.

So—he had become grasping. This slight, new, interesting evaluation occupied his mind for some minutes. Why keep the cone? It would be thrown away even in Saltnatek, even in the poorest, meanest dwelling. Children in their collective vision now wanted buses without drivers, planes without pilots, lessons without teachers. Wanted to come into the world knowing how to write and count, or never to know—it was all the same conundrum. Or to know only a little about everything. He saw helmets on a window ledge, ferns growing out of them. By now, the women had been taught to use pebbles for drainage. Saw children tearing uphill on the motorcycles other visitors had brought. Imagining this, or believing he could see it—the two were identical—he understood that he would never go back, even if they would have him. He would live out his six actuarial years on his own half continent. He would imagine, or think he could see, its pillars rotting, seaweed swirling round the foundations. He would breathe the used-up air that stank of dead sea life. He might have existed a few days past his six more years in the clearer air of Saltnatek. Then? Have fallen dead at the feet of the vacant, thievish children, heard for a second longer than life allows the cadence of their laughter when they mocked him—the decaying, inquisitive old stranger, still trying to trick them into giving away their word for Kingdom Come.

FORAIN

∾❀⌁

*A*bout an hour before the funeral service for Adam Tremski, snow mixed with rain began to fall, and by the time the first of the mourners arrived the stone steps of the church were dangerously wet. Blaise Forain, Tremski's French publisher, now his literary executor, was not surprised when, later, an elderly woman slipped and fell and had to be carried by ambulance to the Hôtel-Dieu hospital. Forain, in an attempt to promote Cartesian order over Slavic frenzy, sent for the ambulance, then found himself obliged to accompany the patient to the emergency section and fork over a deposit. The old lady had no social security.

Taken together, façade and steps formed an escarpment—looming, abrupt, above all unfamiliar. The friends of Tremski's last years had been Polish, Jewish, a few French. Of the French, only Forain was used to a variety of last rites. He was expected to attend the funerals not only of his authors but of their wives. He knew all the Polish churches of Paris, the Hungarian mission, the synagogues on the Rue Copernic and the Rue de la Victoire, and the mock chapel of the crematorium at Père Lachaise cemetery. For nonbelievers a few words at the graveside sufficed. Their friends said, by way of a greeting, "Another one gone." However, no one they knew ever had been buried from this particular church. The parish was said to be the oldest in the city, yet the edifice built on the ancient site looked forbidding and cold. Tremski for some forty years had occupied the same walk-up flat on the fringe of Montparnasse. What was he doing over here, on the wrong side of the Seine?

Four months before this, Forain had been present for the last blessing of Barbara, Tremski's wife, at the Polish church on the Rue Saint-Honoré.

The church, a chapel really, was round in shape, with no fixed pews—just rows of chairs pushed together. The dome was a mistake—too imposing for the squat structure—but it had stood for centuries, and only the very nervous could consider it a threat. Here, Forain had noticed, tears came easily, not only for the lost friend but for all the broken ties and old, unwilling journeys. The tears of strangers around him, that is; grief, when it reached him, was pale and dry. He was thirty-eight, divorced, had a daughter of twelve who lived in Nice with her mother and the mother's lover. Only one or two of Forain's friends had ever met the girl. Most people, when told, found it hard to believe he had ever been married. The service for Tremski's wife had been disrupted by the late entrance of *her* daughter—child of her first husband—who had made a show of arriving late, kneeling alone in the aisle, kissing the velvet pall over the coffin, and noisily marching out. Halina was her name. She had straight, graying hair and a cross face with small features. Forain knew that some of the older mourners could remember her as a pretty, unsmiling, not too clever child. A few perhaps thought Tremski was her father and wondered if he had been unkind to his wife. Tremski, sitting with his head bowed, may not have noticed. At any rate, he had never mentioned anything.

Tremski was Jewish. His wife had been born a Catholic, though no one was certain what had come next. To be blunt, was she in or out? The fact was that she had lived in adultery—if one wanted to be specific—with Tremski until her husband had obliged the pair by dying. There had been no question of a divorce; probably she had never asked for one. For his wedding to Barbara, Tremski had bought a dark blue suit at a good place, Creed or Lanvin Hommes, which he had on at her funeral, and in which he would be buried. He had never owned another, had shambled around Paris looking as though he slept under restaurant tables, on a bed of cigarette ashes and crumbs. It would have taken a team of devoted women, not just one wife, to keep him spruce.

Forain knew only from hearsay about the wedding ceremony in one of the town halls of Paris (Tremski was still untranslated then, had a job in a bookstore near the Jardin des Plantes, had paid back the advance for the dark blue suit over eleven months)—the names signed in a register, the daughter's refusal to attend, the wine drunk with friends in a café on the Avenue du Maine. It was a cheerless place, but Tremski knew the owner. He had talked of throwing a party but never got round to it; his flat was too small. Any day now he would move to larger quarters and invite two hundred and fifty intimate friends to a banquet. In the meantime, he stuck to his rented flat, a standard émigré dwelling of the 1950s, almost a period piece now: two rooms on a court, windowless kitchen, splintered floors, unheatable bathroom, no elevator, intimidating landlord—a figure central to his comic anecdotes and private worries. What did his wife think? Nobody knew, though if he had sent two hundred and fifty invitations she would undoubtedly have started to borrow two hundred and fifty glasses and plates. Even after Tremski could afford to move, he remained anchored to his seedy rooms: There were all those books, and the boxes filled with unanswered mail, and the important documents he would not let anyone file. Snapshots and group portraits of novelists and poets, wearing the clothes and haircuts of the fifties and sixties, took up much of a wall. A new desire to sort out the past, put its artifacts in order, had occupied Tremski's conversation on his wedding day. His friends had soon grown bored, although his wife seemed to be listening. Tremski, married at last, was off on an oblique course, preaching the need for discipline and a thought-out future. It didn't last.

At Forain's first meeting with Barbara, they drank harsh tea from mismatched cups and appraised each other in the gray light that filtered in from the court. She asked him, gently, about his fitness to translate and publish Tremski—then still at the bookstore, selling wartime memoirs and paperbacks and addressing parcels. Did Forain have close ties with the Nobel Prize committee? How many of his authors had received important awards, gone on to international fame? She was warm and friendly and made him think of a large buttercup. He was about the age of her daughter, Halina; so Barbara said. He felt paternal, wise, rid of mistaken ideals. He would become Tremski's guide and father. He thought, This is the sort of woman I should have married—although most probably he should never have married anyone.

Only a few of the mourners mounting the treacherous steps can have had a thought to spare for Tremski's private affairs. His wife's flight from a brave and decent husband, dragging by the hand a child of three, belonged to the folklore, not the history, of mid-century emigration. The chronicle of two generations, displaced and dispossessed, had come to a stop. The evaluation could begin; had already started. Scholars who looked dismayingly youthful, speaking the same language, but with a new, jarring vocabulary, were trekking to Western capitals—taping reminiscences, copying old letters.

History turned out to be a plodding science. What most émigrés settled for now was the haphazard accuracy of a memory like Tremski's. In the end it was always a poem that ran through the mind—not a string of dates.

Some may have wondered why Tremski was entitled to a Christian service; or, to apply another kind of reasoning, why it had been thrust upon him. Given his shifting views on eternity and the afterlife, a simple get-together might have done, with remarks from admirers, a poem or two read aloud, a priest wearing a turtleneck sweater, or a young rabbi with a literary bent. Or one of each, offering prayers and tributes in turn. Tremski had nothing against prayers. He had spent half his life inventing them.

As it turned out, the steep church was not as severe as it looked from the street. It was in the hands of a small charismatic order, perhaps full of high spirits but by no means schismatic. No one had bothered to ask if Tremski was a true convert or just a writer who sometimes sounded like one. His sole relative was his stepdaughter. She had made an arrangement that suited her: She lived nearby, in a street until recently classed as a slum, now renovated and highly prized. Between her seventeenth-century flat and the venerable site was a large, comfortable, cluttered department store, where, over the years, Tremski's friends had bought their pots of paint and rollers, their sturdy plates and cups, their burglarproof door locks, their long-lasting cardigan sweaters. The store was more familiar than the church. The stepdaughter was a stranger.

She was also Tremski's heir and she did not understand Forain's role, taking executor to mean an honorary function, godfather to the dead. She had told Forain that Tremski had destroyed her father and blighted her childhood. He had enslaved her mother, spoken loud Polish in restaurants, had tried to keep Halina from achieving a French social identity. Made responsible, by his astonishing will, for organizing a suitable funeral, she had chosen a French send-off, to be followed by burial in a Polish cemetery outside Paris. Because of the weather and because there was a shortage of cars, friends were excused from attending the burial. Most of them were thankful: More than one fatal cold had been brought on by standing in the icy mud of a graveyard. When she had complained she was doing her best, that Tremski had never said what he wanted, she was probably speaking the truth. He could claim one thing and its opposite in the same sentence. Only God could keep track. If today's rite was a cosmic error, Forain decided, it was up to Him to erase Tremski's name from the ledger and enter it in the proper column. If He cared.

The mourners climbed the church steps slowly. Some were helped by younger relatives, who had taken time off from work. A few had migrated to high-rise apartments in the outer suburbs, to deeper loneliness but cheaper rents. They had set out early, as if they still believed no day could start without them, and after a long journey underground and a difficult change of direction had emerged from the Hôtel de Ville Métro station. They held their umbrellas at a slant, as if countering some force of nature arriving head-on. Actually, there was not the least stir in the air, although strong winds and sleet were forecast. The snow and rain came down in thin soft strings, clung to fur or woolen hats, and became a meager amount of slush underfoot.

Forain was just inside the doors, accepting murmured sympathy and handshakes. He was not usurping a family role but trying to make up for the absence of Halina. Perhaps she would stride in late, as at her mother's funeral, driving home some private grudge. He had on a long cashmere overcoat, the only black garment he owned. A friend had left it to him. More exactly, the friend, aware that he was to die very soon, had told Forain to collect it at the tailor's. It had been fitted, finished, paid for, never worn. Forain knew there was a mean joke abroad about his wearing dead men's clothes. It also applied to his professional life: He was supposed to have said he preferred the backlist of any dead writer to the stress and tension of trying to deal with a live one.

His hair and shoes felt damp. The hand he gave to be shaken must have chilled all those it touched. He was squarely in the path of one of those church drafts that become gales anywhere close to a door. He wondered if Halina had been put off coming because of some firm remarks of his, the day before (he had defended Tremski against the charge of shouting in restaurants), or even had decided it was undignified to pretend she cared for a second how Tremski was dispatched; but at the last minute she turned up, with her French husband—a reporter of French political affairs on a weekly—and a daughter of fourteen in jacket and jeans. These two had not been able to read a word of Tremski's until Forain had published a novel in translation about six years before. Tremski believed they had never looked at it—to be fair, the girl was only eight at the time—or any of the books that had followed; although the girl clipped and saved reviews. It was remarkable, Tremski had said, the way literate people, reasonably well traveled and educated, comfortably off, could live adequate lives without wanting to know what had gone before or happened elsewhere. Even the husband, the political journalist, was like that: A few names, a date looked up, a notion of geography satisfied him.

Forain could tell Tremski minded. He had wanted Halina to think well of him at least on one count, his life's work. She was the daughter of a former Army officer who had died—like Barbara, like Tremski—in a foreign city. She considered herself, no less than her father, the victim of a selfish adventure. She also believed she was made of better stuff than Tremski, by descent and status, and that was harder to take. In Tremski's own view, comparisons were not up for debate.

For the moment, the three were behaving well. It was as much as Forain expected from anybody. He had given up measuring social conduct, except where it ran its course in fiction. His firm made a specialty of translating and publishing work from Eastern and Central Europe; it kept him at a remove. Halina seemed tamed now, even thanked him for standing in and welcoming all those strangers. She had a story to explain why she was late, but it was far-fetched, and Forain forgot it immediately. The delay most likely had been caused by a knockdown argument over the jacket and jeans. Halina was a cold skirmisher, narrow in scope but heavily principled. She wore a fur-and-leather coat, a pale gray hat with a brim, and a scarf—authentic Hermès? Taiwan fake? Forain could have told by rubbing the silk between his fingers, but it was a wild idea, and he kept his distance.

The girl had about her a look of Barbara: For that reason, no other, Forain found her appealing. Blaise ought to sit with the family, she said—using his first name, the way young people did now. A front pew had been kept just for the three of them. There was plenty of room. Forain thought that Halina might begin to wrangle, in whispers, within earshot (so to speak) of the dead. He said yes, which was easier than to refuse, and decided no. He left them at the door, greeting stragglers, and found a place at the end of a pew halfway down the aisle. If Halina mentioned anything, later, he would say he had been afraid he might have to leave before the end. She walked by without noticing and, once settled, did not look around.

The pale hat had belonged to Halina's mother. Forain was sure he remembered it. When his wife died, Tremski had let Halina and her husband ransack the flat. Halina made several trips while the husband waited downstairs. He had come up only to help carry a crate of papers belonging to Tremski. It contained, among other documents, some of them rubbish, a number of manuscripts not quite complete. Since Barbara's funeral Tremski had not bothered to shave or even put his teeth in. He sat in the room she had used, wearing a dressing gown torn at the elbows. Her wardrobe stood empty, the door wide, just a few hangers inside. He clutched Forain by the sleeve and said that Halina had taken some things of his away. As soon as she realized her error she would bring them back.

Forain would have preferred to cross the Seine on horseback, lashing at anyone who resembled Halina or her husband, but he had driven to her street by taxi, past the old, reassuring, unchanging department store. No warning, no telephone call: He walked up a curving stone staircase, newly sandblasted and scrubbed, and pressed the doorbell on a continued note until someone came running.

She let him in, just so far. "Adam can't be trusted to look after his own affairs," she said. "He was always careless and dirty, but now the place smells of dirt. Did you look at the kitchen table? He must keep eating from the same plate. As for my mother's letters, if that's what you're after, he had already started to tear them up."

"Did you save any?"

"They belong to me."

How like a ferret she looked, just then; and she was the child of such handsome parents. A studio portrait of her father, the Polish officer, taken in London, in civilian clothes, smoking a long cigarette, stood on a table in the entrance hall. (Forain was admitted no farther.) Forain took in the likeness of the man who had fought a war for nothing. Barbara had deserted that composed, distinguished, somewhat careful face for Tremski. She must have forced Tremski's hand, arrived on his doorstep, bag, baggage, and child. He had never come to a resolution about anything in his life.

Forain had retrieved every scrap of paper, of course—all but the letters. Fired by a mixture of duty and self-interest, he was unbeatable. Halina had nothing on her side but a desire to reclaim her mother, remove the Tremski influence, return her—if only her shoes and blouses and skirts—to the patient and defeated man with his frozen cigarette. Her entitlement seemed to include a portion of Tremski, too; but she had resented him, which weakened her grasp. Replaying every move, Forain saw how strong her case might have been if she had acknowledged Tremski as her mother's choice. Denying it, she became—almost became; Forain stopped her in time—the defendant in a cheap sort of litigation.

Tremski's friends sat with their shoes in puddles. They kept their gloves on and pulled their knitted scarves tight. Some had spent all these years in

France without social security or health insurance, either for want of means or because they had never found their feet in the right sort of employment. Possibly they believed that a long life was in itself full payment for a safe old age. Should the end turn out to be costly and prolonged, then, please, allow us to dream and float in the thickest, deepest darkness, unaware of the inconvenience and clerical work we may cause. So, Forain guessed, ran their prayers.

Funerals came along in close ranks now, especially in bronchial winters. One of Forain's earliest recollections was the Mass in Latin, but he could not say he missed it: He associated Latin with early-morning hunger, and sitting still. The charismatic movement seemed to have replaced incomprehension and mystery with theatricals. He observed the five priests in full regalia sitting to the right of the altar. One had a bad cold and kept taking a handkerchief from his sleeve. Another more than once glanced at his watch. A choir, concealed or on tape, sang "Jesu, bleibet meine Freude," after which a smooth trained voice began to recite the Twenty-fifth Psalm. The voice seemed to emanate from Tremski's coffin but was too perfectly French to be his. In the middle of Verse 7, just after "Remember not the sins of my youth," the speaker wavered and broke off. A man seated in front of Forain got up and walked down the aisle, in a solemn and ponderous way. The coffin was on a trestle, draped in purple and white, heaped with roses, tulips, and chrysanthemums. He edged past it, picked up a black box lying on the ground, and pressed two clicking buttons. "Jesu" started up, from the beginning. Returning, the stranger gave Forain an angry stare, as if he had created the mishap.

Forain knew that some of Tremski's friends thought he was unreliable. He had a reputation for not paying authors their due. There were writers who complained they had never received the price of a postage stamp; they could not make sense of his elegant handwritten statements. Actually, Tremski had been the exception. Forain had arranged his foreign rights, when they began to occur, on a half-and-half basis. Tremski thought of money as a useful substance that covered rent and cigarettes. His wife didn't see it that way. Her forefinger at the end of a column of figures, her quiet, seductive voice saying, "Blaise, what's this?" called for a thought-out answer.

She had never bothered to visit Forain's office, but made him take her to tea at Angelina's, on the Rue de Rivoli. After her strawberry tart had been eaten and the plate removed, she would bring out of her handbag the folded, annotated account. Outdone, outclassed, slipping the tearoom check into his wallet to be dissolved in general expenses, he would look around and obtain at least one satisfaction: She was still the best-looking woman in sight, of any age. He had not been tripped up by someone of inferior appearance and quality. The more he felt harassed by larger issues, the more he made much of small compensations. He ran his business with a staff of loyal, worn-out women, connected to him by a belief in what he was doing, or some lapsed personal tie, or because it was too late and they had nowhere to go. At eight o'clock this morning, the day of the funeral, his staunch Lisette, at his side from the beginning of the venture, had called to tell him she had enough social-security points for retirement. He saw the points as splashes of ink on a clean page. All he could think to answer was that she would soon get bored, having no reason to get up each day. Lisette had replied, not disagreeably, that she planned to spend the next ten years in bed. He could not even coax her to stay by improving her salary: Except for the reserve of capital required by law, he had next to no money, had to scrape to pay the monthly settlement on his daughter, and was in continual debt to printers and banks.

He was often described in the trade as poor but selfless. He had performed an immeasurable service to world culture, bringing to the West voices that had been muffled for decades in the East. Well, of course, his thimble-size firm had not been able to attract the leviathan prophets, the booming novelists, the great mentors and tireless definers. Tremski had been at the very limit of Forain's financial reach—good Tremski, who had stuck to Forain even after he could have moved on. Common sense had kept Forain from approaching the next-best, second-level oracles, articulate and attractive, subsidized to the ears, chain-smoking and explaining, still wandering the universities and congresses of the West. Their travel requirements were beyond him: No grant could cover the unassuming but ruinous little hotel on the Left Bank, the long afternoons and evenings spent in bars with leather armchairs, where the visitors expected to meet clever and cultivated people in order to exchange ideas.

Forain's own little flock, by contrast, seemed to have entered the world with no expectations. Apart from the odd, rare, humble complaint, they were content to be put up on the top story of a hotel with a steep, neglected staircase, a wealth of literary associations, and one bath to a floor. For recreation, they went to the café across the street, made a pot of hot water and a tea bag last two and a half hours, and, as Forain encouraged them to keep in mind, could watch the Market Economy saunter by. Docile, holding only a modest estimation of their own gifts, they still provided a handicap: Their names, like those of their characters, all sounded alike to barbaric Western ears. It had been a triumph of perseverance on the part of Forain to get notice taken of their books. He wanted every work he published to survive in collective memory, even when the paper it was printed on had been pulped, burned in the city's vast incinerators or lay moldering at the bottom of the Seine.

Season after season, his stomach eaten up with anxiety, his heart pounding out hope, hope, hope, he produced a satirical novella set in Odessa; a dense, sober private journal, translated from the Rumanian, best understood by the author and his friends; or another wry glance at the harebrained makers of history. (There were few women. In that particular part of Europe they seemed to figure as brusque flirtatious mistresses or uncomplaining wives.) At least once a year he committed the near suicide of short stories and poetry. There were rewards, none financial. A few critics thought it a safe bet occasionally to mention a book he sent along for review: He was considered sound in an area no one knew much about, and too hard up to sponsor a pure disaster. Any day now some stumbling tender newborn calf of his could turn into a literary water ox. As a result, it was not unusual for one of his writers to receive a sheaf of tiny clippings, sometimes even illustrated by a miniature photograph, taken at the Place de la Bastille, with traffic whirling around. A clutch of large banknotes would have been good, too, but only Tremski's wife had held out for both.

Money! Forain's opinion was the same as that of any poet striving to be read in translation. He never said so. The name of the firm, Blaise Editions, rang with an honest chime in spheres where trade and literature are supposed to have no connection. When the minister of culture had decorated him, not long before, mentioning in encouraging terms Forain's addition to the House of Europe, Forain had tried to look diffident but essential. It seemed to him at that instant that his reputation for voluntary self-denial was a stone memorial pinning him to earth. He wanted to cry out for help—to the minister? It would look terrible. He felt honored but confused. Again, summoned to the refurbished embassy of a new democracy, welcomed by an ambassador and a cultural attaché recently arrived (the working staff was unchanged), Forain had dared say to himself, Why don't they just give me the check for whatever all this is costing?—the champagne, the exquisite catering, the medal in a velvet box—all the while hoping his thoughts would not show on his face.

The truth was that the destruction of the Wall—radiant paradigm—had all but demolished Forain. The difference was that Forain could not be hammered to still smaller pieces and sold all over the world. In much the same way Vatican II had reduced to bankruptcy more than one publisher of prayer books in Latin. A couple of them had tried to recoup by dumping the obsolete missals on congregations in Asia and Africa, but by the time the Third World began to ask for its money back the publishers had gone down with all hands. Briefly, Forain pondered the possibility of unloading on readers in Senegal and Cameroon the entire edition of a subtle and allusive study of corruption in Minsk, set in 1973. Could one still get away with it—better yet, charge it off to cultural cooperation? He answered himself: No. Not after November 1989. Gone were the stories in which Socialist incoherence was matched by Western irrelevance. Gone from Forain's intention to publish, that is: His flock continued to turn them in. He had instructed his underpaid, patient professional readers—teachers of foreign languages, for the most part—to look only at the first three and last two pages of any manuscript. If they promised another version of the East-West dilemma, disguised as a fresh look at the recent past, he did not want to see so much as a one-sentence summary.

By leaning into the aisle he could watch the last blessing. A line of mourners, Halina and her sobbing daughter at the head, shuffled around the coffin, each person ready to add an individual appeal for God's mercy. Forain stayed where he was. He neither pestered nor tried to influence imponderables; not since the death of the friend who had owned the cashmere coat. If the firm went into deeper decline, if it took the slide from shaky to foundering, he would turn to writing. Why not? At least he knew what he wanted to publish. It would get rid of any further need of dealing with living authors: their rent, their divorces, their abscessed teeth, not to speak of that new craze in the East—their psychiatrists. His first novel—what would he call it? He allowed a title to rise from his dormant unconscious imagination. It emerged, black and strong, on the cover of a book propped up in a store window: *The Cherry Orchard*. His mind accepted the challenge. What about a sly, quiet novel, teasingly based on the play? A former property owner, after forty-seven years of exile, returns to Karl-Marx-Stadt to reclaim the family home. It now houses sixteen hardworking couples and thirty-eight small children. He throws them out, and the novel winds down with a moody description of curses and fistfights as imported workers try to install a satellite dish in the garden, where the children's swings used to be. It would keep a foot in the old territory, Forain thought, but with a radical shift of focus. He had to move sidelong: He could not all of a sudden start to publish poems about North Sea pollution and the threat to the herring catch.

Here was a joke he could have shared with Tremski. The stepdaughter had disconnected the telephone while Tremski was still in hospital, waiting to die; not that Forain wanted to dial an extinct number and let it ring. Even in Tremski's mortal grief over Barbara, the thought of Forain as his own author would have made him smile. He had accepted Forain, would listen to nothing said against him—just as he could not be dislodged from his fusty apartment and had remained faithful to his wife—but he had considered Forain's best efforts to be a kind of amateur, Western fiddling, and all his bright ideas to be false dawns. Forain lived a publisher's dream life, Tremski believed—head of a platoon of self-effacing, flat-broke writers who asked only to be read, believing they had something to say that was crucial to the West, that might even goad it into action. What sort of action, Forain still wondered. The intelligent fellow whose remains had just been committed to eternity was no different. He knew Forain was poor but believed he was rich. He thought a great new war would leave Central Europe untouched. The liberating missiles would sail across without ruffling the topmost leaf of a poplar tree. As for the contenders, well, perhaps their time was up.

The congregation had risen. Instead of a last prayer, diffuse and anonymous, Forain chose to offer up a firmer reminder of Tremski: the final inventory of his flat. First, the entrance, where a faint light under a blue shade revealed layers of coats on pegs but not the boots and umbrellas over which visitors tripped. Barbara had never interfered, never scolded, never tried to clean things up. It was Tremski's place. Through an archway, the room Barbara had used. In a corner, the chair piled with newspapers and journals that Tremski still intended to read. Next, unpainted shelves containing files, some empty, some spilling foolscap not to be touched until Tremski had a chance to sort everything out. Another bookcase, this time with books. Above it, the spread of photographs of his old friends. A window, and the sort of view that prisoners see. In front of the window, a drop-leaf table that had to be cleared for meals. The narrow couch, still spread with a blanket, where Halina had slept until she ran away. (To the end, Barbara had expected her to return saying, "It was a mistake." Tremski would have made

her welcome and even bought another sofa, at the flea market, for the child.)
The dark red armchair in which Forain had sat during his first meeting with
Barbara. Her own straight-backed chair and the small desk where she wrote
business letters for Tremski. On the wall, a charcoal drawing of Tremski—
by an amateur artist, probably—dated June 1945. It was a face that had
come through; only just.

Mourners accustomed to the ceremonial turned to a neighbor to exchange the kiss of peace. Those who were not shrank slightly, as if the touch
without warmth were a new form of aggression. Forain found unfocused,
symbolized love positively terrifying. He refused the universal coming-
together, rammed his hands in his pockets—like a rebellious child—and
joined the untidy lines shuffling out into the rain.

Two hours later, the time between amply filled by the accident, the arrival
and departure of the ambulance, the long admittance procedure, and the
waiting-around natural to a service called Emergency, Forain left the hospital. The old lady was too stunned to have much to say for herself, but she
could enunciate clearly, "No family, no insurance." He had left his address
and, with even less inclination, a check he sincerely hoped was not a dud.
The wind and sleet promised earlier in the day battered and drenched him.
He skirted the building and, across a narrow street, caught sight of lines of
immigrants standing along the north side of central police headquarters. Algerians stood in a separate queue.

There were no taxis. He was too hungry and wet to cross the bridge to the
Place Saint-Michel—a three-minute walk. In a café on the Boulevard du
Palais he hung his coat where he could keep an eye on it and ordered a
toasted ham-and-cheese sandwich, a glass of Badoit mineral water, a small
carafe of wine, and black coffee—all at once. The waiter forgot the wine.
When he finally remembered, Forain was ready to leave. He wanted to argue
about the bill but saw that the waiter looked frightened. He was young, with
clumsy hands, feverish red streaks under his eyes, and coarse fair hair: foreign,
probably working without papers, in the shadow of the most powerful police in France. All right, Forain said to himself, but no tip. He noticed how
the waiter kept glancing toward someone or something at the far end of the
room: His employer, Forain guessed. He felt, as he had felt much of the day,
baited, badgered, and trapped. He dropped a tip of random coins on the tray
and pulled on his coat. The waiter grinned but did not thank him, put the
coins in his pocket, and carried the untouched wine back to the kitchen.

Shoulders hunched, collar turned up, Forain made his way to the taxi rank at the Place Saint-Michel. Six or seven people under streaming umbrellas waited along the curb. Around the corner a cab suddenly drew up and a woman got out. Forain took her place, as if it were the most natural thing in the world. He had stopped feeling hungry, but seemed to be wearing layers of damp towels. The driver, in a heavy accent, probably Portuguese, told Forain to quit the taxi. He was not allowed to pick up a passenger at that particular spot, close to a stand. Forain pointed out that the stand was empty. He snapped the lock shut—as if that made a difference—folded his arms, and sat shivering. He wished the driver the worst fate he could think of—to stand on the north side of police headquarters and wait for nothing.

"You're lucky to be working," he suddenly said. "You should see all those people without jobs, without papers, just over there, across the Seine."

"I've seen them," the driver said. "I could be out of a job just for picking you up. You should be waiting your turn next to that sign, around the corner."

They sat for some seconds without speaking. Forain studied the set of the man's neck and shoulders; it was rigid, tense. An afternoon quiz show on the radio seemed to take his attention, or perhaps he was pretending to listen and trying to decide if it was a good idea to appeal to a policeman. Such an encounter could rebound against the driver, should Forain turn out to be someone important—assistant to the office manager of a cabinet minister, say.

Forain knew he had won. It was a matter of seconds now. He heard, "What was the name of the Queen of Sheba?" "Which one?" "The one who paid a visit to King Solomon." "Can you give me a letter?" "B." "Brigitte?"

The driver moved his head back and forth. His shoulders dropped slightly. Using a low, pleasant voice, Forain gave the address of his office, offering the Saint Vincent de Paul convent as a landmark. He had thought of going straight home and changing his shoes, but catching pneumonia was nothing to the loss of the staunch Lisette; the sooner he could talk to her, the better. She should have come to the funeral. He could start with that. He realized that he had not given a thought to Tremski for almost three hours now. He continued the inventory, his substitute for a prayer. He was not sure where he had broken off—with the telephone on Barbara's desk? Tremski would not have a telephone in the room where he worked, but at the first ring he would call through the wall, "Who is it?" Then "What does he want? . . . He met me *where?* . . . When we were in high school? . . . Tell him I'm too busy. No—let me talk to him."

The driver turned the radio up, then down. "I could have lost my job," he said.

Every light in the city was ablaze in the dark rain. Seen through rivulets on a window, the least promising streets showed glitter and well-being. It seemed to Forain that in Tremski's dark entry there had been a Charlie Chaplin poster, relic of some Polish film festival. There had been crates and boxes, too, that had never been unpacked. Tremski would not move out, but in a sense he had never moved in. Suddenly, although he had not really forgotten them, Forain remembered the manuscripts he had snatched back from Halina. She had said none was actually finished, but what did she know? What if there were only a little, very little, left to be composed? The first thing to do was have them read by someone competent—not his usual painstaking and very slow professional readers but a bright young Polish critic, who could tell at a glance what was required. Filling gaps was a question of style and logic, and could just as well take place after translation.

When they reached the Rue du Bac the driver drew up as closely as he could to the entrance, even tried to wedge the cab between two parked cars, so that Forain would not have to step into a gutter filled with running water. Forain could not decide what to do about the tip, whether to give the man something extra (it was true that he could have refused to take him anywhere) or make him aware he had been aggressive. "You should be waiting your turn. . . ." still rankled. In the end, he made a Tremski-like gesture, waving aside change that must have amounted to 35 percent of the fare. He asked for a receipt. It was not until after the man had driven away that Forain saw he had not included the tip in the total sum. No Tremski flourish was ever likely to carry a reward. That was another lesson of the day.

More than a year later, Lisette—now working only part-time—mentioned that Halina had neglected to publish in *Le Monde* the anniversary notice of Tremski's death. Did Forain want one to appear, in the name of the firm? Yes, of course. It would be wrong to say he had forgotten the apartment and everything in it, but the inventory, the imaginary camera moving around the rooms, filled him with impatience and a sense of useless effort. His mind stopped at the narrow couch with the brown blanket, Halina's bed, and he said to himself, What a pair those two were. The girl was right to run away. As soon as he had finished the thought he placed his hand over his mouth, as if to prevent the words from emerging. He went one further—bowed his head, like Tremski at Barbara's funeral, promising himself he would keep in mind things as they once were, not as they seemed to him now. But the apartment was vacated, and Tremski had disappeared. He had been prayed over thoroughly by a great number of people, and the only enjoyment he might have had from the present scene was to watch Forain make a fool of himself to no purpose.

There were changes in the office, too. Lisette had agreed to stay for the time it would take to train a new hand: a thin, pretty girl, part of the recent, non-political emigration—wore a short leather skirt, said she did not care about money but loved literature and did not want to waste her life working at something dull. She got on with Halina and had even spared Forain the odd difficult meeting. As she began to get the hang of her new life, she lost no time spreading the story that Forain had been the lover of Barbara and would not let go a handsome and expensive coat that had belonged to Tremski. A posthumous novel-length manuscript of Tremski's was almost ready for the printer, with a last chapter knitted up from fragments he had left trailing. The new girl, gifted in languages, compared the two versions and said he would have approved; and when Forain showed a moment of doubt and hesitation she was able to remind him of how, in the long run, Tremski had never known what he wanted.

A STATE OF AFFAIRS

⸙

Owing to his advanced age and a lack of close relatives, M. Wroblewski receives little personal mail. Most of the friends of his youth in Warsaw are dead and the survivors have not much to say, except about their grandchildren, and one cannot keep writing back and forth about total strangers. Even the grandparents know them only through colored snapshots or as shrill, shy voices over the telephone. They barely say anything in Polish and have English-sounding names: Their parents emigrated as soon as they could. M. Wroblewski's wife has a niece in Canberra: Teresa, wife of Stanley, mother of Fiona and Tim. He keeps their photographs filed in large brown envelopes. Should Teresa and her family ever decide to visit Paris, he will spread their cheerful faces all over the flat.

You might imagine that changed conditions in Eastern Europe would stir some hope into the news from Warsaw, but his correspondents, the few who are left, sound dispirited, mistrustful. Everything costs too much. Young people are ignorant and rude. The spoken language is debased. Purses are snatched on church steps. There are no books worth reading—nothing but pornography and translated Western trash. Recently, a friend he has not seen in fifty years but with whom he has kept in touch sent him a long letter. The friend had been invited to describe his wartime ghetto experience in a radio talk. As a result, he was sent messages of insult and abuse. There was even a death threat. He is an old man. Surely enough is enough. "On that score, nothing has changed," he wrote. "It is in the brain, blood, and bone. I don't mean this for you. You were always different."

A compliment, yes, but no one wants to be singled out, tested, examined, decreed an exception. "I don't mean this for you" leads to awkwardness and painful feelings. Perhaps, a long time ago, as a young man, callow and cordial, M. Wroblewski had said the same thing to his friend: "Naturally, you are completely different. I'm talking about all the others." Could he have said it? He would like to be able to send his friend a plane ticket to Paris, find him a comfortable room and discreetly settle the bill, invite him to dinner: M. Wroblewski, his friend, and Magda around the little table in the living room, with the green lampshade glowing and the green curtains drawn; or at Chez Marcel, where he used to go with Magda. The owner would remember them, offer free glasses of cognac with their coffee: jovial, generous, welcoming—One Europe, One World.

There, you see, M. Wroblewski would tell his friend. There are chinks of light.

This is a soft autumn, moist and mild. Between showers the broad boulevards fill up with people strolling as though it were summer. He sits in the Atelier, the new place just next door to the Select, composing and rejecting an answer to his friend. His hat and stick are on a chair; his dog, an obedient one, lies under it. The Atelier opened in the eighties, but he still thinks of it as "the new place." It seems to have been in Montparnasse forever. The table mats depict a mature model posing for a life class some three generations ago. Newspapers are on wooden holders, in the old way. The waiters are patient, except when a customer's reaction to a slopped saucer is perceived as an affront. Across the street the mirrored walls of the building that now rises above the Coupole reflect an Île-de-France sky: watered blue with a thin screen of clouds. If you sit at the front row of tables you may be pestered by foreign beggars, some of them children. M. Wroblewski keeps loose change in his pocket, which he distributes until it runs out. There have been many newspaper articles warning him not to do this: The money is collected for the brutal and cynical men who put the children on the street.

His friend in Warsaw is completely alert, with an amazing memory of events, sorted out, in sequence. If he were here, at this moment, he would find a historical context for everything: the new building and its mirrors, the naked model, the beggar girl with her long braid of hair and the speck of diamond on the side of her nose. Who, after hearing the voice of an old man over the radio, could sit down and compose a threat? All M. Wroblewski can see are a man's hunched shoulders, the back of his thick neck. But no, his friend might say: I have seen his face, which is lean and elegant. What do you still hope for? What can you still expect? So much for your chinks of light.

And so they would exchange visions through the afternoon and into the evening, with the lights inside the café growing brighter and brighter as the trees outside become part of the night. Perhaps his friend would enjoy meeting someone wholly new, remote from the dark riddle of the man and the death letter. Unfortunately, most of M. Wroblewski's Paris acquaintances have vanished or moved away to remote towns and suburbs (everything seems far) or retired to a region of the mind that must be like a twisted, hollow shell. When he reads his wife a letter from Canberra he takes care to translate the English expressions Teresa puts in as a matter of course. Magda used to understand English, but even her French is fading now. Before he reaches the end of the letter she will have asked four or five times, "Who is it from?"—although he has shown her the signature and the bright Australian stamps. Or she may surprise him with a pertinent question: "Are they coming home for Christmas?" There is no telling what Magda means by "home." She may say to him, "Does my father like you?" or even, "Where do you live?"

She uses his diminutive, says "Maciek and I," but knows nothing about him. She can play a game of cards, write a letter—it is never clear to whom—and he pretends to stamp and post it. By the time he has invented a plausible address, the incident has dissolved. She stares at the envelope. What is he talking about? She is poised on the moment between dark and light, when the last dream of dawn is shredding rapidly and awareness of morning has barely caught hold. She lives that split second all day long.

This morning, when he brought in her breakfast tray, he found a new letter astray on the carpet. Her writing is larger than before, easy to read:

> My Dearest Dear!
>
> Maciek is teaching and so am I! At the Polish high school in Paris! He teaches French. I teach algebra and music. Our pupils are well behaved. We have Nansen passports! They open wide, like an accordion. Only a few lucky people are allowed to have Nansen passports! They are very old! Only a few people can have them. Maciek is teaching French.
>
> Your loving
> Magda

Everything in the letter is true, if you imagine that today is unwinding some forty-five years ago. He said, "What a nice letter. Is it for Teresa?"

She sat up in bed, accepted tea. "What is Prussia?"

The Prussia question is new. Perhaps in one of the shredded dreams someone called out "Prussia!" in a dream voice that turned words and names into dramatic affirmations. She looked toward the window, sipped her tea. She could see (if she was taking it in) the big garage at the corner and at least one of the trees on Boulevard Raspail.

"They've cut some trees down," she remarked not long ago, walking with him around the block. She was right: It was he who failed to notice the gaps, even though he goes along the boulevard every day of his life.

Unless you try to keep a conversation alive, nothing shows. When he takes her out in the afternoon for tea and a slice of fruitcake, she looks finer and more self-possessed than most of the old ladies at other tables. They make a mess with crumbs, feed piecrust to their unruly lapdogs, pester the waiter with questions as repetitive and tedious as any of Magda's: Why is that door open? Why doesn't someone shut the door? Well, why can't you get somebody to fix it? The trouble about Magda is only that one can't leave her alone for a minute or she will be out in the street, trying to climb on a bus, on her way to teach a solfège class in a Polish school that no longer exists.

Morning is the slow time, when she refuses to understand the first thing about buttons, zippers, a comb, a toothbrush. Marie-Louise, who was born in Martinique, arrives at nine o'clock, five days a week. She knows how to coax Magda out of bed and into her clothes. (A bath can take three-quarters of an hour.) At last, neatly dressed, holding hands with Marie-Louise, she will watch a program of cartoons or a cooking lesson or a hooded man sticking up an American bank. Still clutching Marie-Louise, she may say, in Polish, "Who is this woman? I don't like this woman. Tell her to go away."

Marie-Louise is sent by the city's social services and costs them nothing. The rules are firm: Household tasks are banned, but she may, as a favor, start the washing machine or make a compote of apples and pears for Magda's lunch. In the meantime, he does the shopping, walks the dog. If Marie-Louise says she can stay until noon he walks up to Montparnasse and reads the newspapers. The white awning and umbrellas at the Atelier bring to mind the south, when Nice and Monaco were still within his means and not too crowded. He and Magda went down every Easter, traveling third class. He can retrace every step of their holiday round: beach in the morning, even when Easter fell in March and the sea was too cold for wading; a picnic lunch of bread, cheese, and fruit, eaten in deck chairs along the front; a rest;

a long walk, then a change into spotless, pressed clothes—cream and ivory tones for Magda, beige or lightweight navy for him. An apéritif under a white awning; dinner at the *pension*. (In the dining room the Wroblewskis kept to themselves.) After dinner, a visit to the casino—not to gamble but to watch the most civilized people in Western Europe throw their money around. You would have to be a millionaire to live that way now.

In Montparnasse, the other day, a woman sitting by herself turned on a small radio. The music sounded like early Mozart or late Haydn. No one complained, and so the waiters said nothing. Against the music, he tried to calculate, in sums that have no bearing on money, his exact due. He would have sworn before any court, earthly or celestial, that he had never crawled. The music ceased, and a flat, cultured voice began describing what had just been played. The woman cut the voice and returned the radio to her hand-bag. For a few seconds the café seemed to have gone dead; then he began to take in conversations, the clink of spoons, footsteps, cars going by: sounds so familiar that they amounted to silence. Of course he had begged. He had entreated for enough to eat, relief from pain, a passport, employment. Shreds of episodes shrugged off, left behind, strewed the roads. Only some-one pledged to gray dawns would turn back to examine them. You might as well collect every letter you see lying stained in a gutter and call the assort-ment an autobiography.

There must have been some virtues, surely. For instance, he had never tried to gain a benefit by fraud. Some people make a whole life out of trick-ery. They will even try to wrangle a box of the chocolates that the mayor of Paris distributes at Christmastime. These would-be swindlers may be in their fifties and sixties, too young to be put on the mayor's list. Or else they have a large income and really ought to pay for their own pleasures. Actu-ally, it is the rich who put on shabby clothes and saunter into their local town hall, waving a gift voucher that wouldn't fool a child. And they could buy a ton of chocolates without feeling the squeeze!

The Wroblewskis, neither prosperous nor in want, get their annual gift in a correct and legal way. About four years ago, a notice arrived entitling Magda Zaleska, spouse Wroblewska, to the mayor's present. She was just beginning to show signs of alarm over quite simple matters, and so he went in her place, taking along her passport, a lease of which she was the cosigner, and a letter of explanation that he wrote and got her to endorse. (Nobody wanted to read it.) He remembers how he trudged upstairs and down be-

fore coming across a hand-lettered sign saying CHOCOLATES—SHOW
VOUCHER AND IDENTITY.

The box turned out to be staggering in size, too large for a drawer or a
kitchen shelf. It remained for weeks on top of the television set. (Neither of
them cared for chocolate, except now and then a square of the bitter kind,
taken with strong black coffee.) Finally, he transferred half the contents to
a tin container that some Polish friends in England had used to send the
Wroblewskis a gift of shortbread and digestive biscuits, and dispatched it
to a distant cousin of Magda's. The cousin had replied that she could find
chocolate in Warsaw but would welcome a package of detergent or some
toilet soap that didn't take one's skin off.

He had used some of last year's chocolates as an offering for the
concierge, packing them attractively in a wicker basket that had come with
a purchase of dried apricots. She removed the ribbon and flowered paper,
folded them, and exclaimed, "Ah! The mayor's chocolates!" He still wonders how she knew: They are of excellent quality and look like any other
chocolates you can see in a confectioner's window. Perhaps she is on the list,
and sends hers off to relatives in Portugal. It hardly seems possible: They
are intended for the elderly and deserving, and she is barely forty. Perhaps
she is one of the schemers who has used deceit—a false birth certificate.
What of it? She is a worthy woman, hardworking and kind. A man he
knows of is said to have filed an affidavit that he was too badly off to be able
to pay his yearly television tax and got away with it: here, in Paris, where
every resident is supposed to be accounted for; where the entire life of every
authorized immigrant is lodged inside a computer or crammed between the
cardboard covers of a dossier held together with frayed cotton tape.

When he brings Magda her breakfast tray he looks as if he were on the
way to an important meeting—with the bank manager, say, or the mayor
himself. He holds to his side of the frontier between sleeping and waking,
observes his own behavior for symptoms of contagion—haziness about
time, forgetting names, straying from the point in conversation. He is fit,
has good eyesight, can still hear the slide of letters when the concierge
pushes them under the door. He was ten months in Dachau, the last winter
and spring of the war, and lost a tooth for every month. They have been replaced, in an inexpensive, bric-a-brac way: better than nothing. The Germans give him a monthly pension, which covers his modest telephone bill,
with a bit over. He is low on the scale of atonement. First of all, as the German lawyer who dealt with the claim pointed out, he was a grown man at

the time. He had completed his education. He had a profession. One can teach a foreign language anywhere in the world. All he had to do when the war ended was carry on as before. He cannot plead that the ten months were an irreparable break, with a before and an after, or even a waste of life. When he explained about the German pension to a tax assessor, he was asked if he had served with the German Army. He feels dizzy if he bends his head—for instance, over a newspaper spread flat—and he takes a green-and-white capsule every day, to steady his heart.

As soon as Marie-Louise rings the front doorbell, the dog drags the leash from its place in the vestibule and drops it at his feet. Hector is a young schnauzer with a wiry coat and a gamesome disposition, who was acquired on their doctor's advice as a focus of interest for Magda. He is bound to outlive his master. M. Wroblewski has made arrangements: The concierge will take him over. She can hardly wait. Sometimes she says to Hector, "Here we are, just the two of us," as if M. Wroblewski were already among the missing. Walking Hector seems to be more and more difficult. Parisians leave their cars along the curbs without an inch of space; beyond them traffic flies by like driven hail. When Magda, of all people, noticed that those few trees were missing, he felt unreasonable dismay, as if every last thing that mattered to him had been felled. Why don't they leave us alone? he thought. He had been holding silent conversations with no one in particular for some time. Then the letter came and he began addressing his friend. He avoids certain words, such as "problem," "difficulty," "catastrophe," and says instead, "A state of affairs."

The Nansen passports are being called in. Three people he knows, aged between eighty-one and eighty-eight, have had letters from the French Ministry for Foreign Affairs: The bureau that handles those rare and special passports is closing down. Polish political refugees do not exist any longer. They have been turned into Polish citizens (this is the first they've heard of it) and should apply to their own embassy for suitable documents. Two of the new citizens are an engraver, who still works in an unheatable studio on the far side of Montmartre, and another artist, a woman, who once modeled a strong, stunning likeness of Magda. She could not afford to have it cast, and the original got broken or was lost—he can't remember. It was through a work of art that he understood his wife's beauty. Until then he had been proud of her charm and distinction. He liked to watch her at the piano; he watched more than he listened, perhaps. The third is a former critic of Eastern European literature who at some point fell into a depression and gave up bothering with letters.

"... and so, ipso facto, Polish citizens," the engraver told M. Wro-blewski, over the telephone. "What are they going to do with us? Ship us back to Poland? Are we part of a quota now? At our age, we are better off stateless." Perhaps it is true. They never travel and do not need passports. Everyone has a place to live, an income of sorts. Two of the three still actually earn money. In a way, they look after one another.

No one has made a move. As the engraver says, when you are dealing with world-level bureaucracy, it is smarter to sit still. By the time you have decided how to react, all the rules may have been changed.

It is true and not true. One can quietly shift a pawn without causing a riot. M. Wroblewski's attitude runs to lines of defense. Probably, some clerk at the ministry is striking off names in alphabetical order and is nowhere close to the W's. After several false starts, he has written and mailed a letter to the Quai d'Orsay asking for French citizenship. He might have applied years ago, of course, but in the old days refusal was so consistent that one was discouraged at the outset. By the time he and Magda had their work, their apartment, their precious passports, the last thing they wanted was to fill in another form, stand in another line. He made no mention in the letter of refugees, status, or citizenship—other than French—but drew attention to the number of years he had lived in France, his fluent French, and his admiration for the culture. He spoke of the ancient historical links between Poland and France, touched briefly on the story of Napoleon and Mme. Waleska, and reminded the ministry that he had never been behind with the rent or overdrawn at the bank.

(He sent the letter more than a month ago. So far, there has been no word from the Quai d'Orsay: an excellent sign. One can coast with perfect safety on official silence.)

In the meantime, something new has turned up. About three weeks ago he received a personal letter from the bank, written on a real typewriter, signed with real ink: no booklets, no leaflets, no pictures of a white-haired couple looking the Sphinx in the eye or enjoying Venice. There was just the personal message and one other thing, a certificate. "Certificate" was printed in thick black letters, along with his name, correctly spelled. A Mme. Car-ole Fournier, of Customers' Counseling Service, entreated him to sign the certificate, ask for an appointment, and bring it to her desk. (Her own signature seemed to him open and reliable, though still untried by life.) According to Mme. Fournier, and for reasons not made clear, he was among a handful of depositors—aristocrats, in their way—to whom the bank was proposing a cash credit of fifteen thousand francs. The credit was not a loan, not an overdraft, but a pool into which he could dip, without paying interest, anytime he needed ready money but did not wish to touch his savings. The sums drawn from that fund would be replaced at the rate of two thousand francs a month, transferred from his current account. There was no interest or surcharge: He read that part twice.

For fifteen thousand francs he could fly to Australia, he supposed, or go on a cruise to the Caribbean. He could buy Magda a sumptuous fur coat. He would do none of those things, but the offer was generous and not to be rejected out of hand. He had opened an account with his first salary check in France: Perhaps the bank wanted to show gratitude for years of loyalty. Besides his current account, he possessed two savings accounts. One of these is tax-free, limited by law to a deposit of fifteen thousand francs—by coincidence, the very amount he was being offered. Some people, he supposed, would grab the whole thing and dribble it away on nonsense, then feel downcast and remorseful as they watched their current account dwindle, month after month. The gift was a bright balloon with a long string attached. The string could be passed from hand to hand—to the bank and back. He saw himself holding fast to the string.

Before he had a chance to do anything about it, he had a dizzy spell in the street and had to enter a private art gallery and ask to sit down. (They were not very nice about it. There was only one chair, occupied by a lady addressing envelopes.) His doctor ordered him to take a week's rest, preferably miles away from home. The preparation that was required—finding someone to sleep at the flat, two other people to come in during the afternoons and on the weekend—was more wearing than just keeping on; but he obeyed, left nothing undone, turned Hector over to the concierge, and caught the train for Saint-Malo. Years before, in an era of slow trains and chilly hotels, he had taken some of his students there. Uncomplaining, they ate dry sandwiches and apples and pitched the apple cores from the ramparts. This time he was alone in a wet season. Under a streaming umbrella he walked the ramparts again and when the sky cleared visited Chateaubriand's grave; and from the edge of the grave took the measure of the ocean. He had led his students here, too, and told them everything about Chateaubriand (everything they could take in) but did not say that Sartre had urinated on the grave. It might have made them laugh.

He left the grave and the sea and started back to the walled city. He thought of other violations and of the filth that can wash over quiet lives. In the dark afternoon the lighted windows seemed exclusive, like careless snubs. He would write to his friend, "I wondered what I was doing there, looking at other people's windows, when I have a home of my own." The next day he changed his train reservation and returned to Paris before the week was up.

Magda recognized him but did not know he had been away. She asked if he had been disturbed by the neighbor who played Schubert on the piano all night long. (Perhaps the musician existed, he sometimes thought, and only Magda could hear him.) "You must tell him to stop," she said. He promised he would.

Mme. Carole Fournier, Customers' Counseling Service, turned out to be an attractive young woman, perhaps a bit thin in the face. Her hollow cheeks gave her a birdlike appearance, but when she turned to the computer screen beside her desk her profile reminded him of an actress, Elzbieta Barszczewska. When Barszczewska died, in her white wedding dress, at the end of a film called *The Leper*, the whole of Warsaw went into mourning. Compared with Barszczewska, Pola Negri was nothing.

The plastic rims of Mme. Fournier's glasses matched the two red combs in her hair. Her office was a white cubicle with a large window and no door. Her computer, like all those he had noticed in the bank, had a screen of azure. It suggested the infinite. On its cerulean surface he could read, without straining, facts about himself: his date of birth, for one. Between white lateral blinds at the window he observed a bakery and the post office where he bought stamps and sent letters. Hector, tied to a metal bar among chained and padlocked bikes, was just out of sight. Had the window been open, one might have heard his plaintive barking. M. Wroblewski wanted to get up and make sure the dog had not been kidnapped, but it would have meant interrupting the charming Mme. Fournier.

She glanced once more at the blue screen, then came back to a four-page questionnaire on her desk. He had expected a welcome. So far, it had been an interrogation. "I am sorry," she said. "It's my job. I have to ask you this. Are you sixty-six or over?"

"I am flattered to think there could be any doubt in your mind," he began. She seemed so young; his voice held a note of teasing. She could have been a grandchild, if generations ran as statistics want them to. He might have sent her picture to his friend in Warsaw: red combs, small hands, zodiac (Gemini) medallion on a chain. Across the street a boy came out of the bakery carrying several long loaves, perhaps for a restaurant. She waited. How long had she been waiting? She held a pen poised over the questionnaire.

"I celebrated my sixty-sixth birthday on the day General de Gaulle died," he said. "I do not mean that I celebrated the death of that amazing man. It made me very sorry. I was at the theater, with my wife. The play was *Ondine*, with Isabelle Adjani. It was her first important part. She must have been seventeen. She was the toast of Paris. Lovely. A nymph. After the curtain calls, the director of the theater walked on, turned to the audience, and said the President was dead." She seemed still to be waiting. He continued, "The audience gasped. We filed out without speaking. My wife finally said, 'The poor man. And how sad, on your birthday.' I said, 'It is history.' We walked home in the rain. In those days one could walk in the street after midnight. There was no danger."

Her face had reflected understanding only at the mention of Isabelle Adjani. He felt bound to add, "I think I've made a mistake. It was not President de Gaulle after all. It was President Georges Pompidou whose death was announced in all the theaters of Paris. I am not sure about Adjani. My wife always kept theater programs. I could look it up, if it interests you."

"It's about your being sixty-six or over," she said. "You'll have to take out a special insurance policy. It's to protect the bank, you see. It doesn't cost much."

"I am insured."

"I know. This is for the bank." She turned the questionnaire around so that he could read a boxed query: "Do you take medication on a daily basis?"

"Everyone my age takes something."

"Excuse me. I have to ask. Are you seriously ill?"

"A chronic complaint. Nothing dangerous." He put his hand over his heart.

She picked up the questionnaire, excused herself once more, and left him. On the screen he read the numbers of his three accounts, and the date when each had been opened. He remembered Hector, stood up, but before he could get to the window Mme. Fournier was back.

"I am sorry," she said. "I am sorry it is taking so long. Please sit down. I have to ask you another thing."

"I was trying to see my dog."

"About your chronic illness. Could you die suddenly?"

"I hope not."

"I've spoken to M. Giroud. You will need to have a medical examination. No, not by your own doctor," forestalling him. "A doctor from the insurance firm. It isn't for the bank. It is for them—the insurance." She was older than he had guessed. Embarrassment and its disguises tightened her face, put her at about thirty-five. The youthful signature was a decoy. "M. Wroblewski," she said, making a good stab at the consonants, "is it worth all this, for fifteen thousand francs? We would authorize an overdraft, if you needed one. But, of course, there would be interest to pay."

"I wanted the fund for the very reason you have just mentioned—in case I die suddenly. When I die, my accounts will be frozen, won't they? I'd like some cash for my wife. I thought I could make my doctor responsible. He could sign—anything. My wife is too ill to handle funeral arrangements, or to pay the people looking after her. It will take time before the will is settled."

"I'm sorry," she said. "I'm truly sorry. It is not an account. It is a cash reserve. If you die, it ceases to exist."

"A reserve of cash, in my name, held by a bank, is an account," he said. "I would never use or touch it in my lifetime."

"It isn't your money," she said. "Not in the way you think. I'm sorry. Excuse me. The letter should never have been sent to you."

"The bank knows my age. It is there, on the screen."

"I know. I'm sorry. I don't send these things out."

"But you sign them?"

"I don't send them out."

They shook hands. He adjusted his hat at a jaunty angle. Everything he had on that day looked new, even the silk ascot, gray with a small pattern of yellow, bought by Magda at Arnys, on the Rue de Sèvres—oh, fifteen years before. Nothing was frayed or faded. He never seemed to wear anything out. His nails were clipped, his hands unstained. He still smoked three Craven A a day, but had refrained in the presence of Mme. Fournier, having seen no ashtray on her desk. There had been nothing on it, actually, except the questionnaire. He ought to have brought her some chocolates; it troubled him to have overlooked a civility. He held nothing against her. She seemed competent, considerate in her conduct.

"Your accounts are in fine shape," she said. "That must be something off your mind. We could allow ... At any rate, come back and see me if you have a problem."

"My problem is my own death," he said, smiling.

"You mustn't think such things." She touched her talisman, Gemini, as if it really could allow her a double life: one with vexations and one without. "Please excuse us. M. Giroud is sorry. So am I."

After the business about the letter and the Prussia question this morning, Magda was quiet. He let her finish her tea (she forgets she is holding a cup) and tried to draw her into conversation about the view from the window.

She said, "The neighbor is still playing Schubert all night. It keeps me awake. It is sad when he stops."

Their neighbors are a couple who go out to work. They turn off the television at ten and there is no further sound until half past six in the morning, when they listen to the news. At a quarter to eight they lock their front door and ring for the elevator, and the apartment is quiet again until suppertime. No one plays Schubert.

He picked up the tray. When he reached the doorway she said in a friendly, even voice, "The piano kept me awake."

"I know," he said. "The man playing Schubert."

"What man? Men can't play anything."

"A woman? Someone you know?"

He stood still, waiting. He said to his friend, If I get an answer, it means she is cured. But she will burrow under the blankets and pillows until Marie-Louise arrives. Once Marie-Louise is here, I will go out and meet you, or the thought of you, which never quits me now. I will read the news and you can tell me what it means. We will look at those mirrored walls across the boulevard and judge the day by colors: pale gold, gray, white, and blue. A sheet of black glass means nothing: It is not a cloud or the sky. Let me explain. Give me time. From that distance, the dark has no power. It has no life of its own. It is a reflection.

Today I shall bring a pad of writing paper and a stamped, addressed envelope. You can think of me, at a table behind the window. (It is getting a bit cold for the street.) I have a young dog. As you can see, I am still boringly optimistic. Magda is well. This morning we talked about Schubert. I regret that your health is bad and you are unable to travel. Otherwise you could come here and we would rent a car and drive somewhere—you, Magda, the dog, and I. I am sorry about the radio talk and its effect on some low people. There are distorted minds here, too—you would not believe what goes on. Someone said, "Hitler lives!" at a meeting—so I am told. I suppose the police can't be everywhere. Please take good care of yourself. Your letters are precious to me. We have so many memories. Do you remember *The Leper*, and the scene where she dies at her own wedding? She was much more beautiful than Garbo or Dietrich—don't you think? I wish I had more to tell you, but my life is like the purring of a cat. If I were to describe it, it would put you to sleep. I may have more to tell you tomorrow. In the meantime, I send you God's favor.

MLLE. DIAS DE CORTA

———

❧

*Y*ou moved into my apartment during the summer of the year before abortion became legal in France; that should fix it in past time for you, dear Mlle. Dias de Corta. You had just arrived in Paris from your native city, which you kept insisting was Marseilles, and were looking for work. You said you had studied television-performance techniques at some provincial school (we had never heard of the school, even though my son had one or two actor friends) and received a diploma with "special mention" for vocal expression. The diploma was not among the things we found in your suit-case, after you disappeared, but my son recalled that you carried it in your handbag, in case you had the good luck to sit next to a casting director on a bus.

The next morning we had our first cordial conversation. I described my husband's recent death and repeated his last words, which had to do with my financial future and were not overly optimistic. I felt his presence and still heard his voice in my mind. He seemed to be in the kitchen, wonder-ing what you were doing there, summing you up: a thin, dark-eyed, non-committal young woman, standing at the counter, bolting her breakfast. A bit sullen, perhaps; you refused the chair I had dragged in from the dining room. Careless, too. There were crumbs everywhere. You had spilled milk on the floor.

"Don't bother about the mess," I said. "I'm used to cleaning up after young people. I wait on my son, Robert, hand and foot." Actually, you had not made a move. I fetched the sponge mop from the broom closet, but when I asked you to step aside you started to choke on a crust. I waited qui-etly, then said, "My husband's illness was the result of eating too fast and never chewing his food." His silent voice told me I was wasting my time. True, but if I hadn't warned you I would have been guilty of withholding assistance from someone in danger. In our country, a refusal to help can be punished by law.

The only remark my son, Robert, made about you at the beginning was "She's too short for an actress." He was on the first step of his career climb in the public institution known then as Post, Telegrams, Telephones. Now it has been broken up and renamed with short, modern terms I can never keep in mind. (Not long ago I had the pleasure of visiting Robert in his new quarters. There is a screen or a machine of some kind everywhere you look. He shares a spacious office with two women. One was born in Martinique and can't pronounce her r's. The other looks Corsican.) He left home early every day and liked to spend his evenings with a set of new friends, none of whom seemed to have a mother. The misteachings of the seventies, which encouraged criticism of earlier generations, had warped his natural feelings. Once, as he was going out the door, I asked if he loved me. He said the answer was self-evident: We were closely related. His behavior changed entirely after his engagement and marriage to Anny Clarens, a young lady of mixed descent. (Two of her grandparents are Swiss.) She is employed in the accounting department of a large hospital and enjoys her work. She and Robert have three children: Bruno, Elodie, and Félicie.

It was for companionship rather than income that I had decided to open my home to a stranger. My notice in *Le Figaro* mentioned "young woman only," even though those concerned for my welfare, from coiffeur to concierge, had strongly counseled "young man." "Young man" was said to be neater, cleaner, quieter, and (except under special circumstances I need not go into) would not interfere in my relationship with my son. In fact, my son was seldom available for conversation and had never shown interest in exchanging ideas with a woman, not even one who had known him from birth.

You called from a telephone on a busy street. I could hear the coins jangling and traffic going by. Your voice was low-pitched and agreeable and, except for one or two vowel sounds, would have passed for educated French. I suppose no amount of coaching at a school in or near Marseilles could get the better of the southern o, long where it should be short and clipped when it ought to be broad. But, then, the language was already in decline, owing to lax teaching standards and uncontrolled immigration. I admire your achievement and respect your handicaps, and I know Robert would say the same if he knew you were in my thoughts.

Your suitcase weighed next to nothing. I wondered if you owned warm clothes and if you even knew there could be such a thing as a wet summer. You might have seemed more at home basking in a lush garden than tramping the chilly streets in search of employment. I showed you the room—mine—with its two corner windows and long view down Avenue de Choisy. (I was to take Robert's and he was to sleep in the living room, on a couch.) At the far end of the avenue, Asian colonization had begun: a few restaurants and stores selling rice bowls and embroidered slippers from Taiwan. (Since those days the community has spread into all the neighboring streets. Police keep out of the area, preferring to let the immigrants settle disputes in their own way. Apparently, they punish wrongdoers by throwing them off the Tolbiac Bridge. Robert has been told of a secret report, compiled by experts, which the mayor has had on his desk for eighteen months. According to this report, by the year 2025 Asians will have taken over a third of Paris, Arabs and Africans three-quarters, and unskilled European immigrants two-fifths. Thousands of foreign-sounding names are deliberately "lost" by the authorities and never show up in telephone books or computer directories, to prevent us from knowing the true extent of their progress.)

I gave you the inventory and asked you to read it. You said you did not care what was in the room. I had to explain that the inventory was for me. Your signature, "Alda Dias de Corta," with its long loops and closed a's, showed pride and secrecy. You promised not to damage or remove without permission a double bed, two pillows, and a bolster, a pair of blankets, a beige satin spread with hand-knotted silk fringe, a chaise longue of the same color, a wardrobe and a dozen hangers, a marble fireplace (ornamental), two sets of lined curtains and two of écru voile, a walnut bureau with four drawers, two framed etchings of cathedrals (Reims and Chartres), a bedside table, a small lamp with parchment shade, a Louis XVI–style writing desk, a folding card table and four chairs, a gilt-framed mirror, two wrought-iron wall fixtures fitted with electric candles and lightbulbs shaped like flames, two medium-sized "Persian" rugs, and an electric heater, which had given useful service for six years but which you aged before its time by leaving it turned on all night. Robert insisted I include breakfast. He did not want it told around the building that we were cheap. What a lot of coffee, milk, bread, apricot jam, butter, and sugar you managed to put away! Yet you remained as thin as a matchstick and that great thatch of curly hair made your face seem smaller than ever.

You agreed to pay a monthly rent of fifty thousand francs for the room, cleaning of same, use of bathroom, electricity, gas (for heating baths and morning coffee), fresh sheets and towels once a week, and free latchkey. You were to keep a list of your phone calls and to settle up once a week. I offered to take messages and say positive things about you to prospective employers. The figure on the agreement was not fifty thousand, of course, but five hundred. To this day, I count in old francs—the denominations we used before General de Gaulle decided to delete two zeros, creating confusion for generations to come. Robert has to make out my income tax; otherwise, I give myself earnings in millions. He says I've had more than thirty years now to learn how to move a decimal, but a figure like "ten thousand francs" sounds more solid to me than "one hundred." I remember when a hundred francs was just the price of a croissant.

You remarked that five hundred was a lot for only a room. You had heard of studios going for six. But you did not have six hundred francs or five or even three, and after a while I took back my room and put you in Robert's, while he continued to sleep on the couch. Then you had no francs at all, and you exchanged beds with Robert, and, as it turned out, occasionally shared one. The arrangement—having you in the living room—never worked: It was hard to get you up in the morning, and the room looked as though five people were using it, all the time. We borrowed a folding bed and set it up at the far end of the hall, behind a screen, but you found the area noisy. The neighbors who lived upstairs used to go away for the weekend, leaving their dog. The concierge took it out twice a day, but the rest of the time it whined and barked, and at night it would scratch the floor. Apparently, this went on right over your head. I loaned you the earplugs my husband had used when his nerves were so bad. You complained that with your ears stopped up you could hear your own pulse beating. Given a choice, you preferred the dog.

I remember saying, "I'm afraid you must think we French are cruel to animals, Mlle. Dias de Corta, but I assure you not everyone is the same." You protested that you were French, too. I asked if you had a French passport. You said you had never applied for one. "Not even to go and visit your family?" I asked. You replied that the whole family lived in Marseilles. "But where were they born?" I asked. "Where did they come from?" There wasn't so much talk about European citizenship then. One felt free to wonder.

The couple with the dog moved away sometime in the eighties. Now the apartment is occupied by a woman with long, streaky, brass-colored hair.

She wears the same coat, made of fake ocelot, year after year. Some people think the man she lives with is her son. If so, she had him at the age of twelve.

What I want to tell you about has to do with the present and the great joy and astonishment we felt when we saw you in the oven-cleanser commercial last night. It came on just at the end of the eight o'clock news and before the debate on hepatitis. Robert and Anny were having dinner with me, without the children: Anny's mother had taken them to visit Euro Disney and was keeping them overnight. We had just started dessert—crème brûlée— when I recognized your voice. Robert stopped eating and said to Anny, "It's Alda. I'm sure it's Alda." Your face has changed in some indefinable manner that has nothing to do with time. Your smile seems whiter and wider; your hair is short and has a deep mahogany tint that mature actresses often favor. Mine is still ash blond, swept back, medium long. Alain—the stylist I sent you to, all those years ago—gave it shape and color, once and for all, and I have never tampered with his creation.

Alain often asked for news of you after you vanished, mentioning you affectionately as "the little Carmencita," searching TV guides and magazines for a sign of your career. He thought you must have changed your name, perhaps to something short and easy to remember. I recall the way you wept and stormed after he cut your hair, saying he had charged two weeks' rent and cropped it so drastically that there wasn't a part you could audition for now except Hamlet. Alain retired after selling his salon to a competent and charming woman named Marie-Laure. She is thirty-seven and trying hard to have a baby. Apparently, it is her fault, not the husband's. They have started her on hormones and I pray for her safety. It must seem strange to you to think of a woman bent on motherhood, but she has financial security with the salon (although she is still paying the bank). The husband is a car-insurance assessor.

The shot of your face at the oven door, seen as though the viewer were actually in the oven, seemed to me original and clever. (Anny said she had seen the same device in a commercial about refrigerators.) I wondered if the oven was a convenient height or if you were crouched on the floor. All we could see of you was your face, and the hand wielding the spray can. Your nails were beautifully lacquered holly red, not a crack or chip. You assured us that the product did not leave a bad smell or seep into food or damage the ozone layer. Just as we had finished taking this in, you were replaced by a picture of bacteria, dead or dying, and the next thing we knew some man was driving you away in a Jaguar, all your household tasks behind you. Every movement of your body seemed to express freedom from care. What I could make out of your forehead, partly obscured by the mahogany-tinted locks, seemed smooth and unlined. It is only justice, for I had a happy childhood and a wonderful husband and a fine son, and I recall some of the things you told Robert about your early years. He was just twenty-two and easily moved to pity.

Anny reminded us of the exact date when we last had seen you: April 24, 1983. It was in the television film about the two friends, "Virginie" and "Camilla," and how they meet two interesting but very different men and accompany them on a holiday in Cannes. One of the men is a celebrated singer whose wife (not shown) has left him for some egocentric reason (not explained). The other is an architect with political connections. The singer does not know the architect has been using bribery and blackmail to obtain government contracts. Right at the beginning you make a mistake and choose the architect, having rejected the singer because of his social manner, diffident and shy. "Virginie" settles for the singer. It turns out that she has never heard of him and does not know he has sold millions of records. She has been working among the deprived in a remote mountain region, where reception is poor.

Anny found that part of the story hard to believe. As she said, even the most forlorn Alpine villages are equipped for winter tourists, and skiers won't stay in places where they can't watch the programs. At any rate, the singer is captivated by "Virginie," and the two sit in the hotel bar, which is dimly lighted, comparing their views and principles. While this is taking place, you, "Camilla," are upstairs in a flower-filled suite, making mad love with the architect. Then you and he have a big quarrel, because of his basic indifference to the real world, and you take a bunch of red roses out of a vase and throw them in his face. (I recognized your quick temper.) He brushes a torn leaf from his bare chest and picks up the telephone and says, "Madame is leaving the hotel. Send someone up for her luggage." In the next scene you are on the edge of a highway trying to get a lift to the airport. The architect has given you your air ticket but nothing for taxis.

Anny and Robert had not been married long, but she knew about you and how much you figured in our memories. She sympathized with your plight and thought it was undeserved. You had shown yourself to be objective and caring and could have been won round (by the architect) with a kind word. She wondered if you were playing your own life and if the incident at Cannes was part of a pattern of behavior. We were unable to say, inasmuch as you had vanished from our lives in the seventies. To me, you seemed not quite right for the part. You looked too quick and intelligent to be standing around with no clothes on, throwing flowers at a naked man, when you could have been putting on a designer dress and going out for dinner. Robert, who had been perfectly silent, said, "Alda was always hard to cast." It was a remark that must have come out of old café conversations, when he was still seeing actors. I had warned Anny he would be hard to live with. She took him on trust.

My husband took some people on trust, too, and he died disappointed. I once showed you the place on Place d'Italie where our restaurant used to be. After we had to sell it, it became a pizza restaurant, then a health-food store. What it is now I don't know. When I go by I look the other way. Like you, he picked the wrong person. She was a regular lunchtime customer, as quiet as Anny; her husband did the talking. He seemed to be involved with the construction taking place around the Porte de Choisy and at that end of the avenue. The Chinese were moving into these places as fast as they were available; they kept their promises and paid their bills, and it seemed like a wise investment. Something went wrong. The woman disappeared, and the husband retired to that seaside town in Portugal where all the exiled kings and queens used to live. Portugal is a coincidence: I am not implying any connection with you or your relations or fellow citizens. If we are to create the Europe of the twenty-first century, we must show belief in one another and take our frustrated expectations as they come.

What I particularly admired, last night, was your pronunciation of "ozone." Where would you be if I hadn't kept after you about your o's? "Say 'Rhône,'" I used to tell you. "Not 'run.'" Watching you drive off in the Jaguar, I wondered if you had a thought to spare for Robert's old Renault. The day you went away together, after the only quarrel I ever had with my son, he threw your suitcase in the backseat. The suitcase was still there the next morning, when he came back alone. Later, he said he hadn't noticed it. The two of you had spent the night in the car, for you had no money and nowhere to go. There was barely room to sit. He drives a Citroën BX now.

I had been the first to spot your condition. You had an interview for a six-day modeling job—Rue des Rosiers, wholesale—and nothing to wear. I gave you one of my own dresses, which, of course, had to be taken in. You were thinner than ever and had lost your appetite for breakfast. You said you thought the apricot jam was making you sick. (I bought you some honey from Provence, but you threw that up, too.) I had finished basting the dress seams and was down on my knees, pinning the hem, when I suddenly put my hand flat on the front of the skirt and said, "How far along are you?" You burst into tears and said something I won't repeat. I said, "You should have thought of all that sooner. I can't help you. I'm sorry. It's against the law and, besides, I wouldn't know where to send you."

After the night in the Renault you went to a café, so that Robert could shave in the washroom. He said, "Why don't you start a conversation with that woman at the next table? She looks as if she might know." Sure enough, when he came back a few minutes later, your attention was turned to the stranger. She wrote something on the back of an old Métro ticket (the solution, most probably) and you put it away in your purse, perhaps next to the diploma. You seemed to him eager and hopeful and excited, as if you could see a better prospect than the six-day modeling job or the solution to your immediate difficulty or even a new kind of life—better than any you could offer each other. He walked straight out to the street, without stopping to speak, and came home. He refused to say a word to me, changed his clothes, and left for the day. A day like any other, in a way.

When the commercial ended we sat in silence. Then Anny got up and began to clear away the dessert no one had finished. The debate on hepatitis was now deeply engaged. Six or seven men who seemed to be strangling in their collars and ties sat at a round table, all of them yelling. The program presenter had lost control of the proceedings. One man shouted above the others that there were people who sincerely wanted to be ill. No amount of money poured into the health services could cure their muddled impulses. Certain impulses were as bad as any disease. Anny, still standing, cut off the sound (her only impatient act), and we watched the debaters opening and shutting their mouths. Speaking quietly, she said that life was a long duty, not a gift. She often thought about her own and had come to the conclusion that only through reincarnation would she ever know what she might have been or what important projects she might have carried out. Her temperament is Swiss. When she speaks, her genes are speaking.

I always expected you to come back for the suitcase. It is still here, high up on a shelf in the hall closet. We looked inside—not to pry but in case you had packed something perishable, such as a sandwich. There was a jumble of cotton garments and a pair of worn sandals and some other dresses I had pinned and basted for you, which you never sewed. Or sewed with such big, loose stitches that the seams came apart. (I had also given you a warm jacket with an embroidered Tyrolian-style collar. I think you had it on when you left.) On that first day, when I made the remark that your suitcase weighed next to nothing, you took it for a slight and said, "I am small and I wear small sizes." You looked about fifteen and had poor teeth and terrible posture.

The money you owed came to a hundred and fifty thousand francs, counted the old way, or one thousand five hundred in new francs. If we include accumulated inflation, it should amount to a million five hundred thousand; or, as you would probably prefer to put it, fifteen thousand. Inflation ran for years at 12 percent, but I think that over decades it must even out to 10. I base this on the fact that in 1970 half a dozen eggs were worth one new franc, while today one has to pay nine or ten. As for interest, I'm afraid it would be impossible to work out after so much time. It would depend on the year and the whims of this or that bank. There have been more prime ministers and annual budgets and unpleasant announcements and changes in rates than I can count. Actually, I don't want interest. To tell the truth, I don't want anything but the pleasure of seeing you and hearing from your own lips what you are proud of and what you regret.

My only regret is that my husband never would let me help in the restaurant. He wanted me to stay home and create a pleasant refuge for him and look after Robert. His own parents had slaved in their bistro, trying to please greedy and difficult people who couldn't be satisfied. He did not wish to have his only child do his homework in some dim corner between the bar and the kitchen door. But I could have been behind the bar, with Robert doing homework where I could keep an eye on him (instead of in his room with the door locked). I might have learned to handle cash and checks and work out tips in new francs and I might have noticed trouble coming, and taken steps.

I sang a lot when I was alone. I wasn't able to read music, but I could imitate anything I heard on records that suited my voice, airs by Delibes or Massenet. My muses were Lily Pons and Ninon Vallin. Probably you have never heard of them. They were before your time and are traditionally French.

According to Anny and Marie-Laure, fashions of the seventies are on the way back. Anny never buys herself anything, but Marie-Laure has several new outfits with softly draped skirts and jackets with a peasant motif—not unlike the clothes I gave you. If you like, I could make over anything in the suitcase to meet your social and professional demands. We could take up life where it was broken off, when I was on my knees, pinning the hem. We could say simple things that take the sting out of life, the way Anny does. You can come and fetch the suitcase any day, at any time. I am up and dressed by half past seven, and by a quarter to nine my home is ready for unexpected guests. There is an elevator in the building now. You won't have the five flights to climb. At the entrance to the building you will find a digit-code lock. The number that lets you in is K630. Be careful not to admit any-one who looks suspicious or threatening. If some stranger tries to push past just as you open the door, ask him what he wants and the name of the ten-ant he wishes to see. Probably he won't even try to give you a credible an-swer and will be scared away.

The concierge you knew stayed on for another fifteen years, then retired to live with her married daughter in Normandy. We voted not to have her replaced. A team of cleaners comes in twice a month. They are never the same, so one never gets to know them. It does away with the need for a Christmas tip and you don't have the smell of cooking permeating the whole ground floor, but one misses the sense of security. You may remem-ber that Mme. Julie was alert night and day, keeping track of everyone who came in and went out. There is no one now to bring mail to the door, ring the doorbell, make sure we are still alive. You will notice the row of mail-boxes in the vestibule. Some of the older tenants won't put their full name on the box, just their initials. In their view, the name is no one's business. The postman knows who they are, but in summer, when a substitute makes the rounds, he just throws their letters on the floor. There are continual complaints. Not long ago, an intruder tore two or three boxes off the wall.

You will find no changes in the apartment. The inventory you once signed could still apply, if one erased the words "electric heater." Do not send a check—or, indeed, any communication. You need not call to make an appointment. I prefer to live in the expectation of hearing the elevator stop at my floor and then your ring, and of having you tell me you have come home.

SCARVES, BEADS, SANDALS

---

*A*fter three years, Mathilde and Theo Schurz were divorced, without a mean thought, and even Theo says she is better off now, married to Alain Poix. (Or "Poids." Or "Poisse." Theo may be speaking the truth when he says he can't keep in mind every facet of the essential Alain.) Mathilde moved in with Alain six months before the wedding, in order to become acquainted with domestic tedium and annoying habits, should they occur, and so avoid making the same mistake (marriage piled onto infatuation) twice. They rented, and are now gradually buying, a two-bedroom place on Rue Saint-Didier, in the Sixteenth Arrondissement. In every conceivable way it is distant from the dispiriting south fringe of Montparnasse, where Theo continues to reside, close to several of the city's grimmest hospitals, and always under some threat or other—eviction, plagues of mice, demolition of the whole cul-de-sac of sagging one-story studios. If Theo had been attracted by her "physical aspect"—Mathilde's new, severe term for beauty—Alain accepts her as a concerned and contributing partner, intellectually and spiritually. This is not her conclusion. It is her verdict.

Theo wonders about "spiritually." It sounds to him like a moist west wind, ready to veer at any minute, with soft alternations of sun and rain. Whatever Mathilde means, or wants to mean, even the idea of the partnership should keep her fully occupied. Nevertheless, she finds time to drive across Paris, nearly every Saturday afternoon, to see how Theo is getting along without her. (Where is Alain? In close liaison with a computer, she says.) She brings Theo flowering shrubs from the market on Île de la Cité, still hoping to enliven the blighted yard next to the studio, and food in covered dishes—whole, delicious meals, not Poix leftovers—and fresh news about Alain.

Recently, Alain was moved to a new office—a room divided in two, really, but on the same floor as the minister and with part of an eighteenth-century fresco overhead. If Alain looks straight up, perhaps to ease a cramp in his neck, he can take in Apollo—just Apollo's head—watching Daphne turn into a laurel tree. Owing to the perspective of the work, Alain has the entire Daphne—roots, bark, and branches, and her small pink Enlightenment face peering through leaves. (The person next door has inherited Apollo's torso, dressed in Roman armor, with a short white skirt, and his legs and feet.) To Theo, from whom women manage to drift away, the situation might seem another connubial bad dream, but Alain interprets it as an allegory of free feminine choice. If he weren't so pressed with other work, he might write something along that line: an essay of about a hundred and fifty pages, published between soft white covers and containing almost as many colored illustrations as there are pages of print; something a reader can absorb during a weekend and still attend to the perennial border on Sunday afternoon.

He envisions (so does Mathilde) a display on the "recent nonfiction" table in a Saint-Germain-des-Prés bookshop, between stacks of something new about waste disposal and something new about Jung. Instead of writing the essay, Alain applies his trained mind and exacting higher education to shoring up French values against the Anglo-Saxon mud slide. On this particular Saturday, he is trying to batter into proper French one more untranslatable expression: "air bag." It was on television again the other day, this time spoken by a woman showing black-and-white industrial drawings. Alain would rather take the field against terms that have greater resonance, are more blatantly English, such as "shallow" and "bully" and "wishful thinking," but no one, so far, has ever tried to use them in a commercial.

So Mathilde explains to Theo as she sorts his laundry, starts the machine, puts clean sheets on the bed. She admires Theo, as an artist—it is what drew her to him in the first place—but since becoming Mme. Poix she has tended to see him as unemployable. At an age when Theo was still carrying a portfolio of drawings up and down and around Rue de Seine, looking for a small but adventurous gallery to take him in, Alain has established a position in the cultural apparat. It may even survive the next elections: He is too valuable an asset to be swept out and told to find a job in the private sector. Actually, the private sector could ask nothing better. Everyone wants Alain.

Publishers want him. Foreign universities want him. Even America is waiting, in spite of the uncompromising things he has said about the hegemony
and how it encourages well-bred Europeans to eat pizza slices in the street.

Theo has never heard of anybody with symbolic imagery, or even half an
image, on his office ceiling outlasting a change of government. The queue
for space of that kind consists of one ravenous human resource after the
other, pushing hard. As for the private sector, its cultural subdivisions are
hard up for breathing room, in the dark, stalled between floors. Alain requires the clean horizons and rich oxygen flow of the governing class. Theo
says none of this. He removes foil from bowls and dishes, to see what
Mathilde wants him to have for dinner. What can a Theo understand about
an Alain? Theo never votes. He has never registered, he forgets the right
date. All at once the campaign is over. The next day familiar faces, foxy or
benign, return to the news, described as untested but eager to learn. Elections are held in spring, perhaps to make one believe in growth, renewal.
One rainy morning in May, sooner or later, Alain will have to stack his personal files, give up Apollo and Daphne, cross a ministry courtyard on the
first lap of a march into the private sector. Theo sees him stepping along
cautiously, avoiding the worst of the puddles. Alain can always teach, Theo
tells himself. It is what people say about aides and assistants they happen to
know, as the astonishing results unfold on the screen.

Alain knows Theo, of course. Among his mixed feelings, Alain has no trouble finding the esteem due to a cultural bulwark: Theo and his work have entered the enclosed space known as "time-honored." Alain even knows about
the Poids and Poisse business, but does not hold it against Theo; according
to Mathilde, one no longer can be sure when he is trying to show he has a
sense of humor or when he is losing brain cells. He was at the wedding,
correctly dressed, suit, collar, and tie, looking distinguished—something
like Braque at the age of fifty, Alain said, but thinner, taller, blue-eyed,
lighter hair, finer profile. By then they were at the reception, drinking
champagne under a white marquee, wishing they could sit down. It was costing Mathilde's father the earth—the venue was a restaurant in the Bois de
Boulogne—but he was so thankful to be rid of Theo as a son-in-law that he
would have hired Versailles, if one could.

The slow, winding currents of the gathering had brought Theo, Alain,
and Mathilde together. Theo with one finger pushed back a strayed lock of
her hair; it was reddish gold, the shade of a persimmon. Perhaps he was mea-

suring his loss and might even, at last, say something embarrassing and true. Actually, he was saying that Alain's description—blue-eyed, etc.—sounded more like Max Ernst. Alain backtracked, said it was Balthus he'd had in mind. Mathilde, though not Alain, was still troubled by Theo's wedding gift, a botched painting he had been tinkering with for years. She had been Mme. Poix for a few hours, but still felt responsible for Theo's gaffes and imperfections. When he did not reply at once, she said she hoped he did not object to being told he was like Balthus. Balthus was the best-looking artist of the past hundred years, with the exception of Picasso.

Alain wondered what Picasso had to do with the conversation. Theo looked nothing like him: He came from Alsace. He, Alain, had never understood the way women preferred male genius incarnated as short, dark, and square-shaped. "Like Celtic gnomes," said Theo, just to fill in. Mathilde saw the roses in the restaurant garden through a blur which was not the mist of happiness. Alain had belittled her, on their wedding day, in the presence of her first husband. Her first husband had implied she was attracted to gnomes. She let her head droop. Her hair slid over her cheeks, but Theo, this time, left it alone. Both men looked elsewhere—Alain because tears were something new, Theo out of habit. The minister stood close by, showing admirable elegance of manner—not haughty, not familiar, careful, kind, like the Archbishop of Paris at a humble sort of funeral, Theo said, thinking to cheer up Mathilde. Luckily, no one overheard. Her mood was beginning to draw attention. Many years before, around the time of the Algerian War, a relative of Alain's mother had married an aunt of the minister. The outer rims of the family circles had quite definitely overlapped. It was the reason the minister had come to the reception and why he had stayed, so far, more than half an hour.

Mathilde was right; Theo must be losing brain cells at a brisk rate now. First Celtic gnomes, then the Archbishop of Paris; and, of course, the tactless, stingy, offensive gift. Alain decided to smile, extending greetings to everyone. He was attempting to say, "I am entirely happy on this significant June day." He was happy, but not entirely. Perhaps Mathilde was recalling her three years with Theo and telling herself nothing lasts. He wished Theo would do something considerate, such as disappear. A cluster of transparent molecules, the physical remainder of the artist T. Schurz, would dance in the sun, above the roses. Theo need not be dead—just gone.

"Do you remember, Theo, the day we got married," said Mathilde, looking up at the wrong man, by accident intercepting the smile Alain was using to reassure the minister and the others. "Everybody kept saying we had made a mistake. We decided to find out how big a mistake it was, so in the evening we went to Montmartre and had our palms read. Theo was told he could have been an artist but was probably a merchant seaman. His left hand was full of little shipwrecks." She may have been waiting for Alain to ask, "What about you? What did your hand say?" In fact, he was thinking just about his own. In both palms he had lines that might be neat little roads, straight or curved, and a couple of spidery stars.

At first, Theo had said he would give them a painting. Waiting, they kept a whole wall bare. Alain supposed it would be one of the great recent works; Mathilde thought she knew better. Either Alain had forgotten about having carried off the artist's wife or he had decided it didn't matter to Theo. That aside, Theo and Theo's dealer were tight as straitjackets about his work. Mathilde owned nothing, not even a crumpled sketch saved from a dustbin. The dealer had taken much of the earlier work off the market, which did not mean Theo was allowed to give any away. He burned most of his discards and kept just a few unsalable things in a shed. Speaking of his wedding gift, Theo said the word "painting" just once and never again: He mentioned some engravings—falling rain or falling snow—or else a plain white tile he could dedicate and sign. Mathilde made a reference to the empty wall. A larger work, even unfinished, even slightly below Theo's dealer's exacting standards, would remind Mathilde of Theo for the rest of her life.

Five days later, the concierge at Rue Saint-Didier took possession of a large oil study of a nude with red hair—poppy red, not like Mathilde's—prone on a bed, her face concealed in pillows. Mathilde recognized the studio, as it had been before she moved in and cleaned it up. She remembered the two reproductions, torn out of books or catalogues, askew on the wall. One showed a pair of Etruscan figures, dancing face-to-face, the other a hermit in a landscape. When the bed became half Mathilde's, she took them down. She had wondered if Theo would mind, but he never noticed—at any rate, never opened an inquiry.

"Are you sure this thing is a Schurz?" said Alain. Nothing else bothered him. He wondered, at first, if Theo had found the picture at a junk sale and had signed it as a joke. The true gift, the one they were to cherish and display, would come along later, all the more to be admired because of the scare. But Theo never invented jokes; he blundered into them.

"I am not that woman," Mathilde said. Of course not. Alain had never supposed she was. There was the crude red of the hair, the large backside, the dirty feet, and then the date—"1979"—firm and black and in the usual place, to the right of "T. Schurz." At that time, Mathilde was still reading translations of Soviet poetry, in love with a teacher of Russian at her lycée, and had never heard of "T. Schurz." In saying this, Alain showed he remembered the story of her life. If she'd had a reason to forgive him, about anything, she would have absolved him on the spot; then he spoiled the moment by declaring that it made no difference. The model was not meant to be anyone in particular.

Mathilde thought of Emma, Theo's first long-term companion (twelve years), but by '79 Emma must have been back in Alsace, writing cookery books with a woman friend. Julita (six years) fit the date but had worn a thick yellow braid down her back. She was famous for having tried to strangle Theo, but her hands were too small—she could not get a grip. After the throttling incident, which had taken place in a restaurant, Julita had packed a few things, most of them Theo's, and moved to the north end of Paris, where she would not run into him. Emma left Theo a microwave oven, Julita a cast-iron cat, standing on its hind legs, holding a tray. She had stolen it from a stand at the flea market, Theo told Mathilde, but the story sounded unlikely: The cat was heavy to lift, let alone be fetched across a distance. Two people would have been needed; perhaps one had been Theo. Sometimes, even now, some old friend from the Julita era tells Theo that Julita is ill or hard up and that he ought to help her out. Theo will say he doesn't know where she is or else, yes, he will do it tomorrow. She is like art taken off the market now, neither here nor there. The cat is still in the yard, rising out of broken flowerpots, empty bottles. Julita had told Theo it was the one cat that would never run away. She hung its neck with some amber beads Emma had overlooked in her flight, then pocketed the amber and left him the naked cat.

When Mathilde was in love with Theo and jealous of women she had never met, she used to go to an Indian shop, in Montparnasse, where first Emma, then Julita had bought their flat sandals and white embroidered shifts and long gauzy skirts, black and pink and indigo. She imagined what it must have been like to live, dress, go to parties, quarrel, and make up with Theo in the seventies. Emma brushed her brown hair upside down, to create a great drifting mane. A woman in the Indian store did Julita's braid, just because she liked Julita. Mathilde bought a few things, skirts and sandals, but never wore them. They made her look alien, bedraggled, like the Romanian gypsy women begging for coins along Rue de Rennes. She did not want to steal from a market or fight with Theo in bistros. She belonged to a generation of women who showed a lot of leg and kept life smooth, tight-fitting, close-woven. Theo was right: She was better off with Alain.

Still, she had the right to know something about the woman she had been offered as a gift. It was no good asking directly; Theo might say it was a journalist who came to tape his memoirs or the wife of a Lutheran dignitary or one of his nieces from Alsace. Instead, she asked him to speak to Alain; out of aesthetic curiosity, she said, Alain acquired the facts of art. Theo often did whatever a woman asked, unless it was important. Clearly, this was not. Alain took the call in his office; at that time, he still had a cubicle with a bricked-up window. Nobody recalled who had ordered the bricks or how long ago. He worked by the light of a neon fixture that flickered continually and made his eyes water. Summoned by an aide to the minister, on propitious afternoons by the minister himself (such summonses were more and more frequent), he descended two flights, using the staircase in order to avoid a giddy change from neon tube to the steadier glow of a chandelier. He brought with him only a modest amount of paperwork. He was expected to store everything in his head.

Theo told Alain straight out that he had used Julita for the pose. She slept much of the day and for that reason made an excellent model: was never tired, never hungry, never restless, never had to break off for a cigarette. The picture had not worked out and he had set it aside. Recently he had looked at it again and decided to alter Julita from the neck up. Alain thought he had just been told something of consequence; he wanted to exchange revelations, let Theo know he had not enticed Mathilde away but had merely opened the net into which she could jump. She had grabbed Theo in her flight, perhaps to break the fall. But Alain held still; it would be unseemly to discuss Mathilde. Theo was simply there, like an older relative who has to be considered and mollified, though no one knows why. There was something flattering about having been offered an unwanted and unnecessary explanation; few artists would have bothered to make one. It was as though Theo had decided to take Alain seriously. Alain thanked him.

Unfortunately, the clarification had made the painting even less interesting than it looked. Until then, it had been a dud Schurz but an honest vision. The subject, a woman, entirely womanly, had been transfigured by Schurz's reactionary visual fallacy (though honest, if one accepted the way his mind worked) into a hefty platitude; still, it was art. Now, endowed with a name and, why not, an address, a telephone number, a social-security number, and a personal history, Theo's universal statement dwindled to a footnote about Julita—second long-term companion of T. Schurz, first husband of Mathilde, future first wife of Alain Poix. A white tile with a date and a signature would have shown more tact and common sense.

All this Alain said to Mathilde that night, as they ate their dinner next to the empty wall. Mathilde said she was certain Theo had gone to considerable trouble to choose something he believed they would understand and appreciate and that would enhance their marriage. It was one of her first lies to Alain: Theo had gone out to the shed where he kept his shortfalls and made a final decision about a dead loss. Perhaps he guessed they would never hang it and so damage his reputation, although as a rule he never imagined future behavior more than a few minutes away. Years ago, in a bistro on Rue Stanislas, he had drawn a portrait of Julita on the paper tablecloth, signed and dated it, torn it off, even made the edges neat. It was actually in her hands when he snatched it back, ripped it to shreds, and set the shreds on fire in an ashtray. It was then that Julita had tried to get him by the throat.

Yesterday, Friday, an April day, Theo was awakened by a hard beam of light trained on his face. There was a fainter light at the open door, where the stranger had entered easily. The time must have been around five o'clock. Theo could make out an outline, drawn in gray chalk: leather jacket, close-cropped head. (Foreign Legion deserter? Escaped prisoner? Neo-Nazi? Drugs?) He spoke a coarse, neutral, urban French—the old Paris accent was dying out—and told Theo that if he tried to move or call he, the intruder, might hurt him. He did not say how. They all watch the same programs, Theo told himself. He is young and he repeats what he has seen and heard. Theo had no intention of moving and there was no one to call. His thoughts were directed to the privy, in the yard. He hoped the young man would not take too long to discover there was nothing to steal, except a small amount of cash. He would have told him where to find it, but that might be classed as calling out. His checkbook was in a drawer of Emma's old desk, his bank card behind the snapshot of Mathilde, propped on the shelf above the sink. The checkbook was no good to the stranger, unless he forced Theo to sign all the checks. Theo heard him scuffing about, heard a drawer being pulled. He shut his eyes, opened them to see the face bent over him, the intent and watchful expression, like a lover's, and the raised arm and the flashlight (probably) wrapped in one of Mathilde's blue-and-white tea towels.

He came to in full daylight. His nose had bled all over the pillows, and the mattress was sodden. He got up and walked quite steadily, barefoot, over the stones and gravel of the yard; returning to the studio, he found some of yesterday's coffee still in the pot. He heated it up in a saucepan, poured in milk, drank, and kept it down. Only when that was done did he look in a mirror. He could hide his blackened eyes behind sunglasses but not the raw bruise on his forehead or his swollen nose. He dragged the mattress outside and spread it in the cold April sunlight. By four o'clock, Mathilde's announced arrival time—for it seemed to him today could be Saturday—the place was pretty well cleaned up, mattress back on the bed, soiled bedclothes rolled up, pushed in a corner. He found a banquet-size tablecloth, probably something of Emma's, and drew it over the mattress. Only his cash had vanished; the checkbook and bank card lay on the floor. He had been attacked, for no reason, by a man he had never seen before and would be unable to recognize: His face had been neutral, like his voice. Theo turned on the radio and, from something said, discovered this was still Friday, the day before Mathilde's habitual visiting day. He had expected her to make the mattress dry in some magical and efficient, Mathilde-like way. He kept in the shed a couple of sleeping bags, for rare nights when the temperature fell below freezing. He got one of them out, gave it a shake, and spread it on top of the tablecloth. It would have to do for that night.

Today, Saturday, Mathilde brought a meal packed in a black-and-white bag from Fauchon: cooked asparagus, with the lemon-and-oil sauce in a jar, cold roast lamb, and a gratin of courgettes and tomatoes—all he has to do is turn on Emma's microwave—a Camembert, a round loaf of that moist and slightly sour bread, from the place on Rue du Cherche-Midi, which reminds Schurz of the bread of his childhood, a carton of thick cream, and a bowl of strawberries, washed and hulled. It is too early for French strawberries. These are from Spain, picked green, shipped palely pink, almost as hard as radishes, but they remind one that it is spring. Schurz barely notices seasons. He works indoors. If rain happens to drench the yard when he goes outside to the lavatory, he puts on the Alpine beret that was part of his uniform when he was eighteen and doing his military service.

Mathilde, moving out to live with Alain, took with her a picture of Theo from that period, wearing the beret and the thick laced-up boots and carrying the heavy skis that were standard issue. He skied and shot a rifle for eighteen months, even thought he might have made it a permanent career, if that was all there was to the Army. No one had yet fallen in love with him, except perhaps his mother. His life was simple then, has grown simpler now. The seasons mean nothing, except that green strawberries are followed by red. Weather means crossing the yard bareheaded or covered up.

Mathilde has noticed she is starting to think of him as "Schurz." It is what his old friends call Theo. This afternoon, she had found him looking particularly Schurz-like, sitting on a chair he had dragged outside, drinking tea out of a mug, with the string of the tea bag trailing. He had on an overcoat and the regimental beret. He did not turn to the gate when she opened it or get up to greet her or say a word. Mathilde had to walk all round him to see his face.

"My God, Schurz, what happened?"

"I tripped and fell in the dark and struck my head on the cat."

"I wish you'd get rid of it," she said.

She took the mug from his hands and went inside, to unpack his dinner and make fresh tea. The beret, having concealed none of the damage, was useless now. He removed it and hung it rakishly on the cat, on one ear. Mathilde returned with, first, a small folding garden table (her legacy), then with a tray and teacups and a teapot and a plate of sliced gingerbread, which she had brought him the week before. She poured his tea, put sugar in, stirred it, and handed him the cup.

She said, "Theo, how long do you think you can go on living here, alone?" (It was so pathetic, she rehearsed, for Alain. Theo was like a child; he had made the most absurd attempt at covering up the damage, and instead of putting the mattress out to dry he had turned the wet side down and slept on top of it, in a sleeping bag. Who was that famous writer who first showed signs of senility and incontinence on a bridge in Rome? I kept thinking of him. Schurz just sat there, like a guilty little boy. He caught syphilis when he was young and gave it to Emma; he said it was from a prostitute, in Montmartre, but I believe it was a married woman, the wife of the first collector to start buying his work. He can't stay there alone now. He simply can't. His checkbook and bank card were lying next to the trash bin. He must have been trying to throw them away.)

Her picture had been on the floor, too, the one taken the day she married Theo. Mathilde has a small cloud of red-gold hair and wears a short white dress and a jacket of the eighties, with shoulders so wide that her head seems unnaturally small, like a little ball of reddish fluff. Theo is next to her, not too close. He could be a relative or a family friend or even some old crony who heard the noise of the party and decided to drop in. The photograph is posed here, in the yard. One can see a table laden with bottles, and a cement-and-stucco structure—the privy, with the door shut, for a change—and a cold-water tap and a bucket lying on its side. You had to fill the bucket and take it in with you.

Schurz never tried to improve the place or make it more comfortable. His reason was, still is, that he might be evicted at any time. Any month, any day, the police and the bailiffs will arrive. He will be rushed off the premises, with just the cast-iron cat as a relic of his old life.

"I'll tell you what happened," he said, showing her his mess of a face. "Yesterday morning, while I was still asleep, a man broke in, stole some money, and hit me with something wrapped in a towel. It must have been his flashlight."

(Oh, if you had heard him! she continued to prepare for Alain. A comic-strip story. The truth is he is starting to miss his footing and to do himself damage, and he pees in his sleep, like a baby. What kind of doctor do we need for him? What sort of specialist? A geriatrician? He's not really old, but there's been the syphilis, and he has always done confused and crazy things, like giving us that picture, when we really wanted a plain, pure tile.)

Schurz at this moment is thinking of food. He would like to be handed a plate of pork ragout with noodles, swimming in gravy; but nobody makes that now. Or stewed eels in red wine, with the onions cooked soft. Or a cutlet of venison, browned in butter on both sides, with a purée of chestnuts. What he does not want is clear broth with a poached egg in it, or any sort of a salad. When he first came to Paris the cheapest meals were the heartiest. His mother had said, "Send me a Paris hat," not meaning it; though perhaps she did. His money, when he had any, went to supplies for his work or rent or things to eat.

Only old women wore hats now. There were hats in store windows, dusty windows, in narrow streets—black hats, for funerals and widows. But no widow under the age of sixty ever bought one. Young women wore hats at the end of summer, tilted straw things, that they tried on just for fun. When they took the hats off, their hair would spring loose. The face, freed of shadow, took on a different shape, seemed fuller, unmysterious, as bland as the moon. There was a vogue for bright scarves, around the straw hats, around the hair, wound around the neck along with strings of bright beads, loosely coiled—sand-colored or coral or a hard kind of blue. The beads cast colored reflections on the skin of a throat or on a scarf of a different shade, like a bead diluted in water. Schurz and his friends ate cheap meals in flaking courtyards and on terraces where the tables were enclosed in a hedge of brittle, unwatered shrubs. Late at night, the girls and young women would suddenly find that everything they had on was too tight. It was the effect of the warm end-of-summer night and the food and the red wine and the slow movement of the conversation. It slid without wavering from gossip to mean gossip to art to life-in-art to living without boundaries. A scarf would come uncoiled and hang on the back of a chair or a twig of the parched hedge; as it would hang, later, over the foot of someone's bed. Not often Schurz's (not often enough), because he lived in a hotel near the Café Mabillon, long before all those places were renovated and had elevators put in and were given a star in some of the guidebooks. A stiff fine had to be paid by any client caught with a late-night visitor. The police used to patrol small hotels and knock on doors just before morning, looking for French people in trouble with the law and for foreigners with fake passports and no residence permits. When they found an extra guest in the room, usually a frantic young woman trying to pull the sheet over her face, the hotelkeeper was fined, too, and the tenant thrown out a few hours later. It was not a question of sexual morality but just of rules.

When dinner was almost finished, the women would take off their glass beads and let them drop in a heap among the ashtrays and coffee cups and on top of the wine stains and scribbled drawings. Their high-heeled sandals were narrow and so tight that they had to keep their toes crossed; and at last they would slip them off, unobserved, using first one foot, then the other. Scarfless, shoeless, unbound, delivered, they waited for the last wine bottle to be emptied and the last of the coffee to be drunk or spilled before they decided what they specifically wanted or exactly refused. This was not like a memory to Theo but like part of the present time, something that unfolded gradually, revealing mysteries and satisfactions.

In the studio, behind him, Mathilde was making telephone calls. He heard her voice but not her words. On a late Saturday afternoon, she would be recording her messages on other people's machines: He supposed there must be one or two to doctors, and one for the service that sends vans and men to take cumbersome objects away, such as a soiled mattress. Several brief inquiries must have been needed before she could find Theo a hotel room, free tonight, at a price he would accept and on a street he would tolerate. The long unbroken monologue must have been for Alain, explaining that she would be much later than expected, and why. On Monday she would take Theo to the Bon Marché department store and make him buy a mattress, perhaps a whole new bed. Now here was a memory, a brief, plain stretch of the past: Love apart, she had married him because she wanted to be Mme. T. Schurz. She would not go on attending parties and gallery openings as Schurz's young friend. Nobody knew whether she was actually living with him or writing something on his work or tagging along for the evening. She did not have the look of a woman who would choose to settle for a studio that resembled a garage or, really, for Schurz. It turned out she could hardly wait to move in, scrape and wax whatever he had in the way of furniture, whitewash the walls. She trained climbing plants over the wire fence outside, even tried to grow lemon trees in terra-cotta tubs. The tubs are still there.

She came toward him now, carrying the bag she had packed so that he would have everything he needed at the hotel. "Don't touch the bruise," she said, gently, removing the hand full of small shipwrecks. The other thing she said today, which he is bound to recall later on, was "You ought to start getting used to the idea of leaving this place. You know that it is going to be torn down."

Well, it is true. At the entrance to the doomed and decaying little colony there is a poster, damaged by weather and vandals, on which one can still see a depiction of the structure that will cover the ruin, once it has finally been brought down: a handsome biscuit-colored multipurpose urban complex comprising a library, a crèche, a couple of municipal offices, a screening room for projecting films about Bedouins or whales, a lounge where elderly people may spend the whole day playing board games, a theater for amateur and professional performances, and four low-rent work units for painters, sculptors, poets, musicians, and photographers. (A waiting list of two thousand names was closed some years ago.) It seems to Theo that Julita was still around at the time when the poster was put up. The project keeps running into snags—aesthetic, political, mainly economic. One day the poster will have been his view of the future for more than a third of his life.

Mathilde backed out of the cul-de-sac, taking care (he does not like being driven), and she said, "Theo, we are near all these hospitals. If you think you should have an X ray at once, we can go to an emergency service. I can't decide, because I really don't know how you got hurt."

"Not now." He wanted today to wind down. Mathilde, in her mind, seemed to have gone beyond dropping him at his hotel. He had agreed to something on Rue Delambre, behind the Coupole and the Dôme. She was on the far side of Paris, with Alain. As she drove on, she asked Theo if he could suggest suitable French for a few English expressions: "divided attention" and "hard-driven" and "matchless perfection," the latter in one word.

"I hope no one steals my Alpine beret," he said. "I left it hanging on the cat."

Those were the last words they exchanged today. It is how they said good-bye.

LINNET

MUIR

THE DOCTOR

❧

*W*ho can remember now a picture called *The Doctor*? From 1891, when the original was painted, to the middle of the Depression, when it finally went out of style, reproductions of this work flowed into every crevice and corner of North America and the British Empire, swamping continents. Not even *The Angelus* supplied as rich a mixture of art and lesson. The two people in *The Angelus* are there to tell us clearly that the meek inherit nothing but seem not to mind; in *The Doctor* a cast of four enacts a more complex statement of Christian submission or Christian pessimism, depending on the beholder: God's Will is manifest in a dying child, Helpless Materialism in a baffled physician, and Afflicted Humanity in the stricken parents. The parable is set in a spotless cottage; the child's bed, composed of three chairs, is out of a doll's house. In much of the world—the world as it was, so much smaller than now—two full generations were raised with the monochrome promise that existence is insoluble, tragedy static, poverty endearing, and heavenly justice a total mystery.

It must have come as a shock to overseas visitors when they discovered *The Doctor* incarnated as an oil painting in the Tate Gallery in London, in the company of other Victorian miseries entitled *Hopeless Dawn* and *The Last Day in the Old Home*. *The Doctor* had not been divinely inspired and distributed to chasten us after all, but was the work of someone called Sir Luke Fildes— nineteenth-century rationalist and atheist, for all anyone knew. Perhaps it was simply a scene from a three-decker novel, even a joke. In museum surroundings—classified, ticketed—*The Doctor* conveyed a new instruction: Death is sentimental, art is pretense.

Some people had always hated *The Doctor*. My father, for one. He said, "You surely don't want *that* thing in your room."

The argument (it became one) took place in Montreal, in a house that died long ago without leaving even a ghost. He was in his twenties, to match the century. I had been around about the length of your average major war. I had my way but do not remember how; neither tears nor temper ever worked. What probably won out was his wish to be agreeable to Dr. Chauchard, the pediatrician who had given me the engraving. My father seemed to like Chauchard, as he did most people—just well enough—while my mother, who carried an uncritical allegiance from person to person, belief to belief, had recently declared Chauchard to be mentally, morally, and spiritually without fault.

Dr. Chauchard must have been in his thirties then, but he seemed to me timeless, like God the Father. When he took the engraving down from the wall of his office, I understood him to be offering me a portrait of himself. My mother at first refused it, thinking I had asked; he assured her I had not, that he had merely been struck by my expression when I looked at the ailing child. *"C'est une sensible,"* he said—an appraisal my mother dismissed by saying I was as tough as a boot, which I truly believe to have been her opinion.

What I was sensitive to is nearly too plain to be signaled: The dying child, a girl, is the heart of the composition. The parents are in the shadow, where they belong. Their function is to be sorry. The doctor has only one patient; light from a tipped lampshade falls on her and her alone.

The street where Dr. Chauchard lived began to decline around the same time as the popularity of *The Doctor* and is now a slum. No citizens' committee can restore the natural elegance of those gray stone houses, the swept steps, the glittering windows, because, short of a miracle, it cannot resurrect the kind of upper-bourgeois French Canadians who used to live there. They have not migrated or moved westward in the city—they have ceased to exist. The handful of dust they sprang from, with its powerful components of religion and history, is part of another clay. They were families who did not resent what were inaccurately called "The English" in Montreal; they had never acknowledged them. The men read a newspaper sometimes, the women never. The women had a dark version of faith for private drama, a family tree to memorize for intellectual exercise, intense family affection for the needs of the heart. Their houses, like Dr. Chauchard's, smelled of cleanness as if cleanness were a commodity, a brand of floor wax. Convents used to have that smell; the girls raised in them brought to married life an ideal of housekeeping that was a memory of the polished convent corridor, with strict squares of sunlight falling where and as they should. Two sons and five daughters was the average for children; Simone, Pauline, Jeanne, Yvonne, and Louise the feminine names of the decade. The girls when young wore religious medals like golden flower petals on thin chains, had positive torrents of curls down to their shoulder blades, and came to children's parties dressed in rose velvet and white stockings, too shy to speak. Chauchard, a bachelor, came out of this world, which I can describe best only through its girls and women.

His front door, painted the gloomy shade my father called Montreal green, is seen from below, at an angle—a bell too high for me during the first visits, a letter box through which I called, "Open the door; *c'est moi,*" believing still that *"moi"* would take me anywhere. But no one could hear in any language, because two vestibules, one behind the other, stood in the way. In the first one overshoes dripped on a mat, then came a warmer place for coats. Each vestibule had its door, varnished to imitate the rings of a tree trunk, enhanced by a nature scene made of frosted glass; you unbuckled galoshes under herons and palm trees and shed layers of damp wool under swans floating in a landscape closer to home.

Just over the letter box of the green door a large, beautifully polished brass plate carried, in sloped writing:

Docteur Raoul Chauchard
Spécialiste en Médecine Infantile
Ancien Externe et Interne
des Hôpitaux de Paris
Sur Rendez-vous

On the bottom half of the plate this information was repeated in English, though the only English I recall in the waiting room was my mother's addressed to me.

He was not Parisian but native to the city, perhaps to the street, even to the house, if I think of how the glass-shaded lamps and branched chandeliers must have followed an evolution from oil to kerosene to gas to electricity without changing shape or place. Rooms and passages were papered deep blue fading to green (the brighter oblong left by the removal of *The Doctor* was about the color of a teal), so that the time of day indoors was winter dusk, with pools of light like uncurtained windows. An assemblage of gilt-framed pictures began between the heron and swan doors with brisk scenes of biblical injustice—the casting-out of Hagar, the swindling of Esau—and moved along the hall with European history: Vercingetorix surrendering to the Romans, the earthquake at Lisbon, Queen Victoria looking exactly like a potato pancake receiving some dark and humble envoy; then, with a light over him to mark his importance, Napoléon III reviewing a regiment from a white horse. (The popularity of "Napoléon" as a Christian name did not connect with the first Bonaparte, as English Canadians supposed—when any thought was given to any matter concerning French Canadians at all—but with his nephew, the lesser Bonaparte, who had never divorced or insulted the Pope, and who had established clerical influence in the saddle as firmly as it now sat upon Quebec.) The sitting-room-converted-to-waiting-room had on display landmarks of Paris, identified in two languages:

Le Petit Palais—The Petit Palais
Place Vendôme—Place Vendôme
Rue de la Paix—Rue de la Paix

as if the engraver had known they would find their way to a wall in Montreal.

Although he had trained in Paris, where, as our English doctor told my mother, leeches were still sold in pharmacies and babies died like flies, Chauchard was thought modern and forward-looking. He used the most advanced methods imported from the United States, or, as one would have said then, "from Boston," which meant both stylish and impeccably right. Ultraviolet irradiation was one, recommended for building up delicate children. I recall the black mask tied on, and the danger of blindness should one pull it off before being told. I owe him irradiation to the marrow and other sources of confusion: It was he who gave my mother the name of a convent where Jansenist discipline still had a foot on the neck of the twentieth century and where, as an added enchantment, I was certain not to hear a word of English. He never dreamed, I am sure, that I would be packed off there as a boarder from the age of four. Out of goodness and affection he gave me books to read—children's stories from nineteenth-century France which I hated and still detest. In these oppressive stories children were punished and punished hard for behavior that seemed in another century, above all on another continent, natural and right. I could never see the right-and-wrong over which they kept stumbling and only much later recognized it in European social fiddle-faddle—the trivial yardsticks that measure a man's character by the way he eats a boiled egg. The prose was stiff, a bit shrill, probably pitched too high for a North American ear. Even the bindings, a particularly ugly red, were repellent to me, while their gilt titles lent them the ceremonial quality of school prizes. I had plenty of English Victorian books, but the scolding could be got over, because there was no unfairness. Where there was, it was done away with as part of the plot. The authors were on the side of morality but also of the child. For a long time I imagined that most of my English books had been written by other children, but I never made that mistake with French; I saw these authors as large, scowling creatures with faces as flushed with crossness as the books' covers. Still, the books were presents, therefore important, offered without a word or a look Dr. Chauchard would not have bestowed on an adult. They had been his mother's; she lived in rooms at the top of the house, receiving her own friends, not often mingling with his. She must have let him have these treasures for a favored patient who did not understand the courtesy, even the sacrifice, until it was too late to say "Thank you." Another child's name— his mother's—was on the flyleaf; I seldom looked at it, concentrated as I was on my own. It is not simply rhetoric to say that I see him still—Fildes profile, white cuff, dark sleeve, writing the new dedication with a pen dipped in a blue inkwell, hand and book within the circle cast by the lamp on his desk. At home I would paste inside the front cover the plate my father had designed for me, which had "Linnet: Her Book" as ex libris, and the drawing of a stream flowing between grassy banks—his memory of the unhurried movement of England, no reflection of anything known to me in Quebec—bearing a single autumn leaf. Under the stream came the lines

> Time, Time, which none can bind
> While flowing fast leaves love
>   behind.

The only child will usually give and lend its possessions easily, having missed the sturdy training in rivalry and forced sharing afforded by sisters and brothers, yet nothing would have made me part willingly with any of the grim red books. Grouped on a special shelf, seldom opened after the first reading, they were not reminders but a true fragment of his twilit house, his swan and heron doors, Napoléon III so cunningly lighted, "Le Petit Palais—The Petit Palais," and, finally, Dr. Chauchard himself at the desk of his shadowy room writing *"Pour ma chère petite Linnet"* in a book that had once belonged to another girl.

Now, how to account for the changed, stern, disapproving Chauchard who in that same office gave me not a book but a lecture beginning "Think of your unfortunate parents" and ending "You owe them everything; it is your duty to love them." He had just telephoned for my father to come and fetch me. "How miserable they would be if anything ever happened to you," he said. He spoke of my *petit Papa* and my *petite Maman* with that fake diminution of authority characteristic of the Latin tongues which never works in English. I sat on a chair still wearing outdoor clothes—navy reefer over my convent uniform, HMS *Nelson* sailor hat held on by a black elastic—neither his patient nor his guest at this dreadful crisis, wondering, What does he mean? For a long time now my surprise visits to friends had been called, incorrectly, "running away." Running away was one of the reasons my parents gave when anyone asked why I had been walled up in such a severe school at an early age. Dr. Chauchard, honored by one of my visits, at once asked his office nurse, "Do her parents know she's here?" Women are supposed to make dangerous patients for bachelor doctors; besotted little girls must seem even worse. But I was not besotted; I believed we were equals. It was he who had set up the equality, and for that reason I still think he should have invited me to remove my coat.

The only thing worth remarking about his dull little sermon is that it was in French. French was his language for medicine; I never heard him give an opinion in English. It was evidently the language to which he retreated if one became a nuisance, his back to a wall of white marble syntax. And when it came to filial devotion he was one with the red-covered books. Calling on my parents, not as my doctor but as their friend, he spoke another language. It was not merely English instead of French but the private dialect of a younger person who was playful, charming, who smoked cigarettes in a black-and-silver holder, looking round to see the effect of his puns and jokes. You could notice then, only then, that his black-currant eyes were never still.

The house he came to remained for a long time enormous in memory, though the few like it still standing—"still living," I nearly say—are narrow, with thin, steep staircases and close, high-ceilinged rooms. They were the work of Edinburgh architects and dated from when Montreal was a Scottish city; it had never been really English. A Saturday-evening gathering of several adults, one child, and a couple of dogs created a sort of tangle in the middle of the room—an entwining that was surely not of people's feet: In those days everyone sat straight. The women had to, because their girdles had hooks and stays. Men sat up out of habit, probably the habit of prosperity; the Depression created the physical slump, a change in posture to match the times. Perhaps desires and secrets and second thoughts threading from person to person, from bachelor to married woman, from mother of none to somebody's father, formed a cat's cradle—matted, invisible, and quite dangerous. Why else would Ruby, the latest homesick underpaid Newfoundland import, have kept tripping up as she lurched across the room with cups and glasses on a tray?

Transformed into jolly Uncle Raoul (his request), Dr. Chauchard would arrive with a good friend of his, divorced Mrs. Erskine, and a younger friend of both, named Paul-Armand. Paul-Armand was temporary, one of a sequence of young men who attended Mrs. Erskine as her bard, her personal laureate. His role did not outlive a certain stage of artless admiration; at the first sign of falling away, the first mouse squeak of disenchantment from him, a replacement was found. All of these young men were good-looking, well brought up, longing to be unconventional, and entirely innocent. Flanked by her pair of males, Mrs. Erskine would sway into the room, as graceful as a woman can be when she is boned from waist to thigh. She would keep on her long moleskin coat, even though like all Canadian rooms this one was vastly overheated, explaining that she was chilly. This may have been an attempt to reduce the impression she gave of general largeness by suggesting an inner fragility. Presently the coat would come off, revealing a handwoven tea-cozy sort of garment—this at a time when every other woman was showing her knees. My mother sat with her legs crossed and one sandal dangling. Her hair had recently been shingled; she seemed to be groping for its lost comfortable warmth. Other persons, my father apart, are a dim choir muttering, "Isn't it past your bedtime?" My father sat back in a deep, chintz-covered chair and said hardly anything except for an occasional "Down" to his dogs.

In another season, in the country, my parents had other friends, summer friends, who drank old-fashioneds and danced to gramophone records out on the lawn. Winter friends were mostly coffee drinkers, who did what people do between wars and revolutions—sat in a circle and talked about revolutions and wars. The language was usually English, though not everyone was native to English. Mrs. Erskine commanded what she called "*good French*" and rather liked displaying it, but after a few sentences, which made those who could not understand French very fidgety and which annoyed the French Canadians present exactly in the way an affected accent will grate on Irish nerves, she would pick her way back to English. In mixed society, such little of it as existed, English seemed to be the social rule. It did not enter the mind of any English speaker that the French were at a constant disadvantage, like a team obliged to play all their matches away from home. Dr. Chauchard never addressed me in French here, not even when he would ask me to recite a French poem learned at my convent school. It began, "If I were a fly, Maman, I would steal a kiss from your lips." The nun in charge of memory work was fiddly about liaison, which produced an accidentally appropriate "*Si j'étaiszzzzzzune mouche, Maman.*" Dr. Chauchard never seemed to tire of this and may have thought it a reasonable declaration to make to one's mother.

It was a tactless rhyme, if you think of all the buzzing and stealing that went on in at least part of the winter circle, but I could not have known that. At least not consciously. Unconsciously, everyone under the age of ten knows everything. Under-ten can come into a room and sense at once everything felt, kept silent, held back in the way of love, hate, and desire, though he may not have the right words for such sentiments. It is part of the clairvoyant immunity to hypocrisy we are born with and that vanishes just before puberty. I knew, though no one had told me, that my mother was a bit foolish about Dr. Chauchard; that Mrs. Erskine would have turned cartwheels to get my father's attention but that even cartwheels would have failed; that Dr. Chauchard and Mrs. Erskine were somehow together but never went out alone. Paul-Armand was harder to place; too young to be a parent, he was a pest, a tease to someone smaller. His goading was never noticed, though my reaction to it, creeping behind his chair until I was in a position to punch him, brought an immediate response from the police: "Linnet, if you don't sit down I'm afraid you will have to go to your room." "If" and "I'm afraid" meant there was plenty of margin. Later: "Wouldn't you be happier if you just went to bed? No? Then get a book and sit down and read it." Presently, "Down, I said, sit down; did you hear what I've just said to you? I said, sit down, *down.*" There came a point like convergent lines finally meeting where orders to dogs and instructions to children were given in the same voice. The only difference was that a dog got "Down, damn it," and, of course, no one ever swore at me.

This overlapping in one room of French and English, of Catholic and Protestant—my parents' way of being, and so to me life itself—was as unlikely, as unnatural to the Montreal climate as a school of tropical fish. Only later would I discover that most other people simply floated in mossy little ponds labeled "French and Catholic" or "English and Protestant," never wondering what it might be like to step ashore; or wondering, perhaps, but weighing up the danger. To be out of a pond is to be in unmapped territory. The earth might be flat; you could fall over the edge quite easily. My parents and their friends were, in their way, explorers. They had in common a fear of being bored, which is a fear one can afford to nourish in times of prosperity and peace. It makes for the most ruthless kind of exclusiveness, based as it is on the belief that anyone can be the richest of this or cleverest of that and still be the dullest dog that ever barked. I wince even now remembering those wretched once-only guests who were put on trial for a Saturday night and unanimously condemned. This heartlessness apart, the winter circle shared an outlook, a kind of humor, a certain vocabulary of the mind. No one made any of the standard Montreal statements, such as "What a lot of books you've got! Don't tell me you've read them," or "I hear you're some kind of artist. What do you really *do*?" Explorers like Dr. Chauchard and Mrs. Erskine and my mother and the rest recognized each other on sight; the recognition cut through disguisements of class, profession, religion, language, and even what poll takers call "other interests."

Once you have jumped out of a social enclosure, your eye is bound to be on a real, a geographical elsewhere; theirs seemed to consist of a few cities of Europe with agreeable-sounding names like Vienna and Venice. The United States consisted only of Boston and Florida then. Adults went to Florida for therapeutic reasons—for chronic bronchitis, to recover from operations, for the sake of mysterious maladies that had no names and were called in obituaries "a long illness bravely borne." Boston seemed to be an elegant little republic with its own parliament and flag. To English Montreal, cocooned in that other language nobody bothered to learn, the rest of the continent, Canada included, barely existed; travelers would disembark after long, sooty train trips expressing relief to be in the only city where there were decent restaurants and well-dressed women and where proper

English could be heard. Elsewhere, then, became other people, and little groups would form where friends, to the tune of vast mutual admiration, could find a pleasing remoteness in each other. They resembled, in their yearnings, in their clinging together as a substitute for motion, in their craving for "someone to talk to," the kind of marginal social clans you find today in the capitals of Eastern Europe.

I was in the dining room cutting up magazines. My mother brought her coffee cup in, sat down, and said, "Promise me you will never be caught in a situation where you have to compete with a younger woman."

She must have been twenty-six at the very most; Mrs. Erskine was well over thirty. I suppose she was appraising the amount of pickle Mrs. Erskine was in. They had become rivals. With her pale braids, her stately figure, her eyes the color of a stoneware teapot, Mrs. Erskine seemed to me like a white statue with features painted on. I had heard my mother praising her beauty, but for a child she was too large, too still. "Age has its points," my mother went on. "The longer your life goes on, the more chance it has to be interesting. Promise me that when you're thirty you'll have a lot to look back on."

My mother had on her side her comparative youth, her quickness, her somewhat giddy intelligence. She had been married, as she said, "for ever and ever" and was afraid nothing would ever happen to her again. Mrs. Erskine's chief advantage over my mother—being unmarried and available— was matched by an enviable biography. "Ah, don't ask me for my life's story now," she would cry, settling back to tell it. When the others broke into that sighing, singing recital of cities they went in for, repeating strings of names that sounded like sleigh bells (Venice, London, Paris, Rome), Mrs. Erskine would narrow her stoneware eyes and annihilate my mother with "But Charlotte, I've *been* to all those places, I've *seen* all those people." What, indeed, hadn't she seen—crown princes dragged out of Rolls-Royces by cursing mobs, duchesses clutching their tiaras while being raped by anarchists, strikers in England kicking innocent little Border terriers.

" . . . And as for the Hun*gar*ians and that Béla *Kun*, let me tell you . . . tore the uniforms right off the Red Cross *nurses* . . . made them dance the Charleston naked on top of *street*cars . . ."

"Linnet, wouldn't you be better off in your room?"

The fear of the horde was in all of them; it haunted even their jokes. "Bolshevik" was now "bolshie," to make it harmless. Petrograd had been their early youth; the Red years just after the war were still within earshot. They dreaded yet seemed drawn to tales of conspiracy and enormous might. The English among them were the first generation to have been raised on *The Wind in the Willows*. Their own Wild Wood was a dark political mystery; its rude inhabitants were still to be tamed. What was needed was a leader, a Badger. But when a Badger occurred they mistrusted him, too; my mother had impressed on me early that Mussolini was a "bad, wicked man." Fortunate Mrs. Erskine had seen "those people" from legation windows; she had, in another defeat for my mother, been married twice, each time to a diplomat. The word "diplomat" had greater cachet then than it has now. Earlier in the century a diplomat was believed to have attended universities in more than one country, to have two or three languages at his disposal and some slender notion of geography and history. He could read and write quite easily, had probably been born in wedlock, possessed tact and discretion, and led an exemplary private life. Obviously there were no more of these paragons then than there might be now, but fewer were needed, because there were only half as many capitals. Those who did exist spun round and round the world, used for all they were worth, until they became like those coats that outlast their buttons, linings, and pockets: Your diplomat, recalled from Bulgaria, by now a mere warp and woof, would be given a new silk lining, bone buttons, have his collar turned, and, after a quick reading of Norse myths, would be shipped to Scandinavia. Mrs. Erskine, twice wedded to examples of these freshened garments, had been everywhere—everywhere my mother longed to be.

"My *life*," said Mrs. Erskine. "Ah, Charlotte, don't ask me to tell you everything—you'd never believe it!" My mother asked, and believed, and died in her heart along with Mrs. Erskine's first husband, a Mr. Sparrow, shot to death in Berlin by a lunatic Russian refugee. (Out of the decency of his nature Mr. Sparrow had helped the refugee's husband emigrate accompanied by a woman Mr. Sparrow had taken to be the Russian man's wife.) In the hours that preceded his "going," as Mrs. Erskine termed his death, Mr. Sparrow had turned into a totally other person, quite common and gross. She had seen exactly how he would rise from the dead for his next incarnation. She had said, "Now then, Alfred, I think it has been a blissful marriage but perhaps not blissful enough. As I am the best part of your karma, we are going to start all over again in another existence." Mr. Sparrow, in his new coarse, uneducated voice, replied, "Believe you me, Bimbo, if I see you in another world, this time I'm making a detour." His last words—not what every woman hopes to hear, probably, but nothing in my mother's experience could come ankle-high to having a husband assassinated in Berlin by a crazy Russian. Mr. Erskine, the second husband, was not quite so interesting, for he merely "drank and drank and *drank*," and finally, unwittingly, provided grounds for divorce. Since in those days adultery was the only acceptable grounds, the divorce ended his ambitions and transformed Mrs. Erskine into someone déclassée; it was not done for a woman to spoil a man's career, and it was taken for granted that no man ever ruined his own. I am certain my mother did not see Mr. Sparrow as an ass and Mr. Erskine as a soak. They were men out of novels—half diplomat, half secret agent. The natural progress of such men was needed to drag women out of the dullness that seemed to be woman's fate.

There was also the matter of Mrs. Erskine's French: My mother could read and speak it but had nothing of her friend's intolerable fluency. Nor could my mother compete with her special status as the only English and Protestant girl of her generation to have attended French and Catholic schools. She had spent ten years with the Ursulines in Quebec City (languages took longer to learn in those days, when you were obliged to start by memorizing all the verbs) and had emerged with the chic little Ursuline lisp.

"Tell me again," my entranced mother would ask. "How do you say 'squab stuffed with sage dressing'?"

"Charlotte, I've told you and told you. '*Pouthin farthi au thauge.*'"

"Thankth," said my mother. Such was the humor of that period.

For a long time I would turn over like samples of dress material the reasons why I was sent off to a school where by all the rules of the world we lived in I did not belong. A sample that nearly matches is my mother's desire to tease Mrs. Erskine, perhaps to overtake her through me: If she had been unique in her generation, then I would be in mine. Unlikely as it sounds today, I believe that I was. At least I have never met another, just as no French-Canadian woman of my period can recall having sat in a classroom with any other English-speaking Protestant disguised in convent uniform. Mrs. Erskine, rising to the tease, warned that convents had gone downhill since the war and that the appalling French I spoke would be a handicap in Venice, London, Paris, Rome; if the Ursuline French of Quebec City was the best in the world after Tours, Montreal French was just barely a language.

How could my mother, so quick and sharp usually, have been drawn in by this? For a day or two my parents actually weighed the advantages of sending their very young daughter miles away, for no good reason. Why not even to France? "You know perfectly well why not. Because we can't afford it. Not that or anything like it."

Leaning forward in her chair as if words alone could not convince her listener, more like my mother than herself at this moment, Mrs. Erskine with her fingertips to her cheek, the other hand held palm outward, cried, "Ah, Angus, don't ask me for my life's story now!" This to my father, who barely knew other people had lives.

My father made this mysterious answer: "Yes, Frances, I do see what you mean, but I have a family, and once you've got children you're never quite so free."

There was only one child, of course, and not often there, but in my parents' minds and by some miracle of fertility they had produced a whole tribe. At any second this tribe might rampage through the house, scribbling on the wallpaper, tearing up books, scratching gramophone records with a stolen diamond brooch. They dreaded mischief so much that I can only suppose them to have been quite disgraceful children.

"What's Linnet up to? She's awfully quiet."

"Sounds suspicious. Better go and look."

I would be found reading or painting or "building," which meant the elaboration of a foreign city called Marigold that spread and spread until it took up a third of my room and had to be cleared away when my back was turned, upon which, as relentless as a colony of beavers, I would start building again. To a visitor Marigold was a slum of empty boxes, serving trays, bottles, silver paper, overturned chairs, but these were streets and houses, churches and convents, restaurants and railway stations. The citizens of Marigold were cut out of magazines: Gloria Swanson was the Mother Superior, Herbert Hoover a convent gardener. Entirely villainous, they did their plotting and planning in an empty cigar box.

Whatever I was doing, I would be told to do something else immediately: I think they had both been brought up that way. "Go out and play in the snow" was a frequent interruption. Parents in bitter climates have a fixed idea about driving children out to be frozen. There was one sunken hour on January afternoons, just before the street lamps were lighted, that was the gray of true wretchedness, as if one's heart and stomach had turned into the same dull, cottony stuff as the sky; it was attached to a feeling of loss, of helpless sadness, unknown to children in other latitudes.

I was home weekends but by no means every weekend. Friday night was given to spoiling and rejoicing, but on Saturday I would hear, "When does she go back?"

"Not till tomorrow night."

Ruby, the homesick offshore import, sometimes sat in my room, just for company. She turned the radiator on so that you saw a wisp of steam from the overflow tap. A wicker basket of mending was on her lap; she wiped her eyes on my father's socks. I was not allowed to say to anyone "Go away," or anything like it. I heard her sniffles, her low, muttered grievances. Then she emerged from her impenetrable cloud of Newfoundland gloom to take an interest in the life of Marigold. She did not get down on the floor or in the way, but from her chair suggested some pretty good plots. Ruby was the inspirer of "The Insane Stepmother," "The Rich, Selfish Cousins," "The Death from Croup of Baby Sister" ("Is her face blue yet?" "No; in a minute"), and "The Broken Engagement," with its cast of three—rejected maiden, fickle lover, and chaperon. Paper dolls did the acting, the voices were ours. Ruby played the cast-off fiancée from the heart: "Don't chew men ever know what chew want?" Chaperon was a fine bossy part: "That's enough, now. Sit down; I said, *down.*"

My parents said, "What does she see in Ruby?" They were cross and jealous. The jealousness was real. They did not drop their voices to say "When does she go back?" but were alert to signs of disaffection, and offended because I did not crave their company every minute. Once, when Mrs. Erskine, a bit of a fool probably, asked, "Who do you love best, your father or your mother?" and I apparently (I have no memory of it) answered, "Oh, I'm not really dying about anybody," it was recalled to me for a long time, as if I had set fire to the curtains or spat on the Union Jack.

"Think of your unfortunate parents," Dr. Chauchard had said in the sort of language that had no meaning to me, though I am sure it was authentic to him.

When he died and I read his obituary, I saw there had been still another voice. I was twenty and had not seen him since the age of nine. *The Doctor* and the red-covered books had been lost even before that, when during a major move from Montreal to a house in the country a number of things that belonged to me and that my parents were tired of seeing disappeared.

There were three separate death notices, as if to affirm that Chauchard had been three men. All three were in a French newspaper; he neither lived nor died in English. The first was a jumble of family names and syntax:

"After a serene and happy life it has pleased our Lord to send for the soul of his faithful servant Raoul Étienne Chauchard, piously deceased in his native city in his fifty-first year after a short illness comforted by the sacraments of the Church." There followed a few particulars—the date and place of the funeral, and the names and addresses of the relatives making the announcement. The exact kinship of each was mentioned: sister, brother-in-law, uncle, nephew, cousin, second cousin.

The second obituary, somewhat longer, had been published by the medical association he belonged to; it described all the steps and stages of his career. There were strings of initials denoting awards and honors, ending with: "Dr. Chauchard had also been granted the Medal of Epidemics (Belgium)." Beneath this came the third notice: "The Arts and Letters Society of Quebec announces the irreparable loss of one of its founder members, the poet R. É. Chauchard." R. É. had published six volumes of verse, a book of critical essays, and a work referred to as "the immortal 'Progress,' " which did not seem to fall into a category or, perhaps, was too well known to readers to need identification.

That third notice was an earthquake, the collapse of the cities we build over the past to cover seams and cracks we cannot account for. He must have been writing when my parents knew him. Why they neglected to speak of it is something too shameful to dwell on; he probably never mentioned it, knowing they would believe it impossible. French books were from France; English books from England or the United States. It would not have entered their minds that the languages they heard spoken around them could be written, too.

I met by accident years after Dr. Chauchard's death one of Mrs. Erskine's ex-minnesingers, now an elderly bachelor. His name was Louis. He had never heard of Paul-Armand, not even by rumor. He had not known my parents and was certain he had never accompanied Dr. Chauchard and Mrs. Erskine to our house. He said that when he met these two he had been fresh from a seminary, aged about nineteen, determined to live a life of ease and pleasure but not sure how to begin. Mrs. Erskine had by then bought and converted a farmhouse south of Montreal, where she wove carpets, hooked rugs, scraped and waxed old tables, kept bees, and bottled tons of pickled beets, preparing for some dark proletarian future should the mob—the horde, "those people"—take over after all. Louis knew the doctor only as the poet R. É. of the third notice. He had no knowledge of the Medal of Epidemics (Belgium) and could not explain it to me. I had found "Progress" by then, which turned out to be R.É.'s diary. I could not put faces to the X, Y, and Z that covered real names, nor could I discover any trace of my parents, let alone of *ma chère petite Linnet.* There were long thoughts about Mozart—people like that.

Louis told me of walking with Mrs. Erskine along a snowy road close to her farmhouse, she in a fur cape that came down to her boot tops and a fur bonnet that hid her braided hair. She talked about her unusual life and her two husbands and about what she now called "the predicament." She told him how she had never been asked to meet Madame Chauchard *mère* and how she had slowly come to realize that R.É. would never marry. She spoke of people who had drifted through the predicament, my mother among them, not singling her out as someone important, just as a wisp of cloud on the edge of the sky. "Poor Charlotte" was how Mrs. Erskine described the thin little target on which she had once trained her biggest guns. Yet "poor Charlotte"—not even an X in the diary, finally—had once been the heart of the play. The plot must have taken a full turning after she left the stage. Louis became a new young satellite, content to circle the powerful stars, to keep an eye on the predicament, which seemed to him flaming, sulfurous. Nobody ever told him what had taken place in the first and second acts.

Walking, he and Mrs. Erskine came to a railway track quite far from houses, and she turned to Louis and opened the fur cloak and said, smiling, *"Viens voir Mrs. Erskine."* (Owing to the Ursuline lisp this must have been "Mitheth Erthkine.") Without coyness or any more conversation she lay down—he said "on the track," but he must have meant near it, if you think of the ties. Folded into the cloak, Louis at last became part of a predicament. He decided that further experience could only fall short of it, and so he never married.

In this story about the cloak Mrs. Erskine is transmuted from the pale, affected statue I remember and takes on a polychrome life. She seems cheerful and careless, and I like her for that. Carelessness might explain her unreliable memory about Charlotte. And yet not all that careless: "She even knew the train times," said Louis. "She must have done it before." Still, on a sharp blue day, when some people were still in a dark classroom writing *"abyssus abyssum invocat"* all over their immortal souls, she, who had been through this and escaped with nothing worse than a lisp, had the sun, the snow, the wrap of fur, the bright sky, the risk. There is a raffish kind of nerve to her, the only nerve that matters.

For that one conversation Louis and I wondered what our appearance on stage several scenes apart might make us to each other: If A was the daughter of B, and B rattled the foundations of C, and C, though cautious and lazy where women were concerned, was committed in a way to D, and D was forever trying to tell her life's story to E, the husband of B, and E had enough on his hands with B without taking on D, too, and if D decided to lie down on or near a railway track with F, then what are A and F? Nothing. Minor satellites floating out of orbit and out of order after the stars burned out. Mrs. Erskine reclaimed Dr. Chauchard but he never married anyone. Angus reclaimed Charlotte but he died soon after. Louis, another old bachelor, had that one good anecdote about the fur cloak. I lost even the engraving of *The Doctor*, spirited away quite shabbily, and I never saw Dr. Chauchard again or even tried to. What if I had turned up one day, aged eighteen or so, only to have him say to his nurse, "Does anyone know she's here?"

When I read the three obituaries it was the brass plate on the door I saw and *"Sur Rendez-vous."* That means "No dropping in." After the warning came the shut heron door and the shut swan door and, at another remove, the desk with the circle of lamplight and R.É. himself, writing about X, Y, Z, and Mozart. A bit humdrum perhaps, a bit prosy, not nearly as good as his old winter Saturday self, but I am sure that it was his real voice, the voice that transcends this or that language. His French-speaking friends did not hear it for a long time (his first book of verse was not sold to anyone outside his immediate family), while his English-speaking friends never heard it at all. But I should have heard it then, at the start, standing on tiptoe to reach the doorbell, calling through the letter box every way I could think of, "I, me." I ought to have heard it when I was still under ten and had all my wits about me.

VOICES LOST IN SNOW

❧

*H*alfway between our two great wars, parents whose own early years had been shaped with Edwardian firmness were apt to lend a tone of finality to quite simple remarks: "Because I say so" was the answer to "Why?" and a child's response to "What did I just tell you?" could seldom be anything but "Not to"—not to say, do, touch, remove, go out, argue, reject, eat, pick up, open, shout, appear to sulk, appear to be cross. Dark riddles filled the corners of life because no enlightenment was thought required. Asking questions was "being tiresome," while persistent curiosity got one nowhere, at least nowhere of interest. How much has changed? Observe the drift of words descending from adult to child—the fall of personal questions, observations, unnecessary instructions. Before long the listener seems blanketed. He must hear the voice as authority muffled, a hum through snow. The tone has changed—it may be coaxing, even plaintive—but the words have barely altered. They still claim the ancient right-of-way through a young life.

"Well, old cock," said my father's friend Archie McEwen, meeting him one Saturday in Montreal. "How's Charlotte taking life in the country?" Apparently no one had expected my mother to accept the country in winter.

"Well, old cock," I repeated to a country neighbor, Mr. Bainwood. "How's life?" What do you suppose it meant to me, other than a kind of weather vane? Mr. Bainwood thought it over, then came round to our house and complained to my mother.

"It isn't blasphemy," she said, not letting him have much satisfaction from the complaint. Still, I had to apologize. "I'm sorry" was a ritual habit with even less meaning than "old cock." "Never say that again," my mother said after he had gone.

"Why not?"

"Because I've just told you not to."

"What does it mean?"

"Nothing."

It must have been after yet another "Nothing" that one summer's day I ran screaming around a garden, tore the heads off tulips, and—no, let another voice finish it; the only authentic voices I have belong to the dead: "... then she *ate* them."

It was my father's custom if he took me with him to visit a friend on Saturdays not to say where we were going. He was more taciturn than any man I have known since, but that wasn't all of it; being young, I was the last person to whom anyone owed an explanation. These Saturdays have turned into one whitish afternoon, a windless snowfall, a steep street. Two persons descend the street, stepping carefully. The child, reminded every day to keep her hands still, gesticulates wildly—there is the flash of a red mitten. I will never overtake this pair. Their voices are lost in snow.

We were living in what used to be called the country and is now a suburb of Montreal. On Saturdays my father and I came in together by train. I went to the doctor, the dentist, to my German lesson. After that I had to get back to Windsor station by myself and on time. My father gave me a boy's watch so that the dial would be good and large. I remember the No. 83 streetcar trundling downhill and myself, wondering if the watch was slow, asking strangers to tell me the hour. Inevitably—how could it have been otherwise?—after his death, which would not be long in coming, I would dream that someone important had taken a train without me. My route to the meeting place—deviated, betrayed by stopped clocks—was always downhill. As soon as I was old enough to understand from my reading of myths and legends that this journey was a pursuit of darkness, its terminal point a sunless underworld, the dream vanished.

Sometimes I would be taken along to lunch with one or another of my father's friends. He would meet the friend at Pauzé's for oysters or at Drury's or the Windsor Grill. The friend would more often than not be Scottish- or English-sounding, and they would talk as if I were invisible, as Archie McEwen had done, and eat what I thought of as English food— grilled kidneys, sweetbreads—which I was too finicky to touch. Both my parents had been made wretched as children by having food forced on them and so that particular torture was never inflicted on me. However, the manner in which I ate was subject to precise attention. My father disapproved of the North American custom that he called "spearing" (knife laid on the plate, fork in the right hand). My mother's eye was out for a straight back, invisible chewing, small mouthfuls, immobile silence during the interminable adult loafing over dessert. My mother did not care for food. If we were alone together, she would sit smoking and reading, sipping black coffee, her elbows used as props—a posture that would have called for instant banishment had I so much as tried it. Being constantly observed and corrected was like having a fly buzzing around one's plate. At Pauzé's, the only child, perhaps the only female, I sat up to an oak counter and ate oysters quite neatly, not knowing exactly what they were and certainly not that they were alive. They were served as in "The Walrus and the Carpenter," with bread and butter, pepper and vinegar. Dessert was a chocolate biscuit— plates of them stood at intervals along the counter. When my father and I ate alone, I was not required to say much, nor could I expect a great deal in the way of response. After I had been addressing him for minutes, sometimes he would suddenly come to life and I would know he had been elsewhere. "Of course I've been listening," he would protest, and he would repeat by way of proof the last few words of whatever it was I'd been saying. He was seldom present. I don't know where my father spent his waking life: just elsewhere.

What was he doing alone with a child? Where was his wife? In the country, reading. She read one book after another without looking up, without scraping away the frost on the windows. "The Russians, you know, the Russians," she said to her mother and me, glancing around in the drugged way adolescent readers have. "They put salt on the windowsills in winter." Yes, so they did, in the nineteenth century, in the boyhood of Turgenev, of Tolstoy. The salt absorbed the moisture between two sets of windows sealed shut for half the year. She must have been in a Russian country house at that moment, surrounded by a large Russian family, living out vast Russian complications. The flat white fields beyond her imaginary windows were like the flat white fields she would have observed if only she had looked out. She was myopic; the pupil when she had been reading seemed to be the whole of the eye. What age was she then? Twenty-seven, twenty-eight. Her husband had removed her to the country; now that they were there he seldom spoke. How young she seems to me now—half twenty-eight in perception and feeling, but with a husband, a child, a house, a life, an illiterate maid from the village whose life she confidently interfered with and mismanaged, a small zoo of animals she alternately cherished and forgot; and she was the daughter of such a sensible, truthful, pessimistic woman—pessimistic in the way women become when they settle for what actually exists.

Our rooms were not Russian—they were aired every day and the salt became a great nuisance, blowing in on the floor.

"There, Charlotte, what did I tell you?" my grandmother said. This grandmother did not care for dreams or for children. If I sensed the first, I had no hint of the latter. Out of decency she kept it quiet, at least in a child's presence. She had the reputation, shared with a long-vanished nurse named Olivia, of being able to "do anything" with me, which merely meant an ability to provoke from a child behavior convenient for adults. It was she who taught me to eat in the Continental way, with both hands in sight at all times upon the table, and who made me sit at meals with books under my arms so I would learn not to stick out my elbows. I remember having accepted this nonsense from her without a trace of resentment. Like Olivia, she could make the most pointless sort of training seem a natural way of life. (I think that as discipline goes this must be the most dangerous form of all.) She was one of three godparents I had—the important one. It is impossible for me to enter the mind of this agnostic who taught me prayers, who had already shed every remnant of belief when she committed me at the font. I know that she married late and reluctantly; she would have preferred a life of solitude and independence, next to impossible for a woman in her time. She had the positive voice of the born teacher, sharp manners, quick blue eyes, and the square, massive figure common to both lines of her ancestry—the west of France, the north of Germany. When she said "There, Charlotte, what did I tell you?" without obtaining an answer, it summed up mother and daughter both.

My father's friend Malcolm Whitmore was the second godparent. He quarreled with my mother when she said something flippant about Mussolini, disappeared, died in Europe some years later, though perhaps not fighting for Franco, as my mother had it. She often rewrote other people's lives, providing them with suitable and harmonious endings. In her version of events you were supposed to die as you'd lived. He would write sometimes, asking me, "Have you been confirmed yet?" He had never really held a place and could not by dying leave a gap. The third godparent was a young woman named Georgie Henderson. She was my mother's choice, for a long time her confidante, partisan, and close sympathizer. Something happened, and they stopped seeing each other. Georgie was not her real name—it was Edna May. One of the reasons she had fallen out with my mother was that I had not been called Edna May too. Apparently, this had been promised.

Without saying where we were going, my father took me along to visit Georgie one Saturday afternoon.

"You didn't say you were bringing Linnet" was how she greeted him. We stood in the passage of a long, hot, high-ceilinged apartment, treading snow water into the rug.

He said, "Well, she is your godchild, and she has been ill."

My godmother shut the front door and leaned her back against it. It is in this surprisingly dramatic pose that I recall her. It would be unfair to repeat what I think I saw then, for she and I were to meet again once, only once, many years after this, and I might substitute a lined face for a smooth one and tough, large-knuckled hands for fingers that may have been delicate. One has to allow elbowroom in the account of a rival: "She must have had something" is how it generally goes, long after the initial "What can he see in her? He must be deaf and blind." Georgie, explained by my mother as being the natural daughter of Sarah Bernhardt and a stork, is only a shadow, a tracing, with long arms and legs and one of those slightly puggy faces with pulled-up eyes.

Her voice remains—the husky Virginia-tobacco whisper I associate with so many women of that generation, my parents' friends; it must have come of age in English Montreal around 1920, when girls began to cut their hair and to smoke. In middle life the voice would slide from low to harsh, and develop a chronic cough. For the moment it was fascinating to me— opposite in pitch and speed from my mother's, which was slightly too high and apt to break off, like that of a singer unable to sustain a long note.

It was true that I had been ill, but I don't think my godmother made much of it that afternoon, other than saying, "It's all very well to talk about that now, but I was certainly never told much, and as for that doctor, you ought to just hear what Ward thinks." Out of this whispered jumble my mother stood accused—of many transgressions, certainly, but chiefly of having discarded Dr. Ward Mackey, everyone's doctor and a family friend. At the time of my birth my mother had all at once decided she liked Ward Mackey better than anyone else and had asked him to choose a name for me. He could not think of one, or, rather, thought of too many, and finally consulted his own mother. She had always longed for a daughter, so that she could call her after the heroine of a novel by, I believe, Marie Corelli. The legend so often repeated to me goes on to tell that when I was seven weeks old my father suddenly asked, "What did you say her name was?"

"*Votre fille a frôlé la phtisie,*" the new doctor had said, the one who had now replaced Dr. Mackey. The new doctor was known to me as Uncle Raoul, though we were not related. This manner of declaring my brush with consumption was worlds away from Ward Mackey's "subject to bilious attacks." Mackey's objections to Uncle Raoul were neither envious nor personal, for Mackey was the sort of bachelor who could console himself with golf. The Protestant in him truly believed those other doctors to be poorly trained and superstitious, capable of recommending the pulling of teeth to cure tonsilitis, and of letting their patients cough to death or perish from septicemia just through Catholic fatalism.

What parent could fail to gasp and marvel at Uncle Raoul's announcement? Any but either of mine. My mother could invent and produce better dramas any day; as for my father, his French wasn't all that good and he had to have it explained. Once he understood that I had grazed the edge of tuberculosis, he made his decision to remove us all to the country, which he had been wanting a reason to do for some time. He was, I think, attempting to isolate his wife, but by taking her out of the city he exposed her to a danger that, being English, he had never dreamed of: This was the heart-stopping cry of the steam train at night, sweeping across a frozen river, clattering on the ties of a wooden bridge. From our separate rooms my mother and I heard the unrivaled summons, the long, urgent, uniquely North American beckoning. She would follow and so would I, but separately, years and desires and destinations apart. I think that women once pledged in such a manner are more steadfast than men.

"*Frôler*" was the charmed word in that winter's story; it was a hand brushing the edge of folded silk, a leaf escaping a spiderweb. Being caught in the web would have meant staying in bed day and night in a place even worse than a convent school. Charlotte and Angus, whose lives had once seemed so enchanted, so fortunate and free that I could not imagine lesser persons so much as eating the same kind of toast for breakfast, had to share their lives with me, whether they wanted to or not—thanks to Uncle Raoul, who always supposed me to be their principal delight. I had been standing on one foot for months now, midway between "*frôler*" and "falling into," propped up by a psychosomatic guardian angel. Of course I could not stand that way forever; inevitably my health improved and before long I was declared out of danger and then restored—to the relief and pleasure of all except the patient.

"I'd like to see more of you than eyes and nose," said my godmother. "Take off your things." I offer this as an example of unnecessary instruction. Would anyone over the age of three prepare to spend the afternoon in a stifling room wrapped like a mummy in outdoor clothes? "She's smaller than she looks," Georgie remarked, as I began to emerge. This authentic godmother observation drives me to my only refuge, the insistence that she must have had something—he could not have been completely deaf and blind. Divested of hat, scarf, coat, overshoes, and leggings, grasping the handkerchief pressed in my hand so I would not interrupt later by asking for one, responding to my father's muttered "Fix your hair," struck by the command because it was he who had told me not to use "fix" in that sense, I was finally able to sit down next to him on a white sofa. My godmother occupied its twin. A low table stood between, bearing a decanter and glasses and a pile of magazines and, of course, Georgie's ashtrays; I think she smoked even more than my mother did.

On one of these sofas, during an earlier visit with my mother and father, the backs of my dangling feet had left a smudge of shoe polish. It may have been the last occasion when my mother and Georgie were ever together. Directed to stop humming and kicking, and perhaps bored with the conversation in which I was not expected to join, I had soon started up again.

"It doesn't matter," my godmother said, though you could tell she minded.

"Sit up," my father said to me.

"I am sitting up. What do you think I'm doing?" This was not answering but answering back; it is not an expression I ever heard from my father, but I am certain it stood like a stalled truck in Georgie's mind. She wore the look people put on when they are thinking, Now what are you spineless parents going to do about that?

"Oh, for God's sake, she's only a child," said my mother, as though that had ever been an excuse for anything.

Soon after the sofa-kicking incident she and Georgie moved into the hibernation known as "not speaking." This, the lingering condition of half my mother's friendships, usually followed her having said the very thing no one wanted to hear, such as "Who wants to be called Edna May, anyway?"

Once more in the hot pale room where there was nothing to do and nothing for children, I offended my godmother again, by pretending I had never seen her before. The spot I had kicked was pointed out to me, though, owing to new slipcovers, real evidence was missing. My father was proud of my quite surprising memory, of its long backward reach and the minutiae of detail I could describe. My failure now to shine in a domain where I was naturally gifted, that did not require lessons or create litter and noise, must have annoyed him. I also see that my guileless-seeming needling of my god-mother was a close adaptation of how my mother could be, and I attribute it to a child's instinctive loyalty to the absent one. Giving me up, my god-mother placed a silver dish of mint wafers where I could reach them—white, pink, and green, overlapping—and suggested I look at a magazine. Whatever the magazine was, I had probably seen it, for my mother sub-scribed to everything then. I may have turned the pages anyway, in case at home something had been censored for children. I felt and am certain I have not invented Georgie's disappointment at not seeing Angus alone. She dis-liked Charlotte now, and so I supposed he came to call by himself, having no quarrel of his own; he was still close to the slighted Ward Mackey.

My father and Georgie talked for a while—she using people's initials in-stead of their names, which my mother would not have done—and they drank what must have been sherry, if I think of the shape of the decanter. Then we left and went down to the street in a wood-paneled elevator that had sconce lights, as in a room. The end of the afternoon had a particular shade of color then, which is not tinted by distance or enhancement but has to do with how streets were lighted. Lamps were still gas, and their soft gradual blooming at dusk made the sky turn a peacock blue that slowly deepened to marine, then indigo. This uneven light falling in blurred pools gave the snow it touched a quality of phosphorescence, beyond which were night shadows in which no one lurked. There were few cars, little sound. A fresh snowfall would lie in the streets in a way that seemed natural. Side-walks were dangerous, casually sanded; even on busy streets you found traces of the icy slides children's feet had made. The reddish brown of the stone houses, the curve and slope of the streets, the constantly changing sky were satisfactory in a way that I now realize must have been aesthetically comfortable. This is what I saw when I read "city" in a book; I had no means of knowing that "city" one day would also mean drab, filthy, flat, or that city blocks could turn into dull squares without mystery.

We crossed Sherbrooke Street, starting down to catch our train. My fa-ther walked everywhere in all weathers. Already mined, colonized by an enemy prepared to destroy what it fed on, fighting it with every wrong weapon, squandering strength he should have been storing, stifling pain in silence rather than speaking up while there might have been time, he gave an impression of sternness that was a shield against suffering. One day we heard a mob roaring four syllables over and over, and we turned and went down a different street. That sound was starkly terrifying, something a child might liken to the baying of wolves.

"What is it?"

"Howie Morenz."

"Who is it? Are they chasing him?"

"No, they like him," he said of the hockey player admired to the point of dementia. He seemed to stretch, as if trying to keep every bone in his body from touching a nerve; a look of helplessness such as I had never seen on a grown person gripped his face and he said this strange thing: "Crowds eat me. Noise eats me." The kind of physical pain that makes one seem rat's prey is summed up in my memory of this.

When we came abreast of the Ritz-Carlton after leaving Georgie's apartment, my father paused. The lights within at that time of day were golden and warm. If I barely knew what "hotel" meant, never having stayed in one, I connected the lights with other snowy afternoons, with stupefying adult conversation (Oh, those shut-in velvet-draped unaired low-voice problems!) compensated for by creamy bitter hot chocolate poured out of a pink-and-white china pot.

"You missed your gootay," he suddenly remembered. Established by my grandmother, *"goûter"* was the family word for tea. He often transformed French words, like putty, into shapes he could grasp. No, Georgie had not provided a *goûter*, other than the mint wafers, but it was not her fault—I had not been announced. Perhaps if I had not been so disagreeable with her, he might have proposed hot chocolate now, though I knew better than to ask. He merely pulled my scarf up over my nose and mouth, as if recalling something Uncle Raoul had advised. Breathing inside knitted wool was delicious—warm, moist, pungent when one had been sucking on mint candies, as now. He said, "You didn't enjoy your visit much."

"Not very," through red wool.

"No matter," he said. "You needn't see Georgie again unless you want to," and we walked on. He must have been smarting, for he liked me to be admired. When I was not being admired I was supposed to keep quiet. "You needn't see Georgie again" was also a private decision about himself.

He was barely thirty-one and had a full winter to live after this one—little more. Why? "Because I say so." The answer seems to speak out of the lights, the stones, the snow; out of the crucial second when inner and outer forces join, and the environment becomes part of the enemy too.

Ward Mackey used to mention me as "Angus's precocious pain in the neck," which is better than nothing. Long after that afternoon, when I was about twenty, Mackey said to me, "Georgie didn't play her cards well where he was concerned. There was a point where if she had just made one smart move she could have had him. Not for long, of course, but none of us knew that."

What cards, I wonder. The cards have another meaning for me—they mean a trip, a death, a letter, tomorrow, next year. I saw only one move that Saturday: My father placed a card faceup on the table and watched to see what Georgie made of it. She shrugged, let it rest. There she sits, looking puggy but capable, Angus waiting, the precocious pain in the neck turning pages, hoping to find something in the *National Geographic* harmful for children. I brush in memory against the spiderweb: What if she had picked it up, remarking in her smoky voice, "Yes, I can use that"? It was a low card, the kind that only a born gambler would risk as part of a long-term strategy. She would never have weakened a hand that way; she was not gambling but building. He took the card back and dropped his hand, and their long intermittent game came to an end. The card must have been the eight of clubs—"a female child."

IN YOUTH IS PLEASURE

─────

❧

*M*y father died, then my grandmother; my mother was left, but we did not get on. I was probably disagreeable with anyone who felt entitled to give me instructions and advice. We seldom lived under the same roof, which was just as well. She had found me civil and amusing until I was ten, at which time I was said to have become pert and obstinate. She was impulsive, generous, in some ways better than most other people, but without any feeling for cause and effect; this made her at the least unpredictable and at the most a serious element of danger. I was fascinated by her, though she worried me; then all at once I lost interest. I was fifteen when this happened. I would forget to answer her letters and even to open them. It was not rejection or anything so violent as dislike but a simple indifference I cannot account for. It was much the way I would be later with men I fell out of love with, but I was too young to know that then. As for my mother, whatever I thought, felt, said, wrote, and wore had always been a positive source of exasperation. From time to time she attempted to alter the form, the outward shape at least, of the creature she thought she was modeling, but at last she came to the conclusion there must be something wrong with the clay. Her final unexpected upsurge of attention coincided with my abrupt unconcern: One may well have been the reason for the other.

It took the form of digging into my diaries and notebooks and it yielded, among other documents, a two-year-old poem, Kiplingesque in its rhythms, entitled "Why I Am a Socialist." The first words of the first line were "You ask ...," then came a long answer. But it was not an answer to anything she'd wondered. Like all mothers—at least, all I have known—she was obsessed with the entirely private and possibly trivial matter of a daughter's virginity. Why I was a Socialist she rightly conceded to be none of her business. Still, she must have felt she had to say something, and the something was "You had better be clever, because you will never be pretty." My response was to take—take, not grab—the poem from her and tear it up. No voices were raised. I never mentioned the incident to anyone. That is how it was. We became, presently, mutually unconcerned. My detachment was put down to the coldness of my nature, hers to the exhaustion of trying to bring me up. It must have been a relief to her when, in the first half of Hitler's war, I slipped quietly and finally out of her life. I was now eighteen, and completely on my own. By "on my own" I don't mean a show of independence with Papa-Mama footing the bills: I mean that I was solely responsible for my economic survival and that no living person felt any duty toward me.

On a bright morning in June I arrived in Montreal, where I'd been born, from New York, where I had been living and going to school. My luggage was a small suitcase and an Edwardian picnic hamper—a preposterous piece of baggage my father had brought from England some twenty years before; it had been with me since childhood, when his death turned my life into a helpless migration. In my purse was a birth certificate and five American dollars, my total fortune, the parting gift of a Canadian actress in New York, who had taken me to see *Mayerling* before I got on the train. She was kind and good and terribly hard up, and she had no idea that apart from some loose change I had nothing more. The birth certificate, which testified I was Linnet Muir, daughter of Angus and of Charlotte, was my right of passage. I did not own a passport and possibly never had seen one. In those days there was almost no such thing as a "Canadian." You were Canadian-born, and a British subject, too, and you had a third label with no consular reality, like the racial tag that on Soviet passports will make a German of someone who has never been to Germany. In Canada you were also whatever your father happened to be, which in my case was English. He was half Scot, but English by birth, by mother, by instinct. I did not feel a scrap British or English, but I was not an American either. In American schools I had refused to salute the flag. My denial of that curiously Fascist-looking celebration, with the right arm stuck straight out, and my silence when the others intoned the trusting ". . . and justice for all" had never been thought offensive, only stubborn. Americans then were accustomed to gratitude from foreigners but did not demand it; they quite innocently could not imagine any country fit to live in except their own. If I could not recognize it, too bad for me. Besides, I was not a refugee—just someone from the

backwoods. "You got schools in Canada?" I had been asked. "You got radios?" And once, from a teacher, "What do they major in up there? Basket
weaving?"

My travel costume was a white piqué jacket and skirt that must have been
crumpled and soot-flecked, for I had sat up all night. I was reading, I think,
a novel by Sylvia Townsend Warner. My hair was thick and long. I wore
my grandmother's wedding ring, which was too large, and which I would
lose before long. I desperately wanted to look more than my age, which I
had already started to give out as twenty-one. I was traveling light; my picnic hamper contained the poems and journals I had judged fit to accompany
me into my new, unfettered existence, and some books I feared I might not
find again in clerical Quebec—Zinoviev and Lenin's *Against the Stream,* and a
few beige pamphlets from the Little Lenin Library, purchased secondhand
in New York. I had a picture of Mayakovsky torn out of *Cloud in Trousers*
and one of Paddy Finucane, the Irish RAF fighter pilot, who was killed the
following summer. I had not met either of these men, but I approved of
them both very much. I had abandoned my beloved but cumbersome an-
thologies of American and English verse, confident that I had whatever I
needed by heart. I knew every word of Stephen Vincent Benét's "Litany for
Dictatorships" and "Notes to Be Left in a Cornerstone," and the other one
that begins:

> They shot the Socialists at half-past five
> In the name of victorious Austria. . . .

I could begin anywhere and rush on in my mind to the end. "Notes . . ." was
the New York I knew I would never have again, for there could be no jour-
neying backward; the words "but I walked it young" were already a gate shut
on a part of my life. The suitcase held only the fewest possible summer
clothes. Everything else had been deposited at the various war-relief agencies of New York. In those days I made symbols out of everything, and I
must have thought that by leaving a tartan skirt somewhere I was shedding
past time. I remember one of those wartime agencies well because it was full
of Canadian matrons. They wore pearl earrings like the Duchess of Kent's
and seemed to be practicing her tiny smile. Brooches pinned to their cashmere cardigans carried some daft message about the Empire. I heard one of
them exclaiming, "You don't expect me, a Britisher, to drink tea made with
tea bags!" Good plain girls from the little German towns of Ontario, chris-

tened probably Wilma, Jean, and Irma, they had flowing eighteenth-century names like Georgiana and Arabella now. And the Americans, who came in with their arms full of every stitch they could spare, would urge them, the Canadian matrons, to stand fast on the cliffs, to fight the fight, to slug the enemy on the landing fields, to belt him one on the beaches, to keep going with whatever iron rations they could scrape up in Bronxville and Scarsdale; and the Canadians half shut their eyes and tipped their heads back like Gertrude Lawrence and said in thrilling Benita Hume accents that they would do that—indeed they would. I recorded "They're all trained nurses, actually. The Canadian ones have a good reputation. They managed to marry these American doctors."

Canada had been in Hitler's war from the very beginning, but America was still uneasily at peace. Recruiting had already begun; I had seen a departure from New York for Camp Stewart in Georgia, and some of the recruits' mothers crying and even screaming and trying to run alongside the train. The recruits were going off to drill with broomsticks because there weren't enough guns; they still wore old-fashioned headgear and were paid twenty-one dollars a month. There was a song about it: "For twenty-one dollars a day, once a month." As my own train crossed the border to Canada I expected to sense at once an air of calm and grit and dedication, but the only changes were from prosperous to shabby, from painted to unpainted, from smiling to dour. I was entering a poorer and a curiously empty country, where the faces of the people gave nothing away. The crossing was my sea change. I silently recited the vow I had been preparing for weeks: that I would never be helpless again and that I would not let anyone make a decision on my behalf.

When I got down from the train at Windsor station, a man sidled over to me. He had a cap on his head and a bitter Celtic face, with deep indentations along his cheeks, as if his back teeth were pulled. I thought he was asking a direction. He repeated his question, which was obscene. My arms were pinned by the weight of my hamper and suitcase. He brushed the back of his hand over my breasts, called me a name, and edged away. The murderous rage I felt and the revulsion that followed were old friends. They had for years been my reaction to what my diaries called "their hypocrisy." "They" was a world of sly and mumbling people, all of them older than myself. I must have substituted "hypocrisy" for every sort of aggression, because fright was a luxury I could not afford. What distressed me was my helplessness—I who had sworn only a few hours earlier that I'd not be vulnerable again. The man's gaunt face, his drunken breath, the flat voice which I assigned to the graduate of some Christian Brothers teaching establishment haunted me for a long time after that. "The man at Windsor station" would lurk in the windowless corridors of my nightmares; he would be the passenger, the only passenger, on a dark tram. The first sight of a city must be the measure for all second looks.

But it was not my first sight. I'd had ten years of it here—the first ten. After that, and before New York (in one sense, my deliverance), there had been a long spell of grief and shadow in an Ontario city, a place full of mean judgments and grudging minds, of paranoid Protestants and slovenly Catholics. To this day I cannot bear the sight of brick houses, or of a certain kind of empty treeless street on a Sunday afternoon. My memory of Montreal took shape while I was there. It was not a random jumble of rooms and summers and my mother singing "We've Come to See Miss Jenny Jones," but the faithful record of the true survivor. I retained, I rebuilt a superior civilization. In that drowned world, Sherbrooke Street seemed to be glittering and white; the vision of a house upon that street was so painful that I was obliged to banish it from the memorial. The small hot rooms of a summer cottage became enormous and cool. If I say that Cleopatra floated down the Chateauguay River, that the Winter Palace was stormed on Sherbrooke Street, that Trafalgar was fought on Lake St. Louis, I mean it naturally; they were the natural backgrounds of my exile and fidelity. I saw now at the far end of Windsor station—more foreign, echoing, and mysterious than any American station could be—a statue of Lord Mount Stephen, the founder of the Canadian Pacific, which everyone took to be a memorial to Edward VII. Angus, Charlotte, and the smaller Linnet had truly been: This was my proof; once upon a time my instructions had been to make my way to Windsor station should I ever be lost and to stand at the foot of Edward VII and wait for someone to find me.

I have forgotten to say that no one in Canada knew I was there. I looked up the number of the woman who had once been my nurse, but she had no telephone. I found her in a city directory, and with complete faith that "O. Carette" was indeed Olivia and that she would recall and welcome me I took a taxi to the east end of the city—the French end, the poor end. I was so sure of her that I did not ask the driver to wait (to take me where?) but dismissed him and climbed two flights of dark brown stairs inside a house that must have been built soon after Waterloo. That it was Olivia who came to the door, that the small gray-haired creature I recalled as dark and towering had to look up at me, that she unhesitatingly offered me shelter all seem as simple now as when I broke my fiver to settle the taxi. Believing that I was dead, having paid for years of Masses for the repose of my heretic soul, almost the first thing she said to me was *"Tu vis?"* I understood *"Tu es ici?"* We straightened it out later. She held both my hands and cried and called me *belle et grande.* *"Grande"* was good, for among American girls I'd seemed a shrimp. I did not see what there was to cry for; I was here. I was as naturally selfish with Olivia as if her sole reason for being was me. I stayed with her for a while and left when her affection for me made her possessive, and I think I neglected her. On her deathbed she told one of her daughters, the reliable one, to keep an eye on me forever. Olivia was the only person in the world who did not believe I could look after myself. Where she and I were concerned I remained under six.

Now, at no moment of this remarkable day did I feel anxious or worried or forlorn. The man at Windsor station could not really affect my view of the future. I had seen some of the worst of life, but I had no way of judging it or of knowing what the worst could be. I had a sensation of loud, ruthless power, like an enormous waterfall. The past, the part I would rather not have lived, became small and remote, a dark pinpoint. My only weapons until now had been secrecy and insolence. I had stopped running away from schools and situations when I finally understood that by becoming a name in a file, by attracting attention, I would merely prolong my stay in prison— I mean, the prison of childhood itself. My rebellions then consisted only in causing people who were physically larger and legally sovereign to lose their self-control, to become bleached with anger, to shake with such temper that they broke cups and glasses and bumped into chairs. From the malleable, sunny child Olivia said she remembered, I had become, according to later chroniclers, cold, snobbish, and presumptuous. "You need an iron hand, Linnet." I can still hear that melancholy voice, which belonged to a friend of my mother's. "If anybody ever marries you he'd better have an iron hand." After today I would never need to hear this, or anything approaching it, for the rest of my life.

And so that June morning and the drive through empty, sunlit, wartime streets are even now like a roll of drums in the mind. My life was my own revolution—the tyrants deposed, the constitution wrenched from unwilling hands; I was, all by myself, the liberated crowd setting the palace on fire; I was the flags, the trees, the bannered windows, the flower-decked trains.

The singing and the skyrockets of the 1848 I so trustingly believed would emerge out of the war were me, no one but me; and, as in the lyrical first days of any revolution, as in the first days of any love affair, there wasn't the whisper of a voice to tell me, "You might compromise."

If making virtue of necessity has ever had a meaning it must be here: for I was independent *inevitably.* There were good-hearted Americans who knew a bit of my story—as much as I wanted anyone to know—and who hoped I would swim and not drown, but from the moment I embarked on my journey I went on the dark side of the moon. "You seemed so sure of yourself," they would tell me, still troubled, long after this. In the cool journals I kept I noted that my survival meant nothing in the capitalist system; I was one of those not considered to be worth helping, saving, or even investigating. Thinking with care, I see this was true. What could I have turned into in another place? Why, a librarian at Omsk or a file clerk at Tomsk. Well, it hadn't happened that way; I had my private revolution and I settled in with Olivia in Montreal. Sink or swim? Of course I swam. Jobs were for the having; you could pick them up off the ground. Working for a living meant just what it says—a brisk necessity. It would be the least important fragment of my life until I had what I wanted. The cheek of it, I think now: Penniless, sleeping in a shed room behind the kitchen of Olivia's cold-water flat, still I pointed across the wooden balustrade in a long open office where I was being considered for employment and said, "But I won't sit there." Girls were "there," penned in like sheep. I did not think men better than women— only that they did more interesting work and got more money for it. In my journals I called other girls "Coolies." I did not know if life made them bearers or if they had been born with a natural gift for giving in. "Coolie" must have been the secret expression of one of my deepest fears. I see now that I had an immense conceit: I thought I occupied a world other people could scarcely envision, let alone attain. It involved giddy risks and changes, stepping off the edge blindfolded, one's hand on nothing more than a birth certificate and a five-dollar bill. At this time of sitting in judgment I was earning nine dollars a week (until I was told by someone that the local minimum wage was twelve, on which I left for greener fields) and washing my white piqué skirt at night and ironing at dawn, and coming home at all hours so I could pretend to Olivia I had dined. Part of this impermeable sureness that I needn't waver or doubt came out of my having lived in New York. The first time I ever heard people laughing in a cinema was there. I can still remember the wonder and excitement and amazement I felt. I was just under fourteen and I had never heard people expressing their feelings in a public place in my life. The easy reactions, the way a poignant moment caught them, held them still—all that was new. I had come there straight from Ontario, where the reaction to a love scene was a kind of unhappy giggling, while the image of a kitten or a baby induced a long flat "Aaaah," followed by shamed silence. You could imagine them blushing in the dark for having said that—just that "Aaaah." When I heard that open American laughter I thought I could be like these people too, but had been told not to be by everyone, beginning with Olivia: *"Pas si fort"* was something she repeated to me so often when I was small that my father had made a tease out of it, called "Passy four." From a tease it became oppressive too: "For the love of God, Linnet, passy four." What were these new people? Were they soft, too easily got at? I wondered that even then. Would a dictator have a field day here? Were they, as Canadian opinion had it, vulgar? Perhaps the notion of vulgarity came out of some incapacity on the part of the refined. Whatever they were, they couldn't all be daft; if they weren't I probably wasn't either. I supposed I stood as good a chance of being miserable here as anywhere, but at least I would not have to pretend to be someone else.

Now, of course there is much to be said on the other side: People who do not display what they feel have practical advantages. They can go away to be killed as if they didn't mind; they can see their sons off to war without a blink. Their upbringing is intended for a crisis. When it comes, they behave themselves. But it is murder in everyday life—truly murder. The dead of heart and spirit litter the landscape. Still, keeping a straight face makes life tolerable under stress. It makes *public* life tolerable—that is all I am saying; because in private people still got drunk, went after each other with bottles and knives, rang the police to complain that neighbors were sending poison gas over the transom, abandoned infant children and aged parents, wrote letters to newspapers in favor of corporal punishment, with inventive suggestions. When I came back to Canada that June, at least one thing had been settled: I knew that it was all right for people to laugh and cry and even to make asses of themselves. I had actually known people like that, had lived with them, and they were fine, mostly—not crazy at all. That was where a lot of my confidence came from when I began my journey into a new life and a dream past.

My father's death had been kept from me. I did not know its exact circumstances or even the date. He died when I was ten. At thirteen I was still expected to believe a fable about his being in England. I kept waiting for him to send for me, for my life was deeply wretched and I took it for granted he knew. Finally I began to suspect that death and silence can be one. How to be sure? Head-on questions got me nowhere. I had to create a situation in which some adult (not my mother, who was far too sharp) would lose all restraint and hurl the truth at me. It was easy: I was an artist at this. What I had not foreseen was the verbal violence of the scene or the effect it might have. The storm that seemed to break in my head, my need to maintain the pose of indifference ("What are you telling me that for? What makes you think I care?") were such a strain that I had physical re-actions, like stigmata, which doctors would hopelessly treat on and off for years and which vanished when I became independent. The other change was that if anyone asked about my father I said, "Oh, he died." Now, in Montreal, I could confront the free adult world of falsehood and evasion on an equal footing; they would be forced to talk to me as they did to each other. Making appointments to meet my father's friends—Mr. Archie McEwen, Mr. Stephen Ross-Colby, Mr. Quentin Keller—I left my adult name, "Miss Muir." These were the men who eight, nine, ten years ago had asked, "Do you like your school?"—not knowing what else to say to chil-dren. I had curtsied to them and said, "Good night." I think what I wanted was special information about despair, but I should have known that would be taboo in a place where "like" and "don't like" were heavy emo-tional statements.

Archie McEwen, my father's best friend, or the man I mistook for that, kept me standing in his office on St. James Street West, he standing too, with his hands behind his back, and he said the following—not recon-structed or approximate but recalled, like "The religions of ancient Greece and Rome are extinct" or "O come, let us sing unto the Lord":

"Of course, Angus was a very sick man. I saw him walking along Sher-brooke Street. He must have just come out of hospital. He couldn't walk upright. He was using a stick. Inching along. His hair had turned gray. No-body knew where Charlotte had got to, and we'd heard you were dead. He obviously wasn't long for this world either. He had too many troubles for any one man. I crossed the street because I didn't have the heart to shake hands with him. I felt terrible."

Savage? Reasonable? You can't tell, with those minds. Some recent threat had scared them. The Depression was too close, just at their heels. Archie McEwen did not ask where I was staying or where I had been for the last eight years; in fact, he asked only two questions. In response to the first I said, "She is married."

There came a gleam of interest—distant, amused: "So she decided to marry him, did she?"

My mother was highly visible; she had no secrets except unexpected ones. My father had nothing but. When he asked, "Would you like to spend a year in England with your Aunt Dorothy?" I had no idea what he meant and I still don't. His only brother, Thomas, who was killed in 1918, had not been married; he'd had no sisters, that anyone knew. Those English mysteries used to be common. People came out to Canada because they did not want to think about the Thomases and Dorothys anymore. Angus was a solemn man, not much of a smiler. My mother, on the other hand—I won't begin to describe her; it would never end—smiled, talked, charmed anyone she didn't happen to be related to, swam in scandal like a partisan among the people. She made herself the central figure in loud, spectacular dramas which she played with the houselights on; you could see the audience too. That was her mistake; they kept their reactions, like their lovemaking, in the dark. You can imagine what she must have been in this world where everything was hushed, muffled, disguised: She must have seemed all they had by way of excitement, give or take a few elections and wars. It sounds like a story about the old and stale, but she and my father had been quite young eight and ten years before. The dying man creeping along Sherbrooke Street was thirty-two. First it was light chatter, then darker gossip, and then it went too far (*he* was ill and he couldn't hide it; *she* had a lover and didn't try); then suddenly it became tragic, and open tragedy was disallowed. And so Mr. Archie McEwen could stand in his office and without a trace of feeling on his narrow Lowland face—not unlike my father's in shape—he could say, "I crossed the street."

Stephen Ross-Colby, a bachelor, my father's painter chum: The smell of his studio on St. Mark Street was the smell of a personal myth. I said timidly, "Do you happen to have anything of his—a drawing or anything?" I was humble because I was on a private, personal terrain of vocation that made me shy even of the dead.

He said, "No, nothing. You could ask around. She junked a lot of his stuff and he junked the rest when he thought he wouldn't survive. You might try . . ." He gave me a name or two. "It was all small stuff," said Ross-Colby. "He didn't do anything big." He hurried me out of the studio for a cup of coffee in a crowded place—the Honey Dew on St. Catherine Street, it must have been. Perhaps in the privacy of his studio I might have heard him thinking. Years after that he would try to call me "Lynn," which I never was, and himself "Steve." He'd come into his own as an artist by then, selling wash drawings of Canadian war graves, sun-splashed, wisteria mauve, lime green, with drifts of blossom across the name of the regiment; gained a reputation among the heartbroken women who bought these impersonations, had them framed—the only picture in the house. He painted the war memorial at Caen. ("Their name liveth forever.") His stones weren't stones but mauve bubbles—that is all I have against them. They floated off the page. My objection wasn't to "He didn't do anything big" but to Ross-Colby's way of turning the dead into thistledown. He said, much later, of that meeting, "I felt like a bastard, but I was broke, and I was afraid you'd put the bite on me."

Let me distribute demerits equally and tell about my father's literary Jewish friend, Mr. Quentin Keller. He was older than the others, perhaps by some twelve years. He had a whispery voice and a long pale face and a daughter older than I. "Bossy Wendy" I used to call her when, forced by her parents as I was by mine, Bossy Wendy had to take a whole afternoon of me. She had a room full of extraordinary toys, a miniature kitchen in which everything worked, of which all I recall her saying is "Don't touch." Wendy Keller had left Smith after her freshman year to marry the elder son of a Danish baron. Her father said to me, "There is only one thing you need to know and that is that your father was a gentleman."

Jackass was what I thought. Yes, Mr. Quentin Keller was a jackass. But he was a literary one, for he had once written a play called *Forbearance*, in which I'd had a role. I had bounded across the stage like a tennis ball, into the arms of a young woman dressed up like an old one, and cried my one line: "Here I am, Granny!" Of course, he did not make his living fiddling about with amateur theatricals; thanks to our meeting I had a good look at the inside of a conservative architect's private office—that was about all it brought me.

What were they so afraid of, I wondered. I had not yet seen that I was in a false position where they were concerned; being "Miss Muir" had not made equals of us but lent distance. I thought they had read my true passport, the invisible one we all carry, but I had neither the wealth nor the influence a provincial society requires to make a passport valid. My credentials were lopsided: The important half of the scales was still in the air. I needed enormous collateral security—fame, an alliance with a powerful family, the power of money itself. I remember how Archie McEwen, trying to place me in some sensible context, to give me a voucher so he could take me home and show me to his wife, perhaps, asked his second question: "Who inherited the——?"

"The what, Mr. McEwen?"

He had not, of course, read "Why I Am a Socialist." I did not believe in inherited property. "Who inherited the——?" would not cross my mind again for another ten years, and then it would be a drawer quickly opened and shut before demons could escape. To all three men the last eight years were like minutes; to me they had been several lives. Some of my confidence left me then. It came down to "Next time I'll know better," but would that be enough? I had been buffeted until now by other people's moods, principles, whims, tantrums; I had survived, but perhaps I had failed to grow some outer skin it was now too late to acquire. Olivia thought that; she was the only one. Olivia knew more about the limits of nerve than I did. Her knowledge came out of the clean, swept, orderly poverty that used to be tucked away in the corners of cities. It didn't spill out then, or give anyone a bad conscience. Nobody took its picture. Anyway, Olivia would not have sat for such a portrait. The fringed green rug she put over her treadle sewing machine was part of a personal fortune. On her mantelpiece stood a copper statuette of Voltaire in an armchair. It must have come down to her from some robustly anticlerical ancestor. "Who is he?" she said to me. "You've been to school in a foreign country." "A governor of New France," I replied. She knew Voltaire was the name of a bad man and she'd have thrown the figurine out, and it would have made one treasure less in the house. Olivia's maiden name was Ouvrardville, which was good in Quebec, but only really good if you were one of the rich ones. Because of her maiden name she did not want anyone ever to know she had worked for a family; she impressed this on me delicately—it was like trying to understand what a dragonfly wanted to tell. In the old days she had gone home every weekend, taking me with her if my parents felt my company was going to make Sunday a very long day. Now I understood what the weekends were about: Her daughters, Berthe and Marguerite, for whose sake she worked, were home from their convent schools Saturday and Sunday and had to be chaperoned. Her relatives pretended not to notice that Olivia was poor or even that she was widowed, for which she seemed grateful. The result of all this elegant sham was that Olivia did not say, "I was afraid you'd put the bite on me," or keep me standing. She dried her tears and asked if there was a trunk to follow. No? She made a pot of tea and spread a starched cloth on the kitchen table and we sat down to a breakfast of toast and honey. The honey tin was a ten-pounder decorated with bees the size of hornets. Lifting it for her, I remarked, *"C'est collant,"* a word out of a frozen language that started to thaw when Olivia said, *"Tu vis?"*

On the advice of her confessor, who was to be my rival from now on, Olivia refused to tell me whatever she guessed or knew, and she was far too dignified to hint. Putting together the three men's woolly stories, I arrived at something about tuberculosis of the spine and a butchery of an operation. He started back to England to die there but either changed his mind or was too ill to begin the journey; at Quebec City, where he was to have taken ship, he shot himself in a public park at five o'clock in the morning. That was one version; another was that he died at sea and the gun was found in his luggage. The revolver figured in all three accounts. It was an officer's weapon from the Kaiser's war, that had belonged to his brother. Angus kept it at the back of a small drawer in the tall chest used for men's clothes and known in Canada as a highboy. In front of the revolver was a pigskin stud box and a pile of ironed handkerchiefs. Just describing that drawer dates it. How I happen to know the revolver was loaded and how I learned never to point a gun even in play is another story. I can tell you that I never again in my life looked inside a drawer that did not belong to me.

I know a woman whose father died, she thinks, in a concentration camp. Or was he shot in a schoolyard? Or hanged and thrown in a ditch? Were the ashes that arrived from some eastern plain his or another prisoner's? She invents different deaths. Her inventions have become her conversation at dinner parties. She takes on a child's voice and says, "My father died at Buchenwald." She chooses and rejects elements of the last act; one avoids mentioning death, shooting, capital punishment, cremation, deportation, even fathers. Her inventions are not thought neurotic or exhibitionist but something sanctioned by history. Peacetime casualties are not like that. They are lightning bolts out of a sunny sky that strike only one house. All around the ashy ruin lilacs blossom, leaves gleam. Speculation in public about the disaster would be indecent. Nothing remains but a silent, recurring puzzlement to the survivors: Why here and not there? Why this and not that? Before July was out I had settled his fate in my mind and I never varied: I thought he had died of homesickness; sickness for England was the consumption, the gun, the everything. "Everything" had to take it all in, for people in Canada then did not speak of irrational endings to life, and newspapers did not print that kind of news: This was because of the spiritual tragedy for Catholic families, and because the act had long been considered a criminal one in British law. If Catholic feelings were spared it gave the impression no one but Protestants ever went over the edge, which was unfair; and so the possibility was eliminated, and people came to a natural end in a running car in a closed garage, hanging from a rafter in the barn, in an icy lake with a canoe left to drift empty. Once I had made up my mind, the whole story somehow became none of my business: I had looked in a drawer that did not belong to me. More, if I was to live my own life I had to let go. I wrote in my journal that "they" had got him but would not get me, and after that there was scarcely ever a mention.

My dream past evaporated. Montreal, in memory, was a leafy citadel where I knew every tree. In reality I recognized nearly nothing and had to start from scratch. Sherbrooke Street had been the dream street, pure white. It was the avenue poor Angus descended leaning on a walking stick. It was a moat I was not allowed to cross alone; it was lined with gigantic spreading trees through which light fell like a rain of coins. One day, standing at a corner, waiting for the light to change, I understood that the Sherbrooke Street of my exile—my Mecca, my Jerusalem—was this. It had to be: There could not be two. It was *only* this. The limitless green where in a perpetual spring I had been taken to play was the campus of McGill University. A house, whose beauty had brought tears to my sleep, to which in sleep I'd returned to find it inhabited by ugly strangers, gypsies, was a narrow stone thing with a shop on the ground floor and offices above—if that was it, for there were several like it. Through the bare panes of what might have been the sitting room, with its deep private window seats, I saw neon striplighting along a ceiling. Reality, as always, was narrow and dull. And yet what dramatic things had taken place on this very corner: Once Satan had approached me—furry dark skin, claws, red eyes, the lot. He urged me to cross the street and I did, in front of a car that braked in time. I explained, "The Devil told me to." I had no idea until then that my parents did not believe what I was taught in my convent school. (Satan is not bilingual, by the way; he speaks Quebec French.) My parents had no God and therefore no Fallen Angel. I was scolded for lying, which was a thing my father detested, and which my mother regularly did but never forgave in others.

Why these two nonbelievers wanted a strong religious education for me is one of the mysteries. (Even in loss of faith they were unalike, for he was ex-Anglican and she was ex-Lutheran and that is not your same atheist—

no, not at all.) "To make you tolerant" was a lame excuse, as was "French," for I spoke fluent French with Olivia, and I could read in two languages before I was four. Discipline might have been one reason—God knows, the nuns provided plenty of that—but according to Olivia I did not need any. It cannot have been for the quality of the teaching, which was lamentable. I suspect that it was something like sending a dog to a trainer (they were passionate in their concern for animals, especially dogs), but I am not certain it ever brought me to heel. The first of my schools, the worst, the darkest, was on Sherbrooke Street too. When I heard, years later, it had been demolished, it was like the burial of a witch. I had remembered it penitentiary size, but what I found myself looking at one day was simply a very large stone house. A crocodile of little girls emerged from the front gate and proceeded along the street—white-faced, black-clad, eyes cast down. I knew they were bored, fidgety, anxious, and probably hungry. I should have felt pity, but at eighteen all that came to me was thankfulness that I had been correct about one thing throughout my youth, which I now considered ended: Time had been on my side, faithfully, and unless you died you were always bound to escape.

BETWEEN ZERO AND ONE

❧

*W*hen I was young I thought that men had small lives of their own creation. I could not see why, born enfranchised, without the obstacles and constraints attendant on women, they set such close limits for themselves and why, once the limits had been reached, they seemed so taken aback. I could not tell much difference between a man aged thirty-six, about, and one forty or fifty; it was impossible to fix the borderline of this apparent disappointment. There was a space of life I used to call "between Zero and One" and then came a long mystery. I supposed that men came up to their wall, their terminal point, quite a long way after One. At that time I was nineteen and we were losing the war. The news broadcast in Canada was flatly optimistic, read out in the detached nasal voices de rigueur for the CBC. They were voices that seemed to be saying, "Good or bad, it can't affect *us*." I worked in a building belonging to the federal government—it was a heavy Victorian structure of the sort that exists on every continent, wherever the British thought they'd come to stay. This one had been made out of the reddish-brown Montreal stone that colors, in memory, the streets of my childhood and that architects have no use for now. The office was full of old soldiers from one war before: Ypres (pronounced "Wipers") and Vimy Ridge were real, as real as this minute, while Singapore, Pearl Harbor, Voronezh were the stuff of fiction. It seemed as if anything that befell the young, even dying, was bound to be trivial.

"Half of 'em'll never see any fighting," I often heard. "Anyway not like in the trenches." We did have one veteran from the current war—Mac Kirkconnell, who'd had a knock on the head during his training and was now good for nothing except civilian life. He and two others were the only men under thirty left in the place. The other two were physical crocks, which was why they were not in uniform (a question demented women sometimes asked them in the street). Mr. Tracy had been snow-blinded after looking out of a train window for most of a sunny February day; he had recovered part of his sight but had to wear mauve glasses even by electric light. He was nice but strange, infirm. Mr. Curran, reputed to have one kidney, one lung, and one testicle, and who was the subject of endless rhymes and ditties on that account, was not so nice: He had not wanted a girl in the office and had argued against my being employed. Now that I was there he simply pretended that he had won. There were about a dozen other men—older, old. I can see every face, hear every syllable, which evoked, for me, a street, a suburb, a kind of schooling. I could hear just out of someone's saying to me, "Say, Linnet, couja just gimme a hand here, please?" born here, born in Glasgow; immigrated early, late; raised in Montreal, no, farther west. I can see the rolled shirtsleeves, the braces, the eyeshades, the hunched shoulders, the elastic armbands, the paper cuffs they wore sometimes, the chopped-egg sandwiches in waxed paper, the apples, the oatmeal cookies ("Want any, Linnet? If you don't eat lunch nobody'll marry you"), the thermos flasks. Most of them lived thinly, paying for a bungalow, a duplex flat, a son's education: A good Protestant education was not to be had for nothing then. I remember a day of dark spring snowstorms, ourselves reflected on the black windows, the pools of warm light here and there, the green-shaded lamps, the dramatic hiss and gurgle of the radiators that always sounded like the background to some emotional outburst, the sudden slackening at the end of the afternoon when every molecule of oxygen in the room had turned into poison. Assistant Chief Engineer Macaulay came plodding softly along the wintry room and laid something down on my desk. It was a collection of snapshots of a naked woman prancing and skipping in what I took to be the backyard of his house out in Cartierville. In one she was in a baby carriage with her legs spread over the sides, pretending to drink out of an infant's bottle. The unknown that this represented was infinite. I also wondered what Mr. Macaulay wanted— he didn't say. He remarked, shifting from foot to foot, "Now, Linnet, they tell me you like modern art." I thought then, I think now, that the tunnel winters, the sudden darkness that April day, the years he'd had of this long green room, the knowledge that he would die and be buried "Assistant Chief Engineer Grade II" without having overtaken Chief Engineer McCreery had simply snapped the twig, the frail matchstick in the head that is all we have to keep us sensible.

Bertie Knox had a desk facing mine. He told the other men I'd gone red in the face when I saw Macaulay's fat-arsed wife. (He hadn't seen *that* one; I had turned it over, like a bad card.) The men teased me for blushing, and they said, "Wait till you get married, Linnet, you haven't done with shocks." Bertie Knox had been in this very office since the age of twelve. The walls had been a good solid gray then—not this drawing-room green. The men hadn't been pampered and coddled, either. There wasn't even a water cooler. You were fined for smoking, fined for lateness, fined for sick leave. He had worked the old ten-hour day and given every cent to his mother. Once he pinched a dime of it and his mother went for him. He locked himself in a cupboard. His mother took the door off its hinges and beat him blue with a wooden hanger. During the Depression, married, down to half pay, four kids in the house, he had shoveled snow for twenty cents an hour. "And none the worse for it," he would always wind up. Most of the men seemed to have been raised in hardship by stern, desperate parents. What struck me was the good they thought it had done them (I had yet to meet an adult man with a poor opinion of himself) and their desire to impose the same broken fortunes on other people, particularly on the young—though not their own young, of course. There was a touch of sadness, a touch of envy to it, too. Bertie Knox had seen Mr. Macaulay and Mr. McCreery come in as Engineers Grade II, wet behind the ears, puffed up with their new degrees, "just a couple more college punks." He said that engineering was the world's most despised profession, occupied mainly by human apes. Instead of a degree he had a photograph of himself in full kilt, Highland Light Infantry, 1917: He had gone "home," to a completely unknown Old Country, and joined up there. "Will you just look at that lad?" he would plead. "Do they come like him today? By God, they do not!" Bertie Knox could imitate any tone and accent, including mine. He could do a CBC announcer droning, "The British have ah taken ah Tobruk," when we knew perfectly well the Germans had. (One good thing about the men was that when anything seemed hopeless they talked nonsense. The native traits of pessimism and constant grumbling returned only when there was nothing to grumble about.) Bertie Knox had a wooden leg, which he showed me; it was dressed in a maroon sock with clocks up the sides and a buckled garter. He had a collection of robust bawdy songs—as everyone (all the men, I mean) had in Canada, unless they were pretending—which I copied in a notebook, verse upon verse, with the necessary indications: Tune—"On, Wisconsin!"; Tune—"Men of Harlech"; Tune—"We Gather Together to Ask the

Lord's Blessing." Sometimes he took the notebook and corrected a word here and there. It doesn't follow that he was a cheerful person. He laughed a lot but he never smiled. I don't think he liked anyone, really.

The men were statisticians, draftsmen, civil engineers. Painted on the frosted glass of the office door was

REVIEW AND DEVELOPMENT
RESEARCH AND EXPANSION
OF
WARTIME INDUSTRY
"REGIONAL AND URBAN"

The office had been called something else up until September 1939; according to Bertie Knox they were still doing the same work as before, and not much of it. "It looks good," he said. "It sounds good. What is its meaning? Sweet bugger all." A few girls equipped with rackety typewriters and adding machines sat grouped at the far end of the room, separated from the men by a balustrade. I was the first woman ever permitted to work on the men's side of this fence. A pigeon among the cats was how it sometimes felt. My title was "aide." Today it would be something like "trainee." I was totally unqualified for this or any other kind of work and had been taken on almost at my own insistence that they could not do without me.

"Yes, I know all about that," I had replied, to everything.

"Well, I *suppose* it's all right," said Chief Engineer. The hiring of girls usually fell to a stout grim woman called "Supervisor," but I was not coming in as a typist. He had never interviewed a girl before and he was plainly uncomfortable, asking me questions with all the men straining to hear. There were no young men left on account of the war, and the office did need someone. But what if they trained me, he said, at great cost and expense to the government, and what if I then did the dreadful thing girls were reputed to do, which was to go off and get married? It would mean a great waste of time and money just when there was a war on.

I was engaged, but not nearly ready for the next step. In any case, I told him, even if I did marry I would need to go on working, for my husband would more than likely be sent overseas. What Chief Engineer did not know was that I was a minor with almost no possibility of obtaining parental consent. Barring some bright idea, I could not do much of anything until I was twenty-one. For this interview I had pinned back my long hair; I wore a hat, gloves, earrings, and I folded my hands on my purse in a conscious imitation of older women. I did not mind the interview, or the furtively staring men. I was shy, but not self-conscious. Efforts made not to turn a young girl's head—part of an education I had encountered at every stage and in every sort of school—had succeeded in making me invisible to myself. My only commercial asset was that I knew French, but French was of no professional use to anyone in Canada then—not even to French Canadians; one might as well have been fluent in Pushtu. Nevertheless I listed it on my application form, along with a very dodgy "German" (private lessons between the ages of eight and ten) and an entirely impudent "Russian": I was attending Russian evening classes at McGill, for reasons having mainly to do with what I believed to be the world's political future. I recorded my age as twenty-two, hoping to be given a grade and a salary that would correspond. There were no psychological or aptitude tests; you were taken at your word and lasted according to performance. There was no social security and only the loosest sort of pension plan; hiring and firing involved no more paperwork than a typed letter—sometimes not even that. I had an unmistakably Montreal accent of a kind now almost extinct, but my having attended school in the United States gave me a useful vagueness of background.

And so, in an ambience of doubt, apprehension, foreboding, incipient danger, and plain hostility, for the first time in the history of the office a girl was allowed to sit with the men. And it was here, at the desk facing Bertie Knox's, on the only uncomfortable chair in the room, that I felt for the first time that almost palpable atmosphere of sexual curiosity, sexual resentment, and sexual fear that the presence of a woman can create where she is not wanted. If part of the resentment vanished when it became clear that I did not know what I was doing, the feeling that women were "trouble" never disappeared. However, some of the men were fathers of daughters, and they quickly saw that I was nothing like twenty-two. Some of them helped me then, and one man, Hughie Pryor, an engineer, actually stayed late to do some of my work when I fell behind.

Had I known exactly what I was about, I might not have remained for more than a day. Older, more experienced, I'd have called it a dull place. The men were rotting quietly until pension time. They kept to a slow English-rooted civil-service pace; no one wasted office time openly, but no one produced much, either. Although they could squabble like hens over mislaid pencils, windows open or shut, borrowed triangles, special and sacred pen nibs used for tracing maps, there was a truce about zeal. The fact is that I did not know the office was dull. It was so new to me, so strange, such another climate, that even to flow with the sluggish tide training men and women into the heart of the city each day was a repeated experiment I sensed, noted, recorded, as if I were being allowed to be part of something that was not really mine. The smell of the building was of school—of chalk, dust, plaster, varnish, beeswax. Victorian, Edwardian, and early Georgian oil portraits of Canadian captains of industry, fleshed-out pirate faces, adorned the staircase and halls—a daily reminder that there are two races, those who tread on people's lives, and the others. The latest date on any of the portraits was about 1925: I suppose photography had taken over. Also by then the great fortunes had been established and the surviving pirates were retired, replete and titled, usually to England. Having had both French and English schooling in Quebec, I knew that these pink-cheeked marauders were what English-speaking children were led to admire (without much hope of emulation, for the feast was over). They were men of patriotism and of action; we owed them everything. They were in a positive, constructive way a part of the Empire and of the Crown; this was a good thing. In a French education veneration was withheld from anyone except the dead and defeated, ranging from General Montcalm expiring at his last battle to a large galaxy of maimed and crippled saints. Deprivation of the senses, mortification of mind and body were imposed, encouraged, for phantom reasons— something to do with a tragic past and a deep fear of life itself. Montreal was a city where the greater part of the population were wrapped in myths and sustained by belief in magic. I had been to school with little girls who walked in their sleep and had visions; the nuns who had taught me seemed at ease with the dead. I think of them even now as strange, dead, punishing creatures who neither ate nor breathed nor slept. The one who broke one of my fingers with a ruler was surely a spirit without a mind, tormented, acting in the vengeful driven way of homeless ghosts. In an English school visions would have been smartly dealt with—cold showers, the parents summoned, at the least a good stiff talking-to. These two populations, these two tribes, knew nothing whatever about each other. In the very poorest part of the east end of the city, apparitions were commonplace; one lived among a mixture of men and women and their imaginings. I would never have believed then that anything could ever stir them from their dark dreams. The men in the portraits were ghosts of a kind, too; they also seemed to be saying, "Too late, too late for you," and of course in a sense so it was: It was too late for anyone else to import Chinese and Irish coolie labor and wring a railway out of them. That had already been done. Once I said to half-blind Mr. Tracy, "Things can't just stay this way."

"Change is always for the worse" was his reply. His own father had lost all his money in the Depression, ten years before; perhaps he meant that.

I climbed to the office in a slow reassuring elevator with iron grille doors, sharing it with inexpressive women and men—clearly, the trodden-on. No matter how familiar our faces became, we never spoke. The only sound, apart from the creaking cable, was the gasping and choking of a poor man who had been gassed at the Somme and whose lungs were said to be in shreds. He had an old man's pale eyes and wore a high stiff collar and stared straight before him, like everyone else. Some of the men in my office had been wounded, too, but they made it sound pleasant. Bertie Knox said he had hobbled on one leg and crutches in the 1918 Allied victory parade in Paris. According to him, when his decimated regiment followed their Highland music up the Champs-Élysées, every pretty girl in Paris had been along the curb, fighting the police and screaming and trying to get at Bertie Knox and take him home.

"It was the kilts set 'em off," said Bertie Knox. "That and the wounds. And the Jocks played it up for all they was worth, bashing the very buggery out of the drums." "Jocks" were Scots in those days—nothing more.

Any mention of that older war could bring the men to life, but it had been done with for more than twenty years now. Why didn't they move, walk, stretch, run? Each of them seemed to inhabit an invisible square; the square was shared with *my* desk, *my* graph paper, *my* elastic bands. The contents of the square were tested each morning: The drawers of my own desk—do they still open and shut? My desk lamp—does it still turn on and off? Have my special coat hanger, my favorite nibs, my drinking glass, my calendar, my children's pictures, my ashtray, the one I brought from home, been tampered with during the night? Sometimes one glimpsed another world, like an extra room ("It was my young daughter made my lunch today"—said with a dismissive shrug, lest it be taken for boasting) or a wish outdistanced, reduced, shrunken, trailing somewhere in the mind: "I often thought I wanted . . ." "Something I wouldn't have minded having . . ." Easily angry, easily offended, underpaid, at the mercy of accidents—an illness in the family could wipe out a life's savings—still they'd have resisted change for the better. Change was double-edged; it might mean improving people with funny names, letting them get uppity. What they had instead were marks of privilege—a blind sureness that they were superior in every way to French Canadians, whom in some strange fashion they neither heard nor saw (a lack of interest that was doubly and triply returned); they had the certainty they'd never be called on to share a washroom or a drawing board or to exchange the time of day with anyone "funny" (applications from such people, in those days, would have been quietly set aside); most important of all, perhaps, they had the distinction of the individual hand towel. These towels, as stiff as boards, reeking of chloride bleach, were distributed once a week by a boy pushing a trolley. They were distributed to men, but not even to *all* men. The sanctioned carried them to the washroom, aired and dried them on the backs of chairs, kept them folded in a special drawer. Assimilated into a male world, I had one too. The stenographers and typists had to make do with paper towels that scratched when new and dissolved when damp. Any mistake or oversight on towel day was a source of outrage: "Why the bejesus do I get a torn one three times running? You'd think I didn't count for anything round here." It seemed a true distress; someday some simple carelessness might turn out to be the final curse: They were like that prisoner of Mussolini, shut up for life, who burst into tears because the soup was cold. When I received presents of candy I used to bring them in for the staff; these wartime chocolates tasted of candle wax but were much appreciated nonetheless. I had to be careful to whom I handed the box first: I could not begin with girls, which I'd have thought natural, because Supervisor did not brook interruptions. I would transfer the top layer to the lid of the box for the girls, for later on, and then consider the men. A trinity of them occupied glass cubicles. One was diabetic; another was Mr. Tracy, who, a gentle alcoholic, did not care for sweets; and the third was Mr. Curran. Skipping all three I would start with Chief Engineer McCreery and descend by way of Assistant Chief Engineers Grade I and then II; I approached them by educational standards, those with degrees from McGill and Queen's—Queen's first—to, finally, the technicians. By that time the caramels and nougats had all been eaten and nothing left but squashy orange and vanilla creams nobody liked. Then, then, oh God, who was to receive the affront of the last chocolate, the one reposing among crumbs and fluted paper casings? Sometimes I was cowardly and left the box adrift on a drawing board with a murmured "Pass it along, would you?"

I was deeply happy. It was one of the periods of inexplicable grace when every day is a new parcel one unwraps, layer on layer of tissue paper covering bits of crystal, scraps of words in a foreign language, pure white stones. I spent my lunch hours writing in notebooks, which I kept locked in my desk. The men never bothered me, apart from trying to feed me little pieces of cake. They were all sad when I began to smoke—I remember that. I could write without hearing anyone, but poetry was leaving me. It was not an abrupt removal but like a recurring tide whose high-water mark recedes inch by inch. Presently I was deep inland and the sea was gone. I would mourn it much later: It was such a gentle separation at the time that I scarcely noticed. I had notebooks stuffed with streets and people: My journals were full of "but what he *really* must have meant was . . ." There were endless political puzzles I tried to solve by comparing one thing with another, but of course nothing matched; I had not lost my adolescent habit of private, passionate manifestos. If politics was nothing but chess—Mr. Tracy's ways of sliding out of conviction—K was surely Social Justice and Q Extreme Morality. I was certain of this, and that after the war—unless we were completely swallowed up, like those Canadian battalions at Hong Kong—K and Q would envelop the world. Having no one to listen to, I could not have a thought without writing it down. There were pages and pages of dead butterflies, wings without motion or lift. I began to ration my writing, for fear I would dream through life as my father had done. I was afraid I had inherited a poisoned gene from him, a vocation without a gift. He had spent his own short time like a priest in charge of a relic, forever expecting the blessed blood to liquefy. I had no assurance I was not the same. I was so like him in some ways that a man once stopped me in front of the Bell Telephone building on Beaver Hall Hill and said, "Could you possibly be Angus Muir's sister?" That is how years telescope in men's minds. That particular place must be the windiest in Montreal, for I remember dust and ragged papers blowing in whirlpools and that I had to hold my hair. I said, "No, I'm not," without explaining that I was not his sister but his daughter. I had heard people say, referring to me but not knowing who I was, "He had a daughter, but apparently she died." We couldn't *both* be dead. Having come down on the side of life, I kept my distance. Writing now had to occupy an enormous space. I had lived in New York until a year before and there were things I was sick with missing. There was no theater, no music; there was one museum of art with not much in it. There was not even a free public lending library in the sense of the meaning that would have been given the words "free public lending library" in Toronto or New York. The municipal library was considered a sinister joke. There was a persistent, apocryphal story among English Canadians that an American philanthropic foundation (the Carnegie was usually mentioned) had offered to establish a free public lending library on condition that its contents were not to be censored by the provincial government of Quebec or by the Catholic Church, and that the offer had been turned down. The story may not have been true but its persistence shows the political and cultural climate of Montreal then. Educated French Canadians summed it up in shorter form: Their story was that when you looked up "Darwin" in the card index of the Bibliothèque de Montréal you found "See anti-Darwin." A Canadian actress I knew in New York sent me the first published text of *The Skin of Our Teeth*. I wrote imploring her to tell me everything about the production—the costumes, the staging, the voices. I've never seen it performed—not read it since the end of the war. I've been told that it doesn't hold, that it is not rooted in anything specific. It was then; its Ice Age was Fascism. I read it the year of Dieppe, in a year when "Russia" meant "Leningrad," when Malta could be neither fed nor defended. The Japanese were anywhere they wanted to be. Vast areas of the world were covered with silence and ice. One morning I read a little notice in the *Gazette* that Miss Margaret Urn would be taking auditions for the Canadian Broadcasting Corporation. I presented myself during my lunch hour with *The Skin of Our Teeth* and a manuscript one-act play of my own, in case. I had expected to find queues of applicants but I was the only one. Miss Urn received me in a small room of a dingy office suite on St. Catherine Street. We sat down on opposite sides of a table. I was rendered shy by her bearing, which had a headmistress quality, and perplexed by her accent—it was the voice any North American actor will pick up after six months of looking for work in the West End, but I did not know that. I opened *The Skin of Our Teeth* and began to read. It was floating rather than reading, for I had much of it by heart. When I read "Have you milked the mammoth?" Miss Urn stopped me. She reached over the table and placed her hand on the page.

"My dear child, what is this rubbish?" she said.

I stammered, "It is a . . . a play in New York."

Oh, fool. The worst thing to say. If only I had said, "Tallulah Bankhead," adding swiftly, "London, before the war." Or, better, "An Edwardian farce. Queen Alexandra, deaf though she was, much appreciated the joke about the separation of m and n." "A play in New York" evoked a look Canada was making me familiar with: amusement, fastidious withdrawal, gentle disdain. What a strange city to have a play in, she might have been thinking.

"Try reading this," she said.

I shall forget everything about the war except that at the worst point of it I was asked to read *Dear Octopus*. If Miss Urn had never heard of Thornton Wilder I had never heard of Dodie Smith. I read what I took to be parody. Presently it dawned on me these were meant to be real people. I broke up laughing because of Sabina, Fascism, the Ice Age that was perhaps upon us, because of the one-act play still in my purse. She took the book away from me and closed it and said I would, or would not, be hearing from her.

Now there was excitement in the office: A second woman had been brought in. Mrs. Ireland was her name. She had an advanced degree in accountancy and she was preparing a doctorate in some branch of mathematics none of the men were familiar with. She was about thirty-two. Her hair was glossy and dark; she wore it in braids that became a rich mahogany color when they caught the light. I admired her hair, but the rest of her was angry-looking— flushed cheeks, red hands and arms. The scarf around her throat looked as though it had been wound and tied in a fury. She tossed a paper on my desk and said, "Check this. I'm in a hurry." Chief Engineer looked up, looked at her, looked down. A play within the play, a subplot, came to life; I felt it exactly as children can sense a situation they have no name for. In the afternoon she said, "Haven't you done that yet?" She had a positive, hammering sort of voice. It must have carried as far as the portraits in the hall. Chief Engineer unrolled a large map showing the mineral resources of eastern Canada and got behind it. Mrs. Ireland called, to the room in general, "Well, is she supposed to be working for me or isn't she?" Oh? I opened the bottom drawer of my desk, unlocked the middle drawer, began to pack up my personal affairs. I saw that I'd need a taxi: I had about three pounds of manuscripts and notes, and what seemed to amount to a wardrobe. In those days girls wore white gloves to work; I had two extra pairs of these, and a makeup kit, and extra shoes. I began filling my wastebasket with superfluous cargo. The room had gone silent: I can still see Bertie Knox's ratty little eyes judging, summing up, taking the measure of this new force. Mr. Tracy, in his mauve glasses, hands in his pockets, came strolling out of his office; it was a sort of booth, with frosted-glass panels that did not go up to the ceiling. He must have heard the shouting and then the quiet. He and Mr. Curran and Mr. Elwitt, the diabetic one, were higher in rank than Chief Engineer, higher than Office Manager; they could have eaten Supervisor for tea and no one would dare complain. He came along easily—I never knew him to rush. I remember now that Chief Engineer called him "Young Tracy," because of his father; "Old Tracy"—the real Tracy, so to speak—was the one who'd gone bust in the Depression. That was why Young Tracy had this job. He wasn't all that qualified, really; not so different from me. He sat down on Bertie Knox's desk with his back to him.

"Well, bolshie," he said to me. This was a long joke: it had to do with my political views, as he saw them, and it was also a reference to a character in an English comic called "Pip and Squeak" that he and I had both read as children—we'd discussed it once. Pip and Squeak were a dog and a penguin. They had a son called Wilfred, who was a rabbit. Bolshie seemed to be a sort of acquaintance. He went around carrying one of those round black bombs with a sputtering fuse. He had a dog, I think—a dog with whiskers. I had told Mr. Tracy how modern educators were opposed to "Pip and Squeak." They thought that more than one generation of us had been badly misled by the unusual family unit of dog, penguin, and rabbit. It was argued that millions of children had grown up believing that if a dog made advances to a female penguin she would produce a rabbit. "Not a *rabbit*," said Mr. Tracy reasonably. *"Wilfred."*

I truly liked him. He must have thought I was going to say something now, if only to rise to the tease about "bolshie," but I was in the grip of that dazzling anger that is a form of snow blindness, too. I could not speak, and anyway didn't want to. I could only go on examining a pencil to see if it was company property or mine—as if that mattered. "Are you taking the day off or trying to leave me?" he said. I can feel that tense listening of men pretending to work. "I was looking over your application form," he said. "D'you know that your father knew my father? Yep. A long time ago. My father took it into his head to commission a mural for a plant in Sorel. Brave thing to do. Nobody did anything like that. Your father said it wasn't up his street. Suggested some other guy. My old man took the *two* of them down to Sorel. Did a lot of clowning around, but the Depression was just starting, so the idea fell through. My old man enjoyed it, though."

"Clowning around" could not possibly have been my father, but then the whole thing was so astonishing. "I should have mentioned it to you when you first came in," he said, "but I didn't realize it myself. There must be a million people called Muir; I happened to be looking at your form because apparently you're due for a raise." He whistled something for a second or two, then laughed and said, "Nobody ever quits around here. It can't be done. It upsets the delicate balance between labor and government. You don't want to do that. What do you want to do that for?"

"Mr. Curran doesn't like me."

"Mr. Curran is a brilliant man," he said. "Why, if you knew Curran's whole story you'd"—he paused—"you'd stretch out the hand of friendship."

"I've been asking and asking for a chair that doesn't wobble."

"Take the day off," he said. "Go to a movie or something. Tomorrow we'll start over." His life must have been like that. "You know, there's a war on. We're all needed. Mrs. Ireland has been brought here from . . ."

"From Trahnah," said Mrs. Ireland.

"Yes, from Toronto, to do important work. I'll see something gets done about that chair."

He stood up, hands in his pockets, slouching, really; gave an affable nod all round. The men didn't see; their noses were almost touching their work. He strolled back to his glass cubicle, whistling softly. The feeling in the room was like the sight of a curtain raised by the wind now sinking softly.

"Oh, Holy Hannah!" Mrs. Ireland burst out. "I thought this was supposed to be a wartime agency!"

No one replied. *My father knew your father. I'll see something gets done about that chair.* So that is how it works among men. To be noted, examined, compared.

Meanwhile I picked up the paper she'd tossed on my desk hours before and saw that it was an actuarial equation. I waited until the men had stopped being aware of us and took it over and told her I could not read it, let alone check it. It had obviously been some kind of test.

She said, "Well, it was too much to hope for. I have to single-handedly work out some wartime overtime pensions plan taking into account the cost of living and the earnest hope that the Canadian dollar won't sink." And I was to have been her assistant. I began to admire the genius someone— Assistant Chief Engineer Macaulay, perhaps—had obviously seen in me. Mrs. Ireland went on, "I gather after this little comic opera we've just witnessed that you're the blue-eyed girl around here." (Need I say that I'd hear this often? That the rumor I was Mr. Tracy's mistress now had firm hold

on the feminine element in the room—though it never gained all the men—
particularly on the biddies, the two or three old girls loafing along to retirement, in comfortable corsets that gave them a sort of picket fence around
the middle? That the obscene anonymous notes I sometimes found on my
desk—and at once unfairly blamed on Bertie Knox—were the first proof I
had that prolonged virginity can be the mother of invention?) "You can
have your desk put next to mine," said Mrs. Ireland. "I'll try to dig some
good out of you."

But I had no intention of being mined by Mrs. Ireland. Remembering
what Mr. Tracy had said about the hand of friendship I told her, truthfully,
that it would be a waste for her and for me. My name was down to do
documentary-film work, for which I thought I'd be better suited; I was to
be told as soon as a vacancy occurred.

"Then you'll have a new girl," I said. "You can teach her whatever you
like."

"*Girl?*" She could not keep her voice down, ever. "There'll not be a girl
in this office again, if I have a say. Girls make me sick, sore, and weary."

I thought about that for a long time. I had believed it was only because
of the men that girls were parked like third-class immigrants at the far end
of the room—the darkest part, away from the windows—with the indignity of being watched by Supervisor, whose whole function was just that.
But there, up on the life raft, stepping on girls' fingers, was Mrs. Ireland, too.
If that was so, why didn't Mrs. Ireland get along with the men, and why did
they positively and openly hate her—openly especially after Mr. Tracy's extraordinary and instructive sorting out of power?

"What blinking idiot would ever marry *her?*" said Bertie Knox. "Ten to
one she's not married at all. Ireland must be her maiden name. She thinks
the 'Mrs.' sounds good." I began to wonder if she was not a little daft sometimes: She used to talk to herself; quite a lot of it was about me.

"You can't run a wartime agency with *that* going on," she'd say loudly.
"That" meant poor Mr. Tracy and me. Or else she would declare that it was
unpatriotic of me to be drawing a man's salary. Here I think the men agreed.
The salary was seventy-five dollars a month, which was less than a man's if
he was doing the same work. The men had often hinted it was a lot for a
girl. Girls had no expenses; they lived at home. Money paid them was a sort
of handout. When I protested that I had the same expenses as any bachelor
and did not live at home, it was countered by a reasonable "Where you live

is up to you." They looked on girls as parasites of a kind, always being taken to restaurants and fed by men. They calculated the cost of probable outings, even to the Laura Secord chocolates I might be given, and rang the total as a casual profit to me. Bertie Knox used to sing, "I think that I shall never see a dame refuse a meal that's free." Mrs. Ireland said that all this money would be better spent on soldiers who were dying, on buying war bonds and plasma, on the purchase of tanks and Spitfires. "When I think of parents scrimping to send their sons to college!" she would conclude. All this was floods of clear water; I could not give it a shape. I kept wondering what she expected me to *do*, for that at least would throw a shadow on the water, but then she dropped me for a time in favor of another crusade, this one against Bertie Knox's singing. He had always sung. His voice conveyed rakish parodies of hymns and marches to every corner of the room. Most of the songs were well known; they came back to us from the troops, were either simple and rowdy or expressed a deep skepticism about the war, its aims and purposes, the way it was being conducted, and about the girls they had left at home. It was hard to shut Bertie Knox up: He had been around for a long time. Mrs. Ireland said she had not had the education she'd had to come here and listen to foul language. Now absolutely and flatly forbidden by Chief Engineer to sing any ribald song *plainly*, Bertie Knox managed with umptee-um syllables as best he could. He became Mrs. Ireland's counterpoint.

"I know there's a shortage of men," Mrs. Ireland would suddenly burst out.

"Oh umptee tum titty," sang Bertie Knox.

"And that after this war it will be still worse. . . ."

"Ti umpty dum diddy."

"There'll hardly be a man left in the world worth his salt. . . ."

"Tee umpty tum tumpty."

"But what I do not see . . ."

"Tee diddle dee dum."

"Is why a totally unqualified girl . . ."

"Tum tittle umpty tumpty."

"Should be subsidized by the taxpayers of this country . . ."

"Pum pum tee umpty pumpee."

"Just because her father failed to paint . . ."

"Oh umpty tumpty tumpty."

"A mural down in . . ."

"Tee umpty dum dum."

"Sorel."

"Tum tum, oh, dum dum, oh, pum pum, oh, oh, uuuum."

"Subsidized" stung, for I worked hard. Having no training I had no shortcuts. There were few mechanical shortcuts of any kind. The engineers used slide rules, and the machines might baffle today because of their simplicity. As for a computer, I would not have guessed what it might do or even look like. Facts were recorded on paper and stored in files and summarized by doing sums and displayed in some orderly fashion on graphs. I sat with one elbow on my desk, my left hand concealed in my hair. No one could see that I was counting on my fingers, in units of five and ten. The system by twelves would have finished me; luckily no one mentioned it. Numbers were a sunken world; they were a seascape from which perfect continents might emerge at any minute. I never saw more than their outline. I was caught on Zero. If zero meant Zero, how could you begin a graph on nothing? How could anything under zero be anything but Zero too? I spoke to Mr. Tracy: What occupied the space between Zero and One? It must be something arbitrary, not in the natural order of numbers. If One was solid ground, why not begin with One? Before One there was what? Thin air? Thin air must be Something. He said kindly, "Don't worry your head," and if I had continued would certainly have added, "Take the day off." Chief Engineer McCreery often had to remind me, "But we're not *paying* you to think!" If that was so, were we all being paid not to think? At the next place I worked things were even worse. It was another government agency, called Dominion Film Center—my first brush with the creative life. Here one was handed a folded thought like a shapeless school uniform and told, "There, wear that." Everyone had it on, regardless of fit. It was one step on: "We're not paying you to think about whatever you are thinking." I often considered approaching Mrs. Ireland, but she would not accept even a candy from me, let alone a question. "There's a war on" had been her discouraging refusal of a Life Saver once.

The men by now had found out about her husband. He had left school at Junior Fourth (Grade Seven) and "done nothing to improve himself." He was a Pole. She was ashamed of having a name that ended in "ski" and used her maiden name; Bertie Knox hadn't been far off. Thinking of it now, I realize she might not have been ashamed but only aware that the "ski" name on her application could have relegated it to a bottom drawer. Where did the men get their information, I wonder. Old "ski" was a lush who drank her paycheck and sometimes beat her up; the scarves she wound around her neck were meant to cover bruises.

That she was unhappily married I think did not surprise me. What impressed me was that so many of the men were too. I had become engaged to be married, for the third time. There was a slight overlapping of two, by which I mean that the one in Halifax did not know I was also going to marry the one from the West. To the men, who could not follow my life as closely as they'd have wanted—I gave out next to nothing—it seemed like a long betrothal to some puppy in uniform, whom they had never seen, and whose Christian name kept changing. One of my reasons for discretion was that I was still underage. Until now I had been using my minority as an escape hatch, the way a married man will use his wife—for "Ursula will never divorce" I substituted "My mother will never consent." Once I had made up my mind I simply began looking for roads around the obstacle; it was this search, in fact, that made me realize I must be serious. No one, no one at all, knew what I was up to, or what my entirely apocryphal emancipation would consist of; all that the men knew was that this time it did look as if I was going through with it. They took me aside, one after the other, and said, "Don't do it, Linnet. Don't do it." Bertie Knox said, "Once you're in it, you're in it, kiddo." I can't remember any man ever criticizing his own wife—it is something men don't often do, anywhere—but the warning I had was this: Marriage was a watershed that transformed sweet, cheerful, affectionate girls into, well, their own mothers. Once a girl had caught (their word) a husband she became a whiner, a snooper, a killjoy, a wet blanket, a grouch, and a bully. What I gleaned out of this was that it seemed hard on the men. But then even Mrs. Ireland, who never said a word to me, declared, "I think it's terrible." She said it was insane for me to marry someone on his way overseas, to tie up my youth, to live like a widow without a widow's moral status. Why were she and I standing together, side by side, looking out the window at a gray sky, at pigeons, at a streetcar grinding up the steep street? We could never possibly have stood close, talking in low voices. And yet there she is; there I am with Mrs. Ireland. For once she kept her voice down. She looked out—not at me. She said the worst thing of all. Remembering it, I see the unwashed windowpane. She said, "Don't you girls ever know when you're well off? Now you've got no one to lie to you, to belittle you, to make a fool of you, to stab you in the back." But we were different—different ages, different women, two lines of a graph that could never cross.

Mostly when people say "I know exactly how I felt" it can't be true, but here I am sure—sure of Mrs. Ireland and the window and of what she said. The recollection has something to do with the blackest kind of terror, as stunning as the bolts of happiness that strike for no reason. This blackness, this darkening, was not wholly Mrs. Ireland, no; I think it had to do with the men, with squares and walls and limits and numbers. How do you stand if you stand upon Zero? What will the passage be like between Zero and One? And what will happen at One? Yes, what will happen?

VARIETIES OF EXILE

———————

❧

*I*n the third summer of the war I began to meet refugees. There were large numbers of them in Montreal—to me a source of infinite wonder. I could not get enough of them. They came straight out of the twilit Socialist-literary landscape of my reading and my desires. I saw them as prophets of a promised social order that was to consist of justice, equality, art, personal relations, courage, generosity. Each of them—Belgian, French, Catholic German, Socialist German, Jewish German, Czech—was a book I tried to read from start to finish. My dictionaries were films, poems, novels, Lenin, Freud. That the refugees tended to hate one another seemed no more than a deplorable accident. Nationalist pigheadedness, that chronic, wasting, and apparently incurable disease, was known to me only on Canadian terms and I did not always recognize its symptoms. Anything I could not decipher I turned into fiction, which was my way of untangling knots. At the office where I worked I now spent my lunch hour writing stories about people in exile. I tried to see Montreal as an Austrian might see it and to feel whatever he felt. I was entirely at home with foreigners, which is not surprising—the home was all in my head. They were the only people I had met until now who believed, as I did, that our victory would prove to be a tidal wave nothing could stop. What I did not know was how many of them hoped and expected their neighbors to be washed away too.

I was nineteen and for the third time in a year engaged to be married. What I craved at this point was not love, or romance, or a life added to mine, but conversation, which was harder to find. I knew by now that a man in love does not necessarily have anything interesting to say: If he has, he keeps it for other men. Men in Canada did not talk much to women and hardly at all to young ones. The impetus of love—of infatuation, rather—brought on a kind of conversation I saw no reason to pursue. A remark such as "I can't live without you" made the speaker sound not only half-witted to me but almost truly, literally, insane. There is a girl in a Stefan Zweig novel who says to her lover, "Is that all?" I had pondered this carefully many years before, for I supposed it had something unexpected to do with sex. Now I gave it another meaning, which was that where women were concerned men were satisfied with next to nothing. If every woman was a situation, she was somehow always the same situation, and what was expected from the woman—the situation—was so limited it was insulting. I had a large opinion of what I could do and provide, yet it came down to "Is that all? Is that all you expect?" Being promised to one person after another was turning into a perpetual state of hesitation and refusal: I was not used to hesitating over anything and so I supposed I must be wrong. The men in my office had warned me of the dangers of turning into a married woman; if this caution affected me it was only because it coincided with a misgiving of my own. My private name for married women was Red Queens. They looked to me like the Red Queen in *Through the Looking-Glass*, chasing after other people and minding their business for them. To get out of the heat that summer I had taken a room outside Montreal in an area called simply "the Lakeshore." In those days the Lakeshore was a string of verdant towns with next to no traffic. Dandelions grew in the pavement cracks. The streets were thickly shaded. A fragrance I have never forgotten of mown grass and leaf smoke drifted from yard to yard. As I walked to my commuters' train early in the morning I saw kids still in their pajamas digging holes in the lawns and Red Queen wives wearing housecoats. They stuck their heads out of screen doors and yelled instructions—to husbands, to children, to dogs, to postmen, to a neighbor's child. How could I be sure I wouldn't sound that way—so shrill, so discontented? As for a family, the promise of children all stamped with the same face, cast in the same genetic mold, seemed a cruel waste of possibilities. I would never have voiced this to anyone, for it would have been thought unnatural, even monstrous. When I was very young, under seven, my plan for the future had been to live in every country of the world and have a child in each. I had confided it: With adult adroitness my listener led me on. How many children? Oh, one to a country. And what would you do with them? Travel in trains. How would they go to school? I hate schools. How will they learn to read and write, then? They'll know already. What would you live on? It will all be free. That's not very sensible, is it? Why not? As a result of this idyll, of my divulgence of it, I was kept under watch for a time and my pocket money taken away lest I save it up and sail to a tropical island (where because of the Swiss Family Robinson I proposed to begin) long before the onset of puberty. I think no one realized I had not even a nebulous idea of how children sprang to life. I merely knew two persons were required for a ritual I believed had to continue for nine months, and which I imagined in the nature of a long card game with mysterious rules. When I was finally "told"—accurately, as it turned out—I was offended at being asked to believe something so unreasonable, which could not be true because I had never come across it in books. This trust in the printed word seems all the more remarkable when I remember that I thought children's books were written by other children. Probably at nineteen I was still dim about relevant dates, plain facts, brass tacks, consistent reasoning. Perhaps I was still hoping for magic card games to short-circuit every sort of common sense—common sense is only an admission we don't know much. I know that I wanted to marry this third man but that I didn't want to be anybody's Red Queen.

The commuters on the Montreal train never spoke much to each other. The mystifying and meaningless "Hot enough for you?" was about the extent of it. If I noticed one man more than the anonymous others it was only because he looked so hopelessly English, so unable or unwilling to concede to anything, even the climate. Once, walking a few steps behind him, I saw him turn into the drive of a stone house, one of the few old French-Canadian houses in that particular town. The choice of houses seemed to me peculiarly English too—though not, of course, what French Canadians call "English," for that includes plain Canadians, Irish, Swedes, anything you like not natively French. I looked again at the house and at the straight back going along the drive. His wife was on her knees holding a pair of edging shears. He stopped to greet her. She glanced up and said something in a carrying British voice so wild and miserable, so resentful, so intensely disagreeable that it could not have been the tag end of a morning quarrel; no, it was the thunderclap of some new engagement. After a second he went on up the walk, and in another I was out of earshot. I was persuaded that he had seen me; I don't know why. I also thought it must have been humiliating for him to have had a witness.

Which of us spoke first? It could not have been him and it most certainly could not have been me. There must have been a collision, for there we are, speaking, on a station platform. It is early morning, already hot. I see once again, without surprise, that he is not dressed for the climate.

He said he had often wondered what I was reading. I said I was reading "all the Russians." He said I really ought to read Arthur Waley. I had never heard of Arthur Waley. Similar signaling takes place between galaxies rushing apart in the outer heavens. He said he would bring me a book by Arthur Waley the next day.

"Please don't. I'm careless with books. Look at the shape this one's in." It was the truth. "All the Russians" were being published in a uniform edition with flag-red covers, on grayish paper, with microscopic print. The words were jammed together; you could not have put a pin between the lines. It was one of those cheap editions I think we were supposed to be sending the troops in order to cheer them up. Left in the grass beside a tennis court *The Possessed* now curved like a shell. A white streak ran down the middle of the shell. The rest of the cover had turned pink. That was nothing, he said. All I needed to do was dampen the cover with a sponge and put a weight on the book. *The Wallet of Kai Lung* had been to Ceylon with him and had survived. Whatever bait "Ceylon" may have been caught nothing. Army? Civil service? I did not take it up. Anyway I thought I could guess.

"You'd better not bring a book for nothing. I don't always take this train."

He had probably noticed me every morning. The mixture of reserve and obstinacy that next crossed his face I see still. He smiled, oh, not too much: I'd have turned my back on a grin. He said, "I forgot to . . . Frank Cairns."

"Muir. Linnet Muir." Reluctantly.

The thing is, I knew all about him. He was, one, married and, two, too old. But there was also three: Frank Cairns was stamped, labeled, ticketed by his tie (club? regiment? school?); by his voice, manner, haircut, suit; by the impression he gave of being stranded in a jungle, waiting for a rescue party—from England, of course. He belonged to a species of British immigrant known as remittance men. Their obsolescence began on 3 September 1939 and by 8 May 1945 they were extinct. I knew about them from having had one in the family. Frank Cairns worked in a brokerage house—he told me later—but he probably did not need a job, at least not for a living. It must have been a way of ordering time, a flight from idleness, perhaps a means of getting out of the house.

✳   ✳   ✳

The institution of the remittance man was British, its genesis a chemical structure of family pride, class insanity, and imperial holdings that seemed impervious to fission but in the end turned out to be more fragile than anyone thought. Like all superfluous and marginal persons, remittance men were characters in a plot. The plot began with a fixed scene, an immutable first chapter, which described a powerful father's taking umbrage at his son's misconduct and ordering him out of the country. The pound was then one to five dollars, and there were vast British territories everywhere you looked. Hordes of young men who had somehow offended their parents were shipped out, golden deportees, to Canada, South Africa, New Zealand, Singapore. They were reluctant pioneers, totally lacking any sense of adventure or desire to see that particular world. An income—the remittance—was provided on a standing banker's order, with one string attached: "Keep out of England." For the second chapter the plot allowed a choice of six crimes as reasons for banishment: Conflict over the choice of a profession—the son wants to be a tap dancer. Gambling and debts—he has been barred from Monte Carlo. Dud checks—"I won't press a charge, sir, but see that the young rascal is kept out of harm's way." Marriage with a girl from the wrong walk of life—"Young man, you have made your bed!" Fathering an illegitimate child: ". . . and broken your mother's heart." Homosexuality, if discovered: Too grave for even a lecture—it was a criminal offense.

This is the plot of the romance: This is what everyone repeated and what the remittance man believed of himself. Obviously, it is a load of codswallop. A man legally of age could marry the tattooed woman in a circus, be arrested for check-bouncing or for soliciting boys in Green Park, be obliged to recognize his by-blow and even to wed its mother, become a ponce or a professional wrestler, and still remain where he was born. All he needed to do was eschew the remittance and tell his papa to go to hell. Even at nineteen the plot was a story I wouldn't buy. The truth came down to something just as dramatic but boring to tell: a classic struggle for dominance with two protagonists—strong father, pliant son. It was also a male battle. No son was ever sent into exile by his mother, and no one has ever heard of a remittance *woman*. Yet daughters got into scrapes nearly as often as their brothers. Having no idea what money was, they ran up debts easily. Sometimes, out of ignorance of another sort, they dared to dispose of their own virginity, thus wrecking their value on the marriage market and becoming family charges for life. Accoucheurs had to be bribed to perform abortions; or else the daughters were dispatched to Austria and Switzerland to have babies they would never hear of again. A daughter's disgrace was long, expensive, and hard to conceal, yet no one dreamed of sending her thousands of miles away and forever: On the contrary, she became her father's unpaid servant, social secretary, dog walker, companion, sick nurse. Holding on to a daughter, dismissing a son were relatively easy: It depended on having tamely delinquent children, or a thunderous personality no child would dare to challenge, and on the weapon of money—bait or weapon, as you like.

Banished young, as a rule, the remittance man (the RM, in my private vocabulary) drifted for the rest of his life, never quite sounding or looking like anyone around him, seldom raising a family or pursuing an occupation (so much for the "choice of profession" legend)—remote, dreamy, bored. Those who never married often became low-key drunks. The remittance was usually ample without being handsome, but enough to keep one from doing a hand's turn; in any case few remittance men were fit to do much of anything, being well schooled but half educated, in that specifically English way, as well as markedly unaggressive and totally uncompetitive, which would have meant early death in the New World for anyone without an income. They were like children waiting for the school vacation so that they could go home, except that at home nobody wanted them: The nursery had been turned into a billiards room and Nanny dismissed. They were parted from mothers they rarely mentioned, whom in some way they blended with a Rupert Brooke memory of England, of the mother country, of the Old Country as everyone at home grew old. Often as not the payoff, the keep-away blackmail funds, came out of the mother's marriage settlement—out of the capital her own father had agreed to settle upon her unborn children during the wear and tear of Edwardian engagement negotiations. The son disgraced would never see more than a fixed income from this; he was cut off from a share of inheritance by his contract of exile. There were cases where the remittance ended abruptly with the mother's death, but that was considered a bad arrangement. Usually the allowance continued for the exile's lifetime and stopped when he died. No provision was made for his dependents, if he had them, and because of his own subject attitude to money he was unlikely to have made any himself. The income reverted to his sisters and brothers, to an estate, to a cat-and-dog hospital—whatever his father had decreed on some black angry day long before.

Whatever these sons had done their punishment was surely a cruel and singular one, invented for naughty children by a cosmic headmaster taking over for God: They were obliged to live over and over until they died the first separation from home, and the incomparable trauma of rejection. Yes, they were like children, perpetually on their way to a harsh school; they were eight years of age and sent "home" from India to childhoods of secret grieving among strangers. And this wound, this amputation, they would mercilessly inflict on their own children when the time came—on sons always, on daughters sometimes—persuaded that early heartbreak was right because it was British, hampered only by the financial limit set for banishment: It costs money to get rid of your young.

And how they admired their fathers, those helpless sons! They spoke of them with so much admiration, with such a depth of awe: Only in memory can such voices still exist, the calm English voice on a summer night— a Canadian night so alien to the speaker—insisting, with sudden firmness, with a pause between words, "My ... father ... once ... said ... to ... me ... ," and here would follow something utterly trivial, some advice about choosing a motorcar or training a dog. To the Canadian grandchildren the unknown grandfather was seven feet tall with a beard like George V, while the grandmother came through weepy and prissy and not very interesting. It was the father's Father, never met, never heard, who made Heaven and Earth and Eve and Adam. The father in Canada seemed no more than an apostle transmitting a paternal message from the Father in England—the Father of us all. It was, however, rare for a remittance man to marry, rarer still to have any children; how could he become a father when he had never stopped being a son?

If the scattered freemasonry of offspring the remittance man left behind, all adult to elderly now, had anything in common it must have been their degree of incompetence. They were raised to behave well in situations that might never occur, trained to become genteel poor on continents where even the concept of genteel poverty has never existed. They were brought up with plenty of books and music and private lessons, a nurse sometimes, in a household where certain small luxuries were deemed essential—a way of life that, in North America at least, was supposed to be built on a sunken concrete base of money; otherwise you were British con men, a breed of gypsy, and a bad example.

Now, your remittance man was apt to find this assumption quite funny. The one place he would never take seriously was the place he was in. The identification of prominent local families with the name of a product, a commodity, would be his running joke: "The Allseeds are sugar, the Bilges are coal, the Cumquats are cough medicine, the Doldrums are coffins, the

Earwigs are saucepans, the Fustians are timber, the Grindstones are beer."
But his young, once they came up against it, were bound to observe that
their concrete base was the dandelion fluff of a banker's order, their commodity nothing but "life in England before 1914," which was not nego-
tiable. Also, the constant, nagging "What does your father really *do*?" could
amount to persecution.

"Mr. Bainwood wants to know what you do."

"Damned inquisitive of him."

Silence. Signs of annoyance. Laughter sometimes. Or something silly:
"What do *you* do when you aren't asking questions?"

No remittance man's child that I know of ever attended a university,
though care was taken over the choice of schools. There they would be, at
eighteen and nineteen, the boys wearing raincoats in the coldest weather, the
girls with their hair ribbons and hand-knits and their innocently irritating
English voices, well read, musical, versed in history, probably because they
had been taught that the past is better than now, and somewhere else better
than here. They must have been the only English-Canadian children to
speak French casually, as a matter of course. Untidy, unpunctual, imperially
tactless, they drifted into work that had to be "interesting," "creative," never
demeaning, and where—unless they'd had the advantage of a rough time
and enough nous to draw a line against the past—they seldom lasted. There
was one in every public relations firm, one to a radio station, two to a publisher—forgetting appointments, losing contracts, jamming typewriters,
sabotaging telephones, apologizing in accents it would have taken elocution
lessons to change, so strong had been paternal pressure against the hard
Canadian r, not to mention other vocables:

"A-t-e is *et*, darling, not *ate*."

"I can't say *et*. Only farmers say it."

"Perhaps here, but you won't always be here."

Of course the children were guilt-drenched, wondering which of the six
traditional crimes they ought to pin on their father, what his secret was,
what his past included, why he had been made an outcast. The answer was
quite often "Nothing, no reason," but it meant too much to be unraveled
and knit up. The saddest were those unwise enough to look into the families who had caused so much inherited woe. For the family was often as not
smaller potatoes than the children had thought, and their father's romantic
crime had been just the inability to sit for an examination, to stay at a university, to handle an allowance, to gain a toehold in any profession, or even

to decide what he wanted to do—an ineptitude so maddening to live with that the Father preferred to shell out forever rather than watch his heir fall apart before his eyes. The male line, then, was a ghost story. A mother's vitality would be needed to create ectoplasm, to make the ghost offspring visible. Unfortunately the exiles were apt to marry absentminded women whose skirts are covered with dog hairs—the drooping, bewildered British-Canadian mouse, who counts on tea leaves to tell her "what will happen when Edward goes." None of us is ever saved entirely, but even an erratic and alarming maternal vitality could turn out to be better than none.

Frank Cairns was childless, which I thought wise of him. He had been to Ceylon, gone back to England with a stiff case of homesickness disguised as malaria, married, and been shipped smartly out again, this time to Montreal. He was a neat, I think rather a small, man, with a straight part in his hair and a quick, brisk walk. He noticed I was engaged. I did not reply. I told him I had been in New York, had come back about a year ago, and missed "different things." He seemed to approve. "You can't make a move here," he said more than once. I was not sure what he meant. If he had been only the person I have described I'd have started taking an earlier train to be rid of him. But Frank Cairns was something new, unique of his kind, and almost as good as a refugee, for he was a Socialist. At least he said he was. He said he had never voted anywhere but that if he ever in the future happened to be in England when there was an election he would certainly vote Labour. His Socialism did not fit anything else about him, and seemed to depend for its life on the memory of talks he'd once had with a friend whom he described as brilliant, philosophical, farseeing, and just. I thought, Like Christ, but did not know Frank Cairns well enough to say so. The nonbeliever I had become was sometimes dogged by the child whose nightly request had been "Gentle Jesus, meek and mild, look upon a little child," and I sometimes got into ferocious arguments with her, as well as with other people. I was too curious about Frank Cairns to wish to quarrel over religion—at any rate not at the beginning. He talked about his friend without seeming able to share him. He never mentioned his name. I had to fill in the blank part of this conversation without help; I made the friend a high-ranking civil servant in Ceylon, older than anyone—which might have meant forty-two—an intellectual revolutionary who could work the future out on paper, like arithmetic.

Wherever his opinions came from, Frank Cairns was the first person ever to talk to me about the English poor. They seemed to be a race, different in kind from other English. He showed me old copies of *Picture Post* he must have saved up from the Depression. In our hot summer train, where every-one was starched and ironed and washed and fed, we considered slum door-ways and the faces of women at the breaking point. They looked like Lenin's "remnants of nations" except that there were too many of them for a remnant. I thought of my mother and her long preoccupation with the fate of the Scottsboro Boys. My mother had read and mooned and fretted about the Scottsboro case, while I tried to turn her attention to something urgent, such as that my school uniform was now torn in three places. It is quite pos-sible that my mother had seldom seen a black except on railway trains. (If I say "black" it is only because it is expected. It was a rude and offensive term in my childhood and I would not have been allowed to use it. "Black" was the sort of thing South Africans said.) Had Frank Cairns actually seen those *Picture Post* faces, I wondered. His home, his England, was every other re-mittance man's—the one I called "Christopher-Robin-land" and had sworn to keep away from. He hated Churchill, I remember, but I was used to hearing that. No man who remembered the Dardanelles really trusted him. Younger men (I am speaking of the handful I knew who had any opin-ion at all) were not usually irritated by his rhetoric until they got into uni-form.

Once in a book I lent him he found a scrap of paper on which I had writ-ten the title of a story I was writing, "The Socialist RM," and some scrawls in, luckily, a private shorthand of mine. A perilous moment: "remittance man" was a term of abuse all over the Commonwealth and Empire.

"What is it?" he asked. "Resident Magistrate?"

"It might be Royal Marine. Royal Mail. I honestly don't remember. I can't read my own writing sometimes." The last sentence was true.

His Socialism was unlike a Czech's or a German's; though he believed that one should fight hard for social change, there was a hopelessness about it, an almost moral belief that improving their material circumstances would get the downtrodden nowhere. At the same time, he thought the poor *were* happy, that they had some strange secret of happiness—the way people often think all Italians are happy because they have large families. I won-dered if he really believed that a man with no prospects and no teeth in his head was spiritually better off than Frank Cairns and why, in that case, Frank Cairns did not let him alone with his underfed children and his na-tive good nature. This was a British left-wing paradox I was often to encounter later on. What it seemed to amount to was leaving people more or less as they were, though he did speak about basic principles and the spread of education. It sounded dull. I was Russian-minded; I read Russian books, listened to Russian music. After Russia came Germany and Central Europe—that was where the real mystery and political excitement lay. His Webbs and his Fabians were plodding and gray. I saw the men with thick mustaches, wearing heavy boots, sharing lumpy meals with moral women. In the books he brought me I continued to find his absent friend. He produced Housman and Hardy (I could not read either), Siegfried Sassoon and Edmund Blunden, H. G. Wells and Bernard Shaw. The friend was probably a Scot—Frank Cairns admired them. The Scots of Canada, to me, stood for all that was narrow, grasping, at a standstill. How I distrusted those granite bankers who thought it was sinful to smoke! I was wrong, he told me. The true Scots were full of poetry and political passion. I said, "Are you sure?" and turned his friend into a native of Aberdeen and a graduate from Edinburgh. I also began a new notebook: "Scottish Labour Party. Keir Hardie. Others." This was better than the Webbs but still not as good as Rosa Luxemburg.

It was Frank Cairns who said to me "Life has no point," without emphasis, in response to some ignorant assumption of mine. This was his true voice. I recall the sidelong glance, the lizard's eye that some men develop as they grow old or when they have too much to hide. I was no good with ages. I cannot place him even today. Early thirties, probably. What else did he tell me? That "Scotch" was the proper term and "Scots" an example of a genteelism overtaking the original. That unless the English surmounted their class obsessions with speech and accent Britain would not survive in the world after the war. His remedy (or his friend's) was having everyone go to the same schools. He surprised me even more by saying, "I would never live in England, not as it is now."

"Where, then?"

"Nowhere. I don't know."

"What about Russia? They all go to the same schools."

"Good Lord," said Frank Cairns.

He was inhabited by a familiar who spoke through him, provided him with jolting outbursts but not a whole thought. Perhaps that silent coming and going was the way people stayed in each other's lives when they were apart. What Frank Cairns was to me was a curio cabinet. I took everything out of the cabinet, piece by piece, examined the objects, set them down.

Such situations, riddled with ambiguity, I would blunder about with for a long time until I learned to be careful.

The husband of the woman from whom I rented my summer room played golf every weekend. On one of those August nights when no one can sleep and the sky is nearly bright enough to read by, I took to the backyard and found him trying to cool off with a glass of beer. He remembered he had offered to give me golf lessons. I did not wish to learn, but did not say so. His wife spoke up from a deck chair: "You've never offered to teach me, I notice." She then compounded the error by telling me everyone was talking about me and the married man on the train. The next day I took the Käthe Kollwitz prints down from the walls of my room and moved back to Montreal without an explanation. Frank Cairns and I met once more that summer to return some books. That was all. When he called me at my office late in November, I said, *"Who?"*

He came into the coffee shop at Windsor station, where I was waiting. He was in uniform. I had not noticed he was good-looking before. It was not something I noticed in men. He was a first lieutenant. I disapproved: "Couldn't they make you a private?"

"Too old," he said. "As it is I am too old for my rank." I thought he just meant he might be promoted faster because of that.

"You don't look old." I at once regretted this personal remark, the first he had heard from me. Indeed, he had shed most of his adult life. He must have seemed as young as this when he started out to Ceylon. The uniform was his visa to England; no one could shut him away now. His face was radiant, open: He was halfway there. This glimpse of a purpose astonished me; why should a uniform make the change he'd been unable to make alone? He was not the first soldier I saw transfigured but he was the first to affect me.

He kept smiling and staring at me. I hoped he was not going to make a personal remark in exchange for mine. He said, "That tam makes you look, I don't know, Canadian. I've always thought of you as English. I still think England is where you might be happy."

"I'm happy here. You said you'd never live there."

"It would be a good place for you," he said. "Well, well, we shall see."

He would see nothing. My evolution was like freaky weather then: A few months, a few weeks even, were the equivalent of long second thoughts later on. I was in a completely other climate. I no longer missed New York and "different things." I had become patriotic. Canadian patriotism is always anti-American in part, and feeds upon anecdotes. American tourists were beginning to arrive in Montreal looking for anything expensive or hard to find in the United States; when they could not buy rationed food such as meat and butter, or unrationed things such as nylon stockings (because they did not exist), they complained of ingratitude. This was because Canada was thought to be a recipient of American charity and on the other end of Lend-Lease. Canadians were, and are, enormously touchy. Great umbrage had been taken over a story that was going around in the States about Americans who had been soaked for black-market butter in Montreal; when they got back across the border they opened the package and found the butter stamped "Gift of the American People." This fable persisted throughout the war and turned up in print. An American friend saw it in, I think, Westbrook Pegler's column and wrote asking me if it was true. I composed a letter I meant to send to *The New York Times*, demolishing the butter story. I kept rewriting and reshaping it, trying to achieve a balance between crippling irony and a calm review of events. I never posted it, finally, because my grandmother appeared to me in a dream and said that only fools wrote to newspapers.

Our coffee was tepid, the saucers slopped. He complained, and the waitress asked if we knew there was a war on. "Christ, what a bloody awful country this is," he said.

I wanted to say, "Then why are you with a Canadian regiment?" I provided my own answer: "They pay more than the Brits." We were actually quarreling in my head, and on such a mean level. I began to tear up a paper napkin and to cry.

"I have missed you," he remarked, but quite happily; you could tell the need for missing was over. I had scarcely thought of him at all. I kept taking more and more napkins out of the container on the table and blotting my face and tearing the paper up. He must be the only man I ever cried about in a public place. I hardly knew him. He was not embarrassed, as a Canadian would have been, but looked all the happier. The glances we got from other tables were full of understanding. Everything gave the wrong impression—his uniform, my engagement ring, my tears. I told him I was going to be married.

"Nonsense," he said.

"I'm serious."

"You seem awfully young."

"I'll soon be twenty." A slip. I had told him I was older. It amazed me to remember how young I had been only the summer before. "But I won't actually be a married woman," I said, "because I hate everything about them. Another thing I won't be and that's the sensitive housewife—the one who listens to Brahms while she does the ironing and reads all the new books still in their jackets."

"No, don't be a sensitive housewife," he said.

He gave me *The Wallet of Kai Lung* and *Kai Lung's Golden Hours*, which had been in Ceylon with him and had survived.

Did we write to each other? That's what I can't remember. I was careless then; I kept moving on. Also I really did, that time, get married. My husband was posted three days afterward to an American base in the Aleutian Islands—I have forgotten why. Eight months later he returned for a brief embarkation leave and then went overseas. I had dreaded coming in to my office after my wedding for fear the men I worked with would tease me. But the mixture of war and separation recalled old stories of their own experiences, in the First World War. Also I had been transformed into someone with a French surname, which gave them pause.

"Does he—uh—speak any French?"

"Not a word. He's from the West." Ah. "But he ought to. His father is French." Oh.

I had disappeared for no more than four days, but I was Mrs. Something now, not young Linnet. They spoke about me as "she," and not "Linnet" or "the kid." I wondered what they saw when they looked at me. In every head bent over a desk or a drawing board there was an opinion about women; expressed, it sounded either prurient or coarse, but I still cannot believe that is all there was to it. I know I shocked them profoundly once by saying that a wartime ditty popular with the troops, "Rock me to sleep, Sergeant-Major, tuck me in my little bed," was innocently homosexual. That I could have such a turn of thought, that I could use such an expression, that I even knew it existed seemed scandalous to them. "You read too damned much," I was told. Oddly enough, they had never minded my hearing any of the several versions of the song, some of which were unspeakable; all they objected to was my unfeminine remark. When I married they gave me a suitcase, and when I left for good they bought me a Victory Bond. I had scrupulously noted every detail of the office, and the building it was in, yet only a few months later I would walk by it without remembering I had ever been inside, and it occurs to me only now that I never saw any of them again.

I was still a minor, but emancipated by marriage. I did not need to ask parental consent for anything or worry about being brought down on the wing. I realized how anxious I had been once the need for that particular anxiety was over. A friend in New York married to a psychiatrist had sent me a letter saying I had her permission to marry. She did not describe herself as a relative or state anything untrue—she just addressed herself to whom it may concern, said that as far as *she* was concerned I could get married, and signed. She did not tell her husband, in case he tried to put things right out of principle, and I mentioned to no one that the letter was legal taradiddle and carried about as much weight as a library card. I mention this to show what essential paperwork sometimes amounts to. My husband, aged twenty-four, had become my legal guardian under Quebec's preposterous Napoleonic law, but he never knew that. When he went overseas he asked me not to join any political party, which I hadn't thought of doing, and not to enlist in the Army or the Air Force. The second he vanished I tried to join the Wrens, which had not been on the list only because it slipped his mind. Joining one of the services had never been among my plans and projects—it was he who accidentally put the idea in my head. I now decided I would turn up overseas, having made it there on my own, but I got no further than the enlistment requirements, which included "... of the white race only." This barrier turned out to be true of nearly all the navies of the Commonwealth countries. I supposed everyone must have wanted it that way, for I never heard it questioned. I was only beginning to hear the first rumblings of hypocrisy on our side—the right side; the wrong side seemed to be guilty of every sin humanly possible except simulation of virtue. I put the blame for the racial barrier on Churchill, who certainly *knew*, and had known since the First World War; I believed that Roosevelt, Stalin, Chiang Kai-shek, and de Gaulle did not know, and that should it ever come to their attention they would be as shocked as I was.

Instead of enlisting I passed the St. John Ambulance first-aid certificate, which made me a useful person in case of total war. The Killed-Wounded-Missing columns of the afternoon paper were now my daily reading. It became a habit so steadfast that I would automatically look for victims even after the war ended. The summer of the Scottish Labour Party, Keir Hardie, and Others fell behind, as well as a younger, discarded Linnet. I lighted ferocious autos-da-fé. Nothing could live except present time. In the ever-new present I read one day that Major Francis Cairns had died of wounds in Italy. Who remembers now the shock of the known name? It was like a flat white light. One felt apart from everyone, isolated. The field of vision drew in. Then, before one could lose consciousness, vision expanded, light and shadow moved, voices pierced through. One's heart, which had stopped, beat hard enough to make a room shudder. All this would occupy about a second. The next second was inhabited by disbelief. I saw him in uniform, so happy, halfway there, and myself making a spectacle of us, tearing a paper napkin. I was happy for him that he would never need to return to the commuting train and the loneliness and be forced to relive his own past. I wanted to write a casual letter saying so. One's impulse was always to write to the dead. Nobody knew I knew him, and in Canada it was not done to speak of the missing. I forgot him. He went under. I was doing a new sort of work and sharing a house with another girl whose husband was also overseas. Montreal had become a completely other city. I was no longer attracted to refugees. They were going through a process called "integrating." Some changed their names. Others applied for citizenship. A refugee eating cornflakes was of no further interest. The house I now lived in contained a fireplace, in which I burned all my stories about Czech and German anti-Fascists. In the picnic hamper I used for storing journals and notebooks I found a manila envelope marked "Lakeshore." It contained several versions of "The Socialist RM" and a few other things that sounded as if they were translated from the Russian by Constance Garnett. I also found a brief novel I had no memory of having written, about a Scot from Aberdeen, a left-wing civil servant in Ceylon—a man from somewhere, living elsewhere, confident that another world was entirely possible, since he had got it all down. It had shape, density, voice, but I destroyed it too. I never felt guilt about forgetting the dead or the living, but I minded about that one manuscript for a time. All this business of putting life through a sieve and then discarding it was another variety of exile; I knew that even then, but it seemed quite right and perfectly natural.

The

CARETTE

SISTERS

About a year after the death of M. Carette, his three survivors—
Berthe and her little sister, Marie, and their mother—had to leave the comfortable flat over the furniture store in Rue Saint-Denis and move to a
smaller place. They were not destitute: There was the insurance and the
money from the sale of the store, but the man who had bought the store
from the estate had not yet paid and they had to be careful.

Some of the lamps and end tables and upholstered chairs were sent to relatives, to be returned when the little girls grew up and got married. The rest
of their things were carried by two small, bent men to the second floor of a
stone house in Rue Cherrier near the Institute for the Deaf and Dumb. The
men used an old horse and an open cart for the removal. They told Mme.
Carette that they had never worked outside that quarter; they knew only
some forty streets of Montreal but knew them thoroughly. On moving day,
soft snow, like graying lace, fell. A patched tarpaulin protected the Carettes'
wine-red sofa with its border of silk fringe, the children's brass bedstead,
their mother's walnut bed with the carved scallop shells, and the round oak
table, smaller than the old one, at which they would now eat their meals.
Mme. Carette told Berthe that her days of entertaining and cooking for
guests were over. She was just twenty-seven.

They waited for the moving men in their new home, in scrubbed, empty
rooms. They had already spread sheets of *La Presse* over the floors, in case
the men tracked in snow. The curtains were hung, the cream-colored blinds
pulled halfway down the sash windows. Coal had been delivered and was
piled in the lean-to shed behind the kitchen. The range and the squat, round
heater in the dining room issued tidal waves of dense metallic warmth.

The old place was at no distance. Parc Lafontaine, where the children had often been taken to play, was just along the street. By walking an extra few minutes, Mme. Carette could patronize the same butcher and grocer as before. The same horse-drawn sleighs would bring bread, milk, and coal to the door. Still, the quiet stone houses, the absence of heavy traffic and shops made Rue Cherrier seem like a foreign country.

Change, death, absence—the adult mysteries—kept the children awake. From their new bedroom they heard the clang of the first streetcar at dawn—a thrilling chord, metal on metal, that faded slowly. They would have jumped up and dressed at once, but to their mother this was still the middle of the night. Presently, a new, continuous sound moved in the waking streets, like a murmur of leaves. From the confused rustle broke distinct impressions: an alarm clock, a man speaking, someone's radio. Marie wanted to talk and sing. Berthe had to invent stories to keep her quiet. Once she had placed her hand over Marie's mouth and been cruelly bitten.

They slept on a horsehair mattress, which had a summer and a winter side, and was turned twice a year. The beautiful stitching at the edge of the sheets and pillows was their mother's work. She had begun to sew her trousseau at the age of eleven; her early life was spent in preparation for a wedding. Above the girls' bed hung a gilt crucifix with a withered spray of box hedge that passed for the Easter palms of Jerusalem.

Marie was afraid to go to the bathroom alone after dark. Berthe asked if she expected to see their father's ghost, but Marie could not say: She did not yet know whether a ghost and the dark meant the same thing. Berthe was obliged to get up at night and accompany her along the passage. The hall light shone out of a blue glass tulip set upon a column painted to look like marble. Berthe could just reach it on tiptoe; Marie not at all.

Marie would have left the bathroom door open for company, but Berthe knew that such intimacy was improper. Although her First Communion was being delayed because Mme. Carette wanted the two sisters to come to the altar together, she had been to practice confession. Unfortunately, she had soon run out of invented sins. Her confessor seemed to think there should be more: He asked if she and her little sister had ever been in a bathroom with the door shut, and warned her of grievous fault.

On their way back to bed, Berthe unhooked a calendar on which was a picture of a family of rabbits riding a toboggan. She pretended to read stories about the rabbits and presently both she and Marie fell asleep.

They never saw their mother wearing a bathrobe. As soon as Mme.

Carette got up she dressed herself in clothes that were in the colors of half mourning—mauve, dove gray. Her fair hair was brushed straight and subdued under a net. She took a brush to everything—hair, floors, the children's elbows, the kitchen chairs. Her scent was of Baby's Own soap and Florida Water. When she bent to kiss the children, a cameo dangled from a chain. She trained the girls not to lie, or point, or gobble their food, or show their legs above the knee, or leave fingerprints on windowpanes, or handle the parlor curtains—the slightest touch could crease the lace, she said. They learned to say in English, "I don't understand" and "I don't know" and "No, thank you." That was all the English anyone needed between Rue Saint-Denis and Parc Lafontaine.

In the dining room, where she kept her sewing machine, Mme. Carette held the treadle still, rested a hand on the stopped wheel. "What are you doing in the parlor?" she called. "Are you touching the curtains?" Marie had been spitting on the window and drawing her finger through the spit. Berthe, trying to clean the mess with her flannelette petticoat, said, "Marie's just been standing here saying 'Saint Marguerite, pray for us.' "

Downstairs lived M. Grosjean, the landlord, with his Irish wife and an Airedale named Arno. Arno understood English and French; Mme. Grosjean could only speak English. She loved Arno and was afraid he would run away: He was a restless dog who liked to be doing something all the time. Sometimes M. Grosjean took him to Parc Lafontaine and they played at retrieving a collapsed and bitten tennis ball. Arno was trained to obey both "Cherchez!" and "Go fetch it!" but he paid attention to neither. He ran with the ball and Mme. Grosjean had to chase him.

Mme. Grosjean stood outside the house on the back step, just under the Carettes' kitchen window, holding Arno's supper. She wailed, "Arno, where have you got to?" M. Grosjean had probably taken Arno for a walk. He made it a point never to say where he was going: He did not think it a good thing to let women know much.

Mme. Grosjean and Mme. Carette were the same age, but they never became friends. Mme. Carette would say no more than a few negative things in English ("No, thank you" and "I don't know" and "I don't understand") and Mme. Grosjean could not work up the conversation. Mme. Carette had a word with Berthe about Irish marriages: An Irish marriage, while not to be sought, need not be scorned. The Irish were not English. God had sent them to Canada to keep people from marrying Protestants.

That winter the girls wore white leggings and mittens, knitted by their mother, and coats and hats of white rabbit fur. Each of them carried a rabbit muff. Marie cried when Berthe had to go to school. On Sunday afternoons they played with Arno and M. Grosjean. He tried to take their picture but it wasn't easy. The girls stood on the front steps, hand in hand, mitten to mitten, while Arno was harnessed to a sled with curved runners. The red harness had once been worn by another Airedale, Ruby, who was smarter even than Arno.

M. Grosjean wanted Marie to sit down on the sled, hold the reins, and look sideways at the camera. Marie clung to Berthe's coat. She was afraid that Arno would bolt into the Rue Saint-Denis, where there were streetcars. M. Grosjean lifted her off the sled and tried the picture a different way, with Berthe pretending to drive and Marie standing face-to-face with Arno. As soon as he set Marie on her feet, she began to scream. Her feet were cold. She wanted to be carried. Her nose ran; she felt humiliated. He got out his handkerchief, checked green and white, and wiped her whole face rather hard.

Just then his wife came to the front door with a dish of macaroni and cut-up sausages for Arno. She had thrown a sweater over her cotton housecoat; she was someone who never felt the cold. A gust of wind lifted her loose hair. M. Grosjean told her that the kid was no picnic. Berthe, picking up English fast, could not have repeated his exact words, but she knew what they meant.

Mme. Carette was still waiting for the money from the sale of the store. A brother-in-law helped with the rent, sending every month a generous postal order from Fall River. It was Mme. Carette's belief that God would work a miracle, allowing her to pay it all back. In the meantime, she did fine sewing. Once she was hired to sew a trousseau, working all day in the home of the bride-to-be. As the date of the wedding drew near she had to stay overnight.

Mme. Grosjean looked after the children. They sat in her front parlor, eating fried-egg sandwiches and drinking cream soda (it did not matter if they dropped crumbs) while she played a record of a man singing, "Dear one, the world is waiting for the sunrise."

Berthe asked, in French, "What is he saying?" Mme. Grosjean answered in English, "A well-known Irish tenor."

When Mme. Carette came home the next day, she gave the girls a hot bath, in case Mme. Grosjean had neglected their elbows and heels. She took

Berthe in her arms and said she must never tell anyone their mother had left the house to sew for strangers. When she grew up, she must not refer to her mother as a seamstress, but say instead, "My mother was clever with her hands."

That night, when they were all three having supper in the kitchen, she looked at Berthe and said, "You have beautiful hair." She sounded so tired and stern that Marie, eating mashed potatoes and gravy, with a napkin under her chin, thought Berthe must be getting a scolding. She opened her mouth wide and started to howl. Mme. Carette just said, "Marie, don't cry with your mouth full."

Downstairs, Mme. Grosjean set up her evening chant, calling for Arno. "Oh, where have you got to?" she wailed to the empty backyard.

"The dog is the only thing keeping those two together," said Mme. Carette. "But a dog isn't the same as a child. A dog doesn't look after its masters in their old age. We shall see what happens to the marriage after Arno dies." No sooner had she said this than she covered her mouth and spoke through her fingers: "God forgive my unkind thoughts." She propped her arms on each side of her plate, as the girls were forbidden to do, and let her face slide into her hands.

Berthe took this to mean that Arno was doomed. Only a calamity about to engulf them all could explain her mother's elbows on the table. She got down from her chair and tried to pull her mother's hands apart, and kiss her face. Her own tears ran into her long hair, down onto her starched piqué collar. She felt tears along her nose and inside her ears. Even while she sobbed out words of hope and comfort (Arno would never die) and promises of reassuring behavior (she and Marie would always be good) she wondered how tears could flow in so many directions at once.

Of course, M. Grosjean did not know that all the female creatures in his house were frightened and lonely, calling and weeping. He was in Parc Lafontaine with Arno, trying to play go-fetch-it in the dark.

THE CHOSEN HUSBAND

$\mathcal{I}$n 1949, a year that contained no other news of value, Mme. Carette came into a legacy of eighteen thousand dollars from a brother-in-law who had done well in Fall River. She had suspected him of being a Freemason, as well as of other offenses, none of them trifling, and so she did not make a show of bringing out his photograph; instead, she asked her daughters, Berthe and Marie, to mention him in their prayers. They may have, for a while. The girls were twenty-two and twenty, and Berthe, the elder, hardly prayed at all.

The first thing that Mme. Carette did was to acquire a better address. Until now she had kept the Montreal habit of changing her rented quarters every few seasons, a conversation with a landlord serving as warranty, rent paid in cash. This time she was summoned by appointment to a rental agency to sign a two-year lease. She had taken the first floor of a stone house around the corner from the church of Saint Louis de France. This was her old parish (she held to the network of streets near Parc Lafontaine) but a glorious strand of it, Rue Saint-Hubert.

Before her inheritance Mme. Carette had crept to church, eyes lowered; had sat where she was unlikely to disturb anyone whose life seemed more fortunate, therefore more deserving, than her own. She had not so much prayed as petitioned. Now she ran a glove along the pew to see if it was dusted, straightened the unread pamphlets that called for more vocations for missionary service in Africa, told a confessor that, like all the prosperous, she was probably without fault. When the holy-water font looked mossy, she called the parish priest and had words with his housekeeper, even though scrubbing the church was not her job. She still prayed every day for the repose of her late husband, and the unlikelier rest of his Freemason brother, but a tone of briskness caused her own words to rattle in her head. Church was a hushed annex to home. She prayed to insist upon the refinement of some request, and instead of giving thanks simply acknowledged that matters used to be worse.

Her daughter Berthe had been quick to point out that Rue Saint-Hubert was in decline. Otherwise, how could the Carettes afford to live here? (Berthe worked in an office and was able to pay half the rent.) A family of foreigners were installed across the road. A seamstress had placed a sign in a ground-floor window—a sure symptom of decay. True, but Mme. Carette had as near neighbors a retired opera singer and the first cousins of a city councillor—calm, courteous people who had never been on relief. A few blocks north stood the mayor's private dwelling, with a lamppost on each side of his front door. (During the recent war the mayor had been interned, like an enemy alien. No one quite remembered why. Mme. Carette believed that he had refused an invitation to Buckingham Palace, and that the English had it in for him. Berthe had been told that he had tried to annex Montreal to the state of New York and that someone had minded. Marie, who spoke to strangers on the bus, once came home with a story about Fascist views; but as she could not spell "Fascist," and did not know if it was a kind of landscape or something to eat, no one took her seriously. The mayor had eventually been released, was promptly reelected, and continued to add luster to Rue Saint-Hubert.)

Mme. Carette looked out upon long façades of whitish stone, windowpanes with beveled edges that threw rainbows. In her childhood this was how notaries and pharmacists had lived, before they began to copy the English taste for freestanding houses, blank lawns, ornamental willows, leashed dogs. She recalled a moneyed aunt and uncle, a family of well-dressed, soft-spoken children, heard the echo of a French more accurately expressed than her own. She had tried to imitate the peculiarity of every syllable, sounded like a plucked string, had tried to make her little girls speak that way. But they had rebelled, refused, said it made them laughed at.

When she had nothing to request, or was tired of repeating the same reminders, she shut her eyes and imagined her funeral. She was barely forty-five, but a long widowhood strictly observed had kept her childish, not youthful. She saw the rosary twined round her hands, the vigil, the candles perfectly still, the hillock of wreaths. Until the stunning message from Fall River, death had been her small talk. She had never left the subject, once entered, without asking, "And what will happen then to my poor little Marie?" Nobody had ever taken the question seriously except her Uncle Gildas. This was during their first Christmas dinner on Rue Saint-Hubert. He said that Marie should pray for guidance, the sooner the better. God had no patience with last-minute appeals. (Uncle Gildas was an elderly priest with limited social opportunities, though his niece believed him to have wide and worldly connections.)

"Prayer can fail," said Berthe, testing him.

Instead of berating her he said calmly, "In that case, Berthe can look after her little sister."

She considered him, old and eating slowly. His cassock exhaled some strong cleaning fluid—tetrachloride; he lived in a rest home, and nuns took care of him.

Marie was dressed in one of Berthe's castoffs—marine-blue velvet with a lace collar. Mme. Carette wore a gray-white dress Berthe thought she had seen all her life. In her first year of employment Berthe had saved enough for a dyed rabbit coat. She also had an electric seal, and was on her way to sheared raccoon. "Marie had better get married," she said.

Mme. Carette still felt cruelly the want of a husband, someone—not a daughter—to help her up the step of a streetcar, read *La Presse* and tell her what was in it, lay down the law to Berthe. When Berthe was in adolescence, laughing and whispering and not telling her mother the joke, Mme. Carette had asked Uncle Gildas to speak as a father. He sat in the parlor, in a plush chair, all boots and cassock, knees apart and a hand on each knee, and questioned Berthe about her dreams. She said she had never in her life dreamed anything. Uncle Gildas replied that anyone with a good conscience could dream events pleasing to God; he himself had been doing it for years. God kept the dreams of every living person on record, like great rolls of film. He could have them projected whenever he wanted. Montreal girls, notoriously virtuous, had his favor, but only up to a point. He forgave, but never forgot. He was the embodiment of endless time—though one should not take "embodiment" literally. Eternal remorse in a pit of flames was the same to him as a rap on the fingers with the sharp edge of a ruler. Marie, hearing this, had fainted dead away. That was the power of Uncle Gildas.

Nowadays, shrunken and always hungry, he lived in retirement, had waxed linoleum on his floor, no carpet, ate tapioca soup two or three times a week. He would have stayed in bed all day, but the nuns who ran the place looked upon illness as fatigue, fatigue as shirking. He was not tired or lazy;

he had nothing to get up for. The view from his window was a screen of trees. When Mme. Carette came to visit—a long streetcar ride, then a bus— she had just the trees to look at: She could not stare at her uncle the whole time. The trees put out of sight a busy commercial garage. It might have distracted him to watch trucks backing out, perhaps to witness a bloodless accident. In the morning he went downstairs to the chapel, ate breakfast, sat on his bed after it was made. Or crossed the gleaming floor to a small table, folded back the oilcloth cover, read the first sentence of a memoir he was writing for his great-nieces: "I was born in Montreal, on the 22nd of May, 1869, of pious Christian parents, connected to Montreal families for whom streets and bridges have been named." Or shuffled out to the varnished corridor, where there was a pay phone. He liked dialing, but out of long discipline never did without a reason.

Soon after Christmas Mme. Carette came to see him, wearing Berthe's velvet boots with tassels, Berthe's dyed rabbit coat, and a feather turban of her own. Instead of praying for guidance Marie had fallen in love with one of the Greeks who were starting to move into their part of Montreal. There had never been a foreigner in the family, let alone a pagan. Her uncle interrupted to remark that Greeks were usually Christians, though of the wrong kind for Marie. Mme. Carette implored him to find someone, not a Greek, of the right kind: sober, established, Catholic, French-speaking, natively Canadian. "Not Canadian from New England," she said, showing a brief ingratitude to Fall River. She left a store of nickels, so that he could ring her whenever he liked.

Louis Driscoll, French in all but name, called on Marie for the first time on the twelfth of April, 1950. Patches of dirty snow still lay against the curb. The trees on Rue Saint-Hubert looked dark and brittle, as though winter had killed them at last. From behind the parlor curtain, unseen from the street, the Carette women watched him coming along from the bus stop. To meet Marie he had put on a beige tweed overcoat, loosely belted, a beige scarf, a bottle-green snap-brim fedora, crêpe-soled shoes, pigskin gloves. His trousers were sharply pressed, a shade darker than the hat. Under his left arm he held close a parcel in white paper, the size and shape of a two-pound box of Laura Secord chocolates. He stopped frequently to consult the house numbers (blue and white, set rather high, Montreal style), which he compared with a slip of paper brought close to his eyes.

It was too bad that he had to wear glasses; the Carettes were not prepared for that, or for the fringe of ginger hair below his hat. Uncle Gildas had said he was of distinguished appearance. He came from Moncton, New Brunswick, and was employed at the head office of a pulp-and-paper concern. His age was twenty-six. Berthe thought that he must be a failed seminarist; they were the only Catholic bachelors Uncle Gildas knew.

Peering at their front door, he walked into a puddle of slush. Mme. Carette wondered if Marie's children were going to be nearsighted. "How can we be sure he's the right man?" she said.

"Who else could he be?" Berthe replied. What did he want with Marie? Uncle Gildas could not have promised much in her name, apart from a pliant nature. There could never be a meeting in a notary's office to discuss a dowry, unless you counted some plates and furniture. The old man may have frightened Louis, reminded him that prolonged celibacy—except among the clergy—is displeasing to God. Marie is poor, he must have said, though honorably connected. She will feel grateful to you all her life.

Their front steps were painted pearl gray, to match the building stone. Louis's face, upturned, was the color of wood ash. Climbing the stair, ringing the front doorbell could change his life in a way he did not wholly desire. Probably he wanted a woman without sin or risk or coaxing or remorse; but did he want her enough to warrant setting up a household? A man with a memory as transient as his, who could read an address thirty times and still let it drift, might forget to come to the wedding. He crumpled the slip of paper, pushed it inside a tweed pocket, withdrew a large handkerchief, blew his nose.

Mme. Carette swayed back from the curtain as though a stone had been flung. She concluded some private thought by addressing Marie: "... although I will feel better on my deathbed if I know you are in your own home." Louis meanwhile kicked the bottom step, getting rid of snow stuck to his shoes. (Rustics kicked and stamped. Marie's Greek had wiped his feet.) Still he hesitated, sliding a last pale look in the direction of buses and streetcars. Then, as he might have turned a gun on himself, he climbed five steps and pressed his finger to the bell.

"Somebody has to let him in," said Mme. Carette.

"Marie," said Berthe.

"It wouldn't seem right. She's never met him."

He stood quite near, where the top step broadened to a small platform level with the window. They could have leaned out, introduced him to Marie. Marie at this moment seemed to think he would do; at least, she showed no sign of distaste, such as pushing out her lower lip or crumpling her chin. Perhaps she had been getting ready to drop her Greek: Mme. Carette had warned her that she would have to be a servant to his mother, and eat peculiar food. "He's never asked me to," said Marie, and that was part of the trouble. He hadn't asked anything. For her twenty-first birthday he had given her a locket on a chain and a box from Maitland's, the West End confectioner, containing twenty-one chocolate mice. "He loves me," said Marie. She kept counting the mice and would not let anyone eat them.

In the end it was Berthe who admitted Louis, accepted the gift of chocolates on behalf of Marie, showed him where to leave his hat and coat. She approved of the clean white shirt, the jacket of a tweed similar to the coat but lighter in weight, the tie with a pattern of storm-tossed sailboats. Before shaking hands he removed his glasses, which had misted over, and wiped them dry. His eyes meeting the bright evening at the window (Marie was still there, but with her back to the street) flashed ultramarine. Mme. Carette hoped Marie's children would inherit that color.

He took Marie's yielding hand and let it drop. Freed of the introduction, she pried open the lid of the candy box and said, distinctly, "No mice." He seemed not to hear, or may have thought she was pleased to see he had not played a practical joke. Berthe showed him to the plush armchair, directly underneath a chandelier studded with lightbulbs. From this chair Uncle Gildas had explained the whims of God; against its linen antimacassar the Greek had recently rested his head.

Around Louis's crêpe soles pools of snow water formed. Berthe glanced at her mother, meaning that she was not to mind; but Mme. Carette was trying to remember where Berthe had said that she and Marie were to sit. (On the sofa, facing Louis.) Berthe chose a gilt upright chair, from which she could rise easily to pass refreshments. These were laid out on a marble-topped console: vanilla wafers, iced sultana cake, maple fudge, marshmallow biscuits, soft drinks. Behind the sofa a large pier glass reflected Louis in the armchair and the top of Mme. Carette's head. Berthe could tell from her mother's posture, head tilted, hands clasped, that she was silently asking Louis to trust her. She leaned forward and asked him if he was an only child. Berthe closed her eyes. When she opened them, nothing had changed except that Marie was eating chocolates. Louis seemed to be reflecting on his status.

He was the oldest of seven, he finally said. The others were Joseph, Raymond, Vincent, Francis, Rose, and Claire. French was their first language, in a way. But, then, so was English. A certain Louis Joseph Raymond Driscoll, Irish, veteran of Waterloo on the decent side, proscribed in England and Ireland as a result, had come out to Canada and grafted on pure French stock a number of noble traits: bright, wavy hair, a talent for public speaking, another for social aplomb. In every generation of Driscolls, there had to be a Louis, a Joseph, a Raymond. (Berthe and her mother exchanged a look. He wanted three sons.)

His French was slow and muffled, as though strained through wool. He used English words, or French words in an English way. Mme. Carette lifted her shoulders and parted her clasped hands as if to say, "Never mind, English is better than Greek." At least, they could be certain that the Driscolls were Catholic. In August his father and mother were making the Holy Year pilgrimage to Rome.

Rome was beyond their imagining, though all three Carettes had been to Maine and Old Orchard Beach. Louis hoped to spend a vacation in Old Orchard (in response to an ardent question from Mme. Carette), but he had more feeling for Quebec City. His father's people had entered Canada by way of Quebec.

"The French part of the family?" said Mme. Carette.

"Yes, yes," said Berthe, touching her mother's arm.

Berthe had been to Quebec City, said Mme. Carette. She was brilliant, reliable, fully bilingual. Her office promoted her every January. They were always sending her away on company business. She knew Plattsburgh, Saranac Lake. In Quebec City, at lunch at the Château Frontenac, she had seen well-known politicians stuffing down oysters and fresh lobster, at taxpayers' expense.

Louis's glance tried to cross Berthe's, as he might have sought out and welcomed a second man in the room. Berthe reached past Mme. Carette to take the candy box away from Marie. She nudged her mother with her elbow.

"The first time I ever saw Old Orchard," Mme. Carette resumed, smoothing the bodice of her dress, "I was sorry I had not gone there on my honeymoon." She paused, watching Louis accept a chocolate. "My husband and I went to Fall River. He had a brother in the lumber business."

At the mention of lumber, Louis took on a set, bulldog look. Berthe wondered if the pulp-and-paper firm had gone bankrupt. Her thoughts rushed to Uncle Gildas—how she would have it out with him, not leave it to her mother, if he had failed to examine Louis's prospects. But then Louis began to cough and had to cover his mouth. He was in trouble with a caramel. The Carettes looked away, so that he could strangle unobserved. "How dark it is," said Berthe, to let him think he could not be seen. Marie got up, with a hiss and rustle of taffeta skirt, and switched on the twin floor lamps with their cerise silk shades.

"There," she seemed to be saying to Berthe. "Have I done the right thing? Is this what you wanted?"

Louis still coughed, but weakly. He moved his fingers, like a child made to wave good-bye. Mme. Carette wondered how many contagious children's diseases he had survived; in a large family everything made the rounds. His eyes, perhaps seeking shade, moved across the brown wallpaper flecked with gold and stopped at the only familiar sight in the room—his reflection in the pier glass. He sat up straighter and quite definitely swallowed. He took a long drink of ginger ale. "When Irish eyes are smiling," he said, in English, as if to himself. "When Irish eyes are smiling. There's a lot to be said for that. A lot to be said."

Of course he was at a loss, astray in an armchair, with the Carettes watching like friendly judges. When he reached for another chocolate, they looked to see if his nails were clean. When he crossed his legs, they examined his socks. They were fixing their first impression of the stranger who might take Marie away, give her a modern kitchen, children to bring up, a muskrat coat, a charge account at Dupuis Frères department store, a holiday in Maine. Louis continued to examine his bright Driscoll hair, the small nose along which his glasses slid. Holding the glasses in place with a finger, he answered Mme. Carette: His father was a dental surgeon, with a degree from Pennsylvania. It was the only degree worth mentioning. Before settling into a dentist's chair the patient should always read the writing on the wall. His mother was born Lucarne, a big name in Moncton. She could still get into her wedding dress. Everything was so conveniently arranged at home— cavernous washing machine, giant vacuum cleaner—that she seldom went out. When she did, she wore a two-strand cultured-pearl necklace and a coat and hat of Persian lamb.

The Carettes could not match this, though they were related to families for whom bridges were named. Mme. Carette sat on the edge of the sofa, ankles together. Gentility was the brace that kept her upright. She had once been a young widow, hard pressed, had needed to sew for money. Berthe recalled a stricter, an unsmiling mother, straining over pleats and tucks for clients who reneged on pennies. She wore the neutral shades of half mourning, the whitish grays of Rue Saint-Hubert, as though everything had to be used up—even remnants of grief.

Mme. Carette tried to imagine Louis's mother. She might one day have to sell the pearls; even a dentist trained in Pennsylvania could leave behind disorder and debts. Whatever happened, she said to Louis, she would remain in this flat. Even after the girls were married. She would rather beg on the steps of the parish church than intrude upon a young marriage. When her last, dreadful illness made itself known, she would creep away to the Hôtel Dieu and die without a murmur. On the other hand, the street seemed to be filling up with foreigners. She might have to move.

Berthe and Marie were dressed alike, as if to confound Louis, force him to choose the true princess. Leaving the sight of his face in the mirror, puzzled by death and old age, he took notice of the two moiré skirts, organdy blouses, patent-leather belts. "I can't get over those twins of yours," he said to Mme. Carette. "I just can't get over them."

Once, Berthe had tried Marie in her own office—easy work, taking messages when the switchboard was closed. She knew just enough English for that. After two weeks the office manager, Mr. Macfarlane, had said to Berthe, "Your sister is an angel, but angels aren't in demand at Prestige Central Burners."

It was the combination of fair hair and dark eyes, the enchanting misalliance, that gave Marie the look of an angel. She played with the locket the Greek had given her, twisting and unwinding the chain. What did she owe her Greek? Fidelity? An explanation? He was punctual and polite, had never laid a hand on her, in temper or eagerness, had traveled a long way by streetcar to bring back the mice. True, said Berthe, reviewing his good points, while Louis ate the last of the fudge. It was true about the mice, but he should have become more than "Marie's Greek." In the life of a penniless unmarried young woman, there was no room for a man merely in love. He ought to have presented himself as *something*: Marie's future.

In May true spring came, moist and hot. Berthe brought home new dress patterns and yards of flowered rayon and piqué. Louis called three evenings a week, at seven o'clock, after the supper dishes were cleared away. They played hearts in the dining room, drank Salada tea, brewed black, with plenty of sugar and cream, ate éclairs and mille-feuilles from Celentano, the bakery on Avenue Mont Royal. (Celentano had been called something else for years now, but Mme. Carette did not take notice of change of that kind, and did not care to have it pointed out.) Louis, eating coffee éclairs one after another, told stories set in Moncton that showed off his family. Marie wore a blue dress with a red collar, once Berthe's, and a red barrette in her hair. Berthe, a master player, held back to let Louis win. Mme. Carette listened to Louis, kept some of his stories, discarded others, garnering information useful to Marie. Marie picked up cards at random, disrupting the game. Louis's French was not as woolly as before, but he had somewhere acquired a common Montreal accent. Mme. Carette wondered who his friends were and how Marie's children would sound.

They began to invite him to meals. He arrived at half past five, straight from work, and was served at once. Mme. Carette told Berthe that she hoped he washed his hands at the office, because he never did here. They used the blue-willow-pattern china that would go to Marie. One evening, when the tablecloth had been folded and put away, and the teacups and cards distributed, he mentioned marriage—not his own, or to anyone in particular, but as a way of life. Mme. Carette broke in to say that she had been widowed at Louis's age. She recalled what it had been like to have a husband she could consult and admire. "Marriage means children," she said, looking fondly at her own. She would not be alone during her long, final illness. The girls would take her in. She would not be a burden; a couch would do for a bed.

Louis said he was tired of the game. He dropped his hand and spread the cards in an arc.

"So many hearts," said Mme. Carette, admiringly.

"Let me see." Marie had to stand: there was a large teapot in the way. "Ace, queen, ten, eight, five . . . a wedding." Before Berthe's foot reached her ankle, she managed to ask, sincerely, if anyone close to him was getting married this year.

Mme. Carette considered Marie as good as engaged. She bought a quantity of embroidery floss and began the ornamentation of guest towels and tea towels, place mats and pillow slips. Marie ran her finger over the pretty monogram with its intricate frill of vine leaves. Her mind, which had sunk into hibernation when she accepted Louis and forgot her Greek, awoke and plagued her with a nightmare. "I became a nun" was all she told her mother. Mme. Carette wished it were true. Actually, the dream had stopped short of vows. Barefoot, naked under a robe of coarse brown wool, she moved along an aisle in and out of squares of sunlight. At the altar they were waiting to shear her hair. A strange man—not Uncle Gildas, not Louis, not the

Greek—got up out of a pew and stood barring her way. The rough gown turned out to be frail protection. All that kept the dream from sliding into blasphemy and abomination was Marie's entire unacquaintance, awake or asleep, with what could happen next.

Because Marie did not like to be alone in the dark, she and Berthe still shared a room. Their childhood bed had been taken away and supplanted by twin beds with quilted satin headboards. Berthe had to sleep on three pillows, because the aluminum hair curlers she wore ground into her scalp. First thing every morning, she clipped on her pearl earrings, sat up, and unwound the curlers, which she handed one by one to Marie. Marie put her own hair up and kept it that way until suppertime.

In the dark, her face turned to the heap of pillows dimly seen, Marie told Berthe about the incident in the chapel. If dreams are life's opposite, what did it mean? Berthe saw that there was more to it than Marie was able to say. Speaking softly, so that their mother would not hear, she tried to tell Marie about men—what they were like and what they wanted. Marie suggested that she and Berthe enter a cloistered convent together, now, while there was still time. Berthe supposed that she had in mind the famous Martin sisters of Lisieux, in France, most of them Carmelites and one a saint. She touched her own temple, meaning that Marie had gone soft in the brain. Marie did not see; if she had, she would have thought that Berthe was easing a curler. Berthe reminded Marie that she was marked out not for sainthood in France but for marriage in Montreal. Berthe had a salary and occasional travel. Mme. Carette had her Fall River bounty. Marie, if she put her mind to it, could have a lifetime of love.

"Is Louis love?" said Marie.

There were girls ready to line up in the rain for Louis, said Berthe.

"What girls?" said Marie, perplexed rather than disbelieving.

"Montreal girls," said Berthe. "The girls who cry with envy when you and Louis walk down the street."

"We have never walked down a street," said Marie.

The third of June was Louis's birthday. He arrived wearing a new seersucker suit. The Carettes offered three monogrammed hemstitched handkerchiefs—he was always polishing his glasses or mopping his face. Mme. Carette had prepared a meal he particularly favored—roast pork and coconut layer cake. The sun was still high. His birthday unwound in a steady, blazing afternoon. He suddenly put his knife and fork down and said that if he ever decided to get married he would need more than his annual bonus to pay for the honeymoon. He would have to buy carpets, lamps, a refrigerator. People talked lightly of marriage without considering the cost for the groom. Priests urged the married condition on bachelors—priests, who did not know the price of eight ounces of tea.

"Some brides bring lamps and lampshades," said Mme. Carette. "A glass-front bookcase. Even the books to put in it." Her husband had owned a furniture shop on Rue Saint-Denis. Household goods earmarked for Berthe and Marie had been stored with relatives for some twenty years, waxed and polished and free of dust. "An oak table that seats fourteen," she said, and stopped with that. Berthe had forbidden her to draw up an inventory. They were not bartering Marie.

"Some girls have money," said Marie. Her savings—eighteen dollars— were in a drawer of her mother's old treadle sewing machine.

A spasm crossed Louis's face; he often choked on his food. Berthe knew more about men than Marie—more than her mother, who knew only how children come about. Mr. Ryder, of Berthe's office, would stand in the corridor, letting elevators go by, waiting for a chance to squeeze in next to Berthe. Mr. Sexton had offered her money, a regular allowance, if she would go out with him every Friday, the night of his Legion meeting. Mr. Macfarlane had left a lewd poem on her desk, then a note of apology, then a poem even worse than the first. Mr. Wright-Ashburton had offered to leave his wife—for, of course, they had wives, Mr. Ryder, Mr. Sexton, Mr. Macfarlane, none of whom she had ever encouraged, and Mr. Wright-Ashburton, with whom she had been to Plattsburgh and Saranac Lake, and whose private behavior she had described, kneeling, in remote parishes, where the confessor could not have known her by voice.

When Berthe accepted Mr. Wright-Ashburton's raving proposal to leave his wife, saying that Irene probably knew about them anyway, would be thankful to have it in the clear, his face had wavered with fright, like a face seen underwater—rippling, uncontrolled. Berthe had to tell him she hadn't meant it. She could not marry a divorced man. On Louis's face she saw that same quivering dismay. He was afraid of Marie, of her docility, her monogrammed towels, her dependence, her glass-front bookcase. Having seen this, Berthe was not surprised when he gave no further sign of life until the twenty-fifth of June.

During his absence the guilt and darkness of rejection filled every corner of the flat. There was not a room that did not speak of humiliation—oh, not because Louis had dropped Marie but because the Carettes had honored and welcomed a clodhopper, a cheapjack, a ginger-haired nobody. Mme. Carette and Marie made many telephone calls to his office, with a variety of names and voices, to be told every time he was not at his desk. One morning Berthe, on her way to work, saw someone very like him hurrying into Windsor station. By the time she had struggled out of her crowded streetcar, he was gone. She followed him into the great concourse and looked at the times of the different trains and saw where they were going. A trapped sparrow fluttered under the glass roof. She recalled an expression of Louis's, uneasy and roguish, when he had told Berthe that Marie did not understand the facts of life. (This in English, over the table, as if Mme. Carette and Marie could not follow.) When Berthe asked what these facts might be, he had tried to cross her glance, as on that first evening, one man to another. She was not a man; she had looked away.

Mme. Carette went on embroidering baskets of flowers, ivy leaves, hunched over her work, head down. Marie decided to find a job as a receptionist in a beauty salon. It would be pleasant work in clean surroundings. A girl she had talked to on the bus earned fourteen dollars a week. Marie would give her mother eight and keep six. She did not need Louis, she said, and she was sure she could never love him.

"No one expected you to love him," said her mother, without looking up.

On the morning of the twenty-fifth of June he rang the front doorbell. Marie was eating breakfast in the kitchen, wearing Berthe's aluminum curlers under a mauve chiffon scarf, and Berthe's mauve-and-black kimono. He stood in the middle of the room, refusing offers of tea, and said that the whole world was engulfed in war. Marie looked out the kitchen window, at bare yards and storage sheds.

"Not there," said Louis. "In Korea."

Marie and her mother had never heard of the place. Mme. Carette took it for granted that the British had started something again. She said, "They can't take you, Louis, because of your eyesight." Louis replied that this time they would take everybody, bachelors first. A few married men might be allowed to make themselves useful at home. Mme. Carette put her arms around him. "You are my son now," she said. "I'll never let them ship you to England. You can hide in our coal shed." Marie had not understood that the mention of war was a marriage proposal, but her mother had grasped it at once. She wanted to call Berthe and tell her to come home immediately, but Louis was in a hurry to publish the banns. Marie retired to the bedroom and changed into Berthe's white sharkskin sundress and jacket and toeless white suede shoes. She smoothed Berthe's suntan makeup on her legs, hoping that her mother would not see she was not wearing stockings. She combed out her hair, put on lipstick and earrings, and butterfly sunglasses belonging to Berthe. Then, for the first time, she and Louis together walked down the front steps to the street.

At Marie's parish church they found other couples standing about, waiting for advice. They had heard the news and decided to get married at once. Marie and Louis held hands, as though they had been engaged for a long time. She hoped no one would notice that she had no engagement ring. Unfortunately, their banns could not be posted until July, or the marriage take place until August. His parents would not be present to bless them: At the very day and hour of the ceremony they would be on their way to Rome.

The next day, Louis went to a jeweler on Rue Saint-Denis, recommended by Mme. Carette, but he was out of engagement rings. He had sold every last one that day. Louis did not look anywhere else; Mme. Carette had said he was the only man she trusted. Louis's mother sent rings by registered mail. They had been taken from the hand of her dead sister, who had wanted them passed on to her son, but the son had vanished into Springfield and no longer sent Christmas cards. Mme. Carette shook her own wedding dress out of tissue paper and made a few adjustments so that it would fit Marie. Since the war it had become impossible to find silk of that quality.

Waiting for August, Louis called on Marie every day. They rode the streetcar up to Avenue Mont Royal to eat barbecued chicken. (One evening Marie let her engagement ring fall into a crack of the corrugated floor of the tram, and a number of strangers told her to be careful, or she would lose her man, too.) The chicken arrived on a bed of chips, in a wicker basket. Louis showed Marie how to eat barbecue without a knife and fork. Fortunately, Mme. Carette was not there to watch Marie gnawing on a bone. She was sewing the rest of the trousseau and had no time to act as chaperone.

Berthe's office sent her to Buffalo for a long weekend. She brought back match folders from Polish and German restaurants, an ashtray on which was written "Buffalo Hofbrau," and a number of articles that were much cheaper down there, such as nylon stockings. Marie asked if they still ate with knives and forks in Buffalo, or if they had caught up to Montreal.

Alone together, Mme. Carette and Berthe sat in the kitchen and gossiped about Louis. The white summer curtains were up; the coal-and-wood range was covered with clean white oilcloth. Berthe had a new kimono—white, with red pagodas on the sleeves. She propped her new red mules on the oven door. She smoked now, and carried everywhere the Buffalo Hofbrau ashtray. Mme. Carette made Berthe promise not to smoke in front of Uncle Gildas, or in the street, or at Marie's wedding reception, or in the front parlor, where the smell might get into the curtains. Sometimes they had just tea and toast and Celentano pastry for supper. When Berthe ate a coffee éclair, she said, "Here's one Louis won't get."

The bright evenings of suppers and card games slid into the past, and by August seemed long ago. Louis said to Marie, "We knew how to have a good time. People don't enjoy themselves anymore." He believed that the other customers in the barbecue restaurant had secret, nagging troubles. Waiting for the wicker basket of chicken, he held Marie's hand and stared at men who might be Greeks. He tried to tell her what had been on his mind between the third and twenty-fifth of June, but Marie did not care, and he gave up. They came to their first important agreement: Neither of them wanted the blue-willow-pattern plates. Louis said he would ask his parents to start them off with six place settings of English Rose. She seemed still to be listening, and so he told her that the name of her parish church, Saint Louis de France, had always seemed to him to be a personal sign of some kind: An obscure force must have guided him to Rue Saint-Hubert and Marie. Her soft brown eyes never wavered. They forgot about Uncle Gildas, and whatever it was Uncle Gildas had said to frighten them.

Louis and Marie were married on the third Saturday of August, with flowers from an earlier wedding banked along the altar rail, and two other wedding parties waiting at the back of the church. Berthe supposed that Marie, by accepting the ring of a dead woman and wearing the gown of another woman widowed at twenty-six, was calling down the blackest kind of misfortune. She remembered her innocent nakedness under the robe of frieze. Marie had no debts. She owed Louis nothing. She had saved him from a long journey to a foreign place, perhaps even from dying. As he placed the unlucky ring on her finger, Berthe wept. She knew that some of the people looking on—Uncle Gildas, or Joseph and Raymond Driscoll, amazing in their ginger likeness—were mistaking her for a jealous older sister, longing to be in Marie's place.

Marie, now Mme. Driscoll, turned to Berthe and smiled, as she used to when they were children. Once again, the smile said, "Have I done the right thing? Is this what you wanted?" "Yes, yes," said Berthe silently, but she went on crying. Marie had always turned to Berthe; she had started to walk because she wanted to be with Berthe. She had been standing, holding on to a kitchen chair, and she suddenly smiled and let go. Later, when Marie was three, and in the habit of taking her clothes off and showing what must never be seen, Mme. Carette locked her into the storage shed behind the kitchen. Berthe knelt on her side of the door, sobbing, calling, "Don't be afraid, Marie. Berthe is here." Mme. Carette relented and unlocked the door, and there was Marie, wearing just her undershirt, smiling for Berthe.

Leading her mother, Berthe approached the altar rail. Marie seemed contented; for Berthe, that was good enough. She kissed her sister, and kissed the chosen husband. He had not separated them but would be a long incident in their lives. Among the pictures that were taken on the church steps, there is one of Louis with an arm around each sister and the sisters trying to clasp hands behind his back.

The wedding party walked in a procession down the steps and around the corner: another impression in black-and-white. The August pavement burned under the women's thin soles. Their fine clothes were too hot. Children playing in the road broke into applause when they saw Marie. She waved her left hand, showing the ring. The children were still French-Canadian; so were the neighbors, out on their balconies to look at Marie. Three yellow leaves fell—white, in a photograph. One of the Driscoll boys raced ahead and brought the party to a stop. There is Marie, who does not yet understand that she is leaving home, and confident Louis, so soon to have knowledge of her bewildering ignorance.

Berthe saw the street as if she were bent over the box camera, trying to keep the frame straight. It was an important picture, like a precise instrument of measurement: so much duty, so much love, so much reckless safety—the distance between last April and now. She thought, It had to be done. They began to walk again. Mme. Carette realized for the first time what she and Uncle Gildas and Berthe had brought about: the unredeemable loss of Marie. She said to Berthe, "Wait until I am dead before you get married. You can marry a widower. They make good husbands." Berthe was nearly twenty-four, just at the limit. She had turned away so many attractive prospects, with no explanation, and had frightened so many others with her skill at cards and her quick blue eyes that word had spread, and she was not solicited as before.

Berthe and Marie slipped away from the reception—moved, that is, from the parlor to the bedroom—so that Berthe could help her sister pack. It turned out that Mme. Carette had done the packing. Marie had never had to fill a suitcase, and would not have known what to put in first. For a time, they sat on the edge of a bed, talking in whispers. Berthe smoked, holding the Buffalo Hofbrau ashtray. She showed Marie a black lacquer cigarette lighter she had not shown her mother. Marie had started to change her clothes; she was just in her slip. She looked at the lighter on all sides and handed it back. Louis was taking her to the Château Frontenac, in Quebec City, for three nights—the equivalent of ten days in Old Orchard, he had said. After that, they would go straight to the duplex property, quite far north on Boulevard Pie IX, that his father was helping him buy. "I'll call you tomorrow morning," said Marie, for whom tomorrow was still the same thing as today. If Uncle Gildas had been at Berthe's mercy, she would have held his head underwater. Then she thought, Why blame him? She and Marie were Montreal girls, not trained to accompany heroes, or to hold out for dreams, but just to be patient.

FROM CLOUD TO CLOUD

⁂

The family's experience of Raymond was like a long railway journey with a constantly shifting point of view. His mother and aunt were of a generation for whom travel had meant trains—slow trips there and back, with an intense engagement in eating, or a game of cards with strangers, interrupted by a flash of celestial light from the frozen and sunstruck St. Lawrence. Then came the dark brown slums of the approach to Montreal, the signal to get one's luggage down from the rack.

To make a short story shorter, his Aunt Berthe (she worked in an office full of English Canadians) would have said Raymond was Heaven and Hell. Mother and aunt, the two sisters had thought they never could love anyone more than Raymond; then, all at once, he seemed to his aunt so steadily imperfect, so rigid in his failings, that the changing prospect of his moods, decisions, needs, life ceased to draw her attention.

He'd had a father, of course—had him until he was eighteen, even though it was Raymond's practice to grumble that he had been raised, badly, by women. His last memories of his father must surely have been Louis dying of emphysema, upright in the white-painted wicker chair, in blazing forbidden sunlight, mangling a forbidden cigar. The partially flagged backyard had no shade in it—just two yellow fringed umbrellas that filtered the blue of July and made it bilious. Louis could not sit in their bogus shadow, said it made him sweat. Behind the umbrellas was the kitchen entrance to a duplex dwelling of stucco and brick, late 1940s in style—a cube with varnished doors—at the northern end of Boulevard Pie IX. "Remember that your father owned his own home," said Louis; also, "When we first moved up here, you could still see vacant lots. It depressed your mother. She wasn't used to an open view."

Where Raymond's sandbox had been stood a granite birdbath with three aluminum birds the size of pigeons perched on the rim—the gift from Louis's firm when he had to take early retirement, because he was so ill. He already owned a gold watch. He told Raymond exactly where to find the watch in his desk—in which drawer. Raymond sat cross-legged on the grass and practiced flipping a vegetable knife; his mother had found and disposed of his commando dagger. His father could draw breath but had to pause before he spoke. Waiting for strength, he looked up at the sky, at a moon in sunlight, pale and transparent—a memory of dozens of other waning moons. (It was the summer of the moon walk. Raymond's mother still mentions this, as though it had exerted a tidal influence on her affairs.)

The silent intermissions, his gaze upturned, made it seem as if Louis were seeking divine assistance. Actually, he knew everything he wished to say. So did Raymond. Raymond—even his aunt will not deny it—showed respect. He never once remarked, "I've heard this before," or uttered the timeless, frantic snub of the young, "I know, I know, I *know.*"

His father said, "There have always been good jobs in Boston," "Never forget your French, because it would break your mother's heart," "One of these days you're going to have to cut your hair," "Marry a Catholic, but not just any Catholic," "With a name like Raymond Joseph Driscoll you can go anywhere in the world," "That autograph album of mine is worth a fortune. Hang on to it. It will always get you out of a tight spot."

In his lifetime Louis wrote to hockey players and film stars and local politicians, and quite often received an answer. Raymond as a child watched him cutting out the signature and pasting it in a deep blue leather-bound book. Now that Raymond is settled in Florida, trying to build a career in the motel business, his whole life is a tight spot. He finds it hard to credit that the album is worth nothing. Unfortunately, it is so. Most of the signatures were facsimiles, or had been dashed off by a secretary. The few authentic autographs were of names too obscure to matter. The half dozen that Louis purchased from a specialized dealer on Peel Street, since driven out of business, were certified fakes. Louis kept "Joseph Stalin" and "Harry S Truman" in a locked drawer, telling Marie, his wife, that if Canada was ever occupied by one of the two great powers, or by both at once, she would be able to barter her way to safety.

Raymond had a thin mane of russet hair that covered his profile when he bent over to retrieve the knife. He wore circus-rodeo gear, silver and white. Louis couldn't stand the sight of his son's clothes; in his dying crankiness he gave some away. Raymond stored his favorite outfits at his aunt's place. She lived in a second-story walk-up, with front and back balconies, a long, cool hall, three bedrooms, on the west side of Parc Lafontaine. She was unmarried and did not need all that space; she enjoyed just walking from room to room. Louis spoke to Raymond in English, so that he would be able to make his way in the world. He wanted him to go to an English commercial school, where he might meet people who would be useful to him later on. Raymond's aunt said that her English was better than Louis's: his "th" sometimes slipped into "d." Louis, panting, mentioned to Raymond that Berthe, for all her pretensions, was not as well off propertywise as her sister and brother-in-law, though she seemed to have more money to throw around. "Low rent in any crummy neighborhood—that's her creed," said Raymond's father. In his last, bad, bitter days, he seemed to be brooding over Berthe, compared her career with his own, said she had an inborn craving for sleeping with married men. But before he died he took every word back, said she had been a good friend to him, was an example for other women, though not necessarily married women. He wanted her to keep an eye on Marie and Raymond—he said he felt as if he were leaving behind two helpless children, one eighteen, the other in her forties, along with the two cars, the valuable autograph album, the gold watch, and the paid-up house.

Louis also left a handwritten inconvenient request to be buried in New Brunswick, where he came from, rather than in Montreal. Raymond's mother hid the message behind a sofa cushion, where it would be discovered during some future heavy cleaning. She could not bring herself to tear it up. They buried Louis in Notre Dame des Neiges cemetery, where Marie intended to join him, not too soon. She ordered a bilingual inscription on the gravestone, because he had spoken English at the office and French to her.

Raymond in those days spoke French and English, too, with a crack in each. His English belonged to a subdivision of Catholic Montreal—a bit Irish-sounding but thinner than any tone you might hear in Dublin. His French vocabulary was drawn from conversations with his mother and aunt, and should have been full of tenderness. He did not know what he wanted to be. "If I ever write, I'm going to write a book about the family," he told his aunt the day of Louis's funeral, looking at the relatives in their black un-natural clothes, soaking up heat. It was the first time he had ever said this, and most likely the last. Poor Raymond could barely scrawl a letter, couldn't spell. He didn't mind learning, but he hated to be taught. After he left home, Berthe and Marie scarcely had the sight of his handwriting. They had his voice over the telephone, calling from different American places (they thought of Vietnam as an American place) with a gradually altered ac-cent. His French filled up with English, as with a deposit of pebbles and sand, and in English he became not quite a stranger: Even years later he still said "palm" to rhyme with "jam."

Raymond behaved correctly at the funeral, holding his mother's arm, seeing that everyone had a word with her, causing those relatives who did not know him well to remark that he was his father all over again. He was dressed in a dark suit, bought in a hurry, and one of Louis's ties. He had not worn a tie since the last family funeral; Berthe had to fasten the knot. He let her give his hair a light trim, so that it cleared his shoulders.

Marie would not hold a reception: The mourners had to settle for a kiss or a handshake beside the open grave. Louis's people, some of whom had come a long way, were starting back with the pieces of a break beyond mending. Marie didn't care: Her family feelings had narrowed to Raymond and Berthe. After the funeral, Raymond drove the two sisters to Berthe's flat. He sat with his mother at the kitchen table and watched Berthe cutting up a cold chicken. Marie kept on her funeral hat, a black straw pillbox with a wisp of veil. No one said much. The chicken was not enough for Ray-mond, so Berthe got out the ham she had baked the night before in case Marie changed her mind about inviting the relatives. She put the whole thing down in front of him, and he hacked pieces off and ate with his fin-gers. Marie said, "You wouldn't dare do that if your father could see you," because she had to say something. She and Berthe knew he was having a bad time.

When he finished, they moved down the hall to Berthe's living room. She opened the doors to both balconies, to invite a cross breeze. The heated air touched the looped white curtain without stirring a fold of it. Raymond took off his jacket and tie. The women had already removed their black stockings. Respect for Louis kept them from making themselves entirely comfortable. They had nothing in particular to do for the rest of the day.

Berthe had taken time off from the office, and Marie was afraid to go home. She believed that some essence of Louis, not quite a ghost, was in their house on Boulevard Pie IX, testing locks, turning door handles, sliding drawers open, handling Marie's poor muddled household accounts, ascertaining once and for all the exact amount of money owed by Marie to Berthe. (Berthe had always been good for a small loan toward the end of the month. She had shown Marie how to entangle the books, so that Louis need never know.)

Raymond stretched out on Berthe's pale green sofa, with a pile of cushions under his head. "Raymond, watch where you put your feet," said his mother.

"It doesn't matter," said Berthe. "Not today."

"I don't want you to wish we weren't here," said Marie. "After we've moved in, I mean. You'll never know we're in the house. Raymond, ask Aunt Berthe for an ashtray."

"There's one right beside him," said Berthe.

"I won't let Raymond put his feet all over the furniture," said Marie. "Not after today. If you don't want us, all you have to do is say."

"I have said," said Berthe, at which Raymond turned his head and looked at her intently.

Tears flooded Marie's eyes at the improbable vision of Berthe ordering her nearest relatives, newly bereaved, to pack and go. "We're going to be happy, because we love each other," she said.

"Have you asked Raymond where he wants to live?" said Berthe.

"Raymond wants whatever his mother wants," said Marie. "He'll be nice. I promise. He'll take the garbage down. Won't you, Raymond? You'll take the garbage out every night for Aunt Berthe?"

"Not every night," said his aunt. "Twice a week. Don't cry. Louis wouldn't want to see you in tears."

A quiver of shyness touched all three. Louis returned to memory in superior guise, bringing guidance, advice. "Papa wouldn't mind if we watched the news," said Raymond.

For less than a minute they stared at a swaying carpet of jungle green, filmed from a helicopter, and heard a French voice with a Montreal accent describe events in a place the sisters intended never to visit. Raymond jumped to an English channel, without asking if anyone minded. He was the male head of the family now; in any case, they had always given in. Vietnam in English appeared firmly grounded, with a Canadian sergeant in the Marine Corps—shorn, cropped, gray-eyed, at ease. He spoke to Raymond, saying that it was all right for a Canadian to enlist in a foreign army.

"Who cares?" said Marie, fatally. English on television always put her to sleep. She leaned back in her armchair and began very gently to snore. Berthe removed Marie's glasses and her hat, and covered her bare legs with a lace quilt. Even in the warmest weather she could wake up feeling chilled and unloved. She fainted easily; it was her understanding that the blood in her arms and legs congealed, leaving her brain unattended. She seemed content with this explanation and did not seek another.

Raymond sat up, knocking over the pile of cushions. He gathered his hair into a topknot and held it fast. "They send you to San Diego," he said. What was he seeing, really? Pacific surf? A parade in sunlight? Berthe should have asked.

When Marie came to, yawning and sighing, Berthe was putting color on her nails (she had removed it for the funeral) and Raymond was eating chocolate cake, watching Rod Laver. He had taken off his shirt, shoes, and socks. "Laver's the greatest man in the modern world," he said.

"Ah, Raymond," said his mother. "You've already forgotten your father."

As Marie had promised, he carried the garbage out, making a good impression on the Portuguese family who lived downstairs. (Louis, who would not speak to strangers, had made no impression at all.) At five o'clock the next morning, Berthe's neighbor, up because he had an early delivery at his fruit store, saw Raymond throw a duffel kit into his mother's car and drive away. His hair was tied back with a white leather thong. He wore one of his rodeo outfits and a pair of white boots.

Before leaving Berthe's flat he had rifled her handbag, forgotten on a kitchen chair—a century before, when they assembled for the funeral feast. Before leaving Montreal he made a long detour to say good-bye to his old home. He was not afraid of ghosts, and he had already invented a father who was going to approve of everything he did. In Louis's desk he found the gold watch and one or two documents he knew he would need—among them the birth certificate that showed him eighteen. He took away as a last impression the yellowed grass in the backyard. Nothing had been watered since Louis's death.

Berthe has often wondered what the Marines in the recruiting office down in Plattsburgh made of Raymond, all silver and white, with that lank brick-dust hair and the thin, cracked English. Nothing, probably: They must have expected civilians to resemble fake performers. There was always someone straggling down from Montreal. It was like joining the Foreign Legion. After his first telephone call, Berthe said to Marie, "At least we know where he is," but it was not so; they never quite knew. He did not go to San Diego: A military rule of geography splits the continent. He had enlisted east of the Mississippi, and so he was sent for training to Parris Island. The Canadian Marine had forgotten to mention that possibility. Berthe bought a number of road maps, so that she could look up these new names. The Mississippi seemed to stop dead at Minneapolis. It had nothing to do with Canada. Raymond should have turned the car around and driven home. (Instead, he left it parked in Plattsburgh. He could not remember, later, the name of the street.)

He has never been back. His excuse used to be that he had nowhere to stay in Montreal. Marie sold the duplex and moved in with Berthe. The last thing he wanted to see on vacation was another standard motel unit, and he knew Berthe wouldn't have him in the house.

He enlisted for four years, then another three. Marie looked upon him as a prisoner, in time to be released. Released honorably? Yes, or he would not have been allowed to settle in Florida: He was still a Canadian in 1976; he could easily have been deported. When he became an American citizen and called Marie, expecting congratulations, she told him that 98 percent of the world's forest fires were started by Americans. It was all she could think of to say. He has been down there ever since, moving like a pendulum between Hollywood North and Hollywood Beach, Fort Lauderdale and the stretch of Miami known as Little Quebec, from the number of French Canadians who spend holidays there. They have their own newspaper, their own radio station and television channel, they import Montreal barbecue. Hearing their voices sometimes irritates him, sometimes makes him homesick for the summer of 1969, for the ease with which he jumped from cloud to cloud.

Marie still believes that "Parris Island" was one of Raymond's famous spelling mistakes. He must have spent part of his early youth, the least knowable, in a place called Paris, South Carolina. She often wonders about other mothers and sons, and whether children feel any of the pain they inflict. Berthe thinks of how easy it must have been for Raymond to leave, with the sun freshly risen, slanting along side streets, here and there front steps sluiced and dark, the sky not yet a burning glass. He must have supposed the rest of his life was going to be like that. When she and Marie ransacked the house on Boulevard Pie IX, looking for clues, imagining he'd left a letter, left some love, they kept the shades drawn, as if there were another presence in the rooms, tired of daylight.

FLORIDA

———

✤

$\mathcal{B}$erthe Carette's sister, Marie, spent eight Christmases of her life in Florida, where her son was establishing a future in the motel industry. Every time Marie went down she found Raymond starting over in a new place: His motels seemed to die on his hands. She used to come back to Montreal riddled with static electricity. Berthe couldn't hand her a teaspoon without receiving a shock, like a small silver bullet. Her sister believed the current was generated by a chemical change that occurred as she flew out of Fort Lauderdale toward a wet, dark, snowy city.

Marie had been living with Berthe ever since 1969, the year her husband died. She still expected what Berthe thought of as husband service: flights met, cabs hailed, doors held, tips attended to. Berthe had to take the bus out to Dorval Airport, with Marie's second-best fur coat over her arm and her high-heeled boots in a plastic bag. Through a glass barrier she could watch her sister gliding through customs, dressed in a new outfit of some sherbet tone—strawberry, lemon-peach—with everything matching, sometimes even her hair. She knew that Marie had been careful to tear the American store and union labels out of the clothes and sew in Canadian ones, in case customs asked her to strip.

"Don't tell me it's still winter," Marie would wail, kissing Berthe as if she had been away for months rather than just a few days. Guiding Marie's arms into the second-best-mink sleeves (paws and piecework), Berthe would get the first of the silvery shocks.

One year, when her son, Raymond, had fallen in love with a divorced woman twice his age (it didn't last), Marie arrived home crackling, exchanging sparks with everything she touched. When she ate a peppermint she felt it detonating in her mouth. Berthe had placed a pot of flowering paper-white narcissi on Marie's dressing table, a welcome-home present reflected on and on in the three mirrors. Marie shuffled along the carpeted passage, still in her boots. She had on her Florida manner, pretending she was in Berthe's flat by mistake. As soon as she saw the plant, she went straight over and gave it a kiss. The flower absorbed a charge and hurled it back. Berthe examined the spot on Marie's lip where the shock had struck. She could find nothing, no trace. Nevertheless Marie applied an ice cube.

She waited until midnight before calling Raymond, to get the benefit of the lower rate. His line was tied up until two: He said the police had been in, investigating a rumor. Marie told about the plant. He made her repeat the story twice, then said she had built up a reserve of static by standing on a shag rug with her boots on. She was not properly grounded when she approached the flower.

"Raymond could have done more with his life," said Marie, hanging up. Berthe, who was still awake, thought he had done all he could, given his brains and character. She did not say so: She never mentioned her nephew, never asked about his health. He had left home young, and caused a lot of grief and trouble.

On Marie's eighth visit, Raymond met her at the airport with a skinny woman he said was his wife. She had dark blond hair and one of those unset permanents, all corkscrews. Marie looked at her, and looked away. Raymond explained that he had moved back to Hollywood North. Marie said she didn't care, as long as she had somewhere to lay her head.

They left the terminal in silence. Outside, she said, "What's this car? Japanese? Your father liked a Buick."

"It belongs to Mimi," he said.

Marie got in front, next to Raymond, and the skinny woman climbed in behind. Marie said to Raymond in French, "You haven't told me her name."

"Well, I have, of course. I introduced you. Mimi."

"Mimi isn't a name."

"It's hers," he said.

"It can't be. It's always short for something—for Michèle. Did you ever hear of a Saint Mimi? She's not a divorced woman, is she? You were married in church?"

"In a kind of church," he said. "She belongs to a Christian movement."

Marie knew what that meant: pagan rites. "You haven't joined this thing—this movement?"

"I don't want to join anything," he said. "But it has changed my life."

Marie tried to consider this in an orderly way, going over in her mind the parts of Raymond's life that wanted changing. "What sort of woman would marry an only son without his mother's blessing?" she said.

"Mom," said Raymond, switching to English, and perhaps forgetting she hated to be called this. "She's twenty-nine. I'm thirty-three."

"What's her maiden name?" said Marie.

"Ask her," he said. "I didn't marry her family."

Marie eased the seat belt and turned around, smiling. The woman had her eyes shut. She seemed to be praying. Her skin was freckled, pale for the climate; perhaps she had come to one of the oases of the heart where there are no extremes of weather. As for Raymond, he was sharp and dry, with a high, feverish forehead. His past had evaporated. It annoyed him to have to speak French. On one of his mother's other visits he had criticized her Montreal accent, said he had heard better French in the streets of Saigon. He lit a cigarette, but before she could say, "Your father died of emphysema," threw it out.

Mimi, perhaps made patient by prayer, spoke up: "I am happy to welcome any mother of Raymond's. May we spend a peaceful and mutually enriching Christmas." Her voice moved on a strained, single note, like a soprano recitative. Shyness, Marie thought. She stole a second look. Her eyes, now open, were pale blue, with stubby black lashes. She seemed all at once beguiling and anxious, hoping to be forgiven before having mentioned the sin. A good point, but not good enough to make her a Catholic.

Raymond carried Marie's luggage to a decent room with cream walls and tangerine curtains and spread. The motel looked clean and prosperous, but so had the others. Mimi had gone off on business of her own. ("I'm feeling sick," she had said, getting out of the car, with one freckled hand on her stomach and the other against her throat.)

"She'll be all right," he told Marie.

Alone with Marie, he called her *Maman*, drew her to the window, showed her a Canadian flag flying next to the Stars and Stripes. The place was full of Canadians, he said. They stole like raccoons. One couple had even made off with the bathroom faucets. "Nice-looking people, too."

"Your father never ran down his own kind," said Marie. She did not mean to start an argument but to point out certain limits. He checked the towels, counted the hangers, raised (or lowered; she could not tell) the air-conditioning. He turned his back while she changed into her hibiscus-patterned chiffon, in case they were going out. In a mirror he watched her buckling her red sandals. Berthe's Christmas present.

"Mimi is the first woman I ever met who reminded me of you," he said. Marie let that pass. They walked arm in arm across the parking lot, and he pointed out different things that might interest her—Quebec license plates, a couple of dying palms. On the floor of the lobby lay a furled spruce tree, with its branches still tied. Raymond prodded the tree with his running shoe. It had been here for a week, he said, and it was already shedding. Perhaps Marie and Mimi would like to trim it.

"Trim it with what?" said Marie. Every year, for seven years, she had bought decorations, which Raymond had always thrown out with the tree.

"*I* don't know," he said. "Mimi wants me to set it up on a mirror."

Marie wondered what Raymond's title in this place might be. "Manager," he'd said, but he and Mimi lived like caretakers in an inconvenient arrangement of rooms off the lobby. To get to their kitchen, which was also a storage place for beer and soft drinks, Marie had to squeeze behind the front desk. Every door had a peephole and chain lock. Whenever a bell rang in the lobby Raymond looked carefully before undoing the lock. Another couple worked here, too, he explained, but they were off for Christmas.

The three ate dinner in the kitchen, hemmed in by boxes and crates. Marie asked for an apron, to protect her chiffon. Mimi did not own one, and seemed astonished at the request. She had prepared plain shrimp and boiled rice and plain fruit salad. No wonder Raymond was drying up. Marie showed them pictures of Berthe's Christmas tree, this year red and gold.

Mimi looked for a long time at a snapshot of Berthe, holding a glass, sitting with her legs crossed and her skirt perhaps a bit high. "What's in the glass?" she said.

"Gin does my sister a lot of good," said Marie. She had not enjoyed her shrimp, washed down with some diet drink.

"I'm surprised she never got married," said Mimi. "How old is she? Fifty-something? She still looks good, physically and mentally."

"I am surprised," said Marie, in French. "I am surprised at the turn of this conversation."

"Mimi isn't criticizing Aunt Berthe," said Raymond. "It's a compliment."

Marie turned to Mimi. "My sister never had to get married. She's always made good money. She buys her own fur coats."

Mimi did not know about Berthe, assistant office manager at Prestige Central Burners—a multinational with tentacles in two cities, one of them Cleveland. Last year Mr. Linden from the Cleveland office had invited Berthe out to dinner. His wife had left him; he was getting over the loss. Berthe intended to tell him she had made a lifetime commitment to the firm, with no leftover devotion. She suggested the Ritz-Carlton—she had been there once before, and had a favorite table. During dinner they talked about the different ways of cooking trout, and the bewildering architectural changes taking place in Cleveland and Montreal. Berthe mentioned that whenever a landmark was torn down people said, "It's as bad as Cleveland." It was hard to reconcile the need for progress with the claims of tradition. Mr. Linden said that tradition was flexible.

"I like the way you think," he said. "If only you had been a man, Miss Carette, with your intellect, and your powers of synthesis, you might have gone . . . ," and he pointed to the glass bowl of blueberry trifle on the dessert trolley, as if to say, "even farther."

The next day Berthe drew on her retirement savings account and made a down payment on a mink coat (pastel, fully let out) and wore the coat to work. That was her answer. Marie admired this counterstroke more than any feat of history. She wanted Mimi to admire it, too, but she was tired after the flight, and the shock of Raymond's marriage, and the parched, disappointing meal. Halfway through the story her English thinned out.

"What's she saying?" said Mimi. "This man gave her a coat?"

"It's too bad it couldn't have worked out better for Aunt Berthe," said Raymond. "A widower on the executive level. Well, not exactly a widower, but objectively the same thing. Aunt Berthe still looks great. You heard what Mimi said."

"Berthe doesn't need a widower," said Marie. "She can sit on her front balcony and watch widowers running in Parc Lafontaine any Sunday. There's no room in the flat for a widower. All the closets are full. In the spare-room closet there are things belonging to you, Raymond. That beautiful white rodeo belt with the silver buckle Aunt Berthe gave you for your fourteenth birthday. It cost Berthe thirty dollars, in dollars of that time, when the Canadian was worth more than the American."

"Ten cents more," said Raymond.

"Ten cents of another era," said Marie. "Like eighty cents today."

"Aunt Berthe can move if she feels crowded," he said. "Or she can just send me the belt." He spoke to Mimi. "People in Montreal move more often than in any other city in the world. I can show you figures. My father wasn't a Montrealer, so we always lived in just the one house. *Maman* sold it when he died."

"I wouldn't mind seeing that house," said Mimi, as though challenging Marie to produce it.

"Why should Berthe move?" said Marie. "First you want to tie her up with a stranger, then you want to throw her out of her home. She's got a three-bedroom place for a rent you wouldn't believe. She'd be crazy to let it go. It's easier to find a millionaire with clean habits than my sister's kind of flat."

"People don't get married to have three bedrooms," said Mimi, still holding Berthe's picture. "They get married for love and company."

"I am company," said Marie. "I love my sister, and my sister loves me."

"Do you think I married Raymond for *space*?" said Mimi.

Raymond said something in English. Marie did not know what it meant, but it sounded disgusting. "Raymond," she said. "Apologize to your wife."

"Don't talk to him," said Mimi. "You're only working him up."

"Don't you dare knock your chair over," said his mother. "Raymond! If you go out that door, I won't be here when you get back."

The two women sat quietly after the door slammed. Then Mimi picked up the fallen chair. "That's the real Raymond," she said. "That's Raymond, in public and private. I don't blame any man's mother for the way the man turns out."

"He had hair like wheat," said Marie. "It turned that rusty color when he was three. He had the face of an angel. It's the first time I've ever seen him like this. Of course, he has never been married before."

"He'll be lying on the bed now, sulking," said Mimi. "I'm not used to that. I hadn't been married before, either." She began rinsing plates at the sink. The slit of a window overlooked cars and the stricken palms. Tears ran down her cheeks. She tried to blot them on her arm. "I think he wants to leave me."

"So what if he does leave," said Marie, looking in vain for a clean dish towel. "A bad, disobedient boy. He ran away to Vietnam. The last man in our family. He should have been thinking about having sons instead of traveling around. Raymond's father was called Louis. My father's name was Odilon. Odilon-Louis—that's a nice name for a boy. It goes in any language."

"In my family we just have girls," said Mimi.

"Another thing Raymond did," said Marie. "He stole his father's gold watch. Then he lost it. Just took it and lost it."

"Raymond never lost that watch," said Mimi. "He probably sold it to two or three different people. Raymond will always be Raymond. I'm having a baby. Did he tell you that?"

"He didn't have to," said Marie. "I guessed it when we were in the car. Don't cry anymore. They can hear. The baby can hear you."

"He's already heard plenty from Raymond."

Marie's English died. "Look," she said, struggling. "This baby has a grandmother. He's got Berthe. *You've* got Berthe. Never mind Raymond."

"He'll need a father image," said Mimi. "Not just a lot of women."

"Raymond had one," said Marie. "He still joined the Marines."

"He or she," said Mimi. "I don't want to know. I want the surprise. I hope he likes me. She. It feels like a girl."

"It would be good to know in advance," said Marie. "Just for the shopping—to know what to buy. Do you want to save the rest of the shrimp or throw it out?"

"Save it," said Mimi. "Raymond hardly ate anything. He'll be hungry later on."

"That bad boy," said Marie. "I don't care if he never eats again. He'll find out what it's like, alone in the world. Without his mother. Without his aunt. Without his wife. Without his baby."

"I don't want him to be alone," said Mimi, showing Marie her streaked face, the sad little curls stuck to her wet cheeks. "He hasn't actually gone anywhere. I just said I thought he was thinking about it."

Marie tried to remember some of the English Berthe used. When she was talking to people from her office, Berthe would say, "All in good time," and "No way he can do that," and "Count on me," and "Not to worry."

"He won't leave you," said Marie. "No way I'll let him do that. Count on me." Her elbow brushed against the handle of the refrigerator door; she felt a silvery spark through the chiffon sleeve. This was the first time such a thing had happened in Florida; it was like an approving message from Berthe. Mimi wiped her hands on a paper towel and turned to Marie.

"Be careful," said Marie, enfolding Raymond's wife and Raymond's baby. "Be careful the baby doesn't get a shock. Everything around here is electric. I'm electric. We'll have to be careful from now on. We've got to make sure we're grounded." She had gone into French, but it didn't matter. The baby could hear, and knew what she meant.

ÉDOUARD,
JULIETTE,
LENA

A RECOLLECTION

―――――

❧

*J*married Magdalena here, in Paris, more than forty years ago. It was at the time when anti-Jewish thoughts and feelings had suddenly hardened into laws, and she had to be protected. She was a devout, lighthearted, probably wayward Catholic convert, of the sort Dominicans like to have tea with, but she was also Jewish and foreign—to be precise, born in Budapest, in 1904. A Frenchman who had grown rich manufacturing and exporting fine china brought her to Paris—oh, a long time ago, even before the Popular Front. He gave her up for the daughter of a count, and for his new career in right-wing politics, preaching moral austerity and the restoration of Christian values. Whenever Magdalena opened *Le Temps* and saw his name, she would burst out laughing. (I never noticed Magdalena actually *reading* a newspaper. She subscribed to a great many, but I think it was just to see what her friends and former friends were up to.) He let her keep the apartment on Quai Voltaire and the van Dongen portraits he'd bought because they looked like her—the same pert face and slender throat.

I never lived with Magdalena. After our wedding we spent part of a week together (to calm my parents down, I went home to sleep) and a night sitting up in a train. I never imagined sharing an address, my name over the doorbell, friends calling me at Magdalena's number, myself any more than a guest in the black-red-and-white-lacquered apartment on Quai Voltaire. The whole place smelled of gardenias. Along the hall hung stills from films she had worked in, in Vienna, Berlin—silent, minor, forgotten pictures, probably all destroyed. (The apartment was looted during the Occupation. When Magdalena came back, she had to sleep on the floor.) Her two pug dogs yapped and wore little chimes. The constant jangling drove them crazy. She washed them with scented soap and fed them at table, sitting on her lap. They had rashes all over their bodies, and were always throwing up.

I was twenty-two, still a student. My parents, both teachers in the lower grades, had made great sacrifices so that I could sit reading books into early manhood. The only home I could have offered Magdalena was a corner of their flat, in the Rue des Solitaires, up in the Nineteenth Arrondissement. Arabs and Africans live there now. In those days, it was the kind of district Jean Renoir and René Clair liked to use for those films that show chimney pots, and people walking around with loaves of bread, and gentle young couples that find and lose a winning lottery ticket. Until she met me, Magdalena had never heard of the Rue des Solitaires, or of my Métro stop, Place des Fêtes. The names sounded so charming that she thought I'd made them up. I begged her to believe that I never invented anything.

She was fair and slight, like all the women in Paris. In my view of the past, the streets are filled with blond-haired women, wearing absurd little hats, walking miniature dogs. (Wait, my memory tells me; not all women—not my mother.) Why had she given up acting? "Because I wasn't much good," she told me once. "And I was so lazy. I could work, really work, for a man in love with me—to do him a favor. That was all." From her sitting room, everything in it white, you saw across the Seine to the Place du Carrousel and part of the Tuileries. Between five and eight, men used to drop in, stand about with their backs to the view, lean down to scratch the ears of the pugs. Raymonde, the maid, knew everyone by name. They treated me kindly, though nobody ever went so far as to scratch my ears.

My parents were anticlerical and republican. In their conversation, Church and Republic locked horns like a couple of battling rams. I was never baptized. It broke their hearts that my marriage to Magdalena had to be blessed, at her insistence. The blessing was given in the church of Saint-Thomas-d'Aquin, in deep shadow, somewhere behind the altar. I had never been in a church before, except to admire windows or paintings; art belonged to the people, whatever the Vatican claimed. The ceremony was quick, almost furtive, but not because of Magdalena: *I* was the outsider, the pagan, unbaptized, unsaved.

My father and mother stayed home that day, eating the most solid lunch they could scrape together, to steady their nerves. They would have saved Magdalena, if only someone had asked—gladly, bravely, and without ruining my life. (That was how they saw it.) I suppose they could have locked her up in the broom closet. She could have stood in the dark, for years and years—as many as she needed. They could only hope, since they never prayed, that there would be no children.

I had already signed our children over to Rome a few days before the wedding, one afternoon just after lunch. Bargaining for their souls, uncreated, most certainly unwished for (I did not separate soul from body, since the first did not exist), went on in the white sitting room. Magdalena, as ever blithe and lighthearted, repeated whatever she'd been told to tell me, and I said yes, and signed. I can still hear the sound of her voice, though not the words she used; it was lower in pitch than a Frenchwoman's, alien to the ear because of its rhythm. It was a voice that sang a foreign song. Did she really expect to have children? She must have been thirty-six, and we were about to be separated for as long as the war might last. My signature was part of an elaborate ritual, in which she seemed to take immense delight. She had never been married before.

She had on a soft navy-blue dress, which had only that morning been brought to the door. This in war, in defeat. There were dressmakers and deliverymen. There was Chanel's Gardenia. There was coffee and sugar, there were polished silver trays and thin coffee cups. There was Raymonde, in black with white organdy, and Magdalena, with her sunny hair, her deep red nails, to pour.

I looked over at the far side of the Place du Carrousel, to some of the windows of the Ministry of Finance. Until just a few months ago, Magdalena had been invited to private ministry apartments to lunch. The tables were set with the beautiful glass and china that belonged to the people. Steadfast, uncomplaining men and women like my father and mother had paid their taxes so that Magdalena could lunch off plates they would never see—unless some further revolution took place, after which they might be able to view the plates in a museum.

I felt no anger thinking this. It was Magdalena I intended to save. As my wife, she would have an identity card with a French name. She would never have to baste a yellow star on her coat. She would line up for potatoes at a decent hour once France had run out of everything else.

Actually, Magdalena never lined up for anything. On the day when the Jews of Paris stood in long queues outside police stations, without pushing and shoving, and spelled their names and addresses clearly, so that the men coming to arrest them later on would not make a mistake, Magdalena went back to bed and read magazines. Nobody ever offered her a yellow star, but she found one for herself. It was lying on the ground, in front of the entrance to the Hôtel Meurice—so she said.

Walking the pugs in the rain, Magdalena had looked back to wave at Raymonde, polishing a window. (A publisher of comic books has the place now.) She crossed the Tuileries, then the Rue de Rivoli, and, stepping under the arcades, furled her silk umbrella. Rain had driven in; she skirted puddles in her thin shoes. Just level with the Meurice, where there were so many German officers that some people were afraid to walk there, or scorned to, she stopped to examine a star—soiled, trodden on. She moved it like a wet leaf with the point of her umbrella, bent, picked it up, dropped it in her purse.

"Why?" I had good reason to ask, soon after.

"To keep as a souvenir, a curiosity. To show my friends in Cannes, so that they can see what things are like in Paris."

I didn't like that. I had wanted to pull her across to my side, not to be dragged over to hers.

A day later we set off by train for the South, which was still a free zone. The only Nazis she would be likely to encounter there would be French; I gave Magdalena a lecture on how to recognize and avoid them. We sat side by side in a second-class compartment, in the near dark. (Much greater suspicion attended passengers in first; besides that, I could not afford it.) Magdalena, unfortunately, was dressed for tea at the Ritz. She would have retorted that nothing could be plainer than a Molyneux suit and a diamond pin. The other passengers, three generations of a single family, seemed to be asleep. On the new, unnatural frontier dividing France North from South, the train came to a halt. We heard German soldiers coming on board, to examine our papers. Trying not to glance at Magdalena, I fixed my eyes on the small overnight case she had just got down from the rack and sat holding on her lap. When the train stopped, all the lights suddenly blazed—seemed to blaze; they were dull and brown. Magdalena at once stood up, got her case down without help, removed a novel (it was *Bella*, by Jean Giraudoux), and began to read.

I thought that she had done the very thing bound to make her seem suspect. Her past, intricate and inscrutable, was summed up by the rich leather of the case and the gold initials on the lid and the tiny gold padlock and key, in itself a piece of jewelry. That woman could not possibly be the wife of that young man, with his rolled-up canvas holdall with the cracked leather straps. The bag was not even mine; it had belonged to my mother, or an aunt. I reached over and turned her case around, so that I could open it, as if I were anxious to cooperate, to get things ready for inspection. The truth was, I did not want the German peasants in uniform to read her initials, to ask what her maiden name was, or to have cause for envy; the shut case might have been offered for sale in a window along the Rue du Faubourg-Saint-Honoré, at extortionate cost. I thought that if those peasants, now approaching our compartment, had not been armed, booted, temporarily privileged, they might have served a different apprenticeship—learned to man mirror-walled elevators, carry trays at shoulder level, show an underling's gratitude for Magdalena's escort's tip. I flung the lid back, against her jacket of thin wool; and there, inside, on top of some folded silk things the color of the palest edge of sunrise, lay a harsh star. I smoothed the silken stuff and palmed the star and got it up my sleeve.

In my terrible fright my mind caught on something incidental—that Magdalena had never owned anything else so coarse to the touch. She had never been a child, had never played with sand and mud. She had been set down in a large European city, smart hat tilted, rings swiveled so that she could pull her gloves on, knowing all there is about gold padlocks and keys. "Cosmopolitan," an incendiary word now, flared in my mind. In the quiet train (no train is so still as one under search), its light seemed to seek out crude editorials, offensive cartoons, repulsive graffiti.

The peasants in uniform—they were two—slid open the compartment door. They asked no more than any frontier inspector, but the reply came under the heading of life and death. "Cosmopolitan" had flared like a star; it dissolved into a dirty little puddle. Its new, political meaning seeped into my brain and ran past my beliefs and convictions, and everything my parents stood for. I felt it inside my skull, and I wondered if it would ever evaporate.

One of the peasants spoke, and Magdalena smiled. She told me later that he had the accent said to have been Wagner's. Seeing the open case, he plunged his hand under the silks and struck a hairbrush. He shut the lid and stared dumbly at the initials. The other one in the meanwhile frowned at our papers. Then the pair of them stumbled out.

Our fellow passengers looked away, as people do when someone with the wrong ticket is caught in first class. I put the case back on the rack and muttered an order. Magdalena obediently followed me out to the corridor. It may have looked as if we were just standing, smoking, but I was trying to find out how she, who had never owned anything ugly, had come into possession of this thing. She told me about the Rue de Rivoli, and that she had thought the star would interest her friends in Cannes: They would be able to see how things were now up in Paris. If she had buried it next to her hairbrush, it would have seemed as though she had something to hide. She said she had nothing to hide; absolutely nothing.

I had been running with sweat; now I felt cold. I asked her if she was crazy. She took this for the anxious inquiry of a young man deeply in love. Her nature was sunny, and as good as gold. She laughed and told me she had been called different things but never crazy. She started to repeat some of them, and I kissed her to shut her up. The corridor was jammed with people lying sprawled or sitting on their luggage, and she sounded demented and foreign.

I wondered what she meant by "friends in Cannes." To women of her sort, "friend" is often used as a vague substitute for "lover." (Notice how soon after thinking "cosmopolitan" I thought "of her sort.") She had mentioned the name of the people who were offering her shelter in Cannes; it was a French name but perhaps an alias. I had a right to know more. She was my wife. For the first and the last time I considered things in that particular way: After all, she *is* my wife. I was leaving the train at Marseilles, though my ticket read Cannes. From Marseilles, I would try to get to North Africa, then to England. Magdalena would sit the war out in an airy villa— the kind aliens can afford.

When I next said something—about getting back to our seats—my voice was too high. It still rises and thins when I feel under strain. (In the 1950s, when I was often heard over the radio, interviewing celebrated men about their early struggles and further ambitions, I would get about two letters a year from women saying they envied my mother.)

It was probably just as well that we were spending our last night among strangers. After our wedding we had almost ceased to be lovers. I had to keep the peace at home, and Magdalena to prepare to leave without showing haste. I thought she was tense and tired; but I appreciate now that Magdalena was never fatigued or wrought-up, and I can only guess she had to say good-bye to someone else. She sent the dogs away to Raymonde's native town in Normandy, mentioning to the concierge that it was for the sake of their health and for a few days only. At the first sign of fright, of hurry, or of furniture removed to storage, the concierge might have been halfway to the police station to report on the tenant who had so many good friends, and whose voice sang a foreign tune.

In the compartment, I tried to finish the thoughts begun in the corridor. I had married her to do the right thing; that was established. Other men have behaved well in the past, and will continue to do so. It comforted me to know I was not the only one with a safe conscience. Thinking this in the darkened, swaying compartment meant that I was lucid and generous, and also something of a louse. I whispered to Magdalena, "What is bad behavior? What is the worst?" The question did not seem to astonish her. Our union was blessed, and she was my wife forevermore, and she could fall back on considerable jurisprudence from the ledgers of Heaven to prove it; but I was still the student who had brought his books to Quai Voltaire, who had looked up to make sure she was still in the room, and asked some question from beyond his experience. She took my hand and said the worst *she* remembered was the Viennese novelist who had taken some of her jewelry (she meant "stolen") and pawned it and kept all the money.

We said good-bye in Marseilles, on the station platform. In the southern morning light her eyes were pale blue. There were armed men in uniform everywhere. She wore a white suit and a thin blouse and a white hat I had never seen before. She had taken a suitcase into the filthy toilet and emerged immaculate. I had the feeling that she could hardly wait to get back on the train and roll on to new adventures.

"And now I am down here, away from all my friends in Paris," she had the gall to say, shading her eyes. It was a way of showing spirit, but I had never known anyone remotely like her, and I probably thought she should be tight-lipped. By "all my friends" she must have meant men who had said, "If you ever need help," knowing she would never ask; who might have said, "Wasn't it awful, tragic, about Magdalena?" if she had never been seen again.

She had left her luggage and jewelry untended in the compartment. I was glad to see she wore just her wedding ring; otherwise, she might have looked too actressy, and drawn attention. (I had no idea how actresses were supposed to look.) Sometimes she used an amber cigarette holder with a swirl of diamond dust like the tail of a comet. She must have sold it during the war; or perhaps lost it, or given it away.

"You look like a youth leader," she said. I was Paris-pale, but healthy. My hair was clipped short. I might have been about to lead police and passengers in patriotic singsong. I was patriotic, but not as the new regime expected its young to be; I was on my way to be useful to General de Gaulle, if he would have me. I saw myself floating over the map of France, harnessed to a dazzling parachute, with a gun under my arm.

We had agreed not to stare at each other once we'd said good-bye. Magdalena kissed me and turned and pulled herself up the high steps of the train. I got a soft, bent book out of my canvas holdall and began to read something that spoke only to me. So the young think, and I was still that young: Poetry is meant for one reader only. Magdalena, gazing tenderly down from the compartment window, must have seen just the shape of the poem on the page. I turned away from the slant of morning sunlight—not away from her. When the train started to move, she reached down to me, but I was too far to touch. A small crucifix on a chain slipped free of her blouse. I stuck to our promise and never once raised my eyes. At the same time, I saw everything—the shade of her white hat brim aslant on her face, her hand with the wedding ring.

I put the star in my book, to mark the place: I figured that if I was caught I was done for anyway. When my adventures were over, I would show it to my children; I did not for a second see Magdalena as their mother. They were real children, not souls to be bargained. So it seems to me now. It shows how far into the future I thought you could safely carry a piece of the past. Long after the war, I found the star, still in the same book, and I offered to give it back to Magdalena, but she said she knew what it was like.

THE COLONEL'S CHILD

⁓❦⁓

I got to London by way of Marseilles and North Africa, having left Paris more than a year before. My aim was to join the Free French and General de Gaulle. I believed the weight of my presence could tip the scales of war, like one vote in a close election. There was no vanity in this. London was the peak of my hopes and desires. I could look back and see a tamed landscape. My past life dwindled and vanished in that long perspective. I was twenty-three.

In my canvas holdall I carried a tobacco pouch someone had given me, filled with thin reddish soil from Algeria. In those days earth from France and earth from Algeria meant the same thing. Only years later was I able to think, I must have been crazy. When you are young, your patriotism is like metaphysical frenzy. Later, it becomes one more aspect of personal crankiness.

Instead of a hero's welcome I was given forms to fill out. These questionnaires left no room for postscripts, and so only a skeleton of myself could be drawn. I was Édouard B., born in Paris, father a schoolteacher (so was my mother, but I wasn't asked), student of literature and philosophy, single, no dependents.

Some definitions seemed incomplete. For instance, I was not entirely single: Before leaving Paris I had married a Jewish-born actress, so as to give her the security of my name. As far as I knew, she was now safe and in Cannes. At the same time, I was not a married man. The marriage was an incident, gradually being rubbed out in the long perspective I've described. So I saw it; so I would insist. You have to remember the period, and France occupied, to imagine how one could think and behave. We always say this—"Think of the times we had to live in"—when the past is dragged forward, all the life gone out of it, and left unbreathing at our feet.

Instead of sending me off to freeze on a parade ground, the Free French kept me in London. I took it to mean they wanted to school me in sabotage work and drop me into France. I did not know special parachute training might be needed. I thought you held your breath and jumped.

Two months later I lay in a hospital ward with a broken nose, broken left arm, and fractures in both legs. They had been trying to teach me to ride a motorbike, and on my first time out I skidded into a wall. The instructor came and sat by my bedside. He was about twice my age, a former policeman from Rouen. He said the Free French weren't quite casting me off, but some of them wondered if I was meant for a fighting force in exile. I was a cerebral type, who needed the peace of an office job, with no equipment to smash—not even a typewriter. I asked if General de Gaulle had been informed about my accident.

"Is he a friend of yours?" said the instructor.

"I've seen him," I said. "I saw him in Carlton Gardens. He came out the door and down some steps, and got into his car. I was carrying a lot of parcels, so I couldn't salute. I don't think he noticed. I hope not."

There was a silence, during which the instructor stared at his watch. Presently, he inquired what I wanted to do with my life.

"I think I am a poet," I said. "I can't be sure."

After that they sent me a regular hospital visitor, a volunteer. Juliette was her name. She was seventeen, from Bordeaux, the daughter of a colonel who had followed de Gaulle to London. She had a precise, particular way of speaking, with every syllable given full value and the consonants treated like little stones. It was not the native accent of Bordeaux, which anyone can imitate, or the everyday French of Paris I'd grown up with, but the tone, almost undefinable, of the French Protestant upper class. I had not heard it before, not consciously, and for the moment had no means of placing it. I thought she had picked up an affectation of some sort while learning English and had carried it over to French. She had, besides, the habit of thrusting into French conversation brief, joyous, and usually irrelevant remarks in English: "You don't say!" "Oh, what a shame!" "How glad I am for you!" "How gorgeous!"

From behind a mask of splints and bandages I appraised her face, which was still childlike, rounded as if over a layer of cream. A beret kept slipping and sliding off her dark hair. "Oh, what a pity!" she remarked, pulling it back on. She was dressed in the least becoming clothes I had ever seen on a young woman—a worn and drooping tunic, thick black stockings, and a navy sweater frayed at the cuffs. She had spent five months in an English girls' school, she told me, and this was the remains of a uniform. She had nothing else to wear, nothing that fitted. Her mother was too busy to shop.

"Can't you shop for yourself?"

"It's not done," she said. "I mean, we don't do things that way."

"Who is we?"—for she still puzzled me.

"Besides, I've got no money." This seemed a sensible explanation. I wondered why she had bothered to make another. "My mother teaches English to French recruits. Actually, she doesn't know much, but she can make them read traffic signs."

"You mean, 'Stop'?"

"Well, there are other things—'No Entry.' " She looked troubled, as if she were not succeeding in the tranquil, sleepy conversation that is supposed to keep a victim's mind off his wounds.

I had lost six front teeth in the accident. Through the gap, Juliette fed me the mess the English call custard. My right arm was fine, but I let her do it. She was grave, intent—a little girl playing. She might have been poking a spoon into a doll's porcelain face. When I refused to swallow any more, she got a bottle of eau de cologne and a facecloth out of a satchel and carefully wiped my hands and wrists and around my neck—whatever was bare and visible. I wondered if she would offer to comb my hair and cut my nails, but the nursing part of the game was over. She sat with her ankles crossed and her hands clasped, a good girl on a visit, and told me that her father, the colonel, was an outcast with a price on his head. From the care she took not to say where he was, I understood they had sent him to France, on a mission. Forgetting about secrets, she suddenly said she yearned to be smuggled into France, too, so that she could join him and they might blow up bridges together.

"I wanted to do that," I said. "That's why I came here. But I'm useless. I may come out of this with a scarred face, or a limp. I'd be at risk."

"Oh, I know," said Juliette. "The Germans would catch you and shoot you. They'd look for a secret agent all covered with scars. Oh, what a nuisance!"

Sweet Juliette. Her dark eyes held all the astonished eagerness of a child of twelve. I often think I should want to be back there, with a Juliette still virginal, untouched, saying encouraging things such as "all covered with scars," but at the age I am now it would bore me.

She came to the hospital twice a week, then every day. Her mother was at work, and I felt the girl had time on her hands and was often lonely. She was with me when they took the last of the mask off. "Well?" I said. "Tell me the worst."

"I can't," she said. "I don't know how you were before." She held up a pocket mirror. My nose was broken, all right, and I had thick, bruised cheekbones, like a Cossack. For someone who had never been to war, I was amazingly the image of an old soldier.

I left the hospital on crutches. There was no such thing as therapy—you got going or you did not. The organization found me a room on Baker Street, not far from where Juliette lived with her mother, as it turned out, and they gave me low-grade and harmless work to do. As my instructor had predicted, I was let nowhere near a typewriter, and once, I remember, someone even snatched a pencil sharpener away. Juliette used to come to the office, though she wasn't supposed to, and sit by my desk as if it were a bed. She had got rid of the uniform, but her new clothes, chosen by her mother, were English and baggy, in the grays and mustards Englishwomen favored. They seemed picked deliberately to make her creamy skin sallow, her slenderness gaunt. The mother was keeping her plain, I thought, perhaps to keep her out of trouble. Why didn't Juliette rebel? She was eighteen by now, but forty years ago eighteen was young. I wondered why she hung around me, what she wanted. I thought I guessed, but I decided not to know. I didn't want it said I had destroyed two items of French property—a motorcycle and a colonel's child. It was here, in London, that I was starting to get the hang of French society. In our reduced world, everyone in it a symbol of native, inborn rank, Juliette stood higher than some random young man who had merely laid his life on the line. She had connections, simply by the nature of how things were ordered.

I asked her once if there was a way of getting a message to my mother, in Paris—just a word to say I was safe. She pretended not to hear but about a month later said, "No, it's too dangerous. Besides, they don't trust you."

"Don't trust me? Why not?"

"I'm not sure."

"Do you?" I said.

"That's different."

Her mother was out most evenings. When Juliette was alone, I brought my rations around, and she cooked our supper. We drank—only because everybody did—replacing the whiskey in her mother's precious Haig bottle with London tap water. Once, Juliette tried restoring the color with cold tea, and there was hell to pay. When the news came from France that her father had been arrested and identified, she came straight to me.

"I'll never see him again," she said. "I haven't even got a decent snapshot of him. My mother has them all. She's got them in a suitcase. I feel sick. Feel my forehead. Feel my cheeks." She took my hand. "Feel the back of my neck. Feel my throat," she said, dragging my hand. We left the office and went to her flat and pulled the blackout curtain. The sun was shining on the other side of the street, where everything was bombed, but she didn't want to see it.

"How do you know your mother's not going to walk in?" I said. "She may want to be alone with you. She may want a quiet place to cry."

Juliette shook her head. "We're not like that. We don't do those things."

I think of the love and despair she sent out to me, the young shoots wild and blind, trusting me for support. She asked me to tell my most important secret, so that we would be bound. The most intimate thing I could say was that I was writing less poetry and had started a merciless novel about the French in London.

"I could tell you a lot," said Juliette. "Heroes' wives sleeping with other men."

"It's not that sort of novel," I said. "In my novel, they're all dead, but they don't know it. Every character is in a special Hell, made to measure."

"That's not how it is," she said. "We're not dead or in Hell. We're just here, waiting. We don't know what Hell will be like. Nobody knows. And some of us are going to be together in Heaven." She put her face against mine, saying this. It never occurred to me that she meant it, literally. I thought her Calvinism was just an organized form of disbelief. "Haven't you got some better secret?" she said. I supposed that schoolgirls talked this way, pledging friendship, and I wondered what she was taking me for. "Well," she said presently, "will you marry me anyway, even without a secret?"

Nobody coerced me into a life with Juliette. There were no tears, no threats, and I was not afraid of her mother. All I had to say was "I don't know yet" or "We'll see." I think I wanted to get her out of her loneliness. When for all her shyness she asked if I loved her, I said I would never leave her, and I am sure we both thought it meant the same thing. A few days later she told her mother that we were engaged and that nothing would keep her from marrying me after the war, and, for the first time since she could remember, she saw her mother cry.

Instead of a ring I gave Juliette some of the Algerian soil. She thanked me but confessed she had no idea what to do with it. Should it be displayed in a saucer, on a low table? Should she seal it up in a labeled, dated envelope? Tactful from infancy, she offered the gift to her mother, her rival in grief.

Now that we were "engaged," I began to see what the word covered for Juliette, and I had no qualms about smuggling her into my room—though never, of course, late at night. We took the mattress off the sagging daybed and put it on the floor, in front of the gas fire. Juliette would take her clothes off and tell me about her early years, though I didn't always listen. Sometimes she talked about the life waiting for us in Paris, and the number of children we would have, and the names we would give them. I remember a Thomas and a Claire.

"How many children should we have?" she said. "I'd say about ten. Well, seven. At least five."

Her clothes were scattered all over the floor, and the room was cold, in spite of the fire, but she didn't seem to feel it. "I hate children," I said. I was amazed that I could say something so definite and so cruel, and that sounded so true. When had I stopped liking them? Perhaps when I adopted the colonel's child, believing she would never grow up. I could have said, "I don't like *other* children," but nothing about this conversation was thought out.

"You will love them," she said happily. "You'll see." She held her spread fingers against the gas flame, counting off their names. Each finger stood for a greedy, willful personality, as tough as a fist. An only child, she invented playmates and named them, and I was supposed to bring them to life.

"I know it sounds stupid," she said, "but I kept my dolls until I was fifteen. My mother finally gave them away."

"Brothers and sisters," I said.

"No, just dolls. But they did have names."

"Is that one of your secrets?" "Secrets" had become charged with erotic meaning, when we were alone.

"You've got a special secret," she said.

"Yes. I've torn up my novel."

"Oh, how lovely for you! Or is that sad?"

"I'm just giving it up. I'll never start another."

"You've got another secret," she said. "You're married to someone." As she said this, she seemed to become aware that the room was cold. She shivered and reached for her dress, and drew it around her like a shawl. "A person went to see your mother. She—your mother—said to tell you your wife was all right. Your *wife*," said Juliette, trying to control her voice, "is in the south of France. She has managed to send your mother a pound of onions. To eat," said Juliette, as I went on staring. "Onions, to eat."

"I did get married," I said. "But she's not my wife. I did it to save her. I've got her yellow star somewhere."

"I'd like to see it," said Juliette, politely.

"It is made of cheap, ugly material," I said, as if that were the only thing wrong.

"I think you should put some clothes on," said Juliette. "If you're going to tell about your wife."

"She isn't my wife," I said. "The marriage was just something legal. Apart from being legal, it doesn't count."

"She may not be your wife," said Juliette, "but she is your mother's daughter-in-law." She drew up her knees and bent her head on them, as if it were disgraceful to watch me dressing. "You mean," she said, after a time, "that it doesn't count as a secret?" I gathered up the rest of her clothes and put them beside her on the mattress. "Does it count as anything?"

"I'll walk you home," I said.

"You don't need to."

"It's late. I can't have you wandering around in the blackout."

She dressed, slowly, sitting and kneeling. "I am glad she is safe and well," she said. "It would be too bad if you had done all that for nothing. She must be very grateful to you."

I had never thought about gratitude. It seemed to me that, yes, she was probably grateful. I suddenly felt impatient for the war to end, so that I could approach her, hand in hand with Juliette, and ask for a divorce and a blessing.

Juliette, kneeling, fastened the buttons of the latest flour sack her mother had chosen. "Why did you tear up your novel?" she said.

Because I can't wrench life around to make it fit some fantasy. Because I don't know how to make life sound worse or better, or how to make it sound true. Instead of saying this, I said, "How do you expect me to support ten children?" The colonel's wife didn't like me much, but she had said that after the war there were a few people she could introduce me to. She had mentioned something about radio broadcasting, and I liked the idea.

Juliette was still kneeling, with only part of the hideous dress buttoned up. I looked down at her bent head. She must have been thinking that she had tied herself to a man with no money, no prospects, and no connections. Who wasn't entirely single. Who might be put on a charge for making a false declaration. Who had a broken nose and a permanent limp. Who, so far, had never finished anything he'd started. Perhaps she was forgetting one thing: I had got to London.

"I could stay all night," she said. "If you want me to."

"Your mother would have the police out," I said.

"She'd never dare," said Juliette. "I've never called the police because *she* didn't come home."

"It would be . . ." I tried to think of what it could be for us. "It would be radical."

Her hands began to move again, the other way, unbuttoning. She was the colonel's child, she had already held her breath and jumped, and that was the start and the end of it.

"We may be in big trouble over this," I said.

"Oh, what a pity," she said. "We'll always be together. We will always be happy. How lovely! What a shame!"

I think she still trusted me at that moment; I hope so.

RUE DE LILLE

―――――――

❧

*M*y second wife, Juliette, died in the apartment on Rue de Lille, where she had lived—at first alone, more or less, then with me—since the end of the war. All the rooms gave onto the ivy-hung well of a court, and were for that reason dark. We often talked about looking for a brighter flat, on a top floor with southern exposure and a wide terrace, but Parisians seldom move until they're driven to. "We know the worst of what we've got," we told each other. "It's better than a bad surprise."

"And what about your books?" Juliette would add. "It would take you months to get them packed, and in the new place you'd never get them sorted." I would see myself as Juliette saw me, crouched over a slanting, shaking stack of volumes piled on a strange floor, cursing and swearing as I tried to pry out a dictionary. "Just the same, I don't intend to die here," she also said.

I once knew someone who believed drowning might be easy, even pleasant, until he almost drowned by accident. Juliette's father was a colonel who expected to die in battle or to be shot by a German firing squad, but he died of typhus in a concentration camp. I had once, long ago, imagined for myself a clandestine burial with full honors after some Resistance feat, but all I got out of the war was a few fractures and a broken nose in a motorcycle accident.

Juliette had thirty-seven years of blacked-out winter mornings in Rue de Lille. She was a few days short of her sixtieth birthday when I found her stretched out on the floor of our bedroom, a hand slackened on a flashlight. She had been trying to see under a chest of drawers, and her heart stopped. (Later, I pulled the chest away from the wall and discovered a five-franc coin.) Her gray-and-dark hair, which had grown soft and wayward with age, was tied back with a narrow satin ribbon. She looked more girlish than at any time since I'd first met her. (She fell in love with me young.) She wore a pleated flannel skirt, a tailored blouse, and one of the thick cardigans with gilt buttons she used to knit while watching television. She had been trained to believe that to look or to listen quietly is to do nothing; she would hum along with music, to show she wasn't idle. She was discreet, she was generous to a sensible degree, she was anything but contentious. I often heard her remark, a trifle worriedly, that she was never bored. She was faithful, if "faithful" means avoiding the acknowledged forms of trouble. She was patient. I know she was good. Any devoted male friend, any lover, any husband would have shown up beside her as selfish, irritable, even cruel. She displayed so little of the ordinary kinds of jealousy, the plain marital do-you-often-have-lunch-with-her? sort, that I once asked her if she had a piece missing.

"Whoever takes this place over," she said, when we spoke of moving, "will be staggered by the size of the electricity bills." (Juliette paid them; I looked after a number of other things.) We had to keep the lights turned on all day in winter. The apartment was L-shaped, bent round two sides of a court, like a train making a sharp turn. From our studies, at opposite ends of the train, we could look out and see the comforting glow of each other's working life, a lamp behind a window. Juliette would be giving some American novel a staunch, steady translation; I might be getting into shape my five-hour television series, *Stendhal and the Italian Experience*, which was to win an award in Japan.

We were together for a duration of time I daren't measure against the expanse of Juliette's life; it would give me the feeling that I had decamped to a height of land, a survivor's eminence, so as to survey the point at which our lives crossed and mingled and began to move in the same direction: a long, narrow reach of time in the Rue de Lille. It must be the washy, indefinite colorations of blue that carpeted, papered, and covered floors, walls, and furniture and shaded our lamps which cast over that reach the tone of a short season. I am thinking of the patches of distant, neutral blue that appear over Paris in late spring, when it is still wet and cold in the street and tourists have come too early. The tourists shelter in doorways, trying to read their soaked maps, perennially unprepared in their jeans and thin jackets. Overhead, there are scrapings of a color that carries no threat and promises all.

That choice, Juliette's preference, I sometimes put down to her Calvinist sobriety—call it a temperament—and sometimes to a refinement of her Huguenot taste. When I was feeling tired or impatient, I complained that I had been consigned to a Protestant Heaven by an arbitrary traffic cop, and that I was better suited to a pagan Hell. Again, as I looked round our dining-room table at the calm, clever faces of old friends of Juliette's family, at their competent and unassuming wives, I saw what folly it might be to set such people against a background of buttercup yellow or apple green. The soft clicking of their upper-class Protestant consonants made conversation distant and neutral, too. It was a voice that had puzzled me the first time I'd heard it from Juliette. I had supposed, mistakenly, that she was trying it on for effect; but she was wholly natural.

The sixteenth-century map of Paris I bought for her birthday is still at the framer's; I sent a check but never picked it up. I destroyed her private correspondence without reading it, and gave armfuls of clothes away to a Protestant charity. To the personal notice of her death in *Le Monde* was attached a brief mention of her father, a hero of the Resistance for whom suburban streets are named; and of her career as a respected translator, responsible for having introduced postwar American literature to French readers; and of her husband, the well-known radio and television interviewer and writer, who survived her.

Another person to survive her was my first wife. One night when Juliette and I were drinking coffee in the little sitting room where she received her women friends, and where we watched television, Juliette said, again, "But how much of what she says does she believe? About her Catholicism, and all those fantasies running round in her head—that she is your true and only wife, that your marriage is registered in Heaven, that you and she will be together in another world?"

"Those are things people put in letters," I said. "They sit down alone and pour it out. It's sincere at that moment. I don't know why she would suddenly be *insincere*."

"After all the trouble she's made," said Juliette. She meant that for many years my wife would not let me divorce.

"She couldn't help that," I said.

"How do you know?"

"I don't know. It's what I think. I hardly knew her."

"You must have known *something*."

"I haven't seen her more than three or four times in the last thirty-odd years, since I started living with you."

"What do you mean?" said Juliette. "You saw her just once, with me. We had lunch. You backed off asking for the divorce."

"You can't ask for a divorce at lunch. It had to be done by mail."

"And since then she hasn't stopped writing," said Juliette. "Do you mean three or four times, or do you mean once?"

I said, "Once, probably. Probably just that once."

Viewing me at close range, as if I were a novel she had to translate, Juliette replied that one ought to be spared unexpected visions. Just now, it was as if three walls of the court outside had been bombed flat. Through a bright new gap she saw straight through to my first marriage. We—my first wife and I—postured in the distance, like characters in fiction.

I had recently taken part in a panel discussion, taped for television, on the theme "What Literature, for Which Readers, at Whose Price?" I turned away from Juliette and switched on the set, about ten minutes too early. Juliette put the empty cups and the coffeepot on a tray she had picked up in Milan, the summer I was researching the Stendhal, and carried the tray down the dim passage to the kitchen. I watched the tag end of the late news. It must have been during the spring of 1976. Because of the energy crisis, daylight saving had been established. Like any novelty, it was deeply upsetting. People said they could no longer digest their food or be nice to their children, and that they needed sedation to help them through the altered day. A doctor was interviewed; he advised a light diet and early bed until mind and body adjusted to the change.

I turned, smiling, to where Juliette should have been. My program came on then, and I watched myself making a few points before I got up and went to find her. She was in the kitchen, standing in the dark, clutching the edge of the sink. She did not move when I turned the light on. I put my arms around her, and we came back to her sitting room and watched the rest of the program together. She was knitting squares of wool to be sewn together to make a blanket; there was always, somewhere, a flood or an earthquake or a flow of refugees, and those who outlasted jeopardy had to be covered.

LENA

❧

*I*n her prime, by which I mean in her beauty, my first wife, Magdalena, had no use for other women. She did not depend upon women for anything that mattered, such as charm and enjoyment and getting her bills paid; and as for exchanging Paris gossip and intimate chitchat, since she never confided anything personal and never complained, a man's ear was good enough. Magdalena saw women as accessories, to be treated kindly—maids, seamstresses, manicurists—or as comic minor figures, the wives and official fiancées of her admirers. It was not in her nature to care what anyone said, and she never could see the shape of a threat even when it rolled over her, but I suspect that she was called some of the senseless things she was called, such as "Central European whore" and "Jewish adventuress," by women.

Now that she is nearly eighty and bedridden, she receives visits from women—the residue of an early wave of Hungarian emigration. They have small pink noses, wear knitted caps pulled down to their eyebrows, and can see on dark street corners the terrible ghost of Béla Kun. They have forgotten that Magdalena once seemed, perhaps, disreputable. She is a devout Catholic, and she says cultivated, moral-sounding things, sweet to the ears of half a dozen widows of generals and bereft sisters of bachelor diplomats. They crowd her bedside table with bottles of cough mixture, lemons, embroidered table napkins, jars of honey, and covered bowls of stewed plums, the juice from which always spills. They call Magdalena "Lena."

She occupies a bed in the only place that would have her—a hospital on the northern rim of Paris, the color of jails, daubed with graffiti. The glass-and-marble lobby commemorates the flashy prosperity of the 1960s. It contains, as well as a vandalized coffee machine and a plaque bearing the name of a forgotten minister of health, a monumental example of the art of twenty years ago: a white foot with each toenail painted a different color. In order to admire this marvel, and to bring Magdalena the small comforts I think she requires, I need to travel a tiring distance by the underground suburban train. On these expeditions I carry a furled umbrella: The flat, shadeless light of this line is said to attract violent crime. In my wallet I have a card attesting to my right to sit down, because of an accident suffered in wartime. I never dare show the card. I prefer to stand. Anything to do with the Second World War, particularly its elderly survivors, arouses derision and ribaldry and even hostility in the young.

Magdalena is on the fourth floor (no elevator) of a wing reserved for elderly patients too frail to be diverted to nursing homes—assuming that a room for her in any such place could be found. The old people have had it drummed into them that they are lucky to have a bed, that the waiting list for their mattress and pillow lengthens by the hour. They must not seem too capricious, or dissatisfied, or quarrelsome, or give the nurses extra trouble. If they persist in doing so, their belongings are packed and their relatives sent for. A law obliges close relatives to take them in. Law isn't love, and Magdalena has seen enough distress and confusion to make her feel thoughtful.

"Families are worse than total war," she says. I am not sure what her own war amounted to. As far as I can tell, she endured all its rigors in Cannes, taking a daily walk to a black-market restaurant, her legs greatly admired by famous collaborators and German officers along the way. Her memory, when she wants to be bothered with it, is like a brief, blurry, self-centered dream.

"But what were you *doing* during those years?" I have asked her. (My mother chalked Gaullist slogans on walls in Paris. The father of my second wife died deported. I joined the Free French in London.)

"I was holding my breath," she answers, smiling.

She shares a room with a woman who suffers from a burning rash across her shoulders. Medicine that relieves the burning seems to affect her mind, and she will wander the corridors, wondering where she is, weeping. The hospital then threatens to send her home, and her children, in a panic, beg that the treatment be stopped. After a few days the rash returns, and the woman keeps Magdalena awake describing the pain she feels—it is like being flogged with blazing nettles, she says. Magdalena pilfers tranquilizers and gets her to take them, but once she hit the woman with a pillow. The hospital became nasty, and I had to step in. Fortunately, the supervisor of the aged-and-chronic department had seen me on television, taking part in a literary game ("Which saint might Jean-Paul Sartre have wanted most to meet?"), and that helped our case.

Actually, Magdalena cannot be evicted—not just like that. She has no family, and nowhere to go. Her continued existence is seen by the hospital as a bit of a swindle. They accepted her in the first place only because she was expected to die quite soon, releasing the bed.

"Your broken nose is a mistake," she said to me the other day.

My face was damaged in the same wartime accident that is supposed to give me priority seating rights in public transport. "It lends you an air of desperate nerve, as if a Malraux hero had wandered into a modern novel and been tossed out on his face."

Now, this was hard on a man who had got up earlier than usual and bought a selection of magazines for Magdalena before descending to the suburban line, with its flat, worrying light. A man who had just turned sixty-five. Whose new bridge made him lisp. She talks the way she talked in the old days, in her apartment with the big windows and the sweeping view across the Seine. She used to wear white, and sit on a white sofa. There were patches of red in the room—her long fingernails and her lipstick, and the Legion of Honor on some admirer's lapel. She had two small, funny dogs whose eyes glowed red in the dusk.

"I heard you speaking just the other day," she went on. "You were most interesting about the way Gide always made the rounds of the bookstores to see how his work was selling. Actually, I think I told you that story."

"It couldn't have been just the other day," I said. "It sounds like a radio program I had in the 1950s."

"It couldn't have been you, come to think of it," she said. "The man lisped. I said to myself, It *might* be Édouard."

Her foreign way of speaking enchanted me when I was young. Now it sharpens my temper. Fifty years in France and she still cannot pronounce my name, Édouard, without putting the stress on the wrong syllable and rolling the r. "When you come to an r," I have told her, "keep your tongue behind your lower front teeth."

"It won't stay," she says. "It curls up. I am sorry." As if she cared. She will accept any amount of petulance shown by me, because she thinks she owes me tolerance: She sees me as youthful, boyish, to be teased and humored. She believes we have a long, unhampered life before us, and she expects to occupy it as my wife and widow-to-be. To that end, she has managed to outlive my second wife, and she may well survive me, even though I am fourteen years younger than she is and still on my feet.

Magdalena's Catholic legend is that she was converted after hearing Jacques Maritain explain neo-Thomism at a tea party. Since then, she has never stopped heaping metaphysical rules about virtue on top of atavistic arguments concerning right and wrong. The result is a moral rock pile, ready to slide. Only God himself could stand up to the avalanche, but in her private arrangements he is behind her, egging her on. I had to wait until a law was passed that allowed divorce on the ground of separation before I was free to marry again. I waited a long time. In the meantime, Magdalena was writing letters to the Pope, cheering his stand on marriage and urging him to hold firm. She can choose among three or four different languages, her choice depending on where her dreams may have taken her during the night. She used to travel by train to Budapest and Prague wearing white linen. She had sleek, fair hair, and wore a diamond hair clip behind one ear. Now no one goes to those places, and the slim linen suits are crumpled in trunks. Her mind is clear, but she says absurd things. "I never saw her," she said about Juliette, my second wife. "Was she anything like me?"

"You did see her. We had lunch, the three of us."

"Show me her picture. It might bring back the occasion."

"No."

They met, once, on the first Sunday of September, 1954—a hot day of quivering horizons and wasps hitting the windshield. I had a new Renault— a model with a reputation for rolling over and lying with its wheels in the air. I drove, I think, grimly. Magdalena was beside me, in a nimbus of some scent—jasmine, or gardenia—that made me think of the opulent, profiteering side of wars. Juliette sat behind, a road map on her knee, her finger on the western outskirts of Fontainebleau. Her dark hair was pulled back tight and tied at the nape of her neck with a dark blue grosgrain ribbon. It is safe to say that she smelled of soap and lemons.

We were taking Magdalena out to lunch. It was Juliette's idea. Somewhere between raspberries-and-cream and coffee, I was supposed to ask for a divorce—worse, to coax from Magdalena the promise of collusion in obtaining one. So far, she had resisted any mention of the subject and for ten years had refused to see me. Juliette and I had been living together since the end of the war. She was thirty now, and tired of waiting. We were turning into one of those uneasy, shadowy couples, perpetually waiting for a third person to die or divorce. I was afraid of losing her. That summer, she had traveled without me to America (so much farther from Europe then than it is today), and she had come back with a different coloration to her manner, a glaze of independence, as though she had been exposed to a new kind of sun.

I remember how she stared at Magdalena with gentle astonishment, as if Magdalena were a glossy illustration that could not look back. Magdalena had on a pale dress of some soft, floating stuff, and a pillbox hat tied on with a white veil, and long white gloves. I saw her through Juliette's eyes, and I thought what Juliette must be thinking: Where does Magdalena think we're taking her? To a wedding? Handing her into the front seat, I had shut the door on her skirt. I wondered if she had turned into one of the limp, pliant women whose clothes forever catch.

It was Juliette's custom to furnish social emptiness with some rattling anecdote about her own activities. Guests were often grateful. Without having to cast far, they could bring up a narrative of their own, and the result was close to real conversation. Juliette spoke of her recent trip. She said she was wearing an American dress made of a material called cotton seersucker. It washed like a duster and needed next to no ironing.

For answer, she received a side view of Magdalena's hat and a blue eye shadowed with paler blue. Magdalena was not looking but listening, savoring at close quarters the inflections of the French Protestant gentry. She knew she was privileged. As a rule, they speak only to one another. Clamped to gearshift and wheel, I was absolved of the need to comment. My broken profile had foxed Magdalena at first. She had even taken me for an impostor. But then the remembered face of a younger man slid over the fraud and possessed him.

Juliette had combed through the *Guide Michelin* and selected a restaurant with a wide terrace and white umbrellas, set among trees. At some of the tables there were American officers, in uniform, with their families—this is to show how long ago it was. Juliette adjusted our umbrella so that every inch of Magdalena was in shade. She took it for granted that my wife belonged to a generation sworn to paleness. From where I was sitting, I could see the interior of the restaurant. It looked cool and dim, I thought, and might have been better suited to the soft-footed conversation to come.

I adjusted my reading glasses, which Magdalena had never seen, and stared at a long handwritten menu. Magdalena made no move to examine hers. She had all her life let men decide. Finally, Juliette wondered if our guest might not like to start with asparagus. I was afraid the asparagus would be canned. Well, then, said Juliette, what about melon. On a hot day, something cool followed by cold salmon. She broke off. I started to remove my glasses, but Juliette reminded me about wine.

Magdalena was engaged in a ritual that Juliette may not have seen before and that I had forgotten: pulling off her tight, long gloves finger by finger and turning her rings right side up. Squeezed against a great sparkler of some kind was a wedding ring. Rallying, Juliette gave a little twitch to the collar of the washable seersucker and went on about America. In Philadelphia, a celebrated Pentecostal preacher had persuaded the Holy Spirit to settle upon a member of the congregation, a woman whose hearing had been damaged when she was brained by a flying shoe at a stock-car race. The deaf woman rose and said she could hear sparrows chirping in High German, on which the congregation prayed jubilant thanks.

Juliette did not stoop to explain that she was no Pentecostalist. She mentioned the Holy Spirit as an old acquaintance of her own class and background, a cultivated European with an open mind.

We were no longer young lovers, and I had heard this story several times. I said that the Holy Spirit might find something more useful to attend to than a ruptured eardrum. We were barely ten years out of a disastrous war. All over the world, there were people sick, afraid, despairing. Only a few days before, the President of Brazil had shot himself to death.

Juliette replied that there were needs beyond our understanding. "God knows what he wants," she said. I am sure she believed it.

"God wanted Auschwitz?" I said.

I felt a touch on my arm, and I looked down and saw a middle-aged hand and a wedding ring.

With her trained inclination to move back from rising waters, Juliette made the excuse of a telephone call. I knew that her brief departure was meant to be an intermission. When she came back, we would speak about other things. Magdalena and I sat quietly, she with her hand still on my arm, as if she had finally completed a gesture begun a long time before. Juliette, returning, her eyes splashed with cold water, her dark hair freshly combed, saw that I was missing a good chance to bring up the divorce. She sat down, smiled, picked up her melon spoon. She was working hard these days, she said. She was translating an American novel that should never have been written. (Juliette revealed nothing more about this novel.) From there, she slid along to the subject of drastic separations—not so much mine from Magdalena as divorcement in general. Surely, she said, a clean parting was a way of keeping life pleasant and neat? This time, it was Magdalena's hearing that seemed impaired, and the Holy Spirit was nowhere. The two women must have been thinking the same thing at that moment, though for entirely different reasons: that I had forfeited any chance of divine aid by questioning God's intentions.

It was shortly before her removal to the hospital that Magdalena learned about Juliette's death. One of her doddering friends may have seen the notice in a newspaper. She at once resumed her place as my only spouse and widow-to-be. In fact, she had never relinquished it, but now the way back to me shone clear. The divorce, that wall of pagan darkness, had been torn down and dispersed with the concubine's ashes. She saw me delivered from an adulterous and heretical alliance. It takes a convert to think "heretical" with a straight face. She could have seen Juliette burned at the stake without losing any sleep. It is another fact about converts that they make casual executioners.

She imagined that I would come to her at once, but I went nowhere. Juliette had asked to be cremated, thinking of the purification of the flame, but the rite was accomplished by clanking, hidden, high-powered machinery that kept starting and stopping, on cycle. At its loudest, it covered the voice of the clergyman, who affirmed that Juliette was eyeing us with great goodwill from above, and it prevailed over Juliette's favorite recordings of Mozart and Bach. Her ashes were placed in a numbered niche that I never saw, for at some point in the funeral service I lost consciousness and had to be carried out. This nightmare was dreamed in the crematorium chapel of Père Lachaise cemetery. I have not been back. It is far from where I live, and I think Juliette is not there, or anywhere. From the moment when her heart stopped, there has been nothing but silence.

Last winter, I had bronchitis and seldom went out. I managed to send Magdalena a clock, a radio, an azalea, and enough stamps and stationery to furnish a nineteenth-century literary correspondence. Nevertheless, the letters that reached my sickbed from hers were scrawled in the margins of newspapers, torn off crookedly. Sometimes she said her roommate had lent her the money for a stamp. The message was always the same: I must not allow my wife to die in a public institution. Her pink-nosed woman friends wrote me, too, signing their alien names, announcing their titles—there was a princess.

It was no good replying that everybody dies in hospital now. The very idea made them sick, of a sickness beyond any wasting last-ditch illusion. Then came from Magdalena "On Saturday at nine o'clock, I shall be dressed and packed, and waiting for you to come and take me away."

Away from the hospital bed? It took weeks of wangling and soft-soaping and even some mild bribery to obtain it. Public funds, to which she is not entitled, and a voluntary contribution from me keep her in it. She has not once asked where the money comes from. When she was young, she decided never to worry, and she has kept the habit.

I let several Saturdays go by, until the folly had quit her mind. Late in April I turned up carrying a bottle of Krug I had kept on ice until the last minute and some glasses in a paper bag. The woman who shares her room gave a great groan when she saw me, and showed the whites of her eyes. I took this to mean that Magdalena had died. The other bed was clean and empty. The clock and the radio on the table had the look of objects left behind. I felt shock, guilt, remorse, and relief, and I wondered what to do with the wine. I turned, and there in the doorway stood Magdalena, in dressing gown and slippers, with short white hair. She shuffled past me and lay on the bed with her mouth open, struggling for breath.

"Shouldn't I ring for a nurse?" I said, unwrapping the bottle.

"No one will come. Open the champagne."

"I'd better fetch a nurse." Instead, I made room on the table for the glasses. I'd brought three, because of the roommate.

Magdalena gasped, "Today is my birthday." She sat up, apparently recovered, and got her spectacles out from under the pillow. Leaning toward me, she said, "What's that red speck on your lapel? It looks like the Legion of Honor."

"I imagine that's what it is."

"Why?" she said. "Was there a reason?"

"They probably had a lot to give away. Somebody did say something about 'cultural enrichment of the media.' "

"I am glad about the enrichment," she said. "I am also very happy for you. Will you wear it all the time, change it from suit to suit?"

"It's new," I said. "There was a ceremony this morning." I sat down on the shaky chair kept for visitors, and with a steadiness that silenced us both I poured the wine. "What about your neighbor?" I said, the bottle poised.

"Let her sleep. This is a good birthday surprise."

I felt as if warm ashes were banked round my heart, like a residue of good intentions. I remembered that when Magdalena came back to Paris after the war, she found her apartment looted, laid waste. One of the first letters to arrive in the mail was from me, to say that I was in love with a much younger woman. "If it means anything at all to you," I said, the coals glowing brighter, "if it can help you to understand me in any way—well, no one ever fascinated me as much as you." This after only one glass.

"But, perhaps, you never loved me," she said.

"Probably not," I said. "Although I must have."

"You mean, in a way?" she said.

"I suppose so."

The room became so quiet that I could hear the afternoon movie on television in the next room. I recognized the voice of the actor who dubs Robert Redford.

Magdalena said, "Even a few months ago this would have been my death sentence. Now I am simply thankful I have so little time left to wander between 'perhaps' and 'probably not' and 'in a way.' A crazy old woman, wringing my hands."

I remembered Juliette's face when she learned that her menopause was irreversible. I remember her shock, her fright, her gradual understanding, her storm of grief. She had hoped for children, then finally a child, a son she would have called "Thomas." "Your death sentence," I said. "Your death sentence. What about Juliette's life sentence? She never had children. By the time I was able to marry her, it was too late."

"She could have had fifteen children without being married," said Magdalena.

I wanted to roar at her, but my voice went high and thin. "Women like Juliette, people like Juliette, don't do that sort of thing. It was a wonder she consented to live with me for all those years. What about her son, her Thomas? I couldn't even have claimed him—not legally, as long as I was married to you. Imagine him, think of him, applying for a passport, finding out he had no father. Nothing on his birth certificate. Only a mother."

"You could have adopted Thomas," said Magdalena. "That way, he'd have been called by your name."

"I couldn't—not without your consent. *You* were my wife. Besides, why should I have to adopt my own son?" I think this was a shout; that is how it comes back to me. "And the inheritance laws, as they were in those days.

Have you ever thought about that? I couldn't even make a will in his favor."

Cheek on hand, blue eyes shadowed, my poor, mad, true, and only wife said, "Ah, Édouard, you shouldn't have worried. You know I'd have left him all that I had."

It wasn't the last time I saw Magdalena, but after that day she sent no more urgent messages, made no more awkward demands. Twice since then, she has died and come round. Each time, just when the doctor said, "I think that's it," she has squeezed the nurse's hand. She loves rituals, and she probably wants the last Sacraments, but hospitals hate that. Word that there is a priest in the place gets about, and it frightens the other patients. There are afternoons when she can't speak and lies with her eyes shut, the lids quivering. I hold her hand, and feel the wedding ring. Like the staunch little widows, I call her "Lena," and she turns her head and opens her eyes.

I glance away then, anywhere—at the clock out the window. I have put up with everything, but I intend to refuse her last imposition, the encounter with her blue, enduring look of pure love.

HENRI GRIPPES

A PAINFUL AFFAIR

⁓✣⁓

*G*rippes's opinion remains unchanged: He was the last author to have received a stipend from the Mary Margaret Pugh Arts Foundation, and so it should have fallen to him—Henri Grippes, Parisian novelist, diarist, essayist, polemical journalist, and critic—to preside at the commemoration of the late Miss Pugh's centenary. (This celebration, widely reported in Paris, particularly in publications that seemed to have it in for Grippes, took place in a room lent by the firm of Fronce & Baril, formerly drapers and upholsterers, now purveyors of blue jeans from Madras. The firm's books reveal that Miss Pugh was the first person ever to have opened a charge account— a habit she brought from her native America and is thought to have introduced into France.) But the honor did not fall to M. Grippes. The Pugh Memorial Committee, made up of old-age pensioners from the American Embassy, the Chase Manhattan Bank (Paris), the French Ministry for Culture, and other intellectual oatcakes, chose instead to invite Victor Prism, winkling him with no trouble out of his obscure post at a university in the north of England. Prism's eagerness to get away from England whatever the season, his willingness to travel under foul conditions, for a trifling sum of money, make him a popular feature of subsidized gatherings throughout the Free World. This is still the way Grippes sees things.

Prism, author of *Suomi Serenade: A Key to the Kalevala*, much praised in its day as an outstandingly skillful performance, also thinks Grippes should have been chairman. The fact that the Pugh centenary celebration coincided with the breakup of the M. M. Pugh Investment Trust, from which the Foundation—and, incidentally, M. Grippes—had drawn considerable funds over the years, might have made Grippes's presence in the chair especially poignant. It could also have tested his capacity for showing humility—an accommodation already strained more than once. Think of Grippes, Miss Pugh's youthful protégé, fresh from his father's hog farm in Auvergne, dozing on a bed in her house (a bed that had belonged to Prism a scant six months before), with Rosalia, the maid, sent along every half hour to see how he was getting on with chapter 2. Think of Grippes at the end, when Miss Pugh's long-lost baby brother, now seventy-something—snappy Hong Kong forty-eight-hour tailoring, silk shirt from Bangkok, arrogant suntan—turned up at her bedside, saying, "Well, Maggie, long time no see."

"She died in his arms," wrote Grippes, in an unusually confidential letter to Prism, "though not without a struggle."

Prism says he had been promised Miss Pugh's library, her collection of autograph letters (Apollinaire to Zola), her matching ormolu-mounted opaline urns, her Meissen coffee service, her father's cuff links, her Louis XVI–period writing table, and the key to a safe-deposit vault containing two Caillebottes and a Morisot. The promise was not kept, but no trick of fortune could possibly erode his gratitude for earlier favors. He still visits Miss Pugh's grave, in a mossy corner of Passy Cemetery, whenever he happens to be in Paris. He leaves a bunch of anemones, or a pot of chrysanthemums, or, when the cost of flowers is really sky-high, merely stands silently with his head bowed. Sunshine flows upon the back of his neck, in a kind of benison. Seeing how the rich are buried imbues him with strengthened faith. He receives the formal promise of a future offered and accepted—a pledge he once believed existed in art. He thinks of Grippes, in his flat across the Seine, scribbling away amid Miss Pugh's furniture and his tribe of stray cats.

Grippes says he visits Miss Pugh's grave as often as he is able. (He has to find someone to stay with the cats.) Each time he goes to the cemetery he gets caught up in a phalanx of mourners shuffling behind a creeping hearse. The hearse parks close to some family mausoleum that is an architectural echo of the mansions that lined Avenue du Bois before it became Avenue Foch. Waiting for the coffin to be unloaded, the mourners stare at one another's collars. Grippes reads inscriptions on tombstones, some of which indicate with astonishing precision what the occupant expected to find on the other side. In this place, where it is never spring, he is conscious of bare branches, dark birds cawing. The day takes on a grainy texture, like a German Expressionist film. The only color glows from the ribbons and rosettes some of the mourners wear on their lapels. (Among the crumbs flicked in Grippes's direction was Miss Pugh's Legion of Honor, after her brother had been assured it would not fetch one franc, his floor price, at auction.) There is nothing extravagant or dangerous about these excursions. They cost Grippes a Métro ticket each way—direct line, Montparnasse-Trocadéro, no awkward change, no transfer, no flight along underground corridors pursued by a gang of those savage children of whom even the police are afraid.

Prism thinks that Grippes started showing signs of infantile avarice and timidity soon after Miss Pugh's death, which left him homeless. For a time Grippes even thought of moving to London. He sent Prism a letter suggesting they take a flat together and live on their memories. Prism responded with a strange and terrifying account of gang wars, with pimps and blackmailers shot dead on the steps of the National Gallery. In Paris, Prism wrote, Grippes could be recognized on sight as a literary odd-jobs man with style. No one would call him a climber—at least, not to his face. Rather, Grippes seemed to have been dropped in early youth onto one of those middling-high peaks of Paris bohemia from which the artist can see both machine-knit and cashmere blazers hanging in Boulevard Haussmann department stores and five-thousand-franc custom tailoring. In England, where caste signs were radically different, he might give the false impression that he was a procurer or a drug pusher and be gunned down at a bus stop.

After reading this letter, Grippes got out a map of London and studied it. It looked crowded and untidy. He cashed in about half the bonds Miss Pugh had made over to him in her lifetime and bought four rooms above a cinema in Montparnasse. While he was showing the removal men where to place Miss Pugh's writing table, a cat came mewing at the door and he let it in.

Grippes denies the imputation of avarice. When Prism gave his famous lecture in Brussels, in 1970, "Is Language a Deterrent?" Grippes traveled by train to hear him, at his own expense. He recalls that Prism was wearing a green corduroy suit, a canary-yellow V-neck sweater, and a tie that must have been a souvenir of Belfast. On his return to Paris, Grippes wrote a lighthearted essay about *le style Anglais*.

Just before the centennial, Prism was interviewed on French television: eighteen minutes of Victor Prism, at a green baize table, with an adulating journalist who seemed to have been dipped in shellac. Prism's French had not deteriorated, though it still sounded to Grippes like dried peas rattling in a tin can. "The fact is," he said, rattling, "that I am the only person who knew

Miss Pugh well—apart from her devoted servant Rosalia, that is. All raise hands, please, who remember Rosalia. *(Camera on studio smiles)* I am the person who called on Miss Pugh after she was evicted from her beautiful house and transported by ambulance to a nursing home in Meudon. She never quite understood that she had bought a house but not the land it stood on. *(Sympathetic laughter)* The last time I saw her, she was sitting up in bed, wearing her sapphire earrings, drinking a bottle of Veuve Clicquot. I have forgotten to say that she was by now completely bald, which did not make her in the least self-conscious. *(Immense goodwill)* I was obliged to return to England, believing I was leaving Miss Pugh in radiant health and in trusted hands." *(Audience delight)*

A heavily edited version of Grippes's answer appeared in *Le Figaro*, under the heading "A PAINFUL AFFAIR: FURTHER CORRESPONDENCE." Mr. Prism had neglected to mention the date of Miss Pugh's transfer to the nursing home: 10 May, 1968. Clouds of tear gas. Cars overturned in Paris streets. Grippes's long-awaited autobiographical novel, *Sleeping on the Beach*, had appeared the day before. His stoic gloom as he watched students flinging the whole of the first edition onto a bonfire blazing as high as second-story windows. Grippes's publisher, crouched in his shabby office just around the corner, had already hung on the wall the photograph of some hairy author he hoped would pass for Engels. The glow from the bonfire tinged bogus Engels pink, investing him with the hearty tone that had quit the publisher's cheeks when, early that morning, a delegation representing what might well turn out to be a New Order had invaded the premises. Grippes, pale trench coat over dark turtleneck, hands clenched in trench coat pockets, knew he was aging, irreversibly, minute by minute. Some of the students thought he was Herbert Marcuse and tried to carry him on their shoulders to *Le Figaro*'s editorial offices, which they hoped he would set on fire. The melancholia that descended on Grippes that evening made him unfit to help and sustain an old lady who was said to be spending all her time sulking under a bed-sheet and refusing to eat. He managed to be with Miss Pugh at the end, however, and distinctly heard her say something coherent about the disposal of her furniture. As for *Sleeping on the Beach*, it was never reprinted, for the usual craven reasons.

Prism says that even before the Pugh Investment Trust filed its bankruptcy petition before a Paris court, the dismantling of Miss Pugh's house had been completed, with the wainscoting on the staircase stripped and sold to a tearoom and what remained of the silver, pictures, and furniture brought under the hammer. (Grippes and Rosalia had already removed some of the better pieces, for safety.) Her will was so ambiguous that, to avoid litigation, Miss Pugh's brother and the Trust split the proceeds, leaving Prism and a few other faithful friends of hers in the cold. Grippes is suspected of having gold ingots under the bed, bullion in the bathtub, gold napoleons in his shoes. The fact is (Grippes can prove it) that Miss Pugh's personal income had been declining for years, owing to her steadfast belief that travel by steamship would soon supersede the rage for planes. "Her private investments followed her convictions as night follows day," writes Grippes, with the cats for company. "And, one day, night fell."

Prism discovered that some of the furniture removed for safety was in the parlor of Rosalia's son, permanent mayor and Mafia delegate of a town in Sicily. He at once dispatched an expert appraiser, who declared the whole lot to be fake. It may have been that on a pink marble floor, against pink wall hangings, in a room containing a bar on which clockwork figures of Bonaparte and Josephine could be made to play Ping-Pong, Miss Pugh's effects took on an aura of sham. Still, the expert seemed sincere to Prism. He said the Boulle chest was the kind they still manufacture on the Rue du Faubourg-Saint-Martin, scar with bleach, beat with chains, then spend years restoring.

About a month after the funeral, a letter appeared in *Le Matin de Paris*, signed "Old-Style Socialist." The writer recalled that some forty years before, a Miss Pugh (correctly spelled) had purchased from an antique dealer a wooden statue said to represent St. Cumula, virgin and martyr. (A brief history of Cumula followed: About to be forced into marriage with a pagan Gaul, Cumula painted herself purple and jumped into the Seine, where she drowned. The pagan, touched by her unwavering detestation of him, accepted Christian baptism, on the site of what is now the Paris Stock Exchange.) Miss Pugh had the effigy restored to its original purple and offered it to the Archbishop of Paris. After several coats of paint were removed, the carving was found to be a likeness of General Marchand, leader of the French Nile Expedition. The Archbishop declined the present, giving as his reason the separation of church and state. "Old-Style Socialist" wondered what had become of the carving, for even if General Marchand stood for nineteenth-century colonial policy at its most offensive, history was history, art was art, and it was easily proved that some persons never ceased to meddle in both.

Prism believes Grippes might have had some talent to begin with but that he wasted it writing tomfool letters. He thinks a note that came in the mail recently was from Grippes: "Dear Ms. Victoria Prism, I teach Creative Journalism to a trilingual class here in California (Spanish/Chinese/some English). In the past you have written a lot of stuff that was funny and made us laugh. Lately you published something about the lingering death of a helicopter pilot. Is this a new departure? Please limit your answer to 200 words. My class gets tired." The letter had an American stamp and a Los Angeles postmark, but Prism has known Grippes to spend days over such details.

Grippes says that Prism's talent is like one of those toy engines made of plastic glass, every part transparent and moving to no purpose. The engine can be plugged in to a power outlet, but it can't be harnessed. In short, Prism symbolizes the state of English letters since the 1950s.

"You ought to write your memoirs," Grippes said to Prism at Miss Pugh's funeral. Prism thought Grippes was hoping to be provided with grounds for a successful libel action. (He concedes that Grippes looked fine that day: dark tie, dark suit, well brushed—he hadn't begun collecting cats yet.)

Actually, Prism is pretty sure he could fill two volumes, four hundred pages each, dark green covers, nice paper, nice to touch. A title he has in mind is *Bridge Building Between Cultures.*

Grippes started his own memoirs about a year ago, basing them on his diaries. He wouldn't turn down a Bibliothèque de la Pléiade edition, about a thousand pages of Bible-weight paper, fifty pages of pictures, full Grippes bibliography, appreciative introductory essay by someone he has not quarreled with, frontispiece of Grippes at the window, back to the light, three-quarter profile, cat on his shoulder. He'd need pictures of Miss Pugh: There are none. She loathed sitting for portraits, photographs, snapshots. Old prints of her house exist, their negatives lost or chewed by mice. The Pugh Memorial Committee donated a few to the Museum of Popular Arts and Traditions, where they were immediately filed under "Puget, Pierre, French sculptor."

"Research might have better luck at the University of Zurich," writes Grippes, at Miss Pugh's Louis XVI–period table. "A tireless Swiss team has been on the trail of Miss Pugh for some time now, and a cowed Swiss computer throws up only occasional anarchy, describing Pugh M. M., Pullman G. M., and Pulitzer J. as the same generous American."

Prism's quiet collaboration with Zurich, expected to culminate in a top-quality volume, *Hostess to Fame*, beige linen cover, ended when he understood that he was not going to be paid anything, and that it would be fifteen years before the first word was transferred from tape to paper.

Grippes says he heard one of the tapes:

"Mr. Prism, kindly listen to the name I shall now pronounce. François Mauriac. The thin, sardonic gentleman who put on a bowler hat every morning before proceeding to Mass was François Mauriac. Right?"

"I don't remember a François."

"Think. François. Mauriac."

"I don't remember a bowler hat."

At the centennial commemoration, Prism stood on a little dais, dressed in a great amount of tweed and flannel that seemed to have been cut for a much larger man. Grippes suspects that Prism's clothes are being selected by his widowed sister, who, after years of trying to marry him off to her closest friends, is now hoping to make him seem as unattractive as possible. Imagining Prism's future—a cottage in Devon, his sister saying, "There was a letter for you, but I can't remember what I did with it"—he heard Prism declare he was happy to be here, in a place obligingly provided; the firm's old boardroom, back in the days when Paris was still; the really fine walnut paneling on two of the; about the shortage of chairs, but the Committee had not expected such a large; some doubtless disturbed by an inexplicable smell of moth repellent, but the Committee was in no way; in honor of a great and charitable American, to whom the cultural life of; looking around, he was pleased to see one or two young faces.

With this, Prism stepped down, and had to be reminded he was chairman and principal speaker. He climbed back, and delivered from memory an old lecture of his on Gertrude Stein. He then found and read a letter Miss Pugh had received from the President of the Republic, in 1934, telling her that although she was a woman, and a foreigner, she was surely immortal. Folding the letter, Prism suddenly recalled and described a conversation with Miss Pugh.

"Those of us who believe in art," Prism had started to say.

Miss Pugh had coughed and said, "I don't."

She did not believe in art, only in artists. She had no interest in books, only in their authors. Reading an early poem of Prism's (it was years since he had written any poetry, he hastened to say), she had been stopped by the description of a certain kind of butterfly, "pale yellow, with a spot like the

Eye of God." She had sent for her copy of the Larousse dictionary, which Rosalia was using in the kitchen as a weight on sliced cucumbers. Turning to a color plate, Miss Pugh had found the butterfly at once. It turned out to be orange rather than yellow, and heavily spotted with black. Moreover, it was not a European butterfly but an Asian moth. The Larousse must be mistaken. She had shut the dictionary with a slap, blaming its editors for carelessness. If only there had been more women like her, Prism concluded, there would be more people today who knew what they were doing.

Grippes says that, for once, he feels inclined to agree. All the same, he wishes Prism had suppressed the anecdote. Prism knows as well as Grippes does that some things are better left as legends.

A FLYING START

―――――

The project for a three-volume dictionary of literary biography, *Living Authors of the Fourth Republic,* was set afloat in Paris in 1952, with an eleven-man editorial committee in the same lifeboat. The young and promising Henri Grippes, spokesman for a new and impertinent generation, waited on shore for news of mass drownings; so he says now. A few years later, when the working title had to be changed to *Living Authors of the Fifth Republic,* Grippes was invited aboard. In 1964, Grippes announced there were not enough living authors to fill three volumes, and was heaved over the side. Actually, he had just accepted a post as writer-in-residence at a women's college in California; from the Pacific shore he sent a number of open letters to Paris weeklies, denouncing the dictionary scheme as an attempt to establish a form of literary pecking order. Antielitism was in the air, and Grippes's views received great prominence. His return to Paris found a new conflict raging: *Two* volumes were now to be produced, under the brusque and fashionable title *Contemporary Writers, Women and Others.* Grippes at once published a pamphlet revealing that it was a police dodge for feeding women and others into a multinational computer. In the event of invasion, the computer would cough up the names and the authors would be lined up and marched to forced labor in insurance companies. He carried the day, and for a time the idea of any contemporary literary directory was dropped.

Grippes had by then come into a little money, and had bought himself an apartment over a cinema in Montparnasse. He wore a wide felt hat and a velvet jacket in cool weather and a panama straw and a linen coat when it was fine. Instead of a shopping bag he carried a briefcase. He wrote to the mayor of Paris—who answered, calling him "Maître"—to protest a plan to remove the statue of Balzac from Boulevard Raspail, just north of the Boulevard du Montparnasse intersection. It was true that the statue was hemmed in by cars illegally parked and that it was defiled by pigeons, but Grippes was used to seeing it there. He also deplored that the clock on the corner near the Dôme no longer kept time; Grippes meant by this that it did not keep the same time as his watch, which he often forgot to wind.

In the meantime the old two-volume project, with its aging and dwindled editorial committee and its cargo of card-index files, had floated toward a reliable firm that published old-fashioned history manuals with plenty of color plates, and geography books that drew attention only to territories that were not under dispute. The Ministry of Culture was thought to be behind the venture. The files, no one quite knew how, were pried away from the committee and confided to a professor of English literature at a provincial university. The *Angliciste* would be unlikely to favor one school of French writing over another, for the simple reason that he did not know one from the other. The original committee had known a great deal, which was why for some thirty years its members had been in continual deadlock.

It seemed to the *Angliciste* that the work would have wider appeal if a section was included on British writers known for their slavish cultural allegiance to France. First on the list was, of course, Victor Prism, lifelong and distinguished Francophile and an old academic acquaintance. He recalled that Prism had once lived in Paris as the protégé of Miss Mary Margaret Pugh, a patroness of the arts; so, at about the same time, had the future novelist and critic Henri Grippes. "Two golden lion cubs in the golden cage of the great lioness," as the *Angliciste* wrote Grippes, asking him to contribute a concise appreciation of his comrade in early youth. "Just say what seemed to you to be prophetic of his achievement. We are in a great hurry. The work is now called *French Authors, 1950–2000,* and we must go to press by 1990 if it is to have any meaning for our time. Don't trouble about Prism's career; the facts are on record. Payment upon receipt of contribution, alas. The ministry is being firm."

Grippes received the letter a week before Christmas. He thought of sending Prism a sixteen-page questionnaire but decided, reasonably, that it might dull the effect of surprise. He set to work, and by dint of constant application completed his memoir the following Easter. It was handwritten, of course; even his sojourn in California had not reconciled Grippes to typewriters. "I feel certain this is what you are after," he wrote the *Angliciste.* "A portrait of Prism as protégé. It was an experience that changed his external image. Miss Pugh often said he had arrived on her doorstep looking as if he had spent his life in the rain waiting for a London bus. By the time he left, a few weeks later, a wholehearted commitment to the popular Parisian idols of the period—Sartre, Camus, and Charles Trenet—caused him to wear a little gray hat with turned-up brim, a black shirt, an off-white tie, and voluminous trousers. At his request, Miss Pugh gave him a farewell present of crêpe-soled shoes. Perhaps, with luck, you may find a picture of him so attired."

Grippes's memoir was untitled.

" 'The drawing room at the Duchess of B—'s overlooked a leafy avenue and a rustic bandstand in the city of O—. There, summer after summer, the Duchess had watched children rolling their hoops to the strains of a polka, or a waltz, or a mazurka, or a sparkling military march, remote indeed from the harsh sound of warfare that assailed her today.'

"Would anyone believe, now, that Victor Prism could have written this? That Prism could have poured out, even once, the old bourgeois caramel sauce?

"He did. The time was soon after the end of the Second World War. They were the first words of his first unfinished novel, and they so impressed Miss Mary Margaret Pugh, an American lady then living in a bosky, sunless, and costly corner of Paris, that she invited Prism to complete the novel in her house.

"His benefactress, if extant, would be well over a hundred. In his unpublished roman à clef, *Goldfinches Have Yellow Feathers*, Prism left a picture of Miss Pugh he may still consider fair: 'Miss Melbourne, from a distance, reminded Christopher of those statues of deposed monarchs one can see at seedy summer resorts along the Adriatic. Close up, she looked softer, middle-class, and wholly alarming. Often as Christopher sat across from Miss Melbourne, trying to eat his lunch and at the same time answer her unexpected questions, he would recall a portrait he had seen of a Renaissance merchant's shrewd, hardy wife. It had something to do with Miss Melbourne's plump shoulders and small pink nose, with her habit of fingering the lockets and laces she wore as though drawing the artist's attention to essentials.'

"Miss Pugh had spent most of her life abroad, which was not unusual for rich spinsters of her generation. She seldom mentioned her father, a common fortune hunter, soon shed by her mother—tactful hostess, careful parent, trusted friend to artists and writers. The ash tree whose shade contributed no little to the primeval twilight of the dining room had grown from a sapling presented by Edith Wharton. As a girl, Miss Pugh had been allowed to peer round the door and watch her renowned compatriot eating sole meunière. She had not been presented to Mrs. Wharton, who was divorced.

"What constituted the difference between Mrs. Pugh, also divorced, and the novelist? It is likely that Miss Pugh never asked herself this question. Most of her interesting anecdotes drifted off in this way, into the haze of ancient social mystery.

"The house that was to be Victor Prism's refuge for a summer had been built in the 1850s, in a quiet street straggling downhill from the Trocadéro. Miss Pugh had inherited, along with the house, a legend that Balzac wrote *Cousine Bette* in the upstairs sitting room, though the prolific author had been buried a good three years before the foundation was dug. *Madame mère* probably bought the house in the 1880s. Soon after that, the character of the street changed. A considerable amount of low-value property changed hands. Most of the small houses were destroyed or became surrounded by seven-story apartment buildings made of stone, sturdily Third Republic in style. The house we are speaking of was now actually at the heart of a block, connected to the world by a narrow carriage drive, the latter a subject of perennial litigation. Tenants of the apartments could look down upon a low redbrick dwelling with a slate roof, an ash tree that managed to flourish without sunlight, dense thickets of indeterminate urban shrubbery, a bronze Italian birdbath, and a Cupid on tiptoe. The path from gate to door was always wet underfoot, like the floor of a forest.

"Inside, the rooms were low and dim, the floors warped and uneven. Coal fires burned to no great effect except further to darken the walls. Half the rooms by the 1940s were shut off. Miss Pugh was no stingier than any other rich woman, nor had there as yet been an appreciable decline in her income. She was taking it for granted there would soon be another war, followed this time by the definitive revolution. Her daydreams were populated by Bolsheviks, swarming up the Trocadéro hill, waving eviction notices. Why create more comfort than one could bear to lose?

" 'To enjoy it, even for a minute' would have been the answer of a Victor Prism, or, for that matter, of any other of the gifted drifters for whom Paris had become a catchall, and to whom Miss Pugh offered conversation and asylum. Some were political refugees of the first postwar wave, regarded everywhere with immense suspicion. It was thought they should go back to wherever they'd come from and help build just, Spartan societies. Not so Miss Pugh, who thought they should sit down in one of the upstairs rooms and write about their mothers. Some were young men on the run from the legend of a heroic father, whose jaunty wartime face, smiling from a mantelshelf, was enough to launch any son into a life of firm and steady goldbricking. Some, like Prism, were trying to climb on the right American springboard for a flying start.

" 'What is your ideal?' Miss Pugh liked to ask. 'At your age, you can't live without one.'

"Thirty, forty years ago, 'ideal' opened the way to tumbledown houses like Miss Pugh's that were really fairy castles. The moat was flooded with American generosity and American contrition. Probably no moat in history was ever so easy to bridge. (Any young European thinking of making that crossing today should be warned that the contrition silted up in the early 1970s, after which the castle was abandoned.) Miss Pugh did not expect gratitude for material favors, and would have considered it a base emotion. But she had no qualms about showing a stern face to any protégé who revealed himself to be untalented, bereft of an ideal in working order, mentally idle, or coarsely materialistic. This our poor Victor Prism was to learn before the summer was out. Miss Pugh belonged to a small Christian congregation that took its substance from Buddhism. She treated most living creatures equally and made little distinction between man and worm.

"How did Prism turn into a protégé? Easily: He rang a doorbell. Rosalia answered to a young man who was carrying a manila envelope, manuscript-size, and a letter. She reached for the letter of introduction but did not let Prism in, even though large drops of rain had started to fall.

"Miss Pugh, upstairs in the Balzac sitting room, addressed, from the window, a troubled-looking patch of sky. 'Hasn't this been going on long enough?' Rosalia heard her say. 'Why don't you do something?'

"The answer to Miss Pugh's cosmic despair, or impertinence, was Victor Prism. She had been acknowledged by the universe before now, but perhaps never so quickly. She sat down with her back to the window, read the letter Rosalia gave her, folded it, thought it over, and said, 'All right. Bring him up.'

"Prism came into her presence with a step that lost its assurance as he drew near. He asked permission to sit down. Having obtained a nod, he placed his manila envelope on a low table, where Miss Pugh could reach it easily, and repeated everything she had just read in the letter: He was promising but poor. He had been staying with Mrs. Hartley-Greene on Avenue Gabriel. Mrs. Hartley-Greene had been indescribably helpful and kind. However, she was interested in painters, not in writers—particularly writers of prose.

"Miss Pugh said, 'Then you aren't that poet.'

" 'No, no,' said Prism. 'I am not that . . . that.'

"He was puzzled by the house, believing that it had deliberately been built at the heart of a hollow square, perhaps by a demented architect, for nonsensical people. Rain poured down on the ash tree and naked Cupid. In a flat across the way a kitchen light went on. Miss Pugh pressed the switch of a green-shaded lamp and considered Prism. He turned his head slightly and observed an oil painting of the martyrdom of St. Sebastian. He thought of mile upon mile of museum portraits—young men, young saints pierced with arrows, with nothing to protect them from the staring of women but a coat of varnish.

"The passage of the envelope from his hands to Miss Pugh's was crucial to his adventure. He wondered if he should speak. At the same time, he hated to let the envelope go. It held his entire capital—two chapters of a novel. He did not know if he would ever write anything better, or even if he could write anything else at all.

"Miss Pugh settled the matter by picking it up. 'It's for me to read, isn't it? I'll do so at once. Perhaps you could come back after dinner tonight.'

"*During* dinner would have suited Prism better: Mrs. Hartley-Greene was under the impression he had already moved out and would not be back except to pick up some luggage. *Goldfinches* gives a vivid account of his retreat: 'Christopher seemed to leave a trail of sawdust. There were arrow wounds everywhere. He did not know what other people thought and felt about anything, but he could sense to a fine degree how they thought and felt about him. He lived on the feelings he aroused, sought acquaintances among those in whom these feelings were not actively hostile, and did not know of any other way to be.'

"Eighty pages were in the envelope, thirty of them blank. Miss Pugh was not forced to spend every minute between tea and dinner reading, though she would have done so gladly. She read anything recommended to her, proceeding slowly, pausing often to wonder if the author was sure of his facts. She had a great fear of being hoodwinked, for she knew by now that in art deception is the rule.

"What Prism had described was an elderly duchess, a loyal old manservant named Norbert, a wounded pigeon, and a nation at war. His fifty completed pages were divided into two chapters.

"Chapter 1: In a city under siege, a duchess wonders how to save the priceless eighteenth-century china presented to her family by the Empress. Whatever food Norbert manages to forage she feeds to her cats. She and Norbert adopt and discard schemes for saving the china. They think about this and discuss it all day long.

"Chapter 2: A pigeon flutters in the window. A cat jumps at it, breaking its wing. The duchess and Norbert hear gunfire moving closer. They discuss a plan for saving the pigeon.

"That was as far as it went. Either Prism did not know what came next or did not want to say. It seemed to Miss Pugh that a good deal had been left in the air. The first thing she asked when he came back that night was if the china was really worth saving. If it was priceless, as he claimed, then Norbert ought to pack it into cases lined with heavy silver paper. The cases could then be buried in the garden, if the ground was soft. That would depend on the season, which Prism had not described.

"She had begun a process that Prism had not foreseen and that was the most flattering success he might have imagined. Everything in the story was *hers*, from the duchess to the pigeon.

"Next, she gave her attention to the duchess's apartments, which seemed to be in the wing of a palace. Prism had not mentioned the style of architecture of the palace, or its condition. Most palaces nowadays were museums. Miss Pugh advised Prism to give the duchess an address more realistic and to eliminate from her life the threat of war.

"Then, at last, she said the only thing that mattered: She was ready to offer Prism the opportunity for creative endeavor Mrs. Hartley-Greene had been obliged to refuse because of her predilection for painters. Prism could return in the morning, by which time Rosalia would have his room ready. In the meantime, Miss Pugh would comb through the manuscript again.

"In *Goldfinches*, Prism skims over the next few hours. We have only the testimony of Rosalia, which is that he turned up in the morning looking as if he had spent the night curled up in a doorway.

"Miss Pugh was eating her breakfast in the sitting room with the green-shaded lamp and the portrait of St. Sebastian. Through a half-open door Prism caught a glimpse of her large, canopied bed. There was an extra place laid at the table.

" 'I was expecting my brother,' said Miss Pugh. 'But he has been delayed.'

"Instead of breakfast, Pugh was to have the manila envelope. In his account of the scene, Prism makes a curious mistake: 'The morning sun, kept from Christopher by the angle of the yellow awning, slid into view and hit him square in the face. His eyes watered, and as if a film of illusion had been removed . . .' and so on. There was no awning, no sun; the house was down a well.

"Miss Pugh asked Prism what he thought of Picasso. He understood the question as a test. Her rooms gave no clue to her own opinion; there were no Picassos in sight, but that was not to say there never could be. He drew a square in his mind, as a way of steadying his thoughts, and put Picasso in it.

"All at once, in a rush of blinding anger, he knew what he believed. His first words were inaudible, but as he regained hold on his feelings the sense of his wild protest became clear: 'All that money. All that *money*. Does he enjoy it? They say he lives in the kitchen, like a squatter. As if the house did not belong to him. He could travel. He could own things. He could have twenty-two servants. He does not deserve to have a fortune, because he doesn't know how to use one.'

"His hostess plucked at her table napkin. She was accustomed to hearing poor young men say what they could do with money. She had heard the hunger in the voice, the incoherence and the passion. She had often aroused this longing, putting out the bait and withdrawing it, which was the only form of wickedness she knew. She seemed to be reflecting on what Prism had just said. There was no denying it was original. Who ever had seen Picasso at an auction of rare furniture? At the races, straining after one of his own horses? Photographed at a gala evening in Monte Carlo? Boarding a yacht for a cruise in Greek waters?

" 'What do you think?' said Prism boldly.

" 'He is the most attractive man in the world. My brother would look good, too, if he could stop drinking and pull himself together. What's your opinion of his goats?' Prism shook his head. 'The sculpture. You can see Picasso doesn't care for animals. Those goats are half starved. I suppose you'll be wanting to get to work.'

"Prism in a very short time came to the conclusion he had climbed on the wrong springboard. He saw that the anxiety and frustration of patronage, the backer's terror of being duped, of having been taken in, was second only to the protégé's fear of being despoiled, stripped, robbed, and left bankrupt by the side of the road. Miss Pugh did not loosen her grip on his two chapters, and even Prism's decision that he wanted to have nothing more to do with them did not lessen the tension.

"He would not claim those two chapters today. If they followed him in the street, he would probably threaten them with an umbrella. And yet the story is his; it is *his* duchess, *his* rustic bandstand. It was also Miss Pugh's. 'Have you moved that poor woman out of that filthy old palace yet?' she would ask Prism at lunch. 'Have you found out any more about the china?' When the leaves of Mrs. Wharton's ash tree began to droop and turn yellow, patroness and protégé were at a stalemate that could be ended only by sincere admission of defeat. Miss Pugh was in her own house; Prism had to play the loser. One day he sat down at the Louis XVI–period table in his room and considered the blank pages still in the manila envelope. He wondered if the time had not come to return to England, try for a good degree, and then teach.

"I can always branch out from there, he said to himself. (How easy it must have sounded.)

"He saw in his mind the museum rooms full of portraits of St. Sebastian, with nothing for protection but a thin coat of varnish. There were two opinions about the conservation of art. One claimed it was a mistake to scour paintings in order to lay bare the original color. The other believed it was essential to do so, even if the artist had made allowances for the mellowing and darkening effect of the glaze, and even if the colors revealed turned out to be harsher than the artist had intended. Prism drew a blank sheet toward him and began to write, 'Are we to take it for granted that the artist thinks he knows what he is doing?' At that moment, Prism the critic was born.

"Miss Pugh was sorry when she heard he wanted to give up the duchess, but it was not her policy to engage the Muses in battle. Prism presented her with the manuscript; she gave him the crêpe-soled shoes. She was never heard to speak of him slightingly, and she read with generous pleasure all the newspaper cuttings concerning himself that he sent her over the years. Whenever he came to Paris Miss Pugh would ask him to tea and rejoiced in the rich texture of his career, which he unfolded by the hour, without tiring speaker or audience. Prism made Miss Pugh the subject of countless comic anecdotes and the central female character of *Goldfinches*. He was always evenhanded."

Another Easter went by before Grippes received an acknowledgment—a modest check in lieu of the promised fee, and an apology: His memoir had been mailed to Victor Prism to be checked for accuracy, and Prism had still not replied. During the year sweeping changes had been made. The *Angliciste* had published a paper on the Common Market as seen through English fiction. It was felt to contain a political bias, and the ministry had withdrawn support. The publisher had no choice but to replace him as editor by the only responsible person who seemed to be free at the time, a famous *Irlandiste* on leave from a university in Belgium. The *Irlandiste* restored the project to its original three volumes, threw out the English section as irrelevant, and added a division with potted biographies of eight hundred Irish poets favorable to France and the Common Market.

Grippes has heard that it is to be published in 2010, at the very latest. He knows that in the meantime they are bound to call on him again—more and more as time goes on. He is the only person still alive with any sort of memory.

GRIPPES AND POCHE

———

⁓❧⁓

𝒜t an early hour for the French man of letters Henri Grippes—it was a quarter to nine, on an April morning—he sat in a windowless, brown-painted cubicle, facing a slight, mop-headed young man with horn-rimmed glasses and dimples. The man wore a dark tie with a narrow knot and a buttoned-up blazer. His signature was "O. Poche"; his title, on the grubby, pulpy summons Grippes had read, sweating, was "Controller." He must be freshly out of his civil-service training school, Grippes guessed. Even his aspect, of a priest hearing a confession a few yards from the guillotine, seemed newly acquired. Before him lay open a dun-colored folder with not much in it—a letter from Grippes, full of delaying tactics, and copies of his correspondence with a bank in California. It was not true that American banks protected a depositor's secrets; anyway, this one hadn't. Another reason Grippes thought O. Poche must be recent was the way he kept blushing. He was not nearly as pale or as case-hardened as Grippes.

At this time, President de Gaulle had been in power five years, two of which Grippes had spent in blithe writer-in-residenceship in California. Returning to Paris, he had left a bank account behind. It was forbidden, under the Fifth Republic, for a French citizen to have a foreign account. The government might not have cared so much about drachmas or zlotys, but dollars were supposed to be scraped in, converted to francs at bottom rate, and, of course, counted as personal income. Grippes's unwise and furtive moves with trifling sums, his somewhat paranoid disagreements with California over exchange, had finally caught the eye of the Bank of France, as a glistening minnow might attract a dozing whale. The whale swallowed Grippes, found him too small to matter, and spat him out, straight into the path of a water ox called Public Treasury, Direct Taxation, Personal Income. That was Poche.

What Poche had to discuss—a translation of Grippes's novel, the one about the French teacher at the American university and his doomed love affair with his student Karen-Sue—seemed to embarrass him. Observing Poche with some curiosity, Grippes saw, unreeling, scenes from the younger man's inhibited boyhood. He sensed, then discerned, the Catholic boarding school in bleakest Brittany: the unheated forty-bed dormitory, a nightly torment of unchaste dreams with astonishing partners, a daytime terror of real Hell with real fire.

"Human waywardness is hardly new," said Grippes, feeling more secure now that he had tested Poche and found him provincial. "It no longer shocks anyone."

It was not the moral content of the book he wished to talk over, said Poche, flaming. In any case, he was not qualified to do so: He had flubbed Philosophy and never taken Modern French Thought. (He must be new, Grippes decided. He was babbling.) Frankly, even though he had the figures in front of him, Poche found it hard to believe the American translation had earned its author so little. There must be another considerable sum, placed in some other bank. Perhaps M. Grippes could try to remember.

The figures were true. The translation had done poorly. Failure played to Grippes's advantage, reducing the hint of deliberate tax evasion to a simple oversight. Still, it hurt to have things put so plainly. He felt bound to tell Poche that American readers were no longer interested in the teacher-student imbroglio, though there had been some slight curiosity as to what a foreigner might wring out of the old sponge.

Poche gazed at Grippes. His eyes seemed to Grippes as helpless and eager as those of a gun dog waiting for a command in the right language. Encouraged, Grippes said more: In writing his novel, he had overlooked the essential development—the erring professor was supposed to come home at the end. He could be half dead, limping, on crutches, toothless, jobless, broke, impotent—it didn't matter. He had to be judged and shriven. As further modification, his wife during his foolish affair would have gone on to be a world-class cellist, under her maiden name. "Wife" had not entered Grippes's cast of characters, probably because, like Poche, he did not have one. (He had noticed Poche did not wear a wedding ring.) Grippes had just left his professor driving off to an airport in blessed weather, whistling a jaunty air.

Poche shook his head. Obviously, it was not the language he was after. He began to write on a clean page of the file, taking no more notice of Grippes.

What a mistake it had been, Grippes reflected, still feeling pain beneath the scar, to have repeated the male teacher–female student pattern. He should have turned it around, identified himself with a brilliant and cynical woman teacher. Unfortunately, unlike Flaubert (his academic stalking-horse), he could not put himself in a woman's place, probably because he thought it an absolutely terrible place to be. The novel had not done well in France, either. (Poche had still to get round to that.) The critics had found Karen-Sue's sociological context obscure. She seemed at a remove from events of her time, unaware of improved literacy figures in North Korea, never once mentioned, or that since the advent of Gaullism it cost twenty-five centimes to mail a letter. The Pill was still unheard-of in much of Europe; readers could not understand what it was Karen-Sue kept forgetting to take, or why Grippes had devoted a contemplative no-action chapter to the abstract essence of risk. The professor had not given Karen-Sue the cultural and political enlightenment one might expect from the graduate of a preeminent Paris school. It was a banal story, really, about a pair of complacently bourgeois lovers. The real victim was Grippes, seduced and abandoned by the American middle class.

It was Grippes's first outstanding debacle and, for that reason, the only one of his works he ever reread. He could still hear Karen-Sue—the true, the original—making of every avowal a poignant question: "I'm Cairn-Sioux? I know you're busy? It's just that I don't understand what you said about Flaubert and his own niece?" He recalled her with tolerance—the same tolerance that had probably weakened the book.

Grippes was wise enough to realize that the California-bank affair had been an act of folly, a con man's aberration. He had thought he would get away with it, knowing all the while he could not. There existed a deeper treasure for Poche to uncover, well below Public Treasury sights. Computers had not yet come into government use; even typewriters were rare— Poche had summoned Grippes in a cramped, almost secretive hand. It took time to strike an error, still longer to write a letter about it. In his youth, Grippes had received from an American patroness of the arts three rent-bearing apartments in Paris, which he still owned. (The patroness had been the last of a generous species, Grippes one of the last young men to benefit from her kind.) He collected the rents by devious and untraceable means, stowing the cash obtained in safe deposit. His visible way of life was stoic and plain; not even the most vigilant Controller could fault his underfurnished apartment in Montparnasse, shared with some cats he had already tried to claim as dependents. He showed none of the signs of prosperity Public Treasury seemed to like, such as membership in a golf club.

After a few minutes of speculative anguish in the airless cubicle, Grippes saw that Poche had no inkling whatever about the flats. He was chasing something different—the inexistent royalties from the Karen-Sue novel. By a sort of divine evenhandedness, Grippes was going to have to pay for imaginary earnings. He put the safe deposit out of his mind, so that it would not show on his face, and said, "What will be left for me, when you've finished adding and subtracting?"

To his surprise, Poche replied in a bold tone, pitched for reciting quotations: " 'What is left? What is left? Only what remains at low tide, when small islands are revealed, emerging ...' " He stopped quoting and flushed. Obviously, he had committed the worst sort of blunder, had been intimate, had let his own personality show. He had crossed over to his opponent's ground.

"It sounds familiar," said Grippes, enticing him further. "Although, to tell the truth, I don't remember writing it."

"It is a translation," said Poche. "The Anglo-Saxon British author, Victor Prism." He pronounced it "Prissom."

"You've read Prism?" said Grippes, pronouncing correctly the name of an old acquaintance.

"I had to. Prissom was on the preparatory program. Anglo-Saxon Commercial English."

"They stuffed you with foreign writers?" said Grippes. "With so many of us having to go to foreign lands for a living?"

That was perilous: He had just challenged Poche's training, the very foundation of his right to sit there reading Grippes's private mail. But he had suddenly recalled his dismay when as a young man he had looked at a shelf in his room and realized he had to compete with the dead—Proust, Flaubert, Balzac, Stendhal, and on into the dark. The rivalry was infinite, a Milky Way of dead stars still daring to shine. He had invented a law, a moratorium on publication that would eliminate the dead, leaving the skies clear for the living. (All the living? Grippes still couldn't decide.) Foreign writers would be deported to a remote solar system, where they could circle one another.

For Prism, there was no system sufficiently remote. Not so long ago, interviewed in *The Listener*, Prism had dragged in Grippes, saying that he used to cross the Channel to consult a seer in Half Moon Street, hurrying home to set down the prose revealed from a spirit universe. "Sometimes I actually envied him," Prism was quoted as saying. He sounded as though Grippes were dead. "I used to wish ghost voices would speak to me, too," suggesting ribbons of pure Prism running like ticker tape round the equator of a crystal ball. "Unfortunately, I had to depend on my own creative intelligence, modest though I am sure it was."

Poche did not know about this recent libel in Anglo-Saxon Commercial English. He had been trying to be nice. Grippes made a try of his own, jocular: "I only meant, you could have been reading *me*." The trouble was that he meant it, ferociously.

Poche must have heard the repressed shout. He shut the file and said, "This dossier is too complex for my level. I shall have to send it up to the Inspector." Grippes made a vow that he would never let natural pique get the better of him again.

"What will be left for me?" Grippes asked the Inspector. "When you have finished adding and subtracting?"

Mme. de Pelle did not bother to look up. She said, "Somebody should have taken this file in hand a long time ago. Let us start at the beginning. How long, in all, were you out of the country?"

When Poche said "send up," he'd meant it literally. Grippes looked out on a church where Delacroix had worked and the slow summer rain. At the far end of the square, a few dark shops displayed joyfully trashy religious goods, like the cross set with tiny seashells Mme. de Pelle wore round her neck. Grippes had been raised in an anticlerical household, in a small town where opposing factions were grouped behind the schoolmaster—Grippes's father—and the parish priest. Women, lapsed agnostics, sometimes crossed enemy lines and started going to church. One glimpsed them, all in gray, creeping along a gray-walled street.

"You are free to lodge a protest against the fine," said Mme. de Pelle. "But if you lose the contestation, your fine will be tripled. That is the law."

Grippes decided to transform Mme. de Pelle into the manager of a brothel catering to the Foreign Legion, slovenly in her habits and addicted to chloroform, but he found the idea unpromising. In due course he paid a monstrous penalty, which he did not contest, for fear of drawing attention to the apartments. (It was still believed that he had stashed away millions from the Karen-Sue book, probably in Switzerland.) A summons addressed in O. Poche's shrunken hand, the following spring, showed Grippes he had been tossed back downstairs. After that he forgot about Mme. de Pelle, except now and then.

It was at about this time that a series of novels offered themselves to Grippes—shadowy outlines behind a frosted-glass pane. He knew he must not let them crowd in all together, or keep them waiting too long. His foot against the door, he admitted, one by one, a number of shadows that turned into young men, each bringing his own name and address, his native region of France portrayed on color postcards, and an index of information about his tastes in clothes, love, food, and philosophers, his bent of character, his tics of speech, his attitudes toward God and money, his political bias, and the intimation of a crisis about to explode underfoot. "Antoine" provided a Jesuit confessor, a homosexual affinity, and loss of faith. Spiritual shilly-shallying tends to run long; Antoine's covered more than six hundred pages, making it the thickest work in the Grippes canon. Then came "Thomas," with his Spartan mother on a Provençal fruit farm, rejected in favor of a civil-service career. "Bertrand" followed, adrift in frivolous Paris, tempted by neo-Fascism in the form of a woman wearing a bed jacket trimmed with marabou. "René" cycled round France, reading Chateaubriand when he stopped to rest. One morning he set fire to the barn he had been sleeping in, leaving his books to burn. This was the shortest of the novels, and the most popular with the young. One critic scolded Grippes for using crude symbolism. Another begged him to stop hiding behind "Antoine" and "René" and to take the metaphysical risk of revealing "Henri." But Grippes had tried that once with Karen-Sue, then with a roman à clef mercifully destroyed in the confusion of May 1968. He took these contretemps for a sign that he was to leave the subjective Grippes alone. The fact that each novel appeared even to Grippes to be a slice of French writing about life as it had been carved up and served a generation before made it seem quietly insurrectional. Nobody was doing this now; no one but Grippes. Grippes, for a time uneasy, decided to go on letting the shadows in.

The announcement of a new publication would bring a summons from

Poche. When Poche leaned over the file, now, Grippes saw amid the mop of curls a coin-size tonsure. His diffident, steely questions tried to elicit from Grippes how many copies were likely to be sold and where Grippes had already put the money. Grippes would give him a copy of the book, inscribed. Poche would turn back the cover and glance at the signature, probably to make certain Grippes had not written something compromising and friendly. He kept the novels in a metal locker, fastened together with government-issue webbing tape and a military-looking buckle. It troubled Grippes to think of his work all in a bundle, in the dark. He thought of old-fashioned milestones, half hidden by weeds, along disused roads. The volumes marked time for Poche, too. He was still a Controller. Perhaps he had to wait for the woman upstairs to retire, so he could take over her title and office. The cubicle needed paint. There was a hole in the brown linoleum, just inside the door. Poche now wore a wedding ring. Grippes wondered if he should congratulate him, but decided to let Poche mention the matter first. He tried to imagine Mme. Poche.

Grippes could swear that in his string of novels nothing had been chipped out of his own past. Antoine, Thomas, Bertrand, and René (and, by now, Clément, Didier, Laurent, Hugues, and Yves) had arrived as strangers, almost like historical figures. At the same time, it seemed to Grippes that their wavering, ruffled reflection should deliver something he alone might recognize. What did he see, bending over the pond of his achievement? He saw a character closemouthed, cautious, unimaginative, ill at ease, obsessed with particulars. Worse, he was closed against progress, afraid of reform, shut into a literary, reactionary France. How could this be? Grippes had always and sincerely voted left. He had proved he could be reckless, open-minded, indulgent. He was like a father gazing round the breakfast table and suddenly realizing that none of the children are his. His children, if he could call them that, did not even look like him. From Antoine to Yves, his reflected character was small and slight, with a mop of curly hair, horn-rimmed glasses, and dimples.

Grippes believed in the importance of errors. No political system, no love affair, no native inclination, no life itself would be tolerable without a wide mesh for mistakes to slip through. It pleased him that Public Treasury had never caught up with the three apartments—not just for the sake of the cash piling up in safe deposit but for the black hole of error revealed. He and Poche had been together for some years—another blunder. Usually Controller and taxpayer were torn apart after a meeting or two, so that the revenue service would not start taking into consideration the client's aged indigent aunt, his bill for dental surgery, his alimony payments, his perennial mortgage. But possibly no one except Poche could be bothered with Grippes, always making some time-wasting claim for minute professional expenses, backed by a messy-looking certified receipt. Sometimes Grippes dared believe Poche admired him, that he hung on to the dossier out of devotion to his books. (This conceit was intensified when Poche began calling him "Maître.") Once, Grippes won some City of Paris award and was shown in *France-Soir* shaking hands with the mayor and simultaneously receiving a long, check-filled envelope. Immediately summoned by Poche, expecting a discreet compliment, Grippes found him interested only in the caption under the photo, which made much of the size of the check. Grippes later thought of sending a sneering letter—"Thank you for your warm congratulations"—but he decided in time it was wiser not to fool with Poche. Poche had recently given him a 33 percent personal exemption, 3 percent more than the outer limit for Grippes's category of unsalaried earners—according to Poche, a group that included, as well as authors, door-to-door salesmen and prostitutes.

The dun-colored Gaullist-era jacket on Grippes's file had worn out long ago and been replaced, in 1969, by a cover in cool banker's green. Green presently made way for a shiny black-and-white marbled effect, reflecting the mood of opulence of the early seventies. Called in for his annual springtime confession, Grippes remarked about the folder: "Culture seems to have taken a decisive turn."

Poche did not ask what culture. He continued bravely, "Food for the cats, Maître. We *can't.*"

"They depend on me," said Grippes. But they had already settled the cats-as-dependents question once and for all. Poche drooped over Grippes's smudged and unreadable figures. Grippes tried to count the number of times he had examined the top of Poche's head. He still knew nothing about Poche, except for the wedding ring. Somewhere along the way, Poche had tied himself to a need for retirement pay and rich exemptions of his own. In the language of his generation, Poche was a fully structured individual. His vocabulary was sparse and to the point, centered on a single topic. His state training school, the machine that ground out Pelles and Poches all sounding alike, was in Clermont-Ferrand. Grippes was born in the same region.

That might have given them something else to talk about, except that Grippes had never been back. Structured Poche probably attended class reunions, was godfather to classmates' children, jotted their birthdays in a leather-covered notebook he never mislaid. Unstructured Grippes could not even remember his own age.

Poche turned over a sheet of paper, read something Grippes could not see, and said, automatically, "We *can't*."

"Nothing is ever as it was," said Grippes, still going on about the marbled-effect folder. It was a remark that usually shut people up, leaving them nowhere to go but a change of subject. Besides, it was true. Nothing can be as it was. Poche and Grippes had just lost a terrifying number of brain cells. They were an instant closer to death. Death was of no interest to Poche. If he ever thought he might cease to exist, he would stop concentrating on other people's business and get down to reading Grippes while there was still time. Grippes wanted to ask, "Do you ever imagine your own funeral?" but it might have been taken as a threatening, gangsterish hint from taxpayer to Controller—worse, far worse, than an attempted bribe.

A folder of a pretty mottled-peach shade appeared. Poche's cubicle was painted soft beige, the torn linoleum repaired. Poche sat in a comfortable armchair resembling the wide leathery seats in smart furniture stores at the upper end of Boulevard Saint-Germain. Grippes had a new, straight metallic chair that shot him bolt upright and hurt his spine. It was the heyday of the Giscardian period, when it seemed more important to keep the buttons polished than to watch where the regiment was heading. Grippes and Poche had not advanced one inch toward each other. Except for the paint and the chairs and "Maître," it could have been 1963. No matter how many works were added to the bundle in the locker, no matter how often Grippes had his picture taken, no matter how many Grippes paperbacks blossomed on airport bookstalls, Grippes to Poche remained a button.

The mottled-peach jacket began to darken and fray. Poche said to Grippes, "I asked you to come here, Maître, because I find we have overlooked something concerning your income." Grippes's heart gave a lurch. "The other day I came across an old ruling about royalties. How much of your income do you kick back?"

"Excuse me?"

"To publishers, to bookstores," said Poche. "How much?"

"Kick back?"

"What percentage?" said Poche. "Publishers. Printers."

"You mean," said Grippes, after a time, "how much do I pay editors to edit, publishers to publish, printers to print, and booksellers to sell?" He supposed that to Poche such a scheme might sound plausible. It would fit his long view over Grippes's untidy life. Grippes knew most of the literary gossip that went round about himself; the circle was so small that it had to come back. In most stories there was a virus of possibility, but he had never heard anything as absurd as this, or as base.

Poche opened the file, concealing the moldering cover, apparently waiting for Grippes to mention a figure. The nausea Grippes felt he put down to his having come here without breakfast. One does not insult a Controller. He had shouted silently at Poche, years before, and had been sent upstairs to do penance with Mme. de Pelle. It is not good to kick over a chair and stalk out. "I have never been so insulted!" might have no meaning from Grippes, keelhauled month after month in one lumpy review or another. As his works increased from bundle to heap, so they drew intellectual abuse. He welcomed partisan ill-treatment, as warming to him as popular praise. Don't forget me, Grippes silently prayed, standing at the periodicals table in La Hune, the Left Bank bookstore, looking for his own name in those quarterlies no one ever takes home. Don't praise me. Praise is weak stuff. Praise me after I'm dead.

But even the most sour and despairing and close-printed essays were starting to mutter acclaim. The shoreline of the eighties, barely in sight, was ready to welcome Grippes, who had reestablished the male as hero, whose left-wing heartbeat could be heard, loyally thumping, behind the armor of his right-wing traditional prose. His reestablished hero had curly hair, soft eyes, horn-rimmed glasses, dimples, and a fully structured life. He was pleasing to both sexes and to every type of reader, except for a few thick-ribbed louts. Grippes looked back at Poche, who did not know how closely they were bound. What if he were to say, "This is a preposterous insinuation, a blot on a noble profession and on my reputation in particular," only to have Poche answer, "Too bad, Maître—I was trying to help"? He said, as one good-natured fellow to another, "Well, what if I own up to this crime?"

"It's no crime," said Poche. "I simply add the amount to your professional expenses."

"To my rebate?" said Grippes. "To my exemption?"

"It depends on how much."

"A third of my income?" said Grippes, insanely. "Half?"

"A reasonable figure might be twelve and a half percent."

All this for Grippes. Poche wanted nothing. Grippes considered with awe the only uncorruptible element in a porous society. No secret message had passed between them. He could not even invite Poche to lunch. He wondered if this arrangement had ever actually existed—if there could possibly be a good dodge that he, Grippes, had never heard of. He thought of contemporary authors for whose success there could be no other explanation: It had to be celestial playfulness or 12.5 percent. The structure, as Grippes was already calling it, might also just be Poche's innocent, indecent idea about writers.

Poche was reading the file again, though he must have known everything in it by heart. He was as absorbed, as contented, and somehow as pure as a child with a box of paints. At any moment he would raise his tender, bewildered eyes and murmur, "Four dozen typewriter ribbons in a third of the fiscal year, Maître? We *can't*."

Grippes tried to compose a face for Poche to encounter, a face above reproach. But writers considered above reproach always looked moody and haggard, about to scream. Be careful, he was telling himself. Don't let Poche think he's doing you a favor. These people set traps. Was Poche angling for something? Was this bait? "Attempting to bribe a public servant" the accusation was called. "Bribe" wasn't the word: It was "corruption" the law mentioned—"an attempt to corrupt." All Grippes had ever offered Poche was his books, formally inscribed, as though Poche were an anonymous reader standing in line in a bookstore where Grippes, wedged behind a shaky table, sat signing away. "Your name?" "Whose name?" "How do you spell your name?" "Oh, the book isn't for me. It's for a friend of mine." His look changed to one of severity and impatience, until he remembered that Poche had never asked him to sign anything. He had never concealed his purpose, to pluck from Grippes's plumage every bright feather he could find.

Careful, Grippes repeated. Careful. Remember what happened to Prism.

Victor Prism, keeping pale under a parasol on the beach at Torremolinos, had made the acquaintance of a fellow Englishman—pleasant, not well educated but eager to learn, blistered shoulders, shirt draped over his head, pages of the *Sunday Express* round his red thighs. Prism lent him something to read—his sunburn was keeping him awake. It was a creative essay on three émigré authors of the 1930s, in a review so obscure and ill-paying that Prism had not bothered to include the fee on his income-tax return. (Prism had got it wrong, of course, having Thomas Mann—whose plain name Prism could not spell—go to East Germany and with his wife start a theater that presented his own plays, sending Stefan Zweig to be photographed with movie stars in California, and putting Bertolt Brecht to die a bitter man in self-imposed exile in Brazil. As it turned out, none of Prism's readers knew the difference. Chided by Grippes, Prism had been defensive, cold, said that no letters had come in. "One, surely?" said Grippes. "Yes, I thought that must be you," Prism said.)

Prism might have got off with the whole thing if his new friend had not fallen sound asleep after the first lines. Waking, refreshed, he had said to himself, I must find out what they get paid for this stuff, a natural reflex— he was of the Inland Revenue. He'd found no trace, no record; for Inland Revenue purposes "Death and Exile" did not exist. The subsequent fine was so heavy and Prism's disgrace so acute that he fled England to spend a few days with Grippes and the cats in Montparnasse. He sat on a kitchen chair while Grippes, nose and mouth protected by a checked scarf, sprayed terror to cockroaches. Prism, weeping in the fumes and wiping his eyes, said, "I'm through with Queen and Country"—something like that—"and I'm taking out French citizenship tomorrow."

"You would have to marry a Frenchwoman and have at least five male children," said Grippes, through the scarf. He was feeling the patriotic hatred of a driver on a crowded road seeing foreign license plates in the way.

"Oh, well, then," said Prism, as if to say, "I won't bother."

"Oh, well, then," said Grippes, softly, not quite to Poche. Poche added one last thing to the file and closed it, as if something definite had taken place. He clasped his hands and placed them on the dossier; it seemed shut for all time now, like a grave. He said, "Maître, one never stays long in the same fiscal theater. I have been in this one for an unusual length of time. We may not meet again. I want you to know I have enjoyed our conversations."

"So have I," said Grippes, with caution.

"Much of your autobiographical creation could apply to other lives of our time, believe me."

"So you have read them," said Grippes, an eye on the locker.

"I read those I bought," said Poche.

"But they are the same books."

"No. The books I bought belong to me. The others were gifts. I would never open a gift. I have no right to." His voice rose, and he spoke more slowly. "In one of them, when What's-His-Name struggles to prepare his civil-service tests, '... the desire for individual glory seemed so inapposite, suddenly, in a nature given to renunciation.' "

"I suppose it *is* a remarkable observation," said Grippes. "I was not referring to myself." He had no idea what that could be from, and he was certain he had not written it.

Poche did not send for Grippes again. Grippes became a commonplace tax-payer, filling out his forms without help. The frosted-glass door was reverting to dull white; there were fewer shadows for Grippes to let in. A fashion for having well-behaved Nazi officers shore up Western culture gave Grippes a chance to turn Poche into a tubercular poet, trapped in Paris by poverty and the Occupation. Grippes threw out the first draft, in which Poche joined a Christian-minded Resistance network and performed a few simple miracles, unaware of his own powers. He had the instinctive feeling that a new generation would not know what he was talking about. Instead, he placed Poche, sniffling and wheezing, in a squalid hotel room, cough pastilles spilled on the table, a stained blanket pinned round his shoulders. Up the fetid staircase came a handsome colonel, a Curt Jurgens type, smelling of shaving lotion, bent on saving liberal values, bringing Poche butter, cognac, and a thousand sheets of writing paper.

After that, Grippes no longer felt sure where to go. His earlier books, government tape and buckle binding them into an œuvre, had accompanied Poche to his new fiscal theater. Perhaps, finding his career blocked by the woman upstairs, he had asked for early retirement. Poche was in a gangster-ridden Mediterranean city, occupying a shoddy boom-period apartment he'd spent twenty years paying for. He was working at black-market jobs, tax adviser to the local mayor, a small innocent cog in the regional Mafia. After lunch, Poche would sit on one of those southern balconies that hold just a deck chair, rereading in chronological order all Grippes's books. In the late afternoon, blinds drawn, Poche totted up Mafia accounts by a chink of light. Grippes was here, in Montparnasse, facing a flat-white glass door.

He continued to hand himself a 45.5 percent personal exemption—the astonishing 33 plus the unheard-of 12.5. No one seemed to mind. No shabby envelope holding an order for execution came in the mail. Sometimes in Grippes's mind a flicker of common sense flamed like revealed truth: The exemption was an error. Public Treasury was now tiptoeing toward computers. The computer brain was bound to wince at Grippes and stop functioning until the Grippes exemption was settled. Grippes rehearsed: "I was seriously misinformed."

He had to go farther and farther abroad to find offal for the cats. One tripe dealer had been turned into a driving school, another sold secondhand clothes. Returning on a winter evening after a long walk, carrying a parcel of sheep's lung wrapped in newspaper, he crossed Boulevard du Montparnasse just as the lights went on—the urban moonrise. The street was a dream street, faces flat white in the winter mist. It seemed to Grippes that he had crossed over to the 1980s, had only just noticed the new decade. In a recess between two glassed-in sidewalk cafés, four plainclothes cops were beating up a pair of pickpockets. Nobody had to explain the scene to Grippes; he knew what it was about. One prisoner already wore handcuffs. Customers on the far side of the glass gave no more than a glance. When they had got handcuffs on the second man, the cops pushed the two into the entrance of Grippes's apartment building to wait for the police van. Grippes shuffled into a café. He put his parcel of lights on the zinc-topped bar and started to read an article on the wrapping. Someone unknown to him, a new name, pursued an old grievance: Why don't they write about real life anymore?

Because to depict life is to attract its ill-fortune, Grippes replied.

He stood sipping coffee, staring at nothing. Four gun-bearing young men in jeans and leather jackets were not final authority; final authority was something written, the printed word, even when the word was mistaken. The simplest final authority in Grippes's life had been O. Poche and a book of rules. What must have happened was this: Poche, wishing to do honor to a category that included writers, prostitutes, and door-to-door salesmen, had read and misunderstood a note about royalties. It had been in italics, at the foot of the page. He had transformed his mistake into a regulation and had never looked at the page again.

Grippes in imagination climbed three flights of dirty wooden stairs to Mme. de Pelle's office. He observed the seashell crucifix and a brooch he had not noticed the first time, a silver fawn curled up as nature had never planned—a boneless fawn. Squinting, Mme. de Pelle peered at the old dun-colored Gaullist-era file. She put her hand over a page, as though Grippes were trying to read upside down. "It has all got to be paid back," she said.

"I was seriously misinformed," Grippes intended to answer, willing to see Poche disgraced, ruined, jailed. "I followed instructions. I am innocent."

But Poche had vanished, leaving Grippes with a lunatic exemption, three black-market income-bearing apartments he had recently, unsuccessfully, tried to sell, and a heavy reputation for male-oriented, left-feeling, right-thinking books. This reputation Grippes thought he could no longer sustain. A Socialist government was at last in place (hence his hurry about unloading the flats and his difficulty in finding takers). He wondered about the new file cover. Pink? Too fragile—look what had happened with the mottled peach. Strong denim blue, the shade standing for *giovinezza* and workers' overalls? It was no time for a joke, not even a private one. No one could guess what would be wanted, now, in the way of literary entertainment. The fitfulness of voters is such that, having got the government they wanted, they were now reading nothing but the right-wing press. Perhaps a steady right-wing heartbeat ought to set the cadence for a left-wing outlook, with a complex, bravely conservative heroine contained within the slippery but unyielding walls of left-wing style. He would have to come to terms with the rightist way of considering female characters. There seemed to be two methods, neither of which suited Grippes's temperament: Treat her disgustingly, then cry all over the page, or admire and respect her—she is the equal at least of a horse. The only woman his imagination offered, with some insistence, was no use to him. She moved quietly on a winter evening to Saint-Nicolas-du-Chardonnet, the rebel church at the lower end of Boulevard Saint-Germain, where services were still conducted in Latin. She wore a hat ornamented with an ivory arrow, and a plain gray coat, tubular in shape, with a narrow fur collar. Kid gloves were tucked under the handle of her sturdy leather purse. She had never heard of video games, push-button telephones, dishwashers, frozen filleted sole, computer horoscopes. She entered the church and knelt down and brought out her rosary, oval pearls strung on thin gold. Nobody saw rosaries anymore. They were not even in the windows of their traditional venues, across the square from the tax bureau. Believers went in for different articles now: cherub candles, quick prayers on plastic cards. Her iron meekness resisted change. She prayed constantly into the past. Grippes knew that one's view of the past is just as misleading as speculation about the future. It was one of the few beliefs he would have gone to the stake for. She was praying to a mist, to mist-shrouded figures she persisted in seeing clear.

He could see the woman, but he could not approach her. Perhaps he could get away with dealing with her from a distance. All that was really needed for a sturdy right-wing novel was its pessimistic rhythm: and then, and then, and then, and death. Grippes had that rhythm. It was in his footsteps, coming up the stairs after the departure of the police van, turning the key in his triple-bolted front door. And then, and then, the cats padding and mewing, not giving Grippes time to take off his coat as they made for their empty dishes on the kitchen floor. Behind the gas stove, a beleaguered garrison of cockroaches got ready for the evening sortie. Grippes would be waiting, his face half veiled with a checked scarf.

In Saint-Nicolas-du-Chardonnet the woman shut her missal, got up off her knees, scorning to brush her coat; she went out to the street, proud of the dust marks, letting the world know she still prayed the old way. She escaped him. He had no idea what she had on, besides the hat and coat. Nobody else wore a hat with an ivory arrow or a tubular coat or a scarf that looked like a weasel biting its tail. He could not see what happened when she took the hat and coat off, what her hair was like, if she hung the coat in a hall closet that also contained umbrellas, a carpet-sweeper, and a pile of old magazines, if she put the hat in a round box on a shelf. She moved off in a gray blur. There was a streaming window between them Grippes could not wipe clean. Probably she entered a dark dining room—fake Henri IV buffet, bottles of pills next to the oil and vinegar cruets, lace tablecloth folded over the back of a chair, just oilcloth spread for the family meal. What could he do with such a woman? He could not tell who was waiting for her or what she would eat for supper. He could not even guess at her name. She revealed nothing; would never help.

Grippes expelled the cats, shut the kitchen window, and dealt with the advance guard from behind the stove. What he needed now was despair and excitement, a new cat-and-mouse chase. What good was a computer that never caught anyone out?

After airing the kitchen and clearing it of poison, Grippes let the cats in. He swept up the bodies of his victims and sent them down the ancient cast-iron chute. He began to talk to himself, as he often did now. First he said a few sensible things, then he heard his voice with a new elderly quaver to it, virtuous and mean: "After all, it doesn't take much to keep me happy."

Now, that was untrue, and he had no reason to say it. Is that what I am going to be like, now, he wondered. Is this the new-era Grippes, pinch-mouthed? It was exactly the sort of thing that the woman in the dark dining room might say. The best thing that could happen to him would be shock, a siege of terror, a knock at the door and a registered letter with fearful news. It would sharpen his humor, strengthen his own, private, eccentric heart. It would keep him from making remarks in his solitude that were meaningless and false. He could perhaps write an anonymous letter saying that the famous author Henri Grippes was guilty of evasion of a most repulsive kind. He was, moreover, a callous landlord who had never been known to replace a doorknob. Fortunately, he saw, he was not yet that mad, nor did he really need to be scared and obsessed. He had got the woman from church to dining room, and he would keep her there, trapped, cornered, threatened, watched, until she yielded to Grippes and told her name—as, in his several incarnations, good Poche had always done.

IN PLAIN SIGHT

❦

*O*n the first Wednesday of every month, sharp at noon, an air-raid siren wails across Paris, startling pigeons and lending an edge to the midday news. Older Parisians say it has the tone and pitch of a newsreel sound track. They think, Before the war, and remember things in black-and-white. Some wonder how old Hitler would be today and if he really did escape to South America. Others say an order to test warning equipment was given in 1956, at the time of the Suez crisis, and never taken off the books. The author Henri Grippes believes the siren business has to do with high finance. (High finance, to Grippes, means somebody else's income.) The engineer who installed the alert, or his estate, picks up a dividend whenever it goes off.

At all events, it is punctual and reliable. It keeps Grippes's rare bursts of political optimism in perspective and starts the month off with a mixture of dread and unaccountable nostalgia: the best possible mixture for a writer's psyche. The truth is he seldom hears it, not consciously. When he was still young, Grippes got in the habit of going to bed at dawn and getting up at around three in the afternoon. He still lives that way—reading and writing after dark, listening to the radio, making repetitive little drawings on a pad of paper, watching an American rerun on a late channel, eating salted hard-boiled eggs, drinking Badoit or vodka or champagne (to wash the egg down) or black coffee so thickly sweetened that it can act as a sedative.

He is glad to have reached an age when no one is likely to barge in at all hours announcing that salt is lethal and sugar poison. (Vodka and champagne are considered aids to health.) Never again will he be asked to hand over the key to his apartment, as a safety measure, or receive an offer to sleep in the little room off the kitchen and never get in the way. In fact, offers to cherish him seem to be falling off. The last he remembers was put forward a few years ago, when his upstairs neighbor, Mme. Parfaire (Marthe), suggested her constant presence would add six years to his life. Since then, peace and silence. Put it a different way: Who cares if Grippes slips into the darkest pocket of the universe, still holding a bitten egg? Now when Mme. Parfaire (no longer "Marthe") meets Grippes in an aisle of the Inno supermarket, on Rue du Départ, she stares at his hairline. Grazing his shopping cart with her own, she addresses a cold apology to "Monsieur," never "Henri." Years of admiration, of fretting about his health and, who knows, of love of a kind have been scraped away; yet once she had been ready to give up her smaller but neater flat, her wider view over Boulevard du Montparnasse, the good opinion of her friends (proud widows, like herself), for the sake of moving downstairs and keeping an eye on his diet. She also had a strong desire to choose all his clothes, remembering and frequently bringing up his acquisition of a green plastic jacket many years before.

What went wrong? First, Grippes didn't want the six extra years. Then, she handed him a final statement of terms at the worst point of the day, five past three in the afternoon—a time for breakfast and gradual wakening. He was barely on his feet, had opened the front door to pick up mail and newspapers left on the mat (the concierge knows better than to ring), and came face-to-face with Marthe. She stood with her back to the stair rail, waiting—he supposed—for Allégra, her small white dog, to catch up. Allégra could be heard snuffling and clawing her way along the varnished steps. There was an elevator now, tucked inside the stairwell, the cost shared by all, but Mme. Parfaire continued to climb. She knew a story about a woman who had been trapped in a lift of the same make and had to be rescued by firemen.

Grippes made his first tactless remark of the day, which was "What do you want?" Not even a civilized, if inappropriate, "I see you're up early" or "It's going to be a fine day." He took in the contents of her nylon-net shopping bag: a carton of milk, six Golden Delicious E.C. standard-size Brussels-approved apples, six eggs, ditto, and a packet of Autumn Splendor tinted shampoo. The tilt of her dark head, her expression—brooding and defiant—brought to mind the great Marie Bell and the way she used to stand here and there on the stage, in the days when "tragedienne" still had meaning. He thought of Racine, of Greek heroines; he hoped he would not be obliged to think about Corneille and the cruel dilemma of making a simple choice. His friend seemed to him elegantly turned out—skirt length unchanged for a decade or so, Chanel-style navy jacket, of the kind favored by wives of politicians in the last-but-one right-wing government. Only her shoes, chosen for comfort and stair climbing, maintained a comfortable, shambling Socialist appearance, like a form of dissent.

As for Grippes, he had on heavy socks, jogging pants, a T-shirt with tiger-head design (a gift), and a brown cardigan with bone buttons, knitted by Mme. Parfaire two Christmases before. She examined the tiger head, then asked Grippes if he had given any more thought to their common future. He knew what she was talking about, she said, a bit more sharply. They had been over it many times. (Grippes denies this.) The two-apartment system had not worked out. She and Grippes had not so much grown apart as failed to draw together. She knew he would not quit the junk and rubble of his own dwelling: His creative mind was rooted in layers of cast-off books, clothes, and chipped ashtrays. For that reason, she was willing to move downstairs and share his inadequate closets. (No mention this time of keeping to the little room off the kitchen, he noticed.) Whenever he wanted to be by himself, she would go out and sit on a bench at the Montparnasse-Stanislas bus stop. For company, she would bring along one of his early novels, the kind critics kept begging him to reread and learn from. At home, she would put him on a memory-preserving, mental-stimulation regime, with plenty of vegetable protein; she would get Dr. Planche to tell her the true state of Grippes's hearing (would he be stone deaf very soon?) and to report on the vital irrigation of Grippes's brain (clogged, sluggish, running dry?). Her shy Allégra would live in harmony with his cats—an example for world leaders. Finally, she would sort his mail, tear up the rubbish, answer the telephone and the doorbell, and treat with sensitivity but firmness the floating shreds of his past.

Grippes recalls that he took "floating shreds" to mean Mme. Obier (Charlotte), and felt called on to maintain a small amount of exactitude. It was true that Mme. Obier—dressed in layers of fuzzy black, convinced that any day was the ninth of September, 1980, and that Grippes was expecting her for tea—could make something of a nuisance of herself on the fourth-floor landing. However, think of the sixties, when her flowing auburn hair and purple tights had drawn cheers in the Coupole. In those days, the

Coupole was as dim as a night train and served terrible food. Through a haze rising from dozens of orders of fried whiting, the cheapest dish on the menu, out-of-town diners used to search for a glimpse of Sartre or Beckett and try to make out if the forks were clean. Now the renovated lighting, soft but revealing, showed every crease and stain on the faces and clothes of the old crowd. Sociable elderly ladies, such as Mme. Obier, no longer roamed the aisles looking for someone to stand them a drink but were stopped at the entrance by a charming person holding a clipboard and wanting to know if they were expected. There might be grounds for calling her a shred, Grippes concluded, but she was the fragment of a rich cultural past. If she seemed on in years, it was only by comparison with Grippes. Not only did Grippes look younger than his age but from early youth he had always preferred the company of somewhat older women, immovably married to someone else. (His reasons were so loaded with common sense that he did not bother to set them out.) Unfortunately, he had never foreseen the time when his friends, set loose because the husband had died or decamped to Tahiti, would start to scamper around Paris like demented ferrets. Having preceded Grippes in the field of life, they maintained an advance, beating him over the line to a final zone of muddle, mistakes, and confused expectations.

The only sound, once Grippes had stopped speaking to Mme. Parfaire, was the new elevator, squeaking and grinding as if it were very old. Allégra waddled into view and stood with her tongue hanging. Mme. Parfaire turned away and prepared to resume her climb. He thought he heard, "I am not likely to forget this insult." It occurred to him, later, that he ought to have carried her net bag the extra flight or invited her in for coffee; instead, he had stepped back and shut the door. Where she was concerned, perhaps he had shut it forever. What had she offered him, exactly? An unwelcome occupation of his time and space, true, but something else that he might have done well to consider: unpaid, unending, unflagging, serious-minded female service. Unfortunately, his bulwark against doing the sensible thing as seen through a woman's mind had always been to present a masculine case—which means to say densely hedged and full of dead-end trails—and get behind it. Anyone taking up residence in his routine seemed to have got there by mistake or been left behind by a previous tenant. The door to Grippes stood swinging on its hinges, but it led to a waiting room.

The difference between Mme. Parfaire and other applicants, he thinks now, was in her confident grasp on time. She never mislaid a day or a minute. On her deathbed she will recall that on the day when Grippes made it plain he had no use for her it became legal for French citizens to open a bank account abroad. The two events are knotted together in her version of late-twentieth-century history. She will see Grippes as he was, standing in the doorway, no shoes on his feet, unshaven, trying to steal a glance at the headlines while she tries to make him a present of her last good years. But then that dishonoring memory will be overtaken by the image of a long, cream-colored envelope bearing the address of a foreign, solvent bank. On that consoling vision she will close her eyes.

No one dies in Grippes's novels; not anymore. If Mme. Parfaire were to be carried down the winding staircase, every inch of her covered up (the elevator is too small to accommodate a stretcher), her presence would remain as a blur and a whisper. Like Grippes, she will be buried from the church of Notre Dame des Champs. Mme. Parfaire as a matter of course, Grippes because he has left instructions. One has to be buried from somewhere. He will attend her funeral, may even be asked to sit with the relatives. Her family was proud of that long literary friendship—that was how they saw it. (She had composed many optimistic poems in her day.) They used to save reviews of his books, ask him courteous questions about sales and inspiration. Leaving the church, narrowing his eyes against the bright street, he will remember other lives and other shadows of existence, some invented, some recalled. The other day he noticed that his father and grandfather had merged into a single strong-minded patriarch. It took a second of strict appraisal to pull them apart.

Grippes needs help with the past now. He wants a competent assistant who can live in his head and sort out the archives. A resident inspiring goddess, a muse of a kind, created by Grippes, used to keep offhand order, but her interest in him is slackening. She has no name, no face, no voice, no visible outline, yet he believes in her as some people do in mermaids or pieces of jade or a benevolent planet or simple luck. Denied substance, she cannot answer the door and stave off bores and meddlers. Mme. Parfaire would have dealt with them smartly, but Grippes made a choice between real and phantom attendance on that lamentable afternoon, when he talked such a lot before shutting the door. The talking was unlike him. He had sounded like any old fool in Montparnasse telling about the fifties and sixties. No wonder she has not encouraged him to speak ever since.

Before turning in at dawn he closes the shutters and heavy curtains. The gurgling of pigeons stirred by early light is a sound he finds disgusting. They roost on stone ledges under his windows, even on the sills, drawn by Mme. Parfaire's impulsive scattering of good things to eat. Instead of trying to look after Grippes, she now fosters urban wildlife—her term for this vexation. Some of the scraps of crumbled piecrust and bits of buttered bread she throws from her dining-room windows shower over the heads or umbrellas of people waiting in cinema queues directly below. The rest seem to be meant for Grippes. Actually, the custom of dropping small quantities of rubbish from a height is becoming endemic in his part of Paris. Not everyone has the nerve to splash paint or call a bus driver names or scribble all over a parking ticket before tearing it into strips, but to send flying a paper filter of wet coffee grounds and watch it burst on the roof of someone else's car is a way of saying something.

On the same floor as Mme. Parfaire lives a public prosecutor, lately retired. His windows face the courtyard at the back of the house. He began to show signs of unappeasable distress in the early eighties, when a Socialist government, newly elected, abolished the guillotine, making his profession less philosophical and more matter-of-fact. For years now he has been heaving into the courtyard anything he suddenly hates the sight of. He has thrown out a signed photograph of a late president of the Court of Appeal, a biography of Maria Callas and all her early records, an electric coffee grinder, a saucepan containing fish soup, and the lid of the saucepan. Grippes's kitchen window seems to be in the line of fire, depending upon whether the prosecutor makes a good strong pitch or merely lets things drop. Only this morning a great blob of puréed carrots struck the kitchen windowsill, spattering the panes and seriously polluting a pot of thyme.

Every so often Grippes types a protest and posts it downstairs in the lobby: "Residents are again reminded that it is against the law to feed pigeons and to throw foodstuff and household objects out of windows. Further incidents will be reported to the proper authorities. Current legislation allows for heavy fines." Occasionally, an anonymous neighbor will scrawl "Bravo!" but most seem resigned. Crank behavior is a large part of city life.

Filling the courtyard with rubbish serves to moderate the prosecutor's fidgety nerves. (Yesterday, Mme. Parfaire dropped two stale croissants, smeared with plum jam, on the stone ledge, street-side. Grippes had to use a long-handled stiff broom to get them off.)

Sometimes a long ribbon of sound unwinds in his sleep. He can see strangers, whole families, hurrying along an unknown street. Everything is gray-on-gray—pavement, windows, doorways, faces, clothes—under an opaque white sky. A child turns toward the camera—toward Grippes, the unmoving witness. Then, from a level still deeper than the source of the scene rises an assurance that lets him go on sleeping: None of this is real. Today is the first Wednesday of a new month. It is sharp noon, the air-raid signal is calling, and he has wrapped up the call in a long dream.

Later, at breakfast, he will remember war movies he saw in his youth. Paris, about to be liberated, shone like polished glass. Nazi holdouts, their collars undone, gave themselves up to actors wearing white bandages and looking reliable. A silvery plane, propeller-driven, droned inland from the Channel. The wisecracking bomber crew was like an element of the dense postwar American mystery, never entirely solved. Films are the best historical evidence his waking mind can muster: He spent much of that indistinct war on his grandfather's farm, where his parents had sent him so he would get enough to eat and stay out of trouble. His father was a schoolmaster in a small town. He believed in General de Gaulle—a heretical faith, severely punished. The young Henri had been warned to keep his mouth shut, never to draw notice to his parents—to behave as if he had none, in fact.

As it happened, his grandfather enjoyed a life of stealth and danger, too. The components were not safe houses and messages from London but eggs, butter, meat, flour, cream, sugar, and cheese. One afternoon Henri left the farm for good, dragging a suitcase with a broken lock, and got on a slow, dirty train to Paris. It was near the end of events. Everyone connected to the recent government was under arrest or in flight, and everything in Germany was on fire. Only the police were the same. It seems to him now that he actually heard the air-raid siren in Paris for the first time a long while later. Nevertheless, it still belongs to black-and-white adventures—in a habitual dream, perhaps to peace of a kind.

Two days ago, the lift stalled between floors. No one was injured, but since then everyone has had to use the stairs, as repairmen settle in for a long stay:

They play radios, eat ham sandwiches, drink red wine out of plastic bottles. Except for Mme. Parfaire, residents have lost the habit of climbing. Grippes and the public prosecutor, meeting by chance on the day of the mishap, took a long time and needed a rest on each landing. The prosecutor wanted to know what Grippes made of the repeated break-ins at Mme. Parfaire's apartment: three in less than two months, the most recent only last night. Two hooded men had entered easily, in spite of the triple-point safety lock and chain, and had departed without taking anything, daunted by the sight of Mme. Parfaire, draped in a bedsheet like a toga and speaking impressively.

Grippes thought it sounded like a dream but did not say so. His attention at the time of the intrusion had been fixed on a late-night documentary about army ants. He supposed the roar and rattle of ants waging war, amplified a hundred thousand times, must have overtaken the quieter sound of thieves hammering down a door. The prosecutor changed the subject, and mentioned a man who had pried open a CD player with a chisel and some scissors, letting out a laser beam that killed him instantly. "I believe it cut him in two," the prosecutor said. Between the third and fourth floors he brought up the nuclear threat. The nuclear threat lately had slipped Grippes's mind, which seemed to be set on pigeons. According to the prosecutor, luxurious shelters had been got ready for the nation's leaders. The shelters were stocked with frozen food of high quality and the very best wines. There were libraries, screening rooms, and gymnasiums, handsomely equipped. One could live down there for years and never miss a thing. A number of attractive rooms were set aside for valuable civil servants, even those in retirement. It was clear from the prosecutor's tone and manner that no place of safety existed for Grippes.

Since that conversation, Grippes had been taking stock of his means of escape and deliverance. The siren may start to wail on the wrong day, at an inconvenient time—signaling an emergency. A silvery plane, propeller-driven, follows its own clear-cut shadow over the heart of Paris. Perhaps they are shooting a film and want the panic in the streets to look authentic. Without waiting to find out, Grippes will crowd his cats into a basket and make for the nearest entrance to the Montparnasse-Bienvenüe Métro station, just after the newsstand and the couscous restaurant. He will buy newspapers to spread on the concrete platform so he can sit down, and a few magazines to provide a harmless fantasy life until the all-clear.

He can imagine the dull lights down there, the transistors barking news bulletins and cheap rock, the children walking on his outstretched legs and dropping cookie crumbs on the cats. He will have just a small amount of cash, enough to appease a mugger. "It's all I have in the world," he hears himself telling the lout holding the blunt side of a knife to his neck. (For the moment, the lout is only playing.) They take banknotes, gold jewelry, credit cards, leather garments: So Grippes has been told. It would be best to dress comfortably but not too well, though it would be worst of all to look down-and-out. Perhaps, then, in worn but quite decent trousers and the apple-green plastic jacket he acquired a whole generation ago. The jacket might seem too decorative for these leaden times—it is the remnant of a more frivolous decade, worth nothing now except to collectors of vintage plastic tailoring, but it is not shabby. Shabbiness arouses contempt in the world outlook of a goon. It brings on the sharp edge of the knife.

Late last night, Grippes hauled the jacket out of the relief-agency collection bag where it had been stored for years. (Every winter, he forgets to have the bag picked up, then spring comes, and the agency closes down.) He wiped it with a soapy sponge and hung it to dry at the kitchen window. The jacket looked fresh and verdant on its wire hanger. He wondered why he had ever wanted to give it away, except to alleviate the distress that the sight of it caused Mme. Parfaire. There must have been a moment of great haste, as well as generosity, at one time, for he had forgotten to search the pockets for stray coins and had almost parted with a newspaper clipping that looked important, a silver coffee spoon, and an unopened letter addressed to himself. On the back of the envelope, an earlier Grippes had written "Utopia Reconsidered," as well as a few scribbled sentences he could not make out. He found his spectacles, put them on but still needed a magnifying glass. I used to write much smaller, he decided.

The words seemed to be the start of a stern and rueful overview of the early eighties, the first years of a Socialist government trying hard to be Socialist. As far as Grippes could recall, he had never completed the piece. He slit the envelope, using the handle of the silver spoon, and discovered a leaflet of the sort circulated by some penniless and ephemeral committee, devoted to the rights of pedestrians or cyclists or rent-paying tenants or put-upon landlords. (Tenants, this time.) Along with the leaflet was a hand-written appeal to Henri Grippes, whose published works and frequent letters to newspapers had always taken the side of the helpless.

"Well, it was a long time ago," said Grippes aloud, as if the sender of the letter were sitting on the edge of a kitchen chair, looking pale and seedy, smoking nervously, displaying without shame (it was too late for shame) his broken nails and unwashed hair. He fixed on Grippes nearsighted gray eyes, waiting for Grippes to show him the way out of all his troubles. The truth is, Grippes announced to this phantom, that you have no rights. You have none as a tenant, none in your shaky, ill-paid job, none when it comes to applying to me.

Perhaps by now the man had come into a fortune, owned a string of those run-down but income-producing hotels crammed with illegal immigrants. Or had lost his employment and been forced into early and threadbare retirement. Perhaps he was an old man, sitting down to meals taken in common in some beige-painted institutional dining room with soft-hued curtains at the windows. A woman said to be the oldest living person in France had frequently been shown in such a place, blowing out birthday candles. She smoked one cigarette a day, drank one glass of port, had known van Gogh and Mistral, and remembered both vividly. Perhaps the writer of the letter, in his frustration and desperation, had joined an extremist movement, right or left, and gone to live in exile. Wherever he was, whatever he had become, he had never received a kind or a decent or even a polite reply from Henri Grippes.

Grippes felt humbled suddenly. Political passion and early love had in common the promise of an unspoilt future, within walking distance of any true believer. Once, Grippes had watched Utopia rising out of calm waters, like Atlantis emerging, dripping wet and full of promise. He had admired the spires and gleaming windows, the marble pavements and year-round unchanging sunrise; had wondered if there was room for him there and what he would do with his time after he moved in. The vision had occurred at eight in the evening on Sunday, the tenth of May, 1981, and had vanished immediately—lost, as one might have read at the time, in the doctrinal night. At the same moment, a computerized portrait of François Mitterrand, first Socialist president of the Fifth Republic, had unrolled on the television screen, in the manner of a window blind. Grippes had felt stunned and deceived. Only a few hours before, he had cast his vote for precisely such an outcome. Nevertheless, he had been expecting a window blind bearing the leaner, more pensive features of the Conservative incumbent. He had voted for a short list of principles, not their incarnation. In fact, he resented having to look at any face at all.

Utopia was a forsaken city now, bone-dry, the color of scorched newsprint. Desiccated, relinquished, it announced a plaintive message. Grippes placed the newspaper clipping, the coffee spoon, and the envelope side by side on the kitchen table, like exhibits in a long and inconclusive trial. He turned the spoon over and read the entwined initials of his ex-friend upstairs. Short of calling Mme. Parfaire to ask if she had ever, in any year, slipped a spoon into his pocket, he had no means of ever finding out how it had got there. Had he taken it by mistake? Only the other day, buying a newspaper, he had left it on the counter and started to walk off with another man's change. The vendor had called after him. Grippes had heard him telling the stranger, "It's Henri Grippes." Respect for authors, still a factor of Paris life, meant that the other man looked chastened as he accepted his due, as if he were unworthy of contemporary literature. Apologizing, Grippes had said it was the first time he had ever done an absentminded thing. Now he wondered if he ought to turn out the kitchen drawers and see how much in them really belonged to other people.

The spoon recalled to Grippes abundant, well-cooked meals, the dining room upstairs with the rose velvet portieres, the Japanese screen, the brass urn filled with silk chrysanthemums, the Sèvres coffee service on the buffet. It was a room that contained at all hours a rich and comforting smell of leek-and-potato soup. Often, as Grippes sopped up the last of the sauce of a blanquette or daube, his hostess would describe enthusiastic reviews she had just read of books by other people, citing phrases he might appreciate or even want to use, such as "Cyclopean vision" (a compliment, apparently) or "the superstructure of essential insincerity," another sort of flattery. Later, she might even coax him into watching a literary talk show. Grippes, digesting, would stare hard at false witnesses, plagiarists, ciphers, and mountebanks, while Mme. Parfaire praised their frank and open delivery and the way they wore their hair. When, occasionally, there was a woman on hand, prepared to be interviewed and to announce in the same straightforward manner, "Well, you see, in *my* book . . . ," Mme. Parfaire would make the comment that the women all looked the same, had terrible legs, and lacked the restraint and distinction of men. Whatever misleading reply Grippes might give when she asked what he was writing—"writing *about*" was the actual phrase—she responded with unflagging loyalty: "At least you always know what you are trying to say."

The night of Utopia had alarmed her, and Grippes had been no help. He remembered now that the tenth of May, 1981, had begun blue and bright and ended under a black cloudburst. It was possible that God, too, had expected a different face on the window blind. Rain had soaked through the hair and shoes of revelers in the Place de la Bastille. Older voters, for whom the victory was the first in a lifetime, wept in the downpour. Their children responded to the presence of television cameras by dancing in puddles. The public prosecutor called Mme. Parfaire to say that Soviet tanks would be rumbling under her windows before next Tuesday. She arrived at Grippes's door, asking for reassurance and an atlas: She thought she might emigrate. Unfortunately, all the foreign maps were unwelcoming and un-French. Grippes offered champagne, so they could toast the death of the middle classes. The suggestion struck her as heartless and she went away.

Left to himself, he had turned his back on the damp, bewildering celebration and stood at the window, imagining tanks, champagne in his hand and disquiet in his mind. He had helped create the intemperate joy at the Place de la Bastille, but why? Out of a melancholy habit of political failure, he supposed. He had never for a moment expected his side to win. By temperament, by choice, by the nature of most of his friendships, by the cross-grained character of his profession he belonged in perpetual opposition. Now a devastating election result had made him a shareholder in power, morally responsible for cultural subsidies to rock concerts and nuclear testing in the Pacific. Unfolding a copy of the left-wing daily *Libération* on the No. 82 bus, which runs through diehard territory, no longer would signify a minority rebellion but majority complacency. Grippes was nearing the deep end of middle age. For the first time he had said to himself, "I'm getting old for all this."

Down in the street, as if the tenth of May were a Sunday like any other, cinema lines straggled across the sidewalk to the curb. It seemed to Grippes that it was not the usual collection of office workers and students and pickpockets and off-duty waiters but well-to-do dentists from the western regions of the city and their wives. The dentists must have known the entrepreneurial game was up and had decided to spend their last loose cash on an action movie set in Hong Kong. Grippes pictured them sorted into ranks, surging along the boulevard, the lights of pizza restaurants flashing off their glasses in red and green. Their women kept pace, swinging gold-link necklaces like bicycle chains. There were no shouts, no threats, no demands but just the steady trampling that haunts the nights of aging radicals. Wistfully, as if it were now lost forever, Grippes had recalled the warm syncopation of a leftist demo: "Step! Shuffle! Slogan! Stop!/Slogan! Step! Shuffle!" How often had he drummed that rhythm of progress on the windowsill before he was forced by the sting of tear gas to pull his head in!

Having set his dentists on the march, Grippes no longer knew what to do with them. Perhaps they could just disband. Those to whom the temptation of power had given an appetite could stroll into Chez Hansi, at the corner of Rue de Rennes, and enjoy one last capitalist-size lobster, chosen from the water tank. What about Grippes? What was he supposed to be doing on the night of change? Reminded of the steadfast role of the writer in a restless universe, he had poured himself another glass and settled down to compose a position piece, keeping it as cloudy and imprecise as his native talent could make it. Visions of perfection emerge and fade but the written word remains to trip the author who runs too fast for his time or lopes alongside at not quite the required pace. He wrote well into the night, first by hand, then after removing a new version of "Residents are again reminded ..." made about fifteen typed revisions of the final text.

The next day (as Grippes recalls the affair), he deposited his article at the editorial offices of the most distinguished newspaper in France. The paper had printed it, finally; not on page I, with nationwide debate to follow, but on 2, the repository for unsolicited opinions too long-winded to pass as letters to the editor. Under a provocative query of some kind—say, "What Tomorrow for Social Anthropology?"—page 2 allowed the escape of academic steam and measured the slightly steadier breathing of neo-monetarists, experts on regional history, and converts to Islam. A footnote in italics described the correspondent's sphere of activity. Grippes's label, "man of letters," confirmed his status and showed he was no amateur thinker.

His entry looked a bit crowded, wedged next to that of a dealer in rare stamps calling for parasocialist reform of his profession, but Grippes was pleased with the two-column heading: "UTOPIA OUR WAY." "Now that the profit motive has been lopped from every branch of French cultural life," his piece began, "or so it would seem," it continued, thus letting Grippes off some future charge of having tried to impoverish the intelligentsia, "surely." After "surely" came a blank: Page 2 had let the sentence die. In the old days (Grippes's prose had suddenly resumed), when he went to the cinema there was room for his legs. He could place a folded jacket under the seat without having it stuck with gum. Ice cream, sold by a motherly vendor, tasted of real vanilla. Audiences at musical comedies had applauded every dance number: Think of "Singin' in the Rain." In spite of a flat cloud of tobacco smoke just overhead one seemed to breathe the purest of air. Now the capacious theater under Grippes's windows had been cut into eight small places, each the size of a cabin in a medium-haul jet. Whenever he ventured inside, he expected to be told to fasten his seat belt and handed a plastic tray. Subtitles of foreign films dissolved in a white blur, while spoken dialogue could not be heard at all—at least not by Grippes. He knew that twenty-three years of right-wing government had produced a sullen and mumbling generation, but he felt sure that a drastic change, risen from the very depths of an ancient culture, would soon restore intelligible speech.

This was the clipping Grippes had found in the jacket pocket, along with the spoon. He had to admit it was not perfect. Nothing had ever been done about the cinemas. The part about rising from the depths made the 1981 Socialist plan of intentions sound like wet seaweed. Still, he had staked a claim in the serene confusion of the era and had launched an idea no one could fault, except owners of theater chains. And "man of letters" had remained on the surface of the waters, a sturdy and recognizable form of literary plant life, still floating.

Last June, it rained every night. Wet clouds soaked up the lights of Montparnasse and gave them back as a reddish glow. At about three o'clock one morning, mild, moist air entered the room where Grippes sat at his writing desk. A radio lying flat on the table played soft jazz from a studio in Milan. A cat slept under the desk lamp. Moths beat about inside the red shade. Grippes got up, pulled a book from the shelf, blew the dust off, found the entry he wanted: "19th June—Half past one. Death of my father. One can say of him, 'It is only a man, mayor of a poor, small village,' and still speak of his death as being like that of Socrates. I do not reproach myself for not having loved him enough. I reproach myself for not having understood him."

It so happened that Grippes had just written the last two sentences: same words, same order. Almost instantly, the cartoon drawing of a red-bearded man wearing a bowler hat had come to mind—not his father, of course. It was Jules Renard, dead for some eighty-odd years. Renard's journals had been admired and quoted often by Grippes's father, dead now for more than forty. A gust of night wind pushed the window wide and brought it to with a bang. The cat made a shuddering movement but continued to sleep. Lifted on a current, a moth escaped and flew straight back.

Grippes wondered how much of the impressive clutter in his imagination could still be called his own. "At least you always know what you are trying to say" referred to unexamined evidence. Like his father, like Jules Renard, he had been carried along the slow, steady swindle of history and experience. Pictures taken along the way, the untidy record, needed to be rearranged by category or discarded for good. Thousands of similar views had been described in hundreds of thousands of manuscripts and books, some in languages Grippes had never heard of. His inspiring goddess had found nothing better to dish up in the middle of the night than another man's journal, and even had the insolence to pass it off as original.

A few notches away from Milan, the BBC was proposing a breakdown in human relations. (Cressida to Quentin: "My cab is waiting, Quentin. I think everything has been said." Quentin to Cressida: "Am I allowed to say good-bye?" Door slams. High heels on pavement. Taxi loud, then fading. Quentin to no one: "Good-bye. I shan't be denied the last word.") The departure of Cressida was stirring dejection or inducing sleep across Europe and the Middle East, down the length of Africa, in India, in Singapore, in Western Samoa. Men and women who had their own cats, moths, lamps, wet weather, and incompetent goddesses were pondering Quentin's solitude and wondering if it served him right. Grippes pulled a large pad of writing paper from under the sleeping cat and drew a picture of a London taxi. He drew a Citroën of the 1960s and a Peugeot with an elegant dashboard, out of some fifties film, set on the Riviera, then a tall Renault, all right angles, built in the thirties, still driven in the early forties by black-market operators and the police. He shaded it black and put inside three plainclothes inspectors.

The Renault, as it approached his grandfather's house, could be heard from a distance; it was a quiet afternoon, close to the end of things. The car turned into the courtyard. Two of the men got out. They had on city suits, felt hats, and creaky, towny shoes. Young Henri's grandfather stood in the kitchen with his arms folded, saying nothing. The two men looked in the usual places, turned up loose tiles and floorboards, slashed all the pillows and bolsters with a knife. As a rule, these sudden descents ended with everyone around the kitchen table. His grandmother had already wiped the faded red-and-blue oilcloth and had begun to set out the thick glasses and plates.

From the window of his wrecked bedroom (the gashed pillows lay on the floor) Henri watched the strangers digging aimlessly outside. They were clumsy, did not know how to use a spade, how to lift the clods they turned up. He saw them the way his grandfather did, cheap and citified. But to hold the law cheap one needed to have powerful allies. His grandfather had physical strength and a native ability to hoard and hang on. The men threw the spades down and came back to the house. Their shoes left mud prints across the kitchen floor and up the scrubbed stairs.

In his room, which had been his father's, down and feathers rose and hovered with every approaching step. One of the visitors took a book down from a shelf over the washstand. He made the remark that he had never seen books in a bedroom before. Henri started to answer that these were his father's old schoolbooks but remembered he was not to mention him. The man gave the book a shake, releasing a shower of handwritten verse: Henri's father's adolescent attempts to reconcile the poetry of sexual craving, as explained in literature, with barnyard evidence. The second stranger offered Henri an American cigarette. It was too precious to waste in smoke. He placed it carefully behind an ear and waited for the question. It was, "Where would you put a lot of contraband money, if you had any?"

Henri answered, truthfully, "In the dark and in plain sight."

They went down to the cellar, pushing Henri, and ran beams of yellow light along racks of wine and shelves of preserved fruit in earthenware crocks. About every fourth crock was stuffed with gold coins and banknotes. The men asked for a crate. Henri, promoted to honest member of the clan, checked the count. He droned, "... four, five, six ..." while his grandmother wept. A few minutes later, he and his grandmother watched his grandfather being handcuffed and hustled into the Renault. He could have brained all three men with his locked hands but held still.

"Forgive me," said Henri. "I didn't know it was down there."

"You had better be a long way from here before he gets back," his grandmother said.

"Won't they keep him, this time?"

"They'll work something out," she said, and dried her eyes.

Today Grippes was wakened abruptly at about eleven-thirty. Two policemen were at the door, wanting to know if he had heard anything suspicious
during the night. There had been another incident concerning Mme. Parfaire. This time, the intruders had broken a Sèvres sugar bowl and threatened the dog. All Grippes could say was that the dog was nineteen years old
and deaf and had certainly not taken the threat to heart. After they went
away, he shuffled along the passage to the kitchen. The cats—a tabby and
a young stray—ran ahead. (He swears they are the last.) The first things he
saw were the jacket on its wire hanger and the soiled windowpanes. At a
window across the court a woman, another early riser according to Grippes
time, parted her curtains. She had nothing on except a man's shirt, unbuttoned. Standing between the flowery folds, she contemplated the sunless enclosure. (The cobblestones below are never dry, owing to a stopped drain.
For years now tenants on the lower floors have been petitioning to have the
drain repaired. Their plight gets not much sympathy from occupants of
upper stories, who suffer less inconvenience or accept the miasma of mosquitoes and flies in summer as the triumph of nature over urban sterility.)

Having observed that nothing had changed during the night, the woman
closed the curtains with a snap and (Grippes supposes) went back to bed.
He had seen her before, but never at that hour. The entrance to her building must be somewhere around the corner. He cannot place it on a map of
Montparnasse, which is half imagined anyway. For a time he supposed she
might be a hostess in a club along the boulevard, a remnant of the Jazz Age,
haunted by the ghost of Josephine Baker. The other day, he noticed that the
club had become an ordinary restaurant, with a fixed-price menu posted
outside. Inquiring, he was told the change had come about in the seventies.

He put some food down for the cats, plugged in the coffeemaker, and
started to clean the window and stone sill. The jacket got in the way, so he
removed it from its wire hanger and put it on. The movement of opinion in
the building concerning Mme. Parfaire and pigeons has turned against
Grippes. She seems to be suffering from a wasting and undiagnosed fatigue
of the nerves—so such ailments of the soul are called. Some think the two
men who keep breaking in are nephews impatient to come into their inheritance. They hope to scare her to death. Others believe they are professional
thugs hired by the nephews. The purpose is to induce her to sell her apart-

ment and move into a residence for the elderly and distribute the money before she dies. Greedy families, the avoidance of death duties are among the
basic certainties of existence. No one can quite believe Grippes does not
know what is taking place upstairs. Perhaps he is in on the plot. Perhaps he
is lazy or just a coward or slumps dead drunk with his head on the typewriter. Perhaps he doesn't care.

Whispered echoes, mean gossip, ignorant assurances reach his ears. Mme.
Parfaire when she descends the curving staircase clutches the banister, halts
every few steps, wears a set expression. Strands of hair hang about her face.
Even in her wan and precarious condition, popular sentiment now runs, she
finds enough strength to open her windows and sustain the life of pigeons.
Garbage-throwing, once seen as a tiresome and dirty habit, has become
a demonstration of selflessness. Once a week she totters across the Seine
to the Quai de la Mégisserie and buys bird food laced with vitamin E,
to ensure the pigeons a fulfilled and fertile span. "Residents are again reminded . . ." is viewed with a collective resentment. Not long ago an anonymous hand wrote "Sadist!"—meaning Grippes.

Yesterday he happened to see her in the lobby, talking in a low voice to
a neighbor holding a child by the hand. She fell silent as Grippes went by.
The women watched him out of sight; he was sure of it, could feel the pressure of their staring. He heard the child laugh. It was clear to him that
Mme. Parfaire was doped to the eyes on tranquilizers, handed out in Paris
like salted peanuts, but he could not very well put up a notice saying so.
People would shrug and say it was none of their business. Would they be
interested in a revelation such as "Mme. Parfaire wants to spend her last
years living in sin, or quasi-sin, or just in worshipful devotion, with the selfish and disagreeable and eminently unmarriageable Henri Grippes"? True,
but it might seem unlikely. As an inventor of a great number of imaginary
events Grippes knows that the reflection of reality is no more than just that;
it is as flat and mute as a mirror. Better to sound plausible than merely in
touch with facts.

He had just finished cleaning the window when the siren began to wail.
He looked at the electric clock on top of the refrigerator: twelve sharp.
Today was a Wednesday, the first one of the month. He could hear two distinct tones and saw them as lines across the sky: a shrill humming—a
straight, thin path—and a lower note that rose and dipped and finally descended in a slow spiral, like a plane shot down. Five minutes later, as he sat
drinking coffee, the warning started again. This time, the somewhat deeper

note fell away quite soon; the other, more piercing cry streamed on and on, and gradually vanished in the bright day.

Stirring his coffee, using his old friend's spoon, Grippes thought of how he might put a stop to the pigeon business, her nighttime fantasies, and any further possibility of being wakened at an unacceptable hour. He could write a note inviting himself to lunch, take it upstairs, and slide it under her door. He would go as he was now, with the plastic jacket on top of a bathrobe. Serving lunch would provide point and purpose to her day. It would stop the downward spiral of her dreams. Composing the note (it would require tact and skill) might serve to dislodge "Residents are again reminded . . ." from his typewriter and his mind.

He pictured, with no effort, a plate of fresh mixed seafood with mayonnaise or just a bit of lemon and olive oil, saw an omelette folded on a warmed plate, marinated herring and potato salad, a light ragout of lamb kidneys in wine. He could see himself proceeding along the passage and sitting down on the chair where, as a rule, he spent much of every night and writing the note. From the window, if he leaned a bit to the right, he would see the shadow of the Montparnasse tower, and the office building that had replaced the old railway station with its sagging wooden floor. Only yesterday, he started to tell himself—but no. A generation of Parisians had never known anything else.

An empty space, as blank and infinite as the rectangle of sky above the court, occurred in his mind, somewhere between the sliding of the invitation—if one could call it that—under her door and the materialization of the omelette. The question was, How to fill the space? He was like someone reading his own passport, the same information over and over. "My dearest Marthe," he began (going back to the first thing). "Don't you think the time has come . . ." But *he* did not think it. "Remember that woman who said she had known van Gogh?" She had no connection to their dilemma. It was just something he liked to consider. "You should not be living alone. Solitude is making you . . ." No; above all, not that. "Perhaps if one of those nephews of yours came to live with you . . ." They were all married, some with grown children. "I think it only fair to point out that I never once made a firm . . ." The whine of the dissembler. "The occasional meal taken together . . ." The thin edge. "You know very well that it is against the law to feed pigeons and that increasingly heavy fines . . ."

How good it would be to lie down on the kitchen floor and let his inspiring goddess kneel beside him, anxiously watching for the flutter of an eyelid, as he deftly lifts her wallet. As it turns out, there is nothing in it except "Residents are again reminded . . ." Like Grippes, like the prosecutor, like poor Marthe, in a way, his goddess is a victim of the times, hard up for currency and short of ideas, ideas of divine origin in particular. She scarcely knows how to eke out the century. Meanwhile, she hangs on to "Residents are again . . . ," hoping (just as Grippes does) that it amounts to the equivalent of the folding money every careful city dweller keeps on hand for muggers.

ABOUT THE AUTHOR

MAVIS GALLANT was born in Montreal and worked as a feature writer there before giving up newspaper work to devote herself to fiction. She left Canada in 1950 and after extensive travel settled in Paris. She is a regular contributor to *The New Yorker* and is currently working on a novel. *The Collected Stories of Mavis Gallant* is the twelfth book of hers to be published in this country.

ABOUT THE TYPE

This book was set in Centaur, a typeface designed by the
American typographer Bruce Rogers in 1929. Centaur was a
typeface that Rogers adapted from the fifteenth-century type
of Nicholas Jenson and modified in 1948 for a cutting by the
Monotype Corporation.